MILA 18
Leon Uris's most powerful novel!

MILA 18
The epic story of Andrei Androfski,
the dashing officer who loved life
but loved freedom more . . .

MILA 18
The passionate story of Gabriela Rak,
whom Andrei loved
but could not marry . . .

MILA 18
The moving story of Alexander Brandel,
a man of peace
who came to terms with war . . .

MILA 18
The romantic story of Wolf and Rachel
who discovered the sweetness of love
in an agony of hatred . . .

MILA 18
The intense story of the journalist,
Christopher de Monti, who found
a reason to live in a holocaust of death . . .

MILA 18
"One of the great novels
of recent years!"
St. Louis Post-Dispatch

MILA 18
LEON URIS

CORGI BOOKS

This book is dedicated to
ANTEK-ITZHAK ZUCKERMAN
ZIVIAH LUBETKIN
*and the others who participated in an immortal
moment on behalf of human dignity and freedom,
and to one in particular*
DR. ISRAEL I. BLUMENFELD

MILA 18
A CORGI BOOK 0 552 08385 2

Originally published in Great Britain by
William Heinemann Ltd.

PRINTING HISTORY
William Heinemann edition published 1961
Fourth impression 1961
Corgi edition published 1963
Corgi edition reprinted 1965
Corgi edition reprinted 1966
Corgi edition reprinted 1967
Corgi edition reprinted 1968
Corgi edition reprinted 1969
Corgi edition reissued 1970
Corgi edition reprinted 1970 (twice)
Corgi edition reprinted 1971 (twice)
Corgi edition reprinted 1972
Corgi edition reprinted 1974 (twice)
Corgi edition reprinted 1975
Corgi edition reprinted 1976
Corgi edition reprinted 1977 (twice)
Corgi edition reprinted 1978
Corgi edition reprinted 1979
Corgi edition reprinted 1980
Corgi edition reprinted 1981
Corgi edition reprinted 1983
Corgi edition reprinted 1984
Corgi edition reprinted 1985
Corgi edition reprinted 1986
Corgi edition reprinted 1988

This book is set in 9pt Monotype Times

Corgi Books are published by Transworld Publishers Ltd.,
61–63 Uxbridge Road, Ealing, London W5 5SA,
in Australia by Transworld Publishers (Aust.) Pty. Ltd.,
15–23 Helles Avenue, Moorebank, NSW 2170, and in New
Zealand by Transworld Publishers (N.Z.) Ltd., Cnr. Moselle
and Waipareira Avenues, Henderson, Auckland.

Printed and bound in Great Britain by
Hazell Watson & Viney Limited
Member of BPCC plc
Aylesbury Bucks

ACKNOWLEDGMENTS

Past experience forewarned me that I would be dependent upon the assistance of tens of dozens of individuals and organizations to research this book. Again, I was fortunate to be the recipient of selfless hours by those who transmitted to me their knowledge of this subject.

Without the devotion of the Ghetto Fighters House International Museum and Shrine, the individual members of the Ghetto Fighters Kibbutz in Israel and their comrades in the International Survivors Association, these pages could scarcely have been written. Sheer weight of numbers precludes my thanking the others, but I would be remiss if I did not acknowledge the contribution of the Yad Vashem Memorial Archives in Jerusalem and the University of Southern California Library.

Within a framework of basic truth, tempered with a reasonable amount of artistic license, the places and events described actually happened.

The characters are fictitious, but I would be the last to deny there were people who lived who were similar to those in this volume.

LEON URIS

part one

TWILIGHT

Chapter One

This is the first entry in my journal. I cannot help but feel that the war will begin in a few weeks. If the lessons of the past three years are any barometer, something awesome is apt to happen if Germany makes a successful invasion, what with three and a half million Jews in Poland. Perhaps the tensions of the moment are making me over-dramatic. My journal may prove completely worthless and a waste of time. Yet, as a historian, I must satisfy the impulse to record what is happening around me.

ALEXANDER BRANDEL

Drops of late summer rain splattered against the high window which ran from the floor to the ceiling.

The big room was violently Polish, in memory of one of the landed gentry who had kept it as a nest for his mistress of the moment during his visits to Warsaw from his estate. All evidence of female occupants had vanished. It was solid and leathery and masculine. Its former grandeur was somewhat qualified by a practical consideration that the present occupant was a working journalist with the particular slovenliness that goes with bachelorhood.

Christopher de Monti was untidy but rather inoffensive about it. It was almost a pleasure for his housekeeper to clean up after him, for he had immaculate taste in records and books and tobacco and liquor and a wardrobe marked with the finest British labels.

In one corner, next to the window, stood a banged-up typewriter and a ream of paper and an overfull ash tray.

The single bedroom was formed by a deep alcove off the living room which could be isolated by drawing a pair of velvet drapes. A night stand beside the huge bed sported an ancient German table-model radio shaped like a church window. From the radio escaped the sad and foreboding notes of Chopin's Nocturne in A Flat.

That was about all one heard on Radio Polskie these days; Chopin performed by Paderewski . . . nocturnes.

It seemed as though night was again to fall on Poland.

Chris grumbled in a state of half sleep and half wakefulness and stretched his lean, wiry limbs to their full reaches and felt across the bed for Deborah. She was gone. His eyes opened and searched the dark corners of the alcove. Then he quieted as he heard her moving about in the other room.

His hand groped automatically on the night stand and found the pack of cigarettes, and in a moment he watched the smoke laze upward as the nocturne raced to a pulsating crescendo.

Chris rolled over on his side and looked at Deborah through an opening in the drapes. Her half-naked body was bathed in late afternoon shadows. Chris loved to watch her dress. She balanced a foot on the end of a chair and stretched her leg and rolled up her stockings and slipped into her blouse and skirt with effortless grace. Then she stood before the mirror, her fingers darting pins into long raven hair and twisting it nervously into a firm knot. He remembered that first time when he had taken the pins from her hair one by one and watched it fall like black silk. She took her trench coat from the coat tree and buttoned it, never acknowledging that she knew Chris's eyes were on her back, and with determined abruptness walked for the door.

"Deborah."

She stopped and pressed her forehead against the door.

"Deborah."

She came into the alcove and sat on the edge of the bed. Chris snuffed out the cigarette, rolled next to her, and lay his head in her lap. Her black eyes filled with melancholy. Her fingers traced his cheek and mouth and neck and shoulders, and Chris looked up at her. How beautiful you are, he thought. She was biblical. Black and olive. A Deborah of the Bible. When she stood, Chris grabbed her wrist and she could feel his hand tremble.

"We can't keep this up. Let me speak to him."

"It would kill him, Chris."

"How about me? It's killing me."

"Please."

"I'm talking to him tonight."

"Oh Lord, why does it always have to end like this?"

"It will until you're my wife."

"You're not to see him, Chris. I mean that."

He released his grip. "You'd better go," he whispered. He turned away, his back toward her.

"Chris . . . Chris . . ."

Pride kept him silent.

"I'll call you," she said. "Will you see me?"

"You know I will."

He threw on a robe and listened to the click-click-click of her footsteps on the marble hall outside. He pulled back the window drapes. The rain had slowed to a miserable drizzle. In a moment Deborah appeared on Jerusalem Boulevard below. She looked up to his window and waved her hand feebly, then ran across the street to where a line of droshkas waited. The horse clip-clopped away from the curb and turned out of sight.

Chris let the drapes fall closed, snuffing out most of the light. He wandered into the kitchen and poured himself a cup of the steam-

ing coffee Deborah had made then slumped into a chair and hid his
face in his hands, shaken by the impact of another parting.

On the radio, a newscaster speaking in nervous Polish recited the
latest diplomatic setback in the growing mountain of them.

Chapter Two

Journal Entry

*On the news we hear that Russia and Germany are about to an-
nounce a non-aggression treaty. It seems impossible that the two
sworn enemies on the planet, pledged to destroy each other have
come to this. Hitler's tactics seem logical. He obviously wants to
neutralize Russia for the time being to avoid the possibility of a two-
front war (that is, if England and France honor their obligations to
Poland). I'm willing to wager that the wages being paid to Stalin
is half of Poland and I think we are being divided up at some long
polished table in Moscow this minute.*

ALEXANDER BRANDEL

In embassies, state departments, chancelleries, foreign offices,
consulates, ministries, war offices, code rooms, newsrooms, frantic
men scurried to all-night conferences, played war games, barked
into telephones of flooded switchboards, cursed, prayed, pleaded.

A trail of broken treaties lay strewn about like corpses after a
Mongol invasion.

Men of good will were stunned at the warped logic behind which
eighty million civilized people rallied and shrieked and strutted like
hysterical robots. Hammered into a hypnotic trance by the well-
timed tantrums that were the mad genius of Adolf Hitler, the men
of good will sank deeper into muck and mire, unable to divest
themselves of the all-consuming monster in their midst.

The geopoliticians had drawn and quartered the world into areas
of labor and raw material and presented the master plan which
stood to make Genghis Khan and every archvillain of every age
pale by comparison.

The German masses gave the edict in a terrifying redundance,
"*Sieg Heil! Sieg Heil! Sieg Heil!*"

"*Lebenstraum* [Land to live]!"

"*Sieg Heil!*"

And they poised ready to act out the role of Teuton war gods to
the strains of Wagnerian Fire Music.

"We must save German citizens living under foreign tyranny! A
German is always a German!"

12

"Sieg Heil!"

Austria and Czechoslovakia qualified. Flushed with bloodless victories, certain that America, France, and England would not fight, the Nazi cancer spread.

"Danzig is German! Return the Polish Corridor! Return the 1914 borders! Halt the inhuman treatment of ethnic Germans!"

"Sieg Heil!"

Once an indifferent world stood by and shrugged as little yellow men fought little yellow men in a place called Manchuria, and once France sputtered feebly as Germany broke the Versailles Treaty and marched into the Rhineland, and once men debated, then sighed as black men in mud huts armed with spears fought for their land . . . a name that children used in games . . . Abyssinia.

A mesmerized world quivered at the proving ground of democratic sterility; the rape of Spain by Italian and Moroccan and German hordes.

Now Austria, now Czechoslovakia, and the righteous cowed and the evil grew bold.

Once the harbingers of peace told their people they had made a bill of peace in a place called Munich. As Poland's hour grew near came that realization that there was no place left to run or to hide, nor words to say, nor treaties to make.

In Moscow, a shrewd chessplayer knew that the long dream of the Allies was to have Russia and Germany maul each other to death. His distrust of England and France was built upon decades of boycott, hard-learned lessons when republican Spain was abandoned, and finally when Russia was not invited to the sellout in Munich.

Hitler, positive of the final timidity of the Allies, positive their string of betrayals would extend to Poland, keyed his war trumpets to shattering highs and was responded to with black drum rolls and pounding boots.

Josef Stalin was no less certain of Allied betrayal. In a desperate bid for time he entered into negotiations with his archenemy. To ensure easy, unimpaired victory for himself, Hitler did business with Stalin, and the Allies cried, "Foul!"

And in the middle a proud and defiant Poland, which hated Russia and Germany with equal vigor, ended all hope of Allied unity by refusing to petition Russia for help.

Chris sped his Fiat down the rain-slickened boulevard and turned into the shop-lined New World Street. It was gray out. The late shoppers clung close to the buildings and moved with haste past the elegant store windows. At the corner of Traugutta Street, where the line of shops ended, the New World Street changed its name to the Krakow Suburb Boulevard for reasons no one seemed to understand. Chris headed toward the semi-faced, semi-elegant

13

Bristol Hotel. The hotel made a good newsman's headquarters. It gave him a twenty-four-hour-a-day switchboard service and it stood at the apex of a triangle that enveloped the Europa Hotel, the Foreign Ministry, the President's Palace, and Warsaw's city hall. Between them, there was always a constant flood of news.

Chris turned the car over to the doorman and brushed past the turmoil of the rumor-filled lobby to the opened-cage Otis elevator of World War I vintage.

On the balcony floor he entered the door of a suite marked *Swiss News Agency*.

Ervin Rosenblum, photographer and journalist and Chris's indispensable man, stood at the worktable, which was spilling over with photographs, cables, stories, and copy.

Chris walked beside him, wordless, and took a fistful of the late dispatches. One by one he let them flutter to the floor. Ervin Rosenblum was a very homely man who stood five feet five inches and was almost sightless without his thick-lens glasses. As Chris read, Ervin searched Chris's pockets for a cigarette.

"Boy," Chris mumbled. "They're surer than hell going to start shooting soon."

Ervin gave up his search for a smoke. "Mark my words, Poland is going to fight," he said.

"Maybe she'll be better off if she doesn't fight."

Ervin looked at his watch nervously. "Where the hell is Susan? I've got to get this stuff to the lab." He picked up his Speed Graphic and jiggled the flash bulbs in his pocket. "Chris, do you think England and France will help us?"

Chris kept reading the dispatches. "When are you and Susan getting married?"

"I can't get her still long enough to ask her. If she's not at the orphanage she's at a Zionist meeting. Did you ever hear of six meetings a week? Only Jews can talk so much. So I'm appointed to the executive council just so I can get dates to see her. Momma asks, are you coming to dinner tonight? She's made potato latkes for you, special."

"Potato latkes? I'll get there between stops."

Susan Geller appeared in the doorway. She was as short and homely as Ervin was. Squat, devoid of almost all features which make women pretty. Her hair was pulled back straight and flat and wrapped into a knot under her nurse's cap. Her hands were large and knobby from the life of lifting sick people and changing bedpans, but the moment she spoke the ugliness faded. Susan Geller was one of the kindest creatures on the earth.

"You're a half hour late," Ervin greeted her.

"Hi, honey," Chris said.

"I like you better," she answered to Chris.

14

Ervin grabbed a batch of negatives, film, bulbs, and his camera. "It's all yours," he said to Chris.

"Can you stop by the President's Palace? See Anton. Maybe he can fix us up for five minutes with Smigly-Rydz. He may be changing his tune now that the Russian-German non-aggression pact is official."

The phone rang. Ervin snatched it off the hook with his free hand. "Hello . . . Just a minute." He held his hand over the mouthpiece. "Wait outside," he said to Susan. "I'll be right there."

Susan and Chris blew good-by kisses to each other.

"Who is it, Rosy?"

"Deborah's husband," he answered, and handed him the phone and left.

"Why, hello, Paul. How are you?"

"I was asking the same question. I was just saying to Deborah how much we and the children have missed you."

"Things have been pretty hectic."

"I can imagine."

"I do owe you an apology for not calling. How . . . uh . . . is Deborah?"

"Fine, just fine. Why don't you break away for dinner tomorrow?"

Chris was finding it unbearable to keep up the masquerade. Every time he saw Paul and Deborah together, every time he thought of them sharing a bed, the revulsion in him grew.

"I'm afraid it's impossible, Paul. I may have to send Rosy to Krakow and——"

Paul Bronski's voice lowered. "It is rather important that you come. I should like to see you on a pressing matter. Say, seven."

Chris was scared. Paul's tone had the authority of a command. Perhaps Paul Bronski himself would call the showdown that Deborah had avoided. Maybe it was all fantasy. They were good friends. Why not invite him to dinner?

"I'll be there," Chris said.

Chapter Three

Journal Entry

I have studied the trend of the behaviour of the ethnic Germans in Austria and Czechoslovakia. They have done a tremendous job in undermining in advance of the German armies. They have certainly been raising all sorts of hell in Danzig. Just before the Austrian "Anschluss" they became strangely quiet. This past week their ac-

tivity here has all but stopped. Could this be on orders? Is this the lull before the storm? Is history about to repeat?

Everyone I know is being called up into the reserve. Smigly-Rydz means to fight. Polish temper and history indicate they will.

ALEXANDER BRANDEL

"We Poles unfortunately got ourselves located between Russia and Germany. The traffic between the two has been busy, indeed," Dr. Paul Bronski, dean of the College of Medicine, said to an auditorium overcrowded with students and faculty. "We have been trampled. We have even ceased to exist, yet Polish nationalism fires a breed of patriot that has always made Poland return."

A spontaneous burst of applause halted his speech.

"Poland is in trouble again. Our two friends are restless. The situation is so urgent that they have even called upon the senior citizens like this specimen before you. . . ."

Polite laughter for Paul's overcritical estimation of himself. Although balding and sporting a scholar's stooped shoulders, Paul Bronski had sharp and handsome features.

"Despite the blunder of the High Command in calling me into the army, I predict that Poland will somehow survive."

In the back of the auditorium, Dr. Franz Koenig stood motionless, looking into the sea of faces. Bronski's leaving filled him with an exhilaration he had never known. His long, patient wait was almost over.

"I leave this university both heavy-hearted and joyous. The prospect of war is enormously real and it saddens me. But I am content for the things that we have done here together and I am happy because I leave so many friends."

Koenig didn't even hear the rest of it. They would all be dripping tears, he knew. Bronski had that facility to put a tremor in his throat that never failed to move the recipients of his milky words.

They were all standing now, and unabashed tears flowed down young cheeks and even grizzly old cheeks of professors in a sloppy indulgence of sentiment as they sang school songs and anthems, which sounded like school songs and anthems everywhere.

Look at Bronski! Engulfed by his adoring staff. Shaking hands, slapping backs until the end. The "beloved" Bronski. "The University of Warsaw without Paul Bronski is not the University of Warsaw." "Your office will remain untouched until you return to us."

Your office, Koenig thought. *Your* office, indeed.

Dr. Paul Bronski, the "beloved" Paul Bronski, had finished the last of his instructions, dictated the last of his letters, and dismissed his weeping secretary with an affectionate buss.

He was alone now.

He looked about the room. Paneled walls covered with the symbols of achievement that one would gather as the head of a great medical college. Diplomas and awards and photos of students and classes. A billboard of glory.

He shoved the final batch of papers into his brief case. All that was left was a photo of Deborah and the children on his desk. He slid that into the top drawer and locked it. And he was done.

A soft, almost apologetic knock on the door.

"Come in."

Dr. Franz Koenig entered. The little gray-haired man with the little gray mustache advanced timidly to the edge of the desk. "We have been together for a long time, Paul. Words fail me."

Paul Bronski was amused. A magnificently understated phrase . . . a lovely play on words. Dr. Koenig was a humorless man who could never believe his sincerity was doubted.

"Franz, I'm going to recommend you fill my office——"

"No one can fill——"

"Nonsense . . ."

And more garble . . . and another farewell.

Franz Koenig waited in his own office across the hall until Paul left, and then he re-entered. His eyes became fixed on the leather chair behind Bronski's desk. He walked behind it and touched it. Yes, tomorrow he would move in and things would look good from here.

My chair . . . dean of medicine! My chair. Bronski gone. Quick-talking, teary-voiced Bronski. Ten years he had waited. The board was blinded by Bronski. They were entranced by the fact they could put a graduate of the university as the dean of medicine for the first time in six decades. That's why they chose Bronski. A whispering campaign against me because I am a German. They were so eager to make Bronski the dean, they even closed their eyes to the fact that he is a Jew.

Franz went to his own office again and got his homburg and tucked his cane over his arm and walked in his half trot down the long corridor. The students nodded and doffed their caps as he sped by.

He approached the big ornate wrought-iron gates. A knot of students blocked his way. For a moment everyone stood still, then the knot dissolved and he passed through, feeling their eyes on him.

How differently they reacted these days, he thought. No longer the vague indifference. He was a man to be respected, even feared. Fear me? The thought delighted him.

Even his fat, nagging Polish wife behaved differently nowadays.

He walked away from the three ponderous main buildings of the university, continuing the fast pace in rhythm to his tapping cane in the direction of Pilsudski Square.

He was happy today. He even made an attempt to whistle. The end of a long, long journey was at hand.

Like most of the million ethnic Germans, Franz Koenig had been born in western Poland in a territory formerly German-occupied, then freed to Poland after the World War. In his youth his family moved to Danzig, which was located in a geographical freak known as the "Polish Corridor." It was a finger of land which split East Prussia away from the German mainland in order to give Poland access to the sea. It was an abnormal division. Danzig and the Polish Corridor filled with ethnic Germans and Poles became a thorn in German pride and the object of bickering and threats from the beginning.

Franz Koenig came from a good merchant family. He had received a classical education in medicine in Heidelberg and in Switzerland. He was a man of total moderation. Although raised in the furor of Danzig, he considered himself neither German nor Polish nor much of anything but a good doctor and teacher; a profession, he felt, that crossed the bounds of nationalism.

Franz Koenig was an adequate man. His appointment to the University of Warsaw was adequate. The Polish girl he had married was adequate. He lived his life in a mild and inoffensive manner, delighting most in the privacy of his study with good music and good books. The early marriage ambitions of his Polish wife failed to stir him. She gave up in disgust and grew obese.

When the Nazis came to power, Franz Koenig was embarrassed by their behavior. In an outburst, rare for him, he referred to the SA Brown Shirts as "thick-necked, pin-headed bullies." He thought himself fortunate to be in Warsaw and clear of the havoc in Germany.

All that changed.

There was a month, a week, a day, and a moment.

The office of dean of the College of Medicine was open. By seniority, competence, and devotion, the position was his. In anticipation of the appointment which should have been routine, he constructed a dull but adequate speech to accept the chair. He never delivered the speech. Paul Bronski, fifteen years his junior, was appointed.

He remembered Kurt Liedendorf, the leader of Warsaw's ethnics, snorting in his ear.

"It's a blow to us—all us Germans, Doktor Koenig. It is a terrible insult."

"Nonsense . . . nonsense . . . "

"Now maybe you understand how the Versailles Treaty has made the German people anonymous. Look, you . . . Heidelberg . . . Geneva. A man of culture. You have been made anonymous too. You are a victim of Jewish cunning. All us Germans are victims of Jewish cunning, Herr Doktor. . . . Hitler says . . ."

18

Jewish cunning . . . Bronski . . . Jewish cunning . . .

All that Franz Koenig ever wanted for a world he served well was to be the dean of medicine at the University of Warsaw.

"Come and spend the afternoon with us, Herr Doktor. Be with your own people," Kurt Liedendorf said. "We have a special guest from Berlin who will give us a talk."

And the guest from Berlin told them, "Perhaps the methods of the Nazis are harsh, but to rectify injustices heaped upon the German people takes men of strong will and vigor. Everything we do is justified because the goal to restore the German people to their rightful way of life is justified."

"Ah, Herr Doktor," Liedendorf said, "Good to see you here. Sit here, sit up front."

"Hitler has seen to it that the German people are not anonymous any more. If you declare yourself as a German, you will not be anonymous!"

He came home from the fourth meeting, and the fifth and the sixth, and he looked at his fat Polish wife and all that was around him. Feudal gentry, universal ignorance. "I am a German," Franz Koenig said to himself. "I am a German."

"Doktor Koenig, you should see it in Danzig. Thousands and thousands of Germans fighting for the Führer. Letting the world know that we will not be abused any more."

How proud he was of the deliverance of the Germans from Austria and Czechoslovakia!

"I've been thinking of it deeply, Liedendorf. I want to join in this work."

He walked along the edge of the Saxony Gardens, past the blocks of government buildings and palaces and art museums. All this granite and marble were not of his sinew. In the beer halls, in the homes of his own people, German people, was where he belonged. Here Dr. Franz Koenig was a respected man. Here they spoke of great things without shame or fear.

He stopped before the Square of the Iron Gates just beyond the Saxony Gardens.

A sickening odor of half-rotted vegetables, unwashed peasants, squalling chickens, haggling, screaming barterers and beggars, and a thousand pushcarts pleaded for the zloty in the most primitive form of trade.

"Used neckties, good as new!"

"Pencils!"

"Buy from me!"

Old women squatted on the cobblestones with a few eggs, thieves and pickpockets roamed about, and lines of pushcarts dangled secondhand shoes and greasy jackets. The noise of the iron rims of the carts roared and echoed over the square.

"Buy from me!"

19

Bearded Jews, bearded Paul Bronskis, argued endlessly to save a half zloty in hand-waving Yiddish, a language cruelly butchering the beautiful German tongue.

A drunken soldier was hurled from a café and fell at Koenig's feet.

Drunk as a Pole—that is what they say, Koenig thought. Drunk as a Pole. Such fitting words.

All of Poland had passed before him in two short squares. How wrong is Hitler's disgust of the Slavs? A nation of thirty million people with only two million newspaper readers. A nation of feudal lords and serfs in this, the twentieth century. A nation which worshiped a black madonna as African Zulus prayed to sun gods.

This was Poland to Franz Koenig. Five per cent Paris, walled behind marble mansions and ruling decadence. Ninety-five per cent Ukrainia . . . abominable ignorance.

What could the good industrious German folk have done with the fertile flat lands and the bursting mineral deposits of Silesia?

"Buy from me!"

Who was this mass of dirty people with their childlike mentality to hold back the German people, who had contributed more to the world's enrichment and knowledge than any other race?

Franz Koenig knew that no matter what small injustices the Nazis perpetrated the final result of a greater Germany justified the means.

Koenig circumvented the confusion of the market place and entered Hans Schultz's bar.

Schultz smiled. *"Guten Tag, Herr Doktor, Guten Tag."*

"Hello, Schultz. Anything new?"

"Ja. Herr Liedendorf is unable to come out these days. He said that our work is done and you should stay home and wait."

Dr. Koenig downed his beer and nodded to Schultz, who smiled as he wiped the bar.

In a few moments he entered his flat and put his hat neatly on the rack and placed his cane directly below it. He looked at his fat Polish wife, whose mouth was sucking in and out like a puckered fish, and he could not hear what she was saying. She walked and her flesh wobbled.

He envisioned her in the bed, which sagged on one side because of her immensity, and he saw her flabby buttocks and her hanging breasts.

Koenig walked to his study and slammed the door behind him.

He turned on the radio. It was always set now on Radio Deutschland.

A rally from Hamburg!

"We Germans cannot tolerate the outrageous treatment of our citizens in Poland, where German women and children are unsafe

20

from Polish vandals . . . where German men are beaten and murdered!"

"*Sieg Heil! Sieg Heil! Sieg Heil!*"

And soon ten thousand voices shattered the air waves, singing
"Deutschland über Alles," and Dr. Franz Koenig closed his eyes
and tears fell down his cheeks, just as they had fallen down the
cheeks of his students.

And he prayed that his liberators would be coming soon.

Chapter Four

Journal Entry

*Wonderful news! Andrei came home on leave unexpectedly! We
of the Bathyran Zionist Executive Council have a lot of things to
talk over and decide. With Andrei here it will give us a chance to
get together.*

ALEXANDER BRANDEL

The army truck came to a halt before the northernmost bridge
that spanned the Vistula River from Warsaw to Praga. Captain
Andrei Androfski hopped out of the cab, thanked the driver, and
walked along the river toward the new northern suburb of Zoliborz.
He tilted back the four-cornered cap worn by officers of the crack
Ulany regiments and he whistled as he walked and received and
returned the smiles and flirtations of young lady strollers. Captain
Andrei Androfski indeed cut the classic figure of an Ulan cavalry
officer. His leather shone, and the short stiletto at his side glinted
when the sun caught it.

He turned away from the river and into a tree-lined street of
lovely new homes in an area stamped with upper-middle-class
wealth. Andrei spotted a large stone on the sidewalk and began to
dribble it with his feet with the dexterity of a trained soccer player,
his leg muscles fairly rippling through his trousers. He gave the
stone a final swift kick of the boot, speeding it down the street
toward an imaginary goal, and turned at the gate of Dr. Paul
Bronski's house.

"Uncle Andrei!" shouted ten-year-old Stephan as he sprinted
over the lawn and leaped on his uncle's back.

"Schmendrick!"

The two "clashed," and the big cavalry officer was "thrown" to
the ground, apparently no match for his eighty-pound nephew. He
surrendered gallantly, got to his feet, and lifted the victor on his
shoulders.

21

"How is Batory?"

"Batory! The finest, the most beautiful, and the most fierce animal in all of Poland."

"What has he done lately, Uncle Andrei?"

"Lately! This week—well, let me see. I took him to England for the Grand National, and he ran so fast he split the air and caused it to thunder. Well sir, those Englishmen thought it was raining and ran for cover and didn't even see the race. Batory lapped the field four times and was coming up for the fifth time when the second fastest horse crossed the finish line. And those stupid Englishmen who were hiding in the stands thought Batory finished last."

"Who takes care of Batory when you are gone?"

"First Sergeant Styka, personally!"

"I wish I could ride him again," Stephan said, recalling the most thrilling incident of his young life.

"You will, just as soon as we clear up some things."

"Can I jump him this time?"

"Yes, I think so. That is, if heights don't make you too dizzy. When Batory jumps, the world below becomes very small. As a matter of fact, I don't enter him in jumping races any more. Batory jumps so high, the other horses are around the track before he comes down."

Andrei walked to the house.

"Uncle Andrei!" cried Rachael Bronski. This meeting was devoid of the previous violence, for the voice belonged to an elegant black-eyed fourteen-year-old young lady whose greeting was limited to an affectionate hug.

"Andrei!" cried Deborah, running in from the kitchen, wiping her hands. She flung her arms around her brother's neck. "You devil. Why didn't you let us know you were coming?"

"I only knew myself last night. Besides, I want to stay clear of Alexander Brandel. He'll call one of those damned meetings."

"How long?"

"Four whole days."

"How wonderful!"

Andrei lifted Stephan from his shoulders as though he were weightless.

"What did you bring me?" Stephan demanded.

"Stephan, shame!" his sister reprimanded.

Andrei winked and stretched his arms out. Stephan began fishing through his uncle's pockets, which had been an unfailing source of booty from his earliest memory. He withdrew a gilded Polish eagle, the insignia whose two spread wings held up the front corner of the Ulany cap.

"Mine?" with apprehension.

"Yours."

22

"Wow!" and Stephan was gone to alert the neighborhood that his great Uncle Andrei was home.

"And for my beautiful niece."

"You spoil them."

"Do me something."

The girl's fingers quickly worked the ribbon open.

"Oh! Oh!" She hugged him and raced to the mirror to fix the pair of ivory combs into thick black hair which was just like her mother's.

"She's beautiful," Andrei said.

"Boys are already starting to look at her."

"What do you mean? What boys?"

Deborah laughed. "She won't be a wallflower like her mother."

Rachel walked to her uncle, whom she adored, and kissed his cheek. "Thank you, Uncle Andrei."

"My reward, please," Andrei said, pointing to the piano.

Rachel played her mood. A bubbling étude. Andrei watched a moment, then Deborah took his hand and led him toward the kitchen. He stopped at the door again. "She plays like an angel— like you used to play."

Deborah shooed Zoshia, the housekeeper, out and set on some water for tea. Andrei sprawled and loosened his tunic. It smelled good in the kitchen. Deborah had been baking cookies. It was like the old flat on Sliska Street on the day before Sabbath. Deborah took off Andrei's cap and ran her fingers through the array of curly blond hair.

"My baby brother."

She set before him a large platter of cookies, which were half finished by the time she poured the tea. He took a long sip. "This is good, this is good. Sergeant Styka brews a lousy tea."

"How are things on the border, Andrei?"

Andrei shrugged. "How should I know? They don't consult me. Ask Smigly-Rydz."

"Be serious."

"Seriously. I'm home for four days——"

"We're all worried sick."

"All right, the German concentrations are very, very heavy. Let me give you an opinion, Deborah. As long as Hitler gets what he wants by bluffing, fine. Well, he isn't bluffing Poland and he may damned well back down."

"Paul has been called up."

Andrei uncrossed his legs. The mention of Paul Bronski struck an obvious note of discord. "I'm sorry to hear that," he said quickly. "I didn't think——"

"None of us did," Deborah said. She walked to the sink and began rolling the thin dough for more cookies. "Have you seen Gabriela yet?"

23

"I came directly here. She is probably still working."

"Why don't you two come to dinner tonight?"

"If Brandel doesn't find me first."

"Try to make it. Christopher de Monti will be over."

"How is my boy Chris?"

"He has been terribly busy since the crisis. We haven't seen him for several weeks," she said, rolling the dough at a furious pace.

Andrei walked up behind his sister, turned her around by the shoulders, and tried to lift her chin so she would look at him. Deborah shook her head and spun away.

"Please don't dream things up between Chris and me."

"Just old friends?"

"Just old friends."

"Does Paul know?"

"There's nothing to know!"

"Did you raise me for an idiot?"

"Andrei, please . . . please, we have enough to worry about these days. And for God's sake, don't pick an argument with Paul."

"Who argues with Paul? He always——"

"I swear, if you two get into another fight——"

Andrei gulped down his tea, stuffed a half dozen cookies into his pocket, and buttoned his tunic.

"Please promise me you'll get along with Paul tonight. He's going away. Do it for me."

Andrei grunted, came up behind Deborah, and gave her a brisk slap on the backside. "See you later," he said.

Andrei Androfski stretched lazily on a park bench on the edge of the Lazienki Gardens facing the American Embassy. The statue of Frédéric Chopin hovered above him, patronized by the local pigeons, and the Belvedere Palace of the former Marshal Pilsudski was immersed in the greenery behind him. It was a nice place to laze. He engaged in his favorite pastime of undressing the female pedestrians with his eyes. He dug into his pocket and found the last of Deborah's cookies and munched.

After a while the main door of the Embassy opened. Gabriela Rak came out and walked up the embassy-lined Aleja Ujazdowska. He caught up to her by the time she reached the first intersection. Sensing a masher behind her, Grabriela stepped quickly from the curb.

"Madam," Andrei said, "would you kindly give me the name of that fortunate young lady who owns the heart of the most dashing officer in the Ulanys?"

She stopped in the middle of the street.

"Andrei? Andrei!" And she spun into his arms. The traffic policeman raised his hand, sending a flood of vehicles swirling around them. They dodged and honked their horns with the irritated understanding one gives to a soldier and his girl kissing in the middle of a street. At last an unpatriotic taxi driver shouted that they were a pair of jackasses and sent them scurrying to the safety of a park bench across the way.

"Oh, Andrei," she said, and lay her head on his chest. "Oh, Andrei," and she sniffled.

"If I knew that I was going to make you so sad, I wouldn't have returned."

She dried her eyes and purred with contentment. "How long?"

"Four days."

"Oh, I'm so happy."

"I almost had to find another woman for myself. I thought you would never get out of the Embassy."

Gabriela toyed with his large hand, which nearly made two of hers. "I've just been in a meeting. We aren't reopening the American school. All the children have been evacuated to Krakow. Even some of the key personnel are leaving."

Andrei grumbled something about the traditional cowardice of Americans.

"Let's not talk about it now," she said. "We only have ninety-six hours, and look at the time we have already wasted. We can't go to my place. I had it repainted. It smells terrible. I didn't know you were coming home."

"And if we go to my place, Alexander Brandel and the whole damned executive council will be camping at the doorstep."

"Let's risk it," Gabriela said with a low-voiced tremor of want that sent her captain to the curb in search of a droshka.

They drove north past the imposing mansions of the "new rich" on the Avenue of the Marshals. Gabriela snuggled against him, her fingers feeling his face and shoulders.

Andrei's flat on Leszno Street sat in a middle-class neighborhood that buffered the rich on the south from the wild slums on the north. They climbed the stairs towards his tiny flat, arms about each other. By the time they reached the third-floor landing, Gabriela stopped to catch her breath.

"My next lover has to live on the ground floor," she said.

Andrei swept her up in his arms and tossed her over a shoulder like a sack of sugar.

"Put me down, you crazy fool!"

He emitted a bloodcurdling cavalry charge and leaped up the final flight of stairs two steps at a time, kicked open his never-locked door, then stood in amazement with Gabriela trying to squirm off his shoulder.

Andrei's eyes went from corner to corner around the flat. He peeked into the kitchen, then looked around again, wondering if he had invaded the wrong apartment. The place was spotlessly clean. For years he had carefully strewn his books and papers about. His

25

desk was always three inches deep in reports. All the wonderful clutter, all the carefully preserved dust—all of the things that make a man a bachelor—were gone.

Andrei kicked open the closet door. Everything pressed and hanging neatly.

The kitchen . . . All those lovely unwashed dishes washed.

There were curtains, lace curtains, at the windows.

"I've been evicted!" Andrei cried. "No, something more horrible than that has happened. A female has been here!"

"Andrei, if you don't put me down I'll scream rape."

He lowered her to the floor.

"I think you owe me an explanation," he said.

"I'd sit in my place night after night waiting for Batory to charge down the street bearing my Ulan warrior. All alone with my ten black cats and my memories. And I came here and sat because you were all around me and I wasn't quite so lonely. But who can sit in such a mess?"

"I know your type, Gabriela Rak. You're going to try to make me over."

"Oh, you know it!"

She leaped at him, and he caught her off the floor and held her and sank his lips into hers. And in a moment Andrei had no more talk to make. They were bringing each other from smoldering dormancy with an urgency that heightened every second.

The phone rang.

It stuck them like a knife. They froze.

It rang again.

"Son of a bitch, Brandel."

It rang again.

"Let it ring, darling," she said.

And it did . . . again and again and again.

Gabriela spun away from him, teary-eyed. "It has eyes, that phone. It never rang the whole time you were gone."

"Well, maybe I'd better answer."

"Oh, you might as well. Every Bathyran in Warsaw knows that Andrei Androfski is home on leave."

He snatched the phone from the hook. "Is that you, you son of a bitch, Brandel?"

A soft voice answered on the other end. "Of course it's me, Andrei. You've been in town for three hours and twenty minutes. Are you snubbing your old friends?"

"Alex, do me something. Go to hell," he said, and slammed the receiver down. The instant he did, he lifted it again and dialed Brandel's number.

"Andrei?"

"I'll call you later. Tell the gang I'm anxious to see them."

26

"I hope I didn't break anything up. Have a nice time. Good Shabes."

Andrei walked to the edge of the bed, where Gabriela sulked. He leaned over and put his lips into her honey hair, and she closed her eyes, reveling in the sensations his touch caused. Andrei went to the window and pulled down the shade, plunging the room into dusk, and he locked the door.

"Don't be angry, Gaby. I didn't know about your place. I would have gotten a hotel room. Don't be angry."

"I'm not angry," she whispered.

They lay beside each other, luxuriating in teasing and touching and whispering.

Suddenly Gabriela broke into a sweat and she was no longer able to control herself. "Oh God, I've missed you so!"

And they fought awkwardly and furiously to get out of their clothing.

The phone rang.

This time it went unanswered.

Chapter Five

Journal Entry

I think I picked the wrong time to call Andrei. Thank goodness his temper goes down as fast as it rises.

I talked to banker friends this evening. Everyone is frantic to convert their securities to American dollars or Swiss and South American bonds. Whole estates are being liquidated.

With the Russian-German alliance a fact, the German propaganda has gone utterly insane with charges of Polish border violations and maltreatment of ethnic Germans.

Meanwhile, why do we keep a deaf ear to England's and France's pleadings that we negotiate for help from Russia? Does our General Staff really think we can beat the Germans?

ALEXANDER BRANDEL

Dr. Paul Bronski filled the large brown envelope with a number of legal and financial papers. There was a will, insurance policies, a variety of securities, some cash in large denominations, and a key to his safe-deposit box. Finally a sealed letter. He scrawled the words, "In the event of my death," and put the letter in with the other papers, wet the flap, and rolled it stuck.

In the dining room, young Rachel Bronski pranced about the table helping the large and rapidly aging Zoshia put the finishing

27

touches on a lush setting. The table was overburdened with heavy silverware and gold-rimmed porcelain.

Rachel touched the flowers in the centerpiece and made them just so.

In his study, Paul Bronski listened to the BBC.

"In an exclusive interview with Polish Marshal Smigly-Rydz, Christopher de Monti of the Swiss News Agency, in a story date-lined Warsaw, said that the Polish position remains as always—no thought of a mutual-aid treaty with the Soviet Union. Later BBC confirmed this seemingly unshakable policy in a news con-ference with Poland's Foreign Minister Beck. Poland's adamance is viewed as bringing war one step closer."

Deborah, putting the finishing touches on herself, entered the study. Paul placed the envelope face down, turned off the news, and smiled at his wife. In their sixteen years of marriage she had never failed to make herself attractive. No man could ask for a more perfect mate for his career.

"You look lovely," he said.

"Thank you, dear," she said. "Paul . . . please try to stay out of an argument with Andrei tonight."

"Andrei makes that difficult at times."

"Please."

"You've got my assurance. Get your brother's."

"I think for the children's sake—and—well, it should be special tonight."

The doorbell rang. Rachel answered. "Hello, Chris, come in."

"You look more like your mother every day."

Rachel blushed. "Momma and Daddy are in the study. Go on in."

Paul and Deborah stood and looked at the door as Chris came through. Then Deborah studiously avoided his eyes. "It's been a long time, Chris," she said.

He nodded. Paul shook his hand, and for the moment the fear of that first moment of the meeting subsided.

"Would you excuse me?" she said. "I've got to see to dinner. I'll be back with cocktails."

Paul offered Chris a seat, then returned to his desk and loaded his pipe. "I've been listening to the news," he said. "I hear you got with the old man."

"Seems strange keeping this position with the clock running out."

"Both Russia and Germany have pushed us around for cen-turies. There's actually little to choose between them. Well, the hell with it. Chris, we've missed you. How have you been?"

"Running."

Much of the tension in Chris had eased. The warm welcome, the small talk. Either Paul was totally ignorant or expedient. Or he was playing some sort of game with great skill. Whatever it was, Paul did not want an ugly scene, and that was a relief.

"I'm leaving tomorrow," Paul said abruptly. "Been called up. More than likely I'll be stationed with the surgeon general's staff in Krakow—paper work. Been so long since I practised medicine, I begged off line duty for the sake of the army. Works out well, they need administrative help."

Chris was both glad and sorry at the pronouncement. Nagging thoughts buzzed around inside him. "See here, Paul," he wanted to say, "Deborah and I love each other very much. It's nothing we planned . . . just happened. I want you to give her her freedom."

The words never found their way beyond nagging thoughts. How can you say to a man who is leaving for war, "I want your wife. Incidentally, have a nice time at the front"?

Why did Paul Bronski have to be such a decent sort? That's what made it so damned lousy. Bronski was a wonderful person. And any desire Chris had to create a scene suddenly melted.

"Chris, you and I haven't known each other tremendously long as some friendships go. You know how it is. With some people you work with them all your life—like myself and Dr. Koenig—and never really know them. Another man can walk into a room and in ten minutes you become friends—real friends. I think you and I are that kind."

"I hope so, Paul."

"I've been a very lucky man. In addition to my position and my family, my father left me a considerable estate which I have been able to enlarge." Paul slid the brown envelope across the desk.

"If something should happen to me . . ." he continued.

"Oh, come now."

"Good friends don't have to make small talk, Chris. Poland doesn't have a chance, does it?"

"No—not really."

"Even if I do get through, which I certainly anticipate, they're going to make it hard on us. With your connections and freedom of movement and with the possibility of an occupied Poland, you are in the best position of anyone I know to convert my estate into Swiss or American holdings."

Chris took the envelope and nodded.

"You'll find everything in order."

"I'll take care of it right away. I have a friend leaving for Bern next week. He can be trusted. Any preference in investments?"

"German munitions seem like a good bet."

They both laughed.

"My bank is good and conservative. They'll know the answers," Chris said.

29

"Good. Well . . . you hold all my fortunes. One more thing. If anything should happen to me, I know you will see to it that Deborah and the children are taken out of Poland."

Chris's mouth went dry. All the rest of it was what one friend does for another. But this seemed as though he were willing Deborah to him. Chris looked into Paul's implacable eyes. Revealing, yet not revealing. If he really knew, he had carried it quietly. He had veiled the pain it must have caused. But isn't this the way Paul Bronski would do things? He was a gentle man as well as a shrewd man. Wouldn't he have thought it out and already forgiven both Deborah and him? Or maybe Chris was overdramatizing everything. Perhaps Paul did feel their friendship deep enough to ask this.

Nothing Paul said or did gave the slightest clue to what was really behind his expression.

Chris folded the envelope and put it in his inside pocket. Deborah entered with two glasses of sherry for herself and Paul and a martini for Chris.

"You two look so grim."

"Chris was explaining the meaning of the news to me, dear."

"Rachel is playing the piano. Come on into the parlor."

They stood around the piano, Paul obviously glorying in the extraordinary talent of his daughter. It was the same melody that was coming over the radio.

Chris felt himself back in bed looking at Deborah's body. Paderewski . . . Chopin . . . a nocturne . . .

Deborah lowered her eyes as her daughter's slender fingers danced over the keys. And Chris lowered his.

Paul looked from one to the other. "Why don't you play, dear?" he said to his wife.

She breathed deeply and slipped beside Rachel and took up the bass. There they were, Deborah and Rachel, beauty and beauty.

The mood of the moment was shattered by a bombastic roar at the door. Uncle Andrei had arrived. He had a second round of battle with Stephan and this time decided to lift fat old Zoshia off the ground and dance her around the anteroom.

"Chris!" he roared, belting de Monti in the back so that he lost half his martini.

Gabriela, filled with the weary happiness of love-making, drifted in almost unseen behind the roaring Ulan. "Keep playing! Keep playing!" ordered Captain Androfski.

Never known as a man adept in stifling emotions, he greeted Paul Bronski in a way that left little doubt of the iciness that existed between them. The words they exchanged testified they were straining for effect for Deborah's sake.

"I hear you've been called up, Paul."

"Yes, they're really scraping the bottom of the barrel."

"No," Andrei retorted, "you'll do a good job for them. You always do a good job."

"Why, thank you, brother-in-law."

There were "ohs" and "ahs" regarding the beauty of the table from Gabriela, Chris, and Paul when dinner was called. Andrei looked up and down for something that was not there. He caught an angry signal from his sister and only then did he seat himself in sulking quiet.

It was a splendid meal, one particularly made to please Andrei. During the gefilte fish and horse-radish the conversation bemoaned the state of the theater in Warsaw. The best plays, always French, were slow reaching Warsaw this summer because of the crisis. Gabriela volunteered that the opera season would suffer too. Rachel hoped that the music would not be affected too much, and Deborah hoped so too, because if things went well the conservatory was going to let Rachel have her debut with a major orchestra.

The chicken soup was loaded with noodles. They talked about the Olympics. Stephan knew almost every statistic. Jesse Owens was great—but Uncle Andrei, who played forward on the Polish soccer team, was greater than Jesse Owens and the rest of the Americans put together. Where would Andrei play this year? Depended upon his situation with the army.

Roast chicken, stuffed helsel and noodle and raisin kugel. Chris reckoned he hadn't had a good Jewish meal in months—he was glad Paul had talked him into coming. Gabriela asked for recipes, which Deborah promised to supply by phone next day. Stephan got restless.

Tea and rice pudding. Reflections of the university. Koenig to the dean's chair? Isn't he mixed up with the Nazis? Well, German or not, Franz Koenig was certainly entitled to the post.

Cognac. Rachel helped Zoshia clear the table. Stephan, who had lost all conversation before and after the Olympics discussion, disappeared.

And then, with the children gone, world politics.

All of this conversation, and Andrei Androfski had not uttered a word.

"Chris, Gabriela," Paul Bronski said, "we have all endured the silent wrath of my brother-in-law, Captain Androfski. Fortunately it was not great enough to ruin my wife's cooking. In his behalf I wish to ask forgiveness for his bad manners."

"I agree with you, Dr. Bronski," Gabriela said hastily. "Your behavior is shameful, Andrei."

Andrei, suddenly exposed, grumbled a low rumble destined to increase in volume. "I promised my sister no arguments. I keep my promises despite the inconveniences it causes me."

"I think it would have been better to argue and get it off your chest rather than sulk like Stephan and try to make everyone at the table as miserable as you," Paul shot back.

"You promised, Paul. Stop baiting him," Deborah said.

"Let Captain Androfski speak before he explodes."

"Paul, you're leaving in the morning. Let's not have an argument tonight," Deborah pleaded.

"Why, dear? Don't you want me to remember home as it always is?"

"I am a man of my word," Andrei said. "But I also remember my home as it always was. Friday night and I sit at my sister's table and there are no candles or benediction."

"Is that what has been bothering you, brother-in-law?"

"Yes, it is the Sabbath."

"We stopped facing east a year ago, Andrei."

"Oh, I knew it was coming. I didn't know you could break her down so quickly. I remember when we lived in the slums on Stawki Street. God, we were poor. But we were Jews. And when we moved to that fancy neighborhood on Sliska Street and Momma died, I had a sister then who was the head of a Jewish house."

"Andrei, let's stop this here and now," Deborah said.

Chris and Gabriela were suddenly trapped in the midst of the flying words of a family feud. They looked helplessly at each other as Andrei sprang to his feet and slammed his napkin down.

"Dr. Bronski started this. Not I. Deborah, I sat with Stephan and talked to him. He does not even know he is a Jew. What happens when he becomes thirteen? Your only son not given a bar mitzvah. I'm glad Momma and Poppa are not alive to see this day."

Paul Bronski seemed to be delighted in having opened Andrei up. "Deborah and I have been married sixteen years. Isn't it about time you got onto the idea we wish to live our own lives without consultation from you?"

"Paul, I am Andrei Androfski, the only Jewish officer in my Ulany regiment. But every man knows who I am and what I am."

"I am Dr. Paul Bronski and they know who I am too. Just a minute, Andrei. I explored your galloping Zionism. It isn't my way to salvation. It didn't appeal to me either."

"And your name didn't appeal to you either, did it, Paul? Samuel Goldfarb. Son of a Parysowski Place peddler."

"You are so right, Andrei. Nothing about Parysowski Place appeals to me. Not its poverty or its smells or the weeping and wailing, waiting for the Messiah to come. The Jews are the ones who have caused their own troubles in Poland, and I want to live in my country as an equal, not as an enemy or a stranger."

"And does that justify your sitting on the council of the Students' Union, those dirty little fascists who throw stones through the windows of Jewish booksellers?"

"I didn't back those actions."

"Nor did you try to stop them. You know why? Well, I'll tell you. You follow a coward's path."

"How dare you!" Deborah said.

"It is you who is the coward and not I, Andrei, because I have enough courage to say that Judaism means nothing to me and I want no part of it. And you go to your holy-roller Zionist meetings not believing what you hear, looking for false salvation."

The words rained down on Andrei like blows. Paul had struck a nerve and his foe turned white and trembled and the room grew breathlessly quiet, waiting for that short fuse to sizzle to the bomb. But Andrei spoke in a deliberate, trembling rattle. "You are a fool, Paul Bronski. Being a Jew is not a matter of choice. And one sweet day soon, I fear, it will crash down on you and destroy all your logic and smart talk. God, you're in for a rude awakening, because you are a Jew, whether you want to be or choose to be—or not."

"Stop it!" Deborah screamed. "This is my home. You will never do this again if you want to set foot in here, nor will you ever see Stephan or Rachel. Paul is my husband. You will respect him."

Andrei hung his head. "I—should do something about my temper," he said softly. "I have caused a scene in front of guests. Why should I care, really, so long as you are happy?"

"I am happy," Deborah said.

"It is only . . . Your words—and your eyes do not march to the same tune."

Andrei walked from the table quickly.

"Andrei!" Deborah called. "Where are you going?"

"To drink. To drink and drink and drink to Dr. Paul Bronski, the king of the converts!"

Deborah started after him. Gabriela quickly stepped from the table and blocked her way. "Let him go, Deborah," she said. "He is all wound up like a piece of spring steel from the tension on the border. You know Andrei, he will be here tomorrow with apologies. Let him go."

The slam of the front door resounded like a cannon shot throughout the house.

"Chris, keep an eye on him, please," Gabriela said.

Chris nodded and followed without a word.

When Chris was gone, Deborah sank into her chair, ashen-faced.

Paul Bronski, feeling contented as a Cheshire cat, soothed, "Don't let him hurt you so, dear."

Deborah looked up through tear-filled eyes. "He knew . . . he knew. And that is what hurts. My husband is going away and I wanted to light the candles tonight like a Jewish mother—and Andrei knew."

And all the cunning of Paul's traps slammed in on him in an

33

unexpected and stunning defeat and he sagged and walked toward the door.

"Paul!" Deborah ordered sharply. "See Gabriela home."

"No, that's all right, Deborah. Let's you and I have another cup of tea and then I'll find my rampaging cavalier in an hour or so. And don't you worry about Andrei—I am the one who loves him. And sometimes, dear Lord, it is almost worth the pain."

Chapter Six

The revolutionary activities of Fryderyk Rak had made it increasingly more dangerous for him to live in a Poland partitioned between Russia, Germany, and the Austro-Hungarian Empire. He went into a self-imposed exile along with many patriots. In France he established himself as one of the leading hydroelectric engineers in Europe.

After the war, in 1918, when Poland had returned to statehood, Fryderyk Rak returned to Warsaw with his wife and daughters, Regina and Gabriela. The new Poland was filled with urgent needs. A hundred years of occupation had left it in a medieval condition. Hydroelectric projects were given an urgent priority. Fryderyk Rak was one of the few Poles with training and experience to cope with the challenge.

He gained neither great wealth nor fame, but a fair measure of each. His most impressive contribution was the part his firm of engineers played in the building of Gdynia. The Versailles Treaty had given new Poland a route to the sea through the Polish Corridor. The only port at the time was Danzig, a so-called "free city" fraught with political dynamite and largely inhabited by unfriendly Germans. Common sense made the building of a Polish seaport a necessity and thus Gydnia was created.

In exile, he had become a rabid skiing enthusiast. With the first snowbursts of winter he would pack the Rak family off to the Alps. His doctor warned him there were slopes for thirty-year-olds and slopes for fifty-year-olds, but he indulged in his inbred stubborn Polish pride by defying the advice and finding the most dangerous, swiftest ways to get down the mountainsides. He died at the age of fifty from a heart attack at the bottom of a treacherous run called K-94, aptly nicknamed "the butcher," and left behind him a well-endowed widow and her two daughters.

In her bereavement, Madam Rak turned to the comfort of her only close living relative, a brother in Chicago. She came out of her period of mourning well stocked with suitors of Polish descent and saw little reason to return to the old country, never having shared

Fryderyk's passion for it. Regina, the oldest daughter, was a rather plain, rather plump girl who was completely content to marry a nice Polish boy whose family imported Polish hams and become an American housewife with a home in Evanston, within gossiping distance of Mother.

Gabriela, the youngest, was of her father's breed; independent, stubborn, and self-centered. Fryderyk Rak had been a liberal man and an indulgent father. Her uncle, however, had taken his position as head of the family and protector of his widowed sister and her offspring with complete seriousness. He had brought with him from Poland much of the old-country traditions of family tyrant. Gabriela rebelled. Warsaw and life with Father were her happiest memories. She received an impressive education from stern nuns in expensive and exclusive Catholic girls' schools, where she prayed each night that the Virgin Mother would help her get back to Warsaw.

As soon as she was of legal age and came into her part of the inheritance, she made straight back. Gabriela's mastery of English, French, German, and Polish and her American education brought her a job with the American Embassy as a teacher. Later she became a nearly indispensable member of the staff and was the only Polish national permitted to work on classified material.

The allowance from her father's estate and her job allowed her to enter that upper echelon of society which had made Warsaw the Paris of the East. There was a never-ending circle of culture and trivia and romance. Gabriela was an extremely pretty girl. Her calendar never lacked for dates. She was a classic Polish beauty with white-blond hair and sparkling blue eyes, but a smaller, petite version.

Like many world travelers, she developed a great degree of sophistication, enjoying flirtations and being romanced. Every few months there was a proposal of marriage to weigh and discard. Gabriela enjoyed her freedom. She measured her relationships with a rather cold-blooded shrewdness. She was content in Warsaw. This was the place—it always was. She realized that she would eventually find the man to go with the place, but life was good and she was in no hurry. Her only indiscretion had been a forgivable girlhood fling with an instructor whose after-school instructions were unforgivable.

When Gabriela left the Bronski house, she began her search for Andrei and Chris at Jerusalem Boulevard, knowing that neither of them did any serious drinking south of there. She checked newsmen's and Zionists' hangouts until she picked up their trail. Once on the scent, she quickened her search, as they had left their calling cards in the form of two medium-sized disturbances and one tiny brawl.

She entered the Bristol Hotel and made straight for the little bar inside the entrance of the night club. A new South American band was playing the latest tangos. Tangos were all the rage now. Perhaps, Gabriela thought, if Andrei is not too far gone, I can bring him back here to dance. He is such a lovely dancer when he wants to be.

She adjusted her eyes to the darkness and warded off the advance of a lone male in a crisp, authoritative voice.

"Yes, ma'am," the bartender said, "they sure were here. Left about a half hour ago."

"In what condition?"

"Soused. Mr. de Monti a little worse off than his officer friend."

Well, there go my tangos, Gabriela thought.

"Any idea of where they were going?"

"Mr. de Monti usually likes to cap off his benders in the Old Town. Says he likes to drink in Polish folklore."

Gabriela stopped for a moment in the lobby and stared into the ballroom. It was filled with elegant Polish officers in uniform and elegant ladies in the latest Paris gowns and bearded, beribboned diplomats. It was a high-ceilinged room with dark mahogany paneling twisted into ornate gingerbread and herringbone parquet floors polished to a dazzle. Floor-to-ceiling mirrors alternated with floor-to-ceiling tapestries depicting grim Polish heroes on statuesque white horses with billowing manes leading determined troops into battle. The immense crystal chandelier sparkled, and the elegant ladies and gentlemen hopped around the room in a counterclockwise circle in step with a lively polka. And when the music stopped, the gentlemen bent from the waist and kissed the ladies' hands. Some responded with flirtatious eyes from behind fans and others by looking off in boredom.

It was as though Gabriela looked at two different centuries from the slinky night club to the grand ballroom. The music faded as she walked north to the Old Town. It was balmy out, and the late theater- and movie-goers wandered along arm in arm and the streetwalkers prowled for business and the droshkas rolled by, holding cuddling couples.

She stopped for a moment on the central bridge and leaned on the rail. Far below, the commuter trains loaded up and sped over the river to Praga.

Gabriela hummed the polka to herself and was soon steeped in nostalgia. It was on a warm night like this that she had met Andrei and it was in a big, brilliant ballroom. Good Lord, Gabriela thought, has it been only two years? It seemed hard to recall a life between her father's death and meeting Andrei. Only two years ... only two years.

The Seventh Ulany Brigade held its annual officers' affair at the

Europa Hotel. This was the eighth in a line of twenty-six events that illuminated the fall and winter season. The Seventh Ulanys had a particularly long string of great cavalry charges which could trace its beginnings back to the first king, Casimir the Great, in the Middle Ages. Therefore, the Seventh Ulany affair always brought out the cream of Warsaw.

Gabriela Rak, as usual, was nearly crushed by the overeager band of bachelor officers. They were particularly out of step, more pompous than the Second and Fourth Ulanys combined, and their humor less amusing than that of any regiment of the season.

At the end of the first hour of violent polkas Gabriela retreated to the sanctity of the powder room to rearrange herself for the second round.

Her closest friend, Martha Thompson, wife of her immediate superior at the Embassy, had a cigarette with her. Martha was a clever woman, a mother of three who retained that particular American chic.

Gabriela was bored. The new season was eight grand balls old and nothing was in prospect for even a mild flirtation.

Martha Thompson, on the other hand, was unvarnished in her enthusiasm. "Aren't they all so beautiful in their boots?" she said.

"Good Lord, Martha, you can't be serious. I've never seen so many fishy-eyed officers in a single brigade."

"Trouble with you, Gaby, you've driven off all the serious contenders. You're a pampered, spoiled little girl."

"I've got an abnormal desire to crack some of them over the skull when they bow and slobber on my hand."

"I kind of like it. Well, young lady, don't wake one morning and find that the only thing left that's any good is much married—or full of complications. Take a stupid one and train him your way."

Gabriela smiled. "Come on, Martha, let's have another go at it."

She braced for the next onslaught and re-entered the ballroom on Martha's arm. Both of them saw him at the same time. In fact, every pair of eyes seemed set on the door as the epitome of a Polish cavalry officer, Lieutenant Andrei Androfski, entered. After that second of awesome silence, which he sensed, he was engulfed by adoring, back-clapping cronies and was soon explaining with bravado how he had performed his latest athletic feat, the winning of the light heavyweight wrestling championship of the Polish Army.

"Isn't he yummy," Martha said.

Gabriela was still staring.

"Who is he?"

"Forget about him, Gaby. You're really bucking city hall. No one has been able to solve him."

"So?"

"Some say he's a Tibetan monk who has taken chastity vows. Others say he has mistresses stashed all over Warsaw."

"Who is he?"

"Lieutenant Androfski."

"The Tarzan of the Ulanys?"

Martha sighed. "Well, back to my drab old reliable husband."

Gabriela took Martha's elbow. "Have Tommy introduce me to Lieutenant Androfski."

"Well, well. A new hat at Madam Phoebe's says you can't get him to see you home."

"I'll meet you there at noon. I know just the one I want."

When Thompson introduced Andrei to Gabriela, he neither bowed nor kissed her hand. He nodded politely and waited for the usual words—"So you're the famous Andrei Androfski!"

"I didn't catch your name," Gabriela said.

A clever opening gambit, Andrei thought. "I know your name, Miss Rak. Like so many, I am an admirer of the work of your late father, so my name is unimportant. You can just snap your fingers and say 'hey you' and I'll know you are addressing me."

It won't be such a dull evening after all, Gabriela thought.

What a lot of nonsense, Andrei thought, to play Victorian fencing games with spoiled brats.

"I have the next set of dances open, Lieutenant."

Brother, he thought, this one doesn't even play coy. Works without a fan. Moving in for the kill already. Well, let's look it over. Pretty little thing all right, a little on the lean side . . .

"You *do* dance, Lieutenant?"

"As a matter of fact, I am an excellent dancer, but frankly I do it only as an accommodation."

Well! Does *he* know it.

"If it annoys you so much, why did you bother to come?"

"My colonel ordered me to come. You see, I have covered my brigade with glory."

Of all the fantastic conceit!

Gabriela was about to walk off but saw Martha Thompson out of the corner of her eye. Martha was nudging Tommy and snickering. The music started.

"I am certain you won't have any trouble finding a partner, Miss Rak," Andrei said. "There's a whole line of stags drooling for you over there."

As he started his retreat Gabriela impulsively snapped her finger and said, "Hey you."

Andrei walked toward her slowly, put his arm about her, and whisked her onto the dance floor. He was not boasting about his prowess as a dancer. Every female eye in the room watched them enviously. Gabriela was furious with herself for behaving as she knew a thousand girls had done before. But she liked being in his

38

arms. They were nicer than any pair of arms she had been in for a year. This made her angrier, because he was managing to convey the feeling that he would just as soon be dancing with a broom.

The thought of bringing this egotistical roughrider to heel began to delight her. What a wonderful idea to torment him! How lovely to end the evening giving Lieutenant Androfski just enough to make him plead . . . then slam the door in his face. First, the hat from Martha Thompson.

"I should like you to see me home later," she said at the end of the set of dances.

Her trap was swift and complete. When one is playing the game at a grand ball and one is a Ulan, it would be an unpardonable discourtesy to reject a lady's "request."

"Perhaps your escort may take exception," he answered.

"I came with Mr. Thompson of the American Embassy—and Mrs. Thompson. I am quite free, Lieutenant—or is it necessary for me to get it in the form of an order from your colonel?"

He smiled weakly. "I will be delighted."

As the automobiles were being driven up to the entrance, Mr. Thompson offered them a ride.

"It is so nice and balmy out, why don't we walk, Lieutenant?"

"If you like."

"Good night, Tommy. Good night, Martha. Don't forget—Madam Phoebe's at noon tomorrow."

It was late and the streets were empty except for a few drunks. There was only the sound of their own footsteps and a very distant droshka.

Gabriela stopped suddenly. "I was terribly silly and rude to you," she said, "and I shouldn't have forced you to bring me home. If you would see me to a droshka——"

"Nonsense. I'll be glad to take you home."

"You don't have to be polite any more—we are off battle limits."

"Matter of fact," Andrei said, "I was a little bit rough on you too. I really don't behave like a pompous ass. I like you better now that I know you work for a living."

He offered her his arm, and she took it and they crossed the street. She smelled good and she felt good and he was wonderfully aware of her. He whistled softly to hide his feelings.

"I knew you were trying to anger me," she said. "I watched you after we danced. You are really very shy and self-conscious, you know."

"I don't want to sound as if I'm bragging, but—I guess everyone expects me to act a certain way."

"And you don't really like it, do you?"

"No, not always. Especially at these dances . . ."

"Why?"

39

"Never mind."

"No, tell me."

"I don't have very much in common with the people who go to grand balls."

"A famous Ulan like you—all those adoring men and women..."

"I don't belong with them."

"Why?"

"I'm not going to spoil your evening with all the serious, complicated things I am."

They walked in silence for the final block. Both of them had moved too quickly to that strange feeling of helplessness at the discovery that they were suddenly infatuated with each other, and it was frightening for them. The game was over for Gabriela. He had behaved nicely and she did not wish to play the tease but wanted to know more about this man who could be a peacock one moment, then sink into boyishness in another.

Her flat was in a large old mansion on the Square of the Three Crosses facing St. Alexander's Church. She stopped before the door and fumbled in her purse for her key and handed it to him. Andrei unlocked the door and handed the key back.

"Good night, Miss Rak," he said.

They shook hands.

"Lieutenant Androfski. I was brought up in America, as you know, and sometimes we do things a little differently. Would you consider me terribly brash if I said I would like to see you again, very soon?"

He took his hand from hers slowly and became pitifully and awkwardly shy. "I am afraid not, Miss Rak," he said quickly, and turned and walked off.

Gabriela was stunned at her own words, more stunned at his action. She ran up the steps, watery-eyed, confused, and hurt and angry.

A large group of American VIPs were flying in from Paris. It included three congressmen and their wives and an advisory board of industrialists for a prospective American loan to build a dam on the Warta River.

"We want to help get this loan pushed through," Thompson said to Gabriela. "I've got to be away in Krakow when they arrive. Can you make up their itinerary and handle them for two days till I get back?"

"Anything special you want them to see?"

"The usual junk around Warsaw. Lunch with the Ambassador, press conference, whatever is going at the opera and theater. Meanwhile, draw up a list for their reception."

"Will do. Don't worry about a thing."

"Here's all the dope. Look this over. Play it to Congressman

Galinowski, big Polish district in Gary. Stay close to Cranebrook; he talks too much."

"Tommy, the last time we had wives, the Ministry of Information sent over a real creep to escort them around. Why don't we try someone else?"

"Like what?"

Gabriela shrugged. "Oh, I don't know. Why not—well, get one of those big Ulany officers. The Seventh Ulanys have a dozen real charmers who speak English."

"Oh, sister," Thompson mumbled. "He's already cost me one hat." He flicked the inter-com and spoke through it. "Mildred. Call up the commanding general at the Citadel. On that group of VIPs coming in day after tomorrow, we're going to need an escort for the wives. Make it important . . . big loan to Poland involved. See if you can get Lieutenant Andrei Androfski—from the Seventh Ulanys—placed on detached duty for PR. Have him report to Miss Rak." He flicked off the switch. Gabriela's face was crimson. "Just call me Cupid Thompson."

If Andrei was livid with rage, which he was, he did nothing to show it. He reported to Miss Rak and took his orders with complete detachment and oozed Polish charm playing escort to the three elderly but appreciative American ladies. Andrei even managed to hold his temper when one of the ladies discovered he was on the national soccer team and insisted he take off his boots so she could see the muscles in his calves.

At the end of the third day he delivered them to their suites and reported to Miss Rak at the Embassy.

"I must say, everyone is commenting on my master stroke of public relations. You have made a noble contribution to a dam on the Warta River."

"Thank you," Andrei said stiffly.

"In fact, Lieutenant, they are so pleased with your company, they particularly asked if you would escort them on a two-day trip to Krakow while the committee surveys the proposed dam site."

"Miss Rak," Andrei said, "I feel I am denying fellow officers a tremendous experience and wish to share this duty with some others——"

"But they particularly asked for you. You *do* want to see that dam on the Warta?"

"Miss Rak. To hell with the dam on the Warta. I hurt your pride the other night and you have made me eat humble pie. You win, I lose. Since I have been taking those—those—nice ladies around Warsaw my brigade has lost an important soccer match and my horse is dying of loneliness. You will have to find someone else to assume this pleasurable duty, because it will take a court-martial to bring me back tomorrow."

"I think that is terribly un-Polish of you."

"Will you let me return to my brigade?"

Gabriela smiled. "If you take me home."

This time when he handed her the key she walked through the door, leaving it open. "Come on up," she said.

Andrei followed awkwardly into a small but tastefully and lavishly furnished living room. The luxury seemed to add to his discomfort. She threw open the french doors and stepped out on the balcony overlooking the Square of the Three Crosses. Andrei stood near the front door, fiddling with his hat.

"Close the door and come on in. I won't bite you."

As he reached the balcony, Gabriela spun around, her eyes ablaze with anger. "You are very right, Lieutenant. I have never suffered such humiliation."

"You've had your revenge."

"No, I haven't."

"I wish you wouldn't make an affair of honor out of this."

"I have never chased a man in my life, nor have I ever been rejected."

"My, what an angry little terrier you are."

"I made it obvious that I found you attractive. I would like to know exactly why you delight in making me feel like some sort of cheap trollop."

"I told you. I don't like places like the grand ballroom of the Bristol—or here. I don't belong here."

"You must certainly know that with a wink of your eye you could obtain the family fortunes of every eligible spinster in Warsaw."

"I have no desire to be anything but what I am."

"And what are you?"

"I am a Jew. I am not inclined to do the things necessary to reach a position I don't covet in the first place. To be sure, I'm one of those good Jew boys. I can throw a javelin farther and jump a horse higher than almost any man in Poland. So, you see, there's a gentlemen's agreement in the Ulanys not to mention publicly my tainted ancestry."

"Is that any reason to treat me as you did?"

"Miss Rak, I don't know how advanced your American education was, but in Poland it is the general consensus we use nice tender young Catholic girls like you for sacrificial offerings."

Gabriela walked back into the living room and braced herself against a lamp table and blew a long, deep breath. "Well, I asked for it. I owe you an apology. At least my pride has been served. I thought you disliked me."

"Not at all. I like you very much."

"Underneath that layer of bluster you are a very sensitive man."

"I'm engaged in serious work. I only serve half time in the army."

"What kind of work?"

42

"You wouldn't be interested."

"I think I would."

"I am a Zionist."

"Oh yes, I've heard something about it. Redemption of Palestine or something like that."

"Yes, something like that."

"Don't be so touchy. What do you do?"

"I'm an organizer and on the executive board of an organization called the Bathyrans."

"Bathyrans? What an odd name."

"It was a group of Jewish warriors sent out by Herod to defend against infiltrators. . . . Look, this doesn't interest you."

"But it does. And what do your Bathyrans do?"

"We follow certain principles of Zionism, which tells us we must re-establish our ancient homeland in Palestine, and we run an orphanage and have a farm outside Warsaw. On the farm we train youngsters in the rededication to the land. When we are able to raise enough money, we buy a piece of land in Palestine and send off a new group to start a colony."

"Why on earth would you do that?"

Andrei's patience snapped. "Because, Miss Rak, the Polish people have not allowed us to own or farm land and——" He stopped short and lowered his voice. "Let's stop this. You don't give a damn about Zionism and I feel like a fool here."

"I am trying to be friendly."

"Miss Rak, between Jerusalem Boulevard and Stawki Street over three hundred thousand people live in a world you know nothing about. Your high and mighty writers call it the 'Black Continent.' It happens to be my world."

He put on his hat and walked toward the door.

"Lieutenant. All this—why does all this mean that we can't be friends?"

Andrei walked toward her slowly. "What do you want from me? I am not interested in a romance."

"Really . . ."

"Stop this silly damned game. I am a poor man, but I don't mind it in the least because I am doing something that makes me happy. I am and never will be anything you consider important. As far as anything in common, we may as well be living on different planets."

Gabriela's voice trembled. "I don't know why I let you get me so angry. You are very presumptuous. Try to be friendly with some-one, and immediately they've got illusions of grandeur."

"I know exactly what's going on in that shrewd little mind of yours and I'll tell you how presumptuous I am. If you annoy me again I am going to rip every stitch of clothing off your body and I am going to make love to you in exactly the way you know I can."

She was small, but her slap was mighty.

Andrei lifted her in his arms. "Scream and I'll blacken both your eyes," he said.

Gabriela was too terrified to know whether he was bluffing or not. He walked in the bedroom to the big canopied, satin-covered bed.

"On second thought," he said, "go out and get a little more flesh on you. You're too skinny for me to trouble with." He flung her on the bed and left.

"Did he do that!" Martha Thompson exclaimed.

Gabriela nodded and poured tea and sliced the apple cake.

"So what did you do?"

"Do? Nothing. I was absolutely terrified. You can imagine."

Martha sipped her tea, nibbled on the cake, and sighed. "Oh dear, why doesn't something like that ever happen to me?"

Suddenly Gabriela pulled out a handkerchief, turned her face, and began to sniffle. "Why, Gabriela Rak, I've never seen you cry."

"I don't know what's gotten into me lately. I've been so jumpy since I've met him. All someone has to do is look at me sideways and I start to cry." And she bawled. "No one has ever been able to get me so angry," she sobbed unevenly. "He's conceited and detestable. Oh God, I hate him!"

Martha sat alongside her on the couch and offered a sympathetic shoulder.

"I hate him!"

"Sure you do," Martha comforted, "sure you do."

Gabriela pulled away and brought herself under control. "I am behaving like a fool."

"Welcome to this world of fools. You took a long time joining us, but you're making up for it all at once. You've had this coming to you, Gabriela. You've been running the show all your life."

"He's a complete opposite of everything I've ever known. Like a stranger from a foreign land."

"You know what your old Aunt Martha always said. The only good ones are either much married or full of complications."

"Complications! The terrible part of it is that I'm scared to death of being snubbed again. I've done just about everything but throw myself at his feet, and that, I'll never do."

"You're going to have to. Alternative, have Tommy send you to Krakow for a long trip."

Gabriela shook her head slowly. "I didn't think anything so simple could be so painful. I want to see him so badly I could burst. I just don't know what to do."

"Well, honey, no matter what this Lieutenant Androfski is, one thing is for certain. He *is* a man."

44

Andrei was stretched out on his bed, his feet propped up on the iron bedstead. He stared blankly at the ceiling, ignoring Alexander Brandel, who was fishing through papers at the old round table in the center of the room.

"I am against appointing Brayloff to edit the paper. He is inclined to lean too much toward the Revisionists' point of view. What do you think, Andrei?"

Andrei grunted.

"Ideally, Ervin Rosenblum would be perfect. However, we can't pay him what he is earning on the outside. Maybe, if we could use Ervin in an advisory capacity . . . I'll talk to him. Now, Andrei, about the Lodz Chapter—you're going to have to give their problems your attention right away." Alexander stopped. "I'm maybe talking to the wall tonight? You haven't heard a thing I've said."

Andrei spun off the bed, shoved his hands in his pockets, and leaned against the wall. "I heard, I heard."

"So what do you think?"

"To hell with Brayloff, to hell with Ervin Rosenblum, to hell with the Lodz Chapter. To hell with the whole goddamned Zionist movement!"

"So now that you've made your great proclamation, maybe you might tell me what is eating you up. You have been uncivilized for a week."

"I've been thinking. Maybe I'll stay in the army."

Alexander Brandel muffled his shock at the pronouncement. "Fine," he said. "I'll predict you'll be the first Jew to become Polish Chief of Staff."

"I'm not joking. Alex. Here I am, twenty-six years old, and what am I? Fighting for a cause that's all but hopeless. Putting on a big front all the time . . . working the clock out . . . living in rooms like this . . . Maybe I'm crazy for not taking the one chance I'll ever have to really be something. I walked today. I walked and I thought. I walked around Stawki Street where I lived when I was a boy, and it scared me a little—maybe that's where I'll end up when all this is over. And I walked to the Avenue of the Marshals and Jerusalem Boulevard. That's where I could be if I set my mind to it."

"And while you were walking, did you walk along the Square of the Three Crosses and past the American Embassy?"

Andrei turned around angrily.

"Thompson at the Embassy called me up and invited me to lunch today. It seems there is a young lady there almost as miserable as you are."

"God Almighty! Can't I even have a broken heart in privacy?"

"Not if you're Andrei Androfski."

"I don't want a lecture about Jewish boys and *shikses*."

Alex shrugged. "If a *shikse* was good enough for Moses, a *shikse*

45

is good enough for Androfski. I know all the things you are think-ing now. Why am I here? Why am I beating my brains out doing this? But if you are able to believe in Zionism the same way some of the priests and nuns believe in Catholicism and the same way the Hassidim believe in Judaism, then you will find the ultimate re-ward of peace of mind greater than any sacrifice."

Andrei knew the words came from a man who could have gained great recognition and economic reward had he not chosen the path of Zionism. Somehow, Alex did not seem to be giving anything up. If only he could believe in Zionism like that.

"Andrei, you stand for something to all of us. We love you."

"So I will lower myself in the eyes of my friends and I will hurt them by taking up with a Catholic girl."

"I said we love you. The only way you could ever hurt your true friends is by hurting yourself."

"Do me a favor and go home, Alex."

Alexander Brandel put all his papers together and stuffed them into his battered brief case. He stuck his cap on his head and wrapped the muffler, which he wore summer or winter, about his neck, and walked to the door.

"Alex!"

"Yes?"

"I'm sorry. I'll—be off duty in a week. I'll take that trip to Lodz right away. Maybe I should also swing around the country and see the chapters in Lublin and Lemberg."

"That may be a good idea," Alex said.

After Alex had left, Andrei poured himself a half glass of vodka, downed it in a single swallow, and took up a caged pacing of the confines of the room.

He stopped and wound up his record player. A scratchy sonata struggled its way flatly out of the sound head. He turned off the lights except the one over the table in the center of the room and walked to his books. He took a book of Hayim Nachman Bialik, the prince of poets of Zionism.

"This is the last generation of Jews which will live in bondage and the first which will live in freedom," Bialik had written.

He was in no mood for Bialik. Another book. One filled with fury. Here. John Steinbeck, his favorite author.

IN DUBIOUS BATTLE

Innumerable force of Spirits armed,
That durst dislike his reign, and, me preferring,
His utmost power with adverse power opposed,
In dubious battle on the plains of Heaven
And shook his throne. What though the field be lost?
All is not lost—the unconquerable will,
The study of revenge, immortal hate,

And courage never to submit or yield;
And what is else not to be overcome?

Andrei filled his glass again. Now there is a man who understands, he thought. Steinbeck knows of fighting for lost causes. In dubious battle . . . His battle . . .

There was a soft, almost imperceptible knock on the door.

"Come in, it's open."

Gabriela Rak stood in the doorway. Andrei seized the edge of the table, daring not to move or speak. She walked across the room into the shadow of the books. "I thought I would take a walk north from Jerusalem Boulevard. I am intrigued by these three hundred and fifty thousand people from the Black Continent." Her fingers ran over the backs of the books. "I see you read in Russian and English as well as Polish. What is this here, this odd script? It must be Yiddish, or Hebrew maybe? A. D. Gordon. They have a volume of A. D. Gordon at the Embassy library. Let me see now. 'Physical labor is the basis of human existence . . . it is spiritually necessary, and nature is the basis of culture, man's elevated creation. However, to avoid exploitation, the soil must not be the property of an individual.' How is that for my first lesson in Zionism?"

"What are you doing here?" Andrei croaked.

She leaned against the books and stiffened, her eyes closed and her teeth clenched, and tears fell down her cheeks. "Lieutenant Androfski. I am twenty-three years old. I am not a virgin. My father left me a considerable endowment. What else would you care to know about me?"

Andrei's hand pawed helplessly around the table. At last his fist smashed down on it. "Why don't you leave me alone?"

"I don't know what has happened to me and I don't seem to care. As you can see, I'm throwing myself at your feet. I beg you, don't send me away."

She turned and wept uncontrollably.

And she felt his hand on her shoulder, and it was gentle. "Gabriela . . . Gabriela . . ."

From that moment when she was consumed by his great and wonderful power, all the things she had considered important to her way of life ceased to be important.

Gabriela knew with no uncertainty that there had never been nor ever would be again a man like Andrei Androfski. Those things which society and its religions and philosophies and economies had imposed upon them as great barriers came crumbling down. Gabriela had been a selfish woman. She suddenly found herself able to give with a power of giving that she did not realize she possessed.

For to her, Andrei was like David of the Bible. He was at one

47

time all that was strong and all that was weak in a single man.

He had within him the power to snuff out a life in an angry fit. Yet there had never been a man who could touch her with such a gentleness.

He was a giant who lived his life for a single ideal. He was a helpless boy who became confused or pouted or angered at a seeming trifle.

He was a symbol of strength to his friends. He would get roaring drunk when the frustrations became too difficult.

But with him there were moments of electric flaring of emotions. There were moments of hurt and pain deeper than any she had known except at the death of her father. There were the great expectations fulfilled with the sensuous thrills of pure physical pleasure.

To her friends it seemed that her willingness to become the mistress of a Jewish pauper was a terrible calamity. For Gabriela, the things she surrendered seemed insignificant and indeed no sacrifice for loving a man who made her happier than she had ever been in her life.

Little by little she divorced herself from the treadmill about which she centered her activities. Gabriela accepted the hard fact that her affair with Andrei might never be resolved in a marriage. She understood that she must never step on the dangerous ground of tampering with his work. She knew he would not be changed over to any of her images. Andrei was Andrei, and she had to take him and everything he was as he was.

Andrei had at last met in Gabriela Rak a woman who could match him fury for fury, passion for passion, anger for anger. She often flared into those stubborn streaks of pride which would be resolved only when he humbled himself or blurted an awkward apology. He sat quietly and took without a whimper the wrath of her anger when he had been out on a binge. He instinctively knew when to back down from a conflict. For his reward he found moments he had never known. Moments when she felt his depression and frustrations over the failures in his work. In those moments she was able to reach him with compassion as he had never been reached before.

He knew he had tamed a wild mare, but one who always kept that streak of rebellion. Gabriela demanded her religious identity. He insisted that she not completely withdraw from all those things which had been her life, and he took many of her friends as his.

And they discovered that they had as many things in common as they once believed had kept them apart. They shared a mutual love of music and books and theater. On occasion he would admit he enjoyed dancing with her.

Gabriela did not strain herself for acceptance among his friends but entered part of his strange world and found those closest to him took to her with sincerity.

His trips around Poland and his leaves from the army always brought him home to days and nights of love-making which never wearied or slackened in intensity.

Only two years ago, Gabriela thought. Only two years since I met my Andrei. She watched from the bridge as the last commuter train left for Praga, then walked north again in pursuit of Andrei and Christopher de Monti.

Chapter Seven

Fukier's ancient Wine Cellar in the Old Town was submerged in noises and smoke and smells. The immense casks leaked age-old wines, which blended with the smells of ales and cheeses. The voices of rowdy bohemians were somewhat buffered by thousands of bottles lining the walls. Amid the uproar, a trio of gypsy musicians inched their way from table to table.

The gypsies stopped and hovered over the table, determined to entertain Andrei and Chris. Andrei emptied his mug, belched, and put a coin on the table. The violinist snatched it and downbeated the accordionist and an unwashed tamborine-rattling female vocalist.

"Jesus Christ," Christopher de Monti mumbled, "Jesus Christ. Even the gypsies play Chopin."

"Chopin is a national hero. Chopin gives us courage!"

"Oh balls! He was a tubercular little wart shacked up with a cigar-smoking French whore who cashed in on Polish misery."

"Is that nice?"

The waitress fought her way to their table, slung down a pair of plates, a loaf of dark rye bread, and a small ham, along with more vodka.

The gypsies played "O Sole Mio."

"Christ, that's worse than Chopin," Chris said.

Andrei gulped down half a pint of vodka and wiped his mouth with the back of his sleeve.

"Let us not digress from our conversation," he said. "The Germans attack, we will counterattack, naturally. My steed, Batory, and I will be the first two into Berlin."

Chris weaved and focused on the ham. He raised his fork, aimed, and plunged it deeply. "This is Poland," he announced. He picked up a knife and cut the ham in two. "One slice goes to Germany. 'Nother slice goes to Russia. No more Poland. All gone.

49

Andrei, tell them goddamn gypsies to blow. So anyhow, all your goddamn poets will write tired sonnets about the good old days when the noblemen kicked the piss out of the peasants and the peasants kicked the piss out of the Jews. Then! Some half-assed piano player will play benefit concerts to the Poles in Chicago. All Chopin concerts. And in a hundred years everybody will say— Jesus Christ, let's put Poland back together—we're sick of hearing Chopin concerts. And in a hundred and two years, the Russians and the Germans will start up again."

Andrei belched again. Chris tried to continue his lecture, but his elbow kept slipping from the table each time he tried to point to Russian Poland. The violin cried. And when a gypsy violin cried in Fukier's, men cried too. "Chris, my dear friend," sniffed Andrei, "take my sister away from that no-good bastard Bronski."

Chris hung his head. "Don't mention a lady's name in a bar, sir. Goddamn broad."

Andrei's sympathetic hand fell on Chris's shoulder. "Damned broad," he agreed.

Andrei emptied, then refilled his mug. "Hitler's bluffing."

"Hell he is."

"He's scared of our counterattack."

"Counterattack, my butt." Chris's fist struck the table. He spread it clean, shoving bottles and plates and glasses into one corner. "This table is Poland."

"I though the ham was Poland."

"The ham is Poland *A*. This is Poland *B*. See the table, stupid? See how nice and flat it is? Perfect for tanks. The Germans have them. They got big ones, little ones, fast ones, heavy ones. Tried and tested in Spain. That General Staff of yours had any sense, they'd pull back now."

"Pull back!" the Ulany officer cried in horror.

"Pull back, I said. Blunt the first German thrust on the Warta River. Then drop everything in back of the Vistula and make your stand."

"Back of the Vistula! You dare insinuate we give up Silesia and Warsaw?"

"Hell yes. They'll take it anyhow. Chopin or no Chopin. If you can hold a Vistula line for three or four months, the British and French will have to start something on the western front."

"Oh, big strategist, de Monti—big strategist!"

"Just common sense and vodka."

Gabriela crossed into the cobblestone square of Stare Miastro, the Old Town. It was surrounded on four sides by perfectly preserved five-story medieval houses that formed the showplace of Warsaw. The historical relics of Poland's glory were preserved in authentic settings. Madam Curie was properly revered in a museum, and shops selling cut glass and national products made it a well-conceived tourist trap as well as a heartstone of Polish sentiment.

At the far end of the square, Gabriela could hear the noise from Fukier's. She walked in and looked around.

There they were, Chris and Andrei, their elbows on the table, their hands clasped, Indian wrestling. The mob had gathered around them, placing bets and rooting them on. Christopher de Monti was deceptively powerful, a carryover from his basketball days. It was he who was pressing Andrei's wrist down slowly. Andrei was humiliated, as befitted a Ulany officer in a contest with a mere mortal. As Chris poured his strength into his hand and pressed downward, a roar went up from the crowd and the odds shifted quickly. Andrei's face turned first red, then purple with strain, and the veins fairly leaped out of his neck.

Their wrists quivered.

Suddenly the innumerable pints of vodka caught up with Chris. He was unable to make the final pin. Andrei, sensing the weakness of his opponent, called on the reserve strength of a great athlete, and Chris wilted.

Utter silence gripped the mob as Andrei came inching back from the brink of defeat. The sweat rolled down Chris's face as he tried to fight off the inevitable. He collapsed. Andrei made the kill with such speed and power that Chris was thrown right out of his chair and went sprawling into the spectators.

The Ulany officer stood up, wavering, and raised both arms over his head to receive his deserved accolades, then bent down to help his victim to his feet. Bloody, but unbowed, Chris's hand lashed out, caught Andrei by the heel of his shiny boot, and sent him crashing to the floor. They both lay on their backs, convulsed with laughter.

"What in the devil are you doing down there!" she demanded.

"Whadda think I'm doing?" Andrei said. "I'm trying to get this drunken slob home."

"It stinks in here," Andrei said.

"I told you it was painted. Now be careful and don't touch anything. It's still wet."

Andrei spilled the unconscious Chris on Gabriela's sofa. He landed with a thud, his legs awry.

"You don't have to be so rough," she admonished. She knelt down and unlaced Chris's shoes. "Take off his coat and tie. He's so drunk, he's liable to choke."

Chris blurted out something about flat tables and Polish hams as Andrei fought him out of his clothing. Gabriela placed a pillow beneath his head, covered him with a blanket, and dimmed the lights.

51

Andrei hovered over him. "Poor Chris. Do you see the way he and Deborah steal looks at each other? As if they are both going to die of broken hearts. Poor Chris."

"Get in there," Gabriela ordered.

He staggered into the bedroom, flopped on the edge of the bed, and held his face in his hands.

"I've got to do something about my temper," he mumbled. Andrei then berated himself roundly, but it was a monotone soliloquy heard only by himself. Gabriela entered with a large mug of steaming black coffee.

Andrei's head dangled with shame. "I'm a son of a bitch," he said.

"Oh, shut up and drink this."

He stole a guilty look at Gabriela. "Gaby . . . baby . . . please don't bawl me out . . . please, baby."

She took his cap off, unbuttoned his tunic, and wrestled his boots off. Andrei had reached that stage of drunkenness where words are thick but thoughts brilliantly clear. The coffee gave him a sudden resurgence. He looked up at his little Gabriela. She was so lovely.

"I don't know why you put up with me," he said.

She knelt before him and lay her head on his lap. Even in this state, his hands touched her hair with amazing tenderness.

"Are you all right, dear? Can we talk?" she asked.

"Yes."

"When you've gone away in the past two years, a week to Krakow, or a week to Bialystok, or a week or two on maneuvers, it was never really too bad because I was always able to live for that moment I knew you would come storming up the stairs into my arms. But now you've been on regular duty—you've been gone nearly two months. Andrei, I almost died. At the Embassy we know how bad things really are. Andrei . . . please marry me."

He struggled to his feet, holding one of the four tall posters. "Maybe you'll hate me the way you hate Paul Bronski for giving up his beliefs, but you mean more to me than being a Catholic does, and I'll give it up and I'll light the candles for you on your Sabbath and I'll try to be all the things——"

"No, Gaby . . . no. No . . . I'd never ask you to do that."

"I know how much you mean to other women. I can see the way they look at you. If you were angry with me and should go away for a night or two, I swear I'll never question you or make a scene."

"You make scenes now. You'd make scenes if we were married. Maybe I wouldn't love you if you didn't make scenes. Dear . . . I . . ."

"What, Andrei?"

"I have never said this to you, but it would be the proudest thing in my life if I were able to take you as my wife. It is only—— I . . .

52

tell myself a hundred times a day that it is not true. It will not happen. But Chris is right. Poland is going to be conquered. God knows what the Germans will do to us. The one thing you don't need now is a Jewish husband."

Andrei's words and their meaning were absolutely clear. "I see," she said, deflated.

"God damn it all. God damn everything." Andrei had that lost look about him that moved Gabriela to forget her own desires, for he was floundering and in trouble and needed her.

"What did Paul Bronski say to you tonight that brought all this on?" she asked.

"That bastard!"

"What did he say to hurt you so?"

Andrei sucked in a deep breath and reeled to the window, where he stared into the darkness. "He called me a phony Zionist—and he is right."

"How can you say that?"

"No, he's right, he's right."

He tried to clear his shrouded thoughts. He looked for Gabriela through bleary eyes. She seemed far away and out of focus. "You've never been on Stawki Street where the poor Jews live. I can see the garbage on the streets and smell it and hear the iron-rimmed wheels of the teamster wagons on the cobblestones. It was a kind of stink and humiliation that drove Paul Bronski out of there. Who can really blame him?"

Gabriela listened with terrible awe as the drunken outpoor increased. Since she had known Andrei he had never spoken a word of his boyhood.

"Like all Jews, we lived through economic boycotts, and blood riots by the same students Paul Bronski leads. My father—you saw his picture?"

"Yes."

"Just another one of those bearded old religious Jews nobody understands . . . sold chickens. My father never got angry, even when they threw stones through his windows. He always said, 'Evil will destroy itself.' You don't know the Krasinski Gardens—nice Polish girls don't go there. It's at the north end, where the poor people go on Saturday to look at trees and eat hard-boiled eggs and onions and pass gas while their kids fall into the fishponds. I had to deliver chickens for my father to the Bristol and Europa. I'd cut through the Krasinski Gardens. The gangs of *goyim* hung out there waiting for us little Jew boys. Every time they beat me up, and stole my chickens we'd have to eat boiled potatoes for a week. I would ask my father, 'Daddy, how long is it going to take for evil to destroy itself?' And all he would answer was, 'Run from the *goyim*, run from the *goyim*.'

"One day I was making my deliveries. I had a pal from the cheder

53

—that's our parochial school. Funny, I don't even remember his name. But I can see his face so plain. He was skinny—half my size. We crossed Krasinski Square, and the *goyim* trapped us right in front of their goddamned cathedral. I started to run. But this kid— wish I could remember his name—he grabbed me and made me set the chickens down in back of us.

"Funny, not running. When the first one came to me I hit him. I could whip most of the kids in my neighborhood, but I never thought of hitting a *goy*. He went down to the pavement—he got up mad, his nose was busted. I hit him again, and he went down again and just lay there and moaned—and I turned and looked at the rest of them, and they backed up and I kept walking forward and I ran at them and they ran away! I caught another one and beat the hell out of him. Me! Andrei Androfski from Stawki Street had beaten up two *goyim*."

And he dropped from the elation of the memory of triumph back to his drunkenness. "That's why I'm a phony Zionist, Gaby. I hate that damned Zionist farm. I don't want to spend my life in little bare rooms over union halls. Bronski knows this—I'm not going to sit in any damned swamp in Palestine."

"Then why, Andrei—why?"

"Because in the Bathyrans I have a dozen, two dozen friends who are together with me. So long as we hang together, no one can steal our chickens. All I want, Gaby, is to be able to live without running."

Spent and weary, Andrei lay back on the bed slowly. "I forced them to make me a Ulany officer. I, Andrei Androfski, a Zionist leader, made them make me a Ulany officer. But I can feel their eyes on my back. Jew, they say to themselves—Jew. But they do not say it to my face. . . ."

"Shhh, darling. You are not fighting now."

"Gaby. I'm so tired. So tired of battling for everyone. I am tired of being the great Andrei Androfski."

"It's all right, dear. You rest now."

She dimmed the lights and lay beside him and soothed him until he fell into a fitful thrashing sleep.

> What is the best Sehora?
> My baby will learn Torah,
> Seforim he will write for me,
> And a pious Jew he'll always be.

Momma's song. Momma's lullaby. Andrei blinked his eyes open. His fingers felt the pillow. There was a bad taste in his mouth.

> What is the best Sehora?
> My baby will learn Torah . . .

54

Andrei sat up quickly. He shook his fuzzy head. Gabriela awoke the instant Andrei did, but she lay motionless and watched him swing his legs to the floor, weave his way into his tunic and walk out of the french doors and stand on the balcony. A quiet, sleeping Warsaw was before him.

Seforim he will write for me,
And a pious Jew he'll always be.

"Poppa," Andrei whispered. "Poppa."
Israel Androfski stood before him. His black coat stained and threadbare. His silver-and-black beard ungroomed because of weariness, and his eyes half closed with the strain of the hard life etched into face and posture.
Andrei could smell the poverty of Stawki Street.
"In cheder you will learn to find comfort in the Torah and the Talmud and the Midrash. You go to school tomorrow to begin your swim in the Sea of Talmud and gather the wisdoms which will give you the strength and understanding to live as a good and pious man all your life."
Little Andrei babbled his excitement in Yiddish, eager to start his training in one of Warsaw's six hundred Jewish schools.
Rabbi Gewirtz stood warming his hands on the fireless stove in a dingy room before a handful of shivering students.
"You see, *Kinder*, we Jews have been in Diaspora since the destruction of the Second Temple and the great dispersion nearly two thousand years ago. . . ."
. . . In the Crimea during the Byzantine era, the Khazars, a warlike people, adopted Judaism, but in the tenth century the Khazars were defeated and dispersed by the Russians much as the Jews were driven from the Holy Land. The Russians swept them out and they have never been heard of since, and their empire was consolidated under Christianity of the Greek Orthodox leaning.
Jews suffered maltreatment during the years of their dispersion in all countries of their dispersion from massacres to expulsions. The fever of Jew baiting heightened to a new level during the Spanish Inquisition, when torture and bestiality were as common as daily prayer.
In the Dark Ages the Jews were blamed for the Black Plague and for witchcraft and for ritual murder.
But it was the Crusaders under the flag of Holy Purification and in the name of God who set out to kill every Jew in Europe. The massacres became so bloody that wave after wave of Jews fled from the fountainhead of butchery in Bohemia to the newly emerging kingdom of Poland.
Here the Jews were welcomed and this was their real beginning, along with the beginning of Poland itself. Jews were needed, for

there was no middle class between the landed gentry and the peasants. The Jews brought with them their arts, crafts, trades, professions, and ability as merchants.

"And how was cheder today, Andrei?"

"The boys tease me because they say Andrei Androfski is not a Jewish name."

"Aha! Well, it is a very Jewish name. It appears all down our family line. Our family were very old in France before they emigrated to Poland during the Crusades."

"Poppa, why must you and Rabbi Gewirtz talk so much about history? I want to know about things happening today. Why do we spend so much time in the past?"

"Why?" Israel Androfski thrust his finger skyward and repeated an old Hebrew phrase. "Know from where you come. Before you know who you are and where you are going, you must know from where you come."

And so Andrei learned that a series of Polish kings granted a number of charters guaranteeing religious freedom and protection to the Jews soon after their arrival in Poland from Bohemia.

However, this condition of security was short-lived, and not long after their arrival there opened a sordid, almost thousand-year parade of oppression against the Jews which never stopped but only varied in intensity from time to time.

It began as the Roman Church grew in power and consolidated its position as the state religion. The Jesuits of Posen and Krakow triggered Middle Age riots against the Jews, persisting in the spreading of lies about ritual murder libels.

The Jesuits received help from immigrant Germans who were the competition with the Jews in commerce. With Church help they managed to obtain a Jew's tax, expulsion from competitive crafts and trades and professions. The feudal *pans* kept Jews from owning or farming land.

And so to Poland came the honor of creating one of the world's first ghettos, an enforced separation of the Jews from the rest of the citizens by walling and locking them in.

Banned from participation in national life and from participation in the normal economic life, they were compelled to be a breed apart.

In their ghettos, limited in their means of livelihood, the Jews began their long tradition of self-rule and self-help. Banded together without choice, they intensified their studies of the Holy Books to find the answers to the thousand-year-old dilemma.

"We are like a bird," Rabbi Gewirtz said. "We are a long way from home and we cannot fly that far, so we circle and circle and circle. Now and again we light upon a branch of a tree to rest, but before we can build our nest we are driven away and must fly again—aimlessly in our circle. . . ."

Polish Jews turned bitter against their homeland. The Poles used the very difference which they had forced on the Jews to prove Jews were not like other people. The Jews had no identity as Poles. They spoke Yiddish, a language carried from Bohemia. They created their own culture and literature apart from the masses around them.

In 1649 the greatest calamity since the falls of the Temples crushed the Jews of Poland. Cossacks of the Ukraine, aided by the Tartars, staged a revolt against the feudal *pans* of Poland. In the wake of gory, savage fighting, the Cossacks became obsessed with the idea of slaying every Jew in Poland, the Ukraine, and the Baltics, and rivers of Jewish blood spurted from the swift-arcing, hissing Cossack sabers. In the frenzy to kill, the Cossacks often buried Jewish babies alive.

And, like the Arab world after the Mongol invasions, the Jews of Poland never recovered from the Cossack massacres.

Numbed from the butchery, they entered an era of desperation and sought a way out of the long black night through their Holy Books.

The cult of the cabala snowballed. The cabala, a study of mystic meanings of the Holy Books, was taught by cabalistic rabbis who preached the Zohar and the Book of Creation. Through cryptic numerology and mystics they sought to overcome the suffering of daily life by finding hidden meanings in the Bible.

Along with the cabalists came a parade of false messiahs. Self-declared messiahs proclaimed themselves the anointed leader to take the Jews back to the Holy Land. A desperate, anguished people disposed of reason and flocked behind them.

King of the frauds was Sabbatai Zvi, a Turkish Jew, who through distortions of the cabala "proved" himself the Messiah. Throughout the world of dispersed Jewry the elders and the rabbis from Amsterdam to Salonika, from Kiev to Paris, argued the validity of Sabbatai Zvi's claims. It was the Polish Jewry who arose, drowning logic with the maddened hope that he could lead them to escape.

A crushing delusion. Sabbatai Zvi was converted to Islam and became a Mohammedan to escape the wrath of the Turkish sultan.

Jacob Frank, a Bohemian rabbi, relit the fires after Sabbatai's death in Albania, but the Frankist sect carried out sex orgies and debasements of the Holy Laws. In the end, Jacob Frank was converted to Catholicism.

And all of the false messiahs fell, and the Jews of Poland sank deeper into a muck of despondency. From the depths of their despair emerged the Hassidim. Israel Baal Shem Tov erupted with yet another new cult which captured the imagination of the enslaved Jews in their ghetto dungeons.

The Hassidim detached themselves from the world of daily tribulation and reality through frenzied prayer that transcended the pain about them. Wild! Leaping! Screaming! Moaning! The joy of prayer!

"Poppa! I don't want to be a tailor or a chicken seller!" Andrei cried. "I don't want to be a Hassid! I want to be like other people in Warsaw."

Israel Androfski's face saddened. He stroked his son's curly bush of hair. "My boy will not be a chicken seller. You will be a great Talmudic scholar."

"No, Poppa, no. I don't want to go to cheder any more!"

His father raised his hand in anger, but the slap never came, for Israel Androfski was too gentle a man. He looked at the burning in his son's eyes with puzzlement.

"I want to be a soldier—a soldier like Berek Joselowicz," Andrei whispered.

Poland, partitioned, at constant war with Germany and Russia, ceased to exist as a state time and again in her long and bloody history. At the end of the 1700s she was again in the throes of one of her numerous rebellions, this time against the Russian Tsar on the east and the King of Prussia on the west. Desperate for manpower, the Poles allowed Berek Joselowicz, a Jew of Vilna, and Josef Aronwicz to organize a Jewish brigade, a radical departure from past principle. Five hundred of them took the field in the defense of Warsaw. Twenty of them survived. With the precedent set, the Jews answered the call to arms in Poland's rebellions against Russia in 1830 and 1863, but as Russia gobbled Poland and the state disappeared from the face of the earth, a huge land ghetto was formed called the Jewish Pale of Settlement. Beyond the Pale, no Jew could travel or live.

And through the 1800s the web of economic strangulation, boycott, excessive taxation, and bestial pogroms continued. Murder of Jews was supported by the Tsar and overlooked by the Russian Orthodox Church. The Jews were driven into a position of mass destitution.

A few fumbling calls for reforms were heard, but the voices were far softer than the gangs of roving Jew killers.

And a new generation in the Pale emerged unsatisfied to continue Jewish existence as it had been through the black centuries. The new generation could not find peace in the cabala or the wild prayer of the Hassidim, nor would they follow false messiahs. To them, the old ideas had failed, and during the mid-1800s dynamic new ideas swept the ghettos of the Pale. Young Jews formed self-defense committees to protect the ghetto against the pogroms as they began to emulate the soldier Berek Joselowicz!

Then came the Lovers of Zion, the first practical move to organize colonies in the Holy Land.

The thousand religious groups, led by their rabbis, fought the new radicals who departed from traditional Jewish living, but the brush fires ran wild and each new pogrom made the desire for freedom more intense. Writers, dreamers, angry young men threw off the shackles of the past.

Theodor Herzl molded the hundred different ideas of a thousand years into a simple paper called "The Jewish State," setting forth the credo that the Jews would never reach a status of equality until the re-establishment of their ancient homeland was achieved.

Herzl was hailed as a new messiah by some, was scorned as a new Sabbatai Zvi by others, but the father of modern Zionism had planted the seed of the new tree of hope for the Jews of the Pale.

As anti-Jewish riots spread over Europe at the end of the century, the urgency of Zionism heightened.

It was into this world of pogrom and flaming new ideas that Israel Androfski was born at close of the century. World War I brought freedom to redeclare the state of Poland behind the legions of Pilsudski. Israel Androfski and most of Poland's Jews listened to the words and ideals of Pilsudski and believed that after nineteen hundred years their emancipation had come. The Socialists and idealists rallied all of Poland behind him.

. . . And then Marshal Pilsudski abandoned the Jews and peasants and the workers of Poland to attain dictatorship with the age-old powers of the feudal gentry, the colonels' clique, and the Church behind him. . . .

To the Jews, another shattering disillusion as riots and unfair taxation and trade restrictions heightened against them.

"Andrei! What is! You carrying rocks in your pockets and fighting *goyim* in Krasinski Gardens?"

"Poppa, they started it. They attacked me when we began our deliveries."

"I told you to run from the *goyim*."

"I will not run."

"God help me! God help me for a son like this. You listen to me. You will go to synagogue and pray and you will be a good Jew!"

They accepted Andrei outside the Jewish area because he could pit his strength against them and win. But behind his back he knew he was always "the Jew." Always the Jew, no matter what he attained. Always the wall between them. Never able to be accepted . . . what he craved the most eluded him.

"I have decided to join the Zionists, Poppa."

"Those radicals! My son, my son. You have not been to

59

synagogue for six months. You are now twenty years of age and you have not found out yet that the price of being a Jew calls for patience and prayer and acceptance of your position."

"I'll never accept it. Oh, Poppa, I cannot find what I want in the Talmud. I must look for myself. . . ."

"Andrei," Alexander Brandel said. "You must accept the commission in the Ulany. Do you realize what it means to all of us to have one of our boys, a Zionist, a Ulany officer? It has never happened. And pray God you'll make the Polish soccer team for the Olympics in Berlin. Andrei . . . do it for us."

"If they would only accept me . . . as . . . not some sort of a freak!"

"I know, Andrei, how hard it is to carry this battle for us, but your back is strong and we need you."

"We are like a bird a long way from home, circling aimlessly . . . looking for a place to light and build a nest. But as soon as we cry we are driven from the tree and we must circle again. . . ."

Israel Androfski lay on his deathbed and rasped to his bereaved boy, "And have you won your great battle for acceptance? Andrei . . . return to a good Jewish life before it is too late. . . ."

> What is best Sehora?
> My baby will learn Torah,
> Seforim he will write for me,
> And a pious Jew he'll always be.

"Know from where you came."

Dawn cast an ugly gray light on Warsaw. Andrei's heavy eyes blinked at the sharpening outlines of the rooftops. He felt the presence of someone behind him.

"It is very chilly. You'd better come inside," Gabriela said.

Chapter Eight

Journal Entry

We are within an inch of war.
The Polish delegation arrived in Berlin for last-minute talks but are without authority to make direct negotiations. It is the consensus that Hitler doesn't really want to negotiate. His pact with Russia puts the Soviet army on the shelf for the time being, and no one is

under the illusion that France and England are going to do very much if Germany attacks us.

I was finally able to get hold of Andrei. Ana Grinspan came up from Krakow, so we will be able to hold an executive meeting later this morning.

ALEXANDER BRANDEL

Throughout Warsaw bells pealed. They pealed from the towers of large and small churches and the cathedral. They pealed from St. Antoine's and St. Anne's and from the Carmelites' and from Notre Dame and the Dominican and Franciscan churches and St. Casimir's and the Jesuits' and from the Holy Cross where Chopin's heart is kept in a little black box near the altar.

Warsaw is filled with churches, and all their bells pealed. For it was Sunday.

A smattering of white sails billowed on the Vistula River to test out the first brisk late-summer breeze, and bathers and sunners packed the shore of the beach at Praga Park.

The Poniatowski Bridge and the Kierbedzia Bridge buckled with the heavy traffic to and from Praga as relatives exchanged visits.

Beneath the Poniatowski Bridge was the Solec district. And this was filled with the odor of freshly dropped horse dung, as most of the teamsters lived in Solec and stabled their horses in the court-yards alongside their homes.

In the winding steps beneath the bridge in Solec the police in-vestigated the knifing of a well-known whore. However, the usual smuggling, mugging, fencing, prostitution, pickpocketing, gam-bling, and thieving which made the Solec the Solec had decreased, for most of the whores and hoodlums were in church.

All of Christian Warsaw, two thirds of its population, piously promenaded in and out of church. The day before, Jewish Warsaw, the other third, had piously promenaded in and out of synagogue.

It was a pleasant day. As Gabriela dressed for Mass she could see beyond her balcony into the square and along the Aleja Ujazdowska, where the elegant promenaded. The men cut fasti-dious figures with their homburgs and canes and spats and pin stripes, and there were the dashing army officers, and women elegant in Paris hats and Paris dresses and fur pieces.

The new rich paraded along Jerusalem Boulevard and the grand Avenue of the Marshals.

The hopeful young lovers and the soldiers of the rank and their girls promenaded up and down New World Street, looking long-ingly into the barred shopwindows.

The visitors from the country flooded the Old Town Square to saturate themselves with Polish lore.

The neither rich nor poor filled the Saxony Gardens. And, since the super-nationalistic marshal, Pilsudski, had died, the crowds were allowed to spill into and examine the wonders of his personal botanical gardens in the Lazienki around his Belvedere Palace.

In the Old Town, boys took photographs of their girls posing on the medieval walls.

And the poor people went to the Krasinski Gardens to look at trees and grass and eat hard-boiled eggs and onions and pull their children out of the lake.

Amid squirting fountains and palaces and church bells, Warsaw promenaded and little girls in knee-length white stockings and bows and pigtails walked before parents who felt rather saintly after their visit to the holy domains and little boys ran after the little girls and pulled their pigtails.

In the middle of the broad sidewalks, life centered about the circular-shaped concrete billboard structures upon which hand-bills were posted announcing cultural events, news, bargains, and Irene Dunne movies.

The monuments of Pilsudski riding his horse, Stefan riding his horse, Casimir riding his horse, Poniatowski riding his horse, and Chopin merely standing were smothered with fresh-cut flowers in the Polish tradition of reverence to her heroes.

Over Pilsudski Square, Warsaw's ground for political and military rallies, stood eleven massive columns forming an entrance to the Saxony Gardens, and in its center the eternal flame to the unknown soldier. This, too, was surrounded with cut flowers.

After church the rich went to the swanky Bruhl House and ate ices and sipped tea after their hour with God, and the poor stared at them from the street through the long, low windows. The rich did not seem to mind.

Not all of Warsaw was so reverent.

The Jews had celebrated their Sabbath a day earlier, and while their Christian brethren purged their sins the Jews quietly circumvented the stringent blue laws. The center of Jewish gangsterism on Wolynska Street smuggled and thieved, the textile workshops on Gensia bartered for raw material, and the stores of the building-materials owners that lined Grzybow Square could be opened with the proper combination of knocks.

In the mixed Christian and Jewish quarters of the smart Sienna and Zlota streets, Jewish professionals and businessmen let their neighbors know they were good Poles and joined in the promenading.

And the bells pealed.

Everything seemed quite in place for a Sunday in Warsaw. That is, if you did not go near the tension-filled ministries or the rumor-riddled lobbies of the Polonia and Bristol and Europa. Or if you were not among those who stopped before the President's Palace and watched and waited for word of a miracle which was not coming. Or if you were not in your home before the radios bringing in voices from the BBC and Berlin and America and Moscow.

For under the normalcy, everyone seemed to know that the bells of Warsaw could well be sounding the death knell of Poland.

The meeting of the Bathyran Council was held in the flat of its general secretary, Alexander Brandel. His place faced the Great Synagogue on Tlomatskie Street and was conveniently near the Writers' Club, which was the meeting place of the journalists, actors, writers, artists, and intellectuals who admitted they were Jewish. The Jewish journalists, actors, writers, artists, and intellectuals who did not admit they were Jewish met in another club a few blocks away.

A dozen routine matters, left unresolved during Andrei's absence, were dispensed with, then the discussion turned to what they should do in the event of war.

"War will bring us to terrible times," Alex said, "I do not think it is too premature to set up on an emergency footing. Perhaps even think about what we will do, God forbid, if the Germans come."

Ana Grinspan, the liaison secretary, was up first. "The very first thing we should do is close ranks as never before. We must establish a system of communications between all our chapters in case of German occupation."

Andrei was looking wistfully out of the window. When Ana began to talk, he turned and looked at her. She was still very attractive, he thought. She had been his girl before Gabriela. Funny, she is a lot like Gabriela. Ana was twenty-five and very Polish in appearance. She lived in Krakow and was from an upper-middle-class family. Most half Jews went to one of two excesses—an abnormal hate of their Jewishness or the embracing of it with an abnormal passion. When Ana discovered her father's Jewishness she became a rabid Zionist. It was this obsession that cooled Andrei towards her. There are times when a woman must be a woman and to hell with Zionism. It's too much to hear it going to bed and waking up. At any rate, their parting was completely civilized.

Ana spoke for ten minutes. No arguments about her point of view. Unity forever.

Tolek Alterman was on his feet. Dear God, please don't let Tolek get wound up, Andrei thought. But Tolek was wound up. He was distinguished by a head of bushy hair, a leather jacket, and a leftish point of view. Tolek was the manager of the Bathyran training farm outside Warsaw. He had been to Palestine with a Poale Zion group and, like all of those who had been to Palestine, he had a holy arrogance about it. "We who have actually been there" was one of his favorite and most-used phrases to press an argument.

"War or no war," Tolek was chanting loudly, "we are banded together because of mutual belief in a set of principles."

63

Now, Andrei thought, he'll ask us what those principles are.

"And what are those principles?" Tolek said. "They are the principles of Zionism. Poland and Russia are the wellsprings of Zionism because of the desire of our people for a homeland after centuries of persecution."

Oh, for Christ sake, Tolek—we know why we are Zionists.

"To remain Zionists, we must continue to function as Zionists." He's snaking into his weird traps of logic.

"The farm is living Zionism. We must continue to keep the farm going and to train our people for their eventual goals—war or no war."

Tolek then shifted into second gear. There was no denying that he had done a great job as manager of the farm. Before he took over, Andrei thought we couldn't grow weeds. Since then we've trained three groups of youngsters and they've established successful colonies in Palestine. If only he wasn't so flushed with his sacred mission.

"Having been there myself . . ." Tolek said.

Talk, talk, talk, talk.

Now it was Susan Geller's turn to talk. "The Bathyran Orphanage in Zoliborz is one of the finest in Poland. We take care of two hundred youngsters. All of them are prospective colonists for Palestine. War will bring us more orphans. Nothing on earth is more important than our children. . . ."

Tolek wants his farm, Susan wants her orphanage, Ana wants unity forever. Each one argues for his own self-interest. Well, Ervin is yawning. Good old Ervin Rosenblum. Our secretary for information and education hasn't anything to say, thank God. Rosy is a social Zionist; he joined us looking for intellectual company—mostly Susan Geller's. I wonder if they'll ever get married.

Did I tell Styka about Batory's left front hoof? It was a little tender after the last patrol. I'm certain I told him to have the veterinarian look Batory over. Maybe I didn't. My leave came so suddenly.

"So, what do you think, Andrei?" Alexander said.

"What?"

"I said—don't you want to add your opinion?"

"Sure. If the Germans come, we go into the forests and fight."

Tolek Alterman's bushy hair flopped as he thrust a finger up and said that Andrei had no restraint. Andrei didn't care to argue today —not with Tolek or Ana or Susan or Ervin or Alexander.

"Who can make plans? Who the hell knows what's going to happen!" Andrei said.

Alexander Brandel stepped in quickly and with his great gift for mediation averted the clash of philosophy spurred on by the gushing rivers of words. He pronounced a few well-chosen, all-con-

64

clusive benedictions about the great wisdom of Zionism in which everyone's point of view was vindicated, and the meeting broke up on a note of unity, unity forever.

When they were all gone, Andrei remained in the home of his closest friend. He and Wolf Brandel, Alex's sixteen-year-old son, engaged in a chess match while Alex worked at his desk.

"As a cavalry officer, I shall show you how to use your horses," Andrei said, moving his knight against Wolf's bishop.

Young Wolf lopped the horse off. Andrei scratched his head. It was no disgrace to lose, for the boy was a chess wizard.

Alex looked over from his desk. "Wolf tells me you commit your horse to battle without proper support. You are a bad officer, Andrei."

"Hah . . . today, schmendrick, you are going to get a lesson."

The mild and graying Brandel smiled and went back to his papers. Being general secretary of an organization with twenty thousand members and a hundred thousand sympathizers kept him busy night and day. Administrator, fund raiser, recruiter. He was overseer of the orphanage, the training farm, and the publication *Kol Bathyran*—Voice of Bathyran.

More than anything, Alexander Brandel was the philosopher of pure Zionism.

There were many types of Zionism, each with its own variants. Alexander Brandel said there was a different type of Zionism for every Jew.

The largest single philosophy, Labor Zionism, emerged from Poland and Russia after terrible massacres of the Jews at the turn of the century. Labor Zionism called for self-sacrifice by a dedicated Jewish labor force as the key to the redemption of Palestine.

The second of the major philosophies was that of the revisionists or activists. These were angry men whose mold demanded retribution. Often super-nationalistic and military-minded, they wanted the injustices of anti-Semitism atoned by "an eye for an eye." From the ranks of the revisionists came many of the terrorists who fought British rule in the Palestine Mandate.

Alexander Brandel's Bathyrans, formed by a small group of intellectuals, were a third group. Their concept was Zionist purity. They believed in a single principle: the establishment of a Jewish homeland was a historic necessity, as proved by two thousand years of persecution.

While the other groups agreed that the Bathyrans indeed had idealism to spare, it was impossible to put ideology into practical use without dogma.

Brandel countered charges that the Bathyrans were an antiseptic social club by taking the best of all the ideas and putting them into practice while being bound by none of them. He did not agree with the restrictions on the individual demanded by the Labor Zionists, nor did he believe in the dedication to force of the Revisionists as a complete answer. Some force and some restrictions—yes, but not completely.

When he had quit his job as an instructor of history at the university to assume leadership of the Bathyrans, the group was struggling and floundering. From chaos he developed concepts and philosophies which brought it into respect.

He lived in abstraction in his personal life. His income was always modest, his person disorganized in a scholar's absent-minded way. The light always burned late in the Brandel flat, for even beyond duty to the Bathyrans, Alexander Brandel was a Polish historian of note.

Wolf knocked off Andrei's second horse when Sylvia, Alex's wife, came in with a pot of tea and some cookies. She was six months pregnant and starting to show very much. Bathyran humor had it that Alex had come home only twice in sixteen years and both times made Sylvia pregnant.

She was the personification of the "good Jewish girl." Plain, pretty with dark and plumpish features, she was sharp in mind and the clever homemaker who created ideal conditions which allowed Alex to pursue his work.

To Sylvia, a Zionist from birth, Alex had achieved the pinnacle of accomplishment for a Jewish man. He was a writer and teacher and historian. Nothing could be greater than that. She had attended her first Labor Zionist meeting in her mother's arms before she could walk and she was completely dedicated to her husband's work. She never complained that they were poor or that he was gone half the time.

In his own lackadaisical way Alex loved Sylvia very much. Almost as much as she loved him.

Alex thrived on work. Only once in a while did he seem to need the comfort of a warm bed and his woman's arms and soothing voice. While the world revolved around him in haste and anger and frustration, he never seemed to vary his pace, never raised his voice, never panicked, never seemed torn by those inner conflicts of other men.

Alexander Brandel had achieved that state of heaven on earth which is called peace of mind.

It seemed paradoxical and almost humorous that it was the team of Brandel and Androfski that made the Bathyrans go. Andrei was fifteen years Alex's junior and his opposite in temper and outlook. Andrei was an activist in thinking. Yet they recognized in each other a particular strength the other lacked. The symbol of strength . . . the symbol of mind.

"You and Gabriela will stay for dinner," Sylvia said.

"If you don't go to any trouble."

"What's trouble? Wolf, the minute you are through with that

66

game, you practice your flute. Money for flute lessons doesn't grow on trees."

"Yes, Momma."

"Andrei, it's a good thing your niece Rachel goes to the same conservatory. He would never practice a note."

Andrei shot a glance at Wolf, who reddened.

So! he thought. You are one of those schmendricks looking over Rachael.

Wolf licked his lips, lowered his eyes, and made a move.

Andrei studied the boy. Gawky, a few straggling hairs on his chin, pimples . . . What could Rachael possibly see in that thing? Not a man, certainly, but on the other hand not quite a boy, Known him since he was a baby. He is a good lad. He will respect Rachael . . . I think.

"Your move."

Andrei made an atrocious play.

"Checkmate," Wolf said.

Andrei glared at the board for three full minutes. "Go practice your flute."

He stretched and yawned and meandered over to Alex, who was writing in a large notebook.

"What's this?" Andrei said, lifting the book and thumbing through it.

"Just a journal of events. Fulfilling my natural calling as a nosy person."

"What do you expect to do with diaries at your age?"

"I don't know if it has any use. Just a wild guess, Andrei, that it might have some importance someday."

Andrei put Brandel's journal back on the desk and shrugged. "It will never take the place of the Seventh Ulany Brigade."

"I wouldn't be too certain of that," Alex said. "Truth used at the right time can be a weapon worth a thousand armies."

"Alex, you're a dreamer."

Alex watched Andrei grow restless. He was really the only person with whom Andrei could speak from the inner reaches of his mind. Alex pushed his papers aside, took a bottle of vodka from his desk, and poured two glasses, a small one for himself and a large one for Andrei.

Andrei took the glass and said, "*Le'chayim!*—to life."

"You were quiet at the meeting today," Alex said.

"The rest of them did enough talking for me."

"Andrei, I've seen you so unhappy only once before. Two years ago, B.G.—before Gabriela. You've had an argument?"

"I always have arguments with her."

"Where is she?"

"In the church most likely, lighting candles and asking forgiveness of Jesus, Mary, the Apostles, and forty Polish saints for living in sin with a Jew."

"It's the coming war, isn't it?"

"Yes, it's the war and it's Gabriela. There are things that a man wants answered before he goes out on a battlefield."

"We talked about these things today for three hours. You weren't with us."

Andrei sipped his vodka and shook his head. "I am a bad Jew, Alex. I am not a Jew my father would have been proud of, may God rest his soul."

Andrei walked to the window and pulled the curtain back and pointed to the great symbol of eastern Europe's Jewry, the Tlomatskie Synagogue. "My father could find comfort for any problem in the words of the Torah."

"But, Andrei, that is why we are Bathyrans and Labor Zionists and Revisionists. We could not find comfort in the Torah alone."

"That is the point, Alex. I am not even a good Zionist."

"My goodness, who's been talking to you?"

"Paul Bronski. He sees right through me. I am a phony Zionist. Alex, now listen to me. I'm not a disciple of A. D. Gordon and that crap of love of the soil. I don't want to go to Palestine, now or ever. Warsaw is my city, not Tel Aviv or Jerusalem. I am a Polish officer and this is my country."

"You told me once very plainly that you don't want anyone to steal your chickens. Isn't that Zionism? Aren't we merely in a struggle for dignity?"

"In dubious battle," Andrei mumbled. Then he sat and his voice became very soft. "I want to live in Poland and I want to be a part of this country as though I belong. But at the same time I want to be what I am. I cannot accept Paul Bronski's terms of giving up what I am. I have wanted to run to the synagogue and believe with my father's faith. I want to believe in Zionism as you believe."

Alexander Brandel tightened the muffler around his neck. He lifted his glass, revealing a big suede patch on his elbow.

"Did you ever read my article when I tried to explain the anatomy of anti-Semitism in Poland? Never mind, it was a bad article." He closed his eyes to intensify his meditation and recited, "All of Poland is divided into three classes. The peasant class, the gentry—those who aim to keep them peasants—and the Jews. Ninety-five per cent Ukrainia and five per cent Paris with a few ethnic groups thrown in to make eternal trouble on our eastern and western borders. We Jews came to Poland at the invitation of a Polish king in the Middle Ages fleeing ahead of the holy swords of purification of the Crusades. We came to establish their merchant and professional class."

"Well said, Professor."

"Andrei, take that poor miserable peasant scratching out an

existence on the land. He is driven to mysticism in his worship in order to justify being able to live in a world he cannot cope with. Now, he has a Jew in his village. The Jew is not allowed to own land, so the Jew makes magic with his hands. The Jew can sew, mend shoes . . . The Jew can read. The Jew reads something in that mysterious script and keeps rituals that frightens the peasant. Or perhaps the Jew becomes the grain merchant. He has to use his wit and cunning to live. He may lend money—this makes him despicable. But what the peasant really does not understand is the Jew who pushes a cart and sells secondhand clothing in order to send his son through college. Now, our peasant goes out once a week to the town and he is very frustrated and confused and he gets drunk. He must hit someone, explode this accumulation of frustration. He cannot hit the nobleman who owns his land and steals half his crop as rent, so he beats up the little Jew who cannot fight back. The nobleman tells him that the Jew who lends the money and is the grain merchant and uses human blood in his rituals has brought him to this state of poverty. He is a victim of Jewish cunning. Now, our nobleman, who robs the peasant blind, does not give them education or medicine or justice, also hates the Jew who is his doctor or lawyer or architect or banker. We are the convenient scapegoat for the serfs and the ones who aim to keep them as serfs."

Andrei grunted. "Wanting to be a Pole in your own land is as futile as wanting to be a Jew in your own land. I am not allowed the luxury of either."

He looked out of the window and saw Gabriela walking toward the flat. At least there is another night with her before I must go back, Andrei thought. At least there is that.

Chapter Nine

The divine feeling which gripped Warsaw on Sunday was, unfortunately, not able to call a truce, to hold back those hands of fate moving toward the twelfth hour. The ministries, the war offices, and the newsrooms were open for business.

Chris turned the bureau over to Rosy and walked to the Foreign Ministry to check out any late announcements in the crisis.

For the moment it was quiet.

He left and, instead of returning to the Bristol, continued past the tall columns of the eternal flame on Pilsudski Square and on into the Saxony Gardens. The Sunday strollers and lazers filled the benches and paths. He passed the big wooden theater which announced the final production of the summer season. New show next week, Chris thought, all German cast. Chris stopped before the lake, checked his watch, and found an empty bench. The warm sun and the gliding swans added to the serenity. He closed his eyes a moment and rubbed his temple. He was queazy and had a slight headache as a result of his binge with Andrei the night before. Lucky Andrei will be going back, he thought, as one more drinking bout with the pride of the Ulanys would do him in.

Deborah appeared down the path. She looked around for him, but he did not signal. For a moment he wanted only to gaze on her. Each time he saw her it was the same as the first. She waved and sat beside him and he quietly took her hand. For a long time they did not speak, nor did they hear the swirl of foot traffic around them or the sounds of giggling from the lake where a soldier stopped rowing his boat and nearly tipped it climbing back to his girl, nor did they hear the swans flutter indignantly to get out of the boat's way.

"I came as soon as I could get away," Deborah said at last.

"Why wouldn't you come to my apartment?"

Deborah merely shook her head. "Chris," she sighed, "what we have been doing has never been right. Only now it seems even more wrong with Paul away."

"It's seemed so long. Just listening for you every minute."

"You know I wanted to come," she said. Her fingers betrayed her nervousness so badly that she withdrew her hand.

"I'm going off tomorrow," Chris said.

She was startled.

"Just a few days. I'm going to make a round of the border."

"I'm glad you called me."

"Since the other night you haven't been off my mind a minute. Deborah, we're sitting here in the sunlight and we can think. We've just got to have this out with Paul."

"No, Chris. Not with him in the army."

"Before that it was another excuse, and before that another. I swear I've been hoping he won't come back."

"Chris!"

"I know, he's a fine fellow."

"I've thought a lot about us too, Chris. When I'm with you—it's —I never thought it would ever come to me. But at the same time I am doing something against everything I've believed in. I'm not going to leave Paul."

"Is there any feeling between you and him?"

"Not the way you mean. There never has been, you know that. There are other ways a man and woman can be something to each other."

"Deborah, I'm not leaving you until you throw me out."

"Then we have come to that. I can't continue to see you and keep what little is left of my self-respect."

His hand touched her cheek and her neck, and she closed her

70

eyes. "Don't, Chris, you know how I am when you touch me. Oh, Chris, all I do is give you problems. I'm no good for you."

She felt his lips touching her face. "Come on up to my place," he whispered. "I'll undress you and we'll lie in bed and listen to music and open a bottle of champagne . . ."

"Chris . . . get up and walk away . . . please."

"I will if you really want me to."

"You know I don't."

The afternoon was filled with a hundred kisses and endearments and a hundred more. Their love-making carried with it an intense sort of desperation, and when they had exhausted each other they fell into deep, glorious naps. When they awoke, Deborah was happy. She bathed and roamed around the kitchen, all but lost in Chris's big terry-cloth robe, and fixed the steaks and iced the champagne while he soaked in a steaming tub.

"Wash my back!" she heard him call.

When she came into the bathroom, his feet were up on the edge of the tub and he was singing a Verdi aria, trying for a high C, which he missed by a full six notes. Deborah whimpered sensuously as she knelt beside the tub and rubbed the soap over his back. He tried to open her robe.

"No peeking," she said.

She grabbed his hair and dunked him, then covered his wet face with kisses.

Toward evening it grew chilly and he lit a fire. They finished their meal and lay contentedly on the big sofa, sipping warming cognac. Deborah opened the robe and closed it over the two of them, and his hand traced the lines of her body from her shoulders to her knees.

"Would you believe that I was such a terrible prude and such a good girl? What have you done to me, Mr. de Monti?"

Deborah Androfski was only eleven when her mother died. She had to assume the role of homemaker for her father and little brother, Andrei. Before and after school, her job never ended. She had to cook and clean and do laundry and shop. They were poor as only a Polish Jew could be. She had to spend hours bargaining and haggling in the filth and poverty of Parysowski Place to save every zloty.

It seemed that all Deborah could remember of her mother after a time was an image of a tired and pain-filled woman waiting for the redemption of death to take her away from the smells and the dirt of Stawki Street. Momma always held her back and groaned as she climbed the stairs. Momma always had a new ache in a never-ending assortment of them.

Israel Androfski, was able to find respite from the struggle of existence in the comforts of a deep-rooted Jewishness which

71

bordered on fanatic joys through prayer. He could detach himself from the misery around him at synagogue. This was denied Momma, for everyday prayer was a privilege of men.

Being a "good Jewish wife" imposed rigid rules of life. As Deborah grew older, all the little vignettes and mosaics began to take form and meaning. Why Momma always complained especially on the Sabbath eve when Poppa came home from synagogue, for a good Jewish wife was supposed to reconsummate the marriage every Friday night. And this was painful and unpleasant for Momma. Momma lost three children by miscarriage; one other died from disease when a year old. This came from what Momma and Poppa did on the Sabbath eve, and it always ended up in pain and suffering.

When Andrei was born, this brought on a new set of ills to Momma's insides.

"Be careful of the boys," Momma told Deborah. "They will make you pregnant and you'll spend your life scrubbing floors and washing and over an oven and giving them babies. Boys are no good, Deborah—boys are no good." Momma went to her grave decrying the suffering connected with being a woman.

Momma's prophecies were borne out when Deborah had to scrub and clean and cook and wash and shop. It was like a voice from the grave always on her shoulder.

By the time she had reached fifteen, her father had worked his way out of the slums and moved the family to the nice Sliska Street neighborhood where Orthodox Jews of means resided.

Although Israel Androfski was a rather kindly man, in the back of her mind Deborah always blamed him for her mother's death. And when she came of an age to understand why her father visited certain women with bad reputations, it further proved, in her mind, the sordidness of what men and women did in bed. Family responsibility had imposed upon her a passive nature. She was always lonely, as long as she could remember, except for Andrei. Her one solace was the piano.

When the burden of being a homemaker lifted after they moved to Sliska Street, Deborah threw all the latent hurts into it, bringing about an artistry that moved her close to dizzying heights of mastery.

Then, as suddenly as she had plunged into it, she rebelled against it when her father demanded she spend more and more time in its study.

A strange and unexplainable phenomenon stirred within her which overpowered the fears of night. A desire for freedom. She wanted to explore that strange world beyond. An instinct of survival let her know she was drowning in a mental ghetto.

In her first act of defiance Deborah quit the piano and demanded to go to the university to study medicine. Her first look at the outside world gave her her first true friend, Susan Geller, a nursing student.

Deborah Androfski was eighteen years old when she met Dr. Paul Bronski, the brilliant young professor for whom every female student in the university carried a secret torch. Deborah was an uncommonly beautiful girl, and as uncommonly naïve as she was beautiful.

Paul Bronski, who had been rather meticulous in every move he made in his life, wanted her for his wife. She had every quality— intelligence and beauty—and would be the perfect mother and hostess. She could supply the needs of a man when he desired, and she would be good for his career.

Deborah stepped into the big wide world too fast. She was completely without sophistication or experience in that game of boys and girls. She was swept off her feet. With shattering accuracy, Momma's dire prediction came true. She was pregnant.

"I love you very much," Paul said. "I want you to become Mrs. Paul Bronski."

"I think I would die if you didn't want me."

"Not want you? Deborah ... dear ... only ... now, we must do something about your pregnancy."

"What——"

"I know this will be difficult for you, but our future depends on it. We are going to have to give you an abortion."

"Paul ... take our baby ..."

"Dear, you're eighteen years old. You are one of my students. Think of what kind of scandal there will be if you are married in your condition. Not only the shame for you and your family, it would ruin my career."

"But ... an abortion ... "

"It will be done carefully—and don't worry. We will have children, lots of them."

The result mired her deep in guilt. Momma was right. Sex was ugly and painful. Her deep religious roots made her bear losing the child as a penance for her sin. She married Paul Bronski and became to him all the things he wished. She was the perfect mother and the clever hostess and she filled his needs as a man.

But it was in darkness in their bed that she served her sentence. The guilt of the sex act was deeply embedded, and she practiced the discipline of pretending to enjoy in order not to offend her husband. She experienced neither fulfillment nor the smaller pleasures of love-making. She was entirely frigid.

What strange and wonderful thing was it that drew her to Christopher de Monti? He took her hand as though she were a little girl and led her through the black evil forest to the golden castle that sat on a cloud.

73

There was that first frightening time they were alone in his apartment and everything between them that had gone before had led to the moment when a man and a woman have nowhere left to go in their relationship but to bed.

She threw an angry tantrum over a seeming trifle. Chris completely understood that she was in reality angry with herself over her fear of an inability to perform.

So many times Chris held her face in his hands.

"Deborah, my love . . . your mother is dead. You are not going to disobey her by letting yourself have the pleasure of a normal woman."

And all the years of frustration burst out when Chris unlocked them and drove them from her.

"I didn't know . . . I didn't know it could be like this."

Deborah blinked her eyes open. The fire was in embers. Chris was rattling around in the kitchen. She looked at her watch. It was very late. He came in, rumpled and smiling, wearing a battered old pair of khaki trousers and holding two cups of coffee.

As wild and wonderful a woman as she had been, Chris watched her change into someone else before his eyes. She fumbled for the telephone and dialed in a nervous, jerky manner. "Hello, Rachael. This is Momma. Darling, I'm sorry I didn't call you. I got held up. Did Zoshia make you a good dinner? Practice your piano, darling. Tell Stephan I'll be home in a little while."

She set the phone down slowly. Chris offered her coffee. She shook her head, avoiding his eyes, and walked away quickly toward her clothing.

"Do we have to play out another remorse-filled scene?"

"Don't."

"But I do——"

"I woke up just now with a terrible start. It is terribly clear that we have done something sinful in the way we have lived. I know we are going to be punished——"

The phone rang.

"Hello."

"It's me, Rosy."

"Yes, Rosy."

"You'd better get down here, right away."

"What's up?"

"Everything out of Berlin has stopped cold. I called Switzerland. They say all the lines from Germany have been cut at the Polish border."

Chapter Ten

August 31, 1939
To: Commander, Company A, Reinforced
From: Commander, 7th Ulany Mounted Brigade—Grudziadz
Subject: Patrol Assignment

Proceed north on the Tczew road at 0700. A special detachment of intelligence scouts has been detailed to your command for the purpose of detecting unusual movements, changes of disposition, or additions of strength to the German Third Army.

Send reports to us by rider in a routine manner.

When you reach Tczew, join battalion and continue with them to Gdynia.

No later than 0600 tomorrow you will encounter Company B coming from Tczew in a patrol which will be the reverse of yours. Send your dispatch with them.

It is emphasized that we are at peace with Germany and an unprovoked incident could have serious repercussions. However, under extraordinary circumstances you are authorized to use your judgment.

Signed: Zygmunt Bozakolski, Brigadier in Command, 7th Ulany Mounted Brigade—Grudziadz.

Captain Andrei Androfski moved Company A out of the large headquarters base at Grudziadz at 0700. It was scheduled as a routine patrol that called for a two-day ride along the eastern border of the Polish Corridor, along a road that ran parallel to German East Prussia. He was to meet another company of his battalion the following morning. For several weeks his brigade had been engaged in these roving patrols covering the area from the Baltic port city of Gdynia to the Grudziadz base. The patrols had been singularly dull and uneventful.

The late-summer day in Pomerania was warmish, and as Company A galloped north they were completely detached from the frantic business taking place in Berlin several hundred kilometers away. The land was green and quiet and, as soldiers do, they looked forward to a blowout in Gdynia.

Berlin, Germany: August 31, 1939

Sir Neville Henderson, the British Foreign Minister, asked for and received a list of demands from the German Chancellery upon which war could be averted. The demands were read to him in a quick unintelligible language. He then demanded to see them in writing. They did not come.

The Germans, instead, demanded direct negotiations with the Polish peace mission upon terms the Poles did not know.

The Polish mission was not authorized to take on a direct negotiation. In last-ditch desperation Sir Neville Henderson pleaded with the Poles to get authorization from Warsaw. The Poles attempted to comply, but when they tried to telephone their capital they discovered the phone lines had been cut.

Sir Neville Henderson, raw-nerved from the tension and lack of sleep, angrily demanded to know why the lines were down. The Germans answered that it was the work of Polish bandits, furthering the already "intolerable" situation and "proving the Poles wanted war."

Berlin was white-hot with war fever. The population was barraged with tales of Polish attacks along the border, of Polish aircraft firing on German commercial planes flying over the corridor, of Poles committing murder and atrocities against "innocent German ethnic families," of Polish mobilization, and of Polish war hysteria.

By the evening of August 31, Captain Androfski's company had made an uneventful ride along the Polish-Prussian border. They came to a halt for the day opposite the German town of Marienwerder, setting up a bivouac in a small woods a few hundred meters from the road. After the evening meal, it turned dark. Normal security was established, then Captain Androfski called together the special detachment of intelligence scouts who had been assigned to him.

In addition to the routine patrol orders, Andrei had also received verbal orders from the brigade intelligence commander concerning the German massing of armor along the corridor in that area, and Andrei's patrol carried the secondary purpose of scouting it. The special detachment of ten men, dressed as civilians, crossed unarmed into Germany with instructions to circle the Marienwerder area during the night and return to camp before dawn. Their observations would be assessed and the data given to Company B.

August 31, 1939
TOP SECRET
To: Commander, Armed Forces
Directive No. 1
... inasmuch as we can find no peaceful means to solve the intolerable situation on the Eastern Frontier ... the attack on Poland is to be carried out in preparations made in CASE WHITE.
Date of attack: September 1, 1939
Time of attack: 0445
Signed: Adolf Hitler

While the men of Company A slept in a wooded area in the Polish Corridor, the epilogue to peace was written hundreds of kilometers to the south, where Germany and Poland faced each other at Gleiwitz and Katowice.

German SS troops, dressed as Polish soldiers, crossed the frontier into Poland, then recrossed into Germany and blew up their own German radio station at Gleiwitz. Therefore, in Nazi logic, a reason had been created to stamp the war as "official."

When First Sergeant Styka shook the men of Company A out of their sleep, they were unaware of CASE WHITE. To them it was to be another boring day of soldiering. They grumbled into wakefulness, cursing as they moved about.

There had been only snatches of sleep for Captain Androfski and First Sergeant Styka. They waited out most of the night until the ten scouts had returned safely. Andrei sifted their information and wrote his dispatch.

September 1, 1939
To: Commander, 7th Ulany Mounted Brigade—Grudziadz
From: Company A, mobile border patrol

Last night we encamped at position L-14 opposite Marienwerder. The area was scouted by the special detachment in accordance with verbal orders.

Abnormal German strength is evident in this area. In addition to units we have previously identified, we have identified two new regiments of armored infantry and at least a portion of a division of Panzer tanks (22nd and 56th Infantry and 3rd Panzer Tanks).

Two battalions of this Panzer tank division moved out of Marienwerder this morning at 0300, apparently for disposition in a southerly direction.

Company A will continue north today. We expect to join the balance of the battalion at Tczew tonight.
Signed: Andrei Androfski, Captain, Company A

Andrei folded the dispatch, then opened it on a sudden impulse. Across the bottom of the paper he scrawled the words, "Long live Poland!"

First Sergeant Styka trotted his mount to Andrei and snapped a salute. "The company is eating, sir. We should be ready to move out in a half hour."

"Any sign of Company B yet?"

"No, sir. No sign of them."

Andrei looked at his watch and wondered. It was half-past five. The deadline was 0600. A half hour to go. Trouble up north? Well, no use speculating about it.

"Morning, sir," the officers said as he moved into their circle.

77

"Morning."

He and Styka sat off to one side and ate. Goddamned ham. My father would roll over in his grave if he could see me eat ham.

"Styka, when the hell are you going to learn to brew tea?" He flipped the contents in the bottom of the cup to the ground.

"I'm afraid never, sir."

"Have the company saddle up and stand by."

"Yes, sir."

Andrei walked to the edge of the woods and stared long and futilely up the empty road, straining to see a telltale whiff of dust or hear the welcome sound of hoofbeats.

0600, the maximum hour, passed. No Company B.

Suddenly the entire movement of the company stopped, and all the men were staring up the road. Andrei walked back to the bivouac area. "Styka!"

"Yes, sir."

"Send me a rider. Make it Tyrowicz."

Company A's best rider, Corporal Tyrowicz, reported.

"Tyrowicz, ride hard back to Grudziadz. I want you back there by noon. Use fields—stay off the main road. Can you do it, lad?"

"I'll try hard, Captain."

"Hand-deliver this dispatch to Brigadier Bozakolski. Tell him that Company B did not show up. We are proceeding north."

"Yes, sir."

He watched Tyrowicz spur out, driving his horse. He wheeled to Styka. "Move the advance scouts out. First platoon take the point. Use flank guards. Be on the road in five minutes, column of twos. Shake it up."

"Yes, sir."

It was chilly in the dawnlight. The men beat warmth into themselves, and darts of frosted air spurted from their mouths. The first rays of light penetrated the woods, changing the world from ugly gray. Up and down, the crisp orders to mount up. There was no cursing or griping. A sobering tension filled them all. Some of the more pious were on their knees saying quick Hail Marys. Strange, Andrei thought, this isn't much of a praying company. He looked at his watch again. It would be fully light in another forty minutes. Where the hell was Company B? Where the hell were they?

Andrei's stomach knotted in much the same way as it did before a soccer match. Was this quiet morning and Styka's bad tea war?

The first sergeant returned. "We are formed up, sir."

Andrei nodded and watched the sergeant trot off out to the road.

The woods were empty now. Andrei checked the saddle buckles on Batory. He chewed a piece of black bread, sipped from the canteen, and slipped it back into the saddlebag. He looked up at his magnificent black beast. The horse was nervous.

Andrei pressed his forehead against Batory's neck. "We render thanks unto Thee for our lives, which are in Thy hands, and for our souls, which are ever in Thy keeping."

Why did I pray? I have not prayed since I was a boy. Batory whinnied and went up on his hind legs. "You feel it too, don't you, boy? Steady, fellow." Andrei swung astride his horse and soon had him calm and trotted out to the road.

"Move out!" Styka barked.

The forward platoon galloped off. The flanks fanned out, and the communicators positioned to keep contact. They advanced in a slow trot, transfixed by the brightening day. North for an hour, then two, three, and each kilometer filled them with greater uneasiness. There was no sign of Company B. It was beyond normal limitations. Either they had had their orders changed or . . . trouble.

Styka heard it first. The column stopped without a command. Everyone's eyes went upward. There was a distant hum in the sky. Then black specks appeared high, high overhead, almost beyond sight.

"Off the road," Andrei ordered quietly.

They went into the ditch on the Polish side of the border road, dismounted, and held their restless horses still. Two hundred pairs of eyes fixed on the sky.

". . . sixty. Sixty-one, sixty-two . . ."

The humming overhead grew louder and louder. And soon the sky was pocked with masses of black spots moving in perfect formation in what appeared to be slow motion.

The only sound in the stunned company was Styka's voice continuing a toll in monotone. ". . . two hundred thirty-four, two hundred thirty-five . . ."

They had never seen such a mass of planes. The awesome display passed and disappeared from sight and sound. Three hundred fifty airplanes. For a very long time no one uttered a sound.

"Captain," Styka said in a cracked voice, "aren't they flying over our territory?"

"East-southeast," Andrei answered.

"Where would the captain say they are heading?"

"Warsaw."

The eyes of every man went from the sky to Captain Androfski. "Well, gentlemen," he said, "the store is open for business." Nervous laughter greeted him. "Styka, bring my officers in and get Private Trzaska from the First Platoon."

They huddled around the map. "Trzaska," Andrei said, "you were a farmer near Starogard, weren't you?"

"Yes, sir."

"Where can we find good cover and an elevation overlooking the road?"

Private Trzaska studied the map a moment, then slid a dirty fingernail up the border and stopped. "There's a small forest here,

79

sir. Runs several hundred meters in all directions and sits on a knoll."

"How far from the road?"

"Oh . . . maybe three hundred meters."

They could make it in an hour of good riding. It was the nearest point with decent cover. "This is where we're going, gentlemen," Andrei said. "Have your men combat-ready, and move single file and stretched out. Quick trot all the way. Second Platoon, take the rear guard and drop your last man a kilometer back. Let's move."

"Mount up!"

"Combat-ready. Load them up."

"Single file. Don't bunch up like a flock of pigeons."

The scouts moved out at a gallop.

This time Captain Androfski was first on the road. He put on his steel helmet, buckled the chin strap, cocked his pistol, and swung Batory up ahead of the company.

Styka's large mustache drooped.

"How you doing, Sergeant?" Andrei asked.

"I'm so scared I could crap my pants," Styka answered.

"Stay close to me. We'll get through today. They say after the first one it's not so bad."

Styka faced the company. "Ride hard!"

Company A moved north again and within an hour found the woods which Private Trzaska had promised. Andrei was pleased. He had cover and an excellent view of the road.

He ordered each of four men to ride out a kilometer in different directions and observe. They were issued flares for warning. Then he sent one rider north to continue to look for Company B and a second rider south back to the Grudziadz base.

By midafternoon a second flight of planes, as large as the first flight in the morning, again blackened the skies, heading toward central Poland.

Andrei sat away from his men, trying to evaluate his situation and its implications. The new German Panzer power they had discovered, the seven hundred airplanes, and the lost Company B —all indicated war had started.

What move?

To continue to Tczew and join the battalion even though there appeared to be trouble up north?

To stand pat and wait for the sign of Germans?

What if the Germans showed up? He had good cover. Should he button up and wait for dark and head back to the main base?

No, impossible. The nature and breeding of the Ulany made the idea of both running and hiding repulsive. He smiled to himself as he thought of Chris. Too bad he won't be the first into Berlin. No doubt we are massing for a huge counterattack into Germany now.

As often happens in war when men are in the field, the decision is made for them.

"Captain," Styka said, "riders coming in from the north!"

Andrei trained his field glasses on them. There were two. One was his, the rider he had dispatched earlier. Another, a stranger. They pulled into the forest with frothing mounts. The stranger was bloody and half senseless.

"Back up, dammit," Andrei said. "Give the man breathing room."

"He's from Company B, sir," Andrei's man said.

"Can you talk, soldier?"

He nodded and gasped. "Holy Mother . . . oh, holy Mother, Captain." Andrei pumped some water down his throat. "Oh, Jesus. We never knew what happened. The Germans . . . heading south . . . right down the road."

"Take this man and keep him calm. Lieutenant Vacek, plant your contact mine on the road. Lieutenant Zurawski, set up all four machine guns in a U-shaped cross fire around the mine. Use the ditches on both sides of the road for cover. Dzienciala, can we use our mortars effectively from this distance?"

"I think so, sir."

"Keep your squad in the woods here as a covering force. The rest of you line out for a single-file charge. I'll lead. If our luck goes right, we can ambush the first batch of them. I want only limited pursuit. Pull back here to the forest for regrouping."

"If we don't pursue, they'll know where we are, Captain."

"Hell, they'll know in Berlin where we are ten minutes after the first shot."

"What does the captain plan to do after we regroup?"

"Sit our asses right here and keep them from getting south on this road. As soon as it turns dark we'll go north to find the battalion."

The single land mine was planted on the road and a cross fire of machine guns established within minutes. The two mortar squads set up in the forest and zeroed in on the road. The rest of Company A stretched nearly the length of the woods . . . and they waited.

A warning flare arched up from the northern advance guard.

"Here they come, Captain."

Out of the north there arose a billow of dust. Andrei lifted his field glasses and watched the cloud of dust grow larger until it could be seen by everyone. And then, the sound of motors. He counted them as they turned a bend into the straight flat stretch of a kilometer and a half directly below him.

"Troop carriers, twenty-two of them. Must have two companies."

And then he could see the swastika markings on their sides. The trucks rambled down the road in an undeterred race. Andrei reasoned that the Germans must have felt there would be no opposition after they had overrun the battalion and Company B.

"Steady the line, dammit!"

He held the glasses to his eyes again. He could see the face of his enemy! In the lead truck the driver looked to be a boy. For some crazy reason he thought of Wolf Brandel at that second, and Batory went up on his hind legs.

"Stand by!"

The lead truck was armored. It struck the mine, and the earth shook and splattered and the truck disintegrated. The second truck, filled with soldiers, attempted to stop short and it careened off the road, rolling into the ditch, bursting into flame. The third and fourth trucks slammed into each other. And then! Rat-a-tat! Rat-a-tat! Streaks of tracers leaped from the machine guns, catching the Germans in a deadly cross fire. German soldiers poured out of the trucks in wild disarray, trying to organize under the frantic shouts of their officers.

Andrei brought his hand down. "Charge! Charge! Kill the sons of bitches! Charge!"

A bloodcurdling battle cry erupted from Company A as they poured down the knoll behind their captain. The horsemen tore into the confused enemy, ripping, hacking, trampling them into a gory massacre.

Unable to organize, the Germans began fleeing on foot, to be run down, shot down, smashed down.

The tail end of the convoy, the last five trucks, were able to turn around and flee back north. The mortars in the woods found one truck, turning it into a torch. The other four escaped.

It was over in ten minutes. A hundred dead and dying Germans lay strewn about the road and ditches, and the air was hot with the burning of the shattered vehicles. Andrei pulled his men back into the forest.

He climbed from Batory and fell to his knees and doubled over to catch his breath. There were howls of the delight of victory among his dripping wet, exhausted men. The first smell of combat had been victory.

Andrei climbed to his feet and leaned against his horse, who was wet with sweat too but excited over the stimulation of carrying his master to a kill.

"Styka, we're not going to throw a victory ball. Calm them down, we've work to do. Medic, what were our casualties?"

"Four dead, sir. Trzaska, Lieutenant Zurawski—I think he got it from our own cross fire—and Wajwod and Lamejko."

"Wounded?"

"Six—one bad."

"Horses?"

"Ten, Captain," Styka said. "All have been executed."

Andrei looked at the wreckage on the road. Nothing could pass. The Germans could not detour, for the ditches were too steep.

"Any orders, Captain?"

"Get the machine gunners back here. No use having them exposed. Just stand by—they'll be back. Let me take a look at the wounded."

The victory had done much to pass the first terrible fear of contact. They waited.

Andrei stood at the farthest edge of the forest, holding Batory's reins. "Well, boy, we're in it now," he said to his horse. "That wasn't so bad after all the times we've practiced it, was it? Too damned easy, if you ask me. Wish we had an alternative to this position. . . . Well, we're committed now. Have to hold them off this road. Think we can keep this position? Sure we can. They'll never get another attack organized today. Easy, boy."

Blam!

An explosion went off at the foot of the knoll, very close to the road, and another and another.

"Styka!"

It was long-range cannon fire. Where? A half dozen more shells exploded, walking up the knoll. Andrei looked at his watch. Only forty-eight minutes since he had regrouped from the attack.

Blam! Blam! Blam! Blam!

"Over there," Andrei said. He pointed in the direction of East Prussia. A dozen iron-treaded monsters were crossing the field, their cannons probing the forest. Andrei grunted. Radio communication and long-range guns had turned a good defensive position into a trap within minutes. Was he going to pay with interest for his ambush? He looked at his pair of puny mortars. They would be unable to reach the tanks until they were fairly near the road. The Germans could lay back out of range and blast them to pieces if they chose. Break for it, maybe? No, dammit, never!

The cannon fire began to find the edge of the woods. The line of horsemen began to waver. "Steady there!"

Two of the tanks reached the road.

"Mortar fire!"

The mortar shells bounced around the tanks. One scored a direct hit. They did nothing to deter the German barrage.

Good God! Andrei thought. How can I stop them?

. . . four-five-six-seven-eight-nine-ten-eleven-twelve. All the tanks were in position now, hitting them from three hundred meters.

"Dismount! Take your horses back and hitch them! Form a staggered firing line."

Blam! Blam! Blam! Blam!

Barks of thin trees burst into flame. A dozen horses cried in terror and several broke from the woods. Company A hid behind the cover of the trees. Only Captain Androfski and Batory stayed forward to observe.

The German tanks groaned into motion toward the bottom of the knoll. "Machine gunners! Give it to them. Shoot for the turrets!"

The machine guns hit into the tanks, and their bullets bounced off like annoying little ant pricks.

"Captain! Airplanes!"

The black vultures streaked over the treetops and screamed down on the woods. The planes flew low, dropping fire bombs, and the woods went up like a torch. A second flight of planes vomited ten thousand machine-gun bullets into them. The instant they passed, the tanks started again. Now truckloads of infantry unloaded, forming up behind the tanks.

Gagging and choking and bleeding, what was left of Company A found what was left of their mounts.

"Charge!" Andrei screamed. Batory, his black mane flying in defiance, led the broken and pathetic line of Ulanys down the knoll and into the German tanks. Andrei's terrible anger could see only the infantry men behind the tanks. I'll get them! I'll get the bastards!

His men were blasted from their saddles before they had gone fifty meters. Andrei whipped around and dragged them to their feet and pulled them on their horses and tried to reorganize the attack. There was nothing left. It was a rout. They went back into the forest, with their captain after them, cursing them to make one more try.

Now the tanks inched forward up the knoll, German infantry-men crouched low behind their iron cover. The line of steel came within a hundred meters—point-blank—and let go again, and the infantry fanned out between the tanks.

In the woods there was the smell of burning flesh and burning wood and the sounds of screaming men and screaming horses. All was havoc. For ten, fifteen, twenty minutes Andrei was able to rally his men to hold off the German infantry. He kicked them to their feet and tried to set them on their horses again, but they were bombed from the saddles and gunned and burned with methodical indifference.

And then he staggered around blindly as a cloud of smoke hit him in the face, and he cried for Batory and felt his horse and struggled into the saddle. "Come on, boy! Let's get them!"

He spurred the animal toward the Germans, then he whirled about and the world began to spin, and when he opened his eyes he felt as though his chest were being crushed and all he could see was the blue sky above him and the tops of the burning trees whirling and whirling. Andrei thrashed about on his hands and knees, semiconscious, crawling to Batory. "Batory! Get up! Get up, boy! Don't lay there! Get up! Let's kill them!"

First Sergeant Styka knelt over Andrei and shook him violently. "Captain, we are finished! Get up, sir! I have two horses. We must make a run for it, sir!"

Andrei lifted the dead horse's head in his hands. "Batory! Get up!"

"Sir, your horse is dead! Nearly all the men are dead!"

The big soldier dragged Andrei to his feet. Andrei broke loose from his grip and kicked his lifeless animal. "Get up, God damn you! Get up! Get up! Get up!"

Chapter Eleven

Humanity had been endowed by the German people with their Beethovens and Schillers and their Freuds and the dubious gifts of a Karl Marx. Now the German people presented humanity with a new set of authors—General von Bock, General von Küchler, General von Kluge, General von Rundstedt, General von Blasko-witz, General List, General Halder, General von Brauchitsch, General von Reichenau. The book they wrote presenting mankind with a new innovation of German culture was called *Blitzkrieg*, lightning war.

Poland formed a huge bulge which fitted into the open jaws of Germany, with Prussia on the north, a common border of many hundred kilometers from the Baltic to Krakow, and in the south newly raped Czechoslovakia beyond the Carpathian Mountains.

The jaws bit down, and saber teeth in the form of armored columns tore deeply into the flesh of Poland. The Poles, arrogant and stubborn and filled with foolhardy national pride and an offensive-minded Polish Staff, doomed whatever small chance there may have been for some sort of stand.

Forgoing logic, Poland did not fall back on her few natural defensive river barriers. Instead, she dreamed in vain of holding a fifteen-hundred-mile border whereon the enemy chose his points of attack. She had further visions of making a counterattack in the form of a hell-bent-for-leather cavalry charge.

Poland's forces were all but immobile, armorless and antiquated, her arsenal better suited to war five decades earlier. Sustained by raw courage, Poland asked the horse to fight the tank.

German land forces ran double and triple envelopments, executed picture-book tactics; massacred, trapped, overwhelmed, sliced, overpowered the near-defenseless but proud enemy. The new book called for the disregard of even the token humanities customarily observed in the organized art of murder known as war.

Death spewed from the skies.

Within hours of the German border violations, the Polish air force, tiny and outdated, was shot to pieces on the ground. Within hours, rail lines were ripped up and supply dumps smoked skyward and hot bridges sizzled as they buckled into rivers. Cities and villages without so much as a gun to fire back were leveled into smoldering rubble heaps.

The Luftwaffe, which had learned to violate open cities in Spain, turned all of Poland into one big turkey shoot. It shot down Polish troops fleeing for cover and Polish peasants working in the fields and Polish children in the schoolyards and Polish women nursing in maternity hospitals and Polish nuns at Mass.

Through the Carpathians from Czechoslovakia, List shoved his armor through the mountain passes and turned the Krakow flank at that place where the Gleiwitz radio-station hoax was perpetrated. In the center, Reichenau was given the honor of unleashing the greatest mass of iron-treaded monsters, and on his left Blaskowitz enveloped a pocket on the flatlands near the industrial heart of Poznan. And Von Bock and Von Küchler lashed out from northern flanking positions in Prussia and Pomerania and there was no more pesky Polish Corridor.

Indeed, the book had been rewritten. It was the ultimate in mechanical and technical murder. The butchery of Poland—the slaughter of two hundred thousand of her army and scores of thousands of her civilians and the rape of her land—was a new German masterpiece.

Captain Andrei Androfski was knocked senseless by his first sergeant and dragged from the scene of the flaming death of Company A. With a half dozen survivors, they found horses and managed to get back to the Grudziadz base, where an even greater catastrophe had befallen the Ulanys. At Grudziadz, one third of Poland's forces had been foolishly concentrated for a counterattack which was never delivered. The Germans enveloped them with ridiculous ease and, having trapped them, chopped them to bits. The large Westerplatte Salient was formed by a double envelopment trapping the Polish marines. Soon, the last of Poland's cavalry charges was made. With the Polish eagle still waving in defiance, a foolhardy attack tried to break the ring of iron around them. The Germans ungallantly ripped the Ulanys to shreds. The Westerplatte Salient collapsed. The remaining Ulanys staggered back from Grudziadz to Torun. And . . . a last weak gasp, one more charge at Wloclawek, and they were done.

There was no rest, for the German monster clamped its jaws tighter and the saber teeth pressed toward Warsaw at the end of only a week.

Captain Andrei Androfski had four horses shot out from under him in seven days. He was gored with arm and leg wounds and his body covered with bruises and filth. He and First Sergeant Styka were two of a handful of survivors when the brigade finally surrendered after Wloclawek.

On the night of September 7, before the Germans could fully organize prisoner compounds and complete the disarming of the Poles, Andrei, Styka, and four others broke out of their area and under cover of darkness gambled they could swim the treacherous upper Vistula River.

Two of them drowned. The remaining four hid in a forest the next day and at night crawled along the ditches of roads filled with German patrols.

At dawn on September 9 the four found refuge in a peasant's hut on the outskirts of Plock, a third of the distance back to Warsaw. Beyond normal exhaustion, hunger, thirst, and close to death from his festering wounds, Captain Andrei Androfski allowed himself the luxury of collapsing.

Styka sent the other two men into Plock to fetch a doctor. He hovered over Andrei, who was terribly still and a chalky yellow shade. Andrei had spent the last ounce of reserve strength pulling Styka across the swift river. The soldier's muddled mind remembered snatches of the past week since dragging Andrei from the burning forest. He saw the vision of his captain leading charge after charge and fighting on even after the end had occurred. He had never seen such anger in a man's eyes as when they were put into the prisoner compound even though Andrei was barely able to stand. "We're swimming the river, Styka, as soon as it turns dark."

The peasant brought Styka bread and lentil soup. The soldier was too weak to lift the spoon or bite through the bread. He lay his head on Andrei's chest. Yes, there were still heartbeats. His eyes began to shut. Must not sleep until the doctor comes . . . must not sleep . . .

"Who is he?" the doctor asked.

"My captain," Styka answered through thick lips. His mind was fuzzy. An ignorant man, Styka was almost illiterate and too exhausted to put into words the horror he had seen in the past week. Only when the doctor promised to remain with Andrei did he fall on the floor by Andrei's bed and drop off to sleep.

When Andrei blinked his eyes open twenty hours later, Styka was hovering over him. Styka managed a small smile. The doctor from Plock had gone and returned. Andrei managed to rise up on his elbows, looked around the cottage, and flopped back on the bed.

"We were wondering if you were ever going to wake up," the doctor said.

"Sure he would! I knew it all along!" Styka roared.

The peasant's wife crossed herself innumerable times and wailed that all her prayers to the Blessed Virgin Mother had been answered.

"What's the scorecard on me?" Andrei asked.

"The wounds are under control. The assortment of cuts and bruises will vanish. Your state of exhaustion will require rest. You are as thoroughly beaten up as any man I have ever examined. You have the constitution of a bull. I don't see how you ever swam that river in your condition."

Styka and the doctor helped him sit up. He took a stiff drink of home-brewed vodka and stuffed a half loaf of bread into his stomach. Despite everyone's objections, he remained sitting.

"Where are we?"

"Plock."

"What is happening?"

"The news is bad all over. We are being beaten everywhere," the doctor said.

"What about Warsaw?"

"The Germans have not reached Warsaw yet. Radio Polskie says Warsaw will fight."

Andrei tried to stand. His legs buckled and he tottered. "Where are the other two, Styka? They got across the river with us—where are they? We must get back to Warsaw and fight."

The doctor and Styka exchanged glances.

"Well, where are they?"

"They have surrendered."

"Surrendered?"

"The Germans have crossed the river in strength. All roads to Warsaw have been cut. I stayed here only until I knew you were all right, Captain, but there is no chance of reaching Warsaw. Every hour we stay here we put these good people in danger. The Germans have been shooting everyone harboring an escaped soldier."

"I am a Pole," the peasant announced. "I will never close my door to a Polish soldier."

"Your sergeant is right," the doctor said. "Now that he knows you are alive, it would be best for him to turn himself in. As for you, I can find you a hiding place for a few days until you get a little of your strength back, and then you must surrender yourself too."

Andrei looked at all four of them. The woman was crossing herself and praying again. "If you will be kind enough to spare me a loaf of bread, a canteen of water, and perhaps some cheese, I will be on my way. I am going to Warsaw."

Styka flopped his arms about helplessly. "Captain, we can't make it."

Andrei managed to walk to his sergeant and put a hand on his shoulder. Styka lowered his eyes. "Look at me, Styka—look at me, I said. You would surrender?"

The big homely man had been a good soldier for fifteen years. Dirt encrusted his once-proud mustache, and beads of sweat broke through the caked mud on his eyebrows and unshaved face. His face dropped in complete dismay. "Yes, sir," he whispered.

"Now you listen here," the doctor said. "Warsaw is a hundred kilometers, the roads are cut, and the place is swarming with German patrols. If you were the strongest and healthiest man in Poland you could not make it. In your condition you won't be strong enough to go ten kilometers."

Styka began to cry, something Andrei had never seen him do. "Captain, sir. We have fought the best we know how. We have not disgraced ourselves."

A sudden dizziness overcame Andrei. He pitched into Styka's arms, then pushed himself free and stumbled into a chair.

Seven days and their war was over. Their fine beautiful brigade pulverized into a disorganized bloody pulp. The vision of the glazed eyes of the soldiers came to him, and he saw the line of thousands of corpses stretched beside the road outside Torun after their cavalry charge and the fields of lifeless horses.

The memory of battle ran together without day or night, beginning or end. The smells and the burns and the agonies. Kicking men to their feet to fire one more round . . . one more round . . . ear-splitting shellbursts and the tank treads cutting into walls of flesh and the cries of the wounded.

. . . The little village north of Rypin. What was its name? He had organized fifty strays for an attack. They stopped in the village for water. The children ran out of the school into the village square to cheer them. The priest came out and the women came out with bread in their hands.

No one heard the airplane, it came so fast. Rat-a-tat-rat-a-tat—and it was gone, and five little children lay bleeding in the square. The priest knelt over them, saying prayers, and the women wailed. The little girl dead, clutching the rag doll. Rat-a-tat—and planes came in again.

"We have fought with honor," Brigadier Zygmunt Bozakolski said. "I am surrendering the Seventh Brigade. I expect you gentlemen to conduct yourselves as Ulany officers."

The prison pen. The accordions of barbed wire. The crisscross of German guards. "Styka, as soon as night falls we are going through the wire and swim the river."

"I'm with you, Captain."

Styka fell on the wire and made himself a human bridge, and the other five ran over the top of him. He followed after them. When they reached the riverbank the air was filled with whistles and sirens and shouts in German.

Flashlights probed the darkness.

The river was swift and pulling them back to shore. The lights streaked over the water. Blam! Blam! Swim for your life! Swim for your life!

A scream! One of them hit. He is dragged by the current like a limp rag.

"I'm going under, Captain. I can't make it."

Styka gurgled and thrashed hopelessly. "Relax, Styka—relax." Andrei's hand was under his chin, his free arm driving at the water.

"I'm drowning! I'm drowning! Mother of God!" Styka screamed.

"Stay calm, you son of a bitch . . ."

Andrei pulled him up on the bank and knelt over him and pumped the water from his lungs and slapped his face until he came around.

. . . And then . . . what happened then?

Andrei looked up. The peasant and his wife. The doctor. And Styka, crying.

"If you wish to surrender, Sergeant, you have my permission."

"What about you, sir?"

Andrei shook his head.

"You are a damned fool!" the doctor said.

"Then I guess I am a damned fool too," Styka said.

"You're going with him? You know he can't make it. Why?"

Styka tried to think. It was hard for him. He shrugged. "Because he is my captain," he said.

Chapter Twelve

For the first few days after the war began, England and France desperately tried to get the German army to withdraw, ready to impose another Munich sellout on Poland. When Germany refused, England and France had to do what they should have done years before; they declared war. With Poland's doom more certain each day, the British and French embassies in Warsaw turned over much of their papers and duties to the neutral Americans.

The Americans were short-staffed, but the spirit remained excellent even with extra burdens.

Well into the second week, complete catastrophe for Poland was evident.

Gabriela left the Embassy after a shift of fourteen hours. Thompson insisted she get some rest. Instead, she got one of the marine guards to drive her to Zoliborz to see the Bronski family, with whom she had lost contact for several days. When she arrived, Zoshia told her that both Rachael and Deborah were at the Bathyran Orphanage. She followed after them.

The bombing raids had increased in intensity as the German armies moved in on Warsaw. The city was determined to fight on. At the orphanage, Susan Geller had sent out an emergency call for help to move the facilities underground so they would at least have food, medicine, and sleeping places during the air raids. Gabriela worked alongside Deborah, Susan, Rachael, and Alex and Sylvia Brandel through the night and all the next day, helping move supplies underground, catching only a few naps whenever they could. She returned to the Embassy. Things had slowed down, and Thompson sent her home again.

She had reached a state of numbness. She looked up at her flat from the street. It was so lonely there. Several buildings near and on the square had been hit by bombs. She found herself doing what she always did when she was lonesome—she walked north to Leszno Street and climbed the four flights to Andrei's flat. As always, the door was open. Just as she arrived the air-raid sirens began. She stood by the window, strangely fascinated by the leaping flames from the slums only a mile away. Some of the fire appeared to be coming from the Old Town. What a tragedy if anything happened to the old square, she thought.

An hour earlier the bombers had started the incendiary attacks to light their way over Warsaw during the night. This time the raiders were hitting acres of workers' homes in Praga across the river.

On the streets below she could hear the confusion as firemen rushed to the slum area, where the houses were so tightly packed and inflammable that the fire could spread all over Warsaw if not contained quickly.

Dull booms from Praga.

There was neither Polish gun nor Polish plane to stop the Germans. But the raiders kept coming back to smash the will of the people to resist.

She shut the window and taped the blackout paper into place, then lit the room with a single lamp beside the bed and stretched out to read herself to sleep with Walt Whitman's *Leaves of Grass*.

A knock on the door startled her.

"Come in."

Alexander Brandel entered the room. She was glad he had come.

"I didn't mean to startle you," he said. "I went to the Embassy and your place first."

"Is everything all right at the orphanage?"

"Fine, fine. The children are so wonderful. We try to keep it like a game. I think they are smarter than we are."

"How is it outside?"

"The whole northern end is burning. Praga is catching hell. So, Mayor Starzynski says to fight on—so, we fight on. Could I have some cognac?"

Gabriela took a bottle from the cabinet and looked at Alex with suspicion. He was mostly a teetotaller, except when Andrei was around. He drank it down very quickly. He coughed as the fire hit his stomach. Perhaps just the air raid, Gabriela thought. It is enough to make anyone nervous. Then Alex began to mop his brow. There was something serious on his mind.

"What is it?" Gabriela said.

"Andrei is in Warsaw."

She closed her eyes and held her stomach as though she had been hit. She tried to ask questions, but her lips would not form words.

"Let me first say that he is all right."

"You swear . . . you swear it now?"

"I swear it. He has been wounded, but it is not serious. Please sit down."

"Where was he wounded, Alex?"

"I tell you it's not serious and I beg you to be calm."

"Where is he?"

"Will you please get control of yourself?"

"Where is he!"

"Gabriela . . . please . . ."

"You're lying! He's been hurt." And then she fought herself into control. "All right, tell me."

"God only knows how he was able to get back to Warsaw. It was a miracle. No one will ever know what he has been through."

"Alex . . . I beg you . . . the truth. How badly is he hurt?"

"His heart is broken, Gabriela."

"Where is he?"

"At the bottom of the stairs."

She lunged for the door, screaming his name. Alex caught her and clamped his hand over her mouth. "Now listen to me, Gabriela! He is broken, without spirit. You are going to have to be a very brave girl."

"Andrei, Andrei," she whimpered.

"He came to me first and asked me to come to you because . . . he does not want you to look at him the way he is. Do you understand that?"

She nodded.

92

"Then make the room dark and I will send him up."

She left the door open and turned out the light. There was a tiny ray from a hall light downstairs. Gabriela listened at the landing for Alexander to reach bottom. She heard Alex's voice. She tensed, waiting for another sound. It seemed like forever. She fought off the agonizing desire to scream out his name and bolt down after him. Then . . . a slow clump, clump, clump. It labored up and up, each step seeming more painful than the last. Clump . . . clump . . . clump . . . clump . . .

Gabriela fell back into the room, her heart throbbing violently. Clump . . . clump . . . clump . . . Dragging and then a deep wheezing breathing.

His hulk cut a shadow on the landing. He stood wavering on his legs and fighting for his breath. He moved for the door, groping in the darkness.

"Andrei?" she whispered.

He groped into the room, stumbling like a blind man, and found the bed and crawled on it and groaned with pain and weariness.

Gabriela burst with desire to turn on the lights, but she dared not. She leaned over the bed quickly and her hand felt around his face. His eyes, his ears, his nose, his mouth. They were all there. Arms, hands, fingers, legs. All of him was there!

He smelled putrid from the smokes of battle and dried blood and sweat, and his hair was matted with dirt. He lay and groaned weakly.

And then Gabriela became calm. She sat on the edge of the bed and lifted his head to her lap and petted him gently. His face burned with fever and he gripped the bedcover and convulsed.

"It's all right, dear, it's all right now."

"Gaby . . . Gaby . . ."

"I'm right here, dear."

And Andrei cried. "They killed my beautiful horse," he sobbed. "They killed Batory."

The shrill screams of the air-raid sirens erupted from Bielany to Rakowiec and from Praga to Kolo as new flames were about to be added to the old as the rape of Warsaw heightened.

"They killed my horse . . . they killed my beautiful horse . . . they killed him . . ."

Chapter Thirteen

Journal Entry—September 17, 1939

The pie has been cut. Poland, the historic whipping boy, is again acting out its ancient historical role. Hitler has paid off in his deal with Stalin. The Soviet armies have jumped us from the rear, obviously moving to pre-set borders.

The German invasion has awed the most advanced military thinkers. Smigly-Rydz, the government, and the foreign legations have fled. They say some of our army has been able to escape.

Somehow Warsaw continues to hold out, but I wonder if Polish courage does not prove that the bloodless collapse of Austria and Czechoslovakia was the better way out?

ALEXANDER BRANDEL

Dateline, Warsaw
September 21, 1939
by Christopher de Monti
(Swiss News)

How long can Warsaw hold out? How long can Mayor Starzynski keep this city rallied? This is the question asked ten thousand times a day.

It is a strange battle, a commuters' war. Soldiers and those civilians pressed into labor battalions take up their positions on Warsaw's outer defense perimeter. When their relief comes, they catch a trolley car back to town to their homes.

Often the front lines begin where the trolley lines end. Troop movements are by red and yellow street cars, taxis, horse-drawn droshkas, and teamster wagons.

On the perimeter there is a strange conglomeration of humanity in the labor battalions digging trenches and preparing fortifications. Old bearded Orthodox Jews, secretaries, housewives in gaily colored babushkas, students in university class caps, children, bankers, bakers.

All over Warsaw long lines queue up for their ration on ever-worsening shortages. Water, in some sections, is doled out by the bucketful. Water priority must go to the fire department for its round-the-clock fight to keep the city from going up in flames.

The women waiting in lines stay put despite artillery fire and air raids. Yesterday nearly a hundred were buried by a collapsing wall.

Around the city, both famous and unknown buildings and landmarks are pocked with shell holes. Warsaw's only skyscraper, the fifteen-story Prudential building, a visible target for German long guns, has suffered better than eighty hits. It still stands intact, although only a single window on the tenth floor remains unshattered.

Poland's pride, the Stare Miasto, the Old Town Square with meticulously preserved Renaissance houses and historic shrines, is being leveled lower each day.

Statues of Poland's heroes which adorn her many squares and parks are now headless, armless, and swordless. The magnificent fountains of the Saxony Gardens and the Lazienki are dry; the swans that filled their lakes have fled, and no one seems to know where.

Despite the situation, a strange calm has fallen over the city. There are amazing semblances of normalcy, and the Poles have not lost their traditional sense of humor. Two papers manage to get published each day. Radio Polskie plays Chopin around the clock between dramatic urgings from Mayor Starzynski. The long-awaited German frontal assault must come sooner or later. How long can Warsaw hold?

Chris pulled his report from the typewriter, hastily marked over the errors with a green grease pencil, and put it into a large envelope.

When the phones went out a week before, Chris was able to obtain a wire until that was broken, then radio. Now Warsaw was completely cut off from communication with the outside world except for the one Radio Polskie station operating for the city on an emergency basis.

There was a sudden break for Chris when arrangements were made for a two-hour truce the next day to allow the balance of the American Embassy personnel to evacuate to Krakow. Chris went to Thompson, who agreed to carry out his reports and Rosy's photos in a diplomatic pouch. Both of them worked feverishly, Rosy shooting up film and Chris doing a series of articles not requiring a dateline but which could run as an "eye-witness" account in papers around the world even after Warsaw's fall. It would stand as a great scoop for Swiss News.

Rosy handed Chris a stack of photographs, and he went through them, marking them and checking their captions. Pictures of broken houses and twisted girders dangling in grotesque shapes and stunned mothers kneeling beside dead children and stunned children kneeling beside dead mothers. War's harvest, a photographer's field day. Dead, bloated animals whose curious expressions asked what they did to be caught in the middle of man's folly, and the images of old ladies praying to Gods and Virgins who do not hear them and trench diggers and exhausted bucket brigades.

Ervin Rosenblum's camera did justice to war. Chris put the pictures into folders.

"Where're the rest of them?" he asked.

"The Kodak lab just went out of action. I'm going to see if I can't get enough junk to rig up a darkroom in my basement."

"Well, if you can't make prints, you'll have to let me send your negatives."

Rosy grumbled. The most horrible thought to any photographer was to surrender exposed film which could not be duplicated if ruined. But Chris was right. It would probably be the last chance to get the pictures out of Warsaw.

Rosy went into his familiar routine of jiggling flash bulbs in his pocket and playing with the shutter stops on his camera. "It's going to be rough on the morale, watching the last of the Americans leave tomorrow," he said. "It will affect us worse than a half dozen bombing raids. You know how it is—everybody has an uncle in Gary or a brother in Milwaukee."

"Yeah," Chris agreed, "it will be rough all right."

"How come you're not evacuating?"

"Why should I? I've got an Italian passport and this is a Swiss News Agency bureau. Switzerland isn't at war. Maybe I want to be on the welcoming committee for my liberators."

"Chris, you don't even make a third-rate Fascist. You think those fellows at the Italian Embassy are going to vouch for you? You're so American you may as well be wearing a sign."

"It happens that America isn't at war either. I'm keeping the bureau open."

"I'll tell you what I know," Rosy answered. "I know that within two weeks the Germans will put us out of business."

"I'll get around it somehow."

"Why?" Rosy persisted. "You won't be able to get any news out but watered-down potato soup."

"You know damned well why I'm staying!" Chris said angrily.

Rosy set his camera down and walked up behind Chris's chair and put a sympathetic hand on his shoulder. "It's not like I don't want you to stay, Chris. I have a good job. I'd really have to struggle if the bureau closed. But . . . when a friend is in trouble, sometimes you don't think too much about yourself. That's why I tell you, pack up and leave with the Americans tomorrow."

"I can't leave her, Rosy."

"My Susan has known Deborah Bronski since college days. When two people like you and she come from different ends of the earth there has to be a great ability on both parts to be able to give. She is controlled by inner forces that make it impossible to change, even if she wanted to."

"It's not true. Bronski has been cutting away at her beliefs for a decade."

"Only on the surface. When the final showdown comes she'll return to them. She doesn't have the ability to do otherwise, and that is why you are walking down a blind alley."

"Oh hell—women in Italy and Spain and Mexico and India and half the damned world are driven to a wall of mysticism and superstitions in order to be able to keep existing in a world which fights them every inch of the way. The trouble with you Jews is that you make yourselves believe you have the priority on suffering——"

"But there is a difference, Chris. In all of the world, no matter how sordid the life, no matter how evil and bare and fruitless, almost every man can open his eyes in the morning in a land in which he had his beginning and a heritage. We can't. And I know what this does to women like Deborah Bronski. I know too many like her."

"No, you're wrong, Rosy. If you really know Deborah, then you'd understand that I am unable to ever leave her."

The bell rang. Rosy answered. It was Andrei. In only a week he had made a remarkable recovery. Much of the pain was still with him and his face showed great weariness, but he pulled himself together for that last battle which had not been fought.

Two days after his return to Warsaw he reported to the commander at the Citadel and was given a spot promotion to the rank of major and placed in charge of a battalion on the southern perimeter. The truce to evacuate the Americans was to take place at his position.

"How is it out there?" Chris asked.

"The same," Andrei answered. "The bastards won't attack."

"Why should they?" Chris said. "They can sit back and blast the city till kingdom come."

"I want to get one more look at them," Andrei said.

"We may be looking at them for a long, long time," Rosy said. "And how are you feeling, Andrei?"

"Never better," he answered, lifting the glass filled with scotch whisky that Chris had poured. "I'm only in for a few hours. I've got to get back. Something has come up that may be of interest to you on that truce tomorrow morning to evacuate the American Embassy personnel."

They both nodded.

"The Germans contacted us a few hours ago by radio. One of our officers just finished speaking to them personally beyond the lines. The Germans have asked for a trade of prisoners of war at the same time the Americans are evacuated."

"How many Germans do you have here?"

"A few hundred, more or less. Most of them are ethnics."

"Seems like a normal procedure," Chris said.

"No, there's something fishy about it," Andrei said. "The Germans are offering us five to one."

"Why would they do that, I wonder?" Rosy asked.

"I don't know—but something's wrong with the whole business."

"We might as well go down there and cover the truce," Chris said. "There may be a story, although God knows when we'll be able to get it out of Poland."

Chapter Fourteen

The American Embassy was closed except for a half dozen token personnel. There had been a final tear-filled farewell with Thompson, who was to evacuate during the truce in the morning, and then Gabriela went to Andrei's flat to wait for him as she had waited for two harrowing nights through shellfire and air raids.

It was just turning dark when he arrived after leaving Chris. They embraced wearily. He slumped into the big armchair while Gabriela poured the last of the vodka. The liquor felt good and warm going down. Gabriela stood behind him and rubbed the knots out of the muscles in his neck.

"I managed to save a large pail of water," she said. "You will feel better when you have washed."

He clumped into the bathroom and dunked his head, trying to wash away the exhaustion, then shaved with a cup of heated water.

Gabriela had the food ready. He shoved some stale bread into a bowl of beans.

"I'm sorry there isn't more to eat," she said. "When we closed down at the Embassy I came straight here. I didn't want to risk standing in line and possibly miss you if you came in. I'll go out and get some things at Tommy's house later and fix you a good warm meal."

"It's fine," Andrei muttered. "I can only stay a few hours anyhow."

He chewed the hard bread without speaking. Gabriela became uneasy. "You'd better take a little nap. You look as if you're ready to cave in."

"Stop nagging me!"

The air-raid sirens cried out. Gabriela turned quickly from his testiness to draw the curtains and put out half the lights.

"Bastards," Andrei mumbled. He pushed the bread through the beans. "Bastards."

In a moment the sky was crackling with the sounds of the motors. Andrei listened for the first whistling screams of the dives and then bombs. He did not have to wait long.

"Mokotow," Andrei said to himself, "the airdrome. Only there's no airdrome left. They're methodical. Every part of Warsaw is like a number on the clock. Mokotow, then Rakowiec, then Ochota, then Wola. Why not? We know where they're coming, but we can't shoot back. Why not? I've seen those sons of bitches face to face. I'll see them again before this siege is over. They won't break us with air raids—they're going to have to make an attack, and when they do——"

"Stop it, please."

Andrei ate and listened. The Germans were passing in from the north, starting their unimpeded diving patterns into the southern fringe of the city from directly over his apartment. As the Stukas and Messerschmitts screamed down on the undefended city, Gabriela became shaken. A miscalculated bombing run dropped a rack just a block away from Leszno Street. Andrei's flat shook from the blast.

"Perhaps we'd better get to the basement," Gabriela said.

"Do I look like a mole or a gopher? I will not live under the ground."

"That arrogant Polish Ulany pride will get us killed."

"Go to the basement, then!"

"No!"

"Well, make up your mind."

It was not a long raid, for there was nothing of military value left to bomb in Warsaw. The Germans had had their sport for the day and departed. Gabriela examined the empty vodka bottle with disappointment. Andrei drew the curtains and watched the dancing flames in the distance. He turned back to her, and she became frightened. He had a strange look on his face that she had never seen before.

"I came to say good-by, Gabriela," he said. "Go home and pack your things. You are allowed one suitcase. You are leaving with the Americans tomorrow."

"I . . . don't believe I understand you."

"Don't make a scene."

"How am I to get through the German lines? Perhaps I should sing 'Swanee River' for them to show them I am an American."

"I spoke to Thompson. He has already made out an American diplomatic passport for you. There is no better way to travel. Tommy will get you to Krakow."

"My, you've been a busy man. Here I thought you were defending Warsaw, and you've been out making diplomatic missions."

"I said I don't want a scene!"

"I'll make up my own mind where and when I want to go."

"So maybe I've condemned you to purgatory! America is such a horrible place? Only a crazy damned fool would want to keep their skinny neck in this city."

"Since when do you tell me what to do?"

"Since now!" he answered, slamming his fist on the table with such force it rattled the bottles and dishes.

Gabriela watched his terrible temper with a bit of a fright and a bit of awe. He seemed to be issuing an ultimatum that if she stayed he would not see her again. She dared not ask. Her eyes were filled with hurt. She whispered, "Andrei, what have I done to make you so angry?"

"You have a mother and a sister in America. That is where you are going."

"Is this good-by?"

"One way or the other . . ."

She waited for him to make some move, some sign. He stood like a lump, glaring at her, unwavering in his intensity.

"All right," she whispered. She picked up her coat and put it on slowly and walked toward the door, waiting, praying for Andrei to call her name. He did not move a muscle or blink an eye. She opened the door and faced him. He was like a stranger. This cruel man was not Andrei . . . to dismiss her as a nobleman dismisses a peasant.

If I walk down these steps I will die, Gabriela thought.

She closed the door and walked across the room to him. She put her arms around him and lay her head on his chest, but he remained emotionless.

"Don't try any female tricks on me."

"All right," she said, "but I didn't believe the day would come when you would not touch me. I will leave you, but you cannot make me leave Warsaw. This happens to be my home too."

"You must leave!"

"Don't shout, Major Androfski. You may frighten away the Stukas."

Andrei flopped his arms hopelessly, and the look of humanity returned to his eyes. "Goddamn but you are one stubborn woman," he said. "I only tried to do it this way because, if I threatened never to see you, you might go. Now let me plead with you. This isn't our country any more. God only knows what the Germans are going to do with three and a half million Jews. I cannot live knowing that because of me harm will come to you. If you love me, then give me my pride. Let me know I have given you life, not taken it from you."

"Oh, Andrei, I should have seen through you right away. I love you. I don't know any other way to love. I cannot leave because I cannot do what I cannot do."

"Oh God . . . Gabriela. I don't want you hurt."

"Shhh, darling, shhh."

"You are a little fool—a terrible little fool."

Warsaw gagged. Clouds of smoke billowed from the ground and then rained down a billion bits of dust and ground-up brick and mortar. An unearthly silence mingled with the fumes of war.

Christopher de Monti and Ervin Rosenblum were already interviewing the evacuees when Major Androfski drove up.

Thompson was the first to reach Andrei.

"Where is Gaby?"

Andrei beat his shoulders to ward off the pre-dawn cold and shifted his feet about. "She wouldn't come, Tommy. Honest to God, I tried."

"I really didn't think she would. Take these papers, she may be able to use them later."

"Thanks, Tommy. Thanks for everything. Gaby sends her love to Martha."

"Take care of her. . . ."

The second-in-command, a captain, approached them, and Andrei assumed a formal pose.

"Have you checked the credentials of all your people?" the captain asked Thompson.

"I have."

"What's the count?"

"Twenty American personnel. Fifteen personnel from mixed neutral embassies, and twelve civilians, miscellaneous."

"Get back with them." Andrei looked at his watch, then strained to see in the darkness. "It will be light in about fifteen minutes. Be ready to move out if everything goes well."

Thompson nodded. They grasped hands, and the American turned and trotted back to the courtyard behind a shattered farmhouse where the evacuees huddled.

Andrei turned to his captain. "How many Germans?"

"We managed to get eighty of them."

"Has this information been radioed to the Germans?"

"Yes, sir. They said they will return three hundred ninety of our people."

Andrei walked down the road to where the German prisoners stamped around restlessly in the cutting chill. They were glum and humiliated. Their faces wore masks of hatred and arrogance. Andrei stared at them for a while. They looked like people he had known all his life. A baker . . . a gentleman with children . . . a teacher . . . What was it that had brought them to this place?

He turned on his heels, followed by the captain, and walked briskly to the forward trenches.

The distant thump-thump-thump of artillery never quit. It was still too dark to see across the field. Another eight minutes. Andrei gave a series of security commands.

Chris climbed down into the trench alongside him.

"Gaby staying?"

"Yes."

"It was a safe bet."

"I tried . . ."

"Don't blame yourself. Be thankful. Find out anything about the prisoner exchange?"

"They're still paying us almost five to one. We're watching for a trick. Lord knows what they're up to."

The thumping stopped.

All eyes strained for the sight of something moving in the ugly grayness over the field. Andrei held his field glasses up and crossed back and forth over the horizon . . . back and forth.

There! A shadow emerging from the clump of trees. Barely make it out. Definitely coming into the field. He waited for five minutes while the figure grew more visible.

You son of a bitch, Andrei thought. How I'd like to blow your filthy head off! The figure stopped. He was holding a makeshift white truce flag.

Andrei jumped out of the trench and walked toward the German over what had once been a potato field. It was pocked with holes and littered with wreckage. From both sides, ten thousand eyes were on them. Andrei stopped a few feet from the German. He was a colonel, but neither beetle-browed nor blond Aryan, but rather nondescript. He seemed uneasy in his exposed position. He and Andrei stared at each other for several moments without a word.

"You are in charge?" the German said at last.

"Yes."

"What is your situation?"

Although Andrei spoke conversational German well, he addressed the colonel in Yiddish. He rattled his Yiddish, staring directly at his enemy.

"We have forty-seven mixed neutral nationals, American Embassy personnel, and eighty of your people. Credentials have been checked."

"Bring them out here. I will escort them through our lines."

"You owe us three hundred ninety Poles. I will bring the evacuees to this point when you bring my people here."

Andrei's implication that he mistrusted the Germans was obvious. There was more the two men wished to say to each other. Andrei longed to break the German's neck with his hands, and the German's eyes told a message of "don't let me find you when we enter Warsaw, Jew boy."

But this part of war was by the rule book. Restraint. The victor had to show majesty. The loser was given his pride.

"I have a message from our commander. He urges surrender of Warsaw to avoid further useless bloodshed."

"I have a message from our Mayor in the event that your commander asks Warsaw to surrender. No."

The German broke off the conversation, looking at his watch. "It will take me approximately six minutes to have your people moving here. They have been assembled in the small woods there."

"I'll wait."

The German snapped his heels together, made a curt short bow from the waist, and walked back across the field.

Andrei stood alone. He heaved a terrible sigh and bit his lip. He watched the figure of the German grow smaller and smaller, and now the thousands of eyes were on him alone. The last of the proud Poles . . . erect as a statue. Still cursing beneath his breath, still praying for his enemy to fight him face to face.

Six minutes passed to the second. The German was efficient. Clusters of men began to emerge slowly from the woods and cross the field toward Andrei. Andrei turned to his own lines and raised his hand.

They came from his side in two groups, one led by Thompson, the other by a German officer in command of the German prisoners. The distance was far shorter to Andrei than to the woods. They came at a trot and were formed up quickly.

Andrei looked toward the woods again, annoyed by the slowness of the Polish prisoners in returning.

"Something is wrong out there," Thompson said.

Andrei lifted his field glasses, and his hand dropped. He kicked a potato on the ground viciously. He lifted the glasses again, and his face contorted with quivers of rage.

"No wonder they wanted to give us five to one," he said. "They're sending back nothing but amputees."

"Oh dear God."

"Must they torment us!" Andrei cried.

"Maybe," Tommy said, "if they torment enough, we will wake up and get off our dead prats in America. Can we leave, Andrei?"

"Go ahead, Tommy. Move slowly. I want to be sure those men are safely in before you reach the woods. They may . . . try something if they were left exposed."

The Americans walked toward the enemy lines, turning their eyes from the macabre marchers coming in the opposite direction.

Andrei returned to the trench.

"What's going on out there?" Chris said.

"Look for yourself."

He took Andrei's glasses. Nearly four hundred armless or legless men straggled toward Warsaw. Men with one arm used their other to carry stretchers of men with no legs, and men with one leg hobbled and fell in the pitholes.

103

Andrei turned to the captain. "Get out there and help those people," he said.

Polish soldiers dropped their weapons and ran over the field and the two forces came together, and in the distance the thump-thump-thump of the cannonading began once more and overhead the first flights of German warplanes ushered in a new day.

It was night when Christopher de Monti reached the Bronski home in Zoliborz. As he approached the house, the familiar sound of music reached his ears. Rachael was playing the piano. How wonderful! How wonderful that Deborah was able to keep them together and functioning, holding back the fear and gloom. Chris was a welcome face these days. Young Stephen let out a large sigh of relief when Chris hugged him, for he knew the duties of "manhood" would be relieved for the time he was there.

Deborah was in the kitchen with Zoshia, who wailed in uncontrolled grief, her fat body wobbling as she cried. Deborah looked up at Chris.

"Poor thing. Her sister was killed in the raid today."

Chris went to the study and found some cognac and made the woman drink it. They helped Zoshia to her feet and led her to Deborah's own bedroom and forced her to lie down and fetched Rachael and Stephan.

"Sit with her, children. Don't let her get up."

Zoshia cried out that she wanted to go to her sister.

"No, dear. It is not safe there. The walls are all tumbling. Now rest . . . rest."

Deborah found a sedative in Paul's study among the medicines he kept for family use and after great difficulty got the maid to drink it. In a while her wails died down to a weaker cry.

Chris led Deborah to the study and locked the door, and for a moment he held her and soothed her. "Poor thing," Deborah said, "poor thing. Her only sister. All she has left is that no-good son, and she may not even have him. Not a word since the war."

"She has you and the children."

Chris poured her a drink, but she refused it. "The children have been so brave—how long can this go on?"

"I talked with Mayor Starzynski just now. It may end at any moment."

"Sometimes I think I will be glad when it is over. Even with the Germans in Warsaw it can't get worse. Have you seen anybody?"

Chris nodded.

"I was at the orphanage," Deborah continued. "Susan Geller is worried about Ervin. She hasn't seen him in three days."

"Rosy is all right. I just left him a few minutes ago."

"That's good. And Gabriela? Did you tell her to come out here with us? It's much safer than in the center of town."

104

"She won't leave Andrei's apartment. You know that."

"Andrei?"

"I was with him this morning, Deborah. The evacuation truce took place through his position on the line. You heard?"

"Yes," she whispered, "they gave us back limbless men . . . I heard."

"Deborah . . . your husband was one of them."

The long storage corridors beneath the National Museum were a crush of cots and mattresses stretched out on the floor. The depth of the cellar gave protection from the shelling. It was converted hastily into a hospital. The power in that section of Warsaw had been blasted out. Even the emergency generators were gone. The musty halls were dimly lit by kerosene lamps. It was damp and it smelled moldy and it was clammy-cold and the smell of wounded flesh and antiseptics mingled with the other smells, and there were the sounds of nurses moving in a gliding kind of silence and there was the sound of continual prayer and moans and now and then a shriek of agony.

In the makeshift maternity ward, infants sucked at empty breasts and screamed angrily at what life had dealt them in their few hours on earth.

Chris led Deborah through the maze of corridors, threading his way among the sick and the dying. He went down another dozen steps into a long corridor storing medieval armor from other, less efficient wars. Here lay the amputees and here knelt their bereaved relatives. A nurse held a flashlight close to Paul Bronski's face.

"Paul . . ."

"He is under heavy sedation."

"Paul . . ."

A legless man next to Bronski spoke. "I was there when he did it. He had operated on about twenty or thirty of us . . . he was working with a flashlight only . . . then he got it . . . direct hit . . . he was the only doctor left alive. He was conscious the whole time, directing the soldiers how to take his arm off. . . ."

"Paul . . ."

Paul Bronski blinked his eyes open. They were glazed, but a small smile cornered his lips to say he knew she was there. She held his hand until he fell back into the drug-induced sleep.

"You Mrs. Bronski?" a doctor asked.

She nodded.

"Lucky he is a doctor. There's every chance he'll get through without infection or serious complication. He's out of shock. He'll pull through all right."

Deborah walked from the house of misery.

Chris waited at the main door of the museum. There were sudden flashes of light, like summer lightning, from the cannon fire on the horizon. The shells arched above them, plunging down on the workers' shacks across the river.

"Let's get out of here," he said, taking her arm to lead her to his car.

She jerked free of him.

"Come on, Deborah. We'll talk about it at home. If one of those shells falls short we'll be blown to kingdom come."

"Get away from me," she snarled.

The skyline lit up in quick, brilliant flashes and he saw her face. Her eyes were those of a madwoman. He grabbed her hard.

"I want to die!"

"Control yourself!"

"We did this to Paul!"

Chris shook her till her head bobbed. "We didn't make this war!"

"God is punishing me! Murderers! We are murderers!" She tore herself out of his grip and ran off into the darkness.

part two

DUSK

Chapter One

Journal Entry—September 27, 1939, Warsaw surrendered.

Poland has been divided into three parts. Germany annexed west-ern Poland to the pre-1918 borders. Soviet Russia has grabbed eastern Poland. The third part has been designated as the General Government Area, which the Germans are going to administrate. It appears this has been set up as a buffer zone against Russia.

The streets of Warsaw trembled beneath the treads of hundreds of tanks moving up Jerusalem Boulevard and the Third of May Boule-vard in parade array. These were followed by tens of thousands of goose-stepping soldiers moving in absolute precision, and overhead, squadron after squadron of planes flew in elements at house-top level.

It was an awesome display. The curbs were lined with stunned people. A few German flags fluttered from the homes of ethnics or cowards.

I think that Andrei and I were the only two of Warsaw's three hundred thousand Jews who watched. The rest sat behind drawn curtains and locked doors. I could not resist the temptation of seeing Adolf Hitler. He glowered at us from an open Mercedes. He looks just like his pictures.

I had to watch after Andrei. He was so enraged I was afraid he might try something foolish and get himself killed. He behaved.

Well, we're in it now, brother.

ALEXANDER BRANDEL

Franz Koenig wiped the peak of his cap with his sleeve to en-hance the shine. What a pity Herr Liedendorf was not here for this moment. Liedendorf, long the leader of Warsaw's ethnics, had been caught shining lights during German night-bombing raids and was shot by a Polish firing squad. He died a true son of Ger-many.

Franz Koenig, a brand-new official, had applied for Nazi membership. He was pure in birth, German all the way down to his great-grandparents. He was certain his membership would come through. He admired himself in the mirror and attached the swastika to his right sleeve and went into the bedroom to collect his plump Polish wife. She was too afraid to laugh when she saw the potbellied little professor decked out in a comic-opera uniform. Franz had changed since he began taking up with the Germans a few years before. Once she had had ambitions for him when he was at the university. She prodded him to try to win the chair of medicine. Now he had suddenly become a powerful man and was showing her a dark side she never knew existed, and she did not particularly like it.

Koenig's wife looked like an overdecorated Christmas tree or perhaps a clove-garnished pig ready for the oven. She made nearly two of him. Franz circled her, reckoned she would have to do, and they went out of their flat to the staff car waiting to take them to the grand ballroom of the Europa.

When they arrived the room was filled with uniformed generals of the land forces and admirals of the sea forces and generals of the sky forces and pin-striped, swallow-tailed, beribboned members of the diplomatic forces. Franz saw many old friends, also in new uniforms, and they looked neither more nor less ridiculous than he did, nor did their wives. There was a fantastic amount of heel clicking, square handshakes, bowing and hand kissing, glass clinking, and merry congratulations to the tune of soft Viennese waltzes ludicrously rendered by a German army band. Bottles popped and there was laughter and monocles. There was an entourage of new Polish mistresses, quick to serve new masters, and they were sized up for bed duty by the new administrators of Warsaw.

The orchestra stopped between two notes.

A single drum roll.

Everyone scrambled to set down his drink and line up on either side of the sweeping staircase.

Adolf Hitler appeared at the top of the stairs and as he stepped down, followed by a mass of black-uniformed men, the orchestra rendered a soul-stirring "Deutschland über Alles." It was indeed a moment for German backs to be ramrod-stiff and German hearts to pound. Unable to contain himself, an overenthusiastic officer of lower rank cried out, "*Sieg Heil!*"

Hitler stopped and nodded and smiled.

"*Sieg Heil!*" cried the officer again.

And the room broke into spontaneous rhythmic chanting, right arms thrust forward.

"*Sieg Heil! Sieg Heil! Sieg Heil!*"

Tears of joy streamed down the cheeks of Dr. Franz Koenig, the enthralled and the hypnotized.

Like the ethnic Germans of Austria and Czechoslovakia, the ethnics of Poland lined up for their reward for the service of spying on Poland and helping to destroy the country of their residence in advance of the German army. In the months before the invasion Dr. Koenig had grown powerful in the movement, second only to the late Liedendorf. He was made a special deputy to the new Kommissar of Warsaw, Rudolph Schreiker.

"Dr. Paul Bronski is here to see you, sir," a secretary told Koenig.

Koenig looked up from his massive, gleaming desk in his new office in the city hall.

"Show him in."

Paul was ushered in. Koenig pretended to be deep in meditation of a paper before him. He allowed Bronski to stand, neither offering recognition, a handshake, a seat, or sympathy for his missing right arm.

Paul Bronski had made a good recovery, but he was still very weak and in constant pain. He stood before Koenig's desk for a full five minutes before the German looked up. He realized that Koenig was basking in the glory of retribution. Koenig looked around the lavish environment, as if to point out the distance he had traveled from the tiny cluttered room he had had at the university.

"Sit down," Koenig said at last. He lit his pipe, rocking his chair back and forth, back and forth. Then, after another few moments, after insatiable sensations oozed from every pore, the delightful pleasures of revenge faded.

"Bronski, I summoned you here because we are in the process of forming a new Jewish Civil Authority. We are disbanding the old Jewish Council as of this afternoon. I am appointing you as deputy in charge of Jewish professionals."

"But . . . Franz . . . my position at the university . . ."

"As of tomorrow, there will be no more Jews at the university."

"I have no choice?"

"That is correct. If you carry out our directives and co-operate, you will be much better off than the other Jews in Warsaw, I can assure you."

"I . . . don't know what to say. It would certainly do no good to plead that . . . I have been divorced from all things Jewish for many years."

"The directives from Berlin clearly state that all new laws regarding Jews refer also to converts to Catholicism and people having one Jewish parent, grandparent, or great-grandparent. Active or inactive practice of Judaism is not a matter of consideration."

"Franz . . . I . . . it is hard to believe what I hear."

"Times have changed, Dr. Bronski. Get used to it quickly."

"We have been friends a long, long time. . . ."

"Never friends."

"Professional colleagues, then. You have always been a compassionate man. You were here this last month. You saw what happened. You are an intelligent human being. I cannot believe that you have completely lost feeling for us."

Koenig set his pipe down. "Yes, Bronski, I have made peace with myself, if that is what you mean. You see, I have been lied to by all those philosophers of righteousness who speak of truth and beauty

110

and the triumph of the lambs. This is real, here and now. It is a victory of lions. Germany has given me in one instant more than a thousand years of piddling through mediocrity and finding comfort in the quotations of false wisdoms."

"Franz . . ."

"Just a minute, Bronski. Your way puts me below your cunning. This way makes me your master. I take it you will serve on the Jewish Civil Authority."

Paul laughed ironically. "Yes, I'll be happy to."

"Very well, then. Tomorrow at ten you will report here to receive your first instructions from the Kommissar, Rudolph Schreiker."

Paul stood up slowly and extended his hand.

Koenig refused it. "It would be wise if you got into the habit of dispensing with amenities which heretofore made us appear as equals. You will address me as Dr. Koenig at all times and otherwise show the respect due a superior."

"Times have changed," Paul said. He started from the room.

"Bronski. One more thing. The Zoliborz suburb is being commandeered for the exclusive use of German officials and officers. Jews are no longer permitted. I shall be moving into your house in about ten days, so you have that length of time to resituate yourself. Before you start crying, I might say that out of deference to past relationships I will make a reasonable settlement on your property, a courtesy that most of the other Jews in Zoliborz will be denied."

Bronski felt weak. He leaned against the door to support himself, then opened it quickly.

"Tomorrow, here at ten to meet Rudolph Schreiker."

Chapter Two

Journal Entry

Warsaw has blossomed with German uniforms of all colors. One must have a program to tell who is über who. The biggest uniform apparently belongs to the new Kommissar, Rudolph Schreiker. We don't know too much about him, but obviously he is not going to try to win a popularity contest here. The old Jewish Council, a quasi-religious government, has been disbanded. A new instrument called the Jewish Civil Authority has been formed. Emanuel Goldman, the musician and a good Zionist, asked me to serve on the executive board. I ducked him because this so-called Civil Authority doesn't seem quite kosher to me.

ALEXANDER BRANDEL

Rudolph Schreiker, the new Kommissar of Warsaw, had come from a small town in Bavaria. He did not wish to spend his life at a cobbler's bench as had his father, his grandfather, and his great-grandfather. It was doubtful that Rudolph would have made a good cobbler, anyhow, for he wasn't very good at very much.

He reached maturity in that post-war Germany bitter over defeat, jobless, confused, floundering for direction. A malcontent in a time of malcontentment, he spent his energy berating a world he did not understand and was unable to cope with. Schreiker's mediocrity left him with two divorces and four children and debts and alcoholic tantrums.

There were rumblings in Bavaria in the twenties which were music to Rudolph Schreiker and all of his breed. Obscure and insignificant people were being offered a status in life they could never have attained for themselves. His failures were explained to him in a way he liked to believe. He was not responsible for his plight but a victim of conspiracies by the world against his people. He became a Nazi at once.

This new status and this brown uniform and this striking insignia and this man who posed as the Christ of Germany did not demand that he earn his way through labor or through study or wisdom. If these had been demanded, then all the Schreikers would have remained anonymous and Nazism's voice would not have sounded so jewel-toned, and that is why Nazism's voice had such jewel-like tones to him.

All he had to do was exert brute force, the same kind of brute force he used in beating his wives. With little in the way of personality or mental capacity he was yet able to understand clearly that his only hope for success or recognition in the world lay in casting his lot with the Nazis.

He instinctively grasped the one basic rule: absolute obedience. In true German tradition he responded to discipline and power. As a drunkard and wife beater, he had demonstrated his absence of personal morality, so morality posed no problem.

All Rudolph Schreiker really wanted was to be somebody, and Adolf Hitler gave him that chance.

The Nazis took bullies and bums and made them heroes. In exchange, the bums gave absolute obedience. There was no qualm or remorse or inner conflicts of conscience when Schreiker was asked to destroy a synagogue or murder an enemy of the party.

And the Nazis did what Hitler promised. Germany became powerful and feared and, as it expanded, the loyal Schreikers were given their rewards. He had served unquestioningly for nearly two decades, and for this he was made the Kommissar of Warsaw in the General Government Area.

This was a large position for a man who had always been a deputy and whose greatest forte was following commands.

Certainly Schreiker was no mental giant and a great deal of the orders would come from Berlin or Krakow or Lublin, where his superiors held office. Nonetheless, it called for more administrative ability and more initiative and authority than he had ever believed he would possess. He did not want to fail. If he were a success in Warsaw, there might be no limit to how far he could advance.

Schreiker learned many lessons intuitively as a Nazi. One of the purest axioms was that intellectuals were weak men. They espoused noble ideas which he did not understand. They argued ideals, but they were not ready to die for them as he was for Nazism. These so-called thinkers were exactly opposite of what they posed to be. They were all talk. They were cowards.

He, Schreiker, could rule them because he could bully them. And they would not fight back. Moreover, he could use them to accomplish for him what he could not do for himself.

The moment he arrived in Warsaw he examined the lists of ethnics who had supported the Germans. Dr. Franz Koenig. Perfect. Middle-aged, physically inept, proven loyalty. A doctor and professor, highly educated, lover of classics, reader of philosophers. An intellectual who was completely controllable. Rudolph Schreiker gave Dr. Franz Koenig a uniform, a title, and nearly unlimited range and power in his operations.

A good little puppy dog who would help him rule his district.

Paul Bronski was led by Koenig through a series of connecting offices to that of the Kommissar of Warsaw. Rudolph Schreiker sat behind the desk. His personal vanity made him a striking figure. He was a large, strong man with square black German features. Franz Koenig took his place at Schreiker's right.

"They are all here," Koenig said.

Paul Bronski recognized the other men. Silberberg, the playwright. There was Marinski, who controlled most of the leather factories around lower Gensia Street, and Schoenfeld, the most brilliant of Warsaw's Jewish lawyers and a former member of the Polish Parliament. Seidman, an engineer, was there and Colonel Weiss, one of the highest-ranking Jews of the Polish army. Goldman, an outstanding musician who had at one time taught both Deborah and Rachael. He was known as a strong Zionist among the intellectuals. Finally, there was Boris Presser. Presser seemed out of place in an otherwise distinguished gathering. He was a merchant, the owner of a large department store, but completely unnoted politically or socially in Warsaw.

The eight of them fidgeted before Schreiker's desk. The Kommissar looked from one to the other slowly, examining each and playing the game of invoking his power and authority by deliberate mannerism.

"For reasons of racial inferiority," Schreiker said, "we deem it

113

necessary for the Jews to govern themselves separately from the other citizens, under our directives. You eight men have been selected as the executive board of the Jewish Civil Authority. Each one of you will be responsible for a specific department—welfare, health, professions, properties, and so forth. Which of you is Goldman?"

The famed musician and idealist stepped forward. Although aged, Goldman showed the flash of color of a virtuoso.

"You will be in charge, Goldman. You will report directly to me. You others will receive your directives from Dr. Koenig."

Koenig spoke. "You will occupy the premises at Grzybowska 28 immediately and set up offices. Your first task will be to take a census of the Jews in the Warsaw district. As soon as each Jew registers with your Civil Authority he will be issued a *Kennkarte*, which will also serve as a basis for a ration book. Any Jew found at the end of three weeks without a *Kennkarte* will be punished by death."

"I expect this registration to be carried out efficiently," Schreiker added, "or there will be a new Civil Authority in short order. You will be advised of further directives. You are dismissed."

They shuffled for the door, dazed.

"One more thing for now," Schreiker said, standing up and walking around to the front of his desk. He was a large and obviously powerful man and wanted to make certain the others saw it. "We have thousands of young virile soldiers in our garrison who require diversion. You will supply a list of women who will take care of their requirements. We will need at least fifty or sixty to start; the choice ones will be fortunate to serve in an officers' brothel."

They looked from one to the other, desperate for one of them to have the courage to speak out.

Schreiker snatched a paper with their names. "Who is Silberberg?"

Silberberg stepped forward, trembling. All his courage went into the words he wrote. "You are a playwright! You must know actresses." Silberberg's thin chest was pained with fear. He drew a deep breath and spat on the floor. Schreiker ran across the room and stopped in front of him. The playwright closed his eyes, waiting for the blow. It came across the bridge of his nose. He sank to his knees, holding his gory face in his hands, temporarily blinded. Goldman knelt beside him quickly.

"Get away from him!"

"Go on, hit me too, you brave man," Goldman challenged.

Schreiker spun around quickly, looking over the others. "You, cripple!" he said, pointing to Bronski. "You will take personal charge of getting the whores!"

"I am afraid I cannot serve under these conditions," Paul Bronski said.

Franz Koenig sensed that Schreiker had gone too far, too fast. He stepped in quickly. "We shall discuss this in due time," he said. "Now get out, all of you."

Schreiker wanted to beat them all up, but he knew Koenig's move was to save him from bumbling. He must not bumble. After they left he paced the room, livid with rage, and cursed every oath he knew, then slumped behind his desk, swearing he would show who was the authority. When he calmed down, Koenig spoke softly and calmly. "Herr Schreiker," he said, "we have touched upon a very sensitive point."

"But they defied me!"

"Herr Kommissar, never mind. Let us not give them issues to unify them. After all now, we have selected them to do a job for us —right?"

"They are privileged!"

"Yes, yes, exactly," Koenig said. "In order for them to carry on for us, they must have a certain amount of authority and weight among the Jews. If we destroy their authority by forcing them to do something to make them lose face with the people—then they can't do the job for us."

Schreiker thought about that. Yes, he had done a stupid thing. He was going to create a power, then destroy it in the same blow. Koenig was shrewd. Intellectuals could always see those things. He would keep Koenig close at hand so he would not make mistakes.

"There are other ways to supply women for brothels," Koenig said. "I suggest we drop the matter so far as the Civil Authority is concerned. That will make them think they have some importance."

"Yes, of course," Schreiker said. "I was only testing them to see if they had enough personal courage to carry out our directives— just testing them."

Journal Entry

Well, we certainly did not have to wait long to find out what is in store for us and what kind of a man Rudolph Schreiker is.

The seat of the government for the General Government Area has been set up in Krakow, which is a surprise. We were certain it would be in Warsaw. A chap named Hans Frank is running the show down there. Each day he publishes a four-page paper called the General Government Gazette. *Pages one, two, and three cover an assortment of things. Page four is dedicated to the "Jewish Problem." We certainly are making news these days.*

ALEXANDER BRANDEL

DIRECTIVE
ALL JEWS MUST REGISTER IMMEDIATELY AT THE JEWISH CIVIL
AUTHORITY AT GRZYBOWSKA 28 FOR ISSUANCE OF KENNKARTEN
AND RATION BOOKS.
FAILURE TO DO SO IS PUNISHABLE BY DEATH.

DIRECTIVE
THE ZOLIBORZ SUBURB IS OUT OF BOUNDS FOR FUTURE JEWISH
RESIDENCE. THOSE JEWS LIVING IN ZOLIBORZ MUST FIND OTHER QUAR-
TERS WITHIN ONE WEEK.

DIRECTIVE
FOR CLARIFICATION. ALL FUTURE DIRECTIVES PERTAINING TO JEWS
ALSO PERTAIN TO THOSE WITH ONE JEWISH PARENT OR GRANDPARENT.
JEWS WHO HAVE CONVERTED TO OTHER RELIGIONS ARE CONSIDERED
JEWS.

DIRECTIVE
JEWS ARE FORBIDDEN IN PUBLIC PARKS AND MUSEUMS.
JEWS ARE FORBIDDEN IN PUBLIC RESTAURANTS IN NON-JEWISH
DISTRICTS.
JEWS ARE FORBIDDEN TO RIDE ON PUBLIC TRANSPORTATION.
JEWISH CHILDREN ARE TO BE WITHDRAWN FROM PUBLIC SCHOOLS
IMMEDIATELY.

DIRECTIVE
THE PRACTICE OF THE JEWISH RELIGION IS FORBIDDEN. ALL SYNA-
GOGUES ARE OUT OF BOUNDS. JEWISH RELIGIOUS SCHOOLING IS
FORBIDDEN.

DIRECTIVE
THE FOLLOWING TRADES AND PROFESSIONS MAY BE PRACTICED BY
JEWS ONLY AMONG THE JEWISH POPULATION: MEDICINE, LAW,
JOURNALISM, MUSIC, ALL GOVERNMENTAL POSITIONS, ALL MUNICIP-
ALLY OPERATED INDUSTRIES.

DIRECTIVE
JEWS ARE FORBIDDEN TO ATTEND THEATER OR CINEMA IN NON-
JEWISH AREAS.
JEWS ARE FORBIDDEN TO ENTER NON-JEWISH HOSPITALS.

As the registration commenced, each *Kennkarte* was stamped
with a large *J*. A directive came out quickly, lowering the ration of
Jews. This brought on a scramble to obtain illegal and false Aryan
Kennkarten. In Zoliborz and other areas confiscated for German
officials, the dispossessed Jews were forced to abandon their properties without compensation.

Each day a new directive.

Meanwhile Rudolph Schreiker returned to work with which he was more familiar. The old street fighter of the early Nazi days in Bavaria organized gangs of Polish hoodlums and put them on the German payroll with the order to terrorize the Jewish population. Within a few weeks of the German entry into Warsaw there was a rash of unmolested window smashing, shop looting, and the beating up of bearded Jews.

On the streets, loudspeaker trucks rolled up and down the Jewish areas, barking out the latest directives and page four of the *General Government Gazette,* and orders from the Warsaw Kommissar and the Jewish Civil Authority were plastered on walls on every street.

A special detachment of SS troopers rounded up people most likely to resist, Jews and non-Jews alike, who had been fingered in advance by Dr. Franz Koenig and other ethnics. They were marched into Pawiak Prison and shot down by firing squads.

On the radio, round-the-clock saturation to educate the Polish public on the causes of the war.

"Germany has come here to save Poland from Jewish war profiteers."

And the billboards which once announced Irene Dunne movies found her replacement with drawings of bearded Jews violating nuns, bearded Jews using the blood of Christian babies for their rituals, bearded Jews sitting atop piles of money and knifing good honest Poles in the back.

For the most part, the German program met with universal success. The Polish people, who could not strike at their noblemen who had now vanished, nor at the Russians who had betrayed them, nor at the Germans who had massacred them, were willing to accept the traditional Jewish scapegoat as the true cause of their latest disaster.

Chapter Three

DIRECTIVE
ALL JEWISH TRADE UNIONS, PROFESSIONAL SOCIETIES, AND ZIONIST ORGANIZATIONS ARE, AS OF THIS DATE, ILLEGAL.

Journal Entry

The Bathyran Executive Council held an emergency session to-day to prepare to go underground. I must find some loopholes in the

117

German directives which will keep us together and functioning, perhaps under a "front" organization.

Ana Grinspan

has made the most progress. She reports the Krakow Chapter is unified. She has a lot of spunk, that girl. Despite the new directives restricting travel by Jews, Ana has already obtained false travel papers (as a nonexistent Tanya Tartinski). Ana's non-Jewish appearance will help her to move around unchallenged. She has contacted Tommy Thompson at the American Embassy now in Krakow, and he has agreed to receive American dollars from our people outside Poland (and especially our chapters in America) and pass the money on to her. Thank God for Tommy. He is a true friend. Ana is going to travel to all our major chapters at once to set up a system of underground communications which we have worked out.

Susan Geller

has the most urgent situation. She estimates that thirty thousand Jewish soldiers were killed in the invasion. (This figure seems fairly accurate. To the best of our estimates, a Polish total of two hundred thousand soldiers were killed, many thousands escaped over the border, and there are uncounted thousands in prisoner-of-war camps.) In addition, hundreds of children were left parentless during the siege of Warsaw. We must take our share of them. Susan has committed the Bathyran Orphanage to take in another two hundred children, which doubles our present capacity. Needless to say what this does to the budget. We need personnel. That means taking our best people off their outside jobs and sending them to work in the orphanage. God knows how we will manage it. With the cut in rations for the Jews, we must have an extra fifty ration cards from the Jewish Civil Authority for the children.

Tolek Alterman

after his usual speech on Zionism, promised Susan that he will open new acreage at the farm to take up the ration cut. He must be encouraged to increase production if the price of food gets out of hand. But to increase the farm's load will take personnel too.

Ervin Rosenblum

is still working for Swiss News on the technicality that it is a neutral agency, while the letter of the German directive forbids Jews to work on non-Jewish Polish papers. (We expect the Jewish press will be closed down any minute, although Emanuel Goldman, the Authority chairman, sold the Germans on letting it run as a means

118

of mass communication to implement German directives. How long can he hold this point?) Ervin does not believe that either he, Swiss News, or Chris de Monti will be around for long. It will be a great loss, because Ervin is very close to news sources and several times already has given us tips that gave us twenty-four hours of grace to set up defenses. One very sour note. I am distressed that Andrei was not present. I lied to the others, saying he was in Bialystok on business. Three or four members have reported he is planning to do something which will hurt us desperately. I must stop him. I close my entry now in order to find him.

ALEXANDER BRANDEL

Gabriela Rak opened the door for Alexander Brandel at her flat on the Square of the Three Crosses.

"Come in, Alex." She closed the door behind him and took his overcoat and cap.

"Is he here?"

Gabriela nodded and pointed to the balcony.

"Before I see him . . ."

She shook her head. "I don't know, Alex. Some days he paces like an animal and curses. Other days, like today, he sits and sulks and drinks without a word. Yesterday and today he has been out seeing people. I don't know what for. He won't confide in me."

"I know," Alex said.

"I have never known anyone could take defeat so hard, Alex. He has such a fierce pride—it seems as though he is taking it upon himself to suffer for thirty million Poles."

She walked to the french doors and opened them. Andrei was looking aimlessly out at the battered ruins. "Andrei," she called a half dozen times before she got his attention. "Alexander Brandel is here."

He walked into the room. He was unshaven and bleary-eyed from too much drinking and too little sleep. He went directly to the liquor cabinet and poured himself some vodka.

"I'll go fix you some tea, Alex," Gabriela said nervously.

"No," Andrei ordered, "you stay. I want you to hear the great dissertations of Zionist logic. Pearls of wisdom are about to drop like spring rain. We should have a bucket so we could catch them all." He downed the vodka and poured himself another. Gabriela uncomfortably edged into a chair while Alexander walked to Andrei and took the glass out of his hand and set it down.

"Why weren't you at the executive council meeting today?"

"Haven't you heard? There are no more Bathyrans. Directive twenty-two by order of the Kommissar of Warsaw."

"It was a terribly important meeting. We have to set up mechanisms to go underground."

Andrei smacked his lips and clapped his hands together and

119

walked to Gabriela. "Gaby, shall I tell you what they said today, verbatim? Let me see now. Susan Geller cried the loudest because the war gave her lots and lots of new orphans and our girl Susy is going to take them all in, each and every one. So tomorrow Herr Schreiker will issue a directive outlawing orphans. But! Don't underestimate us. Our Alexander Brandel will bypass the directive ... he is a wily man. He finds loopholes in everything. 'From now on,' declares Alex, 'we will call the orphans novitiates and the Bathyran Orphanage will become St. Alexander's Convent.' Now then, Tolek Alterman sprang to his feet. 'Comrades,' he said, 'I will increase the production of the farm tenfold because it is living Zionism.' And then Ana . . . dear old Ana. 'I would like to report that the Krakow group is singing "Solidarity Forever." ' "

"Have you finished?"

"No, Alex. I've had a few meetings of my own."

"So I hear. Very interesting plans you've made."

"What plans?" Gabriela said.

"Why don't you tell her, Andrei?" Andrei turned his back. "No? Well, then I'll tell her. He is planning to take fifty of our best people and leave Warsaw."

Andrei spun around. "Let Alex and the rest of that pack of idiots continue their debating societies while the Germans squeeze the life out of them. Yes, I'm taking fifty people and I'm going over the border to Russia and get arms and return and write a few little directives of my own on the Germans' supply lines."

"Why didn't you tell me this?" she demanded.

"I told you to go to Krakow with the Americans. Well, I still have your papers. It will be my present to you when I leave."

"But why didn't you tell me!"

"So you'd team up with him and schlogg me to death with arguments?"

"No one is going to argue, Andrei," Alex said. "Here it is, straight and proper. You are forbidden to do what you plan."

"Listen to him! The new Kommissar has issued a directive."

"You are not going to take fifty of our best people. We need them desperately to keep other people alive."

"Sing, Brother Brandel!"

"Through us and other Zionist groups the people have organizations prepared to function in their behalf. If you and a hundred others like you take fifty men and women away, you're stripping three and a half million Jews of the only buffer they have to protect them."

"Alex, try and stop me."

"We have worked together for a long, long time, Andrei, but I will not hesitate to throw you out of the Bathyrans in disgrace."

"Then you'll have to throw out the other fifty, because they will follow me."

They stopped suddenly, each building to a point of no return. There was anger in Andrei that defied logic. Alex was stunned. He turned to Gaby, who threw up her hands in helplessness.

"I prayed to God that my son Wolf would be half the man Andrei Androfski was. When I saw you crawl in on your hands and knees from battle I said, 'This is the most gallant man who ever lived. No matter what happens in the days to come, we will pull through so long as Andrei is with us.' Now . . . I see you for what you are. A man without true courage."

Gabriela threw herself between them, looking from one to the other in desperation, and suddenly it was Alex who received her wrath. "How dare you say that to him!"

Alex brushed by her and slapped Andrei across the face. He did not even blink.

"Stop it!" Gabriela cried.

"It's all right, Gaby. He hits like a woman and he knows I will not strike him back."

"But the Germans do not hit like women and you do not have the courage to take their blows and keep your hands at your side."

Andrei walked across the room to the sofa. "I will not let it be said that I destroyed the Bathyrans. Keep them here. I will go alone. There are a hundred thousand Polish soldiers who escaped over the borders who will fight again. There will be one more."

Alex hovered over him. "You are a selfish, vengeful man with only desire to fill this great thirst of yours for personal revenge. Forget the woman who loves you . . . forget your sister and her children . . . forget your friends . . . forget the people to whom you're obligated. When we need you the most, run off to join your roving band of Robin Hoods. Hail and farewell to the gallant Major Androfski of the Seventh Ulanys."

"Stop tormenting him," Gabriela cried.

"For God's sake, Alex," Andrei screamed. "I cannot fight your kind of war. I am not a traitor! I cannot fight your kind of war!"

"You have fought your war your way and it was no good. Now the battle is even more unbalanced. This is not strong men against strong men. We are a few people who have in our hands the responsibility of three and a half million helpless people. We have no weapons but faith in each other. Andrei, you've always wanted to know what Zionism is. This is Zionism, helping Jews survive. You must give yourself to us. We cannot do without you."

Andrei sighed and grunted. "Jesus Christ," he mumbled, "what kind of a battle is this?" He looked up at them. "In all those years I carried the pose of being the great Androfski—and I know why. Because we were fighting a hypothetical battle. Everyone was our enemy—yet, no one. We talked about a dream, we talked about our longings, but now . . . I am no longer in a dubious battle. Can't you understand I have seen the enemy face to face? I want to fight

121

him with these," he said, holding up his hamlike fists. "I want to smash in the faces of those German bastards."

"Will that keep us alive?"

"I don't know if I have the courage you speak of, Alex—to watch murder and not lift my hand."

"Don't leave us, Andrei."

Gabriela knelt beside him and tried to comfort him. "Alex is right," she said. "You must stand by your people."

"Didn't you know, Gaby, Alex is always right—didn't you know?"

Andrei looked from one to the other. Yes . . . his war was over. In his war he had been trampled and humiliated. Now he must try to fight Alexander Brandel's war.

"I will try," he muttered at last. "I will try."

Chapter Four

As a member of the executive board of the Jewish Civil Authority, Paul Bronski had several privileges and immunities. The ration for his family was equal to that of a Polish official, half again as much as the Jewish ration. Franz Koenig convinced Kommissar Schreiker that such generosity to the JCA would pay off.

Paul was able to secure a lovely apartment on Sienna Street, which was a mixed district of upper-middle-class professionals and long one of the fashionable streets in Warsaw. Bronski was not truly discomfited by the German occupation. His fortune was intact in Switzerland, beyond German reach, and he had quickly achieved the top status the new society allowed. So long as Chris stayed in Warsaw, it was an easy matter for him to advance Paul money which he was able to import on Swiss News accounts.

Nevertheless, moving day brought a terrible uneasiness in him. Deborah seemed delighted at the idea of leaving Zoliborz to move into a predominantly Jewish area. It was as though their forced identification as Jews gave her some sort of victory. While the boxes and crates were piled high, Paul closed himself in his study because he could not stand another question from the children.

On his desk were armbands his family had to wear from now on. The Germans were so damned thorough, he thought. Their directive called for the armband to be white in color with a blue Star of David no less than three centimeters in height. Paul laughed at the irony of it all and put the armband on, feeling at least he cheated somewhat by losing the specified arm and having to wear the band on his left arm.

There was a knock on the door and Andrei entered.

"Well, hello, brother-in-law," Bronski said. "Deborah is about the house somewhere, packing."

"As a matter of fact, I came to see you, Paul."

"To gloat over your victory? To tell me how foolish I look wearing a Star of David? To raise your finger and tell me how your ill-fated prediction came to pass—'Bronski, you are a Jew whether you want to be or not'—or to ask if I gave the Germans a lesson on galloping Zionism, which I abhor, and tried to convince them I wasn't really a Jew? Dammit all, the most difficult part of having one arm is trying to load and light a pipe—that and buttoning your fly."

Andrei struck a match and held it over the bowl of Paul's pipe while he drew in the fire.

"How do you feel, Paul?"

"Fine. I discovered I'm still a hell of a good doctor. Did you ever give directions to a corporal on how to amputate your arm by flashlight? Good trick if I say so myself. You look fine. Mere bullet wounds wouldn't annoy you."

"How are Deborah and the children taking this move?"

"Deborah? I think she's delighted. The Lord is making divine retribution for the years I forced her to be an agnostic. I am going to brush up on my Hebrew, read the Torah nightly, and spend the rest of my life saying, 'I shall be a good Jew,' so help me Stawki Street."

"I came here to ask you if you and I shouldn't call a truce."

Paul looked surprised. "You are a gallant winner, sir."

"No, it's just that times have grown so serious we don't have the luxury of battling each other for a point already proven. You're sitting in the JCA. You know just how bad things are."

"Oh, no doubt they are bad. It is going to be a rough transition."

Andrei had his opening. He pressed his point. "Are you certain it is only a transition? No one really knows what the Germans are up to or when they will quit."

Paul looked at Andrei with suspicion. The truce was merely a mask behind which he was operating. "And?" he asked.

"Now that the Jews, the half Jews, the converts, and the unadmitting Jews have been labeled, there is a tremendous need to unify all the loose ends."

"Go on," Paul said.

"Paul, we are trying very hard to get a meeting together of every faction of the community, regardless of philosophy, to map out some sort of master policy. You are sitting in one of the key positions. We want to know if you can be counted in."

"Counted in on what?"

"We can't stand by idly and let the Germans keep pouring these directives at us and beating up our people in the streets. We must

123

go to them as a single body to let them know we are going to resist further abuse."

Paul sighed and lay his pipe in the ash tray and rocked his chair back and forth, back and forth. "I might have known you'd still be trying to lead a cavalry charge."

Andrei, who swore to himself he would not get angry, held his temper. "How much do you have to take from them before you show your spine? Where are all your fine students now? Where are all your colleagues from the university now?"

"Andrei," Paul said softly, "you are not the only one who has meditated about this problem. When I lost my right arm, my body underwent a shock but, as you see, I am well recovered. So, the Jews in Warsaw are losing their right arms. It is painful, but the shock will pass and they will live. Not so well as before, perhaps, but that is the way things are, and nothing we can do will change them."

"Are you willing to guarantee me that the Germans are going to stop at merely taking an arm? Can you tell me honestly the directives won't take the other arm, then both legs?"

"I'll tell you what I am willing to do, Andrei. I am willing to accept life for what it is. The Germans are the law. They have won a war. I see no alternative."

"You really think you can do business with them?"

"I really think I have no choice, Andrei. Andrei . . . Andrei . . . You are always charging windmills—you are always looking for the mystical enemy. Before the Germans, you fought Poland. You cannot accept life for what it is. Yes, I've compromised, but I know reality. I've not chased ghosts. I compromise now because I was suddenly made a Jew again and I have no alternative. Andrei, I've been put into a position of responsibility to this community. Didn't ask for it—didn't want it. But I must, you see. I also have a wife and two children to keep alive——"

"And for that you'll forfeit your soul and honor!"

"Try out the catch phrases elsewhere. I know what you are up to. Insurrection . . . agitation . . . an underground. Break your head against a wall just as you did before the war. I know the reality of what is here now and I'm going to bring my family through it."

Andrei was about to roar that Paul was a coward, always looking for the easy path out. The cat who always lands on his feet. The first to sell his soul. It took all the strength he had, but he restrained himself.

"And, so long as we are talking about it, Andrei, your activities are bound to be known. For the safety of Deborah and the children, it may be best if you stay away from us."

"Let my sister decide that!"

"Oh, nothing her darling brother does can be wrong." .

Andrei spun around on his heels and stamped out. He was unable to resist slamming the door as a sign that he had not entirely lost his restraint.

Paul tapped the pipe against his teeth and shook his head. There he goes, Paul thought. Still looking for a fight. Still at the head of a cavalry charge. How long would Andrei last in this atmosphere before he was dragged up before a firing squad?

But then, Andrei would laugh at them while he was being shot. And for a moment Paul was envious of that reckless courage that was unable to give quarter. He, Paul Bronski, had shown an instinctive courage in a single instant when the German bully Rudolph Schreiker demanded Jewish women for prostitutes. There would be other moments of crisis in the days ahead. How he would like to be Andrei Androfski in those moments. Would he be defiant when the challenge came the next time? He did not know. If only he could store that second of courage in a little box and open it again when he needed it.

A ruckus from the direction of the kitchen sent Paul running from his study. Deborah was standing over Zoshia, yelling at her.

"What is going on here?"

"Zoshia stole our silver. Rachael saw her pass it over the fence to that rotten son of hers."

Paul stepped between the two of them.

"Is this true, Zoshia?" he demanded.

"It is true and I'm not sorry," Zoshia screamed.

"She is a dirty thief," Deborah snarled.

"It is mine and more than mine for the years I have cleaned your Jew dirt."

"Oh, dear Lord," Deborah said, "we have treated you kinder than your own son, whom we've bailed out of jail every time he went into one of his drunken rages. I paid the doctor bills for you and your sister when you couldn't work."

"You brought the Germans to Poland," Zoshia cried. "The priest told us so! It is all the fault of the Jews!" She spat in hatred in their faces and waddled from the room.

Deborah leaned against Paul and cried softly, and he tried to comfort her. "I can't believe it," she murmured. "I can't believe it . . ."

"There is nothing we can do. The Germans are encouraging them to do what she did."

One of the moving men came in.

"We have a wagonload. You said you wanted to come with us to Sienna Street and show us where the things go."

"Mrs. Bronski will be out in a moment. She will follow you over."

The teamster tipped his cap and left.

Deborah dried her eyes. He walked to his office and returned

125

with the armbands. "You and the children will have to wear these," he said.

She took them and stared at them, then put one on her right arm. "Isn't it a shame," she said, "that the first time we really must tell the children they are Jews . . . it must be like this. . . ."

Chapter Five

Journal Entry

Andrei warned me that we could not depend on Paul Bronski. How right he was. We continue to canvass the Jewish community to see who among us will come together for a leadership meeting. We are picking up strength, but not fast enough. A few more of these German directives will do more to convince them than any of our arguments.

I am going to see Rabbi Solomon. If we can win his support, it could well put us over the top.

ALEXANDER BRANDEL

The Rabbi Solomon's name was most often preceded by the word "great". He was one of the most learned men not only of Warsaw but of all Poland, and that constituted the heartland of religious Jewry.

He was a humble man who was beloved for giving his life to study and devotion and teaching. His rulings set the vogues among the religious Jews.

Not the least of the man's many qualities was a political agility. When one came to earth from Talmudic and ethical writings to things real, deftness was required in order to be able to get along with all the diversified factions of Jewish opinion and philosophy. It was because of this wizardry that he was often called upon to use his good offices to mediate between extreme thinkers, from Communists to neo-fascists.

All organized Zionists believed that only they were the true standardbearers of Zionism and that the others outside their ranks were merely pseudo Zionists. It was the same with Rabbi Solomon. His Zionism, he felt, was certainly the purest form, for it came from the books of the Bible which told him a "Messiah" would return to earth and lead the scattered children of Israel back to their "Promised Land." This was not so much Zionism to him but rather fundamental Judaism.

All the new ideas—revisionist, socialist, communist, intellectualism—were merely expedient and radical ideas which took the place of the true basic faith.

Although he did not agree with the new ideas, he was compassionate toward them. He understood that it took enormous inner strength not to be able to rebel against the abuses the Jews had suffered. These new forms of Zionism, therefore, were rebellions by weak men who could not suffer in silence and dignity, to pray and to accept as part of life the penalties imposed by God for being worthy of being the chosen guardians of the Holy Law.

After the Germans shut his synagogue, he worked harder than ever keeping up the morale of his people. During the storm of directives his quiet strength and counsel were constantly sought.

It was after such a strenuous day that Alexander Brandel arrived in his study. The old man looked forward to the relaxation and verbal swordplay with the learned Zionist historian.

They recounted the terrible things of the day with mutual sadness, went through all the accepted amenities, then Alex got down to business.

"We feel the urgencies of the day call for us to set aside the things which divide us," Alex said carefully, "and unite in those upon which we agree."

"But, Alexander, two Jews never agree on anything."

"On certain things, Rabbi Solomon. On taking care of orphans. On helping each other."

"And what shall we do on those things which you claim we agree?"

"We shall first hold a meeting. I have many diversified leaders who have agreed to attend. If you would come, it would be a signal for most of the rabbis in Warsaw to follow suit."

"Do you have support from the Bund?"

"Yes."

"And the Federation of Labor Zionists?"

"Yes."

"And the Communists?"

"Yes."

"Such a meeting will be a mess."

"There is another intention."

"Aha."

"We must try to present a unified front to stop these German directives."

"So? Well, Alexander, I am not a social worker. I am also not a politician. I am merely a teacher. As for civil problems, we have a Civil Authority to cope with most of the problems which you pose."

Alex promised himself not to become discouraged. He started again. "The Jewish Civil Authority was hand picked by the Germans. We feel they merely wish to use it as an instrument to carry out their policy."

"But surely with good Zionists like Emanuel Goldman and Schoenfeld and Silberberg on the Authority——"

"But, Rabbi, they are truly without power. These are extraordinary times and call for extraordinary measures."

"What is so extraordinary about these times, Alex?"

"We could be possibly engaged in a struggle for our very survival."

The old man smiled and stroked his big bushy white beard. How dramatic these young people were! "Alexander. Tell me, learned historian, when in the history of the Jewish people has survival not been an issue? Sometimes the degree varies. What is happening today in Poland has happened many times in our history. Now tell me, Brandel the historian, have we not outlived every tyrant in the past?"

"I think there is a difference."

"So?"

"From the time of the First Temple we have been massacred because of scapegoatism, expedience for the ruling politicians, passion outbursts, ignorance. The Crusades, the Inquisition, the Worms massacre, the Cossack uprisings. Never before have we been faced with a cold-blooded, organized, calculated, and deliberate plot to destroy us."

"And how does the learned historian know this to be true?"

"I read Adolf Hitler."

"Aha. Tell me, Alexander, what do you suppose the Germans stand to gain by destroying the Jews? Will they gain territory? Will they gain more than token wealth? What can be the ultimate goal in doing away with some of the world's finest doctors, musicians, craftsmen, scientists, writers? What is the point that they will win by doing it?"

"It is not the matter of winning a point. They started on us the same way a hundred others started on us, but in the case of the Germans, I do not know if they will be able to stop themselves. Like no other people in history, they are psychologically geared to destroy merely for destroying."

"So, what you are saying is that the Nazis are evil. As a historian, surely you know that evil destroys itself."

"It may also destroy us while it is destroying itself. Where does it say in the Talmud and Torah, Rabbi, that we are not supposed to defend ourselves?"

"But we do defend ourselves. We defend ourselves by living in the faith which has kept us alive all of the centuries. We defend ourselves by remaining good Jews. It will bring us through this hour as it has through all the rest of our crises. And the Messiah will come, as He has promised."

"And how do you suppose we will recognize Him?"

"It is not if we will recognize Him. It is if He will recognize us."

The argument was at a dead end. The old man would not budge.

Alex took his armband off and held it in front of the Rabbi's eyes. "Can you wear this with pride?"

"It was good enough for King David."

"But he did not wear it as a badge of humility!"

"Alexander, why must all Zionists shout? The gates of heaven are barred to those who pick up weapons of death. That is what will come ultimately to you if you form a band of rabble. Learn to suffer in humility and faith. That alone will be our salvation."

Chapter Six

DIRECTIVE
ALL GOVERNMENT PENSIONS FOR JEWS ARE HEREBY SUSPENDED.

DIRECTIVE
JEWS ARE FORBIDDEN TO PATRONIZE NON-JEWISH FOOD MARKETS AND DEPARTMENT STORES.

DIRECTIVE
TRAVEL PERMITS ARE REQUIRED FOR JEWS LEAVING WARSAW. JEWS ARE RESTRICTED TO SPECIAL COACHES MARKED "JEWISH."

DIRECTIVE
JEWS ARE FORBIDDEN TO STAND IN RATION LINES EXCEPT AT SPECIFIED JEWISH STATIONS.

Alexander Brandel's quest for solidarity was frustrating. There was confusion among the people. Most of them were not connected with organizations. They wanted merely to be able to take care of their families. The few men whose power and influence could have rallied everyone were marched to Pawiak Prison and shot.

Mayor Starzynski, who had made the epic fight for Warsaw and was one of the few Poles in high positions to give the Jews credit for their contribution to the defense of the country, disappeared. Like many another, he was taken off in the middle of the night without explanation and never returned.

Alex watched his fellow intellectuals disintegrate. These men who had once gushed forth waterfalls of idealism seemed unable to put their words into practice.

He courted Rodel, the Communist, who controlled an important organization. The baldheaded, chain-smoking leader of the Communists spent most of the time explaining how the Soviet Union truly saved eastern Poland by jumping her from the back while the

Polish army fought for its life. Rodel was always amusing to Alex. He had an amazing range of verbal dexterity and political acrobatics. In the spring of that year Rodel had been violently anti-Nazi. In the summer, after the Russian-German pact, he decided the Germans weren't so bad, after all—it was the Western powers who had really sold everyone down the river. Now he was violently anti-German once more but spent most of his time explaining away Russian treachery. Rodel had no use for Zionism simply because he had no use for anything that was not communism. Nonetheless, Alex needed Rodel. To ignore the Communists would be worse than to be refused by them. The Communists, with their non-Jewish members, boasted the closest-knit group for the Jews. But Rodel was having his hands full. The Communists were being hounded by the Nazis even more unmercifully than the Jews. The Gestapo had a single order covering them: FIND THEM AND SHOOT THEM.

Alex couldn't even get to talk with the leader of the Revisionists, Samson Ben Horin. They were traditionally loners who wanted no part of a plan committing them to act with a group. Alex reckoned they were girding for street fighting.

The businessmen were racked with problems. Shelves were bare, prices were rising, there was a continuing pressure by the new directives. They considered Alex's quest for unity as asking for charity. For them, anything outside of normal business activities was deemed "charity." Charity could be considered only after profits, and they were doubtful these days.

The largest single entity, the religious community, simply refused to budge. They took their cue from Rabbi Solomon to resort to the traditional weapons of prayer and patience.

The Jewish Civil Authority treated Alex as though he were a leper. He was branded as a harbinger of doom by Silberberg, the playwright, who had had all the fight knocked out of him by the single blow delivered in the office of Rudolph Schreiker. Silberberg, whose plays had once reeked with slogans of courage . . . The rest of them were jealous of their stations. Only Emanuel Goldman, the pianist, could be counted on.

Outside the Jewish community, pickings were lean. The gentile intellectuals were as terrified as the Jewish intellectuals. Paul Bronski proved a classic example. From the time he returned to Warsaw till the time he moved to Sienna Street, he did not receive a single call from his former colleagues or students at the university.

The majority of the population wanted no part of the German-Jewish war. A minority were actively engaged in activities against the Jews.

The one great voice of power and conscience, the Church, remained silent.

130

As a clever tactician, Alexander realized early that unity was impossible, so he carefully formulated a secondary objective. When it was all thought out, he called together three of the most reliable strong men. These were people who understood the urgency without being preached to and who, like him, were groping for a way to hang together and bypass the dreaded directives.

The four of them picked each other's brains in a series of secret meetings.

There was Alex, and there was Simon Eden, the iron-handed ruler of the Joint Federation of Labor Zionists. He alone was able to form and control ten different middle- to left-wing factions. His Joint Federation accounted for more than sixty per cent of all organized Zionists. Simon had the best qualities of Alexander and Andrei combined and few of their faults. Like Andrei, he had been an officer in the army and was a large and strong man who could rise to fierceness. Like Alex, he was a cool and deliberate thinker. Andrei respected Simon more than any man in Warsaw except Alex.

The third man was Emanuel Goldman, the aging but still flamboyant artist of the piano who had been appointed head of the Jewish Civil Authority.

Goldman was Dr. Franz Koenig's one error in judgment. Koenig believed correctly that the famed musician had a "name" value to the Jews but certainly underestimated his devotion to humanitarian causes. Goldman was realistic. He knew he could not last long on the Civil Authority. The Germans wanted a weak man to carry out their orders. He was grimly determined to find a route for the community before he was dispossessed.

The fourth man was David Zemba, director of the American Relief Society, an organization supported by American Jews. Zemba a Polish Jew, was small in stature, with a closely cropped beard and a mild manner, but he was utterly fearless and brilliantly shrewd. With Poland occupied, the American dollars which he controlled had to be one of the foundations of any adventure.

Together, they worked out a formula.

Stage one: Emanuel Goldman, as head of the Jewish Civil Authority, received an appointment with Dr. Franz Koenig.

"We are faced with a problem, Herr Doktor. By tradition, we Jews have always taken care of our own. Social work was formerly handled by the old Jewish Council, which has been disbanded. As you know, the war has compounded this problem. We have no legal instrument through which to take care of welfare problems."

"I take it you are petitioning me to set up a welfare department in the Jewish Civil Authority?"

"Not exactly. The Authority does not have either trained personnel or funds and we are too busy taking the census."

"I am certain you did not come here without a proposal."

"So. My proposal is such. There are many professional do-gooders. They can collect the money—they can find the people—they can run orphanages and old-age homes."

"Are you suggesting an independent agency?"

"I am."

"Not as a branch of the Civil Authority?"

"Correct."

"Why?"

"On matters of self-help the Jews are nearly always unified, no matter what their other philosophy. Having this traditional service operated by a government agency would cause tremendous grumbling among diverse elements. The raising of funds would be extremely hard, for people are naturally suspicious of government. There would be untold confusion, duplication of work, and administrative hassles which could be avoided by establishment of an independent agency."

Koenig saw sense in Goldman's arguments. He could assign the Civil Authority to watch over this new agency. On the other hand, if the Civil Authority were running welfare work he would always have Goldman fighting with him for more funds. Yet it was not all so black and white. Dr. Koenig was learning that Goldman was a man of character, and although it appeared on the surface that it was a simple matter, he was not coming in with a proposal that would benefit the Germans.

Emanuel Goldman also knew he was not up against a robot like Schreiker. Koenig was probing, looking for a trap.

"Who do you propose to head this new agency?"

"Oh, there are lots of people. Mainly, we must find a man acceptable to all elements. Say, Alexander Brandel."

"Brandel? With his Zionist background?"

Goldman shrugged. "The Bathyrans as a group never achieved Brandel's personal stature. They are disbanded now. He is mild and inoffensive and quite trusted."

"Suppose I let you have your agency, but on one condition?"

"And that condition, Herr Doktor?"

"Brandel does not run the agency."

They had come to the impasse. Goldman had hoped he could push it through without this moment. Now he had to make his gamble. He reached inside his breast pocket and placed a small envelope on Koenig's desk. "The full plans for the agency are in here, Herr Doktor," he said. "I beg you to study them carefully and give me your answer tomorrow."

The old man left the city hall, not knowing whether he was about to spend his last day on earth.

When Koenig opened the envelope he took out five one-thousand-dollar bills.

It was quite clear to him. The Jews wanted to run this agency

132

away from prying eyes. His first inclination was of anger. He snatched the envelope from the desk and started for Rudolph Schreiker's office. Then he stopped. Schreiker would laugh at him and pocket the money.

The very idea that a good German official would accept a bribe! He walked back to his desk slowly. The last few weeks had plunged him from the dreamworld of Teutonic purity. At this moment Schreiker was organizing hoodlum gangs to begin looting Jewish-owned warehouses.

Why shouldn't the Jews play the game also? But where did he fit in? Five thousand dollars! More in a snap of the finger than he had made in an entire year at the university.

While everyone was playing cutthroat, wouldn't it be utterly ridiculous for him to stand alone as a paragon of virtue? And if he did, how long would he last with Schreiker? Schreiker had been playing him for a fool.

Think it over, Franz. Schreiker needs you. You can make yourself indispensable to him. And this game. It is a rough game. The war was rough. The business here is rough.

He paced the floor of his home taken from Bronski in the Zoliborz suburb. Everyone is scheming and conniving. But he, Koenig, was in a key position. This is only the beginning. He was in a position to amass fantastic wealth in the days ahead.

Play the game . . . five thousand dollars . . . play the game . . . Bit by bit the moral foundations upon which Dr. Franz Koenig had built his life had been nibbled away. From the moment he had cast his lot with the ethnics before the war he began compromising and rephrasing the wisdoms and rethinking the thoughts and justifying.

The next day.

"Emanuel Goldman is here to see you, Herr Doktor."

"Send him in."

"I have spoken to the Kommissar. I was able to convince him that a separate agency for Jewish welfare cases would be the best solution for all concerned. Your Civil Authority is authorized to issue a license for its operation."

Goldman nodded.

"I have taken under consideration the appointment of Alexander Brandel. I think he is an excellent choice. He will deal with me directly on matters of rations, personnel, and privileges."

Goldman nodded again. Dr. Koenig was cutting himself in for a nice big slice, he thought. Now he could not back down. Koenig had pocketed the first bribe. He could be had. The gamble was won. In the future the money would come harder to Koenig, for the five thousand dollars had not only bought his silence but had stuck his neck out. There will be some more for you, you rat, Goldman thought, but not so much as you think, or we may tell your

133

friend Schreiker how you have been stealing from him.

Stage two: Formation of the Orphans and Self-Help Society. Alexander Brandel was made its director.

Stage three: American Relief turned over tens of thousands of dollars of emergency funds to Brandel. In the name of the Orphans and Self-Help Society he leased fifteen pieces of property in the northern section of the Jewish area of Warsaw, where it was less expensive.

The houses were set up as soup kitchens, ration stations, aid and medical stations, orphanages, and for whatever welfare work came under the society's jurisdiction.

Although these places functioned legitimately, each one in fact served the secondary purpose as a screen for the continued activities of the Zionist groups, which the Germans had ordered disbanded.

The Zionists had successfully changed their name but in fact were still intact. Personnel for the Orphans and Self-Help Society were all key people from the Zionist groups. They were given special armbands and special immunities. Another thousand dollars to Dr. Koenig made certain the Orphans and Self-Help Society staff was not screened.

One of the master reasons for the Orphans and Self-Help Society was to get money from American Relief to its welfare objectives without first passing through the hands of the Jewish Civil Authority for disbursement. Goldman was certain that if the Authority touched the money it would become an object of graft.

Brandel now had bases of operations, the Zionists intact, money to pay personnel to run the farms, to increase the capacity of the former Bathyran Orphanage, and to get the hungry and homeless fed and clothed.

There was a final purpose. Only some of the houses were used for welfare work. Brandel was able to get choice jobs for his people, and many of them moved into the headquarters house and worked under the authority of the Orphans and Self-Help Society and donated their wages back into a communal pool. This, Tolek Alterman proclaimed, was "living Zionism."

Journal Entry

The Orphans and Self-Help Society is a reality. All of our key people in Warsaw are working for us.

I took the five-story building at Mila 79 as our headquarters. Twenty of our Bathyran youngsters have left their homes and are living on the premises and donating all their earnings into a communal. This makes me terribly proud! Six of the buildings were handed over to Simon Eden's Federated Zionists as "Orphans and Self-Help Agencies". .... Simon chose Leszno 92 as his head-

*quarters. He also reports communals in all six of his places. We are
reserving the other places, for we are certain some of the reluctant
divergent groups who did not want to unify will come over to us now.*

*Self-help has always been our one great source of unity in the past.
It will bring us together now. Incidentally, at my last meeting I
asked Goldman, Zemba, and Eden if they would mind jotting down
notes on things they see and hear. So many things are happening
these days I cannot keep track of them all. I want their impressions
to set down in the journal. May I say that they are tolerant of this
historian. They all promised to collect notes and turn them over to
me at our weekly meetings.*

ALEXANDER BRANDEL

Chapter Seven

Journal Entry

*I had a long talk today with Ervin Rosenblum. I wanted his opin-
ion about what the Germans were really up to and who was actually
running Poland.*

*Ervin says Hans Frank, the Governor General in Krakow, is not
the real boss. His background indicates he is a civil administrator
mainly here to exploit Poland for the German economy.*

*Lublin, not Krakow, is the real capital. The German political
police, concentration-camp administrators, criminal police, special-
duty squads, and all of that personal Nazi contingent of Hitler's,
independent of the German army, have their organizations and duties so intermixed it is nearly impossible to determine where one ends
and the other begins. We do know that there is one boss in Lublin
of SD, SS, and Gestapo for the General Government Area. He is
Gruppenführer Odilo Globocnik. He is an Austrian (like Hitler)
and has a background as a Jew baiter. As an SS major general, he has
only to answer to three people over him—Hitler, Himmler, and the
SD chief in Berlin, Reinhard Heydrich.*

*I think Ervin is right. It is a cinch he has more power than Hans
Frank.*

*As for the true aim of the Germans? There is a Department 4B of
the Gestapo in Berlin which handles "Jewish Affairs." It is being
run by a Lieutenant Colonel Adolf Eichmann, who, I understand,
has been to Palestine and speaks Hebrew. Ervin is sure the directives
are all part of a master plan coming from Department 4B from blueprints drawn up by Reinhard Heydrich.*

*It certainly appears they are going to start draining Jewish wealth
systematically, throw the leaders and intellectuals into concentration*

camps. No one doubts but that the Germans will strike again. Like Pharaoh and Rome, they will need slave labor. I believe the three and a half million Jews in Poland are marked for this.

Ervin thinks Swiss News will be closed any day. Among the new arrivals is a Nazi named Horst von Epp, who will run the Department of Propaganda and Press. It is only a matter of time until Chris de Monti's credentials are checked.

ALEXANDER BRANDEL

Horst von Epp joined the influx of Nazi officials to Warsaw in the winter of 1939. Completely unlike most of his fellow Nazis, he was a sophisticated man with continental charm and a sparkling sense of humor. He did not wear any of the several choices of uniforms but had tailor-made clothing in the latest fashions and bemoaned the fact that war with England caused him to lose his Bond Street clothier.

The scion of a wealthy family of former nobility, he had little in common with fellow Nazis. He found their violent methods personally distasteful, had little regard for their mentality, and thought all the nonsense of super-men theories, geopolitics, land to live and joy through labor completely ridiculous.

He was far more at home in Paris, on the Riviera, or in New York than in Munich (but he adored Berlin). Yet he was a devoted Nazi and promoted the very principles he abhorred. Denied most of his family holdings by mismanagement and overspending, he was shrewd enough to recognize the irresistible and unstoppable surge of Nazism in the early thirties and simply drifted into the stream. He had few ideals and convictions to deter him from the pursuit of his own pleasures. He wanted the most for the least exertion of effort. He knew the bumbling mentality of most of the early Nazis would call for men like him to think for them.

He was a good-looking man in his early forties, a first-rate libertine who was never faithful to his wife for more than a month or so, and he was a genuine snob, intellectually superior to the majority of his confederates.

Horst von Epp grated the nerves of men like Rudolph Schreiker. He made them feel insignificant, and no Nazi should be made to feel that way. Many would have loved to get rid of Von Epp, but those in power realized he was needed for his particular talents and therefore worth the annoyance he caused.

The German propaganda instrument had effects which had never been duplicated. They knew the basic premise that if a lie was repeated often enough even those who knew it was a lie would soon regard it as truth. Then there were half truths based on masterful distortions of facts. Horst von Epp had helped engineer for Josef Goebbels one of the most brilliant propaganda coups of any age during the Spanish civil war, which was no civil war at all. He was

136

able to clutter the true issues so neatly that the world soon came to believe that the Loyalist government was a Communist government and therefore the Spanish war was a war against communism.

While the Propaganda Ministry poured out fantastic distortions, it became Horst von Epp's job to water down the vitriol. In Berlin, clever and unsatisfied newsmen from the outside world always stood ready to pounce on the validity of the Propaganda Ministry's statements and charges. It was impossible to evict all of the journalists who questioned them and still keep world opinion in check.

Horst stilled the troubled waters. He became the pal of the newspapermen. He was always the swell guy, despite the fact that he was a Nazi. The Nazis were never known for being personality boys, so Horst's personal charm was a luxurious departure from the Nazi bureaucrats. He became the front man who shielded the curious from the inner circle. Horst von Epp could fix anything for a journalist, from a speeding citation to a fräulein, any size or specification—for his friends.

Warsaw became a focal point of world observation. World opinion had to be kept in bounds.

During the winter of 1939, France and England engaged in a make-believe war with Germany on the western front. Not a single shot was fired by either side. Trains moved along the border unmolested. Germany embarked on a massive campaign to try to talk England and France out of continuing the war, now that the "Polish issue was settled."

It therefore became a priority issue in the Propaganda Ministry to keep adverse news from getting out of Poland, which could upset their plans. Legions of neutral journalists had descended on the General Government Area from Italy, Switzerland, Sweden, the Orient. A few Americans and South Americans got in. A slick operator like Horst von Epp was needed to "keep things quiet."

He arrived in Warsaw and established an elaborate headquarters in the Bristol Hotel, commandeering half a floor. He stocked his personal suites with the best liquors and foods. Within two weeks he had a line on every model and actress in Warsaw who was not stricken with Polish nationalism and made the propositions very attractive to them. Twenty-five of the most ravishing specimens were set aside for the pleasure of the top foreign newsmen and diplomats. He made up a second-string team of coeds from the university, secretaries, professional women, and attractive wives seeking to augment their incomes.

After the humorless, dull, blustering Rudolph Schreiker, Von Epp was making things bearable for the foreign journalists. Everything was conducted in a rather informal atmosphere, which both eased the tension and tranquillized the extent of their probing.

137

Chris was just finishing dressing when the doorbell of his flat on Jerusalem Boulevard rang. He opened the door, and Horst von Epp stood before him. The man was immaculately dressed and wore a pleasant smile.

"Hello there," he said. "I am Horst von Epp."

"Come in."

The German looked around. "Lovely ... lovely. Ah! That jacket you are wearing." He looked at the label. "Feinberg of Bond Street. The finest tailor in London. I was his customer right up to the war. Of course I had to switch the labels because he's Jewish, but most of those lunkheads can't tell a fine piece of material when they see one. Uniforms! Uniforms! The tailors in Berlin are butchers. Do you suppose you could get me a few things through Switzerland from Feinberg?"

"You didn't come here for that."

"No. I had a reception for the foreign press corps yesterday. I was particularly looking for you."

"Sorry, I was driving back from Krakow. I phoned in my regrets."

"No matter."

"I just finished reading your love letters," Chris said, referring to the new set of censorship regulations and procedures for filing dispatches.

"Oh, that," Von Epp scoffed. "Nazi bureaucracy. You see, we have to put a hundred people to work making orders and then another hundred countermanding them. Another hundred sorting paper clips. That pays off our obligations to the party faithful. We shall rule the world in triplicate. Cigarette?"

"Matter of fact, yes. I drove back from Krakow so fast I forgot to buy some." Chris was impressed with the package of American Camels.

"I'll send you a case, my compliments. I've also made arrangements for certain members of the press corps to draw food supplies, personal articles, liquor, and so forth, from the SS officers' stores at the Citadel."

Well, Chris thought, this *is* something new in Nazi public relations. He studied Von Epp. Why had he been singled out for special treatment? He had heard Von Epp was coming to Warsaw and was a regular guy. Smooth—very smooth. Yet certainly likable.

"I didn't mean to break in on you," Von Epp said, "but I did want to get acquainted and I have a few matters to take up with you."

"Shoot."

"If you want to keep your offices in the Bristol, I probably can arrange it, but frankly, the place is overrun with Nazis. Needless to say, we must put men to work tapping switchboards and phones, but you'll probably be more comfortable elsewhere."

"I can work right here in my apartment. There's an empty store-room connected to my kitchen. It will work fine." Chris was relieved at the idea that Von Epp was going to let him stay in Warsaw. He had dreaded this moment. Now it had come and gone—just like that.

"Now, the phone lines are open to Switzerland. I'll get you a direct connection with your agency—Swiss News, isn't it?"

"That's right."

"Fine agency. I know your boss, Oscar Pecora, quite well. We're putting up a message center for the press corps at the Bristol so you'll be able to have twenty-four-hour service—you might as well let us see your incoming messages first, because we'll see them sooner or later. Now, anything particular that you want?"

"What's the price?"

Horst von Epp smiled. "You're a big boy—you know what you can and can't do. All I want is your gentleman's agreement to keep within reasonable limitations. I don't want to work hard, and the best way to make things easy for myself is to make them easy for you. What do you say?"

Chris shrugged. "I've never had it better."

"I am afraid there is one unpleasant bit of business on the agenda. So far as I am concerned a Jew can take a photograph as well as a blond Aryan and certainly report a story—but——"

"Rosenblum?"

"I'm afraid so."

"He offered to quit several days ago. He knew this would happen."

Horst von Epp flopped his arms. "I wish I knew what to do. It appears that Berlin simply won't let me have room to maneuver on Jewish matters."

Chris wanted to press the point. Rosy knew it would happen. But Rosy had been wrong about the Germans closing out Swiss News. Better hold his tongue . . .

"It's not your fault," Chris said.

"I have an idea. How about dinner tonight? My suite?"

Chris shrugged. Why not? He had nothing better to do.

"Perhaps . . . a little company later on?"

Chris walked to the window. So many times he had seen Deborah standing before that same window . . . had watched her from the alcove. The last time he had looked at Deborah her eyes were mad and she plunged into darkness. Sienna Street was only four blocks away. So near . . . so damned near. She was there with Paul now, on Sienna Street. Another lonely night, and another, and another. Would there ever be a moment of peace for him? He didn't want to face the darkness alone again. Nagging, longing. Lonely. He would stand at the window and look toward Sienna Street and think about her. Rosy told him he was a fool, she would never leave Paul Bronski.

Chris turned and faced the German. "Ladies? Sure, why not? That's just fine with me."

Chris approached the dinner engagement with Horst von Epp with suspicion. It had all come too easily. He thought he would be on a train to Switzerland by this time, booted from Poland. Instead, he and Swiss News were still alive and operating in the middle of a German occupation.

Chris suspected that Horst von Epp would be a perfect host. He was. In fact, he was more comfortable with the German than he had been with anyone for months. Horst knew all the latest stories and had vast amounts of gossip about mutual friends in the newsmen's world. Chris's suspicions began to fade as the evening wore on. For a while he hung on every word, looking for some telltale sign of what Von Epp really wanted from him. The German would not tip his hand. Further, Chris was constantly amazed at Von Epp's open expressions of disdain for many Nazis.

"Well," Von Epp said, "speaking with realism, I am committed to Hitler's policies. If he wins, I shall be an enormous man. If he loses, I'll become a gigolo on the Riviera. I have one terrible aversion, and that is to perform honest labor. I'll do anything to avoid it, and frankly, I'm not suited for much."

Chris admired his candor.

"Now!" Horst said. "I have a surprise for you. Surprises should always go with dessert."

The German handed a *Kennkarte* over the table. Chris opened it. It was a document signed by Kommissar Rudolph Schreiker. Ervin Rosenblum was to be allowed to continue his position with Swiss News. He was not obliged to wear an armband with a Star of David.

"I don't know what to say.".

"Please understand that I can't guarantee that this won't be revoked, but . . . for the time being . . ."

Chris waved away the after-dinner cognac and loaded his glass with scotch. He pocketed Rosy's *Kennkarte* with amused perplexion. The inevitable cigar smoke came from the direction of Von Epp.

"Herr von Epp," Chris said, raising his glass, "I salute a perfect but confusing host. You know, I am a professional observer of the cat-and-mouse game that diplomats play. I am first rate at deciphering the meaning of double talk. Yet here I am in the middle of a squeeze play and I am completely puzzled. Pardon me for not being subtle, but what the hell are you up to? What's your deal? What are the strings? What do you want from me?"

"Bravo, de Monti. All journalists must be suspicious by nature."

"Are you queer? Do you have designs on me?"

Von Epp roared with laughter. "God, no—but confidentially, the city hall is loaded with them. Chris, you see these Nazi clots around here. They bow stiffly from the waist, kiss a lady's hand like a pig, and walk in those ridiculous uniforms as though they had broomsticks up their rectums. You are my kind of man. We drink scotch and have the same tailor in London. I believe your handshake is better than a Nazi pact. I want to be friends."

"No orders?"

Horst shrugged. "You have friends among the Jews. I would guess that everyone in Warsaw does. Just use a reasonable amount of common sense."

"What do your files say about de Monti?" Chris asked.

"Well, now, let me see. According to your passport, you are an Italian national. Your mother is an American. We are certain your leanings are American. The gentlemen at the Italian Embassy think you are a bad Fascist. However, you've covered both the Ethiopian and the Spanish affairs from the Italian side of the lines. You are cautious not to editorialize but only to report news. That is commendable. What else would you like to know about yourself?"

Chris flipped his napkin on the table. "I'll be a son of a bitch! You take the cake."

"Do we understand each other, Chris?"

Chris smiled and held his glass up in salute. "To friendship."

"A good toast."

The ladies of the evening arrived.

They were, as Horst promised, two of Warsaw's loveliest courtesans. Chris knew both of them, in bed. They were minor European film actresses and belonged to a small social clique that ran in a continual circle in Warsaw. Hildie Solna was a striking blonde. He had had an affair with her before he met Deborah. The other one . . . a few one-night adventures . . . her name slipped his mind— Wanda something-or-other.

Horst von Epp kissed their hands in the accepted fashion. Chris was amused. Yes, he thought, Hildie would be quick to jump on the band wagon and switch masters. He wondered if Von Epp knew how shopworn Hildie was under the paint. Well, she still had enough tricks left to get her through one more war.

"Darling!" Hildie cried in delight at seeing Chris. Dear Hildie . . . the body without a soul. Soft words without meaning. He looked at her. Could he lie in bed tonight with her or Wanda something-or-other and not cry out for his true love?

No . . . It was better to spend the night in agony, longing for Deborah, than with one of them. He turned quickly to Von Epp and spoke in Italian. "I think I will take a rain check. Pretend that I am not your guest. I am sure you can dig up a good German officer

141

to take my place. I shall act as though I were an intruder and beg my leave."

"Go ahead," Von Epp answered. "I will arrange everything." Horst watched Chris pat Hildie's cheek and tell her he was sorry he could not stay, but another time . . . Why would he run off, Von Epp thought? It is as I surmised—de Monti has something going for him here in Warsaw and he does not want to leave—almost certainly a Jewess. If it is so, I have found his price.

Chapter Eight

Ervin Rosenblum was homelier than usual when he opened the door to let Chris in. Aroused from a deep sleep, he yawned and stretched in a half-tied monstrous old robe and paddled to the mantel clock in a pair of worn slippers. He squinted at the clock.

"My God, past midnight! Something terrible has happened!"

Chris handed him the *Kennkarte*. Ervin was nearly blind without his glasses. He held it to his nose but could not read it. "Wait, I'll get my glasses."

He returned from the bedroom with a look of complete puzzlement.

"How in the name of God did you arrange this? I thought sure you had come to tell me good-by."

Momma Rosenblum was up with a monstrous old robe to equal Ervin's. She kissed Chris on the cheek. "Bad news?"

"No, Mamma, good news. Chris will be able to keep the agency open, and I have a special work permit."

"A miracle . . . a miracle."

Chris knew better than to try to stop her from making tea and putting out a feed.

He recounted the day with Horst von Epp to Ervin. Rosy kept looking at the *Kennkarte*, shaking his head.

"You're the analyst, Rosy. What do you make of it?"

"Well you have covered the Italian side of two wars. You have never been caught slipping reports out to the free press, but a man like Von Epp should surely know you pass tips and information to others who can use them. Maybe he is neutralizing you. He knows your word is sound and you won't double-cross him."

"I've thought about that. But why would he let me stay here in the first place?"

"To get you on his side. To make a deal with you sooner or later. To use you, somehow."

"That's possible too. He put on a real show for me. Even tried to soften me up with Hildie Solna tonight."

142

Rosy laughed. "Hildie sure has good instincts. The smoke from battle has not yet cleared and the old girl is in German headquarters. So you had a party?"

"I pulled out."

"Before or after?"

"Before. I begged off."

"Maybe that wasn't so smart, Chris."

"Hildie's a good lay, but—you know."

"And by this time so does Von Epp. Why does an unattached bachelor walk out on a party with the most expensive whore in Warsaw? Because he's carrying a torch for a woman. You might as well be wearing a sign."

The whistle of the teakettle sounded from the kitchen. Momma Rosenblum summoned them in. There was enough on the table for ten men to eat.

"I'm sorry, I didn't know you were coming. There's practically nothing here," she said.

"You shouldn't be so extravagant with the ration on, Momma Rosenblum," Chris said.

"I'm only serving an iota of what you've sent over to us the past month. You could stand a little babying." She knew that Chris and Ervin wanted to speak in confidence and took her leave.

Ervin stirred his tea slowly. "The trouble with a man like Von Epp is that you never know what is really going on in his head. We all know what Schreiker wants and what he is. Von Epp is twice as dangerous."

"No one—positively no one—knows about me and Deborah but you. Perhaps Andrei and Gabriela suspect. Perhaps even Bronski suspects, but no one really knows."

"Don't be lulled to sleep by Von Epp's smooth talk. He's a Nazi. If he ever knew, he could blackmail you into doing anything for him. He'll let you stay on now because he thinks he's discovered a blind spot and he wants to know what it is. Keep away from his parties, and for God's sake be careful when you see Deborah. You'll have to find another place to meet."

"Rosy, I haven't seen her for over a month. Can't you see I'm going out of my mind!"

"I know, Chris, but I also know you're going to try to see her."

"Have you seen her?" Chris whispered.

"Yes. She works most of the day at the orphanage in Powazki. Susan is with her most of the time."

"Does she . . . ask for me?"

"No."

Chris gave a hurt little laugh. "Funny, damned funny. I make secret meetings with Paul Bronski to give him his money—funny, isn't it, Rosy?"

"Not particularly. From now on you'd better give me the envelopes to deliver to him."

"Maybe, you're right. Rosy, see her for me. She's got relatives in Krakow. She could make an excuse to see them. I've got to go there in a few days. Sorenson from the Stockholm Press has a place there. He'll let me use it."

Rosy gripped his arm and stopped him. "If you were my own brother I couldn't love you more, Chris. Don't ask me to do this."

Chris pulled away. "I'll wait. I've got time on my side now. Something will happen."

"Drink some tea. Momma will be offended."

Chris drank slowly, drowning his churning anger.

"So long as you are going to Krakow, would you see Thompson at the American Embassy? He has a package for us."

"I wish you wouldn't ask me to carry in any more packages," Chris said sharply.

"I don't think I understand you."

"I made a deal with Von Epp."

"My, you're a regular boy scout. You don't mind being a messenger boy for Paul Bronski."

"That's different. It's coming through on company funds—it can't be traced."

"So what are you doing with the money from Thompson? Feeding orphans. This has become a crime?"

"Rosy, this Bathyran business is your own affair. I don't want to know anything about it. I'm not getting involved."

Chris got up from the table. Rosy wanted to rip the *Kennkarte* in half and throw it in his face, but he could not. It was too important to all of them. He had to continue working on the outside as long as he was able.

"See you in the office in the morning," Chris said.

"Good night, boss."

Chris flopped on his bed and gazed into nothingness. The soft melodiousness of Chopin on Radio Polskie had been largely replaced by a thumping, clanging Wagner. Chris snapped the radio off.

He walked to the window. Only a few blocks away from Deborah. What was she doing now? Combing Rachael's hair . . . keeping time as Rachael played the piano . . . helping Stephan with his studies? No, it was late. Almost one o'clock. She and Paul would be in bed together.

He closed the curtains abruptly.

He lay back on the bed again. Andrei! Good old Andrei! We'll hang one on! He rolled over and had a hand on his phone. No . . . wait. Andrei was wearing that damned Star of David. He couldn't go into any of the hotels or bars. What's the difference?

Andrei could take off the armband. They could hit some dives, have a real blowout. Hell, Andrei would get mad and try to take on the German army. He let his hand drop from the phone.

Maybe I should have stayed with Von Epp, Chris thought. Hildie Solna is good for a few laughs. Von Epp is good company. If I had met Von Epp anywhere else in the world, we would have been friends. Isn't that reason enough to trust a man? No . . . Von Epp couldn't be trusted.

Just how much does he really know about me? He knows about mother. . . . They must have a file on me a foot thick.

Chris's thoughts began to drift back and back and back in time. All the way back to the beginning.

Chapter Nine

Flora Sloan had been described at various times as enchanting, fetching, witty and gay, terribly, terribly chic, charming, clever, empty-headed, flighty, hyperthyroid, and so forth. All of these descriptions fitted in one way or another, at one time or another. She was never still long enough for a comprehensive composite to be made.

Her background was mysterious. Midwesterner, most people thought. Indiana . . . small town in Wisconsin . . . or something like that.

No one knew when she came to Manhattan or about her early failures and affairs. She was suddenly there. Eminently successful as a fashion executive, a financial wizard, a magazine editor, and later as the queen bee in a hive of social-climbers.

The most successful of her profitable ventures was a pair of marriages and subsequent divorce settlements, first with her magazine-publishing husband, then with a real estate operator from whom she extracted a commendable hunk of mid-Manhattan. After the second coup she retired to become a patron of the arts and grand matron of the Flora Sloan clique.

She did nothing worthy with her independent wealth, but Flora had the ability to do nothing in extremely good taste. Her only true dedication was to keep her face unwrinkled and her body beautiful. She ran through a succession of lovers, with whom she became bored in days, weeks, and occasionally months. The moment they began to ooze around to talking stocks and bonds, they were through.

It was inevitable that sooner or later she would get a pasting. She fell in love with a young artist. His paintings showed a rather sketchy talent, but he did have a positive talent in bed. For the first

145

time in her life she behaved silly, lavished her lover with expensive gifts, became fiendishly jealous, and allowed herself to be pushed around. She sponsored a one-man art show at a time when her expression of like or dislike was a command, and he became a "rage."

Everyone seemed to know that Flora was being had, but how does one tell a queen bee? She woke one rainy morning to find her lover flown from the nest after skinning her out of a small mint. When the detectives dragged him back for a tear-filled showdown, there came the revelation that he had a wife and three children "somewhere in Maine."

Comforting friends soothed her. A trip to Europe would be the remedy for her shattering experience. She pulled herself together for "their" sake. Yes, they were right. An ocean voyage and the long-overdue grand tour to put the broken pieces together.

Flora, her traveling companion, secretary, Irish maid, and two poodles got no farther than the second stop, Monaco. In barreled the Count Alphonse de Monti at a hundred and twenty miles per hour in a red Ferrari. He saddled up to a chair opposite her at the Casino and began throwing around ten-thousand-lira notes like kleenex at the baccarat table.

From the second he bowed and kissed her hand Flora knew what a hell of an elegant gentleman he was. And with a title to boot. She shrieked with exhilaration as he buzzed around hairpin turns in his red Ferrari. She listened breathlessly as he whispered his way through Verdi love arias.

"God damn," she told her traveling companion, "this continental charm is the living end. I checked his financial rating and the bastard's loaded, to boot."

Since European titles and rich American divorcees were fascinating subjects, when Flora became the Countess de Monti it almost knocked the World Series off the front pages.

The glitter lasted through two spaghetti dinners. She found that Italians had very, very funny ideas about their womenfolk. His old Kentucky home outside Rome was big and marbly enough, but although she had investigated his solvency she had failed to check into a stable of mistresses stashed in villas all over southern France. Now that she was properly the Countess de Monti, his charm became reserved for rivers yet uncrossed.

In fact, in many respects, he proved a slob.

He had peculiarities that she had not tested before in men. He was saturated with pride from head to foot. He bathed in old tradition. He professed to be deeply religious. And, like many normal and healthy Italian men of means, he fully expected his wife to stay in the old Kentucky home and get quietly plump while he barreled around Europe in his red Ferrari.

One more thing. An heir! Italians considered the production of a male offspring as some sort of monumental feat. With Flora as his mate, it was—but he managed.

She went into wild scenes about her treatment. Alphonse was proud because his wife was so spicy. But when she blurted out her plan to get rid of the unborn baby, it was another matter. He promptly slapped her into a private apartment under lock and key and the watchful eyes of a pair of matrons, then barreled off in his red Ferrari.

The result of this happy union was Christopher de Monti.

The proud father came home and celebrated long and hard. In fact, he dropped his guard so low that Flora was able to bundle Chris up and flee to the United States.

This time the divorce and custody battle did knock the World Series off the front pages.

Final judgment. Momma got another splendid settlement, mostly in olive groves. Chris was to spend summers with Poppa in Italy.

Flora never quite forgave little Chris for lowering her breasts, ruining her eighteen-inch waistline, and turning her stomach muscles to jelly. Unfortunately a society larger than her personal clique imposed certain conditions which called for her to be a "good mother." She smothered Chris in a sea of motherliness—in full view of her friends.

He remembered being displayed by Flora, led into the parlor where he held court, listening to the "ohs" and "ahs" from the waxen-faced people posed about the room. Momma would tussle his hair. Momma would squeeze him. He hated that, because she was always nervous when he was around and her fingernails always dug into his flesh.

But summer! That was different! In summer he would get on a big ship with his current "Nana" and cross the ocean to Italy and Poppa. He traveled with Poppa in the red Ferrari, and they went to museums and the opera and to the Riviera. He loved his father deeply. He did not think he loved his mother. He cried and Poppa cried when summer was over and he had to return to America to school. Flora took Alphonse's pleas to keep the boy as a personal vendetta against her "motherliness."

And so Chris was kept in America nine months of the year. A veteran Atlantic traveler by the age of twelve, he was also an habitué of fashionable schools with names that all sounded like either Exeter or Briarwood.

He was a very quiet boy and a determined student. His true character was formed by teachers who taught in a day when political liberalism, sense of social conscience, and ideals were not frowned upon. He loved Poppa more than anyone in the world—but somehow, Italy was always a playland.

He read Lincoln and Paine and Jefferson. He completely

147

identified himself as an American. He did not like the way the rich people treated poor people in Italy.

The American dream—the American ideal—became the guidepost in his life.

When he was old enough, Chris overlooked Poppa's weakness for women, and often a new mistress formed a threesome on their travels in the summer. And as he grew older he began to see his father's human frailties. Poppa was vain. Poppa was a snob. Poppa was unmoved by the poverty in Naples. Poppa guarded the iniquities of the class system.

Poppa was a Fascist.

Chris did not know what it meant at first, but each year it came more and more into focus and it rubbed against the grain of his American education.

Poppa would get a little drunk and talk about Benito Mussolini returning them to the glory of ancient Rome. Chris knew Mussolini —a pompous ass—but he never said anything to his father about that. The Italian people were warm and kind and they liked to sing and eat and drink and strut and believe they were great lovers. Years of privation as a second-rate power had allowed evil men to perpetrate the hoax of fascism upon them,

Chris was seventeen. At the end of the summer he would return to America and begin college.

Poppa was particularly perplexed. "I was hoping that your mother would let you study here. She promises her usual scandal if you don't return."

Chris said nothing. He wanted very much to return to America to study.

"I think it is time you and I had a long and serious talk about many things. Although an American education will be satisfactory, it is not really what I hoped for you. Where are you planning to go?"

"Columbia University in New York City."

"Hmmm. I trust they have a good college in business administration and law. For the next four years you should be preparing yourself to take over our estates. I have only done a so-so job. I count on you to make the de Monti fortunes what they were when your grandfather was alive."

"Poppa, you don't understand. I am going to Columbia because of their school of journalism."

"Journalism? But what good will journalism do you in running the de Monti estate?"

"Journalism is one of the greatest ways to translate your ideals. It is a way to bring truth to the world."

"What kind of nonsense is this? You are my son. You will take over my duties just as I took them over from my father and his father before him. And while you are about it you will join the

Young Student Fascist League in your college. It is important you begin to identify yourself as a good Italian boy."

"But I don't believe in fascism."

Alphonse de Monti shrieked. He ranted angrily at Flora for what she had done to the boy's eduction. "You will understand, Chris, what Mussolini has done for us. The Italian people have work now. He will lead us to a grandeur we have not seen in two thousand years!"

Chris held his tongue. He knew that Poppa didn't give a damn about the Italian people working, and Chris felt that fascism would lead them to destruction.

"You are my son and you will do as you are ordered!"

"I'm sorry, sir," Chris said. "I am going to be a journalist."

Alphonse struck Chris across the face . . . then again . . . and again and again . . . and again. The boy stood rigid but unflinching. And then his father began to cry. "Since you were a baby, all I have wanted is for my son. My Christopher—a nobleman—to take over our great traditions—to live to see you as an officer in the Italian army bringing us back our glory—all I wanted is for you, Chris."

What traditions? Those poor bastards slaving in Poppa's olive groves? Whoring all over Europe in ten-thousand-dollar cars? Sitting at the Casino, a portrait of decadence? Trying to resurrect a ghost of ancient Rome which would take them on a path to hell?

Chris was sad because he loved his Poppa so.

"Chris . . . Chris . . . my bambino," the old man pleaded.

"I am sorry, Poppa, that I cannot be the son you want."

Even in anguish there was that deep stubborn pride. "Get out of my house and never come back!"

Chris was a brilliant student in journalism at Columbia. He wrote many letters to Poppa, but they were all returned unopened. He knew the deep pain he had caused his father and he hated himself for it, but he knew that he could not live as an instrument of a thing he hated. He was cut off without a cent.

In his junior year things brightened with an athletic scholarship. He was a first-rate forward on the varsity basketball team and highly successful in the new, experimental one-hand shots.

And Flora? She had taken a dumping in the stock market, but Chris didn't want a thing from her, anyhow. Christmas passed without so much as a greeting from her. She did not like to have Chris around at all these days because he served as a reminder that she was turning ripe fast. She had lovers almost as young as her son.

Eileen Burns was a commercial-art major as vibrant as Chris was quiet. She was completely taken by the lean, handsome right forward on the basketball team and his grim ways.

Perhaps Chris was far more intense about Eileen than a college romance would have implied, but with her all his lonely years and frustrations seemed to pour out. There had been other girls before. He was fifteen when he started with the daughter of one of Poppa's housekeepers.

But with Eileen he could talk about things he only remembered speaking about to instructors in private schools a long time ago. It was different, because Eileen became a part of his hopes. He could say, "I want to be a great journalist—it's a wonderful way to serve mankind." And Eileen understood—she understood so well.

In his senior year Chris met Oscar Pecora. Oscar was standing by the window in his room when he came in from basketball practice late one evening. Pecora was a strange-looking little fellow. Stiff Hoover collar, four-in-hand cravat, bowler hat, pin-striped suit. He had the stamp of a European all over him.

"I hope you will forgive me," Pecora said in Italian. "Your door was open."

Chris looked at him for a while. Ten to one he was from the Italian Legation. "If you're here to ask me to join the Student Fascist League, don't waste either of our time."

Pecora opened his wallet neatly and snapped a card to Chris. OSCAR PECORA: INTERNATIONAL DIRECTOR, SWISS NEWS AGENCY, GENEVA.

Chris flung the dirty laundry off one of the room's two chairs. "Sit down, sir."

"You are familiar with Swiss News?"

"Yes, sir." He knew it was a small agency with one of the very best reputations for journalistic standards in the world.

"I shall get right to the point. We are expanding our operations in America. We will need an extra man for overloaded work in our New York and Washington bureaus. If you are familiar with Swiss News you know we select our people carefully. We find you are one of three students in this country whom we wish to train and put on our staff. When you graduate you will immediately leave for Geneva for a training course to get rid of the bad habits you've picked up in college."

Chris and Eileen were married three days before graduation. A week later they were aboard ship for a honeymoon trip.

No more idyllic four months were ever lived by two people. They loved each other with an energy reserved for the very young in a fairyland setting of snowy mountains and roaring fireplaces. Although half oblivious with thoughts of Eileen, Chris managed to learn the practical methods of journalism taught by the veteran Swiss News staff.

At the end of the schooling Chris was assigned, as promised, as a relief man between New York and Washington. Eileen was homesick to return, which seemed entirely natural for a girl who had lived her life in New Jersey.

There was but one short detour he had to take home, and that was through Rome.

The Count Alphonse de Monti had aged. He was a somewhat seedy representative of faded nobility. Yet he put up a lavish front: the cars and the servants and the women were still there. So were the debts. All his failures seemed to make him a more devout Fascist, for it was easy to blame enemies who did not exist.

Alphonse de Monti was a gentleman to the core. He was polite to his son and his son's bride, but his coolness made it completely obvious he would never accept the fact that his son would not be the things he wanted.

Chris left Italy with a feeling that he might never see Poppa again.

Chris and Eileen became members of those faceless legions of Manhattan cliff dwellers who rushed to dinner and theater, washed down too many martinis at lunch, and made certain their "new love and independence" would not be marred by the sudden announcement that a child was on the way. Chris thrived on all of it.

Eileen didn't tell Chris how lonely it was when he was away in Washington. He was happy—so happy. And a new marriage is something large and powerful, the little flaws and cracks often invisible in the over-all magnitude. Each reunion after a week in Washington buried the loneliness.

Six months of it. Then, while he was away in Washington, he was suddenly called to a conference in Denver. Next time she tried tagging along in Washington. It was worse than staying in New York. She was in his way. A journalist had to have mobility and no limitation on hours, no worries about a wife waiting in a hotel room.

"Chris honey, why don't I take a job? You know, Mom and Dad did spend a fortune getting me through Columbia and——"

Enough of the old-country pride had rubbed off on him to make the idea of a de Monti wife working unthinkable.

Oscar Pecora arrived just in time.

"You are one of our bright young stars, Christopher. We have an extraordinary opportunity. Bureau chief in Rio de Janeiro."

Rio! And less than a year with Swiss News!

Chris was so happy that Eileen covered her disappointment, as a good wife will do. This was his life and it was a great opportunity. She was planning to have a talk with Chris about buying a place in Jersey, near Mom and Dad. Maybe starting a family. They'd had their fun. . . .

But Eileen held her tongue and packed and went along.

Chris fitted in every newsmen's bar and in the lobbies of the capitols and in the offices of prime ministers and at the scenes of disasters. Hours of light and darkness and light and spaces of great distance had lost meaning to him when a story was involved.

They had a beautiful apartment on the Avenida Beira Mar that hugged the bay. She came to learn every corner of it and how many squares were in the marble of the entrance hall and how many different colors there were in the drapes.

She tried very, very hard to assimilate herself into that circle of diplomats who seemed to spend their entire lives holding a cocktail glass for the incoming attaché of culture or the outgoing second secretary.

Eileen got a pair of cats and stroked them and paced the floor in lounging pajamas and waited until Chris got back.

And then one day she broke. He wrote:

Dear Oscar,

I must resign this bureau for personal reasons. I should like to return to New York if you've a spot for me there. Otherwise, I am afraid I must quit the agency and find a job in New York.

Dear Christopher,

I understand your plight and I sympathize with it. Try to understand mine. Hold on another six or eight weeks and I'll get things shifted around so that you can break someone in and I'll make an opening in New York.

"Honey, why don't you go on back to the States ahead of me? See your folks. It will do you good."

Eileen was relieved and frightened at the same time. It was an omen, she knew it. The little flaws were turning to deepening cracks.

And Chris was worried, too, because when Eileen left he did not miss her as much as he believed he should. At first he dreaded the thought of coming back from a trip with Eileen not there. But . . . it wasn't so bad. There was always a poker game going at the press club or the Embassy, always a party in session with an open invitation to him.

Dear Chris,

I have taken a job in an advertising firm here. I know how much you are against this, but you won't be when you see how happy I am. It won't interfere with a moment of our being together. . . . I made that clear to them. But, I just can't keep on feeling so useless. Please, darling, don't be angry.

Chris swallowed his pride. Why not? Eileen was too vital to be locked up in a lonely flat. She was too sensible to become a partner to a wasteland of women's clubs. That's one of the things he admired about her from the first. Her desire to be useful—not like his mother.

When he returned to New York there was a wonderful reunion. Oscar Pecora had given him the New York Bureau permanently! He had enough help so that he would have to make only an occasional trip to Washington. For a moment they seemed to have recaptured those first days of their marriage.

And then, the scene:

"Eileen, be reasonable, honey. The conference in Quebec is one of the most important international meetings of the year."

"You promised and Oscar promised. No more traveling."

"Eileen! Dan is sick. He can't work. He's in the hospital."

"Then let them send someone else."

"Swiss News is a small outfit. We haven't got that many men."

"You don't need any more. Good old Christopher de Monti will always go."

"Don't make it so dramatic. It's only ten days."

"Ten days in Quebec . . . ten days in Washington . . . ten days in San Francisco. Do you know what it's like alone here for ten days? I don't ask terribly much, Chris—to work until we decide to have a home and a baby—but what's the use of having a baby who won't know his father! We have so much fun together when you're here. I don't ask much, Chris——"

"Christ! You're making a world revolution out of this. How can you ask me to let Oscar down after all he's done for me?"

"How about me, Chris? Haven't I done something for you too? Do you ever think about letting me down?"

Chris didn't answer. He went into the bedroom.

Eileen trailed in slowly. "Your things are all packed," she said with tears falling into the corners of her mouth. "Your gray suit didn't get back from the cleaner's in time."

"Eileen . . . honey . . ."

"Hurry, Chris. You'll miss your plane."

When he returned from Canada his reception was one of polite coldness. For the first time in their marriage Eileen did not want to be loved when he returned from a trip. It was doubly bad when she played out the role of the accommodating wife.

"I guess we're in a lot of trouble," Chris said the next morning.

Eileen's silence was answer enough.

"I thought about it all during the time in Quebec. About us and where we are going. I've been pretty damned selfish. I guess I've done all the taking . . . none of the giving."

"That's not true, Chris. You've tried. So have I. I really wanted to be the kind of woman you need."

"Do you still love me?"

"Yes . . . and I think, in your way, you love me too. But I'm kind of jealous, I guess, because what you have away from me means

153

more to you than I ever will. It's not your fault or mine."

"Let's try, Eileen, please let's try. I know most of this has been my fault."

"Don't let that Italian pride of yours compound a mistake."

"Why don't we take a ride over to Jersey and look at some of that real estate? Then I'll get a letter off to Oscar——"

"Chris . . . Chris. I do love you, but if I take you away from that world of yours out there you'll grow to hate me."

Both of them tried hard to pull it together. Eileen never did buy that house in New Jersey and she was terribly cautious about having a child.

Restraint and all its murderous aspects came between them.

There were more trips—there always would be, but she never made another scene or shed another tear—and there were no more wild reunions.

For a year they drifted and grew more and more indifferent to each other.

And one day Christopher de Monti had to face that moment when a man's pride grovels to its lowest depths. He found it out by accident, by returning home from a trip early and taking a phone call not meant for him. Eileen had begun sleeping with another man.

Chris never spoke to her about it. He waited until a weekend when she was visiting her parents, and he packed his things and left with only a brief note.

Dear Eileen,

I have learned about you and Daniels at your office. There is absolutely no use of discussing anything. For my part of the guilt, I am sorry, but it will be best for us both if I never see you again. If you will arrange the divorce as quickly and quietly as possible on some semi-civilized grounds, I would be obliged.

After a month of trying to drown his pride across every bar in England and Europe, Chris got himself steamed out and reported to Oscar Pecora in Geneva.

"That's quite a little bar bill you've run up, Christopher. It's a wonder you have a liver left," Pecora said.

"Oh, for God's sake, Oscar, save the sermon."

"Tell me, Chris. Was the pain because you loved Eileen so much, or has your Italian nobility been offended?"

"I don't know, Oscar."

"If you still love Eileen you can have her back. She's written to me a half dozen times. Of course you've got this stack of letters you've never opened. She'll come to you on any condition—on her hands and knees. Now, if your love is so great, it must find forgiveness for her."

154

"I don't know if I can, Oscar. Besides, the same thing will happen again. She's a fine woman, Oscar. She really tried. I've got no right to butcher her life up——"

"And deep in your heart you really don't want her back. Except for the blow to your vanity, you are happy to be free."

For a moment Chris looked offended.

"That's hitting below the belt, Oscar."

"Truth does not offend you, Christopher."

"I guess you're right."

"Well, there's no use of both Eileen and me losing you. I saw it coming for a long time. One of us had to be the big loser, and I'm glad it's not me."

"Let me get back to work, Oscar, right away."

"Fine. How does Ethiopia sound? The legions of Rome are on the march. That Italian passport of yours will come in handy."

"You know how I feel about the Fascists. I can't stomach covering their side of a war against defenseless little black men with spears."

"You are a journalist, Christopher. Leave your personal politics out of it. We can get you attached to the Italian command. Get the best you can out of the latitude they give you to operate."

Chris walked slowly to the big wall map behind Oscar Pecor's desk. "Ethiopia? Why not? That's about as far away as I can get from the goddamned mess I've made."

Chapter Ten

Mussolini's campaign in Ethiopia was a pleasant little war. Sort of reminded one of when the colonizers of the last century directed their armies from campaign chairs in the shade of banana trees with a tall, cool gin and tonic in their hands as they brought "civilization" to the Zulus.

It was, indeed, good practical experience for the aspiring new legions of Rome. The little clay townships made excellent targets for the artillery gunners. The infantry could zigzag about the tall brush, boning up on their efficiency without too much danger, for the natives were mostly armed with spears and the few Ethiopian riflemen were dreadful shots.

Chris made peace with himself and played it straight. He could stand nearly everything except when he interviewed the bragging, strutting aviators after they had returned from their missions of bombing and strafing undefended villages of thatched huts.

Ethiopia was not the real battleground.

The British fleet ordered a muscle-flexing maneuver in the Mediterranean. Mussolini called the bluff. There were indignant pickets in Paris and New York and London against Italian legations by people who had learned only in the last month or so that there was actually a country named Ethiopia.

For one fleeting moment the world had a twinge of conscience. An embargo was called against Italy, but it was really not an embargo at all.

Then, for all its inept and ill-fated existence, the League of Nations was honored by one great moment of human dignity. A small black man who was named the Lion of Judah, Haile Selassie, the Emperor of Ethiopia, made a plea to the souls of men for his people. But Ethiopia was a long way away from about everywhere, and who the hell really cared about Addis Ababa?

Apathy of free men. This was the real victory. The scent of blood made the legions of Rome hungry.

On the Yangtze River an American gunboat named the *Panay* was sunk. Some Americans were able to convince other Americans that the *Panay* had no right being there in the first place. Yellow men in the Orient were battling yellow men—but that was far away too.

There followed the era of appeasement. The Versailles Treaty was broken by the tramping of German boots into the Rhineland.

The bullies grew brave.

The crucible: Spain.

"Christopher, you did a magnificent job in Ethiopia. Your restraint was remarkable. Now, Christopher! Your Italian passport is really going to come in handy," Oscar Pecora said. "I've gotten you credentials to cover the Insurgent side in Spain."

Christopher de Monti went to Spain on the Fascist side as a man obsessed with a mission. This was the climax of his life. This was the meaning of every word he had read about freedom and truth. Spain was not Ethiopia. Now the world would listen!

He joined Franco's forces just after the conquest of Milaga. He became a man with a split personality. On the surface, Christopher de Monti sent out routine dispatches and stories expected of a competent journalist.

All his skill and ingenuity were used in smuggling stories to the free world. Using daring and cunning, he risked his life time and again to get reports over the border to the "neutral" embassies in self-exile in France.

Christopher de Monti secretly reported the arrival of millions of tons of German and Italian war materials—cannons, tanks, airplanes.

Christopher de Monti secretly reported the arrival of the first contingents of German and Italian aviators fighting for Franco.

Christopher de Monti secretly reported that Germany and Italy were using Spain as a testing ground for personnel and equipment.

Christopher de Monti secretly reported the arrival of masses of Italian ground forces.

Christopher de Monti secretly reported the atrocities committed by Franco's Moroccan hordes and wrote the true reports that the ranks of the Catholic Church were, in actuality, with the Loyalist government.

Christopher de Monti was the first to send through a secret report that the "unidentified" submarines blockading Loyalist ports were Italian.

He was the first to send through documentary evidence that the Italian air force was murdering women and children in unde- fended open cities.

And he watched his work drown in a cesspool of German propa- ganda. The rape of Spain, the first of the great sellouts in an age of sellouts, left him a disillusioned man. Fainthearted democracies hid behind shallow words and non-intervention pacts and em- bargoes which penalized a democracy fighting for its life.

The world did not want to hear what Christopher de Monti risked his life to tell them.

Oscar Pecora kept a close eye on Chris and finally decided that he could not go on smuggling out his stories from the Franco side. Afraid for Chris's life, he recalled him from Spain early in 1938.

Christopher de Monti, a quiet boy who had formed a love of truth long before he was a man, had been betrayed by his mother and disillusioned by his father. He had destroyed his own relations with a fine woman and he hated himself for that. But this was to be the cruelest disillusion of all.

He left Spain with his faith in the human race gone.

Chris had always been a sensible and hard-working journalist. He was particularly sober and responsible in a fraternity of the not-so-sober and sometimes irresponsible. His one binge had been with reason—when he broke his marriage with Eileen.

His second was worse. Oscar Pecora bailed him out of a Paris police station after a month's solid drinking and packed him off to his villa on the lake at Lausanne.

Oscar Pecora was a patient man who loved Christopher. Chris- topher was his own protégé. Like a son. Chris sulked bitterly until the boiling within him could not be contained.

And one night it all exploded.

Chris was drunk. Madame Pecora, Oscar's beautiful former- opera-singing wife, had retired. They were sitting on the balcony and there was a full moon on the lake and Chris was coming to the end of a fifth of scotch whisky.

"Why, Oscar, why! Why did they do that?"

"Tell me about it, Chris."

"Saw them killing women and children. Dirty bastard Italian fliers sitting in their dirty bastard clubs bragging about it. . . .

157

Watched them torture soldiers. Ever seen a Moroccan torture someone? By putting his testicles in a squeezer . . . Oscar . . . God dammit . . . I got all that over the border to the Americans!"

"Christopher. Every report that you sneaked out of Spain was planted in newspapers and wire services. All we can do is give the facts to the people. We cannot force them to stage a rebellion in righteous wrath."

"You are so right, Oscar. The whole goddamned human race sat on its hands and watched them murder Spain. Lemme tell you something, brother. They'll pay for not stopping Mussolini and Hitler in Spain. Pretty soon they'll run out of hiding room and, Jesus Christ, will they get clobbered!"

Oscar Pecora's sympathetic hand fell on Chris's shoulder. "We journalists are like garbage cans, Chris. Everybody sends us their filth. Through us comes all that is rotten in man. Christopher, what you are going through now . . . You were a single small voice that cried out for justice in a dark and angry sea and no one heard you. Until a man is struck in his own face he does not want to believe the attack on his brother concerns him."

Chris stumbled from his chair, staggered to the rail, and hung onto it. "Shall I tell you why I became a journalist? Do you know Thomas Paine? 'The world is my country, all mankind are my brethren . . . to do good is my religion.' "

Oscar Pecora recited, " 'In a chariot of light from the region of day, The Goddess of Liberty came. Ten thousand celestials directed the way, And hither conducted the dame. A fair budding branch from the gardens above, Where millions with millions agree, She brought in her hand as a pledge of her love, And the plant she named Liberty Tree . . . from the east to the west blow the trumpet to arms! Through the land let the sound of it flee; Let the far and the near all unite, with a cheer . . . in defense of our Liberty Tree.' "

"Bravo, Brother Pecora! Bravo! And now I give you William Lloyd Garrison . . ." Chris stood upright and thrust his finger into the air. " 'With reasonable men, I will reason; with humane men I will plead; but to tyrants I will give no quarter . . .' Now how's that for a goddamn quote?"

Chris reeled into his seat. "Little Jefferson . . . we need a little Jefferson to round it out. . . . Oscar, I'm drunk . . . God damn I'm drunk."

"Come, Christopher. You're tired. You have lost a hard battle, but you are my best soldier and tomorrow we must go out to the field again."

"She's in Jersey . . . married that guy. They've got two kids . . . nice little home, I hear. Me . . . I'm the real winner, Oscar. I get to bring truth to the people."

158

The next afternoon, after Chris awoke from a deep sixteen-hour slumber, he found his way to Oscar Pecora's study sheepishly.

"Boy, did I hang one on," he said in an apologetic voice.

"For talent, nearly anything can be forgiven."

"It has all been a pretty startling lesson, Oscar. I can see why the men in our business turn crass and cynical. We sound the great trumpet and no one hears us. Free men with full bellies don't want to believe that a black native in Ethiopia concerns them or that the bombing of an open city in Spain is the prelude to the bombing of London."

"Christopher, you've eaten my food, drunk my liquor, and now Madame Pecora is giving you flirtatious glances. I think it is high time you got back to work."

"Doing what, Oscar? Can I go on being a journalist under these conditions? I have learned now that truth is not truth. Truth is only what people want to believe and nothing more."

"But you will continue to seek it as a journalist or as a streetcar driver in Geneva. You have lost sight of the fact that there is a world of decent human beings and a lot of them are listening. They depend on the Christopher de Montis to be their eyes. You are not a man to abandon the human race because you have lost a battle. Now, what do you say, Christopher?"

Chris laughed ironically. "When you come right down to it, I'm not much good for anything else. I can't even operate a streetcar."

"I've called in men from our European bureaus for the past month. We are trying to determine how events will shift. What do you think, Christopher?"

Chris shrugged. "Spain is Italy's show, mainly. The republican government will fall sooner or later. Franco is it." Chris looked at the wall map behind Oscar. "Hitler will start up next."

"Bergman in Berlin thinks so too. How does Warsaw sound to you? We have a small bureau there."

"If you still want me, why not? One place is as good as another."

"Settled. You go to Poland. We have a free-lance man we've been using off and on. An Ervin Rosenblum."

"Photographer, too, isn't he?"

"Yes, a good man. Take him on with you and try him out. Christopher, don't try anything foolish in Poland. Keep us in business as long as you can there."

"You don't have to tell me. I've had my fill of playing cops and robbers. It won't do any more good in Poland than in Spain. Don't worry, Oscar. All you'll get are the straight reports."

Dear Oscar,

Warsaw has been like a tonic. I'm glad one of us had some sense and I thank you. It's like a little Paris here.

Ervin Rosenblum is a crackerjack. I want to keep him on permanently. The bureau is in good shape. The usual government red tape, but nothing earth-shaking. Next week I hope to have a direct phone connection to Geneva. That will speed things up considerably.

Although I'm getting along O.K. in French and English, I'm taking an hour a day of Polish. And—can you believe it?—I've taken on the hobby of coach of several of the army basketball teams.

Chris blew a whistle. He talked to Andrei Androfski in French, and Andrei translated into Polish that the basketball practice for the day was over. The members of the newly formed Seventh Ulany Brigade team thanked their coach and trotted from the floor of the Citadel gymnasium.

Andrei, the team captain, worked with Chris for another half hour. He was intrigued by Chris's wizardry in dribbling and hook shooting. Chris showed him the variations of passing the ball while being guarded and how to fake his pass moving in one direction, flipping the ball in the other.

They sat down drenched with sweat after the brisk workout. Chris wiped his face with a towel and lit a cigarette. "I'm pooped. I haven't done this in years."

"Those cigarettes are no good," Andrei said. "They wind you. Such a wonderful game. I did not realize there were so many fine points to it. But what can I do with these dumb oxen? They have no finesse."

"They're coming along fine. By the end of the season they'll play like the Harlem Globetrotters."

Chris slapped Andrei's knee. "Well, to the showers."

"I think I'll practice foul shots for a while," Andrei said. "Say, by the way, what do you have on tonight?"

"I can be had."

"Good. My colonel gave me his box at the opera. *La Bohème.*"

Opera! It struck a note of joy in Chris. He had neglected it so much lately. It had been a religion with him in New York and with Poppa in Italy.

"You'll have dinner with Gabriela and me and then we'll pick up my sister. She would join us for dinner, but she wants to bring the children and her daughter has a late piano lesson."

"I didn't know you had a married sister."

"Yes, my one and only."

Chris hedged. "Look, I'll be a third wheel breaking in on a family party."

160

"Nonsense. Her husband is in Copenhagen at a medical convention. Besides, the children will be thrilled to have a real live Italian explain the libretto to them. Settled! Be at Gabriela's apartment at six."

"This is my sister, Deborah Bronski. And my niece Rachael, and the schmendrick is Stephan."

"How do you do, Mr. de Monti."

"Call me Chris . . . please."

It was the most strange and awesome sensation Chris had ever experienced. Even as he walked from the car to the house he felt it come over him. The instant he saw her eyes she understood that he was reading a message of a deep inner sadness and frustration.

Good God, she was beautiful!

Chris was an experienced, sophisticated man. He was too wise to be felled suddenly like this. Yet his stability seemed shot. This strange feeling had never happened—not even with Eileen.

During the opera they were both uncomfortable in their awareness of each other. It was as though ectoplasm were leaping from the body of one to the other. There was a quick succession of stolen glances. There was the first accidental brushing of arms that made them twinge. And a few less accidental touchings.

Between the second and third acts Chris and Deborah found themselves standing away from the others, oblivious of the pomp and finery around them. Deborah turned completely pale as they stared wordlessly at each other.

The bell rang and the audience began to drift in to their seats.

Deborah suddenly broke and turned. Chris automatically touched her elbow. "I must see you," he blurted. "Please phone me at Swiss News at the Bristol."

Andrei called across the lobby for them to hurry.

Four days passed.

Chris started each time the phone rang. Then he began to resign himself to the fact that she would never call him and that he had done something foolish. Flirtations were flirtations, but this wasn't. There was in this none of the game men and women play. It was something serious from the very first second. Even though he realized she would not call, he could not shake that strange feeling.

"Hello . . ."

"Is this the Swiss News Agency?"

"Yes . . ."

"Christopher de Monti?"

"Speaking."

"This is Deborah Bronski."

Chris's hand became wet on the phone.

"I will be in the Saxony Gardens in an hour, along the benches beside the swan lake."

They were both quiet and confused and feeling guilty and foolish as they found themselves sitting opposite each other.

"I feel absolutely silly," Deborah said. "I am respectfully married and I want you to know I have never done anything like this before."

"It is all so strange."

"I cannot lie about the fact that I wanted to see you again and I don't know why."

"You know what I think? I think that you and I are a couple of magnets made out of some sort of unique metal. I think I was irresistibly pulled to Warsaw."

And then they were awkwardly quiet, groping for a logical thought.

"Why don't we take a walk," Chris said, "and talk about things?"

She lay awake that night. And she met him again and she lay awake again. All of those little things that make a romance the most wonderful exploration of one human by another had been denied Deborah. Now suddenly she was flooded with them. Flooded with emotions she never believed she would have or knew existed.

The touch of a man's hand. The little duels of small talk to inflict small hurts on each other. The instantaneous thrill the moment he appeared coming down the path. The pangs of jealousy. The color of eyes, the way his dark hair fell over his forehead, the long strong hands, the sensitive expressions, the lanky careless stature.

The pain of being away from him.

The first kiss. She did not know what a kiss was. She did not believe feelings from a kiss were part of the human experience.

"Deborah, I love you."

Each new adventure was like nothing that had ever happened to her before.

"I am not quite certain I know what love is, Chris. I do know that seeing you is wrong and we will get into trouble if we keep it up. But I know I want to see you, regardless. Because . . . being away from you is becoming more and more unbearable. Is this what love is, Chris?"

Chapter Twelve

Journal Entry

*Today, my son was born. Susan Geller was in attendance with
Dr. Glazer from our orphanage. Sylvia came through beautifully
for a woman of forty.*

*Outwardly, I must exhibit unabashed joy. Inwardly, I am worried.
This is a bad time for a Jewish child to be born.*

*Moses is a common name, but I think the historian in me weighed
my decision. The first Moses was also born in an era of duress, and
when Pharaoh ordered all Jewish male infants slain he was hidden
in the bulrushes. With this sentimentality and much luck, Moses
Brandel will come through the difficult days ahead.*

ALEXANDER BRANDEL

Despite the austerity and the outlawing of religious ceremonies,
nothing could diminish the collective happiness of the Bathyrans.
Moses Brandel was born to be spoiled by them all. He was their
baby, and they were damned well going to have a blowout at the
bris.

Tolek Alterman closed down the farm and brought in all the
workers, thirty boys and ten girls, to Warsaw with an extravagance
of food.

Momma Rosenblum took charge of cooking the traditional
dishes. Rabbi Solomon would personally conduct the prayers at
the ceremony.

The event took place at the Writers' Club on Tlomatskie Street,
near Alex's flat, which the Orphans and Self-Help Society had
"leased" as an agency.

On the eighth day after his birth Moses Brandel was passed
around on an ornate velvet pillow from relative to relative, from
Bathyran to Bathyran, and finally ended up in the arms of his
godfather, Andrei Androfski.

Down the street, the Great Tlomatskie Synagogue was boarded
up at the doors and windows and guards posted around it, but in
the Writers' Club a covenant with God was made by this child in a
ceremony over four thousand years old from the command in
Genesis, "He that is eight days old among you shall be circumcised,
every male throughout your generations."

As in ancient times when Abraham circumcised Isaac, symbolic
of a covenant with God, so did Finkelstein, the professional
mohel, circumcise Moses Brandel. It is probable that Finkelstein
did a better job, as he had had far more practice. He had been
mohel at some two thousand *brisim*.

163

Little Moses lost his composure and shrieked.

"Blessed are you, Lord our God, Master of the Universe, who have made us holy with your commands, and have commanded us to bring Moses, the son of Alexander and Sylvia, into the covenant of Abraham our father," chanted Rabbi Solomon.

When Moses' ordeal was over, the infant was returned to his mother in their flat down the street and the celebration began.

"*Mozeltoff!*" everyone congratulated the proud father.

"*Mozeltoff!*"

And the toasts began.

And singing.

And dancing.

And soon the Writers' Club reeled under the impact of a dancing hora ring. The "proud father" was pulled into the center, and one by one the young Bathyran girls whirled with him around the circle in unison with the clapping and stamping. He danced and danced until he could dance no more. It didn't take much wine to get him high; he had been heady since the birth of the baby.

At last he staggered from the dance floor, sweating and gasping for breath.

Ervin Rosenblum and Andrei hooked their hands under Alex's arms and dragged him off to a side room, where he flopped down, wiped his face, and fanned himself.

"Why do Jews have to make such a tsimmes about the birth of a son?" Alex asked.

"Our kids have been pent up so long, they are about to explode with the tension," Rosy said. "This party is doing everybody good."

"So!" roared Andrei. "How does the new father feel now?"

"At my age, to have a son is an unexpected bonus."

Then he looked up glumly from Andrei to Ervin. They could hear the hilarity outside, but they were never a second away from the times. Even in the middle of the celebration it lurked in Alex's mind. "Have you see the new set of German directives?"

They nodded.

"So, they may as well celebrate tonight."

"Why don't you forget it for a night too, Alex?" Andrei said.

"I've been doing a lot of thinking. I am at the headquarters at Mila 19 most of the time now, day and night. As soon as Sylvia is on her feet she'll be working at the orphanage again. I think we will give up our apartment and move to Mila 19. Susan Geller has indicated she'll move over too. I think it will be encouraging for our youngsters to have us living there. We are only using the first floor for offices and the dispensary. We could divide the place into dormitories for boys and girls and bring in another sixty or seventy people."

"I'll move in if I can bring Momma," Ervin Rosenblum said.

164

"No. So long as you are able to work on the outside, it would be better not to be too closely identified."

Alex looked slyly at Andrei. Andrei Androfski at Mila 19 would be a great boost to everyone's morale.

"What are you doing with the basement?" Andrei asked.

"Storage."

"Have you thought about an underground press?"

Andrei had behaved very well for the past weeks. He had shown great restraint, but he was going to be a problem as things grew worse, Alex thought. Ana Grinspan had started publication of a weekly sheet in Krakow. Alex didn't want to face the situation. Discovery of an underground printing plant could destroy the entire Orphans and Self-Help organization.

"I'll help you with your press, Andrei, but not at Mila 19."

"Then you really don't need me there, do you?"

"We had better get out to the dance floor," Ervin said quickly.

The forgotten man—or the forgotten boy—at the *bris* of Moses Brandel was his sixteen-year-old brother, Wolf. He seemed bewildered by everything. When everyone said "*Mozeltoff*" to him, he wondered why he was being congratulated. He was a bit forlorn over the attention the new baby was getting and more confused at suddenly becoming a brother. Wolf was rather shy, anyhow, and leaned against a wall and watched the others dance. Rachael watched him while she played the piano.

Poor Wolf, she thought. He is like a lost soul. When her mother relieved her at the piano she drifted over to him.

"Would you like to dance?" she asked.

"Uh-uh."

"Come on."

"No, I don't care to. Besides, I get all tangled up with my feet."

There was an electrifying moment as the evening reached its highlight when Emanuel Goldman entered the room and it was announced that he would perform at the piano.

He had been in retirement for several years, and his hands and reflexes had become slowed and his technique rusty, but there was still that great personal charm of a real virtuoso. Tonight he had made an exception and was going to perform. The hall became breathless with anticipation as he seated himself at the upright and burst into a thundering polonaise.

Rachael Bronski went out to the balcony where Wolf Brandel stood alone, looking at the Tlomatskie Synagogue down the street. His hands were shoved forlornly into his pockets.

"Don't you want to hear Emanuel Goldman play?" she said.

"I can hear him fine from out here."

She walked up behind him, and that made him uncomfortable. He moved a few feet away, still keeping his back to her.

165

"What's the matter, Wolf? I've never seen you so unhappy."

He turned and shrugged. "Everything, I guess. Mostly the way things are today. Wearing this," he said, touching the Star of David on his arm. "Not being able to go to school. Are you still taking piano lessons?"

"Momma teaches me now. I have a lot of time to practice when I'm not working at the orphanage. Are you still taking flute lessons?"

"No. I never liked it, anyhow"'

"I thought you did."

"No, I just said that."

"Why?"

"To make Momma happy. It wasn't really too bad. I kind of used to look forward to Tuesdays. Sitting in the park with you after lessons."

"I miss that too," she said softly.

"Well, you'll get over that. I'm not much."

"Why do you always pull yourself down?"

"Look at me. I get more stupid-looking every day."

"It's not so, Wolf. You're turning into a man and you will be very, very handsome."

He shrugged. His voice alternated from high to low, and now he had much trouble holding it steady. He cleared his throat formally. "I should like to visit your brother Stephan," he said. "I realize that you and your mother are schooling him, but he needs older masculine company. Someone he can look up to. I could teach him chess and many other things."

"That would be very nice. Stephan does need an older . . . man. Uncle Andrei is not around much, and Father works very late."

"Good. I will come to see him. Rachael . . ."

"Yes?"

"Do you think—I mean—with all the joy around here now——What I mean to say is that everyone is kissing everyone. Do you think it would be proper if we expressed our joy too? I mean, properly. For little Moses."

"I don't know. Seeing how happy everyone is, it might be all right, don't you think?"

He pecked at her cheek and pulled back abruptly. "That was stupid," he said. "It wasn't a real kiss. Have you ever had a real kiss, Rachael?"

"Once," she answered.

"Did you like it?"

"Not too much. I really didn't like him. I only wanted to see what a kiss was like. It was sort of mushy. Have you ever had a real kiss?"

"Lots of them," he threw off nonchalantly.

"Did you like it?"

166

"You know how it is. I can take it or leave it."

Rachael and Wolf looked at each other for ever so long, and their breathing became irregular. There was a burst of applause inside and spontaneous calls for the master to play more. Then the shouts died down. Goldman played a soft Beethoven sonata.

Rachael was becoming frightened at the strange feeling she had all over her body. "We had better get inside," she said.

"Could I—for real?"

She was too scared to talk. She nodded her head and closed her eyes and lifted her chin and parted her lips. Wolf braced himself and leaned over slightly and touched his lips to hers.

He lowered his eyes and jammed his hands in his pockets.

"That was very good," Rachael said, "nothing at all like the other time."

"Could we do it again?" he asked.

"Maybe we shouldn't. . . . Well, just once more."

This time Wolf pulled her gently to him and they felt each other and it was even more wonderful. Her arms reached around him and held him against her and it was so good. "Oh, Wolf," she whispered.

She tugged away from him and walked toward the door.

"Rachael."

"Yes?"

"Shall I see you soon?"

"Yes," she said, and ran inside.

Chapter Thirteen

Paul Bronski generally brought his work home from the Civil Authority after hours. The census had been a demanding task. There had been a wild scramble for "Aryan" *Kennkarten* not stamped with the damning *J*. Many of the Jewish population were trying to buy their way out of the country or otherwise make the census count very difficult. Three hundred and sixty thousand Jews had registered with the Civil Authority.

It was the new directives and continual organizational work that kept Paul busy until late each night.

Deborah, who spent the days at the orphanage and the evenings schooling her children, took time out from their studies to make tea for Paul.

When she entered the study he was slumped over the desk, his eyes red from reading, and he was pale with fatigue. As he sipped the tea she stood behind him and massaged his neck. It always felt so good when Deborah did that.

"Anything bad?" she asked.

"Just weary," he answered. "This stump aches. Acts up in the damp weather."

"Can't you take anything?"

"Don't want to get into the habit of too much pain killer."

"Paul, you've been working too hard. Why don't we take a few days off together? We can slip off somewhere. You can get a travel pass."

"I wish I could. My belated responsibilities to the Jewish community are rather time-consuming."

She sat on the desk. He smiled and pushed his papers back. "We aren't spending much time together," she said. "Orphanage during the day—but they're so short-handed—our children's lessons at night. I'll cut off a few hours at the orphanage."

"No," Paul said. "I won't be able to get home earlier, anyhow. Besides, it makes a good impression to have the wife of a Civil Authority member volunteering in the Orphans and Self-Help program."

There was something Deborah didn't like about that. Paul had reacted with a sense of duty to his new status, but he was still groping for prestige—still thinking in terms of doing the proper thing.

"When is all this going to end?" Deborah said glumly. "Once I was foolish enough to think nothing could be worse than during the siege."

"Well, no one really knows what the Germans are up to. But even they only can go so far. It will level off." He switched the subject quickly. "I saw Chris today."

"Oh . . ."

"He's been able to transfer most of our accounts to American banks." Paul laughed ironically. "There's a paradox for you. We are getting richer all the time."

Deborah worked hard to mask the sudden shock at the mention of Chris's name. "How is Chris?" she said quickly.

"Fine—fine."

"I didn't know that he would be allowed to continue here. Susan Geller told me Ervin Rosenblum was concerned about a possible closing of Swiss News."

"Seems he has gotten himself in thick with this Von Epp fellow. Naturally, his agency wants him to keep operating as long as the Germans let him. Incidentally, we decided that for mutual interests we shouldn't see each other except in emergency. There's no use alerting the Germans that we have business, and I could endanger Chris's position here. We don't need the funds, fortunately, and if we do we can always work through Rosenblum."

"Yes," Deborah said, "that's sensible."

"Dear," Paul said, "while we're about it, I want to speak to you about this business of sending Stephan to Rabbi Solomon for study. Let me say that I am in sympathy with your motives, but it's dangerous business."

Deborah's sweetness suddenly vanished. "Dangerous for whom?"

"For the boy himself."

"Have you thought about the shock he has received in the past few months?"

"Of course I have. Deborah, be sensible. We are very lucky. We have been spared all the harrowing things going on in Warsaw."

"Is that really it, Paul?" she said sharply. "Protecting our position?"

"Did you ever think what would happen to us if I'm thrown off the Civil Authority? I'm not a criminal for wanting to protect my family."

Paul had never seen Deborah look so stubborn. Almost always he had been able to talk her around in the past.

"Our son is being humiliated and persecuted because he is a Jew," Deborah said. "He should at least have some moral fortification to withstand these shocks. We cannot let him stumble through this without knowing why he is a Jew."

Deborah wanted to say more. She wanted to tell Paul that if he assumed his responsibility as a Jewish father he would give his son instruction and training as other Jewish fathers were doing since the outlawing of the cheder schools. But what she said carried an authority he had never heard from her before. She let it stop there because Paul was tired and confused and she did not wish to hurt him.

The doorbell rang.

Paul opened it. Gawky Wolf Brandel dangled before him. "Good evening, sir," he said, his face reddening.

Paul smiled slightly. He quickly tried to change the atmosphere of the argument. "Good evening, Mr. Brandel. Did you come to visit with Stephan or Rachael?"

"Rachael—I mean Stephan, sir."

"I will let you have them both for the price of one chess game."

Oh darn, Wolf thought. Bronski was a tough chessplayer. It would take an hour to beat him. Then a lovely thought occurred. He would throw the game on purpose. This would kill two birds with one stone—please Dr. Bronski's vanity and allow him to see Rachael quicker.

That night Deborah lay awake. The mention of Chris had stirred a restlessness in her. She ached for him. She closed her eyes and began to remember moments of coming up the path in the Saxony Gardens . . . his touch, the warmth of him. The music in his room as they lay in the shadows. She squirmed about the bed.

She had run from him in anger and fright. But always in the back of her mind she knew she would see him again. Now . . . cut off, completely. Not even a stolen glance . . . a touch . . . not even his voice on the phone. He must have been terribly, terribly hurt. But he is still in Warsaw . . . he is still here. She wanted him to touch her. Oh, Chris . . . Chris . . . Chris . . . please touch me.

Her tears fell on the pillow.

Paul reached out for her, and her body turned tense and rigid as it always did. Deborah forced the tears to stop and breathed deeply several times to make herself relax, and she rolled over to her husband.

Paul was in trouble. He was walking a tightrope. In the old days before the war he was so sure of himself, so independent and clever. He was floundering and now he had to lean on her more and more.

"You aren't angry about what I said about Stephan? If it means so much to you, then we will chance it. We'll let the boy continue with Rabbi Solomon."

His hand went beneath her waist. She put her arms about him as he lay his head on her breast.

"I need you so much," Paul said.

After sixteen years of taking her for granted, it was the first confession he had ever made.

Chapter Fourteen

Journal Entry

Something new has been added. As if we don't have enough to worry about, we were presented with Sturmbannführer Sieghold Stutze. Despite the lowly rank of SS major, it looks as if Stutze holds great power.

He came from Globocnik's SS, SD, Gestapo capital in Lublin. Like Globocnik and Hitler, Stutze is an Austrian. He arrived with a detachment of SS troopers who are billed as "specialists in Jewish affairs." We are learning that Globocnik and not Governor General Hans Frank is the real boss of Poland. It may hold true then that Stutze and not Rudolph Schreiker will be the real boss of Warsaw.

Whereas Rudolph Schreiker has shown himself to be a plain and simple pigheaded bully, Stutze is exhibiting a maniacal lust for cruelty. He is small in stature, thus a Napoleonic complex. He is slightly deformed in one leg and has a limp. This is a clue to his sadistic delight in inflicting pain. We are very concerned about this development.

ALEXANDER BRANDEL

170

Although religious study had been banned, this merely meant it would be carried on in secret places, as had been done by the Marranos during the Spanish Inquisition and a hundred times in a hundred places where it had been banned during Jewish history.

Stephan Bronski had entered a most impressionable age. After a lifetime of immunity, the sudden branding of being a Jew made his trips to Rabbi Solomon's home part of a great adventure of discovery. He liked the secrecy of it. He was fascinated by the strange cryptic scrawlings in Hebrew and much awed by the infinite wisdoms of the rabbi. The gradual understanding of the two thousand years of unspeakable persecution did much to alleviate the confusion within him.

His class had six other boys. They studied in the basement beneath the home of Rabbi Solomon. They spoke in whispers. All about them were the treasures taken from the synagogue for safekeeping. The synagogue's library of many thousand books of Talmudic and Jewish literature was there. The menorah, the sacred candelabra, were there. The heart of Judaism, the Torah scrolls from the ark of the synagogue, were there.

The boys learned Hebrew prayers, ethics of the fathers, and prepared for their bar mitzvah.

The old man would walk from one to the other and pick up the chant of their prayer, pat one on the head, twist another's ear who was lagging. Although he was ancient, the boys could not put anything over on him, for it seemed he could see in back of his head and hear all seven of them at the same time.

Stephan Bronski asked the rabbi if he could be excused for a moment and it was granted. He stood up, and then he saw them!

There were three Nazis in black uniforms in the doorway. Major Sieghold Stutze stood before the other two.

"Rabbi!" Stephan cried.

And they all froze in terror.

Sieghold Stutze limped into the room. "Well, well, well, what do we have here?"

The children flocked behind the rabbi, quivering in fright. One vomited. Only Stephan Bronski stood in front of the old man. His eyes burning with anger, he looked at that moment very much like his Uncle Andrei.

Stutze brushed Stephan aside as he tried to "protect" the old rabbi and grabbed him by the beard and flung him to the floor. He took the dagger from his belt, straddled the fallen man, and cut off the earlocks worn by religious Jews because King David had worn them.

The other two Nazis broke into laughter. They walked around the room, throwing the books to the floor, overturning the desks, trampling on the symbolic ornaments from the synagogue.

"These will make a lovely bonfire," Stutze said. His eyes searched

171

the room carefully. "It is here, somewhere—now where is it?" He walked to a large canvas. "Could it be beneath here?"

"No!" shrieked the rabbi.

"Aha!" Stutze said, pulling the canvas away, revealing the Torah scrolls.

"No!" shrieked the rabbi again.

Stutze took off the breastplate, tore off the velvet cover, and took out the scrolls which formed the heart of Judaism, Christianity and Islam—the five books of Moses. Genesis, Exodus, Leviticus, Numbers, and Deuteronomy. "Here it is, the prize."

The rabbi crawled to the Nazi and threw his arms about his knees and begged him not to harm the scrolls. Stutze answered by sending his boot thudding into the old man's ribs.

As he dangled the tree-of-life lambskin Torah before Solomon's nose the old man cried prayers.

Stutze laughed and his troopers laughed. "I understand old Jews often die for this trash."

"Kill me, but do not harm the Torah!"

"Shall we have some amusement? You! Boys! Line up against the wall! Hold your hands over your heads and put your faces to the wall."

The boys did as they were ordered. Stutze dropped the Torah to the floor. Rabbi Solomon crawled quickly to it and covered it with his body.

Stutze took out his pistol and walked to the boys. "All right, old Jew, dance for us. Right on the Torah."

"Kill me first."

The Austrian cocked his pistol and placed the barrel against the back of Stephan Bronski's head. "I shall not kill you, old Jew. Let me see how many of the boys I will have to kill first. Now dance for us."

"Don't do it, Rabbi!" Stephan shouted.

Stutze went into a spasm of hysterics. "Sometimes when I play this game we have to kill two or three before they do their dance."

The old man got to his knees, grunting in anguish.

"Now dance for us, old Jew."

As Stutze tantalized the boys by placing the pistol against their skulls they cried, "Rabbi! Rabbi!"

The tears streamed down the old man's cheeks.

He brought his foot down on the Torah and shuffled a grotesque dance on the sacred lambskin.

"Faster, old Jew, faster! Wipe your feet on them!"

"Now, old Jew—piss on them! Piss on them!"

While the Nazis convulsed in laughter at the desecration of the Law, Stephan Bronski had in the flash of a second made a lightning dash for freedom.

Chapter Fifteen

Never a dull moment since Sturmbannführer Sieghold Stutze has honored us with his presence. He calls his SS detail the "Reinhard Corps" after Reinhard Heydrich, the SD chief in Berlin. This gives us a clue to the chain of command. Hitler, Himmler, Reinhard Heydrich, Globocnik, and, in Warsaw, Stutze. In this week's meeting with Emanuel Goldman, David Zemba, and Simon Eden, they gave me a raft of notes for my journal.

The Reinhard Corps swept into the northern Jewish area in large trucks and emptied Jewish stores of all their merchandise.

The Reinhard Corps has been going into individual homes and taking clothing, pots, pans, lamps, books—which are burned—pillows, blankets.

The Reinhard Corps has emptied supplies from Jewish warehouses, including Zemba's American Relief supplies. This has created shortages in medicine and food. Then Dr. Koenig sold us back the things that Stutze had stolen at a six-hundred-per-cent markup.

Fuel ration has brought on pneumonia this winter, Emanuel Goldman tells me. He says another cut in food ration was ordered by Schreiker yesterday.

Not to be outdone by the Reinhard Corps, Rudolph Schreiker has hundreds of thugs from Solec and even mobs of children and students to roam the Jewish area and smash store windows, beat up Orthodox Jews on the street, and loot. It is understood that no Pole will be punished for a crime against a Jew. Special rewards are offered to Poles who turn over Jews with "Aryan" Kennkarten.

Rabbi Solomon's synagogue was burned to the ground, as he was caught by Stutze teaching cheder in his basement. (I could have sworn young Stephan Bronski was receiving instructions. Maybe not. He did not show up among those turned in at Pawiak Prison.) Rabbi Solomon's congregation was fined twenty thousand zlotys to free the boys and to pay for the petrol which the Germans used to burn the synagogue. Zemba's American Relief put up half the fine in American dollars.

All teen-age orphans in our orphanage in Powazki and a dozen other orphanages were forced to donate blood to the German army. Does Hitler know his Ayrans will be transfused with impure blood?

Simon Eden says the trade in poison is getting large. Everyone is carrying a capsule for suicide. No one gets more than a few hours' sleep these nights. Whistles, rifle butts, pounding boots. We sleep with one eye open. A hundred different rape cases reported. "Juden 'raus [Jews, come out]!" is heard every night, all night.

If we are to hand out prizes for ingenuity, Stutze's Reinhard

Corps must win. They force the old Orthodox to scrub sidewalks under bayonets. They have made them dance naked. They make them exercise with heavy cobblestones. They make them beat each other with galoshes. They make them crap their pants. Still, through it all, I am proud of these Jews. They refuse to shave off their beards or earlocks. They walk with their heads erect in great dignity despite the fact that their very appearance will bring them abuses. They are stubborn and honorable and of Rabbi Solomon's breed, and we Zionists could learn a thing or two from them.

Schreiker, jealous of Stutze and not to be outdone, turned loose mad Gerta, an ethnic with a psychopathic hatred of Jews. She has been allowed to wander through the northern quarters with a lead pipe.

A.B.

Chapter Sixteen

Journal Entry

The German hand is being revealed more each day. The Krakow Gazette keeps hammering on a theme of "segregation of the Jews on reservations." That is fancy talk for ghettos.

More talk about sending Jews from Austria, Czechoslovakia, and Germany into Poland.

Yesterday it became true. A ghetto was decreed in Lodz. Chaim Rumkowski was appointed chairman of a Council of Elders. Ana Grinspan is there now to see if we can organize a "self-help house" like Mila 19. There are around two hundred thousand Jews in Lodz.

At yesterday's meeting with Emanuel Goldman, David Zemba, and Simon Eden, Goldman thinks we are heading into a week of crisis in Warsaw. He says that all the abuses up to date have been merely to soften us up. A new Nazi, Oberführer Alfred Funk, has arrived, and that means trouble because Funk is the direct liaison between Berlin and Globocnik in Lublin and is no doubt carrying a pocketful of candy on new German policy.

ALEXANDER BRANDEL

SS Brigadier Alfred Funk was the young blond blue-eyed Aryan about whom Adolf Hitler bragged. He was an intelligent and industrious man who cut a smart figure and would have been successful in any capacity he sought in life. He was shrewd and astute and dependable, unlike the bumbling bully Rudolph Schreiker, the timid conforming opportunist Franz Koenig, the half-mad Sieghold Stutze, and the cynical, lazy Horst von Epp.

Like Von Epp, he calculated that the rise of Nazism was unstoppable. Unlike Von Epp, he felt that Hitler could bring the German people to their peak position in history. Like most of the German people, he willingly chose to be a part of this "march to destiny." He accepted the traditional German obedience to authority without question. He desired to be a large and important man and he became what he desired. Alfred Funk had a few qualms at first about Nazi methods but soon realized that the political tyranny of the concentration camps, the abolition of civil liberties, and the destruction of the intellectual opposition were merely fundamentals clearing the path for this Greater Germany. He became a deputy of tyranny with conviction. The tools of tyranny were not questions in his mind—only the best methods of using them.

Golden hair, trim body, Alfred Funk was a man of undeniable strength who was able to impose his authority. As the master blueprints came from Berlin from Heydrich and Eichmann of the 4B section of Gestapo, Oberführer Funk received the position of special liaison to Globocnik in Lublin.

When Emanuel Goldman was summoned to the city hall to see Oberführer Alfred Funk, he had already surmised Funk's mission in Warsaw.

Funk spoke impassively. "We are concerned abo : the unsanitary habits of Jews. Your homes are filled with lice. Lice cause typhus."

Funk was, indeed, starting on an interesting tack, Goldman thought. "I am not a doctor like the eminent Frank Koenig," Goldman answered curtly, "but your regulations denying us sanitary facilities are the cause of the outbreak of lice."

Funk stared. He did not blink or budge. The old man is tough. The Nazi picked up a paper. "Our facts scientifically prove otherwise. Everyone knows Jews are filthy. Look at those bearded people. A perfect nesting place for lice."

"We didn't have a bit of trouble with them in the past," Goldman answered.

"But there's trouble now, isn't there, Goldman? Now, Goldman, I want your Civil Authority to help us protect the citizens of Warsaw. Have this Orphans and Self-Help Society of yours set up delousing sheds. Each Jew will get a stamped card when he is deloused. He will have to have the card in order to receive rations. We will carry out extensive inspections of personal dwellings in order to stamp out this scourge."

You mean looting parties under the guise of medical inspection, Goldman thought.

"In order to control this condition which the Jews have brought on Warsaw, we have blacked out certain areas of the city which will be under quarantine."

Goldman knew . . . here it comes.

"All Jews must move into the quarantine area within two weeks under punishment of death." He shoved a map of Warsaw over his desk at the old man. It was blacked out from the northern rail bridge below Zoliborz down to Jerusalem Boulevard. The eastern boundary was a zigzag line past the Saxony Gardens, and the western boundary roughly in a line with the Jewish and Catholic cemeteries. Funk was watching him. There was no use arguing with the German.

"Goldman," Funk continued, "you do agree we are at war with the Jews."

"I cannot disagree."

"Therefore, we consider that Jewish property, personal and otherwise, is legitimate booty—spoils of war. Therefore, when the move is completed into the quarantine area, you will begin a registration of all Jewish property. I have appointed Dr. Koenig as registrar and custodian of Jewish property. That goes for business inventories, bank accounts, jewels, furs, et cetera, et cetera."

Koenig! My, he has come up in the world. . . .

"One final thing, Goldman. Because you Jews have imposed these deplorable dangers and have consistently disobeyed our directives, we are fining all the Jews three hundred thousand zlotys. We are holding fifty people in Pawiak Prison to assure payment of the fine within a week. Your Civil Authority is expected to make the collection. You are to draft directives covering the things we have discussed and you will return here tomorrow for me to study them."

When Goldman returned to the Civil Authority building at Grzybowska 28, he summoned the board immediately. Goldman relayed his conversation with Brigadier Alfred Funk to seven pasty-faced men.

"The quarantine order is merely a thin disguise for a ghetto. If we collect this mass fine for them, there will be others. Registration of property. I don't have to explain that to you. The most dreadful part of their whole scheme is to make us issue the orders. Now, we on the Civil Authority believe we could be of some service to the community and be a protective wall between the community and the Germans. The Germans are converting the Civil Authority into their own tool for carrying out their dirty work."

The room was stricken with fear. Everyone knew what the Germans were up to. Everyone also knew he was facing a moment when he had to search the depths of his own soul to see if it held a hidden reservoir of courage. So long as they carried out German orders, they and their families were safe. Defiance could bring them instant death. Was this worth dying for? Emanuel Goldman, their chairman, thought it was.

One by one they revealed themselves. Weiss, who had been an army officer all his life, had never been much of a practicing Jew. He considered himself an assimilated Pole. He was angry. He banged his fists on the table. "Certainly, as conquerors, they will give us the choice to withdraw in honor," he said.

What nonsense, Goldman thought. Weiss is still playing colonel. "These are not soldiers, but Nazis," Goldman said. "I do not know if they will let us resign."

Now Silberberg. Once he had written plays in which vaunted ideals bounced from the rafters of the theaters. He had been terrified into conformity. He sulked. He hated himself for it. "We are not collaborators," he said, finding his reserve of strength.

Seidman, the engineer, was orthodox. "Misery is nothing new for the Jewish people. We have lived in ghettos before."

As he talked he began to sound like Rabbi Solomon, but Goldman knew that Seidman spoke from conviction and not fear.

Marinski, the factory owner. He had spent a lifetime building his leatherworks. The new orders would end in confiscation of his factories, he was certain of it. He had to calculate. As a member of the Civil Authority, can I save my factory or shall I gamble that the Germans will back down if we have a show of strength? There was another thing worrying Marinski. He was a just and proud man. The right and wrong seemed clear. "We must make a stand," he said.

That was the way Schoenfeld felt too. He was a brilliant lawyer. "No matter how complete the occupation. No matter how strong their authority, they have to base every action on cause. They gave you a cause with the excuse of a quarantine. A determined effort by us, and I am certain we can force them to adhere to the rules of basic decency. Make them negotiate."

And Paul Bronski spoke. "We have no choice. To whom can we appeal? An outside world who won't listen to us? Schoenfeld, you are a fool if you think you can negotiate them out of a ghetto. They want it, they've ordered it in Berlin, and they'll have it. There is nothing we can do."

"Yes there is," Goldman answered. "We can behave like men." Boris Presser, the merchant, who had an art of being anonymous, said nothing except to vote with Paul Bronski and Seidman against making a protest to the Germans.

"It is voted five to three that we protest to Funk."

A sudden wave of nausea hit Paul. He stumbled to his feet. "We are under no bylaws stating that we can vote. We are merely independent department heads. If you want to go to Funk with a protest, do it in the name of the others—not me."

Was it an outburst of cowardice? Was it an outburst of self-preservation? Goldman wondered. He wondered if it was not all a useless gesture. There would be fifty more men like Paul Bronski to replace them and fifty more to replace *them*. What good would a protest do? Bronski was the realist there. The Germans would have what they wanted, regardless.

Emanuel Goldman was very tired. He was seventy-three years old. His children were all married. He lived alone with only his housekeeper.

He had had a good rich life. He had traveled and brought fame to his people and his country. A quirk of fate had put him into a position he did not wish, but he had accepted the position without protest. He had been made the chairman of the Civil Authority because Franz Koenig thought he was a weak man. Goldman was far from weak. He was an idealist who did not know how to back down from the things in which he believed.

He spent the night tying up all the loose ends of his business and took them to his friends, David Zemba of American Relief and Alexander Brandel. He left them knowing he would probably not see them again.

In the morning he reported to Oberführer Alfred Funk. He sat opposite the German very calmly, a picture of self-assurance, with the old flamboyance still in his mannerisms. Funk knew the moment Goldman entered the room, but his icy blue eyes did not betray the thoughts whirling behind them.

"You have drafted the directives?"

The old man shook his head.

Funk registered neither surprise nor anger.

"I won't put my name on a ghetto order," Goldman said.

"Do you speak in behalf of the entire board?"

"I suggest you ask them," he retorted.

"I am curious," Funk said. "Why are you doing it?"

Goldman smiled. "I am more curious. Why are you doing it?"

It was Funk who broke off the staring contest.

Goldman arose, bowed slightly, sending his long white silken hair awry. "Good day," he said, and left.

Alfred Funk thought for a moment about the various possibilities, then shrugged to himself and methodically lifted his desk phone. "Find Sturmbannführer Stutze. Have him report to me instantly."

Journal Entry

Emanuel Goldman was murdered last night. It appears to be the personal handiwork of Sturmbannführer Sieghold Stutze. He was beaten to death with a pipe. His body was dumped on the streets before the Civil Authority building as a clear-cut message.

Boris Presser, whom none of us know, has been appointed Civil Authority chairman and Dr. Paul Bronski given wider powers.

I must now deal with Bronski on all matters concerning the Orphans and Self-Help Society. We cannot expect from Bronski anything near what Goldman did for us.

ALEXANDER BRANDEL

Chapter Seventeen

Journal Entry

It is summer of 1940 already. News from the outside world, our one great source of hope, lists one disaster after another. Norway and Denmark have fallen. The Low Countries and the debacle at Dunkirk. Italy has been dragged into the war. German power is still on the rise, unchecked. France has paid for a decade of appeasement.

Rudolph Schreiker has no more trouble with the Jewish Civil Authority with Boris Presser as chairman. Paul Bronski's co-operation with the Orphans and Self-Help Society is rigidly guided by German directives.

The poor Jews have had their personal property stripped and carted away. They have no choice but to register for slave labor in one of the dozens of new German factories and enterprises springing up all over the Warsaw area. Dr. Franz Koenig owns three or four factories outright. When short of labor they merely pull people off the streets in roundups and they simply disappear.

The rich are able to do better. There is wild trade in gold and jewelry and false Aryan papers. Everyone in the upper classes scrambles for himself. As for our countrymen, we do get superficial help from certain classes, but the bulk of the Poles show us nothing but apathy.

Any questions about who runs Poland? They are answered. SS Gruppenführer Globocnik in Lublin. It is known that Governor General Hans Frank protested to Hitler about having Jews deported from all over Europe into Poland. He was overruled. They are pouring in by the tens of thousands to the sixteen Jewish "reservations" in the curious master plan in Berlin calling for "resettlement" of all Jews in occupied countries.

Some of the German and Austrian Jews are pretty haughty. They have been able to rent themselves nice flats and look down upon us poor Polish Jews as inferior. However, the vast majority arrive destitute. Dr. Glazer, who heads the medical staff of the Orphans and Self-Help, fears epidemic conditions and possibly mass starvation if we get another ration cut. Can Dave Zemba's America Aid keep up with the massive new problems we face?

What is the ultimate aim of the Germans' master plan? As Ger-

179

*man victories increase, their fear of world opinion lessens. I hear
that the 4B section of the Gestapo on Jewish affairs under Adolf
Eichmann on the Kurfürstendamm in Berlin is an empire within an
empire.*

A.B.

It was getting more dangerous for Andrei each time he traveled
outside Warsaw. On his last trip he had a close call when a sudden
inspection was pulled at a siding. He slipped the Pole who spotted
his fake travel pass a three-hundred-zloty bribe and it worked. He
always carried the bills folded and placed in his papers so the
inspector could be bought on the spot.

When Emanuel Goldman headed the Jewish Civil Authority,
Andrei was issued travel permits under the guise of Orphans and
Self-Help business. Now that Paul Bronski was the liaison, he shut
off all but legitimate permits.

Andrei had to travel with false papers as a non-Jew. His *Kennkarte* read "Jan Kowal." Normal hazards were increased by bands
of hoodlums who hung out around the train depots detecting
hidden Jews, whom they either extorted or turned over to the
Gestapo for rewards.

Andrei's Aryan appearance and obvious physical prowess had
got him through six false-permit trips. How long he could evade
capture was a moot question.

He arrived at the central terminal on Jerusalem Boulevard and
walked directly toward Mila 19 to report to Alexander Brandel. He
had gone only a few blocks when he stopped and watched the surge
of humanity pouring into the Jewish quarantine areas. First they
had come from other parts of Warsaw, then from the surrounding
countryside. Now they were transported in from outside Poland.
Barbed-wire accordions were laid across dozens of streets and
placed under guard to define the quarantine districts.

A stream of miserable dazed human beings filled the streets
from the northern terminal for several blocks south. Iron wheels
on the cobblestones set up a din. Some of the wealthier of the new
arrivals had their belongings on horse-drawn wagons. Others had
their goods piled high on bicycle-driven porter carts, still others
on hand push-carts. Most carried their possessions wrapped up
in a single blanket slung over their backs.

Hawkers tried to sell them armbands, pots, pans, books—anything. Self-Help workers were trying to organize the chaos.

"Where are they from?" Andrei asked another onlooker.

"Belgium."

No matter how many times Andrei saw it, the sight disgusted
him. Anger churned him into a hot flush. He abruptly turned away
from the direction of Mila 19 and walked quickly to Leszno 92,
the headquarters of Simon Eden.

Leszno 92 had a line of refugees outside it that ran for a block. Volunteers were aiding in registration and working the soup kitchen for the new arrivals. He walked past the line. They became a blur of faces.

He entered the main room and was recognized immediately.

"I want to see Simon," he whispered to one of the girls behind the counter.

Because Simon Eden was the most powerful Zionist in Warsaw, he lived in semi-seclusion in the attic. Three buzzes would let him know a friend was coming up. A different signal would send him to the safety of the rooftops for hiding.

Andrei climbed the ladder into the attic. Simon pulled up the last step. They slapped each other on the back and went into his small garret quarters. It was wilting from the midday heat which had come through the roof and settled in the airless room. Andrei opened his shirt and took off his hat. Simon smiled as he saw that Andrei was still wearing his boots in symbolic defiance of the enemy.

Simon opened and closed a half dozen desk drawers until he discovered a half-filled bottle of vodka. He took a swig and passed it to Andrei.

"How was the trip?"

Andrei shrugged. "Good and bad."

"Did you see any of my people?"

"Krakow. The underground press is getting important. At least it keeps the people aware of German motives."

"What about the ghetto in Lodz?"

"I don't know if we can set up Self-Help houses there. This bastard Chaim Rumkowski is acting like a mad emperor. He walks around with a pair of German guards."

Simon grunted. Andrei relayed the rest of the events, city by city, and a pall of gloom as thick as the heat settled on them. Simon needed no expert to disseminate the news. His dark rugged features strained with the words of a uniformly worsening situation.

"What does Alex have to say about all this?"

"I haven't seen Alex yet," Andrei answered. "I came straight here from the terminal."

Simon looked at him curiously.

"What's on your mind, Andrei?"

"You were an officer in the army, Simon. We've been friends since I can remember. Out of everyone in this whole business, you and I think the most alike. When all this started I wanted to cross the border and get arms. Alex talked me out of it. I've gone along with everything, but . . . after this last trip . . . Simon, we've got to start hitting back."

Simon took another nip of vodka from the bottle and scratched

181

his unshaven jaw. "Not a day passes by that my stomach doesn't turn over. It is all I can do to keep from exploding."

"If I go to Alex he'll talk me out of starting a resistance movement. He can talk a leopard out of his spots. But if you and I went to him—you, speaking for Federated Zionists—and issued him an ultimatum, he'd have to start giving us some of the funds from American Aid to buy arms. We've got to do it now. Thompson is afraid the Germans are watching him. If they send him out of Poland, one of our chief sources to get dollars in is gone."

Simon Eden wiped the sweat from his forehead with his sleeve and walked to the tiny window which looked straight down for six stories. Hundreds of impoverished refugees lined up before Leszno 92 for a bowl of soup and a *Kennkarte* which would give them the "privilege" of joining slave labor.

"What about them down there?" Simon asked. "We are all they have."

"How long can you get slapped in the face without raising your hand!"

Simon spun around from the window. "What the hell can we do!"

"Kill the bastards! Make life hell for them!"

"Andrei! Denmark, Norway, Poland, France, Belgium, Holland! Will they give in to us? Twenty, thirty, a hundred to one in reprisal for every one we kill, and they'll murder women and babies and old men. Can you take that responsibility?"

"You're a damned fool, Simon, and Alex is a damned fool. Do you really think they will stop with ghettos and slave labor? They mean to wipe us off the face of the earth."

The two giants glared at each other, portraits of anger and frustration. Simon shook his head.

"One of these days we will be at the twelfth hour, and by God you'll know then there is no way but to fight our way out," Andrei said.

Andrei left Simon Eden in a huff. He did not go to Mila 19 to see Alexander. There would be hours of reports and bickering. Alterman and Susan and Rosy would listen to his monotonous repetitions of the fear of new ghettos, the continued murder of intellectuals, the slave-labor camps, the unbelievable abuses. And they would try to put up a new Self-Help house in Bialystok or Lemberg. They would try to print a one-page paper. They would put up a few bags of sand to hold back a rising, rampaging river.

Andrei walked fast for Gabriela's flat, trying to shut out the sight and the sound of the agony around him. Many people were becoming anonymous in Warsaw these days. Gabriela was one of them. It was an unwritten code that if you ignored a friend who recognized you in a public place it was understood.

182

Gabriela had moved from her flat to a smaller one on Shucha Street. Through Tommy Thompson she sent messages to her mother and sister that it would be dangerous for her if they were to communicate with her. She stopped her allowance from coming into Poland and took an inconspicuous job as a tutor in French and English in the small, exclusive school in the Ursuline Convent.

Andrei stopped before her flat on Shucha Street. Across the street stood Gestapo House. It was ironic, but he thought Gaby's flat was probably in the safest place in Warsaw. It was early. She would not be home yet. He dashed off a note and put it in her mailbox so she would not be startled.

Andrei threw off his cap and flopped into a big armchair and fought with himself to relax the burning pains of tension in his chest. It had been a terrible trip. He did not realize until this moment that he had not slept more than a few hours in three days. His eyes closed and he rolled his face into the sun's rays to catch its warmth, and he dozed quickly.

. . . The sound of footsteps brought him sharply awake. Gaby had read his note. She was running up the steps. The door to the flat flung open and closed quickly, and she set down her parcels of food and looked for him in the evening shadows. She curled up on his lap and lay her head on his chest, and they clung to each other with no sound except for her deep sighs and no movement except for her trembling.

She looked at him. His face was so drawn and tired. Day by day she watched the energy being sapped from him. After each trip he was drained. He was eating himself away inside.

Now, at this moment, she could transfuse life back into him. Andrei smiled with pleasure at the feel of her fingertips tracing the lines of his face and her lips brushing his eyes and ears and neck.

"It was very bad this time," he said. "I don't know how much longer I can take it."

"I'll take care of you, dear. . . ."

She unbuttoned his shirt and felt his chest and shoulders, and the knots of tension slowly melted away.

"I'll take care of you," she whispered.

"Gaby . . ."

"Yes, darling . . ."

"When you touch me like this it all seems to go far away. Why are you so good to me?"

"Shhh . . . shhh . . . rest, darling . . ."

"Gaby, when will they stop? What do they want from us?"

"Shhh . . . shhh . . . shhh."

Chapter Eighteen

Journal Entry

> Don't hide your gold ring, Mother,
> Your chances are quite nil,
> That if the Germans do not find it,
> Kleperman, the *goniff*, will.

That verse is attributed to Crazy Nathan, a half-wit who roams the ghetto making rhymes and some rather clairvoyant observations. No one knows where Crazy Nathan comes from, who his parents are, or even what his last name is. He wears filthy rags and sleeps in alleyways and cellars. Everyone looks upon him as a harmless goof and treats him with benevolent tolerance. Crazy Nathan shows up at the best cafés in the Jewish districts and, after a few new verses, earns his meal. He prefers fish so he can share it with the dozen or more alley cats who follow him. He has named his cats after the board members of the Jewish Civil Authority.

A.B.

Max Kleperman was a product of the slums. He learned at a tender age that it was easier to live off his fellow man than, God forbid, bend his back in honest labor.

By the age of five Max was a fast-hand artist. He could wander through the smelly, noisy trade in Parysowski Place and rifle wares off the pushcarts of the old bearded Jews with dazzling deftness. By the time he reached seven he was an expert in fencing his stolen goods.

While good Jewish sons like Andrei delivered chickens for their fathers and were robbed and beaten by hoodlums, naughty Jewish sons like Max Kleperman showed a natural aptitude as middlemen. He would purchase all stolen chickens and other goods from the hoodlums and resell them on the Parysowski open market at stunning markups.

By the age of fourteen he had been a guest of the Pawiak Prison three times. Once for theft. Once for extortion. Once for swindling.

By the age of sixteen he went to his natural habitat, to live in the Smocza area populated by the Jewish underworld of Warsaw.

At seventeen he was accepted as a full-fledged member of the Granada Night Club, the most notorious hangout for thugs and gangsters in Poland.

As Max grew older his varied talents expanded. He became the head of a gang of strong-arm men who muscled in on the building-trade area on Grzybowski Square. The square was lined with building-material shops, craftsmen, contractors, teamsters, ironworks, and brick shops. Plying his talent as a middleman with the help of husky friends, Max elbowed his way into the square until his "clearance" became standard for most normal operations. Only the opposition of the labor unions kept him from absolute czardom.

His hand was in every pie from blueprint to finished product. His little finger bore an eight-carat diamond and his cigar ashes dripped on half the building deals made in Warsaw.

Max was at home at the Granada Night Club or even with the *goyim* underworld in Solec, where he was respected; but strangely, he reached a point in life where he began to wonder what all his hard labor was for. He was, in fact, nothing but a bum.

Max Kleperman did not want to be a bum. He wanted to be as respectable as the "new rich" who promenaded on the Avenue of the Marshals on the Sabbath. He could not muscle himself into their affection, and this annoyed him. So he set about to purchase respectability. First the beautiful old mansion of a nobleman living in France. It did not help. His neighbors looked upon him as a social leper.

Max was determined. He hired an expensive lawyer with a three-word dictum, "Make me respectable."

The lawyer's first move was to buy a pair of seats in the Great Tlomatskie Synagogue. Max could parade in during the High Holy Days when the synagogue was filled to capaciy and uniformed police held back the mobs of onlookers who "ohed" and "ahed" at the elite.

Max was put on a program of philanthropy. He donated to the poor and he patted orphans on the head and sponsored scholarships for students who never did amount to much.

His work was so good that he was accepted into membership by a half dozen professional societies. Then followed a series of lavish parties.

Soon Max Kleperman was so respectable he fired his lawyer.

To consolidate his hard-won position, Max had to get rid of his ignorant wife, who was constantly a source of embarrassment. She was delighted with the settlement. Max then shopped around through the professional matchmakers for a nice homey girl from a good religious family.

One was found for him. Sonia Fischstein filled the bill. Her family was Orthodox, respectable, traditional, and acceptable to a settlement on their daughter. Rabbi Solomon was called in to negotiate the terms.

Rabbi Solomon saw right through Kleperman's fraud. Max was enraged at the rabbi's attitude. He even invited the notion of having him rubbed out. Then he learned that Rabbi Solomon was really respectable—in fact, the most respectable man in Jewish Warsaw. He set out to cultivate the great man.

Rabbi Solomon was not fooled. He considered everything. Max would never change, but his quest for respectability would keep him in check and there was some hope that a little of the decency he was exposing himself to would rub off on him. Besides, Sonia Fischstein was quickly running out of chances to marry. So he agreed to the match.

Rabbi Solomon became the earthly custodian of Kleperman's soul. Max realized under his puffy jowls that his one link with the Maker was through the rabbi.

When the Germans invaded Poland, Max was sad because no one liked Germans. However, he was a realistic man. His past made him perfect for the type of business that was flourishing— black market, smuggling, money exchanging. In fact, opportunities were never so great. Moreover, the Germans could be dealt with. Before the smoke of battle had cleared, Max Kleperman got in touch with Dr. Franz Koenig and impressed him that his organization would be indispensable to the Germans.

At that time, Dr. Koenig had the problem of opening brothels for German soldiers, a venture in which the Jewish Civil Authority had refused to co-operate. Eager to prove his own mettle to Rudolph Schreiker, Dr. Koenig gave Max his first assignment, the rounding up of a hundred whores. Max had pimped in his younger days but not since he became respectable. Nevertheless, his contacts in the Solec were still active and he came through for Koenig in two days.

Dr. Koenig knew he had a real ally.

With a license to operate, Max Kleperman gathered around him the most immoral gang of chiselers in Warsaw. His tentacles spread everywhere.

When the Germans introduced slave labor, Max had at long last broken his enemy, the labor unions. He grabbed firm control of the building-trade industry and from there poached on dozens of legitimate businesses. With the strong arm of the Germans behind him, it became realistic to do business with Max and his partners.

The main windfall was the sale of protection. If a father or son was picked up off the street in a German roundup and taken to the slave-labor camps outside Warsaw, Kleperman could arrange a release for a price.

It was in this area that he posed as a benefactor of the people. When they came to him for a release of a relative, Max treated them with great sympathy, all the while appraising them for how much he could shake them down. He would tell them it took a lot of money to make a fix with the Germans. There is honor among thieves. Max refused compensation until he arranged the release.

Dr. Koenig, Sieghold Stutze, and Rudolph Schreiker had also hit a windfall in kickbacks.

Max's interests became so large that he and his six minor partners leased a building on the corner of Pawia and Lubeckiego streets, opposite the Pawiak Prison, to direct their enterprises. The organization became known as the Big Seven.

When the Germans ordered registration of Jewish property, Dr. Franz Koenig became custodian of all Jewish-owned dwellings in Warsaw. The Big Seven became the agent for Koenig.

During the quarantine directives, Jews had to move from all parts of Warsaw into the new restricted area. Eighty thousand Christians who lived in the quarantine area were to be replaced by a hundred fifty thousand incoming Jews. In the two weeks of the move, with a quarter of a million people suddenly upheaved, the Big Seven made a killing.

Amid the frantic turmoil and the endless streams of wagons and pushcarts, there was a frenzied scramble to find living quarters for a hundred fifty thousand people in an area designed to hold eighty thousand.

Property was at a premium for the Jews. As agent for Koenig's office, Kleperman was able to rent and sell at astronomical figures, even "doing a favor" to those wealthy enough to afford it.

Property values again jumped when the mass deportation of Jews from occupied countries into Poland began.

Dr. Franz Koenig and the other German heads preferred to deal with the Big Seven mostly because of the language barrier that existed with the Poles. Most Jews spoke Yiddish.

Toward the end of the summer of 1940, Max Kleperman was summoned to the city hall to the office of Dr. Franz Koenig. When he was ushered into the office he was surprised to find Rudolph Schreiker and Oberführer Alfred Funk there also. Max did not mind doing business with Koenig, but he did not like Schreiker and he knew that when Funk was in Warsaw trouble was brewing, for Funk carried the messages from Berlin. No matter how decent Max was to Schreiker, Schreiker always bullied him around. Kleperman had made a large donation to the German Winter Relief, yet this did not placate Schreiker.

Max betrayed his nervousness by incessantly squeezing his cigar. He deftly slipped the eight-carat diamond into a vest pocket lest it end up in German Winter Relief.

He had never met Funk before. Funk was arrogant. Max could see immediately the disdain Funk held for him.

Max's upper lip dampened with perspiration, and ashes dropped on his trousers.

Rudolph Schreiker opened a map of Warsaw on a conference table. Max mopped his brow and studied it. A heavy black grease-pencil line was drawn encircling the areas which the Germans had placed under quarantine. Much of it followed the route of the barbed-wire rolls in "epidemic" streets.

"I have studied the past several weeks Warsaw and I am aghast," Alfred Funk said. "You Jews have been guilty of the most blatant infractions of our regulations. We have notified the Jewish Civil Authority that the Jews are fined three million zlotys and they must collect it within a week."

Kleperman nodded and squeezed his cigar.

"As you know, you are a filthy people," Funk continued. "We cannot seem to do anything about your sanitation habits. Typhus is reaching epidemic proportions despite our delousing operations. Therefore, for the protection of the people of Warsaw, and in order to further segregate you dirty Jews, we have decided to build this enclosure around the quarantine areas."

Max dared not take his eyes off the map.

"General Funk is willing to consider having an outside building group construct the enclosure. I suggest the Big Seven, provided your bid is in order," Dr. Koenig said.

Max was able to pick up all the meanings of Koenig's statement. Kickbacks down the line for the Germans. A continuance of the pattern of forcing the Jews to carry out German directives and thereby justifying the German claim that "Jews were doing this to Jews."

Max had an infamously gained knowledge of construction. He clamped the cigar in his teeth, and his fat finger ran down the lines marked by the Germans.

"What type of an enclosure do you have in mind?"

"A brick wall, ten feet high. Triple strands of barbed wire on top."

Max licked his dry lips. The line ran for eleven or twelve miles, more or less. He jotted down a page of figures to approximate the number of bricks, miles of barbed wire, mortar needed.

"About labor costs?"

"The Jewish Civil Authority will recruit three battalions of labor."

Good, Max thought. Slave labor. They worked for rations. He went back to work on his figures. With slave labor, inferior materials, salvaged brick, he could bring it well under the fine of three million zlotys with a huge profit for himself.

"With the price of the zloty," Max whined. "It was five to one—now it is a hundred to one and still climbing."

"Don't steal so much and it may go down," Rudolph Schreiker snapped.

Max toyed with the figures and looked from one to the other. "I am sure I can come up with a satisfactory figure," he said.

"Yes, I am sure you will," Funk agreed.

In ancient days Jewish slave labor built monuments to Egyptian glory. Now we build one to German glory. We pay for it with a fine. We watch it happen with a strange fascination. A lot of people are relieved that the ghetto is coming. Safety in numbers. Well, we've got numbers. The population has swelled to over a half million and they are still pouring in.

Each morning labor battalions are formed in various parts of the quarantine area. They split into a dozen or more smaller groups, all working in different places.

A row of bricks here . . . a row of bricks there. Two rows, three rows. It seems aimless, without a plan. Now and then two groups connect.

The Krakow Gazette has stepped up its tirades on page four with the campaign about the uncleanliness of Jews, asserting that we "sub-humans" must be segregated.

The wall grows higher. Two feet, three feet, four. It follows a weird, unexplainable course. From the slums of Stawki Street and Parysowski Place, which is crammed with refugees, it follows south along the Jewish cemetery and stops at the fashionable Sienna Street, running there to Wielka Street, north again.

The wall is shutting off the Saxony Gardens and the Great Tlomatskie Synagogue. We are even denied the squalid Krasinski Gardens. I do not believe there will be a single tree in the ghetto.

For eleven crooked, reasonless miles. Who planned this? In some places the wall cuts right down the middle of the street, putting half of the houses in the ghetto and half outside. On Leszno Street it slices right through the middle of the courthouse. Chlodna Street is a finger of land on the Aryan side, splitting the ghetto into two parts. The big ghetto is on the north. A smaller ghetto is to the south, and this holds the elite-members of the Civil Authority, Militia, wealthy, German and Austrian deportees. A bridge covered with barbed wire crosses Chlodna Street, connecting the two ghettos. It has been named the "Polish corridor."

Seven, eight, nine, ten feet. The wall is connected in all parts. Tens of thousands of jagged pieces of glass have been cemented on top to rip off the hand of anyone who tries to scale it. A triple strand of barbed wire is on top of the glass.

There are thirteen gates. Never has that unfortunate number had a more sinister use. There are guards at each gate. A few of the Reinhard Corps bossing the unarmed Polish Blue Police. There is a rumor that a Jewish police force will be formed inside the ghetto.

Irony. One Catholic church on Leszno has been included in the ghetto. The Catholics have put it to work. Franciscan Father Jakub has been sent in to take care of Jewish converts who are forced to live as Jews now but still carry on Catholic ritual.

Statistics? The ghetto is a thousand acres, or one hundred square blocks, or fifteen hundred buildings. Any way you cut it, it's pretty rough to find places for a half million people.

On November 7, 1940, the Big Seven had completed the wall and the ghetto was declared. In a fell swoop tens of thousands who were working at jobs outside the quarantine area were jobless.

Sieghold Stutze's Reinhard Corps had the task of ghetto security. True to early rumor, a Jewish Militia was formed. On paper it was under the direction of the Jewish Civil Authority, a guise in keeping with the German policy of trying to create the illusion that the Jews were imposing this upon each other. Stutze was the ruler of the Jewish Militia.

He chose as his chief a former sub-warden of the Pawiak Prison named Piotr Warsinski, who had a long-time reputation of brutality to prisoners, especially Jewish prisoners.

Piotr Warsinski was squat, bald, and sported an immense mustache. A tormented youth filled with fear of a brutal father had left him impotent and seething with hatred. Warsinski blamed his demented soul on being a Jew. He converted. Conversion left him with an unreasonable hatred of Judaism. Now the Germans forced him to be a Jew again and it intensified his hate.

Warsinski gathered about him the dregs of Jewish society. Men and women with limited mentality, criminal records, without conscience. They were given truncheons, special armbands, blue caps, and they were issued black boots, the symbol of power. They were given preferential rations and quarters for themselves and their families.

There was one condition. Warsinski made it utterly clear that their personal survival depended upon complete obedience.

As 1940 closed, a half million people in the Warsaw ghetto formed the largest human stockyard the world had ever known. They were at the complete mercy of the greatest military power ever experienced by man. The Germans had craftily carried out their master plan by forcing Jew to rule Jew through the impotent Jewish Civil Authority backed by the potent Jewish Militia under the sadist Warsinski. To augment their problems, the Big Seven continued their legalized swindles.

All that was left to protect this swell of humanity was a thin line of Zionists, Socialists, and the Orphans and Self-Help Society with American Aid.

Chapter Nineteen

I think that Susan Geller will die of a broken heart. The Germans have ordered her to abandon our orphanage (and pride and joy) in Powazki and move inside the ghetto. Their directives order Susan to leave all equipment attached to the floors and walls, and that constitutes some of our most expensive things. Even the Orphans and Self-Help Society has a hard time renting property these days. Space is at a premium. We were able to find Susan a building on Niska Street, which she must completely convert. It is hardly comparable to the place in Powazki.

Thank the Lord for my dear wife Sylvia and for Deborah Bronski. Between the two of them, they kept Susan from a breakdown on moving day. It is so strange how different Deborah and Paul Bronski are. Yesterday I had to argue for three solid hours to convince Paul Bronski to petition the Germans to allow us to keep our farm in Wework running. You never know how the Germans will react. Paul just phoned me that the farm will be allowed to operate. Tolek Alterman will be overjoyed.

I am sending my son Wolf out to the farm in Wework. It will be good for him out there.

We have received our first group of Dutch Jews. The trip to Poland was very hard. They were jammed in cattle cars. Where can we put them? I don't know. The ghetto has over five hundred fifty thousand people in it now.

Mila 19 has been divided up by the Bathyran Council. On the first floor we have the ghetto administrative offices of the Orphans and Self-Help. We have a soup kitchen that can be entered from the back alley (Orphans and Self-Help now runs sixty soup kitchens), and we have a dispensary for minor ailments and a delousing shed as demanded by our German friends.

Second story. Bathyran families. Our rule is one family to a single room, regardless of the size of the family. The kitchen for the entire house is also on the second floor.

Twenty-one families . . . sixty-two occupants, including Sylvia, me, and baby Moses (now that Wolf is gone).

Third floor. Walls have been broken through. Our dormitory for single girls. We have thirty. Divided right down the middle; fifteen work in the dispensary and soup kitchen and fifteen are hired out as domestics in the small ghetto on the southern end. I cheat by supplying our domestics with green armbands denoting a Self-Help employee in order to allow them to move about unmolested by Warsinski's overeager Jewish Militia.

Fourth floor. Fifty of our boys have a dormitory. Twenty of them work in Mila 19. Thirty work at various jobs around the ghetto, mostly as bicycle porters and riksha drivers.

The problem is shaping up. Of our eighty "kids," most have left families to live with us in the communal. How many members of their families can we take in—the aged, the ill? This is going to become serious.

In the attic we have cut up a dozen cubicles for the married couples. They are living on the second floor, mostly more than two to a room, so they must have a place where they can duck off for a few hours to have privacy. There are pre-set signals on the doors to advise whether the cubicles are in use or not. Sylvia and I are fortunate. With Wolf gone and the baby still an infant, we manage very well in our room.

The unmarried who wish privacy have to work it out for themselves. We neither officially encourage nor discourage it. Off the record, the unmarried know that the basement is available to them.

Irony. David Zemba, who wins more and more respect from me all the time went in to see Schreiker and demanded that American Aid be allowed to open an office in the ghetto. So he gets it. The dollars he receives from American Jews are our main support, but we can't keep up with the flood of refugees, mass fines, and confiscations.

Dr. Glazer says the typhus death rate is becoming alarming. Pneumonia, TB, and malnutrition will be critical problems.

We are able to get passes in and out of the ghetto with relative ease. We know the situation won't last long, so we are lining up people in the Jewish Civil Authority and the Jewish Militia who control passes who can be bribed in the future.

Orphans and Self-Help with American Aid money has taken over another important function, running all the Labor Zionist farms and ours at Wework. We have managed to open two more farms and we can also buy food and transfer through this farm system. The over-all operation is called Toporol.

A straw in the wind? Perhaps, I don't know. For all the astute planning for which the Germans are famous, they are pulling an enormous blunder. In the ghetto we have thousands of building-trade people, craftsmen, tailors, engineers, etc. If used properly, these people would be of tremendous value to the German war effort. There is no rhyme or reason for the way people are slapped into slave-labor battalions. Carpenters are sent to the Brushmaker's factory, doctors are set to digging ditches and building airfields (for an attack on Russia?), and this inconsistency draws me to two conclusions.

1. The Germans are not quite certain why they are herding Jews into Poland.

2. A "final solution" of their "Jewish problem" has not been decided.

ALEXANDER BRANDEL

In the winter of 1940 and the spring of 1941 Wolf Brandel worked on Toporol Farm 2 situated northeast of Warsaw, near the village of Wework.

Each time the produce and milk were taken in to the ghetto the farm workers sent letters in to their loved ones. Wolf wrote to his mother and father and Stephan Bronski, who looked up to him very much. And he wrote to Rachael Bronski.

Dear Rachael,

It is sure different out here on the farm. Like in another world away from the ghetto. There are seventeen girls and thirty of us fellows. I'm one of the youngest. We live in dormitories (separate, boys and girls).

Tolek Alterman, who has been to Palestine, keeps us hustling. He gives us a continual lecture about living Zionism almost every night and we have slogans posted everywhere about keeping production up and getting milk and fresh vegetables in to the children in the orphanage.

We work very hard. I'm milking cows. I'm lousy at it. I like everything, including Tolek. He needs a haircut, however.

Would you write to me? Your mother can give your letters to Susan Geller and they will reach me. Also, please have Stephan write.

> *Your sincere friend,*
> WOLF BRANDEL

Dear Wolf,

It was nice to hear from you. I will write to you regularly. Stephan studies you know what and you know where and he is getting good at it. He misses you. He admires you greatly. I am very happy for you being out of here—if you know what I mean.

> *With fondest regards,*
> RACHAEL BRONSKI

Dear Rachael,

I'm milking better. However, the real important work in the winter is the hogs and I've asked to be transferred. Whatever you do, don't tell anyone we are raising hogs. The rabbis would raise h— if they knew, but with meat so scarce, we must. I'm certain that God will let the kids at the orphanage into heaven, anyhow.

At night it is swell here. We have a kind of game room. We have a community meeting to talk about production, farm problems, and division of work. Then a lecture by Tolek. Afterward we can debate, hear music, study and read and play games. (I'm chess champion.)

Almost always before bedtime we start up a song fest and sing the songs that the Bathyran pioneers sing in Palestine and we dance horas.

We don't even have to wear the Star of David unless we go to the village.

Please write.

Most sincerely,
WOLF BRANDEL

Dear Wolf,

It sounds nice on the farm and I'm glad for you. Winter here has been—well, you can imagine. Momma says things are very bad at the orphanage. We have 100% too many children and 50% too little rations and medicine. That is why your job is important. I suppose you hear about the things happening in the ghetto. I don't want to write you about them, you'll worry.

Fondly,
RACHAEL BRONSKI

Dear Rachael,

Hey, guess what! I am learning to play the accordion and the guitar. Tolek Alterman is teaching me. He knows all the Palestine pioneer songs, as he has been there. I'd like to teach them to you.

Warmest personal regards and kind wishes and thoughts,
WOLF

Dear Wolf,

I would indeed like to learn your songs. But when? When will I ever see you? I mean, Stephan misses you.

I am busy with my music too. I play recitals all the time and quite a few concerts. Sometimes eight or nine a week. I have learned about fifty children's songs and singing games (also in French and German) so I can go around to all the orphanages and entertain them.

Do you dance with the girls? I think I am envious.

Very fondly,
RACHAEL

Dear Rachael,

We are celebrating Succoth in memory of Moses and the ancient tribes in the wilderness and giving thanks for the first fruits of the harvest.

You lived in Zoliborz before the war and they don't allow celebrations now, but ask your mother about how Succoth used to be. Almost all the upper balconies and courtyards in Jewish homes had little "succah" huts built of branches and twigs and leaves to commemorate the way the Jews lived during their wandering.

Out here we have constructed a giant "succah" and it is covered with hundreds of fruits and vegetables and we have all our meals under it. Don't worry, we are sending all the food in to the orphanage just as soon as the holiday is over.

To answer your question candidly—I do dance with girls. However, I play the accordion most of the time for them while they dance.

Most sincerely,
WOLF

Dear Wolf,

Hanukkah has passed. The holidays in the ghetto were terribly gloomy. Everyone spoke of the old days when the Tlomatskie Synagogue was jammed with people in fancy dress and there was an air of gaiety everywhere. Now we can't even see the Tlomatskie Synagogue. Hanukkah seems almost like a mockery. Silly, celebrating the Maccabees storming into Jerusalem, throwing out the tyrants and rebuilding the Temple, when we are cowered in a ghetto.

I think the worse of all was Yom Kippur, earlier. We were all sitting and meditating and atoning for our past sins. The stillness this year was horrible. There was no breath of movement anywhere. Everyone was really asking God what we have done so terrible as to deserve this punishment.

Sorry to be so glum.

RACHAEL

Dear Rachael,

I worry about things in the ghetto all the time. Tolek keeps telling us we are front-line soldiers and how important the farm is. I try to make myself believe him.

I think about you often.

With affection,
WOLF

Dear Wolf,

I think about you, too, but I guess you're really not too lonesome with all those girls out there. If you know what I mean.

Also, with affection,
RACHAEL

Dear Rachael,

I will be frank with you.

I have had offers (not exactly offers) to kiss and play around, but I am not interested. Most of the girls like to neck. I think one or two even will do more (so it is rumored).

I don't know how you will take this, but I miss you more all the time. I didn't think I would, but I do. This sounds awful, but I think mostly about those four different times we kissed and held

195

each other. You'll probably stop writing to me and I won't blame you.

WOLF

Dear Wolf,

You didn't write anything bad at all. I wish you were here right now so I could kiss you.

With deepest affection,
RACHAEL

Dear Rachael,

I sure don't know why anyone would want to kiss me. Especially someone like you, so beautiful. I never said it, but I have always thought so. You are very beautiful.

I look at your picture every chance I get and memorize your letters. The once or twice they didn't come I was pretty miserable.

Candidly speaking, I am pretty certain I am in love with you.

Love,
WOLF

Dear Wolf,

I am not certain what love is, so I can't be sure. I do know that—I have a funny feeling inside me when I think about you and that is almost all the time. I know, too, that it hurts me to be apart. I didn't know anything could be so painful. I cry at night sometimes. That's because I'm a girl, I guess.

Isn't it curious? I liked you very, very much before you left (I wouldn't want you to think I'd kiss a boy I didn't like very, very much), but since you've been away I guess it must be love or something very close to it.

RACHAEL

Dearest Rachael,

If two people feel the same way about each other and are forced to be apart and nothing was decided upon before they parted, then they find they miss each other more and more all the time, I think an understanding could be reached.

I would like you to be my girl, candidly speaking. I promise I won't have another girl or fool around until I see you. I wouldn't impose the same conditions on you except to ask you to promise you will let me know immediately if you feel seriously inclined toward anyone else. Then, when we see each other, we can decide how we really feel.

WOLF

Dearest Wolf,

I think your idea is wonderful, but you can be sure that I am not and won't be interested in anyone else. The thought of any other boy than you touching me makes me shudder.

Love,
Your girl,
RACHAEL

A great deal of that calm and witty shrewdness that was the mark of Dr. Paul Bronski's personality had vanished. It seemed as though he was worried all the time. At home he was often irritable and many times he snapped at the children for trifles. Deborah tried hard to compensate by comforting him, but Paul's burdens were running ahead of her powers to transmit sympathy. As the deputy under the chairman, Boris Presser, Paul had to carry out the German directives, deal directly with both Piotr Warsinski as well as the Orphans and Self-Help Society, and was often the scapegoat for all sides. He got little or no support from Boris Presser, who was a complete robot of conformity.

Deborah waited several days after she and Rachael had had their confidential talk in order to find Paul in a proper restful mood. As they prepared for bed one night, Paul had let it be known by the innuendoes married couples develop that he desired sex. Deborah, as always, prepared to comply. It was in that moment that he seemed a little relaxed as he sat in the big chair near the bed and sipped tea and watched her put up her hair as she sat before the mirror.

As he looked at her he thought it amazing how she managed to keep herself so beautiful. Deborah worked eight, ten, twelve, and often fourteen hours in the orphanage on Niska Street. She had kept up Stephan's studies and Rachael's piano and she had been a good and comforting wife. There was not a line in her face, no gray in her hair, no telltale sagging of her body.

Perhaps there was envy on the part of Paul. Once Deborah had been retiring and obedient and passive. Now she seemed the stronger of the two. Paul resented his growing need for her.

Deborah twisted the long black strands of hair into tight curls on her forehead and deftly darted pins into them to hold them in place. Then she picked up the hairbrush and went into her nightly stroking exercise.

"Paul, dear."

"Yes?"

"I have been thinking that, with both of us gone a good part of the day and conditions as they are, wouldn't it be nice if Rachael were able to get away for a change of scenery? I could take Stephan along with me to the orphanage. There are dozens of boys his own age and he enjoys it there. . . ."

Bronski furrowed his brow. "It would be nice if all of us got a change of scenery. What about your plans for Rachael to debut with the symphony? Besides, this is so much nonsense. There is no place she could go but to another ghetto."

She watched him in the mirror out of the corner of her eye. "We could send her to the Toporol farm in Wework."

He put his cup down. "Wework? The damned place is just a front for Zionists. The whole place is staffed by former Bathyrans."

"But it's healthy and there are girls her age and she will have a chance to look at trees and flowers and something other than misery."

"You know the morals of these Zionist children."

"No, I don't," snapped Deborah.

"They're very loose."

"Has it occurred to you that Rachael is nearly as old as I was when I met you?"

Bronski paled at the verbal slap. Then his eyes narrowed. "Just a minute. Isn't that where the Brandel boy is?"

"Yes. And before you say another word, I think he is a fine young man who would be overly aware of not violating her. Besides, it's something that they will have to work out for themselves whether we like it or not."

"My, listen to the voice of modern sophistication. Have you become a free-love advocate? Are you going to spend the rest of your life throwing up to me your debauching?"

"Paul, she happens to be in love with the boy. Lord only knows they have little or no chance for a normal life, and I cannot see that it is a sin for her to want to be near him."

He stood up abruptly. "There are other considerations. The Toporol farms are open only on a technicality. We have no guarantee the Germans won't take a notion to raid them and ship everyone off to labor. If she is caught out there, I won't be able to help her."

Deborah lay down the hairbrush and spun about on the vanity bench. "Is there a guarantee they won't come in here in the next ten minutes and haul us away? Living itself is a plain and simple day-to-day risk."

The issue was clear. Paul would continue to retrench, to play it close, cautious. Deborah was willing to let her daughter take the risk to pursue a normal, healthy impulse.

Compromise, Paul, compromise! Caution! She had done everything but call him a coward.

He paced the floor, then spurred into one of his more frequent tantrums. "Dammit! There are nearly six hundred thousand people in this ghetto! I have to find place for four thousand new families by the end of the week! There is no space! People are sleeping in courtyards, alleyways, basements, attics, warehouses, hallways!"

"I don't see what one has to do with the other."

"Everything has to do with everything! I'm sick and tired of being chastised by my own wife for trying to protect my family. Isn't it enough that I let Stephan keep on with this whim of yours to study with Rabbi Solomon? He barely escaped with his life once. Do you know one of those children caught was shot? It could have been your own son. I am still the head of this family, and that girl is not going to Wework!"

She nodded and turned and picked up the brush again and stroked her hair. More and more she saw him going down. So long as Mrs. Bronski, wife of the JCA deputy chairman, works in an orphanage and so long as his daughter plays in morale-building concerts and the status is not besmirched, that was all that really mattered. The words never left her lips. She wanted to cry that there had to be an end to the price he was willing to pay for his skin—but she merely stroked her hair and said, "Yes, Paul."

Chapter Twenty

Journal Entry

Wolf wants to come home. I don't know why. I thought he would be happy on the farm. Tolek says he is one of the best people out there. What could it be?

The brief marriage of convenience between Germany and the Soviet Union has been abruptly annulled. Russia was attacked last week (June 21, 1941). This year's casualties have been Greece, Yugoslavia, Crete, and North Africa. Rumania and Bulgaria have declared war against the allies. (What allies?) The news reports that Britain is getting a fearful bombing by the Luftwaffe. London is catching it even worse than Warsaw did. Hard to believe.

The prospects of four to six million Jews in the Soviet Union in the path of Germany's unchecked onslaught is a terrifying prospect.

ALEXANDER BRANDEL

Old Rabbi Solomon entered the headquarters of the Big Seven on the corner of Pawia and Lubeckiego streets opposite the prison. Many of the sleazy characters around the anteroom were accomplished rabbi baiters. They stared at the old man. He carried a holy dignity in his stature, almost as though he had a mystic power to invoke God's wrath.

"Anounce me to Max Kleperman," he ordered sternly.

"Ah, my rabbi," beamed Max. "My own holy rabbi," he cooed

to the personal guardian of his soul. Max rushed from behind his desk and pulled the old man in by the elbow, shoved him in a chair, and raced to the door and shouted, "I am with my rabbi. I am not to be disturbed for anyone. Not for a fire—not even for Dr. Franz Koenig!"

He winked to relay his fearlessness. Rabbi Solomon let him play out the role. "What can I get you? Maybe a chocolate. Hershey's from America—or coffee, Swiss Nestlé's, personal stock."

"Nothing at all."

"You have received my food packages?"

Solomon nodded. Large bundles arrived each week with butter, cheese, eggs, bread, fruit, vegetables, meats, candies. They were promptly turned over to the Orphans and Self-Help Society.

The rabbi said he wouldn't mind if Max smoked in his presence, so Max went through the ritual of nipping the end of a cigar, coddling it, squeezing it, lighting it, puffing it, admiring its taste, pointing it. "Confidentially, I wanted to speak to you, Rabbi. You have been forgetful. This business of teaching Talmud Torah after you were caught twice, and then the Passover seder you conducted in prison yet. Your last trip to Pawiak Prison cost me sixty thousand zlotys in gifts to the German Winter Relief. They take winter relief in the middle of the summer, those *goniffs*."

The old man did not dignify Max with an answer. It seemed as though lightning shot out from his eyes, and his white beard fairly bristled in anger.

"Rabbi, can't you take a joke? You know Max Kleperman stands behind you."

"I should like Max Kleperman to stand beside me. The situation in the ghetto is degenerating. The plight of the street urchins anguishes me. Many of them are starving. Without families, they will turn into wild animals."

"It is terrible, terrible, terrible," Max agreed, his forefinger fishing around up his nose. "Confidentially, Rabbi, I and my partners are bringing a few things into the ghetto to alleviate the situation. For this I ask no thanks, mind you. And my sweet wife Sonia, God love her soul, spends every day working in an Orphans and Self-Help soup kitchen."

Rabbi Solomon's bony hand slammed down on the desk top. "Stop this mockery, man! You have not seen your wife for two months, and in that time you have lived with eight different prostitutes."

"So, I have a few minor weaknesses! You are supposed to tend to my spiritual needs, Rabbi. . . . Only yesterday two of my men were shot at the wall of Muranowski Place trying to bring flour into the ghetto for food for babies."

"I am certain you will arrange appropriate funerals, and when their funeral vans return to the ghetto they will be filled with black-market food which you will sell at a thousand-per-cent profit."

"Shut up, old man!" Max raged suddenly.

"Smuggler, liar, thief!"

Max raised a bulky paperweight. His veins popped from his neck. He grew purple. He would not tolerate such talk from anyone but the Germans. No, not even from Piotr Warsinski. He had warned Warsinski that if the Jewish Militia touched any Big Seven business he would personally break his skull like an eggshell. Warsinski knew Max was not kidding. Why take these insults from this bearded old bastard! Crack his head in! What was this strange power the old man held over him? What was this fear of the beyond Max had?

He slid into his chair and wilted.

"Do you think our God is so shallow in His wisdom that He does not detect your scheme to bribe your way into heaven through me?"

"Rabbi," Max whined, "you don't understand the fundamentals of business matters. Business is business."

He avoided Rabbi Solomon's eyes, mumbling about how misunderstood he was. Suddenly his hand turned the desk key and he withdrew an iron box and opened the lid. Sweat rolled down his face as he dipped his fat hand into the till and peeled off a large number of American dollars.

"Give this to the sick in the name of Max Kleperman!"

"You dare bribe me with this pittance?"

"Pittance! These are American dollars. Two hundred zlotys apiece!"

Rabbi Solomon stroked his beard thoughtfully as he looked at the money. Max watched him, praying that he would pick it up.

Which was the wiser of the decisions? Leave the money and leave Max to fry in hell for eternity? Or take back some of what Max stole? After all, nothing could make the man change his ways, and this could do so much for so many children.

"Is there enough here to open up an orphanage to take a hundred children off the streets and feed them?"

"An entire orphanage? My partners ... the price of the zloty ..."

Max's cigar billowed with the fury of a locomotive.

"It would do much to alleviate some of the unpleasant talk about you and the Big Seven. An orphanage named for Max and Sonia Kleperman."

Max had to think about that. It would look good. He would again become a benefactor of the people. Besides, his new smuggling operations were reaping a fortune. "How much would it cost?" he asked with caution.

"Two thousand dollars a month."

Max slammed his hand on the table. "Done."

"That is, two thousand a month, taking it for granted that the Big Seven will supply food and medicine."

"But—but—but——"

"But what?"

"But of course."

"Now, if you'll be so good as to make a lease assigning one of the properties you manage, I shall make arrangements with Alexander Brandel."

"My own property!"

"I think the house at Nowolipki 10 will be the most suitable."

"Nowolipki 10! Rabbi, you're a worse *goniff* than Dr. Koenig!"

Max Kleperman whined through all the tortures of losing one of his most formidable properties. He, personally, would have to kick back the lease money to Franz Koenig from his own pocket.

Goddamned little orphan bastards! Goddamned old rabbi bastard! God shook you down worse than the Germans did, Max thought.

Rabbi Solomon snatched the money and the papers from Max Kleperman's desk, stuffed them into a big pocket in his long black frock, and asked the good Lord to please forgive his dubious methods.

Alexander Brandel shook his head in disbelief.

"How in the name of God did you manage to shake Max Kleperman down for this property?"

"You're right. It was the name of God."

Alex grunted at the irony. He tied the muffler around his neck as though he had a chill, even though it was the middle of summer and the room was like a furnace. No one, including Alex, seemed to know why he wore the muffler.

"It is a miracle," Alex said. "A hundred children. We will find room there for two hundred—it is a miracle."

"God works miracles, Alex. Believe a little more in him and a little less in Zionism."

Alex put the papers and money in the desk. He had not seen Rabbi Solomon since the *bris* of Moses. The old man seemed in fine fettle. He commented upon it.

"I am kept alive by the Almighty so that I may carry my share of today's burdens," the rabbi answered.

But Alex did not look so good. Rabbi Solomon said nothing. Alex had always been a bit untidy. He was seedy now. He did appear as good as a man could be expected to on three or four or a luxurious six hours' sleep a night. He sat behind that desk day and night, bargaining, pleading, juggling lives, juggling *Kennkarten* and rations, juggling medicine. Fencing with the crushing pressures from all sides. Debating for hours on end with Paul Bronski to wheedle an extra gram on the rations.

"Why have you done this, Rabbi? I came to you once and asked you to help us unify and you refused."

"I do not question the word of God. I merely follow his instructions."

"Are you saying you have done this out of divine revelation?"

"I say that I find nothing in the Torah or the Holy Laws which commands me not to help starving children. It is hard for me to walk in the streets and see them these days. I studied the situation for many hours and I searched my soul as well as the word of the Law. I conclude that self-help has always been a God-meant key to Jewish survival. For some strange reason God has picked a *goy* like you and a *goniff* like Max Kleperman as his instruments of self-help. Mind you, I still do not subscribe to these radical theories of Zionism and physical resistance."

As usual, Alex thought, Rabbi Solomon has all the answers. Perhaps he has an answer that has been nagging at me for weeks now. For a long time Alexander longed to show someone his journal. He desired a concurrent opinion that his notes and hours of work at it really had some significance. He knew that Simon Eden and David Zemba had been more or less indulgent of a former historian. Time and again he was tempted to take someone into his confidence. But whom? Rabbi Solomon? Beneath that crustiness lay a shrewd and brilliant mind. One thing was certain——the man could be trusted. Alex started to clear his throat for the proclamation.

"Alex. Already, what is on your mind? You are like a little boy with a secret. *Nu?*"

Alex smiled and walked to the door and bolted it. He went to the big floor safe behind his desk, dialed the combination, and pulled the heavy iron doors open and took out three volumes of thick notebooks wrapped in a large canvas cloth and placed them before the old man.

"*Nu?*" said Solomon, putting on his thick glasses. "What is the great mystery?" He bent his face down so that his nose nearly touched the page to give vision to his semi-blind eyes. "Alex, you are a *goy*. You even write in Polish."

"You will find some in Yiddish, some in Hebrew."

"Hummm—let me see. Let me see what is so important. 'August 1939. This is the first entry in my journal. I cannot help but feel that war will begin in a few weeks. If the lessons of the past three years are any barometer, something awesome is apt to happen if Germany makes a successful invasion. . . .'" He looked up quickly to Alex and back to the books, and only his mouth moved, forming the words as he read more rapidly.

Rabbi Solomon seemed spellbound as he turned page after page. It was all there. From the first declaration of Alexander Brandel's intuition of a unique event to the daily record from the moment of occupation. There were limericks by Crazy Nathan, gossip, German directives, his personal diary, events of the world outside, ghetto poems, songs, poetry. The names and number of Yiddish theatrical productions. The recording of the sudden departure of friends. The constant groping for an answer.

At the end of the first hour, when he had closed the initial volume of the journal, Rabbi Solomon knew he had read a remarkable history of his people going through another siege of Rome and Greece and Babylon.

His eyes stung and were watery, but he quickly opened the second volume and thumbed through page after page with pulsating wonder.

Then he stopped.

"Who knows about this?" he asked in a hush.

"Eden. Zemba. Emanuel Goldman, before his murder."

The rabbi was on his feet. "When have you had time?"

"At night, in my room."

"Amazing! Your intuition of a holocaust. Your wisdom in putting it all down on paper before the events occurred."

Alex shrugged. "Time and again Jews have written secret histories from intuition."

"Intuition? I wonder. The Lord works in His own ways. Moses was a *goy*, like you. Alex, you must not leave this about. Not even in the safe. Hide it."

"Rabbi, I have never seen you so excited. Are you certain of its importance?"

"Certain! This will sear the souls of men for centuries to come. This journal is a brand that is to be stamped on the German conscience so that a hundred of their unborn generations will have to live with these words with guilt and shame!"

Alex sighed and nodded with contentment. He knew now that all those hours through the night when he had been drugged from lack of sleep and forced his hand to write out another line had not been in vain.

"May God forgive me for saying this, Alex, but that journal is like a new chapter of the 'Valley of Tears Chronicle.' "

Journal Entry

Rabbi Solomon has an infectious enthusiasm for the journal and he has paid me the most magnificent of compliments. He calls it a new chapter in the "Valley of Tears Chronicle!" (The "Valley of Tears" lists fifteen centuries of Jewish martyrdom, particularly detailing the massacres and suffering of the Jews under the Crusaders during the Middle Ages. The lifework of Rabbi Yosef Hacohen was discovered by Rabbi Eibeschutz in 1850 and translated and has become a part of our lore, prayer, and tradition.)

Rabbi Solomon insists I expand the journals and that it should be hidden more carefully and even duplicated in case of the destruction or German discovery of the original. Such precautions! He and I have gone to the basement of Mila 19 and made a hiding place by moving bricks. I think it is nonsense, but so long as it pleases him . . .

We have formed a secret society of contributors. We call ourselves the Good Fellowship Club. Simon Eden and David Zemba are left over from the original contributors.

All of the executive council of the Bathyrans (except Andrei Androfski) are members of the Good Fellowship Club; i.e., Susan Geller, Ervin Rosenblum, Tolek Alterman, and Ana Grinspan.

Other members:
Silberberg, the former playwright, who is on the Jewish Civil Authority and our closest ally there.

Rodel, Communist leader in the ghetto. He has been in semi-hiding since the occupation but has been valuable in both children's aid and contacts on the Aryan side.

Dr. Glazer, chief of medical staff of Orphans and Self-Help.

Rabbi Solomon, of course.

Father Jakub, priest of the Convert's Church. I have known him since 1930. He is one of the few who has had a long record of sympathetic understanding toward us. (Incidentally, Orphans and Self-Help does not have much to do with converts. The converts and half Jews fare much better than most in the ghetto. It seems as though the Catholic Church is determined to take care of "their" Jews.)

From time to time we will vote in new members to the Good Fellowship Club.

Ervin Rosenblum, who still works on the Aryan side and has less demands on his time than we do, has agreed to spend his spare time classifying and cataloguing the information now pouring in.

Rabbi Solomon is making duplicate copies of the first three volumes (in Yiddish and Hebrew only). In the Jewish tradition, special scribes write all our Torah scrolls by hand. That is why they have been so accurate for millennia. Seeing Rabbi Solomon copying the journal reminds me of that.

It is thrilling to see this come alive and the belief that the work is important.

I must admonish everyone to write more neatly, especially Father Jakub.

ALEXANDER BRANDEL

## Chapter Twenty-one

"Rachael."

"Wolf!"

They stood facing each other in the hallway outside the main recreation room of the new Max and Sonia Kleperman Orphanage on Nowolipki Street. Children swirled around them before herding nurses who clapped their hands sternly.

"Wolf, this is such a surprise, seeing you."

"I didn't know I was going to be able to come in. I didn't have any time to write."

"How did you find out where I was?"

"Stephan told me. I was with him all morning. I've been here for an hour. I was watching you give the recital from out here. You were very good."

"Why didn't you come in?"

"I don't know. I got to watching you singing and playing and watching the kids all laughing . . . "

The hallway suddenly became empty. It was shadowy and hard for them to see each other, and they were wordless as the impact of the sudden meeting lessened.

"It's nice to see you again," Wolf said.

"Will you be here long?"

"That depends. I don't know."

Wolf looked about and grunted. "Could we take a walk or something? Here, let me hold your music."

"All right."

Wolf tried to think. There was no place to walk in the ghetto, nor bench to sit upon, nor nightingale to hear. There was only misery and beggars and stone and brick without a leaf of grass or the green of a tree.

"I'd like to sit and talk someplace," Wolf said.

"So would I. We have so much to talk about."

"Where can we go?"

"If we go to my place Stephan won't leave you alone. Then Momma and Daddy will come home and Daddy would make you play chess."

"Sure can't go to Mila 19. The minute we walked in the door there'd be all kinds of gossip. Besides, there's no place there to be alone."

"We can't stand here."

"I'd sure like to talk to you."

"We could try Uncle Andrei's place. I stop there often to talk to him. Most of the time he isn't there and his door is never locked."

"Boy! If he caught me there with you he'd break my neck."

206

"Oh no. Uncle Andrei's bark is much worse than his bite."

"Well . . . all right."

They did not see each other on the entire walk to Andrei's. Wolf's eyes were cast down, looking at the pavement, and Rachael had learned to walk through the streets looking dead ahead to shut out the terrible things happening on all sides. The beggar children were more pathetic every day, and in the last week corpses of starved persons were beginning to appear in the gutters.

Suddenly they found themselves all alone in Andrei's flat. Wolf turned on the light over the table in the center of the room while Rachael caught her breath from the climb up the stairs.

Now they could see each other. Wolf had changed. His elongated, gangly body had filled out and his white, blemished skin was unblemished and deepened to a tan from working in the wind and the sun, and the scraggly hair on his chin had turned to a hard beard which could legitimately be shaved every other day and the shaky voice was now a steady baritone.

Rachael had changed too. She had been more like a girl before. Now she was much different. Round and soft, like her mother. Her eyes were filled with sadness and weariness.

Wolf suddenly turned his back and scratched his head. "Heck! This isn't the way I figured it would be," he blurted.

"It's very strange, isn't it? Almost as if we were just meeting each other for the first time."

Wolf sagged into a chair, disappointed at his own weak performance. How many nights he lay awake at the farm thinking about this very moment when he would see Rachael again and simply sweep her off her feet. Now both of them seemed like strangers to each other and both wondered about all the passion and promises they had written.

"Wolf, you're disappointed."

"Just at myself. Candidly speaking, I'm not one for fancy talking." He stood up slowly, towering over her. "I have missed you," he managed to say. Rachael leaned against him slightly and he put his arm around her shoulders. Her arms found their way about him and she began to tremble, and as they held each other close the terrible uneasiness inside them ebbed. Wolf audibly gulped and sighed with relief. They searched each other out and kissed and then they were both calm.

Rachael and Wolf stood before the window, watching darkness come. They looked down on the street, and from this height they could see beyond the wall into the "Polish corridor" which separated the big and little ghetto and they could see the dome of the forbidden Tlomatskie Synagogue. His arm was about her waist and her head was on his shoulder.

"This is wonderful," Rachael said.

"It sure is."

"You have become terribly handsome and mannish."

Wolf shrugged. "Rachael, I meant all the things I wrote to you."

"So did I. I know that now." She pulled away from him. "Wolf . . ."

"What?"

"Would you answer one thing, honestly?"

"Sure."

"Did you have any girls on the farm?"

"Heck! What kind of a stupid question is that?"

"I think I'm a terribly jealous kind," Rachael answered.

"I'm sure not much to be jealous about."

"You didn't answer me."

"I messed around a little." Then he added quickly, "But that was before we made promises."

"Messed around?"

"You know, messed around."

"More than . . . kissing?"

Wolf patted his flat chest to demonstrate. "Messed around."

"Oh."

"Before we made promises."

"Did you do any other things?"

"Rachael . . ."

"I think I should know everything before we can be certain of our relationship. What else have you done?"

"Rachael, I'm a boy and boys are different, and if I tell you you're liable to get very mad."

"I'm sixteen, almost seventeen. I've been a woman for several years. I know about these things—I mean, Momma and I have had long talks about growing up."

Wolf was flustered. Rachael was adamant.

"Wolf . . ."

"What?"

"Have you ever . . . done it?"

"You sure ask a lot of questions. This isn't something a man wants to discuss with his girl."

"If we are really sweethearts, the way we say we are, then there shouldn't be any secrets."

"I tried it once," Wolf croaked. "Even before I went to the farm. It was on my birthday. My sixteenth—almost two years ago. You don't want to hear about it."

"Yes, I do."

"Well, I was with three of my pals. One of them was older—he was nineteen—and he knew a woman in Solec. One of those kind of women."

"What kind?"

"Who does it for money."

208

"Oh . . . one of *those* kind."

"So, anyhow, it was my birthday and all that and we were at this guy's house and he snitched a bottle of vodka from his parents' liquor cabinet. I never drank before, except a sip now and then. I got to laughing and couldn't stop. Then we started talking about . . . things, and he said he knew this woman in Solec. Next thing you know, it was a date and I was feeling pretty good."

"And you went there?"

Wolf nodded.

"And you did?"

"Well, it wasn't so hot. I got scared as hell and I didn't know what to do. Boy, I'll bet you hate me now."

"No. I admire your honesty. Now I know that you will always be honest with me."

"You're not mad?"

"Momma explained that certain things are very normal for boys—that is, men. And she says I should not suppress my emotions and feelings too much because that can lead to frustration."

"She's sure smart."

"Sometimes I think she says it to me because she's frustrated. I can feel that she hasn't been too happy with Daddy."

"That's too bad. My folks are happy. Poppa doesn't seem to need it too much because he works all the time, but I know he and Momma are happy. Rachael, you sure are understanding."

"Wolf . . . do you ever think about us . . . doing it?"

"Yes . . . I never would try or force my attention on you or ever do anything to hurt you. But it's not my fault that I can't help thinking about it. It's supposed to be a sin to think about it, but I can't help it."

"I think about it too," she whispered.

"I . . . didn't know that girls thought about it. The way boys do."

"Yes . . . the same way. All the time you were away I began to wonder if I would see you again. And I knew that if there wasn't a war and a ghetto and the awful things that are happening, I would grow up a little slower, like we're supposed to. And we could play coquette like girls are supposed to. But this fear hanging over us all the time . . . Waking up in the middle of the night when the whistles are blowing outside during roundups and walking the streets when their sirens blow and the loudspeakers shout . . . Now, those little children dying in the streets—it all made me change. I'm terribly aggressive, aren't I?"

"I think you are the most wonderful person who ever lived."

Rachael threw her arms about Wolf and clutched him desperately. "I love you in a different way than Momma loves Daddy. She is trying to tell me. Wolf, I don't want to die unhappy like Momma!"

This kiss was different from all others, for in the instant of its impact they reached manhood and womanhood, and they wanted each other and there was neither restraint nor control. Her eyes closed and her cheeks were damp with the wonderful feel of him and her teeth found his shoulders and her hands clawed at his back and his fingers fumbled for the buttons on her blouse. . . .

The door slammed!

They looked in terror at Andrei across the room. He took two, three menacing steps toward them.

"You little son of a bitch," he hissed.

Wolf stepped in front of Rachael, and she buried her face against his back and wept.

Andrei looked from one to the other, the fury twitching his face.

"Get out of the room, Rachael," Wolf said softly.

"He'll kill you!" Rachael cried.

Andrei stopped. Wolf Brandel abusing my niece. But look. It is not Wolf any longer. A tall, strong young man waiting like a fool for me to tear him apart. And Rachael . . . Strange. Not until this moment did I realize that she is a woman. Wolf Brandel. I diapered him when he was a baby. Has he ever been anything but a fine person? God, Andrei! What is the matter with you? These two love each other!

Andrei relaxed.

"In the future," he said, "if you leave your armbands in the mail-box I'll know you are up here and won't disturb you. And for God's sake, lock the door."

Chapter Twenty-two

The next day Wolf Brandel returned to Andrei's flat.

"I want you to know," he said to Andrei, "that I am not messing around with Rachael. I feel more deeply for her than I've ever felt for anyone. I love her. I'm sure not much, but she feels that way about me too."

Andrei nodded. "I thought about it. I believe you." He poured himself a short drink of vodka. "Do you drink this stuff?"

"I had it a few times at the farm. I don't care too much for it. I want you to know that—well, how much we appreciate your confidence. There's hardly a place where two people can be alone in the ghetto."

"It was a shock, all of a sudden seeing someone you thought as a little girl in the arms of someone you thought of as a little boy. Under normal conditions things would have happened more slowly. One has to grow up quickly these days, there is no choice."

"Andrei, I don't really want to do anything to her."

"I appreciate your good intentions, but they will become lost in the heat of the moment one day. Just be as gentle as you can and make her be careful."

Wolf blushed violently. "I think I'll try a little vodka." He sipped and made a face as it burned its way to his stomach. "I wanted to see you about something else too. I'm not going back to the farm."

"Oh? Tolek Alterman tells me you are his best worker. I am certain he can arrange for you to come in once a week with the milk so you can see her."

"That's not really why."

"What is it?"

"Life is easy out there. I think I ought to be doing more."

"Don't be so noble."

"I'm not noble. It would be easier if you left Warsaw, but you stay."

"Look, Wolf. Be happy your father is in a position to put you on the farm."

"That's just my point. I'm getting preferential treatment because I'm Alexander Brandel's son. That's not right. I talked to Momma and Poppa last night after I took Rachael home. I told them I wasn't going back."

"How did they take it?"

"Momma cried. Poppa argued. You know how he can argue. Between him and Tolek Alterman I've heard enough Zionist logic to last for six lifetimes. Anyhow, I may not look it, but I can be stubborn. When Poppa knew I wasn't going back he began to blame himself for not being a good father and not spending more time with me. He always does that. So, the baby started screaming and all four of us were going at once. Then later we sat in his office, just the two of us. We don't do that too often. He's convinced that I'm right by wanting to stay. He told me to come to see you. You would have work for me."

"Did he say what kind of work?"

"No. But I know that you must be mixed up in important things. I want to be a runner."

"What makes you think you can be a runner?"

"Well, I don't look too Jewish."

"We use women as runners, Wolf."

"I can do the job as well as a woman."

"You said you don't look Jewish. I say you do. Know what would happen if you got picked up? They'd march you to Gestapo House on Shucha Street and unbutton your pants. Your father put you in a covenant with God when he had you circumcised so that God would recognize you as a Jew. Only trouble is that the Germans use that for recognition too."

The thought did not appeal to Wolf.

211

Andrei looked the boy over. Eighteen. Tall, strong. Smart—smart as a whip. The shyness was a decoy. Wolf Brandel had mastered his studies as a brilliant scholar. Ideals. Wonderful. So many people without them, these days. Taking the hard road to satisfy an inner desire to do right. A good soldier in any army.

"Come on, let's take a walk, son."

They walked down Leszno Street past the Converts' Church and the huge new complex of houses forming a factory to make and repair German army uniforms. "A Franz Koenig Enterprise," the big sign said. Koenig also had part ownership of the woodwork factory in the little ghetto and of the huge Brushmaker's complex at the extreme northern end. Dr. Koenig had become a millionaire.

They waited on the corner until a red and yellow streetcar came along and hopped on the back of it. Its sides and tops showed large Stars of David. The Ghetto lines were operated by the Big Seven.

At Smocza and Gensia, Andrei got off. Wolf walked alongside him until they reached the wall that ran down the middle of Okopowa Street. He was filled with the adventure of it all. They walked up the street to the middle of the block. Over the wall was the Jewish cemetery. This was a neighbourhood for a lot of smuggling. People could hide in the cemetery with black-market goods. In this area the wall was heavily guarded. Andrei stopped at the old abandoned Workman's Theater. Before the war it had been one of the showplaces of the vital Yiddish stage. Now the lobby had been converted into yet another soup kitchen. The rest, empty.

Down the alleyway to the stage door. Andrei looked about quickly, thrust the door open, and shoved Wolf inside. They were on the stage. It took a moment to adjust their eyes to the darkness and their noses to the musty smell. Andrei whispered to be careful of cables and obstacles. The house was ghostlike. The hard-back seats in a state of disrepair. A faded backdrop of a Polish gentry's garden hung behind them.

Andrei listened. He could make out very dim sounds from the soup kitchen. He tiptoed to the light cage and threw a switch. Wolf was entranced. Nothing lit up. Some sort of signal, he was certain.

Above them a trap door opened. Andrei scooted up it quickly, the boy behind him. They were in a large loft. The trap closed after them.

"Ladies and gentlemen," Andrei said, "you all know our newest worker."

Wolf's mouth hung open in awe. There were four people present, all former Bathyrans who lived at Mila 19. Adam Blumenfeld was at a radio receiver with earphones on. "Hello, Welvel," he greeted the boy by his nickname.

Pinchas Silver worked at a box of hand-set print. Beside the small press were copies of the underground paper, *Liberty*. Pinchas smiled and welcomed Wolf in. A forgery table and camera were in one corner.

The Farber sisters, Mira and Minna, were there, studying to become runners.

"Any news?"

Adam Blumenfeld took one earphone off. "I've got BBC. Something about American destroyers being loaned to England."

"How about the Home Army?" Andrei asked in reference to the quickly growing Polish underground force.

"They keep changing frequencies. Unless we can get their schedule, we can only pick them up hit or miss."

Andrei grunted. His most urgent job now was to set up a solid liaison with the Home Army, but he had been unsuccessful. He turned to Wolf. "Two lessons. First, live with access to the top floor. In danger, we go to the rooftops. Second, this work is neither romantic nor exciting. It is dull and exacting."

For the next few weeks Wolf learned to stand radio watch and work the printing press. Then Andrei made him memorize the entire Jewish Militia and know which police would "play" for bribes and how much. One by one he learned the secret rooms behind bakeries, in abandoned synagogue basements, where Simon Eden and Rodel, the Communist, and the small nucleus of the underground carried on their sub rosa business.

His prime duty: to distribute the copies of *Liberty*. Dump them in the market places, drop them at secret rooms, post them on conspicuous walls. As Andrei had warned, it was exacting and tedious work. The streets were more dangerous to travel each day. Piotr Warsinski's police were pulling people in by the hundreds for the continued feeding of the slave-labor factories.

Dr. Franz Koenig took a quick trip to Berlin to be received by Himmler, personally, and brought back with him a contract for a great portion of the German army's brushes. The Brushmaker's complex in the north had to be tripled. When there were no people on the streets, Warsinski ordered indiscriminate raids on homes or the bulging refugee compounds for workers.

Wolf accepted his duties without protest. He envied the Farber sisters. Blonde and blue-eyed, they fitted the bill as "Aryans." Learning the paths of a runner was only a small part of the training.

They had to learn the Catholic Bible forward and backward, how to pray in Latin, how to pray with the rosary. They had to learn to go deaf to the sounds of Yiddish and German, the languages with which they had been raised, in order to "prove" they were not Jewish.

There was one more regular who worked in the loft of the Work-

213

man's Theater, and that was Berchek, a former commercial artist. From time to time "Aryan" *Kennkarten*, travel papers, and even passports were obtained. These had to be doctored for use by underground members. Berchek taught Wolf the principles of forgery and allowed him to work on the simpler tasks of fixing photographs on the papers.

Andrei was terribly proud of his protégé. The boy learned quickly and responded to orders without question. In one or two tight spots while distributing *Liberty*, he kept himself out of trouble by quick thinking.

When Wolf went off duty he spent part of the time at home with his parents and his baby brother at Mila 19. Some of the time was with his "adopted" brother, Stephan Bronski. He taught the younger boy his Hebrew and tutored him in basic subjects and played chess and answered a thousand searching questions.

And two or three nights a week he would meet Rachael in Andrei's flat.

Each time they met, they brought their relationship one step closer to culmination. Each time they chastised themselves and groped and damned. They wanted to try it, desperately. First Wolf, then Rachael took turns in being the stronger to resist. Each time they parted, they parted heartsick but eager for the next rendezvous.

The thought of seeing each other kept them alive. It was able to make them somewhat oblivious of the horror around them. More and more terrible things were happening. So long as there was that electric second when he ran up the final flight of steps into her arms, the rest did not matter so much.

Journal Entry

Last night the Good Fellowship Club met to discuss the latest disaster.

Yesterday morning twenty-five Reinhard Corps Nazis, under the personal direction of Sieghold Stutze, entered the ghetto at the Zelazna Gate. Their barracks are directly outside the wall, so there is little or no warning. They proceeded directly to Nowolipki 24 and surrounded the house. Fifty-three occupants—men, women, and children—were pulled out and loaded aboard two army trucks.

As they drove off, the Jewish Militia posted signs all over the building that it was "contaminated by typhus, rodents, etc. . . . ."

The fifty-three were taken to the Jewish cemetery. On the north wall they were forced to dig a huge ditch, undress, and stand on its edge. They were shot in the back and, after they fell into the ditches, were bayoneted.

The Militia entered the Nowolipki property and carted off every single belonging.

214

We have had mass executions at the cemetery before. Usually a group accused of "criminal" activities or intellectuals. Never have fifty-three people been indiscriminately lopped off without excuse.

Although the property was "condemned as contaminated," I was able to lease it this morning as an orphans' home. Now I hear that the Germans are going to do a series of legal explanations of their actions to "justify" the executions. "Fear of epidemic" is their main reason as well as the catchall phrase "criminal activities."

We in the Good Fellowship Club are rather certain this mass execution was a test case.

Other distressing signs. A further ration cut was ordered this morning. Dr. Glazer says this puts us below starvation level. This means that anyone obtaining enough food to live is a "criminal," according to Nazi logic. Who figures these things out for them?

It is in the Soviet Union where the real terror is going on. More and more word comes back about special SS "Action Kommandos" massacring Jews all over the Baltics, White Russia, and the Ukraine just as quickly as the German army presses forward.

We heard something about a plan to send all the Jews to the island of Madagascar. (It might be a vacation.)

Hans Frank has lost his battle, once and for all. Not only are Jews still pouring into the General Government Area, but criminals, homosexuals, gypsies, "Slavic types," political prisoners, prostitutes, and others deemed as "sub-human." So, the General Government Area has become the "cesspool" for Germany's non-Aryans. Several huge new concentration camps are under construction. One in particular, Auschwitz in Silesia, I hear, is mammoth.

The Good Fellowship Club reasons that this transporting of Jews and "sub-humans" is a burden on the rail system, especially for the Germany army on the Russian front. It is taking tens of thousands of their manpower also.

Conclusion: The Germans have reached their decision for a "final solution" for us. *I fear further executions until they reach the desired level for slave labor.*

The phone interrupted Alex.

"Hello, Alexander Brandel, here."

"Alex. *Shalom aleichem,*" a voice on the other end said. It was a greeting from a contact named Romek on the other side of the wall.

"*Shalom,*" Alex answered.

"Alex, I hope you didn't forget we have a lunch date."

"Ach, what a stoop I am. I forgot to mark it down."

"Yetta's house at two o'clock."

"Good, good, I'll be there."

Alex quickly locked the volume of the journal in the safe and went upstairs to his room. Wolf was playing with baby Moses on the floor.

"Son," Alex said, "get Andrei at once. Wanda has arrived from

Krakow with a package. Tell him to send one of the Farber girls to the Old Town Square. He'll understand. Time is important. Wanda will pass at two o'clock."

When Wolf arrived at the loft over the Workman's Theater, only Adam Blumenfeld was there on radio watch.

"Where is everyone? A runner is in from Krakow."

"Lord," Blumenfeld grunted. "She wasn't expected till tomorrow. Andrei, the Farber sisters, and Berchek are all on the Aryan side. Pinchas Silver can't go. Get back to your father and tell him right away. He'll know what to do."

Alex drummed his fingers on the desk top, trying to think. It was one o'clock. Only an hour to the pickup. It was so unexpected that all four of the Bathyran runners were on the other side.

Think, dammit, think, Alex said to himself.

His usual unalterable calm became thready. Eight to ten thousand dollars were in the package. Nice, wonderful, untraceable dollars from Thompson at the American Embassy.

He looked at the phone. Call up Romek over the wall. No, that would be breaking the cardinal rule. Never phone a contact on the Aryan side under any circumstances.

What if Wanda saw there was no contact? They had completely lost one package like that.

Alex lifted the phone and dialed the Orphans and Self-Help Division at Leszno 92, Simon Eden's headquarters and asked to speak to Atlas.

In several moments Simon Eden was on the phone.

"Atlas, here."

"Brandel."

"Yes?"

"I got an invitation from Romek to be at Yetta's house for lunch at two o'clock. I simply can't get away from my desk. Could you keep it for me?"

"That's less than an hour. Hold on a moment and I'll see if I can rearrange my appointments."

Three more precious minutes ticked off. It was twelve after one.

"Alex."

"Yes!"

"Can't do it. Impossible."

Alex put the receiver on the hook slowly. Lost! The package is lost! He looked up slowly and saw his son at the edge of the desk.

"I'll go, Poppa."

"No."

"I've got false papers and I've been in training——"

"I said no!"

"Poppa . . ."

"It's damned well bad enough I let you talk me into this business of leaving the farm. It has nearly killed your mother."

"I swear," the boy said softly, "I'll never talk to you again."
Wolf turned and walked toward the door and unbolted it.

"Wolf, for God's sake, don't ask me to——" He knew his boy.
Gentle but stubborn. Even more stubborn than Andrei. Alex
steadied himself. "All right. Leave everything identifying you on
the desk. Take only your false papers. Time is running short.
You'll have to go out of one of the three northern gates—there
should be a guard 'playing' at one of them." Alex opened a drawer.
"Here, twelve hundred zlotys, mixed notes. That will get you in
and out of the ghetto. Go to the Madam Curie Museum in the Old
Town Square. Buy some blue violets on the way and wrap them in
a newspaper. Wanda is Rebecca Eisen. You know her."

"Anything else?"

"If . . . anything happens . . . you are not Wolf Brandel."

"Don't worry, Poppa. Nothing will happen."

"Son, we haven't spent enough time together—now, all of a
sudden——"

"Poppa, you mean so much to so many people. I've always been
very proud of you."

Wolf walked briskly for the closest gate at Dzika and Stawki
streets, only a few blocks from Mila 19. He made a false run past
the gate to study the Jewish militiamen on guard. He did not
recognize any of the three, so it was certain they did not know
who he was.

He walked to the man of highest rank and snapped out his
Kennkarte. The guard unfolded the three-part document and deftly
palmed the folded hundred-zloty note. The guard studied the
document. It was obviously a false paper, for it was not marked
with a *J.* A clue that this was underground work or smuggling.
He'd try for more.

"My old mother is very sick," the guard said.

"She should see a doctor," Wolf answered, slipping the man
another hundred zlotys.

A windfall. "What time are you coming back?"

Bastard wants more, Wolf thought. "Few hours."

"Too bad. I won't be on duty. Try my cousin Handelstein at the
Gensia Gate. Tell him you spoke to Kasnovitch."

"Thanks," Wolf said.

Fifty zlotys on the other side of the gate took care of the Polish
Blue Police.

Wolf walked rapidly for the Old Town Square. Time was running out.

For several weeks the Gestapo had been watching the movements of Tommy Thompson at the American Embassy in Krakow.
They knew his sympathies and were relatively certain he was passing money and information to the Jews. The Gestapo allowed

217

him to continue, in the hope that they could trail his contacts successfully and break up the ring at the Warsaw end.

Recently Thompson started a new activity. The Home Army, a large Polish underground, was forming and growing quickly and he had been working with them. This was a more serious matter. He was earmarked to be thrown out of Poland shortly.

The Gestapo decided to make an arrest of the next runner who left Thompson. From the moment that Thompson passed a package of eight thousand dollars to Wanda, the Bathyran runner, they were on her.

Trained and alert, Wanda became suspicious when there had been a dragnet at the Warsaw railroad terminal and she was allowed to pass through the inspection far too easily, her fake papers not scrutinized and her package unchallenged.

She entered the Old Town Square with the intuition she was being tailed. The square was not badly crowded—only thirty or forty people. Yet it was impossible to spot a stake-out because the quadrangle of five-story buildings could have hidden a hundred pairs of searching eyes. She entered on purpose from the corner opposite the Madam Curie Museum and walked cater-corner over the cobblestones. From the corner of her eye she glanced at the partly bombed-out museum. A lanky young man leaned against the wall. She came closer, still moving diagonally, calculated to pass him at a distance of some twenty or thirty meters in order to study him.

Click-click-click went her heels on the cobblestones.

Blue violets wrapped in newspaper. She shot a glance upward. It was Wolf Brandel. Smart boy, Wanda thought. He sees that I am going to pass him by.

Now Wanda had put a block and a half of open space behind her. If she was being tailed they would have to show themselves in the vast square or face the danger of losing her. She wanted to look back but dared not. She could not make her contact with Wolf until she was certain.

Wanda spotted a grate next to a sewer hole. Perfect! She walked over the grate and intentionally jammed her high heel into it so it would stick. She knelt down to free herself and in doing so stole a look behind her. Two men stopped dead in their tracks halfway over the square.

Trap!

Wolf was watching her closely. He saw the men trailing her. He saw her quickly throw the package into the sewer, pull her heel loose, and walk from the square. In a moment the place was flooded with Germans rounding everyone up. Wolf held fast.

"Violets for your mother, sonny?"

Wolf looked into the eyes of a pair of waiting Gestapo.

As a matter of standard operational procedure, any Jew caught on the Aryan side was personally interrogated at Gestapo House by the chief, Gunther Sauer.

A few moments after Rebecca Eisen, known as Wanda, disposed of her package of dollars she was arrested and the forty-two people in the Old Town Square were rounded up and hauled in for questioning. Four hidden Jews were found among them.

Gunther Sauer's appearance was deceptive. Pouchy, elderly, and of medium build, he owned an extraordinarily high forehead with a widow's peak of neat silver hair. His eyes were a bit puffy and half closed and his voice was gentle.

One would easily mistake him for a kindly grandfather instead of a Gestapo chief. He was, indeed, an adoring grandfather.

And Gunther Sauer loved animals. A bright-eyed dachshund named Fritzy sat beside his desk in a cushioned basket all the time. Sauer would break from his work at intervals and go into spasms of laughter when Fritzy performed for a tidbit.

He was, first and last, a policeman utterly devoted to his job, a master of his profession, and living in that world apart, as policemen often do. Sauer was a master at political terror, which became the prime job of the state police after the Nazis took power. The eradication of political and intellectual opposition was a dogma which had to be executed with ruthless objectivity.

He was also a master of the psychological warfare that one uses to break down the nerves and will of the opponent. Intellectuals were putty. Business competitors of the Nazis even easier. The intelligent application of fear could win the battle of a hundred armies.

Unlike many of his Gestapo compatriots, Gunther Sauer never used terror or torture for its own sake, but as a tool of the trade to gain an end. Torture did not always work on some people, nor did psychological fear tactics. In his estimation, it was a waste of time and energy to dismember someone who was not going to help you solve your "police" problem. Sauer abhorred the brutality of Sieghold Stutze, who received personal pleasure from inflicting pain.

One had to be completely objective about the victim. After a study of a person he could fairly well establish the limit of his moral endurance. He never used torture on prisoners who he knew would not break under torture.

On the other hand, he never hesitated when he spotted weakness. And it never annoyed him that he resorted to torture more often than not. Once or twice, early in his career, he had spent sleepless nights after torturing a child in front of its mother, but he learned to harden himself to it as part of a day's work.

Sauer interrogated the first three Jews. All of them were nervous and talky. The first was a smuggler who implied a bribe and friends in high office.

The second, a fool who had escaped from Lemberg, a vagrant.

The third, one of the many thousands of "hidden" Jews living as Christians in Warsaw on the Aryan side. This man gave such a garbled version to cover his tracks and contacts that he was most suspect as the contact for Rebecca Eisen.

Wolf Brandel was shoved into the office. Sauer was leaning over his desk, scratching Fritzy's chest. The dog whined and begged as Sauer teased the animal by opening and closing the drawer containing the box of tidbits. Fritzy won his prize, ran in a happy circle, then settled on the rug and crunched the hard biscuit.

Wolf snatched his cap from his head and stood at attention.

A quick appraisal. Eighteen or so. Not too Jewish in appearance. Strong, well fed, therefore resourceful. A perfect size and shape for a runner. He shifts from one foot to the other, nervously, but his eyes are innocent. He looks forward at me.

"Jew?"

"Yes, sir, I got caught."

"Name?"

"Hershel Edelman."

"Where are you from, Hershel?"

Watch his sweet talk, Wolf. They had the line on Sauer. Deceptive. He'll tie you in knots.

"I'm from Wolkowysk."

"How did you get to Warsaw?"

"My family was taken to the ghetto in Bialystok. I hid in the church during the roundup. After, I walked to Bialystok to look up a friend of my father outside the ghetto."

"What was the name of the church in which you hid?"

"St. Casimir's."

"What was the name of the priest?"

"I don't know, sir. He didn't know I was hiding there."

"Go on."

"So I saw this friend of my father. He used to do business with him."

"What is his name?"

"Wynotski."

"What's your father's business?"

"*Schoychet.*"

"I beg your pardon?"

"It's a man who kills chickens and cows so the meat will be kosher."

"Fritzy, bad boy. Now get in your bed and stay there. . . . But,

Hershel, you said Wynotski did business with your father. If Wynotski sold kosher meat, wouldn't he be in the ghetto?"

"No, sir. Wynotski has a gift shop. You see, sir, my father carved chessmen in his spare time and sold them to Wynotski. If you lived around Wolkowysk and Bialystok, you'd have heard about my father's chessmen."

"Go on."

"So, anyhow, Wynotski got me this Aryan *Kennkarte* and travel pass."

"I take it Wynotski is not Jewish."

"Half Jewish, I think. Anyhow, his house and gift shop was lousy with crucifixes and rosaries and Bibles and stuff like that."

"Where did Wynotski get the Aryan *Kennkarte?*"

"Most likely bought it from a family where someone died and it wasn't recorded. Anyhow, I didn't ask questions. I mean, sir, under the conditions, you just take it and don't ask questions."

Clever young man, Sauer thought. Either a magnificent fake or entirely honest.

"Continue," Sauer said.

"So, I came to Warsaw."

"Why?"

"Why not? It's the biggest city in Poland. I figured I'd have the best chance to stay hidden because I don't know anybody here and wouldn't get recognized."

"How long have you been here?"

"Three days."

"Where have you stayed?"

"I found a loose window in back of the men's room at the railroad station. Anyhow, it's like a storeroom for mops and buckets and stuff and I've been sleeping there."

"What were you doing standing in front of the Old Town Square statue?"

"The Madam Curie Museum," Wolf corrected. "Waiting for someone."

"Who?"

"Well, you can imagine. I've got to figure something out. I start prowling around. My money is running low and stuff. So, pretty soon you hear talk and stuff, and so I went to the Solec because they said you can get fixed up there for just about anything. I went to the Granada Club. Sure got tough guys in there, and I met this —well—whore."

Sauer was entranced.

"So, I find out she is Jewish. Selma is her name. I'm sure it is a fake name. So, anyhow, I'm cautious at first because I think she may be helping look for runaways like me, but it's kind of funny how two Jews can spot each other. So, Selma says she knows someone who can help me but for me not to come back to the Granada because the hoodlums in there are looking for hidden Jews and to meet her next day at the Old Town Square."

"What were you doing with violets?" Sauer snapped.

Wolf scratched his head and blushed. "This whore was sure nice to me, sir. I just wanted to buy her violets."

Sauer talked softly to Wolf for two hours. The questions were masked in huge traps. Every so often Wolf would whimper, "Sir, if you are trying to confuse me, you sure are succeeding. I'm getting mixed up trying to remember the honest truth."

That night Wolf Brandel spent alone in a cell. The screams of torture pierced his eardrums from down the hall.

Gunther Sauer, in his meticulous, grinding way, listened to wire playbacks of the interviews with the four Jews. He was oblivious of the cries of pain coming from Rebecca Eisen in the main interrogation room.

In the morning Sauer called Gestapo in Bialystok. In the afternoon they phoned him back. Yes, there was a gift shop run by a half Jew named Wynotski who had disappeared. There was record of a *schoychet* from Wolkowysk who was sent into the ghetto and who had a son who had escaped. Edelman was, in fact, famous for his hand-carved chessmen.

The whore in Solec? Untraceable. The moment the Nazis approached the Granada Club no one would know anything. Even their informers could not be counted upon. Whores had dozens of names. Selma could be Elma or Thelma.

The weeks of meticulous training were put to the acid test. Each of the underground assumed an identity of an actual person who could not be traced. The identities were taken from information supplied by Bathyran runners in other cities. Wolf Brandel's story had been carefully worked out for weeks before he was given the name of Hershel Edelman. The real Edelman was obviously masquerading as someone else, somewhere in Poland.

"Bring back Hershel Edelman," Sauer said.

The boy seemed no more frightened than a night at Gestapo House would demand. Sauer played for the one possible loophole. He opened his desk drawer and pulled out a chessboard and a set of chessmen.

"Sit down."

"Yes, sir."

"Black or white?"

"Your preference, sir."

"I have seen you defend yourself, Edelman. Now I should like to see your attack. Take the white."

"Sir," Wolf said haltingly. "Sir, this is very awkward. I mean, under the circumstances, I'm rather afraid to win."

"You had better win, young man."

Wolf did. In nine moves.

He was sent into the main interrogation room to sit alone on the single chair beneath the spotlight. There was nothing else in the room. Gunther Sauer had hit a dead end. His only choice was shock identification—or resort to torture. He was puzzled by the boy and not certain he would break down. Even if he did break down, he might have been telling the truth and could reveal nothing.

Sauer proceeded to the booth next to the interrogation room. There, through an arrangement of mirrors, he could watch the interrogation without being seen. Sensitive microphones piped sounds back to him, refined to pick up heartbeats.

"Bring in that woman," Sauer ordered.

He watched closely as Wolf sat fidgeting in the hard chair. All Wolf could think of now was to keep his mind on Rachael and keep thinking of her and keep saying to himself that she would be proud of him, no matter what happened.

The iron door creaked open.

Wolf looked toward it slowly. Two Gestapo men stood on either side of the figure of a woman, holding her up. They let her go. The woman staggered, then fell face first to the floor.

Wolf edged out of the chair toward her.

Sauer watched and listened. . . .

He knelt and rolled the woman over. It was Rebecca Eisen. Her face was bloated and distorted. One eye was locked tight, a multitude of colors, and blood gushed from her broken mouth and her torn fingernails. She quivered the other eye open. They recognized one another.

"Lady," Wolf said, "lady, are you alive? I wish I could do something for you, lady."

"Boy . . . boy . . . water . . . "

A small smile crossed Gunther Sauer's lips. If they were actors, they had played it to perfection. Hershel Edelman was obviously clean, but the story was so pat—so untraceable—the boy mystified him so. . . .

"What do you think, sir?" an assistant asked.

"They don't know each other," Sauer said. "On the other hand, they don't have to if he was actually a contact. The violets—I'm not sure of the violets."

"Shall we send a dog in there?"

"Let me think about it."

The Club Miami on Karmelicka Street inside the ghetto was the Jewish counterpart of the notorious Granada Club in the Solec as the center of smuggling, fencing, and prostitution. At the moment, members of Max Kleperman's Big Seven were the ruling gentry.

The Club Miami had a unique distinction as a "free trading

zone." All activities within the bounds of this unholy sanctuary were looked upon as "off the record." This confidence was respected even by the Germans. The Nazis realized that, as often as not, they too would need the facilities of a "free trading zone" and thus allowed the operation to exist. A half dozen rooms in back of the main bar were used to carry out transactions which were never taped, nor were the transactors followed or photographed. Unwritten law, gentlemen's agreement, honor among thieves.

Max Kleperman knew that something strange was afoot when he received a phone call from Rabbi Solomon to go to the Club Miami.

Max arrived, filled with eager anticipation of a huge deal. The bartender advised him his contact waited in one of the back rooms. He entered and closed the door. Andrei Androfski turned and faced him. Max's inevitable cigar smoke billowed around the room. Extraordinary for Androfski himself to come to him.

"One of our people has been picked up," Andrei said.

Max grunted in disappointment. From time to time the Zionists had come to him to arrange releases for those stupidly picked up by Piotr Warsinski for the labor battalions. Kleperman had made one big killing when Rodel, the Communist, was thrown into Pawiak. It may be a big one again, Max hoped. After all, Rabbi Solomon personally made the call and Androfski personally made the contact.

"Who?"

Andrei halted for a moment. "Wolf Brandel."

Max whistled. It was getting interesting. He polished his outlandish ring hastily on his vest.

"Where is he?"

"Gestapo House."

Max put his cigar down and shook his head. Work camps . . . easy to make a fix. Pay off a few shnook guards. Koenig's factories in the ghetto, a little harder. The money went right to Koenig and cost more. The Jewish Militia, hadn't found one yet who wouldn't go for two hundred zlotys. Pawiak Prison—difficult, but he always came through.

"Gestapo House," Max said. "Brandel's boy. I don't know."

Max calculated the pros and cons quickly. He could rat on the Brandel boy and endear himself to the Germans. It would be genuine proof of his honesty and sincerity. Question was, would they appreciate it? On the other hand, the Big Seven and the Orphans and Self-Help Society were doing more and more business with him all the time. He could lose a lot of face in the ghetto if word of a sellout got around. But . . . suppose he tried to get the Brandel boy out and failed or the Germans got wind of it. He'd be out on his ass, but good.

Max stood up quickly. "Leave me out of it. Hands off. I'll forget everything you said."

"Sit down, Max," Andrei said softly. "Max, that order of flour for the Orphans and Self-Help—just cancel it. We're opening up a new source."

Max slipped into his chair. "Damn you, Androfski, I went to a lot of trouble to ship that wheat in here. I brought in so goddamned much flour that half the bakeries on the Aryan side had to close."

"Just talking off the top of my head, Max, but forty or fifty of our own people think we can run the smuggling operation just as effectively."

The message was clear. The Brandel boy had to be freed at any price. Androfski was one of those bastards who didn't bluff. Max opened his wallet and took out his estimation pad and began to scratch figures down.

"It will cost plenty."

"We'll pay."

"I'll have to work in gold or dollars. We can only move through high-class people."

"I've only got zlotys," Andrei lied.

"So have I got zlotys. A warehouse full of them. They aren't worth the goddamn paper they're printed on. Gold or dollars, three thousand dollars."

"Three thousand dollars!"

"Your hearing is excellent."

Andrei's eyes watered in anger. He turned his back on Kleperman to conceal the rage inside him. Filthy stinking scum. Bargaining for a life as if it were a secondhand suit on the Parysowski market. Goddamned son of a bitch, Kleperman. Rachael's eyes. Day and night she waited in his flat. Could he look at Rachael's eyes again?

"It's a deal," he whispered.

"Let's have the details."

Andrei sat down opposite Max and held his face in his hands. "He got picked up in the Old Town Square carrying an Aryan *Kennkarte* made out for a fictitious Stanislaw Krasnodebski. He was sent out as a contact for a pickup from one of our girls from Krakow. Now the Germans hauled in forty, fifty people. Mass questioning. No doubt they've looked at his penis and know he's Jewish. We've got reason to believe several Jews were grabbed in the dragnet."

"One of my boys was taken in on the same roundup," Max said, and added ironically, "He isn't as lucky as Brandel. Doesn't have his friends."

"So, he goes on a story of being Hershel Edelman from Wolkowysk. If we're lucky, he hasn't been identified."

"He'll need more than luck with Sauer working him over. I'll find out what his status is. If he is under suspicion we can't touch him at Gestapo House. That will only endanger him. Sauer doesn't take bribes. Just hope the boy doesn't crack. We have to wait until he is transferred."

Andrei nodded. Max stood up.

"Max . . . I know the Big Seven can put us out of business, but if there's a double cross you'll get it first from me, personally."

Chapter Twenty-four

Eight days passed.

Rachael Bronski waited in her Uncle Andrei's flat twenty-four hours each day, resisting consolation, eating only enough to keep her alive.

Each time Andrei walked in and shook his head the shock recoiled through her like the jagged glass on the top of the wall. She kept her eyes open in vigil until she collapsed from exhaustion, and then only a few nightmare-filled hours' respite could be found.

She twitched and sweated on the bed and woke up with her heart thumping and the sweat pouring into her eyes, and Wolf would be standing there at the foot of the bed, gory and dismembered, and she would cry out the horror within her and then start her slow, zombie-like pacing of the room.

All of this silly war of morality I fought with him. All this modesty—all this fear . . . Wolf was locked up in that terrible place. I have sent him to his grave, unloved. I have sent him to his grave, unloved. If Andrei comes through the door and tells me Wolf is dead, then I must die too.

Rachael developed a superhuman sharpness for sound. From four flights up she could hear the door of the lobby open and close. Each time it did she would walk to the door of the flat and lean against it and begin to count footsteps.

It took sixty steps to get to Andrei's flat.

She would count. Sometimes the sound of footsteps would stop on the first landing or the second or third. She could tell if they were climbing stairs or walking in a corridor.

She could tell if their sound was taking someone up or down.

The ninth day.

She washed her face with cold water and fixed her hair and sat by the window. The door opened and closed in the lobby. Rachael listened and began her count.

. . . ten . . . eleven . . . twelve . . .

The footsteps had reached the first landing.

. . . sixteen . . . seventeen . . . eighteen . . .

She was able to distinguish between footsteps as they rose higher. The flat, weary shuffle was a man. The sharp sound was a woman's heels. The soft sound, the child.

. . . thirty-three . . . thirty-four . . . thirty-five . . .

Two men! Two men walking up slowly. Everyone walked slowly these days.

. . . forty-three . . . forty-four . . . forty-five . . .

Her heart began to race. Two men on the third-floor landing. Oh God! Please don't let them go into a flat down there. Please, God! Please make them come up to this floor. Please, God! I have never heard two men come up to the fourth floor! Please! Please!

. . . fifty-one . . . fifty-two . . . fifty-three . . .

Rachael backed away.

. . . fifty-nine . . . sixty

The door opened.

Andrei walked in . . . someone behind him.

"Wolf!"

He walked in slowly and took off his cap. Rachael pitched forward into his arms and fought off the consuming blackness that took hold of her.

For many, many moments she was too terrified to look up. Was this another dream?

No . . . no . . . no dream. She looked up. He was fine. Just a scar on his cheek. And then she allowed herself the luxury of breaking wide open in convulsive tears.

"Rachael," he whispered, "I am all right. Please don't cry. I am all right. . . ."

Andrei left them, closing the door behind him.

Alex and Sylvia sat in their room, ghost-faced, drained of life. Neither of them had spoken a word for an hour since Wolf had left to go to Rachael.

Andrei knocked softly and entered.

"Dr. Glazer examined him. None of the dog bites are infected. He'll be all right."

The bit of information brought forth a new burst of crying from Sylvia. And then the baby shrieked and Sylvia picked him up and clutched him to her breast and rocked him back and forth, oblivious of Alex's words of consolation.

Alex nodded to Andrei to leave Sylvia alone. He tiptoed from the room, both of them retreating to his office. Alex began berating himself.

"Stop sniveling," Andrei demanded. "He is a courageous boy."

"Where is he now?"

"Don't you know?"

" Should I ?"

"He is with his girl."

227

"His girl?"

"My niece."

"Oh, I didn't know." Alex began berating himself again for being such a bad father that his own son would not confide his love life.

"Shut up, Alex, the boy is alive and safe."

Alex kept rambling. "All these eight horrible days I said it was right to get Wolf out. We have bought freedom for our people before. Rodel cost us nearly two thousand when they took him to the Pawiak Prison, and he isn't even one of ours. The Communists didn't even pay me back for Rodel's release. It was all right, buying Wolf out. We would have done the same for any of our people."

"You want to hear it, I'll tell you!" Andrei raged. "It was not all right! You should have left your son to die before crawling in front of Max Kleperman!"

"Don't talk like that, Andrei!"

Andrei snatched him from his chair and grabbed his lapels and shook him as though he were weightless. "Grovel! Beg Max Kleperman for mercy! That three thousand dollars could have bought guns to storm the Gestapo House and take your son out like a dignified human being!"

Alex fell against him and wept, but Andrei slung him into his chair. "God damn you, Alex! God damn you! Open your goddamned precious journal and read to me about the Jewish massacres in the Soviet Union!"

"For God's sake, leave me alone!"

"I want money! I've got to buy guns!"

"No—never. Never, Andrei. We keep twenty thousand children alive—not one zloty for guns."

Alexander Brandel gasped violently for air as the room whirled around him. He had never seen the anger of the big man who glowered over him. Cornered and beaten, his soul cried out instinctively for the lives of the children.

"I'm through," Andrei hissed.

"Andrei," Alex cried pathetically.

"Roast in hell!"

"Andrei!"

The door slammed on his plea.

Andrei Androfski wandered in a fog, aimlessly through the ghetto streets. It was done. There was no turning back. He walked and walked and walked in a daze that shut out the sight of corpses and the pitiful moans of the child beggars or the brutal clubs of the Jewish Militia.

And he found himself standing in the lobby of his apartment house before the bank of mailboxes. His hand groped instinctively in slot 18. He pulled out two armbands. Two white armbands with blue stars of shame. The kids were still upstairs. Wolf and Rachael. He shoved the armbands into the slot and dug around in his pocket. Two bills. A hundred zlotys each. Always when he plunged lower and lower one word kept him from reaching the bottom—"Gabriela." Two hundred zlotys. Enough to get him to the Aryan side. He needed her desperately.

"I have quit," Andrei said.

"What are you going to do?" Gaby asked.

"Try to contact the Home Army. They'll give me a command. The Home Army needs men like me. They won't argue and quibble they'll fight—tired of all this damned arguing—all this dealing with Kleperman."

Gaby watched him mumble aimlessly.

"Roman. That's the name of the commander of the Home Army in the Warsaw district. Roman. I'll get to him somehow. You'll stick with me, Gaby?"

"You know I will."

He put his arms about her waist and buried his head in her belly, and she stroked his hair. "Are you certain?"

"I am certain—absolutely certain."

Rachael and Wolf lay side by side on the bed, awed by the magnificence of their experience.

Wolf was completely exhausted. Rachael held him and petted him, and her lips sought him again and again.

She felt so elated from the wonderment of fulfillment.

It was not ugly or difficult. She felt no shame when they saw each other for the first time. Wolf had been so gentle and tender. He knew the awkwardness in her.

He was happy. She had made him happy. He was tired, but he wanted her to touch him.

Poor dear Wolf, Rachael thought. He is so shy he cannot say words he wants to, but I feel every word he wants to tell me by the way he touches my breast and kisses me and whispers to me.

It felt good . . . so good . . . and I am so proud I was able to be a woman for his sake. Now anything can happen and it won't be quite so bad.

I am so sleepy. . . . Uncle Andrei must be furious. I hope he went to see Gabriela, because I'm not going to leave. I'm going to snuggle close and sleep for a little while, then I'll wake him up and try it again. . . .

Chapter Twenty-five

No one has seen Andrei for ten days. We assume that he is living on the Aryan side. After so many years of working together, it is difficult to believe he is really gone. None of us knew till now what a symbol of security he was. It has been a terrible blow to the morale here at Mila 19.

We now operate ninety soup kitchens and have some twenty thousand children under the care of Orphans and Self-Help.

Dr. Glazer tells me we have a new trouble, venereal disease. Before the war, prostitution was never a Jewish social problem. Nowadays I hear more and more of wives and daughters, many from fine old Orthodox families, taking to the streets.

For a family to get a daughter married to a Jewish militiaman is an achievement.

Tommy Thompson has been evicted from Poland. We have lost a dear friend. However, we have been expecting it for a long time. Ana Grinspan has already made a new contact to pass in American Aid funds. Believe it or not, a chap named Fordelli, who is the second secretary at the Italian Embassy. Although he is a good Fascist, he takes exception to the German treatment of the Jews. Is Ana having an affair with him?

ALEXANDER BRANDEL

Alex was instinctive about bad news. The moment Ervin Rosenblum walked into his office he knew something had gone wrong. Ervin paced and wrung his hands.

"Out with it."

"My pass to the Aryan side has been revoked."

"Has de Monti protested?"

"He left for the eastern front four days ago. He doesn't know yet."

"Confidentially, it is as well you are inside the ghetto with us."

"But all the contacts on the Aryan side . . ."

"It is getting more difficult for you to see anyone, and de Monti refused to co-operate. You were being watched every minute. Ervin, I've been thinking. You can fit right in here at Mila 19. We need you in several positions."

"Like for example?"

"Orphans and Self-Help cultural director. *Nu*, don't shrug and make faces. The arrangement of debates, concerts, theater, chess tournaments becomes more and more important to give the people something to think about other than misery. What do you say?"

"I say that you are a good friend."

"Another thing. The Good Fellowship Club. I can't keep up with all the material coming in to the journal. I have been thinking for a long time. Build a secret room in the basement. With you putting time in, we could really expand the archives."

Ervin shrugged at what he felt was charity.

"Think it over, Ervin. Let me know."

That evening Susan Geller came to Ervin's flat. Since the ghetto, they had had little time for each other. Susan was nearly completely married to the orphanage and Ervin was on the Aryan side most of the time. They met about once a week at Good Fellowship Club meetings, usually too weary to pursue personal pleasures. Their unofficial engagement seemed destined to go unresolved.

"Susan!" Momma Rosenblum cried with delight.

"Hello, Momma Rosenblum."

"You heard?"

"Yes."

"So maybe cheer him up a little."

Ervin sat on the edge of his bed, staring glumly at the hole in the toe of his bedroom shoe. She sat beside him, creaking the bed.

"So maybe you've come to pray over the corpse," he said.

"Shut up. Alex had offered you a responsible position. So, stick up your nose. Be a martyr."

"I am glad you stopped by to cheer me up with your tender consolation."

"Ervin, you'll take the job?"

"I have a choice, maybe?"

"Stop krechtzing. Alex is very excited about the plans for a secret room in the basement. You know how important the work on the journal is."

"All right, all right. I'm bubbling with happiness."

"Confidentially, Ervin, I am just as happy that you don't go to the Aryan side any more. I have been afraid for you, even with your fancy super-official papers."

"That's something. I didn't think you had time to think about me."

"Ugh, you are in a mood. Of course I think about you."

"I'm sorry."

"Ervin," she said, taking his hand, "on the way here I was giving this all a great deal of meditation. We're not getting any younger and God knows I'll never grow pretty. With conditions as they are and so forth and so forth and so forth, perhaps we should consider getting married. In addition to the fact that already we should be having a little pleasure now and then, there are very practical reasons. For example, you'll be working at Mila 19 most of the time. It will be difficult for you to keep up this flat. So, why should we waste space? If we are married, Alex will give us our own room

231

on the second floor and you can move Momma in and so forth and so forth."

He reached over and kissed her on the cheek. "How can a man resist a proposal like that?"

Journal Entry

Ervin and Susan were married yesterday by Rabbi Solomon. It is about time.

ALEXANDER BRANDEL

Chapter Twenty-six

Chris returned to Warsaw from the eastern front to find Rosy gone, his office and apartment thoroughly searched and filled with hidden microphones, and his private line to Switzerland unavailable.

He dialed Rosy's number in the ghetto, to learn the phone was disconnected; then stormed to the Press Division at the Bristol Hotel, where his attempt to see Horst von Epp was thwarted by a minor bureaucrat.

"I am sorry, Mr. de Monti. Herr von Epp is in Berlin for a conference."

"When will he be back?"

"I am sorry. I don't have the information."

"Well, where can I reach him in Berlin?"

"I am sorry. I don't have that information."

A second minor official was equally sorry and uninformative about the revoking of Ervin Rosenblum's credentials, and a third minor official was sorry about the suspension of Chris's wire to Switzerland.

"Sorry, Mr. de Monti. Until further instructions you will have to file all dispatches here at the Bureau for Censorship."

Chris was tired and his head was fuzzy from the long trip back from the front lines. He stifled his irritation, knowing nothing could be done until he could put the pieces back in place. A hot bath and a tall drink and the things that a man looks forward to after living in the mud were in order.

While he soaked and sipped he decided not to pursue it any more until he could get his mind straight after a night's sleep.

Chris hid himself at a corner table at Bruhl House to avoid conversation and nibbled his way halfheartedly through a leather-tough schnitzel. The room was filled with guttural sounds of talk about the eastern front, the voices sharp with confidence.

"You are not hungry tonight, Mr. de Monti?" the waiter asked patronizingly as Chris gave up. "It is getting more and more difficult to put together an eatable menu. They . . . get it all."

Chris signed the bill and wandered out into the street. Warsaw was a gay place these days. The city was filled with German troops having their last fling before shipment to the eastern front. Although the Polish people were open in their hatred of the enemy, there were enough women not annoyed with patriotic considerations to give the German lads a good time. Brothels reaped a fortune, beer and vodka and goldwasser flowed in the taverns, and even the ancient streetwalkers struck an unexpected vein of gold.

Most of Warsaw's musicians were Jews. German soldiers and their girls slipped into the ghetto to dance and live it up in one of the fifty night clubs, mainly operated by the Big Seven, for the music on the Aryan side was dreadful.

Chris walked for several blocks. He was weary and unsettled from the shocks of war and hung in limbo by the sudden turn of events in Warsaw.

From the taverns, there was riotous singing from Germans as drunk as Poles and from Poles as drunk as Poles. In order to avoid further accosting by the streetwalkers, he crossed at Pilsudski Square and stopped to get his bearings.

Back to his car and home? No. Damned apartment gave him the creeps.

Track down a party? A good bender and maybe a little action afterward? No.

Chris looked around, then found himself walking up a footpath in the Saxony Gardens, which seemed more delightful with every step because it put the sounds of Warsaw behind him. It grew darker and dimmer as he walked. All he could hear now were occasional squeals from the bushes by roomless couples consummating their deals. Now and then a self-conscious pair emerged from the thickets or down the path, avoiding his eyes.

Chris walked past the swan lake. So often he had waited there for Deborah . . . sitting on the bench . . . waiting for her to appear. That first wonderful instant he would see her . . . That moment never changed, never dulled.

Damned fool, sitting here. Deborah isn't coming up the path— there won't be a tryst. No beautiful Deborah to see through the velvet curtains. Only a roomful of microphones and hidden eyes.

Chris was magnetically drawn to the ghetto wall. He crossed the Saxony Gardens and wandered along Chlodna Street, which divided the big and little ghettos. On both sides of him was the wall. The night lights caught the broken glass cemented on the top, causing it to sparkle like the sudden glint of a rat's eyes.

So dark . . . so quiet. It was hard to comprehend that six hundred thousand people lay in silence on the other side. All that could be heard was the sound of his own steps, and all that could be seen of life was his shadow, which grew longer and longer as the light contorted the angle of his movement.

He stood underneath the bridge. It was covered with barbed wire. He had come there many times during the day and stared at it, watching the Jews cross from one ghetto to the other over the "Polish corridor," hoping beyond hope he could catch a glimpse of Deborah.

He stood for a half hour.

What the hell, he thought, and walked away quickly.

From the corner of his eye he detected movement in an indentation in the wall ahead of him. Quickly two men stepped out and blocked his path. Chris stopped and looked over his shoulder. Two more men were behind him. He could not distinguish their faces, but the bulky cut of their clothing and leather workers' caps and their size intimated that they were thugs.

"Waiting for somebody under the bridge, Jew boy?" a voice came from one of the figures.

Hoodlums out Jew hunting. Big sport, these days. Good source of income. What to do? Show his papers and pass through?

"Come on, Jew boy. Two hundred zlotys or you'll take a walk to Gestapo House."

Chris's blood boiled. "Go to hell," he snapped, and walked straight at the pair ahead of him.

One from behind hooked his arm and turned him around. Chris drove his fist into the figure's mouth and the man fell backward, hit the curb, and landed on the flat of his back.

Damn! Damn my temper!

Two leaped on him, and while he struggled to free himself the third brought a blackjack to the side of his cheek.

A surge of raw strength threw the men from him. As he shook himself free, the first one got up and caught him in the eye with a hamlike fist, and for an instant Chris was blinded. He reeled, then stopped abruptly as his back hit the ghetto wall.

Chris grunted as the blackjack found its mark again. He sank to his hands and knees and wobbled on all fours and the ground spun around him.

"Get up, Jew boy!"

Chris looked up. They hovered over him. One with the blackjack, another with a jagged broken bottle. Another, bloodymouthed from his blow. He could not see the fourth man.

His head cleared and the ground steadied. Chris lurched up, ramming his shoulder into the one with the glass bottle to crack out of the ring. With the air suddenly smacked from his lungs, the hoodlum fell and sat on the ground, gasping.

And then Chris sank under a rain of fists and boots. He was jerked to his feet and propped against the wall, his arms spread-eagled as in the position of a crucifixion. The leader could not resist one last smash into the stomach of his helpless victim. A light was held to Chris's face. His dark Italian features were studied. "He's a Jew, all right."

Chris's head rolled up and his eyes opened and he snarled. The leader pressed the jagged glass close to his eye, so he dared not move.

Chris brought his knee up into the man's groin and the man shrieked and staggered back, then came forward, enraged and intent on cutting up his face.

"Wait. He fights too good to be a Jew. We had better make sure he is."

"What's the difference now? Just take his money."

"Holy Mother! Look at these papers! He isn't a Jew."

"Let's get out of here."

Footsteps . . . faded . . . they're gone . . .

Chris slipped down to the ground, bloody, and pawed around to pull himself up.

Someone stood over him. He managed to hold his head up enough to see the faces of a frightened middle-aged couple.

"Help me . . ."

"Don't touch him, Poppa. Can't you see he's a Jew? He jumped over the wall. Leave—leave before the guard comes."

Chapter Twenty-seven

A week passed before Horst von Epp returned to Warsaw. He entered the Holy Cross Church, spotted Chris kneeling in the first row, and knelt beside him.

"Good Lord," Horst said, "what happened to you?"

"I was mistaken for a Jew."

"Bad mistake, these days."

"You should have seen me a week ago."

"I thought we'd better meet out of the office," Horst said, nodding in the direction of the little black box on the altar containing Chopin's heart. "Let's take a walk. That box may have a microphone hidden in it. Matter of fact, I bit into a microphone planted in my breakfast bun this morning."

They shaded their eyes from the sun. Chris put on dark glasses to cover the bruises, and they strolled down New World Street. Across the street a pair of men began to follow them, and Von Epp's car drifted alongside at a crawl. "Lovely system," Von Epp said. "This way no one knows exactly who is watching who. How did you find the Russian front?"

"Nothing but victory for the Fatherland. Trouble is, I'm having a time getting my dispatches through about your glorious achievements."

"Sorry about that. Your line to Switzerland was restored this morning. Bloody blockheads. I knew the moment I left Warsaw there would be a panic."

"Restoring Rosenblum to me too?"

They crossed the street.

"Your silence is deafening, Horst," Chris pressed.

"Be reasonable."

"He's like my right arm."

"I told you I didn't know how long I'd be able to keep him out of the ghetto."

They walked in quiet unison for the rest of the block, then stopped at the junction where Jerusalem Boulevard turned into the Third of May Boulevard. A screaming set of sirens froze all movement. A pair of motorcycles followed by a command car followed by a convoy of a hundred trucks filled with fresh soldiers poured past them. From two or three of the trucks they were able to catch a note or two of a marching song. The convoy swept toward the newly reconstructed bridge to Praga.

Meat for the eastern front, Chris thought. The blitzkrieg had swept over the steppes. The fantastic military machine was slicing up the vastness of Russia from the Black Sea to the gates of Moscow. Horst and Chris drifted in the wake of the convoy to the bridge, and they stopped in the middle and leaned on the rail.

"Schreiker called me in and questioned me about Rosenblum. They were all on me about him. For both of your welfares it is better this way. It is impossible to have him out of the ghetto without casting all sorts of suspicion on you. Obviously he's mixed up in some sort of contacts around Warsaw and probably two steps ahead of being hauled into Gestapo House. Now don't press me on this matter, Chris."

Von Epp was right. Rosenblum was in thick as a courier. The Germans would be fools to allow him to continue to run loose.

"If you need another man, for Christ sake, find yourself a nice untainted Aryan."

Chris nodded. The Vistula River was filled with barges bearing the tools of war for transfer to the eastern front.

"Any of all this bother you, Horst?"

"Everyone knows the Jews started the war," Horst recited from the principal dogma.

"I saw a few things out there behind your lines that may be pretty hard to explain."

"Believe me, Goebbels will find explanations. And the rest of us? Hell, we'll all shrug with blue-eyed innocence and say, 'Orders

236

were orders—what could we do?' Thank God the world is blessed with short memories."

"Where does it end?"

"End? We can't stop until we either own it all or get blown up into a billion pieces. Besides, don't be too hard on us. Conquerors have never won prizes for benevolence. We are no worse than a dozen other empires when they ran the show."

"Does this make it right?"

"My dear Chris, right is the exclusive property of the winning side. The loser is always wrong. Now, if I were you, I'd string along with us for awhile because the way things are going we may be Rome, Babylon, Genghis Khan, and the Ottomans combined for many hundred years."

"Christ, what a prospect."

Horst laughed and slapped Chris on the back vigorously. "Trouble with you, you bastard, you've been out on the front looking at the seamy side of things. Warsaw is the warriors' reward. Unbend a little. How about a private party tonight? You, me—a pair of ladies. Hildie Solna said you were rather nice to her last time out."

"Once in a while my chemicals get out of balance. Hildie restores them. Usually when I'm tailing off a drunk."

"Tell you what. To hell with Hildie. Tonight I'm lending you number one from my private stock. Eighteen, built like a ripe peach. And where this dear girl picked up so many tricks in her short life—fantastically beautiful muscle control, and she does a thing of rubbing on baby oil . . ."

A roaring truck blotted out further dissertation on the orgy.

Chris again became entranced by the river barges. Horst von Epp was correct. "Right" was the winning side. He sure was with the winner. Five hundred years of Germany? Could be. The trip to the eastern front was the clincher. No matter how dark things had been in Spain, in Poland he always felt that the pendulum would swing back the other way. But would it? A breakthrough in Egypt would put Rommel on an unstoppable path to India. Moscow was digging in for a siege. The frantic preparations in America—too little, too late. He had seen the German power unleash a fury that made the conquest of Poland look like child's play. Kiev, a half million Russian soldiers trapped. What could stop them?

Chris looked at Von Epp, who was enjoying a cigarette. Orders are orders. A wall of indifference built around him that shut out a struggle of good and evil.

And then . . . the thoughts of the massacre outside Kiev seared into his mind. Chris had to make his move. Make it soon. Now . . . now . . .

And Horst von Epp was his only chance.

Do it, Chris prodded himself, do it—tomorrow may be too late.

"I want to go into the ghetto," Chris said quickly, fearing his own courage.

"Come now, Chris," Von Epp said, concealing his delight. "It will put us both in a bad light." All of Horst von Epp's patience was beginning to pay off now. Chris had held a card up his sleeve from the beginning. His desire to stay in Warsaw at any cost. His reluctance to join the parties after a reputation as a lothario in other places at other times. Chris wanted something. Von Epp knew that from the start. Now the card was being played with caution.

"I've got to see Rosenblum and clean up a lot of odds and ends."

"If you insist on this . . ."

"I insist."

Von Epp threw up his hands in "defeat." "All right." He glanced at his watch. Enough for one day, he thought. He looked for his car, which had trailed them and parked at the foot of the bridge. "Can I drive you into town?"

"I'll walk. I'll see you later."

"Try to change your mind about going into the ghetto." Horst turned briskly as he started for his car.

"Horst!"

The German turned to see Chris walking grimly toward him, on the brink of a terrible decision.

"Suppose I want to get someone out of the ghetto?"

"Rosenblum?"

"No."

"A woman?"

"And her children."

"Who?"

"My grandmother."

Horst von Epp smiled. Christopher de Monti had played his card. Every man had his price. Von Epp always found it. With most, petty bribes . . . favors. That was for petty people. Christopher de Monti? Tough. An idealist in the throes of conflict. Blackmail often worked. Almost everyone had dirty tracks they tried to cover. Von Epp found them too.

No matter how tough, how idealistic, how clean, every man had his price. Every man had his blind spot.

"How important is this?" Horst asked.

"Everything," Chris whispered, culminating the decision, putting himself at the mercy of the German.

"It can be done, I suppose."

"How?"

"She can sign papers that she isn't Jewish. We have handy form letters for all occasions, as you know. Marry her, adopt the children. A ten-minute detail. Then send her into Switzerland as the wife of an Italian citizen."

"When can I pick up my pass for the ghetto?"
"After we settle on the price."
"Like Faust? My soul to the devil?"
"That's right, Chris. It will be steep."

Chapter Twenty-eight

Andrei waited for two restless, mood-filled weeks before he
could corner the man known to him as Roman, the Warsaw commander of the fledgling underground Home Army.

Time and again Andrei had to stifle his desire to go back into
the ghetto with his friends. He drank heavily in the evenings, and
when his mind became fuzzed he was filled with remorse. He had
been intolerant of Alexander Brandel's struggle. He had acted
wrongly to friends who believed in him.

He thought about everything since the war had come. Bull-
headed . . . angry. Perhaps he was no good for a command again.
There was a time when he had settled down and moved about
Poland on mission after mission. He had pieced together a secret
press. He had acted with a cool head and a quick mind.

But always, anger surged. Rebellion against tyranny. He was
overpowered by this drive to throw off his containment and fight.

And Gaby. He was remorseful about her too. What kind of life
had he given her? He had taken her from a world in which she
thrived and placed demands upon her, giving little or nothing in
return. When the command in the Home Army comes, maybe I
will get away from Warsaw. Then perhaps she can forget about me
slowly and find the thread of a decent life.

At long last the word came back through super-cautious networks of information that Roman would see him. It was with an
immense feeling of relief that he followed out the instructions. A
contact in Praga. A blindfolded ride back over the river. Two
dozen false turns to throw off his sense of direction. Men whispering, leading him up a dirt path. A door, a room. Where was he?
He did not know exactly.

"You may take off the blindfold," a high tenor voice said in
immaculate Polish.

Andrei adjusted his eyes to the shadows of the room. They were
in a large shed. Crude curtains shutting out light. A kerosene
lantern on a shelf. A cot. A few garden tools.

Roman's face came across the flicker of light. He had seen the
prototype of Roman a thousand times in a thousand places. Tall,
erect, blond, high forehead, curly hair. He wore the unmaskable
glower of perpetual arrogance of a Polish nobleman. It was the

sneer of a Ulany colonel, the innuendo of superiority, the thin mocking lips. Andrei could almost tell Roman's story. The son of a count. Landed gentry. Misused wealth. Medieval mentality. Roman most likely lived in the South of France before the war. He cared damn little about Poland except to bleed his estate dry with the blood of legalized serfdom. He saw damned little of Poland except during the social season.

Andrei's estimation was deadly accurate. Like many of his ilk, Roman had become suddenly smitten with latent Polish "nationalism" after the invasion. He joined the government in exile in London because it was the fashionable thing to do. London was jammed with Poles who gathered to hear Chopin and recite poetry and live memories of Warsaw in the "good old days."

He parachuted into Poland to work with the Home Army, a play of immature romanticism. Despite the guise of workman's clothing, Roman's frailties shone like a beacon. "You are persistent, Jan Kowal," Roman said to Andrei.

"Only as persistent as you are evasive," Andrei answered.

"Cigarette?" American, of course. He'd rough it later with the local product. No use carrying nationalism to extremes.

"I don't smoke."

Roman did. With a long cigarette holder.

"You're Androfski, aren't you?"

"That's right."

"I remember seeing you in Berlin in the Olympics."

Andrei began to have that uneasy feeling he had had a thousand times in the presence of the Romans. He could read the thoughts hidden behind Roman's eyes.

. . . Jew boy. We had Jewish families on our estate. Two of them. One was the village tailor. Had a little Jew son with earlocks. I beat the hell out of him with my horsewhip. He wouldn't fight—only pray. The other Jew . . . grain merchant. Thief. Cheat. Always had my father indebted to him. The inbred hatred of centuries could not be belied by Roman's small, tight smile.

"I am afraid," Roman said, "that our position is such that you cannot expect too much co-operation from us at the present time. Perhaps later, as we are better organized . . ."

"You mistake my mission," Andrei said. "I represent only myself. I wish to place myself at the service of the Home Army. A fighting command, preferred."

"Oh, I see. That puts a different light on everything." Roman's slim elegant fingers caressed the long cigarette holder. "The Home Army does not work under conditions of a peacetime military force, naturally. All our people are volunteers. The maintenance of discipline cannot be as simple as a day in the guardhouse or the loss of pay. Discipline is life and death."

"I don't understand what you are trying to say."

240

"Merely this. We wish to avoid in advance the creation of unnecessary problems."

"Such as?"

"Well, we don't solicit your services. It may be impossible to get our men to respond to your leadership. And . . . you might feel rather uncomfortable with us."

"No room for Jews!"

"As a matter of fact, yes."

"Your army represents the government of Poland. Thirty thousand Jewish soldiers died in Polish uniform during the invasion." Andrei stopped. He knew his arguments were falling on deaf ears. Roman's eyes now said, "If it weren't for the Jews we would not be in this situation." Oh, they'd have a few Jews all right, Andrei knew. A nice quota system like all the quota systems he'd lived with all his life.

"I'll make you a counteroffer. I know my way in and out of all sixteen ghettos. Let me organize my own unit of the Home Army."

Roman turned his back on Andrei. "My dear—er—Jan Kowal. That would only increase the friction. Can't you see?"

"It is disgusting," Gabriela snapped.

"No, I should have known."

"What now?"

"There is no turning back. I am leaving in the morning for Lublin." Gaby's face became drawn. Sooner or later Andrei would reach a fearful conclusion. "The Bathyrans there have a good collection of foreign passports and visas. For old times' sake they will give me one and enough money to travel. I'll pick up the underground railway. We have sent a number of people out of the country that way. Goes into Germany to Stettin. From Stettin it will be a relatively easy matter to make a deal for a boat to Sweden. From Sweden I'll get to England, then join the Free Polish Forces. If they refuse me a command, I'll join the British army."

Gabriela listened to every word with mounting fear. Andrei stopped his pacing. "Someone in this world must let me fight."

She nodded. She knew. There would never be peace for him again until he was able to strike back.

"What about us?" she whispered.

"Go to Krakow to the Americans. Thompson is gone, but you still have friends there. They will get you out. We will meet in England, Gaby."

She bit her finger and brushed the hair back over her shoulder nervously. "I don't want to be parted from you."

"We can't travel together."

"I'm afraid of it all, Andrei."

"There is no choice."

"Andrei, it is such a wild scheme. So many, many things could go wrong. If you leave tomorrow and I never see you again——"

He put his hand over her mouth gently, then wrapped his arms around her in his wonderful way, which he had not done for a very, very long time. "And when we meet in England, do you know the first thing we will do?"

"No."

"Get married, of course, woman!"

"Andrei, I'm so afraid."

"Shhh." He petted her hair and rubbed the back of her neck and she purred and smiled weakly. "I must go into the ghetto. There are a few things in my flat. Nothing of value but sentimental. I should like Rachael and Stephan and Deborah to have them."

He broke from her and put on his cap. "Strange . . . I wanted so badly to see Stephan have his bar mitzvah. Well—no matter now."

"Hurry back, darling. . . ."

The return to the ghetto after his absence was shocking. In the few weeks he had been away the situation had collapsed with fearful speed. With winter coming on, the sight of corpses in the streets was commonplace and the smell of death, the low moan of misery, and the tautness of expectant doom cast a pall of gray in the midday sun.

Andrei shoved his hand into the mail slot in the hope that Rachael's and Wolf's armbands would be there. He might be able to speak to them . . . say a few words . . .

The flat was as he had left it. He looked about. The library. Some to Wolf, some to Stephan to read later—if there would be a later. The trinkets which once had been shined to a dazzling polish and adorned his uniform were tarnished. He threw them with his medals into a box. Stephan would want these.

The records and the player for Rachael.

What else was there? Very little. A Zionist organizer had no time for the accumulation of personal wealth. It was a shame that there were so few bits of tangible evidence of what this shabby room had meant. There had been much happiness here once.

The photograph album. The brown oval-framed pictures of Momma and Poppa. The pictures of his own bar mitzvah. Deborah would want these.

Should he see Alex? Rosy? Susan Geller? He heard Rosy and Susan were married. He really should. Hell, saying good-by is a rotten business. Just skip it. This was no bon voyage.

He sat at the table and wrote a note, which he was certain that Rachael and Wolf would receive, dividing his things and saying farewell.

He blotted and folded it.

The door creaked open and closed. Simon Eden was in the room with him.

"Bad news travels fast," Andrei said.

"We have had a twenty-four-hour watch here. We hoped you'd come back."

Andrei didn't want to get into a discussion with Simon. He wanted nothing to sway his mind, throw him into turmoil, challenge his loyalty, play on his sympathy. He had made his decision.

"I've spent my life arguing," Andrei said quickly. "I don't want one now."

Simon Eden was acquainted with the reality of Andrei's words. Two Jews in a room will give you three opinions. His life had been an endless debate. Minute interpretations. Interpretations of interpretations. The kinds of Zionism, the variations of Judaism. Every man an eminent literary and musical critic. Every man having the personal answer to every problem. Debate . . . talk, talk, talk, talk.

"I didn't come to argue. Just to ask you what you are going to do. My people on the Aryan side tell me you made a contact with Roman. Did he give you a commission in the Home Army?"

"They don't want anyone but tenth-generation red-blooded Polish Catholics."

"I could have told you that. Jews in the ranks of the partisans are getting murdered for their boots and guns. And I could have told you the Home Army won't back Jewish units. Going to make a run for it?"

"I think so."

"Strange damn thing about us, Andrei. We are a race of individuals like none other. We are savage about our right to seek truth as individuals. We are ridiculous sometimes at the numbers of answers we have to the same problem or how we can confuse a simple issue with conversation."

"It was the lack of unity that lost us Jerusalem in ancient times," Andrei said. "It is the same damned thing that will destroy us here."

Their talk was without anger. Simon was one who was always held in esteem by Andrei for his strength and for his unique ability to hold together a dozen factions of Jews engaged in ideological differences. "You say individualism is a weakness. I agree that it has been, at times. At the same time, it is also our greatest source of strength. The constant search for truth by a single man has been the key to survival."

"Don't trick me, Simon. I said I did not want to argue. Now you are trapping me into an argument on my right to argue."

"Can I say that you have expected too much?"

"I? All I've ever wanted to do is——"

"I know damned well what you've wanted to do. Did it ever occur to you that we don't have six hundred thousand Andrei Androfskis in the ghetto? They are just ordinary people clinging to a thread of life. They cling to a magic *Kennkarte* which allows

243

them to work in slave labor. Some even sell their daughters' bodies
—they beg and plead——"

"Without leaders!" Andrei snapped.

"Do you forget that this country was trampled and its leaders
killed? Do you dare say Alexander Brandel is not a leader? And
Dave Zemba? Do you think Emanuel Goldman was not a leader?
Are you ashamed of the courage of Wolf Brandel? Andrei, Alex
hears nothing and sees nothing but the cry of hungry children. His
only dogma is to put food into their bellies. And damn you, he has
fought a hell of a war in his own way."

Andrei shoved out of the chair. "Thanks for the lecture."

Simon grabbed his arm. "Hear me out for one more minute."

Andrei pulled his arm free. Simon was not begging or pleading.
He had too much respect to slough Simon off.

"Go on."

"You have begged to die stupidly, irrationally, unheard, in vain.
No underground army will form until the people want one. We're
coming to the end of 1941, and in 1942 the people will want an
army. They hear about the massacres in the east and they see the
death rate climb to a hundred a day in the ghetto and they are not so
afraid of reprisal any more and not so certain that Brandel has the
answer for survival. Andrei, every idea, every man's thinking is
good or bad because it comes at the correct time. It was not the
correct time for a fighting force before. Now it is becoming the
correct time. People are thinking about it more. They are talking
about it. They are starting to plot. To think in terms of guns."

Andrei slipped back into the chair. Simon hovered over him,
burning his arguments home with intensity.

"So much has been lost," Andrei whispered. "So much to do."

"Recontact Roman."

"That bastard."

"Never mind your personal feelings. Press him for arms."

"Hell, you're crazy, Simon. It's too late. The Home Army will
give us nothing but evasions. Piotr Warsinski has a gang of ghouls,
and the Gestapo has a thousand informers. Our contacts on the
Aryan side are flimsy. There is no real unity. We have no source for
arms."

"Did you ask for victory or the right to fight?"

"Are you with me now, Simon? Are you really with me?"

Simon dug into his pocket and pulled out a fat wad of bills.
Hundred-zloty notes. "Buy guns," he said.

From the moment that Gabriela heard the lightness in his steps,
she knew that something wonderful had happened. He flung open
the door, his face beaming, and he threw the money on the table
and picked her up and whirled her around and around.

For the first time since the war Andrei seemed at peace. There

244

was much to do and his own people would be battling him all the way, but, by God, they were thinking his way. They knew, in some degree, that they had to find means to defend themselves.

Too little . . . too late . . . it did not seem to matter.

Chapter Twenty-nine

Chris parked his car opposite the ghetto gate facing the Square of the Iron Gates. An unshaven Polish Blue policeman picked his teeth with his little fingernail as he examined Chris's pass and waved the barrier up.

A few steps inside the wall Chris was challenged by a pair of huskies in long gray coats and mirror-polished boots of the Jewish Militia.

Chris oriented himself quickly. He knew from Rosy where Deborah was most likely to be. His best chance to see her alone would be at the orphanage on Niska Street. The ghetto was filled with spies and informers, yet he felt that Horst von Epp was both too clever and sophisticated to use the crude tactics of having him tailed. Horst had Chris boxed in, anyhow. If he were to force his luck, the German risked scaring his prey to cover.

Chris walked along the wall beyond which the "Polish corridor" split the big and little ghettos. The streets were sticky with unswept dirt, and the pungent odors of filth filled his nostrils.

He approached the bridge which ran over the "Polish corridor" to the big ghetto. He stopped. There! On the foot of the bridge steps. The corpse of an emaciated woman. Enormous ghastly circles formed on the skin pulled taut by protruding bones. Chris backed away. He had seen corpses on the eastern front by the hundreds—he remembered the massacre—but . . . here . . . dead of starvation. It was different. Foot traffic moved around the dead woman with no one paying the least attention.

Chris edged up the steps to the top of the bridge. He was imprisoned in barbed wire. He looked down into the "Polish corridor." He had stood down there on the street so many times, looking up to where he now stood, hoping for a look at Deborah. He had been caught down there and beaten. He continued quickly over the bridge and down the steps into the big ghetto.

High barbed-wire walls surrounding Dr. Franz Koenig's uniform factory greeted him. Slow movement on the other side of the wire by half-starved slave laborers. Brisk, arrogant movement along the guard posts by the Jewish Militia.

Each step now made him catch a vignette of squalor, of pain. Each step churned his queasy belly close to a vomit. A lice-riddled

245

ragged remnant of what had once been a human being lay in front of him.

The mosaic of misery, the montage of horror became blurred. He was walking on a small square.

"Armbands! Buy armbands!"

"Books for sale. Twenty zlotys a dozen." Spinoza for a penny, Talmud for a dime. A lifetime collection of wisdom. Buy it in gross lots for kindling . . . keep my family alive one more day.

"Mattress for sale! Guaranteed lice-free!"

Two children blocked Chris's way. Warped, inhuman. "Mister, a zloty!" one whined. The second, a smaller brother or sister too weak to cry for food. Only the lips trembled.

"Do you want a lady's company? Nice virgin girl from a good Hassidic family. Only a hundred zlotys."

"My son's violin. Imported from Austria before the war . . . Please, a beautiful instrument."

"Mister, how much for my wedding ring? Solid gold."

A long line of scraggly, ragged humanity getting a dole of watery broth at a soup kitchen. The line pressed forward, stepping wearily over a corpse of one who had died en route to the soup.

An old man collapses in the gutter with hunger. No one looks.

A child sits propped up against a wall, covered with sores and lice bites and burning with fever, moaning pitifully. No one looks.

Loudspeakers boom. "*Achtung!* All Jews in Group Fourteen will report tomorrow to the Jewish Civil Authority at 0800 promptly for deportation for volunteer labor. Failure to report for volunteer labor is punishable by death."

The "kings" from the Big Seven with flour and meat and vegetables make their barters quietly, in whispers against the walls, in the alcoves, in the courtyards.

A Nazi sergeant from Sieghold Stutze's Reinhard Corps stands in the middle of Zamenhof Street. Bike rikshas, the basic mode of transportation, swirl around him. Each riksha comes to a halt before the "master" and doffs his cap and bows.

Clang! Clang! The bulging red and yellow street car with the big Star of David on its front and sides.

"*Achtung!* Jews, listen! Green ration stamps are hereby ruled invalid."

Another corpse . . . another . . . another.

Billboards filled with directives. BY ORDER OF THE JEWISH CIVIL AUTHORITY the building at Gensia 33 is declared contaminated.

Walls hold torn corners of posters and publications of the underground press ripped down by the Jewish Militia.

The Jewish Militia. Fat and brutal, beating a herd of hapless girls with their clubs as they push them north to their destination in the Brushmaker's factory.

Chris doubled over in the seat before the desk in Susan Geller's office at the orphanage. His face was chalky, his stomach churning, ready to rebel at one more sight, one more smell.

Susan closed the door and stood over him. He stumbled to his feet.

"I'm sorry I couldn't get here sooner," Chris said. "I got back from the front and ran into a pile of trouble. You know it's very difficult for me to get in here."

Susan was immobile, wordless.

"I tried to get Rosy back."

"I'm sure you did everything you could," she said coldly. "It is just as well for him to be in the ghetto. With Ervin's Jewish nose, the hoodlums would always attack him, even with his fancy immunity papers."

"Where is he, Susan?"

"We live at Mila 19 with the others."

Chris grunted. "Lord, I didn't even bring you a wedding present."

"It isn't necessary."

"Susan, is there anything I can do? Anything you want or need?"

She walked to the glass door which overlooked a sea of cots jammed together holding a hundred typhus-riddled children. Do? "Surely that must be the understatement of all time."

Her coldness reached him. "Susan, what have I done?"

"Nothing, Chris. There is one thing you can do. It will be a very fine wedding present for me and Ervin. You know what kind of work Ervin does. I beg you not to betray him to the Germans."

"I am sorry that you feel it necessary to say that to me."

Susan turned on him. "Please, Mr. de Monti. No lectures about honor and humanity."

"Rosy is my friend——"

"Horst von Epp is also your friend."

Chris sank into the chair, shattered.

"I am sorry for the unpleasantries, Chris. These are unpleasant times. When a person is trying to survive he is apt to be rude to an old friend. Now, if you'll let me go back to work . . ."

"I want to see Deborah Bronski."

"She isn't here."

"She is here."

"She doesn't want to see you."

"She is going to have to."

"I'll give her your message."

"Susan, before you go . . . You've been close friends for many years——"

"We were the only two Jewesses allowed to study in a class of fifty nurses. We clung together for self-preservation."

"Do you know about——"

"Ervin is my husband. He confides in me."

247

"I have a chance to get her and her children out of Poland."

Susan Geller turned from the door. Her homely face was clearly puzzled. There were many things she did not like about Christopher de Monti. There was something about him that reminded her of a Polish nobleman despite his loyalty to Ervin. The one thing she had no doubt about was his love for Deborah Bronski.

"Can you influence her?"

"I don't know," Susan answered. "Strange things happen to people under this pressure. Most people will do anything to survive. Many completely lose their souls, their sense of morality is shattered, they turn to weak masses of jelly. A very few seem to find sources of unbelievable strength. Deborah has become a single symbol of humanity to many dozens of children. I would say that a lesser woman would grab the chance to flee. . . ."

"Tell her that I am waiting," Chris said.

It took all the restraint he owned to contain the overpowering drive to sweep Deborah into his arms. She was thin, and the signs of weariness were in her face. But she was more beautiful than he remembered. Her eyes spoke a compassion that one can gain only through suffering. They stood before each other with lowered heads.

"I have never stopped hungering for you for a minute in all these months," Chris blurted.

"This is hardly the time or the place for a balcony scene," she answered stiffly. "I only agreed to see you to avoid an embarrassing argument."

"All of this great pity you give. Is there none for me? Is there no word of consolation for the hours I've stood beneath the bridge praying to get a glimpse of you? Is there no iota of sympathy for all those nights I've drunk myself into a stupor from loneliness?"

The hardness flowed out of her. She had been cruel. She sat down and folded her hands in her lap, and they rested like a Mona Lisa's.

"Listen to me without haste or anger," Chris pleaded. "I can get you and the children safely out of Poland."

Deborah blinked her eyes and frowned as though she really did not comprehend what he was saying. She stole a glance at him.

"Do you understand what I am saying?"

"There's so much work here. Every day we lose two or three or four of our babies."

"Deborah, your own people encourage escape. It is no sin. You owe the gift of life to your children."

She became confused; she tried to piece together a line of logic. "My children are strong. We will fight this out as a family. Rachael and I have work . . ."

He knelt before her. "Listen to me. I was at the capture of Kiev.

248

Within a week after the German army entered, Special Action Kommandos rounded up nearly thirty-five thousand Jews. They were dragged out of basements and closets and barns. The Ukrainians helped hound them down for an extra ration of meat. Then they were marched to a suburb called Babi-Yar—Grandmother's Pits. A thousand at a time they were stripped naked—men, women, children. They were lined up at the edge of the pits and shot in the back. Then bayoneted, then covered with lime—then another thousand were marched in. Thirty-three thousand in three days, and the Ukrainians cheered every time the guns went off. An insanity has taken over the Germans."

Deborah was glassy-eyed with disbelief.

"I saw it with my own eyes!"

"Paul will keep us alive."

"Paul has brought you to this. He has dishonored himself and sold himself to them so completely, they will never let him out alive."

"Paul has only done this for us!"

"You don't believe that yourself. He has done it for Paul. Now, listen. You're leaving. I'll have you picked up and forced out beyond your choice before I'd let you die."

"You'll never touch me again."

Chris nodded and stood. "I know that," he said weakly. "I have already resigned myself to the fact that I will never see you. I know that there can never be a life for us if Paul is left here. That doesn't matter to me—all I want is for you to live."

"I can't leave him," Deborah said.

"Ask him! I think he will let you and your son and daughter die before he faces this alone here."

"That's not true."

"Ask him!"

Deborah tried to push her way to the door, but Chris grabbed her arms with a vise-like grip. She started a useless resistance. Then she stiffened.

"I'll haunt you, Deborah. Every day and every night I'm waiting beyond the wall."

"Let me go!"

"Haven't we been punished enough? Do you want the death of your children as part of the penance too?"

"Please, Chris," she begged.

"Tell me you don't love men and you're free of me."

Deborah leaned against him and put her head on his chest and sobbed softly, and his strong arms folded about her gently. "That is my greatest sin," she cried, "still loving you."

Chris's arms were empty. He watched her disappear among the cots in the ward.

Paul dozed in the overstuffed chair. She was sick with worry about him since the Germans closed the Civil Authority and moved their headquarters to the big ghetto at Zamenhof and Gensia, in the former ghetto post office. They would have to move soon, too, she was certain. House by house, the Germans were emptying the little ghetto on the south.

Deborah watched him over the top of her book. Sometimes his mind would go blank in the middle of a sentence and he would stare aimlessly, then try to mumble his way back to reality. He wanted to sleep, only to sleep. He was taking greater doses of pills to block from his mind the torment of the German directives.

The children never said it, but she knew. She knew they were ashamed of him.

God, why did I have to see Chris? No rational human being could avoid being swayed by the thought of leaving this chamber of horrors. There was less and less she could do about the wails of the pitiful ragamuffins. Babi-Yar ... Would it happen in Warsaw? Did she have the right to deny a try for life for Stephan and Rachael?

She doubted that Rachael would leave. She had sent her own daughter to a woman's bed at the age of seventeen. She felt it would be the greater sin to yield to society's dogmas of morality and find some morning the boy was gone forever and her child bear a lonely and unfulfilled cross. They had so little and so little time. But Rachael would not leave the boy. Deborah knew that as surely as she knew she would not leave Paul.

Perhaps she should send Stephan away by himself. He was a tenacious little boy, so much like his Uncle Andrei. So eager to fight. He would rebel.

Suppose she asked Paul. Would he let them go, or would he let them die first? Was Paul's weakness for survival at any price so consuming that he would bring his family to doom out of sheer fear?

Paul blinked his eyes open and saw Deborah's black eyes searching him questioningly.

"I must have dozed," he said groggily. "Dear, what is it? Why do you look at me that way?"

She started at the realization that she had not heard him.

"Is something wrong, Deborah? Is there something you want to ask?"

"No," she said. "I have the answer."

Chapter Thirty

Journal Entry

> If you want to be in movies,
> You don't have to travel far,
> The ghetto is like Hollywood,
> All here, have a STAR.

COMPLIMENTS OF CRAZY NATHAN

Ervin Rosenblum has done a magnificent job as cultural secretary of Orphans and Self-Help. We now have a full Ghetto Symphony Orchestra, fifteen theatrical productions in Yiddish and Polish, a secret school for both primary education and religious training in each orphanage; art exhibitions, debates, poetry readings, etc., etc. Several individual artists perform in roving troupes. Most well known is Rachael Bronski, who has made her debut with the symphony playing Chopin's Second Concerto. She is called the "Angel of the Ghetto." A pity Emanuel Goldman was not there to see her great talent.

But . . . our situation continues to degenerate. The death rate, mainly from typhus and starvation, climbs upward: July, 2200; August, 2650; September, 3300; October, 3800. So far in November, 150 a day. Strange, the suicide rate continues to drop. Conclusion: The weaker ones have killed themselves already. The rest are determined to survive. Each morning families deposit new corpses on the sidewalk. No money for funerals. The "sanitation teams" come along with hand pushcarts, shovel the corpses up, twenty or thirty to a cart, and wheel them to the cemetery for burial in mass graves. The spectacle of death and starvation no longer impresses anyone. We must immunize ourselves. How crass.

Food comes in daily to Transferstelle. There is simply not enough to feed everyone. The Big Seven has shoved prices so high, Orphans and Self-Help is barely able to get bare minimum rations. The Big Seven has a virtual control on the licensed bakeries. The bakers are the "kings" of the ghetto.

Smuggling has become a way of life. No one can stop it. Napoleon tried and failed. The Germans cannot stop it. Even if they were scrupulous and honest, it would be impossible. Every guard is corrupt, Jewish Militia on the inside, The Polish Blues and the Germans on the outside. They all "play" for the right price. Why should the Germans even try to stop smuggling? Payoff money is lining the pockets of their top officials.

Smuggling runs from primitive forms to highly organized operations. In its most basic form, small, quick children dart about and move through small cracks in (or one of a half dozen tunnels under) the ghetto wall. Some of these children are sole providers for their families. They risk going into the Aryan side to scavenge in the garbage cans, barter if they have anything to barter, beg at the squares, or steal. One poor child was stuck in a crack in the wall. He was beaten by police on both sides of the wall.

The main transfer point of smuggled goods is outside the ghetto where the Jewish and Catholic cemeteries have a common wall. It has been breached in a dozen places and is a sort of "free trading zone." Gravediggers who work the detail for mass graves are the main contact people. However, one must be in the upper bracket of smugglers to work the cemeteries.

Needless to say, the Big Seven has the most profitable and highly organized operation. They have paid off all down the line. However, every once in a while the Germans put on a show and catch a Big Seven Smuggler and shoot him. It makes Kleperman appear not to be in league with the Germans. I'm certain he knows in advance.

The Big Seven built an underground pipe under the wall to pipe in milk from the Aryan side. Sacks of flour and other goods are thrown over the wall at given times in given places. Portable ladders come up out of nowhere, go against the wall, and in three or four minutes, while the guard turns his back, in come the goods. The Big Seven has even constructed a portable ramp and brought in a live cow on it.

Epitome of the smuggler's art is the large funeral (which only the wealthy can afford). The Big Seven controls the undertaking licenses. Their funeral vans always re-enter the ghetto with a ton or so of goods. When business is slow, I hear the Big Seven stages fake funerals with empty coffins.

To control prices, the Big Seven sells only part of its goods; a shortage raises prices. Food is stored all over the ghetto in basements. I hear that Mila 18, directly across the street from us, holds one of the largest caches. An "independent" smuggler, Moritz Katz, runs a band from Mila 18.

Oddity. Along Leszno Street is the freak boundary of the "Polish corridor." The wall slices the courthouse in half, so it can be entered from both sides. Jews enter from the ghetto through a basement. Poles use the main entrance on the Aryan side. Meetings are held in certain chambers, offices, and corridors. Kleperman's "authorized" representatives have space in the courthouse much like one buys a seat on the Stock Exchange (or a London prostitute has a station). For a broker's fee, Kleperman's "authorized" representatives trade gold, dollars, and precious stones.

The most horrible of all sights in the ghetto are the "snatchers." Starved children prowl near the bakeries and, driven by hunger, grab bread from people as they leave. They eat it on the run. Often children

252

have been beaten half to death while cramming the bread into their bellies.

The Good Fellowship Club appointed a special committee to analyze the always elusive mystery of what the Germans are really up to. Information from the massacres in the east. There are definitely four main groups of "Action Kommandos," SS men trained for massacre.

Group A. Commanded by SS Major General Franz Stahlecker in the Baltic-Leningrad area.

Group B. Commanded by SS General Artur Nebe, White Russia.

Group C. Otto Rasch (rank?) in Kiev on the southern front. The Babi-Yar massacre of thirty-three thousand in three days seems to be his brain child.

Group D. SS Major General Otto Ohlendorf (is he the noted engineer of pre-war times? Hard to believe) in central Russia.

The method is basic. Roundup, victims dig their own graves, are stripped, shot in the back. This apparently amuses the local populations, who are giving full co-operation. The SS have augmented their ranks with Ukrainians and Lithuanians. Reports of massacres so far at Rovno, Dvinsk, Kovno, and Riga. They say seventy thousand have been shot at Wilno.

We are trying to determine what the shifts in general German policy are and how these massacres will apply to us in Warsaw and the General Government Area. Have the Germans established the number of people they will need to run their slave-labor factories? Obviously the action groups were formed in advance of the invasion of Russia.

Ervin Rosenblum develops the theory of the German "apologetics." They go to extraordinary lengths to prove their "innocence" and establish their "justifications." This, of course, means they know they are doing something evil and feel they must cover their tracks.

The German language has been bastardized by the Nazis with their "joy through labor" ... "Aryan-master race" ... "land to live" ... "German destiny" ... "the true ones" ... "folk people" ... "führer" ... "inhuman treatment of ethnics," etc., etc.

The whole text on behavior toward Jews also has been compounded in this new "language." The basic "theory" is that the Jews have always been the enemies of the German people and are therefore trying to destroy them, so the Germans must destroy the Jews purely out of "self-defense." They point up to the economic competition with classic portraits of the cunning Jew who has "always hated the German" and robs the German of his right to make a living.

Here are examples of their new double-meaning language:
Reservation—ghetto.
Legitimate war booty—wealth stolen or confiscated from Jews.
Contaminated—to be confiscated.
Sanitation measures—an excuse for mass executions.

Unpleasantness—the carrying out of mass murder.

Shot while trying to escape—a common phrase for someone killed in prison.

Resettlement—deportation with confiscation of all property.

Voluntary labor—slave labor.

Sub-humans—Jews, Slavs, gypsies, political and criminal prisoners, clergy, homosexuals (other than German), and others unfit to breathe Aryan air.

Mongrelization—the excuse to "get rid of sub-humans" who will contaminate the pure German blood lines.

Bolshevik-profiteer-warmonger—almost always used before or behind the word "Jew" to pound in the identification.

Now then, theorizes Silverberg, the playwright, the Germans go to fantastic trouble to make themselves truly believe what they are saying. The verbal acrobatics are played out. Basis: In order to live in the ghetto, one must break the law. Therefore, everyone who is alive in the ghetto is a criminal in the German lexicon and can legally be executed. Incredible?

Here are some of their "proofs":

They will go to great trouble to hold a kangaroo court trial, documented fully, to punish a common thief or vagrant. They will make an exhaustive investigation over a single typhus death to "prove" their interest in human lives. They will show "shock" at the brutality of the Jewish Militia, which must be brutal to enforce their rule.

They allowed a few schools to reopen to "prove" German love of freedom of education. Because we are unable to support many schools, have no textbooks, fuel, facilities, and the children are too sick and weak to attend, this "proves" the sub-human Jews will not educate their children.

Ghettos have been made to "isolate" the warmongers and filthy Jews from the Poles. And to protect the Jews from the vengeance of the Poles once the Poles understood what the Jews had brought upon them.

More "proof" of the German case: Special SS film units have entered the ghetto. They film the delousing sheds. Have you ever seen a man fifty pounds underweight, freezing cold, and hairless? German narration shows this is a "sub-human" disease carrier, and the appearance portrays just that.

Bearded rabbis are forced to pose in the warehouses at Transferstelle beside tons of food while the narration "proves" how the Gestapo located secret caches which these old bearded Jews hoarded while their neighbors starved.

The Jewish Militia is always willing to oblige with a show of brutality which, when captured on film, finds the obvious commentary of Jew destroying Jew.

Their prize exhibits are the smugglers' orgies. The smugglers are mostly men of low mentality, lower morality. At their clubs they

254

*gladly pose gorging food, drinking, brawling, in orgies with prosti-
tutes. The Germans then plant garbage cans filled with scraps outside
the clubs and photograph beggar children clawing around in them.*

*Most sinister move in the German master plan is the creation of
the illusion that the Jews are doing all this to one another. The dregs
of society in the Jewish Militia, the emasculated Jewish Civil
Authority, the smugglers. This is "final vindication" for the Germans
—of themselves.*

*What is next on the Nazi blueprint? Who knows? Nothing out of
Berlin comes in the form of written orders (further indication of their
knowledge of their evil). SS General Alfred Funk carries it all in
verbally. Two phrases in the German lexicon appear more and more.
We do not know what they mean and they terrify us.*

1. *En route to unknown destination.*
2. *Final solution of the Jewish problem.*

ALEXANDER BRANDEL

Only a man of Rabbi Solomon's stature would dare risk walking
the ghetto streets alone at midnight. He turned the corner into
Mila Street in a half trot, then slowed to a walk when his ancient
legs rebelled, then took up the trot again.

At Mila 19 he grunted up the steps and pounded on the door.
The girl on night watch opened it, alarmed. "Rabbi, what are you
doing out this hour of night?"

"Where is Alexander Brandel?" he gasped, fighting to regain his
wind.

"Come in."

Through Alex's office, down the corridor to the basement landing. The girl scratched a match and lit a candle and took the old
man's hand. They went down a step at a time. The stairs creaked
beneath their weight. He squinted to adjust his eyes to the sudden
blackness. The basement was musty and dark. An aisle cut through
two rows of packing cases all marked with supplies for the
Orphans and Self-Help Society. She led him down the row and
stopped before a particular crate some four feet in height. She
knocked on the case with six short raps, then pulled open a false
door, lowered her head, and entered the secret room where Alexander and Ervin Rosenblum looked up from the voluminous notes
being prepared for entry in the journal.

"Rabbi! What on earth . . ."

"The news! I have just heard the news on the radio. America is
in the war!"

part three

NIGHT

Chapter One

Since Pearl Harbour, events have occurred with stunning rapidity. Our first natural impulse of gladness has faded to bitter reality. America is being beaten in the Pacific. Suddenly we are cut off from our main source of income, American Aid. Our cash reserve can only hold us for days. We are frantically trying to find new avenues of revenue.

Two days after Pearl Harbor, detachments of Waffen SS from Trawniki Concentration Camp carried out a swift roundup raid at our farm at Wework. In a fell swoop we have lost fifty of the cream of our youth. Was I wrong to keep the farm in operation, knowing this might happen? Where could we have put fifty extra people at Mila 19? I do not know. After the roundup they were put on a cattle car (along with a trainload of deportees from the Baltics).

Then unfolds a most unusual tale. The train took a crooked, uncertain course toward Germany. Obviously slave labor at the end of the line. By some miracle, Ana Grinspan was working in the ghetto of Czenstochowa at the time the train stopped there. (Second thought, Czenstochowa is quite a site of miracles; i.e., Christian versions. This is the home of the "Black Madonna," the "Luminous Mountain," and the "Miracle of the Mount.") Ana (traveling as the Aryan Tanya Tartinski) learned somehow that there were Bathyrans in one of the cattle cars. She followed the train into Germany. The internees were put up at a temporary relocation camp near Dresden. Ana entered the lager armed with false papers, a tall story, and Jewish hutzpah and managed to bring out Tolek Alterman and ten of our youngsters.

This girl, Ana Grinspan, is fantastic! This is the fourth time she has crossed into Germany, walked into concentration camps, and freed key people. Her own story is recorded fully in Volume 4A of the journal. Someday when it is read I wonder if her exploits will be believed?

Tolek and Ana got back here to Warsaw. Tolek immediately went to work for Andrei. The other ten who escaped are scattered. Shall we ever hear from them again? Or the ones in the Dresden lager?

Tolek tells one story of the trip into Germany that I must record here. The train was all open cars; everyone half froze to death. It was a tortuous, stop-and-start trip. It took three days to reach the town of Radomsk near the German border, where they stopped again at a siding to give priority to a military train for the eastern front.

Dozens of curious peasants gathered about the train. Our people,
who had not eaten or drunk for three days, were near dead with
thirst. They begged the peasants to pass them a few handfuls of
snow to quench the thirst. The peasants first made them throw out
their rings, money, and valuables. Then . . . they got a handful of
snow.

Mira and Minna Farber were captured on the Aryan side of War-
saw along with our major contact, Romek. Both girls died under
torture at Gestapo House. Romek is still alive, but I understand he
is blind and badly crippled. This shatters our major contact on the
Aryan side. I am sick about the Farber girls. They were wonderful,
sweet, quiet girls. Twenty-two or -three, I believe. Cursed with non-
Jewish faces which made them natural "runners." Thank God their
parents are both gone.

Ana Grinspan is staying in Warsaw to try to reset our shattered
runner system. Things are black in Krakow, anyhow. Bathyran
House was raided and the underground press there seized.

The day after our farm was raided at Wework all the Toporol
farms were closed. We lost several hundred of our best people and
irreplaceable food supplies.

A.B.

Wolf Brandel, eighteen, wisened and toughened, became the first
lieutenant of Andrei Androfski. Although Andrei and Alexander
made peace with each other, a certain coolness had developed between them.

Alexander had enough of a sense of history to realize that the
initiative and his philosophy were slowly slipping from his control.
Andrei's approach to resistance was creeping over them. From
time to time Alexander held a line, and if Andrei pressed an issue
he retrenched. At first Alexander would permit no illegal activity at
Mila 19. Now Andrei demanded a second secret room in the basement of Mila 19 be dug for the manufacture and storage of arms.
Alex avoided a showdown, afraid of the growing power that Andrei
could gather behind him. He allowed the room to be built.

This second room was carved out so that it ran beneath the
center of Mila Street. Andrei brought in Jules Schlosberg, a pre-
war chemist of note, for the purpose of creating weapons which
could be made cheaply with accessible components. Jules first
weapon was a bottle bomb requiring only low-grade fuel, a wick,
and a plastic detonation cap. It was a foolproof fire bomb. Next
Schlosberg worked to perfect a more complicated weapon; a
grenade which would be built inside the casing of an eight-inch
length of water pipe and exploded by contact percussion.

On the Aryan side, arms were difficult to obtain. As soon as they
came into demand, the price spiraled. The Home Army had the
money and the contacts to cover the market. Roman evaded the

frantic efforts of Simon Eden and the Jews to obtain a share of weapons.

Each purchase of a pistol became a large, involved project. A weapon such as a rifle was almost unheard of. A machine gun did not exist. For his arsenal Andrei concentrated on Schlosberg's "inventions," which were manufactured by Bathyrans in hidden rooms around the ghetto. While Rodel, the Communist, cooperated on matters of Self-Help, he was jealous of his arms sources. The Revisionists at Nalewki 37 remained aloof on both self-help and arms. Andrei was able to obtain ten pistols of six different calibers, each with only a dozen rounds of ammunition. Although it seemed completely ridiculous in the face of a German army that had conquered all of the world it sought, Andrei was content with his work and had a rather pleasant attitude that at the right time and the right place his microscopic might would cause a mighty roar.

Andrei's main source of pistols was a small ordnance shed near the main train depot on Jerusalem Boulevard, where wounded German officers were transferred from the eastern front back to Germany. Their sidearms were checked in for reissue, and in a rush a few could conveniently be "lost" by the German sergeant in charge of the detail.

Immediately after American Aid folded, Alexander Brandel got a radio message to the two Jewish members of the Polish government in exile in London, Artur Zygielboim and Ignacy Schwartzbart, with a plea for emergency funds. A message in Hebrew was radioed back using passages in the Bible as reference to advise them that the funds were being flown in by British aircraft and would be parachuted to the Home Army. A later confirmation of the parachute drop came, and Tolek Alterman was dispatched from the ghetto into the Aryan side to receive the money from Roman.

When Alterman returned to the ghetto, Andrei and Ana Grinspan were called to Alexander Brandel's office.

Tolek came in and took off his worker's cap, appearing strange to them, as they had not yet adjusted to the shaved head. The long floppy hair that had been his trademark had been ordered shorn to give him a more Aryan appearance.

Tolek dramatically placed a bundle of American dollar bills on Alexander's desk. "I was only able to get one third of the amount that was parachuted in for us," he announced.

Alex's face sagged.

Andrei sat with his legs stretched out, the heel of one boot balanced on the toe of the other. He stared at the tip of his toe.

"That arrogant son of a bitch Roman," Tolek snorted in growing rage.

"Don't waste your time chewing up the furniture, Tolek,"

Andrei said softly. "The fact that you were able to contact that bastard Roman and even get him to admit he received the money, much less turn any of it over to you, was an accomplishment."

"I'll tell you why he turned over part of it," Ana Grinspan said. "So we would not stop future parachute drops. Roman knows that so long as we get a crumb we'll keep the money coming."

Alex rubbed his temples, tried to think. "We need more so badly. When will the British fly in more?"

"Ten days. Two weeks," Andrei answered. "As quickly as it arrives from America."

"Then, Andrei, we have to get one of our people there when it is dropped."

"Forget it. Roman won't permit that. Take what he gives us and keep our mouths shut."

"But we can't hold the line," Alex cried. He was about to accuse Andrei of skimming too much off for his fool weapons inventions in the basement but thought better of it. "Dave Zemba told me this morning that he has a plan to obtain zlotys here in the ghetto," he said with desperation in his voice. "But we must have the other money."

"One thing is obvious," Ana Grinspan said. "With Romek gone, we must have a new contact on the Aryan side. As soon as we do we must get in direct contact with our people in London and arrange our own drops."

Andrei looked up from the toe of his boot, sensing Ana's thoughts, anticipating her next words. She stood over him. "What about Gabriela Rak?" she asked.

Andrei did not flick an eye. He shrugged. "Why not?" he said. "I'll ask her."

He left the meeting knowing what he must do. Andrei had always felt that someday he must lose Gabriela, that his time with her was borrowed time. When the ghetto was formed he knew, too, that it would be only a matter of time before someone brought up her name for underground work. The moment had arrived. He had carefully rehearsed for it so that when her name was mentioned he would show no evidence of concern.

Andrei sat alone in his flat, meditating and gathering himself for the task ahead. He began collecting memories of her from that first moment at the grand ball of the Ulanys. It was so very long ago. He had been sitting right here at this table reading—what was it?—Steinbeck, when Gabriela came through the door and begged for the right to love him. And he remembered all the individual episodes of the warmth and comfort always there when he plunged into depths of despair.

The next day, still showing no outward sign to his friends, he went to the basement of Mila 19 where Jules Schlosberg had completed his first pipe grenade. Andrei, of course, was most anxious to

261

test the weapon somewhere in an open field away from the ghetto. He tied the pipe to his left forearm. It had been designed so that it could be hidden on a man, fitted between the elbow and wrist. He told Ana that he would see Gabriela about setting up her place on Shucha Street as a contact point, then left the ghetto.

At Gabriela's apartment, the moment he saw her he thought he would falter. She wore that same expression that told of the strain of listening for him, anxiety, relief at the sight of him. The weak smile. The trembling embrace. When she touched him he thought he would die before being able to go through with it.

"Come, dear," she said, "I have some dinner."

"Sorry. I can't stay."

"You'll be back later tonight?"

"No."

"You look so strange, Andrei. What is it?"

"I want to talk to you about something." He managed to look placid, almost bored. "We've had to do a lot of reorganizing. It's getting more and more difficult for me to get in and out of the ghetto. Today I had to tag onto a labor battalion going out as a road gang. Anyhow, everyone feels I should stay in the ghetto," he lied. "Besides, it's getting extremely dangerous for me to see you. It would be only a matter of time until I'm trailed here."

"Then I'll come into the ghetto with you, of course," she said.

"Well, as a matter of fact, that wouldn't be suitable."

"You never did make a good liar," she said. "What's really on your mind?"

"This is the last time I'll be seeing you, Gaby. I came to say good-by. It's not easy——"

"Why? I have a right to know."

"I don't want a scene."

"I assure you there will be no scene."

He sucked in a deep breath. "Ana has been in Warsaw since a week after Pearl Harbor. We've had a lot of business together and naturally have been seeing a lot of each other."

"Go on."

"I wish you wouldn't insist."

"I do insist."

"Very well. The night that Romek and the Farber sisters were taken to Gestapo House she was at my flat. Ana was pretty tired and upset, as you can imagine. Well, one thing led to another . . ."

Andrei watched Gabriela's back stiffen with the hurt from his words and he watched her eyes grow watery. "I don't have to draw you a diagram. You know that Ana and I were once . . . Well, she's older and better now. All things equal, it is a very good arrangement for both of us."

He stopped when she abruptly slapped his face. Then he shrugged. "I don't see why you have to take that attitude. Frankly,

262

let's admit it. We are getting a little tired of each other. At least I am. Well, that's life. We should be civilized and shake hands and wish each other luck. After all . . ."

"Get out!"

Andrei walked briskly down the street, knowing that her eyes were on his back. He turned the corner out of her sight and stopped and leaned against the building and touched the place where she had slapped him and choked back the tears. Insurmountable grief overcame him, and he sank to a sitting position on the pavement and dropped his head into his arms, which were drawn around his knees.

"Drunk," several people commented, passing him by.

A pair of Polish Blue policemen hovered over him. "Get to your feet," one ordered, prodding him with the club.

"Leave me alone," Andrei mumbled, "just leave me alone."

They bent down on either side of him, grabbed him under the armpits, and pulled him to his feet. "Let's see your *Kennkarte!*"

Andrei grabbed them by the scruffs of their necks and banged their heads together. Both of them reeled about, bloody and half-senseless. Andrei staggered down the street, blinded by his own tears.

Across the street a pair of German soldiers crisscrossed in square movements before the iron gates of the home of a high Nazi. Andrei became aware of the pipe grenade tied to his arm. His right hand fished up the sleeve of his left arm and pulled it free.

He waited until the Germans approached each other and timed his throw to hit at their feet as they crossed. The pipe arched end over end, hit the sidewalk, gave one short clatter. Then a flash and a racket and then screams.

Ana waited in Andrei's flat. His dazed eyes, his incoherent movement alarmed her.

"Andrei!"

He shook his head hard, spiraling back to reality.

"What happened? What's wrong? What did she say?"

Andrei lurched for the cabinet holding his horde of a half bottle of vodka. A stiff drink straightened him up. "What would you expect her to say when I broke in unannounced and found her and her Polish lover rolling around on the bed?"

"Oh, Andrei! I am sorry."

"Never mind—never mind. I've been suspecting it for a long time. No matter. Tomorrow I'll go out and start setting up other contacts."

In the days after, Andrei suffered a torment he did not realize existed. Throughout the nights he sulked in agony, trying to find a secret source of strength to keep him from crawling back to Gabriela. He was unable to eat. He became weak. He slept only when drugged exhaustion came over him, and his sleep was in snatches filled with teasing, hurting dreams. Each memory of his Gabriela plunged him to a new depth of torment. He moved about the ghetto with a listlessness that matched the listlessness of life around him. It was as though the will to live had left him for the first time.

A few days before Christmas, Andrei dragged himself up the stairs to his flat.

Gabriela Rak stood behind the table. He had seen her in dreams with haunting reality. But now—a hallucination in the middle of the day! The end was coming. He knew he was losing his mind. The vision refused to disappear. "Gaby?" he said, half frightened.

"Yes," she answered in a voice so crisp as to dispel the illusion.

"What the hell are you doing in the ghetto!" he roared. "How did you get in?"

"You are not the sole custodian of cleverness in the human race."

"I demand to know——"

"Kindly don't shout."

"—how you got in."

"I work for the Ursuline sisters, remember? The convent has a church. My good friend Father Kornelli is the priest. Father Kornelli told me that Father Jakub at the Converts' Church needed more candles for Christmas day, so I volunteered to bring them. Wasn't that nice of me?"

Suddenly Andrei felt the presence of someone else in the flat. He turned his eyes slowly to the kitchen. Ana stood in the doorway. "Hello, Andrei," she said.

He looked from Ana to Gabriela to Ana to Gabriela. He turned crimson. Caught red-handed!

"Really, Andrei," Ana said, "you have become a frightful liar. I should be angry, for you assault my honor."

"Which do you think is worse, Ana, Andrei's story about you and him or the story about me rolling around in bed with my Polish lover?"

"Actually, both are corkers. By the way, Andrei, did you ever get around to telling Jules Schlosberg that his grenade works? Fortunately for us, the Gestapo has blamed it on Home Army."

"All right—all right," Andrei said, "enough fun. Ana, tell Gaby how Mira and Minna Farber died."

The mood of foolery burst.

"Go on, tell her, Ana. No? Well, I will. After the Gestapo finished with them they were turned over to the Reinhard Corps barracks for sport. Stutze led the parade. A hundred more of his sportsmen followed. They continued raping them for hours after they were dead. Raping their corpses. Ana sent me to ask you to take their place in Warsaw."

"That would never happen to me, dear. I carry a vial of poison."

"I don't want any of it to happen to you. None of it!"

"You're shouting again."

"Ana, for God's sake—tell her."

"I'll tell *you*, Andrei," Gabriela said. "I'll tell you I have watched the only man I have ever loved come to me time after time after time with his heart eaten away because of the indifference of the Polish people. I am ashamed and I am humiliated for the way they have turned their backs on this terrible thing. Now you ask me, too, to be indifferent. I am going to carry my share of this. I am going to work with Ana, whether you forbid it or not."

Andrei turned his back on both of them and stared glumly, blankly, out of the window.

"I guess you don't need me here," Ana whispered to Gabriela. Gabriela saw her to the door. They touched cheeks and she left. Gaby drew the bolt on the door and walked to the center of the room. Andrei continued his sulking for a long, long time, berating himself for the rotten break he had given Gabriela by ever meeting her. Finally he turned around.

Gabriela had taken her dress off. It lay on the floor at her feet. She whisked her slip over her head in a delicate motion and let it crumple on top of her dress.

"Why, Andrei, you're blushing."

"For God's sake, this is no time for . . ."

She retreated to the bed and lay down and beckoned him with her forefinger. "Come," she said, "let me show you how I take care of my other lover."

Andrei Androfski surrendered unconditionally.

It was night. Gabriela came out of her sleep laughing. Andrei sat up, startled. When his heart stopped racing he turned to her. "What's so damned funny at two o'clock in the morning?"

"I forgot to deliver the candles to Father Jakub!"

And Andrei roared. "Hell! They're only converts. In a pinch they can de-kosherize some of Rabbi Solomon's stock."

They settled into each other's arms and spoke with that particular endearment known only to those who are very much in love and who feel they have discovered something unique in the universe.

"We have had something, Gaby. More than most people have in a lifetime."

"There is only one Andrei Androfski. He makes me very sad and he makes me very happy, but I am so glad he is mine. I have more wonderment—more fulfillment—than a hundred ordinary women have in their hundred ordinary lives."

"No regrets?"

"No regrets. I have been happier with you than a woman has a right to expect."

"I feel that way about you, Gaby. I wonder why God has been so good to me."

"Promise me, Andrei, you'll never again try to send me away."

"I promise—never again."

"Because I am prepared to take anything. Whatever lies ahead, we go it together, and if the very worst comes, I am happy."

"Oh, Gabriela ... Gabriela ... Gabriela ..."

"Love ... love ... love ... love ..."

Chapter Two

Gabriela Rak has given us all a shot in the arm. Why didn't we use her earlier? I guess because Andrei tried to shield her. A natural forgivable impulse. Her first action was to have Father Kornelli organize a dozen young priests about Warsaw who agreed not to register the deaths in their parishes with the authorities. In this way Gabriela (through the priests) can purchase the Kennkarten from the families of the deceased. We estimate in the neighborhood of twenty thousand Jews on the Aryan side. With Aryan Kennkarten they can at least get ration books.

The Ursuline Sisters have always been sympathetic and have taken as many children from us as they possibly can. They have enlisted similar help from the Sisters of the Order of the Lady Immaculate and the Sisters Szarytki of the municipal hospitals in Warsaw.

Gaby has rented flats for three more of our runners (code names: Victoria, Regina, Alina), whose main job is to supply money to hidden Jews.

Andrei tells me her flat on Shucha Street contained a windowless alcove two meters deep. A bookcase was built across it on hinges. Andrei says it is impossible to detect there is a hidden room behind the bookcase.

Zygielboim and Schwartzbart in London radioed us that fifteen thousand dollars had been dropped for us to the Home Army. Tolek Alterman was able to get only $1650. We have put an urgent priority— on establishing our own direct contact with England.

Gabriela traveled to Gdynia (where her father was a key engineer in building the port) to see an old friend, Count Rodzinski. He is almost unique, a sympathetic nobleman. His estate includes several kilometers of coast line and he owns several boats. He made a successful trial run to Karlskrona, Sweden. This could be an enormous break for us. From his estate we can smuggle out key people, and from

Sweden we can bring in American funds as well as visas and pass-ports. (Our forgeries here are expensive and crude.)

What could we accomplish with a thousand Poles like Gabriela Rak—or a hundred—or two dozen?

ALEXANDER BRANDEL

Of the two, Father Kornelli was far more nervous than Gabriela Rak as they sat in the anteroom of the office of Archbishop Klondonski. The room had a bare, cold, dark, musty appearance. The walls were lined with expressionless statues.

Father Kornelli was young and highly excitable, one of a hand-ful of priests moved to action by the happenings in the ghetto. To him it was a simple basic rule that the saving of lives was the carry-ing out of Christ's work.

Monsignor Bonifacy opened the door to the archbishop's office. "His Grace will see you now."

Archbishop Klondonski studied them from behind his desk. He was a square, squat man with blond hair, blue eyes, and rugged features that revealed his Slavic peasant ancestry. He was decep-tively simple in appearance.

The monsignor, on the other hand, was a thin, gaunt man with slender, even delicate features and dark, penetrating eyes which hinted a shrewd, probing mind.

Gabriela and Father Kornelli kissed the archbishop's ring, and he waved them into chairs opposite him. Monsignor Bonifacy slipped into a chair across the room, watching, listening, unnoticed.

"Gabriela Rak!" Klondonski said expansively, in the manner of a politician running for office. "By chance the daughter of Fryderyk Rak?"

"Yes, sir."

"A fine man. A great Pole. I remember him when he was one of the engineers building the port of Gdynia. I was a young priest at the time, not much older than Father Kornelli. Gdynia was my first parish."

Gabriela studied his open pleasantness and calculated it was a ruse with which he disarmed his visitors.

"If I am not mistaken," the churchman continued, "he met an untimely death in Switzerland."

"Your Grace has a phenomenal memory."

"And your mother—and sister, was it?"

"They live in America."

"A good place these days. Great Pole, your father. Now, tell me about yourself, young lady."

"After finishing my schooling I returned to Warsaw and until the war I worked as an aide in the American Embassy. I am now teaching at the Ursuline Convent."

"Ah, yes." He leaned back in his chair, smiling like an amiable

267

Friar Tuck, reasonably assured her request would be nominal and in the nature of a personal favor. "And your problem, my child?"

"I am here to speak to Your Grace in behalf of the Jewish Orphans and Self-Help Society in the ghetto."

The momentum of the conversation stopped. Klondonski's blue eyes lost their sweet sparkle. He covered his temporary puzzlement by tapping his fingertips together in mock meditation.

"There is imminent peril that thousands of children will die of starvation in the next few months unless immediate help is forthcoming."

Bonifacy spoke quickly. "Your Grace has studied the report on the situation."

"Oh yes," he said, taking the cue. "Yes, we have been concerned, naturally."

"While His Grace expressed concern," Bonifacy continued to refresh his superior's memory, "and we concluded in our report that there are hardships in the ghetto, it is a reflection of the times in Poland."

"Yes, my dear," said Klondonski, "we are all undergoing hardships."

"It is difficult to comprehend," Gabriela answered swiftly, "that Your Grace could study an impartial report and fail to discern the difference between mass starvation and rampant disease in the ghetto and mere privation out here. People are dying off in there at a rate of over five thousand a month."

Bonifacy spoke in a slow measured whisper now. "Our reports are based on examinations of the ghettos in Poland by a responsible international body, a commission of the Swiss Red Cross. They will be in Warsaw again next week. To date their reports do not bear out your contentions. We feel that the Jews are inclined to a natural tendency to exaggerate."

Gabriela looked to Father Kornelli for support. Wilful cowardice? Closed minds? Fear? A crass expression of anti-Semitism?

"Your Grace... Mo' 'gnor... " Father Kornelli said unevenly. "You must necessarily alize that any Swiss report is based on expediency and fear. While I do not have the details of their investigations I am quite certain they are seeing only what the Germans wish seen, listen, only to those with whom the Germans will let them speak. Switzerland is vulnerable to German invasion and defenseless. They have everything to lose by getting the Germans angry. If you wish the truth, I suggest you call in Father Jakub, who heads our Converts' congregation inside the ghetto."

"You *do* want the truth, Your Grace?" Gabriela asked bluntly.

The round Polish face of Archbishop Klondonski reddened. He did not want the truth. He simmered down and weighed his words with astute care, for his adversaries were sharp and persistent. "We do have a natural humanitarian concern. Yet the Catholic Church is not a political body, a welfare agency, or an underground. Whether or not we like the present occupants of power is a moot point. The fact is, they do constitute the government of Poland. We have a clearly outlined duty to perform. We cannot enter the Church into any schemes in wholesale defiance of authority."

"It seems to me, Your Grace, that our Church was born in defiance of the authority of Rome," Gabriela said. "If you would only see the cardinal in Krakow. If we could organize a thousand convents to take five children each . . . If . . ."

The archbishop held up his hand. "I have closed my eyes and turned my back and shut my ears to those priests and nuns who have engaged in these activities. But my office is for the spiritual welfare——"

"Your Grace, this is basic Christianity we are pleading for."

"——the spiritual welfare of the Polish people," he finished, ignoring the interruption.

"Those are Polish people behind the wall."

"Not really, Miss Rak. The fact of the matter is, we could do more for them if they agreed to conversion. Now, if they allowed us to give their children instructions in Catholicism——"

Gabriela came to her feet. "Your Grace! I am shocked! You cannot demand what God has decided."

"I will overlook your rudeness and forgive because of the tensions of the times. I suggest penance."

What was left of Gabriela's restraint exploded. "I will not forgive yours. And I suggest penance for you, sir! For every child who dies within your power of saving."

The archbishop was on his feet, as was Monsignor Bonifacy. A frightened Father Kornelli knelt and kissed the archbishop's ring. He held it in Gabriela's direction.

She looked at his hand. "You are not the representative of the Jesus Christ my father taught me of," she said, and walked from the room.

Chapter Three

Journal Entry

Strange studies are being initiated. Dr. Glazer told me six months ago that he had cancer and his time was limited. A few weeks ago he became very ill. Subsequent examination also revealed a severe case of malnutrition. Glazer has chosen to starve to death so that the Orphans and Self-Help doctors can initiate through him the world's first comprehensive medical study on starvation. There is a mania to have some good come out of even this basest form of human death. Each day the doctors meet and hold forums on the mental and physical changes of those dying of hunger. Most all of them have malnutrition themselves and discuss their own cases. (The full study of starvation is carried as a separate volume of the journal, 9A.) Dr. Glazer dictates his symptoms, his mental changes. The patterns are shrinking flesh, gauntness, skin changing color, weakness, running sores, depressions, hallucinations, gnarling bones, bloating stomachs. A Jewish gift to posterity—a detailed account of what it is like to starve to death.

Irony. This week a shipment of wheat and tons of potatoes poured in to Transferstelle and was distributed without cost to the orphanages. Our orphanage on Niska Street also received medicines we no longer thought existed and even chocolates (which no one has seen for two years). Then a school was licensed and textbooks arrived. The orphanage was painted; new bedding arrived. Then we discovered why we were being killed with kindness. Elaborate preparations were for the benefit of a delegation of Swiss from the International Red Cross who had arrived to investigate ghetto conditions. Our orphanage was designated as "typical and representative."

The Swiss carried out the sham to a T. They called a committee together at the Jewish Civil Authority building and called witnesses. The JCA, led by Boris Presser and Paul Bronski, dutifully testified to "bettering-leveling" conditions. (Truth: December death by starvation went over 4000.) Silberberg, the last friend left on the JCA board, tried to get to the Swiss to give them the truth. He was hauled off to Pawiak Prison as a "Bolshevik agitator." I was invited to testify and declined. What could I say? Could I endanger these life-giving shipments if I know that the moment the Swiss leave it would all return to as before.

We decided to get Andrei over to the Aryan side to reach Christopher de Monti. It is known that de Monti is escorting the Swiss about Warsaw. Andrei reasoned that it would be better not to attempt to get to de Monti, for even if he were to turn in our report the Swiss would not submit it. It is doubtful the Swiss would stick their necks out or suddenly make overt moves in behalf of humanity. I conceded that Andrei was correct. The Swiss do not wish to anger the Germans. They treat the entire war with indifference. We hear of numerous examples of courage by the Danes, Dutch, French, et al., in behalf of their Jewish communities. Even the Swedes, who are neutral, are harboring thousands of Jewish refugees. Could it be that ghettos could exist only in Poland, the Baltics, and Ukrainia? Our Bathyrans in Hungary and Rumania tell us that Adolf Eichmann is even having trouble extracting the Jews there. Ervin Rosemblum works in the basement, filing more and more documents. It seems that everyone is writing diaries

these days. There is a terrible fear that we will be forgotten.
Jules Schlosberg continues to build weird weapons in the next
room to Ervin. I am certain we'll be blown up someday.

ALEXANDER BRANDEL

It became dangerous in the streets in the winter of 1941 after the American entry into the war. The only regulars on the streets were the corpses deposited each morning for the sanitation squads. Even the sanctity of the Club Miami became suspect.

Andrei seldom showed up in public these days, so when a feeler was sent out by Paul Bronski for a meeting, Bronski was led through a series of blind alleys before he was finally allowed to come face to face with his brother-in-law in a basement somewhere near the Gensia Gate. Bronski's blindfold was removed. He adjusted his eyes to the candlelight.

Andrei stood over him, thinner and wearier. He studied Paul. Paul had aged with a sudden sagging of his face muscles. The thin face was prune-lined, he shook with constant tension, and his fingers were yellow with tobacco stains.

They changed amenities without feeling.

Paul took out a cigarette and went through one-armed contortions of lighting it. "This business of arms smuggling and underground press is putting the entire population in grave danger," he said.

"Go on."

"No matter what you think about us on the Civil Authority, we try our best under very limited conditions. If your activities increase it will only antagonize the Germans."

"Shut up, Paul! For Christ sake—antagonize the Germans. Do you think this death on the streets is a result of any underground? Are you so damned naïve after two years of this as to think the population is in any less danger whether there is an underground or not?"

Bronski shook his head. "I told Presser it was useless to argue with you. Andrei, there is no magic formula for getting rid of the Germans. Your activities are costing us millions of zlotys in fines and the lives of hundreds in reprisals."

"And what about the fines and the executions before the underground existed?"

"I'm trying to do the best I can," Paul whined.

Andrei could not even bring himself to hate Paul Bronski. Once, before the war, he had had a reluctant admiration for the penetrating mind and sharp wit that could run him through mental acrobatics. The thing before him was a mumbling shell.

How very strange, Andrei thought. Little Stephan Bronski had begun as a runner between the orphanage and the Self-Help headquarters over a year ago and increased his sphere of operation each

271

month. The youngster idolized Wolf Brandel, who taught him the routes around the ghetto over rooftops, through courtyards and basements, and all the secret hiding places. Stephan pressed to be given more responsible missions, even begged to be allowed to go to the Aryan side. Stephan was not yet thirteen years old. How can a boy demand to walk like a man and his own father crawl through the mud?

"Andrei, think what you will of me, but the people here only want to survive. You know that, Andrei—survive. The best way to live is through the Civil Authority. No one has answered your call to arms, Andrei. Your way would be mass suicide. Andrei—now listen—Boris Presser and I have been negotiating with Koenig. Koenig is a reasonable man and he can maneuver Schreiker. Koenig promises that if we can get the underground to stop its activities they will make a settlement with us on rations, medicine, and the disposition of the labor force."

"Good God, Paul. Can you believe your own words?"

"It's our only chance!"

There was nothing more to be said. Andrei could not mask his contempt. He handed Paul Bronski a blindfold. "I don't know anything about an underground."

Bronski took the blindfold. "You'll have to tie it on ... I can't do it with one hand."

Ervin Rosenblum worked in the musty room below Mila 19, sorting the notes of the Good Fellowship Club. A rap on the false packing crate which served as an entrance made him douse the lights and freeze. Ana Grinspan entered.

"Susan has just come back," she said. "Get up to your room."

"Is anything wrong?"

"Go on."

Ervin felt his way through an aisle lined with packing cases. In the main office on the first floor he saw everyone staring. Alexander Brandel stood by the door of his office, shaking his head.

Ervin raced up the stairs to the second floor carefully. The rail was gone, chopped up for firewood weeks earlier. Down the corridor to that cell which he shared with his wife and mother.

Momma Rosenblum lay on a cot beneath a pile of quilts. It was icy. There was no heat in the house. The room was ugly and bare except for Momma's cot, double bed for Ervin and Susan, and a single table and two chairs.

Susan's face was distraught. Ervin felt a catch in his heart. Susan had always seemed resilient to tragedy, plodding on, doing her job regardless. He had never seen her like this. He wiped his glasses nervously, trying to adjust his vision to the change of light from the cellar.

"Tell me," he said at last.

272

"Dr. Glazer," she groaned.

In a way, Ervin was relieved. They had been expecting Glazer to go. Another death, another, another. Key people dying in droves. Glazer had been like a father to Susan from the day she graduated from the university. Little Bernard Glazer who had brought so many children into life had watched them die, helpless to save them. Glazer was better off, Ervin thought. But God, he'd be missed. He was the best man in his field.

Ervin flopped his hands. "Too bad," was all he could say.

Susan slung a sheaf of papers on the table. "A farewell present to you, Ervin. A minute-by-minute account of his death."

What a legacy! Ervin stared at the yellowish papers but did not touch them.

"Take it, Ervin!" Her voice rose sharply. "It's Dr. Glazer's gift to you!"

"Susan ... Susan ... please."

"Damn you!" she shrieked. "People die and you write in your lousy journal! God damn you, Ervin!"

Momma Rosenblum stirred. "*Kinder, Kinder,*" she said weakly, "don't shriek at each other."

Susan sat beside the old woman and felt her forehead automatically. "I'm sorry, Momma. I didn't mean it, Ervin."

"It's all right, Susan, I understand."

"God, I don't know what to do with Dr. Glazer gone. God ... Ten children died today ... God ... " Her breath darted out in streams of frosty air.

Journal Entry

As the population is decimated the Germans close off the little ghetto in the south. As soon as a bit of room becomes available in the big ghetto, houses are closed off in the south. Crossing the bridge over the "Polish corridor" are the fancy Jews from Germany, the Jewish Civil Authority people, and the Militia and wealthier smugglers and members of the Big Seven. Only one major factory complex is left in the small ghetto, and that is the woodwork shops. As the small ghetto is abandoned it has become a no man's land where Wild Ones without Kennkarten hide so they will not have to submit to slave labor. The abandoned ghetto has become a rendezvous for smugglers and to carry on prostitution for those still decent enough in appearance to sell their bodies. Raiding parties cross into the little ghetto at night and rip up wooden floors, doors, rails, and anything else that can be used for firewood and cart it off. In the big ghetto the crowding is worse than before. People sleep in hallways, cellars, in outside courtyards.

We continue to attempt to get dollars from British parachute drops, but it is hit-and-miss. With our dollar supply shrinking, the zloty has inflated again. David Zemba has made a simple plan.

Through our people in London we have gotten American Aid to deposit several hundred thousands of dollars in Swiss accounts. Many of the smugglers have enormous collections of zlotys virtually unspendable and useless to them. We buy the zlotys by transferring Swiss dollars into their personal accounts in Geneva. We are able to get a good rate and with enough of these zlotys can buy essentials. We try not to deal with the Big Seven, but it is certain that Max Kleperman has his people in on this. Also, we can make direct barter with our Swiss money for houses, rooms, gold, food, and medicine with those smugglers who have caches. This latter is preferable to the zloty exchange. David Zemba is in conferences, trading for our Swiss dollars all day, every day. He has saved hundreds of lives.

Three major slave-labor factory complexes remain in the ghetto, all belonging to Franz Koenig. In the small ghetto there is a woodwork plant. In the north, the Brushmaker's district. This latter supplies a major part of the brushes for the German army. Most of the people, in their desperation to live, still maintain that a Kennkarte stamped for labor is the key to life.

From the third factory we hear something that is a ray of hope, however faint. It is the uniform factory. Although the Germans claim to be at the gates of Moscow, we sense their first great defeat of the war. Nearly a hundred thousand bloody uniforms have arrived from the eastern front. In the factory the slave laborers clean, patch, and weave them and make them ready for reissue in Germany.

A hundred thousand German casualties? Good news.

ALEXANDER BRANDEL

Chapter Four

Rachael raced through rapid passages of Chopin's Second Concerto in preparation for a concert with what was left of the Ghetto Symphony Orchestra to be held in Franz Koenig's uniform factory.

She turned to the slow lilt of the andante, and her mind strayed from her work. Three more members of the orchestra had died. There were only forty musicians left and they were listless. A spasm of tension gripped her stomach. Wolf had been gone five days this time. It was the third time in a month that Andrei had sent him to the Aryan side. They said they wouldn't, but they needed Wolf, even at the risk. What were they to do? She longed to marry him, but her father would be violently opposed. Wolf's father had once been an active Zionist and many people knew about Wolf's work. Poppa would allow nothing to besmirch his position on the Civil Authority. He was completely unreasonable about it.

274

In the bedroom, Stephan lay on his stomach studying the Haftorah, a reading from the Prophets, in preparation for the coming bar mitzvah. He always remembered the sound of music from his mother and sister. It had a magic quality of transcending him beyond all harm and all ugliness. Rachael stumbled on a passage, then fingered her way through the next bars.

Stephan automatically stopped reading and rolled off the bed and walked to the window. They had just moved to this new place in the big ghetto. He had to share a bedroom with Rachael, and it was a pretty run-down place but far better than most people had. Just across the street stood the old post office building where the Civil Authority had been housed since the Germans closed the place on Grzybowska Street. His father worked in there. In front of the large square, columned structure stood the only tree and plot of grass in the ghetto. It felt cool and soft to roll in.

The music stopped.

Stephan walked back to his bed and flopped on his belly, waiting for Rachael to begin playing again so he could resume his studies.

He had always had an unspoken communication with his sister. They wanted to talk to each other now. She sat on the edge of his bed and mussed his hair. He rebelled slightly.

"How can you read that chicken scratch?" she said, referring to the Hebrew text.

"It's no worse than the chicken scratch you read at the piano." Stephan closed the book. "I wish Wolf would get back and help me with my lessons. Rabbi Solomon—well, we have to be perfect. He's tough."

"Stephan?"

"Yes?"

"Wolf told me you tried to get him and Uncle Andrei to let you distribute the underground paper."

The boy did not answer.

"Is it true?"

"I guess so."

"Does Momma know?"

"No."

"Don't you think you'd better tell her?"

He spun off the bed, away from her inquiries.

"What would we do if anything happened to you?"

"Don't you understand, Rachael?"

"With Wolf and Uncle Andrei doing their work, I can't lose all of you."

"If only Poppa——" Stephan stopped short. "Nothing."

"You can't make up for him, Stephan."

"I'm so ashamed. For a long time I tried to believe what he was telling me."

"Don't be too hard on Poppa. No one knows how much he has suffered. You must be kind."

"How can you say that? If it weren't for Poppa you and Wolf could marry."

"He's still your father, Stephan, and I know that Rabbi Solomon would be the first to tell you to honor him, always."

"Rachael . . . Momma and Poppa don't love each other any more, do they?"

"It's only because of the times, Stephan."

"That's all right. You don't have to try to explain."

She changed the subject quickly. "So, you're going to be a real man next week. Well, let me see if you have a hair on your chin yet." Rachael wrestled him to the floor. He gently allowed himself to be pinned down. Her fingers dug into his ribs and he squirmed, half angry, half laughing.

"Quit it, Rachael! I can't wrestle with you any more."

She bared her claws. "And why not?"

"Because you're a girl and I may grab something by mistake."

"Well! Stephan Bronski! You *are* becoming a man!"

In a moment she went back to the andante movement. Stephan slipped beside her on the bench and rested his head on her shoulder. Rachael put her arm about her brother and kissed his forehead.

"It won't be much of a bar mitzvah for you, will it?"

"Just taking the oath to live as a Jew is important," he answered.

"You are a little man."

"Don't be afraid, Rachael. Wolf will be back. I heard you cry last night. Don't be afraid. Rachael, I think I understand everything about you and Wolf and I want you to know I'm very glad because next to Uncle Andrei he's the finest man who ever lived. He has explained lots of things to me . . . about being a man . . . like things Poppa should have explained . . ."

Rachael blanched, then smiled. "I wish he would come back. I wish he would come back. . . ."

"He said he'd get back for my bar mitzvah. He will, Rachael."

Alexander Brandel's office was converted into a makeshift synagogue, just as a million other places had been converted for illicit worship for two thousand years. Rabbi Solomon donned the ancient vestments of the rabbinate and opened the Torah scroll and chanted to the room where Ervin Rosenblum and Andrei and Alex and three Bathyrans stood near what represented an altar. Beyond Alex's desk, Rachael and Susan and Deborah and many of Stephan's friends jammed together. The shell of the man who was once Dr. Paul Bronski was alone by the door.

Stephan Bronski fidgeted slightly as his mother brushed her hand over the tallis which had belonged to her own father. Since no new shawls had been made since the occupation, the rabbi ruled it fitting for the boy to wear this symbol of one generation passing a tradition to another. Stephan's months of study were coming to a culmination.

He looked about toward the door, hoping that Wolf Brandel would come through it in the last moment, but all he saw was his father. He smiled slightly at Rachael.

Rabbi Solomon faced the assemblage. Another boy was ready to accept his duties as a son of the commandment, a guardian of the Laws, and take upon himself the terrible burden of Jewish life. Only a week earlier there had been another bar mitzvah. The son of Max Kleperman had reached the age of thirteen. He was given the symbols of manhood in a large hall at the Big Seven headquarters amid gluttonous revelry. The old man wanted to turn his back on Kleperman's mockery and walk away, but he didn't, for he was merely the administrator of God's will and not its judge.

His thinning high voice asked the candidate to step forward.

Stephan took a last sigh and felt his mother's hand squeeze his shoulder. He walked forward to receive his new social status. The boy was slight and small like his father.

"Bless the Lord Who is to be praised."

"Praised be the Lord Who is blessed for all eternity," the men in the room answered.

"Blessed art Thou, O Lord our God, King of the universe, Who didst choose us from among all the peoples by giving us Thy Torah. Blessed art Thou, O Lord, Giver of the Laws," Stephan chanted.

The boy and the old man turned to the Torah scrolls which lay on Alexander Brandel's desk. With the tassels of the shawl, Stephan touched the Torah, kissed the shawl, and read from the Laws of Moses. From the benediction he went to the climax of his studies, the chanting of the Maftir Aliya from the Book of Prophets, one of the most difficult of all Hebrew readings.

Stephan faced the room and chanted from memory. His voice was small and high, but it carried with it that cry of anguish born of the oppressions of many Pharaohs in many ages. The room was awed as the lad displayed the full mastery of his accomplishment. Even Solomon delved into memory to try to recall when a young man had read the Haftorah with greater authority, grace and musical perfection.

When the closing benediction was done, the Torah scrolls were closed, to be taken and hidden from desecration by the Germans.

Stephan Bronski faced the room. Uncle Andrei winked. Stephan looked about, hoping that Wolf might have come in, but he hadn't. He cleared his throat. "I would like to thank my mother and father," he said in the traditional opening of the valedictory, "for bringing me up in the Jewish tradition."

The pronouncement seldom failed to bring tears to women.

Deborah and Rachael proved no exception. But in the rear of the office the words struck Paul Bronski like a stiletto. He lowered his eyes as his son continued.

"I realize that becoming a son of the commandment is just a token of manhood. A lot of people told me how sorry they were that I couldn't have my bar mitzvah in peacetime when the Great Tlomatskie Synagogue would have been almost full and relatives would have come from all of Poland and there would have been a large celebration and presents. I thought a lot about all that, but I am really glad to have my bar mitzvah in a place like this room, because in places like this the Jewish faith has been kept alive during other times of oppression. I think, too, it is a special privilege to have your bar mitzvah in bad times. Anyone can live like a Jew when things go well, but to take an oath to be a Jew today is really important. We know that God needs real Jews to protect His laws. Well . . . we have survived everyone who has tried to destroy us before because we have kept this kind of faith. Our God will not let us down. I am very proud to be a Jew and I will try hard to uphold my responsibilities."

Rabbi Solomon held the tallis on Stephan's head and chanted the closing priestly blessing. The room pressed forward to converge on the boy and congratulate him with hearty "*Mozeltoffs.*" Paul Bronski left the place quickly and quietly.

"I guess you are satisfied now," Paul snapped at Deborah. "You've put on your little circus. You've won your battle. You've showed me up as a damned fool in front of the whole ghetto."

Deborah tried to contain herself. His eyes were filled with that half-wild look again.

"Grinding salt into my wounds," he continued. "Making me look ridiculous."

"Stephan did not have a bar mitzvah as a vendetta against you."

"Like hell."

"Paul, let's go to sleep," she pleaded.

"Sleep?" He laughed sardonically. "Who sleeps?"

He tried to light a cigarette, but his hand trembled so violently that he was able to accomplish it only with her steadying hand. "Well, Deborah, now that our son is properly a Jew and you have won your crusade for his holy purification for my sins——"

"Stop it!"

"—now perhaps we can discuss a family matter. We *are* still a family, you know."

"If you speak like a civilized person."

His outburst was done now. He calmed himself. "You've got to give up working at the orphanage and Rachael has to stop giving concerts. As for Stephan, he spends entirely too much time on the streets."

278

She merely narrowed her eyes at his pronouncement.

"We must reappraise all our friends. A continued association with Brandel, Rosenblum, and Susan could become dangerous. Everyone is aware of their past affiliations and no one is sure they are not part of this underground."

"Now you just stop where you are, Paul——"

"Let me finish, dammit, let me finish! I can't guarantee your immunity because of the likes of your goddamned brother and his agitators. They've pulled in the entire family of one of our board members and are holding them all at Pawiak Prison as a warning for us to break up this underground."

All that was left of a desire for honor seemed to drain out of him in that instant. His skin was a horrible gray. "We have decided ——"

"What?"

"We have decided that our families have to come to work inside the Civil Authority building and never be out of our sight."

"Oh, my God, it's come to this." Deborah held her hand over her eyes for only a few tears. "All through this," she whispered, "I have waited patiently for . . . Paul, at first I tried so very, very hard to make myself believe that what you were doing was really the right thing. But each day as you degrade yourself lower and lower you have ceased to be a human being."

"How dare you!"

"Good God, Paul! Didn't you hear your son today? Can't the courage of a little boy touch you, move you?"

"I won't listen!"

"You will listen, Paul Bronski! You will listen!"

He knelt before her desperately and grabbed her arm and shook it. "We can talk aesthetics until hell freezes, but what I am saying to you is reality."

The tears fell down her cheeks. "Reality? My poor man, you are the one who has been hiding from reality. I'm going to tell you what reality is. Your daughter is sleeping with Wolf Brandel, and I sent her to him because her marriage would endanger her father's precious position as a collaborator."

"That son of a bitch——"

"Good! At least you have the decency to show anger. But he is a fine young man and I thank God she is able to find a few moments of happiness in this hell. Shall I tell you more reality? I am working on manufacturing bombs in the cellar of the orphanage, and your son Stephan is delivering the underground newspaper."

Paul Bronski stood up and grunted like a confused, dying animal.

"Do you know why, Paul? He came to me and pleaded—'Momma, I'm going to be thirteen. . . . Momma, someone in our family has to be a man.'"

Paul crumpled into a chair and sobbed. She stood over the groveling, shaking cur, and the disdain ebbed into a terrible weariness. "I only did it for you," he wept, "only for you."

"I'm tired, Paul. . . . I'm all done in." Suddenly, without plan, the words found their way through her. "I have a chance to leave the ghetto with the children."

He looked up at her, blinking. "De Monti . . . De Monti."

She nodded.

"You'd do this to me?"

"I have made my atonements. I have paid, repaid a thousand, thousand times, and I swear I don't know if I was ever wrong even in the beginning. But if I was, I have been punished by you. I promise you, Chris will never touch me. All I want is to find a hole someplace to crawl into where I can't hear starving children cry. Maybe a patch of grass . . . that's all I want . . . just . . . a patch of grass."

Paul slid to the floor on his knees and doubled up before her feet. "Please don't leave me," he wept, "please don't leave me . . . please don't leave me . . ."

Chapter Five

Spring of 1942.

The awesome winter was done, but the smell of death lingered. The little ghetto on the south was all but shrunken. Polish families inched back in as the Jewish decimation increased. All that remained in the south were a few streets of Jews, the woodwork factory, and Wild Areas. The big ghetto became more crammed than ever.

With the reinforcement of the Waffen SS guard, the ghetto fell into a grip of fear worse than any it had experienced. The smug Elite Corps with their lightning streaks on black uniforms entered Warsaw fresh from their jobs as Kommandos in the Special Action massacres on the eastern front. Placed under Sieghold Stutze, they were wild, drinking louts, turned into savages by the sight of the blood of their victims. They filled the barracks at 101 Leszno Street just beyond the ghetto wall, opposite Koenig's uniform factory.

A second set of guards arrived. Latvians and Lithuanians wearing uniforms of Nazi Auxiliaries with insignias of skull and crossbones on their epaulets. These peasants from the Baltics had carried out their share of the eastern massacres with relish.

A third force came in from Globocnik's headquarters in Lublin. Ukrainians. Their men's choir, sober or drunk, sang with such harmony they were dubbed the Nightingales. The Litts, Latts, and

Nightingales took the red brick building cater-corner to the SS barracks.

Each night the sounds of drunken revelry heightened the fear.

SS General Alfred Funk, courier of the verbal messages on "Jewish problems," arrived in Warsaw as a harbinger of doom. Fresh from conferences with Heydrich, Himmler, and Hitler in Berlin, he arrived with Adolf Eichmann, Gestapo 4B, Jewish affairs.

The Krakow *Gazette* increased its build-up of the "final solution to the Jewish problem." Around Poland, the feverish activity of building new camps brought in German experts in transportation and construction. But these new camps were different. They were neither for slave labor nor for the containment of enemies of the Reich. They were built in great secrecy in out-of-the-way locations, and their structures had odd shapes unlike any ever seen.

By midwinter Alfred Funk concluded his conferences in Warsaw and returned to SS headquarters in Lublin and further verbal instructions for Globocnik.

Early in March one of Ana Grinspan's runners reached Warsaw with the information that an Operation Reinhard, named after Heydrich, was taking place for the liquidation of the Lublin ghetto. The ghetto occupants as well as transports of Jews from outside Poland were being sent to a camp named Majdanek on the outskirts of the city.

When Funk came back to Warsaw everyone speculated wildly on the meaning, but after the winter just past no one believed things could get worse.

Rabbi Solomon sat on the floor in another of the makeshift synagogues before his emaciated congregation, which had once been a proud group recognized in the religious circles of Poland. The few stragglers who remained represented the heart of European Jewry. Stephan Bronski, the rabbi's favorite pupil, was near the learned one.

It was the ninth day of the Hebrew month of Ab, the day on which the greatest disasters had befallen the Jews. On Tisha B'Ab the First Temple of Solomon was destroyed by the Babylonians, and centuries later, on the same day, the Second Temple fell to the Romans, starting a series of events which eventually spread the seed of Abraham to the corners of the world as damned and eternal wanderers and strangers.

On Tisha B'Ab an angry Moses had come down from Sinai and smashed the tablets of the commandments upon sight of the reveling tribes of Israel worshiping an idol. It was as though he had cast an eternal curse upon them, for this night of Tisha B'Ab the lights burned late in the offices of Gestapo House, Reinhard Corps headquarters, and the offices of Rudolph Schreiker.

Rabbi Solomon read from the "Valley of Tears" and the Holy Torah was revealed and he swayed and cried Jeremiah's prophecies of doom.

"And the Lord shall scatter you among the nations and ye shall be left few in number."

A mournful response followed his words.

"We looked for peace, but no good came; and for a time of health and behold trouble! For, behold I will send serpents among you which will not be charmed and they shall bite you, saith the Lord . . . the harvest is past, the summer ended and we are not saved . . . for death is come up to our windows and is entered into our palaces to cut off the children from without, and the young men from the streets . . . the carcasses of men shall fall as dung upon the open field."

As Rabbi Solomon lamented, the overture to the most horrible catastrophe in a catastrophe-filled history was playing out.

Black Friday ushered in the Big Action.

The Nazis called in members of their networks of informers and bled them for information during the\ night. By dawn a swift, merciless sweep was plotted to denude the Jews of the last of their leadership.

With sirens screaming in hideous harmony to the rabbi's prayers, the SS and their Litts, Latts, Polish Blues, Jewish Militia, and Ukrainians swept in from every gate and scoured the ghetto, smoking out the resistance people from secret rooms.

Tens of dozens were marched unceremoniously to the cemetery and shot by a firing squad of Nightingales.

Ana Grinspan, Andrei Androfski and Tolek Alterman had the fortune to be on the Aryan side. Other Bathyrans hid in the basement of Mila 19 with Jules Schlosberg and Ervin Rosenblum amid journals of the Good Fellowship Club and homemade fire bombs. Simon Eden spent the day crossing rooftops, and Rodel, the Communist, cringed in a hidden closet.

Alexander Brandel and David Zemba were among the fortunate not on the roundup list.

But dozens of people from the Bathyrans and the Labor Zionists and Revisionists and Bundists were not so fortunate. Black Friday shattered the ghetto and it sank to its lowest depths.

On the Sabbath following the massacre the ghetto was plastered with terrifying orders and the loudspeaker trucks roamed up and down, up and down, booming the edicts.

ORDER OF DEPORTATION NOTICE

1. By order of the German authorities all Jews living in Warsaw, without regard to age or sex, are to be deported to the East.

2. The following are excluded from the deportation order:

(a) All Jews employed by German authorities or in German

enterprises who have their *Kennkarten* properly stamped.
- (b) All Jews who are members and employees of the Jewish Civil Authority as of the day of this notice.
- (c) All Jews belonging to the Jewish Militia.
- (d) The families of the above-mentioned. Families consist only of husband/wives and children.
- (e) Jews employed by social welfare agencies under the Jewish Civil Authority and Orphans and Self-Help Society.

3. Each deportee is entitled to take fifteen kilograms of personal possessions as baggage. All baggage over the weight will be confiscated. (All valuable articles such as money, jewelry, gold, etc., should be taken in order to use it for an orderly resettlement.) Three days' food should be taken.

4. Deportation commences on July 22, 1942, at 11 A.M.

5. Punishments:
- (a) Jews in the published lists not reporting will be shot.
- (b) Jews undertaking activities to evade or hinder orderly deportation will be shot.

JEWISH CIVIL AUTHORITY, WARSAW
Boris Presser, Chairman

ANNOUNCEMENT

Each deportee who reports voluntarily will be supplied with 3 kg. bread and 1 kg. marmalade. Food distribution will be held at Stawki Square.

Staging center for deportation will be the process center at Stawki 6-8 on the Umschlagplatz.

JEWISH CIVIL AUTHORITY, WARSAW
Dr. Paul Bronski, Deputy Chairman

ANNOUNCEMENT

Each day deportations will be clearly posted and announced for the proceeding day. Deportees for July 23 shall come from the following areas:

Elektoralna St. No. 34-42
Chlodna St. No. 28-44 inclusive
Orla St. No. 1-14 and 16-34
Leszno St. No. 1-3, 7-51, 57-77
All Biala Street

BY ORDER OF PIOTR WARSINSKI
Jewish Militia of Warsaw

The underground recoiled from Black Friday and set out to determine what was behind the deportation.

For the first three days the Germans had an unexpected success. Wild Ones who lived in hiding without *Kennkarten* left their secret hovels, unable to resist the temptation of the three kilograms of bread and one kilogram of marmalade promised by the Germans. There were more volunteers than could be processed at the Umschlagplatz.

The deportation center was in a gray four-story concrete structure at Stawki 6-8, just beyond the northern gate. It was out of view of both the ghetto and the Aryan side. Once a school, it had later been an Orphans and Self-Help hospital.

Waffen SS Hauptsturmführer Kutler, in charge of the detail, was a member of the Kommandos who had carried out the massacres on the eastern front. Kutler was in a state of drunkenness, tormented by a continuous nightmare of blood. His gory dreams were shared by most of the other Kommandos, who kept themselves going on liquor and dope.

A pair of thick iron doors hung across the entrance. Inside, a half dozen Nazis made selections, standing in front of the neverending lines of humanity. A few were returned to the ghetto for labor. Most were passed along to the immense cobblestone yard surrounded by a high wall.

The courtyard detail was composed of Nightingales and their Litt and Latt compatriots under the direction of a few SS men who held vicious Alsatian dogs at leash end.

A brick train shed and platform some two blocks in length ran to the extreme end of the courtyard. A train of forty-four cattle and freight cars stood in readiness.

As the selectees came in, their belongings were ransacked for jewelry, money, valuables of any kind. In order to make room for more people on the cars, most of the clothing they carried was confiscated.

A detail of Jews from Koenig's labor pool carted the clothing across the street to a building which served as a warehouse. Linings of coats were ripped apart for hidden valuables. Personal mementos—family letters, pictures, keepsakes—were burned in a large oven alongside the building.

When six thousand people had been gathered, they were loaded on the trains. At three o'clock promptly each afternoon the train pulled out for an "unknown eastern destination."

The Wild Ones who had volunteered in the first days of the Big Action had been cowed to such a state that they offered almost no resistance. But anyone who balked inside the Umschlagplatz courtyard was pounced upon immediately, mercilessly, by the guards.

Outside the courtyard, Polish Blues and Jewish Militia kept order in the lines feeding people into the selection center.

The aged, cripples, and those obviously unfit for labor were taken from the Umschlagplatz and shot by SS firing squads at the cemetery several blocks away. In this way the Germans "proved" they were taking only the healthiest people to the new labor camps.

Despite the passivity of the Orthodox community, men like Rabbi Solomon continued to wield great influence over the people. As more and more rabbis went to an unknown fate, diminishing the numbers leading the Orthodox Jews, the remaining inherited more responsibility.

On the fourth day of the Big Action the remnants of the underground had the Umschlagplatz under observation and scurried desperately around Warsaw trying to learn the destination of the trains.

Alexander Brandel visited Rabbi Solomon in an attempt to convince him to go to the Jewish Civil Authority. The old man had drawn a rigid circle binding his duties. The Civil Authority, he argued, was beyond his sphere of activity. Through Talmudic reasoning and arguments Alex weakened his stand by drawing parallels with ancient exiles. Finally the rabbi agreed to a rabbinical court and allowed Alex to plead before the five rabbis they were able to assemble.

They decided it was morally correct for Rabbi Solomon to petition the Civil Authority.

The old man was partly blind, able to see only in shadowy images. Months before, he had been forced to give up his work on the Good Fellowship notes and Brandel's journal. He entered the Civil Authority building at Zamenhof and Gensia streets on the arm of Stephan Bronski, his favorite student.

Paul Bronski was more nervous than usual. The sight of Stephan with the rabbi in broad daylight in a place which was a rats' nest of informers unnerved him. Stephan was sent home. Although Solomon could not see Paul, he was able to sense the uneasiness in the man's voice.

"Dr. Bronski, there has been much talk about these deportations. In fact, little else is spoken of."

"That is certainly understandable."

"We hear that there are continuations of the eastern massacres in death camps."

"Nonsense. Can't you see it is the same group of agitators we have had to contend with since the first day of the occupation? We

285

have only their propaganda that there have ever been massacres in the east."

"Has the Civil Authority ever questioned the Germans about the validity of the stories of the eastern massacres?"

Of course not. Paul clamped his teeth together. Sightless though the old man was, none of the keen edge had gone from his mind, nor had he lost the acid manner of setting verbal traps.

"My dear Rabbi Solomon, no one claims that life in the ghetto has been easy. We are the losers in a war in which we have been chosen as the scapegoat. Yet, through orderly process, the fact is that we have kept most people alive and here."

"Then, Dr. Bronski, I assume you are ready to assure us that most of us will still be alive and here in three or four weeks?"

Paul had spoken about the deportations only to Boris Presser. His own hopes were that within a week or two the Germans would restock their labor camps and the deportations would stop.

"I am waiting for an answer, Dr. Bronski."

Paul was afraid to take a position. Suppose he said the deportations would stop and they did not. Suppose the rumors of death camps were true and the Civil Authority had taken no stand on them. He had run out of maneuvering room. For two years and seven months he had found one more escape, and one more, and one more. This was the dead end.

"I am reasonably certain the deportations will stop as soon as the Germans decongest the ghetto. Decongestion of the ghetto will alleviate many of our problems here, and the population shifts to strengthen their labor pool closer to the eastern front will obviously satisfy the Germans."

"Would the Civil Authority ask the Germans if your reasonable certainties are reasonable certainties with them also?"

Rabbi Solomon's trap sprang shut. Paul wanted no more of the man. He mumbled quickly that the matter would be pursued.

Boris Presser had performed his duties as chairman of the Jewish Civil Authority almost as a nonentity. He was a quiet little man whose forte was an extraordinary ability to stay out of people's way and to carry out his office in a mechanical manner, without emotional attachment. The murder of Emanuel Goldman, the first Civil Authority chairman in the early days of the occupation, clearly outlined the limitations of his power.

Presser dexterously avoided clandestine meetings with the underground, the social agencies, or the smugglers. He was learned at knowing nothing, seeing nothing, hearing nothing. He kept himself untainted through deftness. He was, in fact, the perfect tool in the Nazi logic which pointed up that Jews were killing each other off. When boxed in from time to time, Presser could always justify the existence of the Civil Authority. Without it, he explained

286

conditions would be far more severe. He made himself believe it was an instrument of survival.

When Paul Bronski confronted Boris with the ground swell of apprehension over the deportations Presser would not be talked into a meeting with the Germans. As he had done a hundred times before, he delegated Paul Bronski.

The choices? Schreiker and the Reinhard Corps were impossible to speak to. Could he move through Max Kleperman? No, the Big Seven wanted to know nothing about the deportations. Move through Brandel and David Zemba? No, it was they who brought the pressure on the Civil Authority.

Dr. Franz Koenig was his only choice.

Koenig's new residence was a forty-room palace, the latest confiscation in his capacity as chief of confiscations. In a few short years he had become a multimillionaire.

Koenig had grown abnormally obese. His body resembled a pear and his head a puffy tomato with an obnoxious flat clipping of fuzz on top.

Power was unbecoming. After the first sweet taste of revenge and fulfillment, he came to loggerheads with the reality that he had placed himself in league with men of a bestiality he did not believe could exist among civilized people. His wonderful Germany, his land of the gifts of culture, was being run by maniacs and sadists. He remembered his very first discussion of the mass murders. Now he wondered what he had done. Yet, irresistibly, he rose higher and higher. Himmler himself received him regularly. All that Franz Koenig had known of truth and beauty was abandoned by him. A victim of fear, he had been purchased—soul, heart, and mind.

Paul's throat was caked dry as he stood before Dr. Koenig. It was a long way from the university to this forty-foot office. Yet Paul's presence always had the disconcerting effect of making Koenig remember that he had once been content to read Schiller and listen to Mozart in the sanctity of his study, away from his fat Polish wife.

Paul managed to blurt out the message of apprehension over the deportations.

"You have a militia at your disposal. Use it," Koenig snapped in irritation.

"But if we use it more than we already have to implement the deportations, it will only serve to confirm the people's suspicions."

Koenig rocked back and forth in his outsized chair. He could turn the matter over to Rudolph Schreiker for a flat and brutal closing of all discussion. Was this wise? Only a few days and the stream of volunteers for deportation had all but dried up. There was risk of a hardening resistance with the growing underground. Koenig had a dozen factories both in and out of the ghetto which needed a constant supply of labor. Schreiker had not changed an iota from his blundering, stupid ways. He had learned to manipulate Schreiker, to make his own position firm by the feeling that he was indispensable. Schreiker was deep in his debt through bribes and loans.

Paul Bronski and Boris Presser had been obedient servants. If they were replaced in a swift purge, it could upset the well-controlled balance he maintained over the ghetto.

"It is reasonable," Koenig said in measured terms, "that the Jewish Civil Authority assure the people of our good intentions."

When Paul had gone, Koenig went to the city hall to convince Rudolph Schreiker of the importance of having the Jewish Civil Authority make a public proclamation for the continuance of orderly deportations. Schreiker was, as usual, too confused by the issues to do other than mumble for Koenig to go ahead.

The next day Paul Bronski, Boris Presser, and the entire board of the Jewish Civil Authority were whisked out of the ghetto for an inspection at Poniatow, Trawniki, and dozens of eastern labor camps which existed to supply road gangs constructing air strips and manufacturing munitions. The railroads had received their first Russian bombings. Gangs of Jews put them back into working order.

The superficial inspection was parallel to the "inspections" held for the Swiss Red Cross in their investigation of ghetto conditions. Yet it served as a face-saving gesture for Presser and Bronski. At the end of the tour, which showed or proved nothing, Koenig distorted it into Nazi logic. The inspection "proved" that the deportations from Warsaw were for the announced purpose of dispersing and decentralizing industry and moving it closer to the eastern battle line.

Neither Boris Presser nor Paul Bronski was able to allow himself the luxury of pursuing the truth. On their return to Warsaw, Koenig had prepared statements for their signature. They affixed their names for the stated reasons and under tolerable working conditions and further urged co-operation in orderly departures.

Copies of the documents were plastered on a thousand walls, but despite them the streams of volunteers had completely dried up by the sixth day of the Big Action.

"Juden! 'Raus!"
"Jews! Outside!"

Whistles! Sirens! Deserted streets. Taut fear behind the drawn shades.

The Nightingales who sang in such beautiful harmony poured from their trucks in another of the sudden strikes to block off a building and pour in and smash down doors and drag the struggling occupants into the streets.

Wolf Brandel slipped into his trousers and shirt at the sounds of

288

the screams across the way and peered from a corner window in Andrei's flat to the scene of horror in the courtyard. Rachael wrapped herself in the bed sheet and tried to look, but Wolf held her back at arm's length.

A drama of violence erupted amid the confusion as a man attempted to break through the cordon of Ukrainians to reach his wife and was bloodily clubbed to the pavement for his efforts. He lay groaning and twitching, drenched in his own blood. Another outburst. A frantic young mother lurched at a huge guard, clawing his face, biting his hand, as she tried to get back her infant. The guard roared with laughter, grabbed her by the hair, and flung her into a circle of flailing clubs. The cordon pushed their captives up the street toward the Umschlagplatz with a steady tattoo of truncheon smashes.

Wolf buttoned his shirt clumsily and replaced his pistol in his belt. Rachael forgot her modesty and let the sheet fall from her, but the blood-burst on the streets had broken the spell of love-making. Wolf braced his back against the iron bedstead and dropped his face on his knees while she dressed. She cuddled up next to him, laying her head on his lap, and they stayed numbed and quiet until the last of the cries faded from their hearing.

"Where are the trains going?" she whispered shakily.

He shook his head.

"My father says they'll stop soon, but I don't believe him. There's talk about death camps."

She began to tremble, and her face and hands felt icy. He tried to comfort her.

"I don't mean to be like this . . . It was only—— I was so frightened when you didn't come back in time for Stephan's bar mitzvah. I'm always dreaming of the trains. I dream they're taking Stephan. Wolf, he's taking too many chances. Make him stop."

"How can I argue with him to be against what we are trying to stand for?"

"What do we stand for? What in God's name do we stand for?"

"I don't know, really. My father might be able to put it into certain words. So can Rabbi Solomon. I just want to live and I want you to live. I guess that's all I really stand for."

In a little while she became calm.

"Someday it will all be over, Rachael. It must end sometime."

"If I could only be your wife. If I could only have your baby. Wolf, if either of us goes on the trains, I want you to know how very much I love you."

"We're going to come through this . . . Rachael." Then his voice saddened. "My father talked to Rabbi Solomon about marrying us secretly, without your father knowing. He won't do it."

"Why? It's only because my father would never agree——"

"To Rabbi Solomon it would mean he would be taking the side of the underground against the Civil Authority. You know how the Orthodox are about finding hidden meanings in hidden meanings. Besides, I would want the world to know you're my wife."

"I try so hard to remember my father the way he used to be, but I think I hate him. I swear, sometimes I almost wish he were——"

"Shhhhh . . ."

Sounds on the roof sent them into a grip of fear. Wolf rolled off the bed, yanked Rachael off, and shoved her behind him into an alcove. Someone was rattling about overhead. An indistinguishable figure appeared at the skylight in the kitchen ceiling. It tugged at the trap door. Wolf withdrew his pistol, cocked it, and aimed it on the skylight. The trap door groaned open, sending in a burst of light and air. A pair of legs lowered and a figure dropped to the floor.

"It's Stephan."

Stephan got to his feet, rubbing his wrist, which was tingling from the impact of breaking the fall. "I'm sorry to have to come here," he apologized, "but Uncle Andrei needs you right away, Wolf."

"Where is he?"

"At the loft over the stage, Workman's Theater."

Wolf fought his way into his shoes, slapped his cap on, and peered out of the window. Nightingales patrolled the street below.

"You'll have to go over the roofs," Stephan said.

"You two get on the roof and stay till after dark," Wolf ordered.

Rachael obeyed silently, fearing words would bring on a betrayal of tears. A kitchen table was shoved under the skylight. Wolf climbed on, leaped up, caught hold, and struggled through. He closed his eyes for a moment as he saw the sheer drop. The sharp heights always brought on dizziness. He lay flat on his belly and reached down into the kitchen. Rachael hoisted Stephan into Wolf's hands. She came through last. Wolf closed the skylight and pointed to cover behind a chimney. Stephan and his sister crouched behind it and watched Wolf disappear over the top of the ghetto.

It took him an hour to negotiate the mile over the roofs, down stairs, sprinting through exposed courtyards and over intersections, diving into the cover of friendly basements.

Wolf knew instantly it was a very important meeting, for Simon Eden was there with Andrei and Tolek Alterman. Andrei and Simon had kept apart to lessen the chance of their both being captured. It was the same with the other leaders. They came together under an urgency, for the informers had unearthed dozens of hiding places on Black Friday.

Simon spoke to Wolf and Tolek. "The Germans are lying about the deportations. One of my people has been able to observe the Umschlagplatz. For six days now the same forty-four cars have come and gone. Figure it. The trains pull out every day at three o'clock. They return by eight o'clock the next morning. Seventeen hours' travel. Eight and a half going. Eight and a half coming back. Subtract an hour's unloading time. Subtract an hour to turn the train around. Consider today's travel conditions."

"Summary," Andrei said. "It is our educated guess this train is not traveling more than seventy or eighty kilometers beyond Warsaw."

Tolek rubbed his jaw, drew a mental picture of Warsaw's environs. "There is no labor camp or combination of them inside this radius which can continue to take six thousand new people every day."

"Exactly."

"As you know," Simon continued, "My runner system was almost shattered on Black Friday. I lost almost all my people on the Aryan side."

Andrei handed Wolf and Tolek packs of money. "There's a guard playing at the Tlomatskie Gate. Go out in fifteen-minute intervals at six o'clock and meet at Gabriela's flat. She will have a railroad maintenance engineer there. He will place you in observation positions along the rail line."

When they had gone Simon Eden asked Andrei about new arms. It was the same story. No arms. No money. No help from Roman or the Home Army. Evasions. Frustration. They had only five hundred soldiers left after Black Friday.

Andrei looked at his watch and said it was time for him to leave too.

"Must you go to Lublin?" Simon asked.

"Yes."

"If there was a way to command you not to go . . ."

"No, Simon."

"Are you certain you can get into this camp?"

"I don't know for certain. Ana tracked down my old company sergeant. A good soldier, that Styka. I have faith in him. He has been working on it for two weeks. Ana brought the message that he can get me in."

"Andrei, if we lose you . . ."

"What's to lose, Simon?"

Simon flopped his big hands to his sides. "What's to lose? I've been in a fog for over two years. I try to tell myself all this is untrue. It is not happening. I'm numb, but we survive on instinct."

Andrei slapped his back.

"Well," Simon said, "wishing you luck inside Majdanek is rather ludicrous these days. Does Gabriela know?"

"No. I promised her not to keep secrets, but I cannot bring myself to talk about this trip to Lublin. But the minute I come through the door tonight, she will no longer be fooled."

"I envy you, Andrei, having that kind of love. Andrei, for God's sake, get back here safely. I can't keep going without you."

"See you around, Simon."

Chapter Seven

Andrei rubbed his eyes wearily and brought them to focus beyond the unwashed window. The train poked past a hamlet of thatched shanties surrounded by the rye fields of the flat Lublin Uplands. It was a long, slow trip. Late afternoon before he would reach Lublin. Good old Styka. He had come through.

Simon's words ran through his mind: "I've been in a fog . . . I'm numb, but we survive on instinct." On those nights before a dangerous assignment Gabriela, too, was instinctive. She had held him all night with her eyes wide open and without a word.

Andrei allowed himself the reward of a sigh and an inner rebellion of his nerves over another close call. There had been an unexpected siding of the train and an inspection. Life and death hinged on an exchange of glances with one of the Polish police, who returned later for his bribe.

Freedom and capture had hung by a thread so many times, he could not count them any more. Every day fate or luck or a proper instinctive move was the difference between life and death. Each night at Mila 19 the Bathyrans related a series of stories of the day's close brushes and miraculous escapes.

Andrei took a canteen from his knapsack and sipped a swallow of water and bit off a small hunk of the staling bread. It was painful to put food into his stomach, which, shrunken by the lack of food, rebelled at the sudden stretching.

The train passed a hamlet. The tracks split a large field in half where men and oxen strained against plow leashes and women bent double in stoop labor. Burly leathered men and wrinkled women in drab black rags carried on in a primitive way, almost unchanged from feudal times. Peasants puzzled Andrei. He wondered how they could go on in poverty, superstition, ignorance, with a complete lack of desire to make either their land or their lives flourish.

Andrei remembered a Bathyran meeting long ago. Tolek Alterman had returned from the colonies in Palestine and, before the national leadership, exalted the miracles of drying up swamps and irrigating the desert. A fund-raising drive to buy tractors and machinery was launched. Andrei remembered that his own reaction had been one of indifference.

Had he found the meaning too late? It aggravated him. The land of the Lublin Uplands was rich, but no one seemed to care.

In the unfertile land in Palestine humans broke their backs pushing will power to the brink.

He had sat beside Alexander Brandel at the rostrum of a congress of Zionists. All of them were there in this loosely knit association of diversified ideologies, and each berated the other and beat his breast for his own approaches. When Alexander Brandel rose to speak, the hall became silent.

"I do not care if your beliefs take you along a path of religion or a path of labor or a path of activism. We are here because all our paths travel a blind course through a thick forest, seeking human dignity. Beyond the forest all our paths merge into a single great highway which ends in the barren, eroded hills of Judea. This is our singular goal. How we travel through the forest is for each man's conscience. Where we end our journey is always the same. We all seek the same thing through different ways—an end to this long night of two thousand years of darkness and unspeakable abuses which will continue to plague us until the Star of David flies over Zion." This was how Alexander Brandel expressed pure Zionism. It had sounded good to Andrei, but he did not believe it. In his heart he had no desire to go to Palestine. He loathed the idea of drying up swamps or the chills of malaria or of leaving his natural birthright.

Before he went into battle Andrei had told Alex, "I only want to be a Pole. Warsaw is my city, not Tel Aviv."

And now Andrei sat on a train on the way to Lublin and wondered if he was not being punished for his lack of belief. Warsaw! He saw the smug eyes of the Home Army chief, Roman, and all the Romans and the faces of the peasants who held only hatred for him. They had let this black hole of death in Warsaw's heart exist without a cry of protest.

Once there had been big glittering rooms where Ulanys bowed and kissed the ladies' hands as they flirted from behind their fans.

Warsaw! Warsaw!

"Miss Rak. I am a Jew."

Day by day, week by week, month by month, the betrayal gnawed at Andrei's heart. He ground his teeth together. I hate Warsaw, he said to himself. I hate Poland and all the goddamned mothers' sons of them. All of Poland is a coffin.

The terrible vision of the ghetto streets flooded his mind. What matters now? What is beyond this fog? Only Palestine, and I will never live to see Palestine because I did not believe.

By late afternoon the train inched into the marshaling yards in the railhead at Lublin, which was filled with lines of cars poised to pour the tools of war to the Russian front.

At a siding, another train which was a familiar sight these days. Deportees. Jews. Andrei's skilled eye sized them up. They were not Poles. He guessed by their appearance that they were Rumanians.

He walked toward the center of the city to keep his rendezvous with Styka. Of all the places in Poland, Andrei hated Lublin the most. The Bathyrans were all gone. Few of the native Jews who had lived in Lublin were still in the ghetto.

From the moment of the occupation Lublin became a focal point. He and Ana watched it carefully. Lublin generally was the forerunner of what would happen elsewhere. Early in 1939, Odilo Globocnik, the Gauleiter of Vienna, established SS headquarters for all of Poland. The Bathyrans ran a check on Globocnik and had only to conclude that he was in a tug of war with Hans Frank and the civilian administrators.

Globocnik built the Death's-Head Corps. Lublin was the seed of action for the "final solution" of the Jewish problem. As the messages from Himmler, Heydrich, and Eichmann came in through Alfred Funk, Lublin's fountainhead spouted.

A bevy of interlacing lagers, work camps, concentration camps erupted in the area. Sixty thousand Jewish prisoners of war disappeared into Lublin's web. Plans went in and out of Lublin, indicating German confusion. A tale of a massive reservation in the Uplands to hold several million Jews . . . A tale of a plan to ship all Jews to the island of Madagascar . . . Stories of the depravity of the guards at Globocnik's camps struck a chord of terror at the mere mention of their names. Lipowa 7, Sobibor, Chelmno, Poltawa, Belzec, Krzywy-Rog, Budzyn, Krasnik. Ice baths, electric shocks, lashings, wild dogs, testicle crushers.

The Death's-Head Corps took in Ukrainian and Baltic Auxiliaries, and the *Einsatzkommandos* waded knee-deep in blood and turned into drunken, dope-ridden maniacs. Lublin was their heart.

In the spring of 1942 Operation Reinhard began in Lublin. The ghetto, a miniature of Warsaw's, was emptied into the camp in the Majdan-Tartarski suburb called Majdanek. As the camp emptied, it was refilled by a draining of the camps and towns around Lublin, then by deportees from outside Poland. In and in and in they poured through the gates of Majdanek, but they never left, and Majdanek was not growing any larger.

What was happening in Majdanek? Was Operation Reinhard the same pattern for the daily trains now leaving the Umschlagplatz in Warsaw? Was there another Majdanek in the Warsaw area, as they suspected?

Andrei stopped at Litowski Place and looked around quickly at the boundary of civil buildings. His watch told him he was still early. Down the boulevard he could see a portion of the ghetto wall. He found an empty bench, opened a newspaper, and stretched his legs before him. Krakow Boulevard was filled with black Nazi uniforms and the dirty brownish ones of their Auxiliaries.

"Captain Androfski!"

Andrei glanced up over the top of the paper and looked into the mustached, homely face of Sergeant Styka. Styka sat beside him and pumped his hand excitedly. "I have been waiting across the street at the post office since dawn. I thought you might get in on a morning train."

"It's good to see you again, Styka."

Styka studied his captain. He almost broke into tears. To him, Andrei Androfski had always been the living symbol of a Polish officer. His captain was thin and haggard and his beautiful boots were worn and shabby.

"Remember to call me Jan," Andrei said.

Styka nodded and sniffed and blew his nose vociferously. "When that woman found me and told me that you needed me I was never so happy since before the war."

"I'm lucky that you were still living in Lublin."

Styka grumbled about fate. "For a time I thought of trying to reach the Free Polish Forces, but one thing led to another. I got a girl in trouble and we had to get married. Not a bad girl. So we have three children and responsibilities. I work at the granary. Nothing like the old days in the army, but I get by. Who complains? Many times I tried to reach you, but I never knew how. I came to Warsaw twice, but there was that damned ghetto wall . . ."

"I understand."

Styka blew his nose again.

"Were you able to make the arrangements?" Andrei asked.

"There is a man named Grabski who is the foreman in charge of the bricklayers at Majdanek. I did exactly as instructed. I told him you are on orders from the Home Army to get inside Majdanek so you can make a report to the government in exile in London."

"His answer?"

"Ten thousand zlotys."

"Can he be trusted?"

"He is aware he will not live for twenty-four hours if he betrays you."

"Good man, Styka."

"Captain . . . Jan . . . must you go inside Majdanek? The stories . . . Everyone really knows what is happening there."

"Not everyone, Styka."

"What good will it really do?"

"I don't know. Perhaps . . . perhaps . . . there is a shred of conscience left in the human race. Perhaps if they know the story there will be a massive cry of indignation."

"Do you really believe that, Jan?"

"I have to believe it."

Styka shook his head slowly. "I am only a simple soldier. I cannot think things out too well. Until I was transferred into the

295

Seventh Ulanys I was like every other Pole in my feeling about Jews. I hated you when I first came in. But . . . my captain might have been a Jew, but he wasn't a Jew. What I mean is, he was a Pole and the greatest soldier in the Ulanys. Hell, sir. The men of our company had a dozen fights defending your name. You never knew about it, but by God, we taught them respect for Captain Androfski."

Andrei smiled.

"Since the war I have seen the way the Germans have behaved and I think, Holy Mother, we have behaved like this for hundreds of years. Why?"

"How can you tell an insane man to reason or a blind man to see?"

"But we are neither blind nor insane. The men of your company would not allow your name dishonoured. Why do we let the Germans do this?"

"I have sat many hours with this, Styka. All I ever wanted was to be a free man in my own country. I've lost faith, Styka. I used to love this country and believe that someday we'd win our battle for equality. But now I think I hate it very much."

"And do you really think that the world outside Poland will care any more than we do?"

The question frightened Andrei.

"Please don't go inside Majdanek."

"I'm still a soldier in a very small way, Styka."

It was an answer that Styka understood.

Grabski's shanty was beyond the bridge over the River Bystrzyca near the rail center. Grabski sat in a sweat-saturated undershirt, cursing the excessive heat which clamped an uneasy stillness before sundown. He was a square brick of a man with a moon-round face and sunken Polish features. Flies swarmed around the bowl of lentils in which he mopped thick black bread. Half of it dripped down his chin. He washed it down with beer and produced a deep-seated belch.

"Well?" Andrei demanded.

Grabski looked at the pair of them. He grunted a sort of "yes" answer. "My cousin works at the Labor Bureau. He can make you work papers. It will take a few days. I will get you inside the guard camp as a member of my crew. I don't know if I can get you into the inner camp. Maybe yes, maybe no, but you can observe everything from the roof of a barrack we are building."

Grabski slurped his way to the bottom of the soup bowl. "Can't understand why the hell anyone wants to go inside that son-of-a-bitch place."

"Orders from the Home Army."

"Why? Nothing there but Jews."

Andrei shrugged. "We get strange orders."

"Well—what about the money?"

Andrei peeled off five one-thousand-zloty notes. Grabski had never seen so much money. His broad flat fingers, petrified into massive sausages by years of bricklaying, snatched the bills clumsily. "This ain't enough."

"You'll get the rest when I'm safely out of Majdanek."

"I ain't taking no goddamned chances for no Jew business."

Andrei and Styka were silent. Grabski looked from one to the other, snarling, bullying. He quickly realized that the men before him were as large and tough as the Death's-Head Corps. He knew, too, Styka would kill him. Grabski grunted, cursed, and shoved the money into his pants pocket. "Be here in the morning at six. We'll get started on the work pass."

A sudden northeast breeze blew the sack curtains into the room, bringing in a terrible stench, nauseating the men. Grabski shoved away from the table and slammed the window shut. "Every time the wind blows we get that smell from Majdanek."

Andrei and Styka stood behind Grabski. Styka pointed to the skyline a few kilometers away where grayish smoke fizzled from a tall chimney.

"That's it," Styka said, "Majdanek."

"Only way the Jews leave that camp is through the chimney," Grabski said. Amused at discovering himself a humorist, he broke into a fit of laughter.

Chapter Eight

Horst von Epp waited with an infinite, knowing patience for Christopher de Monti to unravel after he had made his visit to the ghetto. Horst played it like a puppet master, confident that Chris was sinking closer to that point where he would be abandoned by the ever-shrinking voices of morality within him. As the weeks and months went, Horst saw his calculations coming to pass.

Chris drank hard these days, and women he had once resisted with bored ease were now constant bedmates. He became a per-petual guest at the perpetual parties he once shunned. As the heav-iness inside him compounded, that point of no return would soon be reached. A week, a month, two, it did not matter to Horst, for Chris's downfall had become inevitable in his calculation. One day he would come to Horst and babble a plea for the life of the un-known Jewess inside the ghetto, and the piper would be paid.

Dr. Franz Koenig's parties were uninhibited affairs that generals recalled with affection during the long cold winter nights on the Russian front. Koenig kept an international flavor, spicing the invitations to include the diplomatic corps, the press, and the stars of the moment, as well as the top Nazis. Nothing was spared by Koenig in the pursuit of gluttony and revelry. In addition to Warsaw's courtesans, Koenig continually imported new, young, slim, high-cheekboned blondes from Berlin, playing the role of a degenerated industrialist with great finesse.

Dr. Koenig premiered the newly remodeled ballroom as the first large midsummer event of 1942. It had been redecorated in unabashed elegance. Amid tinkling glasses, bowing, kissing of hands, rumors ran rampant and deals and bribes and barter were made. Much of the talk was about the new depth of the German armed penetrations. El Alamein in North Africa stood before Rommel's magnificent Afrika Korps, and on the Russian front the Don River had been reached. The Japanese guests had an air of cocksure confidence. The Americans had not recovered from the devastation of Pearl Harbor. The Japanese General Staff was positive America had no stomach to make the sacrifice necessary to displace them from the Pacific islands. It was a night for Axis gaiety. America had come into the war with too little, too late. The glitter of Dr. Franz Koenig's new ballroom made the participants so heady, there was even talk of a German breakthrough to India, which had been the long-forbidden dream of a dozen empires in a dozen ages.

Towards one o'clock the more strait-laced had made their departures and the party broke into splinter groups drifting to one of the many lush parlors adjoining the ballroom.

In another hour the guests would include only Dr. Koenig's intimate circle of ten or twenty and the new imports from Berlin. The serious business of an orgy would begin.

Chris's cup had run over. He was in that state of inebriated calm when all of the tensions within him seemed gone for the moment. In the library he rested his head on the shoulder of a young German model. She was delighted to have found an Italian and he said that it was some time since he had had a German girl, so it should be fun. The room was quite dark, lit only by candelabra and some light filtering in from the main ballroom.

His German girl was approached by Koenig's aide and spoke so rapidly that Chris could barely decipher it through the alcoholic haze. Apparently she was essential to an act and could not be dispensed with. She eased away with apologies and promises. Chris yawned and shut his eyes for a moment.

He opened them, smacked his lips, and looked around for a servant. A figure of a small woman framed the doorway. Chris tried to think. He had seen the girl from a distance several times during the evening. He was positive he knew her from somewhere, and it seemed as though she were watching him.

She walked into the library, moving to the uninhabited corner

298

by the candelabra. Chris walked up behind her. "Do I know you?" he asked.

She turned and faced him, holding her chin up to the candlelight. "Once you did."

He squinted, trying to make her out in a sliver of light.

"Gabriela!"

She nodded. He turned chalky.

"What the hell are you doing here? What do you want?"

"An old friend wants to see you. He is in a desperate situation."

"Andrei?"

"Yes."

Chris mopped his wet forehead. "Impossible. What's more, it's dangerous for you to be here. Dangerous for both of us." He grabbed her arm. "Wait. Let me think."

"Hello there, Chris! I've been looking for you."

Chris spun around to see Horst von Epp glower past him, staring at Gabriela. "Sorry, I wasn't able to get here till late, but I understand it was rather dull—up to now, that is. This makes it all worth while. By God, Chris, you have an unfailing talent to find the most magnificent creatures."

Gabriela played her role, acknowledging his interest with a coy smile.

"Well, aren't you going to introduce us, Chris?"

"Yes—certainly."

"I am Victoria Landowski. I've just come to Warsaw from Lemberg for a visit with my cousin. From the many descriptions, I take it you must be Baron von Epp."

"Madam," Horst said, taking Gabriela's hand. He kissed it with a touch and look which embraced all the connotations, and she let her eyes answer him just enough to let him know she understood and welcomed his intentions.

"And where will you be staying, Miss Landowski?"

"I am not quite certain yet, Baron. Why don't I reach you as soon as I'm settled?"

Horst bowed and backed off gracefully, yielding the girl to Chris with her promise of a future relationship. "It should be a wonderful fall season. . . . I say, Chris, are you ill?"

"Dr. Koenig is too generous with his liquor. I think I've had one too many."

"Why don't we get a breath of air, Chris?" Gabriela said.

"Good idea."

Horst von Epp watched them leave, intrigued with the pretty little thing. He sized her up for bed. Koenig's busy aide whispered in his ear that he was invited to the conservatory, where the girls were about to amuse them.

The doorman closed Chris and Gabriela into his Fiat. He

fumbled for the ignition switch. "You're a damned fool walking into this nest," he mumbled.

Chris drove aimlessly at a crawl, checking the rear-view mirror constantly to see if he was being followed.

"What I want to say is, things have changed."

"I should say that's rather obvious."

"Gaby, you don't understand."

"I do understand, quite well. I told Andrei it was a waste of time and that you wouldn't come."

"Gaby . . ."

"If you gave a damn for him you wouldn't have let two and a half years go by," she said.

Chris wanted to tell Gaby he had tried to see her during the past year but had lost track of her when she changed flats. But he could not say it.

"Where is he?" Chris blurted impulsively.

"A hotel room near the yacht club in Saska Kempa."

Chris sucked in a lungful of air, grunted, looked in the rear-view mirror once more, then made a U turn and drove on the Third of May Boulevard directly for the Poniatowski Bridge. In Saska Kempa, Chris concealed his car in a teamster's stable several blocks from the shabby hotel.

A meek handshake, an avoiding of Andrei's eyes. Unbearable small talk. Chris sagged into a hard-backed chair, studying the designs in the linoleum on the floor.

"How have you been?"

"Just fine."

"Seen Deborah?"

"Yes. She is all right."

"The children?"

"They are all right."

"Do you have a glass of water? I'm all dried out." He sipped and looked up at them. "A hell of a reunion, isn't it? Well, I'm here. Gaby said it was something desperate."

"We've needed you many times in the past two and a half years," Andrei said. "But I wouldn't come to you unless it was something so important we had to come to you."

He watched Chris go through uncomfortable mannerisms. "What is it?" Chris looked to Gabriela, but she gave no solace in her expression.

"Chris," Andrei said in a voice filled with an unfamiliar pleading, "tens of thousands of people are being murdered every day in extermination camps. We have put together an authentic report, detailing the locations, the names of the personnel and commanders, the method of operation. We have gone to the Home Army and begged them to get this out to the government in exile, but they won't help us. Every day means twenty, thirty, forty, fifty

300

thousand human beings. Chris—you've got to carry this out for us and get it into the world press. We've got to stop this blood bath. This is the only way."

Chris pulled himself to his feet. "I've heard this talk, but I don't believe it. Germany is a civilized country. The Germans aren't capable of doing what you claim—it's a lie."

"I've just come from inside Majdanek. If you care to interview your friend Baron von Epp, I'll gladly supply you with some very leading questions."

Chris sank back into the chair again in a stupor. Andrei lay a typewritten book of a hundred pages before him. Chris glanced at it out of the corner of his eye but pulled his hand back. "I'm not your man," he whispered.

"Chris, you and I have spent too many hours together putting this lousy world under our microscopes. I know how you've been pulled apart these last two years, but I've always known with all my soul that in the crucible you are unable to walk away from the cries of the anguished without destroying yourself as a human being."

"I told you, no! Why the hell did you ask me here?"

"Chris! Chris! Chris! You and I believe in the final nobility of man! You can't turn your back on us!"

Chris's fist drummed against the table with a monotonous thud-ding repetition. "I've cried for justice before, Andrei! I cried rape and murder in Spain and it fell on deaf ears."

"My God, Chris! Men have always destroyed each other. They always will. You can't pull out because you've been hurt once."

"Do you really believe that goddamned world out there is going to be moved by this report? It's you who is the fool, not me. No one's going to care about murdered Jews or starving Indians or floods in Holland or earthquakes in Japan so long as their stinking bellies are full! Your goddamned conscience of man is a myth, Andrei."

Andrei hovered over Chris. He shook Chris's shoulders, but the man would not unbend. Andrei slowly sank to his knees. "Chris, I beg you on my knees to help us."

Gabriela jerked angrily at Andrei. "Get off your knees!" she commanded. "Get off your knees! You will never do this again before any man!"

Chris turned his sweaty face up to her enraged expression. He tried through bleary eyes to beg her to stop.

"You sanctimonious son of a bitch," Gabriela quivered. "You sit up there on your throne and watch all us little ants scramble in fright to survive and you make your terse comments and your snide observations. I present to you, Christopher de Monti—champion of the press! Oh God, no. Don't dirty your precious hands with our blood."

301

"All I ever wanted is for Deborah to live—that's all—that's all I've ever wanted. I know she'll never see me again, but I want her to live—that's all I've ever wanted."

"Your sister is a very fortunate woman, Andrei. In a single lifetime she has had two upstanding men like Paul Bronski and Christopher de Monti who would sell their souls for her."

Andrei was limp with weakness and humiliation. "My sister is a woman," he whispered. "She will take her life and the life of her children before she allows you to save her at the expense of a betrayal to the Nazis."

"That's enough, Andrei," Gabriela said. "Look at him. He is completely degenerated."

Andrei gave up. He walked to the door. "You were right, Gabriela. We should not have asked him. I'd like to spit on you, Chris, but I must save my strength."

Andrei left the room.

"You're not worthy of his spit," Gabriela said, and followed.

Chris slumped over the table, weeping, choking on his own saliva and tears. His hand fell on the report. He pulled his head up. He gained control of himself and turned the first page.

COMBINED JEWISH ORGANIZATIONS' REPORT ON EXTERMINATION CENTERS IN OPERATION WITHIN THE GENERAL GOVERNMENT AREA OF POLAND, JULY 1942

We are able to authenticate firmly the existence of four centers in the General Government Area created for the sole purpose of conducting mass exterminations. In addition, two combination concentration-extermination camps are in existence. There are five hundred labor camps in Poland, of which a hundred and forty are reserved for Jews. All of them contain some sort of murder facilities.

The only conclusion to be drawn is that a master German plan is in effect for the absolute destruction of the Jewish people. In the beginning, mass starvation, disease, and executions decimated the various ghettos by tens of thousands. After the invasion of Russia, Kommandos of four Special Action groups massacred additional hundreds of thousands. The culmination of this plan is now assembly-line murder. The master plan, it must be concluded, comes from Hitler through Himmler and Heydrich. The actual execution is performed by the so-called 4B section of the Gestapo (Jewish affairs) under the direction of SS Sub-Colonel Adolf Eichmann.

The extermination centers are located at railheads and generally in secluded sites. They are guarded by Waffen SS and Ukrainian and Baltic Auxiliaries. A staggering amount of planning, material, and manpower is being used to carry out this operation at a time when Germany is conducting a war on many fronts. For example, rail cars are at an urgent premium for the purpose of shipping war materials to the Russian front, yet importation of Jews from German-occupied countries into Poland seems to have taken a priority over army needs. In addition, thousands of engineers, scientists, and key personnel are tied up in this operation as well as desperately needed manpower. We can safely estimate that from two to three hundred thousand men are directly or indirectly involved. All of this effort testifies to the insane will of the Nazis as well as to the urgency of our situation.

These camps follow a basic pattern. Deception is carried out and secrecy maintained. This certainly indicates the Nazis are aware of the evil they are perpetrating. At each camp, deportees arrive and are weeded at selection centers. A few are set aside for slave labor. The rest, including women and small children, are moved to a "sanitation center" under the illusion of receiving a disinfectant shower. Hair is shorn. The guards play out the game to the end by issuing bars of soap (which later turn out to be made of stone), and victims are asked to remember the number of the peg on which their clothing is hung. Many women attempt to hide children in their clothing or throw them off trains to peasants, but they are almost always found out.

When the occupants are in, an iron door is sealed and an attendant carries out the gassing. The first gassings were from the carbon monoxide exhaust of engines. This method proved slow and petrol costly, therefore a prussic acid mixture called Cyclon B was developed by the Hamburg Insecticide Company. Death is in minutes.

Jewish slave laborers clean the chambers and remove the corpses to crematoriums, where they are burned. At first cremation was in open pits, but the stench was unbearable. The Jewish laborers generally last only a few weeks before losing their sanity.

There are many variations, but this is the general pattern. Gold teeth are pulled from the corpses before burning. Anything of value is taken for the German war effort. Everything else—clothing, eyeglasses, shoes, artificial limbs, even dolls—is stored in warehouses, then scrutinized for hidden valuables. Hair is baled and shipped to Germany for use in the manufacture of mattresses and to waterproof submarine periscopes. In one camp, bodies have been boiled down for their fat content, to be used in the making of soap.

In addition to the Polish camps, we have reason to believe several camps in Germany have extermination facilities. Dachau, among others, is used as an "experimental medical" center. Humans are compelled to undergo experiments, such as the grafting of bones, transplants of organs, testing beyond human limitations in freezing, electrical shock, etc. In all camps, extermination and labor, the indignities, abuses, torture, and rape are universal. These are amplified in the attached supplementary reports.

The German extermination facilities are capable of murdering a minimum of a hundred thousand persons a day in Poland. We do not have the additional numbers who are killed inside Germany. The Polish camps are currently working at full capacity. New gas chambers and crematoriums are being constructed to increase the rate.

The Polish camps are:

LUBLIN DISTRICT

Belzec—Located on the Lublin–Tomaszow rail line near Rawa Ruska, handling Jews from the Lwow-Lemberg area with a capacity of ten thousand a day.

Sobibor—Near Wlodawa, between Wlodawa and Chelm. Capacity believed to be six thousand a day.

Majdanek—An early concentration camp in the Lublin suburb Majdan-Tartarski under the personal direction of Odilo Globocnik, SS Gruppenführer of Poland. Capacity in excess of ten thousand a day.

WESTERN POLAND

Chelmno—The oldest extermination center (in operation at the end of 1941), nine miles from Kolo, on the rail line between Lodz and Poznan, exterminating Jews in western Poland.

CENTRAL POLAND

Treblinka—Most recently discovered by underground efforts, located in the Sokolow Podlaski province near Warsaw, liquidating Jews from the Warsaw ghetto as well as Radom, Bialystok, Grodno, the Baltics, Czenstochowa, Kielce.

SOUTHERN POLAND

Auschwitz—Located just outside the Silesian village of Oswiencim. The concentration camp has some fifty satellite labor camps. Extermination facilities are in a compound named Birkenau. Capacity in excess of forty thousand a day. Gypsies, Russian POWs, political, criminal, and other prisoners are liquidated here as well as Jews.

SUPPLEMENTARY REPORT No. 1
by "Jan" on the Majdanek extermination camp in Lublin

I was able to enter Majdanek disguised as a Polish laborer, one of hundreds who work on construction jobs in the outer compounds.

At 0700 I left Lublin by horse and cart with a party named "Leopold." We were halted at a rail terminal approximately one kilometer from the main gate of the camp. The terminal is adjacent to the main highway. We sat and waited while several thousand Rumanian Jews were herded over the highway on a march to the camp gate.

A line of Red Cross vans waited alongside the terminal building. German guards loaded these vans with aged, cripples, infants, and others unfit to walk the mile. Leopold told me these Red Cross vans are actually sealed, escape-proof cabins. Once they are in motion, the carbon monoxide from the exhaust is routed back into the van so that by the time they reach Majdanek the occupants are dead.

(*Note:* This same method was used in both Chelmno and Treblinka but ruled out as too slow and costly. It is used only to supplement the main extermination facilities.)

I entered the outer compound at 0800 through a gate which bore a sign: LABOR BRINGS FREEDOM. My crew was working on a brick barrack in the outer camp, fifty meters from the inner camp, for use by a new guard contingent. I was able to place myself on the third-story roof in a hidden spot and in a position of observation through a pair of field glasses which I brought in in my lunch box.

I should estimate that the entire camp area covered six or seven hundred acres. At its closest point it was only a kilometer and a half from Lublin. The outer camp contains guard barracks, the commandant's home, a general store, garage, and other service buildings of a permanent nature.

The inner compound is composed of forty-six barracks made of wood of the type used as German army stables. Air and light came through a narrow row of skylight windows. I was told that each barrack holds nearly four hundred prisoners. Obviously they are crammed with room only for slabs for beds and a narrow passageway to the main door.

The inner compound is surrounded by double walls of barbed wire five meters high. Between the two walls is a continuous patrol by Ukrainians with Alsatian dogs. I am told that the inner wall is electrified at night.

High guard towers with floodlights and machine guns stand every twenty-five meters along the outer wall.

Leopold called my attention to the set of barracks nearest us. He told me these are warehouses. The Rumanian Jews whom I had seen earlier at the rail terminal were already filing into the first barrack, which is a selection center. Only a few were taken into the camp. The rest treked over an open plot to a concrete building marked by signs I could clearly identify as SANITATION CENTER.

The "sanitation center" is very pretty, with lawns and trees and flowers planted around it.

When four hundred people had gathered, the line from the warehouse was halted and the group ordered into the "sanitation center." In approximately ten minutes I heard a burst of hideous screaming which lasted only ten or fifteen seconds. The building was then besieged by Jewish prisoners (*Sonnderkommandos*) who, I am told, clean out the chamber and remove the personal belongings to the second warehouse for sorting.

Ten minutes after the first gassing, the Jewish prisoners brought the corpses out. I saw them clearly. They were the same four hundred who had gone in twenty minutes before. Six to eight corpses were piled on a welded sledlike affair, and each "sled" was pulled by Jewish prisoners. The *Sonnderkommandos* passed out of the inner-camp gate to a side road which ran one kilometer up a hill to a large building with a tall smokestack. I was able to see this clearly also through my field glasses.

The entire gassing process took thirty minutes for four hundred people. On the first day of my observation there were twelve separate gassings, or approximately forty-eight hundred persons. On the second day there were twenty gassings, or eight thousand, and on the third day seventeen gassings, or sixty-eight hundred. I have been told that upward of forty gassings have been accomplished in a twenty-four-hour period and never less than ten.

Leopold and other laborers have worked both in the repair of the gas chamber and crematorium. He tells me the chamber is a low-ceilinged room of four meters by twelve. It resembles a shower room in every detail except that the shower heads are false. An SS man is able to control the volume of gas through a barred observation window. Leopold and a crew of workers must enter the chamber every few weeks in order to resurface the concrete, which is torn up by victims clawing to get out.

Leopold was also instrumental in building the crematorium after open-pit burning of corpses was abandoned because of the stench. After the sleds are run to the crematorium the corpses are placed on a table and examined for gold teeth and slit open (and bled through a drainage pipe) to see if any gold or valuables had been swallowed. Then the corpses are taken into the adjoining room and placed in one of five ovens that hold five to seven corpses apiece. Extending arms and legs are hacked off. Cremation lasts minutes. The bones are removed from grates from the opposite side. Through my field glasses I was able to make out hills of bones some two stories high. Leopold tells me that recently when he went to repair the ovens a bone crushing machine had been installed and the bone meal sacked and shipped to Germany for fertilizer.

Christopher de Monti held his head between his legs and began to vomit. He vomited until his guts screamed with pain. Page after page it went. The full report of Andrei Androfski, the reports of a handful of survivors of Treblinka and Chelmno and the labor camps.

"God! What have I done?" he cried in anguish. "I am a Judas! I am a Judas!"

The puke and the tears and the pain and the liquor crushed on him and he fell to the floor in a dead faint.

Chapter Nine

FELLOW JEWS! WARNING!

DO NOT REPORT TO THE UMSCHLAGPLATZ FOR DEPORTATION! THE DESTINATION IS A DEATH CAMP LOCATED NEAR THE TREBLINKA VILLAGE! HIDE YOUR CHILDREN! RESIST! THIS IS A SIGNAL FOR AN UPRISING! JOIN US!

JOINT FORCES

Journal Entry

Oh, my God, why have you forsaken us! How has man reached such depravity? We are at the bottom of a swill pit, and it is midnight! In all of the long tortured history of our people we have reached the moment of greatest degradation.

ALEXANDER BRANDEL

The immediate result of the revelations brought the long-sought unity among the diversified elements in the ghetto. Simon Eden and the Labor Zionists already had a working agreement with Andrei and the Bathyrans. Now the Communists and many religious fringe groups and individuals went under the single banner of Joint Forces. The Revisionists agreed to a non-binding working agreement. Simon Eden was declared commander and Andrei Androfski his deputy, with the Communists taking charge of activity beyond the wall. Although they were weak inside the ghetto, the Communists on the outside gave them the closest set of allies of any other group on the Aryan side. Wolf Brandel was sent into the Brushmaker's district to organize a fighting unit inside the factory complex.

The Joint Forces counted sixty pistols, thirty-four rifles, and a single automatic weapon.

The guns were of so many different calibers and varieties that some had only a half dozen rounds of ammunition. The tiny arsenal was reinforced somewhat by several thousand homemade bottle bombs and grenades manufactured from water pipes perfected by the chemist, Jules Schlosberg, in the cellar of Mila 19.

The total combat force stood at five hundred sixty young men and women, mostly in their early twenties, almost entirely without military training.

The call for a rebellion has fallen on deaf ears. How can the people rebel? What do they have to rebel with? What help will they receive from the outside? In a final banality of the German language, the Nazis refer to the exterminations as "dispensation of special treatment." The desire to survive has become so intense that the people will not allow themselves to believe there is a death camp at Treblinka. The Jewish Militia and members of the Civil Authority rip down underground posters as quickly as they are put up. Kennkarten stamped for slave labor are still believed by the people to be some sort of magic key to life.

It is amazing how the people will submit themselves to a living death worse than death itself. Even the most decadent societies in past history have understood that a basic minimum must be accorded for a slave or even an animal to be able to produce a reasonable day's work. The Germans have even made an innovation on this by turning all of Poland into one big slave-labor pool. With millions of extra laborers who cannot exist otherwise, the competition for the right to become a slave is fierce.

The slaves in Dr. Koenig's brush and uniform factories are separated from their families, numbered, stamped, beaten at their work. They labor in abysmal conditions for sixteen to eighteen hours a day. There is almost no heat in winter or ventilation or light. They exist with no personal property or human rights. They are terrorized and starved so that the fight for food among them is a further struggle to live. Their sleeping quarters are unfit to be pigsties. Every slave of every time has dreamt of freedom, and every tyrant of every time has recognized that dream. Here the only alternative is death. The slightest defect by protest or sickness brings immediate liquidation and replacement by another who scrambles for the right to be a slave.

The Big Action enters its second week. Yesterday no volunteers showed up at the Umschlagplatz. The Militia and Nightingales surrounded Koenig's Brushmaker's factory and selected half the workers for deportation. Today the Civil Authority called for volunteers to fill the factory openings. It was oversubscribed! Of course this newest German ruse will not last long, but it is fantastic that the people continue to allow themselves to be tricked.

Crazy Nathan stands near the Umschlagplatz and laments and prophesies that he will be the sole survivor in Warsaw. His latest psalm:

The Germans are so good to us.
They even make a raid

To give us free vacations,
With all expenses paid.

ALEXANDER BRANDEL

On the ninth day of the Big Action, Alexander Brandel walked into the barracks of the Jewish Militia, cater-corner to the Civil Authority building at Zamenhof and Gensia streets. The police who had bullied the ghetto around for nearly two years became uneasy at the presence of Brandel. He was more disheveled than ever. His slight stature certainly posed no threat of physical harm, yet they feared him. He was one of the few untouchables. Harm to him would bring savage retribution to them. But more, they feared his calm. He asked to see Piotr Warsinski.

Warsinski, the convert, whose hatred of Jews matched the viciousness of the Reinhard Corps, also feared Alexander Brandel. The flesh on the backs of his hands was always crimson from a nervous itch. At the sight of Alex entering his office, his fingernails dug into them, turning his skin to bleeding scales.

"What do you want here?" he growled.

"I should like to go into the Umschlagplatz and I want a dozen of my nurses around the selection center."

"You're crazy."

"I'll pay for the privilege."

"Get the hell out or you'll be taking a train ride yourself."

That goddamned smile on Brandel's face! That son of a bitch! What he hated more than anything was Brandel's calm. Brandel's refusal to argue. When he had been sub-warden at Pawiak Prison he liked to watch the prisoners cringe, broken at his feet. Then one like Brandel would show up. Unafraid. He hated unafraid bastards. Warsinski's itch worsened and his slitty eyes watered.

This morning he had beaten a woman prisoner to death with his hands. Women pointed up his impotence, his inability to be a man even when he paraded them around naked and made them perform obscenities with male prisoners.

He dropped his hands below the desk and tore at them with his fingernails.

"What do you want?"

"To see Haupsturmführer Kutler and Sturmbannführer Stutze. There are certain people who are taken to the Umschlagplatz whom we want to buy back."

"What are you paying with?"

"American dollars."

"I'll take the message to them. How much a head?"

"Six dollars."

"Whatever deal is made, add on another dollar for the Militia."

"Fine," Alex said, shoving away from the desk, hiding his revulsion. What pearls of wisdom had he gathered in a lifetime of

309

study to pierce the heart of Piotr Warsinski? Seven dollars per life. Warsinski's cruel eyes told him that one day he would stand on a platform and watch Alex ride off to Treblinka in a cattle car.

Hauptsturmführer Kutler was sloppy drunk when Warsinski reached the SS barracks. The sight of Warsinski's bloody hands triggered a quicker guzzling. The nightmare had been particularly bad for several days as Kutler relived the massacre of Babi-Yar and woke up screaming from a dream of drowning in blood. Now his sleep was tormented by visions of little animals tearing at his flesh. Sturmbannführer Stutze tried to pull the captain to his feet. Stutze was sickened at the weak fiber of the Germans who had been Kommandos in the Action Squads. They constantly drank themselves to the DT's and pumped their veins full of dope. Austrians such as he and Globocnik and Hitler were made of sterner stuff. When the war was won, the Austrians would dominate the weaker German species. Kutler was in no condition to talk. Stutze had him taken to his room by a pair of guards, then turned to Warsinski.

"So," Stutze said, "he offered you six dollars a Jew head. How much did you add on for yourself?"

"Only a dollar a Jew, Herr Sturmbannführer, and much of that must be spread among my police."

The crippled Austrian meditated. "Hummm. What is the difference? Let them buy the Jews. We'll get them all back anyhow. Only . . . Jews barter. You are a Jew, Warsinski. Barter."

Warsinski winced at being called a Jew.

"I want ten dollars a Jew, payable at the end of every business day," Stutze said.

"Yes, sir."

"And, by the way, let us keep this transaction between us."

"Yes, sir."

At the final price of eleven dollars and fifty cents a head, Alexander Brandel and his nurses were allowed into the Umschlagplatz. In the next few days they snatched out a few writers, scientists, musicians, poets, historians, teachers, children, engineers, doctors, actors, and rabbis from among the thousands jammed into the daily train.

The ruse of taking factory workers failed because volunteers refused to take their place any more. The next cleanup was a systematic dragnet of the ghetto to bag the thousands of beggar children, Wild Ones, and homeless for deportation. Crazy Nathan was among those picked up, but Alexander purchased his life, for he was a sentimental historian and the "crazy" one had filled his journals with hundreds of poems and anecdotes.

In these days the lines of deportees were not so orderly as in the beginning. Bribe money flashed all over the Umschlagplatz. When

310

there was no money, the deportees offered the guards watches, rings, furs—anything—to buy their way back into the ghetto for another day, another hour. And each day the marches to the trains were halted dozens of times by frantic bursts for freedom which only intensified the brutality of the guards.

And each day when the trains pulled out at three o'clock there were leftovers in the square. These prisoners were taken to the top floor of the selection building, to be first in line for deportation the next day. Each night the Ukrainian guards stripped the prisoners, searching for valuables. Women were taken to the lower floors of the building and raped.

On the twelfth day of the Big Action, the Bathyran Council met and demanded from Alex that he stay out of the Umschlagplatz. Tolek and Ana pleaded that a whim of Kutler or Stutze would cancel their deal and threaten his own life. Alex would have none of it, not even their orders nor, finally, their threats to restrain him. For so many years he had battled to breathe life into the dying. He could not hold back the flood, but he was frantic to salvage the product of a great culture.

And on the next day he milled in the courtyard of the Umschlagplatz, as usual.

"Alex! Come quickly. Rabbi Solomon has passed from the selection center. They're taking him to the cemetery for execution."

Alex raced over the square, stumbling, gasping, into the building, down the corridor, past the guard, into Kutler's office. The captain was more than halfway through his first bottle of schnapps and it was not yet noon. Alexander completely lost his composure.

"The Rabbi Solomon!" he said.

"Don't push your luck, Jew boy," Kutler blurted.

Alex panicked.

"A hundred dollars!"

"Hundred?" He began to laugh. "Hundred for that old Jew carcass? God damn. The price for old Jews is good today. He's all yours, Jew boy."

As Alex sighed and reeled out, Kutler reared back and laughed until the tears came to his eyes.

In the middle of the night Sylvia Brandel tiptoed down to Alexander's office. Mila 19 was asleep except for the guards. Earlier in the day she had tried to go to him, but his door was locked. He refused to answer her calls. She did not know whether to be angry or hurt or to try to approach him with sympathy or to leave him alone. It was indeed strange behavior for Alex. She rattled on the doorknob and knocked again. He opened it and walked away from her.

Sylvia stared at his back, trying to adjust to the awesome experience, for Alexander was not like other men. He had always been a strong stone lighthouse for people to look up to find light and shelter. In twenty years of marriage she could not remember him floundering or crying for help. At first she was troubled that he did not seem to need the compassion that other men needed, but she learned to revere him and to live to serve him. Alex lived in his own world, a strange mixture of ideals and ideas, and he functioned with inexhaustible reservoirs of patience and courage. It was frightening to see him derailed.

"How is Rabbi Solomon?" he asked.

"We have a cot set up for him in the Good Fellowship room in the cellar. Ervin will stay with him tonight. Alex, will you eat something? There is some soup left in the kitchen."

"I'm not hungry," he whispered.

"It's almost three o'clock. Please come up to bed."

He flopped at his desk, and his face dropped into his hands in utter defeat.

"Alex, I have never questioned your decisions, but I beg you—don't go to the Umschlagplatz again. There is a limit to what I can stand too."

Tears welled in the corners of his eyes and rolled to nothing halfway down his cheek.

"No man can continue as you have without breaking up."

"I've failed," he whispered, "I've failed."

"You're a human being, Alex. You've given your life to other people. I can't stand to see you let yourself be destroyed."

"I've failed," he mumbled, "I've failed."

"Alex, for God's sake!"

"I lost my head today. I'll lose it again."

"You're tired . . . so tired."

"No. It's just . . . that I knew today . . . everything I've stood for . . . everything I've tried to do has been wrong."

"Oh no, darling."

"My way? Keep one more body alive for one more day. All my cunning to save a single man, and now thousands flood to their deaths and there is nothing I can do . . . nothing."

Sylvia gripped him awkwardly. "I won't hear you berate yourself after all you have done."

"Done?" He laughed. "What have I done, Sylvia? Trade with swindlers and Nazis? Use trickery and cunning? Done?" He took her hands, and he was again gentle Alex. "They are going to destroy our entire culture. How can I preserve a few voices to show the world who we were and what we have given them? Who will be left?"

He walked away from her. "We don't speak of it here in Mila 19, but Andrei and I have had little to say to each other since the war. Do you know why? When the Germans came here he wanted to take our people to the woods to fight. I stopped him. I took the guns and the bullets from him. My way—I had to have my way."

"Alex please!"

"Wrong! I am wrong and I've always been wrong! Not my journal or Rabbi Solomon's prayers will deliver us. Only Andrei's guns, and it is too late and I did this to him."

Like the catacombs of Rome, an underground city was clawed beneath the ghetto of Warsaw. Every person capable of working joined in a frantic race to build hiding places.

Fifty thousand trap doors, fifty thousand secret entrances led to false rooms in sub-floors, closets, behind bookcases, in attics. In the stores and bakeries they hid in unfired ovens, under counters. They made hiding places by removing the stuffing in couches, under tubs, in garbage dumps.

They lived a second away from their escape hatches. Walking in the streets became a memory. Communication was by rooftop. Behind loose tiles, stoves, toilets, pictures, lay entrances to secret rooms.

Cellars were good to hide in, for they could hold larger stores of food and their entrances were easily concealed, but attics had the advantage of the best escape routes.

The epitome of ingenuity did not deter the Big Action from bagging their quotas for the deportations. The cry of children, the keen noses of trained dogs, the spying of informers continued to flush more and more secret places. Guards in the streets watched guards upstairs break every window in a house, for unbroken windows revealed the presence of a hidden room.

At Mila 19 and at Leszno 92, Andrei and Simon took attic rooms where an alarm bell would send them to the rooftops, where the guards were not so anxious to follow.

The entrance through the packing crates to the secret rooms in the basement of Mila 19 was abandoned as not safe enough, and a false water closet was constructed on the main floor. By removing a loose floor bolt the lavatory swung away, revealing a hole in the wall large enough for a man to crawl through. A ladder led to the new parts of the basement dug out since the Big Action and holding a dozen people Alex had snatched from the Umschlagplatz as well as the archives and arsenal rooms. An exit tunnel was dug to tie into a large drainage pipe which led many meters beyond Mila 19. The underground complex spread until it was halted by the main line of the pipe which ran directly down the middle of Mila Street. The sound of rushing sewage was constantly heard.

At the end of the third week in August the Big Action suddenly ground to a halt. The roundups stopped.

Max Kleperman had not only one of the few Jewish telephones in the ghetto, he had two, the second a direct line to Dr. Franz Koenig, with whom a vast amount of business was transacted. The license to buy and sell gold, agent real estate, smuggle, inform were exclusive rights granted the Big Seven.

Max Kleperman's private phone rang.

"*Ja, Herr Doktor . . . Ja, Herr Doktor . . . Ja, Herr Doktor.*"

After several more "*Ja, Herr Doktors*," Max hung up and called for his secretary. "Dr. Koenig wants to see all the partners here in my office in an hour. Get hold of them right away and have them wait here. I go now to see him at his residence and I will come back with him for the meeting."

Max checked out his appearance, took the diamond ring from his little finger, and clapped hands for his chauffeur and body-guard. They drove from the ghetto through the Krasinski Gate. Max liked to drive to the Aryan side. He enjoyed looking at the trees. There was only one tree in the entire ghetto, and that was in front of the Civil Authority. That particular tree annoyed him, for he always considered the Civil Authority in competition with the Big Seven. Many times he toyed with the idea of planting a half dozen trees in front of his headquarters on Pawia Street but decided it would be provocative.

Max had a particular affection for the Krasinski Gardens. As a boy he had started his career there, hiring Polish hoodlums to steal from the Jewish delivery boys and reselling the merchandise at Parysowski Place. Parysowski Place was closed to trade these days, since the deportations.

Max heaved a sigh of relief now that the deportations had stopped. Even he and the Big Seven people were getting edgy. Certainly the Germans had accomplished what they wanted. Max's mind turned to visions of a new plum awaiting him at Dr. Koenig's. With the deportations over, some new venture was cooking. I've come a long way since the old days, he thought.

Dr. Koenig was the best of the Germans to deal with. He didn't shout or berate one, nor did he try to steal arms and legs off in a deal. All Dr. Koenig wanted was a fair share. A fine man, Dr. Koenig.

Max was ushered into Koenig's office. He sat down and squeezed his cigar in excited anticipation and, when Koenig nodded that it was all right for him to smoke, lit it with the silver lighter on the desk.

"Are your partners waiting at the Big Seven?" Dr. Koenig asked.

"They will be there as ordered, Herr Doktor."

"Now, Max, let's talk a little business."

Kleperman opened his arms graciously. "I am your humble servant."

Koenig put on a pair of bifocals, opened a file, and lifted a sheet of paper and studied it. "You've made quite a killing in the last few years, Kleperman."

The smile vanished from Max's face. Over his shoulder he caught a glimpse of a pair of SS Waffen guarding the door. Max cleared his throat and leaned on his elbow. What was Koenig up to?

"I must say, you were very clever. Bilking us out of a quarter of a million dollars."

Max thrust out his hand in protest. "A terrible exaggeration!"

"One of your partners volunteered the information."

Max's big fingers tugged away to loosen his collar as Dr. Koenig read a terribly correct accounting of his fancy footwork. "And finally," Koenig said, "you have given inflated zlotys to the welfare people through agents in exchange for dollar deposits in Swiss banks. Buildings for which you have acted as agent have been leased to Orphans and Self-Help for dollars also. Now, Max, you know all of this is illegal."

Kleperman was way ahead of Koenig. He looked over his shoulder to see if the guards had miraculously disappeared. They hadn't. The *hutzpah*, the gall of Koenig to sit there with this holier-than-thou attitude when it was he, Kleperman, who set up most of the deals for the German. They had wallowed together in the muck, and now Koenig was going into an act of righteousness. Nothing on earth was worse than a righteous thief!

"As Kommissar of Jewish property," Koenig said, "I am appalled at the state of the affairs conducted by you. You have blatantly betrayed the trust of the occupation authorities."

Think fast! Max Kleperman, you are in a bad position. His brain raced. He'd have to go for a deal. He'd play with the Swiss money and save the South American money. No one knew about the South American money.

"I am in a bad bargaining position." Max smiled.

"I thought you would comprehend the situation."

"But, as always, Max Kleperman is a reasonable man."

Max nodded in the direction of the SS men. Koenig ordered them to wait outside.

"Now, Kleperman, let's make a clean breast. How much do you have sitting in Swiss banks, and which banks?"

"I have forty thousand dollars on demand," Max confided.

"Which banks?"

Max wiped his forehead with his sleeve.

"May I conclude, Herr Doktor, that the various contracts be-

315

tween you and the Big Seven are about to be terminated?"

"You may conclude whatever you wish to conclude."

Max cleared his throat and leaned over the desk to dispense a great confidence. "The fact is, I have a few dollars more. Fifty thousand. Frankly, I am weary of business. I should like to enjoy the fruits of my labor. Now—we make a final deal. I'll sign half this money to you now and half when I arrive in Bern with my family."

Koenig rocked in his chair and smiled slightly. "Ready to jump ship, eh, Max?"

Max winked.

"How about your partners?"

"Believe me, I've tolerated those thieves as long as it is humanly possible. I think this is a reasonable way for two honorable men to end a long and fruitful association."

"But, Max, how will you live?"

"Somehow, I'll struggle by."

"Perhaps with the money in the National Bank in Geneva?"

"Oh—oh yes, I did have an account there."

"And the Bank of South America in Buenos Aires, and the Grain Exchange in Rio de Janeiro."

"*Herr, Herr, Herr . . .*"

Koenig spread six documents before Kleperman and handed him a pen. "Just sign these, Mr. Kleperman. We will fill in the details."

Max's face twitched violently. A belch of misplaced cigar smoke gagged him. "The other partners have money over the border too. If I sign these papers and give you the information on them, do I get a passport?"

Koenig smiled. "You've made yourself a deal."

Max scrawled his signature on the papers, giving away over two hundred thousand ill-earned dollars. Droplets of sweat dripped on the transfers as he signed.

"When I arrive in Switzerland I will give you the information on the others."

Koenig nodded. "We knew we could depend on your co-operation, Max. You will receive information about your departure shortly."

Max was sick, but he still had his life. The pair of SS men led him out of Koenig's palace. He had money in eight banks. There were two places that that righteous thief Koenig had not discovered. Max flopped in the back seat of his car, removed his hat, and fanned himself and groaned.

His eyes bulged in terror! His cigar fell from his mouth. His chauffeur had been replaced by an SS man, and his bodyguard was gone. Before he could budge, a pair of SS were on either side of him and the car whisked out of the driveway. It stopped six minutes later at the entrance to the Jewish cemetery.

Max was white with terror at the sight of Sturmbannführer Sieghold Stutze. The SS men had to help him walk. Stutze tapped a length of pipe in his open palm as Max was dragged before him. Kleperman took off his hat. "Your excellency, Sturmbannführer . . . I . . . I . . ."

Stutze spoke. "I wanted to be here for you personally, Kleperman. You are the filthiest of all the filthy Jews. I have always admired that ring of yours. No, don't bother to give it to me now. I'll get it after the execution."

"Ah, then . . . you did not receive the word. Dr. Koenig and I made a deal. You are in for a hundred thousand dollars . . . you see . . ."

"Shut up. You didn't really think we would let you out of Poland with what you know?"

"My lips are sealed. I swear it."

"You don't have to swear it. We are going to seal them for you."

Six powerful hands gripped him. He dropped to his knees. They began to drag him.

"Wait!" the Austrian said. "Let him crawl."

"Excellency. There is more money. I didn't tell Koenig. You . . . me . . . a private deal . . ."

The lead pipe caught Kleperman behind the ear. He pitched face down on the dirt and crawled to Stutze and threw his arms around his knees. "Mercy! Mercy! Mercy for Max Kleperman!"

The pipe came down and down, again, again, again, until Max's face was squashed like an overripe watermelon. Stutze broke into a sweat. He kicked with his gimpy leg and screamed and ranted until he had exhausted himself on the blood orgy and had to be held upright by his SS troopers.

Max Kleperman's lifeless body was dragged down the long path lined with desecrated grave markers to the west wall and unceremoniously flung into a ditch twenty feet long and twelve feet deep.

Along the edge of the ditch the partners and fifty members of the Big Seven were lined up. They cried, begged, bartered. Below them, Kleperman lay in a bed of lime.

Some fell to their knees and cried for God and for mother. Whoremasters, thieves, informers.

"Mercy!"

"Fire!"

The sound of rifle fire was a cliché within these walls. The Jewish gravediggers watched impassively as the bodies plunged to the bottom of the ditch and stared up at them from grotesque positions. The firing squad advanced to the edge of the ditch and poured gunfire into the twitching bodies until they were still.

Shovels of lime were spread. Another batch of Big Seven people was hauled in.

PROCLAMATION!
IT HAS BEEN DISCOVERED THAT THE BIG SEVEN COMPANY HAS BEEN GUILTY OF INNUMERABLE CRIMES AND WERE THE MAIN PERPETRATORS OF MUCH OF THE JEWISH SUFFERING. IN THE NAME OF COMMON JUSTICE THE GERMAN AUTHORITIES HAVE DISPOSED OF THESE CRIMINALS AFTER INVESTIGATIONS AND TRIALS.
AS OF THIS DATE ALL FURTHER DEPORTATIONS ARE CANCELED. SPECIAL SCHOOLS MAY REOPEN AND AUTHORIZED PUBLIC MEETINGS WITHIN THE GHETTO ARE PERMITTED. THE CURFEW IS AGAIN EXTENDED TO 7 P.M.

> BY ORDER
> RUDOLPH SCHREIKER
> KOMMISSAR, DISTRICT OF WARSAW

Chapter Eleven

Rachael thumbed through a stack of sheet music, selected several numbers, and slipped on her Star of David armband. Deborah, dressed in a gown and robe, entered the room, yawning and stretching.

"Are you certain it is safe to give a recital today? I feel uneasy about it."

"Momma, there haven't been any deportations for four days. Ervin is arranging programs all over the ghetto to get people's minds off the past three weeks. Besides, I'll be playing at your orphanage on Niska and nothing will happen there."

"Well, I suppose it is all right."

"I may see Wolf today. It's been ten days."

Deborah fussed with her daughter's hair. "I wish you wouldn't go to Andrei's."

"We can't any more, Momma. It's being watched all the time."

"You can come here. Your father won't be home till late."

As Rachael turned and faced her mother, Deborah realized for the first time that her child was as tall and mature as she. "Thanks, Momma, but Wolf is terribly proud about that. Besides, it's not the most important thing any more. Just being able to see each other for a few minutes and talking is all we really want."

Deborah patted her cheek.

Stephan burst into the apartment. "Hey, come on. Aren't you ready yet?"

"Be careful, children. Keep your Civil Authority *Kennkarten*
318

handy and forgive me for not coming. I'm dog-tired. I have to get a few hours' sleep before going back to the orphanage. Tell Susan I'll take the night shift."

Stephan and Rachael pecked kisses on Deborah's cheek.

Rachael opened the door and stopped. "Strange," she said. "Being able to walk in the streets again."

"Be careful," Deborah repeated.

The assembly hall in the Niska Street orphanage was capable of holding most of the four hundred children. It was one of the twenty-eight institutions under Alexander Brandel's Orphans and Self-Help Society which somehow managed to feed and secretly educate over twenty thousand parentless youngsters. Unlike the rest of the ghetto, these homes had no hiding rooms, for it would have been impossible to construct them secretly. After all, Brandel concluded, these were children, and he had to believe in the final mercy of the enemy to leave them alone.

Rachael Bronski was the very favorite of the children. They crammed together, filling all the benches, sitting in the aisles and on the floor before her piano on the platform at the end of the hall. The nurses, teachers, and social workers stood along the back wall.

Rachael looked continually to the back door through which Wolf might appear. A long time ago when he returned from the Bathyran farm at Wework, he had come to her during a recital in this very place. Perhaps he would come again today.

Rachael held up her hands for attention and told the children what her first number would be. It was a new one in which she narrated the life of Chopin behind a sampling of waltzes, nocturnes, and etudes, ending with the patriotic crescendo of a polonaise.

The next number was a medley of Yiddish songs. She watched the faces of the children searching their memory for a faint voice in the past which had sung to them.

> "Should I be a rabbi?
> I don't know my Torah,
> Should I be a merchant?
> I have nothing to sell.

> "And I have no hay,
> And I have no oats,
> And I'd like a drink of vodka,
> But my wife will curse me,
> So I'll find a big rock,
> And I'll sit me down and cry.

> "Should I be a *schochet?*
> I cannot use a *chalef,*

319

Should I be a *melamed?*
I don't know an *alef.*

"Should I be a cobbler?
I don't have any last.
Should I be a teamster?
I have no cart or horse.

"Should I be a blacksmith?
I won't have any anvil,
Should I run a tavern?
No, my wife would get too drunk."

"What would you like to hear next?"
"Palestine!"
"Rachael! Sing to us about Palestine!"
"Palestine!"
"Palestine!"

"The roses bloom in Galilee,
And the land rejoices.
Round the day and through the night,
We lift our thankful voice.

"We love you, our Galilee,
Your land makes our hearts sing.
We guard it dear with soul and gun
And fear not what fate brings . . ."

Susan Geller entered at the rear of the hall. She looked around quickly, then whispered to her second nurse. The woman looked startled for an instant, then nodded and whispered to another nurse.

"All together now, children!"

"The roses bloom in Galilee,
And the land rejoices . . ."

Susan Geller looked around once more and spotted Stephan. She wove through the pack of children, took his hand, and led him to a side door. "Make no outcry, Stephan. The building is surrounded by Militia. Get upstairs. There are twenty-five or thirty children in an attic classroom. Do you know where it is?"

Stephan nodded.

"Take them over the roof to Mila 19. Tell Alexander Brandel to get to the Umschlagplatz quickly."

Rachael frowned as she saw Stephan slip out of the hall.

320

> "We love you, our Galilee,
> Your land makes our hearts sing . . ."

Susan sat on the bench beside Rachael. "At the end of this song I will make an announcement. You keep playing. We want no panic. Do you understand?"

"Oh God . . ."

"Keep playing, Rachael, keep playing."

"I . . . understand . . ."

Susan stepped before the piano and held up her hands. "Children!" she said. "Aunt Susan has a most wonderful surprise! Today we are going to the country on a picnic!"

The announcement was greeted with "ohs" and "ahs" of disbelief.

"We are all going on a train ride out of the ghetto and we will see all of those things we have talked about—trees and flowers and farms. All those wonderful things which you have never seen before. This is going to be the greatest experience of your life. Now we will all file out of the hall and to the street. Don't be frightened of the soldiers, because today they are there to help us. Now, Rachael, would you play something while we march out?"

Susan stepped into the corridor just as Piotr Warsinski entered the building. She blocked the door to the assembly hall.

"We are quite ready," Susan said. "If you will kindly tell your men not to alarm the children we will keep them calm."

"We just want the children, not you."

"We choose to go too."

Warsinski shrugged. "Have it your way. Get them out into the streets."

"Quickly," Stephan Bronski ordered two dozen six-year-olds in the attic classroom. Ghetto life had conditioned them to respond to his order with unqualified discipline. Stephan was first up the escape ladder to the roof. He nudged the trap door open an inch and peered around.

A Ukrainian on the roof!

Stephan signaled for the line behind him to be still. The guard paced back and forth, sweating in the heat through his dirty brown, black-sleeved shirt. He turned. Stephan could see his face and the epaulets with the skull and crossbones and the big knobby hands gripped around a rifle.

The guard stopped near the corner of the roof. The ridge was built up fifteen inches over the roof level. The guard knelt on it, peering past a steep tile roof which partly blocked the view to the street five stories down.

Clump . . . clump . . . clump . . .

The man looked around at the thing flying over the roof at him.

321

Before he could gather his wits or straighten up it was on him at a dead run. Stephan slammed his body at the Ukrainian at the same instant the man tried to stand up. It threw him off balance. His legs buckled and he fell onto the overhang, dropping his rifle on the roof.

In a frantic grab he snatched the top of the ridge. Stephan lifted the guard's fallen rifle and with its butt smashed the clinging man's hands.

A shriek!

The guard slid down the tiles, flailing in panic for something to grab. His body swooped over the edge and became smaller, smaller, smaller, until it stopped suddenly on the pavement.

"Quick!" Stephan cried, ruling out fear or revulsion at his deed. One by one the children climbed onto the roof.

Rifle fire crackled from the street. Shouts below! "*Juden Kinder!* Jew children!"

The ghetto rat knew his way well. He fled over the ceiling of the city with the knowledge of a craftsman. Then a dead end.

The line of buildings dropped from five stories to four. A chasm four feet wide separated the buildings. Stephan looked for the mattress which had been laid on the lower roof to break the falls. It had been removed! The decision was already made for him. He could neither stay nor turn back.

"Now we are going to have to jump over to that roof. We will have to stand on the very edge so we can reach the roof. When you land, land on your feet and use your legs as though they were big giant springs. Bend and then throw yourselves on your tummies."

A little girl wept in fear.

"You," he said to the largest youngster, "you be my assistant commander. You stay till last. Everyone choose a partner." He quickly took the crying girl by the hand. "You will be mine." Before she could register a protest they leaped over the drop onto the next roof.

Piotr Warsinski reported to Haupsturmführer Kutler.

"How is it?" Kutler asked.

"The most successful 'kettle' we have ever made. Every orphanage is cleaned."

"How many?"

"Maybe ten, twelve thousand heads."

"That's a lot of Jew babies. Well—they've got no valuables. Start loading them up. Send the leftover bastards to the top floors for storage till tomorrow and the day after. I want all your people around the Umschlagplatz on guard tonight. Bastards in the ghetto liable to try something."

Warsinski turned to leave. "Good job, Chief," laughed Kutler.

Kutler walked out to the selection desks and frowned at the sight of the nurses mingling with the children. "Warsinski!"

"Yes, sir."

"What are all those people doing here?"

"They wanted to come with the children."

Susan Geller came up to them. "Surely you cannot object to having us resettled with our wards," she said.

Kutler sneered. He did not like her homely face. He glanced around at the other nurses, teachers, doctors, and workers holding their tiny flocks together. Goddamned Jews, Kutler thought. They got some kind of strange love for dying like martyrs. He remembered the fathers holding their hands over their sons' eyes on the edge of the pits at Babi-Yar at Kiev.

"You people aren't wanted in this transfer," Kutler said.

"The children will enjoy their picnic in the country so much more if they have us with them to explain everything. You see, many of them do not remember being out of the ghetto."

Kutler turned his eyes away from Susan Geller's insistent stare. "What have you got in that bag?" he asked.

"Chocolates. I've been saving them for a wonderful occasion like this."

Kutler cracked. "Be heroes," he muttered, and dashed back to his office and closed and bolted the door. He yanked viciously at a desk drawer, unable to open it quickly enough, and smashed the top of the schnapps bottle, guzzling until a hot wave of alcohol flooded his blood and crashed into his brain, dulling his thoughts. "Heroes . . . martyrs . . ."

The courtyard bulged with ten thousand ragged, emaciated children with a sprinkling of nurses who kept up a play of gaiety. Some of the older children who knew where they were going kept it to themselves.

"Jew babies, start moving up the ramps!"

"Well, children, now begins our wonderful picnic in the country."

"Aunt Susan, when will we come back?"

"Oh, probably later tonight."

"Keep moving down to the end of the platform to the first car!"

The engine warmed up with a few puffs of steam.

The line of tykes straggled up the ramps. Curses and kicks moved them quicker.

Kutler, in a thick drunk, staggered out to the courtyard and watched the march. He snarled semi-intelligible sounds, screaming to hurry it up. He sighted a dozen small children leaning against a far wall, doubled up from exhaustion and hunger, too weak to drag themselves to their feet. Kutler wove toward them. "Up, you Jew babies!" he shrieked.

323

Two or three nurses converged on them, helping them to their feet.

A rachitic girl of three clad in filthy rags toppled to the cobblestones, dropping a torn baby doll which had neither arms nor legs. Her little hand reached for it.

Kutler's shiny black boot stamped on the doll.

The ragamuffin stared curiously at the tall black-uniformed man hovering over her. "My baby," she whined weakly, "I want my baby." Her hand tugged, trying to pry it from under the Nazi's boot. His Mauser pistol came out of the holster.

A pistol shot echoed.

"Let me through! Let me through!" cried Alexander.

A half dozen bulky Jewish militiamen restrained the desperate Brandel before he could get into the selection center. He was dragged screaming and fighting across Stawki Street to the warehouse where Warsinski had the Umschlagplatz detail office.

"I demand to be allowed in the Umschlagplatz!"

Warsinski let Alexander babble, plead, coax, argue. Then he spoke. "Your immunity is running short, Brandel. Take him back to the ghetto."

Clickety-clack, clickety-clack the train rolled over the countryside.

"Now, children," Susan Geller said, "I have another surprise. Chocolates!"

"Chocolates!"

She passed the bag of poisoned candy about the car.

"Doesn't that taste wonderful?"

The train rolled on.

"Let's all sing together."

> "Onward, onward,
> On to Palestine.
> Onward, onward,
> Join the happy throng . . ."

"I'm sleepy, Aunt Susan."

"Well, why don't you lie down and rest?"

"I'm sleepy too, Tante Susan."

"Well, all of you take a nap. It must be the excitement and the fresh air."

One by one they closed their eyes. Susan Geller snuggled between a pair of her babies and held them close to her and slowly swallowed the last square of chocolate.

Shluf mine faygele,
Mach tzu dine aygele

Eye lu lu lu,
Shluf geshmak mine kind,
Shluf un zai-gezund,
Eye lu lu lu

Sleep my little bird,
Shut your little eyes,
Eye lu lu lu,
Sleep tight my child,
Sleep and be safe,
Eye lu lu lu.

Chapter Twelve

Sturmbannführer Sieghold Stutze was adept at aping his God, Adolf Hitler, down to the slightest gestures. Thumbs in belt, he limped up and down the courtyard holding the massed assemblage of Jewish Militia. He stopped before a microphone and glared at his captive audience with seductive authority. The board of the Jewish Civil Authority was lined up on his right and a company of his Reinhard Corps on his left.

Throwing a hand above his head, he shrieked in a high pitch which echoed off the stones of the yard. "Fat Jews! You are fat because we have rewarded you too much. Despite our loyalty to you, you continue to permit publication of lies about us! You allow these Communist agitators to exist under your noses! They will be found and destroyed! Because of these lies we have not received a single volunteer for four days for orderly deportation for honest labor in the east!" Stutze whirled around to Warsinski. "Read the new orders!"

Warsinski opened a document. " 'From this day forward every member of the Jewish Militia has a personal daily duty to bring three people to the Umschlagplatz for deportation for honest labor. In the event a militiaman fails to meet his quota, he and his family will be deported immediately.' "

The respite in the Big Action, the show of "common justice" by executing the Big Seven, and the reopening of the schools, all became part of a master scheme to lure the people into relaxing their vigil long enough for the Germans to reorganize for the next onslaught.

A terrorized Jewish Militia under Warsinski's obedient haranguing had long ago sold their souls; now they sank to a new depth of decadence. It became a common sight to see them dragging their own relatives to the Umschlagplatz for deportation when they were unable to fill their quotas.

Ghetto *Kennkarten* stamped for labor were long believed to be a magic key to life. In a stroke of the pen they were all declared invalid. All but a handful of people in the ghetto had lost their immunity to deportation.

Each day new "kettles" and "pots" were executed. Streets or blocks of houses were hermetically sealed off and methodically raked from cellar to attic for occupants.

The constant fountain of trickery spouted. The lure of food was used to gain new spies. Children were tortured before the eyes of their mothers to reveal the locations of secret bunkers.

An immunity to tragedy became normal. Yet the roundup of the orphans accomplished what the master planners knew it would. It seemed to crush whatever morale and will to exist remained.

Alexander Brandel, long the symbol of love and dignity, long the symbol of food and medicine, turned into a morose, depressed man overnight. Speechless day followed speechless day. He no longer functioned as the dynamic force for survival.

Rabbi Solomon sat in the dank cellar next to the sewer pipe under Mila 19 and wailed ancient Hebrew prayers day and night to the sound of rushing sewerage.

Deborah Bronski was the sole nurse remaining from the Niska Street orphanage to take care of the two dozen boys and girls Stephan had led over the roofs to Mila 19. Yet another room was dug out alongside the pipe and fitted with bunks and a classroom.

Deborah flicked on the light in her bedroom. She opened the dresser drawers one by one and filled a suitcase. An item or two came from the jewelry box. A few things of a personal nature. Everything else was to be left. She checked the children's room for the mementos they wanted, then walked down the long hall.

There was a light from Paul's study. She entered and could see the back of his head as he sat in his swivel chair in front of his desk.

"I am leaving you, Paul. I should have done so long ago. Stephan and Rachael will be with me."

Paul was motionless.

"Good-bye, Paul."

As she turned to go, she saw that his hand hung limply over the arm of the chair, a crumpled sheet of paper in his fist. On the floor lay a bottle. She recognized it as his sleeping pills. The bottle was empty. It had been filled only a few days earlier. Deborah walked slowly to the front of the desk. Paul was rigid,

326

his eyes closed. She set down the suitcase and felt his hand. It was icy. There was no pulse.

Paul Bronski was dead.

"May God forgive me," she said, "but I wish I could say that I am sorry."

She pried the paper loose from his hand. "My dear Deborah," the note read, "I wish I knew what to say or what I have done to deserve this scorn from you. Boris Presser has an envelope explaining various affairs which I'm sure you'll find in order . . ." And there the scrawling stopped.

The top of the desk was tidy. Paul was meticulous in his habits. Everything would be in order. Even his death. He had closed out a business day by suicide simply because there was no alternative.

Deborah shook her head in a final bewilderment. She looked squarely into his sallow, lifeless face. "Oh, Paul, Paul, Paul. Even this had to be done so properly. Why didn't you write a message for your son and daughter? Why didn't you make this act an outcry for justice and protest? Paul, Paul . . . Why?"

She picked up her suitcase. Without remorse, without tears, without regret, without pity, she left everything that had been between them, forever.

"We must have help!" an impassioned Andrei cried.

Roman, the Home Army commander in Warsaw, listened with head cocked, eyes lazily half shut. The nobleman placed a cigarette in the long holder delicately and lit it. A frustrated Andrei waved off Roman's offer of a smoke.

"Jan Kowal," Roman said softly, "just last week we sent you thirty two rifles."

"Of six different calibres with a hundred and six rounds of ammunition. One of the rifles becomes obsolete the moment it fires its three bullets."

"If there is suddenly a downpour of heavy-caliber automatic weapons from the skies, I'll be the first to let you know."

Andrei smashed his fist on the table.

Roman got up and clasped his hands behind him dramatically. "Just what do you want?"

"We haven't the strength to mount an attack without help from outside. If you had three companies of the Home Army make simultaneous diversified strikes in the suburbs, we can push out of the ghetto."

Roman sighed with frustration. Despite the rigors of living underground, he had lost none of the fine edge that characterized a French-bred snob. "It is impossible," he said.

"Can you be that much of a Jew-hater to watch us cooked alive?"

Roman leaned against the window sill and bit on the ivory

holder with the studied gestures of one who knows he is on stage. His eyebrows raised on his high forehead. "Shall we get coldly realistic? What if I carry through your plan? Where will you go? How many will you break out?"

"As many as you can make provisions for."

"Ah," beamed Roman, "that is the rub. Ninety per cent of the peasants would turn in a Jew for a bottle of vodka. Ninety per cent of the people are quite certain this war is being fought because of international Jewish bankers. Not my personal feelings, mind you, but I am in no position to carry out a program to educate the Polish people." Roman was deadly accurate again.

"Then at least let the fighting force find its way out with the children."

"Children? Those convents and monasteries which take Jewish children are filled to the brim. Most won't. The few others want ten thousand zlotys a head in advance with the right to convert them to Catholicism."

Andrei closed his eyes.

Roman warmed up to his arguments, sliding his tongue over his teeth as he paced. "I cannot allow partisan units made up of Jews. I do not command an army on discipline. The underground depends upon secrecy and loyalty. You know full well you will be betrayed just as you were betrayed when you gave us the report on extermination camps. It was sold by someone to the Gestapo."

"At least—at least give us guns and money. At least the money you've stolen from us."

Roman frowned and sat at the table, lifting some papers to read to demonstrate he was too busy for further bickering. Andrei snatched them out of his hand and flung them to the floor.

"All right, Jan!" Roman snorted. "Your precious report was smuggled out of Poland by someone or other and has been published in London. Have you heard the heads of state make impassioned cries for justice? Has the world suddenly stormed to its feet in indignation? Jan Kowal, no one really gives a damn."

Andrei pushed back from the table. "Don't slop your Polish garbage on the rest of the world, Roman. This is the only corner of the world where extermination camps could exist. The German army doesn't have enough divisions to guard against the people if they tried it in London or Paris or New York. Only in your goddamned Warsaw! All over this continent men and women are behaving with basic Christian decency. You are a Christian, aren't you?"

Roman went through arrogant gestures of indulgent disgust.

"You won't walk away from this free. They're already starting to gas Poles at Auschwitz only because you let them get away with it with us. March into the chamber with your chin up, Roman, your turn is coming."

Andrei stormed out.

Roman broke the shortened cigarette from the holder and squashed the tip out. He looked up at a stunned aide. "If those blasted Jews try to contact me again, I am not to be reached, do you understand?"

"Yes, sir."

"Jews are so emotional. Oh well, at least we won't have a Jewish problem when the war is over."

Simon Eden smashed his fist into his open palm as Andrei related the meeting with Roman. The attic room fell into gloom. Tolek, Alexander Brandel, Ana, Ervin, Wolf Brandel, Simon Eden. A ghastly morbidity crushed them. It was all over. Everyone thought the same thing at the sam moment. It was all over . . . done.

The alarm bell sounded five short rings to indicate a "friend" was coming up. Rodel, the Communist, entered. For an instant everyone looked eagerly with a flickering of hope beyond hope that some miracle had happened. Rodel shook his head. "They can give us four armed men, no more. They can't even really spare that."

Tolek droned the names of writers, doctors, actors, journalists, and Zionists who had been taken to the Umschlagplatz in the last few days. He went on and on, moaning a death march.

"Be quiet," Andrei said.

But he droned on. The last of the rabbis—one saved by the Catholic Church as some sort of relic of a past civilization, the other was in their cellar. The rest, dead. "Dead, all dead," Tolek said. "Farm gone . . . farm gone . . . everyone is dead."

"Shut up," Andrei repeated.

Ana Grinspan, an unwavering symbol of strength, a figure of daring, collapsed and cried hysterically. There was no one in the room who could comfort her.

"Say something, Alex," Simon Eden pleaded.

But Alex said nothing these days.

"Dead . . . all dead. *Nishtdoo, keiner, keiner nishtdoo.*"

"Stop your goddamned crying!" Andrei screamed.

Ervin licked his dry lips. Tears wet his thick glasses, so that the people before him were blurred images. Within five days he had lost his wife Susan and his mother. He had tried gallantly to carry on for Alexander Brandel after the children were rounded up. "Simon . . . Andrei . . . Comrade Rodel . . . I . . . have taken all the notes and volumes of the Good Fellowship Club and hidden them in milk cans and steel boxes. I had occasion to speak to your committees today. They are in full accord with

329

me that if this last try for help was unsuccessful we should burn the ghetto and commit mass suicide."

"You have no right to hold meetings behind my back," Simon said without conviction.

"We had no time for rules of procedure," Ervin said.

"Who among us hasn't thought of suicide?" Ana cried.

And then silence. There were no arguments.

"As a Labor Zionist . . . as a Labor Zionist," Simon mumbled. He brushed the hair back from his eyes. "As a Jew and Labor Zionist," he floundered and fumbled. Oh God, he thought, death would be so sweet, so very sweet. "As commander of Joint Forces, I cannot and will not give an order for a suicide pact. But if this is the wish of everyone, then I will resign my command and also abide by the decision."

Andrei stared up at his comrade. Simon had been a soldier. Simon had been a strong man. Simon had been a leader. His innards were shot. The fine features of his dark face sagged with the loss of will.

Wolf Brandel, the youngest commander in the ghetto, walked slowly toward the door. "I will not obey that order," he said. "My girl and I are going to live, and if we're captured we are going to make them pay. If they want me," Wolf cried, "let them come in and try to get me!"

He slammed the door behind him.

"Well," Andrei whispered, "one of us is left with enough strength to want to live."

Tolek fell on his knees. "Oh God! God! God! Please help us! What have we done? What have we done?"

No one looked at the other. Their faces fell into their hands. All through the night they sat wordless until the dawn broke them with weariness and they dropped off into snatches of nightmare-filled sleep.

And then, as suddenly as it began, the Big Action ended. On September 16, 1942, there were no more deportations or "kettles."

The Warsaw ghetto, the largest human stockyard in man's history, one held nearly six hundred thousand people. That number was decimated by starvation, disease, executions, deportation to slave labor, and finally assembly-line murder in Treblinka. When the Big Action ended, less than fifty thousand remained.

Horst von Epp cut the classic conception of the ramrod German baron as he stood framed before the tall window of Chris's flat, transfixed by the first snowfall of the winter, and the strains of a Chopin record.

Chris came in from outside, slapping the cold from his bones. He nodded to Horst, he was pleased at the unexpected visit.

"Hope you don't mind my breaking in and helping myself to the whisky?" Horst said, fixing a scotch for Chris.

"Why should I mind? There's nothing in this apartment your friends haven't examined twenty times."

The Chopin record came to the end. "I like Chopin. All those blockheads play is Wagner. A tribute to Hitler in absentia. Isn't there something enormously enchanting about the first snow?"

Chris threw open the drapes to the alcove bedroom, tugged off his shoes and wet socks. He fished around under the bed for his slippers.

> "O the snow, the beautiful snow,
> Filling the sky and the earth below,
> Over the housetops, over the street,
> Over the heads of the people you meet,
> > Dancing,
> > Flirting,
> > Skimming along,
> Beautiful snow, it can do nothing wrong."

"Ye gods, Chris, that's horrible."

"James Whittaker Watson, 1824–90. My recitation for the second-grade graduation. My mother didn't come to the graduation. I never forgot snow, beautiful snow."

Horst handed him a tall drink. They clinked glasses. "*Fröhliche Weihnachten*—Christmas cheer," he said.

"I'll be a sad bastard. Christmas. I forgot all about it."

"I toast those poor misled Aryans laying on their wet bellies in snow, beautiful snow on the eastern front for the glory of the Fatherland," Horst said.

"Amen. Well, how does it feel to get clobbered?"

"We are going to lose at Stalingrad, aren't we, Chris?"

"It's going to be a catastrophe, Baron. Your Chief of Staff should have read Napoleon's memoirs and taken a lesson of what mother winter does to trespassers."

"I had it about a week ago. The sudden realization Germany is going to lose the war. It is making a mess out of all the Christmas parties. Everyone is so damned glum. Stalingrad, El Alamein, the landings in North Africa. But you know what really confounds me is those Americans. Guadalcanal. Now there's a romantic name. Everyone underestimates Americans. Why?"

"The mistaking of gentleness as weakness is like underestimating a Russian winter."

"Next year," Horst said, "Berlin is going to be bombed. What a pity. Oh dear, how they are going to pay us back. Well, Christmas cheer."

Horst set down his drink and again became enchanted with the falling snow. "Chris," he said, looking outside, "a report has just been published by the Polish government in exile in London. A nasty White Paper detailing alleged extermination camps operating in Poland. Heard about it?"

"Something or other."

"Tell me," Horst said, "how did you smuggle it out of Poland?"

Chris made only a nominal attempt to cover his deed. "What makes you think it was me?"

"My male vanity. When a beautiful piece of tail, Victoria Landowski from Lemberg, turns out not to be a piece of tail and not even Victoria Landowski, my masculinity was offended."

"Find the woman. They are behind all sinister plots."

"The trouble was, I couldn't find the woman. My friend Christopher de Monti had become deliciously decadent, a quivering alcoholic mass of sponge. Then Victoria Landowski enters and Christopher undergoes a magic transformation. He returns to being—what do you call it?—a clean-cut All-American boy. I began to add this sudden spiritual resurrection. It was not difficult to figure the rest of it."

"By God, Horst, you're downright clairvoyant. Well, does Gestapo Chief Sauer put his dogs on me, feed me a quart of castor oil, or use testicle crushers to make me talk?"

"Oh, cut the nonsense out. Those dreary people at the Gestapo won't figure this thing out for months. How did you get the reports out? Italian diplomats?"

"Something like that," Chris answered.

"See! I told Hitler personally not to trust the Italians. Those people are far too romantic to really carry out a first-class war of annihilation. As soon as we come to the acid tests, they abandon us."

Chris laughed. "I'm only an Italian by passport. Come to think of it, I'm really not much of anything. But I do know the Italian people. They were sold a bill of goods that they were a reincarnation of the noble Romans, twenty centuries removed. So why in hell shouldn't they believe it? All they really wanted was to be somebody again."

"On German coattails."

"The bride awoke to find her maidenhead broken, but the Teutonic god she married had turned into an ugly black gorilla.

Sort of a beauty and the beast in reverse. Horst, the Italian people have no stomach for what you are doing in Poland. It was no chore at all getting five men to carry out five separate copies of the extermination-camp report."

"Archetype German villain that I am," Horst said, "I cannot comprehend why those who are utterly crushed insist on dying gestures of defiance. Martyrs are dreadful. I watched you sink to degeneration. What was that voice that called you out of Satan's arms? What did it say to you?"

"It told me . . . I must become worthy enough to receive the spit of a man who was once my friend."

"Morality." Horst shook his head. "Just before the war I saw that big hammy American baritone—what was his name?—Tibbett. Lawrence Tibbett. He sang in Paris. After a song about mother's southern-fried cake he bellowed some more dreadful poetry. Somehow, the damned verse keeps going through my mind these days.

> "Out of the night that covers me,
> Black as the pit from pole to pole,
> I thank whatever gods may be . . ."

" 'For my unconquerable soul,' " Chris said. "To William Ernest Henley, 1849–1903.

> "Under the bludgeonings of chance
> My head is bloody, but unbowed.

"This immediately brings to mind the question of why all poets have three names and why wasn't my mother at the fifth-grade commencement ceremonies, either?"

"It will never replace Schiller or Heine—that is, before Heine became a Jew. I know, you cannot put man's soul in a ghetto or gas his spirit at Treblinka. It looks fine in the hands of poets but puzzling when it really happens. Why did you do it, Chris? A few sermons by minor bishops, a few editorials by minor newspapers, a few pasty statements by minor politicians, a few protest suicides by minor idealists. What did you hope to gain? *Ach.* Now I have to spend the whole winter writing counterpropaganda."

"I'm sorry it's making you lose so much sleep, Horst. I thought perhaps the report itself might annoy you."

"Don't give me that snide journalist's sneer. I know—how could we do this? The fine, cultured German people, after which I rattle off the names of musicians, poets, doctors, and list all our gifts to mankind. How could we do this? It will take the great philosophical and psychiatric brains a hundred years to find a standard of morals to explain this behavior."

333

"I'll simplify it," Chris said. "You're a pack of beasts."

"Oh no, Chris, we are not even to be classed with beasts. Man is the only animal on this planet which destroys its own species. But how in the devil did I get involved in this? I'm no more guilty than you are. Less, perhaps. I'm trapped. But you, dear Chris, are all the moralists in the world who have condoned genocide by the conspiracy of silence."

"The conspiracy of silence," Chris mumbled. "Yes, I buy that."

"Hell, my own skin isn't important. After the war all this business will be unearthed and mankind will register a proper shock and horror. Then they will say, 'Let us all forget about the past. Let bygones be bygones.' And all over Germany you'll get a chorus of 'Amen.' What will the song be? There was nobody here in Germany but us anti-Nazis. Extermination camps? We knew nothing about them. Hitler? Always did think he was crazy. What could we do? Orders were orders. And the world will say, 'Look at all the good Germans.' They will string up a few Nazis as showpieces, and all the good German folk will slink back to their cobblers' benches and sulk and wait for the next Führer." Horst broke into a sudden sweat and lost his composure. He downed a shot of whisky quickly.

"What's eating you, Horst?"

"The Jews. They'll pin a curse on us. They'll make us a scourge among men for a thousand years."

"History is written by survivors. There will be no Jewish survivors," Chris said.

"Hell! They're uncanny. They have this maddened, insatiable desire to put words on paper. This mania to document their torment." Horst calmed and thought. "Last time they documented their destruction we got a Bible, then a 'Valley of Tears'—now what? You know, Chris, my brother was in a Knight Templar colony in Palestine before the war. Every winter he would climb around in caves near the Dead Sea looking for ancient Hebrew letters."

"Why, Horst, you're afraid of your hereafter. I wouldn't have dreamed it."

"I have a crawling suspicion that inside that ghetto wall are ten thousand diaries buried beneath the ground. And that is what is going to crush us. Not the allied armies, not a few tokens of retribution, but the voices of the dead, unearthed. From this stigma we can never. . . . Forgive me, Christmas has a habit of putting me in a mood."

"What are you going to do with me?" Chris asked sharply.

"I've given it a lot of thought. I can't let you out of Poland. I mean, after all, we have to play the game. We both played fairly and I lost. I made a bad guess. On the other hand, no use letting

334

Sauer get his hands on you. I am a believer in grandiose gestures!
Pack a bag!"

Horst steered his auto down Jerusalem Boulevard. About them
a dismal attempt to find Christmas cheer was being made by the
Poles and despondent German soldiers.

"Chris, one last thing I must know. This Victoria Landowski.
Was she a good piece?"

"The truth? I wouldn't know."

"Amazing. Simply amazing. Well, we will find her one day."

"When you do, do me one last favor. Give her a chance to
finish herself off before Sauer roughs her up."

"Chris, you're asking entirely too much."

"She is very important to me."

"Oh well, it is Christmas. My promise. By God, I'm forgetting
all my good German training and turning into a downright sentimentalist."

The car stopped before the ghetto gate opposite the Tlomatskie
Synagogue. Horst handed Chris a *Kennkarte* and special papers.
"Into the ghetto. These papers will keep you out of police hands
until you find your friends. In three days I'll turn in a report you
are missing. That should give you enough time to get buried in
there."

"I am afraid I have no friends left," Chris said.

"Don't be too sure. Jews have an infallible intelligence system.
They will somehow know how the extermination-camp report
was spirited out of Poland."

Chris got out of the car. "You're one for the books."

"Well, three cheers for the final triumph of morality in men.
If we ever run across one another after the war, put in a good
word for me. There is always a demand for ex-German barons as
gardeners, bartenders, villain parts in movies. I am a man of
many talents." He sped away.

The ghetto streets were devoid of life. Chris turned up his coat
collar and walked aimlessly through the swirls of snow. Eyes were
on him from the rooftops the instant he entered. He wandered
until he grew weary. Where to go? Whom to see? What a strange
ending. Were there people behind the stillness? Was there life left?

Where to go? Where to turn?

"You!"

Chris whirled about. He saw no one in the courtyard from
which the voice came.

"You!" it called again.

Chris walked toward the voice. It was coming from an indentation in the building.

"Turn around and walk," the voice commanded. "Don't look
around. I will give you directions."

He sat alone on the cot in the attic of Mila 19. Andrei Androfski entered.

Finally Chris stood up and turned his back on Andrei. "Divine retribution. The sinner has come to face his makers. Poetic justice in its purest form."

Andrei sat at the wooden table and placed his elbow in the center. "Want to hand-wrestle? I haven't eaten as well as you, but I can still beat you."

"Don't you know me, Andrei? I stood by with my hands in my pockets and my ears deafened to the cries of the dying."

"Must you be so dramatic? All I want to do is hand-wrestle."

"Andrei . . ."

"We know how that report reached London, Chris. Thank you."

Chris bit his lip to hold off tears.

"We got a horse over the wall this morning. Steaks tonight. Take this pistol. Later I'll show you how to move around. I'll put up another cot here for you. When you hear five alarm bells in short rings, it is a friend. Long dashes, we go to the roof. We must be very careful. The roofs are icy."

"Andrei . . ."

"Never mind. I understand."

Chris was alone. He peered out of the slanting garret window. The snow had stopped, revealing the spires of churches beyond the wall. The churches would be filled with kneeling, praying, singing people. Meager gifts would be exchanged, and for an instant the spirit of goodness would pass through people. Would they think for a fleeting moment of those inside the ghetto? Would they remember that Jesus was a Jew? Chris was flooded with a strange, wonderful, warm sensation, and peace filled his body and his heart. It was a comfort he had never known in a restless, searching life. Now he had captured it.

Five short rings.

"Deborah . . ."

"Don't say anything. Just let me hold you, Chris. Don't speak . . . don't speak . . . Just let me hold you."

part four

DAWN

Chapter One

Alexander Brandel continues to be morose and uncommunicative. He has barely spoken to any of us all winter. The Orphans and Self-Help Society still "legally" exists and carries immune Kennkarten. *I have assumed Alexander's duties, such as they "officially" remain. There is still much intercourse with the Civil Authority on rations, etc.*

The ghetto is like a morgue. It is impossible to believe that the face of the moon could be more quiet and deserted than the ghetto streets. During the Big Action the women going to the Umschlag-platz for deportation wanted to carry their silk comforters and feather beds, but they were too bulky. So they cut them open and dumped the feathers and goose down on the roofs so they could carry the outer cover (in hopes of finding something to refill them with at their destination). In some places the feathers are ankle-deep on the roofs, and when a wind blows it looks like snow coming down. Always, feathers drift down to add to the haunting stillness.

We think there are forty thousand of us left. Several thousand are at the Brushmaker's and the uniform factory. There are some of us "authorized" personnel left, a thousand or so. (Why, we do not know.) Mostly there are Wild Ones. The ghetto has been transformed into an underground city with mazes of tunnels, hidden rooms, and cellars dug under cellars. The Militia and Nightingales wrecked all the vacant houses, so they are thoroughly uninhabitable.

We are completely shut off from the little ghetto, which has been devoid of Jews for almost a year, except for the woodwork factory, which has now closed. Poles are moving back into the former little ghetto, scrambling for the fine houses on Sienna and Sliska streets, which they are able to get without compensation to the departed occupants.

This winter we have concentrated in getting key people into the Aryan side. David Zemba reluctantly left the ghetto with his family, but I hear he continues to live in Warsaw, refusing to leave the country. We have been able to place six of the children (who escaped the Niska orphanage and live in the cellar of Mila 19) in the Franciscan Sisters' convent in Laski.

Joint Forces has about seven hundred fighters in training, learning street-fighting tactics, the handling of our various weapons, and the routes over the roofs. We have twenty so-called battle companies, about one third armed. There are seven Labor Zionist companies, two Bund, four Communist, two Bathyran, and religious and mixed groups. The Revisionists outside of Joint Forces have a well-armed group of fifty or more at their bunker under Nalewki 37.

Arms, food, and medical stores are hidden in dozens of alternate store bunkers all over the ghetto. Our standard weapon is the Polish 35 rifle. We have about thirty of these with a thousand rounds of ammunition. Next in importance are the fifty-six various models of 9-mm. pistols (German Mausers, Parabellums and Swedish Lahtis). The odd weapons are a nuisance, but we take them despite the difficulty and cost in obtaining ammunition. We have a few Italian Berettis (cal. 32) and Glisentis 10.35. The two Hungarian Baby Frummer .380's have only eight rounds between them. (A round of ammunition for the Baby Frummer costs two hundred zlotys apiece, whereas 9-mm. ammo runs from eighty to a hundred and twenty zlotys.)

We have several thousand fire bottles and nearly a thousand water-pipe grenades manufactured from a formula by our genius, Jules Schlosberg. We have also three dozen Polish grenades and assorted knives.

Schlosberg's newest concoction is a tin can filled with nuts and bolts. The open end of the can is sealed with plastic percussion caps and covered with a light wax. The theory works. We tested four of them in empty houses. The impact was so great that some of the bolts shot clear through the plaster walls into the next rooms. We call this "weapon" the "matzo ball."

Joint Forces operates out of four primary bunkers. Simon Eden's headquarters (Leszno 92) under Bund House, Gensia 43, and our bunker at Mila 19 (which now holds almost a hundred people, including eighteen children) form the "Central Command." Rodel has a series of small bunkers at the southern end around the uniform factory. His main bunker is under the Converts' Church! Father Jakub hears nothing. A good friend. The other command in the Brushmaker's district is held by Wolf Brandel, who is barely twenty years old. Wolf amazes us all with his imagination and complete calm. His main bunker is at Franciskanska Street, almost at the ghetto wall and under two parts of the factory complex. Rachael Bronski, now a soldier, has gone to live at the Franciskanska bunker. Stephan Bronski, incidentally, is considered the best runner in the ghetto.

The Brushmaker's factory still turns out six thousand brushes a day for the Wehrmacht. This means, of course, a constant flow of raw supplies in from the outside. Wolf has capitalized on this by paying off a few key people in shipping and receiving. Food cans and supplies coming in can be easily marked and used for smuggling in pistols and ammunition.

Before David Zemba went over to the Aryan side we held a final meeting of the Good Fellowship Club (half our original number are

339

left). It was decided that everything except the current volume in progress should be hidden immediately. Fifty completed volumes have been stuffed into fourteen milk cans and sealed and buried in fourteen different places. Ten more milk cans and iron boxes contain unclassified or unentered material, such as photographs, diaries, poetry, essays. Only six people know where the twenty-four cans and boxes are hidden: David Zemba, Andrei Androfski, Gabriela Rak, Alexander Brandel, Christopher de Monti, and myself. David, Andrei, Gabriela, and Alex each know where part of the cache is located, so if captured they cannot possibly reveal the entire archives.

Only Christopher de Monti and I know the location of all the cans and boxes. We have placed the most urgent priority in getting Chris out of Poland, for he alone is our greatest hope of bringing world attention to the holocaust which has befallen us. However, there is an unparalleled man hunt for him on the Aryan side, and getting him out of Poland will be nearly impossible.

One bit of good news. Although Finland is an ally of Germany, she has adamantly refused to turn over her Jewish community (of two thousand) to Eichmann. In fact, old Marshal Mannerheim has threatened to use the Finnish army to protect the Jews. We hear similar reports of defiance, particularly from Denmark. Also, we hear that Bulgaria and Rumania will not yield Jews to Eichmann's fanatical pressure. Lord, Lord, what couldn't we do with the protection of the Polish Home Army, which now has a quarter of a million men!

With the Good Fellowship Club archives hidden, I feel that my work has come to an end. I am so lonely without Susan and Momma. I am almost blind from the years of working in the cellar in bad light with these notes. My hands and shoulders are swollen with arthritis from the dampness. I am in pain all the time. How much longer can we go on? How many of us will escape? Two? Five? Fifty? How many? And what of Joint Forces? A fool's army. No one in their wildest dreams believes we can hold out against assault for more than two or three days. So what is the use? When will we fight? Or will we fight? Who among us will dare to fire the first shot against them? Who?

Entered as the first entry of a new volume by Ervin Rosenblum on January 15, 1943.

## Chapter Two

Blond, blue-eyed, trim, intelligent, industrious SS Oberführer
Alfred Funk stood, posture correct, at the head of a polished table.
Listening in rapt attention on his left sat Rudolph Schreiker and
Dr. Franz Koenig. Opposite them, Gestapo Chief Gunther Sauer
and Sturmbannführer Sieghold Stutze, newly appointed as security
police head for all of Warsaw. Not so rapt in his attention, Horst
von Epp, bored, stared out of the window at the opposite end of
the table.

Funk had carried verbal orders from Berlin to Poland on the
"Jewish question" for so long that meanings were understood
beyond their thin veils. He spoke in an uninspired monotone.

"Those who remain in the ghetto are Communists, criminals,
perverts, and agitators."

Four of them agreed. Von Epp played with a paper clip.

"Himmler has decided that for the sake of common justice we
must erase this blot. We will proceed shortly with the final phase
of the liquidation of the ghetto."

Each of the men immediately translated the order into his own
personal sphere of action.

For Rudolph Schreiker the removal of the Jewish problem in his
area would be a relief. It was getting far too complicated for him
to understand; besides, many of his business dealings could be
buried in the ghetto.

Franz Koenig had been way ahead of it, anticipating the ghetto-
liquidation order. He had already negotiated new war contracts,
using labor at Trawniki and Poniatow.

Sauer took the order with unconcern. A policeman is always
busy. Old problems are solved, new ones pop up. The Gestapo
never rests, never will rest. Put out one fire, two more ignite. It did
not matter.

Horst von Epp wanted the meeting to break up so he could get
to a telephone and check to see if the new girls had come in from
Prague.

Stutze was the most outwardly concerned. To him would fall the
actual job of digging the vermin out. The Jews had shown great
ingenuity in hiding themselves, and with an entire winter to dig in
he would need more help.

"You are, of course, aware that the Jews are subterranean,"
Stutze said. "One can walk in the streets of the ghetto for hours
without a sign of life. They live like moles. According to their
Civil Authority records, there are forty to fifty thousand of them
left. And one cannot overlook the fact that they have been arming
themselves."

Funk cut Stutze short. "You do not suggest that Jews will fight?"

"Of course not, Oberführer," the Austrian said too quickly. "But you yourself said that criminals and Communists have taken refuge in the ghetto."

"I have full faith that your Reinhard Corps will be more than equal to the situation," Funk concluded abruptly.

Stutze blanched. Funk had put him in such a position that he could not request additional troops. "Of course, Oberführer."

"Fine . . . fine," Funk said. "Tomorrow evening I should like to hear your plans for completion of the liquidation."

"Of course, Oberführer."

"You, Dr. Koenig, shall submit your requirements to have the machinery in your factories transferred."

Koenig nodded.

"Until tomorrow evening, gentlemen."

They came to their feet sharply.

"Heil Hitler."

"Heil Hitler."

"Herr Sauer . . . a moment please."

The Gestapo chief returned to his seat. Horst von Epp also remained. When the others were gone, Funk turned to Sauer.

"On this matter of the archives in the ghetto of which I spoke to you on my last visit. What have you been able to ascertain?"

"Not too much. The Jews protect these historians with an uncommon devotion. Not even their Militia will inform on them. Fear of retribution, I suppose."

"What's this about?" Horst asked.

"The Jewish mania for diaries. We have unearthed thousands of them in reservations around Poland and particularly in the special-treatment camps. We have long been aware of an entire organization here writing records."

Well, well! Horst thought.

"We cannot proceed with the final liquidation of the ghetto until these records have been found," Funk continued. "Hitler himself gave me specific instructions to see that these Jew lies are found. We cannot permit their distortions to be published."

Sauer was unmoved by Funk's double talk. The general sensed it. "Isn't it enough," Funk pressed, raising his voice to a sharper pitch, "that this filthy pack of lies about our labor camps was smuggled out of Poland?"

"Perhaps," Sauer said softly, "the Führer should take the matter up with our Italian friends to learn how this was done."

"It is the job of the Gestapo to learn these things and stop them before the crime is committed."

Horst became fascinated at the sudden sharpness of argument. Someone had to give.

"We want positive information on these ghetto archives," Funk snapped.

"Certain people," Sauer answered, "were in such a hurry to cover their business transactions, they did away with the Big Seven prematurely and in a single fell swoop destroyed my entire system of informers." The implication was obvious. Half of Warsaw's Nazis wanted Max Kleperman's lips sealed.

The policeman rubbed his eyes and meditated, speaking as if to himself. "If anyone in the ghetto knows about these papers it would be Alexander Brandel, but he has not been seen all winter. We know there is a bunker under Mila 19. We have not been able to determine the entrance."

Funk, anxious to oversimplify the matter and get rid of Sauer, whom he could not bully, made an abrupt decision. "I shall have Stutze find this Brandel immediately. Then we can proceed with the liquidation of the ghetto."

Later that evening Horst walked down two flights in the Bristol Hotel to where a brace of SS guards flanked the door leading to Alfred Funk's suite. Funk's orderly let him in.

"The Oberführer is taking a bath," the orderly said. He mixed a drink for Von Epp and disappeared into the bedroom.

Funk bathing again. Funk bathed before and after all conferences. Some days he took five or six baths. Often, when a good party was moving into its second stages and the women were getting deliciously vile, Funk would excuse himself and run off to take a shower.

Reading the Jew Freud was legally banned, but Horst had brought several volumes to Warsaw nevertheless. Freud's interpretations afforded him a never-ending, amusing list of clues to the strange behavior of his Nazi cohorts. Alfred Funk's mania for cleanliness, he concluded, was an unconscious effort to wash his soiled soul with soap. However, the ersatz soap was of a very poor quality these days.

Horst reflected on the bizarre reactions at the earlier conference. He had attended many conferences at long polished tables where Funk and other Nazis announced dogma and sent everyone on his merry way with crisp "Heil Hitlers." But today there was a roomful of unusual performances. The first cracks. The minute trace of doubt and fear.

Rudolph Schreiker loosened with a dozen audible sighs of relief that the ghetto was to be liquidated.

One could see the wheels of Koenig's mind spinning to shift his fortune to Argentina, which alone showed a friendship for the Nazis.

Stutze was afraid to execute the final liquidation. In a moment he showed outright cowardice.

Sauer. A fine chap, like myself. Sauer never wavers. Knows his job. Plods on. He and I are true stalwarts.

It was Funk who had put on the real show, reflecting Berlin's panic over some obscure Jewish archives. Funk had backed down from Sauer, something he had never done before.

Funk bundled himself into a large towel robe and padded, still dripping, into the living room.

"You look tired, Alfred," Horst said. "I have just the relaxation the doctor ordered."

Funk's orderly was all over him, trying to dry his master's hair. He dismissed the man curtly and lit a cigarette and flopped into a big chair, stretched his legs and arms, opening the top of his robe enough to reveal the double streaks of lightning tattooed under his left armpit, the mark of an SS Elite.

"I've got a pair of Czech sisters just in from Prague. They come highly recommended. They're not much to look at, but I understand they do fantastic contractions."

"Good. I need a little sport."

Funk left the room with a drink, leaving the bedroom door ajar so that they could speak.

In the beginning of their relationship, Funk had detested Horst von Epp. His cynical attitude, his snide mockery and obvious lack of sincere devotion to Nazi ideals and his constant barbs at the conferences irritated Funk no end. Then Horst began to grow on him.

Horst von Epp ran his office with enviable German efficiency. Moreover, he was the best officers' pimp in Europe, and once one got used to his sense of humor it lost much of its offensiveness. Funk came to understand that Von Epp was actually berating himself most of the time through his jokes.

He liked Von Epp for another reason too. He was reluctant to admit it, but he liked to talk to Horst. Since he had joined the party in 1930 he was in a league of tight-lipped, humorless men who considered it dangerous to speak one's inner thoughts or even admit to having them. He had taken vows as harsh as those of a monk in one of those silent ecclesiastical orders.

After the first shocks of Von Epp's curt observations of the Nazis subsided he found himself looking forward to coming to Warsaw. With Von Epp he could share thoughts, speak, fence verbally, confide frustrations. He could indulge himself in a way he dared not, even with his own wife and children.

Horst leaned against the doorframe while Funk primped himself to his blond Aryan best before the mirror.

"How is our defeat at Stalingrad being taken in Berlin? Graciously, I hope."

Funk dropped the hairbrush and spun around angrily, then contained himself. "We will break through at Stalingrad."

"That is what I was afraid of. You spoilsports will be too bull-headed to see the handwriting on the wall. And the crushing of our Afrika Korps in Tunis?"

Funk quickly spouted the line of Nazi logistics. The Russians would collapse soon. America was too weak-spined to fight a sustained war, give up her sons and her luxuries and make the sacrifices necessary for victory. England? Washed up.

"Oh, for Christ sake, Alfred," Horst said, sitting on the edge of the bed. "I wrote most of that nonsense after Dunkirk. Know what I've been doing lately? Soul-searching. Do you ever soul-search?"

"That is a dangerous avocation reserved exclusively for those whose advanced age makes them otherwise useless. I gave it up twelve years ago when I joined the party."

Funk pulled up his suspender straps and assured his servant he was capable of buttoning his own tunic. Horst followed Funk back into the living room, where they settled down to await the arrival of the sisters from Prague.

"Why is Hitler suddenly concerned over a few Jewish writings? Is it guilt? Is there a realization that Germany will lose the war unless they break through to Stalingrad? Does Hitler liken these writings to the other book the Jews wrote which has tormented the conscience of man for two thousand years? Does he fear two millennia of a Jewish curse gnawing at the souls of unborn German generations, thwarting their growth? Is it a fear of divine retribution?"

"Nonsense," Funk snapped. He was about to recite the Nazi line about the war's being fought because of international Jewry but decided to spare Horst, or rather spare himself from Horst's retorts.

"Would you say this strange desire to find a few books when you own half the world would point out that the pen is indeed mightier than the sword?"

"Nothing of the sort. Every conqueror has justified his actions. In our case the obliteration of the Jews is our holy mission, just as the obliteration of other peoples has been a holy mission for other empires."

"Would you say that this desire to find the archives is more like a dog scratching frantically to cover up his dung pile?"

"Put it away, Horst. You talk as though the German people have committed some sort of crime."

"Haven't they?"

"Of course not. Precedent is all around us. Even the ancient Hebrews destroyed their enemies . . . attributed to the commands of their God. Mongols made pyramids of skulls. The Chinese used human bodies as mortar to build the Great Wall. Napoleon had his Gestapo and the Russians have theirs. We are merely making

345

variations on an ancient theme. Every man wants to be the best. The drive to rule is a completely natural expression of human behavior. In an individual the drive finds its expression by pushing the writer's pen to create a book, by driving the athlete to strain his heart and his muscle. When the drive becomes a national expression it takes the form of conquest. Every people in every age have taken their turn. The world has only one standard for proof that one is better than the other, and that is conquest."

Horst grunted at Funk's cruel but accurate logic. "Granted," he said, "that the desire to dominate is an unalterable trait in the human being. Let us take it a step farther. A woman wants to commit adultery. She has a family, children, position in the community. Does she walk naked in the streets to her lover and perform sex acts in a store window? No. Why? Adultery is a sin we all indulge in, but the woman finds a secluded place, deceives her husband, and avoids scandal. She plays by the rules. You see, Alfred, even the game of sin must be played by the rules. So must war be fought by the rules."

Funk set his glass down. "What you are saying is that when the sloppy aim of the Luftwaffe kills women and children in London it is permissible. When it is deliberate we break the rules. Isn't that a hypocritical double standard? Is it a greater sin for a submarine to kill a man on a ship without warning or to blast him, gentlemen's style, off a battlefield? Your rule says 'Kill soldiers.' Is the killing of an armed man really less a murder than the killing of a child? We have learned that other conquests have failed because one cannot go to war with compassion. Total war means total death. If victory means reducing Poland to a pool of cultureless serfs, then that is what must be done."

"Then why not use poison gas on their armies?"

"This is not a decision of compassion but of expediency. We would certainly not hesitate if we knew they would not do the same to us. You cannot measure brutality by degrees. All conquerors justify their aims on a political theory. In our case the Nazis provide our various frills. No country goes to war without the belief in its own justice—we take it a step farther. We act out what others only theorize. In the concentration camps we reduce our political enemy until he takes the physical appearance of a sub-human. This makes us supermen by comparison."

"Alfred, does any of this ever annoy you as an individual?"

"No. I decided by 1930 that you either become a Nazi or drown. My personal views on this Jewish business fail to be important. Horst, have you witnessed a gassing?"

"No."

"I'll arrange one for you."

"Thanks, anyhow."

"The first time I witnessed one it was with a sense of complete fascination. I slept very well that night. The only thing that annoyed me a little was some of the Jewesses carrying their children into the chambers who looked at me with a mocking Mona Lisa smile."

Horst was sorry he had brought the whole subject up.

"I shall tell you why the German people will be able to achieve what others have failed. It is because we are capable of the perfect state of mind necessary. We can give absolute obedience, respond to total authority, like no others."

Horst spun the ice cubes with his forefinger. He glanced up into Funk's face. The Oberführer was in a state of detachment, the cruel and impersonal monster qualities dominating his appearance.

"Others talk of love of country. We act it out through absolute obedience. Four years ago I was commandant of the Waffen SS youth training school at Dachau. We got boys at the age of sixteen for a year's indoctrination, complete with live prisoners to experiment with. The entire course was geared to teach absolute unquestioned obedience to the Fatherland. Each boy was given an Alsatian puppy of six to eight weeks of age when he entered training. During the year part of their study was to train the animal, live with it, compete it against the other dogs. We encouraged them to develop the natural affection a boy does for a dog."

Funk clasped his hands behind him.

"The last graduation test to see if the boy was worthy to become an SS officer was by calling him into a private room with his dog. As he stood before me at attention with his dog at his side I would say, 'Hans, I order you to strangle your dog this instant.' "

Horst thought he was going to vomit.

"Oh, a few were unable to do it. Some even broke and cried. But! Almost all of them, without a trace of remorse, without a second of hesitation, said, '*Jawohl, Herr Kommandant*,' and proceeded to snap their dog's neck without a trace of emotion. And this, Horst, is the supreme state of absolute obedience which we Germans have attained."

Horst poured himself a triple drink. "Heil Hitler," he said.

Sturmbannführer Sieghold Stutze paced his room in the barracks wildly. Gestapo Chief Sauer had just left him with orders to set up a massive pot around Mila 19 and not to leave until the underground bunker was located and Alexander Brandel found.

It was just like that bastard Prussian, Alfred Funk, to give him the dirty work, he fumed. Where was his promotion to Standartenführer? He had more than earned his colonelcy. It was all part of the German plots against the Austrians.

All winter the Jews had been arming in the ghetto. No telling what those crazy Jews were liable to do. He broke into a sweat.

347

Damned if he'd walk into a trap on Funk's whim. Funk simply didn't understand how dangerous it was.

And then the idea came to him as he heard a shriek down the hall. It was that damned Kutler and his nightmares again. Wait! Kutler. That drunken beast was becoming completely useless. Yes! That was it! Kutler would lead the force into the ghetto. Kutler would set up the kettle. Good idea . . . good idea.

Chapter Three

"Aha!" Andrei cried with fiendish delight, rubbing his hands together. "Aha, you stupid man. You have made a fool's gambit!" Andrei moved his knight over the chessboard. "Check!"

Chris countered immediately, lopping off an exposed castle, putting Andrei's chessmen in an impossible position. "Fool's gambit, all right," he said, "but you have the wrong fool."

Andrei studied the board a moment and cursed under his breath.

Chris pulled back from the table and paced the tiny garret room restlessly.

"What's the matter, Chris?"

"I'm hungry, I want a smoke, I'm sick of being cooped up—I want to see Deborah."

"I have yet to hear the first person speak in favor of ghetto living," Andrei said.

"It has its advantages. It got me out of some bad drinking habits." Chris patted his stomach. "And notice how slim I've become."

"What's bothering you?" Andrei asked again.

"To go or not to go. Hell, I know how important it is to get out of Poland knowing where the archives are buried, but it was impossible to leave Deborah before, even believing she hated me. Now, I swear, I don't know if I have the strength to leave."

"Women," Andrei grunted, "they have a way of getting under one's skin." He walked up behind Chris and put one hand on his shoulder. "I am confident that when the time comes you will make the correct decision, and if you are very lucky the decision will be made for you."

Both men froze at the same instant, trying to hear something that alerted a sixth sense beyond their normal waves of hearing. A few seconds later the alarm bell erupted in a series of dashes.

"I'll never get used to that goddamned bell," Chris said.

Wolf Brandel came in carrying a large suitcase. He looked at the chessboard. "Who played black?" he asked. Chris jerked his thumb at Andrei. Wolf grimaced and went "Tsk, tsk, tsk."

"Got a cigarette?" Chris asked.

"Don't smoke."

"Hell."

"Hey, Andrei. Three Kar 98's came in with seventy rounds of ammo. Pretty good. We got a line on four Mauser 9-mm.'s day after tomorrow."

"Good work," Andrei said. "At this rate we'll have weapons for half our force in another few weeks. How is Rachael?"

"Fine."

"What do you have in the suitcase?"

"I want to get some matzo-ball grenades to take back to my bunker. We tested one yesterday. Blam! Nuts and bolts everywhere. I want to talk to Schlosberg about designing a real big matzo ball." Wolf held his hands out to indicate a four-foot diameter. "Something like a land mine we can detonate with a hot spark. Something packed with a couple thousand nuts and bolts."

"Good idea," Andrei said.

Wolf put the suitcase on the table. "Take a look."

Andrei opened the lid, not knowing what to expect. He unfolded a blanket. An automatic weapon and five clips of ammunition burst into view.

"My God," Andrei said, not believing what his eyes saw, "my God! A Schmeisser machine pistol. My God!" Andrei licked his lips; his hands trembled to pick up the weapon but feared it would disappear like a mirage. "Where on earth did you get it, Wolf?"

"German tank sergeant, lost a leg on the eastern front. Sold it for only four thousand zlotys."

"My God!"

"Go on, Andrei, pick it up."

Andrei lifted the weapon out of the suitcase. He patted it with a gentleness reserved only for Gabriela. He slipped the bolt, sighted in, cradled it against his hip, clicked the trigger.

"It's yours," Wolf said.

"Mine?"

"A gift from the Brushmaker's command."

"I couldn't accept it."

"We had a meeting and a vote. We decided in a democratic manner it would be most effective in your hands. Of course most of the voters were Bathyrans."

Andrei was seized with emotion. "I love it so much there is only one name for her. Gaby! Perhaps Gaby will fire a shot heard around the world! Wolf, I love you!"

The alarm bell sounded again. Simon Eden came in.

"Got a smoke?" Chris asked.

"Only German ersatz, but they're yours."

Chris retreated to the cot, caressing the pack of cigarettes with the same affection Andrei had shown for the Schmeisser.

"Look!" Andrei said, showing Simon the machine pistol.

"Yes, I know," Simon said. "As commander of Joint Forces, I was given the nominal courtesy of being allowed to cast my vote with the Bathyrans for its disposition."

It was immediately clear to Andrei that Simon's dark eyes were trying to shield trouble.

"What's on your mind, Simon? You're a worse faker than I am."

"Funk arrived in Warsaw last night."

It had been long expected. Everyone knew it would come and what Funk's arrival meant. Final liquidation. Yet the silence was long and frightened.

"Alfred Funk," Chris said at last. "The harbinger of spring. The messenger of peace and light."

Andrei patted his Schmeisser. "Gaby, dear girl, you arrived just in time."

The tall, angular commander looked doubtfully from Wolf to Andrei to Chris, then exploded his message. "I am making a change in strategy," he said. "I am pulling our companies out of their exposed positions, breaking them up and putting them into bunkers."

"Why?" Andrei demanded. "To have them wait in the ground like shivering dogs to be hunted down and butchered bunker by bunker?"

Simon shook his head in defeat. "I have reappraised our strength. We cannot make a street fight."

"What? Wasn't it Simon Eden who came to me a year ago oozing Zionist purity from every pore, saying, 'Don't fight now, Andrei. Wait! Make your shots heard! Do not die in silence!'"

"God damn it, Andrei. Do you think I like this decision?"

"Why did you lie to me?"

"Because . . . because I believed with all my soul that we would gather an angry army of ten thousand soldiers. We can't last more than two or three days. There will be no help from the Aryan side. Nothing . . . nothing."

He unfurled a large blueprint and flattened it on the table.

"Look," Simon continued, "a city engineer's map of the sewer system under Warsaw. We move our companies into bunkers which can connect to the sewers. I have sent Rodel over the wall to buy trucks and get drivers. The Communists will set up escape routes and hiding places in the forests. We go under the wall a group at a time and move through the sewers, and we will come up five or six miles beyond the ghetto in prearranged locations."

Andrei snatched the blueprint off the table and crumpled it.

"Do we destroy ourselves with a futile three-day gesture?" Simon screamed. "Or is it our duty—yes, our duty—to get a handful of survivors out? If we stay, we die—all of us. At least this other way a few may get through to tell the story."

"He's right, Andrei," Chris said, stepping between them. "This story must be told."

Andrei looked slowly to Wolf Brandel.

"I don't know," Wolf pleaded.

Andrei sat down slowly and contained his temper. "What story will they tell, Simon Eden? Will they unearth the Brandel journals and read about how five hundred thousand sheep walked silently, without protest, to their deaths and the high-sounding idealists who stood for honor crawled out on their hands and knees through crap-filled sewers to tell the world our heritage? What story, Simon? What story? Have you no shame? Have you no anger to avenge dead children? Simon! One week! Let us stand and fight like men for one week!"

"We cannot hold a week. It is impossible."

"Betar! Masada! Jerusalem! We must show them Jews can still fight, Simon!"

"It is our duty to try to survive," Simon said.

Andrei turned to Wolf. "Order the Bathyrans back to Mila 19. We will not be a partner to this final debasement of our people."

"Don't pull your people out of the command," Simon pleaded.

"Do you hear me, Wolf? I have given you an order!"

Wolf looked again from one to the other in utter confusion.

Ring! Ring! Ring! screamed the alarm bell in long dashes. Ring! Ring! Ring!

Wolf stole a glance at the street. "It's swarming with SS."

The four men quickly checked their weapons and bolted out to the ladder to the roof. Andrei was the last one through. He closed the trap door behind him and rubbed his arms in the sudden burst of January cold.

"Down through Mila 5," Andrei said. "Be careful not to stir up those feathers and give our position away."

They crouched low and stepped on the feathers as though they were walking on eggs. Chris's foot hit a hidden ice slick and he crashed down, unable to contain a pain-racked scream.

"My knee!" he cried, torn with pain.

"What is it?"

"Trick basketball knee. Fine time to jump out."

"Look over the side," Andrei said. Wolf crawled off with Simon.

Chris grimaced as he tried to slip the loose cartilage back into place. It cracked as it found the slot. Chris turned white-lipped.

"Can you move?"

"Wrap it up in something so it won't jump out again," he grunted.

Andrei whipped off his leather jacket, then tore the sleeve from his shirt and with it deftly locked Chris's kneecap into place.

At the edge of the roof Wolf and Simon peered down on a street swarming with Germans. The kettle was set up all the way from Nalewki to Zamenhof streets with the main force concentrating on the Orphans and Self-Help headquarters at Mila 19. They slipped back to Andrei.

"We're boxed in," Simon said.

"Can we make a break for your headquarters?"

"No," Simon answered. "We'd have to cross an open courtyard at Mila 5. We'd never make it."

"Can't stay here," Wolf said. "They'll be all over the roof in minutes."

"I have a hiding place up here," Andrei said. "I think it will hold all four of us."

Chris struggled to his feet. Simon and Wolf draped an arm over his shoulders and Chris was able to hobble. Andrei led them to the last house at Mila and Zamenhof.

The roof slanted at a sharp pitch for fifteen yards to the rain gutters. Near the very edge, before the overhanging eaves, was a large chimney.

"We've got to get down there to the chimney," Andrei said. "Lie absolutely flat and move in a direct line with the chimney so you won't be observed from the street."

Andrei went on his belly, headfirst down the steeply angled tiles, the Schmeisser cradled in his elbows. Inch by inch he wiggled his body downward. Watch the ice, he said to himself, dig your toes in. don't look at the edge—that's a five-story drop—easy . . . easy. The blood poured into his head and made him giddy for a moment, and he was suddenly struck with the weakness of three days without food. The tile nails jammed into his legs and belly and slicked his leather jacket, and the cold cramped his body. A few feet more . . . just a few feet. Andrei lined up the chimney and rolled against it.

With his back braced against the chimney, he waved for the next man to come down. Simon went over. Andrei removed a loose tile nail, the first key to a Chinese puzzle. He slid a tile out and loosened five more, which he set down into the sub-roof. He had made a hole just large enough for a man to get into the sub-roof and eaves.

Simon made the mistake of coming down feet first. Although he was in a better position to grab with his hands. he could not see his direction or the slicks and could conceivably miss the chimney, for Andrei was unable to shout up directions without drawing attention from the street. Midway down, Simon had to turn his body so that he would come headfirst.

Come on, Simon. Come on, for Christ sake, Andrei muttered to himself. Time drawled on. Come on, Simon. If they get on top of us, we'll be clay pigeons.

Simon Eden reached the chimney, put his back against it, and dropped his head between his legs, close to tears of sheer fright.

Next Chris. Wolf crouched in a rear guard, watching the roof-tops.

Chris was racked with pain, dragging the game leg, but he came down fast and without hesitation. Andrei dared a peek around the corner of the chimney to the street. Luck was with them so far.

"Simon, get down there. Crawl forward as far as you can go. Stay on the crossbeams. The flooring under it is rotted away. Chris, follow him in. Move up as close against him as you can so there'll be room for all of us."

Simon went headfirst into the hole. He slid his body over the beams. The joists formed a sharp angle at the beams, so a large man like Simon Eden was all but wedged in a vise. He pushed forward with the greatest effort until he came to a dead end.

Chris followed him, struggling with the painful leg.

Andrei looked up the roof to Wolf and waved to him to begin his descent. Wolf hated the roofs. They made him dizzy. He had moved a few yards when all he could see was the edge below him and all he could think of was his body hurtling down a sheer plunge of five stories to the pavement. He closed his eyes. Everything began to spin. He froze on the spot. Andrei and the chimney seemed miles away.

Andrei snarled. He wanted to shout up to Wolf, curse him, prod him, order him. Time was running out. Should he crawl up after Wolf? No, that would certainly attract attention from the street. But if he allowed Wolf to stay where he was, Germans would be above him at any second.

"Come on, lad," Andrei prayed. "Come on. Move, boy, move."

The sweat in Wolf's eyes turned icy. He lifted his head. "Got to . . . got to . . . got to . . ." He crawled an inch . . . another . . . "Got to . . . got to . . . got to . . ." Closer, closer, closer. Andrei scampered up, snatched his hand, and dragged him down the last six feet. Wolf was shaking.

"Get down there," Andrei said, hurling him headfirst into the hideaway.

Andrei went into the roof last. He was greeted by an accumulation of sixty-five years of filth and cobwebs. He stretched his body downward until he was stopped by Wolf's feet, then eased his upper half down. He lay flush against the chimney. Andrei lifted the tiles from his prone position and slipped them back into place. When the last tile was fitted, the eaves were plunged into darkness.

The four men were locked in a lightless coffin. They lay inside a triangle formed by beams, rafters, and the wall. Each man lay on three two-inch boards which supported his body at his calves, thighs, back, and shoulders. Beneath the beams was a rotted floor, part of which extended into the eaves, directly over the street.

The face of one man touched the feet of another end to end.

Their movement was limited to a few inches. They could turn over from back to stomach only with a slow effort.

"Everybody all right?" Andrei whispered.

They answered in the affirmative.

"How's the leg, Chris?"

"Going up like a balloon."

"Painful?"

"Let me suffer in peace."

A bug bit Wolf under the eye. "How long did you stay here, Andrei?"

"Once for six hours."

"Holy Mother."

"Of course I didn't have such nice company. Don't lie on the sub-floor. It's rotted. Pieces may fall down on the street. And reach up and rub your partner's feet so his blood will circulate."

Andrei tucked the Schmeisser firmly into the apex of the joist and beam and saw a slit of light at the extreme end of the eaves. By the most difficult of straining and contortion, he could lift his head and put his eye to it.

"By God. Some boards are split. I can see the pavement." He worked the blade of a pocketknife back and forth between the boards, separating them a half inch. "I can see Mila 19."

"What's going on?"

"It's swarming with Germans. They must be looking for the bunker."

Wolf and Simon felt Chris writhe as spears of pain lashed up and down his leg. Chris's leg twitched against Wolf's face. Simon handed Chris a handkerchief. "Bite on this," he said.

Luminous eyes peered at the four strangers who had invaded their home. A scraping of claws.

"Rats!"

"Get out of here, you bastards!"

"Oh God, I hate rats," Wolf moaned.

"You'll find them quite friendly in a few hours," Andrei said. "It's the bats at night that get you."

Wolf's skin crawled as he felt the animal dash over his chest and brush up against his face. "Oh God damn it," he cried, "I hate rats."

They became silent. The sound of guttural orders bounced off the deserted houses in the street below and echoed up to them. They had found a Jew on Mila Street and were torturing him for the location of the Mila 19 bunker.

Cries of agony below settled them down to adjust to their own discomfort. And then the automatic silence when one breathes only with controlled quiet, for there was movement on the roof above them.

"No Jews down this way, Sergeant!"

"You can never tell where the vermin hide. Post a guard here and one at the opposite end of the roofs."

"Yes, sir."

Andrei calculated that the guards were at that point where the roof began its pitch, some fifteen yards away. From their speech, they were Ukrainians.

The beams cut into their bodies, but no one dared change his position. The slightest sound now could give them away.

They muted themselves into a deeper stillness at the sound of noises in the attic under them. A smashing of glass. The sound of hatchets and sledge hammers bursting the walls and doors. The building was undergoing a dismantling for secret hiding places.

Each of them touched his weapon at the same instant for a comfort which did not really exist.

Curses penetrated their tomb from the frustrated, grunting hunters.

Screaming whistles in the street. Another Jew had been located cringing in a courtyard sewer.

More men were on the roof above them.

Chris's body convulsed in pain. His eyes rolled back in his head. He clamped his teeth into the cloth in his mouth. Simon was trying to decide whether or not to knock Chris unconscious with the pistol barrel, but at that moment Chris straightened out and was still.

Chris saw his father kneeling at the altar next to the library in their villa outside Rome. So funny to see his father praying. Poppa was a hypocrite! He drank, he gambled, he was a libertine . . . he was a Fascist. But Poppa prayed. Poppa told him to learn to pray. I've wanted to pray but I couldn't. I just couldn't without damning myself.

Oh Mary, Mother of God! Help me! I'm going to scream! My leg! Jesus! Jesus! Help me!

"Have your men smash holes in the roof. Jews hide in the roofs!"

They could feel the vibration of the sledge hammers as they splintered the tiles. The ancient beams rattled under the pounding and shot needles of fear through their bodies. Wolf wept softly to himself. Each new blow brought the enemy closer and closer to the edge of the roof.

All Chris could see was his father's chapel.

Andrei had no thoughts but of that moment when the hammer would burst through and reveal him. He would fire the gun into their rotten faces.

Simon Eden was calm. It did not matter much any more, Simon thought. His parents, his sister and brother were gone. The years as a Labor Zionist organizer had taught him that when the fountains of idealism ran dry one weighed the odds without emotion and accepted reality. This was the end. Trapped in a

355

coffin with rats and spiders. There had been no sweetheart, really. A marriage ended in failure. To be the wife of a Zionist organizer, one had to be a woman like Sylvia Brandel. There had not even been a sweetheart like Gabriela. He envied Andrei. Simon's only marriage was to Zionism.

They were coming down the roof with ropes around their waists. Andrei prayed as he held his machine pistol ready, his finger quivering on the trigger. There was only one hope. Perhaps we are so far out on the edge they won't come down, he thought.

An hour passed. Then two, then three.

At last the hammering above and below them stopped.

The relief from the tension brought on a new realization of physical agony. Their bodies had been cut to a blissful numbness. Chris mumbled hallucinations. They stretched one by one and shifted their positions slightly and massaged themselves and each other to restore circulation.

They had to be quiet; the Ukrainians were still up there. The terror on the streets was unabated.

Wolf played a chess game in his mind. It was the most magnificent jeweled board one could imagine. The black squares were made of solid gold and the white of ivory, each pawn and piece carved of a different precious gem. Move the pawn . . . no, the bishop. He tried to think. Then the board would become muddled and the opponent's chessmen turned to rats and spiders. Why can't I keep the board straight? Why? I've played blindfolded before! The rats ate his chessmen and he could not move his hands to help them. Stop eating my chessmen! Rachael . . . Please don't let me think of Rachael. I'll cry if I do.

Andrei licked his lips. Food! Oh, look at it. Deborah, you shouldn't have cooked so much. You cook just like Momma. The gefilte fish is just right. So tasty.

Andrei sniffed. He came out of his trance slowly. Smoke! The brick chimney next to him was becoming warm. German efficiency. Many fireplaces in the ghetto had false coveys for hiding places. This was countered by burning fires in them so any bricked-up Jews would be smoked out. Their hiding place turned into a stifling furnace. The sweat gushed from their bodies, driving them deeper into agony. Whiffs of smoke slithered into the eaves through the crumbled mortar. Andrei gagged and twisted his head to the slit in the eaves to try to suck in a whiff of pure air.

"The smoke is coming through that one down there!" he could hear someone shout. "Mark it off the list."

Andrei closed his eyes again and dreamed of food.

The high-pitched multi-thousand-cycle cries of bats.

Simon's dream of cold and wet made him urinate.

Andrei opened his eyes. He could hear the flapping wings and the vibrations. Dream or real? Dream or real? Dream or real?

Oh God, I'm hungry. Tiny droplets of light sparkled off and on, off and on. Andrei looked through the slit in the boards. Outside, a glaring, artificial light. He turned over again and watched the sparkling overhead. They were beams of searchlights pushing through cracks in the roof. It must be night. He listened for several moments. He could hear nothing on the roof.

"Simon!" Andrei dared whisper. "Simon!"

"Andrei!"

"Chris!"

"He is unconscious," Simon said. "He passes out and comes to, passes out and comes to."

"Wolf!"

Andrei was answered by a feeble groan. Andrei kicked against Wolf's shoulder. "Wolf!"

The return was an incoherent babbling.

"Must be night. They're using searchlights."

"That's the way I figured it," Simon said.

Andrei looked through the boards again, squinting to see through the glare. There was still a concentration of SS at Mila 19. He groped around for his weapon and toyed with the idea of breaking out of the entombment and firing at the searchlights. No, he'd be shot off the roof in seconds.

"I guess we're no worse off than those poor bastards in the bunker," Andrei said. "At least they're not looking for us."

"Nothing to do but wait," Simon said.

"Yeah . . ."

And then quiet once more as they heard the steps of men patrolling the roof over them, complaining about their bad fortune of night-time duty.

Nothing to do but wait. Andrei slumped back, hoping for a misty dream to take him where there were plates piled with food.

"I didn't catch your name."

"I know your name, Miss Rak. Like so many, I am an admirer of the work of your late father, so my name is unimportant. You can just snap your fingers and say, 'Hey you,' and I'll know you are addressing me."

"You do dance, Lieutenant?"

"As a matter of fact, I am an excellent dancer, but frankly, I do it only as an accommodation."

Gaby! Gaby! I am afraid! Gaby! I am so afraid!

Whistles!

Andrei forced his eyelids apart. I must be dead, he told himself. I am nowhere. In the sky. In hell. I am dead. There was no movement in his body. No feeling. No pain.

But then the cold sent a chill through him and his stomach knotted with hunger.

Like hell! I'm dead! He tried to move his arms. Numb. Neck

and shoulders without feeling from the pressure of the beams. First my fingers . . . just my fingers first. He drew them up like claws, back, forth, back, forth; then he shook his wrists. His fingers scratched against his leg and sides, over and over to make some feeling return. His body tingled as he tore at it harder and harder. He pinched himself again and again and slapped his face. Inch by inch circulation flowed.

"Simon!" he croaked.

"Andrei!"

"The others?"

"Out cold. Neither of them has spoken for two hours. I've been counting seconds. It must be day again."

"I don't know."

"Can you see down on the street?"

His head felt like a lead ball. He pushed it to the crack. The searchlights were gone. It was misty out. Germans were still all over the street.

"They're still down there."

"I think they've left the roof. I heard them ordered down. No sounds for over fifteen minutes."

"Think it may be a trick?"

"We've got to take a chance," Simon said. "We can't hold out here another day."

Andrei rolled over on his back. Sharp needles of pain greeted his effort to raise his arms over his head. He fished around for the key tile and wiggled it. He tugged desperately. It slid away, letting in a show of light, nearly blinding him. Andrei pulled the other five tiles loose. He drew himself up on all fours, his knees resting on a pair of beams, and shoved the upper part of his body through the hole.

"Clear! Simon, it's clear!"

He pulled himself outside to the roof and crouched against the chimney, reaching it until he found Wolf's head. Straining with every sinew, he slid Wolf over the rafters until his body appeared beneath the opening. Next Chris was pushed by Simon until Andrei could hook onto him.

Simon jammed past the two unconscious, prostrate bodies. Simon and Andrei looked at each other. Their faces were swollen and misshapen by bug bites, their clothing ripped to shreds. Blood and bruises were everywhere, and layers of filth hid their features. They stared like strangers.

"Do you look like hell," Andrei said.

"You're no lily of the valley, Androfski." Simon looked at his watch and held it against his ear. "Thirty hours we've been in there."

Andrei looked at Simon again and began laughing. And Simon laughed too. They burst into a hysterical, uncontrolled laughter in

358

each other's arms until they ached and tears fell down their cheeks. And it ebbed slowly, each shaking his head alternately. Andrei wiped his Schmeisser clean and counted the clips of ammunition, then got to his knees and reached down and slapped Wolf's face.

"Is he alive?"

Andrei slapped him again and again.

Wolf groaned convulsively and sucked at the air. He blinked his eyes, shrank away from the light.

At the same time Simon worked on Chris.

Wolf came to enough to look up at his comrades and smile at the sight of them.

"Listen, Wolf. Stay here with Chris. Massage yourself and keep massaging him. There are holes all over the roof, so this one won't draw further attention."

"Where are you going?"

"Up to take a look. They've stopped patrolling the roof, but they're still in the streets. Stay here until we come back for you with ropes."

Andrei crawled up, with Simon close behind him. When the roof flattened, they inched to the edge to get the best possible look down on Mila Street.

Andrei's fists tightened around the Schmeisser, enraged at what met his eyes. A double cordon of bayonet-wielding SS Reinhard Corps men formed a corridor and circle around people straggling out of the building, flushed from the bunker. He saw Rabbi Solomon thrown to the ground. Alex knelt over to help him up. Sylvia Brandel held the child, and Tolek and Ana and Ervin stood by Deborah, keeping the children calm.

Kutler barked orders, clapping his hands in delight that the search was over.

"Schnell!"

"Move quickly, Jews!"

Andrei backed away slowly. "Come on, Simon," he said.

"Where are you going?"

"Where do you think?"

"You'll destroy us all," Simon snapped. He stood up quickly and blocked Andrei's path.

"Let me pass," Andrei hissed.

"You're a damned fool," Simon said, grabbing his shirt.

Andrei's fist smashed into Simon Eden's mouth. The big man went flat on his back. Before Andrei could make a step, he found himself looking into the muzzle of Simon's Luger leveled at his heart.

They glared, neither daring to move.

"Jews . . . move out!"

Simon's face went slack. His pistol hand dropped. "I'm coming with you," he said.

359

The two men moved swiftly over the rooftops to Mila 5. The stairs were clear. They ran down, jumping half a flight at a time, and stopped in the courtyard.

"It's clear."

They sprinted through the courtyard, down into the basement of Mila 1, and into a tunnel that came up on the edge of Muranowski Place. A fast straight run down Niska Street brought them to the intersection ahead of the slower-moving cordon.

Andrei flattened his back against the corner house, gasping for air, his legs wobbly. He looked around the corner. Kutler strutted, laughing and jovial, with a dozen SS men in the lead of the quarry, SS men on either sidewalk, and Nightingales in the rear.

Andrei beckoned Simon to get close to him. "Kutler and some SS men are in front of our people—about ten yards. Let them get past us. We'll hit them from behind."

"How many guards?"

"Hundred."

He shoved a clip of ammunition into the Schmeisser and threw the bolt. Simon unclicked the safety lock on his pistol.

Step by step, as in a funeral procession, the bagged game of Mila 19 walked for the Stawki Gate to the Umschlagplatz. Alexander Brandel stood tall and brave despite the ordeal in the bunker. He walked like a patriarch toward Calvary, and those behind him found courage in his presence.

A dozen black uniforms passed the corner of Niska Street.

Rat-a-tat-tat-a-tat!

A flame erupted from the end of Andrei's machine pistol. Kutler pitched forward on his face, the back of his head shot away. Four of his cohorts tumbled around him.

Rat-a-tat-tat!

Wham! Simon Eden's pistol crackled with deadly accuracy. Wham! Wham! Wham! Shrieks, Germans toppled to the ground.

Andrei stepped into the intersection and blasted at the row of flanking guards.

A wild melee. The Nazis broke and scattered.

"Run, you sons of bitches! Run! Run! Run!"

Rat-a-tat! Rat-a-tat!"

"Run, you lousy bastards! Run! Run! Run!" Andrei screamed, spewing death into them.

A calmer Simon Eden picked his shots, sharp-shooting the stunned Germans. A hidden fire bomb came out of Tolek Alterman's shirt and arched into an alcove filled with cowering SS. They shrieked out into the streets, trying to put out the flames devouring them.

"Scatter!" Simon commanded. "Alex! Tolek! Ana! Move, everybody! Go!"

The captives fled from the street.

"Sons of bitches!" Andrei screamed. "Sons of bitches! Die!" He tore down Zamenhof, looking for the terrified enemy. Bullets came back at him. He knelt and poured fire.

And then he was whirled around with a sudden impact that cracked his head on the side of a building. He slid to the sidewalk. On hands and knees he tried to fight to his feet, but he could not get up and it all became a blur. His face hit the sidewalk . . . blood oozed from the corners of his mouth . . . oblivion.

Chapter Four

"Idiot!"

SS Oberführer Funk slapped Sturmbannführer Sieghold Stutze across the mouth. The Austrian winced, then came stiffly to attention.

"Imbecile!" He slapped Stutze again, leaving streak marks on his cheek. Stutze stood at an even more ramrod posture.

"Swine!" Another slap.

"Herr Oberführer," Stutze whined.

"Chased by Jews! Eleven SS men killed!" Whap! Whap!

"Herr Oberführer. We were attacked by fifty madmen!"

"Liar! Coward! Assemble your officers at the barracks immediately."

"*Jawohl, Herr Oberführer!*" Stutze snapped his heels together. "Heil Hitler!"

"Get out of my sight, you worm."

Horst watched the performance, somewhat amused. "It seems," he said when Stutze had left, "that I detect flaws in the lofty theories of absolute obedience. Oh, I grant you that the German people are the most likely to succeed as robots, but we are still riddled with human frailties. Stutze is a coward, Schreiker a damned fool, Koenig a thief, and myself—well, I'd rather not go into that."

Funk didn't hear a word. He was too immersed in his own sudden dilemma. "Has the world gone entirely mad?" he said. "First Reinhard Heydrich is assassinated by Czech bandits, and now—this."

"Yes, dear Reinhard. We shall all miss his noble soul," Horst said.

Funk kept talking aloud to himself. "*Ach!* Himmler will have a wild tantrum when he learns about this." He lit a cigarette and pressed his fingertips together in a rapid motion, noticing the nails needed trimming and cleaning. Better get it done. Dirt annoyed him. "Tomorrow I personally will direct operations to begin the liquidation of the ghetto."

361

"Do you think that's wise, Alfred?"

"What?"

"To go into the ghetto tomorrow."

Funk took it as an immediate affront to his courage. He was no Stutze!

Before he could answer the challenge Horst held up his hand. "Just a moment. Today the Jews have burst another one of our pet theories like a bubble. They have discovered that we are not supermen at all. Hit a German with a bullet and he will drop dead like any other man. This delicious taste of blood after three years of torment will obviously spur them into greater efforts."

"I have no time for your nonsense today," Funk cracked back with the full cruelty revealed in his eyes. He was incensed with the very idea that the sub-human rabble could present an obstacle, but he did not wish to argue, for Horst had a needle under his skin and was prodding him.

"Do you have any idea of the Jewish strength?" Horst asked.

"What difference does that make!"

"A good general should know the weight of the enemy forces."

"Enemy forces, indeed! Since when do we recognize Jews as a fighting force?"

"I should say that as of today would be a good time."

Funk slammed his fist on the table. Horst refused to be intimidated and obviously was not going to be slapped around like the Austrian. Funk recalled why he had hated Horst von Epp in the beginning. That attitude of knowing something Funk did not know. That ability to operate on a level of shrewdness that eluded the stern, dogmatic, rigid SS devotion. Funk smiled faintly in an attempt to play the game with Von Epp. "And what do you propose might happen if I take the Reinhard Corps into the ghetto tomorrow?"

"I don't propose it, nor do I suggest it. I know it," Horst said. "You will lead three hundred men into a massacre."

"And I say they will flee and bury themselves at the sight of us. Jews won't fight."

"How unfortunate that you have become victimized by our own propaganda. Oh yes, I know. You have proof. We have translated our theories by acting out our superiority on helpless people. You'll find another caliber of man left inside those walls."

"Do you really believe that I would hesitate in the face of Jews?"

"When I was in the ministry in Berlin I spent week after week inventing and expounding the theories of Jewish cowardice, Alfred. The plain and simple fact of the matter is—we are liars."

Funk's entire face reacted with shock.

"I doubt if any warriors in the world were as furious in battle as the ancient Hebrews, nor did any people in man's history fight harder for freedom. Not once, but many times, they made Rome totter. And since their dispersion, because they have not had the opportunity to fight under a Jewish flag, we have been able to isolate them into individual units and riddle them with inferiority complexes. German torment has taken these segregated masses and jelled them together as a people for the first time in two thousand years. We cannot measure their determination to acquit themselves, but we can make an educated guess that we'd better be damned careful from this point on."

Funk sprang to his feet. "I will not listen to this anarchy. You defile the noble purposes of the Third Reich!"

"Oh, stop shouting, Alfred. I invented half the noble purposes of the Third Reich." Horst walked to the window and drew the curtains apart. Across Krakow Boulevard and beyond the Saxony Gardens some of the ghetto roofs could be seen. "Who is left in that ghetto is the one man in a thousand in any age, in any culture, who through some mysterious workings of forces within his soul will stand in defiance against any master. He is that one human in a thousand whose indomitable spirit cannot bow. He is the one man in a thousand who will not walk quietly to the Umschlagplatz. Watch out for him, Alfred Funk. We have pushed him to the wall."

Oberführer Funk became confused. Von Epp, one of the very creators of the Aryan myth, was ripping it apart. Suddenly it became clear to him. "I have been ordered by Himmler to have the ghetto liquidated, and that is what shall be done," he snapped.

Horst flopped his arms to his side in disgust. "Simple, eh? Orders are orders."

"Naturally."

"Alfred, you represent that confounding German idiocy which is unable to improvise from a fixed plan. Forget that orders are orders before you perform a monumental blunder."

"You know, Horst, I really should report your conversation to Himmler. I really should. What possible blunder can I make by fulfilling orders? Say that these noble creatures do fight. So what? We shall destroy them."

"For a decade we have been preaching a gospel of Jewish cowardice. It is Nazi dogma. What happens if the Reinhard Corps is wiped out tomorrow in the ghetto? How shall we explain it to the world? Shall we say that Jews fight, after all? How would we look to those whom we have impressed as supermen to be forced even to admit that Jews were standing up against us?"

"I hadn't thought of that," Funk admitted.

"Suppose this defiance in the ghetto lasts a week . . . ten days . . ."

"Impossible."

"But suppose it does. It could ignite rebellions all over Poland. 'See,' the Poles would say, 'the Germans have lied to us. Let us take a crack at them too.' Perhaps the Czechs and the Greeks may like

363

to have a crack at superman hides. You invite insurrection."

Funk sank to the seat, completely confused now. "Hitler will be out of his mind with rage," he mumbled.

"Get back to Berlin immediately," Horst said. "We must put across to them that this liquidation can be completed only if it can be carried out with no further armed conflict. We could invite a dangerous precedent, otherwise. As for this unfortunate incident today, I will say that it was a band of Communists or bandits. You know, minimize it with the usual stories. Then we proceed carefully. We outwit them. We use cunning to lure them out."

"Very well," Funk agreed, "very well."

Andrei's eyes fluttered open. He was in a bunker cell somewhere. Someone hovered over him. It was Simon.

"My gun!"

"It's under the cot. No ammunition left, mind you, but the gun is there."

Andrei closed his eyes. He tried to separate the blur of events that all ran together. He remembered seeing Kutler fall in the street, parts of the agony in the rafters, snatches of things that might have been dreams or might have happened. Simon fed him a drink of water. Half of it spurted out of his mouth, unable to penetrate the thick dry caking lining his throat. He sipped again.

"What happened?"

"We put on quite a brother act. We make a colorful pair."

"Where is everyone?"

"Scattered in a half dozen bunkers."

"Did Alex get away?"

"He's in the cell across the passage."

"My sister?"

"At the Franciskanska bunker with the children."

"Chris . . . Wolf . . ."

"They are safe."

Andrei forced himself up on his elbows. He ached all over. He pushed himself to a sitting position on the edge of the cot and was stricken with a spell of dizziness. He lowered his head between his legs to let blood circulate.

Simon moved a small crude table beside the cot and placed a bowl of gruel on it with a hunk of stale bread. It was the first food Andrei had eaten in nearly five days. His stomach growled and his hand trembled as he sloshed the bread in the bowl to soften it. The food was taken slowly, carefully.

"Where am I? At your bunker?"

"Yes."

"How did I get here?"

"I scraped you off the sidewalk. You fell short in your one-man effort to annihilate the entire German garrison, but not too bad,

364

eleven SS killed, two Ukrainians. You're the rage of the ghetto."

Andrei felt his pain-racked body. "Did I get hit?"

"Grazed. The doctor said that normally it wouldn't have stopped you from playing soccer an hour later, but combined with hunger, exhaustion, and a few other discomforts, you fainted."

"Fainted? What a ridiculous thing to do. Only women faint." He mopped the bread around in the bowl more rapidly, cleaned the dish, and licked his fingers. Simon was acting strangely, he thought. His voice rang with bitterness and he was avoiding Andrei's eyes. Simon never did that. He could win most of his arguments by his penetrating look alone.

"One of our people didn't make it," Simon said. He set a familiar notebook on the cot beside Andrei. Andrei recognized it as a volume of the Good Fellowship Club's study. Simon laid a pair of thick-lensed glasses on top of the book.

"Ervin?"

"Yes. Stray bullet. He lived long enough to tell me where he had hidden this volume. It was the one he was working on. We went to the Mila 19 bunker immediately to find it. Rest of the bunker is destroyed, but we were able to find many hidden things. We salvaged all the arms stores."

Tears welled up in Andrei's eyes. "You would think that we would get used to our friends dying after a time. I loved Ervin. Lot of years together." Andrei bit his lip, but the tears fell anyway. "Quiet, gentle little man. Believed in what he was doing without shouting, breast-beating. He just stayed in the cellar month in and month out, working on the archives. He never said why. He just did it because somebody had to. Ever see how swollen his hands were from the damp? Blind as a bat, but he stayed and kept working after they took Susan. He stayed and went about his business . . . never raised his voice."

The cot groaned as Simon sat beside Andrei. Simon picked the book up, opened it, and turned the pages, then pulled the candle on the table directly to him. "This was his last entry." He read, " 'When will we fight? Or will we fight? Who among us will dare to fire that first shot against them? Who?' " He closed it and set it down. He bunched his massive frame forward and rubbed the knuckles of one hand against the palm of the other. "I don't deserve to be the commander. I want you to take over."

"No, Simon, no."

"Don't humor me, Andrei. I was the man who was planning to send our companies through the sewers to escape. You were the one who fired the shot—and I pointed my pistol at your heart to stop you."

"Don't you think I know how torn up you are to have to give an order that will turn us into a suicide force?" Andrei said.

"You don't understand," Simon snapped, standing up abruptly

365

with his back to Andrei. "I aimed that pistol at your heart because I was afraid to go down on the street. I was afraid, and I'll be afraid again."

"You were afraid, but you went anyhow, and while I was in a blind rage you brought them to safety, because when the moment was needed you were calm and deliberate, as a good commander must be." Andrei walked up behind him and put his hand on Simon's shoulder. "I had a lot of time to think while we were up in the rafters. I found answers to many questions. I guess when one is close to his Maker many perplexing problems suddenly become amazingly clear and simple. Who fights what kind of war? The quiet courage it took to be a soldier like Ervin Rosenblum. Simon . . . I . . . I'm no damned good for anything but leading cavalry charges."

"Perhaps," Simon whispered, "if you stuck close by me to knock me flat on my back . . ."

"I don't think it will be necessary again."

"There were too many mistakes today," Simon said with a quick surge of excitement. "We have to have scouts in observation posts so that nothing can get into the ghetto before we can move our companies into battle position."

Andrei nodded in agreement.

"And we have to teach them that the cardinal rule is to pick up enemy weapons and strip their uniforms. We missed on that today."

Andrei nodded again and smiled slightly at the knowledge that Simon was again in full control and eager.

"I'm thinking. We should find a new bunker close to the central area for a command post." Simon stopped abruptly, watching Andrei look at the volume of the journal and Ervin's glasses. "Andrei, what made you go into the streets?"

"I don't know. Just that this was the moment which could not pass. It wasn't even seeing my sister. It was Alex. I couldn't let them take Alexander Brandel to the Umschlagplatz." Andrei picked up the book. "So damned much time has gone by, and Alex and I have barely talked to each other. I wish I knew how to apologize."

"Why don't you try?"

"What can I say for being a damned fool?"

"Come," Simon said.

Andrei trailed him haltingly out of the cell and across the narrow passageway to the opposite cell. Simon pulled back the sack curtain. The three of them were there. Sylvia with her little boy on her lap. Moses Brandel at the age of four was disciplined to the silence of underground living; pale, scrawny from the lack of sun and air and nourishment. Alexander gazed emptily at the floor in much the same way as he had since the children were taken to the

366

Umschlagplatz. Sylvia stood and put the boy down. She blocked Andrei's way, but Simon nodded for her to leave the room. She looked from Andrei to Alex, then took the child and led him out.

Andrei hulked helplessly over the dejected man, groping for words. He knelt slowly beside Alex. Alex turned his face, recognized Andrei, and hung his head.

"I . . . uh . . . wanted to give you this," Andrei said, showing the book. "They . . . uh . . . were lucky enough to salvage it from Mila 19."

Alex did not answer.

"I think that—well, with Ervin gone, you'll want to take up the work again."

Again, nothing.

"It's very important that the archives be continued and—— Look, I know something I didn't know. What I mean to say is, it takes many kinds of men and many kinds of battles to fight a war."

Andrei reached out and touched his shoulder, but Alex shrank away.

"Please look at me, Alex," Andrei whispered. "You must hear what I'm saying. Alex, once I told you that the Brandel journal would never take the place of the Seventh Ulany Brigade, and you answered that truth is a weapon worth a thousand armies. I never understood that till now. It's true, all of the divisions of the German army can't defeat these words."

Alex shook his head slowly.

"You . . . you were right. You've won a great battle with this," Andrei said.

The mouth in Alex's bearded face fumbled to form words in a cracked, wavering voice. "I called my dearest friend a man who thirsts for personal revenge. I . . . took the weapons from your hands. I am the vengeful man. Your way has always been the only way."

"You're wrong about that, Alex. My way hasn't been the only way. I would have destroyed us all long ago. You see, only because of men like you and Simon has a moment like today been possible for men like me."

"The children are gone. . . . Everyone is gone. . . . I have failed."

Andrei clutched Alex's arms hard and pleaded with fervor. "Listen to me!" he cried. "We've all done the best with what we've had. No man has ever fought a better fight than you! And it was the only fight. It was, I swear it."

"Don't patronize me, Andrei. It is I who should be on my knees to you."

Andrei released his grip and stood up slowly, and his voice mellowed with softness. "All my life I have believed I walked in the darkness, battling windmills, crying for lost causes, living a life in dubious battle. My father gave me a country which hated me, and

367

you have given your sons a ghetto and genocide. God only knows what kind of a world Wolf will hand to his sons. We enter this world in the middle of a war that is never won. It has always been this way—this endless war. No one of us ever really wins in his life. All you have the right to ask of life is to choose a battle in this war, make the best fight you can, and leave the field with honor."

Alex mumbled, "Make your battle . . . leave the field with honor."

"You've fought your good fight. Now the war goes on. I must fight my way now."

"Oh, Andrei, stop! What is there left but doom?"

"Left? We have a lot left. We can go out like men. . . . 'What though the field be lost? All is not lost—unconquerable will, the study of revenge, immortal hate . . . The courage never to submit or yield.' I never understood those lines till now. But I know—it is not a dubious battle."

Alexander picked up the book, and his fingers caressed it lovingly. He opened it, glanced up at Andrei quickly, then thumbed hungrily through Ervin's notes. He came to the last entry. "Who will fire the first shot?" Alex took out a pencil, and his hand wrote:

Journal Entry

Today a great shot for freedom was fired. I think it stands a chance of being heard forever. It marks a turning point in the history of the Jewish people. The beginning of the return to a status of dignity we have not known for two thousand years. Yes, today was the first step back. My battle is done. Now I turn the command over to the soldiers.

Chapter Five

Piotr Warsinski slammed the phone receiver down. He scratched his scaly hands. Again he had pleaded in vain with Sieghold Stutze to issue firearms to the Jewish Militia. After the outbreak of January 18, Warsinski was positive that the Germans would return to the ghetto immediately with an overpowering force. Instead, several days had passed in silence and his police were becoming afraid to patrol the streets.

Warsinski scoffed at the idea that the ambush at Niska and Zamenhof streets was anything but an insane gesture by a madman. He knew there was no real planned insurrection. He had no fear of this so-called Joint Jewish Forces. But he was afraid of what would happen if Sieghold Stutze decided he was no longer able to command the Militia effectively.

Piotr growled in frustration and became restless. He decided to leave the barracks and go to the Pawiak Prison. A girl had been brought in earlier who was suspected of being a member of the Joint Forces. He would work her over, and that would relieve the tension. Perhaps he could force from her the location of Eden or Andrei Androfski or Rodel. If he could deliver such a prize to Sieghold Stutze it would reaffirm his ability.

But, Piotr mused, it was getting more and more difficult to beat information out of these people as time went along. Those who were left simply could not be tortured for information. But what the devil, he could rip the clothing from the girl and smash her up. That would be a good evening's sport.

Piotr was not afraid to go into the streets alone. He told his men so. Yet it was stupid to invite another attack from a madman. He called in his personal bodyguards, six fat, faithful huskies, to escort him to the Pawiak Prison a few blocks from the barracks.

When he arrived at the ugly reddish brick structure a phone call awaited him. He took it in his office.

"Sturmbannführer Stutze here," the Austrian said.

"Yes?"

"Warsinski, I have been thinking over your request for arms. Perhaps we can supply some guns for a special squad of your men—in exchange for certain new duties."

"When can we talk about it?"

"Tomorrow."

"Fine. I shall expect you at the barracks, then?" Warsinski asked.

"No, no, no," Stutze said quickly. "We meet outside the ghetto at the Stawki Gate at noon."

"Noon. Stawki Gate."

Warsinski unbuttoned his long gray coat and hung it up. He took off his jacket and lowered his suspenders. His big belly, released from restraint, poured over the top of his trousers. His hands itched. He scratched them until they pained, then opened the desk drawer and wiped a thick oozy green salve over them. The ointment stung tears into his eyes. He stretched back on his cot, holding his hands under his head, his underwear gray with sweat stains under the armpits.

What was Stutze up to? Warsinski's bulgy face became mobile with thoughts and counterthoughts. He had to keep the appointment. Was it a trick? Perhaps Stutze was a coward, afraid to come into the ghetto, and wanted the Militia to carry out Reinhard Corps duties. Why else would he give arms? Had Stutze decided that a convert like Warsinski wasn't really a Jew and therefore could be trusted with guns, like the Ukrainians? He brushed his long handle-bar mustache. Why not arm him? He had been loyal. But . . . the Big Seven had been loyal too.

Crash!

A splintering sound bolted him to a sitting position. He saw the door fly open with such impact that it nearly tore off its hinges.

"What the hell!"

Three pistols were leveled at him. One man closed the door, the second went to the desk and tore the phone wire out. Warsinski squinted at the third. Knew him from somewhere. Alterman . . . Tolek Alterman from the Bathyrans.

Warsinski scowled at them fearlessly.

"I have the pleasure of carrying out the judgment of Joint Forces to execute you as a traitor to the Jewish people," Tolek said.

Warsinski laughed in contempt. "Guards!" he roared. "Guards!"

"They don't hear you, Piotr Warsinski. They are all locked up. Pawiak Prison is in the hands of Joint Jewish Forces. The prisoners are being freed at this moment."

The smirk came off Warsinski's face. The guns on him were in steady hands. He folded his hands and closed his eyes and lowered his head. "I don't beg like Jews," he said. "Go on. I am ready."

"It is not so simple," Tolek said. "There are a lot of questions you are going to answer first."

Warsinski snarled at them. He thought so. Yellow Jews unable to carry out the execution. It is all a bluff. Talk . . . negotiate . . . bargain . . .

Tolek's boot suddenly came up into Warsinski's fat stomach, sinking in from toe to heel. The air left Warsinski. He sank from the bed to his knees. A second kick caught him alongside the jaw, thudding his head against the wall. He sat dazed. Tolek nodded to his two comrades. The first, Pinchas Silver, tossed a thumbscrew and a pair of pliers onto the desk. Adam Blumenfeld revealed a barb-tipped whip.

"We picked up a few of your toys from the interrogation room, Warsinski. Get up and sit at the desk."

Warsinski did not move.

The lash cut through his underwear. Piotr crawled quickly on his hands and knees to the desk and sat.

"Thumb . . . let's have your thumb."

The lash ripped once more over his neck.

"Thumb!"

He extended a green-ooze-covered paw. Tolek locked Warsinski's thumb into the screw and slowly turned the top bolt to apply steady pressure.

"You've got no guts for torture," Warsinski snarled in defiance, "no real guts for it. Jews are too weak!"

Tolek slipped his pistol into his belt, grabbed Warsinski's outsized mustache in his fist, and ripped it from his face.

"Yaaaaaahhhh!" Warsinski screamed, clutching a gory upper lip with his free hand.

Tolek slipped the pliers onto a big dirty fingernail of Warsinski's free hand.

"Adam, tighten the thumbscrew. Warsinski can loosen the bolt if he wants to reach for it. It will cost him a fingernail to try."

Adam Blumenfeld tightened the bolt, crunching the vise into Warsinski's knuckle. He gasped. The sweat poured from his face and turned his underwear to a soggy rag. Adam turned the thumbscrew a quarter turn.

"Yahhhh!"

Warsinski suddenly tried to reach for the screw, but Tolek held the pliers tight and a fingernail tore loose.

Mucus spurted from his nose, and his eyes ran.

"Will you co-operate?"

"Stop! Stop! I'll talk!"

As his thumb was freed he stumbled blindly around the room, wailing and bouncing off the walls. He sank in a blubbering, groaning hulk to the floor. A mass of sweaty ugliness.

Tolek and the other two looked down at him with disgust, and Tolek was sick to his stomach with himself for his brutality, but he knew he could not puke in the presence of an enemy who regarded it as a weakness.

"He didn't even last five minutes," Pinchas said. "I didn't think he would."

They dragged him to the cot and flung him on it.

In a few minutes Alexander Brandel came in and after shuddering at the first sight of Warsinski grilled him for twelve hours from questions and knowledge gained from the Good Fellowship archives. Piotr Warsinski revealed his own crimes, the crimes of his officers, his own fortunes, the places of hidden stores, information about Stutze, Schreiker, Koenig, the Nightingales, and the Reinhard Corps.

Next morning Piotr Warsinski was killed in accordance with the Joint Forces' judgment by a single bullet through the back of his head.

Chapter Six

The immediate problem facing Joint Forces was locating a new command bunker in the central area. The other bunkers were already jammed to capacity, and the hundred people from Mila 19 added to the problem. To build a suitable underground complex for two to three hundred people would take weeks.

Alexander Brandel's knowledge through his past dealings became invaluable. By one means or another he knew of most hiding places in the ghetto.

Alex suspected there was a large bunker under Mila 18, across the street from his own former headquarters.

He had often done business with a smuggler named Moritz Katz, a rotund little chap who in pre-war Warsaw had been a furrier. His business was always considered on the fringe; a tightrope between the legal and the unlawful. It was difficult to come right out and say that Moritz fenced stolen goods. His clientele was always high class. He carried an ethical concept with him into the ghetto. He was a decent fellow, as smugglers went. After all, smuggling was an honorable necessity in ghetto life. Moritz bought and sold at reasonable prices. Moreover, he was softhearted. When things got particularly desperate, Alex could always get Moritz to make an urgent delivery of essentials at cost price.

Moritz had two distinguishing features. He was in a never-ending card game, and his mouth always chewed sweets, fruit, cake, candy. For the latter frailty, he was known as Moritz the Nasher.

The Bathyrans who guarded the rooftops around Mila 19 detected Moritz the Nasher entering and leaving Mila 18 so many times that it had to be suspected as his headquarters.

These suspicions were advanced after the bunker at Mila 19 was expanded until its rooms stretched to the sewer under the middle of the street. Deborah Bronski had the room next to the sewer pipe with the children from the orphanage. Many times they heard foreign sounds coming from either the inside of the pipe or beyond it.

From this Alex concluded that Moritz the Nasher had a bunker under Mila 18, separated from his own by the twelve-foot pipe. He discussed this possibility with Simon and Andrei.

"I am positive there is a bunker under Mila 18, and if it is what we think, it will be a large one."

"It would be a perfect location for a command post," Simon said. "Particularly since the Germans have located and wrecked Mila 19, they'd never suspect we'd be in another location so close."

"But," Andrei said realistically, "how the hell do you find the entrance? Moritz Katz is the shrewdest smuggler in the ghetto."

"Can we get a message to him?" Alex suggested.

"No one has seen him for weeks, since his gang was caught at the Gensia Gate and taken to the Umschlagplatz."

They mused and pondered. The idea of a large, ready-made command post was terribly appealing.

"Well. What's to lose if we cut a hole through the children's room and make another on a direct line across the *Kanal*? If we're lucky we might hit the bunker."

372

"You know how tricky sound is in the sewers. The children may have been hearing an echo coming from a hundred meters away."

"What the hell?" Andrei said. "Let's cut through and look around. Nothing to lose."

Simon shrugged a dubious okay. No one had a better suggestion.

"I think I'd better go in alone," Andrei said. "If Moritz is still down there he will panic if he sees an army coming after him."

Later that day Andrei entered the shambled Orphans and Self-Help building at Mila 19. He went to the converted water closet where the false lavatory once covered the secret entrance to their underground rooms. The lavatory was smashed, but the pipe leading to the cellar was still intact.

Andrei tucked a flashlight and short-handled pick and sledge hammer into his belt, strapped the Schmeisser "Gaby" on his back, and slid down the pipe. He flicked on the light. The beam probed over mounds of wreckage. The retaining walls and over-head crossbeams had been knocked loose, caving in the main tunnel in many places. Andrei inched forward, digging away the blockage with his hands.

He came to the room which had belonged to the children. It was a shambles. The layers of bunks had been wrecked with axes and the books torn to shreds and the few toys smashed. Andrei moved along a ten-foot wall which lay against the *Kanal* pipe. Seepings oozed through. He could hear the flow of sewage. He calculated in order to line up Mila 18.

Any decision would most likely be wrong. "Well, I've got to start someplace."

He fixed the flashlight on a single spot, sank his pick into the dirt wall, and hacked it away until it crumpled to the outer shell of the pipe.

Andrei smoothed a place big enough for him to carve out a manhole and bashed at the concrete with the sledge until it cracked under the beating. Once through the outer layer, he jarred loose enough bricks from the inner lining of the pipe so that he could fit through.

He wiped the sweat from his eyes and refixed the tools in his belt, cursing that he was on a wild-goose chase, then knelt at the hole and looked into the *Kanal* with his light. It was not too bad. The tide on the Vistula River was low, as he had calculated, so the sewage was only waist-high.

Andrei squeezed through the hole into the sewer. His feet skidded in the slime. He pulled the strap of his weapon several notches tighter so it would ride higher on his back and not get wet. In both directions dim streaks of light filtered through the manholes, sending an eerie bluish light glistening on the bricks.

He waded to the middle and looked behind him so he would

remain in a line with the children's room. On the opposite side of the sewer he thrust his ear against the brick, hoping for sound. There was none.

His flashlight moved first in one direction for several yards, then another.

Andrei splashed down a dozen yards. A cluster of bricks were not laid in the same pattern as the rest, as though they had been knocked loose and replaced. Could it be! He felt with his fingers. The bricks were definitely not cemented in. There was room for a man to fit through if they were removed. Was there a bunker on the other side? Were the children actually hearing smugglers coming in and out of the sewer?

Andrei hit his sledge against the bricks for a sounding. Hollow ring! It was not solid on the other side. There was a room!

He picked at the bricks. They came out easily.

It was hollow on the other side. Andrei shone the light in.

He crawled in and moved his light in a complete circle. "Holy God!" he muttered, and whistled with disbelief. He stood at his full height in a huge subterranean room. It was the most magnificent underground structure he had ever seen. Along one wall were sacks of rice, flour, sugar, salt. There were crates of medicine. Salted meats. Cases of tins of food. A bin of dried vegetables. Beautiful couches, easy chairs, furniture, bed.

"Holy God!"

He found the exit into a corridor and inched down it. Five more large rooms were on either side of the corridor, and each as big as the first one and each held stores. Overhead an electric line with light bulbs.

Andrei came to the end of the corridor. It turned into a smaller tunnel holding a series of cells.

"Don't move," a voice behind him commanded. "Hands over your head. High!"

Andrei lifted his arms. It had all been too good to be true. He cursed himself for forgetting to unstrap his weapon in the excitement of locating the bunker.

"Put both your hands on the wall," the voice commanded. Andrei did as he was told. "Now turn your face."

He looked into a blinding light.

"Andrei Androfski?"

"Is that you, Moritz?"

"How in the hell did you figure out where this bunker was?"

"We added two and two. Put that goddamned gun away and take the light out of my eyes."

"Don't rush me into any decisions. I'm not sure whether I have to kill you or not." He shifted the light toward one of the cells. "Step into my office. What I'm holding on you, for your information, is a shotgun."

Moritz lit a lantern and settled in back of his desk. He had a grizzly beard and an anemic color. Much of his chubbiness had shrunk away. Underground living had been hard on him. Moritz kept the shotgun leveled at Andrei's chest. Andrei was too busy being awed by the office. In addition to electrical wiring, there was a phone on the desk and a low-wattage radio transmitter.

"What a setup."

Moritz shrugged modestly at the compliment. "We tried to give our customers good service. Only trouble is that we've got no more customers. We got no one. Most my boys were grabbed on a haul. Just me and my wife Sheina and a few others. You've met Sheina? She's asleep in the other room. She sleeps through anything, that woman. Even your banging holes into my bunker. She's sick. She needs a doctor. Change of life."

"How in hell do you run the lights—the radio?"

"Generator, what else? Used to be able to send messages to my contacts on the Aryan side. Simple code."

"Telephone?"

"One of my boys worked for the phone company. There's a million ways to screw the phone company. We tied in on a Ukrainian line from the guards at the Brushmaker's and we speak Yiddish. They've never been able to figure it. No, Andrei. I'm sorry you had to find this place because I've always held you in high esteem. You were a very smart man to locate my bunker, but naturally I've got to kill you."

"Not so fast, Moritz. Obviously I wouldn't pull a move like this without a cover. You've heard of Joint Jewish Forces?"

Moritz screwed up his face. He suspected he was about to be taken. "I still get around."

"They know I'm here and what I'm looking for."

"Oh crap!" Moritz the Nasher said. He lay the shotgun on the desk in disgust. "Minute I saw you barreling through the sewer into the bunker I said to myself that this bastard is too smart to come in exposed. Now you talk to Alexander Brandel. He'll tell you I've been right down the line with his Orphans setup. I always did business on the square with him."

"Moritz, for God's sake, stop apologizing. Do you hear me pushing you around?"

Moritz the Nasher was hungry. He opened the top desk drawer and took out a packet of German chocolate, unwrapped it, nibbled, and decried the lack of fresh fruit. "You want my bunker, no doubt."

"No doubt."

"And seven hundred thousand zlotys' worth of food."

"I feel bad, Moritz—believe me."

"What a kick in the ass life is. If one thief doesn't get you, another will," Moritz opined.

Andrei sympathized with him. Moritz the Nasher was a gambler, a smuggler, a man who existed by wit. But he was also a supreme realist. He knew that he had been caught flat. At least Andrei Androfski and the Joint Forces held him no malice. Maybe he was lucky, after all. Had the Germans or the Militia found him first . . . curtains . . . Umschlagplatz. He had hoped that he and his wife Sheina could ride the war out in Mila 18. They had enough supplies and medicine to see through a year or two without ever coming up. But . . . what kind of a life was it for a man? Never to see the sun. Nobody to play cards with. Candy running out. Always in fear that the next minute or the next or the next those goddamn German dogs would sniff him out.

"Let me ask you something, Androfski," Moritz asked. "This here Joint Forces—you the ones who blasted the SS men at Zamenhof and Niska?"

Andrei nodded.

"You the ones who fixed up Warsinski?"

Andrei nodded again.

"You guys really mean business?"

Andrei nodded for the third time.

"Let me tell you something. You work, you live, you do your best, but you never quite get onto the idea of the way they're kicking you around. In the last week—since the ambush—for the first time in my life I'm proud to be a Jew."

"That's the way we all want to go out."

Moritz shrugged. "So, maybe I'm glad you found me first. Obviously, you realize you have me over a barrel."

"Obviously," Andrei agreed.

Moritz munched on another square of chocolate, somewhat relieved that his long, taut vigil was over.

"Moritz," Andrei said, "the one thing that Joint Jewish Forces really needs is a quartermaster."

"What's a quartermaster?"

"Someone high class to get in supplies."

"You mean a smuggler?"

"No. Quartermaster is a respectable position. Every army has them."

"What's the cut?"

"Well, a regular army—like ours—doesn't work on cuts."

"*Oy vay!* What a day this has been. All I've ever done is run a nice clean business."

"Moritz, you're too much of a gambler to ride this war out in a hole. We've got doctors. Sheina will get treatment. You'll have lots of interesting people here to share this bunker."

"I bet I will. Tell me honest, Androfski. This post of quartermaster. Is it important? I mean, like a Ulany colonel?"

"In our army," Andrei said, "it's the most important."

Moritz sighed in resignation. "One condition. No one inquires into my past finances."

"Done," Andrei said.

They clasped hands, Moritz pulled a faded double deck of cards, shuffled, and began to deal. "Before you move in, one game of sixty-six."

Chapter Seven

An ant line of laborers in a Brushmaker's building bent their backs, pushing large clumsy carts. The line moved in an endless circle from the lumber store to the lathe room to the assembly room.

An emaciated slave named Creamski, who had kept alive somehow for ten months, loaded the cart with finished toilet-brush handles from the lathe room. He grunted down the corridor, pushing the load at a snail's pace.

The assembly room consisted of ten long tables, each forty feet long. Each table had a series of varied drilled holes to stuff bristles, tie the wires, and attach the handles. Fifty men worked each table.

Creamski pushed his cart to table number three; toilet brushes. A "leader" stood at the head of each table. "They are here," Creamski whispered to the "leader."

He pushed his cart along the table, placing several handles before each bench.

"They are here," he whispered.

"They are here."

The word passed down the line and over to the next table and the next—"They are here."

"You there!" the German foreman shouted from the balcony. "Hurry up!"

Creamski moved faster, emptying the cart. He turned it about and pushed it out of the room, down the corridor, past the lathe room, and into the lumber warehouse.

While his cart was being loaded with boards, he stepped into the checker's office.

"Now!" he said to the checker. The two of them shoved the desk aside, revealing a trap door. Creamski pulled it open.

"Now!" Creamski called down into the black hole.

Wolf Brandel's head popped out of the tunnel. He moved quickly out of the checker's office, scrutinizing the long high stacks of lumber. "Move them out," the beardless commander ordered. One by one, forty Jewish Fighters emerged from the underground passage. The Franciskanska bunker a few blocks away connected to the *Kanal*. Wolf's company had followed the sewer to a point inside the Brushmaker's complex and dug the tunnel into the checker's office.

With hand signals he dispersed his force of ten women and thirty men to pre-fixed positions. They ducked behind the lumber with their weapons ready. Wolf blew a long breath and nodded for Creamski to return to the assembly room.

Creamski grunted and strained to put the loaded cart into motion. As he turned into the lathe room he gave a hand signal which could be seen by a table "leader" in the assembly room. Every eye in the room was on the "leader." He nodded.

Clump! Clump! Clump! Clump!

The feet of the inmates thumped against the floor in unison.

Boom! Boom! Boom! Boom!

They took their wooden handles and banged them on the tables, setting up a din.

"What's going on!" shrieked the foreman through a megaphone from his balcony cage. "Stop this noise! Stop it! Do you hear!"

Clump! Clump! Clump! Clump! Boom! Boom! Boom! Boom!

The clatter from the building swelled over the compound.

"Guards!" the foreman shouted into his alarm phone. "Guards! Building number four! Quick!"

Alarm sirens erupted all over the complex in a series of short whistles to draw the guards to assembly building number four.

The foreman locked the barred door of his office. He snatched the pistol from his desk and looked down at the five hundred pairs of maddened eyes staring up at him.

Clump! Clump! Clump! Clump!

"Krebs dies! Krebs dies! Krebs dies! Krebs dies!" they chanted his name.

Ukrainians, Latvians, and Estonians poured out of the guard barracks with whips, guns, and dogs, racing for the spot of the insurrection.

Part of Wolf Brandel's force, hidden around the outside of the building, let them pass through. There was only one entrance, through the main corridor. He watched the first of the guards pass into the assembly room from his position in the lathe room.

"Now!"

Wolf and ten of his Fighters stepped into the corridor and faced a mass of guards. The Ukrainians had trapped themselves. A pipe grenade shattered in their midst, followed by a tattoo of pistol fire.

The Ukrainians outside plunged backward for the exit, but the Jewish Fighters outside moved in to cut them off. A massacre ensued.

A half dozen guards reached the assembly room. The slaves leaped from their benches. In pent-up wrath they attacked their tormentors and their tormentors' dogs with bare hands. Within

378

seconds, the guards and dogs were pummeled to death and their bodies smashed with spit and kicks and disembowelment and decapitation.

Benches were overturned and smashed, lathes broken up by sledge hammers.

"Krebs! Krebs! Krebs! Krebs!"

The foreman was bug-eyed, insane with fright, locked in his own prison. They were coming up the balcony after him. No way of escape!

"Krebs! Krebs! Krebs! Krebs!"

He placed the barrel of the pistol in his mouth and pulled the trigger as the outstretched arms of the slaves reached through the cage for him.

Ana Grinspan, with a company in the central district, was the highest-ranking woman commander in the ghetto. Her company was the most integrated of the various parties and final proof that unity had been achieved. Thirty-two Fighters came from the Bathyrans, Poale Zion, Gordonia, Dror, Communists, Akiva, Hashomer Hatzair, Hechalutz, and the Bund. She even had four members from religious Zionist Mizrachi who could no longer stomach the passive attitudes of the Orthodox Agudah.

The secondary objective at Brushmaker's was the confiscation of the fleet of five trucks. The instant Brushmaker's was secured Wolf turned the trucks over to Ana, who put into operation a pre-set plan. Each truck had a driver, four fighters, and liberated Brushmaker's slaves.

They struck at every known remaining warehouse, store, shop, medical station, bakery, and private cache in the ghetto, holding anything usable for Joint Forces. Loading rapidly under the protective guns of the Joint Fighters, they whisked off to a series of small bunkers scattered all over the ghetto.

No protest or conversation was permitted.

"Load! Move!"

And away.

Every sack of flour, every grain of food was carted off.

One of the bunkers in the central command was located almost beneath the Jewish Militia barracks, where the Fighters kept the barracks under scrutiny. Simon Eden ordered a raid to bring back a half dozen militiamen.

They were dragged off to the new command center at Mila 18 to confront Alexander Brandel, who had drawn up a list of dozens of persons suspected of collaboration, concealing wealth, and illegal operations. The captured militiamen were quick to sing out all they knew about the location of these people.

Squads of Jewish Fighters made forays, unearthing one person after another on the list. The most notorious of the collaborators were executed. The others were fined.

"You are fined ten thousand zlotys for passing information to the Germans."

"You are fined twenty thousand zlotys for collaboration with the Jewish Militia."

"You are fined ten thousand zlotys for failure to protect Jews taken to the Umschlagplatz within your power to warn them."

These fines were collected on the spot, on pain of death, without argument or equivocation.

Rodel, the squat, blocklike commander of the southern area, had been a member in good standing in the Communist party most of his adult life. He deemed it ironic that his command bunker was located under the Converts' Church with the open knowledge of Father Jakub.

Moreover, the war had compelled him to enter strange alliances with Labor Zionists holding completely diverse political views. Zionism was the drug of the Jewish people, he had said on numerous occasions. However, he worked not only with Labor Zionists but Jabotinski Revisionists, whom he considered fascists, and religious elements, whom he considered mentally inept. It was a strange war to Rodel, but no stranger than the Soviet Union and America fighting as allies.

From the moment of Warsinski's assassination, Rodel ordered the workers in the uniform factory to sabotage the product. In the following days, uniforms left Warsaw with flies, armholes, and neckholes sewn shut, buttons with no buttonholes, and seams that would rip away under the slightest stress.

An hour after Wolf Brandel captured Brushmaker's, Ludwig Heinz, the manager of the uniform factory, sent a message to Rodel through Father Jakub that the Lithuanian guards had fled. Heinz, an ethnic German, was one of an infinitesimal number who displayed a measure of humanity toward the slave labor under him. Within the strict limitations permitted, Heinz was credited with saving a number of lives. He walked untouched to the corner of Nowolipki and Karmelicka streets to open the main gates and allow the Jewish Fighters in.

"I'm glad my part in this is over," Heinz said to Rodel.

Rodel shook his shiny, hairless head. "It is a strange war," he said. "You've been decent within your means. Joint Forces has ordered me to see you safely through the ghetto gates."

"I'm glad it's over," Ludwig Heinz repeated.

"Let's go," Rodel said, pointing in the direction of the Leszno Gate two blocks away.

As Ludwig Heinz turned, Rodel whipped out his pistol and struck the man across the back of the ear with the barrel. Heinz pitched forward to the street, unconscious. Rodel leaned down and ripped part of his clothing off and bloodied his face with a series of blows.

"All right," he ordered two fighters, "take him to the Leszno Gate and dump him. I'm sorry I had to beat him up, but it's for his own good. If he walked out unharmed, the Germans would suspect him. This way they may get the impression he barely escaped."

As they hauled Heinz away, he shook his head again. "Strange war," he said.

Samson Ben Horin, commander of the Jabotinski company of Revisionists, had remained outside the jurisdiction of Joint Jewish Forces, but the events of the day compelled him to look upon Eden's army with a new respect. He dispatched a runner to Eden with an offer to keep runner contact with their bunker and join in limited co-operation.

Simon soon found an assignment much to Ben Horin's liking.

On the last day of January, Samson Ben Horin led a combined company, half Revisionists, half Joint Forces, through the sewer pipes under the wall into the Aryan side. He picked the hour of the Vistula's lowest tide, when the sewage was only knee-deep. Using Simon's engineer's map of the sewer system, he had only a mile to negotiate. Ben Horin's party came to a stop beneath a manhole close to Bank Square near the Ministry of Finance.

Three Aryan side contacts waited. One was dressed as a sewer worker, the second sat in the driver's seat of a parked teamster wagon, and the third watched at the corner in a position to observe the German Exchange Bank on Orla Street.

It was the day before payday for the German garrison. At precisely noon an armored truck from the ministry would stop to deposit part of the payroll at the Exchange Bank.

The watchman signaled the arrival of the armored truck.

The horse-drawn wagon moved from the curb and stopped beside the manhole. A long ladder was taken from it and set down in the sewer. Samson Ben Horin led his party out of the sewer. They scattered with startling rapidity so that both ends of the block-long Orla Street could be sealed.

A dozen German soldiers formed a guard around the armored truck before the bank. They passed the money sacks in.

Samson Ben Horin arched a homemade matzo-ball grenade. It landed at the right front tire of the truck.

Nuts and bolts flew everywhere, ripping into the bodies of the Germans.

A second grenade.

A third.

Half of the Germans were on the ground, groveling with iron in them. The truck was disabled, but the guards inside fired back.

381

A fire bottle splattered against the side of the truck, igniting into flame and driving the defenders out.

Samson Ben Horin signaled for his men to converge. They pressed in from both ends of Orla Street. The Germans were pinned against the wall and the flaming truck. A few plunged into the bank for safety.

Half of the raiders grabbed every money sack in sight. The other half pushed into the bank and forced the vaults open. Within eight minutes of the time they had come from the sewer, they disappeared the same way with more than a million zlotys.

Simon Eden referred to the actions as practical field training to teach his army that the invulnerable enemy was indeed vulnerable.

Within a week after Andrei's ambush at Niska and Zamenhof streets, which signaled the uprising, Joint Jewish Forces had purged the ghetto of collaborators, added millions to their treasury, controlled the streets, confiscated tons of food, wrecked the two major slave-labor factories, and freed the workers.

There were two large jobs left. The Jewish Militia, who cowered in their barracks, and the Civil Authority. The act of mere vengeance: doing away with the Jewish Militia was overruled by more practical considerations of settling with the Jewish Civil Authority.

On February 1, 1943, a hundred and fifty men and women of Joint Forces surrounded the Jewish Civil Authority building at dawn. Simon Eden broke down the doors and entered with fifty more Fighters.

From his office on the third floor Boris Presser watched the scene below with Marinski, his assistant.

"Get into the outer office," Presser said quickly. "Stall them. Keep them out of here."

Presser sat behind his desk and tried to think. Every day he had been phoning Rudolph Schreiker to report on the rampaging of the Joint Forces. Murder in the streets, assassinations, looting, extortion. Boris was positive the actions would result in a murderous reprisal from the Reinhard Corps, but another day passed and another and another and nothing happened.

Each day his people cringed in the Civil Authority building with their families, trying to push him into a decision. Boris didn't like decisions or involvements. He had made a career of evasiveness. The Germans had always told him what to do. He did it. He had the ready-made excuse of throwing up his hands and saying, "What could I do?"

Marinski bolted into the room, crying semi-coherently, "Stop them! They're taking our families!"

"Stop shouting. Shouting will do no good. Get out there and delay Eden from coming in."

382

Boris locked the door and ran to the phone. First Schreiker, then the Militia. The line was dead. He clicked it desperately. Nothing. Presser rubbed his throbbing temples and slipped to the window. Women and children, families of the Civil Authority, were being prodded out into the street at gun point. A ruckus in the outer office. Authoritative knocks at his door.

Stall . . . play for time . . . debate . . . stall.

He unlocked the door. Simon Eden stood before him. Black-eyed; long, wiry frame; intense. Simon hovered over the smaller man, shoved the door open wide, and looked around the office. He stepped inside the room and closed the door behind him, shutting out Marinski, who was too terrified to protest the abduction of his wife and daughter.

Boris backed up, bringing everything within him to the fore to maintain control and not show his fear. "I protest this humiliation of the Civil Authority," he said.

Simon ignored him; his eyes showed almost boredom.

"You have no right to barge in here and kidnap our families. You have no right to treat us like collaborators." Boris prodded to find a point of argument.

Simon would not argue. "History will pass judgment on the Civil Authority," he said dryly.

Careful, Presser said to himself, careful. Don't anger him. "You must realize," Boris fenced, "that I have no personal authorization to grant you recognition."

"Just recognize what comes out of the end of this muzzle. It is quite simple. We have your families. We want your treasury."

Beads of perspiration popped out on Boris Presser's upper lip. To refuse would be to admit that he was truly a puppet of the Germans, for in fact Joint Jewish Forces now represented the authority in the ghetto. But if he did recognize Eden, the Germans would eventually punish him when they returned. Boris was in a vise. He opened his arms benevolently. "Surely, Simon, as a man who knows organizational structure, you are aware that I do not control our very insignificant treasury. I have no way of acting."

"Find a way," Simon interrupted. "In an hour we shall deposit three corpses at the doorsteps of this building. One will be a member of your own family. Each hour thereafter, three more hostages will be shot until you deliver two million zlotys to Joint Forces."

Marinski, eavesdropping, burst in, "Give him the damned money!"

Boris was dying to drink a glass of water to relieve his parched throat, but he knew that if he lifted a glass his hand would spill it with trembling. "Let me discuss this with my board," Boris said, continuing the role of a reasonable man. "There are many touchy legal problems. Mind you, I am certain they can be solved, but this is rather sudden. Let us thrash it out. We will come up with a suitable compromise."

Simon Eden looked down at him with final disgust. "You have no alternative," he said, and before Boris Presser could speak again, Simon left.

An hour later the two million zlotys were turned over to Simon, half from the denuded treasury and half confiscated as ransom from personal fortunes.

"I was in favor of dumping you at the Stawki Gate with Piotr Warsinski," Simon said impassively. "But Alexander Brandel is a dreamer. He believes in the poetic justic of making you and your people burrow into the ground and live like rats . . . as the rest of us have."

The Jewish Fighters released the hostages. Boris Presser's action ended any further use the Germans may have had for the Civil Authority.

Boris Presser and the rest who had served as message boys of the Germans were cast loose to spend the rest of their days despised and scorned by both their own people and the enemy.

The next morning posters were nailed over the front door of the abandoned Civil Authority building and posted on the walls throughout the ghetto.

ATTENTION!

AS OF TODAY, FEBRUARY 1, 1943, THE JEWISH CIVIL AUTHORITY IS DISBANDED. THIS GHETTO IS UNDER THE SOLE AND ABSOLUTE AUTHORITY OF JOINT JEWISH FORCES. ORDERS ARE TO BE OBEYED WITHOUT RESERVATION.
SIGNED:

Atlas, Commander, Joint Jewish Forces
Jan, Executive Commander

Chapter Eight

Journal Entry

The Star of David flies over the Warsaw ghetto!
On February 2 1943, the German Sixth Army surrendered at Stalingrad. We feel for the first time that Germany will lose the war. But how quickly will the floodwaters recede?
None of us are so foolish as to believe we will ever live to see a Jewish state in Palestine, but we have sounded the great trumpet of the return. A Jewish army controls the first autonomous piece of Jewish land in nearly two thousand years of our dispersal. Our

"national" is only a few square blocks and we know we shall not hold it long, but, as Tolek Alterman says, *"This is living Zionism."* No matter what happens hereafter, for this moment we are a proud and free people.

The first *"capital"* of our *"Jewish state"* is Mila 18. I shall describe it. There are six main rooms. These are named for the six Polish extermination camps. Rooms: Belzec and Auschwitz hold a hundred and twenty fighters of two companies, one Bund and one Bathyran. This group is under Andrei's personal command (in addition to his other duties).

Majdanek is the room which runs alongside the Kanal. Joint Forces had voted to keep this room (and several others around the ghetto) for the exclusive use of as many children as we can care for. We have rounded up forty. Nothing takes priority over the continuation of the Orphans and Self-Help tradition. As soon as we can place these children on the Aryan side we find others to bring into Majdanek. Although Rachael Bronski lives at the Franciskanska bunker (under Wolf's command—I am very proud of him. To think such a soldier and leader is my son), she spends a great deal of time on the "children" operation. We keep a program of schooling and games. At night they can go out for exercise and fresh air. Pray God a few of them will survive. They are our harvest.

Treblinka holds food stores and is the "hospital" for the central command (two doctors, four nurses.) Sobibor keeps relatives of the Fighters and those few intellectuals we have been able to salvage. A smattering of writers, scientists, artists, theologists, historians, and teachers, who represent the last voice of our dying culture.

Chelmno is the arsenal and munitions works. Jules Schlosberg and a dozen workers manufacture and store fire bombs and grenades. (Actual weapons—i.e., pistols, rifles—are as scarce as ever.)

The second hallway is filled with small cells which are also named in "honor" of the lesser camps.

Stutthof is a closet holding the generator; Poniatow has the office and living quarters of Simon, Andrei, Tolek (operations and training officer), and Christopher de Monti. Stutthof holds two other cots for the radio and telephone operator on watch. Trawniki is a tiny cell for the exclusive quarters of Rabbi Solomon. He is the last rabbi left in the ghetto. Father Jakub tells me the Church is hiding Rabbi Nahum, probably to preserve as a historic relic. Dachau is shared by Moritz and Sheina Katz and Sylvia and me. (What privileged characters we are!)

Our number varies, but two hundred and twenty persons is the limit. We could not fit another in sideways. Thanks to the ingenious engineering by Moritz the Nasher's departed gang, circulation through air vents is not too bad. We use the generator for lights, sparingly. Petrol is hard to get and is needed for fire bombs.

385

Candles are used most of the time. But candles burn oxygen.

Mila 18 has six entrances: the sewer through the children's room, a removable stove in the house above, and four tunnels in different directions running one hundred to three hundred feet away from Mila 18.

Expansion of our army is almost nil. Few left in the ghetto are fit to fight. Secondly, the arms shortage is as bad as ever. Our forces, combined with the three Revisionist groups at Nalewki 37 (Jabotinski, Chayal, and Trumpeldor), give us a total of six hundred soldiers. Less than one in three has a firearm. The operations of the last week have seriously depleted our ammunition. We average less than ten rounds per weapon.

Our "quartermaster." Moritz the Nasher, made his first major acquisition yesterday—several hundred pairs of boots. Boots, long time a symbol of German oppression, have become a symbol of our defiance. In Poland only strong men wear boots these days. Simon knew that the boots would be a great morale factor.

The Joint Jewish Forces work in three operations. One third: duty on the rooftops watch and in roving patrols. One third: constructing underground bunkers. One third: in training. The commanders (Eden, Androfski, and Rondel, sometimes Ben Horin) have set up a system of rooftop fighting based on ambush tactics. Each company has alternate bunkers, so that we continually shift our positions. The key is a continued building of a skilled runner system to keep communications intact. Although we have had simulated combat drills for several days, the main question is yet to be answered. Can this rabble army with few weapons maintain discipline under fire? Is there enough individual courage and ability to improvise among these unskilled soldiers to really tell upon the greatest military power the world has ever known?

The task of holding for a week seems impossible, but there is an unmistakable air of optimism. Morale is splendid. A new feeling of dignity among the surviving population is infectious.

We await the enemy. We know that this fight for freedom is entirely without hope. But does the fight for freedom ever really end? Andrei is right. All we have left is our honor and the historic duty to make our battle at this moment.

ALEXANDER BRANDEL

An ingenious phone circuit had been rigged from Mila 18 through the sewers directly to the other command posts at Wolf Brandel's Franciskanska bunker and to Rodel beneath the Converts' Church. A half dozen phones, mainly in German factories, were used on occasion for contact beyond the wall, along with the low-wattage radio transmitter.

Tolek Alterman dozed on his cot next to the phone in the commander's office in Poniatow at Mila 18.

The phone rang. Tolek swung to a sitting position. He had let his hair grow long again since he stopped going to the Aryan side. He brushed it out of his eyes and fished for the receiver.

"Jerusalem," he said. "Roberto speaking."

"Hello, Roberto. This is Tolstoy in Beersheba." Tolek recognized the bull-horn voice of Rodel. "Get me Atlas."

Andrei, who was standing behind Tolek, walked quickly around the el of the corridor to Chelmno, where Simon fretted over the plans of the matzo ball-land mine being designed by Jules Schlosberg.

"Phone," he said. "Rodel."

"Hello, Beersheba. This is Atlas in Jerusalem."

"Hello, Atlas. Tolstoy, Beersheba. My angels see the Rhine Maidens and their Swans at Stalingrad. One thousand bottles. It looks as if they are coming through the Red Sea."

"Don't take any wine unless it's offered."

"*Shalom.*"

"*Shalom.*"

Simon set the phone down and looked up at Tolek and Andrei.

"I heard," Andrei said. He went quickly to Belzec and Auschwitz. "All right! Let's go! Up to the roofs!"

The Fighters snatched their weapons and crowded to the ladder which would take them through the stove into Mila 18.

"Move along, move along," Andrei prodded.

Alexander Brandel stumbled from his cell, coming out of a deep sleep. "A drill, Andrei?"

"No drill. They're coming."

"Runners!" Simon Eden barked.

A dozen swift, daring boys in their teens clustered around the entrance to Poniatow. Simon towered over them. "The Germans are massing before their barracks with their Auxilaries. We expect them through the Zelazna Gate. One thousand in number. Alert all companies. Hold fire unless fired upon. Move out!"

The ghetto rats scampered through the six exits to alert the scattered bunkers.

Andrei watched the last of his men go up the ladder to the stove upstairs. Stephan, Andrei's personal runner, followed his uncle as though he were glued to him. Andrei poked his head into Poniatow. Simon was afraid. Andrei slapped Simon's shoulder hard. "We won't fire until we can smell their breath," he said. "Don't worry."

"We'll soon find out," Simon said. "I wish I could be up there with you."

Andrei shrugged. "Such are the fortunes of a commander," he said, and was gone with Stephan close behind him.

Tolek ran up and down the tunnel. "Stop the generator! Combat conditions! Deborah, keep the children quiet. Rabbi, I'll have to ask you to pray silently. Moritz, card game's over for now. Button up, everyone—button up!"

Adam Blumenfeld at the radio threw a switch to put the receiver on batteries as the generator ground to a halt and the lights went out.

Beep . . . beep . . . beep . . . beep . . . he heard in his earphones. He pulled the headset off and called out in the darkness.

"Are you there, Simon?"

"I'm here."

"Radio confirmation. The Germans are moving."

Beep . . . beep . . . beep . . . beep . . . warned the mobile transmitter from the Aryan side.

Simon struck a match and found the candle on the desk. He cranked the phone handle.

"Haifa . . . hello, Haifa."

"This is Haifa."

"This is Atlas in Jerusalem. Let me speak to Chess Master."

"Chess Master speaking," Wolf Brandel answered from the Franciskanska bunker.

"The Rhine Maidens and their Swans are at Stalingrad. One thousand bottles. They're coming through the Red Sea. Don't drink any wine unless it's offered."

"Oh boy!"

Simon hung up. He could see Alex and Tolek on the fringe of the candle glow. Now was the commander's agony. Waiting in the dark. The acid test was here. It was deathly still. Even the endless prayers of Rabbi Solomon trailed to a silent movement of the lips.

Across vacant courtyards, flitting over rooftops, sloshing through sewage, darting up deserted staircases, the runners from Mila 18 flashed from cover to cover to alert the Fighters. The companies moved in ghostlike silence to their positions behind windows, on the roofs, from sewer cover. Yes, it was all quite like a drill.

The streets had a stillness like the face of the moon. Some feathers fluttered down from the rooftops in sudden gusts of wind. Hidden eyes watched the ethereal stillness.

A dim sound of heels cracking against cobblestones. Clump . . . clump . . . clump . . . clump . . . clump.

The SS at the Zelazna Gate, barricaded behind machine-gun nests, darted out to remove the barbed-wire blocking the entrance.

Rodel looked from the window in the uniform factory out to the picket fence where the black-uniformed marchers flickered past with the broken motion of a film running to a halt. The bootless brown uniforms of the Auxiliaries made a softer tread. Rodel watched, his teeth tightening in his moon-shaped face. On and on they passed.

"Hello, Beersheba," Rodel phoned to his bunker. "This is

Tolstoy. Advise Jerusalem that the Rhine Maidens and their Swans have passed the Land of Goshen. Brunhilde is leading them. They are going up the Jordan River."

Andrei Androfski looked up and down the rooftops at his dispersed Fighters. He was satisfied that they were deployed properly. Once on the roofs, the Joint Command was able to keep their companies in communication by signal posts from roof to roof. A message was relayed from Ana Grinspan's company that the Germans were marching up Zamenhof Street almost at the same moment that Rodel's command had phoned the information to Simon Eden. Andrei crawled on his belly to the corner overlooking the interesection of Mila and Zamenhof streets, with Stephan at his heels. He wiggled into a position to observe Zamenhof Street through a pair of field glasses.

Andrei grumbled to himself and sharpened his focus. "Brunhilde himself," he said. "Stutze. How nice."

Clump! Clump! Clump! Clump! The boot heels cracked, their echoes reverberating off the hollow shells of the buildings.

"Halt!"

The SS, Wehrmacht, and Auxiliaries broke ranks and scattered at the corner of Zamenhof and Gensia streets under the eyes and guns of Ana Grinspan's company.

With the enemy three blocks away, Andrei shifted his position, risking a little more exposure to get a better view. He saw the Germans surrounding the Civil Authority building and the Jewish Militia barracks. SS men smashed into the abandoned Civil Authority. In a few minutes Andrei watched a confused command meeting in the middle of Zamenhof Street. Stutze pointed and ranted.

"Hello, what's this?" Andrei whispered.

Jewish militiamen appeared in the streets for the first time since they had been terrorized into their barracks, but now they came at the end of Wehrmacht bayonets. Several Jewish militiamen, obviously of rank, were pulled from the herd and beaten into the Civil Authority building.

The sounds of machine pistol shots split the air.

"Runner!" Andrei snapped. Stephan crawled alongside him.

"Get a message to Simon. The Germans are rounding up the Jewish Militia. Some of them are being executed in the Civil Authority building. Apparently the Germans don't know that the Civil Authority has defected. We can anticipate the Germans taking the Militia straight up Zamenhof to the Stawki Gate and the Umschlagplatz. We want instructions."

Stephan repeated the message, then scooted down the middle of the roof for the short run through the skylight of Mila 18 and down the stairs to the bunker. Stephan appeared at the same moment that Ana Grinspan's runner appeared with an identical message.

Simon looked to Tolek and Alex.

"Andrei wants instructions," Stephan said.

The Germans would march the Jewish Militia under the massed guns of Andrei's companies and a company of Wolf's Fighters near the Stawki Gate. There were a thousand Germans in the street. They would be sitting pigeons. Should the rebellion begin on a note of saving Jewish traitors? Would it not be poetic and historic justice to see those ghouls marched off to the Umschlag-platz just as they had taken their own blood and flesh? An out-burst which would give these bastards a chance to spread and hide would all but deplete the ammunition stores of the Joint Forces.

Command decision! God. If only Andrei were down here to knock me on my back. Tolek and Alex continued to watch him in the dim light. Simon sucked in a deep breath, then another. The Germans were in a box such as they might never be caught in again. But . . . did it not take just as much courage to make the decision to let them pass out of the ghetto to give his Fighters a day, a week, ten days to find more ammunition?

"Tell Andrei . . . to keep absolute discipline. Let them pass." He spun the crank of the phone to confirm his opinion, to assure him-self. "This is Jerusalem. Atlas speaking. The Rhine Maidens are at Herod's Palace and are taking Korah and Absalom to Egypt. Let them pass."

In the bunker of the Revisionists at Nalweki 37, Samson Ben Horin faced the commander of his Chayal group who were spread along the roofs over Zemenhof near Ana Grinspan's company. The Chayal officer, Emanuel, snorted at Ben Horin.

"We will not let them pass!"

Samson Ben Horin stroked his newly grown beard. He liked it. The liaison runner from Eden's headquarters looked from Ben Horin to his officer.

"We are not obligated to carry out orders from Eden," the officer prodded.

"You are obligated to take my orders," Ben Horin answered. "By coincidence they are exactly the same. Let the Germans pass through."

Emanuel was enraged. "The Germans are in a box!"

Ben Horin shrugged.

"You are a flunky of the Labor Zionists," Emanuel cried.

"I shall relieve you of your command this instant if you cannot obey," Ben Horin threatened angrily.

Emanuel sulked, simmered, calmed, and was returned to his post, distressed that Ben Horin had taken a position concurrent with that of the Joint Forces.

Clump! Clump! Clump! Clump!

Andrei crawled as close to the roof's edge as he dared. He looked over his people. Their sweaty hands tightened around their weapons. Black eyes blazed from hidden corners. Andrei poked his fist into the air in a "hold fire" signal.

Beneath him the Germans took the Jewish Militia toward the Umschlagplatz and Treblinka.

Andrei licked his lips. He sighted "Gaby," the Schmeisser, on Sieghold Stutze's heart. "Ah," he whispered to himself. "What a lovely, magnificent target. So full of nice plump syphilitic blood." He clenched his teeth, pulling his itching, wiggling finger off the trigger.

The Fighters strewn out above Zamenhof Street looked down on their tormentors, gnawing pains of restraint holding them from unleashing their wrath.

"Look at that juicy Austrian. Ah, Stutze . . . Will I ever get such a lovely shot at you?" Andrei half cried to himself. "What a god-damn war!"

"Hello, Jerusalem," Wolf Brandel said. "The Angel from Lebanon advises us that the Rhine Maidens have taken Korah and Absalom into Egypt. They are boarding the train for hell. All is clear."

As the tail end of the German force disappeared out of the Stawki Gate, the hands gripping the guns and grenades and bottle bombs relaxed and their bodies slumped in exhaustion, drained by tension.

A waving of signal flags, rooftop to window, window to rooftop to street. A scampering of the runners. "All is clear."

The generator in Mila 18 sputtered and spun into life. The lights flickered on. The children in Majdanek, lying tightly against Deborah on the floor, resumed their reading game and Rabbi Solomon lifted the chant of his prayer and Moritz the Nasher cut the double deck of cards for another round of sixty-six and Alexander wrote down the notes in the journal.

Simon Eden was doubled over the desk with exhaustion. Andrei came in and slammed him across the back. "Simon! Did I have that syphilitic Austrian in my gun sights! I ached from head to toe to blast his head off. What discipline! Not a whisper up there! Not a sign. Not for a single second did Stutze know he was under our guns! Simon! Simon! By God, we have an army!"

Simon nodded weakly.

"You know," Andrei whispered confidentially, "I will wager anything you own that we can hold them for a week."

Chapter Nine

Oberführer Funk arrived in Berlin somewhat regretful that he had allowed Horst von Epp to muddle his thinking. It was preposterous to suggest a new set of tactics for the liquidation of the ghetto. He should have followed orders and returned with heavily armed men the day after the January 18 act of banditry. But it was too late. He had no choice. When Funk proposed Von Epp's theory of pacifying the Jews he was chagrined that Himmler thought it an excellent idea. In fact, it was so well received that Funk took full credit for thinking up the entire scheme.

In Berlin, problems were cropping up everywhere. The shock of the catastrophe at Stalingrad rocked the High Command, which was now facing a mammoth Russian winter counteroffensive.

In North Africa, Rommel's magnificent Afrika Korps was engaged in furious actions with the ever-strengthening Allied forces. A second disaster seemed in the making.

Italy was all but militarily impotent. One could smell that Italy was about to defect politically, as well.

In the air, the Luftwaffe had failed in its mission to crush the morale of the dogged Englishmen, and now all of England was being transformed into a gargantuan air field poised to return German bombs tenfold.

In the Pacific, the Americans had wrested the initiative. They seized island after island, which the Japanese had been certain was beyond the stamina of the American fighting men. The Japanese had not reckoned the extent of the uncommon valor of the United States Marine Corps.

Throughout the German Empire one could sense the restless awakening of the conquered. Despite brutal reprisals for underground activities, secret armies continued to grow. Indeed, Yugoslavia was gathering a force potent enough to divert badly needed German divisions off the eastern front. The policing of Greece and Poland required men and arms needed elsewhere.

To a lesser degree, sabotage, assassination, harassment, espionage flared up from Prague to Copenhagen to Oslo to Amsterdam to Brussels. Pin pricks, indeed, but enough stings were causing a painful swelling. Even in northern Italy a partisan army was forming.

This was the sudden realization of the brute who thought himself invincible being felled and stunned for the first time and crawling to his feet with a new appraisal of his adversary. Germany was stunned and smarted. The contemptuous smile was wiped from his lips. He was in pain.

Funk's visits with Eichmann at Gestapo 4B showed that

Eichmann was still going about his job of rounding up the Jews with uncommon zeal, but he was hitting stone walls. Finland flatly defied German orders to turn over the Jews and threatened to use the Finnish army to defend them. A second flat refusal came from the Bulgarians. Then Denmark. King Christian of Denmark responded to the German order for Jews to wear the Star of David by putting on the first one himself and ordering all Danes to follow suit in a display that one Dane was the same as another.

In France and Belgium and Holland, Jews were hidden in convents and attics, and even the Rumanians balked and the Hungarians split on the issue. Italy refused to become a partner to genocide.

Although Eichmann's agents were able to flush out Jews, get them through subterfuge and threat and strong-arm methods, nowhere in western Europe were they for sale for extra rations as they were in Poland, Ukrainia, and the Baltics.

Funk arrived in Berlin during a period of agonizing reappraisals. Himmler, Eichmann, and those most interested in the final solution agreed that the Warsaw ghetto, largest symbol of European Jewry, had to be liquidated quietly. It would indeed be a terrible propaganda setback for Berlin to admit the Jews were capable of fighting. It would be worse if Jews were to conduct the first rebellion against the Nazis that could start a chain reaction among the restless undergrounds.

Alfred Funk returned to Warsaw just long enough to turn the matter of peaceful liquidation over to the district Kommissar, Rudolph Schreiker. He left immmediately for Denmark, where the pesky Danish underground was chopping the rail system to bits and leading in British bombers. Denmark, symbol of the "little Aryan" brother, was behaving badly.

Throughout February 1943, Rudolph Schreiker bumbled through a fruitless campaign to lure the forty thousand survivors out of the ghetto. Joint Jewish Forces had a standing order that anyone volunteering for deportation or attempting to leave under German auspices would be shot.

Joint Jewish Forces allowed small numbers of Germans to enter the ghetto unmolested. Schreiker's emissaries went to the factories, attempting to win "labor transferrals" by guaranteeing good working conditions in Poniatow or Trawniki. To back up his intentions of good faith, Schreiker shipped in some food and medicine.

A few prominent Jews in prison in Warsaw were sent into the ghetto to form a new Jewish Civil Authority to open schools and hospitals and resume cultural activities.

But no one budged from his hiding place.

In a week Schreiker realized the new Civil Authority was powerless and in an angry rage over his own failure had them executed in the bloody Civil Authority building.

The newspapers and the radio decried the lack of Jewish co-operation in the resettlement for "honest labor." The Polish people were fed a line that it was Jewish behavior that was to blame for the Polish misfortunes, for if Jews reported for "honest labor," then Poles would not be needed. It was a "logic" the Poles accepted.

Simon Eden had the one thing he wanted most, time. It was time he had played for when he held fire when the Militia was taken to the Umschlagplatz. Time gave him the chance to augment his meager forces.

The Revisionists made firm contact with a small right-wing underground group, the ND Brigade, on the other side. Through the ND Brigade, the Revisionist groups—Chayal, Jabotinski, and Trumpeldor—were the best-armed company in the ghetto.

The Communist underground People's Guard was ill armed and could not spare a bullet for the ghetto, but they gave Joint Forces a strong liaison on the Aryan side with radio contact and hiding places in Warsaw.

By March of 1943 the tiny Jewish Forces were deeply hidden in the catacombs of the ghetto, were quick in their response to discipline, had as good observation and communications and contacts as circumstances allowed. The small teams of Fighters had shown extraordinary restraint in holding fire and maneuvering without being seen and had developed leadership to such a degree that even the pessimistic Simon Eden was beginning to feel they could hold the Germans at bay for a week.

Mid-March. Two months had passed and the Jews still held the ghetto. Alfred Funk roared into Warsaw, locked Rudolph Schreiker in his office, and berated him with obscenities for an hour. Schreiker was stripped of the duty. He was allowed to retain his post, for the Nazis could not admit failure in Jewish matters, but ghetto liquidation was turned over to Horst von Epp and Dr. Franz Koenig.

On March 17 a single German staff car drove through the Leszno-Tlomatskie Gate with a pair of large white flags attached to either fender. It moved at a crawl up Zamenhof Street and stopped before the Civil Authority building. A single soldier without rank stepped from behind the wheel and held up another white flag.

The car was under observation by Jewish Fighters the instant it entered the ghetto. The soldier shifted nervously from one foot to the other, unnerved by the quiet.

Heads began popping out from behind doorways, crevices, windows, courtyards, in a circle around him. He waved the white flag vigorously. Then his eyes narrowed as a woman holding a German rifle and wearing German boots approached him, leading a dozen men.

Ana Grinspan had seen Germans in her rifle sights before, but this was different. The mutual curiosity of enemy looking at enemy. The practical application of Andrei's continued lectures that these were not supermen. Hit them with a bullet and they will go down. The soldier was clearly puzzled at the face of his enemy. The "sub-human" was a tall handsome woman leading men whose prowess he had no desire to contest.

"I have a message for your commander from Dr. Franz Koenig representing the German authorities," he recited.

"Runner," Ana commanded, "go to Atlas in Jerusalem and tell him that Pharaoh has sent a messenger under truce. We will hold him at Herod's Palace."

A runner dashed off down Zamenhof Street.

"Blindfold him," Ana ordered.

Moments later Simon Eden spoke to the back of the soldier. "I am the commander," he said.

"Dr. Koenig wishes to have a meeting under truce with you and your command. He guarantees complete safety——"

Simon interrupted. "Tell him that if he wishes a conference he will walk alone through the Leszno-Tlomatskie Gate holding a white flag and he will stop before the Civil Authority building. He will come between twelve and twelve-ten o'clock."

The single obese figure of Franz Koenig waddled into the unearthly stillness. He quaked with fear, waving an oversized white flag back and forth with each step.

Down the middle of the empty street. The eerie sensation that a thousand pair of eyes were on him. Hidden. Looking at him. He stole glances at the windows and the roofs. Not a stir. How could anything be so deserted?

Koenig had wanted to wear civilian clothing, but he feared the Nazis would think he was afraid to wear a uniform. He did slip off the swastika armband the instant he was inside the ghetto. No use antagonizing them, he thought.

He inched farther up the street, past Dzielna, past Pawia. Still no sign of life. He stopped at the intersection of Gensia and looked in all four directions. Nothing. Only a snowball of feathers. The structure of the Civil Authority building was behind him.

"Anyone here?" Anyone here . . . anyone here . . . anyone here? echoed his voice.

"Hello!" Hello . . . hello . . . hello.

Ten minutes passed. Koenig was numbed with fear.

"Koenig!"

He looked for the voice.

"Koenig!"

The front door of the Civil Authority building was ajar. He walked gingerly up the steps and shoved the door open. It groaned.

He narrowed his eyes to slits to see down the shadowed corridor and waved the white flag.

"Truce!" he called. "Truce!"

The door slammed behind him. He turned and looked into the bearded face of Samson Ben Horin.

"Hands up," Ben Horin said. He frisked Koenig. "March!" Down the corridor. The walls were stained with dried blood from German executions. The plaster chipped away. Debris everywhere.

"Turn in there. Sit."

Franz didn't like the sordid room. It was overturned and smashed. It smelled bad. He swallowed to loosen his throat and stared at the table, afraid to look into the eyes of Samson Ben Horin. Samson smirked.

"So you are a superman," he said.

Koenig felt inept before the lean, fierce, black-eyed young Jew who could obviously rip him to shreds. Samson sat in the window sill and swung his leg back and forth. "So you are a superman," he repeated.

The door opened. Simon Eden towering over six feet three inches and like a band of steel, Andrei Androfski with the power of a lion, Rodel with the build of a tank—all came in and leaned against the wall.

Koenig knew instantly that not only were the Joint Forces not a myth, but the survivors were a fierce breed.

Alexander Brandel helped Rabbi Solomon into the room. He and the old man sat opposite Koenig.

"Stand up in the presence of our rabbi," Andrei said, "and cover your head."

Koenig pushed the chair back from the table and arose.

Rodel did not particularly subscribe to the idea of having Samson Ben Horin and Rabbi Solomon attend the conference. To him, Ben Horin's Revisionists were akin to fascists. Moreover, Ben Horin would not bind himself to Joint Forces. As for Solomon, it was sentimentality and nonsense. But for the sake of unity he did not protest.

"Talk," Simon said.

"On behalf . . . on behalf of the German authority, I am authorized to negotiate a settlement of our difficulties."

The pronouncement was made without reaction. Koenig cleared his throat and continued.

"We would like to put the past behind us. Let bygones be bygones. I mean, there is no use dragging out old skeletons in the closet. Let us forget yesterday and talk about tomorrow."

Still no reaction from the six men he faced.

"What we wish to do is complete the resettlement of the ghetto. Now, before you say anything, let me assure you that I came here fully prepared to guarantee excellent working conditions at camps you are free to examine."

Ben Horin swung his leg back and forth from his seat in the window. Rodel glared hatred. Simon and Andrei looked aimlessly at the floor. Only Alex registered some amazement.

Koenig cleared his throat again.

"We are prepared to sign a pact. Our word. A treaty, if you please . . ." He stopped. All six pairs of hard eyes were on him now, registering disdain. He was making no progress whatsoever and he was getting more nervous.

"All right. I ask you, under what conditions will you consider abandoning the ghetto?"

There were no German tricks left, no more cunning or wile or ruses.

"You must consider it," Koenig continued. "Mind you, I am not making threats, but surely you must know that your position is impossible."

Still no reply. Koenig had come to barter, prepared to fall back to a line of retreat to get what he wanted; peaceful liquidation. Their continued silence had left him with no choice but to make the final offer at once.

"You men here represent the leadership of what we estimate to be forty to fifty thousand people. To show you we mean business, we are prepared to pay you a handsome indemnity. Several hundred thousand zlotys. We will deposit it in Swiss francs, American dollars, or however you desire, and we will give you two thousand visas to Sweden. We guarantee safe conduct under Swedish or Swiss auspices. If you wish, you can leave in lots of one hundred and arrange coded messages to assure each other of safe arrivals. Now, gentlemen, what could be fairer than that?"

Koenig's offer was absolutely clear. It was a bribe for freedom. They would allow the leaders and part of the Jewish Forces to escape and, not only that, pay them to escape in exchange for leaving the rest of the survivors undefended and at the mercy of the Germans. Without Joint Jewish Forces there would be no further danger of resistance. The rest would go quietly.

"Don't keep Dr. Koenig waiting, Alex," Simon said. "I'm sure you have an answer for him."

Alexander Brandel stood up face to face with Franz Koenig. He expectorated a large wad of spit which landed on Franz Koenig's nose and dribbled down the German's lips and chin.

"Get out," Simon hissed.

Samson Ben Horin jumped down from the window sill and cocked his pistol. "Let's give the Germans a real answer."

"No," Rabbi Solomon said. "He has entered our house under truce. We are bound to protect him."

"Rabbi! This is Pharaoh! The blood of Jewish slaves is on his

397

hands. His fat pockets bulge with gold from Jewish sweat."

"No, Samson," the rabbi admonished softly. "As elder of this community, I will not permit it."

Samson jammed the barrel against Koenig's temple and snarled. Neither Andrei nor Simon nor Rodel cared to stop him.

"Only one side in this war is the Nazis'. Let this miserable cur crawl out of here with the memory of honorable men engraved on his wretched soul living in fear of the moment the wrath of God will avenge us!" Solomon said.

Simon heaved a sigh and grasped the gun barrel and lowered it from Koenig's temple. "Let him go," he said.

Samson Ben Horin whirled around and smashed the wall with his fist.

"Get out before I change my mind," Simon said to Koenig.

Franz Koenig bolted out of the room, tripped and tumbled from his awkward fat, and crawled halfway down the corridor in a panic to escape. He ran out into the street, waving the white flag.

"Truce! Truce! Truce!"

Simon and Samson and Andrei and Rodel and Alex gathered about the window and watched Koenig stumble over the intersection and out of sight.

"Truce! Truce! Truce!"

Andrei put his hand on Alex's shoulder. "*Nu*, how does it feel to be a man of violence?"

"Not bad, Andrei. Not bad at all."

Chapter Ten

Journal Entry

For the entire month of March the Germans have made a frantic effort to lure Jews into the open. The Gestapo has initiated a "visa" scheme designed to make "foreigners" register at the Polonia Hotel. The unwritten understanding is that Jews in hiding will be given passage to Sweden if they can purchase their freedom.

The Gestapo has gone to extraordinary lengths to make the visa selling appear legitimate. A fake Red Cross unit is at the Polonia to administrate the plan. (Note: Fake Red Cross establishments have been used again and again by the Germans throughout Europe to bait escaped prisoners of war and others in hiding. They also use fake undergrounds with collaborators operating them.)

Apparently they are allowing a few of the visa purchasers to reach Sweden to "prove" to the others that this is the real thing.

We were astonished to learn that David Zemba has put so much credence in the visa scheme that he has come out of hiding and is actually at the Polonia Hotel for the purpose of contacting world Jewry to get money to buy visas. Visas go at from ten to twenty thousand zlotys each.

We are certain it is an over-all scheme to lure us into complete complacency. The leopard does not change his spots. We are even more sure the visa scheme is a fraud and that most of those who register will end up in Treblinka.

Strange that a man with the experience of David Zemba could be duped so easily. I suppose the desperation is so great that people are ready to fool even themselves with a slim hope there may be a thread of truth.

Consistent with the German "peace" offensive, we have not had an overt act against the ghetto in two and a half months. There is still electricity in many areas and tap water is available. Food deliveries continue to the factories, although the factories no longer are productive. Smuggling goes on with comparative ease. Moritz Katz has built a "Quartermaster Corps" with a dozen former smugglers. They have stocked enough food for a two-week supply for the Fighters and our immediate dependents. We store water for drinking purposes as quickly as we can find containers and storage space. (We estimate we have a ten-day supply.)

One thing is certain. The Germans do not wish to fight with us. The ghetto is plastered with "peace" posters urging the people to come out and report for labor. Joint Forces continues to warn of the dangers. We permit no volunteers for deportation.

How long will the Germans continue to tolerate our behavior? It is already the first week in April. We expect the ax to fall at any moment.

ALEXANDER BRANDEL

Dusk, the quiet transition to darkness, brought Deborah Bronski and forty children from the ages of three to ten years through a tunnel beneath Mila 18 to a courtyard near Muranowski Place.

They emerged singly from beneath the earth, gasping deeply to fill their lungs with pure air, and they blinked at the intensity of the dying daylight.

Jewish Fighters on the roof above them crisscrossed back and forth to guard the precious ones from a sudden attack. Sylvia Brandel was the last to emerge. They ran and jumped and rolled around and skipped and clapped hands with the joy of the release from bondage. Soon . . . soon it would be springtime.

In a few moments the children played games that children play in a ghetto. They played the game of "smuggler," hiding an object from the searching "Nazis and Nightingales." They played "escape," weaving in and out of passages of the abandoned house to reach the "Aryan side" past the "Polish Blues." They played

"Jewish Fighters and Germans," peppering each other with imaginary bullets and bombs.

Everyone wanted to be Atlas and Jan and Chess Master and Tolstoy. The girls wanted to be Tanya, like Ana Grinspan, or Rachael Bronski. No one wanted to be Pharaoh or Brunhilde or Nazis or Nightingales or Polish Blues.

"Bang! Bang! I caught you, Jew!"

A little boy tripped and fell in the courtyard and his nose bled. He did not cry although he was in pain, for he was taught not to cry when he was hurt. Nazis and their dogs listened for crying children, to find hiding places.

Deborah hugged the boy and stopped the bleeding. In a moment he darted up the steps to resume the game.

She looked at her watch. In a moment Rachael would be coming. Strange, Deborah thought, that after a time a person would begin to take on the characteristics of a rat or a mole. Living beneath the earth should dim human values. Tragedy should immunize one to pain. Darkness should ease loneliness. It was not that way at all. Her heart ached again and again when the Fighters brought a warped little body to the children's room in Mila 18. A whimpering skeleton salvaged from the cold sidewalk or dark alley or abandoned, shattered room. Deborah cried when it was dark for their wild little eyes and their sharp nails which lashed out like those of frightened animals. She cried at the slow, torturous inability to respond to tenderness.

How she missed Rachael. That loneliness never left her.

And Stephan. The gnawing fear each time he left the bunker with Andrei. How many times can a person die without the nerves dying too?

If only Rachael could stay with her. It was dangerous for the girl to come out of the Franciskanska bunker at night to visit. But Rachael should be with Wolf. There was no room for the children other than at Mila 18.

"Saska Kempa," a Fighter called down from the roof.

"Grochow," a girl's voice called up from the street, answering the password.

Rachael was coming diagonally across the courtyard. Deborah could not distinguish her face from the distance. She wore new knee-length boots and a leather jacket crisscrossed with a pair of bandoliers. Grenades were hooked into the belts, a rifle was slung over her shoulder, and her black hair was knotted up under a worker's cap. In her hand she carried Wolf's guitar. Despite the subterfuge, it was still Rachael. Nothing could keep her from walking like a woman. Nothing could taint her softness.

"Hello, Momma."

"Hello, darling."

They kissed cheeks.

"Where is Stephan?"

"Out with Andrei. Why isn't Wolf with you?"

"He's holding pistol drill at the factory."

"Maybe you shouldn't come out alone at night."

"Momma, I'm a soldier."

Deborah took off her daugher's cap and unpinned her hair and let it fall down on her shoulders. "Don't be a soldier for a while," she said.

Rachael nodded.

"I caught you," cried the voice of a child. "Off to the Umschlag-platz!"

"Such wonderful games they play," Deborah sighed. She sat down with her daughter on the top step and watched the children dart in and out of the courtyard. "You look fine," Deborah said aimlessly.

"You don't, Momma. Are you sick?"

"No. Just that . . . every once in a while this unreality becomes real and you stop working long enough to think. You're in a hole under the ground, and the only way out is death. When I have time to think I become frightened. Just plain frightened."

Rachael patted her mother's hand. "It's strange, Momma, but being with Wolf . . . He has a way about him. I've always the feeling that we will get through."

"That is a good way to feel," Deborah said.

"Yes," Rachael said quickly. "He makes everyone around him feel that way. I can hardly believe it sometimes because he's just like a little boy. He didn't let me go on the Brushmaker's raid, but everyone told me afterward how he was. Calm—like ice. A real leader. I just know we can get through anything together." Rachael stopped short. What was she saying? Speaking of the hope of freedom to her mother, when her mother's position was hopeless. "I'm sorry, Momma . . . I didn't mean . . ."

"No, dear. It's nice to hear a voice filled with hope."

"Tell me about it, Momma."

"With Susan gone, I have no girl friends to talk to. You are my best girl friend now."

"I'm glad."

"Simon and Alex and Andrei are moving heaven and earth to get Chris out of the ghetto. He's the most important man here now. Alex calls him our passport to immortality. One day he will have to run for it. He must go alone, of course. It's killing him, and it's killing me."

Deborah lay her head on her daughter's shoulder and sobbed softly, and Rachael comforted her.

How terrible for Momma to love without hope. Each day a hell of torture and the knowledge of inevitable doom. The inability to combat it, cry out against it. With Wolf there was hope, always hope.

"It's all right, Momma . . . it's all right . . ."

Deborah was wound up like a spring.

"It's all right, Momma . . . it's all right . . . shhh . . . shhh."

"I don't know what's come over me. It's just that being shut in that bunker all day with the children . . . pretending to them . . . making believe everything will be all right. They know I'm an awful liar."

"Tante Rachael!" Moses Brandel cried at discovering the visitor from Franciskanska.

"Tante Rachael is here!"

Children converged toward them from all corners of the building. Deborah dried her eyes. "It's time for us to get back," Deborah said.

They crawled through the tunnel into the Majdanek room. Rachael and Sylvia and Deborah lifted the children into layers of straw bunks and tucked them in. They lay close to the edge, tiny little faces looking to the lone candle on the wooden table near Rachael. Rachael strummed Wolf's guitar, and her thin voice sang about a never-never land of milk and honey.

And soon they fell asleep and Rachael left and Deborah dozed, waiting for Andrei and Stephan to return.

"Deborah."

She blinked her eyes open. Andrei stood over her. She smiled.

"Stephan is asleep in my office," he assured her at once. "Come out into the corridor. I want to tell you something."

From the rooms of the Fighter companies, the voices of singing, joking, storytelling. A beep-beep-beep from the radio. A howl of laughter as Moritz the Nasher slapped the cards of a winning hand of sixty-six on the table.

Andrei and his sister found a quiet place just inside one of the escape tunnels.

"Chris is waiting for you," he said. "Muranowska 24. There's a guard at the other end of the tunnel on the lookout for you."

"Thanks," she whispered.

"Before you go, Gabriela found places for three more children. You'll have to make a selection. It's an excellent place with a childless couple. Woodcutter and his wife."

Make a selection! Deborah hurt at the thought. She felt as though she were at the selection center in the Umschlagplatz. The power to give three children the right to life. How to choose? Three sick ones? Three with the saddest eyes? Three with the most pitiful wails? How do you choose? By seniority as subterraneans?

"Their chances of survival are excellent. Pick strong children," Andrei said.

402

"Very well."

She and Andrei looked at each other and passed thoughts without words. Both of them had the same instantaneous impulse. Send Stephan. No one would blame them or accuse them of favoritism. The boy had more than earned his right to freedom. But Deborah and Andrei were trapped by the very things with which they had infused Stephan. How do you tell your son that dignity and honor are things for other people to die for?

Thoughts which never became words.

Andrei patted his sister's cheek and handed her a flashlight.

"Will Chris be leaving soon?"

"Any day," Andrei answered.

She plunged into the tunnel, inching along with the dim light poking ahead of her through the narrow dirt walls beneath the dead ghetto above. The last twenty yards were on hands and knees.

The Fighter on watch at Muranowska 24 pulled her through the trap door and helped her to her feet. She caught her breath and wiped the perspiration from her cheeks and stretched her back.

"Is there water here?"

He pointed to the storage basins. It was a ghetto and it was war, but Deborah was a woman about to go to her lover and she was going to make herself desirable. She washed the streaks of dirt from her face and brushed her hair and fixed it the way Chris liked it and was extravagant with a drop of a gram of perfume that Gaby had sent in with Andrei. Then she ascended the stairs to find him.

When Chris had first returned to her Deborah was riddled with a feeling of sordidness. She was ashamed she could desire Chris in such a place. Their trysts were in cellars and attics, cold straw, oppressive heat, in hidden tunnels or on floors. In the torn-up bunker at Mila 19, next to rushing sewer waters. Bodies sweaty or shivering and pimpled with cold.

She was ashamed of the sensuous pleasures. The shame never faded, but neither did her desire for those pleasures.

Deborah pushed open the attic door.

Chris watched the lights of Warsaw blink on one by one as darkness swept the city. She slipped beside him quietly and watched them too.

"A zloty for your thoughts," she said.

"My thoughts? They aren't worth a zloty, even with today's inflation."

"Then a kiss for your thoughts?"

Chris smiled a smile that was not a smile. "I've been thinking of man, God, and the universe—all those damned things no one ever really understands."

"That is worth a kiss," she said.

Chris could not be appeased. "Today, in a bunker at Mila 18,

Christopher de Monti of Swiss News listened to two men arguing philosophy over a minute point to which each adamantly clung. They clung to their points, although it will never make a bit of difference. It will never affect the price of tea in China. Alexander Brandel argues for Rabbi Solomon to make a statement in support of Joint Forces as a morale factor for the survivors of the ghetto. Rabbi Solomon quotes the Torah, Midrash, and Mishna opinions that an act of vengeance is a form of suicide which is roundly forbidden. So there you have it, Deborah. Two men in a hole in the ground debating a question that is going to be solved for them anyhow. Frankly, man, God, and the universe give me a large pain."

"My, you *are* in a mood. Here I get all prettied up to make myself alluring and I cannot even seduce a kiss from you."

"Sex should never get in the way of man, God, and the universe. I think right now I'd give up sex forever for a cigarette and a good belt of scotch."

Chris walked away from the window, patting his pockets for cigarettes that were not there. "Why the hell doesn't Andrei bring in a few packs of cigarettes from Gabriela?"

"Some of us have been living this way for quite a few years now," Deborah answered sharply.

Chris sagged to the cot and mumbled that he was sorry.

"What's really bothering you, Chris?"

"Don't you know?"

"Perhaps we'd better talk about it."

"I don't want to." He shook his head slowly. "I just don't want to." They were at a dead end. In a few days Gabriela would find a route for him to take out of the country. Deborah would be left behind. There was no way for her to leave the children or Rachael or Stephan. There was no way for her to take them. He had to go and she had to stay. Simple and absolute.

"I never felt sorry for those poor bastards I preyed upon for my bread and butter. The generals, the admirals, the heads of state. The great doers. Many of them looked upon themselves as pawns of fate. Not me. I said to myself: They deserve everything they get. They really crave this destiny bit. They beg for martyrdom. So, now I feel sorry for them. Look at me, Christopher de Monti, the great white hope of the battered tribes of Israel. I am the voice beyond death which must not be stilled."

"None of us has a choice, Chris. Be grateful you may be able to walk in the sun again."

"Without you . . . Deborah . . . All I want is to come home at the end of a day to you. I'm not made of the sterner stuff of Andrei and Alex and Rabbi Solomon."

"You'll find it when the time comes."

"I cannot reconcile myself to what I have given you, Deborah. Torment. Love in the catacombs. I can't make peace with it."

"Chris, listen to me. When I die——"

"Stop it!"

"When I die, Chris, dying will be very painful. I will want to live because I have known what ecstasy is. If we had never met, there would be no regrets. How lonely and empty it would be never to know giving and receiving love and, yes, all the pain it brings."

Deborah knelt beside him. He lifted her face in his hands and smiled. "And on flows the Vistula," he said.

"For these moments we can make it stand still. You and I have the magic power to transcend the flowing river and the guns and the cries. Right now love . . . they are all far away . . . far away."

Chapter Eleven

Alfred Funk looked down at a blown-up map of the ghetto and rubbed his hands together with childlike glee and anticipation. He lifted a magnifying glass and moved it about, stopping at the displacement of troops, armor, and artillery marked with various colored pins. He changed a pair of pins indicating high-powered searchlight batteries.

He was honored that Berlin was forgiving enough to give him the chance to vindicate himself. This time there would not be failure.

His plan was simple. Every seven meters around the wall he would alternate a "foreign racial watchman" with a Polish Blue policeman. An SS officer would patrol each section of two hundred meters behind the Ukrainians to make certain their weapons could not be purchased by the Jews. The circle of soldiers around the ghetto wall would make a breakthrough impossible and reduce the possibility of a single man sneaking through.

The city engineers as well as army engineers advised him against blowing up the sewers. The huge *Kanal* pipes could cave in parts of the city as well as wreck the drainage to the Vistula. Instead, every manhole leading out of the ghetto would be under watch. Accordions of barbed wire would be dropped down the manholes. This would not impede the flow of sewage but would trap the Jews trying to escape through the sewers. Poison-gas smoke candles would be used both in the sewers and the bunkers inside the ghetto.

With all exits blocked, Funk would then move in the Reinhard Corps, Wehrmacht and Waffen SS with armored pools held in readiness. Most of the forty thousand Jews were in the factory compounds. He would nip these off quickly and get them on the way to Treblinka.

The magnifying glass stopped at a bank of searchlight positions pinned on the map on the Aryan side near Muranowski Place. Master stroke, Funk complimented himself on the night lights. By working two shifts of troops day and night, the Jews would not have a chance to rest or alternate their positions. Once the factory workers were gone, he'd move in the dogs and special sound detectors to flush out the bunkers with dynamite, flame throwers, or poison gas.

Water and electricity would be shut off the same night his troops moved into position.

It was a marvelous, simple, and efficient foolproof plan.

Everything was ready at Treblinka to give "special treatment." The entire process would take three to four days. Five days at the absolute most.

Now, about the Jewish Forces, he thought. He wanted them to open fire first and commit themselves to combat. This way he could clean them out in a few hours. Once they were gone, the liquidation of the rest would be much easier. But would they fire at heavily armed troops? Damn it, no—they'd cower.

If these Jews did open fire it would cost him troops. Ten or twenty casualties. Should he send in Ukrainians the first day and let them take the casualties? No. The honor had to go to the Reinhard Corps! Shame to risk blooding the Elite Corps, but such were the fortunes of war. They would be insulted if they did not enter the ghetto first.

He ran over the map again, replaced his tanks for reserve, and set his artillery in positions to effect better cross fire, then set the magnifying glass and picked up the roster of troops being placed at his disposal.

SS UNITS
  SS staff and officers, Warsaw
  Reinhard Corps, Warsaw
  Special Waffen SS, Trawniki and Poniatow
  SS Panzer Grenadier Battalion
  SS Mobilized Cavalry Battalion
  SS Police Regiment, Lublin
  SS Dog Company, Belzec
  All Gestapo units, Warsaw
WERHMACHT UNITS
  Battalion, Infantry
  Engineer companies, detached
  Flame-throwing companies, detached
  Battalion plus battery, artillery
  Special detachment anti-aircraft searchlight units
  Medical Corps company
LOCAL UNITS
  All companies, Polish Blue Police

All companies, Polish fire brigades
FOREIGN RACIAL GUARDS
   One battalion mixed, Baltic guards
   One battalion, Ukrainian guards

Alfred Funk sighed with contentment. His special brigade of eight thousand men was being assembled rapidly. Those from outside the Warsaw district were en route. It was a nicely rounded force. He muttered his unhappiness at having to expose SS people to the first fire, but . . . no choice . . . simply no choice.

Horst von Epp returned from his regular four-day monthly trip to Krakow with the knowledge that Oberführer Funk had been in Warsaw for three days. The instant he entered Funk's office the Oberführer snapped up from his desk. "Aha!" Funk cried with obvious delight. "Aha! Enter Neville Chamberlain, the great negotiator. The great appeaser!"

"From the tremors of joy in your voice, I should say that you have come on a mission of annihilation."

"Look!" Funk said, proudly pointing to the map. "I am grateful for this chance to vindicate myself." He clasped his hands behind his back snappily and paced with a jaunty step. "The instant I returned from Denmark, Himmler called me in. 'Enough of all this nonsense,' Himmler told me. 'Der Führer commands you to obliterate the Warsaw ghetto immediately. This symbol of Jewry must be wiped off the earth. You, Alfred, have priority on all troops in the General Government Area.' "

Horst von Epp grimaced and swung open the liquor cabinet.

Funk had his knuckles on the desk and bent forward rigidly, his blue eyes alive with vehemence. "You know, Horst, you actually had me fooled for a moment with your silky talk. Negotiate with the Jews, indeed! I was a fool to listen to you. I should have carried out my orders to the letter in January."

One quick jigger of scotch roared down von Epp's throat, and a second followed, and a third was poured. Then he turned and faced Funk and began to laugh ironically. Funk's face quivered as his expression changed from anger to puzzlement.

" 'With reasonable men. I will reason; with humane men I will plead; but to tyrants I will give no quarter . . .' "

"What in the name of hell are you babbling about, Horst?"

"As a good propagandist, I studied the art of another good propagandist. We should all study our predecessors, don't you think?"

"I don't recall the phrase, nor do I see the occasion for your laughter."

"I give you William Lloyd Garrison, master American propagandist."

407

The muscles in Funk's face knotted with anger. "Perhaps it would be more fitting if you quoted Nietzsche."

"Ah yes. That great humanitarian, Friedrich Wilhelm Nietzsche. To enter into a higher civilization, a super-race must ruthlessly destroy the existing inferior civilizations. We must divest, purge, cleanse ourselves of Judeo-Christian perversions in order to achieve this ultimate form of life. Now, how's that for Nietzsche, Alfred?"

"It is men like you, who compromise with sub-human forms of life, who will keep the German people from reaching their goals."

Horst flopped his hands. "Here we go, underestimating the Americans again. A chronic, incurable illness of ours, underestimating Americans." Horst settled opposite Funk's chair, tilting the bottle of scotch once more. "I paraphrase an underestimated American. Reasonable men reason. Compassionate men show mercy. Tyrants destroy. We destroy because we must destroy because we must destroy."

"You are playing dangerous games with this radical thinking, Horst. Take my advice. Change your tune. Berlin is not so happy over some of your attitudes."

"Save it, Alfred. You will need apologists around like me after the Third Reich is crushed to expound the theories of apologetics. What shall I say? Ah yes, there was no one here but us anti-Nazis. What could we do? Orders were orders."

"You speak treason against the Fatherland," Funk said menacingly.

Horst jumped up from his seat and slammed the bottle on the desk. It was the first show of temper Alfred Funk had ever seen him make, and he was clearly startled into silence.

"Damn you!" Horst cried. "I am neither damned fool nor coward enough to keep smiling and pretending and clicking my heels and bowing from the waist in the face of absolute disaster. Say it, Alfred! Germany has lost the war!"

Funk's eyes bulged with disbelief.

"We have lost the war! We have lost the war! We have lost the war!" Horst bellowed.

Funk paled and sat down.

"Now we have the opportunity to soften the blows of defeat if we have the intelligence to recognize defeat and prepare for it carefully. So, what do we do? Step up the murders at Auschwitz. Five thousand more Poles and Slavs a day . . . We respond to the reality of defeat by throwing open the doors for our own destruction."

Funk mopped his brow and smiled weakly. He thought he had better change the subject. Von Epp always tied him in knots when they argued. He was like the devil himself! One lovely day

408

Himmler would tell him to get rid of von Epp. What a pleasure that would be.

Alfred Funk cleared his throat. "One of the things I discussed with Goebbels concerns you. Next week we are to meet in Lublin and design a campaign to minimize the unpleasantness in Poland. We start by understating the numbers of Jews involved in the final solution. Then we deny the special-treatment camps have facilities for other than labor. Bone-crushing machines are being installed in all special-treatment centers to eliminate the evidence. In fact, those given special treatment by firing squads are being exhumed for cremation. Eichmann has full-time staffs at 4B making a duplicate set of records—court trials, epidemics, and such—which can account for a good part of the deaths. In Czechoslovakia, at Theresienstadt, we have established a model camp for Jews and invited the Red Cross to inspect it. . . ."

"Shut up, Alfred! We scratch like dogs to cover dung piles while we proceed to drown ourselves in our own vomit."

Alfred Funk had that queasy feeling in his stomach again. He tested his words carefully. "The world has a short memory."

"I think this time they are not going to forget. Jews have a long memory. They weep for temples lost two thousand years and they repeat old wives' stories of liberations and rituals from the dawn of time. Do you know what an old Jew rabbi told me once when I asked him about Jewish memory?"

"What?"

"The words 'I believe' mean 'I remember.' Even Nietzsche is puzzled over their ability to outlive everyone who has tried to destroy them. I believe . . . I remember. So you see, Alfred, a thousand years from now old Jews will wail in remembrance of the Nazi pharaoh who held them in bondage in Warsaw."

Terrifying thoughts ran through Alfred Funk's mind. Damn Eichmann and his mania for rounding up Jews. Damn Globocnik! Damn Himmler! Damn Hitler! They had all gone too far with this Jewish business. But what could he say? What could he do? He looked at the map on the desk. In a few days his army would be assembled. Perhaps . . . perhaps when he destroyed the last of the Jews he could enter into the higher form of life the Nazis promised. He restored his calm. To hell with Horst von Epp!

"Shall I tell you something, Alfred?" Horst said, bleary from a rapid emptying of the bottle. "You are a man who understands the mathematics of checks and balances. We Germans respect mathematics. The punishment always balances the crime. We have only eighty million Germans. It is not a sufficient number to bear our guilt. To balance the scale, we pass on our sentences to be served by a hundred unborn generations."

Alfred Funk began to shake visibly. Words he dared not speak but thoughts he could not squelch were being hammered at him.

"Our names will be synonymous with the brotherhoods of evil. We shall be scorned and abused with no more and no less an intensity than the scorn and abuse we have heaped upon the Jews."

Alfred Funk pushed away from his desk. He was perspiring badly. He had to take a bath.

Chapter Twelve

Andrei sat in the back row of the small church of a village on the northern fringe of the Lublin Uplands.

Gabriela Rak knelt before the altar, whispering prayers before a crudely hewn image of a bleeding Christ on the crucifix. She stood, lit a candle on the right side of the altar, knelt at the aisle, crossed herself, and retreated back to Andrei just as Father Kornelli entered.

"The children were exhausted," Father Kornelli said. "The two girls fell right to sleep. The boy is waiting for you," he said to Andrei.

"When will they leave?" Gabriela asked.

"In the morning Gajnow and his wife will come and fetch them. It is about ten miles into the forest to their home. Gajnow is a good man. The children will be safe with him. You must of course tell them that they have to learn Catholicism for their own protection."

"I have told the girls," Gabriela said. "They are bright children. They understand."

"I'll talk to the boy now," Andrei said.

"You will find him in my room," Father Kornelli said.

Andrei crossed a dirt courtyard filled with flitting geese and wallowing pigs. He entered the priest's home. The door to the bedroom was ajar. He opened it a bit wider and looked at the two sleeping girls. One child had only a name they had invented for her. She did not know her name when they had found her. The other was a twelve-year-old daughter of one of the members of the Civil Authority. Deborah had been right. Children were children. This one deserved to have the second chance for life. Andrei shut the door and walked down the short hall to the sitting room and entered. A bed had been made on the couch, but his nephew Stephan was still dressed.

"It has been a long day, Stephan," Andrei said. "You should get some sleep."

Stephan looked at him with suspicion.

"Tomorrow you and the girls will be taken on the next stage of your journey."

"What about you, Uncle Andrei?"

"I must be getting back to Warsaw with Gabriela."

"You said I had a mission. What is it?"

"Yes . . . I've come to give you your orders now. Your orders are to survive."

"I don't understand you, Uncle Andrei."

"Stephan, you and the girls will be staying in the forest at the home of a very wonderful old couple."

"Staying?"

"Yes Stephan. I've come to say good-by."

The boy's eyes grew wide with astonishment. "You tricked me!"

"I told you to obey orders without question. That is not trickery."

"You tricked me. You promised me you were taking me on a special mission."

"You have a very special mission."

"No. I won't stay. I'll run away if you don't take me back to Warsaw!"

"This was a decision of your elders, Rabbi Solomon and Alex."

Andrei walked to the boy slowly and put his hand on his shoulder. Stephan twisted away from him abruptly. "You lied to me, Uncle Andrei! I'll get back to Warsaw myself!"

"I overestimated you, Stephan. I thought you were a good soldier. I guess you're still a little boy."

"I am a good soldier! I am as good as any runner in the ghetto!"

Andrei shrugged. "Not really. A good soldier knows how to obey orders even though they may not please him."

"It is not a soldier's assignment to hide in the woods like a coward."

The boy was too clever to fool with games of words. Andrei had no alternative but to give him the hard facts in all their naked cruelty. Perhaps he should have done so earlier.

"Are you man enough to hear the truth? Can you take it, Stephan?"

"I can take it," the boy answered firmly.

"Your momma is going to die. There is no way out for her."

"No!"

"Truth, Stephan. Momma is going to die. She cannot leave those children and she cannot get them out. She is trapped and she is doomed."

"Momma will live!"

"Only if you survive and preserve her memory."

"I'll go back and die with Momma!"

"I said are you man enough to hear the truth? I have not finished."

Stephan's eyes burned with an anger that told his uncle he had

411

the courage to see it through. Andrei pointed for him to sit down on the sofa.

"Your sister and Wolf and I are in an impossible situation. The odds on reaching a star are better than the odds on any of us coming through. Do you think I lied to you when I told you I have a mission? It is the job of your mother and your sister and me to die for the honor of our family. It is your job to live for our honor. I say this with all my soul Stephan. It is you who has the more difficult mission. You must go from this battle to fight your way into Palestine, and you will have to fight again for your freedom."

Stephan looked up at his uncle, who was pleading for a sign of affection. The boy bit his lip hard to hold back the tears, but his eyes still showed anger.

"Stephan, one of us must get through this to show who we were and what we stood for. It is a big job, son! Only the best soldier can do it. You must live for ten thousand children killed in Treblinka and a thousand destroyed writers and rabbis and doctors. It's a hell of a big mission."

Stephan flung his arms around his uncle's waist and buried his head on Andrei's chest, and Andrei patted his head. "I'll try," Stephan wept.

Andrei comforted him and knelt beside him and held his tear-stained cheeks in his hands and winked. "You won't let me down, Stephan . . . I know it."

Andrei removed the large gold ring which had been given to him as a member of the Polish team. "To seal the bargain," he said.

Stephan looked at it in disbelief and tried to slip it on a finger. It was even too large for his thumb.

"Well now, don't worry about that. Once you get out at that woodcutter's cottage and get fresh air and food and exercise, that damned ring will be too small for you. See if I'm not right."

Stephan tried to smother his tears, but he could not. He wept convulsively. "I'll try . . . I'll try . . ."

"Come on now, let's get you undressed. It's been a long trip for any soldier."

Stephan submitted as his uncle unbuttoned his shirt and trousers and lifted him in his arms and carried him to the sofa. He clutched the ring in his fist and buried his head in the pillow.

"Now there are parts of the orders which you will understand as a good soldier whose duty it is to survive. You've got to learn all this Hail Mary business, but it's not so bad as you may think. You know Gabriela has been doing it all her life and she is a fine woman. We Jews have had to pray like that before—during the Inquisition, to fool the Spaniards——"

Andrei stopped short. The pillow was wet with the boy's tears.

"Tell me about Batory."

412

"Batory! Hah! Now there's a horse for you. The blackest, fiercest animal in all of Poland. Only a few weeks ago I took him to England for the Grand National and he ran so fast he split the air and caused it to thunder. Well, sir, those Englishmen . . ."

Father Kornelli and Gabriela waited in the tiny vestry. The priest poured two fingers of kirchwasser. She sipped it with controlled slowness, capturing its warmth.

"I was filled with unpriestly forlorn when the archbishop exiled me to limbo or purgatory or what have you. May the Holy Mother forgive me, but I am quite certain that the Lord won a battle with the archbishop. My little church has become a vital link to the partisans in the forests." He winked with slyness. "There are grenades stored beneath the altar."

"Shame on you, Father."

"Gabriela Rak! I was delighted that I was able to make contact with you. I want to find places for more children. Dozens of them. Gajnow is a good man. I must find others."

Suddenly Gabriela grimaced, paled, and drank the rest of the cherry brandy in a single swallow.

"Is anything wrong?"

"Just a little queasy spell."

"Do you think you should be making such strenuous trips in your condition?"

Gabriela was startled at the sudden unmasking. "I didn't realize I was being so obvious."

"There is nothing in my vows which says I cannot recognize a pregnant woman when I see one. The first month or two is always the worst, I understand."

Gabriela fumbled nervously with the empty glass. He poured her another drink. "I don't want a sermon, Father. I don't seek forgiveness, nor do I confess to sin."

"I am offended that you look upon me as an old fishwife in whom you cannot confide."

"I'm sorry, Father. Yes, I would like to hear my own voice speaking the thoughts I've held locked for so long."

"Having a child under your circumstances is a very difficult task."

"I'm fully aware of the consequences."

"Does Andrei know?"

"Perhaps and perhaps not."

"I don't understand."

"We have had to adapt our lives to each other in a strange way. It's full of unsaid things."

"It is a constant source of amazement," Father Kornelli broke in. "The capacity of the human being to live with tension. The way nerves can be controlled, thoughts and fears locked——"

413

"Not really, Father. Andrei and I know each other's thoughts. A look, a touch, a sigh. A way he avoids my eyes. A way I avoid his. We read each other's fears, though we never speak them. The sound of his breath in the darkness, the touch of his fingers are all silent couriers."

"What a wonderful experience to be able to communicate with another human being that way."

She sighed deeply, unevenly, and sipped the drink once more. "Yes, I suppose he knows that I am carrying his child."

"He should hear it from your lips."

"No, Father. It's all part of silent understanding. Andrei returns to the ghetto now, and he will never leave it again. I accept it. I don't challenge it and I cannot burden him with worry about me."

"You speak against every concept we hold sacred. You cannot live without hope. That is a sin."

Her eyes brimmed with sadness. "I know it and he knows I know. But we have never said it and we never shall. My Andrei is a man so full of pride it would be utterly impossible for him to leave so long as there is a bullet to be fired, and when the last bullet is fired he will fight them with his fists. That's my Andrei, Father."

The priest patted her hand. "My dear. My poor child."

She shook off his sympathy and her own self-pity. "Don't feel sorry for me. I don't think you understand. I'm deliberately having this baby."

His expression betrayed the idea that he was immune to shock.

"I planned this with cold-blooded, meticulous calculation. Each time we part there has always been that gnawing fear that this is the last time. But you even harden to that. Now that the end has really come it is almost anticlimactic. This is the last time. I think he was hoping I'd do this, and I think he's proud of me."

"Do you realize what you're doing?" he cried in panic.

"I must have his life in my body. I cannot let Andrei be destroyed. This is the only way to preserve his life. I regret I cannot bear him a hundred children."

"This is not an act of love. It is an act of vengeance."

"No, Father. It is an act of survival. I will not let Andrei be destroyed!"

He studied the animal fury in her eyes. She was a savage with the most basic of all instincts. And then he was puzzled. Had the absence of a prescribed ritual made their union less pure? Could a man and a woman cherish each other more deeply, sacrifice, give fidelity, truth, with a greater ability and depth because of a prescribed ritual? Had not Andrei and Gabriela behaved in a manner completely sacred to the eyes of God? He did not like these questions of himself.

414

Gabriela stood and turned her back to Father Kornelli as the defiance ebbed from her, and her voice was shaky. "I have one terrible regret. I must leave the Church. Andrei's child must be raised as a Jew."

He was dazed and hurt, but at the same moment of anger there was admiration for the completeness of her giving. He walked to her. "I cannot condone that and I cannot be your priest," he whispered. "But I can be your friend and I want you to know that I will help you."

She nodded and remained rigid, then suddenly spun around and faced him in anguish. "Will I be forgiven?"

"I shall pray for you and your child as I have never prayed before."

Andrei suspected that Gabriela and Father Kornelli would be immersed in a deep and intimate conversation. When he left Stephan he made sufficient noise upon entering the church to alert them of his presence. He entered the vestry chalky-faced.

"How is Stephan?"

"How? His heart is broken."

"What is he doing now?"

"He's trying very hard to be a man, but he's doing what any fourteen-year-old boy would do. He's crying himself to sleep."

"Please know, Andrei, that Gajnow will protect those children. I will personally do everything in my power."

He patted the priest on the shoulder. "I am very grateful, Father."

Father Kornelli changed the tone by opening the curtain to the storage closet for his vestments. He took out a bottle of vodka. "Look! I have been saving this for a special occasion. Take it, Andrei."

"Father . . . I couldn't . . ."

"No. Go on. I want you to have it."

Andrei looked towards Gabriela, who nodded that it was all right.

"You two children look completely done in. Now Count Borslawski's hunting lodge is vacant and at your disposal. Just a mile into the woods. The horse cart is hitched up. You'll find a roaring fire in the fireplace and a meal fit for royalty. Be off! Go on, get out of my sight."

"By God, Father Kornelli," Andrei said, "if there were a few more priests like you around, I'd seriously consider becoming a convert!"

Chapter Thirteen

All week detachments of special troops have been arriving in Warsaw from Globocnik's headquarters in Lublin, the labor camps of Trawniki and Poniatow, and the extermination camps. They are staging in Praga over the river. Oberführer Funk has issued them extra schnapps and promised a mere three to four days' work in liquidating the ghetto. They have named themselves the Death's-Head Brigade after Globocnik's Lublin butchers.

Strange. The two extreme political philosophies in the ghetto have been able to get the closest co-operation on the Aryan side. The Communists and the People's Guard on the left, the Revisionists and ND Brigade on the right are in close alliance. Unfortunately both undergrounds are small and semi-effectual. We can expect no further help from the Home Army.

The ND Brigade is even discussing trying to get the Revisionists out of the ghetto to form a partisan unit. (It would weaken our forces badly if they left, but they are not under our command.)

The Communists have two trucks in hiding in the Targowek suburb. We have heard rumors of Jewish partisan units forming in the Machalin Forest. The Communists have agreed to transport any people we can slip out of the ghetto to the forest.

We have two short-range transmitters. One is at Mila 18 and the other at the Franciskanska bunker. We only transmit messages in case of emergency. We know that German direction finders are trying to get bearings on our bunkers when we transmit, so we must go through the cumbersome business of taking the radios out of the bunkers and moving them from place to place in order to send messages. As a last-ditch measure we have worked out a series of codes with the People's Guard, who stand radio watch on the Aryan side. We transmit on a low frequency which can be received by an ordinary radio. Our code tells them the number of people coming through the sewers and through which manhole. Andrei informs me that Gabriela Rak is in contact with the People's Guard in the hopes she will find places for more children. She stands a radio watch of several hours a day also.

The Germans have dropped barbed wire into the sewers at most of the manholes leading from the ghetto. However, the sewer networks are so vast and tricky, we can bypass the wire. We have also formed a special squad called the "Sewer Rats," whose duty it is to duck beneath the running sewage and cut the barbed wires in the main sewers.

Jules Schlosberg delivered the land mine to my son Wolf. It took

longer than expected to manufacture because Wolf was adamant
about wanting to be able to control the detonation. Wolf reasons
he can get the maximum number of enemy this way. It is fixed to
be discharged by a spark from a hundred and fifty yards' distance.
The mine is a true curiosity; flat and nearly five feet in diameter.
Jules says it has the power of a one-ton bomb, and there are so many
nuts and bolts stacked in it that he calls it the "kasha bowl." I think
Jules likens all of his inventions to food simply because he is hungry;
the pipe grenade is called "long strudel," the nut-and-bolt grenade
"matzo ball," and the fire bottles "borscht soup."

Simon, Andrei, and Wolf argued lengthily over the placement of
the "kasha bowl." Wolf wants to plant it squarely under the Brush-
maker's main gate. He reasons that the Germans are too arrogant
to enter the factory in spread formations and they'd march right in
on top of the mine. Both Andrei and Simon, who are military men,
doubt if the Germans have such a lack of judgment. But Wolf won
out. Under the gate it goes. Wolf is quite stubborn in his own quiet
way—like his mother.

We have not been able to find a safe route for Christopher de
Monti. We cannot take any chances of his being captured. He is fit
to be tied; particularly because he must stay with the "women and
children" in the bunker when the Fighters go to the roofs on alerts.
Simon assures him it is far more difficult to stay than be upstairs.
Simon almost dies with tension during the alerts.

Optimism continues, but my own personal view is that we cannot
hold for a week in light of the power the Germans have massed in
Praga.

ALEXANDER BRANDEL

Oberführer Alfred Funk glowered majestically before the assemblage of officers of his Death's-Head Brigade. The swastika and
the skull and crossbones were in evidence everywhere. With
pointer in hand, he crisply explained the disposition of troops.

"Are there questions?"

Naturally, there were none.

"I read you now a message from Reichsführer Heinrich Himmler."

Everyone leaned forward in anticipation.

" 'This is a page of glory in our history, which has never been
written and is never to be written. We have the moral right, we
have the duty, to our people to destroy the sub-humans who want
to destroy us. Only through the ruthless execution of our duty will
we attain our rightful place as masters of the human race.' " Alfred
Funk breathed deeply, awed by the words. He folded the document and placed it in his breast pocket. "Sturmbannführer Sieghold
Stutze. You will step forward."

417

The Austrian limped crisply to the general and cracked his heels together with vigor.

"To your Reinhard Corps has fallen the great honor of leading the Death's-Head Brigade into the ghetto to initiate its liquidation. Befitting this monumental occasion of the obliteration of the largest European Jewish reservation, I am pleased to notify you that you have been promoted from Sturmbannführer to Obersturmbannführer!"

Stutze was hit with a wave of nausea. Not even for the rank of Obergruppenführer did he wish to enter the ghetto first. For weeks he had been thinking of ways and means to attain a transfer to an extermination camp. He snapped his heels together once more, bowed to Funk, and then drew himself up straighter. "I am honored!"

"Heil Hitler!" barked Funk.

The room stormed to its feet. "Heil Hitler!" they responded.

Moved by the enormity of the moment, several officers burst into a spontaneous singing of the "Horst Wessel" song.

> "Close ranks! Raise the swastika!
> Storm troops, march with calm determination!
> Soon Hitler's flags will fly over all!
> Soon Germany will take its rightful place."

"Hello, Jerusalem. This is Tolstoy at Beersheba."

"Atlas in Jerusalem. What is it, Tolstoy?"

"Water and electricity have been cut off in our sector."

"We have the same report from Haifa. We are awaiting an Angel from Canaan for a full report. Have your Angels give a blue alert."

"*Shalom* and . . . good *yontof*."

"Happy holidays to you too."

Simon set down the phone. Strange, he thought, that Rodel, a Communist and devout atheist, should wish him a "good holiday" for Passover. Simon faced Andrei, Tolek, Alex, and Chris. "Power and water are off in Rodel's area too. He wished us a happy Passover. . . . Tolek, send out the runners. Spread a blue alert."

It became abysmally glum. The last-minute decision to bring in another forty children crammed Mila 18 beyond its capacity. Air circulation sufficient for two hundred twenty persons was inadequate for nearly three hundred packed into the catacomb. The rooms had no place for movement. The corridors were crushed with sweaty bodies, stripped to undergarments, sucking at the oxygen scarcely enough to keep the candles lit.

"Passover," Andrei said sardonically. "The feast of liberation. What a damned joke."

Simon nodded in agreement. "Oh, where is Moses to lead us

418

through the Red Sea and drown Pharaoh's army! The only pillars of fire are the ones that will devour us."

"Well," Andrei said, "we have to have the seder."

Chris shook his head. "You Jews astonish me. In the pits of hell, about to be destroyed, and you mumble rituals to freedom."

"Doesn't one cry out more desperately for freedom when it is taken from him? What better time can there be than tonight to renew faith?" Alexander Brandel said.

"Come now, Alex," Chris prodded. "Andrei, you, Simon . . . most of those out there are not renewing a faith they've ever kept. Rodel, the Communist, wishes you well. What was his synagogue?"

"Yes, Chris, you are right in a way. And it is very strange that we who have not lived like Jews have chosen to die like Jews."

"There is no reason and there is every reason," Simon said. "We only know . . . we must have the seder."

Passover. The night of the seder. The retelling of a story from the ancient Hagada as old as recorded history. The liberation from Pharaoh's bondage.

How Jewish Warsaw would have reverberated with the weeks of unabated excitement before the war! Alex tried to remember the Tlomatskie Synagogue . . . crowds jammed to watch the elite fill the marble temple.

In the homes of the poorest, brass and silver candlesticks shone to a glisten and the white tablecloths and shining dishes dazzled the eye and the kitchens smelled of baking and candies prepared with the very soul of the homemaker.

The tables were fixed with special foods symbolizing the suffering of Moses and the tribes. The diced nuts and bitter herbs for the mortar of Pharaoh's bricks which the Jews laid in bondage.

What the hell kind of bitter vetch could there be for the ghetto in the future, Alex thought! What symbol would there be for sewer water!

Watercress for the coming of spring, and the egg for the symbol of freedom. Well, spring was coming to Warsaw. There was no egg, no watercress. Forty thousand terrified people mumbling ancient prayers, begging of an unhearing God to fill His promises to bring forth . . . to deliver . . . to redeem . . . to take the tribes of Israel. In six hundred bunkers the ritual was repeated in numbed and tear-filled voices while the Polish Blue Police took their positions around the ghetto walls every seven meters.

But . . . the story had to be told. Was it ever to be told with greater futility? Alexander wondered. Still . . . it had to be told.

A tiny bench stood at the junction of the two corridors of Mila 18. They held a pair of candlesticks Moritz Katz had managed to salvage. Substitutes took the place of the prescribed symbolic foods.

Alexander pushed his way past the jam of humanity into Rabbi Solomon's cell.

"We are ready to begin the seder," he said. He helped the old man to his feet. Solomon was no longer able to see except in shadowy outlines, nor was he able to read. But that did not matter. His voice was yet clear and he knew the Hagda by memory. He was led to the bench and seated upon a pillow, for the pillow symbolized the free man who relaxes while he feasts. From rooms Auschwitz, Belzec, Chelmno, Majdanek, Treblinka, and Sobibor, the Fighters and the children pressed to the door in bated breath to hear—Zionists plain and fancy, infants, Communists, Bundists, Orthodox, and smugglers.

One could hear gasping in the silence. The air was putrid and the heat oppressive.

The silver goblet in the center of the bench was called Elijah's cup. When the Prophet who had foretold the second coming of Israel drank from the Passover goblet, the prophecy would be fulfilled. Solomon's ancient hands felt over the bench for the cup. He lifted it and jiggled it. It was empty, for there was no wine.

"Perhaps," he said, "this is a way we are being told that Israel will come again. Perhaps Elijah has come and drunk."

Someone began to sob, but one sob was melted into another. All a shimmering mass of bodies. Another sobbed, and another.

"A learned man walks through a maze searching for rooms marked 'truth.' Bits of the puzzle are given us in our Torah and our Mishna and the Midrash and the Talmud. But how strange that the real clues come to us at a time when we least expect them."

"Momma . . . Momma," a child wept.

Another began praying, and another and another.

The old man's voice cried out again. "Why are we in this place? What is God trying to tell us? Why have I been spared when all my colleagues are gone? Is there a message for us here?"

Alexander Brandel had never heard Rabbi Solomon rant like this. Why? The weeping was becoming universal. People were remembering candlesticks and tables bending beneath the weight of food. People remembered the faces with smiles of tenderness and lullabies. Sister . . . brother . . . lover . . . they remembered. . . .

"Remember the stories of our people!" cried Rabbi Solomon. "Remember Betar and Masada and Arbel and Jerusalem. Remember the Maccabees and Simon Bar Kochba and Bar Giora and Ben Eliezer! No people upon this earth have fought for their freedom harder than we have. Tonight we are on the eve of another fight. Forgive an old man who told you not to use arms, for he realizes now that the truest obedience to God is the opposition to tyranny!"

The bunker was galvanized. Yes! Yes! Alexander trembled. He

has found a great key to all of life—to obey God is to fight the tyrant!

The bony hand lifted Elijah's cup. "Elija has drunk our wine tonight. Israel will come!" He chanted a prayer of the ages, and the bunker trembled.

And then it was silent once more.

"Let us begin the seder," he said. "Let us begin our feast of liberation."

The youngest Fighter in Joint Jewish Forces, an eleven-year-old runner named Benjamin, opened the Hagda to ask the questions.

He asked, "Why is this night different from all other nights of the year?"

And Rabbi Solomon answered firm and unwavering, "This night is different because we celebrate the most important moment in the history of our people. On this night we celebrate their going forth in triumph from slavery into freedom."

The Fighters in the Franciskanska bunker were tired and dreamy. Wolf and a squad of his people had just finished planting the "kasha-bowl" mine in the middle of the Brushmaker's Gate and returned in time to conduct a symbolic seder. After the seder, the not-yet-twenty-year-old commander announced a great treat.

When he had captured the Brushmaker's he had found a case of schnapps in the office of Krebs, the disposed overseer. Wolf had hidden it for just such an occasion. Almost all of the eighty Fighters at Franciskanska had no knowledge of liquor, only passing forays with wine and vodka. It was not long before they were all suffused with a lovely, peaceful glow. Wolf, cross-legged on the earthen floor of the main room, began the song fest, playing his accordion. A squad of Communists attached to his command insisted upon singing Russian folk songs hailing victories of the proletariat. Wolf had to show impartiality to his command. He played for them and what they lacked in numbers, they made up in vigor. The Zionists answered with songs of how the pioneers in Palestine had redeemed eroded land. They played and they sang until they were hoarse, and then they hummed nostalgically. Wolf's accordion was very beaten up and wheezed along with great effort.

The guard changed. Everyone was at peace. The phone rang.

Wolf retreated to his small three-by-six "office." He lifted the receiver. "Haifa. Chess Master speaking."

"This is Atlas at Jerusalem. Is the 'kasha bowl' in place?"

"Yes, sir."

A pause at the end of the line. "Chess Master, the Angel has just returned from Canaan. Blue boys are all around the walls of Jericho. We expect the Rhine Maidens to come at dawn. Change the alert from blue to gray. *Shalom.*"

"Shalom."

Wolf hung up. They were crowded about his office. Eighty pairs of eyes on him. "Runners. Change the alert to gray. Polish Blue Police have the ghetto surrounded. We anticipate the Germans at dawn."

As the runners scampered off to warn the satellite bunkers, the stunned soldiers continued to stare at him. Wolf nonchalantly shrugged, picked up his accordion again, and began to play.

> *"Havenu shalom aleichem!*
> *Havenu shalom aleichem!*
> *Ve-nu ve-nu*
> *Shalom aleichem!"*

And with a snappy hora he got everyone to clap in rhythm and he passed around the last four bottles of the schnapps he had been hoarding. When the shock had passed, they became mellow again and dreamy. Wolf set down the accordion.

"We'd better get some sleep. We want to be wide awake for our house guests."

He walked around the bunker, quietly checking last-minute details, giving looks and smiles of encouragement. In one part of the bunker he had to kneel, for he was too tall to stand straight.

The Fighters were dozing off one by one. Only emergency candles at the exits. It was still. . . . Those awake were at least fighting the battle within them in silence.

Being commander had its small compensations. Wolf had his own private cubbyhole off the main bunker and a sacking curtain over it. It was large enough to contain a table for the phone, a chair, and a bed of straw.

Rachael's rifle was propped against the wall. She unloosened her hair and let it fall. Wolf knelt in the straw, then squirmed his way close to her. With a free hand he snuffed out the candle. They had learned to lie together so tightly so that when either spoke only the other could hear.

"I'm so proud," Rachael said. "You are so brave."

Wolf didn't answer. He felt icy. He crushed even more tightly against her.

"Don't worry, Wolf. You will get us through. Everyone trusts you. . . . Did you see the way they all calmed down after being so frightened?"

Even in their room, privacy was limited. At any instant a messenger could poke a flashlight in. She carefully unbuttoned her blouse enough to draw his head against her breast, and she wrapped him in her arms and soothed him. As a commander, he never showed fear before his Fighters. But now, alone with her, he was cold and he trembled and it was she who was not afraid. Wolf

422

would get up in the morning and lead them to their positions as though he had not a care in the world. Her fingers stroked his hair and his face. . . .

"I'm scared," he said.

"Shhh . . . shhh . . . shhh . . ."

Chapter Fourteen

Five o'clock. The first light of day. The only movement, a snow-fall of feathers cascading from the roofs.

Andrei wiggled up to his forward observation point and through binoculars scanned the intersection. His four companies were well concealed. Less than half of them were armed. Cardinal rule: take guns from the enemy or from a fallen comrade. Distant sounds beyond the wall. Andrei took a borscht fire bomb-bottle from his jacket and shook it to wet the wick. It would be the signal to open fire if the Germans came into his area.

Andrei heard movement behind him. He looked over his shoulder. A figure moved in his direction. Andrei put the binoculars on the figure. "Dammit! What's he doing here?" he muttered as Alexander Brandel, on hands and knees, muffler straggling, crawled toward him.

"Who told you to leave the bunker?" Andrei snorted as Alex came alongside him.

"Since I have become a man of violence, I was certain you would not deny me the pleasure of this moment."

"Get down below."

"Please let me stay, Andrei."

"Write your journal."

"It's up to date."

"Shhh . . . here they come."

"I don't hear anything."

"Well . . . it's too late to send you down. Stay close to me and keep quiet."

Andrei signaled to his people, then strained to hear.

"I don't see them," Alex whispered.

"Shhh . . . shhh."

Clump! Clump! Clump! Clump!

Andrei looked around for a return signal. A blue flag waved in a window on Zamenhof Street. "They're coming down Gensia Street between the factory compounds. I hope Wolf lets them pass."

Clump! Clump! Clump! Clump!

Andrei fixed the binoculars at the intersection of Gensia and

Zamenhof, site of the abandoned Jewish Civil Authority building. The first of the black-helmeted, black-uniformed troops appeared. Stutze was leading them. They would be under the guns of Ana Grinspan's company now. He signaled over the roof to hold fire, guessing they would come up Zamenhof into the central area.

"Halt!" The command broke the silence.

"Daggers ready?" The Nazi knives were unsheathed.

"Parade march!"

Clump, clump, clump, clump, they goose-stepped up Zamenhof Street.

"Look at those arrogant syphilitic whores," Andrei hissed. "All bunched up like a rat pack, goose-stepping. We'll scatter them, eh, Alex?"

Clump! Clump! Clump! Clump!

Andrei handed Alex the binoculars. He pushed his glasses up on his forehead and focused on the black waves of uniforms filling the width of Zamenhof Street, pouring around the corner at them in row after row. Alex felt a knotting of his stomach. He wished he had stayed in the bunker. Andrei was more concerned with the discipline of his troops. So far no one moved or made a sound.

On they came around the corner of Gensia. The line of Nazis stretched for a block, and still they came.

"Sing!"

A thousand hairy hands thrust a thousand daggers skyward. Clump, clump, clump, clump, they goose-stepped.

> "When Jewish blood is squirting from our
> daggers!
> Only then the Fatherland will be free,
> When Jewish corpses rot and putrefy,
> We'll glory in Hitler's victory."

Clump! Clump! Clump! Clump!

Their voices and their boots grew louder, and the marrow of the Jews was chilled.

> "When Jewish blood squirts from our
> daggers!
> It shall make us doubly glad,
> When Jewish skulls are stacked to the sky,
> Good Germans shall not be sad."

"Halt!"

The massed Reinhard Corps stopped at the intersection of Zamenhof and Mila Streets. Sieghold Stutze called his officers together and huddled over a map and discussed the first phase of the operation. They stood directly below Andrei and Alexander.

The Reinhard Corps was in the gun sights of the four companies of Jews awaiting the signal.

Andrei took out a pack of matches. He began to light the bottle but stopped. "I am a sentimentalist, Alex. I believe in historic justice. Have you ever lit one of these bottles?"

"Me? God in heaven, no."

"I hereby commission you to signal the uprising," Andrei said, thrusting the bottle into Alex's hand.

Alex merely stared at it. "Well . . . what do I do?"

"Light the wick and throw the bottle down on the street."

"Light . . . and throw . . ."

"Yes, it's very simple. You're bound to hit one of those syphilitic whores. But hurry, before they disperse."

Alex licked his lips. The challenge was too tempting, the honor too great. "I'll try," he said shakily. He carefully placed the bottle flat and struck a match. The wind blew it out.

He struck another and tried to touch the flame to the wick hurriedly, and the wind blew that one out too.

"Come along, Alex. Men of violence must act deliberately."

Alex struck a third match and sheltered the flame by cupping his hands, but his hands trembled so violently that he could not steady it on the wick.

He gave up. "We all battle in our own ways. I can't do it."

"Try once more," Andrei said.

Alex clenched his teeth, fired with determination, and struck the match. Andrei held his wrists, steadying his hands like a kindly father, and the flame touched the wick. It fizzed.

"Throw it!"

Alex flung it over the edge like a hot rock and it spiraled down to the street.

Whommmmmmm! Plow! Fzzzzzzzztttt!

The bottle smashed on the helmet of an SS man and erupted!

"Yaaaaaaahhhh!" the human torch screamed. The ranks around him split apart and became transfixed on him as he twitched and kicked and rolled in the streets, being consumed by fire. "Yaaaahhhh! Yahhh! Yaaaaaaahhhhhh!"

They all looked up to the roofs simultaneously.

Blam! Blam! Blam! Blam!

Blue flames spurted from hidden rifles and pistols, behind windows, doorways, the roofs.

Wissshhhh! Whoom! blew the fire bombs.

Sieghold Stutze's eyes looked upward as Jewish guns vomited into their midst, spewing three years of pent-up rage. "Hans!" Stutze shrieked. "Look! A woman is firing!" He pitched forward on his face as a bullet tore at his chest. He crawled on his knees. The earth rumbled with deafening shocks of grenades. Nuts and bolts blew apart Sieghold Stutze's stomach. He clutched at his guts spilling into the street. A fire bomb fell at his feet and whisshed up his boots, and he groveled and screamed and gagged and died. Human torches and bullet- and grenade-riddled Germans turned the intersection into a pond of carnage.

Oberführer Alfred Funk soaked luxuriously in a deep warm sudsy tub and sniffed the rising scented steam. The tones of Wagner's *Tannhäuser* "Overture" crashed in from the phonograph in the living room. Between low points in the crescendo Funk could hear the sound of gunfire from the ghetto. He hummed in tune. "Da dam dam dam."

His orderly lay a tray containing his shaving gear on the rim of the tub. Funk sharpened the razor, looking up with disdain at the orderly, who never did it properly. He flicked his thumb over the edge and was satisfied. "Dum de dum dum," he sang, "dum de dum dum dum dum dum . . . de da da da," as he lathered his face.

"Hold the mirror still," he snapped.

"*Ja*, Herr Oberführer."

Horst von Epp appeared in the doorway, bleary-eyed, wearing a dressing gown over his pyjamas. Funk looked contemptuously at him and snorted. "What gets you up at this hour of the morning?"

"You'd better drink this," Horst said, thrusting the glass of schnapps forward.

Funk screwed up his face. "At six o'clock in the morning? Never. Dum de dumm. Da da da." He stretched his skin so the razor could bite off the stiff chin hairs.

Horst took the mirror out of the orderly's hand. "Alfred, put the razor down. You're liable to cut your throat after what I tell you."

Funk merely glowered.

"The Reinhard Corps has been massacred. Your men have been thrown out of the ghetto."

"Damn you, Horst! This is the last of your nonsense I am going to tolerate!" He lifted the razor to resume shaving.

Horst lowered Funk's hand slowly. "We have succeeded very well in drawing their fire. A hundred SS men have been killed. At least that number wounded. Our forces have fled beyond the wall."

Funk blinked in disbelief, then smiled weakly. "There must be a mistake. Those are Jews in there."

"I have prepared a press release that it wasn't Jews but that we discovered gangs of Polish bandits hiding in the ghetto and have gone in to clean them out. The gunfire was not from Jews but from the bandits, et cetera, et cetera, et cetera."

"Jews? Jews threw the Reinhard Corps from the ghetto? Jews?"

"Jews," Von Epp answered.

Funk threw over the tray and slushed to his feet, half slipping.

426

He leaped from the tub and ran into the living room. A bloody, trembling officer stood before him.

"Untersturmführer Dolfuss," he said, snapping his heels before the naked, dripping general.

"Speak, God damn you!"

"We were caught in a terrible cross fire."

"Where?"

The confused lieutenant tried to find Zamenhof and Mila streets on the table map filled with pretty colored pins. Funk's orderly threw a large towel over his master.

"What the good officer is attempting to say, Alfred . . . it was here," Von Epp said.

"So," he snarled. "So. They want the taste of the whip." He lifted the phone. "Get me field headquarters. . . . Hello . . . Oberführer Funk here. Send the tank officer to my suite immediately."

Noon.

Six medium panzer tanks rumbled through the Swientojerska Gate and hugged the wall as they proceeded toward Zamenhof Street and into the central area. Their cannons and machine guns pointed at the buildings.

Their motors set up a din, and their weight caused the streets and the buildings to tremble.

The Fighters of Ana Grinspan's company became frozen with fear at the sight on the street. What could one do with pistols? The panzers passed under the muzzles of ineffective guns and turned into Zamenhof Street.

The gun turrets swung menacingly and aimed at the upper stories of the buildings on both sides of them. Gunners peered through the slits, looking at the lifeless, motionless windows and roofs. Now where was this army of the Jews? Now let them fire!

Andrei tried to think as the tanks rumbled toward his area. If they blasted his people to cover or if his people cowered, the Germans would own the ghetto immediately. But how to stop tanks? For an instant an agonizing thought tantalized him. Perhaps we are cowards. Perhaps all the fight was gone from us after the first ambush.

As the first tank rolled over the intersection of Kupiecka Street a lone figure darted out into the street so quickly that the German gunners could not train their guns on it. The figure ran directly in front of the lead tank.

Andrei watched the single Jewish Fighter attack the panzer. The fighter's cap fell off, revealing a long head of flaming red hair. It was a girl! With the tank almost on top of her, she jammed a pipe grenade into its treads. The tank rolled on the grenade and exploded it. With a resounding shudder the tread unsnapped and lashed from its moorings and the tank spun around, helpless. The redheaded girl was crushed.

Fighters watching on both sides turned the panzers into iron coffins. As from the tops of ravines, they rained down a hailstorm of borscht bottles. The tanks spun crazily, firing wildly at an enemy they could not see, trying to wipe the pricks of fire from their steel skins, but the rain of bottles increased. The tanks became engulfed in flame and turned into infernos. Fighters crept up close to make their hits more certain.

One by one the hatches were thrown open and gagging, blinded, burned Germans stumbled out onto the streets, to be raked by cross fire.

Dusk.

The German corpses were stripped of uniforms and guns and ammunition and stacked at the curbstones as Jewish corpses had once been stacked in the ghetto.

The tanks were silent and smoldering and wrecked.

The streets became quiet again.

Tolek Alterman was the first up from Mila 18. He shouted at the top of his lungs, "The Germans have quit! The Germans have quit! Condition green!"

"Condition green!" a voice echoed.

Hand signals . . . runners flashed from block to block.

"Hello, Haifa. The Germans have quit the ghetto! Condition green!"

"Beersheba! Condition green!"

The cries of joy and whoops bounced from building to building.

A Fighter appeared in the street, running up and down, calling the all-clear.

They poured out of the buildings and threw their arms about each other and skipped and somersaulted and hugged each other and cried and shouted and wept for joy.

In a few moments hora rings were dancing in the middle of the street and civilians cringing from the sounds of battle came up one by one in shock and amazement and kissed the Fighters.

Andrei and the other commanders were tolerant of the breakdown in discipline. Nothing could dim the exultation of those who had waited three years for this moment of triumph.

Gabriela Rak heard the voice of Alexander Brandel on her radio, as did all of Warsaw. "Fellow Poles. Today, April 19, 1943, we have struck a blow for freedom as the first to rebel against Nazi tyranny. By ejecting the Nazi butchers from the ghetto, the Joint Jewish Forces tonight hold the only piece of sovereign Polish territory. In the past we have begged you to join us, and we beg you again. The Germans are murdering Polish citizens at a staggering rate in the gas chambers at Auschwitz. They intend to reduce

Poland to a slave-labor pool by murdering more than half its citizens. No matter what our differences have been, the struggle for survival is mutual. Join us. Help us destroy the tyrant!"

In Warsaw, things were rather gay. For a while there was concern over the noise and shooting from the ghetto, but the newspapers and radio quickly explained that bandit gangs were hiding there and the Germans had begun action to get them out. The Germans confessed to a half dozen or so casualties, but the noise was certainly nothing to get excited about. As for this repeated broadcast from a clandestine radio—well, it was typical Jewish exaggeration and really, who cared, anyhow?

Chapter Fifteen

The weary Fighters of Joint Forces slept deeply with delicious dreams of their victory. It was a victory largely belonging to a single girl who threw herself beneath a tank at the right moment to galvanize them into action, but she had done it and they had won the day. Tomorrow or the tomorrow after they would be asked to do the same as the redheaded girl, but tonight it did not matter. Victory is a balm. Alexander Brandel, a man of violence, celebrated longer and harder than anyone. He said he had two thousand years of defeats to make up for.

While the rabble army slept, their commanders worked far into the night on more practical matters than celebrations. They assessed the day. It had been a good day mostly. Only six of the twenty-two battle groups had been committed to action. Casualties from stray bullets were nominal. They had captured sixty rifles and pistols from fallen German soldiers. They had administered a wicked defeat to the best of Hitler's Elite.

Yet the balance sheet added up to a minus based on one simple fact. Joint Fighters had expended more ammunition than they could replace. There would not be many more victories like today's. It was a war of diminishing returns. A rather sober judgment said they'd shot themselves out of business quickly. The victory broadcast from the ghetto failed to stir the population or the Home Army. A dozen Polish youths tried to get into the ghetto to help but were shot for their effort.

Tomorrow . . . another day. The commanders guessed that the Germans would go for the factories. Here was the largest pool of Jews in the most vulnerable place and most difficult to defend.

Simon shifted two companies under Andrei to help Wolf at Brushmaker's. Ana took her company from the central area and

Tolek brought three groups down to Rodel at the uniform complex.

They argued till dawn. Simon and Andrei demanded that Wolf remove the kasha-bowl land mine. The Germans surely would not dare march through the gates in close formation again after the lesson of the first day. Wolf reckoned differently. He was certain they had not learned or would not admit respect for the Jewish fighting force. Wolf filibustered until it was too late to replant the mine.

The second morning.

Andrei and Wolf lay side by side in a second-story window which looked down at Brushmaker's main gate. The plunger to set off the kasha bowl was at Wolf's hand. He trusted no one else with the mine ignition switch.

Half of Wolf's Fighters crouched inside the main factory buildings behind barricades placed there for the protection of the workers. Their position was vulnerable, for they had to meet a German attack head on. The second half, along with Andrei's two companies, were scattered in a ring around the Brushmaker's in order to hit the Germans from the rear. The gamble was completely upon the guess that the Germans would make a try for Brushmaker's.

Ten o'clock in the morning.

"What's holding them up?" Wolf wondered.

"Confusion. They're making their plans outside this time," Andrei said. "Germans can't improvise too well. They must fix their plan."

Wolf patted the handle of the plunger. "We'll unfix them."

"A waste. They'll never come in through the main gate."

"We'll see."

At eleven o'clock runners reached them with the word that the Germans had concentrated a large force in the Krasinski Gardens. Eden had anticipated properly. The Germans were out to snip off the northeastern corner of the ghetto containing the Brushmaker's complex.

By eleven-fifteen runners reported movements outside the wall along Bonifraterska Street and opposite Muranowska Street. A ring of soldiers on the entire sector.

"Hello, Jerusalem. This is Haifa. Troop concentration to cut off Brushmaker's. They'll be entering at any moment."

"This is Jerusalem. I have two companies ready to move at their backs if you need them."

"Hold them."

The Germans entered the ghetto in three places: the two Swientojerska gates opposite the gardens and at the Przebieg Gate touching Muranowski Place.

They strung out quickly on Nalewki Street from the gardens for

430

two full blocks to Muranowski Place. The Brushmaker's compound was completely cut off. Its eastern boundary was the ghetto wall along Bonifraterska Street.

"They've a positive talent for walking into traps," Andrei said. The Revisionists were also on top and behind the Germans. Andrei dispatched a runner to Ben Horin to hold fire.

Now deployed, the Germans moved toward the main gate. A company down Gensia Street, a company up Walowa set to converge.

Opposite the main gate, the Germans took cover near the buildings. A loudspeaker unit was set up.

"*Juden 'raus!* Jews come out!"

Five minutes passed. There was no movement from inside the factory. Fixed bayonets, battle ready, the Germans edged for the main gate.

"See?" Andrei snorted. "I told you they wouldn't march in."

"Wait."

With caution a squad poked inside the gate. A courtyard of forty meters of open space awaited them before they could reach the main building. They edged into the courtyard unmolested, but squarely in the sights of the barricaded fighters inside.

A second squad of Germans followed into the courtyard. They fired blindly into the main building. Glass shattered, brick chipped away, bullets echoed. No fire was returned. They fired again and again. No return.

A third squad entered and set up a machine gun pointing at the main building, and the other two deployed to give cover to the main German force.

"I'll be goddamned!" Andrei said as he watched a German battalion mass to march in.

The protection squads gave an all-clear signal.

Clump! Clump! Clump! Clump!

Trawniki SS unsheathed their daggers and marched at the gate. The first line passed over the kasha bowl . . . the second . . . the third.

Andrei licked his lips and looked at the ignition plunger. Wolf's hands toyed with it.

"Now . . . now," Andrei said.

"Just a few, few more," Wolf said. "Just . . . a . . . few . . ." His hand thrust the plunger down.

Warsaw bounced from the impact.

Blood and sinew and muscle and shrieks soared skyward. Nuts and bolts erupted like an angry volcano. Disintegrated bits of a hundred Germans floated back to earth. The near living, the half living whimpered with shock, and the neatly deployed living were terrified.

The three German squads in the courtyard were met with a

barrage from the factory, but the land mine had already thrown them into disarray.

From the rooftops Samson Ben Horin's Revisionists—Chayal, Jabotinski, and Trumpeldor—poured a murderous fire at the backs of the Germans stretched out along Nalewki Street.

It was a rout!

Fighters from Andrei's and Wolf's commands tore into the streets at the fleeing enemy with a vengeance. Confused Germans guarding the ghetto gates fired into their own troops pouring out. Other Germans tried to leap the ghetto walls. Their hands were sliced to ribbons on the cemented broken glass, their bodies tangled in the barbed wire.

Wolf's judgment on the planting of the kasha bowl was confirmed.

Chapter Sixteen

Journal Entry

THE THIRD DAY

Today we administered to the Germans their most humiliating defeat of our infant rebellion. I shall describe it.

The Reinhard Corps who survived the first day and Ukrainians, Litts, Latts, and Estonians assembled at their parade ground off 101 Zelazna Street and crossed and marched along the wall along Leszno Street, apparently to enter at the Tlomatskie Gate. Rodel has been anticipating such a move against the uniform factory. The Germans moved in the former "Polish corridor", a slot between two sets of walls. Rodel's Fighters had rounded up twenty ladders. With the Germans singing and marching in the "protected" corridor, they rushed the ladders against the wall, climbed, and pelted pipe grenades down on the Germans. The enemy never even got into the ghetto!

Later in the afternoon Germans poured through four gates behind heavy machine-gun and mortar barages. Our strategy: let them in. Their protective barrage must lift quickly after their troops penetrate. Then we hit them from the rear. All four times we drove them out.

Two events to hearten us! The first Russian bombers passed overhead for an air raid (on Germany, we hoped). We cheered them wildly!

Tonight the Germans admit on the radio broadcasts that the "Polish bandits" have been joined by Jewish gangs (perverts, subhumans, nun rapists, etc., etc.). This admission that they are fighting Jews is bound to have an impact on the people.

THE FOURTH DAY

Our friends arrived at dawn. This time they neither sang nor marched in formation. They moved in dispersed, heavily armed formations. After artillery, mortars, and machine guns drove us to cover, they came in slowly. They crept along in the shadows of the buildings. We no longer suffer from fright. It is they who show fear. We allow them to get deep into the ghetto, and then we hit them with cross fires at intersections, hurl fire bombs and grenades down from the roofs, shout at them in German to confuse them, jump them from the rear.

Today they concentrated on the uniform factory. We estimate they used a thousand troops to seal it off. Rodel's forces harassed them unmercifully, but they managed to get a few hundred workers out. Frantic for a victory, they blew up a hospital near Pawiak Prison. All but the bed patients had long been evacuated.

THE FOURTH NIGHT

Banks of floodlights in tall buildings over the wall lit up large sections of the ghetto. Their troops moved in to continue with a night attack on the uniform factory. Simon and Andrei have spoken of this possibility (night action) for some time. Simon tried our most daring foray. Broken into three groups, our people dressed in German uniforms taken from the factory and trimmed (leather belts, helmets, even decorations) from fallen enemy. Group 1 was led by Andrei, Group 2 by Simon, and Group 3 by Tolek Alterman. Our "Germans" merely marched out of the ghetto. The enemy mistook us. We got them completely off guard. Simon's group attacked the floodlights and artillery. They wrecked twenty floodlights and five cannons. Tolek's group raided the arsenal at SS barracks, captured a machine gun and twenty rifles and several thousand rounds of ammunition (desperately needed).

Group 3, Androfski split into two parts. Part one raided the central market and "confiscated" three trucks loaded with food. The second unit raided the Citadel Hospital for medical supplies.

We know we have reached our high-water mark. We cannot use German uniforms at night again, as they will undoubtedly think of using a password to prevent future occurrences. (Further testimony to their respect for us as a fighting force.) Nevertheless, we can continue to confuse them in the day by sudden attacks, wearing their uniforms.

THE FIFTH DAY

We took inventory. Ammunition is very, very low. Schlosberg has manufactured four more smaller versions of the kasha bowl. We have planted them at key intersections, hoping for the best.

Simon called in all commanders and called for less concentrated

433

fire on the enemy and more "individual improvisation." Translated, this means more acts of individual heroism.

Our Fighters responded today with incredible acts of courage. A tank blew up on one of the planted mines on Nowolipki, but another tank and armored car were stopped literally barehanded. A Fighter from Rodel's command leaped on the tank, threw open the hatch, and hurled a bottle inside! The armored car was stopped by Fighters leaping on it from a second-story window with grenades in their hands.

The Germans sense we are running short of ammunition. They are pressing us harder. Thank God they have not been able to replace the floodlights we destroyed. Tonight the ghetto was dark. Our fighters need sleep desperately.

THE SIXTH DAY

Incredible acts of heroism continue to save the day. Wolf's command reports the following.

Two Fighters without guns leaped on a German squad with knives; killed two, three fled. They took the weapons.

Rachael Bronski was caught by a squad of Germans as she tended a wounded Fighter. She reached inside her skirt and flung a hidden grenade at them.

In the central area, Andrei tells me that his people are making the Germans fight house by house, room by room. We start at the ground floor and make the Germans pursue us up, step by step, to the roof. We hurl bombs and grenades on them and we continue to fight clear up to the roof. The Germans quit. They will not come on the roofs.

From Rodel's command: Saul Sugarman, an old-time Bundist, was badly wounded. He refused to die until he crawled back to his bunker and gave his rifle to his brother.

Simon has called for hit and run only when we are behind the Germans; not to meet them head on. We don't have the ammunition. We should adjust our positions so that we can retreat and lead them into dead ends to use our bombs with the most effect.

The Germans have managed to unearth a few bunkers of civilians. They have been marched out of the ghetto. I hear that Boris Presser and his family were taken to the Umschlagplatz today. Well? What can one say? Has there ever been a doubt of Jewish courage? I suppose we all have wrestled with that. Andrei confided to me that it crossed his mind on the first day when he saw the six tanks come up Zamenhof Street. I hope these past six days answer that question forever. Sacrifice is commonplace. Not a single Fighter has surrendered.

THE SIXTH NIGHT

Still no replacement for the destroyed floodlights. The Germans press in on night patrols to keep us from sleeping. We butchered them.

Our Fighters shout in the darkness and the Germans fire blindly at our voices, revealing their positions and their fear.

A report from the Aryan side tells us that Funk asked for SS volunteers for night patrols and no one volunteered!

The report also says that the Polish people are awed by our fight. To hell with awe! Less awe and more help is what we need.

As I write this I realize that tomorrow begins the seventh day of the rebellion. The four days' work Alfred Funk promised the Death's-Head's Brigade has proved false. This week we have prayed for will come to pass. God! Will we get help?

THE SEVENTH DAY

Simon Eden spoke to his commanders before dawn. We are to drop back to even more desperate tactics. We are to stay in hiding until the German is so close we can smell his breath, count the hairs on his head. Attack by knife, leap on him barehanded, and choke him to death. Fire only at point-blank range. We cannot afford the luxury of missing a single round. We cannot make a bad throw of a single grenade. We must constantly shift our positions at night to alternate bunkers. Finally, a further cut in rations. Water: one glass per day per Fighter.

Today the Germans finally cleaned out the uniform factory. Rodel's people did not have the fire power to stop them. We had managed to take most of the laborers from the Brushmaker's factory into buildings and bunkers.

The bunkers are becoming unbearable. Mila 18 has four hundred people (capacity 220). It is only an iota above suffocation level. The thermometer today read 140 degrees.

THE SEVENTH NIGHT

The Germans have had enough of the ghetto in the dark. We own the night. We are the kings of darkness! They do not come in here out of sheer cowardice and fear. Like college boys making drunken vows, we have fulfilled our "goal" of holding the ghetto for a week. Israel reborn has lived for seven days under fire! Ridiculous, isn't it? We are perilously low on ammunition. Food and water are not going to improve. We cannot replace a fired round of ammunition. We cannot replace a killed fighter. Our wounded die quietly with no complaints about the little aid we can give them. But I am ashamed of my past cynicism. I have never seen morale so high. I have never been so proud to be a Jew. At night we walk tall and straight as free men. We sing and we dance. We tell jokes about our hunger and we laugh about our fear. Strange, so very strange, how a hopeless cause can be the cause of the most exhilarating experience I have ever known (forgive me, Sylvia).

ALEXANDER BRANDEL

Chapter Seventeen

Simon Eden was chagrined. A week was over and his army was still intact and full of fight. Simon, who had dreaded the burden of command, had reacted to a hundred crises without hesitation. When in doubt, he personally led his troops on foray after foray. He had become transformed into a symbol of leadership.

The week's end called for a reappraisal. His Fighters no longer had the luxury of concentrating gunfire. This meant that the Germans could cut off and fine-comb surrounded areas with a determined effort. No longer able to protect the civilians in the southern area, Simon ordered Rodel to abandon a suicidal position and pull his Fighters into the central area.

Wolf was ordered to cut and destroy the phone line between Mila 18 and the Franciskanska bunker despite the fact that runners often needed hours to negotiate a few blocks during the daytime. There was too great a risk of the Germans finding the phone line and using it to lead them into the bunkers.

A new standing order: all Fighters were to scour for food and water during the night in bunkers which the Germans had discovered during the day.

In his favor was his continued night control of the ghetto, plus the fact that the Germans gave up using tanks and armored cars. And Andrei Androfski, his workhorse, his nonpareil warrior. The sight of Andrei nearby never failed to calm him.

Simon worked throughout each night, having developed a remarkable facility to sleep in short snatches. Rodel came to Mila 18, to the first floor, where Simon stayed during the night to escape the heat of the bunker.

Rodel reported that all his Fighters were moved and deployed in the central area.

"Good. Get some sleep," Simon said. "It's four o'clock in the morning."

"I wanted to talk to you about something else. I hear rumors that Samson Ben Horin is taking the Revisionists out of the ghetto."

"That's right," Simon answered. "I'm going to see him now."

"Take me with you."

"Why? You and Ben Horin haven't passed a civil word to each other for five years."

"They've no right to leave!" Rodel roared.

This was what Simon had expected of the hotheaded Communist. No matter how many times a man must come to a decision, there is no immunity to the shock of a new decision. This was the most difficult he had faced the entire week.

"The Revisionists are not obligated to our command," Simon answered softly.

"But they do have a duty."

"What is their duty, Rodel? Glorious death? They've fought well. We've all done what we set out to do. We can no longer protect civilians—you know that."

"But each day we can hold out, our monument grows higher. With the Revisionists here we can buy time. A day . . . two . . ."

Simon did not know how to answer. "I've thought about this moment long and hard. There is a line which we cross when it is no longer our duty to die but to live. Each man has his line set in a different place. I cannot command what a man must choose for himself."

"All right then, but you don't have to help them by approval. Simon, think! You're setting a dangerous precedent. Others may decide to go."

"Yes . . . I know . . ."

The rendezvous with Samson Ben Horin was held at Nalewki 37 in a lantern-lit room. It would be daylight in two hours. Samson's neatly trimmed beard was in straggly disarray, and his hollow features made his weariness more pronounced.

"Did you bring me a map of the sewers?"

Simon spread it on the table. "Do you still plan to try it before dawn?"

"Yes. It shouldn't take more than an hour to reach the Vistula. They'll have a barge waiting for us."

"I don't want to interfere, but you're taking your people right under the heart of Warsaw by staying in the main line. It's dangerous. I seriously suggest that you consider using small cross lines . . . here . . . here . . . here . . ." he said, pointing. "This way you come out a few miles north in Zoliborz."

"We can't change plans now. They'll be waiting for us."

"Delay it for a day. Recontact your people on the outside and set up a safer route."

Samson hemmed and hawed, then sprang from his seat. He had thought of a safer route, but it would cost him twenty-four hours. "It's a greater risk to stay," he said. "We don't think we can hold for another day."

Simon showed no reaction to the shock he felt. "Do you have a compass?"

"Yes."

He penciled in the route. "It's almost perfectly straight. Watch for barbed wire here. Tides won't be too bad. Hold hands, keep conversation down. Be careful with lights."

Samson Ben Horin studied the map for several moments, then folded it and put it in his breast pocket. Simon arose. "I've got to get back to my bunker," he said. "We have a meeting scheduled in ten minutes. Our German friends are bringing up another battalion of artillery."

"Thanks for everything, Simon. Listen, I want you to know. What I mean to say is . . . this is a group decision to leave."

"No explanation is necessary."

"It's not as if we are running away."

"No one has accused you of that."

"Simon, when the ghetto was started we had five hundred people in Warsaw. There are fifty-two of us left. I want you to know that I personally voted to remain. But . . . as their leader, I am obligated to take them out to the forests."

"I figured it was that way."

"Eleven of my people have decided to remain with you. We have also voted to leave you half our guns and eighty per cent of our ammunition. You'll find it all in our bunker."

He extended his hand. Simon shook it. Samson Ben Horin, a rebel among rebels, headed quickly for his bunker.

In ten minutes the forty-one remaining Revisionists were in the main sewer line under Gensia Street. They passed near Wolf's Franciskanska bunker, under the Brushmaker's compound, and they were beneath the wall. Every ten yards Samson flicked on his flashlight for a two-second bearing. A chain, hand to hand, moved silently.

The light found the barbed-wire trap.

Five men with wire cutters bit their pliers into the barrier and worked it apart slowly.

Samson peered at his watch. It was going too slowly. It would be light in fifty minutes. "Hurry," he whispered.

"It's very thick."

"Hurry!"

They grunted as their rusty instruments tried to break the wire. Samson flashed his light again. They were only a third of the way through. He pushed past the wire-cutting team and with his hands squeezed the accordions flat. The barbs tore his flesh in a dozen places, but he batted at the wire until there was a partial clearance. They slugged through. The wire ripped their flesh and their clothing and they were bloodied and in pain.

Overhead, a Polish Blue policeman patrolling the area was drawn to the manhole by foreign sounds. He knelt and lay his ear against the manhole, then darted off to the Citadel gate only a block away, where the Wehrmacht had a camp.

"There are people in the *Kanal*. I'm sure of it. I could hear them grunting."

The last of the Revisionists passed the entanglement. Their bloody legs were washed with sewage. The manhole cover behind them clunked open. A blasting light probed in. German voices! The Revisionists flattened against the slimy side of the bricks, just out of reach of the beams.

"See? Some of the wires have been cut!"

"Get a ladder!"

Samson was dizzy. Simon's warning about going through an arterial flashed through his mind. Trapped in a black fetid coffin. Oh God! He could feel the tremors of fear running up and down the line. Stay? Fight when they come into the sewer after us? Run back to the ghetto? Bolt for the river?

"Let's go, we can't stay here!" He pushed on down Franciskanska Street, slushing as fast as his feet could hold in the slime and muck. Samson wanted to flash his light to study the map and find a small connecting *Kanal*, but there was no time to stop. Two mains converged. Freta Street. Large intersection. We are halfway there. The sewage ran swiftly.

Behind them they could hear the Germans lowering a ladder and they could see a crisscross of lights searching for them.

"We have to change our course," Samson said.

"No."

"Yes, I say. Up Freta Street."

"No. We won't make the river."

"Come on. Up Freta Street!"

"Samson!" someone shrieked at the end of the line. "Samson! Poison gas!"

Samson turned on his flashlight and saw the billows of smoke rolling at them.

There! A built-in iron ladder leading up to the street! Coughing, screaming at the end of the line! Samson climbed the ladder and put his shoulder against the manhole and shoved the lid off. He poked his head out, then squirted onto the street. Two, three, four, five, six seven, they fled after him.

Blinding lights!

Red streaks of tracer bullets from an arc of German machine gunners shot them down. Some scampered back to the sewer and were shot down the hole into the poison gas. And then, after a few more shattering screams as the gas converged from four directions, it was still.

The longest-sought German breakthrough came just before dawn on the eighth day with the destruction of the Revisionists whose attempt to break down a main *Kanal* proved as foolhardy as Simon Eden had feared.

On the eighth day the Germans roared into the ghetto, inspired by the victory. It had a strange reaction on the Jewish Fighters. It brought to them a full and final realization that there was no escape, that the fight would have to be fought to the very end on

439

this ground. The Jews turned savage, hurling themselves into German ranks as living grenades and torches. Cornered, out of ammunition, they fought with rocks and clubs and bare hands.

Each step the Germans took into the central area, they paid more heavily. The Jews were on top of them, behind them, beneath them, and they fought like maniacs.

On the eighth day they drove the Germans out.

The calculated concealment of news of the uprising burst apart. The word rolled over the length and breadth of Poland.

Jews have rebelled in the Warsaw ghetto!

Jews have been holding against onslaught after onslaught for over a week!

Tales of the fanatical Jewish courage dribbled out. The myth of Jewish cowardice was burst.

Berlin was shocked.

Jews fighting, routing the Elite Corps! It was catastrophic, a humiliation as bad a propaganda defeat as Stalingrad was a military defeat.

On the ninth day Funk mounted his most furious assault, using six thousand troops, and at the end of the ninth day he received his officers, who babbled stories of yet another defeat.

"Herr Oberführer, they strike like phantoms!"

"And you strike like cowards," Funk shouted. "You disgrace the SS, the Fatherland. You disgrace our Führer, Adolf Hitler."

Funk threw them all out except Horst von Epp. He loathed the man personally but had to rely on him more and more in the past days. Von Epp could make up the most magnificent excuses.

Funk sat at his desk to write his report. Six hundred Jews had been taken out of the ghetto on this, the ninth day. In all, only eight thousand removed in ten days and most of them from the uniform factory. There were still over thirty thousand of them hidden, and it was getting more difficult to locate them each day. At this rate it could take forever. His promise of four days to liquidate the ghetto was haunting him like a joke—like Göring's promise that no bomb would drop on Germany. He could sense the disdain of the officers. No, they would not dare replace him, for that would be admission that the Jews had defeated the SS.

Horst concentrated heavily on which woman to bring in for a weekend. Alfred Funk wrote his daily report. The report was concise and boasted of progress which had not been made and exaggerated enemy strength and expanded the myth of a large army of Polish bandits helping the Jews. Crisp, dull, military. Copies to Police General Kruger in Krakow, to Globocnik in Lublin, and to Himmler. Ultra-secret.

Horst walked over to him in a turmoil between a redhead and a blonde and lifted the report and scanned it. "Have you ever heard of the Ass of Balaam, Alfred?"

"The what of what?"

"The Ass of Balaam in the Bible."

"Of course not."

"The Ass of Balaam attempts to curse the sons of Israel and ends up praising them. I think the Americans call it a left-handed compliment."

"Must you always talk in riddles?"

"Look at these phrases in your report. You refer to the 'enemy.' Since when do we admit the Jews are a military enemy? And here— 'Jewish disregard for death and the unshakable decision to resist'— why don't you recommend we decorate them with Iron Crosses?"

Funk took the report and tore it in half. "I'll do it over."

"They tell me it's like a nightmare in there," von Epp said.

"I don't understand this at all. Most of these troops have performed well on the eastern front . . . I simply don't understand it." Horst's mind was back on the women. Alfred Funk's was not. "We have to get them off the roofs," he said. "Must get them down on the ground . . ."

The phone rang. Funk answered. He turned sallow and clapped his hand over the mouthpiece. "Himmler calling from Berlin." Alfred Funk lifted his latest reports and read passages, spoke of German devotion and courage, gave assurances. Then he became quiet and listened and listened. His shading turned to crimson and then to gray. He placed the receiver on the hook very, very slowly.

"News of this insurrection has spread all over Europe. Hitler has been in a rage all day."

Horst von Epp's hand clutched his throat unconsciously.

"Damn! Damn!" Funk walked to the window in a violent anger. "Damn their filthy Jew souls!"

He whirled to Horst. His face was a mask of evil. Von Epp was frightened.

"What are you going to do, Alfred?"

"I'll get these filthy animals down from the roof. I shall burn the ghetto to the ground!"

Chapter Eighteen

"Heinkel bombers!" cried the Fighters on the roofs.

The German airplanes swooped in at a height of two hundred feet over the Brushmaker's and slowed their speed. Tons of black bombs fell from their opened wombs on the crush of buildings. They hurled down, tore through the roofs, splattered on the streets, ignited.

The incendiaries smoldered and their groping flames licked

around for fuel. The wood spurted into sudden fire and roared up the stair wells to the roofs.

"The ghetto is burning!"

The Heinkels zoomed in on a second and a third pass. There was nothing to shoot back and deter their "drill" with human targets. Palls of smoke billowed and spiraled heavenward and flames leaped on the roofs, turning them into frying pans. Glass windows exploded and scattered on the streets, and orange-and-red fingers of flame leaped violently through the windows.

A scorched runner spilled into the bunker at Mila 18, holding his blackened hands, and another with wild eyes came in, and another. All of them had the same story.

"We have to abandon the roofs."

The ghetto burned crisply, concisely, and hopelessly, for there was not so much as a single drop of water to stop the conflagration. Fire, a hungry beast, devoured all that would succumb and relentlessly searched for more.

Warsaw's fire brigades surrounded the ghetto with power hoses ready. Orders: keep the flames locked in on the Jews. Occasionally an angry spark would leap the wall and ignite on the Aryan side. These fires beyond the wall were quickly stamped out. Not a single drop of water went into the ghetto.

At the end of the tenth day of the uprising the northern quarter of the ghetto was in flames.

On the tenth night the new artillery battalions went to work. They poured five thousand rounds of artillery fire from the mouths of their cannons over the wall at point-blank range. Debris flew in the wake of the shell fire. Walls that refused to fall to fire were blasted apart.

Blam! Blam! Blam! Blam! bellowed the German guns.

The earth shook and windows rattled and the muzzles flashed lightning and no one slept in Warsaw.

Blam! Blam! Blam! Blam! they reached out at the silhouettes outlined in the fire. Blam! Blam! Blam! Blam! until daylight.

And then the Heinkels came back and showered more coals into the inferno, and the fire raced from house to house, leaped over intersections, block to block. The tightly packed poor Stawki area raged, and the fire raced down Zamenhof, up Niska, along Mila, along Nalewki, devoured the Brushmaker's complex.

Immense belches of violently twisting columns of smoke streamed skyward and turned into yellow-black clouds and blocked the sun and turned day into night. Showers of soot rained down thickly, covering the city with a snowfall of ashes. Everything was an ugly disintegrating gray.

One by one Simon called his groups down from the roof. The very key to their defenses was burned from under them. Fighters

442

whom the Germans had been unable to force down were now driven out by the ever-probing, darting flames.

The wall of fire billowed down Zamenhof and encircled and ate the Civil Authority building and ran down Gensia, once a commercial artery of Warsaw, and the Pawiak Prison erupted like an immense torch.

Easter Sunday!

The mighty organ of the cathedral bellowed a tribute to the resurrection of the Son of God. The confines of the cathedral and of every church in Warsaw were overrun with pious who knelt, crossed, prayed, Hailed Mary, dipped holy water. Choir boys with shiny faces sang out to the glory of the Lord in falsetto voices.

The flames from the ghetto warmed them and caused the pious to perspire profusely, but they pretended no discomfort, for this was a joyous time.

"Hail Mary, full of grace . . . Mother of God . . ."

Gabriela Rak knelt in the last row of the mighty tabernacle. She had wept until she had no more tears. A coughing broke out in the cathedral as a wind shift sent gusts of smoke from the ghetto racing down to the altar.

Gabriela looked up at the bleeding, limp Christ. The archbishop chanted prayers rapidly in Latin.

"Oh my God," Gabriela whispered to herself. "My hatred for these people around me knows no bounds. Help me, God. Help me not to hate them . . . help me not to hate . . . please let my child live. My child must live, but I am afraid because of my hatred. O Jesus . . . how can you do this to your own people?"

Gabriela knelt alone after the cathedral was empty.

It was a bad day for an Easter Sunday. The gardens and the Vistula River and the places where one celebrates the resurrection and the coming of spring were simply unbearable because of the damned fire inside the ghetto. Soot poured down on their clothing, and it was humid and dark. A perfectly wonderful day was being ruined.

"O Jesus, Jesus, Jesus. Why are you making them suffer?" Gabriela moaned. "Help me, help me. Help me not to hate."

In deference to the holy day, the fire brigade poured their water jets over the ghetto wall to keep the Converts' Church from falling to the flames as they reached the southern boundary.

Easter night.

Fires lit the sky from the Converts' Church on the south to Muranowski Place on the north; from the cemetery on the west to the Brushmaker's on the east. All of the ghetto blazed.

Horst von Epp stood transfixed before his window and watched. A naked oil-covered girl lolled on the bed behind him. He was drunk as he had never been drunk. He hung onto the curtain.

443

"Fire is fascinating," the girl observed.

"That is no fire. That is hell. That is hell the way the devil meant it to be!"

"Horst, be a good boy. Close the curtain and come to bed."

"Hell!" He poured a drink sloppily. It ran over the edge of his glass and down his arm. "I salute our thousand-year empire! See it! See it! We shall live in fires like that for a thousand years! We are cursed!"

He turned and looked at the girl wildly. "Cursed, damned . . ." The shadows of the flames crisscrossed her body.

"You frighten me," she whimpered.

"Get out, you slut!"

Inferno! Inferno! Inferno!

Large beams devoured by the fire plunged from the roofs through floors. Choking, gagging, blinded Jews scrambled dazed into the streets and walked in helpless circles. Jews hurled their children from windows and then themselves. Jews were crushed and buried under collapsing walls.

On the thirteenth night of the rebellion the artillery began again to make up for its one-day Easter holiday.

Jews were charred into unrecognizable smoldering corpses.

Jews were roasted in bunkers which were turned into coffins by wind shifts and downdrafts.

Jews were choked to death in clouds of smoke which crushed their lungs.

Jews leaped from their hiding places into the sewers and were boiled to death in bubbling, sizzling waters.

On the fifteenth day the ghetto burned.

On the sixteenth day the ghetto burned.

On the seventeenth day it burned. Pillars of smoke continued to reach for the sky, and for miles in every direction it was black. Undraped skeletons defiantly remained standing.

Searchlights picked out the dissenters and the guns rankled and the walls fell.

Because of the extreme depth of Mila 18, it had been spared direct contact with the fire. But the bunker was a continued scene of the epitome of agony. Heat reached 170 degrees. Naked people collapsed atop each other in exhaustion. The Treblinka room, the central area hospital, was loaded with groaning, charred ruins of human beings. Many were burned beyond recognition. Deborah Bronski and the other nurses had no salve for their wounds and but a drop of water for their parched lips. Day and night they begged to be put to death to escape their misery, but not even a bullet could be spared for that.

And when they died they were taken through the Majdanek

444

room, the children's part of the bunker connected to the sewer. Their bodies were floated out in the sewer to make room for more near death to be brought down from the inferno above.

His voice grew weaker and weaker, but day and night Rabbi Solomon wailed in a stupor the chant "Eli, Eli."

> "My God, my God, why hast Thou forsaken me?"
> In fire and flame our race did they burn,
> With shame our masses brand.
> Yet none turned away from thee,
> Not from Thee, my God, nor Thy Torah. . . .

On the nineteenth day nearly everything that could be burned had burned. Now was a time for smoldering. Iron beams sizzled out their stored-up heat. Pavements could not be walked on. The boiling sewers ran cool again.

And when the sizzling slowed on the twentieth day, the Germans returned to probe the enemy strength, hoping that their work had been complete.

But most of the Fighters lived and throughout their agony begged to see the face of the enemy once more. Rodel and ten of his people moved behind the broken walls, searching out bunkers of Fighters, when the Germans came in.

He hid his men in a rubble pile as a patrol advanced toward him along Lubecka Street.

The Germans moved cautiously, fearfully, hopefully expecting every Jew would be gone.

An officer pointed to his sub-machine gunner to check the rubble pile on his right.

Rodel had a quick decision to make. The Germans had twenty men spread on the street. His people did not have the equipment to attack them. Yet the soldier would surely discover them if he kept coming. Rodel tightened his fat lips and felt his pistol. His eyes became glued to the soldier's weapon. A lovely sub-machine gun, and then he saw the soldier's water canteen.

The German had almost reached Rodel's group.

"Stay under cover," Rodel ordered, and in the same instant leaped out of the rubble.

"Jew!" screamed the startled German in his last word. Rodel's knife slit him in half. He snatched the sub-machine gun, jerked off the ammunition belt, and drew the German patrol away from his own Fighters.

"After him!"

The Waffen SS fired.

Rodel dropped back into the skeleton of a building. Half its walls had fallen away, exposing the stairway up to the top floor, which was still burning. He crouched and let go a burst which

445

scattered them and he began to climb the exposed stairs. Half of the twenty Germans raced in after him, and the second half stayed in the street and fired into the denuded building.

Up one flight, up two. He crouched and shot down on his pursuers.

His own Fighters used that moment to make their escape.

Rodel came to the top floor. The rooms were burning. He retreated to a dead end. Fire lapped all around him. The Germans came up the steps and forced him to break ground with a grenade lobbed at his feet. He reeled back, his machine pistol spewing defiantly. Curses poured from his mouth. The fire caught his shirt and flared up his back. He snarled and moved into his tormentors and fired, and they began retreating down the stairs, awed by his rage.

A human torch spit at them from a landing. His gun went empty. He pulled his pistol out and fired.

A German bullet struck him, two, three. He staggered and crashed out of the building, flaming down to the sidewalk, and his body smashed on the pavement. With broken bones protruding from his body, he kept crawling toward the Germans on the street and firing his pistol.

On the twentieth day the Germans returned with sound detectors, engineers, and dogs. Thirst-crazed Fighters leaped at them with vengeance, but the tide of war had turned unalterably.

While the ghetto burned, Oberführer Funk meticulously planned the block-by-block extermination of what remained of the ghetto. With military efficiency the Germans set up barricades over a block and then took it apart house by house, room by room. They were able to unearth one bunker after another and find people cowering in the rubble. Once a bunker was located, the engineers moved in efficiently and set dynamite charges in them. The blasts were followed up by teams of flame throwers, and finally the last of the "experts" pumped poison gas in.

Manhole covers were thrown open and poison gas filled the sewers. They were flooded to the height of the pipes. Soon the putrid waters were clogged with corpses entangled in the barbed-wire traps.

On the twenty-first and twenty-second days, bunkers fell by the dozens. Still the pesky, arrogant Jewish Fighters continued their attacks. The Germans detested running into the Fighters because it called for a struggle to the death.

By the twenty-third day a hundred fifty bunkers had been methodically located.

A next tactic was tried.

Five-gallon cans of drinking water and freshly baked bread were set out by the Germans at intersections to lure the starved, thirst-crazed survivors into the open. Once a child was captured, he was tortured before his mother to reveal the location of a bunker. The bestial dogs forced their share of confessions.

Fifteen thousand near dead were uncovered and marched to the Umschlagplatz by the end of the twenty-third day.

On the twenty-fourth day the Germans were certain they had won the hardest battles and it was now a downhill fight. During the night Andrei Androfski, whose job was to reorganize the Joint Fighters after each day, pulled together two hundred sixteen fighters and the entire stock of firearms and waited for the enemy. Fighting out of rubble, they audaciously threw the Germans out of the ghetto in a series of ambushes, captured the planted food and water, and crashed through the Gensia Gate into the Aryan side, where they raided a small arsenal and threw the arms over the wall to their waiting comrades. They had captured enough food, ammunition, and water to sustain them for another angry gasp.

Sylvia Brandel was killed in this action, trying to tend to a fallen Fighter.

So great was Oberführer Funk's frustration, he shot one of his officers to death in a rage.

"German patrol overhead."

Mila 18 went into a familiar pattern of silence. Deborah Bronski kept the remaining twenty children quiet. The Fighters did not breathe. The wounded prayed silently, daring not to shriek out their pain.

An hour passed . . . two . . .

The Germans still hovered over them, pressing in to find the elusive headquarters of the Joint Fighters.

On the third hour Rabbi Solomon began to weep prayers. Simon Eden nearly choked him to death to silence him.

Overhead, dogs sniffed up and down Mila Street; sound detectors begged to hear a cough, a cry.

At the end of the third hour the tension became unbearable. Heat added to the stillness. One by one they pitched forward in dead faints. Christopher de Monti yanked Deborah's hair to keep her awake.

And then a cry!

Simon and Andrei and Tolek Alterman pistol-whipped the weepers into silence before a mass outbreak of hysteria.

Fix hours . . . six . . .

The utter collapse as the Germans left the street.

Journal Entry

Tomorrow our battle goes into its twenty-fifth day. I want death to take me. I cannot stand more of it. Till yesterday I managed, but now Sylvia is gone and Moses is close to death. What has he had? What has he had?

447

Our boys and girls still fight fiercely. The enemy cannot claim the ghetto. I will die with pride. There is only one thing I wish now. Christopher de Monti must be taken out of the ghetto. He alone knows where the entire works of the Good Fellowship Club are buried. We cannot risk keeping him here any longer. I have not prayed in synagogue since I have been a boy. I have taken a position of convenience by calling myself an agnostic. I therefore did not have to submit to the hypocrisy of dogma, but on the other hand it spares me from exposing myself by saying I am an atheist and do not believe in God. Yes, a true position of convenience. Now I ask God to prove Himself. I beg him to let Christopher de Monti live so that this history will not die.

ALEXANDER BRANDEL

Chapter Nineteen

Andrei rolled his tongue over his gritty teeth and peered out from behind the rubble pile. Muranowski Place before him was lit up with arc lights. It looked like day. Andrei thought, this night life is killing me. There was no chance of getting into the bunker from the Muranowski entrance. The square had at least two companies of Germans in it. He scratched his beard. Got to remind Simon to trim my beard tomorrow. I looked like hell in the mirror. Come to think of it, I owe Simon a trim too.

Andrei patted the Schmeisser, "Gaby," and sized up the opposition. He had only one clip of twenty bullets and a grenade. Poor Gaby, Andrei said to himself. I can't keep you clean any more. I'm all out of oil. Your pretty little sights are all rusted. Sorry, Gaby, we simply can't take on a hundred of these whores by ourselves.

Well, they're not moving, Gaby, so we'd better move, because I'm tired. I'd love to brush my teeth again before I die.

Each night since the beginning of the rebellion Andrei made a round of the Joint Fighters' positions and reset them with orders for the next day. After the Germans were driven out of the ghetto in the first days the job was not too difficult. He could travel walking upright with runners at his side. During the fires it was nightmarish. Leaping flames, crumbling walls, and those damned artillery shells.

Now the communications between bunkers were all but broken. Two days ago he carried an order from Simon that each group was independent to act and improvise against the conditions in the immediate area. Each commander was responsible for forming his own hit-and-run attacks and, even more urgent, finding the food and ammunition and medical supplies to continue the fight.

Each night Andrei left Mila 18 to regroup the diminishing army. The Germans were getting bolder and bolder. Their night patrols increased. It took Andrei almost all night to find his scattered people, although their area was becoming smaller and smaller. Caution every damned step of the way. The Germans owned the southern end of the ghetto. Now at Muranowski Place they had a foothold in the north. On arterials like Zamenhof and Gensia, they dug in with permanent positions.

Joint Fighters shrank their area. Two bunkers holding half the force formed the extreme boundaries. At one end was Mila 18 and at the other end Wolf Brandel in the Franciskanska bunker.

Between these two bunkers the balance of the Joint Fighters had an interlacing network of a dozen smaller bunkers and two hundred people.

Ana's company pulled back into Franciskanska. Tolek Alterman was sent out of Mila 18 to take over Rodel's command of the small bunkers on the northern fringe.

Tonight Andrei pulled them in tighter again.

A month was coming to an end. It was a miracle, but over half the Joint Fighters were alive and armed. They had captured enough to sustain the rebellion into a second month!

"Filthy whore," Andrei grunted, realizing the Germans had a permanent hold in Muranowski Place. His mind ventured the thought of a hit-and-run attack on them tomorrow night. He was very weary. He slid out of his hiding place and crept over the rubble piles down Nalewki Street through a puzzle of broken walls. He prowled with the deftness of a large cat playing with shadows and sped in his search to find one of Mila 18's six entrances out of sight of the enemy.

The entrance from Muranowski Place was out of the question. The drainage pipe on Nalewki 39 was too close to German activity to try. He went for the third entrance in what had been a courtyard in the rear of a house on Kupiecka Street, which had a tunnel connecting to an air-raid shelter. Andrei peered out from the wreckage at the shelter. It looked clear, then he narrowed his eyes.

Something out there . . .

Andrei's eyes could penetrate the darkness with the sharpness of the large cat he was when he moved in the night. He saw the outlines of German helmets. They were in an emplacement of some kind past the courtyard and they were facing Mila Street with their backs to him.

Andrei calculated the odds. If he ran for the air-raid shelter and its tunnel entrance, there was every chance he would make it without being sighted. But any risk involving German discovery of Mila 18 had to be avoided.

His choice was to move on to the fourth entrance on Zamenhof Street or the sewers. Neither choice appealed. Zamenhof Street would be filled with the enemy, and the sewers were dangerous. He decided to have a closer look at the German emplacement.

Andrei slithered on his belly over the courtyard and crept up behind the enemy. Andrei observed what seemed to be a squad of six men fixed in an emplacement which looked over part of Mila Street from behind a barricade of fallen bricks.

He studied the area around them. On their left, a fallen building. On their right, a partially standing building. Andrei calculated that if he could reach the half-ruined structure he could get over the top of them, but any movement beyond his present position would be detected.

He felt about for a brick and threw it to the left. It skittered over the rubble.

"What was that!"

The Germans turned a machine gun on it.

Rat-a-tat! Rat-a-tat!

Andrei sprinted in the opposite direction. He made a flying belly flop in the ruined structure and began to climb up while the Germans continued to be occupied with the decoy.

"Stop your fire. It is only falling rubble," someone ordered.

"Yes. Don't be so nervous."

The Germans laughed jumpily.

Andrei was above them now. He inched up so he could count helmets. Four . . . five, six. Bastards! Whores! They had set up a machine gun to cover part of Mila Street as a permanent emplacement. Filthy whores! Andrei squinted. Regular army, Wehrmacht. Good, they were less willing to die bravely than the SS. It was a stupid position. What audacity to put up this gun without flanking cover, he thought. Well . . . I shall have to give them a lesson on how to be soldiers. Too bad they shall not be around afterward to benefit. Look at the fools, all clustered up as if they were at a Hitler rally. How lovely.

Andrei unhooked the hand grenade from his belt, placed the handle in his teeth, and with his free hands slipped his clip of ammunition into the machine pistol. Now, Gaby, don't you be a naughty girl and jam on me.

He calculated his moves. I'll have to hit them very fast. Unfortunately my grenade will ruin their machine gun. I must throw at the fat one and go for the three on the right with my machine pistol. Remember, Andrei . . . first I go for their pistols and the privates with the rifles. Then I yank off their ammunition belts, then their water. One, two, three, four; pistols, rifles, ammo, water. He looked back over his shoulder to the air-raid shelter. A twenty-five-yard dash back. Won't have more than a half minute to do the job. Okay . . . ready . . .

He pulled the pin from the grenade, steadied the machine pistol, and counted ... one ... two ... three ... and lobbed the pineapple down on the fat soldier on the left.

Startled shrieks! A flash! Men held ripped faces!

Andrei counted ... one ... two ... three ... four ... while the bits of the grenade spent their wrath, and he leaped.

Straight down, fifteen feet, into the writhing Germans. Gaby spit a blue flame at the three soldiers on the right side of the machine gun, and they were still. The gun jammed before he could turn it on the other three.

One lay groaning under the gun, and a second leaped wounded into Mila Street, screaming, "Jews! Jews! Help! Help!"

The last soldier was knocked against the wall. He crawled to his feet. Andrei pulled the trigger of his weapon. It was jammed. He hit it with his fist, but it was stuck tight. The soldier jerked his pistol out of his holster. Andrei flung his weapon at the helmetless redheaded enemy, and the barrel cracked against his skull and caused him to fire wild. Andrei's fist smashed the German's mouth and shattered his jaw. A kick in the groin, and he sank to his knees, and Andrei brought the flat of his hand on the German's neck and it broke with a loud pop.

He was dead.

The wounded soldier crawled for a pistol. Andrei's boot smashed into his jaw and he too was still. Half a minute gone. Hurry! Pistols, rifles, ammo, water ... Where's that goddamned rifle? Can't find it.

The sounds of boots converging from both ends of Mila Street. Andrei tried to turn the machine gun on them, but the grenade had wrecked it.

He leaped out of the wrecked emplacement and scampered into the air-raid shelter and into the secret entrance to Mila 18.

"Where in the hell have you been!" Simon Eden greeted him with relief and anger.

Andrei shrugged. "It's slow moving up there."

Then Simon saw the guns and belts and water canteens draped over Andrei. "What happened?"

"Nothing much. Just routine." Andrei treated himself to a couple of swallows of water, took enough ammunition to fill three clips, and turned the rest over to Simon, grumbling that he wished he could find some oil to lubricate the Schmeisser.

After seeing Deborah to tell her Rachael was all right, he saw Alex to report that Wolf was fine, then went upstairs with Simon to a small closetlike room which they felt was safe during the night hours, and there they rehashed their diminishing position. Over three hundred Fighters remained, but the circle of bunkers was shrinking. There was enough food and water to hold out for another five or six days. Ammo? One sharp encounter and they would be depleted. What to do when the ammo was gone? Dig deeper and hide? Suicide? No thought of surrender. Attempt escape or fight barehanded.

"Maybe Moritz Katz will come in with ammunition," Simon said, hoping beyond hope.

Andrei yawned. "Moritz will do it if anyone can."

"If he brings in a couple hundred rounds, I want you to make a raid on the Przebieg Gate. There's a field kitchen and some loose arms supplying the troops in Muranowski Place."

Andrei stretched out on the floor. "Przebieg Gate . . . good idea. Holy Mother, I've got to get some sleep. Tomorrow you have to clip my beard. I'm a mess. Wake me up at daybreak."

It seemed to Andrei that he had no more than closed his eyes when he felt a sharp slap across the soles of his boots. He and his machine pistol awoke at the same instant. Simon was over him. His finger slid off the trigger. "What . . . hell . . . Simon . . . it isn't daybreak yet."

Then he rubbed the thick cakes of sleep out of his eyes and saw Alexander Brandel next to Simon. Andrei propped up on an elbow. "What's wrong?"

"Moritz and two of the smugglers got captured very close to the Kupiecka entrance to the bunker. They were taken away alive."

Andrei was fully awake in a second. "We'd better start moving the Fighters to some of Tolek's bunkers."

"Can't," Simon answered. "Mila Street is crawling with Germans. Movement is impossible. We've been lying frozen all night. I'm afraid hysteria is going to break out down there any minute."

"De Monti," Andrei said.

"That's right," Alex answered. "We've got to get Chris moved immediately."

"Have you heard anything from the Ayran side? Any word from Gabriela?"

"No, but we can't wait. The Germans are all but breathing on Mila 18. I want you to take Chris over to Wolf's bunker. We'll try to reach the Aryan side to set up an emergency hiding place for him."

"What time is it?"

"Almost five o'clock."

"It's going to be a tricky business getting him over there in daylight."

"I think we're out of extra chances, Andrei."

Andrei nodded.

"Get him over there and get back here."

Andrei was already on his feet.

Chris and Deborah stood in the tunnel exit through the Auschwitz room which led to Nalewki Street. Farther down the tunnel

Andrei probed about to make certain there were no Germans near the entrance. Chris tucked his pistol into his belt and flicked the flashlight a couple of times and knelt and tightened the rags wrapped around his feet which would assure greater silence in their movements. And then there was nothing left to check and he was forced to search for Deborah's face in the half darkness.

"It's so terribly, terribly strange"—his voice trembled—"how you wait for a moment and dread it. You dread it every living moment of the day and night. Now it is here. Somehow I'm almost glad—it's almost better to bear the agony than live with the tension."

"I've always known," Deborah said, her fingers feeling for his face and tracing the contours of his lips and chin. "I've known you'd be able to do it, Chris."

"Oh God, Deborah . . . help me . . . help me . . ."

"I've always known you'd be able to make the right decision, Chris . . . you must . . ."

Then all she could hear were deep futile sighs. "My anger against them is nearly as great as my love for you. All day and all night I've memorized the places where the journals are buried. I'll be tormented until I can unearth them and hold them up for the world to see. I'll never rest, Deborah . . . it's like a brand seared on my soul."

They felt a closeness of each other and were softly holding each other.

"Thanks for everything," Chris said.

"Thanks for . . . life," she whispered.

They could hear the shuffle of Andrei's rag-covered boots coming toward them and they seized each other desperately. Andrei cleared his throat.

Deborah gasped and spun out of Chris's arms and bit her hand hard. Chris grabbed her from behind and she sagged and writhed to keep from breaking down.

"We have to go," Andrei said sternly.

Chris still held her. "Go," she cried, "please go!"

"Christ!" Chris wailed.

"We have to go," Andrei repeated. He took Chris's arms from Deborah and she plunged out of the tunnel into the Auschwitz room of the bunker. Chris started after her, but Andrei grabbed him and his hold was like a vise.

"Steady, Chris."

Chris collapsed and buried his head in Andrei's chest. "Steady . . . steady," Andrei said as he dragged the grieving man up toward the entrance.

It was turning light outside. They poked their heads out of the drainage pipe in the Nalewki 39 courtyard and sprinted to cover. Around them, fires continued to sizzle. They could hear a rumble of trucks assembling in Muranowski Place.

453

Andrei gestured that they had to move along under cover to the intersection of Nalewki and Gensia, a single block. They were almost completely hidden by the few walls, shell holes, immense rubble piles.

At the intersection they were in for trouble. It was a main cross street which ran parallel to the ruins of the Brushmaker's and was filled with patrols and movement. It would be hell to get across the street without being seen.

Andrei crept along a few feet, signaled Chris to follow, crept another few feet, signaled Chris again.

They inched along for fifty yards. It took two hours.

Clump! Clump! Clump! Clump!

They lay flat as a company of soldiers passed. The boots seemed to be only inches away from them.

A hundred feet north, the Germans had discovered a bunker of civilians. A little emaciated boy and two girls no more than six years old crawled out of a pile of bricks, holding their hands over their heads. They stood trembling under the guns and bayonets of the German soldiers, who were amused with their find. An officer ordered the children to hold their hands higher so he could properly photograph his "prisoners."

Dogs were moved into the area along with sound detectors.

Freeze or go? Andrei did not like his present position. His only cover was out toward Nalewki Street. The Germans were fanning out and would be behind him. He nudged Chris and pointed to a shell hole a few yards away.

Andrei slid up to it cautiously. It was perfect. The bottom was covered with fallen timber, mud, and muck. He plunged down six feet headfirst and Chris made his move in a leap and dive atop him. They squirmed under the charred timbers to cover their bodies. And they lay.

An hour passed. The sounds of activity overhead never faded.

Grrrrrrr! Grrrrrrrr!

They heard a dog's claws padding around, sniffing. Andrei opened an eye just a slit.

A dog crouched on the rim of the shell hole. He could see fangs. The animal sniffed and growled.

"What do you see, Schnitzel?" a soldier said.

"Jews down there, Schnitzel boy? I see nothing."

The soldier unhooked the dog's leash and the animal skittered down to Chris and Andrei.

The animal poked his nose through the boards and sniffed. Chris felt the dog's wet nose against his face. The animal's jaws opened and the teeth pressed close to Chris's throat.

"Schnitzel! Up here, boy!

"Up here I say!"

The dog backed slowly off the buried bodies. The soldier hooked

454

his leash again and knelt and squinted into the shell hole. He called another soldier.

"Schnitzel smells Jews down here. Do you see anything?"

"No ... Wait. Is that a hand?"

"Where?"

"In the mud there."

"Ah yes ... I see it now."

"It looks like they are dead."

"Well, let's make certain. Stand back. I throw a grenade."

... the grenade slowly rolled down the hole.

Andrei lifted his head, snatched the grenade in a lightning motion, and threw it back up.

Blam!

The dog yelped.

"Jews!"

"Move your ass, Chris! Move your ass!"

Chapter Twenty

The Germans were in Mila 18, directly over the bunker, smashing around to find the entrance.

In the dark catacomb the hidden could hear guttural orders being snapped, the clumping of boots, the crash of axes. Simon Eden slipped from the cot to the floor. The cot creaked too much. It could send up a sound. He propped his back against the dirt wall, and his bleary black-ringed eyes went upward in his head. Alex sat against the wall opposite him, bent double with tension, exhaustion, and grief for his wife. The stunted, lily-pale boy Moses Brandel, who had spent most of his life in silence, was silent again.

For five hours the hidden tried to make their breathing soundless and their hearts stop, for surely the detectors would catch a sound of life. Alex raised his head long enough to look at his watch. It was three more hours till darkness.

Oh Lord ... what then? Even when darkness comes they would be locked in this, their tomb, their final coffin. Four hundred lungs gasped for the meager ration of air. Four hundred of the damned—numbed, sweaty, half naked, half dead.

The sixty Fighters who remained still had enough anger in their heart to spoil for the making of a gesture of defiance.

Simon tried to rationalize. It was difficult to do that any more. The sewers were deadly and filled with bloated gassed corpses. There was no door open to them beyond the wall. We are finished, anyhow. Why not take my Fighters up and make a final attack? What would happen to the children and the civilians if we went up? What would happen to them?

Either way, doomsday was at hand. Well, Simon, make the choice, he said to himself. Be baked alive in this catacomb or destroy some of the enemy along with us? So hard to think. So hard. I wish Andrei would get back.

The noise above them stopped. For that instant everyone's heart in the bunker stopped too. They waited ... a moment ... two ... three.

"They're gone," Alex whispered ever so softly. "Do you suppose Chris and Andrei got to Wolf?"

Simon didn't hear Alex. His stomach churned with anger. The instant Andrei returned he would split into two forces. He would take one and Andrei the other, and they would throw every last grenade, fire every last shot in a suicide attack. Goddamn Germans! Dirty bastard animals! Dirty bastard animals!

Deborah Bronski slipped into the cell. They learned to speak and hear the other by barely whispering. "Will I be able to take the children up tonight? They've been lying still for two solid days and nights without speaking. They must have some air . . . some water . . ."

Simon was detached. Alex and Deborah tried to speak to him, but he was in his own fuzzy world of logistics, trying to organize an attack with knives against cannons.

"Simon, don't do it," Alex begged. "Don't do what you're thinking."

"At least we'll die looking at the sky," Simon said.

Oberführer Alfred Funk's field headquarters were in the Citadel, a few blocks from the northern gates of the ghetto. His goading obsession for several days had been focused on a blown-up sectional map of the central area filled with markings where sounds had been detected along Mila Street. Trails of underground sounds indicating tunnels, all in the proximity of the middle of the block. He knew it led to the Jews' main bunker. Two entrances had been located. One in an air-raid shelter on Kupiecka Street, the other in a house on Muranowski Place. But he could not attack yet, for there were certain to be three or four more entrances and the Jews could either escape or hide in the other exits.

A large black grease-pencil mark was drawn around the houses from Mila 16 to Mila 22.

Funk walked to the second-story window and looked out at his handiwork. Most of the ghetto had been leveled. Engineers were systematically dynamiting the standing buildings one by one to flush out those Jews who had hidden themselves in sub-floors. It had gone well in the last few days. Since the final action more than twenty thousand Jews had been taken to the Umschlagplatz and another five thousand were known dead. How many were burned or gassed? Impossible to tell, but the total indicated that victory over the invisible army of the Jews was at hand. He could not foolishly declare victory until the Mila Street bunker had been found.

Funk was desperate to find it quickly, for soon the rebellion would be in its second month and that would look very, very bad. Polish Home Army activity had been spurred by the Jewish rebellion, and unrest among the occupied countries could be felt as a direct result. He simply had to finish it off before it went over a month's duration.

A knock on the door.

"Enter."

An eager young Waffen SS officer from Trawniki entered, snapped his heels together, unable to contain his joy. "Heil Hitler!" Untersturmführer Manfred Plank crackled.

"Heil Hitler," Funk grunted.

"Herr Oberführer! We are certain we have located another entrance to the main Jew bunker!"

"*Ja?*"

"*Jawohl!*"

Funk showed the man the map. The young officer snapped off his cap and tucked it under his left arm, and his right forefinger shot out and pointed to the location of Nalewki 39. "Here we have discovered a drainage pipe. It runs in this direction . . . so. Along with the tunnel on Muranowski Place and the tunnel on Kupiecka Street, it converges on the same location . . . here . . ."

"Mila 18."

"We may also have found the location in Mila 18 itself. A large removable oven on the first floor of the building which still stands is extremely suspicious. We did not wish to take action until we received your personal orders."

Funk rubbed his hands together eagerly. "Four possible entrances. Good."

In a few moments Oberführer Alfred Funk emboldened his troops by another of his personal appearances in the ghetto. Surrounded by two squads of sub-machine-gun-bearing Nazi guards, he marched alongside the exuberant Untersturmführer Plank until they came to a place which had once been a building, now a rubble heap. Manfred Plank showed where the drainage pipe had been uncovered.

"We sent a man twenty meters deep into it. It becomes a tunnel at that point and turns sharply toward Mila 18."

Funk looked at his watch. Two and a half hours of daylight left.

A staff car at the Przebieg Gate whisked him across town to Shucha Street and Gestapo House. Gunther Sauer was in a foul mood. His dog Fritzie had developed a cataract and was going blind. Moreover, his wife wrote complaining letters about the shortages of butter and meat developing at home.

457

Now Funk. These SS people were impossible. Himmler's saving grace was his love for animals. Poor Himmler couldn't bear to see a hurt dog. It was confided to him at one of the gassings at Treblinka that he had attended with Himmler. Himmler despised Göring, who was cruel to animals.

Sauer gave Fritzie an affectionate pat on the head and looked up to Alfred Funk in his grandfatherly way.

"I want to see the three Jews from the bunker. The Moritz Katz man and the others."

"So?"

"We have located three entrances to their precious bunker. Faced with these facts, perhaps they will talk."

Sauer reached in the drawer and gave the dog a tidbit. "Can't see them," he said.

"And why not?"

"They're dead. Tried to break them down. Turned them over to the dogs last night. There, Fritzie . . . good boy . . . good boy."

"Simon, come quickly."

He pushed down the dark corridor. Alex opened the curtain to Rabbi Solomon's cell. The last doctor left in the ghetto knelt over the old man's prostrate body. The rabbi presented little more than a weightless bag of bones. His eyes were opened like a defiant Elijah doing combat with the wicked priests of Jezebel. His bony fingers clutched Torah scrolls.

Simon lifted his body and placed it on the cot and closed Rabbi Solomon's eyes, and he looked inquiringly at the doctor.

"Don't ask me why he died. Old age, lack of air . . . grief . . . who knows?"

"Last night he told me he would die today," Alex said.

"And what did he say?" Simon snapped. "To fight tyrants is to honor God?"

"No . . . in fact, he said he wished he were like King David with a young wench to warm his bed."

Simon spun around and into the corridor. "Fighters up!" he called. "We're moving up for an attack!"

"Fighters up!"

"Fighters up!"

A hideous shriek came from the arsenal in the Chelmno room simultaneously with an explosion of the stored munitions.

Jules Schlosberg's body was hurled into the corridor.

"Germans!"

Simon plunged over the bodies of confused, frantic civilians into the turn of the corridor. The bunker was in a dark panic. He smashed his way into the Belzec room, where half of the Fighters were housed. A blinding light probed through the secret entrance from the tunnel up to Kupiecka Street.

"Germans!"

"*Juden 'raus!*" a voice commanded from the other end of the tunnel.

Simon dived over the corridor to the Auschwitz room. Another light penetrated from the tunnel at Muranowski Place.

Mass screaming and wailing and praying and crushing broke loose among the scrambling, aimless ants who battered forth from the tunnels. Simon and the Fighters used pistols and clubs on them to force them back and into silence. He was crushed against a wall. A dozen broke out in the Auschwitz room up the tunnel.

"We surrender," they cried.

Rat-a-tat! The German machine gun blasted them down.

Simon kicked his way clear and drove into the Majdanek room, where a dozen of his Fighters already blocked the room to keep the children from getting trampled.

Simon handed his flashlight to Deborah and pulled the bricks away which led into the sewer. He poked his head through and flashed the light up and down. There were no Germans, but billows of poison gas floated in from both directions.

With Alex and a dozen Fighters forming a chain across the *Kanal* to Mila 19, Simon and Deborah passed the children out of the room one by one to the old bunker across the *Kanal*. Some of them were swept up by the rushing sewer waters. Others doubled over, gagged and blinded, as the cloud of gas enveloped them.

Outside Majdanek, frantic people tried to batter past the bayonets of the Fighters to get to the dubious safety of the death-filled sewers.

"Hold your breath, children! Duck under the water! Keep your eyes closed!"

German machine gunners at the head of the entrances shot down the panicked civilians, and then poison gas and lashes of fire from flame throwers ate up what little oxygen was left in Mila 18 and the bunker became a huge gas chamber filled with a screaming, frantic doomed mass.

Chapter Twenty-one

Chris and Andrei froze for the rest of the day in the second floor of a gutted structure from which they could watch the Germans methodically move over the area inch by inch, dragging the dregs of humanity from beneath the ground. The Germans were finding bunkers quickly now. Thirst-maddened people who had to live in silence for days on end broke.

Often at dusk there was a respite as the Germans pulled their forces off the streets and out of the ghetto to give it a working over with artillery, picking out for target practice the diminishing numbers of skeletons of buildings.

Andrei used this lull to make the final lunge for the Franciskanska bunker. Andrei always looked forward to seeing Wolf, for there was always an air of frivolity, jokes, songs, poems.

Not this night.

When Chris and Andrei arrived, Wolf and Rachael and Ana were sprawled glassy-eyed on the floor of the big room. Andrei looked around. There were only twenty-odd Fighters present. Everyone seemed only half conscious. There was no greeting for them. There had been no guard at the bunker entrance.

Wolf's head hung between bunched-up knees, and Rachael lay on the floor beside him, her face in his lap. Ana looked up for an instant and half recognized Andrei and sagged again.

"What happened?" Andrei demanded.

No one answered.

Andrei turned to Ana. He didn't like looking at her these days. All the tall fine hard round woman that had once been Ana was gone. She was wasted.

"Ana! What happened!"

Ana sniffled and mumbled incoherently.

"Momma . . . Daddy . . . Momma . . . Daddy . . ." wailed a woman Fighter. "Momma, I'll be with you soon."

Andrei turned abruptly in all directions. Living dead.

He reached down and jerked Wolf Brandel to his feet. Wolf slumped at the end of Andrei's arms like a rag doll. Andrei shook him. Wolf blinked his eyes.

"Fool's gambit," he mumbled. "Fool's gambit . . . fool's gambit."

Andrei's hands let Wolf go, and Wolf fell to the ground again and he lolled on the floor, smacking his lips for water. Rachael groveled for her canteen, turned it over. It was empty. Wolf pulled Rachael to him and propped his back against the wall and looked up at Andrei.

"What the hell do you want?" Wolf said. "The canteen is empty. We have no ammunition left." His hand flopped and hit the accordion beside him. "Even this thing won't work any more."

"Get on your feet, you son of a bitch," Andrei bellowed in a tone that shook the bunker. "Get on your feet! You're a commander of the Jewish Fighters!"

Wolf Brandel was shocked back to life. He dragged himself up and hung laboriously before Andrei Androfski, swaying back and forth . . . back and forth.

"Now, what happened?"

Wolf licked his lips. "Germans . . . got close to the bunker . . . we all came up. We were committed to fire by a fool who opened up on them. In ten minutes we were out of ammunition . . . not a

460

thing left . . . so we started throwing stones! Know how well stones stop the German army! Know that, Andrei! Stones! Stones!" Wolf caught his breath and puffed to fill his lungs with air. "They hit us with mortars and flame throwers. I watched . . . I watched while they turned my soldiers into torches and I threw stones at them . . ."

"Leave him alone, for Christ sake," Christopher de Monti demanded.

Andrei kept at Wolf. "Is this what is left?"

Wolf blinked like a drunkard and looked at his people. Last night seventy-four of them had sat in the bunker and laughed about wanting to take a bath and how the twenty girls could hardly service the men and if only the men had money what fortunes could be made! And they sang about the Galilee until the accordion broke.

Only a few scraggly scarecrows left . . .

"Stop it!" Ana screamed. "Stop it, Andrei!"

Andrei lifted her up and slapped her across the face with a sound that struck everyone in the bunker.

"Stand up, damn you all!" he bellowed unrelentingly. "Stand up, you bastards."

One by one they struggled to their feet.

"Now hear me. So long as your lungs breathe, you fight. We move back to Mila 18 and we find weapons."

Christopher de Monti was paralyzed by Andrei's wrath. Yes, Andrei had the mystic power to take this punch-drunk crowd for yet one more attack.

"Ssshhh . . . someone is coming!"

Silence.

Tolek staggered into the bunkers. His long hair was caked with innumerable layers of dirt and muck. He looked like a wild hairy ape from another age. His clothing was torn and his head was bloodied from the reopening of an old wound. He wavered to Andrei and jerked his head towards the commander's cell.

Andrei and Tolek were alone in Wolf's room.

"They've got Mila 18," Tolek said.

"Are you sure?"

"Yes. I am sure."

Simon! Deborah! Rabbi Solomon! Alex! Andrei covered his face in his hands and bit his lip so hard that blood poured from it and he shook so hard that Tolek grabbed his hair and wrenched it. "Hold on, Andrei . . . hold on . . ."

And then things became very, very clear.

"How many Fighters do you have left, Tolek?" he asked softly.

"A hundred thirty-two."

"There must be twenty or thirty more on the southern boundary," Andrei said quickly, his mind calculating and making

461

decision upon decision. He fished around the table top for Wolf's duplicate map of the sewer system. He marked in a routing. . . .

"I'm going back to Mila 18," he said. "You stay here. At four o'clock I will have rounded up your people and any survivors around Mila 18. We are going to make a diversionary attack on the western side of the ghetto to draw the Germans away long enough for you to take to the sewers. There is only one thing important now. Christopher de Monti must be saved."

"I'll go with you to Mila 18," Tolek said. "Wolf will take them through the sewers."

"We've got no time for this nonsense. You'll take them through the sewers!"

Tolek clenched his teeth and nodded in obedience.

"At four o'clock when we make our attack you will break radio silence and send a message to the Aryan side that you will be coming out at Prosta Street."

Tolek's eyes narrowed.

"Prosta Street! But . . . through this course it is over five miles through small connecting pipes! It's impossible. It will take six or seven hours!"

"Every damned fool who tries the sewers obliges the Germans by walking down main lines. These small laterals are your only chance."

"The Vistula is running high. We'll have to go on our hands and knees in the small pipes. We'll drown."

Andrei punched Tolek on the shoulder. "You'll make it, Tolek. Living Zionism, you know."

Tolek took the map from Andrei. "I'll try."

Andrei stepped out to the main room. He collected the half dozen bulletless guns and pistols and strapped them on his back and tucked them into his waist.

"Well," he said, "you go to the sewers at four o'clock. Tolek and Wolf will take you through a new route. Have a good trip. See you next year in Jerusalem."

Wolf and Chris and Rachael stood at the ladder leading out of the Franciskanska bunker, blocking Andrei's way.

"We heard," Chris said. "Mila 18 has been attacked. We're going back with you."

"Uh-uh," Andrei answered.

"Don't try to stop us," Chris threatened.

In a single motion Andrei jerked Chris's pistol from his belt and knocked Wolf Brandel flat on his back and shoved his niece sprawling.

"Tolek!" he said, flipping the pistol to him. "If either of these two move, use the pistol. You have my orders to put one through Wolf's brain. As for Chris, just wing him—but not too seriously, or else he will be a horrible burden dragging through the sewers."

462

Chris made an angry pass at Andrei, but Tolek was between them and the cocked pistol was leveled on him. There was no doubt in Chris's mind that Tolek would follow Andrei's orders. He snarled, then backed off.

"Chris . . ." Andrei said softly. "Don't forget where those journals are buried . . . will you?"

"I won't forget," Chris answered hoarsely. "I won't forget."

Andrei took two steps up the ladder.

"Uncle Andrei!" Rachael cried.

He stepped down for an instant, and she flung her arms around him and wept.

"It is good," Andrei said, "that even in this place we still have tears left for each other and broken hearts. It is good that we are still human. Rachael . . . you will go from this place and become a fine woman."

"Good-by, Uncle Andrei."

Outside, Andrei wrapped the rags on his feet tightly and began darting over the rubble, playing cat-and-mouse with the crisscrossing searchlights, flopping flat ahead of the hurling bombs. A few things left that would burn seared and sizzled. A wall tottered behind him and crashed, sending flying debris about his head. He groped and stumbled and fell and ran in the holocaust.

In an hour he reached Mila 18.

The Germans were gone. As always, they left a bunker after they had poured gas and gunfire and bullets into it, returning in two or three days to send in their dogs before they dared enter themselves. Andrei climbed down the main entrance from the demolished Mila 18. The poison gas had spent its fury.

He was in the small corridor lined with tiny cells. He was standing on a mass of entwined corpses. His flashlight played over them. He pushed into the commander's cell. It was empty. He found Rabbi Solomon in his cell, still and stretched on his cot, a Torah in his waxy hands.

Andrei stepped over the bodies into the main corridor. The Chelmno room with its ammunition stores was a sight of devastation. Bodies were charred, unrecognizable from the explosions of the bottle bombs.

Wait!

Coughs!

Weak . . . weak coughs!

Sounds of gagging and gasping from the Majdanek room.

Andrei plunged over the bodies.

"Simon! Deborah! Alex!" his lone voice called in the dark.

His light sped frantically over the bodies in Majdanek. Two or three of them were breathing with the desperation of fish out of water.

"Simon!"

463

Andrei rolled over the body of his commander. Simon Eden was dead. And then the light fell on the lifeless face of Alexander Brandel holding his infant Moses against his chest.

He turned the corpses over one by one. Fighters who had tried to hold back the civilians. Children . . . children . . . children . . . and the light poked at the bricks removed to the sewer.

"Deborah!"

He knelt behind the body of his sister, who hung half in, half out of the room, stricken down while passing a child through the sewer to the safety of Mila 19. As he touched her she gasped. There was yet life!

"Deborah!"

"Don't . . . don't . . ."

"Deborah . . . you're alive!"

"Don't . . . look at me . . . I am blind."

"Oh God! Deborah . . . oh, my sister . . . oh, my sister . ."

He lifted her in his arms and found a corner and held her and rocked her back and forth and kissed her cheeks.

She coughed and gagged in terrible pain. "Some children are alive in Mila 19," she rasped.

"Ssshhhh . . . don't talk . . . don't talk."

"Chris . . . Rachael . . . Wolf . . ."

"Yes, darling . . . yes. They have escaped. They are safe."

She made a sound of relief and groaned as the sharpness of the gas jabbed her lungs.

"Andrei . . . pain . . . children in pain. Kill them . . . put them out of their misery . . ."

"Deborah! Deborah! Deborah!"

"So good . . . you holding . . . me . . . Andrei . . . I lost my pill . . . please . . . give . . . me . . . one."

Andrei reached in his breast pocket and took a small cyanide capsule and put it against his sister's parched lips.

"So good . . . you holding me . . . I was afraid I'd be alone. Andrei . . . sing Momma's song . . . when we were children . . ."

"What is the best Sehora?
My baby . . . will . . . learn the Torah. . . ."

Chapter Twenty-two

Gabriela bolted upright in bed, her heart pounding unmercifully. A dream of a chill wind passing through the room was unfounded. She perspired from the clarity of the nightmare. Andrei was a ghost floating over the smoldering rubble of the ghetto. She rolled to one side and squinted to read the luminous dial of the bedside clock. Three forty-five.

She flicked on the radio automatically, as she always did during the waking hours. Perhaps there would be a radio signal from the ghetto transmitter today. There had been none for twenty-six days, since the last time they fetched four children out of the sewers and took them to Father Kornelli. Twenty-six days of silence.

She slipped into a dressing gown and walked out to the fifth-story balcony. Far from the dream of cold, it was warmish out, fighting its way into late spring. Moonlight threw light on the ghetto. She watched for ever so long, just as she had stood and watched for hour after hour during the day. She had taken the new apartment because of its view of the ghetto.

The artillery fire had stopped. Almost nothing remained standing. The moonbeams played on disorganized heaps of brick.

Beep . . . beep . . . beep . . .

A weak sound came from her radio.

She ran into the room.

Beep . . . beep . . . The signal faded and became drowned in static and re-emerged. Beep . . . beep . . . beep.

It stopped.

She sat with bated breath for a repeat. There was no further sound.

Then from the ghetto a sudden crackle of gunfire startled the stillness. She ran once more to the balcony but could see nothing. The gunfire sounds heightened.

Gabriela closed the balcony door, pulled down the blackout curtain, and flicked on the lamp beside the phone stand. She hedged for several moments, hoping that the transmission from the ghetto would be repeated. She lit a cigarette and pulled at it nervously, then with an impulsive spur of decision dialed a number.

A half-sleeping voice answered at the other end of the line.

"Kamek. This is Alena," Gabriela said.

"Yes?"

"Did you hear it?"

"Yes, but I could not understand it."

"Neither could I," Gabriela said. "What should we do?"

"There is nothing we can do until after curfew. Come over to my place as soon as it turns light."

Oberführer Funk blinked sleepily over the report. It was almost four o'clock in the morning, yet he wanted it for Kruger, Globocnik, and Himmler, finished and en route by dawn. It was preciously close to the one month marking the uprising. He wanted to give assurances that the bulk of the action was over. Any further action was merely the formality of a mop-up. Soon, quite soon, victory could be formally declared.

465

He yawned, bleary-eyed, affixing his signature to the report. A last sip of schnapps and then some sleep.

Four o'clock.

Funk untied his silk night robe.

The sound of gunfire! What the devil! It was not possible. He had ordered the artillery to cease fire at two-thirty and for the patrols to resume their fixed positions.

He tied his robe quickly and started to lift the phone, then let his hand drop. A sudden grip of fear encompassed him. Could it be possible that the Jews were attacking? No ... it was ... discovery of another bunker, that was all. Don't let your imagination run wild. Calm ... calm, now. Another large belt of schnapps and he sat slowly behind his desk again.

The crackling gunfire was sharper now. His hand once more touched the phone, fell from it. He licked his dry lips, sagged in the chair, and waited. The report to Berlin, Lublin, and Krakow lay face up before his eyes.

From: The SS and Police Führer, Warsaw District, Special Actions.

Ref. NO: 1 ab/ST/Gr–16 07–Journal No. 663/43 SECRET

Re: Large-scale Ghetto Operation

To: Reichführer Der Schutzstaffel Himmler, Berlin
SS Obergruppenführer, Police General, Krakow
Gruppenführer General Government SS, SD, Lublin

I beg to advise the following information:

1. A total to date of 34,795 Jews and other sub-humans caught for deportation, 7,654 known destroyed in former residential area. Estimate another 11,000 destroyed in bunkers by asphyxiation, flames, etc.

Conclusion:

Except for sporadic resistance from the few remaining Jews and sub-humans, we have succeeded in our mission.

2. Account of reduction of Jewish residential compound.

(a.) 612 bunkers destroyed.

(b.) So-called Jewish residential area is nonexistent. Three buildings remain standing; that is, the Converts' Church, parts of the Pawiak Prison, the *Jewish Civil Authority building* (former post office convenient for us to make immediate on-the-site executions of those we do not desire to transport).

3. Booty captured to date:

(a.) 7 Polish rifles, 1 Russian rifle, 7 German rifles.

(b.) 59 pistols of various calibers.

(c.) Several hundred hand grenades, including Polish and home-made.

(d.) Several hundred incendiary bottles.

(e.) Homemade explosives and infernal machines with fuses.

(f.) A variety of explosives, ammunition of all calibers. (In destroyed bunkers we were not able to capture further booty, which was destroyed. The captured hand grenades were used by us against the bandits.)

Furthermore, I beg to report

1. 1200 used German uniforms (tunics) and 600 pair of used trousers. (Some uniforms were equipped with medals.)

2. Several hundred assorted German helmets.

3. Four million zlotys (from deportees). Fourteen thousand dollars, nine thousand dollars in gold; an undetermined value in gold, rings, watches, jewelry.

I beg to report that today the principal Jew-bandit bunker was located at a place known as Mila 18 and it was summarily destroyed by gas, flame throwers, dynamite, and small-arms fire.

The ruins of the Jewish residential reservation will give us vast amounts of scrap material and used brick which can be salvaged for future building projects.

May I make mention of the valiant SS Waffen and Wehrmacht troops attached to this command whose uncommon devotion in the face of the "invisible" enemy has brought about this success. They went into the sewers, crawled into bunkers, and otherwise exposed themselves to the gunfire of the enemy. These comrades will not be forgotten.

Under separate cover I recommend the following decorations:

Iron Cross, Second Class—SS Haupsturmführer Zisensis.

Cross of War Merit, Second Class with Swords—SS Untersturmführer Manfred Plank, SS Rottenführer Joseph Blesche.

IT IS MY FIRM OPINION THAT I WILL BE ABLE TO ADVISE YOU OFFICIALLY OF THE FINAL EXTERMINATION OF THE JEWS IN WARSAW WITHIN SEVENTY-TWO HOURS.

Heil Hitler!

> *Signed:*
> SS Oberführer Alfred Funk

Certified copy:
(Jesuiter)
SS Sturmbannführer

Horst von Epp entered the room but did not speak. The two of them listened and listened and listened for nearly an hour until the gunfire in the ghetto stopped.

Five o'clock.

The moments before dawn of the second month of the uprising came. Neither Alfred Funk nor Horst von Epp dared lift the telephone. A knock.

"Enter!"

Untersturmführer Manfred Plank, showing the effects of battle, stood wild-eyed before his general. "Heil Hitler," he said with somewhat less than his usual vigor.

"Heil Hitler," Alfred Funk answered.

"What happened out there?" Horst von Epp asked.

It seemed as though Plank's fine young Aryan body would collapse.

"Speak!" ordered Funk.

Plank's lips quivered. "We were moving into our fixed position at the western end of Niska Street . . ."

"Speak!"

"Like . . . like ghosts, they leaped out of the ruins on us! They did not fight like human beings . . ."

"Speak!" Funk screamed again at the faltering man.

"We were compelled to abandon our positions."

"Swine!"

"Herr Oberführer!" cried Manfred Plank. "I have been decorated twice for valor on the eastern front. As a result of my fearless attitude in combat I was sent to SS Waffen training. I tell you, sir . . . I tell you . . . there are supernatural forces in there!"

"Get out," Funk hissed.

He did not hear the Untersturmführer click his heels and make his squarely conceived exit.

Funk's hands were so slippery with sweat, he could not hold his drink. He took his report promising victory and dropped it in the wastebasket after tearing it to shreds, and he looked up at Horst with dazed puzzlement.

"Even from their graves . . ."

"Tonight we have really lost this battle."

On his hands and knees, his shoulders rubbing against the top of the pipe, Wolf Brandel crawled first into the sewer pipe that cut diagonally down the eastern end of the ghetto. Rachael, second in line, grabbed his ankle with one hand and followed. Tolek, next in line, took Rachael's ankle and Chris took Tolek's and Ana took Chris's. The chain spread down for the twenty-three who left the bunker after sending the radio signal to the Aryan side.

Eight beeps, a pause, six more beeps. Repeat the message twice. Decoded, it meant: "Twenty coming through the Prosta Street manhole."

Ten seconds after Andrei started his diversionary attack in the western ghetto, Wolf and Tolek began their perilous journey.

The lateral pipes connecting to the large ones were slightly more than a yard in diameter, and to move in them one had to crawl laboriously on hands and knees.

Silence—absolute, complete, utter silence—was commanded by the leaders.

They inched into the pitch-blackness while overhead Andrei leaped out at Manfred Plank's SS company and threw the Germans into confusion to draw attention from the evacuees. Andrei had chosen the desperation route carefully. No one was apt to watch the smaller laterals under the ground simply because it was not believed that a human could move for long through them.

They came to Nalewki Street. Their small pipe dumped into the big *Kanal*. Wolf halted the line and sloshed around in the darkness, feeling the walls to find the continuation of the small pipe on the other side. Corpses floated swiftly down and hit against him and knocked his feet from beneath him and he went under in the sewer water. He got to his feet after being swept ten or twenty yards and again slogged upstream to feel for the lateral. An hour passed before his hands found it.

He recrossed the *Kanal* and took Rachael's hand. Hand in hand, the chain crossed the big line and re-entered the lateral on their hands and knees.

For another agonizing hour of step by step, the chain pressed on in measured progress. Their backs were breaking, their knees raw and bloody from the dragging. The stench blinding and numbing.

The pipe ran into the Zamenhof *Kanal*.

Three tortured hours had passed since the beginning.

Again Wolf had to cross alone and grope around from memory. Another hour passed.

When he had gotten the chain over the Zamenhof *Kanal* the lateral pipe was running high and fast. They crawled on hands and knees, ever southward, with the sewage splashing up to their chins, floating into their eyes and noses and ears and hair.

Six hours later they were under the Converts' Church and the site of the demolished uniform factory . . . now under the wall in the "Polish corridor."

Along the chain one Fighter after the other fainted. They had to stop long enough to slap them into consciousness and drag them further. Silence could not be broken even when someone pitched flat into the sewage and drowned. The line tightened. There were twenty-two left instead of twenty-three.

Another went under and another.

After they crawled eight hours on hands and knees the pipe widened. They were able to stand bent over. The water running in this direction was only a few feet high. Wolf did not give them a chance to glory in the respite. He drove them on while the chance for making progress was good. The strong dragged the weak to their feet. Pain . . . nausea . . . numbness . . . half sanity . . . half life . . . they trudged on, on, on through the bilge and filth, until in the ninth hour they had passed out of the ghetto and the "Polish cor-

469

ridor," and now they looked for the main *Kanal* which would take them down Zelazna Street.

Somehow in the darkness they had taken a wrong turn and veered back north. Then they splashed around in aimless circles. Wolf stopped them, trying to find his bearings and the main *Kanal*. Without compass, light, conversation, and using only a hazy memory of a few hours' study, he was utterly and completely lost. There was no use pushing on. Three more had fainted, including Ana. Unless he gave them rest they would all be done in. Wolf crawled back to Tolek and broke the nine-hour silence.

"Rest," he said.

Rest . . . rest . . . rest . . . the magic word fired back along the line.

They sat in the pipe with the sewage waters swirling around their chests and they gasped and groaned with hunger and thirst and weariness and bloody hands and knees.

Tolek and Chris held the head of Ana, who was unconscious from falling into the water.

Wolf crawled away alone, counting each step carefully until he came to a large *Kanal*. He was utterly confused, for the Twarda Street line veered into the system at an angle. He could not understand. They were more than a mile away from the designated Prosta Street manhole and completely confused as to direction, but the big *Kanal* had ledges and would give them a place to recover their strength.

Wolf retraced his steps and led them to the Twarda main, and they crawled on to the ledges and collapsed.

Wolf and Tolek and Chris stayed half awake, trying each in his own mind to comprehend the situation, and the same set of questions crossed their minds without conversation. Had their message to the Aryan side been received? Would someone be waiting for them on Prosta Street . . . if they reached Prosta Street?

As commander, Wolf Brandel had other decisions to reach. He tried to reason out their proximity. He guessed rightly that they were under the former little ghetto area which was now largely reinhabited by Poles. The area, he knew, was under close watch of the police because of its proximity to the ghetto. Overhead they could hear motor vehicles and the marching of soldiers. Perhaps we are near Grzybow Square, Wolf thought. It was an assembly point for the Germans to enter the southern end of the ghetto.

Daylight showed through manholes on either end of their ledge. Wolf looked his people over. It was a battle of endurance against exhaustion more than anything at this point. One by one his people had passed out into semi-consciousness. If his guess of location was right, they would now be safe from poison gas and out of reach of the prying sound detectors. The tides were going high again. Water splashed over the ledge. Nothing to do but wait until darkness . . . nothing to do but wait.

470

Kamek's house in Brodno was the first stop in the underground railway to the Machalin and Lublin forests. Gabriela arrived shortly after the morning curfew was lifted.

"They're down there!" she cried.

Kamek was unexcitable. He put his hands behind his back and deliberately pieced everything together. "Where are they? We do not know. Neither you nor I got the signal clearly. It could be one of fifteen manholes."

Gabriela pressed her temples and tried to reason.

"Moreover," Kamek continued, "both of our trucks are gone. The Gestapo raided our headquarters last night; our people are dispersed."

"The Home Army . . . Roman . . ."

"We cannot depend upon them. Someone may sell out."

Gabriela knew he was right. She winced. Kamek, once Ignacy Pownicki, had been a journalist and an ardent supporter of both the ruling colonels' clique and the reactionary pre-war noblemen's caste. Events during the war changed his thinking. Humanity overpowered nationalism. Kamek was one of the few who were revolted by and ashamed of the behavior of the Polish people toward the things happening in Poland's ghettos. He did not embrace the leftists' philosophy personally, but he joined them, for they were the ones who gave the fullest support to those in the ghetto. Kamek lost his identity as Ignacy Pownicki to immerse himself fully in the underground work of the People's Guard.

He was a cool man, seeming almost lazily detached from the urgency.

"They're under there somewhere," Gabriela mumbled again.

"Keep calm, Gabriela. You and I are the only two who are aware of it and who are left in a position to help. The Jewish Fighters' leaders all know your address. Certainly they will attempt to contact you. The best thing you can do is go home and wait."

The cuckoo chirped the hour. "Ah, time for the news."

Kamek flicked on the radio and closed his eyes to concentrate on the true meanings, for the real news was between the lines and filled with cryptic clues. The war since Stalingrad continued to go badly for the Germans, and their double talk could not fully cover it. There was not a single mention of the ghetto action. This also was a good indication, for they were quick to brag of victories. He flicked off the radio.

Gabriela was already on her feet, walking toward the door.

"Keep calm," he said once more.

The light filtering through the manholes was turning dimmer and dimmer. Wolf watched it fade. Soon it would be night again. He slipped off the ledge and inched along where the nineteen survivors lay entwined like a net full of freshly caught fish. During the day

471

they had passed out and awakened, slept in snatches and gained back an ounce of strength from what they lost during the terrible crawling of the night before.

Wolf satisfied himself that all of them could be marched again. The instant darkness fell he alerted them to stand by. Soon the movement overhead thinned to silence and then, a break. Ack-ack guns in the distance popped at another Russian air raid. This would keep the Germans busy in the streets.

"Let's go," he said.

The water ran chest-high. Wolf first, Tolek second, Chris third, they pushed against the current, moving southward in a direction which they knew was leading them away from the ghetto. Some of the shorter girls had to go up on tiptoes to keep the sewage out of their mouths and noses.

Hand in hand, they inched down the *Kanal,* hoping desperately to find another arterial. Wolf counted steps.

In three hours, he estimated, they had moved two and a half blocks. Someone was always slipping or collapsing or breaking silence.

And then the luxurious sound of loud rushing water farther down the line met his ears. It meant another large *Kanal!* This sound spurred the half-dead line of marchers to another effort. The two sewer lines merged in swirls and whirlpools battering together.

Wolf halted the line. From his memory of the maps, he tried to remember where two such intersections merged at such an angle. There was no place like it in the ghetto. A *Kanal* the size of the one before him must be near the Jerusalem Boulevard area. If so, they were entirely beyond both the big and little ghettos. Wolf decided to gamble with his flashlight. It was soaked and unworkable. Chris had dry matches in a pipe pouch.

A single match sent a dullish yellow glow on the moist bricks. It also revealed the shocking condition of his people. Wolf knew the race for life had to be speeded, more gambles taken. He lit a second match and sloshed nearer the intersection. A third match found him what he was looking for, an iron ladder leading to the street.

"Hold the line still," Wolf told Tolek and Chris. "I'm going up to find out where we are."

"Wolf . . . don't . . ." Rachael cried.

"It will be all right. There's an air raid going on up there."

He climbed the ladder and shoved hard to wiggle the manhole cover loose. It gave after a fifth renewal of effort. He held it open just enough to look out to the streets. Good luck! Pitch-black in a blackout! Streets deserted!

"Help me lift this manhole cover."

Chris, Tolek, and Wolf hung on the narrow ladder and grunted together and dislodged it. Wolf darted for the cover of a building, worked toward the corner, and sprinted back, replacing the lid. He huddled with Tolek. Chris was too occupied holding Ana and Rachael erect. Rachael fainted again. Ana had been in a bad way for hours.

"We are directly under the intersection of Twarda and Zelazna."

"That means we are just two and a half blocks from Prosta Street." Would someone from the People's Guard be waiting for them there? Both agreed that it was a small chance. It was twenty-four hours since they had sent the signal and entered the sewer. Moreover, in daylight this present intersection would be too crowded. Wolf decided to try a push for the quieter Prosta Street and at the same time send Tolek to Gabriela's flat.

"Careful, and bring back water."

Tolek and Wolf once again dislodged the manhole cover and shoved it back into place.

Wolf lowered himself once more and went back to the other sixteen.

"We are three hours from Prosta Street. We can make it by daylight if everyone tries with all they have. Tolek has gone out for water. He will be waiting for us."

"No! No!" a girl shrieked. "We'll never make it! No!"

"Keep her quiet," Wolf barked.

"No!" the girl screamed again. She began drinking the sewage in her thirst madness.

Wolf went back and lit a match and fished for her head and jerked it out of the contaminated bilge. The girl was insane. In a moment the poison hit her stomach and she gave a last two or three writhes of agony and was dead.

Wolf let her loose, and she was washed into the merging waters, spun in a whirlpool, and swept into the larger *Kanal*.

"Listen, all of you! We're going to live! I promise you we'll live! Two more hours and there will be water to drink! Fight! Live!" he pleaded.

They took hands and pressed north into the whirlpools. The rushing water broke their line, and before they could pull it together another Fighter who was moving in a coma was swept under and drowned.

"Together!" rasped Wolf. "Hands together . . . push . . . push . . . we'll be through this intersection in a minute."

They pressed north again in foggy oblivion. Each agony-filled step, each one called upon God unknown.

"I'll live . . . I'll live . . . I'll live . . ."

"Survive . . . survive . . . survive . . ."

"God help me live . . . live . . . live . . . live . . ."

Tolek Alterman wove his way through the streets of Warsaw with the skill of an alley cat. Years of moving around in the ghetto, later in rubble and flame and falling walls, made this trek seem like child's play by comparison.

It was four-thirty in the morning when he stopped before an apartment door on the top floor of Dluga 4. The name read "Alena Borinski." He knocked sharply. The door opened a crack, stopped by the night latch.

"Who is it?" Gabriela asked cautiously from the other side.

"Don't scream when you see me. I've been in the sewers."

Gabriela flung the door open. Tolek tumbled in and looked around desperately for the kitchen. He stumbled to it and turned on the water faucet and let the water spill into his throat and guzzled it like a lunatic. She locked the door behind her and looked at the scene of madness. He emitted animal-like grunts as the water found its way to his caked innards.

A gray stinking creature from another planet, unrecognizable as human, sucking at the faucet. He drank too fast and began vomiting in the sink and drank again, and sharp pains hit his belly. At last he was appeased and he slipped to the floor, weeping hysterically.

Gabriela ran to the phone. "Kamek! Come to my flat as soon as the curfew is over. Bring clothing and any food you have."

"Have they arrived?"

"Yes."

Gaby dipped a rag in alcohol and wiped Tolek's forehead and comforted him.

"I'm sorry," he whispered. "I'm sorry . . ."

"Please tell me about it . . . please."

"Twenty-two or twenty-three of us went into the sewer. . . . Did you get our signal?"

"Yes, but we couldn't distinguish it. Good Lord, have you been in the sewer for twenty-four hours?"

"Yes. Maybe sixteen, seventeen left. Few went crazy from thirst . . . drank the sewage . . . told them not to . . . some others drowned."

"Where are they now?"

"Trying to make Prosta Street. We've got to get water to them."

"There's nothing we can do for another hour and a half, until it turns light and the curfew is lifted. Kamek will be here by then."

Gabriela studied the thing before her. "Your voice. Don't I know you?"

"Tolek."

474

"Oh, my poor dear. I didn't even recognize you."

"Don't suppose anyone could."

"Who else is down there?"

"Christopher de Monti. We must get him out."

She nodded and her eyes widened. "Who else?"

"Rachael . . . Wolf . . . Ana . . ."

He stopped, and the pained expression she bore both asked the wordless question and answered it. She stood up and walked to the kitchen chair and sagged into it. She bit her lip. The last tears she had left in her trickled down her cheeks. Andrei was still out there in the ghetto . . . leading cavalry charges . . . Andrei would never come out. She knelt beside Tolek once more and helped him to his feet.

"Come," Gaby said, "let's steam you out so you look presentable."

Gabriela filled the last of four shopping bags with bread, cheese, and bottles of water. Each bag had a rope tied to the handles so it could be lowered quickly into the *Kanal*.

Kamek was a picture of his usual calm. "Today is Sunday," he recited for his own benefit. "Sunday is trouble. We cannot ride through the streets with a load of hay on Sunday. I must get a covered truck and try for the best."

Tolek came in from the bathroom. He had been soaking and scrubbing for two full hours. It brought him back to the semblance of a man. He tucked a short crowbar into his belt for lifting the manhole cover quickly and took two of the shopping bags from Gabriela.

"I hope they made it," Tolek mumbled. "They were in a bad way when I left them."

Kamek stood up. "After you get that food and water down to them, wait in the café down the street. Watch for my truck."

"Hurry with that truck," Gabriela said. "They've been down there almost thirty hours."

"Leave it to Kamek," Kamek said.

"It's day," Wolf said, looking up to the manhole cover atop him. "It's day and we're at Prosta Street. Today we'll be saved."

Weeping . . .

"Our Father which art in heaven."

"O Merciful God . . . save us . . . save us . . ."

Christopher de Monti leaned against the bricks. He held Ana with one arm and Rachael with the other. Both of them were semiconscious.

Death closed in with each passing second. There were only twelve left.

"O help us, merciful God . . ."

"Today we'll be saved," Wolf cried. "Today we'll be saved."

475

Christopher skidded to his knees and struggled to his feet, pull-ing the girls up. Feverish fire tore through his body.

Shadows over them!

"Shh . . . someone's up there . . . silence . . ."

"Merciful . . . merciful . . ."

"Sshhh!"

Their eyes looked up in terror. The cover slipped off. "It's me, Tolek! It's me, Tolek! Are you down there? Are you down there?"

"Help . . . help . . ."

"Tolek . . . help . . . us . . ."

"Thank God! They're alive. Listen, down there. We are lowering bread and water. We will remain close by until the truck arrives. Do you hear me?"

"Water . . . water . . ."

"Water!"

"Water!"

"Water!"

"Quiet," Tolek commanded. The bags were lowered. "There are smelling salts in one of the bags."

Mass weeping broke out as the bottles were opened and they gurgled and wetted their dehydrated bellies. They tore at the bread and the cheese with the savagery of starved animals and grunted and wept and prayed.

Even the calm Kamek was worrying. He was running out of chances. Two covered-truck owners had their vehicles in repair. Three others were out of the city in the countryside to bring in food from villages.

It was almost eleven o'clock.

Church bells pealed. The pious were coming and going to Mass.

Kamek walked into the Solec to the house of Zamoyski, the teamster of thieves. He did not like to do business with Zamoyski. He was a slimy crook. Kamek had no choice. From time to time on desperate occasions the People's Guard used Zamoyski's truck . . . for a price.

When Kamek came to his house Zamoyski was in his usual Sunday pose—coming out of a bombastic Saturday-night hang-over.

"Sunday?"

"Special load."

Must be important, Zamoyski thought. I'll take him for plenty. He grunted disdainfully. "It's heathen to drive on Sunday. Be-sides . . ."

A roll of green American dollars from Kamek's pocket to the center of the table cut short the oration and bargaining.

"Wait till I get my shirt on."

"Bring a ladder."

476

"A ladder?"

"Yes. The guns we are running are up in a loft."

Noon.

Gabriela and Tolek drank their fourth cup of tea in a café on Prosta Street. Bells pealed. Tolek was a nervous wreck.

The pious paraded in their finery after their hour with God. "What the hell is holding Kamek up?" Tolek sputtered. "They've been down in that hole almost thirty-six hours."

Gabriela patted his hand. "Kamek won't let us down," she said.

In the sewer the food and drink had restored the twelve survivors to a state of consciousness and gave them enough strength to cling to life for another few hours.

They could hear the church bells.

Children played in the street almost directly above them. The children stood in a circle and threw a ball and sang a song and clapped hands

"Raz! dwa! trzy! One! Two! Three!"

The ball was thrown.

> "The Roman king had many sons,
> Until one born became a Caesar,
> Low to the ground, high to the air,
> *Raz! dwa! trzy!* One! two three!
> Yes he was, yes he was,
> The great Caesar."

Zamoyski's truck rumbled up Jerusalem Boulevard.

"Where to?" he asked.

"Prosta Street."

He turned up Zelazna, then into Prosta.

"Where?"

"Stop by the manhole halfway up the block opposite the café."

Zamoyski's face opened with the sudden discovery. "What's this all about, Kamek? I don't like this business. Wait a minute. Jews! I'm not getting mixed up in Jew business!"

Zamoyski felt something cold against the side of his face. It was the barrel of Kamek's pistol.

The truck screeched to a halt beside the manhole. Kamek held Zamoyski at bay. Tolek and Gabriela sprinted out of the café. Tolek knocked the cover off the manhole, ran to the back of the truck, and pulled the ladder off. Gabriela took a short-barreled shotgun from inside her trench coat.

The burst of light from the street blinded those in the *Kanal* for an instant. Chris held one side of the ladder, Wolf the other. They

477

dragged the other ten and literally threw them up. Tolek reached down and pulled them through.

> *"Raz! dwa! trzy! One! Two! Three!*
> The Roman ..."*

The children stopped and gawked at the things emerging from the sewer. Gabriela's shotgun menaced them back.

People stopped their Sunday stroll and looked at the sight.

Stunned customers of the café gaped in amazement.

Zamoyski cried and cursed. "I am ruined! I am trapped! Holy Mother! I am dead!"

Wolf Brandel tumbled out last and hobbled heavily. He was thrown bodily atop the others in the back of the truck, and within two minutes of their stopping they sped away toward the bridge and Brodno.

Chapter Twenty-four

Journal Entry—December 1943

I, Christopher de Monti, shall make the final entry in the Brandel journals of the Good Fellowship Club. After months of hiding I have arrived here in Sweden with Gabriela Rak, whose child is due at any moment. She does not want it to be born on Polish soil. I shall see to it that neither she nor her child shall ever want.

Little is known here about the uprising despite the fact that Artur Zygielboim, a Jewish member of the Polish government in exile in London, committed suicide last June in protest to the world's indifference to the genocide of his people.

What of the Warsaw uprising? How does one determine the results of such a battle? Jewish casualties were in the tens of thousands while the Germans merely lost hundreds.

I look through the books of history and I try to find a parallel. Not at the Alamo, not at Thermopylae did two more unequal forces square off for combat. I believe that decades and centuries may pass, but nothing can stop the legends which will grow from the ashes of the ghetto to show that this is the epic in man's struggle for freedom and human dignity.

This rabble army without a decent weapon held at bay the mightiest military power the world has ever known for forty-two days and forty-two nights! It does not seem possible, for many nations fell beneath the German onslaught in hours. All of Poland was able to hold for less than a month.

Forty-two days and forty-two nights! At the end of that time SS Oberführer Alfred Funk ordered the Great Tlomatskie Synagogue dynamited to the ground to symbolize the destruction of Polish Jewry. He received the Iron Cross for valor.

But Alfred Funk failed, just as all the other Pharaohs failed.

The new year will see Nazi Germany crushed. Germany's cities are destined to be dismantled brick by brick and her people to perish in flames in much the same way as they destroyed the Warsaw ghetto.

What of the murderers? What of Horst von Epp and Franz Koenig? No doubt their ilk will die in bed of old age, for the world is a forgiving world and they will say they were merely following orders. And the world will say . . . let us forget the past. Let bygones be bygones. Even the Alfred Funks may escape. Already we hear the verbal gymnastics of the Polish government in exile spouting theories of apologetics in behalf of their people who committed the conspiracy of silence.

I, Christopher de Monti, swear on the eternal soul of my late friend, Andrei Androfski, that I shall not let the world forget. I shall return to Poland. I shall find the Brandel journals and I shall make it a brand on the conscience of man forever.

Wolf Brandel and Rachael Bronski, Tolek Alterman and Ana Grinspan are fighting in a Jewish partisan unit near Wyszkow. Stephan Bronski is alive and well in the home of a woodcutter named Gajnow in the Lublin Uplands. We shall all meet again someday.

I shall close this final entry with the words of the man who wrote the first entry and who is responsible for the historical documents of the Good Fellowship Club. On our last night together in the bunker of Mila 18, this is what Alexander Brandel told me:

"If the Warsaw ghetto marked the lowest point in the history of the Jewish people, it also marked the point where they rose to their greatest heights. Strange, after all the philosophies had been argued, the final decision to fight was basically a religious decision. Rodel would decry my words; Rabbi Solomon would be outraged if I told him this. But those who fought, no matter what their individual reasons, when massed together obeyed God's covenant to oppose tyranny. We have kept faith with our ancient traditions to defend 'the laws.' In the end we were all Jews." And Alexander Brandel, always mystified by ways of God and strange ways of men, shook his head in puzzlement. "Isn't it odd that the epitome of man's inhumanity to man also produced the epitome of man's nobility?" Alexander Brandel told me something else. "I die, a man fulfilled. My son shall live to see Israel reborn. I know this. And what is more, we Jews have avenged our honor as a people."

CHRISTOPHER DE MONTI

A SELECTED LIST OF FINE NOVELS
AVAILABLE FROM CORGI BOOKS

THE PRICES SHOWN BELOW WERE CORRECT AT THE TIME OF GOING
TO PRESS. HOWEVER TRANSWORLD PUBLISHERS RESERVE THE
RIGHT TO SHOW NEW RETAIL PRICES ON COVERS WHICH MAY
DIFFER FROM THOSE PREVIOUSLY ADVERTISED IN THE TEXT OR
ELSEWHERE.

☐ 12569 5	THE FOURTH PROTOCOL	*Frederick Forsyth*	£3.95
☐ 12140 1	NO COMEBACKS	*Frederick Forsyth*	£2.95
☐ 11500 2	THE DEVIL'S ALTERNATIVE	*Frederick Forsyth*	£2.95
☐ 10244 X	THE SHEPHERD	*Frederick Forsyth*	£1.95
☐ 10050 1	THE DOGS OF WAR	*Frederick Forsyth*	£2.95
☐ 09436 6	THE ODESSA FILE	*Frederick Forsyth*	£2.50
☐ 09121 9	THE DAY OF THE JACKAL	*Frederick Forsyth*	£2.95
☐ 12612 8	POLAND	*James A. Michener*	£3.95
☐ 08299 6	THE BRIDGES AT TOKO-RI	*James A. Michener*	£1.95
☐ 09766 7	THE BRIDGE AT ANDAU	*James A. Michener*	£2.50
☐ 08406 9	RETURN TO PARADISE	*James A. Michener*	£3.50
☐ 08404 2	THE FIRES OF SPRING	*James A. Michener*	£2.95
☐ 12283 1	SPACE	*James A. Michener*	£3.95
☐ 08502 2	CARAVANS	*James A. Michener*	£2.95
☐ 09945 7	CENTENNIAL	*James A. Michener*	£3.95
☐ 11320 4	CHESAPEAKE	*James A. Michener*	£3.95
☐ 11755 2	THE COVENANT	*James A. Michener*	£3.95
☐ 08000 4	SAYONARA	*James A. Michener*	£1.95
☐ 08501 4	TALES OF THE SOUTH PACIFIC	*James A. Michener*	£2.95
☐ 08405 0	RASCALS IN PARADISE	*James A. Michener*	£2.50
☐ 09240 1	THE DRIFTERS	*James A. Michener*	£3.95
☐ 07594 9	HAWAII	*James A. Michener*	£4.95
☐ 07500 0	THE SOURCE	*James A. Michener*	£3.95
☐ 12614 4	THE HAJ	*Leon Uris*	£2.95
☐ 10565 1	TRINITY	*Leon Uris*	£3.95
☐ 08866 8	QB VII	*Leon Uris*	£3.50
☐ 08384 4	EXODUS	*Leon Uris*	£3.95
☐ 08091 8	TOPAZ	*Leon Uris*	£2.95
☐ 07300 8	ARMAGEDDON	*Leon Uris*	£3.50
☐ 08521 9	THE ANGRY HILLS	*Leon Uris*	£1.95

All Corgi/Bantam Books are available at your bookshop or newsagent, or can be ordered from the following address:

Corgi/Bantam Books,
Cash Sales Department,
P.O. Box 11, Falmouth, Cornwall TR10 9EN

Please send a cheque or postal order (no currency) and allow 60p for postage and packing for the first book plus 25p for the second book and 15p for each additional book ordered up to a maximum charge of £1.90 in UK.

B.F.P.O. customers please allow 60p for the first book, 25p for the second book plus 15p per copy for the next 7 books, thereafter 9p per book.

Overseas customers, including Eire, please allow £1.25 for postage and packing for the first book, 75p for the second book, and 28p for each subsequent title ordered.

Fodor's 99

Cancún, Cozumel, Yucatán Peninsula

The complete guide, thoroughly up-to-date

Packed with details that will make your trip

The must-see sights, off and on the beaten path

What to see, what to skip

Vacation itineraries, walking tours, day trips

Smart lodging and dining options

Essential local do's and taboos

Transportation tips

Key contacts, savvy travel advice

When to go, what to pack

Clear, accurate, easy-to-use maps

Books to read, videos to watch, background essays

Fodor's Travel Publications, Inc.
New York • Toronto • London • Sydney • Auckland
www.fodors.com

II

EDITOR: Alison B. Stern

Editorial Contributors: Patricia Alisau, Michele Back, David Brown, Richard Harris, Christina Knight, Wendy Luft, Dan Millington, Helayne Schiff, M.T. Schwartzman (editor), Stephen Wolf
Editorial Production: Linda K. Schmidt, Nicole Revere
Maps: David Lindroth, *cartographer*; Steven K. Amsterdam, *map editor*
Design: Fabrizio La Rocca, *creative director*; Guido Caroti, *associate art director*; Jolie Novak, *photo editor*
Cover Photograph: Joan Iaconetti
Production/Manufacturing: Rebecca Zeiler

Copyright

Special Sales

CONTENTS

IV   **Contents**

Maps

ON THE ROAD WITH FODOR'S

WE'RE ALWAYS THRILLED to get letters from readers, especially one like this:

It took us an hour to decide what book to buy and we now know we picked the best one. Your book was wonderful, easy to follow, very accurate, and good on pointing out eating places, informal as well as formal. When we saw other people using your book, we would look at each other and smile.

Our editors and writers are deeply committed to making every Fodor's guide "the best one"—not only accurate but always charming, brimming with sound recommendations and solid ideas, right on the mark in describing restaurants and hotels, and full of fascinating facts that make you view what you've traveled to see in a rich new light.

About Our Writers

Our success in achieving our goals—and in helping to make your trip the best of all possible vacations—is a credit to the hard work of our extraordinary writers.

Patricia Alisau, who updated the Caribbean Coast, Campeche, and Mérida and the State of Yucatán chapters, is a psychologist-turned-journalist and archaeology buff. She was so drawn to the surrealism of Mexico City—"Where in the U.S. can you find pyramids?" she asks—that she moved to the capital; what began as a one-week vacation became a 20-year sojourn. She was restaurant-and-nightclub columnist for the *News,* Mexico's English-language daily, worked as a photo stringer for the Associated Press during the Nicaragua Revolution, and has written for Mexico's *Vogue* magazine.

Former Berkeley Guides writer and editor **Michele Back** careened around Yucatán's Caribbean coast in a battered Nissan Tsuru rental. After a variety of escapades that included bribing a Chetumal policeman, downing mass quantities of papaya milkshakes, and comparing mosquito bites with her partner in crime (future human rights lawyer and Supreme Mack Daddy of Brazil, Mauricio Claudio).

Michele is now attempting to adopt a professional attitude for her job with the U.S. Information Agency.

Richard Harris, who wrote "The Three Faces of the Yucatán" essay in our Portraits section, left a law practice in 1981 to study pre-Columbian Indian ruins. He is the author of two books on the archaeology and ecology of the Yucatán Peninsula. As president of PEN New Mexico, the only English-Spanish bilingual chapter of the writers'-rights group PEN International, he spends much of his time in Mexico as an advocate for imprisoned or threatened Latin American writers.

A freelance writer and photographer based in Laguna Beach, California, **Dan Millington** has traveled extensively in Mexico and is familiar with many regions of the country. This past year he updated the chapters on Cancún, Isla Mujeres, and Cozumel. We'd also like to thank Burson-Marsteller and Aeroméxico for their help with travel arrangements.

This book was originally written by freelance writer and translator **Erica Meltzer,** who first visited the Yucatán in 1967. It was then that she learned the truth of the old Mexican proverb "He who has been touched by the dust of Mexico will never again find peace in any land." She moved to Mexico City for three years, and from her current base in New York gets back to the country as frequently as possible.

Connections

We're pleased that the American Society of Travel Agents (ASTA) continues to endorse Fodor's as its guidebook of choice. ASTA is the world's largest and most influential travel trade association, operating in more than 170 countries, with 27,000 members pledged to adhere to a strict code of ethics reflecting the Society's motto, "Integrity in Travel." ASTA shares Fodor's devotion to providing smart, honest travel information and advice to travelers, and we've long recommended that our readers—even those who have guidebooks and traveling friends—consult ASTA member agents for the experience and professionalism they bring to your vacation planning.

On Fodor's Web site (www.fodors.com), check out the new Resource Center, an online companion to the Gold Guide section of this book, complete with useful hot links to related sites. In our forums, you can also get lively advice from other travelers and more great tips from Fodor's experts worldwide.

How to Use This Book

Organization

Up front is the **Gold Guide,** an easy-to-use section divided alphabetically by topic. Under each listing you'll find tips and information that will help you accomplish what you need to in Cancún, Cozumel, and the Yucatán Peninsula. You'll also find addresses and telephone numbers of organizations and companies that offer destination-related services and detailed information and publications.

The first chapter in the guide, Destination: Cancún, Cozumel, Yucatan Peninsula, helps get you in the mood for your trip. New and Noteworthy cues you in on trends and happenings, What's Where gets you oriented, Pleasures and Pastimes describes the activities and sights that make Cancún, Cozumel, and the Yucatán Peninsula really unique, Fodor's Choice showcases our top picks, and Festivals and Seasonal Events alerts you to special events you'll want to seek out.

Chapters in Fodor's *Cancún, Cozumel, Yucatán Peninsula '99* are arranged geographically, moving clockwise in a rough circle from the peninsula's prime destination, Cancún (Chapter 2). Nearby Isla Mujeres, a popular day trip from Cancún, is covered in Chapter 3, and Cozumel, an easy boat ride from both, is the focus of Chapter 4. We travel down the Caribbean coast in Chapter 5, then hop over to the gulf coast to Mérida and the state of Yucatán in Chapter 6. Directly south, Campeche comprises Chapter 7.

Each island chapter and major city section begins with an Exploring section, followed by a recommended walking or driving tour and a list of sights in alphabetical order. Each regional chapter is divided by geographical area. Within each area, towns are covered in logical geographical order, and within town sections all restaurants and lodgings are grouped together. The A to

Z section that ends all chapters covers getting there and getting around. It also provides helpful contacts and resources.

At the end of the book you'll find Portraits, including a chronology of the Maya and the history of Yucatán and "The Three Faces of the Yucatán," a lively, in-depth essay on the region by Richard Harris. Finally, there's also a **Spanish vocabulary** to help you learn a few basics.

Icons and Symbols

★ Our special recommendations
✕ Restaurant
🏨 Lodging establishment
✕🏨 Lodging establishment whose restaurant warrants a special trip
🕓 Good for kids (rubber duckie)
☞ Sends you to another section of the guide for more information
✉ Address
☎ Telephone number
🕐 Opening and closing times
💲 Admission prices (those we give apply to adults; substantially reduced fees are almost always available for children, students, and senior citizens)
⚴ Indicates a pre-Columbian site of note (a Maya temple, for example)

Numbers in white and black circles that appear on the maps, in the margins, and within the tours correspond to one another.

The restaurants and lodgings we list are the cream of the crop in each price range. Price charts appear in the Dining and Lodging sections of island chapters, and in the Pleasures and Pastimes section that follows each regional chapter introduction.

Hotel Facilities

We always list the facilities that are available—but we don't specify whether they cost extra: When pricing accommodations, always ask what's included. In addition, assume that all rooms have private baths unless otherwise noted.

Assume that hotels operate on the **European Plan** (EP, with no meals) unless we note that they use the **Continental Plan** (CP, with a Continental breakfast daily), **Modified American Plan** (MAP, with breakfast and dinner daily), or are **all-inclusive** (all meals and most activities).

Restaurant Reservations and Dress Codes

Reservations are always a good idea; we note only when they're essential or when they are not accepted. Book as far ahead as you can, and reconfirm when you get to town. Unless otherwise noted, the restaurants listed are open daily for lunch and dinner. We mention dress only when men are required to wear a jacket or a jacket and tie. Look for an overview of local habits in the Gold Guide and in the Pleasures and Pastimes section that follows each chapter introduction.

Credit Cards

The following abbreviations are used: **AE**, American Express; **DC**, Diners Club; **MC**, MasterCard; and **V**, Visa.

Please Write to Us

You can use this book in the confidence that all prices and opening times are based on information supplied to us at press time; Fodor's cannot accept responsibility for any errors. Time inevitably brings changes, so always confirm information when it matters—especially if you're making a detour to visit a specific place. In addition, when making reservations be sure to mention if you have a disability or are traveling with children, if you prefer a private bath or a certain type of bed, or if you have specific dietary needs or other concerns.

Were the restaurants we recommended as described? Did our hotel picks exceed your expectations? Did you find a museum we recommended a waste of time? If you have complaints, we'll look into them and revise our entries when the facts warrant it. If you've discovered a special place that we haven't included, we'll pass the information along to our correspondents and have them check it out. So send us your feedback, positive *and* negative: email us at editors@fodors.com (specifying the name of the book on the subject line) or write the Cancún, Cozumel, Yucatán Peninsula editor at Fodor's, 201 East 50th Street, New York, New York 10022. Have a wonderful trip!

Karen Cure
Editorial Director

Golfo de México

Dzilam
de Bravo

Dzilan
González

Progreso

Yucalpetén

Sisal

Punta Baz

Dzibilchaltún

Motul

Ter

Tekanto

Izama

172

25

261

Mérida

80

Citilcúm

Celestún

281

Umán

180

Hoctún

Holca

Punta Nimun

Chuncucmil

Maxcanú

Mayapán

18

Y U C A

Muna

Santa Cruz

Uxmal

Ticul

Kabah

184

Ozkutzcab

Sayil

Tzucacab

Tenabó

Labná

Tinúm

261

Campeche

180

Hopelchén

Punta Seybaplaya

261

Edzná

QU

La Joya

Champotón

C A M P E C H E

Río Champotón

Sabancuy

180

Escárcega

186

Río

186

Xpujil

186

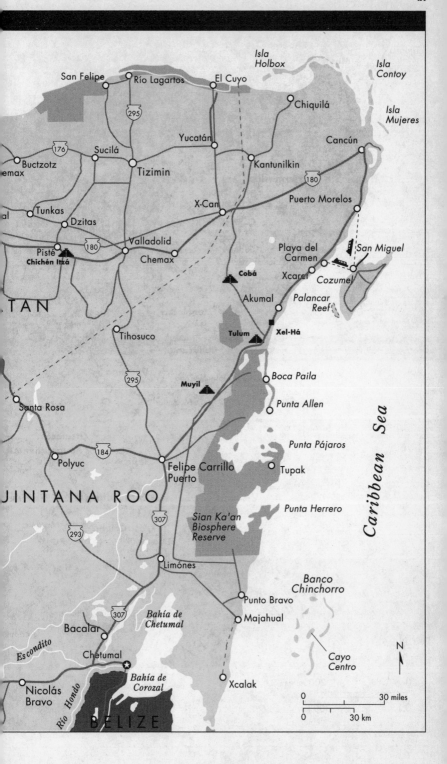

Isla
Holbox

Isla
Contoy

San Felipe

Río Lagartos

El Cuyo

Chiquilá

Isla
Mujeres

295

Yucatán

Cancún

Buctzotz

176

Sucilá

emax

Tizimin

Kantunilkin

180

Tunkas

X-Can

Puerto Morelos

al

Dzitas

Valladolid

Playa del
Carmen

San Miguel

Pisté

180

Chichén Itzá

Chemax

Cobá

Xcaret

Cozumel

T A N

Akumal

Palancar
Reef

Tihosuco

Tulum

Xel-Há

295

Muyil

Boca Paila

Santa Rosa

Punta Allen

Punta Pájaros

184

Polyuc

Felipe Carrillo
Puerto

Tupak

JINTANA ROO

Punta Herrero

307

Sian Ka'an
Biosphere
Reserve

293

Caribbean Sea

Limónes

Banco
Chinchorro

Punto Bravo

307

Bahía de
Chetumal

Majahual

Bacalar

Cayo
Centro

N

Escondito

Chetumal

Bahía de
Corozal

Nicolás
Bravo

Xcalak

Río Hondo

0   30 miles
0   30 km

B E L I Z E

x

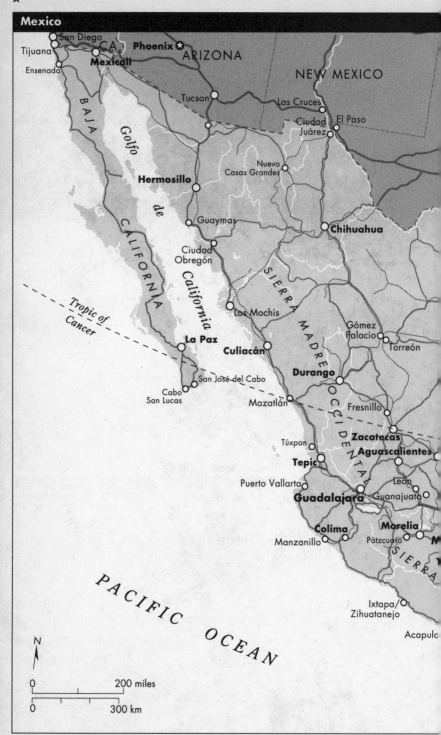

Mexico

San Diego
Tijuana
Ensenada
Mexicali
CA
Phoenix ✪ ARIZONA
NEW MEXICO
Tucson
Las Cruces
Ciudad
Juárez
El Paso
BAJA
Golfo
Nuevo
Casas Grandes
Hermosillo
de
Chihuahua
Guaymas
CALIFORNIA
Ciudad
Obregón
California
SIERRA
Los Mochis
Gómez
Palacio
Torreón
Tropic of
Cancer
La Paz
Culiacán
MADRE
Durango
San José del Cabo
Cabo
San Lucas
Mazatlán
Fresnillo
OCCIDENTAL
Túxpan
Zacatecas
Aguascalientes
Tepic
León
Puerto Vallarta
Guadalajara
Guanajuato
Colima
Morelia
M
Manzanillo
Pátzcuaro
SIERRA
PACIFIC
OCEAN
Ixtapa/
Zihuatanejo
Acapulco

N

0   200 miles
0   300 km

SMART TRAVEL TIPS A TO Z

Basic Information on Traveling in Cancún, Savvy Tips to Make Your Trip a Breeze, and Companies and Organizations to Contact

AIR TRAVEL

BOOKING YOUR FLIGHT

Price is just one factor to consider when booking a flight: frequency of service and even a carrier's safety record are often just as important. Major airlines offer the greatest number of departures. Smaller airlines—including regional and no-frills airlines—usually have a limited number of flights daily. On the other hand, so-called low-cost airlines usually are cheaper, and their fares impose fewer restrictions, such as advance-purchase requirements. Safety-wise, low-cost carriers as a group have a good history—about equal to that of major carriers.

When you book, **look for nonstop flights** and **remember that "direct" flights stop at least once.** Try to **avoid connecting flights,** which require a change of plane. Two airlines may jointly operate a connecting flight, so ask if your airline operates every segment—you may find that your preferred carrier flies you only part of the way. International flights on a country's flag carrier are almost always nonstop; U.S. airlines often fly direct.

Ask your airline if it offers electronic ticketing, which eliminates all paperwork. There's no ticket to pick up or misplace. You go directly to the gate and give the agent your confirmation number. There's no worry about waiting on line at the airport while precious minutes tick by.

CARRIERS

When flying internationally, you must usually choose between a domestic carrier, the national flag carrier of the country you are visiting, and a foreign carrier from a third country. You may, for example, choose to fly Aeroméxico to Cancún. National flag carriers have the greatest number of nonstops. Domestic carriers may have better connections to your hometown and serve a greater number of gateway cities. Third-party carriers may have a price advantage.

➤ MAJOR AIRLINES: **Aeroméxico** (☎ 800/237–6639) to Cancún, Cozumel. **American** (☎ 800/433–7300) to Cancún. **Continental** (☎ 800/231–0856) to Cancún, Cozumel. **Delta** (☎ 800/241–4141) to Cancún. **Lacsa** (☎ 800/225–2272) to Cancún. **Mexicana** (☎ 800/531–7921) to Cancún, Cozumel. **TWA** (☎ 800/892–4141) to Cancún. **US Airways** ☎ 800/428–4322) to Cancún.

➤ REGIONAL AIRLINES: For air packages from local charter operators, *see* Tour Operators, *below.*

➤ FROM THE U.K.: **American Airlines** (☎ 0345/789–789) via Miami and Dallas. **British Airways** (☎ 0345/222–111) daily from Gatwick or Heathrow via Mexico City. **Continental** (☎ 0800/776–464) from Gatwick via Newark. **Northwest** (☎ 0990/561–000) via Minneapolis. **TWA** (☎ 0181/814–0707) via St. Louis.

➤ WITHIN THE YUCATÁN: **Aerocaribe** (reserve through Mexicana, ☎ 800/531–7921) services Cancún, Cozumel, Mérida, Chichén Itzá, Villahermosa, Palenque, Ciudad del Carmen, and Playa del Carmen. **Aviacsa** (☎ 5/448–8900 in Mexico City) services Cancún, Chetumal, and Mérida.

CHARTERS

Charters usually have the lowest fares but are the least dependable. Departures are infrequent and seldom on time, flights can be delayed for up to 48 hours or can be canceled for any reason up to 10 days before you're scheduled to leave. Itineraries and prices can change after you've booked your flight.

In the U.S., the Department of Transportation's Aviation Consumer Protection Division has jurisdiction over charters and provides a certain degree of protection. The DOT requires that money paid to charter operators be held in escrow, so if you can't pay with a credit card, **always make your check payable to a charter carrier's escrow account.** The name of the bank should be in the charter contract. If you have any problems with a charter operator, contact the DOT (☞ Airline Complaints, *below*). If you buy a charter package that includes both air and land arrangements, remember that the escrow requirement applies only to the air component.

CHECK IN & BOARDING

Airlines routinely overbook planes, assuming that not everyone with a ticket will show up, but sometimes everyone does. When that happens, airlines ask for volunteers to give up their seats. In return these volunteers usually get a certificate for a free flight and are rebooked on the next flight out. If there are not enough volunteers, the airline must choose who will be denied boarding. The first to get bumped are passengers who checked in late and those flying on discounted tickets, so **get to the gate and check in as early as possible,** especially during peak periods.

Although the trend on international flights is to drop reconfirmation requirements, many airlines still ask you to reconfirm each leg of your international itinerary. Failure to do so may result in your reservation being canceled.

Always **bring a government-issued photo ID to the airport.** You may be asked to show it before you are allowed to check in.

CONSOLIDATORS

Consolidators buy tickets for scheduled international flights at reduced rates from the airlines, then sell them at prices that beat the best fare available directly from the airlines, usually without restrictions. Sometimes you can even get your money back if you need to return the ticket. Carefully read the fine print detailing penalties

for changes and cancellations, and **confirm your consolidator reservation with the airline.**

➤ CONSOLIDATORS: **Cheap Tickets** (☎ 800/377–1000). **Up & Away Travel** (☎ 212/889–2345). **Discount Travel Network** (☎ 800/576–1600). **Unitravel** (☎ 800/325–2222). **World Travel Network** (☎ 800/409–6753).

COURIERS

When you fly as a courier, you trade your checked-luggage space for a ticket deeply subsidized by a courier service. It's all perfectly legitimate, but there are restrictions: You can usually book your flight only a week or two in advance, your length of stay may be set for a certain number of days, and you probably won't be able to book a companion on the same flight.

CUTTING COSTS

The least-expensive airfares to Cancún are priced for round-trip travel and usually must be purchased in advance. It's smart to **call a number of airlines, and when you are quoted a good price, book it on the spot**—the same fare may not be available the next day. Airlines generally allow you to change your return date for a fee. If you don't use your ticket, you can apply the cost toward the purchase of a new ticket, again for a small charge. However, most low-fare tickets are nonrefundable. To get the lowest airfare, **check different routings.** Compare prices of flights to and from different airports if your destination or home city has more than one gateway. Also price off-peak flights, which may be significantly less expensive.

Travel agents, especially those who specialize in finding the lowest fares (☞ Discounts & Deals, *below*), can be especially helpful when booking a plane ticket. When you're quoted a price, **ask your agent if the price is likely to get any lower.** Good agents know the seasonal fluctuations of airfares and can usually anticipate a sale or fare war. However, waiting can be risky: The fare could go *up* as seats become scarce, and you may wait so long that your preferred flight sells out. A wait-and-see strategy works best if your plans are flexible.

THE GOLD GUIDE / SMART TRAVEL TIPS

If you must arrive and depart on certain dates, don't delay.

ENJOYING THE FLIGHT

For better service, **fly smaller or regional carriers,** which often have higher passenger-satisfaction ratings. Sometimes you'll find leather seats, more legroom, and better food.

For more legroom, **request an emergency-aisle seat.** Don't sit in the row in front of the emergency aisle or in front of a bulkhead, where seats may not recline.

If you don't like airline food, **ask for special meals when booking.** These can be vegetarian, low-cholesterol, or kosher, for example.

When flying internationally, try to maintain a normal routine, to help fight jet lag. At night, **get some sleep.** By day, **eat light meals, drink water (not alcohol), and move around the cabin** to stretch your legs.

Many carriers have prohibited smoking on all of their international flights; others allow smoking only on certain routes or certain departures, so **contact your carrier regarding its smoking policy.**

FLYING TIMES

Cancún is 3½ hours from New York and Chicago, 4½ hours from Los Angeles. Flights to Cozumel and Mérida are comparable in length.

HOW TO COMPLAIN

If your baggage goes astray or your flight goes awry, complain right away. Most carriers require that you **file a claim immediately.**

➤ AIRLINE COMPLAINTS: U.S. Department of Transportation **Aviation Consumer Protection Division** (✉ C-75, Room 4107, Washington, DC 20590, ☎ 202/366–2220). **Federal Aviation Administration Consumer Hotline** (☎ 800/322–7873).

AIRPORTS

The major gateways to the Cancún area are **Cancún Airport** and **Cozumel Airport.** Mérida, Campeche, Chetumal, and Playa del Carmen have smaller airports served primarily by domestic carriers. Some ruins have airstrips that can handle small planes.

➤ AIRPORT INFORMATION: **Cancún Airport** (☎ 98/860049). **Cozumel Airport** (☎ 987/24081).

BIKE TRAVEL

BIKES IN FLIGHT

Most airlines will accommodate bikes as luggage, provided they are dismantled and put into a box. Call to see if your airline sells bike boxes (about $5; bike bags are at least $100) although you can often pick them up free at bike shops. International travelers can sometimes substitute a bike for a piece of checked luggage for free; otherwise, it will cost about $100. Domestic and Canadian airlines charge a $25–$50 fee.

BOAT & FERRY TRAVEL

The Yucatán is served by a number of ferries and boats, ranging from the spiffy, usually efficient hydrofoils (motorized catamarans) between Playa del Carmen and Cozumel to the more modest launches plying the waters from Puerto Juárez and Cancún to Isla Mujeres, and the tiny craft and catamarans heading out to the smaller offshore islands (Isla Holbox, Isla del Carmen, the Alacranes Reef).

Schedules are approximate and often vary with the weather and the number of passengers. Prices are generally quite reasonable.

BUS TRAVEL

Bus travel in Yucatán, as throughout Mexico, is inexpensive by U.S. standards, with rates averaging about $3 per hour. Buses run the gamut from comfortable air-conditioned coaches with bathrooms, televisions, and hostess service (*especial,* deluxe, and first-class) to dilapidated "vintage" buses (second- and third-class) on which pigs and chickens travel and stops are made in the middle of nowhere. While a lower-class bus ride can be interesting if you are not in a hurry and want to see the sights and experience the local culture, these fares are only about 10% to 20% lower than those in the premium categories. Therefore, travelers planning a long-distance haul are well advised to **buy the first-class or *especial* tickets** when traveling by bus within Mexico; unlike tickets for the other classes, these can be reserved in advance. ADO (Auto-buses del Oriente) is the principal first-class bus company serving the Yucatán peninsula.

The Mexican bus network is extensive, far more so than the railroads. Buses go where trains do not, service is more frequent, tickets can be purchased on the spot (except during holidays and on long weekends, when advance purchase is crucial), and first-class buses are faster and much more comfortable than trains. **Bring something to eat on all overnight bus rides** in case you don't like the restaurant where the bus stops, and **bring toilet tissue,** as rest rooms vary in cleanliness. Smoking is prohibited on a growing number of Mexican buses, though the rule is occasionally ignored.

BUSINESS HOURS

Most businesses are open weekdays 9–2 and 4–7. Banks are open weekdays 9–5. Some banks open on Saturday mornings.

CAMERAS & COMPUTERS

EQUIPMENT PRECAUTIONS

Always **keep your film, tape, or computer disks out of the sun.** Carry an extra supply of batteries, and **be prepared to turn on your camera, camcorder, or laptop** to prove to security personnel that the device is real. Always **ask for hand inspection of film,** which becomes clouded after successive exposure to airport X-ray machines, and **keep videotapes and computer disks away from metal detectors.**

TRAVEL PHOTOGRAPHY

Photo Help: KODAK INFORMATION CENTER (☎ 800/242–2424). *KODAK GUIDE TO SHOOTING GREAT TRAVEL PICTURES,* available in bookstores or from Fodor's Travel Publications (☎ 800/533–6478; $16.50 plus $4 shipping).

CAR RENTAL

Rates in Cancún begin at $50 a day and $300 a week for an economy car with air-conditioning, a manual transmission, and unlimited mileage. This does not include tax on car rentals, which is 10%.

➤ MAJOR AGENCIES: **Alamo** (☎ 800/522–9696, 0800/272–2000 in the U.K.). **Budget** (☎ 800/527–0700, 0800/181181 in the U.K.). **Hertz** (☎ 800/654–3001, 800/263–0600 in Canada, 0345/555888 in the U.K., 03/9222–2523 in Australia, 03/358–6777 in New Zealand). **National InterRent** (☎ 800/227–3876; 0345/222525 in the U.K., where it is known as Europcar InterRent).

CUTTING COSTS

To get the best deal, **book through a travel agent who is willing to shop around.**

Also **ask your travel agent about a company's customer-service record.** How has the company responded to late plane arrivals and vehicle mishaps? Are there often lines at the rental counter? If you're traveling during a holiday period, does a confirmed reservation guarantee you a car?

Be sure to **look into wholesalers,** companies that do not own fleets but rent in bulk from those that do and often offer better rates than traditional car-rental operations. Prices are best during off-peak periods. Rentals booked through wholesalers must be paid for before you leave the United States.

➤ RENTAL WHOLESALERS: **Auto Europe** (☎ 207/842–2000 or 800/223–5555, FAX 800–235–6321). **Kemwel Holiday Autos** (☎ 914/835–5555 or 800/678–0678, FAX 914/835–5126).

INSURANCE

Regardless of any coverage afforded you by your credit-card company, **you must have Mexican auto-liability insurance.** This is usually provided by car-rental agencies and included in the cost of the car. Be sure that you have been provided with proof of such insurance: If you drive without it, you are not only liable for damages, but are breaking the law. When driving a rented car you are generally responsible for any damage to or loss of the vehicle. You also are liable for any property damage or personal injury that you may cause while driving. Before you rent, **see what coverage you already have** under the terms of your personal auto-insurance policy and credit cards.

REQUIREMENTS

In Mexico your own driver's license is acceptable. An International Driver's Permit is a good idea; it's available from the American or Canadian automobile association, and, in the United Kingdom, from the Automobile Association or Royal Automobile Club. These international permits are universally recognized, and having one in your wallet may save you a problem with the local authorities.

SURCHARGES

Before you pick up a car in one city and leave it in another, **ask about drop-off charges or one-way service fees,** which can be substantial. Note, too, that some rental agencies charge extra if you return the car before the time specified in your contract. To avoid a hefty refueling fee, **fill the tank just before you turn in the car,** but be aware that gas stations near the rental outlet may overcharge.

CAR TRAVEL

AUTO CLUBS

➤ IN AUSTRALIA: **Australian Automobile Association** (☎ 06/247–7311).

➤ IN CANADA: **Canadian Automobile Association** (CAA, ☎ 613/247–0117).

➤ IN NEW ZEALAND: **New Zealand Automobile Association** (☎ 09/377–4660).

➤ IN THE U.K.: **Automobile Association** (AA, ☎ 0990/500–600), **Royal Automobile Club** (RAC, ☎ 0990/722–722 for membership, 0345/121–345 for insurance).

➤ IN THE U.S.: **American Automobile Association** (☎ 800/564–6222).

EMERGENCY SERVICES

The Mexican Tourism Ministry operates a fleet of some 275 pickup trucks, known as *Los Angeles Verdes,* or the Green Angels, to render assistance to motorists on the major highways. The bilingual drivers provide mechanical help, first aid, radio-telephone communication, basic supplies and small parts, towing, and tourist information. Services are free, and spare parts, fuel, and lubricants are provided at cost. Tips are always appreciated.

The Green Angels patrol fixed sections of the major highways twice daily 8–8, later on holiday weekends. If your car breaks down, **pull as far as possible off the road,** lift the hood, hail a passing vehicle, and ask the driver to **notify the patrol.** Most bus and truck drivers will be quite helpful. If you witness an accident, do not stop to help, but instead find the nearest official.

➤ GREEN ANGELS: In Mexico City, call ☎ 5/250–8221.

GASOLINE

PEMEX, Mexico's government-owned petroleum monopoly, franchises all gas stations, so prices throughout the Yucatán will be the same. Gas prices tend to be slightly higher than those in the United States; some stations in Mexico now accept American credit cards and dollars. Fuel quality is not up to United States standards—fuel-injected engines are likely to have problems after a while. Unleaded fuel, known as *Magna Premio* and *Magna Sin* (lower octane), is available at most PEMEX stations. When filling your tank, ask for a specific peso amount of gas rather than for a number of liters. **Keep the tank full,** because gas stations are not plentiful.

INSURANCE

Make sure there is proof of Mexican liability insurance in your rental car; if you're driving your own car, be sure to purchase Mexican insurance at the border. Do not rely on credit-card companies' assurances that you do not have to purchase auto insurance in Mexico unless you are ready to fork over large sums and be reimbursed later. If you are involved in an accident and don't have liability insurance, Mexican authorities will demand that damage be paid for on the spot, in cash; you might also land in jail.

PARKING

Always park your car in a parking lot, or at least in a populated area. Never leave anything of value in an unattended car.

ROAD CONDITIONS

The road system in the Yucatán Peninsula is extensive and generally in good repair. **Route 307** parallels most of the Caribbean coast from Punta Sam, north of Cancún, to Tulum; there it turns inward for a while before returning to the coast at Chetumal and the Belize border. **Route 180** runs west from Cancún to Valladolid, Chichén Itzá, and Mérida, then turns southwest to Campeche, Isla del Carmen, and on to Villahermosa. From Mérida, there is also the winding, more scenic **Route 261,** which provides good access to some of the more off-the-beaten track archaeological sites on the way south to Campeche and Francisco Escárcega, where it joins **Route 186** going east to Chetumal. These highways are two-lane roads. **Route 295** (from the north coast to Valladolid and Felipe Carrillo Puerto) is also a good two-lane road.

The *autopista,* or *carretera de cuota,* an eight-lane toll highway between Cancún and Mérida, was completed in 1993. It runs roughly parallel to Route 180 and cuts driving time between Cancún and Mérida—formerly around 4½ hours—by about one hour. Tolls between Mérida and Cancún can run as high as $10, and there are long stretches between highway exits.

Once off the main highways, motorists will find the roads in varying conditions. Some roads are unmarked, which makes it confusing to reach a given destination. Many are unpaved and full of potholes. If you must take one of the smaller roads, the best course is to **allow plenty of daylight hours and never travel at night.** Always slow down when approaching towns and villages—which you are forced to do by the ubiquitous *topes* (speed bumps)—because you will find small children and animals in abundance. Children selling oranges, nuts, or candies will almost certainly approach your car. Some people feel that it is best not to buy from them, reasoning that if they can make money this way, they will not go to school. Others choose to buy from them on the theory that they would probably go to school if they could afford it, and need the meager profits to survive. Judge for yourself.

RULES OF THE ROAD

Mileage and speed limits are given in kilometers. One kilometer is approximately ⁹⁄₁₀ mile. In small towns, observe the posted speed limits, which can be as low as 20 kph (12 mph).

CHILDREN & TRAVEL

CHILDREN IN CANCUN

All children, including infants, must have proof of citizenship for travel to Mexico. Children traveling with a single parent must also have a notarized letter from the other parent stating that the child has his or her permission to leave the home country. In addition, parents must fill out a tourist card for each child over 10 years of age traveling with them.

The advisability of traveling with children in the Yucatán will depend on the age and maturity of your child. Infants may be bothered by the heat, and finding pure water or fresh milk in remote areas may be a problem. Because children are especially prone to diarrhea, special care must be taken with regard to food. If they enjoy travel in general, children will do well in the Yucatán, where, as in the rest of Mexico, children are welcome almost everywhere.

Be sure to plan ahead and **involve your youngsters** as you outline your trip. When packing, include things to keep them busy en route. On sightseeing days try to schedule activities of special interest to your children. If you are renting a car don't forget to **arrange for a car seat** when you reserve.

FLYING

If your children are two or older, **ask about children's airfares.** As a general rule, infants under two not occupying a seat fly at greatly reduced fares or even for free.

In general the adult baggage allowance applies to children paying half or more of the adult fare. When booking, **ask about carry-on allowances for those traveling with infants.** In general, for babies charged

THE GOLD GUIDE / SMART TRAVEL TIPS

10% of the adult fare you are allowed one carry-on bag and a collapsible stroller, which may have to be checked; you may be limited to less if the flight is full.

Experts agree that it's a good idea to use safety seats aloft for children weighing less than 40 pounds. Airlines, however, can set their own policies: U.S. carriers allow FAA-approved models but usually require that you buy a ticket, even if your child would otherwise ride free, since the seats must be strapped into regular seats. Airline rules vary, so it's important to **check your airline's policy about using safety seats during takeoff and landing.** Safety seats cannot obstruct the movement of other passengers in the row, so get an appropriate seat assignment as early as possible.

When making your reservation, **request children's meals or a free-standing bassinet** if you need them; the latter are available only to those seated at the bulkhead, where there's enough legroom. Remember, however, that bulkhead seats may not have their own overhead bins, and there's no storage space in front of you—a major inconvenience.

GROUP TRAVEL

When planning to take your kids on a tour, look for companies that specialize in family travel.

➤ FAMILY-FRIENDLY TOUR OPERATORS: **Families Welcome!** (✉ 92 N. Main St., Ashland, OR 97520, ☎ 541/482–6121 or 800/326–0724, ℻ 541/482–0660).

HOTELS

Most hotels in Cancún allow children under a certain age to stay in their parents' room at no extra charge, but others charge them as extra adults; be sure to **ask about the cutoff age for children's discounts.**

➤ BEST CHOICES: Several hotel chains provide services that make it easier to travel with children. The **Fiesta Americana Coral Beach Cancún** and **Condesa** (☎ 800/343–7821) offer free activities for children and teenagers in high season. The **Cancún Sheraton Resort & Towers** (☎ 800/334–8484) provides connecting "family rooms".

Camino Real (☎ 800/7–CAMINO), **Westin Regina** (☎ 800/228–3000), and the **Presidente Inter-Continental** (☎ 800/327–1200) offer children's "clubs" during school vacations.

CONSUMER PROTECTION

Whenever possible, **pay with a major credit card** so you can cancel payment or get reimbursed if there's a problem, provided that you can provide documentation. This is the best way to pay, whether you're buying travel arrangements before your trip or shopping at your destination.

If you're doing business with a particular company for the first time, **contact your local Better Business Bureau and the attorney general's offices** in your state and the company's home state, as well. Have any complaints been filed?

Finally, if you're buying a package or tour, always **consider travel insurance** that includes default coverage (☞ Insurance, *below*).

➤ LOCAL BBBs: **Council of Better Business Bureaus** (✉ 4200 Wilson Blvd., Suite 800, Arlington, VA 22203, ☎ 703/276–0100, ℻ 703/525–8277).

CRUISE TRAVEL

Cozumel and Playa del Carmen have become increasingly popular ports for Caribbean cruises. Cruise lines that depart from Miami include **Caribbean** (☎ 800/327–6700), **Dolphin** (☎ 800/222–1003), **Fantasy/Celebrity** (☎ 800/423–2100), **Majesty** (☎ 800/532–7788), and **Norwegian** (☎ 800/327–7030). Lines with Caribbean cruises stopping in the Yucatán from other Florida ports (principally Fort Lauderdale, Port Manatee, and Tampa) include **Cunard** (☎ 800/221–4770), **Norwegian** (☎ 800/327–7030), **Princess** (☎ 800/421–0522), **Regal** (☎ 800/270–SAIL), and **Royal** (☎ 800/227–4534). From New Orleans: **Commodore** (☎ 800/237–5361) and **Holland America** (☎ 800/426–0327); and from Galveston, TX: **Sun** (☎ 800/872–6400).

DISCOUNT CRUISES

Usually, the best deals on cruise bookings can be found by consulting a cruise-only travel agency. Contact the **National Association of Cruise Only Travel Agencies (NACOA)** (✉ 3191 Coral Way, Suite 622, Miami, FL 33145, ☎ 305/446–7732, FAX 305/446–9732) for a listing of such agencies in your area.

CUSTOMS & DUTIES

When shopping, **keep receipts** for all of your purchases. Upon reentering the country, **be ready to show customs officials what you've bought.** If you feel a duty is incorrect, appeal the assessment. If you object to the way your clearance was handled, get the inspector's badge number. In either case, first ask to see a supervisor, then write to the appropriate authorities, beginning with the port director at your point of entry.

IN CANCUN

Entering Mexico, you may bring in (1) 400 cigarettes or 50 cigars or 250 grams of tobacco, (2) one photographic camera and one nonprofessional film or video camera and 12 rolls of film for each, and (3) gift items not exceeding a combined value of $300. You are not allowed to bring meat, vegetables, plants, fruit, or flowers into the country.

IN AUSTRALIA

Australia residents who are 18 or older may bring back $A400 worth of souvenirs and gifts (including jewelry), 250 cigarettes or 250 grams of tobacco, and 1,125 ml of alcohol (including wine, beer, and spirits). Residents under 18 may bring back $A200 worth of goods.

➤ INFORMATION: **Australian Customs Service** (Regional Director, ✉ Box 8, Sydney, NSW 2001, ☎ 02/9213–2000, FAX 02/9213–4000).

IN CANADA

Canadian residents who have been out of Canada for at least 7 days may bring in C$500 worth of goods duty-free. If you've been away less than 7 days but more than 48 hours, the duty-free allowance drops to C$200; if your trip lasts 24–48 hours, the allowance is C$50. You may not pool allowances with family members. Goods claimed under the C$500

exemption may follow you by mail; those claimed under the lesser exemptions must accompany you. Alcohol and tobacco products may be included in the 7-day and 48-hour exemptions but not in the 24-hour exemption. If you meet the age requirements of the province or territory through which you reenter Canada, you may bring in, duty-free, 1.14 liters (40 imperial ounces) of wine or liquor *or* 24 12-ounce cans or bottles of beer or ale. If you are 16 or older you may bring in, duty-free, 200 cigarettes and 50 cigars.

You may send an unlimited number of gifts worth up to C$60 each duty-free to Canada. Label the package UNSOLICITED GIFT—VALUE UNDER $60. Alcohol and tobacco are excluded.

➤ INFORMATION: **Revenue Canada** (✉ 2265 St. Laurent Blvd. S, Ottawa, Ontario K1G 4K3, ☎ 613/993–0534, 800/461–9999 in Canada).

IN NEW ZEALAND

Although greeted with a "Haere Mai" ("Welcome to New Zealand"), homeward-bound residents with goods to declare must present themselves for inspection. If you're 17 or older, you may bring back $700 worth of souvenirs and gifts. Your duty-free allowance also includes 4.5 liters of wine or beer; one 1,125-ml bottle of spirits; and either 200 cigarettes, 250 grams of tobacco, 50 cigars, or a combo of all three up to 250 grams.

➤ INFORMATION: **New Zealand Customs** (✉ Custom House, ✉ 50 Anzac Ave., Box 29, Auckland, New Zealand, ☎ 09/359–6655, 09/309–2978).

IN THE U.K.

From countries outside the EU, including Mexico, you may import, duty-free, 200 cigarettes or 50 cigars; 1 liter of spirits or 2 liters of fortified or sparkling wine or liqueurs; 2 liters of still table wine; 60 milliliters of perfume; 250 milliliters of toilet water; plus @136 worth of other goods, including gifts and souvenirs.

➤ INFORMATION: **HM Customs and Excise** (✉ Dorset House, ✉ Stamford St., London SE1 9NG, ☎ 0171/202–4227).

IN THE U.S.

U.S. residents may bring home $400 worth of foreign goods duty-free if they've been out of the country for at least 48 hours (and if they haven't used the $400 allowance or any part of it in the past 30 days).

U.S. residents 21 and older may bring back 1 liter of alcohol duty-free. In addition, regardless of your age, you are allowed 200 cigarettes and 100 non-Cuban cigars. Antiques, which the U.S. Customs Service defines as objects more than 100 years old, enter duty-free, as do original works of art done entirely by hand, including paintings, drawings, and sculptures.

You may also send packages home duty-free: up to $200 worth of goods for personal use, with a limit of one parcel per addressee per day (and no alcohol or tobacco products or perfume worth more than $5); label the package PERSONAL USE, and attach a list of its contents and their retail value. Do not label the package UNSOLICITED GIFT, or your duty-free exemption will drop to $100. Mailed items do not affect your duty-free allowance on your return.

➤ INFORMATION: **U.S. Customs Service** (Inquiries, ✉ Box 7407, Washington, DC 20044, ☎ 202/927–6724; complaints, Office of Regulations and Rulings, ✉ 1301 Constitution Ave. NW, Washington, DC 20229; registration of equipment, Resource Management, ✉ 1301 Constitution Ave. NW, Washington, DC 20229, ☎ 202/927–0540).

DINING

Eating breakfast or having cocktails in a variety of hotels is a good way of getting to know different properties. For lunch and dinner, however, in such areas as Cancún, it is generally best to **stay away from restaurants in the large chain hotels** because prices tend to be exorbitant. (That said, some of the best restaurants may be located in such hotels; they are reviewed when that's the case.) Also, when buying fish from beachside and roadside palapas, **make sure the facilities are sanitary** so you don't get food poisoning. Be especially careful with shellfish and anything to which mayonnaise may have been added.

Restaurants in the Yucatán, including those in hotels, are for the most part very casual. The exceptions will be noted within reviews. Most restaurants are open daily for lunch and dinner during high season (Dec.–Apr.), but opening hours tend to be more erratic during the rest of the year. It's always a good idea to **phone ahead.**

DISABILITIES & ACCESSIBILITY

ACCESS IN CANCUN

For people with disabilities, traveling in the Yucatán can be both challenging and rewarding. Travelers with mobility impairments used to venturing out on their own in the United States should not be surprised if locals try to prevent them from doing things. This is mainly out of concern; most Mexican families take complete care of relatives who use wheelchairs, so the general public is not accustomed to such independence. Additionally, very few places in the Yucatán have handrails, let alone special facilities and means of access. Not even Cancún offers wheelchair-accessible transportation. Knowing how to ask for assistance is extremely important. If you are not fluent in Spanish, be sure to **take along a pocket dictionary.** Travelers with vision impairments who have no knowledge of Spanish will probably need a translator; people with hearing impairments who are comfortable using body language usually get along very well.

MAKING RESERVATIONS

When discussing accessibility with an operator or reservations agent, **ask hard questions.** Are there any stairs, inside *or* out? Are there grab bars next to the toilet *and* in the shower/tub? How wide is the doorway to the room? To the bathroom? For the most extensive facilities meeting the latest legal specifications, **opt for newer accommodations,** which are more likely to have been designed with access in mind. Older buildings or ships may have more limited facilities. Be sure to **discuss your needs before booking.**

TRANSPORTATION

➤ COMPLAINTS: **Disability Rights Section** (✉ U.S. Department of Justice, Civil Rights Division, ✉ Box 66738, Washington, DC 20035–6738, ☎ 202/514–0301 or 800/514–0301, TTY 202/514–0383 or 800/514–0383, FAX 202/307–1198) for general complaints. **Aviation Consumer Protection Division** (☞ Air Travel, *above*) for airline-related problems. **Civil Rights Office** (✉ U.S. Department of Transportation, Departmental Office of Civil Rights, S-30, ✉ 400 7th St. SW, Room 10215, Washington, DC 20590, ☎ 202/366–4648, FAX 202/366–9371) for problems with surface transportation.

TRAVEL AGENCIES & TOUR OPERATORS

As a whole, the travel industry has become more aware of the needs of travelers with disabilities. In the U.S., the Americans with Disabilities Act requires that travel firms serve the needs of all travelers. Note, though, that some agencies and operators specialize in making travel arrangements for individuals and groups with disabilities.

➤ TRAVELERS WITH MOBILITY PROBLEMS: **Access Adventures** (✉ 206 Chestnut Ridge Rd., Rochester, NY 14624, ☎ 716/889–9096), run by a former physical-rehabilitation counselor. **Accessible Journeys** (✉ 35 W. Sellers Ave., Ridley Park, PA 19078, ☎ 610/521–0339 or 800/846–4537, FAX 610/521–6959), for escorted tours exclusively for travelers with mobility impairments. **Flying Wheels Travel** (✉ 143 W. Bridge St., Box 382, Owatonna, MN 55060, ☎ 507/451–5005 or 800/535–6790, FAX 507/451–1685), a travel agency specializing in customized tours and itineraries worldwide. **Hinsdale Travel Service** (✉ 201 E. Ogden Ave., Suite 100, Hinsdale, IL 60521, ☎ 630/325–1335), a travel agency that benefits from the advice of wheelchair traveler Janice Perkins.

DISCOUNTS & DEALS

Be a smart shopper and **compare all your options** before making any choice. A plane ticket bought with a promotional coupon may not be cheaper than the least expensive fare from a discount ticket agency. For high-price travel purchases, such as packages or tours, keep in mind that what you get is just as important as what you save. Just because something is cheap doesn't mean it's a bargain.

CLUBS & COUPONS

Many companies sell discounts in the form of travel clubs and coupon books, but these cost money. You must use participating advertisers to get a deal, and only after you recoup the initial membership cost or book price do you begin to save. If you plan to use the club or coupons frequently, you may save considerably. Before signing up, find out what discounts you get for free.

➤ DISCOUNT CLUBS: **Entertainment Travel Editions** (✉ 2125 Butterfield Rd., Troy, MI 48084, ☎ 800/445–4137; $20–$51, depending on destination). **Great American Traveler** (✉ Box 27965, Salt Lake City, UT 84127, ☎ 801/974–3033 or 800/548–2812; $49.95 per year). **Moment's Notice Discount Travel Club** (✉ 7301 New Utrecht Ave., Brooklyn, NY 11204, ☎ 718/234–6295; $25 per year, single or family). **Privilege Card International** (✉ 237 E. Front St., Youngstown, OH 44503, ☎ 330/746–5211 or 800/236–9732; $74.95 per year). **Sears's Mature Outlook** (✉ Box 9390, Des Moines, IA 50306, ☎ 800/336–6330; $19.95 per year). **Travelers Advantage** (✉ CUC Travel Service, ✉ 3033 S. Parker Rd., Suite 1000, Aurora, CO 80014, ☎ 800/548–1116 or 800/648–4037; $59.95 per year, single or family). **Worldwide Discount Travel Club** (✉ 1674 Meridian Ave., Miami Beach, FL 33139, ☎ 305/534–2082; $50 per year family, $40 single).

CREDIT-CARD BENEFITS

When you use your credit card to make travel purchases you may get free travel-accident insurance, collision-damage insurance, and medical or legal assistance, depending on the card and the bank that issued it. American Express, MasterCard, and Visa provide one or more of these services, so **get a copy of your credit** card's travel-benefits policy. If you are a member of an auto club, always **ask hotel and car-rental reservations agents about auto-club discounts.** Some clubs offer additional discounts on tours, cruises, and admission to attractions.

DISCOUNT RESERVATIONS

To save money, **look into discount-reservations services** with toll-free numbers, which use their buying power to get a better price on hotels, airline tickets, even car rentals. When booking a room, always **call the hotel's local toll-free number** (if one is available) rather than the central reservations number—you'll often get a better price. Always ask about special packages or corporate rates.

When shopping for the best deal on hotels and car rentals, **look for guaranteed exchange rates,** which protect you against a falling dollar. With your rate locked in, you won't pay more, even if the price goes up in the local currency.

➤ AIRLINE TICKETS: ☎ **800/FLY–4–LESS.** ☎ **800/FLY–ASAP.**

➤ HOTEL ROOMS: **Players Express Vacations** (☎ 800/458–6161).

PACKAGE DEALS

Packages and guided tours can save you money, but don't confuse the two. When you buy a package, your travel remains independent, just as though you had planned and booked the trip yourself. Fly/drive packages, which combine airfare and car rental, are often a good deal.

ELECTRICITY

Electrical converters are not necessary because the country operates on the 60-cycle, 120-volt system; however, many Mexican outlets have not been updated to accommodate three-prong and polarized plugs (those with one larger prong), so **bring an adapter.**

GAY & LESBIAN TRAVEL

➤ GAY- AND LESBIAN-FRIENDLY TRAVEL AGENCIES: **Corniche Travel** (⊠ 8721 Sunset Blvd., Suite 200, West Hollywood, CA 90069, ☎ 310/854–6000 or 800/429–8747, FAX 310/659–7441). **Islanders Kennedy Travel** (⊠ 183 W. 10th St., New York, NY

10014, ☎ 212/242–3222 or 800/988–1181, FAX 212/929–8530). **Now Voyager** (⊠ 4406 18th St., San Francisco, CA 94114, ☎ 415/626–1169 or 800/255–6951, FAX 415/626–8626). **Yellowbrick Road** (⊠ 1500 W. Balmoral Ave., Chicago, IL 60640, ☎ 773/561–1800 or 800/642–2488, FAX 773/561–4497). **Skylink Travel and Tour** (⊠ 3577 Moorland Ave., Santa Rosa, CA 95407, ☎ 707/585–8355 or 800/225–5759, FAX 707/584–5637), serving lesbian travelers.

HEALTH

FOOD & DRINK

In the Yucatán, the major health risk is posed by the contamination of drinking water, fresh fruit, and vegetables by fecal matter, which causes the intestinal ailment known as *turista,* or traveler's diarrhea. Bad shellfish can also be a culprit. To prevent such an unpleasant interruption to your vacation, **watch what you eat.** Stay away from ice, uncooked food, seafood that may not have been refrigerated, and unpasteurized milk and milk products, and **drink only bottled water or water that has been boiled** for at least 20 minutes. When ordering cold drinks at untouristed establishments, skip the ice—ask for your beverage "*sin hielo.*" (You can usually identify ice made commercially from purified water by its uniform shape and the hole in the center.) Hotels with water-purification systems will post signs to that effect in the rooms. If these measures fail, try paregoric, a good antidiarrheal agent that dulls or eliminates abdominal cramps—it requires a doctor's prescription in Mexico—or Imodium (loperamide), which can be purchased over the counter. In mild cases, try Pepto-Bismol. Drink plenty of purified water or tea; chamomile tea (known as *te de manzanilla,* and readily available in restaurants throughout Mexico) is a good folk remedy for diarrhea. In severe cases, rehydrate yourself with a salt-sugar solution (½ tsp. salt and 4 tbsp. sugar per quart/liter of water).

MEDICAL PLANS

No one plans to get sick while traveling, but it happens, so **consider signing up with a medical-assistance** company. Members get doctor referrals, emergency evacuation or repatriation, 24-hour telephone hot lines for medical consultation, cash for emergencies, and other personal and legal assistance. Coverage varies by plan, so **review the benefits of each carefully.**

➤ MEDICAL-ASSISTANCE COMPANIES: **International SOS Assistance** (⊠ 8 Neshaminy Interplex, Suite 207, Trevose, PA 19053, ☎ 215/245–4707 or 800/523–6586, ℻ 215/244–9617; ⊠ 12 Chemin Riant-bosson, 1217 Meyrin 1, Geneva, Switzerland, ☎ 4122/785–6464, ℻ 4122/785–6424; ⊠ 10 Anson Rd., 14-07/08 International Plaza, Singapore, 079903, ☎ 65/226–3936, ℻ 65/226–3937).

SHOTS & MEDICATIONS

According to the U.S. government's National Centers for Disease Control (CDC) there is a limited risk of malaria and dengue fever in certain rural areas of the Yucatán Peninsula, especially the states of Campeche and Quintana Roo. Travelers in most urban or easily accessible areas need not worry. However, if you plan to visit remote regions or stay for more than six weeks, **check with the CDC's International Travelers Hotline.** In areas where malaria and dengue, both of which are carried by mosquitoes, are prevalent, use mosquito nets, wear clothing that covers the body, apply repellent containing DEET, and use spray for flying insects in living and sleeping areas. Also **consider taking antimalarial pills.** There is no vaccine to combat dengue.

➤ HEALTH WARNINGS: **National Centers for Disease Control** (⊠ CDC, National Center for Infectious Diseases, Division of Quarantine, Traveler's Health Section, ⊠ 1600 Clifton Rd. NE, M/S E-03, Atlanta, GA 30333, ☎ 404/332–4559, ℻ 404/332–4565).

HOLIDAYS

Banks, government offices, and many businesses close on these days, so plan your trip accordingly: January 1, New Year's Day; February 5, Constitution Day; January 6, the Feast of the Epiphany and the celebration of the founding of Mérida; March 21, Benito Juárez's birthday; May 1, Labor Day; September 16, Independence Day; November 20, Revolution Day; and December 25, Christmas Day.

Banks and government offices close during Holy Week, especially the Thursday and Friday before Easter; on May 5, anniversary of the Battle of Puebla; May 10, Mother's Day; September 1, opening of Congress; October 12, Día de la Raza; November 1 and 2, Day of the Dead; December 12, Feast of the Virgin of Guadalupe. Some private offices close from Christmas to New Year's Day; government offices usually keep a skeleton staff.

INSURANCE

Travel insurance is the best way to **protect yourself against financial loss.** The most useful plan is a comprehensive policy that includes coverage for trip cancellation and interruption, default, trip delay, and medical expenses (with a waiver for preexisting conditions).

Without insurance, you will lose all or most of your money if you cancel your trip, regardless of the reason. Default insurance covers you if your tour operator, airline, or cruise line goes out of business. Trip-delay covers unforeseen expenses that you may incur due to bad weather or mechanical delays. It's important to compare the fine print regarding trip-delay coverage when comparing policies.

For overseas travel, one of the most important components of travel insurance is its medical coverage. Supplemental health insurance will pick up the cost of your medical bills should you get sick or injured while traveling. U.S. residents should note that Medicare generally does not cover health-care costs outside the United States, nor do many privately issued policies. Residents of the United Kingdom can buy an annual travel-insurance policy valid for most vacations taken during the year in which the coverage is purchased. If you are pregnant or have a preexisting condition, make sure you're covered. British citizens should buy extra medical coverage when traveling overseas, according to the Association of British Insurers. Australian travelers should buy travel insurance, including extra medical coverage, whenever they go abroad, according to the Insurance Council of Australia.

Always **buy travel insurance directly from the insurance company**; if you buy it from a cruise line, airline, or tour operator that goes out of business you probably will not be covered for the agency or operator's default, a major risk. Before you make any purchase, **review your existing health and home-owner's policies** to find out whether they cover expenses incurred while traveling.

➤ TRAVEL INSURERS: In the U.S., **Access America** (⊠ 6600 W. Broad St., Richmond, VA 23230, ☎ 804/285–3300 or 800/284–8300). **Travel Guard International** (⊠ 1145 Clark St., Stevens Point, WI 54481, ☎ 715/345–0505 or 800/826–1300). In Canada, **Mutual of Omaha** (⊠ Travel Division, ⊠ 500 University Ave., Toronto, Ontario M5G 1V8, ☎ 416/598–4083, 800/268–8825 in Canada).

➤ INSURANCE INFORMATION: In the U.K., **Association of British Insurers** (⊠ 51 Gresham St., London EC2V 7HQ, ☎ 0171/600–3333). In Australia, the **Insurance Council of Australia** (☎ 613/9614–1077, FAX 613/9614–7924).

LANGUAGE

Spanish is the official language of Mexico, although Indian languages are spoken by approximately 20% of the population, many of whom speak no Spanish at all. This is the case in Mérida and much of the state of Yucatán, where a number of modern languages derived from Maya are spoken. In the beach resorts of Cancún and Cozumel, English is understood by most people employed in tourism; at the very least, shopkeepers will know the numbers for bargaining purposes. Mexicans welcome even the most halting attempts to use their language, and if you are in Mérida, you may even be introduced to a few Maya words and phrases.

The Spanish that most U.S. and Canadian citizens learn in high school is based on Castilian Spanish, which is different from Latin American Spanish. In terms of grammar, Mexican Spanish ignores the *vosotros* form of the second person plural, using the more formal *ustedes* in its place. As for pronunciation, the lisped Castilian "c" or "z" is dismissed in Mexico as a sign of affectation. The most obvious differences are in vocabulary: Mexican Spanish has thousands of indigenous words, and the use of *¿mande?* instead of *¿cómo?* (excuse me?) is a dead giveaway that one's Spanish was acquired in Mexico. Words or phrases that are harmless or commonplace in one Spanish-speaking country can take on salacious or otherwise offensive meanings in another. Unless you are lucky enough to be briefed on these nuances by a native coach, the only way to learn is by trial and error. Some recommended language schools in Mérida are listed in Chapter 6.

LANGUAGES FOR TRAVELERS

A phrase book and language tape set can help get you started.

➤ PHRASE BOOKS AND LANGUAGE-TAPE SETS: Languages for Travelers: Fodor's Spanish for Travelers (Audio Set), $16.95. Languages for Travelers: Fodor's Spanish for Travelers (Phrase book), $7. Call 800/733–3000 from the U.S.; 800/668–4247 from Canada; and 410/848–1900 from other destinations.

LODGING

If you plan to stay in Cancún or Cozumel, you'll have a variety of accommodations to choose from. There are luxurious and expensive internationally affiliated properties with numerous food and beverage outlets, the latest room amenities, boutiques, and sports facilities. These beach resorts also have more modest hostelries—usually a short walk or a shuttle ride from the water. As you get into the less-populated and less-visited areas of the Yucatán, particularly the cities, accommodations tend to be simpler and more "typically Mexican." The hotels discussed in this book all meet a minimum standard of cleanliness, and most have a certain rustic charm. Inexpensive bungalows, campsites, and places to hang a hammock along many of the beaches are other options.

APARTMENT & VILLA RENTALS

If you want a home base that's roomy enough for a family and comes with cooking facilities, **consider a furnished rental.** These can save you money, especially if you're traveling with a large group of people. Home-exchange directories list rentals (often second homes owned by prospective house swappers), and some services search for a house or apartment for you (even a castle if that's your fancy) and handle the paperwork. Some send an illustrated catalog; others send photographs only of specific properties, sometimes at a charge. Up-front registration fees may apply.

➤ RENTAL AGENTS: **Europa-Let/Tropical Inn-Let** (⊠ 92 N. Main St., Ashland, OR 97520, ☎ 541/482–5806 or 800/462–4486, ℻ 541/482–0660). **Property Rentals International** (⊠ 1008 Mansfield Crossing Rd., Richmond, VA 23236, ☎ 804/378–6054 or 800/220–3332, ℻ 804/379–2073). **Rent-a-Home International** (⊠ 7200 34th Ave. NW, Seattle, WA 98117, ☎ 206/789–9377 or 800/488–7368, ℻ 206/789–9379). **Vacation Home Rentals Worldwide** (⊠ 235 Kensington Ave., Norwood, NJ 07648, ☎ 201/767–9393 or 800/633–3284, ℻ 201/767–5510). **Villas International** (⊠ 605 Market St., San Francisco, CA 94105, ☎ 415/281–0910 or 800/221–2260, ℻ 415/281–0919). **Hideaways International** (⊠ 767 Islington St., Portsmouth, NH 03801, ☎ 603/430–4433 or 800/843–4433, ℻ 603/430–4444; membership $99) is a club for travelers who arrange rentals among themselves.

MAIL

POSTAL RATES

It costs 2.70 pesos to mail a postcard or letter weighing less than 20 grams to the United States or Canada. The cost to Great Britain is 3.40 pesos.

RECEIVING MAIL

Mail can be sent either to your hotel, to the post office, or, if you are an American Express card member, to the local branch of American Express. American Express offices in the Yucatán are located in Campeche City, Mérida, Cancún, and Cozumel. Another option is the Mexican postal service's *lista de correos* (poste restante) service. To use this service, you must first register with the local post office in which you wish to receive your mail. Mail should be addressed to: your name; a/c Lista de Correos; town name; state, postal code; Mexico. Mail is held at post offices for 10 days, and a list of recipients is posted daily. Postal codes for the main Yucatán destinations are as follows: Cancún, 77500; Isla Mujeres, 77400; Cozumel, 77600; Campeche, 24000; Mérida, 97000. Be forewarned, however, that mail service to and within Mexico is notoriously slow and can take anywhere from 10 days to three weeks. **Never send anything of value to Mexico through the mail.**

MONEY

COSTS

Mexico has a reputation for being inexpensive, particularly compared with other North American vacation spots such as the Caribbean. Cancún, however, is probably the most expensive destination in Mexico. In Mérida and the other cities in the Yucatán, where fewer American tourists visit, you will find the best value for your money. For obvious reasons, if you stay at international chain hotels and eat at restaurants geared to tourists (especially hotel restaurants), you may not find the Yucatán such a bargain.

Rates in the Yucatán decrease in the off-season by as much as 30%. Speaking Spanish is helpful in bargaining and when asking for dining recommendations. As a general rule, the less English spoken in a region, the cheaper things will be (☞ Language, *above*).

Sample costs are as follows: cup of coffee, 6–15 pesos; bottle of beer, 15–45 pesos; plate of tacos with trimmings, 15–55 pesos; grilled fish platter at a tourist restaurant, 25–75 pesos; 2-km (1-mi) taxi ride, 15 pesos.

Off-season, Cancún hotels cost one-third to one-half what they cost during peak season. Cozumel is a bit less costly than Cancún, and Isla Mujeres is slightly less expensive than Cozumel.

CREDIT & DEBIT CARDS

Should you use a credit card or a debit card when traveling? Both have benefits. A credit card allows you to delay payment and gives you certain rights as a consumer (☞ Consumer Protection, *above*). A debit card, also known as a check card, deducts funds directly from your checking account and helps you stay within your budget. When you want to rent a car, though, you may still need an old-fashioned credit card. Although you can always *pay* for your car with a debit card, some agencies will not allow you to *reserve* a car with a debit card.

Otherwise, the two types of plastic are virtually the same. Both will get you cash advances at ATMs worldwide if your card is properly programmed with your personal identification number (PIN). (For use in Cancún, your PIN must be four to six digits long.) Both offer excellent, wholesale exchange rates. And both protect you against unauthorized use if the card is lost or stolen. Your liability is limited to $50, as long as you report the card missing.

➤ ATM LOCATIONS: **Cirrus** (☎ 800/424–7787). **Plus** (☎ 800/843–7587).

CURRENCY

At press time, the peso was still "floating" after the devaluation enacted by the Zedillo administration in late 1994. While exchange rates were as favorable as one U.S. dollar to 8.5 Mexican pesos, one Canadian dollar to 6.25 pesos, and a pound sterling to 14.6 pesos, the market and prices are likely to continue to adjust. **Check with your bank or the financial pages of your local newspaper for current exchange rates.**

Mexican currency comes in denominations of 10, 20, 50, 100, 200 and 500 peso bills. Coins come in denominations of 20, 10, and 5 pesos and 50, 20, 10, and 5 centavos. Some denominations of bills and coins are very similar, so check carefully. To avoid fraud, it's wise to **make sure that "pesos" is clearly marked on all credit-card receipts.**

Dollar bills, but not coins, are widely accepted in many parts of the Yucatán, particularly in Cancún and Cozumel. Many tourist shops and market vendors, as well as virtually all hotel service personnel, take them, too.

Traveler's checks and all major U.S. credit cards are accepted in most tourist areas of Mexico. The large hotels, restaurants, and department stores accept cards readily. Most of the smaller, less expensive restaurants and shops, however, will only take cash. Credit cards are generally not accepted in small towns and villages, except in tourist-oriented hotels. When shopping, you can usually get better prices if you **pay with cash.**

EXCHANGING MONEY

For the most favorable rates, **change money through banks.** Although fees charged for ATM transactions may be higher abroad than at home, Cirrus and Plus exchange rates are excellent, because they are based on wholesale rates offered only by major banks. You won't do as well at exchange booths in airports or rail and bus stations, in hotels, in restaurants, or in stores, although you may find their hours more convenient. To avoid lines at airport exchange booths, **get a bit of local currency before you leave home.**

➤ EXCHANGE SERVICES: **Chase *Currency To Go*** (☎ 800/935–9935; 935–9935 in NY, NJ, and CT). **International Currency Express** (☎ 888/842–0880 on the East Coast, 888/278–6628 on the West Coast). **Thomas Cook Currency Services** (☎ 800/287–7362 for telephone orders and retail locations).

TRAVELER'S CHECKS

Do you need traveler's checks? It depends on where you're headed. If you're going to rural areas and small towns, go with cash; traveler's checks are best used in cities. Lost or stolen checks can usually be replaced within 24 hours. To ensure a speedy refund, buy your own traveler's checks—don't let someone else pay for them: irregularities like this can cause delays. The person who bought the checks should make the call to request a refund.

PACKING

LUGGAGE

How many carry-on bags you can bring with you is up to the airline. Most allow two, but the limit is often reduced to one on certain flights. Gate agents will take excess baggage—including bags they deem oversize—from you as you board and add it to checked luggage. To avoid this situation, make sure that everything you carry aboard will fit under your seat. Also, get to the gate early, and request a seat at the back of the plane; you'll probably board first, while the overhead bins are still empty. Since big, bulky baggage attracts the attention of gate agents and flight attendants on a busy flight, make sure your carry-on is really a carry-on. Finally, a carry-on that's long and narrow is more likely to remain unnoticed than one that's wide and squarish.

If you are flying internationally, note that baggage allowances may be determined not by piece but by weight—generally 88 pounds (40 kilograms) in first class, 66 pounds (30 kilograms) in business class, and 44 pounds (20 kilograms) in economy.

Airline liability for baggage is limited to $1,250 per person on flights within the United States. On international flights it amounts to $9.07 per pound or $20 per kilogram for checked baggage (roughly $640 per 70-pound bag) and $400 per passenger for unchecked baggage. You can buy additional coverage at check-in for about $10 per $1,000 of coverage, but it excludes a rather extensive list of items, shown on your airline ticket.

Before departure, **itemize your bags' contents** and their worth, and label the bags with your name, address, and phone number. (If you use your home address, cover it so that potential thieves can't see it readily.) Inside each bag, **pack a copy of your itinerary.** At check-in, **make sure that each bag is correctly tagged** with the destination airport's three-letter code. If your bags arrive damaged or fail to arrive at all, file a written report with the airline before leaving the airport.

PACKING LIST

Pack light, because you may want to save space for purchases: the Yucatán is filled with bargains on clothing, leather goods, jewelry, pottery, and other crafts.

Resort wear is all you will need for the Caribbean beach towns: Bring lightweight sports clothes, sundresses, bathing suits, sun visors, and cover-ups for the beach and a jacket or sweater to wear in the chilly, air-conditioned restaurants, or to tide you over a storm or an unusual cool spell. If you plan to visit any ruins, **bring comfortable walking shoes** with rubber soles. Lightweight rain gear is a good idea during the rainy season. Cancún is the dressiest spot on the peninsula, but even fancy restaurants don't require men to wear jackets. Women may wear shorts at the ruins, on the beaches, and in the beach towns but should not do so in cities such as Mérida.

Insect repellent, sunscreen, sunglasses, and umbrellas are musts for the Yucatán. Other handy items—especially if you will be traveling on your own or camping—include toilet paper, facial tissues, a plastic water bottle, and a flashlight (for occasional power outages or use at campsites). Snorkelers should consider bringing their own equipment unless traveling light is a priority; shoes with rubber soles for rocky underwater surfaces are also advised. For long-term stays in remote rural areas, *see* Health, *above.*

In your carry-on luggage **bring an extra pair of eyeglasses or contact lenses** and **enough of any medication you take** to last the entire trip. You may also want your doctor to write a spare prescription using the drug's generic name, since brand names may vary from country to country. **Never put prescription drugs or valuables in luggage to be checked.** To avoid customs delays, carry medications in their original packaging. And don't forget to copy down and carry addresses of offices that handle refunds of lost traveler's checks.

PASSPORTS

When traveling internationally, **carry a passport even if you don't need one** (it's always the best form of I.D.), and make **two photocopies of the data page** (one for someone at home and another for you, carried separately from your passport). The best time to apply for a passport or to renew is during the fall and winter. Before any trip, be sure to check your passport's expiration date and, if necessary, renew it as soon as possible. (Some countries won't allow you to enter on a passport that's due to expire in six months or less.) If you lose your passport, promptly call the nearest embassy or consulate and the local police.

U.S. CITIZENS

For stays of up to 180 days, you must prove citizenship through either a valid passport, certified copy of a birth certificate, or voter registration card (the last two must be accompanied by a government-issued photo ID). Minors traveling with one parent need notarized permission from the absent parent. All U.S. citizens, even infants, need a valid passport to enter Mexico for stays of more than 180 days.

➤ INFORMATION: **National Passport Information Center** (☎ 900/225–5674; calls are charged at 35¢ per minute for automated service, $1.05 per minute for operator service).

CANADIAN CITIZENS

You need only proof of citizenship (either a valid passport, certified copy of a birth certificate, or voter registration card—the latter two must be accompanied by a government-issued photo ID) to enter Mexico for stays of up to 180 days.

Information: PASSPORT OFFICE (☎ 819/994–3500 OR 800/567–6868).

U.K. CITIZENS

Citizens of the United Kingdom need only a valid passport to enter Mexico for stays of up to 180 days.

➤ INFORMATION: **London Passport Office** (☎ 0990/21010), for fees and documentation requirements and to request an emergency passport.

AUSTRALIAN CITIZENS

You must have a valid passport and a multiple-entry Visa to the U.S.

➤ INFORMATION: **Australian Passport Office** (☎ 13/1232).

NEW ZEALAND CITIZENS

You must have a valid passport and a multiple-entry Visa to the U.S.

➤ INFORMATION: **New Zealand Passport Office** (☎ 04/494–0700 for information on how to apply, 0800/727–776 for information on applications already submitted).

SAFETY

When visiting the Yucatán, even in such resort areas as Cancún and Cozumel, **use common sense.** Wear a money belt, make use of hotel safes when available, and carry your own baggage whenever possible. Reporting a crime to the police is often a frustrating experience unless you speak excellent Spanish and have a great deal of patience.

Women traveling alone are likely to be subjected to catcalls, although this is less true in the Yucatán than in other parts of Mexico. Avoid direct eye contact with men on the streets—it invites further acquaintance. Don't wear tight clothes if you don't want to call attention to yourself. Also be aware that clothing that seems innocuous to you, such as sleeveless shirts or Bermuda shorts, may be inappropriate in more conservative rural areas. If you speak Spanish and are being harassed, pretend you don't understand and ignore would-be suitors or say "no" to whatever they say. Don't enter street bars or cantinas alone.

SENIOR-CITIZEN TRAVEL

To qualify for age-related discounts, **mention your senior-citizen status up**

front when booking hotel reservations (not when checking out) and before you're seated in restaurants (not when paying the bill). Note that discounts may be limited to certain menus, days, or hours. When renting a car, **ask about promotional car-rental discounts,** which can be cheaper than senior-citizen rates.

➤ EDUCATIONAL PROGRAMS: **Elderhostel** (✉ 75 Federal St., 3rd floor, Boston, MA 02110, ☎ 617/426–8056). **Interhostel** (✉ University of New Hampshire, ✉ 6 Garrison Ave., Durham, NH 03824, ☎ 603/862–1147 or 800/733–9753, FAX 603/862–1113).

SHOPPING

Shopping is convenient in such resort areas as Cancún and Cozumel, but often you'll be paying top peso for items that you can find in smaller towns for less money. As for bargaining, it is widely accepted in the markets, but you should understand that in many small towns the locals earn their livelihoods from the tourist trade, and not all will start out with outrageous prices. If you feel the price quoted is too high, start off by offering no more than half the asking price and then slowly go up, usually to about 70% of the original price. Bargaining is not accepted in most shops, except when you are paying cash.

STUDENT TRAVEL

TRAVEL AGENCIES

To save money, **look into deals available through student-oriented travel agencies.** To qualify you'll need a bona fide student I.D. card. Members of international student groups are also eligible.

➤ STUDENT I.D.s & SERVICES: **Council on International Educational Exchange** (✉ CIEE, ✉ 205 E. 42nd St., 14th floor, New York, NY 10017, ☎ 212/822–2600 or 888/268–6245, FAX 212/822–2699), for mail orders only, in the United States. **Travel Cuts** (✉ 187 College St., Toronto, Ontario M5T 1P7, ☎ 416/979–2406 or 800/667–2887) in Canada.

➤ STUDENT TOURS: **Contiki Holidays** (✉ 300 Plaza Alicante, Suite 900, Garden Grove, CA 92840, ☎ 714/740–0808 or 800/266–8454, FAX 714/740–2034).

TAXES

AIRPORT

An air departure tax of $17 or the peso equivalent must be paid in cash at the airport for international flights from Mexico, and there is a domestic air departure tax of around $10. Traveler's checks and credit cards are not accepted as payment for these taxes.

HOTEL

Hotels in the state of Quintana Roo are now charging a 2% lodging tax, the income from which is to be used for tourism promotion.

VALUE-ADDED TAX (V.A.T.)

Mexico has a value-added tax (V.A.T.) or I.V.A. (*impuesto de valor agregado*), of 15% (10% along the Cancún–Tulum corridor). Many establishments already include the I.V.A. tax in the quoted price. Occasionally (and illegally) it will be waived for cash purchases.

TELEPHONES

COUNTRY CODES

The country code for Mexico is 52. When dialing a Mexican number from abroad, drop the initial 0 from the local area code.

INTERNATIONAL CALLS

International phone calls can be made from many hotels, but excessive taxes and surcharges—on the order of 60% to 70%—usually apply. Cancún, Cozumel, and Mérida are putting up more and more "LADATEL" phone booths on streets and in some hotel lobbies; these phones accept prepaid electronic cards (sold at pharmacies and grocery stores), which are inserted into the phone and debited for the cost of the call. LADATEL phones also allow you to make collect and calling-card calls to the United States. Throughout Mexico, **dial 09 to place an international call; 02 for long-distance calls; and 04 for information.** When calling the United States or Canada, dial 001 before the area code and phone number. When calling Europe, Latin America, or Japan, dial 00 before the country and city codes.

SMART TRAVEL TIPS / THE GOLD GUIDE

AT&T, MCI, and Sprint international access codes make calling the United States relatively convenient, but you may find the local access number blocked in many hotel rooms. First ask the hotel operator to connect you. If the hotel operator balks, ask for an international operator, or dial the international operator yourself. One way to improve your odds of getting connected to your long-distance carrier is to travel with more than one company's calling card (a hotel may block Sprint, for example, but not MCI). If all else fails, call from a pay phone in the hotel lobby.

➤ ACCESS CODES: **AT&T Direct** (☎ 800/435–0812; 001–800/462–4240 in Mexico). **MCI WorldPhone** (☎ 800/444–4141; 001–800/674–7000 in Mexico). **Sprint International Access** (800/877–4646; 001–800/877–8000 in Mexico).

TIPPING

At restaurants it's customary to leave a 10%–15% tip (make sure, however, that a service charge has not already been added). Bellhops and porters should be given $1 to $2; hotel maids, $1 per day, per room. Tour guides warrant about $1 per person for a half-day tour, $2 for a full day, and $10 per person for a week. Tour-bus drivers should receive $1 per person per day. Car watchers and windshield wipers (usually young boys), as well as gas station attendants and theater ushers, should be satisfied with 3–5 pesos. Taxi drivers (unless extraordinarily helpful) and shoe shiners do not expect tips.

TOUR OPERATORS

Buying a prepackaged tour or independent vacation can make your trip to Cancún less expensive and more hassle-free. Because everything is prearranged, you'll spend less time planning.

Operators that handle several hundred thousand travelers per year can use their purchasing power to give you a good price. Their high volume may also indicate financial stability. But some small companies provide more personalized service; because they tend to specialize, they may also be more knowledgeable about a given area.

BOOKING WITH AN AGENT

Travel agents are excellent resources. In fact, large operators accept bookings made only through travel agents. But it's a good idea to **collect brochures from several agencies,** because some agents' suggestions may be influenced by relationships with tour and package firms that reward them for volume sales. If you have a special interest, **find an agent with expertise in that area;** ASTA (☞ Travel Agencies, *below*) has a database of specialists worldwide.

Make sure your travel agent knows the accommodations and other services. Ask about the hotel's location, room size, beds, and whether it has a pool, room service, or programs for children, if you care about these. Has your agent been there in person or sent others you can contact?

Do some homework on your own, too: Local tourism boards can provide information about lesser-known and small-niche operators, some of which may sell only direct.

BUYER BEWARE

Each year consumers are stranded or lose their money when tour operators—even very large ones with excellent reputations—go out of business. So **check out the operator.** Find out how long the company has been in business, and ask several travel agents about its reputation. If the package or tour you are considering is priced lower than in your wildest dreams, **be skeptical.** Try to **book with a company that has a consumer-protection program.** If the operator has such a program, you'll find information about it in the company's brochure. If the operator you are considering does not offer some kind of consumer protection, then ask for references from satisfied customers.

In the U.S., members of the National Tour Association and United States Tour Operators Association are required to set aside funds to cover your payments and travel arrangements in case the company defaults.

It's also a good idea to choose a company that participates in the American Society of Travel Agent's Tour Operator Program (TOP). This gives you a forum if there are any disputes between you and your tour operator; ASTA will act as mediator.

➤ TOUR-OPERATOR RECOMMENDA-TIONS: **American Society of Travel Agents** (☞ Travel Agencies, *below*). **National Tour Association** (⊠ NTA, ⊠ 546 E. Main St., Lexington, KY 40508, ☎ 606/226–4444 or 800/755–8687). **United States Tour Operators Association** (⊠ USTOA, ⊠ 342 Madison Ave., Suite 1522, New York, NY 10173, ☎ 212/599–6599 or 800/468–7862, FAX 212/599–6744).

COSTS

The more your package or tour includes, the better you can predict the ultimate cost of your vacation. Make sure you know exactly what is covered, and **beware of hidden costs.** Are taxes, tips, and service charges included? Transfers and baggage handling? Entertainment and excursions? These can add up.

Prices for packages and tours are usually quoted per person, based on two sharing a room. If traveling solo, you may be required to pay the full double-occupancy rate. Some operators eliminate this surcharge if you agree to be matched with a roommate of the same sex, even if one is not found by departure time.

PACKAGES

Like group tours, independent vacation packages are available from major tour operators and airlines. The companies listed below offer vacation packages in a broad price range.

➤ AIR/HOTEL: **American Airlines Vacations** (☎ 800/321–2121). **Certified Vacations** (☎ 954/522–1440 or 800/233–7260). **Continental Vacations** (☎ 800/634–5555). **Delta Vacations** (☎ 800/872–7786). **US Airways Vacations** (☎ 800/455–0123).

➤ FROM THE U.K.: **Club Med** (⊠ 106 Brompton Rd., London SW3 1JJ, ☎ 0171/581–1161, FAX 0171/581–4769). **Kuoni Travel** (⊠ Kuoni

House, Dorking, Surrey RH5 4AZ, ☎ 01306/740–050, FAX 01306/744–222). **Sunset Travel** (⊠ 4 Abbeville Mews, 88 Clapham Park Rd., London SW4 7BX, ☎ 0171/498–9922, FAX 0171/978–1337).

THEME TRIPS

➤ ADVENTURE: **TrekAmerica** (⊠ Box 189, Rockaway, NJ 07866, ☎ 973/983–1144 or 800/221–0596, FAX 973/983–8551).

➤ ART AND ARCHAEOLOGY IN THE YUCATÁN: **Far Horizons Archaeological & Cultural Trips** (⊠ Box 91900, Albuquerque, NM 87199-1900, ☎ 505/343–9400 or 800/552–4575, FAX 505/343–8076). **Maya-Caribe Travel** (⊠ 7 Davenport Ave., #3F, New Rochelle, NY 10805, ☎ 914/235–2221). **Sanborn's Viva Tours** (⊠ 2015 S. 10th St., McAllen, TX 78505, ☎ 956/682–9872 or 800/395–8482, FAX 956/682–0016).

From the U.K.: **Journey Latin America** (⊠ 16 Devonshire Rd., Chiswick, London W4 2HD, ☎ 0181/747–8315, FAX 0181/742–1312).

➤ BICYCLING: **Backroads** (⊠ 801 Cedar St., Berkeley, CA 94710-1800, ☎ 510/527–1555 or 800/462–2848, FAX 510/527–1444).

➤ FISHING: **Anglers Travel** (⊠ 1280 Terminal Way, #30, Reno, NV 89502, ☎ 702/324–0580 or 800/624–8429, FAX 702/324–0583). **Cutting Loose Expeditions** (⊠ Box 447, Winter Park, FL 32790, ☎ 407/629–4700 or 800/533–4746). **Fishing International** (⊠ Box 2132, Santa Rosa, CA 95405, ☎ 707/539–3366 or 800/950–4242, FAX 707/539–1320). **Mexico Sportsman** (⊠ 14542 Brook Hollow, #124, San Antonio, TX 78232, ☎ 210/494–9916 or 800/633–3085). **Rod & Reel Adventures** (⊠ 566 Thomson La., Copperopolis, CA 95228, ☎ 209/785–0444, FAX 209/785–0447).

➤ NATURAL HISTORY: **Victor Emanuel Nature Tours** (⊠ Box 33008, Austin, TX 78764, ☎ 512/328–5221 or 800/328–8368, FAX 512/328–2919).

➤ SPAS: **Spa-Finders** (⊠ 91 5th Ave., Suite 301, New York, NY 10003-3039, ☎ 212/924–6800 or 800/255–7727).

THE GOLD GUIDE / SMART TRAVEL TIPS

SMART TRAVEL TIPS / THE GOLD GUIDE

TRAVEL AGENCIES

A good travel agent puts your needs first. Look for an agency that has been in business at least five years, emphasizes customer service, and has someone on staff who specializes in your destination. In addition, **make sure the agency belongs to a professional trade organization,** such as ASTA in the United States. If your travel agency is also acting as your tour operator, *see* Buyer Beware in Tour Operators, *above*).

➤ LOCAL AGENT REFERRALS: **American Society of Travel Agents** (ASTA, ☎ 800/965–2782 24-hr hot line, FAX 703/684–8319). **Association of Canadian Travel Agents** (✉ Suite 201, 1729 Bank St., Ottawa, Ontario K1V 7Z5, ☎ 613/521–0474, FAX 613/521–0805). **Association of British Travel Agents** (✉ 55–57 Newman St., London W1P 4AH, ☎ 0171/637–2444, FAX 0171/637–0713). **Australian Federation of Travel Agents** (☎ 02/9264–3299). **Travel Agents' Association of New Zealand** (☎ 04/499–0104).

TRAVEL GEAR

Travel catalogs specialize in useful items, such as compact alarm clocks and travel irons, that can **save space when packing.** They also offer dual-voltage appliances, currency converters, and foreign-language phrase books.

➤ CATALOGS: **Magellan's** (☎ 800/962–4943, FAX 805/568–5406). **Orvis Travel** (☎ 800/541–3541, FAX 540/343–7053). **TravelSmith** (☎ 800/950–1600, FAX 800/950–1656).

U.S. GOVERNMENT

Government agencies can be an excellent source of inexpensive travel information. When planning your trip, **find out what government materials are available.**

➤ ADVISORIES: **U.S. Department of State** (✉ Overseas Citizens Services Office, ✉ Room 4811 N.S., Washington, DC 20520; ☎ 202/647–5225 or FAX 202/647–3000 for interactive hot line; ☎ 301/946–

4400 for computer bulletin board); enclose a self-addressed, stamped, business-size envelope.

➤ PAMPHLETS: **Consumer Information Center** (✉ Consumer Information Catalogue, Pueblo, CO 81009, ☎ 719/948–3334 or 888/878–3256) for a free catalog that includes travel titles.

VISITOR INFORMATION

For general information contact the government tourist office nearest you.

➤ TOURIST OFFICES: **Mexican Government Tourist Offices (MGTO)**U.S. Nationwide: (☎ 800/446–3942). New York City: (✉ 405 Park Ave., Suite 1402, New York, NY 10022, ☎ 212/838–2949 or 212/421–6655, FAX 212/753–2874). Chicago: (✉ 70 E. Lake St., Suite 1413, Chicago, IL 60601, ☎ 312/606–9252, FAX 312/606–9012). Los Angeles: (✉ 1801 Century Pk. E., Ste 1080, Los Angeles, CA 90067, ☎ 310/203–8191, FAX 310/203–8316). Houston: (✉ 5075 Westheimer, Suite 975W, Houston, TX 77056, ☎ 713/629–1611, FAX 713/629–1837). Coral Gables: (✉ 2333 Ponce de Leon Blvd., Suite 710, Coral Gables, FL 33134, ☎ 305/443–9160, FAX 305/443–1186). Canada: (✉ 1 Place Ville Marie, Suite 1626, Montréal, Québec H3B 2B5, ☎ 514/871–1052, FAX 514/871–3825; ✉ 2 Bloor St. W, Suite 1801, Toronto, Ontario M4W 3E2, ☎ 416/925–0704, FAX 416/925–6061; ✉ 999 W. Hastings St., Suite 1610, Vancouver, British Columbia V6C 2WC, ☎ 604/669– 2845, FAX 604/669–3498). U.K.: ✉ 60 Trafalgar Sq., London WC2N 5DS, ☎ 0171/734–1058, FAX 0171/930–9202).

WHEN TO GO

High season along the Mexican Caribbean runs from mid-December through Easter week. Seasonal price changes are less pronounced in Mérida and other inland regions than at the beach resorts, but it still may be difficult to find a room during Christmas and Easter, as well as the last week of July and the first three weeks of August, when most Mexicans take their vacations.

CLIMATE

Spring and summer are usually pleasant along the coast, although you may experience some afternoon rain and evening breezes; in autumn, storms are common. The steamiest time of year inland is late spring, just before the May–October rainy season. What follows are the average daily maximum and minimum temperatures for Cancún; the rest of the Yucatán follows the same general pattern.

Climate in Cancún

Jan.	84F	29C	May	91F	33C	Sept.	87F	31C
	66	19		73	23		75	24
Feb.	85F	29C	June	92F	33C	Oct.	87F	31C
	68	20		75	24		73	23
Mar.	88F	31C	July	91F	33C	Nov.	86F	30C
	69	21		73	23		71	22
Apr.	88F	31C	Aug.	91F	33C	Dec.	84F	29C
	71	22		75	24		66	19

➤ FORECASTS: **Weather Channel Connection** (☎ 900/932–8437), 95¢ per minute from a Touch-Tone phone.

1 Destination: Cancún, Cozumel, Yucatán Peninsula

A PLACE APART

THE YUCATÁN PENINSULA has captivated travelers since the early Spanish explorations. "A place of white towers, whose glint could be seen from the ships. . . temples rising tier on tier, with sculptured cornices" is how the expeditions' chroniclers described the peninsula, then thought to be an island. Rumors of a mainland 10 days west of Cuba were known to Columbus, who obstinately hoped to find "a very populated land," and one that was richer than any he had yet discovered. Subsequent explorers and conquistadors met with more resistance there than in almost any other part of the New World, and this rebelliousness continued for centuries.

Largely because of their geographic isolation, Yucatecans tend to preserve ancient traditions more than many other indigenous groups in the country. This can be seen in such areas as housing (the use of the ancient Maya thatched hut, or *na*); dress (*huipiles* have been made and worn by Maya women for centuries); occupation (most modern-day Maya are farmers, just as their ancestors were); language (while the Maya language has evolved considerably, basically it is very similar to that spoken at least 500 years ago); and religion (ancient deities persist, particularly in the form of gods associated with agriculture, such as the *chaacs*, or rain gods, and festivals to honor the seasons and benefactor spirits maintain the traditions of old).

This vast peninsula encompasses 113,000 square km (43,630 square mi) of a flat limestone table covered with sparse topsoil and scrubby jungle growth. Geographically, it comprises the states of Yucatán, Campeche, and Quintana Roo, as well as Belize and a part of Guatemala (these two countries are not discussed in this book). Long isolated from the rest of Mexico and still one of the least Hispanicized (or Mexicanized) regions of the country, Yucatán catapulted into the tourist's vocabulary with the creation of its most precious man-made asset, Cancún.

Mexico's most popular resort destination owes its success to its location on the superb eastern coastline of Yucatán, which is washed by the exquisitely colored and translucent waters of the Caribbean and endowed with a semitropical climate, unbroken stretches of beach, and the world's fifth-longest barrier reef, which separates the mainland from Cozumel. Cancún, along with Cozumel and to a lesser extent Isla Mujeres, incarnates the success formula for sun-and-sand tourism: luxury hotels, sandy beaches, water sports, nightlife, and restaurants that specialize in international fare.

Although Cancún is no longer less expensive than its Caribbean neighbors, it can be reached via more nonstop flights and it offers a far richer culture. With the advent of Cancún, the peninsula's Maya ruins—long a mecca for archaeology enthusiasts—have become virtual satellites of that glittering star. The proximity of such compelling sites as Chichén Itzá, Uxmal, and Tulum allows Cancún's visitors to explore the vestiges of one of the most brilliant civilizations in the ancient world without having to journey too far from their base.

Yucatán offers a breathtaking diversity of other charms, too. The waters of the Mexican Caribbean are clearer and more turquoise than those of the Pacific; many of the beaches are unrivaled. Scuba diving (in natural sinkholes and along the barrier reefs), snorkeling, deep-sea fishing, and other water sports attract growing numbers of tourists. They can also go birding, camp, spelunk, and shop for Yucatán's splendid handicrafts. There is a broad spectrum of settings and accommodations to choose from: the high-rise, pricey strip of hotels along Cancún's Paseo Kukulcán; the less showy properties on Cozumel, beloved by partying college-age scuba divers; and the relaxed ambience of Isla Mujeres, where most lodgings consist of rustic bungalows with ceiling fans and hammocks.

There are also the cities of Yucatán. Foremost is Mérida, wonderfully unaltered by time, where Moorish-inspired, colonnaded colonial architecture blends handsomely with turn-of-the-century French-style pomposity. In Mérida the *zócalo* or playa principal is still the hub of tradition, and in the surrounding villages the Maya still live proudly as Maya. Campeche, one of the few walled cities in North America, possesses an eccentric charm; it is slightly out of step with the rest of the country and not the least bothered by the fact. Down on the border with Belize stands Chetumal, a ramshackle place of wood-frame houses that is pervaded by the hybrid culture of coastal Central America and the pungent smell of the sea. Progreso, at the other end of the peninsula on the Gulf of Mexico, is Chetumal's northern counterpart, an overgrown fishing village turned commercial port. Hotels in these towns, while for the most part not as luxurious as the beach resort properties, range from the respectable if plain 1970s commercial buildings to the undated fleabags so popular with detective novelists (one thinks especially of Raymond Chandler) and filmmakers.

Wildlife is another of Yucatán's riches. Iguanas, lizards, tapirs, deer, armadillos, and wild boars thrive on this alternately parched and densely foliated plain. Flamingos and herons, manatees and sea turtles, their once-dwindling numbers now rising in response to Mexico's newly awakened ecological consciousness, find idyllic watery habitats in and above the coastline's mangrove swamps, lagoons, and sandbars, acres of which have been made into national parks. Both Río Lagartos and the coast's Sian Ka'an Biosphere Reserve sparkle with Yucatán's natural beauty. Orchids, bougainvillea, and poinciana are ubiquitous; dazzling reds and pinks and oranges and whites spill into countless courtyards—effortless hothouses. And while immense palm groves and forests of precious hardwood trees slowly succumb to fire and encroachment by man, the region's edible tropical flora—coconuts, papaya, bananas, and oranges—remains a succulent ancillary to the celebrated Yucatecan cuisine.

But perhaps it is the colors of Yucatán that are most remarkable. From the stark white, sun-bleached sand, the sea stretches out like some immense canvas painted in bands of celadon greens, pale aquas, and deep dusty blues. At dusk the sea and the horizon meld in the sumptuous glow of a lavender sunset, the sky just barely tinged with periwinkle and violet. Inland, the beige, gray, and amber stones of ruined temples are set off by riotous greenery. The colors of newer structures are equally intoxicating: Tawny, gray-brown thatched roofs sit atop white oval huts. Colonial mansions favor creamy pastels of bisque, salmon, and coral tones, again highlighted by elegant white: white arches, white balustrades, white rococo porticos. Brilliant colors glimmer in carved hardwood doors, variegated tile floors, brown and green pottery and rugs affixed to walls, and snatches of bougainvillea rushing down the sides of buildings.

YUCATÁN'S COLOR extends beyond the physical to the historical. From the conquistadors' first landfall off Cape Catoche in 1517 to the bloody skirmishes that wiped out most of the Indians to the razing of Maya temples and burning of their sacred books, the peninsula was a battlefield. Pirates wreaked havoc off the coast of Campeche for centuries. Half the Indian population was killed during the 19th-century uprising known as the War of the Castes, when the enslaved indigenous population rose up and massacred thousands of Europeans; Yucatán was attempting to secede from Mexico, and dictator Porfirio Díaz sent in his troops. These events, like the towering Maya civilization, have left their mark throughout the peninsula: in its archaeological museums, its colonial monuments, and the opulent mansions of the hacienda owners who enslaved the natives to cultivate their henequen.

But despite the past's violent conflicts with foreigners, the people of Yucatán treat today's visitors with genuine hospitality and friendliness, especially outside the beach resorts. If you learn a few words of Spanish, you will be rewarded with an even warmer welcome.

— Erica Meltzer

NEW AND NOTEWORTHY

The crisis triggered by the late-1994 peso devaluation was tempered by a U.S.-led bailout of Mexico's economy, but the recovery is tenuous at best. Travelers should be aware of the financial desperation of many Mexicans and avoid wearing expensive jewelry or displaying large sums of cash. While creating hardship for residents, the devaluation has resulted in increased purchasing power for visitors (though prices of chain hotels, calculated in dollars in resort areas like Cancún, have remained stable). However, many projects in progress during the early 1990s—including tourist developments—are getting back into gear again.

At the same time, new types of tourism ventures are being developed. The opening of the first of several planned environmentally friendly jungle lodges in the Xpujil area of the state of Campeche (☞ Chapter 7) has made possible extended visits to the ruins at Becán, Xpujil, Hormiguero, Río Bec, and Calakmul, all of which are undergoing restoration. And in addition to the hotels, shopping malls, and golf courses that *have* been completed in the '90s, a new marina, San Buenaventura, is under construction in Cancún.

WHAT'S WHERE

Cancún

The jewel of Mexico's Caribbean coast, Cancún is for those who want dazzle for their dollar: The hotel zone is lined with high-rise lodgings, glitzy discos, air-conditioned malls, and gorgeous beaches. For a taste of the real Mexico, go downtown, where Yucatecan specialties are served at casual eateries.

Isla Mujeres

Only 8 km (5 mi) across the bay from Cancún, Isla Mujeres is an ocean away in attitude, as sleepy and unassuming as its neighbor is outgoing. Snorkeling and lazing under a *palapa* (thatched roof) are about as energetic as it gets here, though there are some interesting remnants of the island's pirate past to explore.

Cozumel

A morning's boat ride from Cancún and Isla Mujeres, Cozumel strikes a balance between the two in tone. Mexico's largest cruise-ship port, the island is at once commercial and laid back. Along with day trip-

pers, Cozumel draws sportfishing enthusiasts and divers who come to explore some of the world's best reefs.

The Caribbean Coast

Although the eastern shore of the Yucatán is no longer as pristine as it was in the past—what's been termed the Cancún–Tulum corridor is getting increasingly developed—it still offers plenty of secluded beaches to escape to. Visit the Sian Ka'an Biosphere Reserve to see the area's abundant wildlife, including crocodiles, jaguars, and wild boars, as well as more than 300 species of birds.

Campeche

Ruins of the fortifications built to fend off the pirates who ravaged Yucatán's gulf coast make the walled city of Campeche well worth exploring. Among the remnants of Maya settlements that dot the rest of this little-explored state, Edzná is the best known, but ancient cities in southern Campeche, such as Calakmul, Xpujil, and Becán are just as interesting.

Mérida and the Yucatán Peninsula

Long a favorite of archaeologists, the state of Yucatán hosts the two most spectacular Maya ruins, Chichén Itzá and Uxmal. Many travelers are also coming to appreciate the charms of Mérida, with its excellent restaurants and markets and its unique mix of Spanish and French architectural styles.

PLEASURES AND PASTIMES

Beaches

Cancún and the rest of Yucatán offer a wonderful variety of beaches: There are white sands, rocky coves and promontories, curvaceous bays, and murky lagoons. Those who thrive on the resort atmosphere will probably enjoy Playa Chac Mool and Playa Tortugas on the bay side of Cancún, which is calmer if less beautiful than the windward side. On the north end of Isla Mujeres, Playa Cocoteros and Playa Norte offer handsome sunset vistas. Beaches on the east coast of Cozumel— once frequented by buccaneers—are rocky, and the swimming is treacherous, but they offer privacy. On the relatively sheltered leeward side are the widest and best sand beaches.

The Caribbean coast abounds with hidden and not-so-hidden beaches (at Xcaret, Paamul, Chemuyil, Xcacel, Punta Bete, south of Tulum, and along the Boca Paila peninsula). There are also long stretches of white sand, usually filled with sunbathers, at Puerto Morelos, Playa del Carmen, and especially Akumal.

Travelers to Campeche and Progreso will find the waters of the Gulf of Mexico deep green, shallow, and tranquil. Such beaches as Payucán, Sabancuy, Isla del Carmen, and Yucalpetén are less visited by North Americans; facilities are minimal, but some prefer it that way.

Bird-Watching

The Yucatán Peninsula is one of the finest areas for birding in Mexico. Habitats range from wildlife and bird sanctuaries to unmarked lagoons, estuaries, and mangrove swamps. Frigates, tanagers, warblers, and macaws inhabit Isla Contoy (off Isla Mujeres) and the Laguna Colombia on Cozumel; an even greater variety of species are to be found in the Sian Ka'an Biosphere Reserve on the Boca Paila peninsula south of Tulum. Along the north and west coasts of Yucatán—at Río Lagartos, Laguna Rosada, and Celestún—flamingos, herons, ibis, cormorants, pelicans, and peregrine falcons thrive.

Dining

The mystique of Yucatecan cooking has a lot to do with the generous doses of local spices and herbs, although generally the food tends not to be too spicy. Among the specialties are *sopa de lima* (chicken broth spiked with lime juice); *cochinita píbil* and *pollo píbil* (succulent pork or chicken baked in banana leaves with a spicy, pumpkin-seed-and-chili sauce); *poc chuc* (Yucatecan pork marinated in a sour-orange sauce with pickled onions); *tikinchic* (fried fish prepared with sour orange); *carne asada* (broiled beef); *panuchos* (fried tortillas filled with black beans and topped with turkey, chicken, or pork, pickled onions, and avocado); *papadzules* (tortillas piled high with hard-boiled eggs and drenched in a sauce of pumpkin seed and fried tomato); and *codzitos* (rolled tortillas in pumpkin-seed sauce). *Achiote* (an-

natto), cilantro (coriander), and the fiery *chile habanero* are highly favored condiments. You'll also find occasional dishes drenched in mole *poblano,* a spicy sauce of chili, chocolate, sesame, and almonds).

Yucatecans are renowned for—among other things—their love of idiosyncratic beverages. *Xtabentún,* a liqueur made of fermented honey and anise, dates back to the ancient Maya; like straight tequila, it's best drunk in small sips between bites of fresh lime. Local brews, such as the dark bock León Negra and the light Montejo, are excellent. On the healthier side, *chaya* is the bright-green juice of a local plant resembling spinach. Yucatecan *horchata,* a favorite all over Mexico, is made from milled rice and water flavored with vanilla. Also try the *licuados,* either milk- or water-based smoothies, made from the tropical fruits of the region (but avoid outdoor stands, because they often use unpasteurized milk and unpurified water).

Fishing

Sportfishing is popular in Cozumel and throughout the Caribbean coast. The rich waters of the Caribbean and the Gulf of Mexico support hundreds of species of tropical fish, making the Yucatán coastline and the outlying islands a paradise for deep-sea fishing, fly-fishing, and bone-fishing. Particularly between the months of April and July, the waters off Cancún, Cozumel, and Isla Mujeres teem with sailfish, marlin, red snapper, tuna, barracuda, and wahoo, among other denizens of the deep. Bill fishing is so rich around Cozumel and Puerto Aventuras that each holds an annual tournament.

Farther south, along the Boca Paila peninsula, banana fish, bonefish, mojarra, shad, permit, and sea bass provide great sport for flat fishing and fly-fishing, while oysters, shrimp, and conch lie on the bottom of the Gulf of Mexico near Campeche and Isla del Carmen. At Progreso, on the north coast, sportfishing for grouper, dogfish, and pompano is quite popular.

Ruins

Amateur archaeologists will find heaven in the Yucatán, where the ancient Maya most abundantly left their mark. Pick your period and your preference, whether for well-excavated sites or overgrown, out-of-the-way ruins barely touched by a scholar's shovel. The major Maya sites are Cobá and

Tulum (☞ Chapter 5) and Chichén Itzá and Uxmal (☞ Chapter 6), but smaller ruins scattered throughout the peninsula are often equally fascinating.

Oxkintok, just off the main road between Mérida and Campeche, is one of the more rewarding "unrestored" Maya sites in the Yucatán; at press time (spring 1998) it was being restored. Only a few structures have been excavated at this rarely visited spot, but the magnitude of overgrown ruins is impressive, and the presence of sculptures, pottery shards, and other on-site artifacts lets adventurous sightseers experience a more direct link with the ancient past.

Scuba Diving and Snorkeling

Underwater enthusiasts come to Cozumel, Akumal, Xcalak, Xel-Há, and other parts of Mexico's Caribbean coast for the clear turquoise waters, the colorful and assorted tropical fish, and the exquisite coral formations along the Belize reef system. Currents allow for drift diving, and both reefs and offshore wrecks lend themselves to dives, many of which are safe enough for neophytes. The peninsula's cenotes, or natural sinkholes, provide an unusual dive experience. Individual chapters will direct you to the dive sites that will best suit you.

Water Sports

All manner of water sports—jet skiing, catamaran sailing, sailboarding, waterskiing, sailing, and parasailing—are practiced in Cancún, Cozumel, and along the Caribbean coast, where you'll find well-equipped water-sports centers.

FODOR'S CHOICE

Archaeological Sites

★ **Chichén Itzá.** The best-known Maya ruin, Chichén Itzá was the most important city in the Yucatán from the 11th to the 13th centuries. Its eclectic architecture is evidence of a complex intermingling of several different Maya groups.

★ **Cobá.** Once a central city-state in the Maya domain, this site has long languished in a lush, tropical setting. Only about 5% of its more than 6,000 structures have been excavated.

★ **Dzibanché.** This remote ruin, hidden behind miles of fields, is a beautifully restored series of temples and plazas from the Classic period. Its architectural features bear the distinct style of Río Beca. Stop by neighboring Kinichna for a stunning view of the surrounding area.

★ **Edzná.** Archaeologists consider this remote and little explored ruin crucial for its transitional role among several Maya architectural styles. This ruin has been remarkably restored.

★ **Tulum.** The spectacular backdrop of the Caribbean and proximity to Cancún explain why Tulum is the most visited archaeological site in the Yucatán.

★ **Uxmal.** Arguably the most beautiful of Mexico's ruins, Uxmal represents Maya style at its purest, including ornate stone friezes, intricate cornices, and soaring arches.

Beaches

★ **Akumal.** Long stretches of this popular section of the Caribbean coast are filled with shells, crabs, and migrant birds. Protected coves with tranquil water are ideal for swimming or snorkeling.

★ **Playa Norte.** A white-sand beach on the northern tip of Isla Mujeres, Playa Norte—sometimes called Cocoteros or Cocos—is both scenic and social.

★ **Punta Celerain.** The lighthouse at the southern end of Cozumel affords wonderful views of pounding waves, swamps, and jungle.

★ **Xcalak peninsula.** One of the Caribbean coast's still-remote spots, this peninsula is lush with mangrove swamps, tropical flowers, and wildlife.

Nature Reserves and Natural Beauty

★ **Isla Contoy.** An unspoiled island preserve off the coast of Isla Mujeres, Isla Contoy is especially notable for its birds; more than 70 species pass through in the fall.

★ **Laguna de Bacalar.** The second-largest lake in Mexico is known as "The Lake of Seven Colors" because of the stunning hues that a mix of seawater, freshwater, and seaweed produce.

★ **Loltún Caves.** This largest of the many limestone caverns that honeycomb the central Yucatán Peninsula has colorful rock formations as well as pictographs left by the Maya, who lived here for thousands of years.

✯ **Parque Natural del Flamenco Mexicano.** One of the biggest colonies of flamingos in North America rests here from September through April; deer and armadillo roam this huge wildlife preserve, too.

✯ **Río Lagartos National Park.** Another beautiful place in the Yucatán to view flamingos, Río Lagartos also attracts green turtles, who lay their eggs on the beach at night.

✯ **Sian Ka'an Biosphere Reserve.** At this 1.3-million-acre preserve, you can see half-submerged Maya ruins in mangrove canals or bird-watch for exotic species in the jungle.

Shopping

✯ **Casa de Artesanías, Mérida.** Browse for hand-painted furniture, leather goods, hammocks, wax candles, and hand-embroidered blouses in the setting of an old colonial home.

✯ **Los Cinco Soles, Cozumel.** Cruise-ship passengers with limited time to shop can find a large array of well-priced clothing and crafts here.

✯ **Mercado Municipal, Mérida.** The best general market in the Yucatán sells everything from live birds and food to intricate local crafts.

Dining

✯ **La Dolce Vita, Cancún.** Terrific Italian food and a romantic atmosphere draw beach lovers to this restaurant, recently re-located to Laguna Nichupte in the hotel zone. *$$$*

✯ **Casa Cenote, Mexico's Caribbean Coast.** This unique restaurant near the ruins of Tulum allows diners to plunge into a large natural pool before enjoying tasty American and Mexican fare. *$$*

✯ **La Bella Epoca, Mérida.** At this gracious converted mansion, diners indulge in platters of Middle Eastern specialties along with well-prepared versions of French and Yucatecan dishes. *$$*

✯ **La Choza, Cozumel.** The super-fresh Mexican entrées at this friendly, family-run place include chicken mole and

grilled lobster; tortillas are baked on the premises. *$$*

✯ **La Parrilla, Playa del Carmen and Cancún.** This fun bar and grill serves up superb Mexican specialties with flair, in an excellent location. *$$*

✯ **Marganzo, Campeche.** The food at this popular, low-key place typifies the distinctive seafood dishes known as *estilo campechano* (Campeche-style) all over Mexico. *$*

✯ **Velazquez, Isla Mujeres.** This quintessential palapa-style eatery is right on the beach. Don't be misled by the simple, rustic ambience; here you'll find the best seafood on the island. *$*

Lodging

✯ **Casa Turquesa, Cancún.** This small luxury hotel offers the ultimate in taste, culture, and personal attention. Also on the property is the internationally known restaurant **Celebrity**. *$$$$*

✯ **Presidente Inter-Continental Cozumel.** A great water-sports center, a fine beach for snorkeling, and bright, contemporary-style rooms make this the luxury-class choice on Cozumel. *$$$$*

✯ **Rancho Encantado, Bacalar (Mexico's Caribbean Coast).** The sounds of Lake Bacalar lapping up against the shore will lull you to sleep in your private cabaña. Excellent meals, unique guided tours to little-known Maya ruins, and a relaxing massage by the lake will further enhance your stay. *$$$$*

✯ **Ritz-Carlton Cancún.** The Cancún link of this international chain adds class to the beachfront hotel zone. Its facilities and restaurants are superb. *$$$$*

✯ **Na Balam, Isla Mujeres.** The rooms here are attractive in a simple, folk-art fashion, and their proximity to sea and sand is hard to beat. *$$$*

✯ **Gran Hotel, Mérida.** The oldest hotel in Mérida combines character—an Art Nouveau courtyard, high-ceiling, balconied rooms—with reasonable prices. *$$*

✯ **Ramada Ecovillage Resort, Campeche.** Comfort and even a bit of luxury can be found at this jungle lodge on the fringe of the Calakmul rain forest and near a little-explored archaeological zone. *$$*

FESTIVALS AND SEASONAL EVENTS

Traditional religious and patriotic festivals rank among Yucatán's most memorable activities. Towns throughout the region host a number of additional annual fairs, shows, and local celebrations.

Hotel rooms may be hard to get in some places during festival times; be sure to book far in advance, for example, if you want to be near Chichén Itzá around the equinoxes or in Mérida in early January, when the city's founding is commemorated.

WINTER

JAN. 1➤ **New Year's Day** is celebrated throughout the region.

JAN. 6➤ **El Día de Los Reyes** (Feast of the Epiphany, or Three Kings Day) coincides with the anniversary of the founding of Mérida (1542). In that city, the traditional day of gift-giving is also one of parades, fireworks, and outdoor parties.

FEB.–MAR.➤ **Carnaval** (Mardi Gras) festivities take place the week before Lent, with parades, floats, outdoor dancing, music, and fireworks. They are especially spirited in Mérida, Cozumel, Isla Mujeres, Campeche, and Chetumal.

SPRING

MAR. 21 AND SEPT. 21➤ At the **Equinoxes,** Kukulcán, the plumed serpent deity, appears to emerge from his temple atop El Castillo Pyramid at Chichén Itzá and slithers down to earth.

LATE APR.➤ The **Sol a Sol International Regatta,** launched from St. Petersburg, Florida, arrives in Isla Mujeres, sparking regional dances and a general air of festivity.

LATE APR.–JUNE➤ **Billfish Tournaments** take place in Cozumel, Puerto Aventuras, and Cancún.

APR. 28–MAY 3➤ **Holy Cross Fiestas** in Chumayel, Celestún, Hopelchén—all in Yucatán state—include cockfights, dances, and fireworks.

EARLY MAY➤ **Regatta al Sol** brings a fleet of sailboats from Pensacola, Florida, to Isla Mujeres.

MAY 20–27➤ **Hammock Festival,** hailing the furnishing that originated here, is held in Tecoh, on the southern outskirts of Mérida.

MEMORIAL DAY WEEKEND➤ The **Cancún Jazz Festival,** an annual event since 1991, has featured such top musicians as Wynton Marsalis and Gato Barbieri.

AUTUMN

SEPT. 14➤ *Vaquerías* (traditional cattle-branding feasts) attract aficionados to rural towns for bullfights, fireworks, and music.

SEPT. 14–28➤ **Fiesta of San Román** attracts 50,000 people to Campeche to view the procession carrying the Black Christ of San Román—the city's most sacred patron saint—through the streets.

SEPT. 15–16➤ **Independence Day,** the commemoration of a historic speech, known as the *grito* (shout), by Independence leader Padre Miguel Hidalgo, is celebrated throughout Mexico with fireworks and parties.

SEPT. 27➤ **Fiesta of Our Lord of the Blisters** (Cristo de las Ampollas) begins two weeks or more of religious events and processions in Mérida; dances, bullfights, and fireworks take place in Ticul and other small villages.

OCT. 18–25➤ **Fiesta of the Christ of Sitilpech** in Izamal, an hour from Mérida, heralds a week of daily processions in which the image of Christ is carried from Sitilpech village to Izamal; dances and fireworks accompany the walks.

Nov. 1–2➤ On the **Day of the Dead,** or All Saints' Day, Mexicans all over the country visit cemeteries to construct marigold-strewn altars on the graves of loved ones and ancestors, and to symbolically share a meal with them by leaving offerings and having graveside picnics. Bakers herald the annual return of the departed from the spirit world with pastry skulls and candy.

Nov. 29–Dec. 8➤ **Fiesta of Isla Mujeres** honors the island's patron saint, as members of various guilds stage processions, dances, and bullfights. Also, on Dec. 1, Mérida has a display of altars in the main square.

Nov. 30–Dec. 8➤ **Fiesta of the Virgin of the Conception** is held each year in Champotón, Campeche.

Early Dec.➤ **Cancún Fair** serves as a nostalgia trip for provincials who now live along the Caribbean shore but still remember the small-town fiestas back home.

Dec. 3–9➤ **Day of the Immaculate Conception** is observed for six days in the village of Kantunilkin, Quintana Roo, with processions, folkloric dances, fireworks, and bullfights.

Dec. 8–12➤ The **Aquatic Procession** highlights festivities at the fishing village of Celestún, west of Mérida.

Dec. 16–25➤ **Christmas** is celebrated in the Yucatán villages of Espita and Temax with processions culminating in the breaking of candy-filled piñatas.

2 Cancún

The rhinestone of Mexico's Caribbean coast, Cancún is for those who want dazzle for their dollar: The hotel zone is lined with high-rise lodgings, glitzy discos, air-conditioned malls, and gorgeous beaches. For a taste of the real Mexico, go downtown, where Yucatecan specialties are served at casual eateries.

Updated by
Dan Millington

FLYING INTO CANCÚN, Mexico's most popular destination, you see nothing but green treetops for miles. It's clear from the air that this resort was literally carved out of the jungle. When development began here in 1974, the beaches were deserted except for their iguana inhabitants. Now, luxury hotels line the oceanfront, and nearly 2 million visitors a year come for the white-sand beaches and crystalline Caribbean waters. They also come for the sizzling nightlife and, in some cases, for proximity to the Yucatán ruins. Although the resort is too glitzy and tourist-oriented for many, it draws thousands of repeat visitors.

Cancún City is on the mainland, but the hotel zone is on a 22½-km (14-mi) barrier island off the Yucatán Peninsula. The resort is designed to please American tastes; most people speak English, and devotees of cable TV and Pizza Hut will not be disappointed. Beach lovers can bask in Cancún's year-round tropical warmth and sunny skies. The sun shines an average of 240 days a year, reputedly more than at almost any other Caribbean spot. Temperatures linger appealingly at about 80°F. You can sample Yucatecan foods and watch folkloric dance demonstrations as well as knock back tequila slammers at the myriad nightspots.

But there can be more to the resort than plopping down under a *palapa* (thatched roof). For divers and snorkelers the reefs off Cancún, nearby Cozumel, and Isla Mujeres are among the best in the world. Cancún also provides a relaxing home base for visiting the stupendous ruins of Chichén Itzá, Tulum, and Cobá on the mainland—remnants of the area's rich Maya heritage—as well as the Yucatán coast and its lagoons.

The most important buildings in Cancún, however, are modern hotels. The resort has gone through the life cycle typical of any tourist destination. At its inception the resort drew the jet set; lately, it has attracted increasing numbers of less affluent tourists, primarily package-tour takers and college students, particularly during spring break, when hordes of flawless, tanned young bodies inhabit the beaches and restaurants.

As for the island's history, not much was written about it before its birth as a resort. It does not appear on the early navigators' maps, and little is known about the Maya who lived here; apparently Cancún's marshy terrain discouraged development. It is recorded that Maya settled the area during the Preclassic era, in about AD 200, and remained until about the 14th or 15th century. In the mid-19th century minor Maya ruins were sighted; however, they were not studied by archaeologists until the 1950s. In 1970 then-president Luis Echeverría first visited the site that had been chosen to retrieve the state of Quintana Roo from obscurity and abject poverty.

Cancún's natural environment has paid a price. Its lagoons and mangrove swamps have become polluted, and a number of species, like conch and lobster, are dwindling. Although the beaches still appear pristine for the most part, an increased effort will have to be made in order to preserve the physical beauty that is the resort's prime appeal.

Pleasures and Pastimes

Archaeological Sites

Would-be archaeologists can start their exploration of the Maya world in Cancún, which is dotted with the vestiges of an AD 900–AD 1520 settlement. The resort also serves as a gateway for the magnificent Maya site at Tulum, an easy day trip away.

Beaches

Although the Mexican government designed the resort, nature provided its most striking features—its cool, white, porous limestone sand and clear blue waters. Except for the tip of Punta Cancún, Cancún Island is one long beach. The beaches along the island's windward side—those fringing the Bahía des Mujeres—have the calmest water and are ideal for water sports and swimmers of all levels of proficiency. On the eastern coast, facing the open Caribbean, things pick up a bit—waves are bigger and the pounding surf can sometimes surprise the unwary with currents and riptides. Beaches are federal property in Mexico and anyone with stamina can walk for miles, either along the more popular beaches, like Playa Chac Mool and Playa Tortugas, which have restaurants, bars, and sports facilities, or along the less trafficked eastern strand, where Playa Delfines offers spectacular views near the tip of the island.

Dining

One of the most appealing aspects of Cancún's dining options is their diversity. Many restaurants offer a hybrid cuisine that combines fresh fish from local waters, elements of Yucatecan and Mexican cuisines, and a fusion of French, Italian, and American influences. Fiesta dinners are a weekly staple at many hotels, so you can sample a variety of Mexican favorites without venturing out. Those who enjoy high drama at dinner will find places where the waiters artistically prepare meals table-side or where cocktails are served flaming.

For a description of Mexican culinary terms, *see* Dining *under* Pleasures and Pastimes *in the* Destination: Cancún, Cozumel, Yucatán Peninsula chapter.

Lodging

Cancún's hotels presently number more than 110. The resort's architecture, especially in the hotel zone, tends to be a cross between Mediterranean and Maya. In many cases the combination yields an appealing, if sometimes kitschy, style. Typical Mediterranean structures—low, solid, rectangular, with flat, red-tile roofs, Moorish arches, and white stucco walls covered with exuberantly pink bougainvillea—acquire palapas and such ornamental devices as colonnettes, latticework, and beveled cornices. Inside, you'll find bland contemporary-style furniture and lots of pastel hues.

Set back from the principal boulevard, Paseo Kukulcán, in nicely landscaped tropical settings highlighted by palm trees, waterfalls, or tiered pools, the hotels pride themselves on offering endless opportunities for fun. Water sports, marinas, golf, tennis, kids' clubs, fitness centers, spas, shopping, entertainment, excursions, several dining options—are all infused with inimitable Mexican friendliness and attentive service. To keep costs down, choose more modest digs downtown, where local color far outweighs resort facilities.

Nightlife

Cancún is the place for party animals, especially during spring break, when the ultramodern discos and nightclubs pound from late night to early dawn. Entertainment centers like Planet Hollywood and the Hard Rock Cafe, which has recently moved to the Forum Plaza, are also magnets for a younger crowd. A less frenetic nighttime sport is barhopping in the big resort hotels; some lobby bars offer 2-for-1 drinks at happy hour, and most provide live music—everything from classic guitar or flute to mariachi, salsa, reggae, jazz, and rock. You can admire the architecturally diverse hotel interiors as you barhop. For a taste of old Mexico spend an evening at the folkloric ballet dinner show at the convention center. And for a waterborne night out, take a dinner cruise on the *Cancún Queen* or *Columbus*, featuring dancing under the stars.

Water Sports

Cancún is one of the water-sports capitals of the world, and the athletically minded can make optimum use of the Caribbean and the still waters of Laguna Nichupté. Visitors can go fishing, sailing, swimming, jet skiing, windsurfing—the list seems endless. Snorkeling or diving among the host of tropical fish and colorful marine creatures that live along the coral reefs hugging Mexico's Caribbean coast is an incomparable experience. If you want to view the mysterious underwater world but don't want to get your feet wet, a glass-bottom boat or "submarine" is the ticket.

EXPLORING CANCÚN

The island of Cancún, which is shaped roughly like the numeral seven, is divided into two zones, with the hotel zone the much larger of the two. Picture the horizontal leg as extending east from the mainland into the Caribbean; Punta Cancún is where the vertical leg takes over, going north–south. Hotel development began at the north end (close to the mainland), headed east toward Punta Cancún, and is moving south to Punta Nizuc, where the tip of the seven almost joins up again with the mainland. The other zone—Cancún City or downtown Cancún, known as *el centro*—is actually 4 km (2½ mi) west of the hotel zone on the mainland. The seven is separated from the mainland by a system of lagoons: Nichupté, the largest (about 29 square km, or 18 square mi), containing both fresh and salt water; Bojórquez, at the juncture of the two legs of the seven; and Río Inglés to the south. North of the horizontal leg lies Bahía de Mujeres, the 9-km- (5½-mi-) wide bay that separates Cancún from Isla Mujeres. Regularly placed kilometer markers on the roadside help indicate where you are; they go from Km 1 on the mainland, near downtown, to Km 20 at Punta Nizuc.

Paseo Kukulcán is the main drag in the hotel zone, and because most of the seven is less than 1 km (½ mi) wide, both the Caribbean and the lagoons can be seen from either side of it. The hotel zone consists entirely of hotels, restaurants and shopping complexes, marinas, and time-share condominiums; there are no residential areas as such. It's not the sort of place you can get to know by walking. Paseo Kukulcán is punctuated by driveways with steep inclines turning into the hotels, most of which are set at least 100 yards from the road. The lagoon side of the boulevard consists of scrubby stretches of land, many of them covered with construction cranes, alternating with marinas, shopping centers, and restaurants. What is most scenic about Cancún is the dramatic contrast between the vivid turquoise-and-violet sea and the blinding alabaster-white sands. Because there are so few sights, no orientation tours of Cancún are offered: Simply ride the local bus circuit to get a feel for the island's layout.

When you first visit Cancún City (downtown), you may be confused by the layout. There are four principal avenues: Tulum and Yaxchilán, which run north–south; and Uxmal and Cobá, which go east–west. Streets bounded by those avenues and running perpendicular to them are actually horseshoe-shaped, so you will find two parallel streets named Tulipanes, for instance. However, street numbers or even street names are not of much use in Cancún; the proximity to landmarks, such as specific hotels, is the preferred way of giving directions.

Numbers in the text correspond to numbers in the margin and on the Cancún map.

A Good Tour

Cancún's scenery consists mostly of its beautiful beaches and crystal-clear waters, but there are also a few intriguing historical sites tucked away among the modern hotels. In addition to the attractions listed below, two modest vestiges of the ancient Maya civilization are worth a visit, but only for dedicated archaeology buffs. Neither is identified by name. On the 12th hole of Pok-Ta-Pok golf course (Paseo Kukulcán, between Km 6 and Km 7), whose Maya name means "ball game," stands a ruin consisting of two platforms and the remains of other buildings. And the ruin of a tiny Maya shrine is cleverly incorporated into the architecture of the Hotel Camino Real (on the beach at Punta Cancún).

You don't need a car in Cancún, but if you've rented one to make extended trips, it might be worth starting in the southern hotel zone at **Ruinas del Rey** ① and **San Miguelito** ②, driving north to **Yamil Lu'um** ③ and then stopping in at the **convention center** ④ before heading west to **El Centro** ⑤.

Sights to See

❹ **Cancún Convention Center.** This strikingly modern venue for cultural events is the jumping off point for a 1-km-long (½-mi-long) string of shopping malls that extends west to the Presidente Inter-Continental Cancún. In the convention center complex itself, **Inter Plaza** contains 15 restaurants, 21 boutiques, a bank, and several airline offices. At press time a 525-ft observation tower was still under construction. Originally scheduled for completion in late 1994, and now set for 1999, it will feature the highest viewing platform in Latin America. ⊠ *Paseo Kukulcán, Km 9,* ☎ *98/830199.*

The **National Institute of Anthropology and History,** the small museum on the ground floor of the convention center, traces Maya culture by showcasing a fascinating collection of 1,000- to 1,500-year-old artifacts collected throughout Quintana Roo. ☎ *98/830305.* ☜ *About $3, free Sun.* ☉ *Tues.–Sun. 9–7. Guided tour in English, French, German, and Spanish.*

❺ **El Centro** (Downtown Cancún). The main thoroughfare is **Avenida Tulum,** which begins at the spot where Paseo Kukulcán turns into Avenida Cobá. Many restaurants and shops are located along here, as is Ki Huic, the largest crafts market in Cancún. Life-size reproductions of ancient Mexican art, including the Aztec calendar stone, a giant Olmec head, the Atlantids of Tula, and the Maya *chac mool* (reclining rain god), line the grassy strip dividing Tulum's northbound and southbound lanes. Visitors looking for shopping bargains, however, generally find better prices on the parallel **Avenida Yaxchilán.**

⛏ ❶ **Ruinas del Rey** (Ruins of the King). Located on the lagoon side at Cancún Island, roughly opposite El Pueblito and Playa de Oro hotels, these small ruins have been incorporated into the Caesar Park Beach & Golf Resort complex; large signs point out the site. First mentioned in a 16th-century travelogue and then in 1842 when they were sighted by American explorer John Lloyd Stephens and his draftsman, Frederick Catherwood, the ruins were finally explored by archaeologists in 1910, though excavations did not begin until 1954. In 1975 archaeologists, along with the Mexican government, began the restoration of Ruinas del Rey and San Miguelito (☞ *below*), a nearby ruin that is now inaccessible.

Del Rey may not be particularly impressive when compared to major archaeological sites such as Tulum or Chichén Itzá, but it is the largest ruin in Cancún and definitely worth a look. It's notable for its unusual architecture: two main plazas bounded by two streets. Most of the other

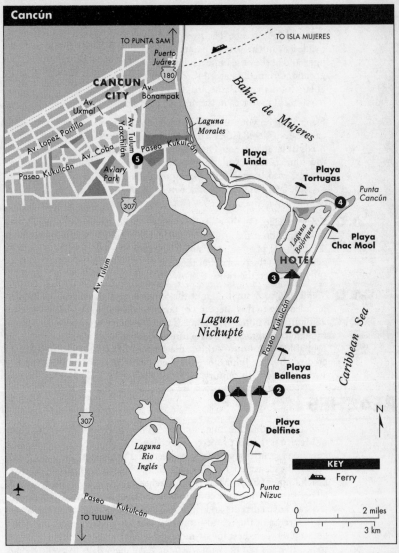

Cancún

TO PUNTA SAM

TO ISLA MUJERES

Puerto
Juárez
180

CANCÚN
CITY
Av.
Uxmal
Av.
Bonampak

Av. Lopez Portillo

Av. Tulum Yaxchilán

Av. Coba

Paseo Kukulcán

Aviary
Park

307

Laguna
Morales

5

Bahía de Mujeres

Playa
Linda

Playa
Tortugas

Punta
Cancún

4

Playa
Chac Mool

Laguna
Bojórquez

HOTEL

3

Paseo Kukulcán

ZONE

Av. Tulum

307

Laguna
Nichupté

Playa
Ballenas

1   2

Playa
Delfines

Laguna
Rio
Inglés

Caribbean Sea

N

Paseo Kukulcán

TO TULUM

Punta
Nizuc

KEY
🚢 Ferry

0   2 miles

0   3 km

Cancún Convention
Center, **4**
El Centro, **5**
Ruinas del Rey, **1**
San Miguelito, **2**
Yamil Lu'um, **3**

Maya cities, which were not in any sense planned but had developed over centuries, contained one plaza with a number of ceremonial satellites and few streets. The pyramid here is topped by a platform, and inside its vault are stucco paintings. Skeletons found buried both at the apex and at the base indicate that the site may have been a royal burial ground. Originally named Kin Ich Ahau Bonil, Maya for "King of the Solar Countenance," the 3rd- to 2nd-century BC site was linked to astronomical practices in the ancient Maya culture.

Depending on your attitude toward reptiles, one aspect of these ruins can be considered either a drawback or a draw: They're home to hundreds of large iguanas. One reader reported that, when he and his fellow tourists stood still, they were approached by about a dozen of the lizards, who begged food like squirrels, and that two of them licked his shoes. ⊠ *Paseo Kukulcán, Km 17,* ☎ *no phone.* ⌦ *About $3, free Sun.* ☉ *Daily 8–5.*

🏛 ❷ **San Miguelito.** On the east side of Paseo Kukulcán is a very small stone building (about the size of a shack) with a number of columns about 4 ft high. At press time this modest Maya site was fenced off and not accessible to the public, but this may change after archaeologists have fully examined the ruins. ⊠ *Paseo Kukulcán, Km 16.5,* ☎ *no phone.*

🏛 ❸ **Yamil Lu'um.** A small sign at the Sheraton will direct you to the dirt path leading to this site, which stands on the highest point of Cancún, adjoining the hotel—the name Yamil Lu'um means "hilly land." Although it comprises two structures—one probably a temple, the other probably a lighthouse—this is the smallest of Cancún's ruins. Discovered in 1842 by John Lloyd Stephens, the remains date from the late 13th or early 14th century. ⊠ *Paseo Kukulcán, Km 12,* ☎ *no phone.*

BEACHES

Cancún Island is one long, continuous beach. By law the entire coast of Mexico is federal property and open to the public; in practice, however, hotel security guards keep peddlers off the beaches, and hotel guests are easily identified by the color of the towels they place on their beach lounge chairs. Most hotel beaches have lifeguards, but, as with all ocean swimming, use common sense—even the calmest-looking waters can have currents and riptides. Overall, the beaches on the windward stretch of the island—those closest to the city, facing the Bahía de Mujeres—are best for swimming; farther out, the undertow can be tricky. It's best not to swim when the red danger flags fly; yellow flags indicate that you should proceed with caution; green or blue means waters are calm. On shore be sure to protect yourself from the searing tropical sun, an obvious precaution once you feel the heat or see the scorched bodies here. Avoid prolonged exposure during peak sunlight hours (11–3) and always use sunscreen or sunblock.

Two popular areas, **Playa Tortugas** (Km 7) and **Chac Mool** (Km 10), have restaurants and changing areas, making them especially appealing for vacationers who are staying at the beachless downtown hotels. Be careful of strong waves at Chac Mool, where it's tempting to walk far out into the shallow water. South of Chac Mool are the usually deserted beaches of **Playa Ballenas** (between Km 15 and Km 16) and **Playa Delfines** (between Km 20 and Km 21), noted for its expansive views. Swimming can be treacherous in the rough surf of Ballenas and Delfines, but they offer a breezy, restful venue for solitary sunbathing.

DINING

At last count there were more than 1,200 restaurants in Cancún, but—according to one successful restaurateur—only about 100 are worth their salt, so to speak. Finding the right restaurant in Cancún is not easy. The downtown restaurants that line the noisy Avenida Tulum often have tables spilling onto pedestrian-laden sidewalks; however, gas fumes and gawking tourists tend to detract from the romantic outdoor-café ambience. Many of the hotel-zone restaurants, on the other hand, cater to what they assume is a tourist preference for bland, not-too-foreign-tasting food.

One key to good dining in Cancún is to find the haunts—mostly in the downtown area, near and around *La Palapa Parque*—where locals go for Yucatán-style food prepared by the experts. A cheap and filling trend in Cancún's dining scene is the sumptuous buffet breakfasts offered by an increasing number of restaurants and hotels on the island. These are especially pleasant when served at palapa restaurants on the beach. At about $15, the brunches are a good value—eat on the late side and you won't be hungry until dinner.

When reviewing Cancún's restaurants, we looked for places where you will get the best values and enjoy your meal the most. Only the truly exceptional hotel restaurants are listed, allowing for more comprehensive coverage of independently operated cafés. Unless otherwise stated, restaurants serve lunch and dinner daily.

What to Wear

Generally speaking, dress is casual here, but many restaurants will not admit diners with bare feet, short shorts, or no shirts. The more up-scale restaurants expect that pants, skirts, or dresses be worn instead of shorts for dinner.

CATEGORY	COST*
$$$$	over $35
$$$	$25–$35
$$	$15–$25
$	under $15

per person, excluding drinks and service

Hotel Zone

$$$$ ✕ **Blue Bayou.** Seven levels of snug dining areas, decorated in wood, rattan, bamboo, and flourishing greens, create the atmosphere for a memorable evening. Sounds from the cascading waterfall and waiters dressed in black pants, white shirts with colorful armbands, and straw boaters heighten a sophisticated New Orleans riverboat tone, set off by jazz that drifts in from the adjoining bar. Blackened meat, fish, and lobster—Cajun and Creole style—are featured on the menu, which is nicely balanced by a number of Mexican specialties. ⊠ *Hyatt Cancún Caribe, Paseo Kukulcán,* ☎ *98/830044. AE, DC, MC, V. No lunch.*

$$$$ ✕ **Bogart's.** Whether you consider it amusingly elaborate or merely pretentious, it's hard to be neutral about Bogart's, probably the most expensive and talked-about restaurant in town. A takeoff from the film *Casablanca,* the place is decorated with Persian rugs, fans, velvet-cushioned banquettes, and fountains; waiters wear fezzes and white suits. A menu as eclectic as the patrons of Rick's Cafe features many seafood and Mediterranean dishes. The food is okay, but don't expect large portions, as servings are nouvelle style. ⊠ *Paseo Kukulcán, Hotel Krystal,* ☎ *98/831133. Reservations essential. AE, DC, MC, V. No lunch.*

18

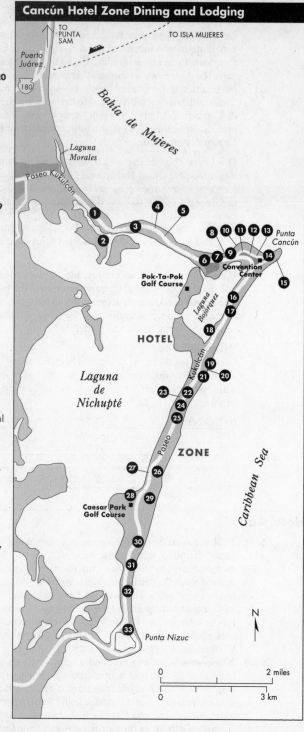

Cancún Hotel Zone Dining and Lodging

$$$$ ✕ **Celebrity Restaurant.** One of Cancún's best restaurants can be found
★ in the **Casa Turquesa** (☞ Lodging, *below*), a small luxury hotel that
does indeed cater to many celebrities. The nautically themed dining room
has both a street and hotel lobby entrance. Subtly lit, with a soaring
palapa roof, swirling ceiling fans, potted palms, rattan furniture, and
an elegantly polished dark-wood floor, it scores high on the romance
scale. Live classic and Spanish guitar music add to the ambience. The
creative cuisine accents local seafood: The culinary delectation here is
the lobster-stuffed chicken breast in coriander sauce. There's also an
interesting selection of other poultry dishes and meats and a good choice
of wines. The Mexican coffee, with vanilla ice cream, orange peel, and
sugar, flambéed table-side with Xtabentum, an anise-based liqueur, is
excellent. ⊠ *Paseo Kukulcán, Casa Turquesa,* ☎ *98/852924. AE,
MC, V. No lunch.*

$$$$ ✕ **Club Grill.** Cancún's hands-down favorite for gourmet dining and
★ a prime choice for that romantic, special-occasion dinner, the **Ritz-
Carlton** (☞ Lodging, *below*) fine dining room is divided into intimate
chambers; one of them has a dance floor and a small stage for live
music in the evening. Walls are trimmed with rich wood, fresh flower
arrangements abound, and tall windows look out onto a bubbling courtyard fountain and the Caribbean beyond. European grill is the house
specialty, and rich sauces and decorative touches give a distinctly
Mexican spin to the grilled chops, steaks, chicken, and seafood. Corn
cream soup, lobster ravioli, and blackened rib-eye steak with Yucatecan spices are popular menu choices. Try the *chipotle* (a smoked
pepper) duck in honey tequila sauce. Their Cigar Dinner features
peppered rack of venison with wild mushrooms foie gras along with
Cuba's best for after-dinner smoking pleasure. Service is attentive
and discreet. ⊠ *Paseo Kukulcán (Retorno del Rey 36),* ☎ *98/850808.
AE, DC, MC, V.*

$$$$ ✕ **La Dolce Vita.** Over the past decade, this appealing restaurant de-
★ veloped a strong and well-deserved local following at its original downtown location on Avenida Cobá. In its present incarnation in the hotel
zone, across from the Marriott CasaMagna and overlooking Laguna
Nichupté, La Dolce Vita has nearly doubled in size, but still maintains
a romantic atmosphere, with lots of hanging plants, candlelit tables
with lace cloths, and soft live trumpet music accompanying dinner. Favorites from the excellent Northern Italian and Continental menu include seafood antipasto, *boquinete* dolce vita (a local white fish stuffed
with shrimp and mushrooms and baked in puff pastry), and creamy
tiramisu. ⊠ *Paseo Kukulcán, Km 14.5,* ☎ *98/850150 or 98/850161.
AE, MC, V.*

$$$ ✕ **Casa Rolandi.** Authentic northern Italian and Swiss dishes are skill-
★ fully prepared by the Italian owner-chef, who grew up near the Swiss
border. If it's on the menu, start with the lobster-stuffed black ravioli,
and go on to grilled seafood garnished with a zesty olive oil. Alterna-
tively, try the homemade lasagna, baked in the large stucco oven; ac-
companied by a lavish antipasto bar, it makes for a satisfying dinner.
In addition, the restaurant serves the best salmon gazpacho in the city.
Many fish and beef dishes are also on the menu. Service is friendly and
efficient, and prices are surprisingly reasonable for this level of cuisine.
The decor is appropriately Mediterranean—white walls, lots of plants,
and copper plates decorating the tables—and the back room offers a
view of the beach. ⊠ *Plaza Caracol,* ☎ *98/831817. AE, MC, V.*

$$$ ✕ **Hacienda El Mortero.** Pampering waiters, strolling mariachis, lush
hanging plants, fig trees, and candlelight make this reproduction plan-
tation home a popular spot to dine. The menu offers a selection of country cooking, and the chicken fajitas and rib steaks are first class. The
favorite among locals here is the *Arrachera* (dried beef) tacos. ⊠ *Paseo*

Kukulcán, Hotel Krystal, ☎ *98/831133. Reservations essential. AE, DC, MC, V. No lunch.*

$$$ ✕ **La Fisheria.** George Savio did such a booming business with his Italian place on the opposite side of the mall (☞ *Savio's, below*) that he decided to branch out and try a seafood restaurant. Not wanting to forsake a proven formula, he offers his popular wood-oven pizzas in addition to seafood standards such as New England clam chowder, steamed mussels, smoked salmon, and, of course, lobster. The setting is ultramodern, with polished stone floors, galvanized steel stairs, and glass walls. There is often live entertainment in the evenings. ⊠ *Plaza Caracol,* ☎ *98/831395. AE, MC, V.*

$$$ ✕ **Lorenzillos.** Perched on its own peninsula in the lagoon, this nautical spot provides a pleasant place to watch the sun set, sip a drink on the outdoor patio while lounging in comfortable handcrafted chairs made by the owner, or sample excellent seafood. Specialties include grilled or broiled lobster (you can pick your own) and whole fish Veracruz style. The seafaring theme extends to the names of the dishes (like Jean Laffite beef) and the restaurant itself (Lorenzillo was a 17th-century pirate). ⊠ *Paseo Kukulcán, Km 10.5,* ☎ *98/831254. MC, V.*

$$$ ✕ **Mikado.** Sit around the grill and watch the utensils fly as the chef prepares steaks, seafood, vegetables, and rice. As is true of Japanese steak houses everywhere, the showy preparation makes the meal. The sushi here is surprisingly good, especially an interesting concoction of rice and grilled eel rolled in avocado. ⊠ *Marriott CasaMagna, Paseo Kukulcán,* ☎ *98/81200. AE, DC, MC, V.*

$$ ✕ **Augustus Caesar.** In spite of the shopping-center location and the constant stream of shoppers passing by, this restaurant produces classic Italian specialties with an emphasis on seafood in a sophisticated, impressive setting. The gray, pink, and white color scheme, enhanced by white stucco columns, potted palms, tile floors, and soft jazz, creates a romantic ambience at night. ⊠ *La Mansión–Costa Blanca Shopping Center,* ☎ *98/833384. AE, MC, V.*

$$ ✕ **Carlos 'n Charlie's.** A lively atmosphere, a terrific view of the lagoon, and good food make this newly remodeled restaurant—part of the popular Anderson chain—Cancún's best-known hot spot. You'll never run out of bric-a-brac to look at: The walls are catchalls, with tons of photos; sombreros, birdcages, and wooden birds and animals hang from the ceilings. For dinner you may be tempted by the barbecued ribs sizzling on the open grill, or one of the steak or seafood specials. After your meal dance off the calories under the stars at the restaurant's **Pier Dance Club.** ⊠ *Paseo Kukulcán, Km 5.5,* ☎ *98/830846. Reservations not accepted. AE, MC, V.*

$$ ✕ **The Cove.** Both waterfront locations serve vast, inexpensive breakfast buffets under palapa roofs. The decor is decidedly nautical, with rigging draped on the walls and chandeliers in the shape of ships' steering wheels. The restaurant near the Casa Maya Hotel overlooks the Caribbean toward Isla Mujeres; the other is beside the Nichupté Lagoon. Both offer lunch and dinner menus filled with seafood dishes and charbroiled steak and chicken. Parents appreciate the lower-priced children's menu, an unusual feature in Cancún. ⊠ *Paseo Kukulcán, Km 16.5, lagoon-side across from Royal Mayan Hotel,* ☎ *98/850016;* ⊠ *beach-side next to Casa Maya Hotel,* ☎ *98/830669. Reservations not accepted. No credit cards.*

$$ ✕ **El Mexicano.** This restaurant seats 300 for a folkloric dinner show in a room resembling the patio of a hacienda. Details such as elaborately hand-carved chairs created by Indians from central Mexico and numerous regional Mexican dishes convey a feeling of authenticity. Be forewarned, however: Though indisputably popular, this is a touristy spot, and the dancing-girl show is not a window into Yucatecan culture. For your meal try the *empanxonostle* (steamed lobster, shrimp, fish, and herbs); it's as extravagant as El Mexicano's surroundings. ⊠ *La Mansión–Costa Blanca Shopping Center,* ☎ 98/832220 or 98/832220. *Folkloric ballet at 8. AE, MC, V.*

$$ ✕ **Jalapeños.** Folks crowd this place in the morning for its inexpensive breakfast buffet and in the evening for the dinner party package, which includes Mexican carnival games, an open bar, a Mexican buffet dinner, and dancing under the stars to Caribbean, marimba, and mariachi music. Six TV screens broadcast major sports events, while bartenders whip up tropical fruit drinks and margaritas to go along with jalapeños stuffed with shrimp or grouper prepared with wine, cilantro, and garlic. ⊠ *Paseo Kukulcán, Km 7,* ☎ 98/832704. *Reservations not accepted. AE, MC, V.*

$$ ✕ **Savio's.** The sea-green, white, and peach decor, a central staircase, floor-to-ceiling windows, and a sleek design with lots of greenery make this mall restaurant a fresh, lively spot for lunch. Early evening, their bar is known as the place to be. For dinner, candlelight and guitar and flute music create a romantic setting. The menu's focus is homemade pastas and seafood. ⊠ *Plaza Caracol,* ☎ 98/832085. *Reservations not accepted. AE, MC, V.*

$$ ✕ **Splash.** Art Deco furnishings, lots of purple and aqua, and neon lights
★ add to the sleek atmosphere of this restaurant. During high season the outside terrace with its peekaboo view of the lagoon is usually full. Never mind—the inside bar area and dining room are cooler. The downstairs area offers the most intimate dining experience. You can't go wrong with any of the homemade pastas or the charcoal-grilled grouper Bora Bora style (in a rich sauce of peaches and clarified butter). Splash has great happy hour specials and all-you-can-eat breakfast, lunch, and dinner deals. ⊠ *Paseo Kukulcán at Kukulcán Plaza,* ☎ 98/853011. *Reservations not accepted. AE, MC, V.*

$ ✕ **100% Natural.** Looking for something light? Head to one of the
★ four locations of this cheery open-air eatery, all done up in colorful tropical colors and featuring the green neon 100% NATURAL sign. Two are in the hotel zone, one at Kukulcán Plaza, and the other in the Plaza Terramar across from the Fiesta Americana; the latter location is open 24 hours. The newest location is in the recently opened Forum Plaza mall, across the street from Dady O disco. Identical menus at all three restaurants appeal to vegetarians, with a broad array of soups, fruit and veggie salads, fresh fruit drinks (39 at last count), and other nonmeat menu items. Egg dishes, sandwiches, grilled chicken and fish, and Mexican and Italian fare are available as well. The three- and four-course breakfast, lunch, and dinner specials are a bargain. ⊠ *Paseo Kukulcán at Kukulcán Plaza,* ☎ 98/852904; ⊠ *Plaza Terramar,* ☎ 98/831180; ⊠ *Av. Sunyaxchen 62,* ☎ 98/843617; *Forum Plaza Km 9.5 Paseo Kukulcan,* ☎ no phone. *Reservations not accepted. AE, MC, V.*

$ ✕ **Shooters Waterfront Cafe, U.S.A.** Popular with tourists year-round for its reasonably priced breakfast, lunch, and dinner specials, this casual restaurant overflows during spring break with college-age revelers who come here as much for the good food as for the frosty margaritas and raucous atmosphere. The decor of the spacious thatched-roof dining room is functional, with dark-wood furnishings; most prominent are the three TVs playing the day's sports events. There is a deck overlooking Lagoon Nichupté, an outdoor bar with informal white plastic café tables, and a pool where diners can have a quick swim before eating. This is not the place to come if you're offended by bikini contests. Shooters is across Paseo Kukulcán from the Omni Hotel. ⊠ *Paseo Kukulcán, Km 16.5,* ☎ 98/850267. *AE, DC, MC, V.*

Downtown

$$$ ✕ **Bucanero.** Quiet dining in a candlelit marine atmosphere is the drawing card for this seafood restaurant, built to resemble the interior of a Spanish galleon, and the seafood—particularly the lobster specialties—is tops. Start the meal with lobster bisque or black bean soup, and round it out with the seafood combination, which includes lobster in garlic sauce, shrimp brochette, and fish fillet. Heaping servings are enough to feed two (which puts this in the $$ price range if you don't mind sharing your meal). Piano music played throughout the evening and waiters dressed as pirates add character to the place. ⊠ *Av. Cobá 88,* ☎ *98/842280. AE, MC, V. No lunch.*

$$$ ✕ **La Habichuela.** This charmer—once an elegant home—is perfect for hand-holding romantics or anyone looking for a relaxed, private atmosphere. Located next to La Palapa Park, this candlelit garden, with white wrought-iron chairs, pebbled ground, and thick tropical greenery, exudes peacefulness while a statue of Pakal, the Maya god of astronomy and culture, surveys the scene. A must on the menu is fresh fish in *Guanabaná* (sweet white Mexican fruit) sauce. Try the *cocobichuela* (lobster and shrimp in a light Indian sauce served on a bed of rice inside a coconut), a specialty of the house. ⊠ *Margaritas 25,* ☎ *98/843158. AE, MC, V.*

$$ ✕ **Carrillo's.** This cheerful restaurant, with a sweeping veranda and pink-and-purple palm trees, specializes in lobster—brochettes, thermidor, and Mexican style. Other house favorites include broiled red snapper smothered with ham, cheese, bacon, shrimp, and a red sauce; a seafood platter massive enough to feed two; and strong Spanish coffee. Carrillo's also provides entertainment and festivities, including a musical trio that plays nightly. ⊠ *Claveles 33,* ☎ *98/841227. AE, MC, V.*

$$ ✕ **El Pescador.** It's first-come, first-served, with long lines, especially
★ during high season. But people still flood into this rustic Mexican-style restaurant with nautical touches; the open-air patio is especially popular. Heavy hitters on the menu include red snapper broiled with garlic and freshly caught lobster specials. For dessert consider sharing the cake filled with ice cream and covered with peaches and strawberry marmalade. **La Mesa Del Pescador** (☎ 98/850505), a newer offshoot in Plaza Kukulcán, is not usually as crowded as this place. ⊠ *Tulipanes 28,* ☎ *98/842673. Reservations not accepted. AE, MC, V.*

$$ ✕ **La Parrilla.** If you're looking for the place where local Mexicans—young and old—hang out, you've found it in this popular downtown spot, a classic by Cancún standards (it opened in 1975). Everything from the food to the bougainvillea and palapa roof is authentic. Popular dishes include the grilled beef with garlic sauce and the tacos *al pastor* (with pork, pineapple, coriander, onion, and salsa). ⊠ *Av. Yaxchilán 51,* ☎ *98/845398. Reservations not accepted. AE, MC, V.*

$$ ✕ **Perico's.** Find the antique car perched atop the palapa roof and you've spotted this zany, eclectic restaurant and bar. Saddles top bar stools, caricature busts of political figures from Castro to Queen Elizabeth line the walls, and waiters dressed as *zapatas* (revolutionaries) serve flaming desserts. The Mexican menu, including Pancho Villa (grilled beef with Mexican side dishes), is reliable, but the real reason to come here is the party atmosphere that begins nightly at 7 when the mariachi and marimba bands play. ⊠ *Av. Yaxchilán 61,* ☎ *98/843152. AE, MC, V.*

$$ ✕ **Pizzeria Rolandi's.** Bright red-and-yellow decor, plants, wood beams, ceiling fans, and visible wood-burning ovens have turned this otherwise simple sidewalk pizza place into a quick-dining treat. You can choose among 10 homemade pasta dishes and 15 different pizzas, with the star attraction being the delicious *Che* (a three-cheese pizza). The

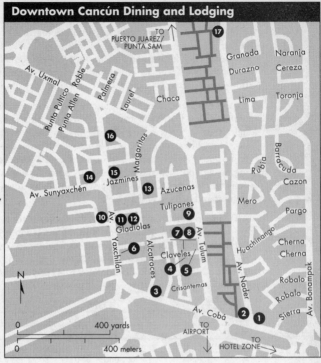

Downtown Cancún Dining and Lodging

Dining
Bucanero, **1**
Carrillo's, **7**
El Pescador, **9**
El Tacolote, **3**
La Habichuela, **13**
La Parrilla, **16**
Perico's, **10**
Pizzeria Rolandi's, **2**
Rosa Mexicano, **4**

Lodging
Antillano, **5**
Caribe Internacional, **14**
Holiday Inn Centro Cancún, **17**
Margarita Cancún, **15**
María del Lourdes, **6**
Mex Hotel, **11**
Plaza Carrillo's, **8**
Posada Lucy, **12**

restaurant will deliver to your hotel. ⊠ *Av. Cobá 12,* ☎ *98/844047. Reservations not accepted. MC, V.*

$$ ✕ **Rosa Mexicano.** One of Cancún's prettiest Mexican colonial-style
★ restaurants presents waiters dressed as *charros* (Mexican cowboys), pottery and embroidered wall hangings, floor tiles with floral designs, and a cozy, softly lighted atmosphere. For extra romance make a reservation for the candlelit patio. Savory appetizers include *nopalitos* (cactus strips sautéed with corn, cilantro, and cheese). Specialties are *filete* Rosa (beef and onions in a tequila-orange sauce) and *camarones al ajillo* (shrimp sautéed in olive oil and garlic, with chili peppers). ⊠ *Calle Claveles 4,* ☎ *98/846313. AE, MC, V. No lunch.*

$ ✕ **El Tacolote.** A lively neighborhood *taquería* (taco stand), El Tacolote has successfully expanded on its original tacos offerings and now serves fajitas, grilled kebabs, and other traditional Mexican favorites. You get three tacos with a standard order. Mix and match fillings, and don't overlook the filet mignon taco. Any doubts about what to order from the menu, choose a Mexican combination dish and you can't go wrong. Bowls of sliced limes and salsa come with your order, in keeping with the very casual tone of this brightly tiled and comfortable place. ⊠ *Av. Cobá 19,* ☎ *98/873045. Reservations not accepted. MC, V.*

LODGING

You may find it bewildering to choose from the variety of hotels in Cancún because in brochures most sound—and look—alike. If proximity to downtown is a priority, then you'll probably want to stay at one of the hotel zone properties at the island's northern end. Many of the malls are within walking distance, and taxis to downtown and to the ferries at Puerto Juárez cost less than from hotels farther south. If, however, you seek something more secluded, there is less development at the southern end.

For the most part the downtown hotels don't offer anything near the luxury or amenities of the hotel zone properties. They will, however, give you the opportunity to stay in a popular resort without paying resort prices, and many accommodations offer free shuttle service to the beach. In addition at a downtown property you'll be closer to Cancún's crafts market (Ki Huic) and restaurants that are more authentic—and less costly—than those you'll find in the hotel zone.

Expect minibars, satellite TV, laundry and room service, private safes (check to see if there is an extra charge for safe use), and bathroom hair dryers in hotels in the $$$$ category; in addition almost every major hotel has suites, rooms for people with disabilities, no-smoking rooms, an in-house travel agency and/or a car-rental concession, guest parking, water-sports facilities, and a daily schedule of planned games and activities for guests. Unless otherwise noted, all hotels have air-conditioning and private baths.

All Cancún hotels are within the 77500 postal code. Price categories are based on nondiscounted rates in the peak winter season, December–early May. For more information, but *not* for reservations, contact the **Cancún Hotel Association** (⌨ Av. Ign. García de la Torre, SM 1, Lote 6, Cancún, QR 77500, ☎ 98/842853 or 98/847083, ℻ 98/847115).

CATEGORY	COST*
$$$$	over $175
$$$	$120–$175
$$	$50–$120
$	under $50

All prices are for a standard double room, excluding 12% tax.

Hotel Zone

$$$$ 🏨 **Caesar Park Beach & Golf Resort.** Liberal use of Mérida marble, Mexican tile murals, and colorful oil paintings give this appealing Westin property, one of Cancún's newest luxury resorts, a distinctly Mexican flavor. Rooms, too, carry out the theme, with terra-cotta tile floors, rattan furniture, woven fiber headboards, and local artwork; some have a private balcony with a view of the ocean, and a few let you see the resort's championship 18-hole golf course across Paseo Kukulcán. Lavish interconnecting pools (*seven* of them) and streams wind through palm-dotted lawns; a terraced fountain in the cavernous central atrium brings the dancing water into the hotel's interior. The Royal Beach Club section comprises 80 oceanfront villas with extra-spacious rooms. ⌨ *Paseo Kukulcán, Km 17 (Box 1810),* ☎ *98/818000 or 800/228–3000,* ℻ *98/818080. 426 rooms, 4 suites. 3 restaurants, 3 bars, lobby lounge, 7 pools, beauty salon, 2 hot tubs, 2 saunas, 18-hole golf course, 2 tennis courts, aerobics, exercise room, shops, children's programs. AE, DC, MC, V.*

$$$$ 🏨 **Casa Turquesa.** The tranquil atmosphere of this small, elegant re-
★ treat belies its central location next to the bustling Plaza Kukulcán. The hotel's entrance is unassuming, but the public rooms are palatial, with high ceilings, stone bas-reliefs, marble floors, and oversize sofas. The 33 spacious suites are decorated individually in pastel tones, with modern furnishings; all have ocean-view private balconies with whirlpool baths. The Royal Suite, with a full kitchen and its own beach, and the duplex Presidential Suite, are the priciest accommodations. The privacy and discreet service afforded at this intimate retreat have made it the choice for celebrities such as Ivana Trump and the Planet Hollywood crew. For dinner the Celebrity (☞ Dining, *above*) and La

Palapa Frida restaurants offer imaginatively prepared seafood and Oaxacan dishes. ⊠ *Paseo Kukulcán, Km 13.5,* ☎ *98/852924,* FAX *98/852922. 33 suites. 3 restaurants, 3 bars, pool, beauty salon, sauna, tennis court, exercise room. AE, MC, V.*

$$$$ ☷ **Fiesta Americana Cancún.** The first of three Fiestas in Cancún, this intimate-feeling hotel is a perennial favorite among Europeans and Mexicans as well as Americans. A warm atmosphere and colorful design—painted villas in rose, yellow, and sand—make it a standout. The lobby, with its potted plants, ceiling fans, and rattan furniture, is a lovely, eclectic mix of Mexican, South Seas, and Mediterranean designs. Eat lunch at the poolside Bikini Bar or slumber by the calm northern waters of Bahía de Mujeres on this palapa-dotted beach. Rooms, which all have balconies, are spacious; they're brightly furnished with rattan and white wood furnishings complemented by white, cobalt-blue, and sea-foam green hues. ⊠ *Paseo Kukulcán, Km 9.5 (Box 696),* ☎ *98/831400 or 800/343–7821,* FAX *98/832502. 281 rooms. 3 restaurants, 3 bars, pool. AE, DC, MC, V.*

$$$$ ☷ **Fiesta Americana Condesa.** This sprawling, friendly hotel offers the same casual elegance and luxurious amenities as its older sister, the Fiesta Americana Coral Beach Cancún (☞ *below*). Situated toward the southern end of the hotel zone, the Condesa has a Mediterranean-style facade featuring balconies, rounded arches, and alternating ocher, salmon, and sand-colored walls. But it's the huge palapa fronting the structure that makes it hard to miss. An attractive and spacious lobby bar has Tiffany-style stained-glass awnings, tall palms, and ceiling fans. Three seven-story towers overlook a tranquil inner courtyard with hanging plants and falling water. The rooms, highlighted by dusty-pink stucco walls and Mexican tile floors, offer the same tranquillity. Balconies are shared by three standard rooms; the costlier accommodations have their own. Oceanfront suites have a private hot tub on the terrace. ⊠ *Paseo Kukulcán, Km 16.5 (Box 5478),* ☎ *98/851000 or 800/343–7821,* FAX *98/851650. 502 rooms. 5 restaurants, 2 bars, pool, beauty salon, 3 tennis courts, health club, shops. AE, DC, MC, V.*

$$$$ ☷ **Fiesta Americana Coral Beach Cancún.** The newest of the Cancún Fiesta properties, this all-suite hotel lies just in front of the convention center and shopping malls at the rotary opposite the Hyatt Regency. The large salmon-color structure—built in Mediterranean style with blue wrought-iron balconies—houses a lobby with marble-tile floors, potted palms, and a stained-glass skylight. All rooms are ample in size, with oceanfront balconies and marble floors; slate-blue, lavender, and beige tones create a soothing, pleasant mood. The hotel's **La Joya** restaurant, serving nouvelle-style Mexican fare, is a fine spot for dinner. As for outdoor activities, choose between the 1,000-ft beach and the 660-ft pool. This is Cancún's largest convention hotel; expect the clientele and occasional slow service to match. ⊠ *Paseo Kukulcán, Lote 6 (Box 14),* ☎ *98/832900 or 800/343–7821,* FAX *98/833173. 602 suites. 3 restaurants, 3 bars, pool, 3 tennis courts, health club, shops. AE, DC, MC, V.*

$$$$ ☷ **Hyatt Cancún Caribe Villas & Resort.** Intimate yet endowed with modern conveniences, this semicircular property was one of the first hotels in Cancún, but it was remodeled after suffering damage from Hurricane Gilbert in 1998. An attractive, contemporary room decor with Mexican accents now predominates: colorful stenciled borders on the walls near the ceilings, tile floors, curtains and bedspreads in dusty pinks and pale green prints, and light wood furniture. Beach-level rooms have gardens, and all rooms in the main tower offer ocean views. ⊠ *Paseo Kukulcán (Box 353),* ☎ *98/830044 or 800/223–1234,* FAX *98/831514. 201 rooms, including 26 beachfront villas. 3 restaurants, 2 bars, 3 pools, beauty salon, 3 hot tubs, 3 tennis courts, jogging, dock, shop. AE, DC, MC, V.*

$$$$ 🏨 **Marriott CasaMagna.** The six-story Marriott is rather eclectically designed: In the lobby modern furnishings are set in an atrium with Mediterranean-style arches, crystal chandeliers, and hanging vines. Three restaurants overlook the handsome pool area and the ocean. The rooms, decorated in contemporary Mexican style, have tile floors and ceiling fans and follow a soft rose, mauve, and earth-tone color scheme. You can learn to prepare Mexican dishes if you attend cooking lessons (one of many guest activities), or you can sit back and watch the chef do the work at **Mikado** (☞ Dining, *above*), the hotel's fine Japanese steak house. ⊠ *Paseo Kukulcán (Retorno Chac L-41),* ☎ *98/852000 or 800/228–9290,* ℻ *98/851385. 414 rooms, 36 suites. 3 restaurants, bar, beauty salon, 2 hot tubs, sauna, 2 tennis courts, health club, dock, shops. AE, DC, MC, V.*

$$$$ 🏨 **Meliá Cancún.** The Meliá Cancún is a boldly modern version of a Maya temple, fronted by a sheer black marble wall and a sleek waterfall. The spacious, airy atrium, filled with lush tropical flora, is dappled with sunlight flooding in from corner windows and from the steel-and-glass pyramid skylight overhead. Public spaces exude elegance; the boutiques could not be more chic. Ivory, dusty-pink, and light-blue hues softly brighten rooms (all with private balcony or terrace); ivory-lacquered furniture and wall-to-wall carpeting create a luxurious ambience. There's an upscale spa, with modern cardiovascular and strength-training equipment and an array of pampering and rejuvenating body treatments. To the chagrin of some guests, the hotel strictly enforces a policy against bringing in outside food or beverages (except bottled water). The **Meliá Turquesa,** a 408-room sister property across the street from Flamingo Plaza, is not as glitzy, but has a more intimate, friendlier atmosphere. ⊠ *Paseo Kukulcán, Km 16,* ☎ *98/85114 or 800/336–3542,* ℻ *98/851263. 450 rooms. 5 restaurants, 3 bars, 2 pools, spa, 18-hole golf course, 3 tennis courts, health club, paddle tennis, shops. AE, DC, MC, V.*

$$$$ 🏨 **Omni Cancún.** This 10-story pink hotel, topped off by a Spanish-style orange tile roof, offers an all-inclusive option, though European plan rates are still available if you don't care to take all your meals at the hotel. The small lobby conveys the same elegant but comfortable feel as the guest rooms, which feature marble floors, sea-green and pink color schemes, and tasteful wood furniture. Some rooms have balconies, but all have either ocean or lagoon views (the former are more expensive). Ranking as a primary attraction is the three-level pool, divided by a bar. ⊠ *Paseo Kukulcán, Lote 48 (Box 127),* ☎ *98/850714 or 800/843–6664,* ℻ *98/850059. 331 rooms and 15 villas. 3 restaurants, 2 bars, pool, 2 tennis courts, exercise room, dock, shops. AE, DC, MC, V.*

$$$$ 🏨 **Presidente Inter-Continental Cancún.** It's hard to miss the striking Mexican-yellow entryway of this hotel, five minutes from Plaza Caracol. During the last several years the hotel has made refurbishments in its rooms to that of Spanish colonial style, with Talavera pottery decorating the hotel throughout. It boasts a quiet beach and a waterfall in the shape of a Maya pyramid by the pool. Well-appointed, larger-than-average rooms are done in royal blue or beige and have light wicker furniture and area rugs on stone floors. Even larger suites offer contemporary furnishings, in-room video equipment, and spacious balconies. ⊠ *Paseo Kukulcán, Km 7.5,* ☎ *98/830200 or 800/327–0200,* ℻ *98/ 832602 or 98/832515. 298 rooms. 2 restaurants, bar, 2 pools, beauty salon, 6 hot tubs, tennis court, exercise room, shops. AE, DC, MC, V.*

$$$$ 🏨 **Ritz-Carlton Cancún.** This ultraposh, peach-colored property with
★   a Spanish-tile roof, wrought-iron railings, and splashing fountains in open courtyards opened in 1993, setting new standards for luxury and service in Cancún. The air-conditioned lobby and public areas are richly appointed with fine European and American antiques, thick car-

pets, and marble floors; the fourth-floor atrium is topped by a massive stained-glass dome. Stylish rooms, done in comfortable shades of blue, beige, and peach, offer all the amenities—wall-to-wall carpeting, travertine marble bathrooms with telephones, separate tub and shower, plush terry robes, and large balconies overlooking the Caribbean. The hotel's elegant restaurants, especially the **Club Grill** (☞ Dining, *above*) and the recently opened **Fantino** (serving Northern Italian dinners), are standouts. ⊠ *Paseo Kukulcán, Retorno del Rey 36,* ☎ *98/850808 or 800/241–3333,* ꜰꜹ *98/851015. 369 rooms. 3 restaurants, 2 bars, 3 pools, beauty salon, hot tub, spa, 3 tennis courts, health club, pro shop, shops. AE, DC, MC, V.*

$$$$ ⬚ **Sierra Cancún.** Formerly the Maeva, this pleasant, all-inclusive resort hotel has the advantage of being closer to town than the hotels on the southern end, while still seeming to be away from it all. Rooms are decorated in tropical colors, with light-wood furnishings and tile floors; all have a sunken lanai or private balcony. The poolside palapa restaurant is a serene spot for lunch. Meals are included in the room rate, and the hotel management strictly prohibits guests from bringing onto the premises any food or beverage purchased outside. The hotel has a resident doctor. ⊠ *Paseo Kukulcán, Km 10,* ☎ *98/832444 or 800/544–46486,* ꜰꜹ *98/833486. 261 rooms. 2 restaurants, bar, 2 pools, beauty salon, tennis court, dock, shop. AE, DC, MC, V.*

$$$$ ⬚ **Sun Palace.** The water pressure in the showerheads is fantastic, and in case you have trouble figuring out how to turn on the whirlpool, it's the little white button behind you in the bathtub. The resort's marble-floored suites, delicate desert pastel appointments, and spare, cool furnishings are a virtual massage to the senses. Every suite overlooks the Caribbean's sparkling, aquamarine water, and windows open to the sea breeze. All-inclusive means convenience: There are unlimited food and beverages (but meals are a disappointment), day-and-night entertainment, and activities—including use of an above-ground diving tank and a variety of nonmotorized water-sports equipment and tours to Maya ruins and to Isla Mujeres. There's a three-night minimum stay. ⊠ *Paseo Kukulcán, Km 20,* ☎ *98/851555 or 800/346–8225. 227 rooms. 3 restaurants, indoor and outdoor pools, outdoor hot tub, tennis court, exercise room, Ping-Pong, billiards, recreation room. AE, MC, V.*

$$$$ ⬚ **Villas Tacul.** The accommodations in this large complex (23 villas on 5 acres), set on its own stretch of beach en route to downtown, are appointed with red-tile floors and authentic Mexican colonial–style furniture, wagon-wheel chandeliers, and tin-work mirrors. Each villa has a kitchen and from two to five bedrooms, making this a good place for families and couples traveling together. An individual housekeeper keeps each unit spotless and serves private breakfasts for an extra charge. There are a few modestly priced studio rooms without kitchen facilities. The grounds are beautifully landscaped, with well-trimmed lawns and islands of palm trees in the pool. ⊠ *Paseo Kukulcán, Km 5.5,* ☎ *98/830000, 98/830080, or 800/842–0193,* ꜰꜹ *98/830349. 23 villas. Restaurant, bar, pool, 2 tennis courts, basketball. AE, DC, MC, V.*

$$$$ ⬚ **Westin Regina Resort Cancún.** This luxury property stands at the southern end of the island, on Punta Nizuc. It is one of the few hotels with direct access to both a 1,600-ft beach and Laguna Nichupté. The low-rise, postmodern-style hotel was designed and decorated by one of Latin America's leading architects. In the public areas stark-white stucco walls contrast with brilliant pink or blue recessed areas framing an array of sculptures and other artwork. From the lobby you can look down on a stylish restaurant with stunning ocean views. In the spacious guest rooms, handsome rustic furnishings and colorful Mexican folk art stand out against white walls and pale marble floors. Con-

cierge tower rooms are available. ⊠ *Paseo Kukulcán, Km 20 (Box 1808),* ☎ *98/850086, 98/850537, or 800/228–3000,* FAX *98/850074. 385 rooms. 4 restaurants, 3 bars, 5 pools, hot tub, 5 outdoor hot tubs, 2 tennis courts, exercise room, children's programs. AE, DC, MC, V.*

$$$ 🏨 **Club Las Velas.** Once you go past the wrought-iron gates of this all-
★   inclusive property, you'll be in a delightfully private enclave. The complex is a replica of a Mexican village, complete with central plaza, fountains, a natural aquarium, and lush gardens. Winding stone pathways connect the Mexican colonial–style attached villas and four five-story towers with the Laguna Nichupté beachfront, palapa restaurant, and pools. Nonmotorized water sports, children's programs, and a water taxi to a nearby ocean beach are part of the package. Rooms are light and airy, with white stucco walls, tropical-print bedspreads, and rattan furniture. Tower rooms from the second floor up all have balconies. The duplex villas are especially suited to families, as adjoining bedrooms can easily form two- or three-bedroom suites. The food—served buffet style at breakfast, and buffet style or à la carte at dinner—is plentiful and good. Nightly theme parties with live entertainment fill the plaza after dinner. ⊠ *Paseo Kukulcán and Galeon,* ☎ *98/832222 or 800/707–8815,* FAX *98/832118. 226 rooms, 59 villas. 2 restaurants, 2 bars, snack bar, 2 pools, 2 tennis courts, aerobics, exercise room, shops, children's programs. AE, MC, V.*

$$$ 🏨 **Hyatt Regency Cancún.** A cylindrical 14-story tower with the Hyatt trademark—a striking central atrium filled with tropical greenery and topped by a sky-lighted dome—affords a 360° view of the sea and the lagoon. Plants spill over the inner core of the cylinder, at the base of which is a bar. Soothing blue, green, and beige tones prevail in the rooms, which also feature contemporary Mexican furniture and striking green or rose-color marble vanities. This hotel, much larger and livelier than its sister property, has an enormous two-level pool with a waterfall. **Cilantro,** the hotel's pretty waterfront dining room, offers a good breakfast buffet. The Punta Cancún location is convenient to the convention center and several shopping malls. ⊠ *Paseo Kukulcán (Box 1201),* ☎ *98/830966, 98/ 831234, or 800/233–1234,* FAX *98/831438. 300 rooms. 2 restaurants, 3 bars, pool, health club, recreation room. AE, MC, V.*

$$$ 🏨 **Krystal Cancún.** Its lobby tends to be hectic, but the location of this hotel, part of a Mexican chain, can't be beat. At the tip of Punta Cancún, within walking distance of three major shopping malls and across the street from the convention center, the Krystal affords spectacular views of the entire ocean coast of the island, the lagoon, and parts of downtown. A 1994 renovation perked up rooms with window planter boxes, rattan furniture, and pastels, but the hotel also went time-share at the time, and guests may be exposed to the sales push. The property hosts **Bogart's** and **Hacienda El Mortero,** two of the best-known restaurants in town (☞ Dining, *above*), as well as the popular **Christine** disco (☞ Nightlife, *below*). ⊠ *Paseo Kukulcán, Lote 9,* ☎ *988/ 31133 or 800/232–9860. 322 rooms. 4 restaurants, 4 bars, pool, hot tub, sauna, 2 tennis courts, exercise room, shops. AE, DC, MC, V.*

$$$ 🏨 **Royal Solaris Caribe.** This all-inclusive property comprises two separate hotel buildings; the grounds between them are covered with lush tropical foliage. A number of the units are time-share apartment suites, with large living rooms, kitchenettes, and bathtubs (as opposed to the shower stalls in the smallish standard rooms). Studio rooms, which also have kitchenettes, offer twice the space of "superior" rooms. The hotel bills its swimming pool as the largest in Cancún. ⊠ *Paseo Kukulcán, Km 20,* ☎ *98/850600, 98/850100, or 800/221–5333,* FAX *98/850354. 488 rooms. 7 restaurants, 5 bars, pool, 2 hot tubs, tennis court, basketball, exercise room, shops, dance club, children's programs. AE, DC, MC, V.*

$$ 🏨 **Calinda Viva Cancún.** This beige stucco eight-story building—part of the Quality hotel chain—is not one of the most attractive in town, but it makes a reliable standby and is in a good location, on the north beach near many malls. Redecorated in late 1994, the functional, moderate-size rooms have marble floors and contemporary pastel decor; half have private balconies and ocean views. The property also has a small garden, a beach, and a Mexican restaurant. ⊠ *Paseo Kukulcán, Km 8.5 (Box 673),* ☎ *98/830800 or 100/221–2222. 216 rooms. Restaurant, bar, pool, 2 tennis courts, dock, shops. AE, DC, MC, V.*

$$ 🏨 **El Pueblito Beach Hotel.** El Pueblito, meaning "little town," is an
★ apt name for this all-inclusive property, which consists of clusters of guest rooms in tri-level units with arches, terraces, balconies, and other architectural details that invoke Old Mexico. Interconnecting pathways lined with tropical foliage lead to intriguing terrace pools with waterfalls and stone archways; there's even a long water slide for kids. Rooms, which are large for the price, have marble floors and simple rattan furnishings; a few have kitchenettes. ⊠ *Paseo Kukulcán, Km 17.5,* ☎ *98/850422,* FAX *98/850731. 239 rooms. 3 restaurants, bar, 5 pools, tennis court, shops, travel services. AE, MC, V.*

$ 🏨 **Villa Deportiva Juvenil Cancún.** This government-run youth hostel on the beach has glass walls, a cable TV room, a pool, and dormitory beds (separate rooms for men and women). A lounge lends itself to the sort of congenial mingling one expects of a youth hostel. There is also an area for camping. ⊠ *Paseo Kukulcán, Km 3,* ☎ *98/831337. 33 rooms (300 beds) with shared baths. Basketball, Ping-Pong, volleyball. No credit cards.*

Downtown

$$$ 🏨 **Holiday Inn Centro Cancún.** The place to stay if you want to be down-
★ town and have all the amenities, this is the newest (built in 1990) and most upscale hotel in the area. It's less expensive than similar properties in the hotel zone and provides free transportation to the beach of the Crown Princess Club. The attractive pink four-story structure, with a Spanish-tile roof, affords easy access to restaurants and shops. Although rooms are generic motel modern, with mauve and blue color schemes, they have appealing Mexican touches. ⊠ *Av. Nader 1, SM 2,* ☎ *98/84455 or 800/465–4329,* FAX *98/847954. 246 rooms. 2 restaurants, 2 bars, pool, beauty salon, tennis court, exercise room, nightclub, coin laundry, travel services, car rental. AE, DC, MC, V.*

$$ 🏨 **Antillano.** This old but prettily appointed property features wood
★ furnishings, a cozy little lobby bar, and a tiny pool. Extras such as tiled bathroom sinks and air-conditioning in the halls and rooms make this hotel stand out from the others in its league. ⊠ *Av. Tulum at Calle Claveles,* ☎ *98/841532 or 98/841132,* FAX *98/841878. 48 rooms. Pool, shops. AE, DC, MC, V.*

$$ 🏨 **Caribe Internacional.** Located on a major traffic circle downtown, this relatively modern hotel can be somewhat noisy. The concrete exterior is covered by stucco and the rooms—although on the small side and sparsely furnished—are pleasant enough and have pastel-color walls. The small pool in a garden at the back adds a bit to this otherwise average property, and the free beach shuttle is a plus. ⊠ *Yaxchilán 36, at Sunyaxchén,* ☎ *98/843999,* FAX *98/841993. 55 rooms, 25 suites. Restaurant, cafeteria, pool, travel services. AE, MC, V.*

$$ 🏨 **Margarita Cancún.** This five-story hotel, just across from the Caribe Internacional, is Mission-style white stucco with yellow-tile trim. Rooms, done in monochromatic tones of blue or beige, have tile floors. Ask for a room with a view of the pool. ⊠ *Av. Yaxchilán 41, SM 22,* ☎ *98/849333,* FAX *98/841324. 100 rooms. Restaurant, lobby lounge, snack bar, pool, travel services. AE, MC, V.*

$$ ⊞ **María del Lourdes.** The María del Lourdes has some nice touches throughout, such as the colonial-style restaurant with rust-and-white stucco walls and the garden surrounding a small pool in the back. The rooms are uninspired, however, with dark brown furnishings and small windows. ⊠ *Av. Yaxchilán 80,* ☎ *98/844744,* ℻ *98/841242. 81 rooms. Restaurant, bar, pool, coin laundry. AE, MC, V.*

$$ ⊞ **Mex Hotel.** This three-story Spanish colonial–style hotel, a block south of the Margarita Cancún, reopened in 1995 after a floor-to-ceiling renovation. Long popular with students, Europeans, and Canadians, it has rooms done in tasteful tones of brown. A pretty courtyard entrance leads to the reception desk. ⊠ *Av. Yaxchilán 31,* ☎ *98/843078 or 98/843–3690,* ℻ *98/849209. 81 rooms. Restaurant, bar, pool. AE, DC, MC, V.*

$$ ⊞ **Plaza Carrillo's.** One of the first hotels to be built in Cancún City,
★ this one is conveniently located in the heart of the downtown area next to the Plaza Carrillo shopping arcade and **Carrillo's** restaurant (☞ Dining, *above*), which are under the same ownership. The hotel corridors are exceptionally clean and well maintained. Rooms are bright, with simple functional decor. ⊠ *Calle Claveles 35,* ☎ *98/841227,* ℻ *98/842371. 43 rooms. Restaurant, pool. AE, MC, V.*

$ ⊞ **Posada Lucy.** This place isn't much to look at outside, but its location, on a quiet side street, is good. The rather seedy pink-and-beige rooms in the main building are small, with no views, but some include kitchenettes. Another 12 rooms, in an adjacent building behind Restaurant Pericos, are available for monthly rental. Expansion added eight third-floor rooms and a Mexican restaurant to the property. ⊠ *Gladiolas 8, SM 22,* ☎ *98/843888. 33 rooms. Restaurant. AE.*

NIGHTLIFE AND THE ARTS

The Arts

Festivals

Cancún's **Jazz Festival** premiered in 1991 and featured Wynton Marsalis and Gato Barbieri. It's an annual event that takes place in late May. The **Cancún Hotel Association** (⊠ Av. Ign. García de la Torre, SM 1, Lote 6, Cancún, QR 77500, ☎ 98/847083) can provide information about this popular gathering. Each November the state of Quintana Roo hosts the **Caribbean Culture Festival.** Cancún and other regional cities present a series of events ranging from Caribbean music to recitals by Mexican poets. Latin American painters and sculptors exhibit here as well. The real draw, however, is the variety of Salsa music. Salsa groups from countries throughout the Caribbean come to Cancún to perform the best this music has to offer. If you're in Cancún at this time, check with the concierge of your hotel to find out when and where these events take place.

Film

Local movie theaters showing American and Mexican films include **Telecines Kukulcán** (⊠ Plaza Kukulcán, ☎ 98/853021) and **Tulum Plus** (⊠ Av. Tulum, SM 2, ☎ 98/843451).

Performances

The **ballet folklórico** dinner show (⊠ Hotel Continental Villas Plaza, Paseo Kukulcán, Km 11, ☎ 98/831095) consists of stylized performances of regional Mexican dances including the hat dance and *la bamba.* By comparison with the renowned Ballet Nacional Folklórico of Mexico City, this troupe suffers, but if it's all you'll get to see of the brilliant Mexican dance traditions, which blend pre-Hispanic and Iberian motifs, then go for it. An admission price of about $50 includes the buffet—a sampling of regional Mexican cooking—the show, and one drink. Performances are held Monday through Saturday; dinner is at 7, the show at 8:30.

The **convention center** hosts a popular ballet folklórico dinner show nightly (⊠ Paseo Kukulcán, Km 9, ☎ 98/830169). Cocktails are at 6:30; dinner, a typical Mexican buffet, is at 7; and the dance production goes on at 8.

Mexican fiesta dinner shows are held once a week at the **Westin Regina** (☎ 98/850086, ext. 193/194) and the **Meliá Turquesa** (☎ 98/832544). Both include folkloric ballet, mariachi music, a Mexican buffet, and drinks. Call for dates, prices, and reservations.

A Mexican *charreada,* or rodeo show (⊠ El Corral de JF, Km 6, Prolongación Av. Lopez Portillo, ☎ no phone), is performed Monday–Saturday at 7 PM. In addition to the show you get dinner and domestic drinks. You can book reservations through your hotel.

Nightlife

The multistory **Party Center** (⊠ Paseo Kukulcán, Km 9, ☎ 98/830351), next to the convention center, is an entertainment complex that hosts several clubs, a sports bar, and two discos (**Tequila Rock** and **Baja Beach Club**), as well as numerous restaurants, specialty boutiques, and a money exchange. Live folkloric bands perform nightly in the central courtyard that provides access to the clubs, bars, discos, and restaurants.

Dinner Cruises

The *Cancún Queen* (☎ 98/852288), a paddle wheeler departing from the AquaWorld Marina (⊠ Paseo Kukulcán, Km 15.2), has a full lobster or steak spread with an open bar and dancing for $65. **Aqua Tours Adventures** (⊠ Paseo Kukulcán, Km 6.25, ☎ 98/830400) offers a pleasantly romantic lobster dinner and sunset cruise to Isla Mujeres that includes dancing under the stars and an open bar. Departures are at 6 PM on Monday, Tuesday, Thursday, and Saturday. On evening cruises with **Asterix Party Fishing** (⊠ Paseo Kukulcán, Km 5.5 at Carlos 'n Charlies, ☎ 98/864847) you catch the fish and the crew prepares it for you. The price is $50, including an open bar and fishing gear; boats depart weekdays at 6 PM and return at midnight. **Pirates Night,** departing from Playa Langosta Dock (⊠ Paseo Kukulcán, ☎ 98/831488), offers a three-course buffet dinner with trips to Treasure Island. Kids under 12 sail at half price and those under five sail free. Cruises are Tuesday and Thursday, leaving at 6:30 PM and returning at 11:30. It's wise to be at the dock 30 minutes before departure time. The galleon *Columbus* (⊠ Paseo Kukulcán, Km16.5, in front of the Omni Hotel at the Royal Mayan Marina, ☎ 98/831488) sets sail every night at 7:30 and 10:30 for a cruise around the lagoon. Lobster or steak dinners are served along with salad and dessert. All drinks are included in the $55 per person ticket.

Discos

Cancún wouldn't be Cancún without its glittering discos, which generally start jumping about 10:30. **Azucar** (⊠ Hotel Camino Real, ☎ 98/844814) sizzles to a salsa beat nightly; the beautiful people don't turn up here until *really* late. Dress properly, though; the club doesn't allow shorts. **Dady'O** (⊠ Paseo Kukulcán, Km 9.5, ☎ 98/833134) has been around for a while but is still a very "in" place, especially with the younger set. The **Dady Rock** (⊠ Paseo Kukulcán, Km 9.5, ☎ 98/831626) bar and grill, next door to Dady'O, opens at 6 PM, and draws a high-energy clientele, with live music, a giant screen, contests, and food specials. **Christine** (⊠ Krystal Cancún hotel, ☎ 98/831133) attracts a slightly older, elegantly attired crowd and puts on an incredible light show. **La Boom** (⊠ Paseo Kukulcán, Km 3.5, ☎ 98/831152) includes a video bar with a light show and is not always crowded, although it can squeeze in 1,200 people. Those who want to party hardy can let loose with live reggae and rock and roll at **Señor Frog's** (⊠ Paseo Kukulcán, Km 12.5, ☎ 98/832188) into the early morning hours.

Music

Batacha (⊠ Hotel Miramar Misión, ☎ 98/831755), a small Caribbean nightclub, is a low-key spot to enjoy some Latin sounds. Visit the **Hard Rock Cafe** (⊠ Forum Plaza, Km 9.5, ☎ 98/832024) for live rock bands (generally six nights a week) and molto music nostalgia. You can hear Caribbean beat dance music (marimba, mariachi, reggae, etc.) at **Jalapeños** (⊠ Paseo Kukulcán, Km 7, ☎ 98/832896) nightly from 8. The place to go for hot live reggae is **Mango Tango** (⊠ Paseo Kukulcán, Km 14.2, ☎ 98/850303), which sits lagoon-side across the street from the Ritz-Carlton. **Planet Hollywood** (⊠ Flamingo Plaza, Paseo Kukulcán, Km 11.5, ☎ 98/850723) is currently the top ticket in town; crowds push their way in for the Hollywood memorabilia—and hope to catch a glimpse of such stars as Demi Moore and Arnold Schwarzenegger, who occasionally check in on their investment. Jazz lovers will want to trek downtown to **Roots Bar** (⊠ Tulipanes Av. 26, near La Palapa park, ☎ no phone) for an evening of outstanding jazz. Varying nights also include Flaminco Blues and modern Brazilian music. Newly opened **La Palapa Frida** (⊠ Casa Turquesa Hotel, Km 13.5, ☎ 98/852924) starts jumping around 9 PM with live salsa to the oldies but goodies.

OUTDOOR ACTIVITIES AND SPORTS

Bullfighting

The Cancún **bullring,** a block south of the Pemex station, hosts year-round bullfights. A matador, *charros* (Mexican cowboys), a mariachi band, and flamenco dancers entertain during the hour preceding the bullfight (from 2:30 PM). ⊠ *Paseo Kukulcán and Av. Bonampak,* ☎ *98/845465 or 98/848248.* ▣ *About $40.* ☉ *Fights Wed. at 3:30.*

Golf

The main course is at **Pok-Ta-Pok** (⊠ Paseo Kukulcán between Km 6 and Km 7, ☎ 98/830871), a club with fine views of both sea and lagoon, whose 18 holes were designed by Robert Trent Jones, Sr. The club also has a practice green, a swimming pool, tennis courts, and a restaurant. The greens fees are $70 ($55 after 2 PM); electric cart, $25; clubs, $15; caddies, $20; and golf clinics, $25 per hour. Playing hours are 6–6 (last tee-off is at 4). There is an 18-hole championship golf course at the **Caesar Park Beach and Golf Resort** (⊠ Paseo Kukulcán, Km 17, ☎ 98/818000); greens fees are $95 ($75 for hotel guests), carts are included, and club rentals run from $20 to $30. The 18-hole executive course (par 53) at the **Hotel Meliá Cancún** (⊠ Paseo Kukulcán, Km 12, ☎ 98/851160) forms a semicircle around the property and shares its beautiful ocean views. The greens fee is about $20.

Health Clubs

Most of the deluxe hotels have their own health clubs, although few of them are very large. There are, however, two gyms in Cancún: Both **Gold's Gym** (⊠ Av. Ixcun, SM 32, ☎ 98/846948 or 98/847092) and **Star's Gym** (⊠ Av. Sayil 22, in the Holiday Inn, ☎ 98/874455) have modern equipment and exercise facilities.

Jogging

Although to some people the idea of jogging in the intense heat of Cancún sounds like a form of masochism, fanatics should know that there is a 14-km (9-mi) track extending along half the island, running parallel to Paseo Kukulcán from the Punta Cancún area into Cancún City.

Water Sports

There are myriad ways you can get your adrenaline going while getting wet in Cancún. The most popular ones are detailed below. In addition you'll also be able to find places to go parasailing (about $35 for eight minutes); waterskiing ($70 per hour); or jet skiing ($70 per hour, or $60 for Wave Runners, double-seated Jet Skis). Paddleboats, kayaks, catamarans, and banana boats are also readily available. **Aqua Tours** (⊠ Paseo Kukulcán, Km 6.25, ☎ 98/830400, FAX 98/830403) and **AquaWorld** (⊠ Paseo Kukulcán, Km 15.2, ☎ 98/852288, FAX 98/852299) maintain large fleets of water toys. **Wet n' Wild** (⊠ Paseo Kukulcán Km 25, ☎ 98/851855), Cancún's newest attraction, is a water theme park offering swimming pools with waves, seven different water slides, a slow-moving river with an ecological viewing area, pools for children, and several bars and restaurants. Those with nerves of steel will want to try the harrowing "Montana Swinger." This thrill-packed ride takes you as high as 180 ft and descends with speeds of up to 60 mi per hour (not recommended for people with heart conditions). Admission is $25.

Fishing

Some 500 species of tropical fish, including sailfish, bluefin, marlin, barracuda, and red snapper, live in the waters adjacent to Cancún. Deep-sea fishing boats and other gear may be chartered from outfitters for about $350 for four hours, $450 for six hours, and $550 for eight hours. Charters generally include a captain, a first mate, gear, bait, and beverages. **Aqua Tours, AquaWorld,** and the **Royal Yacht Club** (⊠ Paseo Kukulcán, Km 16.5, ☎ 98/852930) are just a few of the companies that operate large fishing fleets.

Pelican Pier Fishing Excursions (⊠ Paseo Kukulcán, Km 5.5—across from the Casa Maya Hotel, ☎ 98/830315) offers six hours on their six-person charter boats for $99 per person. Price includes soft drinks, bait, and fishing gear. Also available are deep-sea charters starting at $318 for four hours.

Marinas

A new marina, **San Buenaventura,** between Bahía de Mujeres and Laguna Nichupté, was scheduled for completion in late 1995, but the facility only now is approaching completion. Other marinas include **Aqua Tours Adventures** (☎ 98/830227, FAX 98/830403), **AquaWorld** (☎ 98/852288, FAX 98/852299), **Blue Bay Club & Marina** (☎ 98/801070), **Club Lagoon** (☎ 98/833109), and **Scuba Cancún** (☎ 98/831011).

Sailboarding and Kayaking

Although some people sailboard on the ocean side in the summer, activity is limited primarily to the bay between Cancún and Isla Mujeres. If you visit the island in July, don't miss the National Windsurfing Tournament (☎ 98/843212). The **International Windsurfer Sailing School** (☎ 98/842023), at Playa Tortugas, rents equipment and gives lessons; the **Windsurf Association of Quintana Roo** (☎ 98/871771) can provide information about the tournament. Sailboards are available for about $50 an hour; classes go for about $35 an hour. Although Cancú doesn't offer much in the way of kayaking, you can rent kayaks at **Solo Buceo** (☎ 98/ 830100) in front of the Camino Real Hotel for about $30 per hour.

Snorkeling and Scuba Diving

Snorkeling is best at Punta Nizuc, Punta Cancún, and Playa Tortugas, although you should be especially careful of the strong currents at the last; gear can be rented for $10 per day. Some charter-fishing companies offer a two-tank scuba dive for about $100. As the name implies, **Scuba Cancún** (☎ 98/831011) specializes in diving trips and offers NAUI, CMAS, and PADI instruction. **Aqua Tours Adventures** (☎ 98/830227) offers scuba tours and a resort course, as well as snorkeling trips. **Aqua-World Adventures** (☎ 98/852288) runs 2½-hour daily jungle tours through dense mangroves. A guide leads the way as you drive your own Aqua Ray motorboat on Laguna Nichupté. The $40 price includes snorkeling and light refreshments. Trips leave daily at 8, 9, and 11 AM, noon, and 2 and 3 PM. If you've brought your own snorkeling gear and want to save money, just take a city bus down to Club Med and walk along the resort's beach for less than 1 km (½ mi) until you get to Punta Nizuc. **Blue Peace Diving** (✉ Paseo Kukulcán, Km 16.2, ☎ 98/851447) offers two-tank dives for $85 with NAUI, SSI, and PADI instruction. The areas explored are Cozumel, Akumal, Xpu-ha, and Isla Mujeres. Extended three-day diving trips are available for about $280.

SHOPPING

Resort wear and handicrafts are the most popular purchases in Cancún, but the prices are high and the selection standard. "Caveat emptor" applies as much to Cancún as it does to the "bargain" electronics stores on 5th Avenue in New York City or in Hong Kong. If you're traveling elsewhere in Mexico, it's best to postpone your shopping spree until you reach another town. Still, you can find a respectable variety of Mexican handicrafts ranging from blown glass and hand-woven textiles to leather goods and jewelry made from local coral and tortoiseshell. (Don't be tempted by the tortoiseshell products: The turtles they come from are endangered species, and it is illegal to bring tortoiseshell into the United States and several other countries.)

Throughout Mexico you will often get better prices by paying with cash (pesos or dollars) or traveler's checks. This is because Mexican merchants are averse to the commissions charged by credit-card companies, and frequently tack that commission—6% or more—onto your bill. If you can do without the plastic, you may even get the 12% sales tax lopped off.

Bargaining is expected in Cancún, but mostly in the market. Suggest half the asking price and slowly come up, but do not pay more than 70% of the quoted price. Shopping around is a good idea, too, because the crafts market is very competitive. But closely examine the merchandise you are purchasing: Some "authentic" items—particularly jewelry—may actually be shoddy imitations.

In Cancún shopping hours are generally weekdays 10–1 and 4–7, although more and more stores are staying open throughout the day rather than closing for siesta between 1 and 4 PM. Many shops keep Saturday morning hours, and some are now open on Sunday until 1 PM. Shops in the malls tend to be open weekdays from 9 or 10 AM to 8 or 10 PM.

Shopping Districts, Streets, and Malls

Shopping can be roughly categorized by location: In the malls and in-house boutiques in the hotel zone, prices are generally—but not always—

higher than in the shops and markets downtown. However, at the markets you'll have to sift through lots of overpriced junk and haggle a bit in order to land some good deals in silver or handicrafts.

Downtown

The wide variety of shops downtown along Avenida Tulum (between Avs. Cobá and Uxmal) includes **Fama** (✉ Av. Tulum 105, ☎ 98/846586), a department store offering clothing, English reading matter, sports gear, toiletries, liquor, and *latería* (crafts made of tin). Also on Tulum is the oldest and largest of Cancún's crafts markets, **Ki Huic** (✉ Av. Tulum 17, between Bancomer and Banco Atlantico, ☎ 98/843347), which is open daily from 9 AM to 10 PM and houses about 100 vendors.

Hotel Zone

Fully air-conditioned malls (known as *centros comerciales*), as streamlined and well kept as any in the United States or Canada, sell everything from fashion clothing, beachwear, and sportswear to jewelry, household items, video games, and leather goods.

Kukulcán Plaza (✉ Paseo Kukulcán, Km 13) is a mall that never seems to end, with around 130 shops (including Izod, Benetton, and Harley Davidson boutiques), 12 restaurants, a bar, a liquor store, a bank, a cinema, bowling lanes, and a video arcade.

Flamingo Plaza (✉ Paseo Kukulcán, Km 11.5, across from the Hotel Flamingo) includes an exchange booth, some designer emporiums and duty-free stores, several sportswear shops, two boutiques selling Guatemalan imports, a drugstore, and a Planet Hollywood boutique. At the food court, in addition to the usual McDonald's, Domino's Pizza, and fried chicken concessions, you'll find Checándole, offering what might be the only fast-food mole enchiladas around.

Forum Plaza (✉ Paseo Kukulcán, Km 9.5) across from Dady Rock, has just opened with its centerpiece being the newly moved **Hard Rock Cafe.** It features ACA Joe Beach, Diesel Jeans, Chic Fashion Beachware, and a multitude of jewelry shops. On the second level is the Disney-esque restaurant, the Rain Forest Cafe. There is also a supermarket deli that carries fine Cuban cigars.

Just across from the convention center site, **Plaza Caracol** (✉ Paseo Kukulcán, Km 8.5) is the largest and most contemporary mall in Cancún, with about 200 shops and boutiques, including two pharmacies, art galleries, a currency exchange, and folk art and jewelry shops, as well as cafés and restaurants. Fashion boutiques include Benetton, Bally, Gucci, and Ralph Lauren; in all these stores prices are lower than in their U.S. counterparts. Weary shoppers can rest their feet at the café tables near the first-floor frozen yogurt stand or the fast-food court nearby.

To the back of—and virtually indistinguishable from—Plaza Caracol are two outdoor shopping complexes. The pink stucco **La Mansión–Costa Blanca** specializes in designer clothing and has several restaurants, art galleries, a bank, and a liquor store. **Plaza Lagunas** has some fast-food places (KFC, Subway, Dunkin' Donuts); sportswear shops, such as Ellesse; and a number of souvenir stands. Also near Plaza Caracol, **Plaza Terramar** (opposite the Hotel Fiesta Americana) sells beachwear, souvenirs, and folk art, and has a restaurant and a pharmacy.

Specialty Shops

Galleries

Orbe (✉ Plaza Caracol, ☎ 98/831571) specializes in sculptures and paintings by contemporary Mexican artists. **Mordo's** (✉ La Mansión–Costa Blanca mall, ☎ 98/830838) is the local outlet for a small

Mexico City chain that sells handcrafted leather jackets, belts, and boots, and can customize your purchase with decorative patches, needlework, or metallic trim. **Turquesa Gallery** (⊠ Paseo Kukulcán Km 13.5, ☎ 98/852924) carries the works of world-renowned artists Jose Luis Cuvas (painter) and Juan Soriano (sculptor), whose works are collected the world over. **Mayart** (⊠ La Mansión–Costa Blanca mall, ☎ 98/841272 or 98/841569) displays replicas of Maya art, temple rubbings, and contemporary painting and sculpture. Those interested in contemporary art should stop by the **Xamanek Gallery** (⊠ Plaza Caracol, ☎ no phone) to see the work of Sergio Bustamante, one of the most popular Mexican artists today.

Grocery Stores

Major supermarkets include **Comercial Mexicana** (⊠ Av. Lopez Portillo at Libramiento Kabah, ☎ 98/871303); **San Francisco de Asís** (⊠ Av. Tulum 18, ☎ 98/841155); **Super Deli** (⊠ Av. Tulum at Xcaret, ☎ 98/841122, ext. 149; ⊠ Plaza Nautilus, ☎ 98/831903); **Comercial Mexicana de la Glorieta** (⊠ Av. Tulum at Av. Uxmal, ☎ 98/843330 or 98/844258); and the newest and largest, **Chadraul** (⊠ Av. Tulum 58–59 at Av. Cobá, ☎ 98/841036).

CANCÚN A TO Z

Arriving and Departing

By Bus

The **bus terminal** (⊠ Av. Tulum and Av. Uxmal, ☎ 98/841378 or 98/843948) downtown serves first-class buses making the trip from Mexico City and first- and second-class buses arriving in Cancún from Puerto Morelos, Playa del Carmen, Tulum, Chetumal, Cobá, Valladolid, Chichén Itzá, and Mérida. Public buses (Rte. 8) make the trip out to Puerto Juárez and Punta Sam for the ferries to Isla Mujeres, and taxis will take you from the bus station to Puerto Juárez for about $2.

By Car

Cancún is at the end of Route 180, which goes from Matamoros on the Texas border to Campeche, Mérida, and Valladolid. The road trip from Texas to Cancún can take up to three days. Cancún can also be reached from the south via Route 307, which passes through Chetumal and Belize. There are few gas stations on these roads, so try to keep your tank filled. Route 307 has a Pemex station between Cancún and Playa Del Carmen. Construction is ongoing, changing this route from two to four lanes.

By Plane

Cancún International Airport is 16 km (9 mi) southwest of the heart of Cancún City, 10 km (6 mi) from the southernmost point of the hotel zone. **Aeromexico** (☎ 98/841097 or 98/843571) flies nonstop from Houston, Miami, and New York. **American** (☎ 98/860086) has nonstop service from Dallas and Miami. **Continental** (☎ 98/860040) offers daily direct service from Houston. **Mexicana** (☎ 98/874444 or 98/834881) nonstops depart from Los Angeles, Miami, and New York. In Cancún Mexicana subsidiaries **Aerocaribe** (downtown, ☎ 98/842000; airport, ☎ 98/860083) and **Aerocozumel** (downtown, ☎ 98/842000; airport, ☎ 98/860162) offer flights to Cozumel, the ruins at Chichén Itzá, Mérida, and other Mexican destinations.

BETWEEN THE AIRPORT AND HOTELS

A counter at the airport exit sells tickets for vans (called *colectivos*) and for taxis; prices for the latter range from $15 to $25, depending on the exact destination. Buses, which cost about $9, are air-conditioned and sell soft drinks and beer on board, but may be slow if they're carrying a lot of passengers and need to stop at many hotels. Approximate taxi fares: from the airport to the hotel zone, $22; from the hotel zone to the airport, $10.

Getting Around

Motorized transportation of some sort is necessary, as the island is somewhat spread out. Public bus service is good, and taxis are relatively inexpensive.

By Bus
Public buses operate between the hotel zone and downtown from 6 AM to midnight; the cost is about 3 pesos. There are designated bus stops, but drivers can also be flagged down along Paseo Kukulcán. The service is a bit erratic, but buses run frequently and can save you considerable money on taxis, especially if you're staying at the southern end of the hotel zone.

By Car and Moped
Renting a car for your stay in Cancún is probably an unnecessary expense, entailing tips for valet parking, as well as gasoline and rather costly rental rates (on a par with those in any major resort area around the world). What's more, driving here can be harrowing when you don't know your way around. Downtown streets, being cobblestoned to give the area an "Old Mexico" look, are frequently clogged with traffic. However, if you plan to do some exploring, using Cancún as a base, the roads are excellent within a 100-km (62-mi) radius.

By Ship
Boats leave Puerto Juárez and Punta Sam—both north of Cancún City—for Isla Mujeres every half hour or so (☞ Chapter 3).

By Taxi
Taxis to the ferries at Punta Sam or Puerto Juárez cost $15–$20 or more; between the hotel zone and downtown, $8 and up; and within the hotel zone, $5–$7. All prices depend on the distance, your negotiating skills, and whether you pick up the taxi in front of the hotel or go onto the avenue to hail a green city cab (the latter will be cheaper). Since taxi rates fluctuate according to gasoline taxes and the drivers' whims, check with your hotel. Most list rates at the door; confirm the price with your driver before you set out. If you lose something in a taxi or have questions or a complaint, call the **Sindicato de Taxistas** (☎ 98/886985).

Contacts and Resources

Banks
Generally, banks in Cancún are open weekdays 9–5, with money-exchange desks open 9–1:30. To exchange or wire money try **Banamex** (⊠ Av. Tulum 19, next to City Hall, ☎ 98/843115). Other centrally located banks downtown include **Banco del Atlantico** (⊠ Av. Tulum 15, ☎ 98/841095) and **Bancomer** (⊠ Av. Tulum 20, ☎ 98/870000).

Car and Moped Rentals
Rental cars are available at the airport or from any of a dozen agencies in town, and most are standard-shift subcompacts and Jeeps; air-conditioned cars with automatic transmissions should be reserved in advance. Rental agencies include **Avis** (airport, ☎ 98/860222; ⊠ Hotel Calinda Viva, ☎ 98/830800; ⊠ Mayfair Plaza, ☎ 98/830803); **Budget** (8 locations; airport, ☎ 98/860026; ⊠ Av. Tulum 231, ☎ 98/840204); **Econo-Rent** (airport, ☎ 98/876487; ⊠ Av. Bonampak, ☎ 98/860171); **National** (airport, ☎ 98/860153 or 98/864490); or **Hertz** (9

locations; airport, ☎ 98/860150; ⊠ Reno 35, ☎ 98/876644). The **Car Rental Association** (☎ 98/842039) can help you arrange a rental as well. Rates average around $45 per day.

Mopeds and scooters are also available throughout the island. While fun, they are risky, and there is no insurance available for the driver or the vehicle. The accident rate is high, especially downtown, which is considered too congested for novice moped users. Rates start at around $25 per day.

Consulates

U.S. Consulate (⊠ Av. Nader 40, SM 2A, Edificio Marruecos 31, ☎ 98/830272) is open weekdays 9–1.

Canadian Consulate (⊠ Plaza Mexico Local 312, upper floor, ☎ 98/843716) is open daily 11 AM–1 PM. For emergencies outside office hours, call the Canadian Embassy in Mexico City (☎ 5/254–3288).

Doctors and Dentists

Hospital Americano (⊠ Calle Viento 15, ☎ 98/846133) and **Total Assist** (⊠ Claveles 5, ☎ 98/848082 or 98/848116), both with English-speakers on staff, provide emergency medical care.

Emergencies

Police (☎ 98/841913). **Red Cross** (⊠ Av. Xcaret and Labná, SM 21, ☎ 98/841616). **Highway Patrol** (☎ 98/841107).

English-Language Bookstores

Fama (⊠ Av. Tulum 105, ☎ 98/846586) specializes in books on the Yucatán Peninsula and offers a large selection of English-language magazines. Another outlet for Fama can be found at the Kukulcán Plaza. **La Surtidora** (⊠ Av. Tulum 17, ☎ 98/841103) sells a variety of English- and Spanish-language books.

Guided Tours

AIR TOURS

Trans Caribe (☎ 98/871599 or 98/871692) sea planes offer panoramic tours of Cancún that depart daily from Laguna Nichupté. Prices vary according to the length of the ride, starting at about $35 for 20 minutes. Trans Caribe also will take you island-hopping to Isla Mujeres or Cozumel for diving, and sightseeing to the archaeological sites at Tulum and Chichén Itzá.

Aerolatino (⊠ Plaza México, Av. Tulum 200, ☎ 98/871353 or 98/843938), a small Guatemalan carrier, flies between Cancún and Guatemala City, continuing on to Flores and the ruins at Tikal, for $290 round-trip.

DAY CRUISES

Day cruises to Isla Mujeres are popular; they include snorkeling in El Garrafón, time for shopping downtown, as well as Continental breakfast, open-bar buffet lunch, and music. **Aqua Tours Adventures** (⊠ Paseo Kukulcán, Km 6.25, ☎ 98/830227) books the "Isla Mujeres Adventure," which is particularly popular with locals; it departs at 10 AM from the pier in front of Fat Tuesday's, returns at 5 PM, and costs about $55. The **Tropical Cruiser** (⊠ Playa Langosta, ☎ 98/831488) runs an excursion cruise to Isla Mujeres Monday through Saturday, departing from Playa Langosta.

Dolphin Discovery (⊠ Playa Langosta, ☎ 98/830779 or 98/830780) sails daily from Playa Langosta and Playa Tortugas to the company's dock on Isla Mujeres. The day's program includes an instruction video, a 30-minute swim session with the dolphins, and time to explore the island. The excursion costs about $69.

SUBMARINE CRUISES

Nautibus (☏ 98/833552 or 98/832119), or the "floating submarine," has a 1½-hour Caribbean-reef cruise that departs the Playa Linda marina four times daily. The $30 price includes music and drinks. Tours aboard one of the **Sub See Explorer** (☏ 98/852288) "yellow submarines" depart from AquaWorld in the central hotel zone and can be combined with snorkeling for a full day's outing; the cost with snorkeling is about $40, $35 without. Latest to join the underwater ranks is **Atlantis** (☏ 98/833021), Cancún's first true submarine (the others float on the surface and have window seats below). Tours, available every hour from 10 to 3, include an hour-long cruise from Playa Linda to and from the submarine site, and 50 minutes dive time in the sub. The basic price is $80; add $10 and more time if you want to include lunch (not advised if you're prone to motion sickness).

Late-Night Pharmacies

Farmacia Turística (✉ Plaza Caracol, ☏ 98/831894) and **Farmacia Extra** (✉ Plaza Caracol, ☏ 98/832827) deliver to hotels 9 AM–10 PM, and **Farmacia Paris** (✉ Av. Yaxchilán, Marrufo Bldg., ☏ 98/840164) also fills prescriptions.

Mail

The **post office** (✉ Av. Sunyaxchén at Xel-há, ☏ 98/841418) is open weekdays 8–5, Saturday 9–1; there's also a **Western Union** office (☏ 98/841529) in the building. Mail can be received here if marked "Lista de Correos, Cancún, QR 77500, México." Bear in mind, however, that postal service to and from Mexico is extremely slow and may take two weeks or more. If you have an American Express card, you can have mail sent to you at the **American Express Cancún Office** (✉ Av. Tulum 208, at Agua, ☏ 98/844554 or 98/841999), open weekdays 9–6, Saturday 9–1.

Publications

At the state tourism office, at the airport, and at many hotels, you can pick up a copy of **Cancún Tips,** a free pocket-size guide to hotels, restaurants, shopping, and recreation that usually contains a discount card for use at various establishments. Although it's loaded with advertising, the booklet, published four times a year in English and Spanish editions, has useful maps and up-to-date information. The magazine staff also runs information centers around town, including one at Plaza Caracol (☏ 98/832745) that is open daily 10–10. Several similar publications, among them *Cancún Nights, Cancún Restaurants,* and *Passport Cancún,* are also available at the airport, as well as at malls and hotels around town.

Telephones

Phones set up by Mexico's long-distance service, Ladatel, which enable you to pay for calls by credit card, are in many hotels and on downtown streets. From these phones, you can also dial 01 and reach an AT&T operator in the states, allowing you to charge calls to an AT&T card or call collect. The operator can connect you to any 800 number, a useful service if you must report lost or stolen credit cards. Direct-dial international calls can be made through AT&T operators from most of the hotels on Paseo Kukulcán, but the hotels also charge $3–$5 per call extra for this service. Bypassing the Mexican phone system is worthwhile, however, even if it means calling collect, because of the 60% tax on overseas calls. Be sure to always go through an AT&T operator or you may find your call to the United States costing up to $15 per minute.

Travel Agencies and Tour Operators

American Express (✉ Av. Tulum at Agua, ☎ 98/841999); **Intermar Caribe** (✉ Av. Bonampak at Calle Careza, ☎ 98/844266); **Turismo Aviomar** (✉ Calle Venado 30, ☎ 98/846433).

Visitor Information

Cancún Tips (✉ Av. Tulum 29, Suites 1–5, ☎ 98/841458), open daily 9–9.

The Mexican Ministry of Tourism has established a 24-hour English-language **help line** for tourists: ☎ 800/90392.

Informatel (☎ 98/812345) has a general information number for assistance with anything from hotels, restaurants, and attractions to where to find the best doctor in Cancún. The staff speaks English.

3 Isla Mujeres

Only 8 km (5 mi) across the bay from
Cancún, Isla Mujeres is an ocean away
in attitude, as sleepy and unassuming as
its neighbor is outgoing. Snorkeling and
lazing under a palapa (thatched roof)
are about as energetic as it gets here,
and there are some interesting remnants
of the island's pirate past to explore.

Updated by
Dan Millington

A TINY, FISH-SHAPE ISLAND 8 km (5 mi) off Cancún, Isla Mujeres (*ees*-lah moo-*hair*-ayce) is a tranquil alternative to its bustling western neighbor. Only about 8 km (5 mi) long by 1 km (½ mi) wide, Isla has flat sandy beaches on its northern end and steep rocky bluffs to the south. Because of its proximity to Cancún, it has turned into a small-scale tourist destination, but it is still a peaceful island retreat with a rich history and culture centered on the sea.

Part of that history is blessed by the presence of Isla's first known inhabitants, the ancient Maya. Their legacy lies in the names, features, and language of their descendants here, but not, unfortunately, in the observatory they built on the southern tip—Hurricane Gilbert obliterated the well-preserved ruin in '88 (restoration efforts are ongoing).

The Spanish conquistadors followed: After setting sail from Cuba in 1517, Hernández de Córdoba's ship blew here accidentally in a storm. Credited with "discovering" the island, he and his crew dubbed their find "Isle of Women." One explanation of the name's origins is that Córdoba and company came upon wooden idols of Maya goddesses. Another theory claims the Spaniards found only women when they arrived—the men were out fishing.

For the next several centuries, Isla, like many Caribbean islands, became a haven for pirates and smugglers, then settled into life as a quiet fishing village. In this century it started out as a vacation destination for Mexicans; the '60s witnessed a hippie influx; and since the late '70s, day-trippers from Cancún increasingly disembark here, bringing Isla's hotel, restaurant, and shop owners more business than ever.

Most important, the laid-back island life attracts a crowd that prefers beach pleasures to nightlife—scuba diving, snorkeling, and relaxation to the cable TV and rollicking discos of Cancún. Thanks to concerned locals like Ramon Bravo, a renowned expert on sharks, underwater filmmaker, and author, isleños themselves are working to preserve the island's ecology and tranquillity so that those arriving here for the first time will still find an unusually peaceful, authentically Mexican retreat.

As part of this effort, plans are currently afoot to have the Mexican government declare Isla Mujeres a national park. A fee would be levied on tourists who visit the island—money that would be used, it is argued, to keep the island's fragile ecology intact and to provide better services for visitors without damaging the site's unique character. As of summer 1998 this plan has not been realized, and arriving tourists are not charged a fee.

Pleasures and Pastimes

Beaches

The island's finest and most popular beach is **Playa Norte,** where you can wade far out in the placid waters or relax at congenial palapa bars for drinks and snacks. The view at sunset is truly spectacular. **Playa Paraíso** and **Playa Lancheros** on the western shore are both pleasant spots for beachcombing.

Bird-Watching

About 45 minutes north of Isla Mujeres is **Isla Contoy** (Isle of Birds), a national wildlife park and bird sanctuary. The tiny island—a place of sand dunes, mangroves, and coconuts—is a beautiful and unspoiled spot. Birders come to see the more than 70 species of bird life.

Dining

Dining on Isla Mujeres offers what you would expect on a small island: plenty of fresh-grilled seafood—lobster, shrimp, conch, and fish. If you prefer more familiar fare, you can opt for pizza, steak, or shish kebab. For a description of Mexican culinary terms, *see* Dining *under* Pleasures and Pastimes *in the* the Destination: Cancún, Cozumel, Yucatán Peninsula chapter.

Fishing

Billfish are a popular catch in spring and early summer; the rest of the year, you can fish for barracuda and tuna, as well as for shad, sailfish, grouper, red snapper, and Spanish mackerel.

Lodging

The island's 25 or so hotels offer a surprisingly broad range of options. Most expensive are the charming beachfront hotels that provide a perfect island getaway complete with modern comforts. Budget accommodations, in the heart of the town, are clean and simple.

Snorkeling and Scuba Diving

Even though there is widespread concern over loss of reef, ocean lovers will still be impressed by the underwater spectacle here. From the surface and below, plenty of fascinating sea life can be observed. During the summer months fish are attracted to the mild temperatures and calm waters that prevail between 8 AM and 3 PM. However, the decrease of minute algae in the slightly cooler water in winter produces better visibility.

EXPLORING ISLA MUJERES

For orientation purposes think of Isla Mujeres as an elongated fish: The southern tip is the head and the northern prong the tail. The minute you step off the boat, it's clear how small Isla is. The smaller street names and addresses don't matter much here (islanders have been known to look up their own addresses, and signs are virtually nonexistent). One main paved road, Avenida Rueda Medina, runs the length of the island.

The island's only town, known simply as *el pueblo,* extends the full width of Isla's northern "tail." The village is sandwiched between sand and sea to the north, south, and east; no high-rises block the view. Activity centers around the waterfront piers, where the ferries from Puerto Juárez arrive, and on the coastal main drag, Avenida Rueda Medina. Two blocks inland, past the commercial T-shirt and souvenir shops, you'll find the other spot where everyone gathers—the main square (bounded by avenidas Morelos, Bravo, Guerrero, and Hidalgo). Also called (*la placita* or *el parque*), the main square is the ideal place to take in the daily life of the town—basketball games on the permanent courts, children running around the playground, and locals gathered to chat in front of the Government Palace. On holidays and weekends the square gets set up for dances, concerts, and fiestas.

From town you can easily walk to the island's northwest beaches and to the historical cemetery, but you'll have to rent a moped or hire a taxi to see the rest of Isla's sights.

Numbers in the text correspond to numbers in the margin and on the Isla Mujeres map.

A Good Tour

Start out in the island's little town and walk north on Avenida Lopez Mateos to reach Isla's historical **cemetery** ①. To explore the rest of the island, you'll need to take a moped or taxi south along Avenida Rueda Medina, which leads out of town. The first landmark you'll pass after the piers is the Mexican naval base. It's off-limits to tourists, but from the road you can see the modest flag-raising and -lowering ceremonies at sunrise and sunset (no photo-taking permitted). Continue south and you'll see the **Laguna Makax** ② on your right.

At the end of the lagoon, a dirt road to the left leads to the remains of the **Hacienda Mundaca** ③. About a block southeast of the hacienda, turn right off the main road at the sign that says SAC BAJO to a smaller, unmarked side road, which loops back north. Approximately ½ km (¼ mi) farther on the left is the entrance to the **Tortuga Marina Turtle Farm** ④. When you return to the main Avenida Rueda Medina and go south past Playa Lancheros, you'll soon see **El Garrafón National Park** ⑤. Slightly more than ½ km (¼ mi) along the same road, on the windward side of the tip of Isla Mujeres, is the site of a small **Maya ruin** ⑥, which stood for centuries but was destroyed by Hurricane Gilbert in 1988. You've now come to one of the island's most scenic patches of coastline. Follow the paved perimeter road north into town; it's a beautiful drive, with a few rocky pull-off areas along the way, perfect for a secluded picnic since this road sees little traffic.

Sights to See

❶ **Cemetery.** You'll find Isla's unnamed cemetery, with its 100-year-old gravestones, on Lopez Mateos, the road parallel to Playa Norte. Among the lovingly decorated tombs, many in memory of children, is that of Fermín Mundaca (☞ Hacienda Mundaca, *below*). A notorious 19th-century slave trader (often billed more glamorously as a pirate), Mundaca is said to have carved his own tombstone with a skull and crossbones. On one side of the tomb an inscription reads in Spanish AS YOU ARE, I ONCE WAS; the other side warns, AS I AM, SO SHALL YOU BE. Mundaca's grave is empty, however; his remains lie in Mérida where he died. The monument is not easy to find—ask a local to point out the unidentified marker.

❺ **El Garrafón National Park.** The snorkeling mecca for day-trippers from Cancún is still lovely, but Garrafón—which lies at the bottom of a bluff—was once almost magical in its beauty. Now, as a result of the hands and fins of eager divers, Hurricane Gilbert, and anchors cast from the fleets of tourist boats continually arriving from Cancún, the coral reef here is virtually dead. There has been talk of closing the park to give the coral time to grow back (it's estimated that coral grows at the rate of about 1 centimeter every 40 years), but too many locals make their living from the park for this solution to be feasible. Still, nearly 25,000 visitors each year are impressed by the scenery—parrot fish, angelfish, and the rich blue-green water. Arrive early if you want to avoid the crowds, which start to form about 10 AM. There are food stands and souvenir shops galore, as well as palapas, lockers, equipment rental, rest rooms, and a small aquarium. Recently the park was taken over by the people who run Xcaret (☞ *see* Chapter 5), and plans are under way to attempt to preserve the remaining coral formations at El Garrafón. At press time (summer 1998) it is unknown if the park will be temporarily closed for renovation. ⊠ *Av. Rueda Medina, 2½ km (1½ mi) south of Playa Lancheros,* ☎ *no phone.* 🎫 *Less than $2.* ☉ *Daily 9–5.*

❸ **Hacienda Mundaca.** A dirt drive and stone archway mark the entrance to the remains of the mansion built by Fermín Mundaca de Marechaja, the 19th-century slave trader–cum–pirate. When the British navy began cracking down on slavers, he settled on the island and built an ambitious estate with resplendent tropical gardens. The story goes

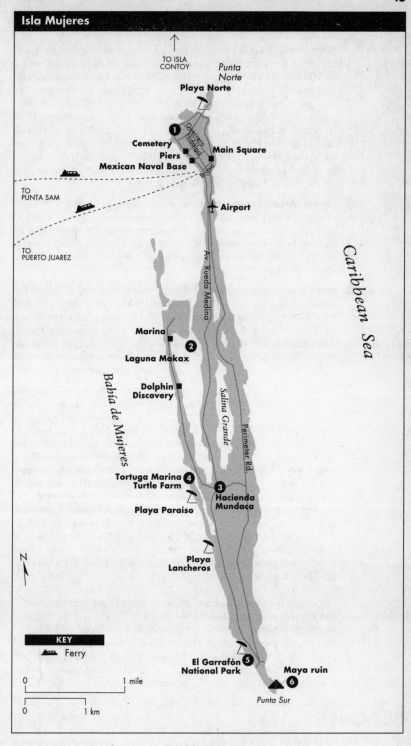

that he constructed it to woo a certain island maiden who, in the end, chose another man.

What little remained of the hacienda has mysteriously vanished, except for a sorry excuse of a guardhouse, an arch, a pediment, and a well. Locals say that the government tore down the mansion, or at least neglected its upkeep. If you push your way through the jungle—the mosquitoes are fierce—you'll eventually come to the ruined stone archway and triangular pediment, carved with the following inscription: *Huerta de la Hacienda de Vista Alegre MDCCCLXXVI* (Orchard of the Happy View Hacienda, 1876). To get here continue south from town along the main road until you come to the "S" curve at the end of Laguna Makax (☞ *below*). You'll see the dirt road to your left. ⊠ *East off Av. Rueda Meina*, ☎ *no phone.* 🎫 *Free.*

❷ **Laguna Makax.** Heading south from town along Avenida Rueda Medina, you'll pass a Mexican naval base and see some *salinas* (salt marshes) on your left; across the road is this lagoon, where pirates are said to have anchored their ships as they lay in wait for the hapless vessels plying the Spanish Main (the geographical area in which Spanish treasure ships trafficked).

🏕 ❻ **Maya ruin.** The sad vestiges of a temple once dedicated to Ixchel, the goddess of fertility, are about 1 km (½ mi) below El Garrafón National Park, at the southern tip of Isla. Though Hurricane Gilbert walloped the ruin and succeeded in blowing most of it away, restoration efforts are under way. The adjacent **lighthouse** still stands, and the keeper sometimes allows visitors to ascend it. The island's most scenic patches of coastline lie along the perimeter road between the lighthouse and town.

❹ **Tortuga Marina Turtle Farm.** Run by an outfit called Eco Caribe, this facility is devoted to the study and preservation of sea turtles. During working hours visitors can examine tanks that contain hundreds of hatchlings and young turtles of various species. The farm's budget is small, but because the turtle population of the Mexican Caribbean continues to dwindle toward extinction, these dedicated ecologists have devoted themselves to care for the hatchlings until they are large enough to be let out to sea; they release about 6,000 infant turtles each month during the hatching season (May through September). Within the confines of the turtle farm are various fenced-in beachfront areas where turtles can be viewed swimming and feeding in the ocean. ⊠ *Follow the main road to fork, about a block southeast of Hacienda Mundaca. Take right-hand fork, the smaller road that loops back north. About ½ km (¼ mi) to the left is the entrance to the turtle farm.* ☎ *987/70595.* 🎫 *$2.* ☉ *Daily 9–5.*

NEED A BREAK?	Walk north from the Turtle Farm along the lovely beach past the Cristalmar Hotel to reach **Hacienda Gomar** (☎ 987/70541), a good Mexican restaurant featuring a buffet lunch and marimba music. If you'd rather not put your shoes back on, try the excellent barbecued grouper, snapper, or barracuda at **Blacky's** (⊠ Playa Paraíso, ☎ no phone) open grill on the beach. Also in the area you'll find handicraft and souvenir shops, a beach bar, and small palapas for shade.

BEACHES

The island's finest and most popular beach is on the northwest part of the island: Follow any of the north–south streets in town to **Playa Norte** (sometimes called Playa Cocoteros, or Cocos). You can wade far out in the placid waters. Hurricane Gilbert's only good deed, according to isleños, was to widen this and other leeward-side beaches by blowing sand over from Cancún. You can sit at congenial palapa bars for drinks and snacks. Try **Chimbo's,** on the beach, where locals come to drink beer, play dice, and chat. There are lots of stands where you can rent snorkel gear, Jet Skis, floats, sailboards, and sometimes parasails. A glorious setting at the end of the day, Playa Norte is a great place to talk to isleños, who are clearly happy to share the beauty of this place. Another great beach in this area is out in front of the Na-Balam hotel. After Hurricane Gilbert slammed the island it created a beautiful and tranquil lagoon, where you can walk or snorkel in 4 ft of water for hundreds of yards offshore.

On the western side of Isla you'll find **Playa Paraíso** and **Playa Lancheros,** good spots for lunch or for shopping for handicrafts, souvenirs, and T-shirts at the small stands. Also housed at Playa Lancheros, in a sea pen, are some pet sea turtles and harmless *tiburones gatos* (nurse sharks). On the ocean side live the carnivorous *tintorera* (female sharks), which have seven rows of teeth and weigh as much as 500 kilograms (1,100 pounds). Also in this area is **Playa Indios** (look for the ATLANTIS sign and head down the road to the beach), with Indio's restaurant, an open-air eatery serving up the best conch ceviche and salsa music.

DINING

As in the rest of Mexico, locals eat their main meal during siesta hours, between 1 and 4, and have a light dinner in the evening. Unless otherwise stated, restaurants are open daily for lunch and dinner.

What to Wear

Generally, restaurants on the island are informal, though shirts and shoes are required at most indoor dining rooms. Some, but not all, outdoor terraces or palapas request that swimsuits and feet be covered.

CATEGORY	COST*
$$$	$15–$20
$$	$8–$15
$	under $8

per person, excluding drinks and service

$$$ ✕ **Chez Magaly.** A pleasant establishment on the grounds of the Nautibeach Condo-Hotel, this poolside restaurant is eclectically decorated with wood floors, plants, plastic chairs, Chinese blinds, and traditional cloth place settings. The menu is hybrid, too, with elements of French, Caribbean, and Mexican fare. Seafood grills, lobster quiche, jambalaya (Caribbean seafood and rice), and tequila-flambéed mangos are among the specialties. ✉ *Av. Rueda Medina, Playa Norte,* ☎ *987/70259 or 987/70436. MC, V. Closed Mon. and 2 wks in June.*

$$$ ✕ **Maria's Kan Kin.** Near El Garrafón, at the southern end of the island, this appealing beach restaurant has a choice location and attractive decor: Wrought-iron tables are set with peach-color linens on three levels of flagstone terraces. Hand printed on straw place mats, the menu itself is a work of art, illustrated with lovely, colorful drawings. Choose a live lobster—which locals trap off the dock in front—or try one of the specialties, such as lobster bisque and coconut mousse, prepared with a French twist. It's the perfect spot for a long lunch that extends to sunset. At press time (summer 1998) Maria's was up for sale, but will hopefully maintain its excellence. ✉ *Main road to Garrafón,* ☎ *987/70015. AE, MC, V.*

48

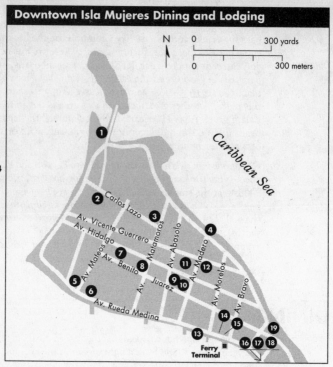

Downtown Isla Mujeres Dining and Lodging

$$$ ✕ ★ **Zazil-Ha.** This fine restaurant, on the grounds of the **Hotel Na Balam** at Playa Norte, offers well-prepared regional specialties as well as interesting vegetarian dishes. The service is friendly and the setting is relaxing; you can eat indoors in the cozy palapa dining room or outdoors on a shady terrace. Light-wood furnishings, Mexican tile floors, and walls decorated with pottery create a charmingly rustic ambience. Try the shrimp ceviche for the first course, followed by the seafood special of the day: maybe fresh lobster meat sautéed in butter with lots of garlic; *chaya* (Maya spinach) with pasta; or *caracol Caribe*, a Caribbean seashell stuffed with seafood. At breakfast the restaurant features homemade bread, tropical fruits, and good coffee, plus a full array of egg dishes. ⊠ *Hotel Na Balam,* ☎ *987/70279. AE, MC, V.*

$$ ✕ **Bucanero.** With a prime location, on one of the main pedestrian drags near the main square, this appealing restaurant has attractive wood tables with blue-and-white inset tiles and terra-cotta floors. For breakfast the *huevos motuleños* (fried eggs served on a corn tortilla heaped with beans, ham, cheese, peas, marinated red onions, all drenched in tomato sauce) are excellent and cheap; lunch and dinner specialties include avocado stuffed with shrimp and *mar y cielo* (fish fillet and chicken breast with french fries and onions). Simple pastas and pizza are also available. The palapa-roofed section is a good choice for quiet conversation away from the busy street front. ⊠ *Av. Hidalgo 11,* ☎ *987/70210. Reservations not accepted. MC, V.*

$$ ✕ **Cafécito.** This airy café is a popular hangout for locals and Europeans who come for coffee, ice cream, crepes, and waffles. Artfully decorated with glass-topped turquoise wood tables, shells, and mobiles, Cafécito serves full dinners during high season. If you would like advance notice of your future, request a tarot card reading from owner Sabrina. ⊠ *Avs. Juárez and Matamoros,* ☎ *987/70438. Reservations not accepted. No credit cards. No lunch Fri.–Wed.*

$$ ✕ **Pizza Rolandi.** Red tables, yellow director's chairs, and green walls
★   and window trim set an upbeat tone at this very "in" chain restau-
     rant. Select from a broad variety of Italian food: lobster pizzas, cal-
     zones, and pastas. Grilled fresh fish and shrimp are highly recommended,
     and salads are excellent. Or just stop in for a drink at one of the out-
     side tables; the margaritas, cappuccino, and espresso are the best in
     town. ⊠ *Av. Hidalgo between Avs. Madero and Abasolo,* ☎ *987/70430.*
     AE, MC, V.

 $ ✕ **La Casita.** Log tables and colorful brush strokes along the walls mark
     this petite coffee house–bakery. The emphasis here is fresh: baked pas-
     tries, breads, and cakes highlight the menu, along with hearty sand-
     wiches. Coffee and cappuccino are among the best on the island. ⊠
     Av. Madero 10 between Avs. Hidalgo and Guerrero,☎ *no phone.*
     Reservations not accepted. No credit cards.

 $ ✕ **Lonchería La Lomita.** With a bright aqua interior and plastic table-
★   cloths, this simple, home-style diner isn't much to look at, but you'll
     find hearty servings of chicken, steak, and seafood cooked to order (grilled,
     fried, or sautéed). The octopus sautéed in butter and garlic is particu-
     larly tasty. Amazingly low-priced lunch and dinner set menus include
     beans, rice, and tortillas or bread; breakfast is also available. On Avenida
     Juárez between Avenidas Madero and Morelos, is La Lomita II, like its
     sister establishment, a no-frills eatery that offers daily specials featur-
     ing generous servings and good value. ⊠ *Av. Juárez 25-B, past Av.
     Allende,* ☎ *no phone. Reservations not accepted. No credit cards.*

 $ ✕ **Mirtita's** and **Villa del Mar.** Next to each other on Avenida Rueda
     Medina across from the ferry dock, these are favorite local hangouts.
     Both serve fresh seafood and Yucatecan specialties. ⊠ *Av. Rueda Med-
     ina,* ☎ *no phone. No credit cards.*

 $ ✕ **Red Eye Café.** A bright red awning marks this open-air café where
     Gus and Inga serve hearty American-style breakfasts with a German
     flair. Fresh sausage, made by a German sausage maker in Cancún, ac-
     companies the egg dishes. ⊠ *Av. Hidalgo,* ☎ *no phone. No credit cards.*
     Closed Tues.

 $ ✕ **Velazquez.** This family-owned palapa-style restaurant on the beach
★   serves the freshest seafood on the island. Don't forget to duck your
     head before entering. *No credit cards.*

LODGING

The approximately 25 hotels (about 600 rooms) on Isla Mujeres gen-
erally fall into one of two categories: The older, more modest places
are situated right in town, and the newer, more costly properties tend
to have beachfront locations around Punta Norte and, increasingly, on
the peninsula near the lagoon. Most hotels have ceiling fans; some have
air-conditioning, but few offer TVs or phones. Luxurious, self-contained
time-share condominiums are another option, which you can learn more
about from the tourist office (☎ 987/70316). All hotels share the
77400 postal code.

CATEGORY	COST*
$$$	$60–$90
$$	$25–$60
$	under $25

All prices are for a standard double room, excluding 12% tax.

$$$ ▦ **Cristalmar.** Although the location of this condo-hotel (a five-minute
     drive from town) is inconvenient for those without their own trans-
     portation, the property—situated on a peninsula by the lagoon on lovely
     Playa Paraíso—boasts a stunning sea view. Spacious one-, two-, and
     three-bedroom suites open to the courtyard, which has a pool and a

palapa bar. Local artwork adorns the walls and dark brown or white wicker furnishings and glass-top tables decorate the rooms. ⊠ *Paraíso Laguna Mar, Lot 16,* ☎ *987/70007 or 987/70390. 38 suites. Restaurant, bar, air-conditioning, kitchenettes, pool, beach, dive shop. AE, MC, V.*

$$$ 🏨 **Na Balam.** This intimate, informal hostelry set on Playa Norte will
★ fulfill all your tropical-paradise fantasies. Three corner suites with balconies affording outstanding views of sea and sand are well worth the price (approximately $90). The simple, attractive rooms have turquoise-tile floors, carved-wood furniture, dining areas, and patios facing the beach; photos of Mexico in its bygone days and Mexican carvings grace the walls. A swimming pool and eight more rooms were added in 1995. Breakfast at the hotel's newly remodeled Zazil Ha restaurant (☞ Dining, *above*) is a delightful way to kick off the day. ⊠ *Calle Zazil Ha 118,* ☎ *987/70279 or 800/552–4550,* FAX *987/70446. 31 rooms. Restaurant, bar, air-conditioning, pool, beach. AE, MC, V.*

$$$ 🏨 **Perla del Caribe.** On the eastern edge of town facing the new sea wall and promenade, the three-story Perla has rooms that look out either on the open sea or town, priced accordingly. All rooms have balconies and are comfortable and functional but not palatial. You can listen to music in the restaurant/bar most evenings. ⊠ *Av. Madero 2,* ☎ *987/70444,* FAX *987/70011. 91 rooms. Restaurant, bar, air-conditioning, pool. AE, MC, V.*

$$ 🏨 **Belmar.** Right in the heart of town, above Pizza Rolandi, this small hotel shares a charming plant-filled inner courtyard with the restaurant, which means it can occasionally be noisy here until 11 PM. Standard rooms are pretty, with tiled baths and light-wood furniture. One enormous suite features a private whirlpool bath on a patio, a tiled kitchenette, and a sitting area. All rooms have phones, satellite TV, and air-conditioning. ⊠ *Av. Hidalgo 110, between Avs. Madero and Abasolo,* ☎ *987/70430,* FAX *987/70429. 11 rooms. Air-conditioning. AE, MC, V.*

$$ 🏨 **Cabañas Maria del Mar.** A rather mind-boggling assortment of
★ rooms is available in this friendly beachfront hotel, but all have a great deal of character, and the place as a whole has a unique Mexican atmosphere. Some of the rooms are rather spare, but those in the slightly more expensive "castle" section have hand-carved wood furnishings by local artisans in a combination of Spanish and Maya styles, folk art, tiled baths, and hand-painted sinks. The hotel has a prime location on Playa Norte, next to Na-Balam, and its reasonable room rates include Continental breakfast. ⊠ *Av. Carlos Lazos 1,* ☎ *987/70179 or 800/552–4550,* FAX *987/70213. 41 rooms, 14 cabañas. Restaurant, bar, air-conditioning, pool, motorbikes, travel services. MC, V.*

$$ 🏨 **Mesón del Bucanero.** This Spanish colonial–style hotel features attractive contemporary wood furnishings in bright rooms. Reasonably priced suites have small sitting areas and balconies, and large closets. Standard rooms are unusually diminutive but functional. ⊠ *Av. Hidalgo 11,* ☎ *987/70210,* FAX *987/70126. 6 rooms. Restaurant. MC, V.*

$$ 🏨 **Posada del Mar.** This hotel's assets include its prime location between town and Playa Norte and its reasonable prices. Rooms have balconies overlooking a main road and beyond to the waterfront. The simple wood furnishings appear somewhat worse for wear, although baths are clean, with cheerful color tiles. Private bungalows in the $ price category are also available. A recently added bar next to the pool is as popular as the street-front palapa-roof restaurant. ⊠ *Av. Rueda Medina 15A,* ☎ *987/70300, 987/70044, or 800/552–4550,* FAX *987/ 70266. 40 rooms. Restaurant, bar, pool. AE, MC, V.*

$ 🏨 **Poc-Na.** The island's youth hostel at the eastern end of town rents bunks or hammocks (which cost less) in dormitory-style rooms (with showers and lockers) that sleep eight. The management requires guests to leave their passports as a deposit for the length of their stay. Proximity to the beach is a bonus. The hotel offers hammocks and mattresses in a dormitory setting. Both men and women can stay here. ⊠ *Av. Matamoros 15,* ⊠ *Av. Matamoros 15,* ☎ *987/70090 or 987/70059. Dining room. No credit cards.*

Private Bungalows

Several pretty, small bungalows near Garrafón are available for rent for the long term and short term, when available. Inquire at **Mexico Divers** (☎ 987/70131).

Marinas

Puerto Isla Mujeres Resort & Yacht Club (☎ 98/833208 or 800/960-4752, FAX 987/70093), located within the Laguna Macax, has recently been completed. This is a full-service marina for vessels up to 90 ft. The cost of mooring is 80¢ to $1.25 per ft, per day. Rates include TV connection, telephone, and 3 gallons of water per ft, per day. In addition the marina has a fueling station for gas and diesel and a boatyard for repairs, along with a 150-ton lift. Also, on the property is the El Mangle restaurant serving up Caribbean and seafood specialties coupled with a 30-room luxury resort.

NIGHTLIFE AND THE ARTS

The Arts

Festivals and cultural events are held on many weekends, with live entertainment on the outdoor stage in the main square. The whole island celebrates the spring regattas and the Caribbean music festivals. **Casa de la Cultura,** near the youth hostel, offers folkloric dance classes year-round. The center also operates a small public library and book exchange. ⊠ *Av. Guerrero,* ☎ *987/70639.* ☉ *Mon.–Sat. 9–1 and 4–8.*

Nightlife

Most restaurant bars feature a happy hour, offering two drinks for the price of one, from 5 to 7; the palapa bars at Playa Norte are an excellent place to watch the sun set. The current hot spot is **YaYa's** (⊠ Av. Rueda Medina 42, near the lighthouse and Playa Norte, ☎ no phone), which serves up huge Texas steaks, chili dogs, and shrimp étouffée along with live jazz, rock, and reggae jam sessions until 2 or 3 AM. The bar at the **Posada del Mar** (⊠ Av. Rueda Medina 15A, ☎ 987/70300) can be subdued or hopping, depending on what's going on in town. **Buho's,** the bar/restaurant at Cabañas María del Mar (⊠ Av. Carlos Lazo 1, ☎ 987/71479), serves food and is a good choice for a relaxing drink at sunset or later at night. **Restaurante La Peña** (⊠ Av. Guerrero 5, ☎ 987/70309) has music and dancing on its open-air terrace overlooking the sea. **Palapa Disco** (⊠ Playa Norte off Av. Rueda Medina) has music and dancing from midnight until 4 AM.

OUTDOOR ACTIVITIES AND SPORTS

For any water sport, beaches on the north and west sides are the calmest.

Fishing

Bahía Dive Shop (⊠ Av. Rueda Medina 166, across from pier, 987/70340) charges $250 for a day of deep-sea fishing, $200 a day for cast fishing (tarpon, snook, and bonefish), and $20 an hour for offshore fishing (barracuda, snapper, and smaller fish).

Snorkeling and Scuba Diving

The famous coral reefs at **El Garrafón** have suffered tremendously from negligent tourists, the effects of Hurricane Gilbert, and the constant dropping of anchors, now outlawed. Though still a beautiful sight (you can spot parrot fish, angelfish, and schools of sergeant majors), the reef is far from its past splendor. Get there early; Cancún day-trippers start churning up the waters at around 10. Good snorkeling continues near Playa Norte on the north end. Underneath the waters near *el farolito* (lighthouse) is a partially buried but still visible statue of the Virgin.

Offshore, there's excellent diving and snorkeling at **Xlaches** (pronounced *ees*-lah-chay) reef, due north on the way to Isla Contoy (☞ Side Trip to Isla Contoy, *below*). Another one of the island's most alluring diving attractions is the **Cave of the Sleeping Sharks,** east of the northern tip. The caves were discovered by an island fisherman known as Vulvula and extensively explored by Ramon Bravo, a local diver, cinematographer, and Mexico's foremost expert on sharks. *National Geographic* and the late Jacques Cousteau had also studied the curious phenomena of the snoozing black tip, bull, and lemon sharks—it's a fascinating site for experienced divers.

At the extreme southern end of the island on the leeward side lies **Los Manchones.** At 30–40 ft deep and 3,300 ft off the southwestern coast, this coral reef makes a good dive site. During the summer of 1994, an ecology group hoping to divert divers and snorkelers from El Garrafón commissioned and sunk a statue called the Cruz de la Bahía (Cross of the Bay) near the southern end of Los Manchones. **Los Cuevones,** to the southwest near La Bandera, reaches a depth of 45 ft. On the windward side of the islet north of Mujeres is an unnamed site complete with two shipwrecked galleons. Dive shops will be able to direct you to this spot and others. They're also described in detail in *Dive Mexico,* a colorful magazine readily available in local shops.

Bahía Dive Shop (⊠ Av. Rueda Medina 166, across from the pier, 987/70340) rents snorkeling and scuba equipment and runs three-hour boat and dive trips to the reefs and the Cave of the Sleeping Sharks. Snorkel gear goes for $5 a day; tanks, $45–$60, depending on the length of the dive. **Mexico Divers** (⊠ Av. Rueda Medina and Av. Medaro, 1 block from ferry, ☎ 987/70131), also called Buzos de México, runs three-hour snorkeling tours for $15; two-tank scuba trips start at $55 for a reef dive and $75 for the shark-cave dive. Rental gear is available. Dive master Carlos Gutiérrez also gives a resort course for $80 and open-water PADI certification for $350 (his prices are generally negotiable). **Coral Scuba Dive Center** (⊠ Av. Matamoros 13-A, ☎ 987/70371) offers Manta Ray dives during the months of May, June, and July for $80, which include a two-tank dive. The company also offers five different shipwreck dives ranging from $50 to $125.

Swimming with Dolphins

If you're fascinated by Flipper and his ilk, **Dolphin Discovery** (☎ 987/70742) will give you the chance to sport in the water with them in a small, supervised group. There are four swims daily, at 9 and 11 AM and 1 and 3 PM. Each session is one hour, consisting first of a half-hour instruction video, and then 30 minutes in the water; the cost is $79 if arriving by boat, which includes an all-you-can eat Mexican buffet.

SHOPPING

Shopping on Isla Mujeres used to be limited to basic resort wear, suntan lotions, and groceries. Now more Mexican crafts shops offering good deals on silver, fabric bags, and handcrafted objects are opening here. Even the smaller shops often accept credit cards. Shopping hours are generally daily 10–1 and 4–7, although many stores now stay open through siesta.

Crafts

Artesanías Glenssy (⊠ Av. Lopez Mateos, ☎ no phone), in Playa Norte, has a wonderful collection of hand-painted, papier mâché figurines and masks. Don't be fooled by the look of the store (it's basically a shack) or some of the other items for sale. The dichotomy is that artist Emilio Medina is creating this amazing work out front of his shop, while also selling film and bathing suits. Haggling with him is futile, as he holds firm on the price of the work he creates.

Casa del Arte Mexica (⊠ Av. Hidalgo 6, ☎ 987/70459) has a good choice of clay reproductions, silver jewelry, batiks, rubbings, wood carvings, leather, and hammocks.

La Sirena (⊠ Av. Morelos, 1 block from the ferry dock through the pine arch marking the way to the island's shopping area, ☎ 987/70223) is set apart from neighboring shops by its extensive array of handcrafted goods. The owners of this small store have collected masks, textiles, and other fine Mexican crafts—including unusual clothing, pottery, and jewelry. While the prices are not low, they are fair for the quality of items offered.

Van Cleef & Arpels (⊠ Aves. Juárez and Morelos, ☎ 987/70299, has an impressive jewelry selection in a large corner shop.

Tienda Paulita (⊠ Avs. Morelos and Hidalgo, ☎ 987/70014) features a standard selection of folk art and handmade clothing in a fairly large space.

Grocery Stores

There are two fair-size groceries: **Super Betino** (⊠ Av. Morelos 3) and **Super Mirtita** (⊠ Avs. Juárez and Bravo). Food, including fresh fruit, can also be purchased in the municipal market on Avenida Guerrero Norte.

SIDE TRIP TO ISLA CONTOY

About 30 km (19 mi) north of Isla Mujeres, Isla Contoy (Isle of Birds) is a national wildlife park and bird sanctuary and a perfect getaway, even from Isla Mujeres. Birders, snorkelers, and fishing aficionados come here to enjoy the setting and the numerous varieties of animal life. This lovely spot enjoys protected sanctuary status, and the number of visitors is carefully regulated. The island, which is only 6½ km (4 mi) long and less than 1 km (about ½ mi) wide, is officially open from 9 to 5:30; overnight visits are not allowed.

In order to land on Contoy it is necessary to purchase an authorization ticket ($5) in Isla Mujeres; this is included in the cost of guided tours. If landing on Contoy is important to you, be sure to specify this when booking a day trip. Many operators simply cruise around Contoy to view the wildlife and land on other islands for lunch. However, government officials may at some point stop all landings on the island in order to protect the fragile environmental balance.

Some 70 species of bird life—including gulls, pelicans, petrels, cormorants, cranes, ducks, flamingos, herons, frigates, sea swallows, doves, quail, spoonbills, and hawks—fly this way in late fall, some of them to breed and make their nests. Although the number of species is diminishing, Contoy is still a rare treat for bird-watchers.

Anyone with an interest in nature will be fascinated by the sea life around this nearly deserted island. For snorkelers the coral and fish are dazzling. Immense rays, occasionally visible in the shallows, average about 5 ft across and can sometimes be seen jumping out of the water. The island's waters also abound with mackerel, barracuda, flying fish, trumpet fish, and shrimp; in December, lobsters pass through in great (though diminishing) numbers as their southerly migration route takes them past.

Black rocks and coral reefs fringe the island's east coast, which drops off abruptly 15 ft into the sea; at the west are sand, shrubs, and coconut palms. At the north and the south you find nothing but trees and small pools of water. The sand dunes inland on the east coast rise as high as 70 ft above sea level. Other than the birds and the dozen or so park rangers who make their home on Contoy, the island's only denizens are iguanas, lizards, turtles, hermit crabs, and boa constrictors.

Visit the outdoor museum, which displays about 50 photographs depicting the island, with captions in English, French, and Spanish. An observation tower offers a superb view of the surroundings.

See Guided Tours, *in* Isla Mujeres A to Z, *below,* for details on getting to Contoy from Isla Mujeres. From Cancún **Asterix** (☎ 98/864270) offers Isla Contoy cruises that depart from the Playa Caracol dock next to the Coral Beach Hotel Monday through Saturday at 9 AM and return at 5 PM. The package, which costs $70, includes Continental breakfast, swimming or snorkeling (equipment rental $5, or bring your own), and an open-bar lunch.

You can ask about the island at the Isla Mujeres tourist office (☞ Visitor Information *in* Isla Mujeres A to Z, *below*). **SEDESOL** (Cancún, ☎ 98/845955), the national ecology and urban-development ministry, can also provide information about Isla Contoy.

ISLA MUJERES A TO Z

Arriving and Departing

By Boat

TO ISLA MUJERES

The **Caribbean Express** and the **Caribbean Miss** (☎ 987/70254 or 987/70253), both air-conditioned cruisers with bar service, make several 30-minute crossings daily. They leave Puerto Juárez on the mainland for the main ferry dock in Isla Mujeres from 6:30 AM to 8 PM at approximately 20-minute intervals; the fare is under $3 per person. Late-night revelers will be glad to know that there now is one ferry departing Puerto Juárez in Cancún for Isla Mujeres at 11:30 PM. Check schedules at the ferry docks, as this particular schedule may only be running November through early April.

There are three slower **passenger ferries** that leave every hour 7:30–7:30 and at 10 AM; the schedule varies depending on the season, so check the times posted at the dock. The one-way fare is only about $1.50 and the trip takes 45 minutes, but delays and crowding are frequent.

A convenient, more expensive service, the **Shuttle** (Cancún, ☎ 98/83448) runs directly from the Playa Tortugas dock in Cancún's hotel zone at least four times a day and costs about $15 round-trip.

Cars are unnecessary on Isla, unless you want to explore the far reaches of the island, but **municipal ferries** that accommodate vehicles as well as passengers leave from Punta Sam and take about 45 minutes. Check departure times posted at the pier, but you can count on the schedule running from about 7 AM to 9 PM. The fare is under $2 per person and $10 per vehicle. In addition a number of tour companies offer day trips to Isla Mujeres from Cancún (☞ Chapter 2).

The **Caribbean Express** and the **Caribbean Miss** (☎ 987/70254 or 987/70253) make the trip from Isla Mujeres to Puerto Juárez between 7 AM and 8 PM at approximately 30-minute intervals; the fare is under $3 per person. The slower **passenger ferry** departs from the main dock at Isla Mujeres to Puerto Juárez at approximately 5, 6, 6:30, 7:30, 8:15, 8:45, 9:30, 10:30, and 11:30 AM, and at 12:30, 1:30, 2:30, 3:30, 4:30, 5, 5:30, 6:30, and 7:30 PM. The first **car ferry** from Isla Mujeres to Punta Sam leaves at about 6 AM and the last departs at about 7:15 PM. Again, schedules change often, so you should call ahead or check the boat schedule posted at the pier.

Getting Around

By Bicycle
Bicycles are available for hardy cyclists, but don't underestimate the hot sun and the tricky road conditions. Watch for the many speed bumps, which can give you an unexpected jolt, and avoid riding at night; some roads have no streetlights. **Rent Me Sport Bike** (⊠ Avs. Juárez and Morelos, 1 block from main pier, ☎ no phone) offers five-speed cycles starting at less than $3 for an hour; a full day costs about $7. You can leave your driver's license in lieu of a deposit; the place is open daily 8–6.

By Bus
Municipal buses (☎ 987/70529 or 987/74173) run at 20- to 30-minute intervals daily between 6 AM and 10 PM (generally following the ferry schedule) from the Posada del Mar hotel on Avenida Rueda Medina out to Colonia Salinas on the windward side. There is also service from the dock to Playa Lancheros on the leeward side, toward the south end of the island. As you might expect, however, the service is slow, because the buses make frequent stops.

By Car
There is little reason for tourists to bring cars to Isla Mujeres, because there are plenty of other forms of transportation that cost far less than renting and transporting a private vehicle. Moreover, though the main road is paved, speed bumps abound, and some areas are poorly lighted.

By Golf Cart
The newest way for tourists to explore Isla is by golf cart. **P'pe's Rentadora** (⊠ Av. Hidalgo 19, ☎ 987/70019) and almost all of the moped rental shops listed below, as well as some hotels, rent them for about $10 an hour.

By Moped
The island is full of moped rental shops. **Motorent Kankin** (⊠ Av. Abasolo 15, ☎ no phone) will provide a two-seater, three-speed Honda for about $5 per hour or $20 per day ($40 for 24 hours); a $20 deposit—or a credit card or passport left behind—is required. **P'pe's Renta-**

dora (⊠ Av. Hidalgo 19, ☎ 987/70019) offers two-seater, fully automatic Honda Aeros, starting at $5 per hour, for a minimum of two hours; it's under $35 for 24 hours. **Ciro's Motorent** (⊠ Av. Guerrero Norte 11 at Av. Matamoros, ☎ 987/70578) has two-seater Honda Tact 50 mopeds. **Richa's Mopeds** (⊠ Av. Abasolo 13, ☎ 987/53566) is a convenient place to rent a moped not only for his prices but Richa's has the cheapest fluff-and-fold laundromat right next door. To beat the standard price of a moped rental try haggling: after all, a moped rented is better than a moped not rented.

By Taxi

If your time is limited, you can hire a **taxi** (⊠ Av. Rueda Medina, ☎ 987/70066) for a private island tour at about $15 an hour. Fares will run about $1 from the ferry or downtown to the hotels on the north end, at Playa Norte. Taxis line up right by the ferry dock around the clock.

Contacts and Resources

Banks

Banco del Atlántico (⊠ Av. Rueda Medina 3, ☎ 987/70104 or 987/70005), the only bank on the island, is open 9–1:30 and exchanges money 10–noon.

Emergencies

Medical Service (☎ 987/70195 or 987/70607). **Hospital** (☎ 987/70017). **Police** (☎ 987/70082). **Red Cross** (☎ 987/70280).

Guided Tours

BOAT TOURS

Cooperativa Lanchera (⊠ waterfront, near the dock, ☎ no phone) offers four-hour launch trips to the Virgin near Playa Norte, the lighthouse, the turtles at Playa Lancheros, the coral reefs at Los Manchones, and El Garrafón for about $10 without meals, $12 with meals. **Cooperativa Isla Mujeres** (⊠ Av. Rueda Medina, ☎ 987/70274), next to Mexico Divers, rents boats at $120 for a maximum of four hours and six people, and $15 per person for an island tour with lunch (minimum six people).

At least two of Isla Mujeres's boating cooperatives sell day tours to Isla Contoy (☞ Side Trip to Isla Contoy, *above*). **Sociedad Cooperativa "Isla Mujeres"** (⊠ pier, ☎ 987/70274) and **La Isleña** (⊠ ½ block from the pier, corner of Avs. Morelos and Juárez, ☎ 987/70036) launch boats daily at 8:30 AM; they return at 4 PM. Tour operators provide a fruit breakfast on the boat and stop at Xlaches reef on the way to the island for snorkeling (gear is included). The tour of Contoy's leeward side includes views from the water of Bird Beach and Puerto Viejo Lagoon. Along the way your crew trolls for the lunch they'll cook on the beach at the Contoy National Park Station—you may be in for anything from barracuda to snapper (unlimited beer and soda are also included). While they barbecue the catch, you'll have time to explore the island, snorkel some more, check out the small museum and biological station, or just laze under a palapa. The size of the group depends on the boat, but it's usually a minimum of six and a maximum of 12. The trip from Isla Mujeres to Isla Contoy takes about 45 minutes, again depending on the boat, and the day tours run about $30 to $40.

TOUR OPERATORS

Club de Yates de Isla Mujeres (⊠ Av. Rueda Medina, ☎ 987/70211 or 987/70086), open daily 9–noon.

Late-Night Pharmacies

Farmacia Isla Mujeres (✉ Av. Juárez, next to the Caribbean Tropic Boutique, ☎ 987/70178) and **Farmacia Lily** (✉ Avs. Madero and Hidalgo, ☎ 987/70164) are open Mon.–Sat. 8:30 AM–9:30 PM and Sunday 8:30–3.

Mail

The **post office** (✉ Av. Guerrero, ½ block from the market, ☎ 987/70085) is open weekdays 8–7 and Sat. 9–1.

Publications

At the tourist office (☞ Visitor Information, *below*) or at your hotel, you can pick up a copy of the monthly *Islander* magazine, which has a wealth of tourist information.

Telephones

Ladatel phones allow you to reach an AT&T operator in the United States by dialing 01 or to charge calls using major credit cards. They may be found at various places around the island, including Avenida Rueda Medina, across from the ferry; outside Bucanero's restaurant (☞ Dining, *above*); across from the taxi stand; and outside the post office. In addition long-distance phone service is available in the lobby of the **Hotel María José** (✉ Av. Madero 21) or at **Club de Yates** (☞ *above*). **Internet Cafe** (✉ Av. Juarez 5 [upstairs], ☎ 987/70652) is the place for those who want to stay in touch electronically. You can fax, E-mail, or get on line for around $3 per half hour. Although it says café, no coffee is served.

Visitor Information

Tourist office (✉ Plaza Isla Mujeres, north end of main shopping street, ☎ 987/70316), open weekdays 9–2 and 7–9.

4 Cozumel

Mexico's largest cruise-ship port, Cozumel is at once commercial and laid back. Along with day-trippers, the island draws sportfishing enthusiasts and divers who come to explore some of the world's best reefs.

Updated by
Dan Millington

COZUMEL PROVIDES A BALANCE between Cancún and Isla Mujeres: Though attuned to North American tourism, the island has managed to keep development to a minimum. Its expansive beaches, superb coral reefs, and copious wildlife—in the sea, on the land, and in the air—attract an active, athletic crowd. Rated one of the top destinations in the world among underwater enthusiasts, Cozumel is encircled by a garland of reefs entrancing divers and snorkelers alike. Despite the inevitable effects of docking cruise ships (shops and restaurants actively recruit customers on an increasingly populous main drag), the island's earthy charm and tranquillity remain intact. The relaxing atmosphere here is typically Mexican—friendly and unpretentious. Cozumel's rich Maya heritage is reflected in the faces of 60,000 or so isleños; you'll see people who look like ancient statues come to life, and occasionally hear the Maya language spoken.

A 490-square-km (189-square-mi) island 19 km (12 mi) to the east of Yucatán, Cozumel is mostly flat, its interior covered by parched scrub, dense jungle, and marshy lagoons. White sandy beaches with calm waters line the island's leeward (western) side, which is fringed by a spectacular reef system, while the powerful surf and rocky strands on the windward (eastern) side, facing the Caribbean, are broken up here and there by calm bays and hidden coves. Most of Cozumel is undeveloped, with a good deal of the land and the shores set aside as national parks; a few Maya ruins provide what limited sightseeing there is aside from the island's glorious natural attractions. San Miguel is the only established town.

Although distant cousins of the Maya first inhabited the island, it was the Maya who transformed it into a key center of trade and navigation as well as the destination for pilgrimages honoring Ixchel, the goddess of fertility, childbirth, and the moon; it is said that every Maya woman was required to visit the site at least once in her lifetime. The Maya called the island *Ah-Cuzamil-Peten* (Place of the Swallows).

In 1518 Spanish explorer Juan de Grijalva arrived on Cozumel in search of slaves. His tales of gold and other treasures inspired Hernán Cortés, Mexico's most famous Spanish explorer, to visit the island the following year and, shortly thereafter, to settle two missionaries there to convert the Indians. Although the Spaniards never succeeded in colonizing Cozumel, disease eventually wiped out much of the native population that had not already been massacred. By 1600 the island was abandoned.

During the 17th and 18th centuries Cozumel became a hideout for pirates and buccaneers, including Jean Laffite and Henry Morgan, who found the catacombs and tunnels dug by the Indians useful for burying their treasure. These corsairs also laid siege to numerous cargo ships, many of which still lie at the bottom of the surrounding waters. In the 19th century Cozumel was primarily a fishing village and supply port for shipping routes to Central America.

At the start of this century the island began to capitalize on its abundant supply of *zapote* (sapodilla) trees, which produce chicle, prized by the chewing-gum industry. Forays into the jungle in search of chicle led to interest in the archaeological remains. Many of the ruins still stand, but Cozumel's importance as a seaport and a chicle-producing region diminished with the advent of the airplane and the invention of synthetic chewing gum.

For some decades Cozumel was just another backwater, where locals hunted alligators and iguanas and worked on coconut plantations to produce *copra* (dried kernels from which coconut oil is extracted). Cozumeleños subsisted largely on the fruits of the sea, including lobster, conch, sea turtles, and fish, which remain staples of the economy. In the 1950s the island eked out an existence as a health resort for wealthy Yucatecans. It was not until the 1960s and the arrival of late oceanographic explorer Jacques Cousteau, who had learned of its magnificent diving opportunities, that Cozumel began its climb out of oblivion.

Pleasures and Pastimes

Beaches

Inviting, sandy beaches line the leeward side of the island. The most popular, **Playa San Francisco**, a 5-km (3-mi) expanse, has restaurants, a bar, and water-sports equipment for rent. On the windward side, where the rough surf of the Caribbean pounds, are mostly rocky coves and narrow beaches. It's fine for sun worshipers, but usually too rough for swimming along here.

Dining

Cozumel's restaurants offer Yucatecan specialties with an emphasis on seafood, fine cuisine with a Mediterranean accent, and everything in between. Regional dishes employing savory lobster, king crab, grouper, and red snapper fillets are highlights.

For a description of Mexican culinary items, *see* Dining *under* Pleasures and Pastimes *in the* Destination: Cancún, Cozumel, Yucatán Peninsula chapter

Fishing

The waters off Cozumel swarm with more than 230 species of fish, the numbers upholding the island's reputation as one of the world's best locations for trolling, deep-sea fishing, and bottom fishing. Beaky jawed billfish—including swordfish, blue marlin, white marlin, and sailfish—are plentiful here from late April through June, their migration season. World records for catches are frequently set on the island in these months.

Deep-sea fishing for tuna, barracuda, wahoo, and kingfish is productive year-round. Aficionados also enjoy Cozumel's bottom fishing (grouper, yellowtail, and snapper) on the shallow sand flats at the northern end of the island, which also harbor bonefish, tarpon, snook, cubera, and small sharks. The best times to fish are sunrise and sunset, just before a full moon.

Lodging

The selection of appealing options includes modern beachfront resorts with sybaritic creature comforts and all-inclusive properties with the barefoot ambience of a secret island hideaway. Since most accommodations cater to divers, expect the focus to be lighter on poshness, but more on diver-related needs. Those with tighter budgets can stay in town, where homey atmosphere and modest facilities prevail.

Scuba Diving

Because of the diversity of coral formations and the dramatic underwater peaks and valleys, divers rank Cozumel's **Palancar reef** among the top five in the world. With more than 30 charted reefs whose average depths range 50–80 ft and a water temperature that hits about 75°F–80°F during peak diving season (June–August, when hotel rates are coincidentally at their lowest), Cozumel is far and away Mexico's number-one diving destination. Sixty thousand divers come here each year to explore the underwater coral formations, caves, sponges, sea fans, and tropical fish.

Shopping

Shopping is an even bigger industry for Cozumel than diving, principally because of the lucrative trade with cruise-ship passengers (Cozumel is Mexico's largest cruise-ship port). Thousands disembark each year in San Miguel, and consequently prices are relatively high compared to, say, Mérida. The variety of folk art ranges from downright schlocky curios to some excellent silver jewelry, pottery, painted balsa-wood animals, blown glass, and *huipiles* (embroidered cotton dresses).

Snorkeling

Snorkeling ranks just after diving among the island's popular sports. There is good snorkeling in the morning off the piers at the Presidente Inter-Continental and La Ceiba hotels, where fish are fed. The shallow reefs in Chankanaab Bay, Playa San Francisco, and the northern beach at the Club Cozumel Caribe also provide clear views of brilliantly colored fish and sea creatures, among them fingerlings, parrot fish, sergeant majors, angelfish, and squirrel fish, along with elk coral, conch, and sand dollars.

EXPLORING COZUMEL

Cozumel is about 53 km (33 mi) long and 15 km (9 mi) wide, but only a small percentage of its roads—primarily those in the southern half—are paved. You can explore dirt roads with care, in a four-wheel-drive vehicle. Beware of flash flooding during the rainy season: A number of the dirt roads can become difficult to navigate in minutes.

Aside from the 3% of the island that has been developed, Cozumel is made up of expanses of sandy or rocky beaches, quiet little coves, palm groves, scrubby jungles, lagoons and swamps, and a few low hills (the maximum elevation is 45 ft). Brilliantly feathered tropical birds, lizards, armadillos, coati, deer, and small foxes populate the undergrowth and the marshes. In addition to the sites detailed in the Sights to See section, *below,* several minor **Maya ruins** dot the eastern coast of the island. One of them, **Tumba del Caracol,** may have served as a lighthouse. There are also a couple of minuscule ruins, **El Mirador** and the **Throne,** identified by roadside markers.

San Miguel, Cozumel's hub, is simply laid out in characteristically Mexican grid fashion. **Avenida Benito Juárez** stretches east from the pier for 16 km (10 mi) across the island, dividing north from south. Running perpendicular is **Avenida Rafael Melgar,** the coastal road on the island's leeward side (the walkway across the street, on the ocean side, is known as the *malecón*). Avenues, which are labeled "norte" or "sur" depending on where they fall in relation to Juárez, parallel Melgar and are numbered in multiples of five. This means that the avenue after Avenida 5a Sur is Avenida 10a Sur, but if you were to cross Juárez on Avenida 5a Sur it would turn into Avenida 5a Norte. The side streets are even-numbered north of Avenida Juárez (2, 4, 6, etc.) and odd south of the avenue (3, 5, 7, etc.). This is less confusing than it sounds; it will be clear once you've walked around town.

The main strip of shops and restaurants is Avenida Rafael Melgar, along the waterfront. The **Plaza del Sol** is the main square, most often simply called *la plaza* or *el parque.* Directly across from the docks, it's hard to miss. A number of government buildings are here, including the large and modern convention center (used more for local functions than for formal conferences) and the state tourist office. The square is the heart of the town, where everyone congregates in the evenings. Heading inland (east) from the malecón takes you away from the touristy zone and toward the residential sections.

The commercial district is concentrated in the 10 blocks between Calle 10 Norte and Calle 7 Sur. North of that point, you find almost no development until you reach the stretch of hotels beyond the airport. South of town, development continues almost uninterrupted to **La Ceiba,** one of a second cluster of hotels and shops and adjacent to the international passenger terminal for cruise ships.

Numbers in the text correspond to numbers in the margin and on the Cozumel map.

A Good Tour

It's worth renting a Jeep to explore Cozumel, which has more sights than either Cancún or Isla Mujeres. If you head south from Cozumel's principal town, **San Miguel** ①, in about 10 minutes you'll come to **Chankanaab Parque Natural** ②. Continue past Chankanaab and past Playa Corona, Playa San Francisco, and Playa del Sol. At Km 17.5 a turnoff leads about 3 km (2 mi) inland to the village and ruins of **El Cedral** ③ (take this detour only if you have a four-wheel-drive vehicle). Backtrack to the coast and go south past Playa de Palancar (the famous reef lies offshore) to the island's southern tip, where you'll find a dirt trail to **Laguna Colombia** ④.

If you head east on the paved road, you'll come to the eastern Caribbean coast. Make a right turn onto a dirt road and follow it for 4 km (2½ mi) south to get to the **Punta Celerain Faro** ⑤. When you return to the paved road and head north, you will first pass the Tumba del Caracol, another Maya ruin that may have served as a lighthouse; a bit farther on are the minuscule ruins of El Mirador and the Throne. Beyond Punta Chiqueros, Playa Bonita, Playa Chen Río, and Punta Morena you'll see Playa Oriente, where the cross-island road meets the east coast. You can take the cross-island road west toward town or continue north. If you choose the latter route, you'll need a four-wheel-drive vehicle to travel on a rough dirt road that dead-ends past Punta Molas; eventually you'll have to turn around. A sign at this junction warns that drivers proceed at their own risk. This pothole-ridden road is the preferred sunbathing spot of boa constrictors, crocodiles, and other jungle denizens.

If you're headed toward town, it's worth making a detour inland to view the ruins of **San Gervasio** ⑥; take the cross-island road west to the army airfield and turn right; follow this road north for 7 km (4½ mi). The road to the ruins is a good one, but a nearly unmaneuverable dirt road leads northeast of San Gervasio back to the unpaved coast road. At the junction is a marvelously deserted beach where you can camp. Heading north along this beach, you'll come to **Castillo Real** ⑦, another Maya site. A number of other minor ruins are spread across the northern tip of Cozumel, which terminates at the **Punta Molas Faro** ⑧.

Sights to See

⚓ ⑦ **Castillo Real** (Royal Castle). A Maya site on the eastern coast, near the northern tip of the island, the *castillo* (castle) comprises a lookout tower, the base of a pyramid, and a temple with two chambers capped by a false arch. The waters here harbor several shipwrecks, remnants from the days when buccaneers lay in wait for richly cargoed galleons en route to Europe. It's a fine spot for snorkeling because there are few visitors to disturb the fish.

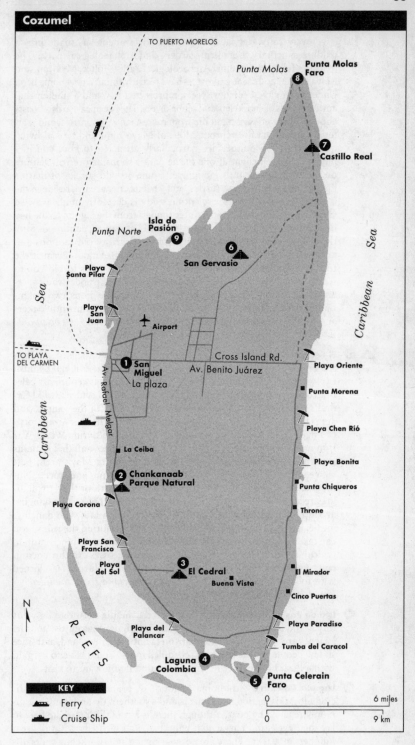

Cozumel

TO PUERTO MORELOS

Punta Molas

Punta Molas Faro 8

7 **Castillo Real**

Isla de Pasión 9

Punta Norte

Sea

6

San Gervasio

Playa Santa Pilar

Playa San Juan

✈ **Airport**

Cross Island Rd.

Av. Benito Juárez

TO PLAYA DEL CARMEN

1 **San Miguel**
La plaza

Playa Oriente

Punta Morena

Playa Chen Río

Caribbean

Av. Rafael Melgar

■ **La Ceiba**

2 **Chankanaab Parque Natural**

Playa Bonita

Punta Chiqueros

Playa Corona

Throne

Caribbean

Playa San Francisco

Playa del Sol

3 **El Cedral**

Buena Vista

■ **El Mirador**

Cinco Puertas

N

R E E F S

Playa del Palancar

Playa Paradiso

Tumba del Caracol

4 **Laguna Colombia**

5 **Punta Celerain Faro**

KEY

⛴ Ferry

🚢 Cruise Ship

0 _____ 6 miles
0 _____ 9 km

⚓ ☕ ❷ **Chankanaab Parque Natural** (Chankanaab Nature Park). Chankanaab (the name means "small sea"), a 10-minute drive south of San Miguel, is a lovely saltwater lagoon that the government has made into a wildlife sanctuary, botanical garden, and archaeological park. The treasures from the Cozumel Archaeological Park—Toltec, Mexican, and Maya statues and stone carvings—have recently found a new home here. Underwater caves, offshore reefs, a protected bay, and a sunken ship attract droves of snorkelers and scuba divers. The botanical garden boasts about 350 varieties of plant life from more than 20 countries, and scattered throughout are reproductions of Maya ruins and typical living quarters. (If mosquitoes are particularly attracted to you, consider buying insect repellent at one of the park's shops before you venture on the nature walk into the jungle.) Some 60-odd species of marine life, including fish, coral, turtles, and various crustaceans, reside in the lagoon; however, a major scientific study is currently under way, so swimming through the underwater tunnels from the lagoon to the bay or walking through the shallow lagoon is no longer permitted. Still, there's plenty to see in the bay, which hides crusty old cannons and anchors as well as statues of Jesus Christ and chac mool. Because the reef's ecological system is extremely fragile, park rules forbid you to wear tanning lotion, feed the fish, or touch any of the underwater specimens. An interactive educational museum, four dive shops, two restaurants, two gift shops, a snack stand, and a dressing room with lockers and showers are on the premises. ⊠ *Carretera Sur, Km 9,* ☎ *no phone.* 🎫 *$7.* ⊙ *Daily 6–5:30.*

⚓ ❸ **El Cedral.** Once the tiny village and ruins comprised the largest Maya site on Cozumel: This was the temple sighted by the original Spanish explorers in 1518, and the first Mass in Mexico was reportedly celebrated here. These days, there's little archaeological evidence of El Cedral's past glory. Conquistadors tore down much of the temple, and at the turn of this century the site was uninhabited. The U.S. Army Corps of Engineers destroyed most of the rest of the ruin during World War II to make way for the island's first airport, and now all that remains is a small structure capped by jungle growth; its Maya arch, best viewed from inside, is covered by faint traces of paint and stucco. Numerous small ruins are hidden in the heavy growth of the surrounding area, but you'll need a guide (there are usually one or two hanging around the main ruin) to find them. Every May a fair, with dancing, music, and a cattle show, is held here. After exploring the ruins, you can take a rest nearby in a small green-and-white cinder-block church, typical of rural Mexico. Inside, a number of crosses are shrouded in embroidered lace. During religious festivals the simple room is adorned with folk art. ⊠ *Turn at Km 17.5 of main island road, then drive 3 km (2 mi) inland to site,* ☎ *no phone.*

❾ **Isla de Pasión.** Beyond Punta Norte, in the middle of Abrigo Bay, this tiny island is now part of a state reserve. Fishing is permitted and the beaches are secluded, but there are no facilities on the island, and since so few people go, there are no scheduled tours. You'll have to bargain with a local boat owner for transportation if you want to visit.

❹ **Laguna Colombia** (Colombia Lagoon). A prime site for jungle aficionados, this lagoon lies at the island's southern tip and is most commonly reached by boat, although there is a trail. Fish migrate here to lay their eggs, and barracuda, baby fish, and birds show up in great numbers in season. There are popular diving and snorkeling spots offshore in the reefs of Tunich, Colombia, and Maracaibo.

❺ **Punta Celerain Faro** (Punta Celerain Lighthouse). Located on the southernmost tip of the island, the lighthouse is surrounded by sand dunes at the narrowest point of land. It affords a misty, mesmerizing view of pounding waves, swamps, and scraggly jungle. Alligators were once hunted nearby; nowadays you may spot a soldier or two from the adjacent army post catching an iguana. The point comes to life at midday when the lighthouse keeper serves fried fish and beer, and locals and tourists gather to chat; Sundays are particularly popular. The lighthouse is at the end of a 4-km-long (2½-mi-long) dirt road—you'll need a four-wheel-drive vehicle if you plan to visit.

8 Punta Molas Faro (Punta Molas Lighthouse). If you are going to attempt to reach the northernmost tip of the island, be sure you have plenty of time and a reliable four-wheel-drive vehicle. While exploring this area keep alert for possible sightings of crocodiles, boa constrictors, and scorpions. They prefer not to have contact with humans, so it's unlikely that they would interfere with your visit, but the unexpected can happen. The lighthouse is an excellent spot for sunbathing, birding, and camping. Although this entire area is accessible only by four-wheel-drive vehicles or by boat, the jagged shoreline and the open sea offer magnificent views, making it well worth the trip.

6 San Gervasio. These ruins of the largest existing Maya and Toltec site on Cozumel are worth visiting. San Gervasio was once the island's capital and probably its ceremonial center, dedicated to the fertility goddess Ixchel. The Classic- and Post-Classic–style site was continuously occupied from AD 300 to AD 1500. Typical architectural features from the era include limestone plazas and masonry superstructures atop stepped platforms, as well as stelae, bas-reliefs, and frescoes. What remains today are several small mounds scattered around a plaza and several broken columns and lintels that were once part of the main building or observatory. Each of the ruins is clearly identified and explained on three-language plaques (Maya, Spanish, and English) and placed in context with individual maps. There are a snack bar and some gift shops at the entrance. To get here take the cross-island road (Av. Juárez) to the San Gervasio access road; follow this road north for 7 km (4½ mi). More likely than not the ruin will close during October. ✉ *Access to road $1, to ruins $3.50.* ☉ *Daily 8–5.*

1 San Miguel. Cozumel's only town retains the laid-back tenor of a Mexican village, although its streets are dotted with an interesting variety of shops and restaurants. Avenida Rafael Melgar, San Miguel's waterfront boulevard, has a wide cement walkway, called the malecón. The malecón separates Avenida Rafael Melgar from the town's narrow sandy beach. As in most Mexican towns, the main square, here called the **Plaza del Sol,** is where townspeople and visitors hang out, particularly on Sunday nights when mariachi bands join the nightly assortment of food and souvenir vendors.

Museo de la Isla de Cozumel (Museum of the Island of Cozumel) is housed on two floors of what was once the island's first luxury hotel. Four permanent exhibit halls of dioramas, sculptures, and charts explain the island's history and ecosystem. Well laid-out and labeled displays cover pre-Hispanic, colonial, and modern times and detail the local geology, flora, and fauna. Among the highlights is a charming reproduction of a Maya house. The museum also presents temporary exhibits, guided tours, and workshops. ✉ *Av. Rafael Melgar between Calles 4 and 6 Norte,* ☎ *987/21475.* ✉ *$3.* ☉ *Daily 10–6.*

NEED A BREAK? On the terrace off the second floor of the Cozumel museum, the **Restaurante del Museo** (☎ 987/20838) offers breakfast, drinks, or a full meal of fajitas or grilled red snapper, all enhanced by a great waterfront view.

BEACHES

Cozumel's beaches vary from long, treeless, sandy stretches to isolated coves and rocky shores. Virtually all development remains on the leeward (western) side, where the coast is relatively sheltered by the proximity of the mainland 19 km (12 mi) to the west. Reaching beaches on the windward (eastern) side is more difficult and requires transportation, but you'll be rewarded if you are looking for solitude.

Leeward Beaches

The best sand beaches lie along the southern half of Cozumel's leeward side, some 5 km (3 mi) long.

Just south of Chankanaab Nature Park (☞ Exploring Cozumel, *above*), **Playa Corona,** which shares access to the Yucab reef, offers the same brilliant marine life as the park. Snorkeling equipment is available for rent, and the restaurant here serves conch and shrimp ceviche, fajitas, and more. The crowds that visit Chankanaab haven't yet discovered this tranquil neighbor.

South of Playa Corona lies **Playa San Francisco,** an inviting 5-km (3-mi) stretch of sandy beach that's considered one of the longest and finest on Cozumel. Comprising the beaches known as Playa Maya and Santa Rosa, San Francisco gets especially crowded during high season, on weekends (with cruise-ship passengers), and on Sunday (when locals come to eat fresh fish and hear live music). Environmental concerns have halted plans to build four or five new luxury hotels here. In the meantime, however, the beach has everything beachgoers need (though costs run higher here than on other, less frequented beaches): two outdoor restaurants, a bar, dressing rooms, gift shops, volleyball nets, beach chairs, and a variety of water-sports equipment for rent. Divers also use this beach as their jumping-off point for dives to the San Francisco reef and the Santa Rosa wall. An abundance of turtle grass in the water makes swimming less popular.

Just south of San Francisco, **Playa del Sol** has complete facilities, including a restaurant-bar, shops, and snorkeling and Jet Ski equipment; you can also rent horses and trot down the beach. One drawback, however, is Playa del Sol's popularity with cruise-ship passengers.

The beach at **Palancar,** with a gently sloping shore enlivened by palm trees, is far more deserted than San Francisco to the north. Offshore lies the famous Palancar Reef (☞ Outdoor Activities and Sports, *below*), which is practically Cozumel's raison d'être. There is a water-sports center and a bar-café on the beach here.

Among Cozumel's most lovely and marvelously secluded beaches are those beaches around **Punta Celerain,** near the lighthouse at the island's southern point.

Santa Pilar and San Juan beaches, which run along the northern hotel strip, sell soft drinks and rent water-sports equipment. Playa San Juan culminates in Punta Norte.

Windward Beaches

The east coast of Cozumel presents a splendid succession of mostly deserted rocky coves and narrow, powdery beaches—sadly garbage-strewn in spots—posed dramatically against astoundingly turquoise water. Swimming can be treacherous here if you go too far out or if a southwestern wind is blowing, but there is nothing to prevent solitary sunbathing on any of the several beaches.

The southernmost of the windward beaches, which lies near the small Maya ruin known as Tumba del Caracol, **Playa Paradiso** hosts the **Paradise Café**, a good place for a snack, some cold beer, and reggae tunes.

To the north of Playa Paradiso, **Punta Chiqueros** is a moon-shape cove sheltered from the sea by an offshore reef. Part of a longer stretch of beach that most locals call Playa Bonita—it's also known as Playa San Martin or Tortuga Desnuda (Naked Turtle)—it boasts fine sand, clear water, and moderate waves. You can swim and camp here, watch the sun set and the moon rise, and dine at the **Playa Bonita** restaurant-bar, which has fine fresh fish.

A little less than 5 km (3 mi) north of Punta Chiqueros is **Playa Chen Río,** another good spot for camping or exploring, where the waters are clear and the surf is not too strong, thanks to the rock formation that protects the small bay. Dining here means excellent fresh fish, shrimp, and lobster dishes at Chen Rio restaurant. This is a perfect spot to spend a casual afternoon.

Nearly 1 km (½ mi) north of Chen Río along the main road is **Punta Morena,** where waves crash on the rocky beach and, on June nights when the moon is full, turtles come to lay their eggs. If you're on the beach then, you may be stopped by soldiers who are stationed here to control poaching. This is also the site of the eastern coast's only hotel, also called Punta Morena, which has a small restaurant and bar.

The cross-island road meets the east coast at the **Mezcalito Café** on **Playa Oriente,** a typical windward side beach with pounding surf. The café is a pleasant place for light meals and drinks. If you want to continue farther north, make sure you have a sturdy vehicle, since the paved road ends here.

There is a string of nameless beaches on the dirt road leading to **Punta Molas** (☞ Punta Molas Faro *in* Exploring Cozumel, *above*), at the island's northern tip. The point itself is a lovely, unspoiled spot for sunbathing and nature viewing, reachable only by boat or four-wheel-drive vehicle.

DINING

Dining options on Cozumel reflect the nature of the place as a whole, with some harmless pretension at times but mainly the insouciant, natural style of the tropical island. More than 80 restaurants in the downtown area alone offer a broad choice, from air-conditioned fast-food outlets—Dairy Queen, Domino's, KFC, Pizza Hut, and Subway—and Americanized places serving Continental fare and seafood in semiformal "nautical" settings to simple outdoor eateries that specialize in fish. For the most part, the more established restaurants accept credit cards, while the café-type places accept only cash. Resort hotels offering buffet breakfasts and dinners are good values for bottomless appetites. A dining tip: Don't be wholly influenced by your cab driver's dining suggestion: It may mean that his restaurant-of-choice is paying him to get you there.

Reservations and What to Wear

Casual dress and no reservations are the rule in most $$ and $ Cozumel restaurants. In $$$ restaurants you would not be out of place if you dressed up, and reservations are advised.

CATEGORY	COST*
$$$	$25–$35
$$	$15–25
$	under $15

per person, excluding drinks and service

$$$ ✕ **Arrecife.** A well-trained staff, impeccably prepared seafood, and
★ Mediterranean fare put this hotel restaurant in a class by itself. Tall
windows and excellent views of the sea complement the stylish
decor—potted palms, white wicker furniture, pink walls—while mu-
sicians, who play regularly, further enhance the romantic mood. You
might find Arrecife's doors unlocked on the weekends if the hotel is
hopping during low season, but the restaurant is officially open only
from November through Labor Day weekend. ✉ *Presidente Inter-
Continental Cozumel hotel,* ☎ *987/20322. AE, DC, MC, V. Closed
Sept. and Oct.*

$$$ ✕ **La Cabaña del Pescador.** To get to this rustic palapa-covered hut,
you've got to cross a gangplank, but it's worth it if you're looking for
well-prepared fresh lobster. The crustaceans are sold by weight, and
the rest—including a delicious eggnog-type drink served at the end of
the meal—is on the house. Seashells and nets hang from the walls of
this small, dimly lit room; geese stroll outside, hoping to be fed by diners seated next to the windows. Another local seafood favorite, king
crab, is the feature at La Cabaña's sister establishment, **El Guacamayo
King Crab House,** right next door. With the less-expensive king crab
the focus of the menu, El Guacamayo falls into the $$ category. ✉ *Carre-
tera San Juan, Km 4, across from Playa Azul Hotel north of town,* ☎
no phone. No credit cards. No lunch.

$$$ ✕ **Pepe's Grill.** This large, bustling restaurant follows the nautical
mode, from the model ships and ship wheels to the weather vanes cov-
ering the walls. Tall windows provide exceptional views of the malecón.
You can choose between the quiet setting upstairs and the livelier
atmosphere in the dining room downstairs. This restaurant caters to
the cruise-ship clientele, so most North Americans will feel right at home,
but with the comforts of home come long lines and high prices.
Caribbean seafood dishes—lobster, shrimp flambé, shellfish grill, and
king crab—are featured as specials, and the steaks—particularly the
chateaubriand in béarnaise sauce, from the state of Chihuahua—are
superb. The grouper fish is fresh and good, as are the Caesar salad and
the salad bar. Live music is played nightly. ✉ *Av. Rafael Melgar Sur
at Calle Rosada Salas,* ☎ *987/20213. AE, MC, V. No lunch.*

$$ ✕ **Carlos 'n' Charlie's.** Rock and roll, a Ping-Pong table, and drinking
contests are the status quo here. American-style ribs, chicken, and
beef selections taste good, but the drinks are better. You can recognize
this place by the red wall just north of the ferry pier. ✉ *Av. Rafael Mel-
gar 11, between Calles 2 and 4 Norte,* ☎ *987/20191. AE, MC, V.*

$$ ✕ **El Capi Navegante.** Locals say you'll find the best seafood in town
here: The captain's motto is "The fish we serve today slept in the sea
last night." Specialties like whole red snapper and stuffed squid are skill-
fully prepared and sometimes flambéed at your table. Highly recommended dishes include conch ceviche and deep-fried whole snapper.
Nautical blue-and-white decor, accented by the life preservers on the
walls, adds personality to this place. ✉ *Av. 10a Sur 312, at Calle 3,*
☎ *987/21730. MC, V.*

$$ ✕ **La Choza.** Home-cooked Mexican food—primarily from the capi-
★ tal and among the best in town—is the order of the day at this fam-
ily-run establishment. A complimentary bowl of guacamole and chips
are brought out with the menu. Start off your meal with soup (onion
and mushroom are the best) and fresh tortillas. Dona Elisa Espinosa's

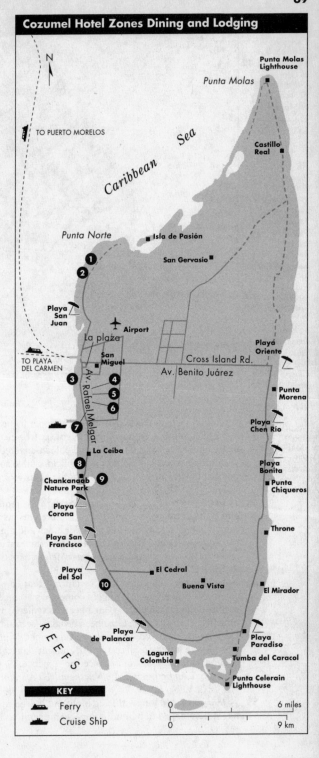

Cozumel Hotel Zones Dining and Lodging

Dining
Arrecife, **8**
La Cabaña del
Pescador, **2**

Lodging
Casa del Mar, **6**
Crown Paradise Sol
Caribe Cozumel, **7**
Diamond Hotel &
Resort, **10**
Fiesta Americana
Cozumel Reef, **9**
Fiesta Inn, **5**
Galápago Inn, **4**
Meliá Mayan
Peradisus, **1**
Plaza Las Glorias, **3**
Presidente
Inter-Continental
Cozumel, **8**

Punta Molas
Lighthouse
Punta Molas
Castillo
Real
Caribbean
Sea
Punta Norte
Isla de Pasión
San Gervasio
Playa
San
Juan
Airport
La plaza
Playa
Oriente
San
Miguel
Cross Island Rd.
TO PLAYA
DEL CARMEN
Av. Benito Juárez
Punta
Morena
Playa
Chen Rio
La Ceiba
Playa
Bonita
Chankanaab
Nature Park
Punta
Chiqueros
Playa
Corona
Throne
Playa San
Francisco
Playa
del Sol
El Cedral
El Mirador
Buena Vista
R E E F S
Playa
de Palancar
Playa
Paradiso
Laguna
Colombia
Tumba del Caracol
Punta Celerain
Lighthouse
TO PUERTO MORELOS
Av. Rafael Melgar

KEY
Ferry
Cruise Ship

0   6 miles
0   9 km

70

Dining

Café Caribe, **27**

Carlos 'n' Charlie's, **5**

Diamond Café, **12**

El Capi Navegante, **25**

El Foco, **21**

El Moro, **9**

Esquisse Café, **16**

La Choza, **22**

La Veranda, **3**

Las Palmeras, **10**

Morgan's, **8**

Pancho's Backyard, **2**

Pepe's Grill, **17**

Pizza Rolandi, **1**

Plaza Leza, **11**

Prima Pasta, **19**

Prima Trattoria, **15**

Santiago's Grill, **23**

Sports Page Video Bar and Restaurant, **6**

Tony Rome's, **24**

Lodging

Bahía, **20**

Bazar Colonial, **14**

Bed & Breakfast Caribo, **28**

Bed & Breakfast Tamarindo, **4**

Mary Carmen, **13**

Mesón San Miguel, **7**

Suites Elizabeth, **18**

Villas Las Anclas, **26**

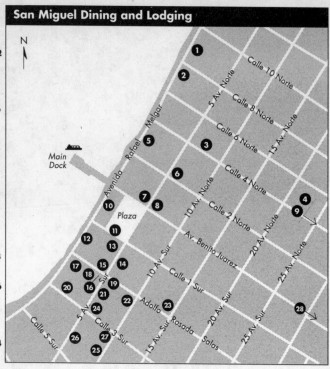

San Miguel Dining and Lodging

specialties include chicken mole, red snapper in sweet mustard sauce, and grilled lobster. To finish, you might try frozen avocado pie—cool, dense, and refreshing. The informal palapa-covered patio is furnished with simple wood tables and chairs, oilcloth table coverings, and hand-painted pottery dishes. ⊠ *Calle Rosada Salas 198, at Av. 10a Sur,* ☎ *987/20958. AE, MC, V.*

$$ ✕ **Las Palmeras.** The redbrick patios with the requisite potted palms and ceiling fans set the mood at this unpretentious waterfront restaurant, where breakfast is a bargain. For lunch and dinner expect seafood specialties and some Mexican dishes. The restaurant also sells margaritas and piña coladas to go. ⊠ *Av. Rafael Melgar, across from pier,* ☎ *987/ 20532. AE, MC, V.*

$$ ✕ **La Veranda.** This charming restaurant that emphasizes Caribbean cuisine feels like you're dining in someone's home. Begin with shrimp scampi and graduate to the Caribbean fish fillet in a mango sauce. Another local favorite is the Caribbean delight—seafood in a teriyaki sauce. Desserts are made daily and vary every night. With comfortable rattan chairs, a lush tropical courtyard, and soft classical music in the background, this is an obvious choice for romance. ⊠ *Calle Norte 4 140 between 5 Av between 5 Av. Norte and 10 Av. Norte,* ☎ *987/24132. AE, MC, V. No lunch.*

$$ ✕ **Morgan's.** No longer the big night out it used to be, this restaurant has still managed to maintain impeccable service, a quiet atmosphere with candlelight, and an international cuisine. Located in the former customs house and done up in honor of its namesake—the seafaring pirate Henry Morgan, who once plied these waters—the restaurant is decorated with ship paneling, portholes, and compasses. The menu offers such appetizers as avocado cocktail and ham with melon, in addition to a selection of steak and fish entrées. ⊠ *Av. Benito Juárez and Calle 5a, north side of plaza,* ☏ *987/20584. AE, MC, V.*

$$ ✕ **Pancho's Backyard.** A jungle of greenery, trickling fountains, ceil-
★ ing fans, and leather chairs set the tone at this inviting restaurant, located on the cool patio of Los Cincos Soles shopping center. The menu highlights local standards such as black bean soup, *camarones al carbon* (grilled prawns), and fajitas. Round out your meal with coconut ice cream in Kahlua. ⊠ *Av. Rafael Melgar Norte 27, at Calle 8 Norte,* ☏ *987/22141. AE, MC, V. Closed Sun. No lunch Sat.*

$$ ✕ **Prima Trattoria.** Considered to be one of the best Italian restaurants on the Island, this pleasant open-air eatery—situated on the second level—offers views of Cozumel's bustling nightlife. Outstanding is the angel hair pasta with lobster and sun-dried tomatoes special. Broiled or blackened grouper steak is a must, along with delectable blueberry cheesecake for dessert. The bottom level is a store where one can find Mexico's finest wines along with pricey Cuban cigars. ⊠ *Av. Rosado Salas 109 A,* ☏ *987/24242 or 987/22477. AE, MC, V. No lunch.*

$$ ✕ **Santiago's Grill.** Beautiful American cuts of meat, including T-bones and sirloins, as well as beef brochettes and fresh shrimp, draw long lines nightly. This small outdoor restaurant with only 10 tables is included on a list given to cruise-ship passengers, so it's not surprising that it's popular with tourists. ⊠ *Calle Rosada Salas 299, at Av. 15a Sur,* ☏ *987/22137. MC, V. No lunch.*

$$ ✕ **Tony Rome's.** Finger-licking, Texas-style barbecued ribs and Las
★ Vegas–style crooning (courtesy of owner Tony Rome) are the drawing cards of this open-air eatery wrapped around a palapa-covered dance floor. In addition to the ribs and the live entertainment, you'll find chicken, lobster, Kansas City steaks, and great happy hour specials. Tony now produces daily fresh pasta to accompany his delicious chicken Parmesan. ⊠ *Av. 5 Sur 21, between Av. Rosado Salas and Calle 3 Sur,* ☏ *987/20131. MC, V.*

$ ✕ **Café Caribe.** Coffee junkies and folks with a serious sweet tooth flock to the little L-shape Café Caribe for the mouthwatering selection of coffees (Cuban, Irish, espresso, cappuccino), along with Belgian waffles, yogurt, ice cream, and freshly baked cakes, pies, and muffins. Cheerfully decorated with colorful art posters, this little café is open only in the morning and evening. The owners have made a few changes recently, including expanding the sandwich menu and adding a pleasant courtyard in the back. It is the perfect spot for both breakfast and after-dinner coffee and dessert. ⊠ *10 Av. Sur 215,* ☏ *987/23621. No credit cards. Closed Sun.*

$ ✕ **Diamond Café.** A discreet signboard at the pink terra-cotta storefront
★ of the elegant Diamond Creations jewelry shop advertises this airy retreat, located in the back of the store. There's a separate entrance as well on Avenida Rafael Melgar. Artfully decorated like a typical Mexican patio, with a central fountain, hanging plants, and terraced seating at wrought-iron tables, the café specializes in home-baked pastries to accompany the espresso and cappuccino brewed on the premises. The café is open all day, serving breakfast, lunch, and light snacks until 10 PM. ⊠ *Av. Rafael Melgar 131,* ☏ *987/23869. No credit cards. Closed Sun.*

$ ✕ **El Foco.** At this *taquería* (taco stand) serving soft tacos stuffed with pork, *chorizo* (spicy Mexican sausage), and cheese, you can also get a good rack of ribs or a steak. Graffitied walls and plain wood tables make it a casual, fun spot to grab a bite and a *cerveza* (beer). ⊠ *Av. 5*

Sur 13-B, between Calle Rosado Salas and Calle 3, ☎ *no phone. No credit cards.*

$ ✕ **El Moro.** This family-run restaurant on the eastern edge of town specializes in low-priced local cuisine—seafood, chicken, and meat. Inside, the decor follows the regional theme, beginning with Yucatecan baskets hanging on the walls. Divers flock to this place, so you know portions are hearty and the food is delicious. Take a taxi; El Moro is too far to walk to and too difficult to find. ⊠ *Calle 75 Norte between Calles 2 and 4,* ☎ *987/23029. MC, V. Closed Thurs.*

$ ✕ **Esquisse Café.** With a delightful French twist, this petite café centers around an artistic theme (Esquisse means "first sketch"), with photographs of Paris and the French countryside adorning the walls. The polished wood tables with directors chairs and soft sofas make this a comfortable place for coffee and catching up on some reading. Espresso and cappuccino along with vegetarian baguettes, quiche-of-the-day, and an assortment of crepes comprise the menu. The café is open 7 AM–11 PM, but closed for siesta 4–6 PM. ⊠ *Av. Rosado Salas at Av. 5 Sur,* ☎ *987/25747. No credit cards.*

$ ✕ **Pizza Rolandi.** This trendy chain restaurant is a good choice for casual Italian fare. Top sellers from the signboard menus carried by the wait staff include lasagna, Four Seasons pizza (with ham, zucchini, mushrooms, and black olives), and pitchers of homemade sangria. Tables in the dining room on the main waterfront drive tend to be noisy, so you'll be better off selecting one beneath the trees on the stucco-walled patio out back. ⊠ *Av. Rafael Melgar 23,* ☎ *987/20946. AE. No lunch Sun.*

$ ✕ **Plaza Leza.** If you're craving the low-key, unpretentious atmosphere of a Mexican sidewalk café, stop here, where you can dawdle for hours over a cup of coffee or a beer. Choose a table on the plaza, or for more privacy, go indoors to the somewhat secluded, cozy inner patio. Plaza Leza serves everything from *poc chuc* (pork chops grilled Yucatán style), enchiladas, and lime soup to chicken sandwiches and coconut ice cream. ⊠ *South side of main plaza,* ☎ *987/21041. AE, MC, V.*

$ ✕ **Prima Pasta.** Since Texan Albert Silmai opened this Northern Italian diner just off the plaza in 1992, he's attracted a strong following of patrons who come for hearty, inexpensive pizzas, calzone, sandwiches, and pastas. To this winning formula the chef has added whole king crab and catch-of-the-day seafood dishes. The breezy dining area on the second-floor terrace above the kitchen smells heavenly and has a charming Mediterranean mural painted on two walls. ⊠ *Calle Rosado Salas 109,* ☎ *987/24242. AE, MC, V.*

$ ✕ **Sports Page Video Bar and Restaurant.** Signed team T-shirts and pennants line the walls and ceilings of this popular restaurant and watering hole. The main attraction is the sports coverage—large TVs simultaneously broadcast at least four athletic events—but the food's good, too. Cheeseburgers are juicy and served with generous portions of crispy fries. Mexican specialties as well as seafood and steak dinners are offered. The place is open from 9 AM for breakfast, so you can have your eggs with ESPN. ⊠ *Av. 5a Norte and Calle 2 Norte,* ☎ *987/ 21199. MC, V.*

LODGING

Cozumel's hotels are located in three main areas, all on the island's western, or leeward, side: in town, and north and south of town. Because of the proximity of the reefs, divers and snorkelers tend to congregate at the southern properties. Sailors and anglers, on the other hand, prefer the hotels to the north, where the beaches are better. Most budget hotels are in town.

Cozumel offers about 3,200 hotel rooms in more than 60 properties. Before booking you should call around, because you will find many bargains in the form of air, hotel, and dive packages, especially off-season; some packages combine Cozumel and Cancún stays, with free airfare between the two. Christmas reservations must be made at least three months ahead of time. The majority of the resort hotels (north and south of town) are affiliated with international chains and offer all the usual amenities; they also generally rent water-sports equipment and can arrange excursions. All hotels have air-conditioning unless otherwise noted. The more costly properties generally offer no-smoking rooms and on-site travel agencies and transportation rentals, and include in-room hair dryers, safes, minibars, satellite TV, and telephones as part of their amenities. All hotels share the 77600 postal code.

The **Cozumel Island Hotel Association** (⊠ Box 228, Cozumel, QR 77600, or 15a Calle 2 Norte, ☎ 987/23132, FAX 987/22809), with 15 member properties, functions unofficially as the island's tourist information bureau.

CATEGORY	COST*
$$$$	over $160
$$$	$90–$160
$$	$40–$90
$	under $40

All prices are for a standard double room, excluding service charges and the 12% tax.

$$$$ 🏨 **Diamond Hotel & Resort.** This large, all-inclusive resort is the southernmost of the island's properties. The hotel is far from town and there is no shuttle service, but because the Diamond's beach is close to Palancar and other reefs there are lots of water-based activities. There's also good nightly entertainment, consisting of of Mexican folkloric ballet and Broadway show tunes in the theater. Accommodations, set in bi-level palapa-roof units spread across the grounds, are furnished in light wood and tropical pastels. Standard rooms are not very large (those on the second floor feel larger because of the high palapa ceiling), but duplex suites easily accommodate three or four people. Pack your bug spray to keep the nightly mosquitoes from nearby swamps at bay. The buffet meals are fairly institutional, but two à la carte restaurants offer decent Italian and Mexican fare. ⊠ *San Francisco Palancar, Km 16.5,* ☎ *987/23554 or 800/858–2258,* FAX *987/24508. 300 rooms. 4 bars, 2 pools, beauty salon, 4 tennis courts, aerobics, basketball, shuffleboard, volleyball, snorkeling, motorbikes, shops, children's programs, car rental. AE, MC, V.*

$$$$ 🏨 **Meliá Mayan Peradisus.** Lush tropical foliage and spectacular sunsets over the beach combine with modern architecture and amenities to make this property north of town a memorable place to stay. Large windows in the light, cheerful lobby look out onto a pool and swim-up palapa snack bar. Standard rooms, some with small patios opening out onto the lawn, are attractively decorated with colorful tropical print bedspreads and light-wood furniture; superior rooms are larger and have balconies overlooking the water. This all-inclusive resort has an international staff and activity coordinators to keep guests happily busy. On the premises is a disco, kids program and playground, horseback trails, health club with steam room and fitness equipment, and an array of nonmotorized water-sports equipment. ⊠ *Box 9, Carretera a Sta. Pilar 6,* ☎ *987/20411 or 800/341–5993,* FAX *987/21599. 200 rooms. 3 restaurants, 5 bars, 2 pools, hot tub, 2 tennis courts, health club, horseback riding, bicycles, shops, dance club, children's programs. AE, MC, V.*

$$$$ 🏨 **Plaza Las Glorias.** A Mediterranean atmosphere prevails inside and out: This large, salmon-colored building has Mexican tiles, marble floors, and wrought-iron details in its public areas. The modern all-suites property, within walking distance of town, has private terraces and ocean views from each of its light, spacious units. You can enjoy live music in the lobby bar several nights a week. One caveat: There is a strong time-share contingent here, and hotel guests are often pestered to sit through the sales pitch. ⊠ *Av. Rafael Melgar, Km 1.5,* ☎ *987/22000 or 800/342–AMIGO,* 🆖 *987/21937. 170 suites. 2 restaurants, 2 bars, pool, dive shop, shops. AE, MC, V.*

$$$$ 🏨 **Presidente Inter-Continental Cozumel.** This hotel exudes luxury,
★   from the courteous, prompt, and efficient service to the tastefully decorated interior. The Presidente is famed not only for possessing one of the best restaurants on the island, **Arrecife** (☞ Dining, *above*), but also for its respectable and professional water-sports center. Located on its own broad, white beach south of the town of San Miguel, the property ranks among the best on the island for snorkeling—barracuda, angelfish, octopus, and more are visible in the waters a few feet off the beach. All rooms are done in bright, contemporary colors with white cedar furnishings. Deluxe rooms, with their own private terraces fronting the beach or gardens, are huge. Complimentary coffee is delivered to your room at the time of your wake-up call. In high season there are weekly theme parties. ⊠ *Carretera a Chankanaab, Km 6.5,* ☎ *987/20322 or 800/327–0200,* 🆖 *987/21360. 253 rooms. 2 restaurants, 3 bars, coffee shop, pool, hot tub, 2 tennis courts, dive shop, motorbikes, children's program, shops, car rental. AE, DC, MC, V.*

$$$ 🏨 **Crown Paradise Sol Caribe Cozumel.** Just across the street from its own small beach (accessible by underground footpath) is the largest all-inclusive resort in Cozumel, consisting of a 10-story main building (currently being remodeled), with a dramatically designed, wood-beamed, palapa-roofed lobby and an adjoining tower. Rooms in the tower, all with balconies and considered deluxe, are slightly more expensive, but those in the main building—reached by a glass-encased elevator—are the same size (sans balcony) and furnished in a lighter, more cheerful fashion. Nicely landscaped grounds and a large pool with a swim-up bar are among the hotel's greatest amenities. ⊠ *Box 259, Playa Paraíso, Km 3.5,* ☎ *987/20700,* 🆖 *987/21301. 321 rooms. 3 restaurants, 3 bars, pool, beauty salon, 3 tennis courts, dive shop, dock, bicycles, shops, travel services, car rental. AE, MC, V.*

$$$ 🏨 **Fiesta Americana Cozumel Reef.** This property, situated on the less developed southern end of the island, is ideally situated for snorkeling and scuba diving. The hotel's beach, although fairly narrow for sunbathing, offers easy access to spectacular underwater scenery. The hotel building itself is across the road from the beach and the restaurant that overlooks the water; guests either have to cross the road at street level (traffic is usually sparse) or use the walkway over the road to reach them. The high-ceilinged lobby, with its polished marble floors, hosts a glitzy silver shop with some unusual pieces. Standard rooms are large, with sea-green headboards and well-made light-wood furnishings; all have balconies looking out on the ocean. There's a semicircular cluster of villas with 56 rooms facing the hotel's main entrance. Reasonable prices and a good location have made the Fiesta Americana one of the most popular hotels on the island. ⊠ *Carretera a Chankanaab, Km 7.5,* ☎ *987/22622 or 800/343–7821,* 🆖 *987/22666. 228 rooms. 3 restaurants, 3 bars, 2 pools, 2 tennis courts, dive shop, motorbikes, car rentals, travel services. AE, MC, V.*

$$$ 🏨 **Fiesta Inn.** This three-story Spanish-roofed structure, south of town and across the street from the beach, has all the trademarks of the Fiesta brand name: a comfortable lobby with a fountain and garden, brightly decorated modern rooms with Moorish archways, a large pool, and an international dining facility. Fully carpeted rooms are painted light blue, with cream-color wicker furniture and private balconies (many have safes as well). Request a room on the third floor— for the same price you get an ocean view. The sing-along **Laser-Karaoke Bar** draws exhibitionists from all over town. ✉ *Carretera a Chankanaab, Km 1.7,* ☎ *987/22900 or 800/343–7821,* 𝔽𝔸𝕏 *987/80100. 180 rooms. Restaurant, 2 bars, pool, hot tub, tennis court, dive shop, motorbikes. AE, MC, V.*

\$\$\$ 🏨 **Galápago Inn.** This pretty white stucco hotel just south of town primarily accommodates divers. The simply furnished, brightly tiled rooms are not rented by the night but exclusively as part of dive packages—booked through the 800 number or your travel agent—that take full advantage of the hotel's expert diving staff and advanced certification diving school. The central garden, with tiled benches and a small fountain, contributes to the inn's Mediterranean feel. The staff here are cheerful and accommodating. ✉ *Carretera a Chankanaab, Km 1.5,* ☎ *987/20663 or 800/847–5708. 58 rooms. 2 restaurants, bar, pool. MC, V.*

\$\$ 🏨 **Bahía.** The lobby here is small but the hallways are pleasant enough, with white walls and red-tile floors. The large accommodations, decorated with the standard stucco, wood, and tile, come with sofa beds and kitchenettes. Ask for a room with a sea view; the balconies overlook the malecón and go for the same price as those facing town. Two penthouse suites are available. ✉ *Av. Rafael Melgar and Calle 3 Sur,* ☎ *987/20209,* 𝔽𝔸𝕏 *987/21387. 27 rooms. Kitchenettes. AE, MC, V.*

\$\$ 🏨 **Bed & Breakfast Tamarindo.** The owners of this five-room charmer have created a lodging that combines European and old-Mexican style. They've decorated each room (some are air-conditioned) with artful imagination and ambience. You'll sit down to a breakfast of fresh breads, fruits in season, homemade yogurt, and french-dripped coffee. Everyone can use the communal kitchen area with cooking facilities and a full-size fridge. The staff will arrange diving expeditions and there is a rinse tank and gear storage facility on the premises. ✉ *Calle 4 Norte 421 between Av. 20 and Av. 25, 987/23614. Massage, bicycles, shops, laundry, bicycles, baby-sitting. MC, V.*

\$\$ 🏨 **Casa del Mar.** Divers frequent this three-story hotel, located south
★ of town near several boutiques, sports shops, and restaurants. An unpretentious but tasteful lobby, which has natural wood banisters and overlooks a small garden, exemplifies the overall simplicity of the place. Cheerful rooms feature yellow-tiled headboards, nightstands, and sinks; Mexican artwork; and small balconies with views of the pool just outside or the sea across the road. The bilevel cabañas, which sleep three or four, are a very good buy at \$115 (especially if you split the cost). ✉ *Box 129, Carretera a Chankanaab, Km 4,* ☎ *987/21944 or 800/437–9609,* 𝔽𝔸𝕏 *987/21855. 98 rooms, 8 cabañas. 2 restaurants, 2 bars, pool, hot tub, dive shop, travel services, car rental. AE, MC, V.*

\$\$ 🏨 **Villas Las Anclas.** Conveniently located parallel to the malecón, these
★ villas are actually furnished apartments for rent by the day, week, or month. The duplexes include a downstairs sitting room, dining area, and kitchenette, which is fully stocked with dishes, refrigerator, and hot plate; a spiral staircase leads up to a small bedroom with a large desk (but no phone or TV) and inset shelves over the double bed. Rooms are extremely attractive, with tastefully bright patterns set off against white walls; they all overlook a quiet courtyard garden. This property is owned and operated by brother and sister Claus and Eva Reinking, who also roast the best coffee on the island. Each apartment is stocked with fresh coffee and a coffeemaker. If you run out, you can buy fresh-ground at the front desk. ✉ *Box 25, Av. 5a Sur 325, between Calles*

3 and 5 Sur, ☎ *987/21403,* ﬁ *987/25476. 7 units. Kitchenettes, refrigerators. No credit cards.*

$ ⌂ **Bazar Colonial.** This attractive, modern three-story hotel, located over a small cluster of shops, has pretty red-tile floors and bougainvillea, which add splashes of color. Natural-wood furniture, TVs (a recent addition), kitchenettes, bookshelves, sofa beds, and an elevator make up for the lack of other amenities, such as a restaurant and a pool. Pick up your freshly brewed coffee in the lobby during morning hours. ⌧ *Av. 5a Sur 9, near Calle 3 Sur,* ☎ *987/20506,* ﬁ *987/21387. 18 rooms. Kitchenettes, shops. AE, MC, V.*

$ ⌂ **Bed & Breakfast Caribo.** Operated in the friendly and comfortable tradition of B&B inns, this one was formerly a doctor's residence. It was totally renovated and restored by a family from Michigan, and the nine air-conditioned rooms are spacious and well furnished, featuring white wicker, blue floral upholstered chairs, and matching serape bedspreads. All rooms have private baths. There's cable TV for guests in the first-floor sitting room. The full (meatless) breakfast buffet, served on the screened-in porch, is included in the price. Weekly and monthly rates are available. One caveat: Avenida Juárez is a main thoroughfare and traffic sounds are audible in the front bedrooms. ⌧ *Av. Juárez 799,* ☎ *987/23195 or 800/830–5558. 4 apartments. MC, V.*

$ ⌂ **Mary Carmen.** Functional and clean, this hotel rents rooms on the ground floor with both air-conditioning and ceiling fans (but no phones or TVs); on the first floor, only air-conditioning is offered. Although the furniture and rugs are rather worn, the double bed and two chairs are adequate considering the price. A drawback is the antiseptic smell throughout the place. ⌧ *Av. 5a Sur 4,* ☎ *987/20581. 27 rooms. MC, V.*

$ ⌂ **Mesón San Miguel.** Situated right on the square, this hotel sees a
★ lot of action from locals who come to the large public bar and outdoor café. The architecturally eclectic San Miguel, with four stories and an elevator, has a burgundy-and-white-tiled lobby floor and a contemporary-style game room with a pool table. The remodeled rooms are clean and functional, with air-conditioning, satellite TV, phones, and balconies overlooking the plaza—amenities unusual in a budget hotel, making this a good bet for your money. Sip a drink in the evenings at **Video Bar Aladino,** the hotel's bar on the square. ⌧ *Av. Juárez 2 Bis,* ☎ *987/20323 or 987/20233,* ﬁ *987/21820. 97 rooms. Bar, café, pool, recreation room. AE, MC, V.*

$ ⌂ **Suites Elizabeth.** This basic hotel offers rooms with fans or with air-conditioning. The latter include large balconies with a view of the rooftops, and many rooms come with refrigerators and hot plates (but no phones or TVs). The vintage '70s furnishings, including light-orange chenille bedspreads, look dated but are still functional. ⌧ *Box 70, Calle Rosada Salas 44,* ☎ *987/20330. 19 rooms. Refrigerators. No credit cards.*

NIGHTLIFE AND THE ARTS

The Arts

Although Cozumel doesn't have much in the way of highbrow performing arts per se, there are performances that reflect the island's heritage, including Fiesta Mexicana nights at the **Crown Paradise Sol Caribe** (☎ 987/20700). Catch the show Friday night only from 7 to 10 PM during high season. Included are folkloric dancers, mariachis, an open-bar buffet dinner, and tequila shots; the cost is about $20.

Movies

Cine Cozumel (✉ Av. Rafael Melgar, between Calles 2 and 4 Norte, ☎ 987/20766) and **Cine Cecillo Borge** (✉ Av. Benito Juárez, between Avs. 30 and 35, ☎ no phone) both show films in English (generally with subtitles) and Spanish nightly at 9.

Nightlife

Cozumel offers enough daytime activities to make you want to retire early, but the young set keeps the island hopping late into the night. There is plenty of nightlife, but a word to the wise: Avoid the temptation to buy or use drugs here. A foreigner involved with drugs will have a particularly difficult time with the Mexican authorities.

Bars

For a quiet drink and good people-watching, try **Video Bar Aladino** at the Mesón San Miguel, at the northern end of the plaza. Serious barhoppers like **Carlos 'n' Charlie's** (✉ Av. Rafael Melgar 11, between Calles 2 and 4 Norte, ☎ 987/20191) for hang-off-the-rafters, raucous fun; don't come here if you're the retiring type. Folks are always spilling out over the outdoor patio (sometimes literally) at **Sharkey's** (✉ Av. Rafael Melgar near Av. Benito Juárez, ☎ 987/21832), where a papier-mâché Marilyn Monroe in a *Some Like It Hot* pose surveys a rowdy crowd. The **Hard Rock Cafe** (✉ Av. Rafael Melgar 2A, near Av. Benito Juárez, ☎ 987/25271) includes all the nostalgic music memorabilia that characterizes the international chain. You and your friends provide the entertainment at the sing-along **Laser-Karaoke Bar** (✉ Fiesta Inn, ☎ 987/22811). The Terminator and Rambo have done it again with a new **Planet Hollywood** (✉ Rafael Melgar 161, ☎ 987/25795). Jock types can play video games or check football scores at the **Sports Page Video Bar and Restaurant** (✉ Corner 5 Av. Norte and Calle 2 Norte, ☎ 987/21199).

Discos

Scaramouche (✉ Av. Rafael Melgar at Calle Rosada Salas, ☎ 987/20791) features a fantastic laser show and a large dance area. **Neptuno** (✉ Av. Rafael Melgar at Calle 11 Sur, ☎ 987/21537), preferred by the teenage set and locals, can be loud and fun. However, both of these discos are often empty except on weekends.

Live Music

Sunday evenings, 8–10 PM, locals head for the *zócalo* (plaza) to hear mariachis and island musicians playing tropical tunes. The piano bar in **La Gaviota** (✉ Crown Princess Sol Caribe Cozumel, ☎ 987/20700, ext. 251) is well attended, and trios and mariachis perform nightly in the lobby bar from 5 to 11 during high season. For romantic piano or guitar serenades, try the dining room of **Arrecife** (✉ Presidente Inter-Continental Cozumel hotel, ☎ 987/20322; low season only). If Frank Sinatra–style entertainment turns you on, check out **Tony Rome's** (✉ Av. 5 Sur 21, between Av. Rosado Salas and Calle 3 Sur, ☎ 987/ 20131), where the owner holds forth at the microphone. In addition to tasty lobster dishes, **Joe's Lobster House** (✉ Av. 10 Sur 229, between Calle Rosada Salas and Calle 3 Sur, ☎ 987/23275) serves up lively reggae and salsa every night at 10:30; this is *the* hot spot for live entertainment.

OUTDOOR ACTIVITIES AND SPORTS

Most people come to Cozumel to take advantage of the island's water-related sports—scuba diving, snorkeling, and fishing are particularly big, but jet skiing, sailboarding, waterskiing, and sailing remain popular as well. You will find services and rentals throughout the island, especially through major hotels and water-sports centers such as **Del Mar Aquatics** (⊠ Carretera a Chankanaab, Km 4, ☎ 987/21665 or 800/877–4383, FAX 987/21833) and **Aqua Safari** (⊠ Av. Rafael Melgar 429, between Calles 5 and 10 Sur, ☎ 987/20101).

Fishing

For the past 22 years the annual **International Billfish Tournament,** held the last week in April or the first week in May, has drawn anglers from around the world to Cozumel; for more information contact the International Billfish Tournament (⊠ Box 442, Cozumel 77600, ☎ 800/253–2701, FAX 987/20999).

You must obey regulations forbidding commercial fishing, sportfishing, spear fishing, and the collection of any marine life between the shore and El Cantil Reef and between the cruise-ship dock and Punta Celerain. As part of a growing conservation movement, it's forbidden to kill certain species, including billfish, so be prepared to return prize catches to the sea. (Regular participants in the annual billfish tournament have seen some of the same fish—notched by successful anglers—caught over and over again.) U.S. Customs allows you to bring up to 30 pounds of fish back into the country.

Charters

High-speed fishing boats can be chartered for $300 for a half day or $350 for a full day, for a maximum of six people, from the **Club Náutico de Cozumel** (⊠ Puerto de Abrigo, Av. Rafael Melgar, Box 341, ☎ 987/20118 or 800/253–2701, FAX 987/21135), the island's headquarters for game fishing. Full-day rates include the boat and crew, tackle and bait, and lunch with beer and soda (lunch isn't included on half days). You can also book three- and four-day trips from the United States at discounted rates. Daily charters are easily arranged from the dock or at your hotel, but you might also try **Aquarius Fishing and Tours** (⊠ Calle 3 Sur, ☎ 987/21092) or **Dive Cozumel** (⊠ Av. Rosado Salas 72, at Av. 5 Sur, ☎ 987/24110, FAX 987/21842). The latter's general manager, Mariano Miguel Mendoza, is a font of knowledge about fishing and diving on the island. All rates vary with the season.

Scuba Diving

The diversity of options for divers in Cozumel includes deep dives, drift dives, shore dives, wall dives, and night dives, as well as theme dives focusing on ecology, archaeology, sunken ships, and photography. With all the shops to choose from (there are now over 100) divers, especially those with less experience or who don't bring their own equipment, should look for high safety standards and documented credentials. Make sure your instructor has PADI certification (or FMAS, the Mexican equivalent) and is affiliated with the **SSS recompression chamber** (⊠ Calle 5 Sur 21B, between Av. Rafael Melgar and Av. 5a Sur, next to Discover Cozumel, ☎ 987/22387 or 987/21848) or the recompression chamber at the **Hospital Civil** (⊠ Av. 11 Sur, between Calles 10 and 15, ☎ 987/20140 or 987/20525). These chambers, which aim for a 35-minute response time from reef to chamber, treat decompression sickness, commonly known as "the bends"; it occurs when divers surface too quickly and nitrogen is absorbed into the bloodstream. Other injuries treated here include nitrogen narcosis, collapsed lungs, and overexposure to the cold. Most of the dive shops in town offer complete dive accident coverage for just $1 per day.

Diving requires that you be reasonably fit. It should also go without saying that—particularly if you are new to diving—you should find a qualified instructor. Another caveat: Always stay at least 3 ft above the reef, not just because the coral can sting or cut you, but also because coral is easily damaged and grows very slowly: It has taken 2,000 years for it to reach its present size.

Dive Shops and Tour Operators

Most dive shops can provide you with all the incidentals you'll need, as well as with guides and transportation. You can choose from a variety of two-tank boat trips and specialty dives ranging from $45 to $60; two-hour resort courses cost about $50–$60, and 1½-hour night dives, $30–$35. Basic certification courses, such as PADI's Discover Scuba or Naui's introductory course, are available for about $350, while advanced certification courses cost as much as $700. Equipment rental is relatively inexpensive, ranging from $6 for tanks or a lamp to about $8–$10 for a regulator and B.C. vest; underwater camera rentals can cost as much as $35, video camera rentals run about $75, and professionally shot and edited videos of your own dive are priced at about $160.

Because dive shops tend to be competitive, it is well worth your while to shop around when choosing a dive operator. In addition to the dive shops in town, many hotels have their own operations and offer dive and hotel packages starting at about $350 for three nights, double occupancy, and two days of diving. You can also pick up a copy of the *Chart of the Reefs of Cozumel* in any dive shop. Before choosing a shop among the many choices, check credentials, look over the boats and equipment, and consult experienced divers who are familiar with the operators here. Here's a list to get you started on your search: **Aqua Safari** (⌧ Av. Rafael Melgar 429, between Calles 5 and 10 Sur, ☎ 987/20101); **Black Shark** (⌧ Av. 5 Sur between Rosado Salas and 3 Sur, ☎ 987/25657); **Blue Angel** (⌧ Av. Rafael Melgar, next to Hotel Villablanca, ☎ 987/21631), for PADI certification; **Blue Bubble** (⌧ Av. 5a Sur at Calle 3 Sur, ☎ 987/21865), for PADI instruction; **Chino's Scuba** (⌧ Av. Adolfo Rosado Salas 16A, ☎ 987/24487); **Dive Cozumel** (⌧ Av. Rosado Salas 72, at Av. 5 Sur, ☎ 987/24110, ℻ 987/21842); **Dive Paradise** (⌧ Av. Rafael Melgar 601, 987/21007); **Michelle's Dive Shop** (⌧ Av. 5 Sur 201, at Calle Adolfo Rosado Salas, ☎ 987/20947); **Ramone Zapata Divers** (⌧ Chankanaab Nature Park, ☎ 987/20502); **Scuba Du** (⌧ Presidente Inter-Continental Cozumel hotel, ☎ 987/20322 or 987/21379, ℻ 987/24130); **Studio Blue** (⌧ Calle Rosado Salas 121, between Calles 5 and 10, 987/24330); **Tico's Dive Center** (⌧ Av. 5 Norte 121, between Calles 2 and 4, ℻ 987/20276).

Nitrox Solutions. This operation offers Nitrox air produced by the DNAx Membrane System, which allows divers considerably longer bottom time with less fatigue. Their training facility includes PADI, ACUC, and IANTD specializing in Nitrox certification. They also offer certification using Cochran Re-Breathers. Their standards of safety are impeccable. ⌧ *Calle 3 Sur between the waterfront and Av. 5, for dives; Av. 65 Sur y Morelos, for main store, classroom, fill station,* 987/25666 for both locations.

Reef Dives

The reefs stretch for 32 km (20 mi), beginning at the international pier and continuing on to Punta Celerain at the southernmost tip of the island. The following is a rundown of Cozumel's main dive destinations.

CHANKANAAB REEF

This inviting reef lies just south of Chankanaab Nature Park, about 350 yards offshore. Crabs, lobster, tang, and angels inhabit the coral formations at about 55 ft. Drift a bit farther south to see the **Balones de Chankanaab,** balloon-shape coral heads at 70 ft.

COLOMBIA REEF

This reef, reaching 82–98 ft, is excellent for experienced divers who want to take some deep dives. Its underwater structures are as labyrinthine and varied as those of Palancar (☞ *below*); large groupers, jacks, eagle rays, and even an occasional sea turtle cluster at the mouths of caves and near the overhangs.

MARACAIBO REEF

Generally considered the most difficult of all the Cozumel reefs for divers, this one—located off the southern end of the island—lends itself to drift dives because of its length. You don't even see the ledge of the reef until you go 121 ft below the surface. Although there are shallow areas, only advanced divers who can cope with the current should attempt Maracaibo.

PALANCAR REEF

This reef system, situated nearly 2 km (1 mi) offshore, offers about 40 dive locations. Black and red coral and huge elephant-ear sponges and barrel sponges are among the attractions at the bottom. The reef, which begins at about 15 ft below the surface, is particularly suitable for drift dives. A favorite of divers is the section called **Horseshoe,** comprising several coral heads at the top of the drop-off. Towering coral columns and deep caves, tunnels, and canyons make for some of the most sensational dives in the Caribbean.

PARAÍSO REEF

Just north of the cruise-ship pier, about 328 ft offshore and up to 30 ft deep, Paraíso provides a practice spot for divers before they head to deeper drop-offs. Also a wonderful site for night diving, this reef is inhabited by star coral, brain coral, sea fans and other gorgonians, and sponges, as well as sea eels and yellow rays. From Paraíso you can swim out to the drop-offs called **La Ceiba** and **Villa Blanca.**

PASEO EL CEDRAL

Also known as Cedar Pass, this seldom-dived reef, just northeast of Palancar Reef, contains a spectacular series of small caverns full of fish. At depths ranging 35–55 ft, you're likely to see sea turtles, moray eels, eagle rays, and groupers among the larger specimens.

PLANE WRECK

During a 1977 Mexican motion picture production, this airplane was sunk about 300 ft away from the La Ceiba pier. Because of its reassuring proximity to the shore and because the average depth of the water is only 9–30 ft, it has been a favorite training ground for neophyte divers ever since. Enormous coral structures and colorful sponges surround the reef, while an underwater trail guides divers by the marine life.

SAN FRANCISCO REEF

Considered Cozumel's shallowest wall dive, this 1-km (½-mi) reef at the end of Old San Francisco Beach is teeming with marine life. It is best dived between 35 and 50 ft.

SANTA ROSA WALL

A renowned spot for deep dives and drift dives, this wall—just north of Palancar—drops off abruptly at 50 ft to enormous coral overhangs and caves below. Sponges are especially populous here, as are angelfish, groupers, and eagle rays—along with a shark or two.

TORMENTOS REEF

Sea fans and other gorgonians and sponges live on this variegated reef, where the maximum depth reaches about 70 ft. One of the best locations for underwater photography, Tormentos hosts sea cucumbers, arrow crabs, green eels, groupers, and other marine life, which provide a terrifically colorful backdrop.

YUCAB REEF

About 400 ft long and 55 ft deep, this reef is less than 1½ km (1 mi) from shore, near Chankanaab. Coral, sponge, sea whips, and angelfish swim in these waters, where the currents can reach 2 or 3 knots.

Snorkeling

Snorkeling equipment is available at the Presidente Inter-Continental, La Ceiba, Chankanaab Bay, Playa San Francisco, and Club Cozumel Caribe hotels, and directly off the beach near the Fiesta Americana Cozumel Reef and Playa Corona for less than $10 a day.

Tour Operators

Snorkeling tours run from $25 to $50, depending on the length, and take in the shallow reefs off Palancar, Colombia, and Yucab. Contact **Apple Vacations** (⌧ Av. 11 and Av. 30, ☎ 987/24311 or 987/20725) for snorkeling, sunset cruises, or tours around the island, or **Caribe Tours** (⌧ Av. Rafael Melgar at Calle 5 S., FAX 987/23100 or 987/23154) for information and reservations. **Fiesta Cozumel** (⌧ Calle 11 Sur 598, between Avs. 25 and 30, ☎ 987/20725, FAX 987/21389) runs snorkeling tours from the 45-ft catamaran *El Zorro*. Rates begin at about $50 per day and include equipment, a guide, soft drinks and beer, and a box lunch. The *Zorro* and the 60-ft catamaran *Fury* are also used for sunset cruises; the cost is under $35 for unlimited domestic drinks and live entertainment. You can book either of these sunset cruises through Caribe Tours.

SHOPPING

As in other Mexican resort destinations, Cozumel's shops accept dollars as readily as pesos, and many goods are priced in dollars. You'll get a better price everywhere on Cozumel if you pay with cash or traveler's checks, although credit cards—MasterCard and Visa more often than American Express, Diners Club, or Discover—are widely accepted. If you use plastic, however, you may be asked to pay a surcharge. Authorities and experienced travelers alike warn against buying from street vendors, because the quality of their merchandise leaves much to be desired, although this may not be apparent until it's too late.

Cruise ships traditionally dock at Cozumel on Monday, but there is traffic here almost every weekday, and the shops are the most crowded 10–11 and 1–2. Traditionally, stores are open 9–1 and 5–9, but a number of them, especially those nearest the pier, tend to disregard siesta hours and even open on weekends, particularly during high season. Don't pay much attention to written or verbal offers of "20% discounts, today only" or "only for cruise-ship passengers," because they're nothing but bait to get you inside. Similarly, many of the larger stores advertise "duty-free" wares, but these are of greater interest to Mexicans from the mainland than to North Americans since the prices tend to be higher than retail prices in the United States.

A last word of caution: Cruise-ship activities directors tend to push the black coral "factories." These should be avoided, not only because they are usually overpriced but also because coral is an endangered species.

Department Stores

Relatively small and more like U.S. variety stores than department stores, the following nevertheless carry a relatively wide array of goods, from the useful to the frivolous. **Chachy Plaza** (⊠ Av. Benito Juárez 5, near church at the back of plaza, ☎ 987/20130) sells everything from liquor and perfume to snorkeling gear and snack food. **Duty Free Mexico** (⊠ Av. Rafael Melgar at Calle 3 Sur, ☎ 987/20796) emphasizes top-line fragrances. **Pama** (⊠ Av. Rafael Melgar Sur 9, ☎ 987/20090), near the pier, carries imported food, luggage, snorkeling gear, jewelry, and crystal. **Prococo** (⊠ Av. Rafael Melgar Norte 99, ☎ 987/21875 or 987/21964) offers a good selection of liquor, jewelry, and gift items.

Shopping Districts, Streets, and Malls

Cozumel has three main shopping areas: **downtown** along the waterfront, on Avenida Rafael Melgar, and on some of the side streets around the plaza (there are more than 150 shops in this area alone); at the **crafts market** (⊠ Calle 1 Sur, behind the plaza) in town, which sells a respectable assortment of Mexican wares; and at the cruise-ship **passenger terminal** south of town, near the Casa Del Mar, La Ceiba, and Sol Caribe hotels. There are also small clusters of shops at **Plaza del Sol** (on the east side of the main plaza), **Villa Mar** (on the north side of the main plaza), the **Plaza Confetti** (on the south side of the main plaza), and **Plaza Maya** (across from the Sol Caribe). As a general rule the newer, trendier shops line the waterfront, while the area around Avenida 5a houses the better crafts shops. The **town market** (⊠ Calle Rosada Salas, between Avs. 20a and 25a) sells fresh produce and other essentials.

Specialty Stores

Clothing

Several trendy sportswear stores line Avenida Rafael Melgar (between Calles 2 and 6). **Miro** (⊠ Av. Rafael Melgar, 1 block from town pier, ☎ 987/20260) has a wide variety of Mexican resort wear in the latest styles. **Explora** (⊠ Av. Rafael Melgar 49, ☎ 987/20316) offers a casual line of modish cotton sports clothing.

La Fiesta Cozumel (⊠ Av. Rafael Melgar Norte 164-B, ☎ 987/22032), a large store catering to the cruise ships, sells a variety of T-shirts as well as souvenirs.

Jewelry

Jewelry on Cozumel is pricey, but it tends to be of higher quality than the jewelry you'll find in many of the other Yucatán towns. **Casablanca** (⊠ Av. Rafael Melgar Norte 33, ☎ 987/21177) specializes in gold, silver, and gemstones, as well as expensive crafts. The elegant **Diamond Creations** (⊠ Av. Rafael Melgar Sur 131, ☎ 987/25330 or 800/322–6476, FAX 987/25334) lets you custom design a piece of jewelry from an extensive collection of loose diamonds—or emeralds, rubies, sapphires, or tanzanite. Customers can select a stone and pick out a mounting, and the store will have it set in an hour in a ring, earrings, necklace, or bracelet. Nothing but fine silver, gold, and coral jewelry—particularly silver bracelets and earrings—is sold at **Joyería Palancar** (⊠ Av. Rafael Melgar Norte 15, ☎ 987/21468). Quality gemstones and striking designs are the strong point at **Rachat & Romero** (⊠ Av. Rafael Melgar 101, ☎ 987/20571). The toney **Van Cleef & Arpels** (⊠ Av. Rafael Melgar Norte 54, ☎ 987/21143) offers a superlative collection of high-end silver and gold jewelry.

Mexican Crafts

El Sombrero (✉ Av. Rafael Melgar 29, ☎ 987/20374) stocks a fine selection of leather clothing and accessories.

Gordon Gilchrist (✉ Studio I, Av. 25 Sur 981, at Calle 15 Sur, ☎ 987/22659), a local artist, displays—by appointment—limited editions of his black-and-white etchings of local Maya sites. He also sells handsome boxes of notepaper featuring these etchings.

Hammocks (✉ Av. 5a Norte and Calle 4, ☎ no phone) are made by Manuel Azueta and sold from his front porch.

Los Cinco Soles (✉ Av. Rafael Melgar Norte 27, ☎ 987/20132 or 987/22040) is your best bet for one-stop shopping. The nearly block-long store stocks an excellent variety of well-priced, well-displayed items, including blue-rim glassware, brass and tin animals from Jalisco, tablecloths and place mats, cotton gauze and embroidered clothing, onyx, T-shirts, papier-mâché fruit, reproduction Maya art, Mexican fashions, silver jewelry, soapstone earrings and beads, and other Mexican wares.

Na Balam (✉ Av. 5a Norte 14, ☎ no phone) sells high-quality Maya reproductions, batik clothing, and jewelry.

Talavera (✉ Av. 5a Sur 349, ☎ 987/20171) carries beautiful ceramics from all over Mexico—including tiles from the Yucatán—as well as masks from Guerrero, brightly painted wooden animals from Oaxaca, and carved chests from Guadalajara.

Unicornio (✉ Av. 5a Sur 1, ☎ 987/20171) specializes in Mexican folk art, including ceramic notions and etched wooden trays, but you'll have to sift through a lot of souvenir junk to find the good-quality items.

COZUMEL A TO Z

Arriving and Departing

By Cruise Ship

At least a dozen cruise lines call at Cozumel and/or Playa del Carmen, including, from Fort Lauderdale, **Chandris/Celebrity** (☎ 800/437–3111), **Cunard/Crown** (☎ 800/221–4770), and **Princess** (☎ 800/568–3262); from Miami, **Carnival** (☎ 800/327–9501), **Costa** (☎ 800/327–2537), **Dolphin/Majesty** (☎ 800/222–1003), **Norwegian** (☎ 800/327–7030), and **Royal Caribbean** (☎ 800/327–6700); from New Orleans, **Commodore** (☎ 800/327–5617); and from Tampa, **Holland America** (☎ 800/426–0327).

By Ferry

Passenger-only ferries depart from the dock at **Playa del Carmen** (☎ no phone; ☞ Chapter 5) for the 40-minute trip to the main pier in Cozumel. They leave approximately every hour between 5:15 AM and 8:45 PM and cost about $5 one way, $7 round-trip. Return service to Playa operates roughly from 4 AM to 7:45 PM. Verify the regularly changing schedule. The car ferry from **Puerto Morelos** (☎ 987/21722), on the mainland to the north of Playa del Carmen, is not recommended unless you *must* bring your car. The three- to four-hour trip costs about $30, depending on the size of the car, or $4.50 per passenger. Again, schedules change frequently, so we advise you to call ahead. Tickets can be bought up to a day in advance.

By Hydrofoil

A water-jet catamaran and two large speed boats make the trip between Cozumel (downtown pier, at the zócalo) and Playa del Carmen. This service, operated by **Aviomar** (✉ Av. 5a, between Calles 2 and 4, ☎

987/20588 or 987/20477), costs the same as the ferry and takes almost as much time, but the vessel is considerably more comfortable and offers on-board videos and refreshments. The boats make at least 10 crossings a day, leaving Playa del Carmen approximately every one to two hours between 5:15 AM and 8:45 PM and returning from Cozumel between 4 AM and 8 PM. Tickets are sold at the piers in both ports one hour before departure; call to confirm the schedule as it tends to be erratic.

By Plane

The **Cozumel Airport** (☎ 987/20928) is 3 km (2 mi) north of town. **Continental** (☎ 987/20487) provides nonstop service from Houston. **Mexicana** (☎ 987/20157) flies nonstop from Miami and San Francisco; **Aerocaribe** (☎ 987/20503) and **Aerocozumel** (☎ 987/20928), both Mexicana subsidiaries, fly to Cancún and other destinations in Mexico, including Chichén Itzá, Chetumal, Mérida, and Playa del Carmen. The airport departure tax is $16.

BETWEEN THE AIRPORT AND HOTELS

Because of an agreement between the taxi drivers' and the bus drivers' unions, there is no taxi service from the airport; taxi service is available *to* the airport, however. Arriving passengers reach their hotels via the *colectivo,* a van with a maximum capacity of eight. Buy a ticket at the airport exit: the charge is $5 per passenger to the hotel zones, a little under $3 into town. If you want to get to your hotel without waiting for the van to fill and for other passengers to be dropped off, you can hire an *especial*—an individual van costing a little under $20 to the hotel zones, about $8 to the city. Another alternative is walking out of the terminal to where the road begins and flagging a taxi exiting the airport after a drop-off. Taxis to the airport cost about $8 from the hotel zones and approximately $5 from downtown. Most car rental agencies (☞ Contacts and Resources, *below*) maintain offices in the terminal.

Getting Around

By Bicycle, Moped, and Motorcycle

Mopeds and motorcycles are very popular here, but also extremely dangerous because of heavy traffic, potholes, and hidden stop signs; accidents happen all too frequently. Mexican law now requires all passengers to wear helmets; it's a $25 fine if you don't. For mopeds go to **Auto Rent** (✉ Carretera Costera Sur, ☎ 987/20844, ext. 712), **Rentadora Caribe** (✉ Calle Rosada Salas 3, ☎ 987/20955 or 987/20961), or **Rentadora Cozumel** (✉ Calle Rosada Salas 3 B, ☎ 987/21503; Av. 10a Sur at Calle 1, ☎ 987/21120). Mopeds go for about $25 per day; insurance is included.

By Bus

Because of a union agreement with taxi drivers, no public buses operate in the north and south hotel zones; local bus service runs mainly within the town of San Miguel, although there is a route from town to the airport. Service is irregular but inexpensive.

By Car

Open-air Jeeps and other rental cars, especially those with four-wheel drive, are a good way of getting down dirt roads leading to secluded beaches and small Maya ruins (although the rental insurance policy may not always cover these jaunts). The only gas station on Cozumel, at the corner of Avenida Juárez and Avenida 30a, is open daily 7 AM–midnight.

By Taxi

Taxi service is available 24 hours a day, with a 25% surcharge between midnight and 6 AM, at the main location (⊠ Calle 2 Norte, ☎ 987/20041 or 987/20236) or at the malecón, (the oceanside walkway), at the main pier in town. You can also hail taxis on the street, and there are taxis waiting at all the major hotels. Fixed rates of about $3 are charged to go between town and either hotel zone, about $8 from most hotels to the airport, and about $6–$12 from the northern hotels or town to Chankanaab park or San Francisco beach. However, cruise-ship passengers taking taxis to or from the international terminal are often charged about twice as much as tourists staying on the island. **Taxi Tip:** When taking a cab into town from a cruise ship, remember that the driver is answering your question about the price in pesos and not in dollars. The cost from the cruise-ship terminal to San Miguel is about $4. For half that fare, simply cross the street and hail a cab into town. Also, take down the cab number in case you leave anything behind, otherwise it's gone for good.

Contacts and Resources

Banks

Banks are open weekdays 9–1:30. Hours for foreign currency exchange vary; your best bet is between 10 AM and noon. Banks include **Banpaís** (⊠ Across from main pier, ☎ 987/21682); **Bancomer** (⊠ Av. 5a at the plaza, ☎ 987/20550); **Banco del Atlántico** (⊠ Av. Rafael Melgar 11, ☎ 987/20142); and **Banco Serfín** (⊠ Calle 1 Sur between Avs. 5a and 10a, ☎ 987/20930).

MONEY EXCHANGE

If you need to exchange money after banking hours, go to **Promotora Cambiaria del Centro** (⊠ Av. 5a Sur between Calle 1 Sur and A.R. Salas), which provides service Monday–Saturday 8 AM–9 PM.

Car Rentals

Following is a list of rental firms that handle two- and four-wheel-drive vehicles (all the major hotels have rental offices): **Budget** (⊠ Av. 5a at Calle 2 Norte, ☎ 987/2090, 987/21732 cruise-ship terminal, 987/21742 airport), **Hertz** (☎ 987/23888 airport), **National Interrent** (⊠ Av. Juárez, Lote 10, near Calle 10, ☎ 987/23263 or 987/24101), and **Rentadora Aguilla** (⊠ Av. Rafael Melgar 685, ☎ 987/20729). Rental rates start at $50 a day.

Doctors and Dentists

The **Centro de Salud clinic** (⊠ Av. 20 at Calle 11, ☎ 987/20140) provides 24-hour emergency care, and the **Medical Specialties Center** (⊠ Av. 20 Norte 425, ☎ 987/21419 or 987/22919) offers 24-hour air ambulance service and a 24-hour pharmacy. Cozumel's newest medical treatment outlets are the **Cozumel Walk-In Clinic** (⊠ Calle 6 Norte and Av. 15, ☎ 987/24070) and **Cozumel Chiropractic** (⊠ Av. 5 Sur 24-A, between Calles 3 and 5, ☎ 987/25099); the latter offers bargain-priced therapeutic massage for overworked or injured muscles.

Emergencies

Police (⊠ Anexo del Palacio Municipal, ☎ 987/20409). **Red Cross** (⊠ Av. Rosada Salas at Av. 20a Sur, ☎ 987/21058). **Air Ambulance** (☎ 987/24070). **Recompression Chamber** (⊠ Calle 5 Sur 21-B, between Av. Rafael Melgar and Av. 5a Sur, ☎ 987/21430).

English-Language Bookstore

Publiciones Gracia (east side of the plaza, ☎ 987/20031) carries a limited selection of guidebooks and English-language publications and is open Monday–Saturday 8–2 and 4–10, and Sunday 9–1 and 5–10.

Guided Tours

See Travel Agencies and Tour Operators, *below,* for addresses and telephone numbers of the companies mentioned here.

A plane trip to **Chichén Itzá** (☞ Chapter 6) is offered by **Caribe Tours;**
the price of $145 includes the flight, transfers to the ruins, buffet
lunch, and a guide. The company also flies to the **Sian Ka'an Biosphere
Reserve** (☞ Chapter 5); in addition to lunch, this $160 plane trip in-
cludes a boat ride through the biosphere's mangroves for a closer look
at the flora and fauna of the region.

Rancho Buenavista (☎ 987/21537) runs four-hour guided horseback
tours that visit three Maya ruins tucked away in Cozumel's tropical
forest. The tour departs from Restaurant Acuario (⊠ Av. Rafael Melgar at Calle 11), weekdays at noon and Saturday at 11; the price ($60)
includes transportation to the ranch and soft drinks or beer during the
tour.

Tours of the island's sights, including San Gervasio ruins, El Cedral,
Chankanaab Park, and the museum and Archaeological Park, cost about
$35 and can be arranged through a travel agency such as **Fiesta
Cozumel. Caribe Tours** sells a similar tour, focusing on the botanical
gardens, archaeological replicas, and reef snorkeling at Chankanaab;
the cost is about $40 and includes an open-bar lunch. Another option
is to take a private taxi tour of the island; they range from $30 to $50
per day depending on which parts of the island you wish to visit.

Glass-bottom-boat trips are provided by **Turismo Aviomar** to people
who don't want to get wet but do want to see the brilliant underwater life around the island. The air-conditioned semi-submarine *Mer-
maid* glides over a number of reefs that host a dazzling array of fish;
the daily tour, which costs about $30, lasts 1 hour and 45 minutes and
includes soft drinks. A similar trip aboard the *Nautilus IV* is available
through **Fiesta Cozumel.**

Off-island tours to **Tulum and Xel-Há** (☞ Chapter 5), run by **Turismo
Aviomar** and **Caribe Tours,** cost about $75 and include the 30-minute
ferry trip to Playa del Carmen, the 45-minute bus ride to Tulum, 1½–
2 hours at the ruins, entrance fees, guides, lunch, and a stop for snorkeling at Xel-Há lagoon.

Day trips to the eco-archaeological theme park of **Xcaret,** about halfway
between Playa del Carmen and Tulum are offered by **Fiesta Cozumel.**
The $50 price includes round-trip ferry to Playa del Carmen, entrance
to the park, and a bilingual guide.

Late-Night Pharmacy

Farmacia Joaquín (⊠ North side of the plaza, ☎ 987/22520) is open
Mon.–Sat. 8 AM–10 PM and Sun. 9–1 and 5–9.

Mail

The local **post office** (⊠ Calle 7 Sur at Av. Rafael Melgar, ☎ 987/20106),
six blocks south of the square, is open weekdays 8–8, Saturday 9–5,
and Sunday 9–1. If you are an American Express cardholder, you can
receive mail at **Fiesta Cozumel/American Express** (⊠ Calle 11 Sur
598, between Avs. 25 and 30, ☎ 987/20725) weekdays 8–1 and 5–
8, and Saturday 8–5.

Publications

At the tourist office and at most shops and hotels around town, you can pick up the *Blue Guide, Cozumel Today Guide, Vacation Guide to Cozumel,* and *Cozumel Island's Restaurant Guide.* These publications, all free, tend to be heavily advertiser driven, but they are helpful all the same and contain good maps of the island and the downtown area.

Telephones

Long-distance calls can be placed from the well-signed **blue phones** around town. However, you'll save 10%–50% by making your calls at the **Calling Station** (⊠ Av. Rafael Melgar 27 and Calle 3 Sur, ℻ 987/21417). You can also exchange money and get one-day dry cleaning done at this handy outlet; it's open 8 AM–11 PM daily during high season (mid-December–April), Monday–Saturday 9 AM–10 PM and Sunday 9–1 and 5–10 the rest of the year.

Travel Agencies and Tour Operators

Apple Vacations (⊠ 11 and Av. 30th 598, ☎ 987/24311 or 987/20725), **Caribe Tours** (⊠ Av. Rafael Melgar at Calle 5 Sur, ℻ 987/23100 or 987/23154), **Fiesta Cozumel Holidays/American Express** (in all major hotel lobbies; ⊠ Calle 11 Sur 598, between Avs. 25 and 30, ☎ 987/20725), **Turismo Aviomar** (in several hotel lobbies, including El Presidente; ⊠ Av. 5 Norte 8, between Calles 2 and 4, ☎ 987/20588).

Visitor Information

State tourism office (⊠ Upstairs in the Plaza del Sol mall, at the east end of the main square, 987/20972), open weekdays 9–2:30. A good source of information on lodgings (and many other things) is the **Cozumel Island Hotel Association** (⊠ Calle 2 Norte at 15a, ☎ 987/23132, ℻ 987/22809), open weekdays 8–2 and 4–7. But *avoid* the "tourist information" booths on the main square: They're actually trying to sell time-share tours.

5 Mexico's Caribbean Coast

Although the eastern shore of the Yucatán from Cancún to Chetumal is no longer as pristine as it was in the past—what's been termed the Maya Riviera is becoming more and more developed—it still has plenty of secluded beach escapes. Get your fill of the social scene and Euro beach culture in Playa del Carmen, then head to more isolated spots such as the mangrove-filled Sian Ka'an Biosphere Reserve and the tranquil Xcalak peninsula. Visit the Maya ruins of Tulum and rub elbows with iguanas and cruise-ship passengers, or examine ancient civilizations in solitude at the Río Bec sites of Dzibanché and Kinichná, near Chetumal.

Updated by
Michele Back

ABOVE ALL ELSE, beaches are what define the eastern coast of the Yucatán peninsula. Soft, blindingly white strands of sand caressing clear turquoise waters filled with offshore coral reefs make the coastline of Quintana Roo a marvelous destination for lovers of the outdoors. The scrubby limestone terrain is punctuated by sinkholes and jungle foliage filled with wildlife, and the shores curve into calm lagoons or crash against cliffs.

The various destinations on the coast cater to different preferences. The once laid-back town of Playa del Carmen is now host to resorts as glitzy as those in Cancún and Cozumel, while Puerto Morelos retains the relaxed atmosphere of a Mexican fishing village. Rustic-themed but comfortable fishing and scuba diving lodges on the even more secluded Boca Paila and Xcalak peninsulas have a well-deserved reputation for bone fishing and superb diving on virgin reefs. The beaches, from Punta Bete to Sian Ka'an, south of Tulum, are beloved of scuba divers, snorkelers, birders, and beachcombers, and offer accommodations to suit every budget, from campsites and bungalows to condos and luxury hotels. Ecotourism is on the rise, with special programs designed to involve visitors in preserving the threatened sea-turtle population.

Then there are the Maya ruins at Tulum, superbly situated on a bluff overlooking the Caribbean, and, a short distance inland, at Cobá, whose towering jungle-shrouded pyramids evoke its importance as a leading center of commerce in the Maya world. South of Tulum, archaeological sites showing elements of the distinct Río Bec architectural style have been beautifully restored but are still largely unvisited by foreign tourists. At the Belizean border is Chetumal, a modern port and the capital of Quintana Roo; with its dilapidated clapboard houses and sultry sea air, it is more Central American than Mexican. The waters up and down the coast, abundant with shipwrecks and relics from the heyday of piracy, are dotted with mangrove swamps and minuscule islands where only the birds hold sway.

During your sojourn along the coast, you'll run into expats from around the world, running lodges and restaurants where you'd least expect to find them. Chat with them for a bit and they'll surely tell you how they succumbed to the spellbinding charm of the Caribbean coast, unable to resist the urge to stay.

Pleasures and Pastimes

Beaches
The Caribbean coast beaches—most blessed with white sand, clear, calm waters, and fringed by dense jungle foliage—are so various that they attract everyone from amateur archaeologists to professional divers and devoted sun worshipers.

Dining
Most of the restaurants along the Mexican Caribbean coast are simple beachside affairs with outdoor tables and *palapas* (thatched roofs). Decor is more quirky than elaborate, and casual attire is accepted, although reservations are not. In addition to their generally casual ambience, restaurants here offer bargains, especially when it comes to seafood, provided it is fresh and local, such as grouper, dorado, and sea bass. Shrimp, lobster, oysters, and other shellfish are usually flown in frozen from the Gulf or Pacific coast, and often you can taste the difference. Tourism and an expatriate presence mean that you'll find

a variety of flavorful cuisines in some surprising places, such as Bacalar and Puerto Morelos. And a number of places that have sprung up where tourists congregate, especially in Playa del Carmen and Puerto Aventuras, cater to North American tastes with pizza, burgers, and spaghetti.

Many restaurants have limited hours or close down in summer and during the hurricane season (September). For a description of Mexican culinary terms, *see* Dining *under* Pleasures and Pastimes *in the* Destination: Cancún, Cozumel, Yucatán Peninsula.

CATEGORY	COST*
$$$$	over $20
$$$	$15–$20
$$	$8–$15
$	under $8

per person, excluding drinks and service

Diving and Snorkeling

Quintana Roo attracts scuba divers and snorkelers with its transparent turquoise and emerald waters strewn with rose, black, and red coral reefs and sunken pirate ships. Schools of black, gray, and gold angelfish, luminous green-and-purple parrot fish, earth-colored manta rays, and scores of other jewel-toned tropical species seem oblivious to the clicking underwater cameras. The visibility in these waters reaches 100 ft, so you can see the marine life and topography without even getting wet. There is particularly good diving in Akumal and Punta Bete. Those who want to get away from all distractions except fish head for Banco Chinchorro.

A series of cenotes (sinkholes) lies just off the highway between Playa del Carmen and Tulum, and are favorites with divers, snorkelers, and swimmers. They sport such colorful names as **Car Wash, Dos Palomas, Dos Ojos,** and **Cenote Azul.** Highway signs identify them so they can be visited easily.

Fishing

Fishing ranks with diving and snorkeling as one of the most popular activities along the coast. For fly-fishing, boats can be rented from locals who run beachside stalls. Many local marinas run charters catering to those interested in Caribbean deep-sea fishing for such catches as marlin, bonito, and sailfish. Generally, larger hotels and specialist resorts have dive shops on the premises. Serious anglers often book a week or more on the Boca Paila peninsula.

Lodging

Accommodations on the Caribbean coast run the gamut from campsites to simple palapas and bungalows to middle-range, strictly functional establishments to luxury hotels and condominiums. Many of these hotels include two or three meals in their prices. The fanciest accommodations are in Playa del Carmen, Akumal, and Puerto Aventuras, while the coastline (including the Tulum area) is sprinkled with small campgrounds and hotels on solitary beaches. Note that hotel rates drop as much as 25% in the low season (September to approximately mid-December). In the high season, it's virtually impossible to find hotels in the $ price range, especially in Playa del Carmen, unless you opt to camp out.

South of Tulum, accommodations are more scarce and thus more pricey. However, some good deals for your money are available. Chetumal offers a respectable number of quality lodging options, as well as several hotels that appear to have been last renovated during the War of the Castes. These lodgings reflect the town's origins as a pit stop for traders en route to or from Central America and are popular with backpackers.

CATEGORY	COST*
$$$$	over $100
$$$	$70–$100
$$	$30–$70
$	under $30

All prices are for a standard double room in the high season (Dec.–Aug.), excluding service and the 12% tax.

Maya Ruins

Lovers of archaeology will not be disappointed here, as the magnificent remains of sacred cities attest to the power held by the coastal Maya in controlling trade routes along the Caribbean. Tulum, a walled city spread before the sea; Cobá, the largest inhabited city of the Maya peninsula; and the majestic stucco masks of Kohunlich are breathtaking. Mysterious temples with hidden chambers, stelae carved with images of deities, and the sounds of wildlife hidden in the jungles intermingle at these sites. One word of warning: If you plan to visit any of the ruins, don't forget your bug repellant, and slather it on at every opportunity.

Nature-Watching

The wildlife on the Caribbean coast is unsurpassed in Mexico, except perhaps in Baja California. Along the more civilized stretches of road, wild pigs, foxes, turkeys, iguanas, lizards, and snakes appear in the clearings. Jaguars, monkeys, white-tail deer, armadillos, tapir, wild boars, peccaries, ocelots, raccoons, and badgers all inhabit the tropical jungle's most isolated retreats. Birders come to stare into the jungle and seaside marshes for glimpses of parrots, toucans, terns, herons, and ibis. Onlookers are entertained by yellow, blue, and scarlet butterflies, singing cicadas and orioles, sparkling dragonflies, kitelike frigates, and night owls nesting in the trees.

The reefs, lagoons, cenotes, and caves along the Caribbean and down the Hondo river—which runs along the borders between Mexico, Belize, and Guatemala—are filled with alligators, giant turtles, sharks, barracuda, and manatees. During July and August sea turtles throng the beaches, laying thousands of eggs. Colorless crabs scuttle sideways toward the coconut groves, over pale white limestone and sand. Tiny mosquitoes and gnats bore through the smallest rips in window screens, tents, and mosquito nets.

Exploring the Caribbean Coast

The coast is divided into two areas: Puerto Morelos to Tulum, which has the most sites and places to lodge; and Tulum to Chetumal, where civilization thins out quite a bit and you find the most alluringly beautiful but remote beaches, coves, inlets, lagoons, and tropical landscapes.

Numbers in the text correspond to numbers in the margin and on the Mexico's Caribbean Coast map.

Great Itineraries

Stays of three to five days will give you enough time to visit the Puerto Morelos to Tulum area, seven days can be spread out along the entire coast, and longer visits will allow you to visit every attraction and village mentioned in this chapter. Playa del Carmen is a convenient base from which to explore, as it is closest to the major ruins of Tulum and Cobá, and has the best bus, taxi, and rental car service outside of Cancún. Venturing south of Tulum on a seven-day or longer trek requires a car, preferably a Jeep or other vehicle that will efficiently negotiate ruts and puddles the size of small Maya settlements.

IF YOU HAVE 3 DAYS

Get a room in **Playa del Carmen** ③ and start out by visiting **Akumal** ⑧ for a diving or deep-sea fishing excursion, snorkeling, or swimming. Later in the day cycle on a rented mountain bike or drive to the tiny lagoon of **Yalkú** ⑨, which was around during the time of the Maya traders. On day two, head out to the cenote at **Xel-Há** ⑫, where you can snorkel, swim, sunbathe, and see some more modest ruins. Day three, head for **Tulum** ⑭ to view the cliffside Castillo temple. Afterward, climb down to the small beach alongside it for a dip in the ocean.

IF YOU HAVE 5 DAYS

Again, stay in **Playa del Carmen** ③. Begin your travels by visiting **Xcaret** ④, an ecological theme park where you can swim with dolphins, snorkel in a cenote, and take in a Maya-themed folkloric performance at night. Spend the morning of day two at **Tulum** ⑭; you can then spend the afternoon cooling off at **Xel-Há** ⑫ or at one of the numerous cenotes along Highway 307. On day three, head for **Akumal** ⑧ and Yalkú ⑨. Spend day four at the archaeological ruins of **Cobá** ⑮. On day five, take a tour of the **Sian Ka'an Biosphere Reserve** ⑯.

IF YOU HAVE 7 DAYS

Follow the first five days of the above itinerary; on day six drive to the enormous **Laguna de Bacalar** ㉑ to marvel at its transparent layers of turquoise, green, and blue waters (it should take about three hours if you drive straight through). Visit the colonial San Felipe Fortress in the village of Bacalar and overnight in **Chetumal** ㉓, visiting the Museum of Maya Culture in the evening. On day seven, visit **Kohunlich** ㉔, which has huge stucco masks of its Maya rulers, surrounded by jungle ruins. Head into the nearby farmlands to do the StairMaster, Maya-style, at the pyramids of **Dzibanché** ㉕ and **Kinichná,** and then drive back up the coast to **Playa del Carmen** ③, stopping at the **Cenote Azul** ㉒, the largest sinkhole in Mexico, and at **Muyil** ⑰, with its small Maya temple and remote lagoon.

When to Tour the Caribbean Coast

If driving your own vehicle, get an early start to travel to the various destinations before the tour buses arrive. This is true practically the whole year round, as nearby Cancún, which is responsible for most of the tours, is the most popular resort in the country. Reach your overnight destination before dark as the majority of the main coastal highway is only two lanes and is not lit at night—nor does it have road reflectors. A four-lane segment is currently under construction between Cancún and Tulum, but until then, follow proper road etiquette—vehicles in front of you that have their left turn signal on are saying "pass me," not "I'm going to turn." If you venture south of Tulum, keep an eye out for military and immigration checkpoints. Have your passport handy, be friendly and cooperative, and don't carry any items that might land you in jail.

THE CARIBBEAN COAST

Quintana Roo, Mexico's youngest state and the one that geographically enfolds the Caribbean coast, entered the modern era in the 1970s, when Mexican politicians decided to develop the area for tourism. (It did not become a state until 1974, the same year that the first two hotels popped up at Cancún.) From Cancún to Tulum at most points the road is 1 or 2 km (½ to 1 mi) from the coast, thus there is little in sight but dense vegetation, assorted billboards, roadside artisans' markets,

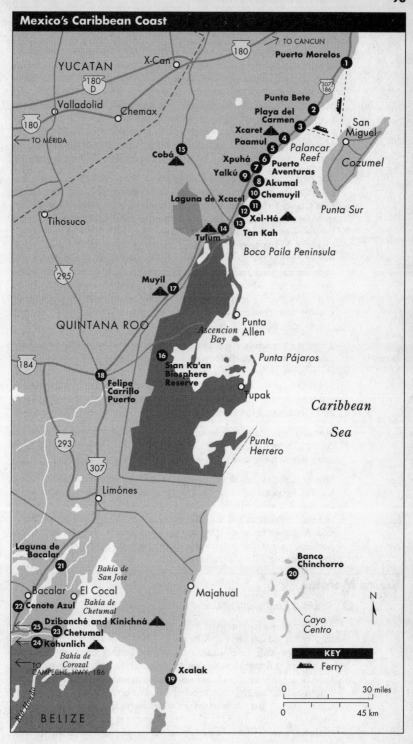

Mexico's Caribbean Coast

and signs marking the dirt-road entrances to the ruins, resorts, beaches, and campgrounds hidden off the road.

It won't stay that way for long. The Mexican government now allows development along the 130-km (81-mi) stretch of coastline known as the Cancún–Tulum Corridor. New hotel developments for the rest of the coastline south to Chetumal have also been announced. Each year more picture-coded international tourist signs crop up, pointing the way to more restaurants, gas stations, and hotels. Still, thanks to the federal government's foresight in setting aside a 36-km (22-mi) strip of coastline and jungle called Sian Ka'an Biosphere Reserve, wildlife and travelers who seek the Yucatán of old still have somewhere to go.

The music, food, and cultural traditions of the Caribbean coast are Yucatecan. The northern portion has a decided European influence. Cancún's transformation into a world-class resort has brought an international flair to the region. The Continental restaurants and glitzy shopping malls of the beach resort now flourish within 16 km (10 mi) of small Maya settlements. The coastline south of Tulum is more purely Maya: Seaside fishing collectives, jungles, and close-knit communities carry on ancient traditions. The far south, particularly Chetumal, is influenced by its status as a seaport and its proximity to Belize and Guatemala. The language spoken here is mainly Spanish and some Caribbean patois, and most visitors to the area are passing through to cross the border.

There isn't much in the way of nightlife on the coast unless you happen upon some entertainment in a luxury hotel bar. More and more restaurants in Playa del Carmen have live music at night on weekends, but there are no discos or nightclubs to speak of in the area. Xcaret offers an evening show Monday–Saturday that's chock full of folk dances and lore about Maya culture.

Nor are there many high-quality crafts available along the Caribbean coast, although the shopping situation has improved in Playa del Carmen, where more and more good folk-art shops are opening.

Our exploration of the Caribbean coast takes you from Puerto Morelos to Chetumal, with brief detours inland to the ruins of Cobá and the Río Bec sites. Highway 307, also known as Route 186, parallels the entire coastline for the 382 km (237 mi) from Cancún to Chetumal. Although buses do traverse the region and are popular with backpackers, a rental car or four-wheel-drive vehicle allows you to explore more thoroughly and creatively.

Puerto Morelos

❶ *36 km (22 mi) south of Cancún on Hwy. 307.*

Most people know Puerto Morelos only as the small coastal town where they catch the car ferry to Cozumel. It has been left remarkably free of the large-scale development so common farther south, though each year more and more tourists escape from Playa del Carmen to take in the easygoing pace, cheap accommodations, and convenient seaside location near a superb offshore coral reef. For obvious reasons this place is particularly attractive to divers, snorkelers, and anglers. The reef at Morelos is about 1,800 ft offshore. The caves of the sleeping sharks of documentary movie fame are only 8 km (5 mi) east of the town.

Morelos was once a point of departure for Maya women making pilgrimages by canoe to Cozumel, the sacred isle of the fertility goddess, Ixchel; today it is not very different from many small towns in the Spanish-speaking Caribbean. There is not much to it beyond a gas station,

In case you want to see the world.

At American Express, we're here to make your journey a smooth one. So we have over 1,700 travel service locations in over 120 countries ready to help. What else would you expect from the world's largest travel agency?

do more .

http://www.americanexpress.com/travel

Travel

In case you want to be welcomed there.

We're here to see that you're always welcomed at establishments everywhere. That's why millions of people carry the American Express® Card – for peace of mind, confidence, and security, around the world or just around the corner.

do more®

Cards

In case you're running low.

We're here to help with more than 118,000 Express Cash locations around the world. In order to enroll, just call American Express before you start your vacation.

do more

Express Cash

And just in case.

We're here with American Express® Travelers Cheques and Cheques *for Two*.® They're the safest way to carry money on your vacation and the surest way to get a refund, practically anywhere, anytime.

Another way we help you...

do more

Travelers Cheques

a central square, and auto repair shops. If you wander down the dirt streets north and south of town, you will notice neighborhoods of Mediterranean-style houses and condos, home to part-time residents who enjoy the town's laid-back mode. Nature endowed Puerto Morelos with a fine deep-sea port (the principal port for the area until the road to Puerto Juárez was built), so today ferries and freight ships call regularly. Most of the action is centered on the long pier south of the square, where vehicles line up for hours waiting for the ferry to depart. Three lighthouses from different eras break up the long stretch of beach, and boats to take out to the surrounding reefs can be rented on the beach.

Dining and Lodging

$ ✕ **Los Pelícanos.** If you're looking for good fresh fish or seafood—fried, grilled, steamed, or enhanced with garlic or tomato sauces—stop by this thatch-roofed restaurant on the beach where you can spend hours feasting on the catch of the day and watching the boats go by. ⊠ *Oceanfront near main plaza,* ☎ 987/10014. *MC, V.*

$$$$ ✕🏨 **Caribbean Reef Club at Villa Marina.** This sophisticated yet un-
★ pretentious little hideaway is one of the best escapes on the coast. The colonial-style suites and studios have marble floors, air-conditioning, ceiling fans, blue-tile kitchenettes, floral pastel linens, and arched windows. Sliding glass doors lead to balconies outside, where you can slip in an afternoon nap on your own private hammock. The adjacent restaurant is easily the most picturesque in town, with a balcony overlooking the sea, hand-painted tile tables, and candlelight at night. A Jamaican chef prepares superb coconut shrimp, seafood gumbo, jerk chicken, and other Caribbean specialties. A full-service PADI dive shop is on the premises, and hotel director Charles McLemore is nearly always around to make sure everything is up to par. ⊠ *South of ferry dock in Villa Marina,* ☎ 987/10191 *or* 800/3–CANCUN *in the U.S.,* ℻ 987/10190 *or* 98/83–2244 *in Cancún. 21 suites and studios. Restaurant, bar, pool, hot tub, dive shop, snorkeling, fishing. MC, V.*

$ ✕🏨 **Posada Amor.** One of Puerto Morelos's first hotels, this family-run property near the pier has been operating for more than 15 years. The humble rooms in several small buildings behind the restaurant have screened windows with dark blue draperies (helpful for late sleepers) and cement-slab beds. Only eight rooms offer private baths. The restaurant, a neighborhood gathering spot, serves great home-style Mexican meals, including a superb breakfast buffet, and has a full bar. ⊠ *Av. Xavier Rojo Gómez (1st street on right as you enter town),* ☎ 987/10033, ℻ 987/10178. ⊠ *Reservations: Box 806, Cancún, Quintana Roo 77580. 19 rooms. Restaurant. No credit cards. No traveler's checks.*

$$ 🏨 **Hotel Ojo de Agua.** Visitors looking for friendly lodging in a peaceful atmosphere right on the beach will be pleased with this family-run hotel. Half of the guest rooms have kitchenettes, and all rooms have ceiling fans and views of the sea or the courtyard gardens. An openair restaurant serves up great burgers, fish, and fun conversation near the small pool. ⊠ *2 blocks north of town,* ☎ 987/10027. *24 rooms. Restaurant, pool, dive shop. AE.*

$$ 🏨 **Los Arrecifes.** Located on an isolated (and sometimes windy) beach, Los Arrecifes is an older hotel that's been remodeled and redecorated. Its 12 one-bedroom apartments with kitchenettes, large living rooms, and balconies are in an ideal, private setting. ⊠ *8 blocks north of town on street closest to beach,* ☎ 987/10196, ℻ 987/10140, *goalship@cancun.rce.com.mx. 12 apartments. Kitchenettes. No credit cards.*

Outdoor Activities and Sports

WATER SPORTS

Snorkeling gear, fishing tackle, and boats can be rented from **El Faro Trips** (☎ 987/10275) on the town's main beach, by the plaza. The **Posada**

Amor hotel can also fix you up with diving and deep-sea fishing excursions. The **Caribbean Reef Club** can arrange diving, fishing, snorkeling, or mountain biking.

Side Trips

Croco-Cun. The biologists running this crocodile farm and miniature zoo just north of Puerto Morelos have collected specimens of most of the animals and reptiles indigenous to the area, and offer immensely informative tours to visitors willing to spend an hour or two learning about the jungle's wildlife. Self-guided tours, a coffee shop, and a gift shop are also on the premises. ✉ *Hwy. 307, Km 30,* ☎ *98/844782.* 🎫 *$4.* ⊘ *Daily 8:30–5:30.*

Dr. Alfredo Barrera Marín Botanical Garden. This 150-acre tropical forest a few miles south of Puerto Morelos off Highway 186 is the largest of its kind in Mexico. Named for a local botanist, the botanical garden is framed by mangroves on the east, facing the ocean, and harbors endangered species such as spider monkeys, toucans, and parrots. There's also a tree nursery, an orchid garden, a reproduction of a *chiclero* (gum collector), an authentic Maya house, and an archaeological site. ✉ *Hwy. 307, look for signs for turnoff to garden,* ☎ *no phone.* 🎫 *$3.* ⊘ *Daily 9–5.*

Punta Bete

❷ *22 km (14 mi) south of Puerto Morelos on Hwy. 307, then about 2 km (1 mi) off main road.*

The roads into Punta Bete may be paved with good intentions, but they aren't paved with anything resembling asphalt. However, once you finish the bumpy 2⅓-km (1½-mi) ride through the jungle, you'll arrive at a 6½-km (4-mi) long isolated beach dotted with bargain bungalow-style hotels and thatched-roof restaurants. Those who would prefer less grit in their personal belongings will find more comfortable accommodations up the road at the Posada del Capitán Laffite (☞ *below*).

Lodging

$$$$ 🔆 **Posada del Capitán Lafitte.** Set on an invitingly long stretch of
★ beach just 10 km (6 mi) north of Playa del Carmen at Punta Bete, this lodging is known for its genuinely chummy atmosphere; the "cute staff" factor figures in heavily here. The three-unit cabañas are clustered around various parts of the point, and each has its own private bath and ceiling fan; 31 units have air-conditioning. Four duplexes at the south end of the property have two-bedroom, two-bath units, ideal for families. If you have a choice, opt for the newer cabañas on the north end of the beach, which are furnished Mexican style as opposed to late-80s Miami style. Breakfast, dinner, tax, and tips are included in the room rate, so you rarely need to carry money. Group activities include snorkeling trips, horseback riding, fishing, and birding. All reservations must be prepaid. ✉ *Box 92, Playa del Carmen, Quintana Roo 77710. Dirt road (follow signs), about 3 km (2 mi) off Hwy. 307, Km 62,* ☎ *987/30214,* 📠 *987/30212, lafitte@diario1.sureste.com or lafitte@turqreef.com.* ✉ *Reservations: Turquoise Reef Group, Box 2664, Evergreen, CO 80439,* ☎ *303/674–9615 or 800/538–6802,* 📠 *303/674–8735. 62 rooms. Restaurant, bar, beach, pool, dive shop, shops, game room, airport shuttle, car rental. AE, MC, V.*

Outdoor Activites and Sports

WATER SPORTS

Posada del Capitán Lafitte (☎ *987/30214 or 800/538–6802*), off Highway 307 just north of Playa del Carmen, has an excellent, full-service dive shop called Treasure Hunters. Services include PADI certification courses, diving, snorkeling, and fishing excursions and specialty courses.

Playa del Carmen

❸ *10 km (6 mi) south of Punta Bete and 68 km (42 mi) south of Cancún.*

Only a few decades ago, Playa del Carmen was a deserted beach where Indian families raised coconut palms to produce copra and the odd foreigner wandered in to get away from it all. There are still a few foreigners-gone-native around, but the town—now the fastest growing on the coast, with a population of over 30,000—has become the preferred destination of travelers who want easy access to gorgeous beaches and the archaeological sights of the peninsula. Playa's alabaster-white beach and small offshore reefs lend themselves to excellent swimming, snorkeling, and turtle-watching. Those traveling the coast by car can stock up on supplies here, while those taking the bus often use Playa as their base camp, since it's the easiest jumping-off point for nearby sights. But Playa is no longer a budget destination, as prices, particularly at the hotels, have been increasing steadily. At the rate the town is growing, you might come back to Playa in two years and find it unfamiliar.

The village of Playa del Carmen, which lies midway between Cancún and Tulum, has undergone not only a tourist boom but also a beautification effort that has greatly enhanced its natural charms. A new water and sewage system was completed in 1994, and many of the main streets in town have been paved. **Avenida 5,** the first street running parallel to the beach, has been closed to vehicular traffic from the plaza to Calle 6 and turned into a pedestrian walkway with quaint little cafés and lots of street art and entertainment. Driving to the beachfront hotels is difficult unless you know exactly where you're going, and parking has become a nightmare. Restaurants and shops are multiplying faster than you can say *Kukulcán,* and many new businesses are branches of Cancún establishments whose owners have taken up permanent residence in Playa or commute daily between the two resorts. **Avenida Juárez,** running from the highway to the beach, is the main commercial zone for the Cancún–Tulum corridor. Here, locals escape the throngs of tourists in small food shops, hotels, pharmacies, auto-parts and hardware stores, and banks lining the curbs. The bus station marks the end of Avenida Juárez.

The busiest parts of Playa are down by the ferry pier, Avenida Juárez, and along the pedestrian walkway. Take a stroll north from the pier along the beach and you'll find a more peaceful part of town: simple restaurants roofed with palm fronds, where people sit drinking beer for hours; a few campgrounds; and overgrown tropical foliage. On the south side of the pier is the **Continental Plaza Playacar,** a first-class, lavish hotel that brought a sense of luxury and style to Playa del Carmen in 1991. Several more all-inclusive hotels, including the **Diamond Resort** and the **Royal Maeva,** have opened in the immense Playacar complex. Within the development is an 18-hole championship golf course.

Playa has acquired the confident veneer of an up-and-coming beach destination, which can be attributed, in part, to the amiability of the locals (including the growing number of expatriates who manage many of the hotels and restaurants). Peace and quiet may not be the operative words here, but the town does provide a fun introduction to the Caribbean coast, and, at least for now, is more low key than Cancún or Cozumel.

Dining and Lodging

$$ ✕ **Da Gabi.** If you can tolerate the slightly pretentious air at this restaurant, you'll be rewarded with high-quality Italian cuisine. Visitors flock here at night to dine on remarkable Italian cuisine under a romantic candlelit palapa. Enjoy the Maya chef's homemade fettuccine, spinach ravioli, angel hair pasta with fresh tomatoes, or oven-baked pizza. You can't go wrong with the daily specials either—salmon antipasto or carpaccio with capers and Parmesan cheese slices, for example. Top your meal off with an espresso or cappuccino. ⊠ *Av. 1 and Calle 12, Da Gabi Hotel,* ☎ *987/30048. No credit cards. No lunch.*

$$ ✕ **La Parrilla.** This deservedly popular chain wins the prize for qual-
★ ity Mexican food served with a unique flair. The open-air restaurant sits a few feet above the street, and the smell of the sizzling *parrilla mixta* (a grilled, marinated mixture of lobster, shrimp, chicken, and steak) makes it hard to resist grabbing one of the few available tables. Other Mexican-inspired dishes, such as fajitas, are available. Friendly service, strong margaritas, and live music help keep things lively until the wee hours of the morning. ⊠ *Av. 5, at Calle 8,* ☎ *987/ 30687. AE, MC, V.*

$$ ✕ **Limones.** A romantic little spot right off Avenida 5, this restaurant offers dining by candlelight, either alfresco in a courtyard or under the shelter of a palapa indoors. Wine bottles hanging from the ceiling and soft guitar music add to the amorous atmosphere. House favorites include copious entrées such as fettuccine, lasagna, and lemon-sautéed beef scaloppine. The daily dinner special is the best bargain in town. ⊠ *Av. 5 at Calle 6,* ☎ *no phone. MC, V.*

$$ ✕ **Máscaras.** The wood-burning brick oven here produces exception-
★ ally good thin-crusted pizzas and breads; the homemade pastas are also excellent. Fresh-squeezed, sweetened lime juice, margaritas, wine, and beer help wash down the rich Italian fare. Be sure to try the smoked salmon pizza or calamari in garlic and oil or—the most popular item on the menu—the four-cheese pizza. The wine cellar stocks good Italian reds. Masks from throughout the world cover the walls. Since it opened in 1983, Máscaras has been unfailingly popular with locals and the workers from the hotels, and is a central gathering spot with a view of the goings-on at the main plaza. ⊠ *Av. Juárez, across from plaza,* ☎ *987/31053. MC, V. No lunch.*

$$ ✕ **Zulu Lounge.** Despite the odd combination of African decor, Thai food, techno music, and pool tables, this funky restaurant keeps visitors coming back with its savory food and laid-back service. Thai dishes such as spring rolls, stir-fried vegetables, and *pad thai* (a noodle dish) are available, but those with bold palates should definitely try the curries, ranging from yellow (slightly spicy) to red (powerfully spicy). Finish off your meal with a decidedly un-Thai but nevertheless tasty slice of cheesecake and cappuccino. ⊠ *Av. 5, near Calle 8,* ☎ *no phone. MC, V. No lunch.*

$ ✕ **El Tacolote.** Meat, margaritas, and mariachi music define this two-story eatery made cheery with bold primary colors and Christmas tree lights. Street bands playing a variety of Mexican music entertain diners feasting on platters of grilled meats, fajitas, or tacos with all sorts of fillings. You can eat cheaply or splurge on a multicourse feast while watching the action on the plaza from an outdoor table. ⊠ *Av. Juárez, across from plaza,* ☎ *987/31363. MC, V.*

$ ✕ **Sabor.** Owner Melinda Burns tried several locations for her café/bakery before she settled on the pedestrian-only stretch of Avenida 5, where patrons have a good view of local goings-on. Its homemade baked goods—chocolate cakes, brownies, and apple pies—have made this place famous. It's hard to find a seat at breakfast time, when locals and travelers drop by for granola, fruit salads, and whole-wheat muffins. You may also be enticed by the giant goblets of blended fruit drinks. Stick with breakfast and snacks here, as the burgers, sandwiches, and other main dishes tend to be a bit dry. ⊠ *Av. 5 between Calles 3 and 4,* ☎ *no phone. No credit cards.*

$$$$ 🏨 **Allegro Resort.** Opened in 1992 as part of the Playacar development, Allegro is an all-inclusive resort that sprawls down a sloping hill to the sea. The guest rooms are spread out in thatch-roofed villas along winding paths; the dining room, bar, lobby, and entertainment areas are housed in a gigantic multipeaked palapa. Unlike many all-inclusive resorts, Allegro's design allows peace and privacy. One pool is used for games and activities, while another is reserved for quiet lounging. Guests get a bit rowdy at the karaoke bar and outdoor stage, but the noise does not reach the guest rooms. Buffet-style meals are plentiful and imaginatively prepared; there are also two à la carte restaurants. Playa del Carmen is a 20-minute walk or a $4 cab ride north. ✉ *Playacar development*, ☎ *987/30339*, FAX *987/30346*. ✉ *Reservations: 901 Ponce de León Blvd., Suite 400, Coral Gables, FL 33134*, ☎ *800/ 858–2258*, FAX *305/444–4848. 296 rooms. 3 restaurants, bar, 2 pools, 4 tennis courts, dive shop, shops, children's program (ages 4–12), car rental. AE, MC, V.*

$$$$ 🏨 **Continental Plaza Playacar.** Playa del Carmen became a first-class tourism destination when the Playacar hotel opened in October 1991. The centerpiece of an 880-acre master-planned resort, Playacar faces the sea on the south side of the ferry pier. A blush-color palace, it possesses all the amenities of its competitors at the larger resort towns. The tropical-style rooms have ocean views and balconies or patios, marble baths, blonde-wood furnishings, satellite TV, and in-room safes. The beach is one of the nicest in Playa del Carmen, and far less crowded than those to the north. Mexican and international dishes are served at a restaurant in the main building and a palapa by the pool. A full-scale scuba and water-sports facility offers diving, snorkeling, sailing, and waterskiing. There's also an 18-hole championship golf course; ask about golf packages. ✉ *Fraccionamiento Playacar (north end of Playacar development), Playa del Carmen, Quintana Roo 77710*, ☎ *987/30100 or 800/882–6684. 188 rooms, 16 suites. 2 restaurants, bar, pool, 18-hole golf course, tennis court, dive shop, beach, shops, travel services, car rental. AE, MC, V.*

$$$$ 🏨 **Mayan Paradise.** The architecture of this hotel at the northern end
★ of town is a successful updating of old Maya style; the rooms are set in two-story bungalows with thatched roofs, terraces, and dark hardwood siding, and they surround a pretty pool and jungle palms. Local hardwood from the sapodilla tree also lines the walls of the guest rooms, which have all the amenities of a luxury hotel at reasonable prices (low end of $$$$). Each has a small kitchenette, color satellite TV, two double beds, room safe, and air-conditioning. Suites even have whirlpool baths. The restaurant and bar are under a palapa and meals are served at a fixed time each day; a buffet breakfast is included in the price of the room. Although not on the ocean, the hotel has its own private beach club and complimentary shuttle service for guests. ✉ *Av. 10 between Calles 12 and Bis, 987/30933. 40 rooms, 3 suites. Restaurant, bar, pool, travel services, free parking. AE, MC, V.*

$$$$ 🏨 **Royal Maeva Playacar.** This all-inclusive Mexican club opened in 1996 in the Playacar development south of the ferry pier and draws plenty of Italian and German vacationers. The complex looks like a small, salmon-color Mexican village sprinkled liberally with red-tiled roofs and colonial arches. Several pools surround a thatched pavilion restaurant in the middle of the tropical garden, beyond which is a powder-sand beach that stretches several miles north to town. The friendly staff of guest pleasers called "Maeva Amigos" hail mainly from Europe and are fluent in several different languages. Free room service, in-room minibars, scuba diving (additional cost), and snorkeling trips keep the Maeva in step with its all-inclusive neighbors down the beach. ✉ *Playacar development*, ☎ *987/31150*, FAX *987/31169. 286 rooms.*

4 *restaurants, 4 bars, 4 pools, 4 tennis courts, basketball, exercise room, volleyball, beach, snorkeling, theater, children's program (ages 5–10), convention center, meeting rooms, travel services, car rental, free parking. AE, DC, MC, V.*

$$$$ 🔟 **Shangri-La Caribe.** Similar to Las Palapas (☞ *below*) next door, Shangri-La's attractive whitewashed bungalows, capped with palapa roofs, have hammocks out front and ceiling fans inside; the oceanfront cabañas also have sitting areas. Music blares from the tropical-style bar, where the French, German, and American clientele gather around the pool table. You can order American or Mexican food à la carte at the spacious restaurant. ⊠ *Dirt road off Hwy. 307, midway between Punta Bete and Playa del Carmen.* ⊠ *Reservations: Turquoise Reef Group, Box 2664, Evergreen, CO 80439,* ☎ *303/674–9615 or 800/538–6802,* 🖷 *303/674–8735. 70 bungalows. Restaurant, bar, coffee shop, pool, beach, dive shop, snorkeling, fishing, shops, car rental. AE, MC, V.*

$$$–$$$$ 🔟 **Baal Nah Kah.** This home-away-from-home is tucked along a sandy
   ★   street just off the main drag. Baal Nah Kah, which means "home hidden among the gum trees" in Maya, offers guests the use of a big kitchen, sitting/living room, and barbecue pit. A convenient block from the beach, the guest house has five bedrooms and one studio on various levels, affording complete privacy. Two rooms have spacious balconies with a panoramic view of the ocean; all come with tile baths, two fans or air-conditioning, double or king-size beds, and Mexican decor. A small café serving breakfast, snacks, and light meals is next door. ⊠ *Calle 12 between Av 5 and Av. 1,* ☎ *987/30110,* 🖷 *987/30050.* ⊠ *Reservations: Turquoise Reef Group, Box 2664, Evergreen, CO 80439,* ☎ *303/674–9615 or 800/538–6802,* 🖷 *303/674–8735. 5 rooms, 1 apartment. No credit cards.*

$$$ 🔟 **Albatros Royale.** The nicest complex right on the beach, the Royale opened in 1991 but still looks brand new. Two-story palapa-covered buildings face each other along a pathway to the sand, resembling a small village. Sea breezes and ceiling fans cool the small rooms, simply decorated with white walls and tile floors; five have a view of the ocean. If you choose, a breakfast buffet across the street at the sister **Pelicano Inn** hotel (☞ *below*) will be included in your room rate. The Royale fills up quickly; advance reservations are advised. ⊠ *Calle 8 between beach and Av. 5,* ☎ *987/30001,* 🖷 *987/30002.* ⊠ *Reservations: Turquoise Reef Group, Box 2664, Evergreen, CO 80439,* ☎ *303/ 674–9615 or 800/538–6802,* 🖷 *303/674–8735. 31 rooms. Restaurant, in-room safes, dive shop, travel services, car rental. MC, V.*

$$$ 🔟 **El Tucan Condotel Villas and Beach Club.** This lodging in the residen-
   ★   tial north end of town looks like a very exclusive and expensive hotel but actually is the best deal for your money in Playa. Catering to an eclectic European crowd, it is set around a huge jungle garden with a pool, winding flagstone paths, even a cenote, and offers the ultimate in tranquility well away from the noise of downtown Avenida 5; however, it's a mere 10-minute walk to get there. All rooms and suites in the slate-colored buildings are fairly well separated from one another and have attractive accents such as burnished tile floors and painted wood furniture. Each has a private terrace, overhead fan, and tiny kitchenette; groceries can be purchased at a small store on the premises. A buffet breakfast is included at the Tukan Maya restaurant across the street, which also offers lunch and dinner à la carte. ⊠ *Av. 5 between Calles 14 and 16, Quintana Roo 77710,* ☎ *987/30417,* 🖷 *987/30668. 56 rooms, 55 suites. Restaurant, bar, grocery, pool, beach club, bicycles. MC, V.*

$$$ 🔟 **Las Palapas.** German manager Gunter Spath has made Las Pala-
   ★   pas into an ideal get-away-from-it-all destination resort with his friendly personality and attention to detail; many guests stay for 10 days or more. White cabañas are trimmed in blue, and duplexes have balconies

or porches and hammocks. The thatch roofs and hexagonal shape of the buildings enhance the ocean breezes, making air-conditioning unnecessary. German tour groups keep the hotel's occupancy up to 80% year-round; make reservations early. Room rates include creative and tasty breakfasts and dinners. ⊠ *Hwy. 307, Km 292, Box 116, Playa del Carmen, Quintana Roo 77710,* ☎ *987/3–0582 or 800/433–0885,* FAX *987/3–0458. 75 cabanas. 2 restaurants, 2 bars, in-room safes, pool, beach, shops. AE, MC, V.*

$$$ 🏨 **Molcas.** This colonial-style hotel has been in business for 20 years, dating back to when Playa was a quaint fishing village. The hotel has aged gracefully, offering air-conditioned rooms graced with dark-wood furniture facing the pool, the sea, or the street. Rooms are well insulated from any outside noise. Your shopping needs—from gold jewelry to Cuban cigars—can be met right outside on the street that slopes down toward the ferry pier. ⊠ *Av. 5 at Calle 1, Box 79, Quintana Roo 77710,* ☎ *987/30070,* FAX *987/30138. 24 rooms. Restaurant, bar, pool, shops, travel services, car rental. AE, MC, V.*

$$$ 🏨 **Pelicano Inn.** Formerly Cabañas Albatros, this sister hotel to the Albatros Royale (☞ *above*) is a peaceful enclave of white stucco and plants. The entrance is an odd tunnel painted with scenes from the deep. Six rooms face the ocean directly; the other 32 have peekaboo views of the sea. All are spacious and offer ceiling fans, private bathrooms, and double beds. Breakfast is included in the price of the room. ⊠ *On beach at Calle 8,* ☎ *987/30997,* FAX *987/30998.* ⊠ *Reservations: Turquoise Reef Group, Box 2664, Evergreen, CO 80439,* ☎ *303/674–9615 or 800/538–6802,* FAX *303/674–8735. 38 rooms. Restaurant. MC, V.*

$$ 🏨 **Alejari.** This two-story complex set amid lush gardens is one of the most pleasant accommodations on Playa's north beach and the best deal, although noise from the nearby bars could disturb light sleepers late into the night. Some rooms have kitchenettes, while all offer fans or air-conditioning. A hearty breakfast comes with the room, and the Mexican family that owns the hotel is extremely friendly and accommodating. ⊠ *Calle 6N, on the beach,* ☎ *987/30372,* FAX *987/30005.* ⊠ *Reservations: Box 166, Playa del Carmen, Quintana Roo 77710. 29 rooms. Restaurant, kitchenettes. AE, MC, V.*

$$ 🏨 **Delfín.** Though not on the beach, the Delfín is a good choice for its bright, airy rooms decorated with colorful mosaics and cooled by sea breezes and fans or air-conditioning. Safety deposit boxes are available inside each room, while everything you need or want in Playa is within immediate walking distance. The management is exceptionally helpful. ⊠ *Av. 5 at Calle 6, Playa del Carmen, Quintana Roo 77710, 987/30176. 14 rooms. MC, V (5% fee).*

$$ 🏨 **Maya-Bric.** Tucked away a few blocks from the hustle and bustle of the main drag, the Maya-Bric offers a tranquil escape in its landscaped courtyard and pool area; the staff, however, could benefit from charm school. The rooms have fans and are comfortable and basic, with few frills. Try to avoid the rooms overlooking the parking lot as they get all the street noise at night. The gates are locked at night, making this one of the most private places around. The on-site dive shop runs snorkeling, diving, and sightseeing trips to the nearby reefs. ⊠ *5a Av. Norte between Calles 8 and 10, Playa del Carmen, Quintana Roo 77710, 987/ 30011. 29 rooms. Breakfast room, pool, dive shop. MC, V (6% fee).*

$ 🏨 **Elefante.** Three blocks from the beach, this three-story, family-run hotel is well kept and the best deal around for the price; the only sore spot is the unkempt field you pass on the way to the rooms. All the bare-bones units overlook a small plant-filled walkway and have tile floors and bathrooms, two double beds, and fans; some have kitchenettes. There's a restaurant down the street. ⊠ *Av. 12 and Calle 10,* ☎ *987/91987. 38 rooms. No credit cards.*

Nightlife and the Arts

With few exceptions, Playa closes down around 11 most nights. Until then, however, you'll have no problem finding something to do on Avenida 5. Many restaurants, such as **Pez Vela** (✉ Av. 5 at Calle 2, ☎ 987/30999) and **Karen's Pizza** (✉ Av. 5 between Calles 2 and 4, ☎ no phone) on this main strip have nightly live music, and the people-watching along the Avenida is entertainment in itself. Of course, no Mexican beach resort would be complete without **Señor Frog's** (✉ next to the ferry dock, ☎ 987/30930), a well-known favorite for cute waiters, beer, and dancing on the table.

Outdoor Activities and Sports

DIVING

Playa del Carmen's scuba scene has grown considerably in the past few years. Most shops offer similar services, but the quality of the equipment and dive instructors varies; those listed below are known to be reliable. The oldest shop in town, **Tank Ha** (✉ Maya-Bric and Albatros Royale hotels, 987/31355), with PADI-certified teachers, arranges diving and snorkeling trips to the reefs and caverns. Other dive shops are at the Shangri-La Caribe, Las Palapas, Pelicano Inn, El Tucan Condotel, and Continental Plaza Playacar hotels.

GOLF

The **Casa Club de Golf** clubhouse (✉ Continental Plaza Playacar Hotel, ☎ 987/30100) can arrange for golf.

HORSEBACK RIDING

Rancho Loma Bonita (☎ 987/845465) offers horseback expeditions on the beach and in the jungle. Trips include food, drinks, and bilingual guides.

MOUNTAIN BIKING

There are bike paths between Playa del Carmen and Xcaret. Contact the El Tucan Condotel (☞ Dining and Lodging, *above*) for bike rentals.

Shopping

Avenida 5 between Calles 4 and Calle 10 is definitely the best place to shop in Playa, if not along the whole coast. Pretty shops and boutiques have sophisticated offerings from all of Mexico and hand-painted batiks from Indonesia. Except where indicated, the shops listed below are open from about 10 in the morning to 9 or 10 at night.

El Ogún (✉ Av. 5 at Calle 8, ☎ 987/31638) is probably the only place on the coast where you can buy *árboles de la vida* (painted wood sculptures that represent the "tree of life," complete with Adam, Eve, and the snake), as well as quality stone and wooden masks and Talavera pottery from the state of Pueblo. **El Vuelo de los Niños Pajaros** (✉ Rincón del Sol, Av. 5 at Calle 8, ☎ 987/30445) has a great selection of regional music on CD and tape, along with handcrafted paper, cards, incense, and beaded baskets. **Amber Museum Shop** (✉ Av. 5 between Calles 4 and 6, FAX 987/30446) has simple but elegantly crafted amber jewelry by a German designer who also keeps a shop in Chiapas near the mines that provide the raw material. **La Calaca** (✉ Av. 5 between Calles 6 and 8 and Av. 5 and Calle 4, ☎ 987/30177 for both locations) has an eclectic collection of wooden masks and other carvings; of note are the playful devils and angels. Off Avenida 5 try **Telart** (✉ West side of main plaza next to Restaurant El Tacolote, ☎ 987/30066), a small store stocked with attractive and original indigenous weavings such as blankets, place mats, and wall hangings from the states of Chiapas, Michoacán, and Oaxaca. **Promoshow** (✉ Calle 6 between Av. 5 and Av. 10, ☎ 987/31202) sells pre-Hispanic music instruments such as tambours, flutes, ocarinas, rain sticks, and a *teponaztle* (a bamboo instument); it also stocks famous handmade guitars from Paracho, Michoacán. **Artesanías Margarita** (⊠ Calle 2 and Av. 5, ☎ no phone) has exquisite hand-painted sun hats and wind chimes designed by Luis de Ocampo. **El Dorado** (⊠ Calle 1 between Av. 5 and the ferry pier in the Las Molcas Hotel shopping arcade, ☎ no phone) has replicas of pre-Hispanic Inca and Maya jewelry fashioned in silver dipped in gold.

Xcaret

🏖 ❹ *6 km (4 mi) south of Playa del Carmen and 72 km (45 mi) south of Cancún.*

A paved road off Highway 307 leads to Xcaret, a sacred Maya city and port that has been developed into a 250-acre ecological theme park on a gorgeous stretch of coastline. Maya ruins are scattered over the lushly landscaped property, a vivid green oasis set against gray limestone and the turquoise sea.

One highlight of the park is the underground river ride, where visitors don life jackets (snorkels, masks, and fins come in handy as well) and float with the cool water's currents through a series of caves. At the educational Dolphinarium, visitors can attend a dolphin workshop ($30) and even swim with the dolphins ($50 for 30 minutes); only 36 people are allowed in the water with them each day, so arrive early to sign up for your slot. An artificially created beach, breakwater, and lagoons are perfect for snorkeling and swimming. Instruction and water-sports equipment rentals are available. Xcaret also includes a botanical garden, a museum with reproductions of the Yucatán peninsula's main archaeological sites, a tropical aquarium, wild bird sanctuary, stables with riding demonstrations, a dive shop, and several restaurants. Its Butterfly Pavilion is one of the world's largest. Plan on spending the entire day. Transportation is available from Cancún and Playa del Carmen on colorfully decorated buses.

A new nighttime attraction is a sound-and-light show and walk through a candlelit Maya village, altar, and underground passageway. The evening winds up with a folkloric flourish, its highlight an exhibition by the famed Flying Indians of Papantla who swing by their feet from a tall pole in an ages-old mystical prayer to the sun god. Most tourists are unaware that the ritual has nothing to do with Maya culture, as it comes from indigenous tribes in Veracruz. The show is presented daily at 6 PM; tickets can be purchased in advance from travel agencies and major hotels at Playa del Carmen or Cancún. ☎ 987/14000. 💲 *Theme park, Mon.–Sat. $39, including show; Sun. $30, no show.* ⊙ *Apr.–Oct., daily 8:30 AM–10 PM; Nov.–Mar., daily 8:30 AM–9 PM.*

Dining

$ ✕ **Bar and Restaurant Marganzo Xcaret.** This small palapa restaurant serves conch ceviche, lobster, poc chuc, and french fries, with gracious service, at prices far lower than those inside the Xcaret theme park. ⊠ *Hwy. 307 at Xcaret turnoff,* ☎ *no phone. No credit cards.*

Paamul

❺ *10 km (6 mi) south of Xcaret.*

Beachcombers and snorkelers are fond of Paamul, a crescent-shape lagoon with clear, placid waters sheltered by the coral reef at the lagoon's mouth. Shells, sand dollars, and even glass beads—some from the sunken pirate ship at Akumal—wash onto the sandy parts of the beach. Trailer camps, cabañas, and tent camps are scattered along the shore; a restaurant sells cold beer and fresh fish; and in June and July visitors may view one of Paamul's chief attractions: sea turtle hatchlings on the beach. You can also take the jungle path to the north, which leads to a lagoon four times the size of the first and even more private.

Lodging

$$ ⊡ **Cabañas Paamul.** If you're looking for seclusion and comfort, you'll be thrilled with this small hostelry on a perfect white-sand beach. Seven bungalows painted white and peach face the sea. All have two double beds, ceiling fans, and hot-water showers. The hotel turns Mexican holidays into fiestas for the guests. A large palapa houses the restaurant, and there is a small market just off the main highway at the road to the hotel. The property includes 140 full-service hookups (gas, water and drainage) for motor homes and tents, and a full-service dive shop. ⊠ *Hwy. 307, Km 85.* ⊠ *Reservations: Box 83, Playa del Carmen, Quintana Roo 77710,* ☎ *987/62691,* ℻ *987/256913. 10 rooms. Restaurant, dive shop. No credit cards.*

Puerto Aventuras

❻ *5 km (3 mi) south of Paamul.*

Puerto Aventuras attempts to offer visitors the opportunity to get away from it all without really leaving it. The 900-acre self-contained resort contains a beach club, 18-hole golf course, several restaurants and shops, an excellent dive shop, and a 95-ship marina. Ultimately, there are plans for a 250-ship marina, tennis club, beach club, shopping mall, movie theater, and five deluxe hotels with a total of 2,000 rooms. In addition the **underwater archaeology museum,** on the marina, displays models of old ships as well as coins, canons, sewing needles, and nautical devices recovered from Mexican waters by CEDAM (Mexican Underwater Explorers Club) members. It's supposed to open daily 10–1 and 2–6, but hours are irregular. Currently, development of Puerto Aventuras seems to be at a standstill, so take advantage of the tranquility while you can, before this mellow marina becomes overrun with Cancún-esque thrill seekers.

Lodging

$$$$ ⊡ **Club Oasis Puerto Aventuras.** Opened in 1992 by the Spanish company that owns luxury hotels worldwide, this large hotel bustles with European tour groups on great package deals. The hotel is all-inclusive, with meals, domestic drinks, and most activities included in the rates. Sparkling-clean rooms with views of the marina have whirlpool baths on their balconies and kitchenettes with microwaves. A shuttle bus runs to the golf course, commercial center, and marina. ⊠ *On beach at north end of complex.* ⊠ *Reservations: Travel America, 4505 Peachtree Lakes Dr., Duluth, GA 30096,* ☎ *770/448–7700,* ℻ *770/448–6911. 286 rooms. 3 restaurants, 3 bars, deli, kitchenettes, 2 pools, dive shop, shops, travel services, car rental. AE, MC, V.*

$$$$ ⊡ **Continental Plaza Puerto Aventuras.** Situated on the marina a short distance from the beach, the Continental Plaza has a variety of rooms, many with kitchenettes. Most guest quarters are decorated in soft shades of blue and peach and feature French doors opening onto balconies overlooking the pool. The hotel has a shuttle service to the beach; restaurants, shops, and water-sports services are within walking distance. ⊠ *Calle Caleta Xel-Ha, Puerto Aventuras, Quintana Roo 77710,* ☎ *987/35133,* ℻ *987/35134. 56 rooms. Restaurant, bar, pool, bicycles, car rental. AE, MC, V.*

$$$$ ⊡ **Omni Puerto Aventuras.** This hotel is one of the best places to get
★ seriously pampered without having to share your relaxation with hordes of tour groups. Hallways lined with antique colonial furniture give way to spacious rooms. Each room has a Jacuzzi on the balcony

or terrace, as well as appreciated touches such as hair dryers and coffeemakers. The calm beach, edged with talc-soft sand, is only a few steps away from the rooms, and the swimming pool seems to flow right into the sea. A complimentary Continental breakfast and newspaper arrive at your room every morning by way of a secret cubbyhole to avoid disturbing your slumber with a knock on the door. To top it all off, one of the coast's best dive shops is on the property. ⊠ *On beach near marina,* ☎ *987/35100,* FAX *987/35102, maymarpave@mail.sybcom.com. 30 rooms. 2 restaurants, bar, in-room safes, minibars, pool, exercise room, beach, dive shop. AE, MC, V.*

Outdoor Activities and Sports

DIVING

Mike Madden's CEDAM Dive Centers (⊠ Club Omni Puerto Aventuras Hotel, ☎ 987/35129) is a full-service dive shop with certification courses; cave and cenote diving are specialties.

Xpuhá

❼ *3 km (2 mi) south of Puerto Aventuras.*

The little fishing village of Xpuhá can be found along a narrow sandy road off Highway 307. Most people come here to fish, snorkel, drink beer on the beach, and add another layer of sand to their camping gear. A cluster of pastel-color hotel buildings sit on the beach; inexpensive rooms are available on a first-come, first-served basis, although don't expect much in the way of friendly conversation from the locals.

Akumal

❽ *37 km (23 mi) south of Playa del Carmen and 102 km (63 mi) south of Cancún.*

The name Akumal, meaning "Place of the Turtle," recalls ancient Maya times, when the beach was the nesting ground for thousands of turtles. The place first attracted international attention in 1926, when explorers discovered the *Mantanceros,* a Spanish galleon that sank in 1741. Three decades later, Akumal became headquarters for the Mexican Underwater Explorers Club (CEDAM) and a gathering spot for wealthy underwater adventurers who flew in on private planes and searched the waters for sunken treasures. Mexican diver/businessman Pablo Bush Romero, a lover of this pristine coast, was the founder of both CEDAM and of the first resort in the area, which predated the development of Cancún.

The long curved bay and beach are rarely empty now, especially at lunchtime, when tour buses stop here en route from Tulum. Even so, it's far less crowded than Cancún or Playa del Carmen. Those who stay here are seeking the comforts of an international resort without the high-rises. Europeans—who tend to gravitate toward Mexico's quieter side—are coming in ever greater numbers.

Akumal consists of three distinct areas. Half Moon Bay to the north is lined with private homes and condominiums and has some of the prettiest beaches and best snorkeling in the area. Akumal proper consists of a large resort and small Maya community with a market, grocery stores, laundry facilities, and pharmacy. There's also an ecology center next to the dive shop with a staff of ecologists. More condos and homes and an all-inclusive resort are at Akumal Aventuras to the south. People come to this part of Akumal simply to gaze out over the sea and to walk on the deliciously long beaches.

First and foremost, however, Akumal is famous for its diving. Area dive shops sponsor resort courses and certification courses, and luxury hotels and condominiums offer year-round packages comprising airfare, accommodations, and diving (hotel rooms are at a premium during the high season, mid-December–April, and reservations should be made well in advance. Lower prices can be had during the medium season from early May to mid-September and low season from mid-September to mid-December). The reef, which is about 425 ft offshore, shelters the bay and its exceptional coral formations and sunken galleon; the sandy bottom invites snorkelers to wade out at the rocky north end, where they can view the diverse underwater topography. Deep-sea fishing for giant marlin, bonito, and sailfish is also popular.

⑨ Devoted snorkelers may want to walk to **Yalkú,** a blessedly undeveloped lagoon a couple of miles north of Akumal along an unmarked dirt road. Wending its way out to the sea, Yalkú hosts throngs of parrot fish in superbly clear water with visibility to 160 ft, but it has no facilities.

Dining and Lodging

$$ ✕ **La Lunita.** Locals and enterprising tourists congregate at the indoor and patio tables of this converted one-bedroom condo at Half Moon Bay for good conversation and innovative cuisine. The menu changes daily, but expect to find such eclectic dishes as the fresh fish served with a lime and cilantro sauce or chicken with grilled eggplant and zucchini. The conversation typically includes everyone in the place, and you're sure to pick up a few tips on local events and secret beaches. You'll need a car, a cab, or strong legs to reach this place, but it's worth it. ⊠ *Hacienda de la Tortuga; go through entranceway at Club Akumal Caribe, then turn left (north) at dirt road to Half Moon Bay,* ☎ *987/ 22421 for condo office. No credit cards.*

$$$$ 🏨 **Club Oasis Akumal.** An all-inclusive luxury hotel managed by the Spanish hotel group Oasis, this sprawling property started as the private preserve of millionaire Pablo Bush Romero, a friend of the late Jacques Cousteau. Today, the beach—protected by an offshore reef— and the pier are used as the starting point for canoeing, snorkeling, diving, fishing, and windsurfing jaunts. The U-shape building, with nautical decor, has handsome mahogany furniture and sunken blue-tile showers between Moorish arches. Apartments have full kitchens and dining areas. All rooms have balconies (you can choose a sea view or a garden view) and air-conditioning or ceiling fans (same price). The clientele consists primarily of Americans and Canadians on package deals, though nongroup guests are also welcome. ⊠ *South of Akumal off Hwy 307. Reservations: Travamérica,* ☎ *770/448–7700 for reservations, 987/59000 for guests;* FAX *770/448–6911 for reservations, 987/59009 for guests. 120 rooms, 4 apartments. Restaurant, 2 bars, 2 pools, tennis court, beach, dive shop, bicycles, shops, recreation room, travel services, car rental. AE, MC, V.*

$$$$ 🏨 **Hacienda de la Tortuga.** One of several condominium projects lining the shores of Half Moon Bay north of Akumal, this small complex on the beach has one- and two-bedroom units with tile kitchens and baths. Housekeeping service is part of the arrangement. The dive shops and restaurants at Club Akumal Caribe (☞ *below*) are within walking distance. ⊠ *Dirt road about 10 min north of Club Akumal Caribe. Reservations:* ⊠ *Box 18, Puerto Aventuras, Quintana Roo 77710,* ☎ *987/59068,* FAX *987/59070. 9 condos. Restaurant, kitchenettes, pool, beach. AE, MC, V.*

$$$ 🏨 **Club Akumal Caribe & Villas Maya.** Accommodations at this resort, situated on the edge of a cove overlooking a small harbor, range from rustic but comfortable bungalows with red-tile roofs and garden views

(Villas Maya) to beachfront rooms in a modern three-story hotel building. All have air-conditioning, ceiling fans, and refrigerators. Also available are the more secluded one-, two-, and three-bedroom condominiums called the Villas Flamingo, on Half Moon Bay and 1 km (½ mi) from the beach. The bungalows and hotel rooms are cheerfully furnished in rattan and dark wood, with attractive tile floors; the high-domed, Mediterranean-style condominium units have kitchens and balconies or terraces overlooking the pool and beach. Two dive shops offer resort courses, PADI certification, and cenote or cave diving; snorkeling, windsurfing, kayaking, and deep-sea fishing are also available. The best of the three restaurants is **Lol Ha**: The grilled steak and seafood dinner entrées are bountiful. An optional meal plan includes breakfast and dinner. ⊠ *Hwy. 307, Km 104,* ☎ *987/59012. Reservations:* ⊠ *Akutrame, Box 13326, El Paso, TX 79913,* ☎ *800/351–1622 or 800/343– 1440 in Canada. 21 rooms, 40 bungalows, 4 villas, 5 condos. 3 restaurants, bar, grocery, ice cream parlor, pizzeria, snack bar, pool, beach, 2 dive shops, shops, children's program (5–14). AE, MC, V.*

Outdoor Activities and Sports

DIVING

Akumal Dive Center rents equipment, runs dive trips, and has certification programs. For dive packages, including accommodations, contact Akutrame Inc. (⊠ Box 13326, El Paso, TX 79913, ☎ 915/ 584–3552 or 800/351–1622; 800/343–1440 in Canada).

Chemuyil and Laguna de Xcacel

10 **11** *7 km (4½ mi) south of Akumal.*

You can stop for lunch and a swim at the little cove at Chemuyil. The crescent-shape beach, which has been declared an official sea turtle reserve, is popular with tour groups and campers who pitch their tents under the few remaining palms (most were destroyed by disease and have not been replaced). Fresh seafood is served here for lunch by a modest eatery on the beach.

The Laguna de Xcacel perches next to Chemuyil on a sandy ridge overlooking yet another long white beach. A tranquil place boasting calm waters, a nearby cenote, and visits by sea turtles during the summer, Xcacel has recently been tagged by the government for development. At press time the beach was expected to be closed to the public; locals are wary that the upcoming development will seriously harm the beach's appeal, not to mention the turtle nesting sites.

Xel-Há

12 *3 km (2 mi) south of Laguna de Xcacel.*

Now managed by the same people that run Xcaret (☞ *above*), Xel-Há (pronounced shel-hah) is a natural aquarium cut out of the limestone shoreline. The national park consists of several interconnected lagoons where countless species of tropical fish breed. The rocky coastline curves into bays and coves in which enormous parrot fish cluster around an underwater Maya shrine. Several low wooden bridges over the lagoons have benches at regular points, so you can take in the sights at leisure. Though much of the fauna used to be threatened by suntan oil and garbage, 1995's hurricane Roxanne cleaned out the pollution, and wearing suntan lotion is strictly forbidden, so now the waters are remarkably clear. Certain areas are off-limits to swimmers, but because the lagoons are quite large, in places you can swim fairly far out, or you can explore one of the underwater caves or the cenotes deep in the jungle. Lockers and dressing rooms are available, and you can rent snorkel gear ($7) and buy underwater cameras (the $20 fee includes a roll of film).

The park holds other attractions as well. A shrine stands at the entrance, and there are other small Maya ruins throughout, including one named **Na Balaam** for a yellow jaguar painted on one of its walls. There is also a huge but overpriced souvenir shop, food stands, and a small museum housing artifacts from pre-Hispanic days. The enormous parking lot attests to the number of visitors who come here; you should plan to arrive in the early morning before all the tour-bus traffic hits. For a pleasant breakfast or lunch you may want to try one of the five restaurants, which all serve reasonably good ceviche, fresh fish, and drinks. ☎ 987/54070 or 987/54071. 🗺 $15. ⊙ Daily 8–8.

If you're sick of tour buses, head across the road to the little-visited **Xel-Ha Archaeological Site.** A small site composed of squat structures, it was thought to be inhabited from the Late Preclassic until the Late Postclassic period. The most interesting sights are on the north end of the ruins, where remains of a Maya *sacbe* (road) and mural paintings in the **Jaguar House** sit near a tranquil, deep cenote. ☎ No phone. 🗺 $1.50, free Sun. and holidays. ⊙ Daily 8–5.

Tan Kah

⓭ 9½ km (6 mi) south of Xel-Há on dirt road off Hwy. 307.

Tan Kah offers a tranquil beach and a shaded cenote that feels remote and is surprisingly undiscovered for now. There is one notable hotel and restaurant, however. Tan Kah should be enjoyed before it is snatched up by the hungry jaws of Yucatán peninsula resort development.

Dining and Lodging

$$ ✕ **Casa Cenote.** Don't miss this outstanding restaurant in front of a
★ large cenote—this one's a minipool of fresh and salt water full of tropical fish. In fact, work up an appetite with a pre-meal swim in the sinkhole. With luck you may spot one of the three resident manatees, bashful critters who would prefer to be left in peace. Follow up with a quick snorkeling trip in the sea, then rest in the shade while you wait for your meal. The restaurant's beef, chicken, and cheese are imported from the United States, and the burgers, chicken fajitas, and nachos are superb. On Sunday afternoon the expats living along the coast gather at Casa Cenote for a lavish barbecue featuring ribs, chicken, beef brisket, or lobster kebabs. The restaurant operates without electricity or a generator (perishables are packed in ice coolers) and closes at 5 PM. ⊠ Left at the end of dirt road into Tan Kah (look for Casa Cenote sign on Hwy. 307), ☎ no phone. Reservations not accepted. No credit cards.

$$$ ✕🖼 **Tan Kah Inn.** A friendly East Texas family left the States to run
★ this exquisite guest house, located on a sunny strip of sand just up the road from Casa Cenote. The inn is mostly frequented by divers, who come in small groups to take advantage of the nearby reefs, top-notch equipment, and full-service, personal attention (dive groups are no more than 10 people). The five spacious rooms, some with breathtaking ocean views, each have their own balcony or terrace. An upstairs restaurant serves a wide variety of food, including Yucatecan cuisine; group rates include all three meals. Evening activities feature presentations on Maya culture and celebrations of Mexican festivals. ⊠ Tan Kah Bay 16, Quintana Roo 77780, ☎ 987/42188. Reservations: ⊠ Box 5, Tulum, Quintana Roo, ☎ 409/636–7721, FAX 409/636–7111. 5 rooms. Restaurant. No credit cards.

Tulum

 2 km (1 mi) south of Tan Kah, 130 km (81 mi) south of Cancún.

One of the Caribbean coast's biggest attractions, Tulum is the Yucatán Peninsula's most visited Maya ruin, attracting more than 2 million people annually. Unfortunately, this means you'll be sharing the site with roughly half of the tourist population of Quintana Roo on any given day, even if you arrive early. The amount of attention that Tulum receives is not entirely undeserved. Though the architecture is of mostly unremarkable Postclassic (AD 900–1541) style, the location of the ruins by the blue-green Caribbean waters is indeed riveting.

Tulum entered a new phase in 1994 when an ecological park project was launched by private investors to save the site from further deterioration. The entrance and parking lot were moved away from the ruins. In the past tour buses and cars spewed noise and fumes just a few feet away from the crumbling temples. Now even the highway turnoff is new, and an enormous paved lot has separate designated areas for cars ($1 fee) and buses. Aesthetically speaking, however, the new entrance is an eyesore. An enormous cement slab building is filled with burger joints and tacky shops selling the requisite overpriced T-shirts and junky souvenirs. An electric shuttle car costing $1 each way hustles visitors to the temples; otherwise it's a ½-km (¼-mi) hike. Clay reproductions of Maya gods, machine-produced serapes with pyramid designs, and wood carvings are laid out on the side of the road where the shuttle stops.

You can hire a guide to the ruins at the stand near the shuttle stop. He may attempt to titillate you with mostly false stories of virgin sacrifices and other quirky Maya customs. Visitors are no longer allowed to climb or enter Tulum's most impressive buildings (only three, described below, really merit close inspection), so you can see the ruins in two hours. You may, however, wish to allow extra time for a swim or a stroll on the beach, where it's likely that the ancient Maya beached their canoes.

The modern name for the site, "Tulum" means "wall." The pre-Hispanic name was "Zama" from *zamul* (dawn), because the city faced the sunrise over the ocean. Tulum is the only Maya city known to have been inhabited when the conquistadors arrived. Juan de Grijalva and his men, who spotted it from their ships in 1518, were so intimidated by the enormity of its vivid 25-ft-high blue, white, and red walls that they were reluctant to land. What they had seen was four towns so close to one another that they appeared to be one continuous metropolis. The Postclassic architecture at Tulum evinces strong influences of the Toltecs as a result of the encroaching empire of central Mexico. Although artistic refinements found elsewhere in the Maya world are missing here, the site is well preserved.

Tulum has long held special significance for the Maya. A key city in the League of Mayapán (AD 987–1194), it was never conquered by the Spaniards, although it was abandoned about 75 years after the Conquest. For 300 years thereafter, it symbolized the defiance of an otherwise subjugated people; it was one of the last outposts of the Maya during their insurrection against Mexican rule in the 1840s War of the Castes. Uprisings continued intermittently until 1935, when the Maya ceded Tulum to the government.

Tulum's fortifications attest to its military importance. It may once have been home to 2,000 people living in houses set on man-made platforms along the main artery. John L. Stephens, an American explorer, came upon Tulum in 1842, and his traveling companion, Frederick Cather-

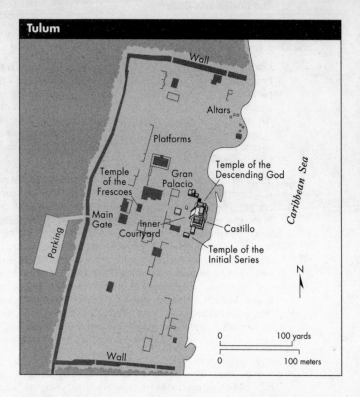

Tulum

Wall

Altars

Platforms

Temple of the Frescoes

Gran Palacio

Temple of the Descending God

Main Gate

Parking

Inner Courtyard

Castillo

Temple of the Initial Series

Caribbean Sea

N

0   100 yards

0   100 meters

Wall

wood, sketched its magnificence. Those sketches eventually illustrated a book by Stephens, which became the archaeological bible of its time.

Visitors enter the archaeological site through a low limestone gateway in a crumbling wall. Even the Maya, who are typically short of stature, have to duck their heads. Apparently the design forced those who entered to bow in deference to the divinities within. Low-lying structures dot the site's 60-acre grassy field, wrapped on three sides by a 3,600-ft-long wall.

The first significant structure is the two-story **Temple of the Frescoes**, to the left of the entryway. The temple's vaulted roof and corbeled arch are examples of Classic Maya architecture. Faint traces of blue-green frescoes outlined in black on the inner and outer walls refer to ancient Maya beliefs (the most clear frescoes are hidden from sight now that visitors aren't allowed to walk into the temple). Reminiscent of the Mixtec style, the frescoes depict the three worlds of the Maya and their major deities, and are decorated with stellar and serpentine patterns, rosettes, and ears of maize and other offerings to the gods. One scene portrays the rain god seated on a four-legged animal—probably a reference to the Spaniards on their horses.

The largest and most famous building, the **Castillo** (castle), looms at the edge of a 40-ft limestone cliff just past the Temple of the Frescoes. Atop the castle, at the end of a broad stairway, sits a temple with stucco ornamentation on the outside and traces of fine frescoes inside the two chambers. (The stairway has been roped off, so it's no longer possible to walk through the top temple.) The front wall of the Castillo has faint carvings of the Descending God and columns depicting the plumed serpent god, Kukulcán, who was introduced to the Maya by the Toltecs. The regal structure overlooks the rest of Tulum and an expanse of dense jungle to the west; the blue Caribbean blocks access from the east. Footpaths are etched at the sides of the Castillo wherever it's possible to catch a snapshot of the ruins against the sea. Researchers think the Castillo may have functioned as a watchtower to monitor enemy approaches by sea.

To the left of the Castillo is the **Temple of the Descending God**—so called for the carving of a winged god plummeting to earth over the doorway. The same deity is seen in stucco masks in the corners, and is thought either to be Ab Muzen Cab, the bee god, or to be associated with the planet Venus, guardian of the coast and of commerce.

The other buildings at the site typically have flat roofs resting on wood beams and columns. The architecture is considered commonplace, with few distinguishing features. Buildings were laid out along straight streets running the length of the site with a slight dip, or culvert, between two gentle slopes. The tiny cove to the left of the Castillo and Temple of the Descending God is a good spot for a cooling swim, but there are no changing rooms. A few small altars sit atop a hill at the north side of the cove and have a good view of the Castillo and the sea. ☒ *$2, free Sun. and holidays, parking $1, use of video camera $4.* ◷ *Daily 8–5.*

Tourist services are clustered at the old turnoff, called the *crucero*, which leads from Highway 307 to the ruins. The new road is a few yards farther south and is clearly marked with overhead signs. Still farther south is the turnoff for the Boca Paila Peninsula, the Sian Ka'an preserve, and several small waterfront hotels. On the highway about 4 km (2½ mi) south of the ruins is the present-day village of Tulum. The highway running through town has been widened to four lanes, and street lamps placed down the middle. As Tulum's importance as a commercial center increases, markets, auto-repair shops, and other businesses continue to spring up along the road. Growth has not been kind to the pueblo, however, and it has become rather unsightly and congested.

Dining and Lodging

$$$ ✕⊡ **Cabañas Ana y José.** Several two-story buildings face the beach at this small, well-loved hotel south of the ruins. All rooms have fans, tile floors, and hot-water showers; those on the second floor are cooler, thanks to the sea breeze. Unfortunately, the generator from the hotel next door runs until late and may disturb light sleepers. Mountain bikes are available for rent, and the English-speaking management can arrange for diving trips with the Aktún Dive Center, in town. The restaurant ($), complete with an aviary full of parrots and parakeets, serves unique Mexican cuisine in a sandy palapa. Electricity goes on only four hours a day between 6:30 in the evening and 10:30 at night. Ana and José also own a modest hotel and restaurant, **El Mesón,** located on the main highway. ☒ *Dirt road off Hwy. 307 between ruins entrance and Tulum pueblo, 6 km (4 mi) south of ruins,* ☎ *98/806022,* 📠 *98/ 806021, anayjose@cancun.rce.com.mx. Reservations: C/O Ms. Judith Ivarra,* ☒ *9501-C Siempre Viva Rd. 8-135, San Diego, CA 92173-3528. 16 rooms. Restaurant. MC, V.*

$$ ✕⊡ **Cabañas Tulum.** This property, idyllically situated in a coconut grove on the beach, is 7 km (4½ mi) south of the Tulum ruins on the dirt road leading to Boca Paila. Beachfront palapa bungalows with private bathrooms, and an indoor-outdoor restaurant, bar, and game room make a good package. ☒ *Box 10, Tulum, Quintana Roo 77780,* ☎ *98/ 258295. 18 cabanas. Restaurant, bar, beach, recreation room. No credit cards.*

$ ✕⊡ **Acuario.** This hotel and restaurant at the turnoff for the Tulum ruins has large, clean rooms with satellite TV, screen windows, ceiling fans, and hot water; the pool isn't well maintained and may not even be filled when you're here. The adjoining **Restaurant Cristina** ($) is well worth a visit because the owner takes pride in the preparation and quality of the food. Acuario offers a menu that includes above-average seafood, soup, tacos, nachos, guacamole, salads, and tasty coconut ice cream. Buses to and from Playa del Carmen stop at Acuario's parking lot, and the management can arrange rental cars. ✉ *Crucero Ruinas de Tulum, Hwy. 307, Km 127, Tulum, Quintana Roo 77780,* ☎ *987/ 12194. 30 rooms. Restaurant, bar, grocery, pool, shops. No credit cards.*

Cobá

 ⑮ *49 km (30 mi) northwest of Tulum and 167 km (104 mi) southwest of Cancún.*

Beautiful but barely explored, Cobá was once one of the most important city-states in the entire Maya domain. It now stands in solitude: The spell this remoteness casts is intensified by the silence at the ruins, broken occasionally by the shriek of a spider monkey or the call of a bird. Processions of huge army ants cross the footpaths, and the sun penetrates the tall hardwood trees, ferns, and giant palms with fierce shafts of light. Cobá exudes the still, eerie ambience of a dead city.

The site is not inaccessible, however. Cobá is a 35-minute drive northwest of Tulum, down a well-marked and well-paved road that leads straight through the jungle. A few rest stops dot the road en route to Cobá, among them **Restaurant Lolche** (open daily 6–6), marked by a parking lot and two wooden statues. Inside, a large artisan's market is packed with pottery and hammocks. Check out the carved wooden jaguars, Cobá's signature souvenir. The restaurant serves tasty Yucatecan cuisine at low prices. Water and snacks are available at the small stand next door.

Archaeologists estimate that some 6,500 structures are present in the Cobá area, but only 5% have been uncovered, and it will take decades before the work is completed. Discovered by Teobert Maler in 1891, Cobá was subsequently explored in 1926 by the Carnegie Institute but not excavated until 1972. At present there is no restoration work under way.

The city flourished from AD 800 to AD 1100, probably boasting a population of as many as 55,000 inhabitants. Situated on five lakes between coastal watchtowers and inland cities, its temple-pyramids towered over a vast jungle plain. One of them is 138 ft tall, the largest and highest in northern Yucatán. Cobá (meaning "ruffled waters") exercised economic control over the region through a network of at least 16 *sacbeob* (white stone roads), one of which measures 100 km (62 mi), and is the longest in the Maya world. Cobá's massive, soaring structures and sheer size—the city once covered 70 square km (44 square mi)—made it a noteworthy sister nation to Tikal in northern Guatemala, to which it apparently had close cultural and commercial ties.

The main groupings are separated by several miles of intense tropical vegetation, so the only way to get a sense of the immensity of the city is to scale one of the pyramids. Maps and books about the ruins are sold at the makeshift restaurants and shops that line the parking lot. None of the maps are particularly accurate, and unmarked side trails lead temptingly into the jungle. Stay on the main, marked paths unless you have a guide. Several men with guide licenses congregate by the entrance and offer their services. When you go, bring plenty of bug repellent, and, if you plan to spend some time here, bring a canteen of water (you can also buy sodas and snacks at the entrance).

The first major grouping, off a path to your right as you enter the ruins, is the **Cobá Group,** whose pyramids are built around a sunken patio. At the near end of the group, facing a large plaza, you'll see the 79-ft-high Iglesia (church), where some Indians still place offerings and light candles in hopes of improving their harvests.

Farther along the main path to your left is the **Chumuc Mul Group,** little of which has been excavated. The principal pyramid here is covered with the stucco remains of vibrantly painted motifs (*chumuc mul* means "stucco pyramid").

A kilometer (approximately ½ mile) past this site is the **Nohoch Mul** (Large Hill) **Group,** the highlight of which is the pyramid of the same name, the tallest at Cobá. The pyramid, which has 120 steps—equivalent to 12 stories—shares a plaza with Temple 10. The Descending God (also seen at Tulum) is depicted on a facade of the temple atop Nohoch Mul, from which the view is excellent. The temple seems to have been erected much later than the pyramid itself. It was from the base of this pyramid that the longest sacbe started. It extended all the way to Yaxuná, 20 km (12 mi) southwest of Chichén Itzá. Because of their great width (up to 33 ft), there is considerable speculation about the function of the sacbeob. The Maya had no beasts of burden, so they carried all cargo on their own backs. Thus the roads may have been designed to allow people to walk abreast in processions, suggesting that they played a role in religion as well as in trade. The unrestored **Crossroad Pyramid** opposite Nohoch Mul was the meeting point for three sacbeob.

Beyond the Nohoch Mul Group is the **Castillo** (castle), with nine chambers that are reached by a stairway. To the south are the remains of a ball court, including the stone ring through which the ball was hurled. From the main route follow the sign to **Las Pinturas Group,** named for the still-discernible polychromatic friezes on the inner and outer walls of its large, patioed pyramid. An enormous stela here depicts a man standing with his feet on two prone captives. Take the minor path for 1 km (½ mi) to the **Macanxoc Group,** not far from the lake of the same name. The main pyramid at Macanxoc is accessible by a stairway. The portal of the temple at its summit is divided by a column; there are also a molded lintel and the remains of a stucco painting. Many of the stelae here are intricately carved with dates and other symbols of the history of Cobá.

Devotees of archaeology may wish to venture farther to the small **Kukulcán Group,** one of the larger satellites of Cobá, positioned just 5½ km (3½ mi) south of the Cobá group. Only five structures remain, and they are among the more puzzling ruins in the Maya world; their design and use have yet to be explained by archaeologists. The three-story temple is particularly intriguing because it is the only Maya structure in which the top story does not rest on filled-in lower stories.

Cobá can be comfortably visited in a half day, but if you want to spend the night, opt for the Villa Arqueológica Cobá (☞ Dining and Lodging, *below*), operated by Club Med and only a 10-minute walk from the site along the shores of Lake Cobá. Spending the night is highly advised—the nighttime jungle sounds will lull you to sleep, and you'll be able to visit the ruins in solitude when they open at 8 AM. Even on a day trip, consider taking time out for lunch at the Villa, after the intense heat and mosquito-ridden humidity of the ruins. Buses depart Cobá for Playa del Carmen and Valladolid twice daily. Check with your hotel and clerk at the ruins for times, which may not be exact. 🖃 *$1.75, free Sun. and holidays.* ⊙ *Daily 8–5.*

Dining and Lodging

$$ ✕▥▦ **Villa Arqueológica Cobá.** This Club Med property, a 10-minute walk from the entrance to the Cobá ruins, overlooks one of the region's vast lakes, where turtles swim to the hotel's dock for a breakfast of bread and rolls. Tastefully done in white stucco and red paint, with bougainvillea hanging from the walls and museum-quality pieces throughout the property, the hotel has a clean, airy feel; corridors in the square, two-story building face a small pool and bar. The air-conditioned rooms are small but they feel cozy, not claustrophobic. A handsome library, housing books on the Maya and paperback novels, also contains a large-screen TV (with VCR) and a pool table. The restaurant food is very good, but it's not included in the room rates as at most Club Med properties. For regional fare try the ceviche, shrimp, *pollo píbil* (chicken baked in banana leaves), or enchiladas. On the more international side are pepper steak, marinated artichokes, and chocolate mousse. *Reservations:* ☎ 5/254–7077, ᶠᴬˣ 5/255–3164. *40 rooms, 3 suites. Restaurant, bar, pool, tennis court, shops. AE, MC, V.*

$ ✕▥▦ **El Bocadito.** Though not as lavish as the Villa Arqueológica (☞ *above*), El Bocadito is a friendly, satisfactory budget alternative and only a five-minute walk from the ruins. The simple, tiled rooms fill up quickly—if you're thinking of spending the night, stop here before visiting the ruins. There is no hot water, and only fans to combat the heat, but the camaraderie of the clientele and staff make up for the discomforts. The restaurant is decent, clean, and popular with tour groups. ✉ *On road to ruins,* ☎ 987/42087. *10 rooms. AE, V.*

Sian Ka'an and the Boca Paila Peninsula

⑯ *15 km (9 mi) south of Tulum to Punta Allen turnoff, located within Sian Ka'an; 137 km (85 mi) south of Cancún.*

Sian Ka'an, meaning "where the sky is born," was first settled by the Maya in the 5th century AD. In 1986 the Mexican Government established the 1.3-million-acre Sian Ka'an Biosphere Reserve as an internationally protected area; the next year it was named a World Heritage Site by the United Nations Educational, Scientific, and Cultural Organization (UNESCO). In 1996 the reserve was extended by 200,000 acres.

The Man and the Biosphere program at UNESCO, of which this is part, was created to preserve biologically rich areas of the earth and to promote the sustainable use of their natural resources. The reserves are particularly important in developing countries, where, for large segments of the population, encroaching on dwindling resources is the only way they know to survive. Maintaining and preserving the ecological diversity of these areas while educating the local people to do likewise is the challenge of the biosphere program.

Under the program the land is divided for various purposes, including research, preservation, and economic activities in conjunction with conservation. Assisted by scientists, the local population makes a living through fishing, lobster harvests, and small farming and receives support from the low-impact tourism, biological research, and sustainable development programs.

The Sian Ka'an reserve constitutes 10% of the land in Quintana Roo and covers 100 km (62 mi) of coast. Freshwater and coastal lagoons, mangrove swamps, watery cays, savannahs, tropical forests, a barrier reef, hundreds of species of local and migratory birds, fish, other animals and plants, and fewer than 1,000 local residents—primarily Maya—share this area, one of the last undeveloped stretches of coastline in North America. Some of the approximately 27 sites of ruins scattered about are linked by a unique canal system—the only one of its kind in the Maya world in Mexico.

It's recommended that you see the reserve via guided tour: This can be arranged through the private, nonprofit **Amigos de Sian Ka'an** organization (✉ Plaza América, Av. Cobá 5, Suites 48–50, Cancún, QR 77500, ☎ 98/849583, FAX 98/873080). You'll get an excellent, informed tour. Highlights include visiting the Maya ruins of Xlapak and jumping off the boat into one of the channels to float downstream in the current. The three-hour tour leaves from Cabañas Ana y Jose Monday–Thursday and Saturday morning and includes a bilingual guide and binoculars.

The most convenient way to explore on your own is to enter via the Punta Allen turnoff, south of Cancún on the coastal road; you'll be on a secluded 35-km (22-mi) coastal strip of land that is part of the reserve. If you are exploring on your own, you will be confined to swimming, snorkeling, and camping on the beaches, as there are no trails into the surrounding jungle.

The narrow, extremely rough dirt road down the peninsula is lined with lush vegetation and several small trails to the beach. Deserted fishing lodges, palapas, and copra farms lend an eerie air to the area. The road ends at **Punta Allen,** a fishing village whose main catch is spiny lobster, which was becoming scarce until ecologists taught the local fishing cooperative how to build and lay special traps to conserve the species. There are several small guest houses, but the road is filled with potholes. In the rainy season it may be completely impassable. Most fishing lodges along the way close for the rainy season in August and September, and accommodations are hard to come by. If you haven't booked ahead and want to explore, start out early in the morning so you can get back to civilization before dark.

Many species of the once-flourishing wildlife have fallen into the endangered category, but the waters here still teem with rooster fish, bonefish, mojarra, snapper, shad, permit, sea bass, and crocodiles. Fishing the flats for the wily bonefish and fly-fishing are especially popular, and the peninsula's few lodges run deep-sea fishing trips. The beaches are wide and white, and although many of the palms have succumbed to the yellowing palm disease imported from Florida, the beautiful vegetation is growing back.

Lodging

$$$$ 🏨 **Boca Paila Fishing Lodge.** This enclave of nine spacious cottages in the midst of the Sian Ka'an Biosphere Reserve offers clean, bright, and cheerful accommodations that include the basics: bed, dresser, and nightstand on tile floors. Catering principally to anglers, the lodge provides boats and guides for fly-fishing and bonefishing; guests can bring their own tackle or rent some at the lodge. Maya specialties, such as pollo píbil, are served at mealtime. (Meals are included in room rate.) A transfer service to and from the Cancún airport is available at an extra charge, or clients can rent a car in Cancún and drive to the lodge. A one-month advance reservation with 50% payment is recommended in the high season; bookings may be for less than a week during the low season. ✉ *Boca Paila peninsula,* ☎ *no phone. Reservations:* ✉ *Frontiers, Box 959, Wexford, PA 15090,* ☎ *412/935–1577 or 800/245–1950,* FAX *412/ 935–5388. 9 cottages. Restaurant, bar. No credit cards, unless arranged with Frontiers.*

$$$$ 🏨 **Caphé-Ha.** Built as a private home by an American architect, this
★ small guest house—between a lagoon and the ocean—is a perfect place

to stay if you're interested in bonefishing or bird-watching. A two-bedroom house with kitchen, bath, and living room or a two-unit bungalow with shared bath are your choices; though neither has fans or electricity, all the windows have screens and catch the ocean breeze. A caretaker/chef from Mérida cooks meals that are served in the solar-powered community palapa; he will prepare vegetarian meals upon request. Fishing tackle and snorkeling gear are available from the property's small dock, but there's an extra charge for bonefishing. The room rates include breakfast and dinner; advance reservations must be accompanied by a 50% deposit, and a three-day or longer stay is required during high season. ⊠ *30 km (19 mi) south of Tulum, on road to Sian Ka'an, 5 km (3 mi) past bridge at Boca Paila and around next rocky point,* FAX *610/912–9392 for reservations. 1 villa, 1 bungalow. Dining room, fishing. No credit cards.*

$$$$ 🏨 **Casa Blanca Lodge.** Punta Pájaros, to which this remote fishing re-
   ★   sort provides unique access, is reputed to be one of the best places in the world for light-tackle saltwater fishing. The American-managed, all-inclusive lodge—just 100 ft from the ocean—is set on a rocky outcrop covered with palm trees. Bonefish swarm in the mangrove swamps, flats, and shallow waters. The lodge's 10 large, modern guest rooms, painted white with turquoise trim, and featuring slatted windows and tile and mahogany bathrooms, provide a pleasant tropical respite at dusk. An open-air thatched bar and a large living and dining area welcome anglers with drinks, fresh fish dishes, fruit, and vegetables at the start and end of the day. Rates are highest from March through June, lowest from January through March. During the high season, Sat.–Sat. stays and a 50% prepayment are required, but you may stay fewer days during the low season. Rates include a charter flight from Cancún to the lodge, all meals, a boat, and a guide. *Reservations:* ⊠ *Frontiers, Box 959, Wexford, PA 15090,* ☎ *412/935–1577 or 800/ 245–1950,* FAX *412/935–5388, or Outdoor Travel,* ☎ *713/526–3739 or 800/533–7299. 10 rooms. Restaurant, bar, fishing. MC, V.*

Muyil

 ⑰ *24 km (15 mi) south of Tulum on Hwy. 307.*

The name of the archaeological site of Chunyaxché has been changed back into its ancient name of Muyil. Dating from the Late Preclassic era (300 BC–AD 200), it was connected by road to the sea and served as a port between Cobá and the Maya centers in Belize and Guatemala. A 15-ft-wide sacbe, built during the Late Postclassic period (AD 1250–1600), extended from the city to the mangrove swamp; today the remains of the sacbe get flooded during the rainy season. Structures were erected at 400-ft intervals along the white limestone road, almost all of them facing west. At the beginning of this century, the ancient stones were used to build a chicle (gum) plantation, which was managed by one of the leaders of the War of the Castes. Today, the most notable site at Muyil is the remains of the 56-ft **Castillo temple-pyramid**—one of the tallest on the Quintana Roo coast—at the center of a big patio. During excavations of the Castillo, jade figurines representing the moon goddess Chichén were found here. Recent excavations at Muyil have uncovered some smaller structures, but these excavations were halted by the death of the archaeologist in charge. The ruins are located near the edge of a deep-blue lagoon and are surrounded by a nearly impenetrable jungle—bring bug repellant. You can drive down a dirt road on the side of the ruins to swim or fish in the lagoon. 🎫 *$1, free Sun. and holidays.* ⊘ *Daily 8–5.*

Felipe Carrillo Puerto

18 *99 km (61 mi) south of Tulum.*

The town of Felipe Carrillo Puerto is named for a local hero who preached rebellion. In 1920 Carrillo Puerto became governor of Yucatán and instituted a series of reforms to help the impoverished campesinos; these led to his assassination by the alleged henchman of the presidential candidate of an opposing party. Formerly known as Chan Santa Cruz, this town also played a central role in the 19th-century War of the Castes, during which it was not only a significant political and military center but also a religious capital. It was here that what became known as the Talking Cross first appeared, carved into a cedar tree near a cenote. The Indian priest Manuel Nahuat, translating from behind a curtain, interpreted the cross as a sign for the Indians to attack the *dzulob* (white Christians). Although Mexican soldiers cut down the tree and destroyed the cross, the Indians made other crosses from the trunk and placed them in neighboring villages, including Tulum. By 1904 half the local population had been annihilated in the war.

Today, the town exists primarily as the hub of three highways, and the only vestige of the momentous events of the last century is the small, uncompleted temple (on the edge of town in an inconspicuous, poorly marked park) begun by the Indians in the 1860s and now a monument to the War of the Castes. The church where the Talking Cross was originally housed also stands. Several humble hotels, some good restaurants, and a gas station may be incentives for stopping here on your southbound trek.

Dining and Lodging

$ ✕🏨 **El Faisán y El Venado.** Given the paucity of hotels in Felipe Carrillo Puerto, this Pepto-Bismol pink one is your best bet. It's bare bones, but you can choose between rooms with air-conditioning or with ceiling fans. Some also come with color TV and refrigerator. The pleasant restaurant does brisk business with locals at lunchtime because it is so centrally located. Yucatecan specialties such as poc chuc, *bistec a la yucateca* (Yucatecan-style steak), and pollo píbil are served in a simple but rustically decorated setting. Beware of the run-down bathrooms. ✉ *Av. Juárez 781, 77200,* ☎ *983/40702 (hotel) or 983/40043 (restaurant). 21 rooms. Restaurant. No credit cards.*

Xcalak

19 *71 km (44 mi) southeast of Felipe Carrillo Puerto on Hwy. 307 to the Majahual exit south of Limones; turn left and go 56 km (35 mi) to Majahual, where you'll reach the beach; turn right and take dirt road for 54 km (33 mi) to Xcalak.*

Devoted divers and tranquility seekers who don't mind putting up with dirt, sand, and ruts to get to Xcalak will be aptly rewarded when they get here. A fishing village near the tip of the Xcalak peninsula, which divides Chetumal Bay from the Caribbean Sea, Xcalak offers a landscape lush with mangrove swamps, tropical flowers, birds, foxes, and other wildlife. The Xcalak area offers some wonderfully deserted beaches, but the few small resorts here cater mostly to divers who come
20 to visit **Banco Chinchorro,** a 42-km (26-mi) coral atoll and national park some two hours by boat from Xcalak. Strewn with shipwrecks, it's an undersea explorer's dream. Fishing is not permitted here.

Though much care is being taken to preserve the peninsula's natural wonders, recent developments have made the peninsula more accessible for visitors. The **La Aguada-Chetumal ferry** shuttles passengers between Chetumal and Xcalak Fri.–Mon., leaving Chetumal at 8 AM and Xcalak at 4 PM ($5). Transportation from Xcalak to the ferry dock is available from Las Conchitas restaurant in Xcalak. In addition **Servicios Aeréos Ejecutivos** (✉ Av. 5 de Mayo No. 67, Chetumal, ☎ 983/21294, FAX 983/22038) will fly you to Xcalak from Chetumal, Majahual, or elsewhere on the Caribbean coast.

Lodging

$$$$ 🏨 **Costa de Cocos.** For the ultimate in privacy and gorgeous scenery,
★ you can't beat Costa de Cocos, located 2 km (1 mi) from town. Here, divers and explorers congregate for trips to the famed Chinchorro Banks (weather permitting); Bird Island; and San Pedro, Belize. Costa de Cocos is one of the precious few resorts in this area and is easily the most hospitable and comfortable. Stay here for even a few days and you will feel like family. Twelve cleverly crafted cabañas offer 24-hour wind-powered electricity and an eclectic selection of paperback books. Room rates include delicious breakfasts and dinners. The proprietors, Dave and Maria Randall, are immensely knowledgeable about the peninsula and the reef offshore. The full-service dive shop offers NAUI certification courses (more comprehensive than PADI). Other activities include sea kayaking and fishing trips. It's best to make room reservations in advance, but if you plan to drop by unannounced, be sure to start out for Xcalak early in the day so you can make it back to the main road before dark if the cabañas are full. ✉ *Xcalak Peninsula, 54 km (33 mi) south of Majahual*, ☎ *no phone, www.costadecocos.com. Reservations:* ✉ *Turquoise Reef Group, Box 2664, Evergreen, CO 80439,* ☎ *303/674–9615 or 800/538–6802,* FAX *303/674–8735. 12 cabanas. Restaurant, dive shop. No credit cards.*

Bacalar

112 km (69 mi) south of Felipe Carrillo Puerto, 320 km (198 mi) south of Cancún, and 40 km (25 mi) northwest of Chetumal.

㉑ The spectacularly vast **Laguna de Bacalar,** also known as the Lake of the Seven Colors, is the second-largest lake in Mexico (56 km, or 35 mi, long) and is frequented by scuba divers and other lovers of water sports. Seawater and fresh water mix in the lake, intensifying the aquamarine hues, and the water contrasts starkly with the dark jungle growth. If you drive along the lake's southern shores, you'll enter the affluent section of the town of Bacalar, with elegant waterfront homes. Also in the vicinity are a few hotels and campgrounds.

Founded in AD 435, **Bacalar** appears to be the oldest settlement in Quintana Roo. Of some historical interest is the **Fuerte de San Felipe,** a stone fort built by the Spaniards during the 18th century to ward off marauding pirates and Indians and later used by the Maya during the War of the Castes. The monolithic structure is right on the plaza and overlooks the lake. Presently it houses government offices and a museum with exhibits on local history (ask for someone to bring a key if museum doors are locked). ☎ *No phone.* 🖃 *$1.* ☉ *Tues.–Sun. 10–6.*

㉒ Just beyond Bacalar exists the largest sinkhole in Mexico, the **Cenote Azul,** 607 ft in diameter, with clear blue waters that afford unusual visibility even at 200 ft below the surface. Surrounded by lush vegetation and underwater caves, the cenote attracts divers who specialize in this somewhat tricky type of dive. There's a restaurant at the foot of the cenote where you can linger over fresh fish and a beer while gazing out over the deep, blue waters. Swimming can be done just beyond the restaurant from a rocky shore. ☉ *Daily 8–8.*

Lodging

$$$ ☷ **Rancho Encantado.** On the shores of Laguna Bacalar, 30 minutes
★   north of Chetumal, the Rancho comprises 12 Maya-themed *casitas* (cot-
tages), each with its own patio and hammocks, kitchenette, sitting area,
and bathroom. The casitas and public areas have hand-carved hard-
wood furnishings, woven Oaxacan rugs, and sculptures of Maya gods;
lush green lawns border the water. Both breakfast and dinner are in-
cluded in the room rate, and guests applaud the homemade breads and
ice creams, curries, gumbo, lasagna, and other exotic fare (no red
meat is served). You can swim and snorkel off the private dock lead-
ing into the lagoon, or take in a Jacuzzi or massage while looking out
over the water. Adventure tours to the ruins in southern Yucatán,
Campeche, and Belize are available, and the ranch's staff are well in-
formed on changes at the nearby archaeological sites. The ranch is also
available for group retreats and meetings. When traveling south on High-
way 307, watch for the road sign on your left. *Reservations:* ✉ *APDO
40, Chetumal, Quintana Roo 77930,* ☎ *983/80427.* ✉ *Reservations
in U.S., Box 1644, Taos, NM 87571,* ☎ *800/505–MAYA,* ℻ *505/751–
0972, www.encantado.com. 12 casitas. Restaurant, bar, hot tub, mas-
sage, meeting, travel services. No credit cards.*

Chetumal

❷❸   *58 km (36 mi) south of Bacalar and 382 km (237 mi) south of Cancún.*

Chetumal is the last town on Mexico's southern Caribbean shore. It was
founded in 1898 as Payo Obispo, in a concerted and only partially suc-
cessful effort to gain control of the lucrative traffic in the region's pre-
cious hardwoods, arms, and ammunition, and also as a base of operations
against the rebellious Indians. The city, which overlooks the Bay of
Chetumal at the mouth of the Río Hondo, was devastated by a hurri-
cane in 1955 and rebuilt as the capital of Quintana Roo and the state's
major port. Though Chetumal remains the state capital to this day, it
attracts few visitors other than those en route to Central America.

Overall, Chetumal feels more Caribbean than Mexican; this is not sur-
prising, given its proximity to Belize. Run-down (but often charming)
clapboard houses interspersed with low-lying ramshackle commercial
establishments line the quiet streets. The mixed population includes
many black Caribbeans, and the arts reflect this eclectic combina-
tion—the music includes reggae, salsa, and calypso (but little mariachi).
The many Middle Eastern inhabitants have influenced the cuisine,
which represents an exotic blend of Yucatecan, Mexican, and Lebanese.
Although Chetumal's provisions are modest, the town has a pleasant,
extended waterfront, since the city is surrounded by the Bay of Chetu-
mal on three sides.

The town's most attractive thoroughfare, the wide **Boulevard Bahía,**
runs along the water and is a popular gathering spot at night (though
on the weekend Chetumal practically shuts down). The main plaza sits
between the boulevard and Avenidas Alvaro Obregón and Héroes. Un-
remarkable modern government buildings and patriotic statues and mon-
uments to local heroes wall in the plaza on two sides. The water
lapping at the dock creates a melancholy rhythm, but if you sit at one
of the sidewalk cafés by the square, you will have an appealing view
of the huge, placid bay.

Downtown Chetumal is getting spruced up to attract more tourists.
Mid-range hotels and tourist-friendly restaurants are popping up near
and along the main thoroughfare, Avenida Héroes, and travel agen-
cies hype the fascinating and unique nearby ruins of Kohunlich, Dz-

ibanché, and Kinichná (☞ *below*). In town, the **Museum of Maya Culture** provides a comprehensive introduction to Maya civilization. The interactive museum comprises three levels, each containing relevant exhibits; sky (devoted to the "higher learning" of Maya arts, writing, and arithmetic), earth (showing Maya daily life in trade, food, architecture, and politics), and the underworld (dealing with Maya spirituality). A replica of a typical Maya dwelling sits in the patio outside. Vivid videos, stellae, multimedia displays, and models of major Maya cities guide the visitor through the early beginnings to the final demise of the civilization with the arrival of the Spanish conquistadors. ⊠ *Av. Héroes and Calle Mahatma Ghandi,* ☎ 983/26838. ☞ *$2.* ☉ *Tues.– Thurs. 9–7, Fri. and Sat. 9–8, Sun. 9–2.*

Laguna Milagrosa, a lovely lagoon with an island in the center and a shoreline graced by palms and bougainvillea, is 15 km (9 mi) west of Chetumal on the road to Bacalar. Restaurants and shops that rent out diving equipment are in the vicinity, too.

Dining and Lodging

$$ ✕ **Cactus Restaurant.** This lively restaurant just off Avenida Héroes is characterized by fake cacti and bumping dub reggae music. Fajitas, salads, fish and lobster are served on rickety balconies overlooking the street. For dessert try one of the various crepes (caramel, banana, or coconut). ⊠ *Av. 5 de Mayo 61,* ☎ 983/29588. *AE, MC, V.*

$$ ✕ **Emiliano's.** The seafood is excellent here, as evidenced by the packed house most days at lunchtime. Try the shrimp pâté (a smooth blend of cream cheese and grilled shrimp) and the huge chili relleno stuffed with seafood. For an all-out feast for two or more, go for the seafood platter. ⊠ *Av. San Salvador 557, at Calle 9,* ☎ 983/70267. *MC, V.*

$$ ✕ **Mandinga.** One of the best places in town for the freshest seafood, Mandinga is best known for its octopus and conch seafood soup, a spicy blend of the daily catch. ⊠ *Av. San Salvador 182, between Héroes and Belice,* ☎ 983/24824. *No credit cards. No dinner.*

$$ ✕ **Sergio's Pizzas.** This pizza parlor became so popular that the owners had to convert the small frame house into a bigger place while they added more dishes to the menu. Locals rave about the grilled steaks, barbecued chicken (made with Sergio's own sauce), and garlic shrimp, along with smoked oyster and seafood pizzas. Avoid the pastas. ⊠ *Av. Alvaro Obregón 182, at Av. 5 de Mayo,* ☎ 983/20882. *MC, V.*

$$$ 🏨 **Holiday Inn Chetumal Puerta Maya.** The best thing about Chetu-
★ mal's best hotel is its staff, whose cheerfulness and accommodating ways make coming back from a business meeting or a sweaty trip to the ruins a welcome experience. All of the comfortable rooms have air-conditioning units, satellite color TV, and modern furnishings in pastel colors. No-smoking rooms and rooms for people with mobility problems attest to the hotel's willingness to serve. A large swimming pool is on the lobby level. The hotel's restaurant, **Nah Balam,** serves buffets as well as an international menu. The hotel has the largest banquet and conference facilities in town—it can accommodate 1,600 persons in the banquet room. ⊠ *Av. Héroes 171, 77000,* ☎ 983/21050 *or* 800/ 465–4329, ℻ 983/21676. *75 rooms, 10 suites. Restaurant, bar, pool, meeting rooms, travel services, car rental. AE, MC, V.*

$$ 🏨 **Hotel-Suites Arges.** This mid-size, charming hotel is probably the best deal for your money in Chetumal (it's on the low end of the $$ range). Moorish-style hallways lead to huge rooms with air-conditioning, TVs, telephones, and refrigerators. The master suite contains a dining area and two bedrooms. The downstairs restaurant offers tasty local fare; a gym, Jacuzzi, and travel agency are also on the premises. ⊠ *Lázaro Cárdenas 212, off of Av. Héroes,* ☎ 983/29525, ℻ 983/24911, arges@200.33.110.20. *24 rooms. Restaurant, bar, hot*

tub, exercise room, recreation room, conference room, travel services, car rental. MC, V.

$$ 📺 **Los Cocos.** The lush, jungle-themed decor of this hotel's outdoor restaurant and lobby ends when you enter the rooms. Disturbingly pink walls aside, however, the hotel does offer comfortable rooms with powerful air-conditioning, in-room phones and TVs, and a pleasant garden area with a large swimming pool. The waterfront is within easy walking distance, and the restaurant is popular with both locals and travelers. ✉ *Av. Héroes 134, at Calle Chapultepec, 77000,* ☎ *983/20544,* 📠 *983/20920. 80 rooms. Restaurant, bar, pool, shops. AE, MC, V.*

Kohunlich

 42 km (26 mi) west of Chetumal, on Route 186.

Kohunlich is renowned for the giant stucco masks on its principal pyramid, the creatively named **Edificio de los Mascarones** (Mask Building), for one of the oldest ball courts in Quintana Roo, and for the remains of a great drainage system at the **Plaza de las Estelas** (Plaza of the Stelae). The masks—about 6 ft tall—are set vertically into the wide staircases; first thought to be representations of the Maya sun god, they are most likely the faces of actual rulers of Kohunlich, according to new theories. Archaeologists say there are over 500 mounds on the site, most unexplored, and believe that Kohunlich was built and occupied during the Early and Late Classic periods, about AD 300–AD 1200. Recent excavations have turned up 29 individual and multiple burial sites inside a residence building called **Templo de Los Viente-Siete Escalones** (Temple of the Twenty-Seven Steps). This site is usually deserted, and in the vicinity are scores of unexcavated mounds, stelae, and thriving flora and fauna. ☎ *No phone.* 🎟 *$2.* ☉ *Daily 8–5.*

Dzibanché and Kinichná

 1 km (½ mi) east of turnoff for Kohunlich on Rte. 186, follow signs for 24 km (15 mi) north to fork for Dzibanché (1½ km, or 1 mi, from fork) and Kinichná (3 km, or 2 mi from fork).

Dzibanché and its sister city Kinichna are considered to have been the most powerful alliance ruling southern Quintana Roo during the Classic period of the state. The fertile farmlands surrounding the ruins are still being used today as they no doubt were hundreds of years ago, and the winding drive deep into the fields makes visitors feel as if they are coming upon something undiscovered. Indeed, the area's ruins have not yet been fully restored—on your way back from these two sites, look for a large hill on your right-hand side. The stone structures protruding from the hill suggest that it contains another enormous temple, buried under layers of vegetation.

Despite the absence of visitors, these ruins have been well restored and are very accessible. Dzibanché, named "writing on wood" for a quebracho wood lintel discovered at the site, has several plazas surrounded by temples, palaces, and pyramids, all bearing the Río Bec style of architecture. The famed lintel of **Temple IV**, with eight glyphs dating to AD 618, is currently housed in the Museo de la Cultura Maya in Chetumal (☞ *above*), but there is still a great deal to see at the site, including the carved stone steps at **Edificio 13** and **Edificio 2**, which still bears some traces of stone masks. ☎ *No phone.* 🎟 *$1.* ☉ *Daily 8–5.*

Before or after seeing Dzibanché, make your way back to the fork in the road and head over to Kinichná ("House of the Sun," in Maya). The site consists of a two-level pyramidal mound split into Acropolis B and Acropolis C, apparently dedicated to the sun god. The two levels of stone temples show typical Río Bec architectural styles and the stone supports from what could have been stuccoed masks similar to those found at Kohunlich. Two mounds at the foot of the pyramid suggest that the temple was a ceremonial site. At its summit Kinichná offers the finest views of any archaeological site in the area. ☎ *No phone.* ✉ *$1.* ⊙ *Daily 8–5.*

THE CARIBBEAN COAST A TO Z

Arriving and Departing

By Bus

CHETUMAL

The bus station (✉ Av. Salvador Novo 179) in Chetumal is served by **ADO** (☎ 983/29877), **Caribe Express** (☎ 983/27889), and other lines. Buses run regularly from Chetumal to Cancún, Villahermosa, Mexico City, Mérida, Campeche City, and Veracruz, as well as Guatemala and Belize.

PLAYA DEL CARMEN

There is first-class and deluxe service on the **ADO** line (✉ Av. Juárez at Av. 5, ☎ 987/30109) between Playa del Carmen and Cancún, Valladolid, Chichén Itzá, Chetumal, Tulum, Xel-Há, Mexico City, and Mérida daily. **Mayab** (✉ Av. Juárez, ☎ no phone) runs second-class buses to the above destinations, and deluxe express buses to Chetumal. **Autotransportes Oriente** (✉ Av. Juárez, ☎ no phone) has express service to Mérida eight times daily, and one bus daily to Cobá. **TRP** (✉ Av. Juárez at Av. 5, ☎ no phone) offers first-class service about every 15 minutes to Cancún.

By Ferry

Ferries and jet foils—which can be picked up at the dock—run between Playa del Carmen and Cozumel about every hour (more frequently in the early morning and evening). **Water Jet Service** (✉ near the ferry dock, ☎ 987/2108) makes the 35–40 minute trip for about $5.

By Plane

Almost everyone who arrives by air into this region flies into Cancún (☞ Chapter 2).

Getting Around

By Car

The entire coast, from Punta Sam near Cancún to the main border crossing to Belize at Chetumal, is traversable on Highway 307. This straight road is entirely paved and is being widened into four lanes to Playa del Carmen. Eventually, it will be widened as far south as Chetumal (but be careful—many motorists see the road's straightness as an opportunity to speed). Gas stations are becoming more prevalent, but it's still a good idea to fill the tank whenever you can; there are gas stations in Cancún, Puerto Morelos, Playa del Carmen, Tulum, Felipe Carrillo Puerto, and Chetumal.

Good roads that run into Highway 307 from the west are Route 180 (from Mérida and Valladolid), Route 295 (from Valladolid), Route 184 (from central Yucatán), and Route 186 (from Villahermosa and, via Route 261, from Mérida and Campeche). There is an entrance to the *autopista* toll highway between Cancún and Mérida off Highway 307 just south of Cancún. Approximate driving times are as follows: from Cancún to Felipe Carrillo Puerto, 4 hours; from Cancún to Mérida, 4½ hours (3½ hours on the new *autopista* toll road, $27); from Carrillo Puerto to Chetumal, 2 hours; from Carrillo Puerto to Mérida, about 4½ hours; from Chetumal to Campeche, 6½ hours. Be sure to stock up on groceries, pharmacy items, hardware, and auto parts in Puerto Morelos, Playa del Carmen, Felipe Carrillo Puerto, or Chetumal.

By Plane
In **Chetumal** the airport is on the southwestern edge of town, along Avenida Alvaro Obregón where it turns into Route 186. **Aerocaribe** (☎ 983/26675) has daily flights to Cancún and frequent flights to Belize, Tikal, Veracruz, and Villahermosa.

The airstrip in **Playa del Carmen** is near the Continental Plaza Hotel, and there is occasional shuttle service to Cozumel. A small airline called **Aero Saab** (Playa del Carmen airstrip, ☎ 987/30501) offers daily scheduled air tours to Tulum, Uxmal, and Chichén Itzá if enough passengers turn up to fill the four- and five-seat Cessnas. The company also offers charter flights to Cozumel, Mérida, Belize, and Guatemala.

By Taxi
Taxis can be hired in Cancún to go as far as Playa del Carmen, Tulum, or Akumal, but the price is steep unless you have many passengers. Fares run about $55 or more to Playa alone; between Playa and Tulum or Akumal, expect to pay at least $25. It's much cheaper from Playa to Cancún, with taxi fare running about $30; negotiate before you hop into the cab. Taxis wait eagerly for passengers by the bus station in Playa, and there's a taxi stand at the entrance to Akumal.

Contacts and Resources

Banks
CHETUMAL
Banco del Atlántico (✉ Av. Héroes 37, ☎ 983/22776) and **Bancomer** (✉ Av. Alvaro Obregón 222 at Av. Juárez, ☎ 983/25300 or 983/25318) provide banking services, including foreign currency exchange.

PLAYA DEL CARMEN
Banco del Atlántico (✉ Av. Juárez between Avs. 10 and 15, ☎ 987/30404 or 987/30064) cashes traveler's checks weekdays 10–noon; a new **Bancomer** (✉ Av. Juaréz between Calles 25 and 30, ☎ 987/30402 or 987/30406) does the same. Both banks have ATM machines that accept some U.S. bank cards.

Car Rental
In **Playa del Carmen** car rental agencies proliferate around the ferry pier and Avenida Juárez. Rental agencies include **Budget** (✉ Hotel Continental Plaza Playacar, ☎ 987/30100); **Hertz** (✉ White Sands Travel, ☎ 987/31130 or 987/30703; ✉ Hotel Continental Plaza Playacar, ☎ 987/30033); and **National** (✉ Hotel Molcas, ☎ 987/30360 or 987/30883). If you want air-conditioning, reserve your car at least one day in advance.

In addition most of the first-class hotels in Puerto Aventuras, Akumal, and Chetumal offer car rental service.

Emergencies
CHETUMAL
Police (✉ Av. Insurgentes and Av. Belice, ☎ 983/21500). **Red Cross** (✉ Av. Héroes 279, ☎ 983/20571).

PLAYA DEL CARMEN
Police (✉ Av. Juárez between Avs. 15a and 20a, next to post office, ☎ 987/30291). **Red Cross** (✉ Av. Juárez at Av. 25, ☎ 987/31233).

English-Language Bookstores

Your best bet for the widest selection of English-language books is in **Puerto Morelos,** where Jeanine Kitchel keeps **Alma Libre** humming along. Over 10,000 books on a variety of topics are available, and Jeanine's yearly trips to the States keep the supply plentiful. ✉ *Av. Tulum 3, on main plaza,* 987/10264. ☉ Tues.–Wed. 6–9:30, Thurs.–Sat. 10:30 AM– 1:30 PM. Closed May–Aug.

In **Playa del Carmen,** Duty Free (✉ main plaza, ☎ no phone) has English-language periodicals. The **gift shop** at the Playacar hotel (☎ 987/ 21583) has a modest selection of magazines and paperbacks. However, expect to pay double what you pay in the United States.

Guided Tours

Although some guided tours are available in this area, the roads are quite good for the most part, so renting a car is an efficient and enjoyable alternative: Most of the sights you'll see along this stretch are natural, and you can hire a guide at the ruins sites.

ECOTOURISM

Naviera Asterix (☎ 98/864847 or 99/864270 in Cancún) offers guided yacht tours to Contoy Island. **Ecolomex Tours** (☎ 98/843805 or 98/ 871776 in Cancún) does off-the-beaten-path trips to little-known areas along the coast. **Ava Tours** (☎ 98/848676 or 98/848696 in Cancún) specializes in aerial tours of the coast. All will pick up at hotels along the coast from Puerto Morelos to Playa del Carmen.

MAYA RUINS

Mayaland Gray Line Tours (✉ Hotel America, Av. Tulum at Calle Brisa, ☎ 98/872450 or 800/235–4079, FAX 98/872438 in Cancún or ✉ Las Molcas Hotel, Calle 1 Sur between Av. 5 and the ferry pier, ☎ 987/31106 or 800/235–4079 in Playa del Carmen), one of the Yucatán's leading tour companies, is now running tours to Chichén Itzá from hotels around Punta Bete, Playa del Carmen, and Akumal. Tours include pickup at your hotel, transportation on a deluxe bus, lunch at the Mayaland hotel, and use of the hotel's facilities (including swimming pool), and free beer, wine, and soft drinks on the ride home. The first-class hotels in Playa del Carmen and Puerto Aventuras can arrange **day tours** to Tulum, Chichén Itzá, and Cobá.

In Chetumal try **Turistica Maya de Quintana Roo** (✉ Av. Héroes No. 165-A, ☎ 983/20555 or 983/22058, FAX 983/29711, holimaya@mp-snet.com.mx) for tours to Kohunlich, Dzibanché, the Laguna de Bacalar and Fort of San Felipe, and Belize.

In Playa del Carmen, **Aero Fénico** Airlines (☎ 987/30636) has full-day and half-day tours to Uxmal, Chichén Itzá, Palenque, Mérida, and Tikal in Guatemala; entrance fees, tour guide, and lunch are included.

Mail

The **Chetumal post office** (✉ Plutarco Elias Calles No. 2, ☎ 983/ 22578) is open weekdays 8–7, Saturday 8–noon. The **Playa del Carmen post office** (✉ Av. Juárez, next to police station, ☎ 987/30300), is open weekdays 8–7.

Medical Clinics

Chetumal: Hospital General (✉ Av. Andres Quintana Roo, ☎ 983/ 21932). **Playa del Carmen:** Centro de Salud (✉ Av. Juárez at Av. 15a, ☎ 987/21230, ext. 147) or **Dr. Victor Macias,** a bilingual physician (✉ Calle 2 Norte and Av. 35, ☎ 987/30493).

Pharmacies

Chetumal: Farmacia Social Mechaca (⊠ Av. Independencia 134C, ☎ 983/20044). **Playa del Carmen:** There's a pharmacy at the **Plaza Marina** shopping mall and several on **Av. 5** between Calles 4 and 8.

Telephones

In **Chetumal** the government-run telephone office, TELMEX, is at Avenida Juárez and Lázaro Cárdenas. For long-distance and international calls, you might also try the booths on Avenida Héroes: One is on the corner of Ignacio Zaragoza and the other is just opposite Avenida Efraín Aguilar, next to the tourist information booth.

In **Playa del Carmen** there are Ladatel long-distance phone booths in front of the post office on Avenida Juárez and at the corner of Avenida Juárez and Avenida 5.

Many of the more remote places on the Caribbean coast rely on E-mail and the Internet as their major form of communication. In Playa del Carmen, Internet service is available, though expensive (about $1 a minute at most places). There are several Internet providers near Avenida 5; try **Caseta Telefónica Phone-Fax 2** (⊠ Calle 8 and Av. 5, in the Rincon del Sol Plaza, ☎ 987/31246), which provides fax, E-mail, Netscape navigator, and long-distance phone service.

Travel Agencies

There are more major travel agencies and tour operators up and down the coast than before, and first-class hotels in Playa del Carmen, Puerto Aventuras, and Akumal usually have their own in-house travel services.

CHETUMAL

Turística Maya de Quintana Roo (⊠ Holiday Inn Chetumal Puerta Maya, ☎ 983/20555 or 983/22058, FAX 983/29711).

PLAYA DEL CARMEN

White Sands Travel (⊠ Av. 5 between Calle 6 and 8, ☎ 987/31080) and **Amazing Tours** (⊠ Av. Juárez between Calles 2 and 4, ☎ 987/30925).

Visitor Information

CHETUMAL

The **tourist information booth** (⊠ Av. Héroes, opposite Av. Efraín Aguilar, ☎ 983/23663) is open weekdays 8:30–2:30 and 6–9.

PLAYA DEL CARMEN

The **tourist information booth** (⊠ Av. 5, 1 block from beach, ☎ no phone) is open 8–1 and 5–8. In both Playa del Carmen and Chetumal, you might have to cool your heels for a while until someone actually shows up to run the booth.

6 Mérida and the State of Yucatán

Long a favorite of archaeologists, the state of Yucatán contains two of the most spectacular Maya ruins, Chichén Itzá and Uxmal. Travelers are also coming to recognize the charms of Mérida, with its excellent restaurants and markets and its unique mix of Spanish, Maya, and French architectural styles.

BONUS MILES MAKE GREAT SOUVENIRS.

Earn Miles With Your MCI Card.

Take the MCI Card along on this trip and start earning miles for the next one. You'll earn frequent flyer miles on all your calls and save with the low rates you've come to expect from MCI. Before you know it, you'll be on your way to some other international destination.

Sign up for MCI by calling 1-800-FLY-FREE

Earn Frequent Flyer Miles.

Is this a great time, or what? :-)

Easy To Call Home.

1. To use your MCI Card, just dial the WorldPhone access number of the country you're calling from.
2. Dial or give the operator your MCI Card number.
3. Dial or give the number you're calling.

American Samoa	633-2MCI (633-2624)
# Antigua	1-800-888-8000
(Available from public card phones only)	#2
# Argentina (CC)	0-800-5-1002
# Aruba ÷	800-888-8
# Bahamas	1-800-888-8000
# Barbados	1-800-888-8000
# Belize	557 from hotels
	815 from pay phones
# Bermuda ÷	1-800-888-8000
# Bolivia ♦(CC)	0-800-2222
# Brazil (CC)	000-8012
# British Virgin Islands ÷	1-800-888-8000
# Cayman Islands	1-800-888-8000
# Chile (CC)	
To call using CTC ■	800-207-300
To call using ENTEL ■	800-360-180
# Colombia (CC) ♦	980-16-0001
Collect Access in Spanish	980-16-1000
# Costa Rica ♦	0800-012-2222
# Dominica	1-800-888-8000
# Dominican Republic (CC) ÷	1-800-888-8000
Collect Access in Spanish	1121
# Ecuador (CC) ÷	999-170
El Salvador	800-1767
# Grenada ÷	1-800-888-8000
Guatemala (CC) ♦	9999-189
Guyana	177
# Haiti ÷ Collect Access	193
Collect Access in French/Creole	190
Honduras ÷	8000-122
# Jamaica ÷ Collect Access	1-800-888-8000
(From Special Hotels only)	873
From payphones	★2
# Mexico (CC)	
Avantel	01-800-021-8000
Telmex ▲	001-800-674-7000
Mexico Access in Spanish	01-800-021-1000
# Netherlands Antilles (CC) ÷	001-800-888-8000
Nicaragua (CC)	166
(Outside of Managua, dial 02 first)	
Collect Access in Spanish from any public payphone	★2
# Panama	108
Military Bases	2810-108
# Paraguay ÷	00-812-800
# Peru	0-800-500-10
# Puerto Rico (CC)	1-800-888-8000
# St. Lucia ÷	1-800-888-8000
# Trinidad & Tobago ÷	1-800-888-8000
# Turks & Caicos ÷	1-800-888-8000
# Uruguay	000-412
# U.S. Virgin Islands (CC)	1-800-888-8000
# Venezuela (CC) ÷ ♦	800-1114-0

You've read the book. Now book the trip.

For all the best deals on flights, hotels, rental cars, and vacation packages, book them online at www.previewtravel.com. Then click on our Destination Guides featuring content from Fodor's and more. You'll find hotels, restaurants, attractions, and things to do around the globe. There are even interactive maps, videos, and weather forecasts. You'll have everything you need to make your vacation exactly what you want it to be. All it takes is a trip online.

Travel on Your Terms™
www.previewtravel.com
aol keyword: previewtravel

preview travel℠

Updated by
Patricia Alisau

THE YUCATÁN IS one of the most culturally rich parts of the country. It is the heart of a fascinating juxtaposition of two powerful civilizations—that of the Maya and that of transplanted Europeans. Vestiges of the past are evident in this land of oval thatched-roof huts and stately old mission churches, and in its people—particularly the women who still dress in traditional garb. Mysterious "lost cities" lie hidden in the forests. Small fishing villages dot beaches that are so far unjaded by the tourist industry. In the midst of this exotic landscape stands the elegant old city of Mérida, for centuries the main stronghold of Spanish colonialism in the land of the Maya.

There is a marvelous eccentricity about Mérida. Fully urban, with maddeningly slow-moving traffic, it has a self-sufficient, self-contented air that would suggest a small town more than a state capital of some 1.5 million inhabitants. Gaily pretentious turn-of-the-century buildings have an Iberian-Moorish flair for the ornate, but most of the architecture is low-lying, and although the city sprawls, it is not imposing. Grandiose colonial facades adorned with iron grillwork, carved wooden doors, and archways conceal marble tiles and lush gardens that hark back to the city's heyday as the wealthiest capital in Mexico.

Mérida is a city of subtle contrasts, from its opulent facades to its residents, very European yet very Maya. The Indian presence is unmistakable: People are short and dark-skinned, with sculpted bones and almond eyes; women pad about in *huipiles* (hand-embroidered, sacklike white dresses), and craftsmen and vendors from the outlying villages come to town in their huaraches. So many centuries after the conquest, Yucatán remains one of the last great strongholds of Mexico's indigenous population. To this day, in fact, many Maya do not even speak Spanish, primarily because of the peninsula's geographic and, hence, cultural isolation from the rest of the country. Additionally, the Maya—long portrayed as docile and peace-loving—for centuries provided the Spaniards and the mainland Mexicans with one of their greatest challenges. Yucatán tried to secede from the rest of Mexico in the 1840s and, as late as the 1920s and 1930s, rebellious pockets of Maya communities held out against the outsiders, or *dzulobs*. Yucatecans speak of themselves as *peninsulares* first, Mexicans second. It could well have been this independent attitude that induced Gov. Salvador Alvarado, in 1915, to convene the first feminist congress in the country (and Latin America as well) with the idea of liberating women "from being social wards and from the traditions that have suppressed them for years." This congress, which Alvarado described as "brilliant," was so successful that it was followed by the second congress in Mexico City in 1921 where women asked for the right to vote. (Finally, in 1953, they were granted the right).

The Maya civilization—one of the great ancient cultures—had been around since before 1500 BC, but it was in a state of decline when the conquistadors arrived in AD 1527, burning defiant warriors at the stake, severing limbs, and drowning and hanging women. Huge agricultural estates brought riches to the Spaniards, and Mérida soon became a strategic administrative and military foothold, the gateway to Cuba and to Spain. Francisco de Montejo's conquest of Yucatán took three gruesome wars, a total of 24 years. "Nowhere in all America was resistance to Spanish conquest more obstinate or more nearly successful," wrote the historian Henry Parkes. By the 18th century, huge maize and cattle plantations flourished throughout the peninsula, and the wealthy *hacendados* (plantation owners), left largely to their own devices by the viceroys in faraway Mexico City, accumulated fortunes under a semi-feudal system. As the economic base shifted to the export of dyewood, henequen, and chicle, the social structure—based on Indian peonage—barely changed.

Insurrection came during the War of the Castes in the mid-1800s, when the enslaved indigenous people rose up with religious fervor and massacred thousands of whites. The United States, Cuba, and Mexico City finally came to the aid of the ruling elite, and between 1846 and 1850 the Indian population of Yucatán was effectively halved. Those Maya who did not escape into the remote jungles of Quintana Roo or get sold into slavery in Cuba found themselves worse off than before under the dictatorship of Porfirio Díaz, who brought Yaqui prisoners from Northern Mexico to the peninsula as forced labor under the rapacious grip of the hacendados. Díaz's legacy is still evident in the pretentious French-style mansions that stretch along Mérida's Paseo de Montejo.

Yucatán was then and still is a largely agricultural state, although tourism, and the *maquiladora* (assembly plants, usually foreign-owned) now play more prominent roles in the economy. There are more than 50 factories. The capital accounts for more than half the state's population, but the rest of the inhabitants live in villages, maintaining conservative traditions and lifestyles. The state exports honey, textiles, henequen, orange-juice concentrate, fresh fish, hammocks, and wood products.

Physically, too, Yucatán differs from the rest of the country. Its geography and wildlife have more in common with Florida and Cuba—with which it was probably once connected—than with the central Mexican plateau and mountains. A mostly flat limestone slab possessing almost no bodies of water, it is rife with underground cenotes (sinkholes), caves with stalactites, small hills, and intense jungle. Wild ginger and spider lilies grow in profusion, and vast flamingo colonies nest at swampy estuaries on the northern and western coasts, where undeveloped sandy beaches extend for 370 km (230 mi). Deer, turkeys, boars, ocelots, tapirs, and armadillos flourish in this semitropical climate (the average temperature is 82°F, or 28°C).

But it is, of course, the celebrated Maya ruins, Chichén Itzá and Uxmal especially, that bring most tourists to Mérida. Indeed, the Puuc hills south of Mérida have more archaeological sites per square mile than any other place in the hemisphere. The roads in this region rank among the best in the country, and local travel agencies are adept at running tours.

Pleasures and Pastimes

Beaches
Although Yucatán's beach resorts are no match for those of Cancún and the Caribbean coast, the north coast of the peninsula has long stretches of wide, soft white-sand beaches shared by sunbathers and fishermen. Progreso, where Mérida residents go to beat the heat, is unpretentious and affordable, and on summer weekends it can be as lively as any place on the Mexican Caribbean. Empty beaches stretch for about 64 km (40 mi) to the east, punctuated by small fishing villages that are catching the eye of developers as tourism takes off. Other popular beach destinations are Celestún and Sisal.

Bird-Watching
More than 300 bird species are abundant in the Yucatán, both along the coast and inland. The most extraordinary are flamingos, which can

be seen in the natural parks at Celestún and Río Lagartos at any time of year. The largest flocks of both flamingos and birding enthusiasts can be found during the spring months, when thousands of the birds—90% of the entire flamingo population of the Western Hemisphere—come to Río Lagartos to nest.

Dining

Dining out is a pleasure in Mérida. The city's 50-odd restaurants offer a superb variety of cuisine—primarily Yucatecan, of course, but also Lebanese, Italian, French, Chinese, and Mexican—at very reasonable prices. Generally, reservations are advised for those places marked $$$, but only during the high season. Casual but neat dress is acceptable at all Mérida restaurants. Avoid wearing shorts in the better places, however.

Beach towns north of Mérida like Progreso, Yucalpetén, Sisal, Telchac Puerto, and Río Lagartos to the east and Celestún to the west offer the most mouthwatering seafood around, always fresh-caught the same day. A real gourmet dish is the blue crab at Celustún. However, you can't go wrong with most restaurants, whether they be thatched-roof affairs along the beach or in-town eateries.

Beware the restaurants in Pisté, the village nearest to Chichén Itzá. They're overpriced, and the food is only fair. It's better to try one of the *palapa* (pre-Hispanic thatched roof) cafés along the main road or the small markets and produce stands, which can provide the makings for a modest picnic.

The restaurants near the ruins in Uxmal are nothing to write home about, either. The exception is Los Almendros, in Ticul, which is well worth the 15-minute drive.

All restaurants are open for breakfast, lunch, and dinner unless otherwise noted. People who like eating with the locals might stop in at one of the many *loncherías* (diners) in the small towns and downtown districts of cities for *panuchos* (cooked tortillas stuffed with beans and topped with shredded meat or fish), *empanadas* (meat-filled turnovers), tacos, or *salbutes* (fried tortillas smothered with diced turkey, pickled onion, and sliced avocado). However, take care with the *habanero* chilies. This native species will have smoke coming out of your ears if not used in moderation.

For more on Mexican culinary items, *see* Dining *in the* Destination: Cancún, Cozumel, Yucatán Peninsula chapter.

CATEGORY	COST*
$$$$	over $20
$$$	$15–$20
$$	$8–$15
$	under $8

per person, excluding drinks and service

Fishing

Those interested in sportfishing for such catch as grouper, red snapper, and sea bass, among others, will be sated in **Yucalpetén,** west of Progreso. **Río Lagartos** also offers good fishing in its murky waters. In the Parque Natural del Flamenco Mexicano in **Celestún,** you have your choice of river or gulf fishing.

Lodging

Outside of Mérida you'll find that accommodations fit the low-key, simple pace of the region. Internationally affiliated properties are the exception rather than the rule. Instead, charmingly idiosyncratic old mansions or former haciendas like the Hacienda Katanchel (☞ Dining and Lodging *in* Mérida, *below*), restored and opened as a hotel in 1996, offer visitors a base from which to explore the countryside. However, the new environmentally friendly Eco Paraiso in Celestún has diversified the hotel offerings.

Mérida's 60-odd hotels offer a refreshingly broad range, from the chain hotels at the top end and the classic, older hotels housed in colonial or turn-of-the-century mansions suffused with genteel charm, to fleabags adequate only for the budget traveler unconcerned with creature comforts. As in the rest of Mexico, the facade rarely reveals the character of the hotel behind it, so check out the interior before turning away.

Location is very important in your choice of hotels: If you plan to spend most of your time enjoying Mérida, stay in the vicinity of the main square or along Calle 60. If you're a light sleeper, however, choose a hotel away from the plaza and parks or one that has double-pane windows to cut out traffic noise. You may be better off staying in one of the places along or near Paseo de Montejo, about a 30-minute stroll from the *zócalo* (main square). If being assured of hot water is a major concern, test the faucets before renting a room. In general the public spaces in Mérida's hotels are prettier than the sleeping rooms. All hotels have air-conditioning unless otherwise noted. More budget hotels are installing air-conditioning in at least a few rooms nowadays to keep up with the competition.

Properties in Mérida have a Yucatán 97000 mailing address.

CATEGORY	COST*
$$$$	over $90
$$$	$60–$90
$$	$25–$60
$	under $25

All prices are for a standard double room, excluding service and the 15% tax.

Ruins

Ancient Maya ruins from the Classic period, about AD 250 to AD 900, are Yucatán's greatest claim to fame. The Maya-Toltec city of Chichén Itzá, midway between Cancún and Mérida, was the first Yucatán ruin to be excavated and extensively restored for public viewing in the late 1930s. Its main pyramid has become one of the most familiar images of Mexico. Uxmal, south of Mérida, is at least equally spectacular. Public interest in these ruins has inspired a boom in ruins restoration since the early 1980s. The archaeological sites along the Puuc Route south of Uxmal, though not large, are among the most beautiful in Mexico, and recently discovered sites such as Aké and X-tambo invite adventuresome travelers to explore where few visitors have set foot in recent centuries.

NOTE: New discoveries about the Maya, one of the most mysterious cultures of Mesoamerica, are constantly coming to light through the diligent work of many archaeological investigators. The Mexican government has earmarked several million dollars for research since 1992, and it is paying off. So keep in mind that many dates of major events reported in the Exploring sections, *below,* are only good estimates unless precise dates have been found in Maya writings. Unfortunately, with the near total destruction of the Maya codices (or books) by a fanatic bishop in the 16th century, many of these historical records have been lost.

Maya temples are not the only ruins that tug at the imagination in Yucatán. Grandiose Spanish colonial mission churches, built—often on the same site—with stones scavenged from ancient pyramids, dominate Maya villages throughout the state. The opulence of a more recent era can be seen at haciendas where wealthy plantation owners grew *henequen,* a fiber used to make rope. Originally, there were 500 haciendas. Some plantations still operate on a small scale today, and some of the lavish mansion houses either have become museums, have been allowed to crumble or, most recently, are now being restored as lodging alternatives.

Shopping

Yucatecan artisans produce some of the finest crafts in Mexico. For the most part, Mérida is the best place in Yucatán to buy local handicrafts at reasonable prices. The main products include *hamacas* (hammocks), *guayaberas* (loose dress shirts for men), *huaraches* (woven leather sandals), *huipiles* (hand-embroidered dresses), baskets, *jipis* (Panama hats made from guano palm) that can be rolled up in your suitcase, leather goods, gold and silver filigree jewelry, masks, painted gourds, vanilla, and piñatas. A word about hammocks, one of the most popular craft items sold here: They are available in cotton, nylon, and silk as well as in the very rough and scratchy henequen fiber. Silk, which is very expensive, is unquestionably the best choice but is hard to find. Double-threaded hammocks are sturdier and stretch less than single-threaded ones, a difference that can be identified by studying the loop handles. Hammocks come in different sizes: *sencillo,* for one person; *doble,* very comfortable for one but crowded for two; *matrimonial,* which will decently accommodate two; and *familiares* or *matrimoniales especiales,* which can theoretically sleep an entire family. Unless you're an expert, avoid the hammocks sold by street vendors and head for one of the specialty shops in Mérida.

Exploring the State of Yucatán

Mérida is the hub of Yucatán and the best base for exploring the rest of the state. From there, highways radiate in every direction. To the east, along Route 180 to Cancún, are the famous Chichén Itzá ruins and the low-key colonial city of Valladolid. Heading south on Route 261, you come to Uxmal and the Puuc Route, a series of the most beautiful ruins in Yucatán. If you follow Route 261 north, it will take you to the seaport and beach resort of Progreso. To the west, separate secondary highways go to Celestún and Sisal, two fishing villages with white-sand beaches on the edge of the Parque Natural Celestún wildlife preserve.

Most roads in the state are narrow, paved two-lane affairs that pass through small towns and villages, with the exception of two toll roads in operation—one from Mérida to Cancún and the other from Mérida to Campeche City. There is rarely heavy traffic on them and they are in very good shape, devoid of potholes and unexpected bumps. But you have to watch out for unattended children and stray dogs. Plans are in the works for more toll roads to be built, but the government doesn't seem to be in any hurry.

Numbers in the text correspond to numbers in the margin and on the State of Yucatán and Mérida maps.

Great Itineraries

IF YOU HAVE 3 DAYS

Spend two days in Mérida, savoring the city's unique character as you make your way among the historic churches and mansions and enjoy the parks and restaurants. You can easily devote a full day to exploring the **zócalo** ① and its surrounding colonial bank, religious, and government buildings. Proceed up Calle 60 to **Parque Hidalgo** ⑨, the neighboring **Museo de la Ciudad** ⑧ and **Iglesia de Jesús** ⑩, finally working your way back past the zócalo to the **Mercado de Artesanías "García Rejón"** ⑥ and the nearby **Mercado Municipal** ⑦, where it's easy to get pleasantly lost for hours. In the evening you're likely to find a theater or dance performance at the **Teatro Peón Contreras** ⑪, the atrium of the **Universidad Autonoma de Yucatán** ⑫, or (on Thursday) **Parque de Santa Lucía** ⑬ or (on Sunday) the main square. Take a second, more leisurely day to visit the Museum of Anthropology and History in the **Palacio Cantón** ⑮ and perhaps the **Museo de Artes Populares** ⑯ or the El Centenario Zoo. On the third day drive or take a tour to one of Yucatán's most famous Maya ruins—either **Chichén Itzá** ⑳ or **Uxmal** ㉔. Each is within about two hours of Mérida, making for an ideal day trip.

IF YOU HAVE 7 DAYS
First explore the sights of **Mérida** ①–⑰, and then take two separate overnight excursions from the city. Spend the night at one of the archaeological hotels near **Uxmal** ㉔, and the next day explore the Ruta Puuc, the series of lost cities south of Uxmal that includes **Kabah** ㉕, **Sayil** ㉖, and **Labná** ㉗, as well as the fascinating **Loltún Caves** ㉘, returning to Mérida through **Ticul** ㉙. On the second excursion, to **Chichén Itzá** ⑳, allow as much as a full day en route to explore some of the recently discovered ruins along the way: There's **Aké** ⑱ and the present-day Maya villages along the way, such as **Izamal** ⑲. After visiting Chichén Itzá, you may wish to beat the afternoon heat by exploring the **Cave of Balancanchén** ㉒ or swimming in one of the cool subterranean cenotes nearby. You might also head north from **Valladolid** ㉓ to see the flamingo nesting grounds at **Río Lagartos National Park** ㊶.

IF YOU HAVE 10 DAYS
In addition to visiting the sights noted above, you may also want to add one or more beach days into your itinerary. An obvious choice is nearby **Progreso** ㉟, with a stop en route from **Mérida** ①–⑰ to see the ruins of **Dzibilchaltún** ㉞, and perhaps side trips to explore smaller, more traditional North Coast beach towns such as **Yucalpetén** ㊱, **Telchac Puerto** ㊲, and **Dzilám de Bravo** ㊳. If you prefer a secluded fishing village, try either **Celestún** ㉜ or **Sisal** ㉝. Guided boat trips are available from both villages into Parque Natural del Flamenco Mexicano, a tropical wetlands teeming with birds and sea life.

When to Tour Mérida and the Yucatán
Sundays are special in Yucatán. Mérida blocks off traffic in the downtown area as what seems to be the entire population of the city mingles in the zócalo and other parks and plazas for entertainment, food, and celebration of life. Sidewalk cafés along this route are perfect vantage points from which to watch the passing parade of people as well as the folk dancers and singers. Sunday is also the day when admission to archaeological sites is free, an important consideration if you plan to explore the Puuc Route, where you can visit seven Maya sites, each of which charges a separate admission on other days of the week.

Thousands of visitors ranging from international sightseers to Maya shamans swarm to Chichén Itzá for the vernal equinox (the first day of spring) to witness the optical illusion that makes a representation of the plumed serpent god Kukulcán appear to descend the stairway of the main pyramid. The phenomenon also occurs on the first day of fall, but the rainy weather typical at that time of year tends to discourage visitors. Another good time is November 1, Mexico's traditional Day

133

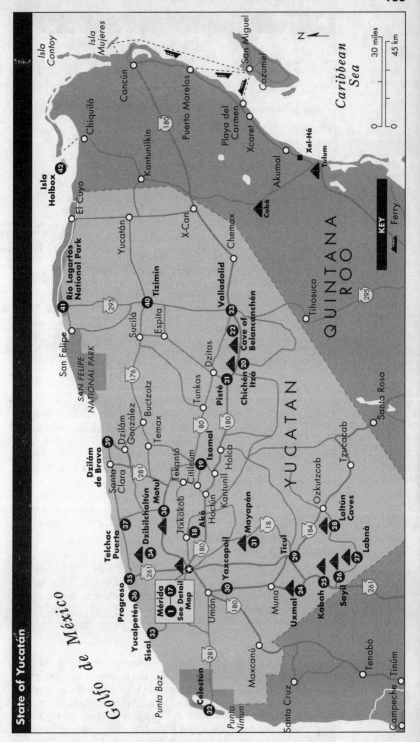

State of Yucatán

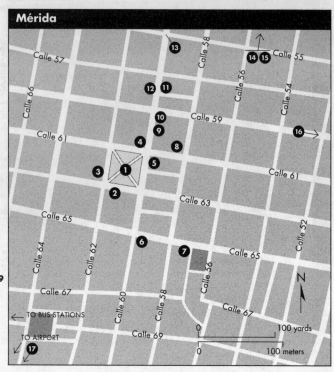

of the Dead celebration, which, in Merida, is called by its Maya name, *Hanal Pixan,* or "food for departed souls." On its eve favorite foods of the dead are put out by the family. Mérida dresses up its main square with dozens of "huts" representing different villages around the state and inside are small altars filled with the time-honored offerings to the departed souls of children and adults. Don't miss the *Otoño Cultural* or "Autumn Cultural Festival" either, if you happen to be in Merida the last week of October through the first week of November. Free classical music concerts, dance performances, and art exhibits take place nightly at the Daniel Ayala Perez and Peón Contreras theaters (☞ Nightlife and the Arts, *below*).

High season generally corresponds to high season in the rest of Mexico: the Christmas period, Easter week, and the months of July and August. Rainfall is heaviest between June and October, bringing with it an uncomfortable humidity. The best months for visiting are the coolest: November–April.

MÉRIDA

Travelers to Mérida are a loyal bunch, content to return again and again to favorite restaurants, neighborhoods, and museums. The city's traffic and noise are frustrating, particularly after a peaceful stay on the coast or at one of the archaeological sites, but its merits far outweigh its flaws. Mérida is the cultural and intellectual center of the peninsula, with museums, schools, and attractions that greatly enhance the traveler's insights into the history and character of Yucatán. Consider making it one of the first stops in your travels, and make sure your visit includes a Sunday, when traffic is light and the city seems to revert to a more gracious era.

Most streets in Mérida are numbered, not named, and most run one way. North–south streets have even numbers, which ascend from east to west; east–west streets have odd numbers, which ascend from north to south. Street addresses are confusing because they don't progress in even increments by blocks; for example, the 600s may occupy two or even 10 blocks. A particular location is therefore usually identified by indicating the street number and the nearest cross street, as in "Calle 64 at Calle 61" (the "at" may appear as "x") or "Calle 64 between 61 and 63."

Zócalo and Surroundings

The zócalo is the oldest part of town and has now been officially dubbed the *Centro Historico* (Historic Center) by city officials. The city is restoring all colonial buildings in the area to their original splendor, and it's not uncommon to see work proceeding on facades on several streets at once.

A Good Walk

Start at the **zócalo** ①; the **Casa de Montejo** ② is on the south side, the **Palacio Municipal** ③ on the west side, the **Palacio del Gobierno** ④ on the northeast corner, and the **catedral** ⑤ catercorner to the Governor's Palace. Step out on Calle 61 from the cathedral and walk east to the **Museo de la Ciudad** ⑧; then double back west on Calle 61 and walk a half block north on Calle 60 to the **Parque Hidalgo** ⑨ and the **Iglesia de Jesús** ⑩ in the same block. Continue north along Calle 60 for a short block to the **Teatro Peón Contreras** ⑪, which lies on the east side of the street; the **Universidad Autonoma de Yucatán** ⑫ is directly across the street on the west side of Calle 60. A block farther north on the west side of Calle 60 is the **Parque de Santa Lucía** ⑬. From the park, walk due north three blocks and turn right on Calle 47 for two blocks to **Paseo de Montejo** ⑭. Once on this street, continue north for two blocks to the **Palacio Cantón** ⑮. From here you can either hire a *calesa* (horse-drawn carriage) or cab parked outside the museum to take you back past the zócalo to the **Mercado de Artesanías "García Rejón"** ⑥ and the **Mercado Municipal** ⑦, or walk if you are up to it.

Sights to See

❷ **Casa de Montejo.** This stately palace sits on the south side of the plaza, on Calle 63. Francisco de Montejo—father and son—conquered the peninsula and founded Mérida in 1542; they built their "casa" 10 years later. The property remained with the family until the late 1970s, when it was restored by banker Agustín Legorreta and converted into a bank. Built in the French style during Mérida's heyday as the world's henequen capital, it now represents the city's finest—and oldest—example of colonial Plateresque architecture, which typically features elaborate ornamentation. It also incorporates a great deal of *porfiriato*, architectural details characteristic of the reign of dictator Porfirio Díaz that mimicked 19th-century French style in such traits as mansard roofs, gilded mirrors, and the use of marble. A bas-relief on the doorway—which is all that remains of the original house—depicts Francisco de Montejo the younger, his wife and daughter, and Spanish soldiers standing on the heads of the vanquished Maya. Even if you have no banking to do, step into the building weekdays between 9 and 5 to glimpse the lushly foliated inner patio, which resembles a small jungle.

❺ **Catedral.** Begun in 1561, this is the oldest cathedral on the North American mainland and it sits on the east side of the plaza. It took several hundred Maya laborers, working with stones from the pyramids of the ravaged Maya city, 36 years to complete it. Designed in the somber Renaissance style by an architect who had worked on the Escorial in

Madrid, its facade is stark and unadorned, with gunnery slits instead of windows, and faintly Moorish spires. Inside, the black **Cristo de las Ampollas** (Christ of the Blisters), now occupying a side altar to the left of the main one, is a replica of the original, which was destroyed during the Revolution (this was also when most of the gold that typically burnished Mexican cathedrals was carried off). According to one of many legends, the Christ figure burned all night yet appeared the next morning unscathed, but the statue was covered with the blisters for which it is named. For those who are fond of near-superlatives, the crucifix above the side altar is reputedly the second largest in the world.

El Centenario Zoological Park. Mérida's great children's attraction, this is a large, somewhat tacky amusement complex consisting of playgrounds; rides (including ponies and a small train); a roller skating rink; snack bars; and cages with more than 300 marvelous native monkeys, birds, reptiles, and other animals. There are also picnic areas, pleasant wooded paths, and a small lake where you can rent rowboats. Come on Sunday if you enjoy the spectacle of people enjoying themselves. The French Renaissance–style arch (1921) commemorates the 100th anniversary of Mexican independence. ⊠ *Av. Itzaes between Calles 59 and 65, entrances on Calles 59 and 65,* ☎ *no phone.* ▣ *Free.* ⊙ *Daily 9–6.*

⑰ Ermita de Santa Isabel. At the far south of the city stands the hermitage (circa 1748), part of a Jesuit monastery also known as the Hermitage of the Good Trip, which was restored in 1966. A resting place in colonial days for travelers heading to Campeche, and the most peaceful place in the city, the restored chapel is an enchanting spot to visit at sunset (when it is open) and perhaps a good destination for a ride in a calesa. Next door there's a huge garden with botanical species, a waterfall, and footpaths bordered with bricks and colored stones. ⊠ *Calles 66 and 77.* ☎ *No phone.* ▣ *Free.* ⊙ *The church hrs are irregular. The garden is almost always open during the day.*

⑩ Iglesia de Jesús. Facing Parque Hidalgo on the north side is one of Mérida's oldest buildings and the first Jesuit church in the Yucatán. The church was built in 1618 of limestone from a Maya temple that had previously stood on the site, and faint outlines of ancient carvings are still visible on the stonework of the west wall. Although it is a favorite place for society weddings because of its antiquity, the church's interior is not very ornate. The former convent rooms in the rear of the building now host a pair of small art museums—the **Juan Gamboa Guzmán Painting Museum** and the adjoining **Gottdiener Museum.** You might pass on the former, which contains oil paintings of past governors and other public figures but rarely identifies them. The latter, on the other hand, displays striking bronze sculptures of the Yucatán's indigenous people by its most celebrated 20th-century sculptor, Enrique Gottdiener. The museums' hours are sporadic, and they often do not keep to their published schedule. ⊠ *Calle 59, between Calles 60 and 58,* ☎ *no phone.* ▣ *Free.* ⊙ *Tues.–Sun. 8–8.*

⑥ Mercado de Artesanías "García Rejón." Shops, somewhat sterile in appearance, selling dry goods, straw hats, and hammocks occupy both sides of Calle 65. Here you'll find local handicrafts and souvenirs. ⊠ *Calles 60 and 65.* ⊙ *Daily 8–7.*

⑦ Mercado Municipal. Here stand two picturesque 19th-century edifices housing the main post office and telegraph buildings. Behind them sprawls the pungent, labyrinthine Mercado Municipal, a place filled with local color, where almost every patch of ground is occupied by Indian women selling chilies, herbs, and fruit. On the second floor of the main building is the **Bazar de Artesanías Municipales,** the principal handicrafts market, where you can buy jewelry (gold or gold-dipped filigree earrings), pottery, embroidered clothes, hammocks, and straw bags. ⊠ *Calle 65, between Calles 56 and 58.* ⊙ *Daily 8–7.*

⓰ Museo de Artes Populares. Those who love Mexican crafts may want to trek several blocks east of the main square to this museum. Housed in a fine old mansion, the museum has a ground floor devoted to Yucatecan arts and crafts, displaying weaving, straw baskets, filigree jewelry, carved wood, beautifully carved conch shells, exhibits on huipil manufacture, and the like. The second floor focuses on the popular arts of the rest of Mexico. ⊠ *Calles 59 and 50,* ☎ *no phone.* ⊒ *Free.* ⊙ *Tues.–Sat. 9–8, Sun. 8–2.*

⓼ Museo de la Ciudad. History lovers should stop in at the small but informative museum. Once a hospital chapel for the only convent in the entire bishopric, it now houses prints, drawings, photographs, and other displays that recount the history of Mérida. ⊠ *Calles 61 and 58,* ☎ *no phone.* ⊒ *Free.* ⊙ *Tues.–Sun. 8–1 and 4–8.*

⓯ Palacio Cantón. The most compelling of the mansions on Paseo de Montejo, the pale peach palacio presently houses the **Museum of Anthropology and History.** Its grandiose airs seem more characteristic of a mausoleum than a home, but in fact it was built for a general between 1909 and 1911 and was designed by Enrique Deserti, who also did the blueprints for the Teatro Peón Contreras. Marble shows up everywhere, as do Doric and Ionic columns and other Italianate Beaux Arts flourishes. From 1948 to 1960 the mansion served as the residence of the state governor. In 1977 it became a museum dedicated to the culture and history of the Maya. Although it's not as impressive as its counterparts in other Mexican cities, it can serve as an introduction to ancient Maya culture before you visit nearby Maya sites. Exhibits explain the Maya practice of dental mutilation and incrustation. A case of "sick bones" shows how the Maya suffered from osteoarthritis, nutritional maladies, and congenital syphilis. The museum also houses conch shells, stones, and quetzal feathers that were used for trading. There's also a bookstore. ⊠ *Calle 43 and Paseo de Montejo,* ☎ *99/230557.* ⊒ *$2.* ⊙ *Tues.–Sat. 9–6, Sun. 8–2; bookstore weekdays 9–3.*

❹ Palacio del Gobierno (State House). Occupying the northeast corner of the main square is this structure, built in 1885 on the site of the Casa Real (Royal House). The upper floor of the State House contains Fernando Castro Pacheco's vivid murals of the bloody history of the conquest of the Yucatán, painted in 1978. On the main balcony stands a reproduction of the **Bell of Dolores Hidalgo,** where Mexican independence was rung out on September 16, 1810, in the town of Dolores Hidalgo near Mexico City. Every year on that date, the state governor tolls the bell to commemorate the great occasion. ⊠ *Calle 61, between Calles 60 and 62.* ⊒ *Free.* ⊙ *Daily 8 AM–11 PM.*

❸ Palacio Municipal (City Hall). The west side of the main square is occupied by this 17th-century building, which is painted yellow and trimmed with white arcades, balustrades, and the national coat of arms. Originally erected on the ruins of the last surviving Maya structure, it was rebuilt in 1735 and then completely reconstructed along colonial lines in 1928. It remains the headquarters of the local government. ⊠ *Calle 62, between Calles 61 and 63.* ⊙ *Weekdays 8–7, Sat. 8–2.*

⓭ Parque de Santa Lucía. The rather plain park at Calle 60 and Calle 55 draws crowds to its Thursday-night serenades, performed by local musicians and folk dancers. The small church opposite the park dates from 1575 and was built as a place of worship for the African and

Caribbean slaves who lived here. The churchyard functioned as the cemetery until 1821.

9 Parque Hidalgo. Only half a block north of the main plaza, at Calle 60 and Calle 59, is the small, cozy park, officially known as Cepeda Peraza. Renovated mansions-turned-hotels and sidewalk cafés stand at two corners of the park, which comes alive at night with marimba bands and street vendors.

14 Paseo de Montejo. North of downtown, the 10-block-long street known by this name exemplifies the Parisian airs the city took on in the late 19th century, when wealthy plantation owners were building opulent, impressive mansions. The broad boulevard, lined with tamarinds and laurels, is sometimes wistfully referred to as Mérida's Champs-Elysées. Inside the mansions the owners typically displayed imported Carrara marble and antiques, opting for the decorative and social standards of New Orleans, Cuba, and Paris over styles that were popular in Mexico City. (At the time there was more traffic by sea via the Gulf of Mexico and the Caribbean than there was overland across the lawless interior.) Although the once-stunning mansions have fallen into disrepair, they are being restored to stateliness by a citywide beautification program.

11 Teatro Peón Contreras. This Italianate theater was designed in 1908 along the lines of the grand European turn-of-the-century theaters and opera houses. In the early 1980s the marble staircase and the dome with frescoes were restored to their past glory. Today, in addition to performing arts, the theater also houses temporary art exhibits and the main **Centro de Información Turistica** (☏ 99/249290), which is to the right of the lobby. The information center distributes maps and can provide details about local attractions. A café serving cappuccino and other coffees, plus light snacks and some meals, spills out to a patio from inside the theater to the right of the information center. ✉ *Calle 60, between Calles 57 and 9.*

12 Universidad Autonoma de Yucatán. The arabesque university plays a major role in the city's cultural and intellectual life. The folkloric ballet performs on the patio of the main building. A Jesuit college built in 1618 previously occupied the site, but the present building, dating from 1711, features Moorish-style crownlike upper reaches and uncloistered archways. ✉ *Calle 60, between Calles 57 and 59.*

1 Zócalo (main square). The Meridanos also traditionally call it the Plaza Principal and Plaza de la Independencia, and it's a good spot from which to begin any tour of the city. Ancient, geometrically pruned laurel trees and *confidenciales* (S-shape benches designed for tête-à-têtes) invite lingering. The plaza was laid out in 1542 on the ruins of T'hó, the Maya city demolished to make way for Mérida, and is still the focal point around which the most important public buildings cluster. The plaza is bordered to the east and west by Calles 60 and 62, and to the north and south by Calles 61 and 63.

Dining and Lodging

$$ ✕ **Alameda.** Middle Eastern and vegetarian specialties share the menu with standard Yucatecan fare at this side-street café, where businessmen linger over grilled beef shish kebab, pita bread, and breakfast coffee. The street action is visible from tables at the front; those in the back patio are quieter. Everything is served without side dishes—if you want beans or potatoes with your eggs, you must ask for them. Meatfree dishes include tabbouleh and spinach and cauliflower casseroles. Only open until 6:30 PM. ✉ *Calle 58, No. 474, across from Posada Toledo,* ☏ *99/283635. No credit cards.*

$$ ✕ **Alberto's Continental Patio.** You can probably find this restaurant
★ praised in just about every guidebook, and it merits the kudos: The set-
ting is romantic and the food is excellent. The building, which dates
from about 1727, is adorned with such fine details as mosaic floors from
Cuba. Two beautiful dining rooms are tastefully decorated with dark-
wood trim, copper utensils, stone sculpture, and candles in glass lanterns
on the tables. An inner patio surrounded by rubber trees is ideal for star-
lit dining. Most of the guests are tourists, but that need not detract from
the surroundings or the food. If you order Lebanese food, your plate
will be heaped with servings of shish kebab, fried kibi, cabbage rolls,
hummus, eggplant, and tabbouleh, accompanied by pita bread, almond
pie, and Turkish coffee. Black bean soup, enchiladas, fried bananas, and
caramel custard make up the Mexican dinner. There are also a Yucatecan
dinner, a Lebanese dinner, and à la carte appetizers and entrées. ⊠ *Calle
64, No. 482, at Calle 57,* ☎ *99/285367. AE, MC, V.*

$$ ✕ **Amaro.** This historic home, where statesman Andres Quintana Roo
was born in 1787, takes on a romantic glow at night with candlelit ta-
bles in the open patio beneath a big tree. Once strictly vegetarian, Amaro
has expanded its menu to include poultry and red meats. Still, the menu
is heavy on health drinks, made mostly with local vegetables, fruit, and
herbs. Regular coffee and Yucatecan beers are also served, and the salads are made with fresh local veggies washed with purified water. Recommended dishes include eggplant curry and soup made with *chaya,*
a local vegetable that looks like spinach. ⊠ *Calle 59, No. 507, between
Calles 60 and 62,* ☎ *99/282451. No credit cards. Closed Sun.*

$$ ✕ **La Bella Epoca.** For a truly special dinner, nothing matches the ele-
★ gance and style of the second-story dining room, the former ballroom
of an old mansion that has been restored well beyond its original
grandeur. Crystal chandeliers sparkle over tiny balcony tables overlooking
Parque Hidalgo. An ambitious menu includes French, Mexican, Mid-
dle Eastern, Yucatecan, vegetarian, and unusual Maya dishes—try the
sikil-pak, a dip with ground pumpkin seeds, charcoal-broiled toma-
toes, and onions; or the succulent *pollo píbil* (chicken baked in banana
leaves). Arrive for dinner before 8 PM to claim one of the small bal-
cony tables overlooking the street. The restaurant has taken over the
building's ground floor, which is outfitted more casually with plain
wooden tables and chairs but which has the same fine menu and win-
dows overlooking the street. ⊠ *Hotel del Parque, Calle 60, between
Calles 57 and 59,* ☎ *99/281928. AE, MC, V.*

$$ ✕ **La Casona.** This pretty mansion-turned-restaurant near Parque
Santa Ana has an inner patio, arcade, and swirling ceiling fans. A bar
features live romantic music weekends. The accent is Yucatecan, with
poc chuc (slices of pork marinated in sour orange juice and spices),
pollo píbil, and *huachinango* (red snapper baked in banana leaves) among
the recommended dishes. Some Italian offerings include homemade
pasta—ravioli, manicotti, and linguine. Vegetables or pasta accompany
most orders. ⊠ *Calle 60, No. 434, between Calles 47 and 49,* ☎ *99/
239996. AE, MC, V. Closed Sun.*

$$ ✕ **Los Almendros.** A Mérida classic, this restaurant—a spin-off from
an original location in the Maya village of Ticul—takes credit for the
invention of poc chuc. The food tends to be on the greasy side, and
some international travelers may feel that local spices such as achiote
overwhelm the main ingredients. Nonetheless, the restaurant provides
a good introduction to the variety of Yucatecan cuisine, including *con-
chinita píbil* (pork baked in banana leaves), panuchos, pork sausage,
papadzules (corn tortillas with pumpkin-seed sauce), and *pollo ticuleño*
(boneless, breaded chicken in tomato sauce filled with fried beans, peas,
red peppers, ham, and cheese). All dishes are described in English with
pictures on the paper menus. Sangria—with or without alcohol—

washes it all down. The two dining rooms have both ceiling fans and air-conditioning. ✉ *Calle 50-A, No. 493, between Calles 57 and 59,* ☎ *99/238135 or 99/285459. AE, MC, V.*

$$ ✕ **Pancho's.** The waiters in this steak and seafood restaurant—Mérida's version of the Carlos 'n' Charlie's chain—dress in what looks like Hollywood's idea of "Bandito" costumes. The bar, with its fancy drinks, attracts the international singles set; dancing is possible some nights on the outdoor patio. People go here more for the atmosphere than for the food, which is standard Mexican fare like fajitas, tacos, and enchiladas. ✉ *Calle 59, No. 509, between Calles 60 and 62,* ☎ *99/ 230942. AE, MC, V. No lunch.*

$$ ✕ **Pórtico del Peregrino.** A red-tile floor, iron grillwork, and lots of plants
★ set the tone in both the indoor and outdoor patio sections of this old colonial home with only 10 tables. The house special is a robust *zarzuela de mariscos* (seafood casserole cooked in white wine); otherwise the menu features lime soup, baked eggplant with chicken, chicken pibil, shish kebab, mole enchiladas, chicken liver brochettes, and spaghetti. For dessert try the coconut ice cream with Kahlúa. ✉ *Calle 57, No. 501, between Calles 60 and 62,* ☎ *99/286163. AE, MC, V.*

$ ✕ **Bar La Ruina.** Perfect for a quick pick-me-up, this spotlessly clean watering hole behind the new ADO bus terminal has an old-fashioned cantina atmosphere. Free hot and cold *botanas,* or snacks, are served nonstop from 11 AM opening to 7 PM closing with beer or mixed drinks. In keeping with Mexican tradition, only men are allowed in the front bar; women and families are ushered to the back rooms. ✉ *Calles 69 and 72,* ☎ *no phone. No credit cards.*

$ ✕ **Cafetería Pop.** This crowded, student hangout, decorated with passé
★ pop art posters and wood tables is situated across from the university (and filled with cigarette smoke). The busiest time is 8 AM–noon, but for late risers the breakfast menu can be ordered à la carte all day, and the noteworthy coffee is freshly brewed around the clock. In addition sandwiches, hamburgers, spaghetti, chicken, fish, beef, and tacos are available. Beer, sangria, and wine are served only with food orders. ✉ *Calle 57, No. 501, between Calles 60 and 62,* ☎ *99/286163. No credit cards.*

$ ✕ **Express.** This plain café-style restaurant is where dignified Méridano men in guayaberas come to bond and where they spend hours in a Madrid café-style ambience (complete with cigar smoke). The mood is reinforced by the paintings of old Spain and old Mérida, ceiling fans, and old-fashioned globe lights. On the menu are broiled garlic chicken, sandwiches, shrimp, and red snapper. Its name notwithstanding, service at this restaurant can be slow: Express is a place for lingering. ✉ *Calle 60, No. 502, at Calle 59,* ☎ *99/281691. No credit cards.*

$ ✕ **Nicte-Ha.** Metal chairs and tables with plastic tablecloths sit under an arcade right on the main square, making this modest eatery a fine place for people-watching. A good selection of Yucatecan fare—soups, *huevos motuleños* (eggs with peas and ham), poc chuc, seafood, *antojitos* (appetizers), and a combination platter—is offered at budget prices. Afterward, stop in at the *sorbetería* next door for a sherbet. ✉ *Calle 61, No. 500, at Calle 60,* ☎ *99/230784. No credit cards.*

$ ✕ **Pizza Bella.** In the same arcade in the main square as Nicte-Ha (☞ *above*), this restaurant serves Mexican and American breakfasts, espresso, and cappuccino as well as pizza. Checkered tablecloths atop wooden tables and an eclectic collection of wall decorations (from maps to beer advertisements) add atmosphere to this otherwise standard pizza joint. ✉ *Calle 61, No. 500, Depto. E-2,* ☎ *99/236401. No credit cards.*

$ ✕ **Santa Lucía.** At lunch time, locals crowd this small five-table din-
★ ing room, a few steps below the sidewalk. The bargain three-course lunch usually includes such Yucatecan specialties as *sopa de lima* (lime soup) and *pollo píbil* (chicken baked in banana leaves in a tangy sour

orange sauce). Before you order, browse through the book of guests' comments to get tips on favorite meals—the pepper steak constantly wins rave reviews. Soft tropical music plays in the background, and the service is friendly and efficient. There's a live band Thursday through Sunday nights. ✉ *Calle 60, No. 481, next to Parque de Santa Lucía,* ☎ *99/285957. MC, V.*

\$\$\$\$ ✕⛨ **Hacienda Katanchel.** Katanchel is a rambling 17th-century henequen
★ hacienda on 740 acres that was lovingly restored to its former splendor by Anibal Gonzalez and his wife Monica Hernandez who opened it as a period-piece hotel in 1996. Concurrently, the couple is replanting the property with endangered Maya plants, trees, and medicinal herbs and restoring a small ruin they found on the estate. The guest rooms, set in small, individual pavilions along a garden walkway, have floors made of local tiles, roofs of red Marseilles tile, overhead fans (air-conditioning on request), hammocks, and four-poster beds that look like pieces of modern sculpture. The eclectically decorated common areas are filled with elegant antique furnishings in the manner of haciendas in the old days. The former *Casa de Maquinas* (machine shop) is now the restaurant where cuisine is contemporary Mexican with a definite Yucatecan flair. If you are not already awestruck by the hacienda, the superb kitchen will win you over for sure. For starters there is chilled sour orange soup or eggplant mousse in peanut sauce, followed by such main dishes as quails in *X'tabentun* (anisette liqueur) sauce or fillet of grouper in sour lime sauce. The height of the dessert menu is *ciricote* (Maya fruit that resembles a red plum) with English cream. A nice selection of Italian, Chilean, French, German, and Portuguese vintages are available to compliment the meal. Katanchel also has day tours at extra cost led by local scholars to local Maya ruins, convents, and colonial villages and wildlife reserves. A meal plan is also available. ✉ *25 km (16 mi) east of Mérida on Hwy. 180 toward Izamal,* ☎ *99/234038 or 888/882–9470 in the U.S.,* ℻ *99/234000. 21 rooms, 13 suites. Restaurant, bar, pool, mineral baths, meeting room. AE, MC, V.*

\$\$\$\$ ⛨ **Fiesta Americana Mérida.** Situated across the street from the Hyatt
★ Regency, this is the town's newest posh hotel, catering to business travelers, groups, and conventions, but also attracting the locals who come to see and be seen. Its lovely pink facade mirrors the architecture of Paseo de Montejo mansions on an epic scale. The echoes of classic grandeur carry into the spacious upper lobby with its massive columns and gleaming marble and brass work and its 300-ft-high glass-roof atrium. Rich floral prints, dark-wood furnishings, and slightly larger-than-life proportions maintain the theme of bygone elegance in the guest rooms, but the units are carpeted and have all the modern conveniences, including modems. They all offer L-shape conversation areas, separate dressing rooms, and remote-control TVs concealed in armoires. Five concierges serve hotel guests and there's a small city of luxury shops and boutiques on the street level to answer any traveler needs. ✉ *Paseo de Montejo and Av. Colón,* ☎ *99/421111,* ℻ *99/421112. 325 rooms, 25 suites. 2 restaurants, 2 bars, air conditioning, no-smoking rooms, room service, pool, tennis, health club, shops, concierge floor, business services, meeting rooms, travel services, car rental, free parking. AE, DC, MC, V.*

\$\$\$\$ ⛨ **Hyatt Regency Mérida.** The north end of Paseo de Montejo is the new hotel district, and this 17-story Hyatt was the first to open in 1994, bringing a new level of service to Mérida. Guests staying on one of the two Regency Club floors receive complimentary Continental breakfast, beverages, and snacks, as well as concierge service. The rooms are regally decorated with russet-hued bed quilts and rugs set off by modern blond-wood furniture and cream-color walls. Satellite TV, direct-dial long-distance phone service, and minibars have been artfully integrated into each unit; club floor rooms also contain personal safes. Amenities not commonly found in Mérida include 24-hour room service and a state-of-the-art business center, plus the city's only tapas bar. Each evening guests head to the piano bar in the marble lobby for live entertainment. The **La Peregrina** restaurant has sporadic presentations of a Yucatecan folk dance troupe along with a buffet (check with the concierge). One of the country's most exclusive silver shops, **Tane**, is also on the premises. ⊠ *Calle 60, No. 344, at Av. Colón,* ☎ *99/ 420202 or 800/228–9000,* ℻ *99/257002. 296 rooms, 4 suites. 2 restaurants, 2 bars, air-conditioning, no-smoking rooms, room service, pool, tennis, exercise room, shops, travel services, car rental, free parking. AE, DC, MC, V.*

$$$ 🏨 **Casa del Balam.** This very pleasant hotel on well-heeled Calle 60
★   was built more than 60 years ago as the home of the Barbachano family, pioneers of Yucatán tourism. Today the hotel—owned and managed by Carmen Barbachano—has a lovely courtyard ornamented with a fountain, arcades, ironwork, and a black-and-white tile floor. Rocking chairs in the hallways impart a colonial feeling, as do the mahogany trimmings and cedar doorways. The rooms are capacious and well maintained, with painted sinks, wrought-iron accessories, and minibars. The suites are especially agreeable, with large bathrooms, tiny balconies, arched doorways, and mahogany bureaus. All rooms now have hair dryers and were soundproofed in 1996 with double-pane windows. Cocktails and light meals are served in the lobby courtyard. ⊠ *Calle 60, No. 488, Box 988,* ☎ *99/248844, 99/242150, or 800/624– 8451,* ℻ *99/245011. 51 rooms, 3 suites. Restaurant, 2 bars, minibars, air-conditioning, no-smoking rooms, room service, pool, travel services, car rental. AE, MC, V.*

$$$ 🏨 **Holiday Inn.** The beautifully remodeled and redecorated hotel, which opened 17 years ago, is a half block from Paseo de Montejo, near the swanky Hyatt and Fiesta Americana (☞ *above* for both), and has reasonable room rates for this part of town. The lodge has a faithful following of Mexican businessmen and a decidedly Mexican flavor. The staff—from bellboys to waiters—exhibit good old-fashioned Mexican warmth and courtesy. There's a nightly Fiesta Mexicana in the patio. This is probably the most light-filled hotel in Mérida, with floor-to-ceiling windows throughout the lobby area and tiled dining room, which are set off with gay Mexican yellows and pinks. Rooms and suites face an open Mexican-style courtyard. Modern units have floral-print bedspreads, a small table, comfy arm chairs, minibars, marble bathrooms, and color TVs with U.S. channels. A business center and meetings wing opened in 1996. ⊠ *Av. Colon and Calle 60, No. 468, 97127,* ☎ *99/256877 or 800/465–4329,* ℻ *99/257755. 209 rooms, 5 suites. 2 restaurants, bar, air-conditioning, no smoking rooms, room service, shops, business services, meeting rooms, travel services, car rental, free parking. AE, DC, MC, V.*

$$$ 🏨 **Hotel El Conquistador.** Located on the Paseo de Montejo, the El Conquistador is within easy walking distance of the Fiesta Americana and the Hyatt (☞ *above* for both) and caters to German tour groups. Don't expect the top-notch amenities of those hotels—however, the contemporary-style rooms have been freshened up with new pillows and yellow floral bedspreads, tile floors, and painted walls. Views of the city from the rooftop solarium and pool area are superlative, the dining room is renowned for its daily breakfast buffet, the staff is helpful, but the prices are high. This hotel will do in a pinch if the better-value Holiday Inn (☞ *above*) is full. ⊠ *Paseo de Montejo, No. 458,* ☎ *99/ 262155 or 99/269199,* ℻ *99/268829. 157 rooms, 4 suites. Restaurant, coffee shop, 2 bars, room service, pool, shops, travel services, free parking. AE, DC, MC, V.*

$$ ⊞ **Caribe.** An old Mérida standard, the Caribe is done in typical colonial style, including tile floors, dark-wood furniture, and a large inner courtyard with arcades. It is on Parque Hidalgo, but most of its rooms overlook the inner courtyard and restaurant, as do the open balconies, which are lined with comfortable chairs. The rooftop sundeck and swimming pool have a great view of the plaza and downtown. The hotel's outdoor café, **El Meson,** is one of the better restaurants in Parque Hidalgo. Most rooms have air-conditioning, but be sure to request one if you want it. ⊠ *Calle 60, No. 500,* ☎ *99/249022 or 800/826–6842,* ℻ *99/248733. 55 rooms, 1 suite. Restaurant, outdoor café, pool, travel services, free parking. AE, DC, MC, V.*

$$ ⊞ **Casa Mexilio.** Two partners—one Mexican, one American—have brought the best of their respective architectural and decorating traditions to bear on this choice bed-and-breakfast with eight guest rooms (four have air-conditioning). Once you enter, you are in an exotic ambience of vine-draped walls, hidden terraces and sundecks, numerous private stairways, and an altogether private feeling to each room. Charming Middle Eastern wall hangings, French tapestries, colorful tile floors, black pottery, tile sinks, rustic furniture, and white walls make up the eclectic decor, which reaches its pinnacle in an immensely cozy sitting room on the second floor. A new wing of this organic (constantly restructuring itself) house was opened in 1997 with even more private terraces for guests along with modest renovations to rooms like adding more windows and air-conditioning. A phone that accepts credit cards has been added to the lobby. Casa Mexilio lacks the amenities of the larger hotels, but if you enjoy a casual ambience and the feeling of staying in a private home with a sumptuous breakfast to start the day, you'll be happy here. This place fills up fast; reservations as well as a minimum three nights' stay are required Christmas week, the month of February, and Easter week. ⊠ *Calle 68, No. 495, between Calles 59 and 57,* ☎ *303/674–9615 or 800/538–6802 for reservations in the U.S., 99/282505. 8 rooms. Breakfast room, pool. MC, V .*

$$ ⊞ **Gran Hotel.** Cozily situated on Parque Hidalgo, this legendary 1901
★ hotel is the oldest in the city, and it still lives up to its name. The three-story neoclassical building exudes charm. Its centerpiece is an Art Nouveau courtyard complete with wrought-iron bannister, variegated tile floors, Greek columns, and myriad potted plants. High ceilings in rooms drenched in cedar antique furniture provide a sense of spaciousness. Thirteen units have balconies—request one of these if you don't mind noise from the park; most of the others have no windows at all. The rooms on the second floor in the back are the quietest. Porfirio Díaz and Fidel Castro stayed in sumptuous Room 17, and Room 13 has an enormous sitting room. The hotel's **Patio Español** serves good sopa de lima plus paella on Sunday. ⊠ *Calle 60, No. 496,* ☎ *99/236963 or 99/247632,* ℻ *99/247622. 25 rooms, 6 suites. Restaurant, bar, air-conditioning, room service. MC, V.*

$$ ⊞ **María del Carmen.** This modern Best Western hotel with the striking, salmon-color tile entrance caters to business travelers, bus groups, and those traveling by car who desire secured parking. The plaza, market, and other major sights are within easy walking distance. The modern remodeled rooms are decorated with ornate Oriental-style lamps and lacquered furniture. ⊠ *Calle 63, No. 550, between Calles 68 and 70,* ☎ *99/239133 or 800/528–1234,* ℻ *99/239290. 87 rooms, 2 suites. Restaurant, bar, air-conditioning, no-smoking rooms, room service, pool, travel services, parking. AE, DC, MC, V.*

$$ ⊞ **Mérida Misión Park Inn Plaza.** Part of the city's landscape for decades (in its earlier incarnation it was the Hotel Mérida), the Misión has two major assets: an excellent location in the heart of downtown and a genuine colonial ambience, with chandeliers, wood beams, archways, patios, and fountains in public areas, along with a pool and a bar with romantic music nightly. Rooms in the modern 11-story annex don't have as much character, but the ones on the upper floors offer good city views. Forty-five units in the old colonial section are set around a pretty courtyard, which gives them much more appeal. In addition all rooms in the hotel have been remodeled with new paint jobs, carpeting, curtains, and bed covers. ⌧ *Calle 60, No. 491,* ☎ *99/239500,* FAX *99/237665. 137 rooms, 8 suites. Restaurant, bar, snack bar, no-smoking rooms, room service, pool, shop, meeting rooms, travel services, car rental, free parking. AE, DC, MC, V.*

$$ 🖬 **Posada Toledo.** This inn occupies a beautiful old colonial house with high ceilings, floors of exquisite Moorish patterned tile, and old-fashioned carved furniture that evoke its former elegance. The dining room, where breakfast is served, is particularly fine, with stained-glass door frames. Antiques clutter the halls, along with warm, faded portraits of 19th-century family life, so that one feels more like a personal guest of the establishment than another nameless hotel client. However, guest room quality varies much more than the rates do, so be sure to inspect your room before checking in. If you're traveling with a few people, consider No. 5, an elegant two-room suite that was originally the mansion's master bedroom. The posada's popularity is becoming a drawback; as in many hotels in converted mansions, noise reverberates through the halls. If you're a light sleeper, ask for a room away from the courtyard. You have a choice of a ceiling fan or air-conditioning (in 20 rooms). ⌧ *Calle 58, No. 487, at Calle 57,* ☎ *99/231690. 22 rooms, 1 suite. Breakfast room. MC, V.*

$$ 🖬 **Residencial.** Location is the major draw at this classy bright pink hotel. It sits on Calle 59, the main entrance to town, and has a gated parking lot. The decor's French colonial theme is most evident in the small dining room with its silken drapes, linen cloths, and high-backed chairs. The food is fine for breakfast but choose to eat the rest of your meals elsewhere. Rooms have powerful showers, comfortable beds, satellite color TV, and mirrored doors on the spacious closets. While the small swimming pool in the central courtyard is pleasant for encountering fellow guests, it's far from private. ⌧ *Calle 59, No. 589, at Calle 76,* ☎ *99/243899 or 99/243099,* FAX *99/240266. 64 rooms, 2 suites. Restaurant, bar, air-conditioning, room service, pool, free parking. AE, MC, V.*

$ 🖬 **Casa San Juan.** This new bed-and-breakfast inn is housed in a beautifully restored colonial mansion built by a Portuguese family in the 1860s, after having been granted the land by Emperor Maximillian. Designated an historical monument by the government, the house has many original components like high ceilings decorated with Belgium railroad ties—a fluke of fashion of the time—tile floors, a stone fountain, and 10-ft-high mahogany doors. Three patios and a sitting room surround an inside garden overflowing with tropical fruit trees, flowers, and vines. All guest rooms (there are six; one has air-conditioning) are extra large with double beds, ceiling and floor fans, and Latin American handicrafts. The Casa, named after the San Juan Park a block away, is now owned by Pablo da Costa, your affable Cuban host in Mérida. Pablo is a former hotelier, has service down to a T (there's even soaps and shampoos stocked in the bathrooms), will give you insider tips on Mérida, and speaks English and French. He's also teamed up with German anthropologist, Jurgen Kremer, who offers guided tours to major Maya sites at affordable prices. A full breakfast of eggs, fruit, juice, rolls, and coffee is included in the room price, and, in addition, Pablo keeps the pantry full of complimentary fruit, lemonade, and bottled water for his guests. A stay of more than three days will also get you cooking privileges in the kitchen. The location is another plus—three blocks from the main plaza and four blocks from both bus stations. ⊠ *Calle 62, No. 545A, between Calle 69 and Calle 71,* ☎ *99/236823,* FAX *99/862937. 6 rooms. Breakfast room, fans. No credit cards.*

$ 🏨 **Dolores Alba.** A comfortable, friendly standby at the high end of the inexpensive range, the Dolores Alba is owned by the Sanchez family, who lives on the premises and who also owns the Dolores Alba in Pisté (☞ *below*). The basic rooms, some with air-conditioning, frame a courtyard where guests' cars can be parked. A full breakfast ($3.50) is served in the dining room; guests can keep cold drinks in the lobby refrigerator. ⊠ *Calle 63, No. 464, between Calles 52 and 54,* ☎ *99/285650,* FAX *99/283163. 40 rooms. Breakfast room, pool. No credit cards.*

$ 🏨 **Hotel el Español.** This three-story hotel is ideal if you want to be practically next door to the Mérida bus stations and have your comforts, too. It's pretty, clean, has good service, and could be charging much more for what it offers. Completely redone at the end of 1996 in tasteful rose and white tones, even down to the floor tiles, it has a small, seven-table restaurant, covered atrium with lots of hanging greenery, faux wrought-iron trimmings, and a pleasant receptionist. Modern-style rooms are outfitted with double beds, color TV, air-conditioning, overhead fans, big closets, and bathrooms. ⊠ *Calle 69, No. 503, at Calle 70,* ☎ *99/234319,* FAX *99/232854. 27 rooms, 1 suite. Restaurant, air-conditioning, fans, room service, free parking. MC, V.*

$ 🏨 **Hotel Mucuy.** Mérida's budget hotels have become affordable again because of favorable foreign exchange rates, but the Mucuy still remains one of the best bargains around. The delightful owners make you feel like part of the family and are eager to share information about the city, as well as some good tips on inexpensive tours to the ruins. The rooms, which are always immaculate, have no air-conditioning but they do have overhead fans and good screens on the windows. Rooms face a tranquil, flower-filled garden perfect for reading or sunning. There's a book exchange and communal refrigerator in the lobby, and the owners live at the front of the hotel. ⊠ *Calle 57, No. 481, between Calles 56 and 58,* ☎ *99/285193,* FAX *99/237801. 22 rooms. No credit cards.*

$ 🏨 **Trinidad Galería.** Eccentricity holds sway at this impossibly original, slightly ramshackle little hotel, nearly unidentifiable unless you are looking for it. In its previous lives it has been a hacienda, an auto rental shop, and a furniture store, but in the late 1980s owner Manolo Rivero made it into a hotel, or more precisely, "a post-contemporary museum hotel." An adjacent art gallery has four yearly expositions of new, young talent to which all hotel guests receive formal invitations. The large, chaotic lobby is filled with modern art such as oil paintings of some distinction, plants, a fountain, and yellow wicker furniture. Making your way through the maze that is the rest of the hotel, you'll encounter painted wooden angels, curved columns, and even a green satin shoe mounted on a pedestal. The rooms are small and equally odd; they have neither phones nor TVs, and only two offer air-conditioning ($$). (Rivero has a second 17-room hotel, the Trinidad, a block away; guests have access to the Trinidad Galería's swimming pool). ⊠ *Calles 60 and 61,* ☎ *99/232463,* FAX *99/242319. 35 rooms. Pool. No credit cards.*

Nightlife and the Arts

Mérida enjoys an unusually active and diverse cultural life, including free government-sponsored music and dance performances nightly, plus sidewalk art shows in four local parks. For information on these and other performances, consult the tourist office, the local newspapers, or the billboards and posters at the **Teatro Peón Contreras** (⊠ Calle 60 at Calle 57) or **Café Pop** (⊠ Calle 57, between Calles 60 and 62).

Dancing

A number of restaurants feature live music and dancing, including **El Tucho** (⊠ Calle 60, No. 482, between Calles 55 and 57, ☎ 99/242323), **Xtabay** (⊠ Above El Tucho, ☎ 99/280961), and **Pancho's** (⊠ Calle 59, between Calles 60 and 62, ☎ 99/230942).

Film

Downtown movie theaters include **Cine Fantasio** (⊠ Calle 59 at Calle 60) and **Cine Rex** (⊠ Calle 57, No. 553); sometimes English films with Spanish subtitles are shown.

Folkloric Shows

The **Hyatt Regency Hotel** (⊠ Calle 60, No. 344, at Av. Colon, ☎ 99/420202) stages sporadic folkloric dances (check with the concierge for schedule) and a buffet dinner beginning at 8 PM at the **La Peregrina** restaurant. Among a variety of performances presented at the **Teatro Peón Contreras** is "The Roots of Today's Yucatán," a combination of music, dance, and theater presented by the Folkloric Ballet of the University of Yucatán on Tuesday at 9 PM. Another theater that regularly hosts cultural events is the **Teatro Daniel Ayala** (⊠ Calle 60, between Calles 59 and 61).

Outdoor Activities and Sports

Baseball

Baseball is played with enthusiasm from February or March through July at the stadium in the **Kukulcán Sports Center** (⊠ Calle 14, No. 17, ☎ 99/240306), next to the Carta Clara brewery. Tickets can also be purchased through the local Lion's Club (☎ 99/253809 or 99/253409).

Bullfights

Bullfights are most often held from November through January, or during other holiday periods at the **Plaza de Toros**, or bullring (⊠ Paseo de la Reforma near Avenida Colón, ☎ 99/257996). Contact the travel desk at your hotel or one of the tourist information centers; prices range from $6 to $9 for seats in the sun and from $10 to $15 for seats in the shade.

Golf

There is an 18-hole championship golf course (and restaurant, bar, and clubhouse) at **Club de Golf La Ceiba** (⊠ Carr. Mérida-Progreso, Km. 14.5, ☎ 99/220053 or 99/220054), 16 km (10 mi) north of Mérida on the road to Progreso.

Tennis

The **Holiday Inn** (⊠ Av. Colón, No. 498, at Calle 60, ☎ 99/256877) and the **Hyatt Regency** (⊠ Calle 60, No. 344 at Av. Colon, ☎ 99/420202) have tennis courts, as do the **Club Campestre de Mérida** (⊠ Calle 30, No. 500, ☎ 99/442552), the **Centro Deportivo Bancario** (⊠ Carr. a Motul s/n, Frac. del Arco, ☎ 99/430382 or 99/430550), and the **Deportivo Libanés Mexicano** (⊠ Calle 1-G, No. 101, ☎ 99/442940 or 99/442942).

Shopping

Malls

Mérida now has several shopping malls; the largest is **Gran Plaza,** with more than 90 shops. It's just outside of town, on the highway to Progreso (called Carretera a Progreso beyond the Mérida city limits).

Markets

On the second floor of the **Mercado Municipal** (⊠ Between Calles 65 and 67 and Calles 54 and 56) you'll find crafts, food, flowers, and live birds, among other items. Note: Men and boys often approach tourists by this market, offering to provide a guided tour or introduction to a shopkeeper with the "best" of whatever you're looking for. These unofficial guides will expect a tip from you (and will receive a commission from the seller if you buy anything), and won't necessarily guide you to the best deals. You're better off visiting some specialty stores first to learn about the quality and types of hammocks, hats, and other crafts; then you'll have an idea of what you're buying—and what it's worth—if you want to bargain in the market.

If you're interested solely in handicrafts, visit the **Bazar García Rejón** (⊠ Corner of Calles 65 and 62), which has neat rows of indoor stalls with leather items, palm hats, and handmade guitars, among other things. On Sunday in Mérida you will find an array of wares. Starting at 9, the **Handicraft Bazaar** (⊠ In front of the Municipal Palace across from the main square) is filled with huipiles, hats, and costume jewelry. Also starting at 9, the **Popular Art Bazaar** (⊠ Parque Santa Lucía, corner of Calles 60 and 55), a very small flea market, offers paintings, engravings, and woodcuts by local artists.

Specialty Stores
CLOTHING
Tastefully designed batik dresses and pillow covers with Maya motifs, along with a nice selection of white *manta* (Mexican cotton) clothing and silver jewelry, can be found at **El Paso** (⊠ Calle 60, No. 501, corner of Calle 61, ☎ 99/285452). You might not wear a guayabera to a business meeting as some men in Mexico do, but the shirts are cool, comfortable, and attractive; for a good selection, try **Camisería Canul** (⊠ Calle 62, No. 484, between Calles 57 and 59, ☎ 99/230158). Pick up a jipi at the well-known **El Becalenö** (⊠ Calle 65, No. 483, between Calles 56A and 58, ☎ 99/850581), where the famous hats are made at Becal, Campeche, by the González family. For stunningly beautiful embroidered dresses inspired by the old-fashioned Yucatecan dresses of the haciendas, visit **Georgia Charukas** (⊠ Fiesta Americana Hotel, Paseo de Montejo and Av. Colon, ☎ 99/257671); the U.S. designer has become an icon of high fashion in Mérida over the last 25 years.

CRAFTS
The best place for hammocks is **Hamacas El Aguacate** (⊠ Calle 58, No. 604, at Calle 73, ☎ 99/286429), a family-run establishment selling a wide variety of sizes and designs. **Tejidos Y Cordeles Nacionales** (⊠ Calle 56, No. 516-B, ☎ 99/285561) is another good hammock emporium.

Casa de Artesanías (⊠ Calle 63, No. 503, between Calles 64 and 66, ☎ 99/235392) purveys folk art from throughout Mexico, such as hand-painted, wooden mythical animals from Oaxaca; handmade beeswax candles and leather bags from Mérida; and hand-embroidered vests, shawls, blouses, and place mats from Chiapas. The streets north of the main square, especially **Calle 60**, are lined with crafts and jewelry stores.

GALLERIES
The **Teatro Daniel Ayala** (⊠ Calle 60, between Calles 59 and 61, ☎ 99/214391) showcases contemporary paintings and photography. **Galería Manolo Rivero** (⊠ Hotel Galería Trinidad, Calle 60 at Calle 61, ☎ 99/232463) displays paintings and sculptures by young, new wave contemporary artists from all over the world.

JEWELRY
La Perla Maya (⊠ Calle 60, No. 485–487, between Calles 59 and 61, ☎ 99/285886) is one of the few jewelry shops selling difficult-to-find,

old-fashioned Yucatecan filigree earrings and bracelets—in silver dipped in gold. The store also stocks lots of quality silver jewelry in modern designs. **Tane** at the Hyatt Regency Hotel (⊠ Calle 60, No. 344, at Av. Colon, ☎ 99/420202) is an outlet for exquisite (and expensive) silver earrings, necklaces, and bracelets, some using ancient Maya designs.

TO CHICHÉN ITZÁ AND VALLADOLID

Although it's possible to reach Chichén Itzá (120 km, or 74 mi, east of Mérida) along the shorter Route 180, it's far more scenic to follow Route 80 until it ends at Tekantó, then head south to Citilcúm, east to Dzitas, and south again to Pisté. These roads have no signs, but are the only paved roads going in these directions. Among the several villages you'll see along Route 80 is Tixkokob, a Maya community famous for its hammock weavers. A short detour southeast from Tikkokob are ruins of Aké (☞ *below*).

Aké

 35 km (22 mi) southeast of Mérida, 5 km (3 mi) southeast of Tixkokob.

This tiny jewel of a site was opened to the public at the end of 1996 and is a convenient stop along the Merida–Izamal route. The bizarre sight of the remains of a hacienda built next to a Maya temple is the most striking feature here. In fact, the site is named after the Hacienda of San Lorenzo Aké, which owes its construction along with that of the local church to the temple stones of Aké. Estimates put occupation of the site at around 200 BC to AD 900. A wall surrounding the city, along with several temples and roads—one of which measured 33 km (20 mi) long and leads directly to Izamal (☞ *below*)—have been discovered so far. All that's excavated is a pyramid with rows of columns at the top, very reminiscent of the Toltec columns at Tula, outside Mexico City. You can easily climb to the top of the ruins to view the surrounding fields being cultivated by farmers. ☜ *$1.* ☉ *Daily 9–5.*

Izamal

⑲ 68 km (42 mi) southeast of Mérida.

One of the best examples of a Spanish colonial town in the Yucatán, Izamal is nicknamed Ciudad Amarillo (Yellow City) because its buildings are painted earth-tone yellow by city ordinance. In the center of town stands the enormous 16th-century **Monastery of St. Anthony de Padua,** perched on—and built from—the remains of a pyramid devoted to Itamná, god of the heavens. The monastery's church, which was visited by Pope John Paul II in 1993, boasts a gigantic atrium (supposedly second only to that of the Vatican in size), frescoes of saints discovered in 1996, and rows of 75 yellow arches. The Virgin of the Immaculate Conception to whom the church is dedicated is the patron saint of the Yucatán and was brought here from Guatemala in 1562 by the fanatic Bishop Landa; miracles are ascribed to her, and a yearly pilgrimage takes place in her honor. Pony traps surround the town's large **main square,** which fronts the cathedral. There are far worse ways to spend an afternoon than to trot around this pleasant town and then lounge in the square enjoying the local action. **Kinich Kakmó,** a pyramid that's all that remains of a royal Maya city that flourished here hundreds of years ago, is located a few blocks from the monastery. It's currently under excavation, but it's worth walking over for a look. If you're traveling here via Route 80 from Mérida, cut south at Tekantó and east again at Citilcúm (the road has no number, and there are few signs).

Chichén Itzá

 ⑳   *116 km (72 mi) southeast of Mérida.*

Probably the best-known Maya ruin, Chichén Itzá was the most important city in Yucatán from the 10th through the 12th centuries. Its architectural mélange encapsulates pre-Hispanic Mexican history and shows the influence of several different Maya groups. What before was deduced to be foreign domination by the Toltecs from central Mexico, indeed, never happened, according to the latest research by Maya scholars, particularly epigraphers who are now able to read 85 percent of the Chichén inscriptions. But Chichén was altered by each successive wave of inhabitants, and archaeologists are able to date the arrival of new inhabitants by the changes in the architecture and the deciphering of hieroglyphics. (There is no mention of Toltecs in the inscriptions.) However, they have yet to explain the long gaps of time when the buildings seem to have been uninhabited. The site is believed to have been first settled in AD 432, abandoned for an unknown period of time, then rediscovered in 964 by the Maya-speaking Itzás, who came from the southern Maya region of the Petén rain forest around Tikal, in what is now northern Guatemala; *Chichén Itzá* means "the mouth of the well of the Itzás." The Itzás may have also abandoned the site but they were the dominant group until 1224 when the site apparently was abandoned for all time. Francisco de Montejo established a short-lived colony here in the course of his conquest of Yucatán in the mid-1500s. At the turn of this century, U.S. Consul General Edward Thompson, an engineer by training with a sharp eye for hidden pyramids, purchased Chichén Itzá and carried out some of the earliest excavations at the site, basing himself at a hacienda on the grounds (now the Hacienda Chichén) and carting most of the treasure away to the Peabody Museum at Harvard University. Years later, when the Mexican government realized what he had in his possession, they made him give it back.

The majesty and enormity of this site is unforgettable. It incarnates much of the fascinating and bloody history of the Maya, from the steep temple stairways down which sacrificial victims may have been hurled, to the relentlessly ornate beauty of the smaller structures. Its audacity and vitality are almost palpable. Chichén Itzá encompasses approximately 6 square km (3½ square mi), though only 20 to 30 buildings of the several hundred at the site have been fully explored. These buildings include the largest ball court in Mesoamerica; a sacrificial well once filled with precious offerings (it was dredged by Mexican diver Pablo Bush Romero, and many of its treasures are now at Harvard); and a round building—one of the only ones in the Maya lands—that was possibly the most elegant and sophisticated of the Maya observatories. Other features of the site include stone sculptures of the feathered serpent god, reclining *chac mools,* steam baths for ritual purification, ruined murals, astronomical symbols, and broad *sacbeob,* sometimes referred to as sacbe (literally "white roads" used for ceremonial purposes and as trade arteries) leading to other ancient centers.

Chichén Itzá is divided into two parts, called Old and New, although architectural motifs from the classical period are found in both sections. A more convenient distinction is topographical, since there are two major complexes of buildings separated by a dirt path. The martial, imperial architecture of the Itzás and the more cerebral architectural genius and astronomical expertise of the earlier Maya are married in the 98-ft-tall pyramid called **El Castillo** (the castle), which dominates the site and rises above all the other buildings.

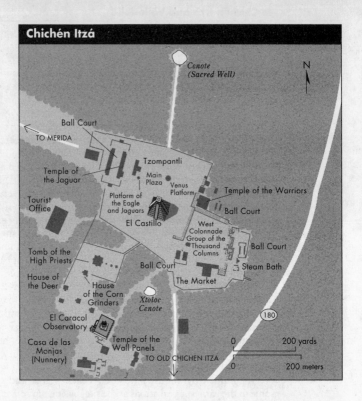

Chichén Itzá

Atop the castle is a temple dedicated to Kukulcán (the Maya name for
Quetzalcóatl), the legendary priest-king from Tula in the Valley of Mexico who was incarnated by the plumed serpent. According to ancient
lore, Quetzalcóatl went into exile, disappearing to the east, but promising to return one day. The Spaniard, Hernán Cortés—whom the Aztecs
(who adopted the cult of Quetzalcóatl after the Toltecs) mistook for
this god—transformed that prophecy into a nightmarish reality. Four
stairways, each facing a different cardinal point, provided access to the
temple; two are used today. Those who fear heights can hold on to a
rusty chain running down the center. Each access way consists of 91
very steep and narrow steps, which, when one adds the temple platform itself, makes a total of 365 (one for each day of the Mayas' extraordinarily accurate solar calendar). Fifty-two panels on the sides stand
for the years of a sacred cycle, while the 18 terraces symbolize the months
of the year. An open-jawed plumed serpent rests on the balustrade of
each stairway, and serpents reappear at the top of the temple as sculptured columns. This is one of the rare examples of a temple with four
stairways in the Maya world, which represents the symbolic partitioning
of the world into four parts, according to mythic lore.

At the spring and fall equinoxes (March 21 and September 21), the afternoon light and shadow strike one of these balustrades in such a way
as to form a shadow representation of Kukulcán undulating out of his
temple and down the pyramid to bless the fertile earth. Back then as
now, this phenomenon is viewed from the broad plaza on the northern side of the pyramid, a space reserved for ritual ceremonies by the
Maya. The sound-and-light show in the evening was completely re-
vamped in 1993, with a new computerized light system that highlights
the architectural details in the Castillo and other buildings with a clarity the eye doesn't see in daylight. An entirely new sound system en-
ables visitors to understand the formerly incomprehensible accompanying

narration, drawn rather loosely from the works of Bishop Landa and from the few surviving Maya texts, including the Books of Chilam Balam and Popul Vuh. Some of the data is incorrect showing a blatant lack of respect for historical detail. Landa initially burned all the Maya manuscripts he collected but later, overcome with remorse and admiration for the Maya, wrote their history. Regardless of the flaws of the show, do try to catch it on the night of a full moon when the narration and setting are particularly powerful. Tens of thousands of people travel to Chichén Itzá for the equinoxes, particularly in the spring when there is little likelihood of rain. Hotel reservations for the event should be made well in advance; a year ahead is not unreasonable.

In 1937 archaeologists discovered a more ancient temple inside the Castillo. A humid, slippery stairway leads upward to an altar that once held two statues: a chac mool and a bejeweled red tiger. The tiger, which had jade-encrusted discs embedded into its body and a turquoise disc laid on top of it, probably as an offering, is now housed in the Anthropology Museum in Mexico City. The inner temple is open to the public for only a few hours in the morning and again in the afternoon. Claustrophobes should think twice before entering: The stairs are narrow, dark, and winding, and there is often a line of tourists going both ways, making the trip somewhat frightening.

The temple rests on a massive trapezoidal square, on the west side of which is Chichén Itzá's largest **ball court,** one of seven on the site. Its two parallel walls are each 272 ft long, with two stone rings on each side, and 99 ft apart. The game played here was something like soccer (no hands were used), but it had a strictly religious significance. Bas-relief carvings at the court depict a player being decapitated, the blood spurting from his severed neck fertilizing the earth. Other bas-reliefs show two teams of opposing players pitted against each other during the ball game. Originally it was thought one team represented the invader Toltecs but new evidence points up the fact that the wardrobe design of the "Toltecs" has very Maya elements and that there never was a ball game between the two. Acoustics are so good that someone standing at one end of the court can hear the whispers of another person clearly at the other end. Sadly, the western wall of the court has been blackened by exhaust fumes from tour buses.

Between the ball court and El Castillo stands a **Tzompantli,** or stone platform, carved with rows of human skulls. In ancient times it was actually covered with stakes on which the heads of enemies were impaled. This motif was, however, known in the Maya region, although a similar platform was found at the Templo Mayor or religious center of Tenochtitlán, the Aztec capital (modern-day Mexico City).

The predilection for sacrifice was once believed to have been unknown to the Maya but recent research verifies that they had been indulging in their own forms of the ritual for hundreds of years. Legend has it that the **Sacred Well,** a cenote (sinkhole) 65 yards in diameter that sits 1 km (½ mi) north of El Castillo at the end of a 900-ft-long sacbe ("white road" in Maya) was used for human sacrifices; another cenote at the site supplied drinking water. Skeletons of about 50 people were found in the first well. The sacrificial victims, many of them children of both sexes, were drugged before being dropped into the well. It is said that, if any of the victims survived, they were fished up out of the well in the hopes that they would recount the psychic visions they had experienced. (Hunac Ceel, the notorious ruler of Mayapán in the 1250s, hurled himself into its depths to prove his divine ascendancy, and survived.) Many archaeologists now believe that nonhuman sacrifices were carried out by local chiefs hundreds of years after Chichén Itzá was abandoned. Thousands of artifacts made of gold, jade, and other precious materials, most of them not of local provenance, have been recovered from the brackish depths of the cenote. Long on display at Harvard's Peabody Museum, many of the finds have now been returned to the Mexican government. Trees and shrubs have washed into the well over the centuries, and their remains have prevented divers from getting to the bottom; because the cenote is fed by a network of underground rivers, it cannot be drained. More treasure undoubtedly remains. The well's excavation launched the field of underwater archaeology, later honed by the late Jacques Cousteau.

Returning to the causeway, you will see on your left the **Group of the Thousand Columns** with the famous **Temple of the Warriors,** a masterful example of the Itzá influence at Chichén Itzá. We know today that the temple was used as a meeting place for the high lords of the Council who ruled Chichén Itzá. The sculpture of the reclining Chaac Mool, god of rain, atop the temple is probably the most photographed figure representing the Maya history. This temple also resembles Pyramid B at Tula (sans Chaac Mool), the Toltecs' homeland, north of Mexico City—that this is what led scholars to believe originally that there was a Toltec connection to the site. However, the carvings of the lords found here are equivalent to carvings discovered at Copán in Honduras. Masonry walls carved with feathered serpents and frescoes of eagles and jaguars consuming human hearts are among the unmistakably Itzá details. Note the impressive feathered serpents columns with their jaws open. They were used to symbolize the ancient War Serpents of the Itza and the vehicle to communicate with the underworld. Using columns and wood beams instead of the Maya arches and walls to divide space enabled the Maya architects to expand the interior and exterior spaces dramatically. These spaces were also used for ritual dancing and processions associated with the council meetings. Murals of everyday village life and scenes of war can be viewed here, and an artistic representation of the defeat of one of the Itzás Maya enemies can be found on the interior murals of the adjacent **Temple of the Jaguar.**

To get to the less visited cluster of structures at "New" Chichén Itzá—often confused with "Old" Chichén Itzá (☞ *above*)—take the main road south from the Temple of the Jaguar past El Castillo and turn right onto a small path opposite the ball court on your left. Archaeologists are currently working in this area, restoring several buildings including the **Tomb of the High Priest,** where several tombs with skeletons and jade offerings were found and the northern part of the site which was used for military training and barracks for the army. Some smaller abodes not yet reconstructed are found to have been guest houses or sleeping quarters for nobles who lived in the center of the city. The work of the Maya epigraphers is leading to the discovery of the function of each of the structures. As work continues, certain ruins will be roped off and closed to tourists.

The most impressive structure within this area is the astronomical observatory called **El Caracol.** The name, meaning "snail," refers to the spiral staircase at the building's core. Built in several stages, El Caracol is one of the few round buildings constructed by the Maya. Although definitely used for observing the heavens (judging by the tiny windows oriented toward the four cardinal points, and the alignment with the planet Venus), it also served a religious function, since the Toltec cult of Kukulcán (Quetzalcóatl), the god of wind, often involved circular temples.

After leaving El Caracol, continue south several hundred yards to the beautiful **Casa de las Monjas** (Nunnery) and its annex, which have long panels carved with flowers and animals, latticework, hieroglyph-covered lintels, and Chaac masks (as does the nunnery at Uxmal). It was the Spaniards who gave the structure this sobriquet; no one knows how the Maya used it.

At "Old" Chichén Itzá, south of the remains of Thompson's hacienda, "pure Maya" style—a combination of Puuc and Chenes styles, with playful latticework, Chaac masks, and gargoylelike serpents on the cornices—dominates. (This style also crops up at Uxmal, Kabah, Labná, and Sayil, among other sites.) Highlights include the **Date Group** (so named because of the complete series of hieroglyphic date inscriptions), the **House of the Phalli,** and the **Temple of the Three Lintels.** Maya guides will lead you down the path by an old narrow-gauge railroad track to even more ruins, barely unearthed, if you ask. A fairly good restaurant and great ice-cream stand are in the entrance building, and there are refreshment stands by the cenote and on the pathway near El Caracol. ☎ *Site and museum $4, free Sun. and holidays; sound-and-light show $3 in Spanish, $5 in English; parking $1; use of video camera $8.* ☉ *Daily 8–5; sound-and-light show (Spanish) at 7, English at 8.*

Lodging

$$$$
★ 🏨 **Mayaland.** The hotel closest to the ruins, this charming 1920s lodging belongs to the Barbachano family, whose name is practically synonymous with tourism in Yucatán. In addition to a main hotel building, there are a wing and several bungalows set in a large garden on the 100-acre site. You can actually see part of "Old Chichen-Itza" from the gardens and the hotel has its own private walkway into the ruins. All units are colonial style and have decorative tiles, ceiling fans, air-conditioning, and television. Eighteen bunglalows were added in 1996, 10 in 1997. Tour buses fill the road in front of the hotel, so choose a room at the back. Light meals served poolside and at tables overlooking the garden are a far better choice than the fixed-price meals served in the dining room. Guided horseback riding tours are offered at extra cost. ⊠ *Carretera Mérida–Cancún, Km 120,* ☎ *985/10129. Reservations:* ⊠ *Mayaland Tours, Av. Colón 502, Mérida,* ☎ *99/250621 or 800/235–4079,* 🆑 *99/250087. 91 rooms, 4 suites. 3 restaurants, bar, air-conditioning, 3 pools, free parking. AE, DC, MC, V.*

$$$
★ 🏨 **Hacienda Chichén.** A converted 17th-century hacienda, this hotel once served as the home of U.S. Consul General Edward S. Thompson. Later it was the headquarters for the Carnegie expedition to Chichén Itzá. The rustic cottages were modernized in 1996 with hand-woven bedspreads and air-conditioning, and all rooms, which are simply furnished in colonial Yucatecan style, have private bathrooms and verandas. Rooms have no phones or TVs; there's a color satellite TV in the lobby area. Three suites were added in 1997. An enormous old pool as well as an old family chapel now used for guest weddings sits in the midst of the landscaped gardens. Fairly good meals are served on the patio overlooking the grounds, and there's an air-conditioned restaurant; stick with the Yucatecan specialties. ⊠ *Km 120 Carretera Mérida, Juarez, Yucatán 97000,* ☎ *985/10045, 99/248844, 99/242150, or 800/223–4084,* 🆑 *99/245011. 18 rooms, 3 suites. Restaurant, bar, air-conditioning, pool, free parking. AE, MC, V.*

Pisté

㉑ *About 1 km (½ mi) west of Chichén Itzá on Route 180.*

The town of Pisté serves mainly as a base camp for travelers to Chichén Itzá. Hotels, campgrounds, restaurants, and handicrafts shops tend to be cheaper here than south of the ruins. At the west end of town are a Pemex station and a bank. On the outskirts of Pisté, a short walk from the ruins, **Pueblo Maya,** a pseudo Maya village, provides a shopping and dining center for tour groups. The restaurant serves a bountiful buffet at lunch ($10).

Lodging

$$ **Pirámide Inn Resort.** The rooms (27 air-conditioned) in this American-owned, two-story motel in Pisté were completely refurbished in 1997 with painted walls, new curtains, and rugs, but they don't have phones or TVs. The garden contains a small Maya pyramid, a swimming pool, and a tennis court, and the restaurant is one of the best in Pisté. The RV park has been closed. ⊠ *Km 117 Carretera Mérida–Cancun.* ⊠ *Reservations: Box 433, Mérida,* ☎ *985/10115. 40 rooms. Restaurant, pool, tennis court, travel services. MC, V.*

$ **Dolores Alba.** The best low-budget choice near the ruins is this family-run hotel, a longtime favorite in the area south of Pisté. The rooms are simple, clean, and comfortable; half have air-conditioning. Hammocks hang by the small pool, and breakfast and dinner are served family-style in the main building. Free transportation to the ruins is provided. ⊠ *Km 122 Carretera Mérida–Cancún, 3 km (2 mi) south of Chichén Itzá. Reservations:* ⊠ *Calle 63, No. 464, Mérida,* ☎ *99/285650,* **FAX** *99/ 283163. 28 rooms. Dining room, pool. No credit cards.*

Cave of Balancanchén

🔺 ㉒ *4½ km (3 mi) northeast of Chichén Itzá.*

The Cave of Balancanchén, a shrine whose Maya name translates as "hidden throne," remained virtually undisturbed from the time of the Conquest until its discovery in 1959. Inside is a large collection of artifacts—mostly vases, jars, and incense burners once filled with offerings. Although there are seven chambers, only three are open to visitors. You'll walk past tiers of stalactites and stalagmites forming the image of sacred ceiba trees until you come to an underground lake. The lake is filled with blindfish (small fish with functionless eyes), and an altar to the rain god rises above it. In order to explore the shrine you must take one of the guided tours, which depart almost hourly, but it's necessary to be in fairly good shape, because some crawling is required; claustrophobes should skip it, and those who go should wear comfortable shoes. Also offered at the site is a sound-and-light show that fancifully recounts Maya history. A small museum at the entrance is very informative. You can catch a bus or taxi to the caves from Chichén Itzá. 🖭 *Caves (including tour) $3, free Sun.; show $3.* ☉ *Daily 9–5; English tour at 11, 1 and 3, Spanish at 9 and noon, French at 10.*

Valladolid

㉓ *44½ km (28 mi) east of Chichén Itzá.*

The second-largest city in the State of Yucatán, Valladolid is a picturesque, pleasant provincial town (population 70,000). It's enjoying growing popularity among travelers en route to or from Chichén Itzá or Río Lagartos who are harried by more touristy places. Montejo founded Valladolid in 1543 on the site of the Maya town of Sisal. The city suffered during the Caste War, when virtually the entire Spanish population was killed by the rebellious Maya, and again during the Mexican Revolution.

Today, however, placidity reigns in this agricultural market town. The center is mostly colonial, although it has many 19th-century structures. The main sights are the colonial churches, principally the large **cathedral** on the central square and the 16th-century **San Bernardino Church and Convent** three blocks southwest. Both were pillaged during the Caste

War. A briny, muddy cenote in the center of town draws only the most resolute swimmers; instead, visit the adjacent **ethnographic museum.** Outside town you can swim in **Cenote Dzitnup,** located in a cave lit by a small natural skylight ($3).

Valladolid is renowned for its cuisine, particularly its sausages; try one of the restaurants within a block of the square. You can find good buys on sandals, baskets, and the local liqueur, Xtabentún, flavored with honey and anise.

Lodging

$$ 🏨 **El Mesón del Marqués.** This building, on the north side of the main square, is a well-preserved, very old hacienda built around a lovely court-yard. All rooms have air-conditioning, phones, and cable TV and are attractively furnished with rustic and colonial touches; 10 new suites were added in 1997. Unusually large bathrooms boast bathtubs—a rarity in Mexican hotels; the new suites also have bidets. ⊠ *Plaza Principal, Calle 39, No. 203, 97780,* ☎ *985/62073,* FAX *985/62280. 22 rooms, 26 suites. Restaurant, bar, pool, shops. AE.*

$ 🏨 **María del Luz.** Another choice by the main plaza, this hotel is built around a small swimming pool and courtyard. The rooms were reno-vated in 1996 with new floors, fresh paint, and tiled bathrooms; air-conditioning and color televisions (local channels only) were also added. The street-side restaurant is attractively furnished with high-backed rattan chairs and linen cloths; Mexican dishes are predictable and inexpensive. ⊠ *Plaza Principal, Calle 2, No. 195, 97780,* ☎ *985/ 62071. 41 rooms. Restaurant, bar, pool. MC, V.*

TO UXMAL AND THE PUUC ROUTE

As soon as you pass through the large Maya town of Uman on Mérida's southern outskirts, you'll find yourself in one of the least populated areas of the Yucatán. From the highest point on the peninsula, the 500-ft crest between the present village of Muna and the ruins of ancient Uxmal, an unbroken expanse of low tropical forest reaches all the way to the southern horizon. The highway to Uxmal and Kabah is a fairly traffic-free route through uncultivated woodlands, punctuated here and there by oval thatched-roof huts and roadside stands where women sell hand-embroidered white cotton dresses.

The forest seems to become more dense beyond Uxmal, which was in ancient times the largest and most important city of the Puuc region. Raised and cobbled ceremonial roads connected it to a number of smaller ceremonial centers that, despite their apparent subservience to the Lords of Uxmal, boasted lofty pyramids and ornate palaces of their own. Several of these satellite sites, including Kabah, Sayil, and Labná, are open to the public along a side road known as the "Ruta Puuc," which winds eastward and eventually joins busy Route 184, a major highway linking Mérida with Felipe Carrillo Puerto, Quintana Roo, on the Caribbean coast, and serving the largest concentration of present-day Maya agricultural towns on the peninsula. From the east end of the Ruta Puuc near Loltún Caves, it takes motorists less than an hour to either retrace their route back to Uxmal or return to Mérida on Route 184.

Uxmal

🏛 ② *78 km (48 mi) south of Mérida on Route 261.*

If Chichén Itzá is the most impressive Maya ruin in Yucatán, Uxmal is arguably the most beautiful. Where the former has a Maya Itzá

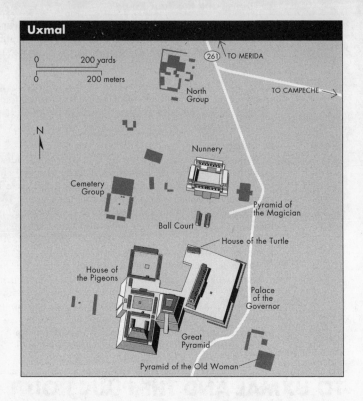

Uxmal

0 ——— 200 yards
0 ——— 200 meters

N

TO MERIDA
261

TO CAMPECHE →

North Group

Nunnery

Cemetery Group

Pyramid of the Magician

Ball Court

House of the Turtle

House of the Pigeons

Palace of the Governor

Great Pyramid

Pyramid of the Old Woman

grandeur, the latter seems more understated and elegant—pure Maya. The architecture reflects the late-classical renaissance of the 7th–9th centuries and is contemporary with that of Palenque and Tikal, among other great Maya metropolises of the southern highlands. Although the name translates as "thrice built" (referring to the three levels of the Pyramid of the Magician, in which older temples were buried), the site was actually rebuilt, abandoned, and reoccupied in several stages, for reasons still unknown. Itzá invaders briefly occupied Uxmal in the 10th century. The site reemerged as a Maya ceremonial center in the Post-Classic era and was deserted for the last time some 90 years before the Conquest. When John Lloyd Stephens came upon Uxmal in 1840, it was owned by a descendant of the same Montejo family that had conquered Yucatán three centuries earlier.

The site is considered the finest and largest example of Puuc architecture, which embraces such details as ornate stone mosaics and friezes on the upper walls, intricate cornices with curled noses, rows of columns, and soaring vaulted arches. Lines are clean and uncluttered, with the horizontal—especially the parallelogram—preferred to the vertical. Many of the flat, low, elongated buildings were built on artificial platforms and laid out in quadrangles. The cult of the rain god, Chaac, who is depicted here with a long curled nose and whose image appears throughout Yucatán, became obsessive in this parched region. But the area lacks cenotes. Though the Maya dug cisterns, called *chultunes,* for collecting rainwater, drought may be the reason that Uxmal was so often occupied and then abandoned. Some phallic figures—very common in Maya art because of the importance of fertility—are found here.

While most of Uxmal remains unrestored, three buildings in particular merit attention. The most prominent, the **Pyramid of the Magician,** is, at 125 ft high, the tallest structure at the site. Unlike most Maya pyramids, which are stepped and angular, it has a strangely elliptical design. Built five times, each time over the previous structure, the pyramid has a stairway on its western side that leads through a giant mask of Chaac with its mouth wide open to two temples at the summit. The mask motif is repeated on one side of the stairs. You get a magnificent panoramic view of Uxmal and the hills by climbing up to the top. According to legend, the pyramid derived its name from a dwarf magician who built it overnight. It is especially lovely at night, when its pale beige slope glows in the moonlight.

West of the pyramid lies the **Nunnery,** or Quadrangle of the Nuns, considered by some to be the architectural jewel of Uxmal. The name was given to it by the Spanish conquistadors because it reminded them of a convent building in Old Spain. However, recent research says it was the palace and living quarters of the high lord of Uxmal by the name of Chaan Chak, which means "abundance of rain." You can see his carved figure on stella No. 14, now on exhibit at the museum at the entrance to the site. Chaan Chak also inaugurated the ball court at Uxmal on January 15 and 16, AD 901, inscriptions say. You may enter the four buildings; each comprises a series of low, gracefully repetitive chambers that look onto a central patio. The building on the southern side is broken by a tall corbeled arch that is formed by placing ceiling stones increasingly close to and on top of one another until they meet at a central supporting capstone. Elaborate decoration—in the form of stone latticework, masks, geometric patterns reminiscent of ancient Greek ornamentation, representations of the classic Maya thatched hut (*na*), coiling snakes, and some phallic figures—blankets the upper facades, in contrast with the smooth, sheer blocks that face the lower walls. The mosaics that thrust into the upper facade are huge, sometimes surpassing several feet in size.

Continue walking south; you'll pass the ball court before reaching the **Palace of the Governor,** which archaeologist Victor von Hagen considered the most magnificent building ever erected in the Americas. Interestingly, the palace faces east while the rest of Uxmal faces west. Archaeologists believe this is because the palace was used to sight the planet Venus. Covering 5 acres and rising over an immense acropolis, the palace lies at the heart of what must have been Uxmal's administrative center. Its 320-ft length is divided by three corbeled arches, which create narrow passageways or sanctuaries. Decorating the facade are intricate friezes (along the uppermost section), geometrically patterned carvings overlaid with plumed serpents, stylized Chaac masks, and human faces. These mosaics required more than 20,000 individually cut stones.

First excavated in 1929 by the Danish explorer Franz Blom, the site served in 1841 as home to John Lloyd Stephens, who wrote of it: "The whole wears an air of architectural symmetry and grandeur. If it stood at this day on its grand artificial terrace in Hyde Park or the Garden of the Tuileries, it would form a new order . . . not unworthy to sit side by side with the remains of Egyptian, Grecian, and Roman art." Today a sound-and-light show recounts Maya legends, including the kidnapping of an Uxmal princess by a king of Chichén Itzá, and focuses on the people's dependence on rain—thus the cult of Chaac. The artificial colored light brings out details of carvings and mosaics that are easy to miss when the sun is shining—for example, the stone replicas of nas, which bear a remarkable resemblance to contemporary huts, on one facade of the nunnery. The show is performed nightly in English and is one of the better productions of this type. ✉ *Site and museum $4, free Sun. and holidays; sound-and-light show in Spanish $3,* *in English $5; parking $1; use of video camera $8.* ⊙ *Daily 8–5; sound-and-light show (Spanish) at 8, English at 9.*

Dining and Lodging

$ ✕ **Nicte-Ha.** This café beside the Hacienda Uxmal hotel is the least expensive dining option by the ruins, serving pizzas, sandwiches, and Mexican snacks. Diners are welcome to use the swimming pool by the restaurant. Stop by after your morning tour, have lunch and a swim, and return to the ruins in late afternoon when the groups are gone and the sun is less intense. ⊠ *Hacienda Uxmal, Hwy. 261,* ☎ *no phone. No credit cards.*

$ ✕ **Las Palapas.** A great alternative to the hotel dining rooms at Uxmal, this family-run restaurant specializes in delicious Yucatecan dishes served with homemade tortillas. When tour groups request it in advance, the owners prepare a traditional feast, roasting the chicken or pork pibil-style in a pit in the ground. If you see a tour bus in the parking lot, stop in—you may chance upon a memorable fiesta. ⊠ *Hwy. 261, 5 km (3 mi) north of ruins,* ☎ *no phone. No credit cards.*

$$$$ ▦ **Hacienda Uxmal.** The oldest hotel at the Maya site, built in 1955 and still owned and operated by the Barbachano family, this pleasant colonial-style building has lovely floor tiles, ceramics, and iron grillwork. The rooms—all with ceiling fans, color TV, and air-conditioning—are tiled and decorated with worn but comfortable furniture. Inside the large courtyard are a garden and pools. Across the road and about 100 yards south you'll find the ruins. Ask about packages that include free or low-cost car rentals for the nights you spend at Uxmal and at the Mayaland hotel in Chichén Itzá. ⊠ *Within walking distance of ruins,* 99/494754. Reservations:⊠ Mayaland Tours, Av. Colón 502, Mérid, ☎ 99/250621 or 800/235–4079, ⅎ𝔸𝕏 99/250087. *78 rooms, 2 suites. 2 restaurants, bar, air-conditioning, room service, 2 pools. AE, DC, MC, V.*

$$ ▦ **Villa Arqueológica Uxmal.** The hotel closest to the ruins is this two-story Club Med property built around a large Mediterranean-style pool. The functional rooms have cozy niches for the beds, tiled bathrooms, and powerful air-conditioners. Maya women in traditional dress serve well-prepared Continental and French cuisine in the restaurant, and large cages around the hotel contain tropical birds and monkeys. For a fee, day-trippers can use the pool, then dine in the restaurant. ⊠ *Km 76 Carrerera (within walking distance of ruins) Uxmal, Yucatán 97000,* ☎ 985/10034, ⅎ𝔸𝕏 985/10018. *44 rooms. Restaurant, bar, air-conditioning, room service, pool, tennis court, free parking. AE, MC, V.*

Kabah

⚒ ㉕ *23 km (14 mi) south of Uxmal on Route 261.*

Kabah, which experts estimate was first inhabited around AD 250, is the largest restoration project currently under way in the Yucatán. A ceremonial center of soft, almost Grecian beauty, it was once linked to Uxmal by a sacbe, at the end of which looms a great independent arch across the highway from the main ruins. The 151-ft-long **Palace of the Masks** (also known as **Codz-Pop** or "coiled mat") is so called because of its 250 Chaac masks, most without curled noses, which from afar look like a rolled-up mat. ▱ *$1.25, free Sun.* ⊙ *Daily 8–5.*

Sayil

⚒ ㉖ *5 km (3 mi) south of Kabah on Route 261.*

Sayil, or "home of ants," is the oldest site of the Puuc group, renowned primarily for its majestic three-story **palace** with 70 rooms. The structure recalls Palenque in its use of multiple planes, its columned porticoes and sober cornices, and in the play of its long, graceful horizontal masses. ▦ *$1.25, free Sun. and holidays.* ⊙ *Daily 8–5.*

Labná

🔺 ㉗ *9 km (5½ mi) south of Sayil on Route 31 East.*

The striking, monumental structure at Labná, called *La Puerta* or "The Gateway," is a fanciful corbeled arch rising high into a near peak with elaborate latticework and a small chamber on each side of it. One theory says the arch was the entrance to an area where religious ceremonies were staged. One of the true curiosities of Maya civilization is that the Maya never discovered the true, or curved, arch. ▦ *$1.25, free Sun.* ⊙ *Daily 8–5.*

Loltún Caves

🔺 ㉘ *18 km (11 mi) northeast of Labná.*

The Loltún Caves is the largest known cave system in the Yucatán. This series of caverns contains wall paintings and stone artifacts from Maya and pre-Maya times (around 2500 BC), as well as stalactites and stalagmites. You can enter the caves only on a guided tour. ▦ *$3, free Sun.* ⊙ *Tues.–Sun. 9–4, tour at 9:30, 11, 12:30, 2, and 3.*

Ticul

㉙ *27 km (16½ mi) northwest of the Loltún Caves, 28 km (17 mi) east of Uxmal.*

Most of the pottery you'll see around the Yucatán is produced in Ticul, where huipiles and shoes are also made. Many descendants of the Xiu dynasty, which ruled Uxmal before the Conquest, still live here. One of the larger towns in Yucatán, Ticul has a handsome 17th-century church.

Dining

$$ ✕ **Los Almendros.** If you're traveling along the Puuc route, it's a good
★ idea to save your appetite for this place, considered by many the best regional restaurant in the Yucatán. It offers fresher and tastier foods than do the other members of the Los Almendros chain. Although the interior is simple and clean, with whitewashed walls, the scenery behind the restaurant gives you a real taste of Yucatán: It's not unusual to see old Maya women in their huipiles and baseball hats patting corn tortillas by hand. The poc chuc and cochinita pibil are good choices, and the prices are the same as in the other branches. This is one place, however, where you can expect to wait in line for a table, especially during high season. ⊠ *Calle 23, No. 196,* ☎ *99/20021. MC, V.*

Yaxcopoil

㉚ *62 km (38 mi) north of Uxmal.*

Yaxcopoil, a restored 17th-century hacienda, offers a nice change of pace from the ruins. The building, with its distinctive Moorish double arch out front, has been used as a film set and is the best-known henequen plantation in the region. Visit the inside, which has been turned into a museum showing rooms with their original furnishings, and the machine room with machinery used in the processing of henequen; the family chapel used for worship is in the garden. ⊠ *Km 33, Rte. 261.* ▦ *$2.* ⊙ *Mon.–Sat. 8–sunset, Sun. 9–1.*

Mayapán

 31 *49 km (30 mi) east of Ticul.*

Those who are really enamored of Yucatán and the ancient Maya can detour at Ticul on Route 18 to the ruined city of Mayapán, the last of the great city-states on the peninsula until AD 1450, when it was demolished by war. It's surmised that it was as big as Chichén Itzá and there are over 4,000 mounds to bear this out. At its height, the population could have been well over 12,000. A half dozen are currently being vigorously excavated, including the palaces of Maya royalty and temple of the benign god Kukulcán. The ceremonial structures that were faithfully described in Fray Diego de Landa's writings will look like they have jumped right out of his book when the work is completed. The access road to the ruin is also being widened at the same time. ⊠ *Before Telchaquillo, Mayapán is off road to left; follow signs.* ▣ *$1.25, free Sun.* ☉ *Daily 8–5.*

PROGRESO AND THE NORTH COAST

Three separate routes lead from the Mérida area to towns along the north coast, covering a distance of 380 km (236 mi). Less traveled roads dead-end at the forgotten former seaport of Sisal and the laid-back fishing village of Celestún, gateway to a flamingo reserve at the western end of the coast. The busiest route leads due north from Mérida to the modern shipping port and local beach playground of Progreso. All three towns have wide, white shadeless beaches that are crowded with bathers from Mérida on weekends, during Holy Week, and in the summer, but nearly vacant on winter weekdays.

The terrain in this part of the peninsula is absolutely flat. Tall trees are scarce, because the region was almost entirely cleared for coconut palms in the early 19th century and again for henequen in the early 20th century. Today local Maya people still tend some of the old fields of henequen, a spike-leaf agave plant, even though there is little profit to be made from the rope fiber it produces. Other former plantation fields have run wild, overgrown with scrub and marked only by the low, white stone walls erected to mark their boundaries. Bird life is abundant in the area, and butterflies swarm in profusion throughout the dry season.

Celestún

32 *90 km (56 mi) west of Mérida.*

If you're going to spend any time at the coast, spend it at this fishing village, with its air of unpretentiousness and gulf-coast flavor. Celestún sits at the end of a spit of land separating the Celestún estuary from the gulf on the western side of Yucatán. It is the only point of entry to the **Parque Natural del Flamenco Mexicano**, a 147,500-acre wildlife reserve with extensive mangrove forests and salt flats and one of the largest colonies of flamingos in North America. From June through March clouds of pink wings soar over the pale blue backdrop of the estuary, up to 18,000 at a time. It's also the fourth-largest wintering ground for ducks of the gulf coast region, with over 200 other species of birds and a large sea turtle population. Conservation programs sponsored by the United States and Mexico not only protect the birds and turtles but other species like the blue crab and endangered crocodiles. Rocks, islets, and white-sand beaches enhance the park's lovely setting. There is good fishing in both the river and the gulf, and you can see deer and armadillo roaming the surrounding land. Bring your bathing suit if you want to enjoy a swim in one of the cenotes. Most Mérida travel agencies offer boat tours of the *ría* (estuary) in the early morning or late afternoon.

Popular with Mexican vacationers, the park's sandy beach is pleasant during the day but tends to get windy in the afternoon, with choppy water and blowing sand. To see the birds, hire a fishing boat at the dock outside town for around $40 for up to six people for a 45-minute tour or book a trip through a Mérida travel agency.

Dining and Lodging

$ ✕ **La Palapa.** A pretty facade made entirely of conch shells leads you to the best seafood place in town, famous for its *camarones a la palapa*— fried shrimp smothered in a garlic and cream sauce. There's a roofed-in area plus open-air terrace for lunching and observing the sea. The menu is full of fresh fish like sea bass and red snapper plus crab, squid and other denizens of the deep. ⊠ *Calle 12, No. 105, between Calle 11 and Calle 13,* ☎ *991/62063. No credit cards. No dinner.*

$$$$ 🏨 **Hotel Eco Paraíso Xixim.** This eco hotel, which opened in December 1996, is built on a nature reserve outside town and is definitely a cut above the other lodges on the Yucatán coast. "Xixim," by the way, means "seashells" in ancient Maya and takes its name from the thousands of seashells lining the beach. The hotel is built on an old coconut plantation and follows certain environmental guidelines: all wastes are recycled and used to irrigate plants or as compost in organic gardening, electrical consumption is kept low, guests separate all their non-biodegradable substances, only nonchemical bug repellant is permitted and sold at the hotel, and strict vigilance is kept at the shore where sea turtles deposit their eggs. Guests stay in thatched-roof beach bungalows with porches and hammocks. The accommodations are like small, private hideaways in the middle of a tropical paradise, with no phones or TVs. The small suites done up in a yellow, blue, and white color scheme, have tiled floors and attractive wicker, cedar, and pine furniture, some inlaid with hand-painted tiles from Tlaquepaque, where some of the country's best handicrafts are made. There's also a sitting area and writing desk. All tariffs include breakfast and dinner—very good Continental cuisine—served in the Club House. Special-interest tours to see the flamingos, old haciendas, archeological sites, bird-watching— even night tours to see sleeping birds—swimming in cenotes, and mountain biking are offered at extra cost. ⊠ *Km 9, del camino viejo a Sisal, Celestún 97367,* ☎ *991/62100,* 𝙵𝙰𝚇 *991/62111. 15 cabañas. Restaurant, bar, fans, in-room safes, pool, Ping-Pong, beach, billiards, library, travel services, free parking. AE, MC, V.*

$ 🏨 **Hotel María del Carmen.** Even though the rooms are a little shabby (but dirt-free) here, this hotel's saving grace is that it's right on the beach with tiny balconies catching the sea breeze and looking out over the fishing boats. The plain units have double beds, tile floors and bathrooms, no air-conditioning, and there are cement stairs leading up to the second- and third-floor levels. The owner, María del Carmen, after whom the hotel was named, lives on the premises and does some of the tidying up herself. ⊠ *Calle 12, No. 111, between Calles 13 and 15, 97367,* ☎ *993/62051. 14 rooms. Fans, free parking. No credit cards.*

$ 🏨 **Hotel Sol y Mar.** Gerardo Vasquez, the friendly owner of this new seven-room hotel, also owns the local paint store next door and chose a tasteful combination of gray and rose for the walls and curtains of these cool, spacious units. Located a half block from the town beach, this is definitely the best hotel of this category around. Rooms are spare but clean with two double beds, small table and chairs, tiled bathroom, and either air-conditioning (in three rooms) or overhead fans; there's no phone or TV. There's also no restaurant but six small eateries are within walking distance. ⊠ *Calle 12, No. 104, corner of Calle 10, Celestún, 97367,* ☎ *no phone. 7 rooms. No credit cards.*

Sisal

㉝ *79 km (49 mi) northwest of Mérida.*

Sisal gave its name to the henequen that was shipped from this port in great quantity during the mid-19th century. With the rise of Progreso, Sisal dwindled into little more than a fisherman's wharf. However, it may take on importance again because of a large, exclusive residential development being built (albeit slowly) here by a Mexican company. (The original company planning the development, the same people who created the Continental Plaza Playacar (☞ Chapter 5), shelved the plans because of near bankruptcy). Sisal livens up in July and August when Méridanos come to swim and dine. Attractions include a **colonial customs house** and the private 1906 **lighthouse. Madagascar Reef,** one of three offshore reefs, offers excellent diving.

Lodging
$ 🏨 **Hotel Felicidades.** A few minutes' walk up the beach east of the pier, this somewhat dingy hotel caters to tourists during the vacation months and can be fun when a crowd arrives. ⊠ *Calle 8, No. 1004, 97367,* ☎ *no phone. 10 rooms. No credit cards.*

Dzibilchaltún

⚒ ㉞ *14 km (9 mi) north of Mérida.*

Dzibilchaltún ("the place where there is writing on flat stones") is one of the largest archaeological sites in the north Yucatán area, occupying more than 65 square km (39½ square mi) of land cluttered with thousands of mounds, low platforms, piles of rubble, plazas, and stelae. It is also the longest-occupied city of this area, established around 375 BC in the Preclassic era and abandoned only when the conquistadors arrived in the 16th century.

For now Dzibilchaltún's significance lies in the stucco sculpture and ceramics, from all periods of Maya civilization, that have been unearthed here. The **Temple of the Seven Dolls** (circa AD 500) is the only structure excavated on the site to date. Low and trapezoidal, the temple exemplifies the late Preclassic style, which predates such Puuc sites as Uxmal. The remains of stucco masks adorn each side, and there are vestiges of sculptures of coiled serpents representing Kukulcán. During the spring and fall equinoxes, sunbeams fall at the exact center of two windows opposite each other inside one of the temple rooms, an example of the highly precise mathematical calculations for which the Mayas were known. The stone cube atop the temple and the open chapel built by the Spaniards for the Indians are additional points of interest. Twelve sacbeob (or sacbe) lead to various groups of structures. Bones and ceremonial objects unearthed by divers from the National Geographic Society between 1957 and 1959 suggest that the **Xlacah cenote** was used for ceremonial offerings. These days, it's ideal for taking a dip if you're walking around the ruins in the heat.

An excellent museum called **Pueblo Maya** opened in December 1994 at the entrance to the site. It's part of a national program dedicated to establishing museums devoted—and accessible—to the country's native peoples. It's fronted by a long rectangular garden featuring a number of the artifacts found on the site plus botanical species common to the area. In the back two thatched-roof huts (*nas*) let you see how the Maya live today. The museum's collection (marked in English as well as Spanish) includes figurines, bones, jewelry, and potsherds found in the cenote as well as the seven crude dolls that gave the temple its name. It also traces the area's Hispanic history and highlights contemporary crafts from the region. ✉ *$3, free Sun. and holidays (free guided tours; ask at the entrance).* ⊙ *Daily 8–8.*

Progreso

🏃 *16 km (10 mi) north of Dzibichaltún, 30 km (19 mi) north of Mérida.*

Progreso, the waterfront town closest to Mérida, is not particularly historical; it's also noisy with traffic and not at all picturesque. On weekdays during most of the year the town is deserted, but when school is out (Easter week, July, and August) and on summer weekends it becomes a popular vacation destination for families from Mérida. More and more retired Canadians are renting apartments here between December and April because of it's low prices). Progreso has fine sand and shallow waters that extend quite far out, making for nice walks, although its beaches are inferior to those of Quintana Roo. Because it is so close to Mérida and because its interest is limited, there is really no reason to spend the night here. The hotels are dismal and smell musty for the most part, but a couple of attractions in the small town may interest you.

The approach requires crossing some foul-smelling swamps, and these remind you of Progreso's main raison d'être: It has been the chief port of entry for the peninsula since its founding in 1872, when the shallow port at Sisal, to the southwest, proved inadequate for handling the large ships that were carrying henequen cargo. Since 1989 the 2-km-long (1-mi-long) pier has been extended 9 km (5½ mi) out to sea to accommodate the hoped-for cruise-ship business and to siphon some of the lucrative tourist trade from Cozumel, but at the moment only a trickle of cruise ships are berthing here. It looks as though all the millions invested have produced a white elephant because most cruise ships require deeper waters. A proposed project for ferry service between Tampa and Progreso is also on hold because the company that was to operate the concession went bankrupt in 1997.

Progreso's attractions include its **malecón** (waterfront walkway), Calle 19, which is lined with seafood restaurants. Fishermen sell their catch on the beach east of the city between 6 and 8 AM. Some 120 km (75 mi) offshore are the **Alacranes Reef,** where divers can explore sunken ships, and **Pérez Island,** which is part of the reef and which supports a sizable population of sea turtles and seabirds.

Dining and Lodging

$$ ✕ **Le Saint Bonnet.** This new, thatched-roof restaurant-bar with the open-air terrace on the malecón has become the "in" place for locals since it opened. It gets its pretentious French name from a French partner who has seen to it that all dishes have Gaelic monikers like the popular shrimp St. Bonnet—jumbo shrimp stuffed with cheese, wrapped with bacon, breaded, fried, and served with crab sauce. Other inventions include *filete al Nomandie* (fish fillet grilled with shrimp and covered with a mushroom/cheese sauce and sprinkled with bacon bits and walnuts). You can wash it down with a French, German, Italian, Portuguese, or Chilean red or white. If you have room for dessert, there's caramel crepes and mango or chocolate mousse. A live band plays lilting tropical music 1–5 each afternoon. ✉ *Av. Malecón 150 D at Calle 78,* ☎ *993/52299. AE, MC, V.*

$ 🏨 **Tropical Suites.** If you're not put off by the gruff receptionist/owner, this clean-but-modest Progreso standby has an ideal location by the ocean and the price is right ($19–$23). The tiled rooms and suites are spacious, and the suites can fit up to four people and have breezy balconies and a quasi kitchen with small fridge for extended stays. The furniture is nothing to write home about—basic double beds, sparse decor, and white plastic chairs; overhead fans and some air-conditioning (in four rooms) help beat the heat; 10 rooms have kitchenettes. There's a guest terrace/sundeck that takes up half the fourth floor and numerous eateries in the vicinity for meals. ⊠ *Malécon and Calle 70, 97320,* ☎ *993/51263,* ℻ *993/53093. 20 rooms, 10 suites. Fans. No credit cards.*

Yucalpetén

❸❻ *3 km (2 mi) west of Progreso.*

If you approach Yucalpetén—lying at the end of a narrow, marshy promontory—from the west, you'll pass a number of dead palm trees that were obliterated by the yellowing palm disease that has swept the peninsula in recent years. The harbor here dates only from 1968, when it was built to provide shelter for small fishing boats during the hurricane season. Little goes on here other than some activity at the yacht marina, where sportfishing for such catch as grouper, red snapper, dogfish, sea bass, and pompano is popular. Just beyond Yucalpetén, the even tinier village of **Chelem** has a few beachfront bungalow hotels.

Dining and Lodging

$$ 🏨 **Sian Ka'an.** These thatched-roof, two-story villas, right on the beach in Chelem (just west of Yucalpetén), all come with kitchenettes, ceiling fans, and terraces that overlook the water. Decorated in rustic Mexican-Mediterranean style, the suites have handwoven bedspreads, *equipales* (leather chairs from Jalisco), and blown glassware. Ask about discounts during the week. ⊠ *Calle 17, s/n, Carretera Yucaltepén–Chelem. Reservations:* ⊠ *Apartado Postal no. 38, Yucaltepén 97320,* ☎ *9099/471571, 993/54017. 8 suites. Restaurant, pool, beach. No credit cards.*

Telchac Puerto

❸❼ *43 km (27 mi) east of Progreso.*

This poverty-stricken little fishing village is worth visiting for its proximity to **Laguna Rosada,** where the flamingos come to nest, and it also has lovely, empty beaches. A new luxury hotel that keeps changing owners has brought some measure of prosperity back to the area. Several smaller luxury hotels are in the planning stages.

More and more foreigners are getting wind of the inexpensive rental homes in the nearby fishing village of **Chicxulub Puerto,** with its inviting beach and low winter rates. Chicxulub has also gotten press among scientists who theorize that debris raised by an asteroid that landed here some 65 million years ago may have caused the extinction of the dinosaurs.

Dining and Lodging

$$$$ ✕🏨 **Club Mayan Resort.** This Mexican all-inclusive, which was bought by a Mexican banker in 1997 after a short period as part of the Club Maeva (Mexican version of a Club Med) chain, is trying to attract the local market with all the food and drink you can consume included in the price of a room. So far this is the only full-service hotel in town. The nightly musical revues along with the children's program operate only from December 25 through April. Rooms are airy and beautifully laid out with tiled floors, blue and pink floral bedspreads that blend with lilac walls, modern furniture, overhead fans, air-conditioning, and

balconies. ⊠ *Telchac Puerto, domicilio conocido, Telchac Puerto.*
Reservations: ⊠ *Calle 58, Paisaje Camino Real, between Calles 49 and*
51, Depto. 124, Merida 97000, ☎ *991/74001,* ℻ *991/74006. 150*
rooms. 2 restaurants, 2 bars, coffee shop, air-conditioning, fans, room
service, 2 pools and 1 children's pool, 3 tennis courts, exercise room,
volleyball, beach, kayaking, children's program (ages 5–12), car rental.
AE, MC, V.

Motul

㊳ *32 km (20 mi) south of Telchac Puerto, 51 km (32 mi) northeast of*
Mérida.

Motul is the birthplace of the assassinated Socialist governor of Yucatán, Felipe Carrillo Puerto, who is also known for his romance with
U.S. journalist Alma Reed in the 1930s. His former house is now a museum containing displays on his life and times. 🎫 *Free.* ☉ *Daily 8–*
noon and 4–6.

Dzilám de Bravo

㊴ *40 km (25 mi) east of Telchac Puerto, 113 km (70 mi) northeast of*
Mérida.

The pirate Jean Laffite supposedly lies buried just outside the village of
Dzilám de Bravo. At least there's a grave so marked, and two locals claim
to be his descendants. Stop here for a swim in the gentle waters, or hire
a boat from a local fisherman to view the seabirds that congregate around
the small strip of land offshore about 10 minutes away.

Tizimín

㊵ *108 km (67 mi) southeast of Dzilam de Bravo.*

Tizimín, renowned as the seat of an indigenous messianic movement
during the 1840s Caste War, is situated at the junction of highways
176 and 295. The town boasts a 17th-century church dedicated to the
Three Wise Men, who are honored here during a festival that is held
December 15 to January 15.

Río Lagartos National Park

㊶ *52 km (32 mi) north of Tizimín.*

If you're a flamingo fan (flamingo season runs from June through March),
don't miss Río Lagartos National Park. Actually encompassing a long
estuary, not a river, the park was developed with ecotourism in mind,
though most of the alligators for which it and the village were named
have long since been hunted into extinction. In addition to flamingos,
birders can spot egrets, herons, ibis, cormorants, pelicans, and even
peregrine falcons flying over these murky waters. Fishing is good, too,
and hawksbill and green turtles lay their eggs on the beach at night.
You can make this a day trip from Valladolid (1¼ hours by road) or
Mérida (2½ hours by road) or one of the resorts along the coast west
of here or you can lodge in San Felipe, 10 km (6 mi) west of Río Lagartos because Río Lagartos has no hotels, just a few restaurants. To get
here you can opt for driving or taking a bus or a tour out of Merida
or elsewhere. Buses leave regularly from Merida and Valladolid from
the second-class bus terminals to either Río Lagartos or San Felipe. A
boat tour to see the flamingos is available from either point. If you drive,
stop in Tizimím first at the offices of the **Reserva** (Flamingo Reserve;
⊠ *Calle 47, No. 415A, between Calles 52 and 54,* ☎ *986/32854),* open
weekdays 9–2 and 6–9, for information. They can arrange for a bilin-

gual guide with three days advance notice. If you miss the Tizimím office, a ½ km (¼ mi) from the entrance into Río Lagartos, you'll spy an information module with the name *Estacion* (Station) written on it. This is the official entrance to the reserve. The helpful folk who work here can also call up a guide with a boat for you. If you've missed both places, once in town, head for the **Isla de Contoy** restaurant (☞ *below*) and ask for Diego. Diego runs the place and is also a guide with a boat. Three-hour boat tours cost $13 an hour for the boat, not per person; you can fit in eight to 10 persons. The boat glides up the estuary east of the dock and in 10 minutes is deep into mangrove forests; another hour and the boat is at the flamingo feeding grounds.

Once you walk into the reserve, you won't see any marked paths with signs for bird-watching. Bilingual birding guides are also on hand but you must reserve at least three days in advance with the Reserve office in Tizimí. The shortest circuit is a little over a mile long and goes west along the estuary in a straight line to the ocean. The cost is $7–$14 an hour.

Dining and Lodging

$ ✕ **Isla de Contoy.** Run by an amicable family, this strictly seafood place offers generous helpings of fish soup, fried fish fillets, shrimp, squid, and crab. It's common practice to wash seafood down with a Yucatecan beer. ✉ *Calle 19, No. 12, 2 blocks from the estuary in Río Lagartos,* ☎ *986/32668.*

$ ✕⌸ **Hotel San Felipe.** This three-story white hotel in the beach town of San Felipe opened at the end of 1996 to cater to the growing number of visitors who want to overnight in the Río Lagartos area. The rooms are pretty basic—white walls with red trim, either with two twin beds or a double bed with a concrete base, overhead fans, reading lamps, and private tiled bathrooms with hot and cold water. There are no phones or TVs, but for $14.50 a double, you can't go wrong. The restaurant serves only fish and seafood dishes for all meals with the exception of breakfast. ✉ *Calle 9, No. 13, between Calles 14 and 16 (2 blocks from the main square), San Felipe 97720,* ☎ *986/633738 or 986/6320891, ext. 127. 18 rooms. Restaurant, fans, free parking. No credit cards.*

Isla Holbox

㊷ *141 km (87 mi) northeast of Valladolid.*

The tiny Isla Holbox (25 km, or 16 mi, long) sits at the eastern end of the Río Lagartos estuary and just across the Quintana Roo state line. A fishing fan's heaven because of the pompano, bass, barracuda, and shark thronging its waters, the island also pleases seekers of tranquillity who don't mind rudimentary accommodations (rooms and hammocks for rent) and simple palapa restaurants. Seabirds fill the air, the long sandy beach is strewn with seashells, and the swimming is good on the gulf side. To get here from Río Lagartos, take Route 176 to Kantunilkin, then head north on the unnumbered road for 44 km (27 mi) to Chiquilá. Continue by ferry to the island; schedules vary, but there are two crossings (time: one hour) a day.

MÉRIDA AND THE STATE OF YUCATÁN A TO Z

Arriving and Departing

Getting around the state is fairly easy, either by public bus or car. There are many more bus lines than before, including the new super deluxe lines that get to your destination unfrazzled—in an air-conditioned coach with spacious seats. There is even some air-conditioning on second-class bus lines if you demand it. In any event all bus lines have at least one round-trip run daily to the main archaeological sites and colonial cities. Connections by bus from smaller towns is also very easy. If you're visiting for the first time, a guided tour booked through one of the many Mérida travel agencies is a good bet until you get your sea legs. If you're just independent and adventurous, by all means hire a rental car and strike out on your own. Just take plenty of bottled water, and find out where the gas stations are along your route.

By Bus

The **main bus station** (✉ Calle 69, No. 544, between Calles 68 and 70, ☏ 99/247868) in Mérida offers frequent second-class service to Akumal, Cancún, Chichén Itzá, Playa del Carmen, Puerto Morelos, Tulum, Uxmal, Valladolid, and Xel-Há. There's the **ADO bus terminal, called CAME** (✉ nearby at Calle 70, between Calles 69 and 71, ☏ 99/247868). Several lines, such as **Expreso del Oriente** (☏ 99/232287) and **Super Expreso** (☏ 99/248391) now offer deluxe service with air-conditioning, refreshments, and movies shown en route. The ADO GL or UNO buses, both operated by ADO, also offer roomy, airline-type reclinable seats. **Autotransportes del Sureste** (☏ 99/281595) at the second-class bus station has the best coverage for out-of-the-way destinations, with daily service to the Guatemalan border, Palenque, and San Cristóbal de las Casas, and four buses daily to Uxmal. As its name suggests, the **Progreso bus station** (✉ Calle 62, No. 557, between Calles 65 and 67, ☏ 99/281344) has departures for Progreso. Buses for Dzibilchaltún and Celestún leave regularly from the San Juan Plaza. A travel agency called **Nuevos Horizontes,** with deluxe ADO service to Valladolid ($5), Cancún ($11), Campeche City ($8), Tuxtla Gutiérrez ($30), Villahermosa ($35), Playa del Carmen ($12.50), Mexico City ($49) and Palenque ($19.50), leaves conveniently from the Fiesta Americana Hotel (✉ Calle 56A and Av. Colon, local no. 56, ☏ 99/200100), where you can also buy your ticket. The Viajes Carmen travel agency (☏ 99/200126), in the lobby of the same hotel, will sell you ADO bus tickets for all routes, but departure is from the downtown bus terminal. The exception is the evening (7:15 PM) run to Campeche, Cuidad del Carmen, Villahermosa, and Mexico City.

By Car

Route 180, the main road along the gulf coast from the Texas border to Cancún, runs into Mérida. Mexico City lies 1,550 km (960 mi) to the west; Cancún, 320 km (200 mi) due east.

The *autopista* is a four-lane toll highway between Mérida and Cancún. Beginning at the town of Kantuníl, 55 km (34 mi) southeast of Mérida, it runs somewhat parallel to old Route 180 and cuts driving time between Mérida and Cancún—formerly around 4½ hours—by about one hour. Access to the toll highway is off old Highway 180 and is clearly marked. The highway has clearly marked exits for Valladolid and Pisté (Chichén Itzá), as well as rest stops and gas stations. At press time (summer 1998), tolls between Mérida and Cancún totaled about $16. From Campeche it takes a little more than two hours to reach Mérida via Route 180, which is the fastest route. Another option is the three-hour drive along Route 261 from Campeche, which passes the ruins of Uxmal and other ancient Maya sites as well as present-day Maya villages. From Chetumal the most direct way—it takes approximately nine hours—is Route 307 to Felipe Carrillo Puerto, then Route 184 to Muna, continuing north on Route 261. These highways are in very good condition.

By Plane

The Mérida airport is 7 km (4½ mi) west of the city's central square, about a 20-minute ride. The following airlines serve Mérida: **Aeromexico** (☎ 99/201260, 99/201293) flies direct from Miami with a stop (but no plane change) in Cancún; **Mexicana** (☎ 99/461332) has a connecting flight from Newark via Cancún, and a number of connecting flights from the United States via Mexico City; **Aerocaribe** (☎ 99/286790), a subsidiary of Mexicana, has flights from Cancún, Chetumal, Cozumel, Oaxaca, Tuxtla Gutiérrez, and Villahermosa. There is additional service to Veracruz, Monterrey, and Havana; **Aviateca** (☎ 99/461296), a Guatemalan carrier, flies from Houston and Guatemala City; and **Taesa** (☎ 99/202077) flies from Mexico City. **Bonanza** (☎ 99/277999), another local carrier, flies to Palenque, Chetumal, and Belize City.

BETWEEN THE AIRPORT AND CITY CENTER
A private taxi costs about $7; there is only collective service for groups (usually a Volkswagen minibus), about $3. For both, pay the taxi-ticket vendor at the airport, not the driver. The inexpensive but irregular No. 79 bus goes from the airport to downtown. If you're driving into town, take the airport exit road, make a right at the four-lane Avenida Itzaes (the continuation of Route 180), and follow it to the one-way Calle 59, just past El Centenario Zoo. Turn right on Calle 59 and go straight until you reach Calle 62, where you again turn right, and drive a block to the main square. (Parking is difficult here.)

Getting Around

By Bus

Mérida's municipal buses run daily from 5 AM to midnight, but service is somewhat confusing until you master the system. In the downtown area buses go east on Calle 59 and west on Calle 61, north on Calle 60 and south on Calle 62. You can catch a bus heading north to Progreso on Calle 56. Unfortunately, there is no bus service from the hotels around the plaza to the long-distance bus station.

By Car

Driving in Mérida can be frustrating because of the one-way streets (many of which end up being one-lane because of the parked cars) and because traffic is dense. But having your own wheels is the best way to take excursions from the city. Prices are sometimes lower if you arrange your rental in advance through one of the large international companies.

By Carriage

Horse-drawn calesas (pony traps) can be hailed along Calle 60. A ride to the Paseo de Montejo and back will cost about $7 to $9, and you can bargain.

By Taxi

Taxis don't cruise the streets for passengers; instead, they are available at 13 taxi stands around the city, from the main taxi office (☎ 99/231317), or in front of the Hyatt Regency/Holiday Inn and Fiesta Americana hotels, which are strung out on the same block. Individual cabs cost $3 minimum.

Contacts and Resources

Banks

Most banks throughout Mérida are open weekdays 9–1:30. **Banamex** has its main offices, open weekdays 9–5 and Saturday 9–1:30, in the handsome Casa de Montejo, on the south side of the main square, with a branch at the airport and the Fiesta Americana Hotel. The downtown and Fiesta Americana Banamex now have automatic teller machines that can be accessed with Cirrus, MasterCard, and Visa bank cards. Several other banks can be found on Calle 65, between Calles 62 and 60, and on Paseo Montejo, and most have the same automatic teller service for the same cards.

MONEY EXCHANGE

There are several exchange houses, including **Del Sureste** (⊠ Calle 56 at Calle 57), open weekdays 9–5 and Saturday 9–1; **Centro Cambriano Canto** (⊠ Headquarters at Paseo de Montejo at corner of Av. Perez Ponce; downtown branch at Calle 61 at Calle 52), both open weekdays 9–1 and 4–7; **Casa de Cambio del Pasaje Pichetti** (⊠ On the main square), open weekdays 9–5 and Saturday 9–1; and two on the ground level of the Fiesta Americana Hotel (Calle 56A and Av. Colon), open weekdays 9–5. By all means avoid the exchange house operated by GBM Atlantico in the same building complex as Centro *Cambiario* Canto as it's under investigation for possible fraudulent practices.

Car Rentals

There are almost 20 car-rental agencies in town, including **Budget** (⊠ Hyatt Regency, Calle 60, No. 344, at Av. Colon, ☎ 99/421226; the Holiday Inn next to the Hyatt, ☎ 99/255453; and airport, ☎ 99/461380); **Dollar** (⊠ Hotel Mérida Misión, ☎ 99/286759; airport, ☎ 99/461323); **National** (⊠ Fiesta Americana, ☎ 99/257524; airport, ☎ 99/461394); **Hertz** (⊠ Fiesta Americana, ☎ 99/277595; ⊠ Calle 60, between Calles 55 and 57, ☎ 99/242834); and **Thrifty** (⊠ Calle 60, between Calles 51 and 49, ☎ 99/232440; airport, ☎ 99/462515).

Consulates

United States (⊠ Paseo de Montejo 453, ☎ 99/255011, 99/258677, or 99/255409). **United Kingdom** (⊠ Calle 58, No. 450, at Calle 53, ☎ 99/286152).

Emergencies

In Mérida: **Police** (☎ 99/252555); **Red Cross** (Calle 68, No. 583, at Calle 65, ☎ 99/249813); **Fire** (☎ 99/249242); **general emergency** (☎ 06).

Hospital O'Horan (⊠ Av. Internacional and Av. Itzaes, ☎ 99/244111, 99/242911, or 99/244800).

English-Language Bookstores

Librería Dante has several branches around Mérida (⊠ Calle 59 at Calle 68; Parque Hidalgo; in Teatro Peón Contreras, at corner of Calles 60 and 57; and on main square, next to Pizza Bella), all of which carry a small selection of English-language books and a Mexico City daily newspaper. All branches are open Monday–Saturday 8–9:30 and Sunday 8–8. For newspapers and magazines from Mexico City and the United States, visit the newsstand under the portals in Plaza Pichetti on the main square.

Guided Tours

There are more than 50 tour operators in Mérida, and they generally offer the same destinations. What differs is how you go—in a private car, a van, or a bus—and whether or not the vehicle is air-conditioned. A two- to three-hour city tour, including museums, parks, public buildings, and monuments, will cost between $7 and $20. Or you can pick up an open-air sightseeing bus at Parque de Santa Lucía for $7; departures are Monday–Saturday at 10, 1, 4, and 7 and Sunday at 12:30 and 5. A day trip to Chichén Itzá, with guide, entrance fee, and lunch, runs approximately $50. For about the same price you can see the ruins of Uxmal and Kabah in the Puuc region, and for a few more dollars you can add on the neighboring sites of Sayil, Labná, and the Loltún Caves. Afternoon departures to Uxmal allow you to take in the sound-and-light show at the ruins and return by 11 PM, for $50–$60 (including dinner). There is also the option of a tour of Chichén Itzá followed by a drop-off in Cancún for about $60. Most tour operators take credit cards.

SPECIAL-INTEREST TOURS

Several of the tour operators in Mérida run overnight excursions to archaeological sites farther afield, notably Cobá, Tulum, Edzná, and Palenque. Tours of the Ruta Maya including sites in Mexico, Guatemala, and Belize are offered by **VN Travel** (⊠ Calle 58, No. 488, ☏ 99/239061 or 99/245996) and **Mayaland Tours** (⊠ Fiesta Americana, Av. Colón, No. 502, ☏ 99/250621 or 800/235–4079, FAX 99/250087), which also offers self-guided tours with economical rental car rates. **Ecoturismo Yucatán** (⊠ Calle 3, No. 235, at Col. Pensiones, ☏ 99/202772, FAX 99/259047) specializes in nature tours, including bird-watching, natural history, anthropology, treking, kayaking, diving in cenotes, and the Mundo Maya. Owners Roberta and Alfonso Escobedo are especially adept at organizing group and individual trips to out-of-the-way archaeological sites and natural parks in Yucatán, Campeche, Chiapas, Tabasco, Belize, and Guatemala.

Emerald Planet (⊠ 4076 Crystal Court, Boulder, CO 80304, ☏ 303/541–9688 or 800/883–3260, FAX 303/449–7805) offers bird-watching and orchid tours and other trips into wildlife reserves—often combined with archaeological ruins—in the state of Yucatán. Tours combining the wildlife reserves in the Yucatán, Campeche, Chiapas, and Quintana Roo are also available. Part of the profits go toward funding Mexico's Pronatura projects. Occasionally, **Pronatura** (⊠ Calle 1-D, No. 254-A, Campestra, 99/443390 and 99/443580), a wildlfe conservation program, will arrange guided one- or two-day trips to Celustún or Río Lagartos accompanied by a bilingual biologist. A donation is expected, based on the time and effort involved in setting it up.

Mail

In addition to the **main post office** (⊠ Calle 65 at Calle 56, ☏ 99/243590), there are branches at the airport (☏ 99/211556) and at the main bus station (⊠ Calle 69, between Calles 68 and 70, ☏ no phone), all open weekdays 7–6, Saturday 9–noon.

Spanish-Language School

Intensive Spanish classes for foreigners are available in Mérida through the **Centro de Idiomas** (⊠ Calle 14, No. 106, at Calle 25, Col. Mexico 97128, Mérida, Yuc., Mexico, ☏ 99/230954 or 99/261156) and the **Academia de Cultura e Idiomas de Mérida** (⊠ Apdo. Postal 78-4, 97100 Mérida, Yuc., Mexico, 99/443148). Classes last a minimum of two weeks; advanced classes in special areas of study are available. Students stay with local families or in hotels.

Telephones

Local phone numbers are gradually changing throughout Mérida, causing much confusion. If you need information, talk with the operator or your hotel staff. There are many long-distance **Ladatel phone booths** around town: at the airport, at all bus stations, at Avenida Reforma and Avenida Colón, Calle 57 at Calle 64, Calle 59 at Calle 62, and Calle 60 between Calles 55 and 53. Both local and international direct calls can be made at some of these public phones, which accept new peso coins. Almost all phones accept Ladatel cards, electronic phone cards that can be purchased at most hotels and at the newsstands by the main square on Calle 61.

Travel Agencies and Tour Operators

Mérida's local agencies and operators include **American Express** (⊠ Calle 56-A, No. 494, ☎ 99/244326, FAX 99/284373), **Buvisa** (⊠ Paseo de Montejo, No. 475, ☎ 99/277933, FAX 99/277414), **Ceiba Tours** (⊠ at the Holiday Inn, Av. Colon 498 and Calle 60, ☎ 99/204477 or 99/203444, FAX 99/256389), **Betanzos Internacional** (⊠ Calle 60, No. 466, Dept. 01, between Calles 53 and 55, ☎ 99/239966 or 99/238594, FAX 99/239966), **Mayaland Tours** (⊠ Av. Colón, No. 502, ☎ 99/250621 or 800/235–4079, FAX 99/250087; Casa del Balam hotel, Calle 60, No. 488, ☎ 99/244919), **Turismo Aviomar** (⊠ Calle 58A, 500-C, ☎ 99/200444 or 99/200443, FAX 99/255064), **Viajes Novedosos** (⊠ Calle 58, No. 488, ☎ 99/245996, FAX 99/239061), and **Yucatán Trails** (⊠ Calle 62, No. 482, ☎ 99/285913 or 99/282582, FAX 99/241928).

24-Hour Pharmacies

Farmacia Yza Centro (⊠ Calle 63, No. 502-A, between Calles 60 and Calle 62, ☎ 99/249510), **Farmacia Yza Tanlum** (⊠ Glorieta Tanlum, ☎ 99/251646), and **Farmacia Canto Centro** (⊠ Calle 60, No. 514, at Calle 63, ☎ 99/285027)

Visitor Information

MÉRIDA

State Tourist Information Center (⊠ Teatro Peón Contreras, Calle 60, between Calles 57 and 59, ☎ 99/249290), open daily 8–8. **Information kiosks:** At the airport (☎ 99/246764), open daily 8–8; at the second-class bus station (⊠ Calle 69, between Calle 68 and Calle 70 , ☎ 99/232287) and **City Tourist Information Center** (⊠ Calle 59 and 62, ☎ no phone), open weekdays 8–8 and weekends 9–7.

PROGRESO

Tourist office (⊠ Calle 80, No. 176, at Calle 37, ☎ 993/50104), open weekdays 9–2 and 4–7.

7 Campeche

Ruins of the fortifications built to fend off the pirates who ravaged Yucatán's gulf coast add Old World romance to the walled city of Campeche. Among the remnants of Maya settlements that dot the rest of this little-explored state, Edzná is the best known and most interesting.

CAMPECHE, THE LEAST-VISITED PART of the Yucatán,
and the most underrated, is for the adventuresome
visitor, who will discover both charm and mystery

Updated by
Patricia Alisau

here. Three-hundred-year-old cannons point across the Gulf of Mexico from fortress battlements, recalling pirate days and lending an air
of romance to the walled capital city of Campeche. This city definitely
exudes the aura of a warrior tradition. Beyond the city, ancient pyramids and ornate temple facades from the area's Maya past—some of
the most important discoveries in the Maya empire to date—lie hidden deep in tropical forests.

Most of the State of Campeche is flat—never higher than 1,000 ft above
sea level—but more than 60% of its territory is covered by jungle, where
precious mahogany and cedar abound. The Gulf Stream keeps temperatures at about 26°C (78°F) year-round; the humid, tropical climate is
eased by evening breezes. Campeche's economy is based on agriculture,
fishing, logging, salt, tourism, and—since the 1970s—hydrocarbons, of
which it is the largest producer in Mexico. But most of the oil industry
is concentrated at the southern end of the state, near Ciudad del Carmen. In the last few years, there's been talk of developing more offshore
drills at Campeche City but the move is being delayed so that studies on
the impact of the aquatic environment, particularly the fishing industry,
can be completed. Over 90 oil platforms dot the Campeche coast.

Campeche City's location on the gulf has played a pivotal role in its
history. Ah-Kin-Pech (Maya for "Lord of the Serpent Tick")—from
which the Spanish name of Campeche is derived—was the capital of
an Indian chieftainship long before the Spaniards arrived in 1517.
Earlier explorers had visited the area, but it was not until 1540 that
the conquerors—led by Francisco de Montejo and, later, his son—established a real foothold at Campeche (originally called San Lazaro),
using it as a base for their conquest of the peninsula.

Because Campeche City was the only port and shipyard on the gulf,
the Spanish ships, with their rich cargoes of plunder from the Maya,
Aztec, and other indigenous civilizations, dropped anchor here en
route from Veracruz to Cuba, New Orleans, and Spain. News of this
wealth spread, and soon the shores were overrun with pirates. From
the mid-1500s to the early 1700s, such notorious corsairs as Diego the
Mulatto, Lorenzillo, Peg Leg, Henry Morgan, and Barbillas swooped
down repeatedly from their base on Tris—or Isla de Términos, as Isla
del Carmen was then known—pillaging and burning the city and massacring its people.

Finally, after appealing for years to the Spanish crown, the citizens of
Campeche received funds that enabled them to build a protective wall
(with four gates and eight bastions). For some time thereafter, the city
thrived on its exports, especially *palo de tinte*—a dyewood used by the
nascent European textile industry—but also hardwoods, chicle, salt,
and henequen. However, when the port of Sisal on the northern Yucatán coast opened in 1811, Campeche's monopoly of the gulf traffic
ended, and its economy fell into decline.

The shape of modern-day Campeche is still defined by history. Remnants of the wall and other military structures divide it into two main
districts, intramural (the old city) and extramural (the new). Because
the city was long preoccupied with defense, colonial architecture is less
developed here than elsewhere in Mexico. Churches are more somber;
streets (a few still paved with flagstones) are narrow because of the confines of the walls; houses are more practical than aesthetic in their de-

sign. Although the face of the city has altered over the centuries, as landfill was added and walls and bastions demolished to make room for expansion, it still retains an aura of antiquity. No more colonial structures are allowed to be damaged according to a government decree, so the air of antiquity will most likely remain for a long, long time.

The state as a whole has a population of only about 635,000, most of it scattered through villages and small towns. Maya traditions still reign in the countryside, which is dotted with windmills and fields of tobacco, sugarcane, rice, indigo, maize, and cocoa. Wildlife flourishes here, too: Jaguars and deer (though diminished in number), tapir, and armadillos roam free, while the sea provides fishing boats with butterfly shrimp, barracuda, swordfish, and other catch.

Thousands of Guatemalan refugees who fled to Campeche were settled into four camps, one of which was involved in excavating the Maya archaeological site of Edzná. Since the Guatemalan government granted an armistice to the refugees in 1993, many of them have returned home. Recently, however, settlements of Chol Maya homesteaders relocated from Chiapas after the Zapatista uprising have appeared on the edge of southern Campeche's Calakmul Biosphere Reserve.

Pleasures and Pastimes

Architecture
Nowhere in the Yucatán does Spanish colonial history feel more immediate than in the city of Campeche. The architecture of the Old City remains pretty much unchanged since the 17th century and is constantly being restored and repainted. The present-day population is predominantly Maya, a race of people with considerable experience at living among the ruins of past glories. In Campeche they've left behind a few of their most impressive royal cities. Heritage blends easily with pragmatism in the capital. You are likely to come across colonial mansions being used as auto body shops and karate studios. Yet the constant proximity of architecture from an earlier era makes this charmingly decrepit city more evocative in its own way than many self-consciously preserved historic districts around the world.

Dining
There is nothing fancy about Campeche's restaurants, but the regional cuisine is renowned throughout Mexico—particularly the fish and shellfish stews, shrimp cocktails, squid and octopus, crabs' legs, panuchos, and other Yucatecan specialties. Unusual seafood delicacies include the famous Champotón baby shrimp from the coastal town of Champotón, which are a highly rated delicacy in other parts of the world; *pan de cazon* (red snapper wrapped in banana leaves); baby shark, cooked, shredded, and served over tortillas and tomato sauce); *moro* crab, hard to find because it's a hot export item; and crayfish claws. *Botanas,* or canapés, include cooked eggs with pumpkin seed and tomato sauce, fruit conserves in syrup with chili, ceviche (raw marinated fish), and *chicharrón* (fried pork rind). The addition of cumin, marjoram, bay leaf, cayenne pepper, and allspice imparts an exotic flavor to entrées. Fruits are served fresh, added to breads, made into liqueurs, or marinated in rum or vinegar. Look for mango, papaya, *zapote* (sapodilla), mamey, guanabana, tamarind, watermelon, jicama, melon, pineapple, and coconut, to name only a few. Because regional produce is plentiful, most restaurants—including all those listed below—fall into the $ to $$ price categories. Casual dress—though not always shorts—is fine in restaurants throughout Campeche, and reservations are not required.

For a description of other Mexican culinary items, *see* Dining *under*
Pleasures and Pastimes *in the* Destination: Cancún, Cozumel, Yucatán
Peninsula chapter.

CATEGORY	COST*
$$	$8–$15
$	under $8

per person, excluding drinks and service

Ecotourism

Southern Campeche contains one of the last vestiges of primeval rain
forest in Mexico, now legally protected under UNESCO's Man and
the Biosphere program as the Calakmul Biosphere Reserve. It adjoins
the much larger Maya Biosphere Reserve across the Guatemalan
border, as well as a smaller reserve in Belize. The deep forest in the
heart of the reserve is almost impossible to reach, but the outskirts
offer plenty of opportunity to see a wide range of orchids and jungle wildlife including spider monkeys, peccaries, boa constrictors, and
hundreds of species of birds. The state is one of the most environmentally correct regions of the country, due in part to the fact that
there's never been mass urban or tourism infrastructure of any kind
to unsettle its basic agrarian culture and due otherwise to the efforts
of the current state government, which has made it a top priority.
Ecotourism in the area is still in its infancy, but already there's rapid
growth in environmentally aware tourism in southern Campeche. For
example, Calakmul (☞ *below*) is the first ruin in the country to in-
stall ecological bathrooms.

Lodging

Most of Campeche City's hotels are old (and several are in disrepair),
reflecting the city's lackadaisical attitude toward tourism. Hotels tend
to be either luxury accommodations along the waterfront, with air-conditioning, restaurants, and other standard amenities, or basic downtown accommodations offering only ceiling fans and a no-credit-card
policy. Those in the latter category tend to be either seedy and unde-
sirable or oddly charming, with some architectural and regional detail
unique to each.

CATEGORY	COST*
$$$	over $90
$$	$40–$90
$	under $40

*All prices are for a standard double room, excluding service and the 15%
tax.*

Ruins

A thousand years ago, as today, the Maya people were a diverse race.
In Campeche, archaeology buffs will find several styles of ruins that
are completely different from any in the states of Yucatán or Quintana
Roo. The Chenes style, found in central and southern Campeche, features facades in the shape of giant masks of jaguars, birds, and other
creatures, often called "monster mouth" temples. Secret passageways
let priests emerge suddenly from the jaws of the beast. The Río Bec
style, found in the southern rain forest where the temples are only one
or two stories high, features two or three false towers attached to the
facades, to give them an illusion of height. An architectural trick called
false perspective makes them appear far larger and more imposing than
they actually are. Visiting most Campeche ruins is much easier now
than a few years ago as, with a few exceptions, they are reachable via
good paved roads. A few do require driving hundreds of highway
miles to the most remote part of the Yucatán Peninsula—not for the

faint-hearted, but ideal for adventurous souls. All ruins are free on Sunday and holidays.

Exploring Campeche

Campeche City, the most accessible place in the state, makes a good hub for exploring other areas, many of which lack restaurants and lodging. For purposes of exploration, the sights in the state of Campeche are arranged in three distinct regions: the northern interior along Routes 261 and 180, containing the ruins of Edzná and other ancient cities as well as many modern Maya villages that can be visited easily en route between Campeche City and Mérida or Uxmal; the southern coast along Route 180—the only part of the Campeche coastline that is accessible by a continuous road—with several small beach resorts and fishing villages that are all but eclipsed by oil industry development; and the southern interior along Route 186, a remote rain forest area with numerous large Maya ruins that have started to get more visitors after opening to the public a few years ago. Route 186 also runs through to the coast of Quintana Roo, linking the ruins of southern Campeche with the ancient Maya cities of southern Quintana Roo, which are definitely worth visiting. These ruins are under extensive research through a 1995 government grant. Previous to this, visitors to the Yucatán Peninsula rarely reached these areas because of their remoteness.

Numbers in the text correspond to numbers in the margin and on the State of Campeche and Campeche City maps.

Great Itineraries

Our Campeche itinerary highlights attractions in Campeche City, then takes you into the countryside. While it may sound dauntingly ambitious to accomplish the city tour in one day, many of the sights described here can be seen in just a few minutes. The more leisurely visitor may wish to schedule two days. Traveling throughout the State of Campeche could take from two to five days, depending on how much time you devote to some of the towns that are farther off the beaten path.

IF YOU HAVE 1 DAY

The city of Campeche is easy to explore in a day, as almost all sights of interest to visitors are located within the compact historical district. Start out at the **Baluarte San Carlos** ⑪ at the southern edge of the **Ciudad Viejo** for an overview of the history of the port. Then head north into the heart of the old city center and take in its time-worn bastions, museums, and colonial buildings, ending up at the pretty **Parque Principal** ② for a stop at the **catedral** ③. Take a break for lunch at the Miramar restaurant. After lunch browse in the **Mercado Municipal** ⑮, then (around 4, after the siesta when everything including taxi service comes to life again) hop in a cab for a late afternoon visit to the **Fuerte de San Miguel** ⑰ and its new Museum of Maya Culture. Come evening, join the locals in a breezy walk along the **malecón** ⑭.

IF YOU HAVE 3 DAYS

After spending the first day in Campeche City, head inland the next morning to visit **Edzná** ㉔, a magnificently restored ceremonial center an hour's drive from the city. Return to your Campeche City hotel—accommodations are crude or nonexistent in the area—and set out the next day to the **Hopelchén** ㉕ region, beyond Edzná, where you can explore the little-known Maya temples at **Hochob** ㉗ and **Dzibilnocac** ㉘, as well as **Bolonchén de Rejón** ㉖, one of the large cave systems on the peninsula. From Hopelchén it is as easy to continue north toward Uxmal and Mérida (☞ Chapter 6) as it is to return to Campeche City.

In addition to the capital and the northern region, you'll have time to explore the southern part of the state. Follow the coast highway and plan to spend the night on **Isla del Carmen** ㉜, hardly a great beach resort but far more pleasant than the only real alternative—the grimy truck stop town of Escárcega. As you head east along Highway 186, across the base of the Yucatán Peninsula toward Chetumal, you will find a number of impressive Maya sites. To appreciate the natural beauty of the rain forest and the myriad ruins, plan to spend at least two or three days at the one small ecotourism resort in the area. **Becán** ㉝, **Chicanná** ㉞, and **Xpujil** ㉟ are just off the highway and can all be explored in a single full day. Local guides can take you to more remote sights such as **Hormiguero** ㊱ and **Río Bec** ㊲ on day trips, or on more ambitious journeys to sites such as **Calakmul** ㊳ deep in the forests of the Calakmul Biosphere Reserve and **El Tigre** ㊴, hidden in the jungle south of Escárcega. From the Xpujil area it is easy now to return to Campeche City via the new Xpuhil–Hopelchén highway avoiding the Campeche coast, or you can just as easily continue to the Caribbean coast since you are right across the state line from Quintana Roo.

When to Tour Campeche

Both the capital and outlying villages of Campeche state, with their predominantly Maya population, celebrate the Day of the Dead (November 1 and 2) with special fervor because it corresponds to a similar observance in ancient Maya tradition. Colorfully embroidered regional dress, street celebrations, special meals, and altars of offerings to deceased loved ones are typical. If you can't make it to one of the small towns for this celebration, stop in at the main plaza in Campeche City where altars from different regions of the state are set up for the two-day observance.

An event called *Sabados Alegres*or Happy Saturdays, was introduced in November 1997 by the tourist office; starting at 6 in the evening, the streets around the main square are roped off to traffic and filled with folk dance performances, handicraft, and food and drink stands.

November also marks the end of the rainy season (the strongest rains fall July–September), when the risk of hurricanes is over and the rain forests of the interior are at their most luxuriant. Any time from November through March is good for traveling, though as everywhere in Mexico, the Christmas and Holy Week holidays mean extremely crowded hotels and public transportation. The rainy season often renders unpaved side roads impassable in central and southern Campeche unless you're in a four-wheel-drive vehicle.

CAMPECHE CITY

The city of Campeche has a time-weathered and lovely feel to it: No self-conscious, ultramodern tourist glitz here, just a friendly city by the sea (population 270,000), proud of its heritage and welcoming all to share in it. That good-humored, open-minded attitude is enshrined in the Spanish adjective *campechano,* meaning easygoing and cheerful. The city gets only about 20,000 tourists a year, its strongest attraction being its sense of history. You can easily imagine pirates attacking the formidable stone walls that surround the downtown, and several Maya ruins and undisturbed Maya towns are within easy driving distance. The city's coastline is cluttered with commercial fishing operations, and there are a few popular public beaches. It is possible to see much of Campeche City in a day or two, but you will probably want to stay

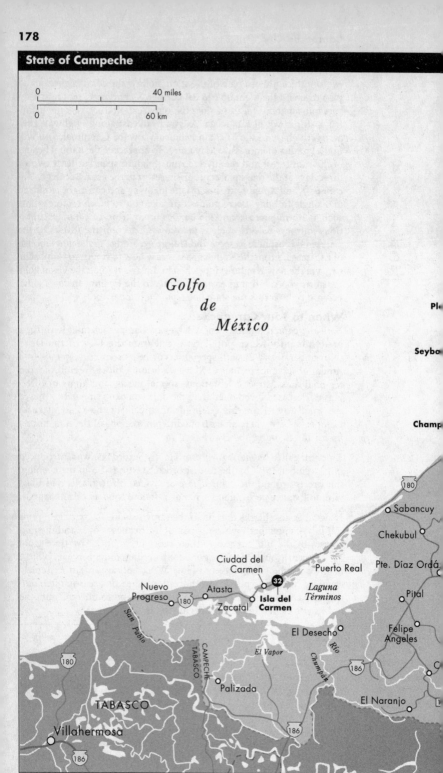

0   40 miles

0   60 km

Golfo de México

Pl⊙

Seyba

Champ

180

Sabancuy

Chekubul

Ciudad del Carmen

32

Puerto Real

Pte. Díaz Ordá

Laguna Términos

Nuevo Progreso

Atasta

180

Pital

Zacatal

Isla del Carmen

Sian Pablo

El Desecho

Felipe Ángeles

El Vapor

CAMPECHE

TABASCO

Río Champtón

186

Palizada

TABASCO

El Naranjo

Villahermosa

186

186

TO MÉRIDA

180 261

Oxkintoc Kopoma

23

Halachó Muna

22 **YUCATAN**

Tancuché 21

Becal 20 **Calkiní** Santa Elena

Hecelchacán 19

Pomuch Chunyaxnic Tzucacab

Campeche Tenabo **Bolonchén**
1—18 **de Rejón**
See Detail 26
Map

180 San Juan
Bautista

aya Bonita Castamoy YUCATAN
29 Cayal CAMPECHE

China 261 25

Bobola Crucero de **Hopelchén**
San Luis

aplaya 188 24 269 28 **Dzilibnocac**
30 **Edzná**

Hool Tabasqueño

La Joya Dzibalchén

180 **Hochob** QUINTANA
27 ROO

potón Río **Chal-Tuni**
31

San Providencia
Pablo
Pixtún Yohaltún QUINTANA ROO
CAMPECHE

Santa María

261 Chunjabin

Centenario Xbonil **Becán** **Xpujil**
33 35 TO
z 186 Conhuas CHETUMAL
34
Escárcega **Hormiguero** **Chicanná**
36 N
Chan Laguna 37
Río Bec

Narciso
Merdoza

andelaria **Calakmul**
39 **El Tigre** **Biosphere**
Reserve 38
Monclova Altamira
BELIZE
5 Baranda Las Golondrinas
Nueva
Coahuila Playa
Bonita
MEXICO
GUATEMALA

GUATEMALA

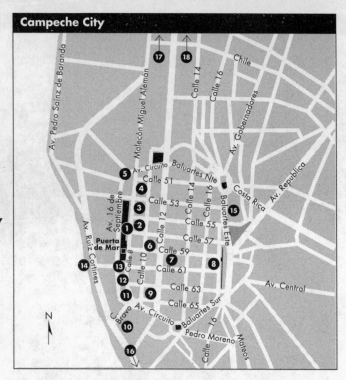

Campeche City

longer to absorb the traditional lifestyle, whiling away the hours at a café near the plaza.

Because it has been walled (though not successfully fortified) since 1686, most of the historic downtown is neatly contained in an area measuring just five blocks by nine blocks. Today, for the most part, streets running north–south are even-numbered, and those running east–west are odd-numbered. The city is easily navigable (on foot, at least); the historical monuments and evocative name plaques above street numbers serve as handy guideposts. The old city looks fresh and pretty with newly painted and remodeled buildings and new signs guiding tourists to attractions along the streets. Lacking the large-scale tourism that has sustained Cancún and Mérida, Campeche was hit harder than any other part of the Yucatán by Mexico's 1995 recession but is showing definite signs of recovery.

On various corners in the old city, or Viejo Campeche, stand seven *baluartes* (bastions) in various stages of disrepair or reconstruction. These were once connected by a 3-km (2-mi) wall in a hexagonal fortification that was built to safeguard the city against the pirates who kept ransacking it. Only short stretches of the wall exist, and two stone archways—one facing the sea, the other the land—are all that remain of the four gates that provided the only means of access to Campeche. Although these walls helped protect the residents, it was not until 1771, when Fuerte San Miguel was built on a hilltop on the outskirts of town, that pirates finally ceased their attacks for good.

Campeche was one of few walled cities in North or Central America and was built along the traditional lines of defensive Spanish settlements, such as Santo Domingo in the Dominican Republic, Cartagena in Colombia, and Portobelo in Panama. The walls also served as a class demarcation. Within them lived the ruling elite. Outside were the barrios of the Indians who aided the conquistadors, and whose descendants continued to serve the upper class. The mulattoes brought as slaves from Cuba also lived outside.

A Good Walk

The Ciudad Viejo, the old city center, is the best place to start a walking tour, beginning with the **Baluarte de la Soledad** ① and its fascinating Maya stelae museum. From the nearby **Parque Principal** ②, the city's central plaza, a short stroll will show you some of the Yucatán Peninsula's most stately Spanish Colonial architecture, including the **catedral** ③ and the **Mansión Carvajal** ④, as well as the remaining sections of the **baluartes** ⑤ ⑪, fortress walls built to protect the city. Walk up **Calle 59** ⑥ past the **Iglesia de San Francisquito** ⑦ to the **Puerta de Tierra** ⑧, then follow the walls around the south side of the historic district to search out some more masterpieces of colonial religious architecture—the **Ex-Templo de San José** ⑨ and the **Iglesia de San Román** ⑩—juxtaposed against the strange modernistic designs of the **Congreso del Estado** ⑫ and the **Palacio del Gobierno** ⑬. End your tour with a stroll along the **Malecón** ⑭.

Sights to See

① **Baluarte de la Soledad.** On the south side of Parque Principal, this old bastion houses the **Museo de los Estela Dr. Roman Pina Chan** in a separate section. The largest of the bastions, this one has comparatively complete parapets and embrasures that offer a sweeping view of the cathedral, the municipal buildings, and the Gulf of Mexico. Artifacts housed inside its three rooms and around the outside of the museum—named for a renowned archaeologist from the State of Campeche—include 20 beautiful and well-proportioned Maya stelae and other pieces from various periods, such as a sculpture of a man wearing an owl mask, columns from Edzná and Jaina, a perfectly sculpted pumpkin, and a phallus. This museum is a real find and not to be missed. ⊠ *Calles 8 and 57,* ☎ *no phone.* 🎟 *50¢.* ⊙ *Tues.–Sat. 8–8, Sun. 8–1.*

⑪ **Baluarte San Carlos.** This bastion, where Avenida 16 de Septiembre curves around and becomes Circuito Baluartes, houses the **Sala de las Fortificaciones** (Chamber of the Fortifications), containing scale models of the original defense system, and the **Museo Graficode la Ciudad,** or City Museum, with photographs and maps of the city as it developed. Don't miss the dungeon inside the bastion, where captured pirates were jailed. ⊠ *Circuito Baluartes and Justo Sierra,* ☎ *no phone.* 🎟 *Free.* ⊙ *Tues.–Sat. 8–8, Sun. 8–2.*

⑤ **Baluarte Santiago.** The last of the bastions to be built (1704) has been transformed into a botanical garden. A film explaining the garden's 250 plant species is shown throughout the day (when the projector is working). The original bastion was demolished at the turn of the century, but it was rebuilt in the 1950s. Architecturally this fort looks much the same as the others in Campeche: a stone fortress with thick walls, watchtowers, and gunnery slits. ⊠ *Calles 8 and 49,* ☎ *981/66829.* 🎟 *Free.* ⊙ *Weekends 9–2 and 5–8.*

⑥ **Calle 59.** On this city street, between Calles 8 and 18, once stood some of Campeche's finest homes, many of them two stories high, with the ground floors serving as warehouses and the upper floors as residences. Geometric motifs decorate the cornices, and the windows are gaily adorned with iron latticework. The richest inhabitants built as close to the sea as possible, in case escape became necessary. (Legend has it that beneath the city a network of tunnels crisscrossed, linking the eight bastions and providing temporary refuge from the pirates. Although the tunnel network has never been found, rumors still persist that it once existed.) These days, behind the genteel lace curtains of some of the homes, you can glimpse equally genteel scenes of Campeche life, with faded lithographs on the dun-colored walls and plenty of antique furniture and clutter.

❸ Catedral. An exception to the generally somber architecture rule of colonial Campeche is the cathedral, which took two centuries (from 1650 to 1850) to build and incorporates neoclassic and renaissance elements. The present cathedral occupies the site of Montejo's original church, which was built in 1540 on what is now Calle 55, between Calles 8 and 10. The simple exterior lines terminate in two bulbous towers rising to each side of the gracefully curved stone entrances, the fluted pilasters echoing those on the towers. Sculptures of saints set in niches recall the French Gothic cathedrals. The interior is no less impressive, with a single limestone nave, supported by Doric capitals and Corinthian columns, arching toward the huge octagonal dome above a black-and-white marble floor. The pièce de résistance, however, is the magnificent Holy Sepulchre, carved from ebony. ⊠ *West side of the Plaza Principal.*

⓬ Congreso del Estado. A modernistic building resembling a flying saucer, the State Congress building is where government activities take place. ⊠ *Calle 8 between Calles 61 and 63.*

❾ Ex-Templo de San José. The Jesuits built this fine Baroque church in 1756, and today its block-long facade stands as an exception to the rather plodding architectural style of most of the city's churches. Its immense portal is completely covered with blue Talavera tiles and crowned by seven narrow, stone finials that resemble the roof combs on many Maya temples. (The roof combs, in turn, are reminiscent of the combs Spanish women used to wear in their elaborate hairdos.) The convent-school next door is now used for cultural events and art exhibitions. Campeche's first lighthouse, built in 1864, sits atop a brick pillar next to the church. ⊠ *Between Calles 10 and 12 and Calles 63 and 65.* ☉ *Tues.–Fri. 9–2 and 5–10.*

⓱ Fuerte de San Miguel. A well-marked scenic drive turns off Avenida Ruíz Cortines near the south end of the city and winds its way to a hilltop, where the fort commands one of the grandest views in the Yucatán, overlooking the city and the Gulf of Mexico. Built in 1771, the fort was positioned to bombard enemy ships with cannonballs before they could get close enough to attack Campeche. As soon as it was completed, pirates stopped attacking the city without a fight. Its impressive cannons were fired only once, in 1842, when General Santa Anna used Fuerte San Miguel to put down a revolt by Yucatecan separatists seeking independence from Mexico. More recently, the hilltop location has made the fort's parking lot a nighttime hangout for amorous local teenagers. Besides a great view and imposing architecture, the fort now houses the **Museo Cultura Maya,** for which you should allow at least two hours. Dedicated solely to the Campeche Maya and with explanations in English, the archaeological collection should not be missed. Six exquisite jade funeral masks found at various tombs at Calakmul comprise the most striking exhibit. Other Calakmul discoveries include urns decorated with cleverly worked king-buzzard, tapir, monkey, turtle, and other animal figures. Yet other museum pieces include a sizeable collection of the small, well-proportioned human funerary figures from the island of Jaina and stucco masks from the Río Bec ruins. A gift shop sells some reproductions of museum pieces. ⊠ *South of downtown on Av. Resurgimiento s/n,* ☎ *no phone.* 🎟 *50¢.* ☉ *Tues.–Sun. 8–8.*

⑱ Fuerte San José. This lofty fortress at the opposite end of town from the Fuerte San Miguel is now home to a new museum—the **Museo de Armas y Barcos,** which is half of the exhibit that used to be in the Museo Regional. The display focuses on the 18th-century military weapons of siege and defense in the many wars fought against the pirates. Scale ships-in-a-bottle, manuscripts, and religious art can also be seen. The view is terrific from the top of the ramparts, which were used for spotting the ships of the invaders. ⊠ *Av. Francisco Morazon s/n, north of town,* ☏ *no phone.* ⊡ *50¢.* ☉ *Tues.–Sun. 8–8.*

⑯ Iglesia de San Francisco. Away from the city center, in a residential neighborhood, stands the beautifully restored church, the oldest one in Campeche. It marks the spot where, some say, the first Mass on the North American continent was said in 1517 (the same claim has been made for Veracruz and Cozumel). One of Cortés's grandsons was baptized here, and the baptismal font still stands. ⊠ *Avs. Gustavo Díaz Ordaz and Francisco I. Madero.*

⑦ Iglesia de San Francisquito. Just east of Calle 12, this tiny, architecturally exquisite church does justice to historic Calle 59's old-fashioned beauty. ⊠ *Calle 59 and Calle 12.*

⑩ Iglesia de San Román. This church sits just outside the intramural boundary in the barrio of the same name at Calle 10 and Calle Bravo. San Román, with a bulbous bell tower typical of other Yucatán churches, was built to house the *naboríos* (Indians brought by the Spaniards to aid in the Conquest and later used as household servants). The barrio, like other neighborhoods, grew up around the church. Though it was built earlier in the 16th century, the church became central to the lives of the Indians only when an ebony image of Christ, the "Black Christ," was brought in about 1565. The Indians had been skeptical about the Christian saints, but this Christ figure came to be associated with miracles. The legend goes that a ship that refused to carry the tradesman and his precious statue was wrecked, while the ship that did take him on board reached Campeche in record time. To this day, the Feast of San Román—when the icon is carried through the streets as part of a colorful and somber procession—is the biggest such celebration in Campeche. People still come to see the black wood Christ mounted on a silver filigree cross. There's a Saturday Mass at 7:30 PM and Sunday Masses at 10 AM and 7:30 PM. ⊠ *Calle 10 and Calle Bravo.*

⑭ Malecón. This is Campeche's waterfront boulevard along Avenida Ruíz Cortines. The broad sidewalk runs the length of the waterfront, from the Ramada Inn south to the outskirts of town, and is popular with joggers and strollers enjoying the cool sea breezes and view at sunset. On weekend nights the malecón turns into an extended college mixer, with hundreds of university students hanging out around their cars, which line the boulevard from end to end.

④ Mansión Carvajal. Built in the early 20th century by one of the wealthiest plantation owners in Yucatán, the eclectic mansion did time as the Hotel Señorial before arriving at its present role as an office for the Family Institute run by the state governor's wife and her staff. Take a stroll: The black-and-white tile floor, Art Nouveau staircase with Carrara marble steps and iron balustrade, and blue-and-white Moorish arcades speak volubly of the city's heyday, when Campeche was the peninsula's only port. ⊠ *Calle 10 s/n, between Calles 53 and 55,* ☏ *no phone.* ⊡ *Free.* ☉ *Mon.–Sat. 8–2:30 and 5–8:30.*

⑮ Mercado Municipal. To take in the heart of a true Mexican inner city, stroll through the market where locals congregate en masse to shop for seafood, produce, and housewares. Beside the market is a small bridge aptly named **Dog Bridge**—four bright yellow plaster dogs guard the area. The market is open daily from dawn to dusk. Try to arrive early, before it gets uncomfortably crowded. ⊠ *Baluartes Este between Calle 51 and Calle 54.*

⑬ Palacio del Gobierno. One block inland from the malecón, on Avenida 16 de Septiembre, the Congreso del Estado shares a broad plaza with this much taller building, dubbed *El Tocadiscos* ("The Jukebox") by locals because of its outlandish facade. The eccentric architecture of these two state capital buildings stands in odd contrast to the graceful colonial skyline of the adjacent Ciudad Viejo historic district. ⊠ *Av. 16 de Sepiembre and Calle 61.*

❷ Parque Principal or Plaza de la Independencia. This is the centerpiece of the old city, the southern side of which—Calle 57—is lined with several agreeable cafés and hotels. The park is the focal point for the town's activities. Concerts are held on Sunday evenings, when it seems all the city's residents come out for a stroll. ⊠ *Bounded by Calles 10, 8, and 55.*

❽ Puerta de Tierra. This is where old Campeche ends—the only one of the four city gates that still stands with its basic structure intact. The walls, arches, and gates were refurbished in 1987. This stone arch intercepts a long stretch of the partially crenelated wall, 26 ft high and 10 ft thick, that once encircled the city; looking through it, you can just barely see across town to its counterpart, the **Puerta de Mar,** through which all seafarers were forced to pass. Because the latter stands alone, without any wall to shore it up, it looks like the Arc de Triomphe. The wall that is standing today around the Puerta de Tierra was built in 1957 to replace the one demolished in 1893. There is a light show offered most nights. ⊠ *Calles 18 and 59.* 🎦 *Light-and-sound show in French and English $2.* ☉ *Show Tues., Fri.–Sat., except Dec. 20–Jan. 4 when it's daily (no show Dec. 24 and 31), 8:30 PM.*

Dining and Lodging

$$ ✕ **La Pigua.** A favorite with local professionals lingering over long
★ lunches, La Pigua is perhaps the best seafood restaurant in town, with the most pleasant ambience. The long, glass-walled dining room is surrounded by trees and plants. A truly ambitious lunch would start with a seafood cocktail or plate of cold crab claws, followed by *pescado relleno,* a fish fillet stuffed with finely diced shellfish, and then local peaches drenched in sweet liqueurs. ⊠ *Av. Miguel Alemán 197-A,* ☎ *981/13365. MC, V. No dinner.*

 $ ✕ **La Cenaduría.** Traditionally, this is where Campechano couples and families came in the evenings (only open evenings after 7) to enjoy a light supper of *sandwich claveteado* (honey–flavored ham or turkey sandwich) or *panuchos* (tortillas stuffed with refried beans and topped with chopped onion and shredded turkey or chicken), for example, washed down with a typical drink —*horchata* (cold rice water flavored with cinnamon). Dining takes place in a colonial courtyard with tables decked out in checkered tablecloths. If you happen in on a Saturday, try the famous coconut ice cream made and sold from a cart by Don Nico, who's been vending it for 30 years and who's become somewhat of a local celebrity. ⊠ *Calle 10 no. 86 at Portales San Francisco (8 blocks northeast of the Plaza Principal),* ☎ *No phone . No credit cards.*

 $ ✕ **La Parroquia.** This is the best place in town for people-watching from it's huge open-air entrance facing Calle 10. The only restaurant open 24 hours a day, La Parroquia is a real locals den with plastic tablecloths and a huge TV hanging from the ceiling and tuned to Mexican soap operas. Beneath its plain facade, however, it's a friendly place where other diners are apt to strike up a conversation with you. The menu is large (the service is slow) and you can feast on inexpensive fried pampano fish, breaded shrimp, *pan de cazon* (baby shark), and spaghetti, as well as Americanized club sandwiches and hamburgers. For dessert try the house specialties—fried bananas and cream or *flan* (caramel pudding). Mixed drinks, beer, and tequila can also be ordered. ⊠ *Calle 55 no. 8,* ☎ *981/68086. No credit cards.*

$ ✕ **La Perla.** Right down the street from the Instituto Campecheño university, this is a popular student hangout. Fresh *licuados* (fruit drinks), soups, salads, and sandwiches are priced for student budgets. ⊠ *Calle 10, No. 345,* ☎ *981/64092. No credit cards.*

$ ✕ **Marganzo.** This rustically furnished restaurant, conveniently situated
★ a half block south of the plaza, is a popular tourist spot—which is not to its detriment. It's impeccably clean, with a colorful decor, wait help dressed in gaily festooned outfits, and the seafood dishes served at lunch and dinner are characteristic of the cuisine for which this region is known. You can't go wrong with such specials as *pan de casón* (tortillas with shredded baby shark). Waitresses dressed in colonial Mexican–style skirts and embroidered blouses keep in step with Marganzo's regional theme. ⊠ *Calle 8, No. 267,* ☎ *981/13898. AE, MC, V.*

$ ✕ **Miramar.** This restaurant across from Hotel Castelmar attracts locals and foreign visitors with its fabulous *huevos motuleños* (fried eggs smothered in refried beans and garnished with peas, chopped ham, shredded cheese, and tomato sauce), red snapper, shellfish, soups, and meat dishes. The heavy wooden tables and chairs and the paintings of coats-of-arms give Miramar a colonial feel. ⊠ *Calle 8, No. 293A,* ☎ *981/62883. MC, V.*

$$ ▥ **Debliz.** Those traveling by car may wish to stay outside town at this modern hotel in a residential area north of the city. The four-story, elevator-equipped property is refreshingly decorated with cream-color walls, beige carpets, dark-wood furnishings, and paintings of flowers. Room amenities include color TV, reading lamps, and double beds. The bar and garden are popular gathering places for hotel guests, most of whom seem to be Europeans. The Debliz can seem deserted and lonely—until the tour buses that frequent the place pull into the parking lot. ⊠ *Av. Las Palmas 55, off Av. Pedro Sainz de Baranda, near baseball stadium,* ☎ *981/52222,* ☎ *981/52277. 114 rooms, 6 suites. Restaurant, bar, coffee shop, air-conditioning, room service, pool, free parking. AE, MC, V.*

$$ ▥ **Ramada Inn.** This is the most luxurious hotel in town and it has
★ undergone major renovations: In 1997, 35 rooms and junior suites were added, and previous to this, in 1994, 30 new rooms were built and improvements were made to the swimming pool and grounds. The rooms are fairly large, with tasteful soft beige–color tile floors and walls, pastel bedspreads and drapes, and some rattan furniture, plus color TV; balconies overlook the pool or the bay across the street. The lobby coffee shop, **El Poquito,** is extremely popular with locals at breakfast and at night before the disco Atlantis opens. ⊠ *Av. Ruíz Cortines 51, on waterfront,* ☎ *981/62233 or 800/228–9898,* ☎ *981/11618. 138 rooms, 11 suites. Restaurant, coffee shop, air-conditioning, room service, pool, exercise room, dance club, business services, meeting rooms, travel services, free parking. AE, MC, V.*

$ ▥ **Alhambra.** A great choice away from the bustle of the city, the Alhambra is a modern hotel facing the waterfront near the university. A wide-screen TV plays softly in the lobby. TVs in the rooms get U.S. stations, sometimes including CNN. Rooms look like standard motel–type units and are carpeted and clean, with king- and double-size beds. ⊠ *Av. Resurgimiento 85, between Avs. Universidad and Augusto Melgar,* ☎ *981/66822,* ☎ *981/66132. 96 rooms, 2 suites. Restaurant, bar, air-conditioning, room service, pool, tennis court, free parking. MC, V.*

$ 🏨 **Baluartes.** This big, square hotel which isn't quite as luxurious as it claims to be, has been going through a lengthy refurbishing since 1995. About half the rooms have been redecorated in cool blue tones and have had their worn carpeting replaced with new terra-cotta tile and new bathroom plumbing; air-conditioning has been installed in all of them. All have double-size beds, in-room phones, and TVs that receive one U.S. network. The renovation has not reached the dismal hallways, lobby, pool areas, or filthy creaking elevators; the restaurant, happily, is no longer drenched in smells of cigarettes. Still, there is a halfway decent sandwich shop, and the location is ideal. Ask to see your room before checking in. Sandwiched between the waterfront malecón and the Puerto del Mar gateway to the old city, Baluartes is within easy walking distance of everything in the historic district. ✉ *Av. Ruíz Cortines 61,* ☎ *981/63911,* FAX *981/65765. 94 rooms, 8 suites. Restaurant, bar, coffee shop, air-conditioning, pool, travel services, free parking. MC, V.*

$ 🏨 **Colonial.** This building—the former home of a high-ranking army
★   lieutenant—dates back to 1850 but was made over as a hotel in the 1940s, when its wonderful tiles were added. There's a plaque outside the front door identifying it as an important historical monument of the town. All rooms are delightfully different in structure, as befits a colonial mansion, but they are also pastel color and spacious, with ceiling fans or air-conditioning (in four of the rooms), cool cotton bedding, good mattresses, tile bathrooms, window screens, and phones. In addition, Rooms 16, 18, 28, and 27 have lots of windows with ambient light and wonderful views of the cathedral and city at night. The well-kept public areas include two foliated patios, a small sun roof, and a sitting room on the second floor for reading. Guests breakfast at a small eatery down the street. ✉ *Calle 14, No. 122, between Calles 55 and 57,* ☎ *981/62222 or 981/62630. 30 rooms. No credit cards.*

$ 🏨 **Del Paseo.** Located in the quiet San Román neighborhood, a block from the ocean, this pretty hotel, which opened in 1995, is cheerful and well lit. Rooms, painted in a soft rose, with tasteful rattan furniture, have balconies, cable TV, and air-conditioning. A glass-roofed atrium next to the lobby is lovely, with its globe lamps, park benches, and many plants. ✉ *Calle 8, No. 215,* ☎ *981/10084 or 981/10100,* FAX *981/10097. 38 rooms, 2 suites. Restaurant, bar, air-conditioning, room service. MC, V.*

$ 🏨 **El Regis.** This new seven-room hotel a mere two blocks from the plaza has to be the best bargain in town with prices at the low end of the $ category. Opened in March 1996, the Regis is a lovely old two-story colonial home with a humongous wooden entrance door, wrought-iron staircase, high ceilings, balconies, and an airy inner atrium. All rooms are spic-and-span with new black-and-white tile floors, two double beds with floral-print bedspreads, a cupboard closet, shower in the bathroom, and cream-color walls. Four rooms come with air-conditioning—the rest have overhead fans—and a TV with Spanish channels. The front doors close at 11 at night but there's a night watchman who opens up for guests who come in later. There's a coffee shop a half block away. ✉ *Calle 12, No. 148, between Calles 55 and 57,* ☎ *981/53175. 7 rooms. Fans. No credit cards.*

$ 🏨 **Lopez.** Cheerful pink, yellow, and white walls and an open, airy ambience make this little two-story hotel a pleasant place to stay. Located five blocks from the main square, standard rooms (on the small side) include colonial-style desks and armoires, luggage stands, easy chairs, and tiled bathrooms. Although the restaurant was closed for remodeling at press time (date of reopening uncertain), it serves basic Continental fare and it's a convenient enough stop for breakfast, lunch, or dinner. ✉ *Calle 12, No. 189, between Calles 61 and 63,* ☎ *981/ 63344,* FAX *981/62488. 39 rooms. No credit cards.*

Nightlife and the Arts

Discos

If you're in the mood to dance, try Campeche's two discos, **Atlantis** (⊠ Ramada Inn, ☎ 981/62233), the only chic club in town, where politicians go to party, or the more student-oriented **El Dragon** (⊠ Sajuge complex, on Av. Resurgimiento, ½ block from the Alhambra Hotel, ☎ 981/11810 or 981/64289). Both places are open Thursday through Saturday nights only.

Movies

Campeche has five movie theaters. Two of the most conveniently located are **Cine Estelar** (⊠ Av. Miguel Alemán and Calle 49-B) and **Cine Alhambra** (⊠ At the shopping center at the Hotel Alhambra, Av. Resurgimiento 85). Both show films made in the United States, with Spanish subtitles, and are only open on weekend nights.

Outdoor Sports and Activities

Hunting, fishing, and birding are popular throughout the State of Campeche. Contact **Don Jose Sansores** at his office in the Hotel Castelmar (⊠ Calle 61, No. 2, ☎ 981/62356, FAX 981/10624). Doves, ducks, and ocellated turkey are hunted October through the end of January, brocket deer and peccary in March and April. Sansores also can arrange sportfishing excursions for snook and tarpon through his Campeche office or his Snook Inn hotel in Champotón (☎ 982/80018, FAX 981/10624), an area with good fishing. In 1997 Sansores also started offering photo safaris to the Capotón area to photograph the wildlife that is otherwise hunted the rest of the year. Licenses and gun permits are required for big game—and arrangements for bringing any firearm and ammunition into Mexico are daunting—so make your inquiries well in advance.

Shopping

Because Campeche is a seaport, folk art here varies somewhat from the rest of Yucatán's handicrafts. Black coral and mother-of-pearl jewelry, seashells, and ships-in-a-bottle are everywhere. You can also find basketry, leather goods, embroidered cloth, and clay trinkets. With a few exceptions, listed below, most of the shops sell cheap-looking trinkets.

Local Crafts

For handicrafts try the newly located **Casa de Artesanía Tukulna** (⊠ Calle 10 no. 333 between Calle 59 and Calle 61, ☎ 981/69088), situated in a lovely old mansion and operated by the government-run Family Institute. Here's where you'll find well-made embroidered dresses, blouses, pillow coverings, regional dress for men and women, hammocks, Campeche's famous jipijapa (Panama) hats (and the replica of a cave showing how they are made), wicker furniture, CDs of ancient Maya songs, posters, books on Campeche ecology in Spanish, jewelry, baskets, leather goods, stucco reproductions of Maya motifs, and much more. The house is so beautiful with its arched doorways, black-and-white tiled floors, and chandeliers that it's worth a visit if only to admire the interior. **Veleros** (⊠ Ah-Kin-Pech shopping center, ☎ 981/12446) is owned by craftsman David Pérez. It stocks his miniature ships, lots of black and red coral jewelry, seashells, furniture with nautical motifs, and, new to the market, jewelry fashioned from sanded and polished bull's horns. The horn looks a lot like tortoise shell (it is no longer legal to hunt the turtles nor to import tortoise to the United States) in thickness and color; although it's not as beautiful, it's a good, legal substitute. Pérez's first shop, **Artesanía Típica Naval** (⊠ Calle 8, No. 259, ☎ 981/65708), is still thriving, but it's much smaller and more cramped than the mall store. Neither shop accepts credit cards.

Shopping Districts and Malls

Campeche City has three large, modern shopping malls: the **Plaza Comercial Ah-Kin-Pech** (⊠ Between Calles 51 and 49), on the stretch of the waterfront boulevard known as Avenida Pedro Sáinz de Baranda; **Plaza del Mar** (⊠ across the parking lot from Ah-Kin-Pech on Av. Ruíz Cortines); and the newest, **El Mexicano** (⊠ Av. Agustin Melgar and). Between them they house a supermarket, a pastry shop, a beauty salon, a travel agency, a sporting-goods store, and clothing shops. The newest is **El Mexicano** (⊠ Av. Agustín Melgar and Av. Universidad). Visit the **municipal market** (⊠ Baluartes Estes at Calle 53), at the eastern end of the city, for crafts and food.

ALONG ROUTE 180 TOWARD MÉRIDA

The so-called short route to or from Mérida takes you past several villages and minor archaeological sites. After Halochób the rest of the way to Mérida consists of relatively monotonous terrain, with the occasional clusters of white thatched-roof huts, speed bumps, windmills, and spearlike henequen plants.

Hecelchacán

⑲ *75 km (47 mi) north of Campeche, along Route 180 toward Mérida.*

Although the pretty 15th-century town of Hecelchacán boasts a lovely church and former convent, it is known primarily for the **Museo Arqueológico del Camino Real.** This museum holds an impressive collection of clay figurines from the island of Jaina (a giant cemetery for the Maya) and stelae of the Puuc style. Don't make a special trip just to tour the museum, since the hours are erratic; it's often closed when it should be open. But if you're en route to Mérida and are an archaeology buff, it's worth the short detour off the highway to check out. Jaina itself is still off limits to walk-in visitors but can be visited with prior written permission from the National Institute of Anthropology and History in Campeche; the tourist office can help with the request. Even then, it may take weeks to get permission and it can be visited on guided boat only. ⊠ *Rte. 180 to Hecelchacán,* ☎ *no phone.* ☞ *Free.* ☉ *Daily 8–4.*

Calkiní

⑳ *24 km (15 mi) north of Hecelchacán.*

Inside the fortress-convent built in Calkiní by the Franciscans between 1548 and 1776 is an exquisite cedar altarpiece on which the four Evangelists have been carved, and the columns and cornices adorning the convent have been painted in rich gold, red, and black. The portal is Plateresque (a 16th-century Spanish style whose elaborate ornaments suggest silver plate), while the rest of the structure is Baroque. Interestingly enough, Calkiní dates back much earlier, to the Maya Ah-Canul dynasty. According to a local codex, the Ah-Canul chieftainship was founded here in 1443 beneath a ceiba, a tree sacred to the Maya and frequently mentioned in their legends. The Ah-Canul was the most important dynasty at the time of the Conquest; the fighters rebelling against Montejo were put down in Mérida, dealing a great blow to the Maya spirit. ☞ *Free.* ☉ *Daily 8–5*

Becal

㉑ *10 km (6 mi) north of Calkiní.*

The small town of Becal is noted for the famous jipijapa (Panama-style) hats made here by local residents. They weave reeds of the guano palm in caves beneath their houses, because the humidity there keeps the reeds flexible. First produced in the 19th century by the García family, the hats have become a village tradition. Who can resist photographing the statue of three giant hats in the center of the town plaza? For a tour of a family hat workshop, just wander into any of the hat establishments on the town's main street and ask; the merchants will be more than happy to take you to their caves.

Halachó

㉒ *6 km (4 mi) north of Becal.*

Just across the Yucatán state line from Becal, in Halachó, townspeople weave motifs from central Mexico into their baskets. The centerpiece of this dusty little Maya town is a magnificent white 18th-century mission church dedicated to Santiago Matamoros, the patron saint of the Spanish conquistadors. Thousands of pilgrims come to Halachó each year to pay homage to the equestrian statue of the saint, located up a flight of stairs behind the altar.

Oxkintoc

㉓ *14 km (9 mi) north of Halachó.*

The archaeological site of Oxkintoc, which is actually in the state of Yucatán, is 2 km (1 mi) off the main highway near the present-day village of Maxcanú and contains the ruins of an important Maya capital that dominated the region from about AD 300 to 1100. Little was known about Oxkintoc until excavations began there in 1991. Bearing a pure Puuc architectural style, structures that have been excavated so far include two tall pyramids, a palace with stone statues of several ancient rulers, and a temple that serves as the entrance to a mysterious subterranean labyrinth, the *Tzat Tun Tzat.* ✉ Off Rte. 184, 1½ km (1 mi) west of Rte. 180, ☎ no phone. 🎫 $2, free Sun. ☉ Daily 8–5.

ALONG ROUTE 261 TOWARD MÉRIDA

This is by far the longer—and more interesting—way to reach the Yucatán capital. The highway takes you through green hills covered by low scrub with occasional stands of tall, dark forest. In the valleys, cornfields and citrus orchards surround the occasional thatched-roof hut.

Edzná

㉔ *55 km (34 mi) southeast of Campeche City.*

The Maya ruin of Edzná deserves more fame than it has. Archaeologists consider it one of the peninsula's most important ruins because of the crucial transitional role it played among several architectural styles. Its obscurity can be attributed to two factors: Excavation began here relatively recently (in 1943), and restoration work is going ahead now. A new tourist facility with a cafeteria, rest rooms, and bookshop went up in 1996 here as well as at the rest of Campeche's major ruin sites. To make touring easier, in 1997 small explanation plaques in English, Spanish, and Maya were placed in front of all excavated structures here as well as at other major sites.

Edzná, occupied from 300 BC to AD 1450, reached its pinnacle between AD 600 to AD 900 and was discovered in 1927. The 6-square-km (2-square-mi) expanse of savanna, broken up only by the occasional tall tree, is situated in a broad valley prone to flooding and flanked by low hills. Surrounding the site are vast networks of irrigation canals, the remnants of a highly sophisticated hydraulic system that channeled rainwater and water from the Champotón River into human-made *chultunes,* or wells. Over the course of several hundred years, Edzná grew from a humble agricultural settlement into a major politico-religious center. It's now known that Edzná was the collection point for agricultural products grown in the region. Some products were sent to the Peté in Guatemala in exchange for hand-carved ritual objects and adornments for the site.

Commanding center stage in the **Gran Acrópolis,** or Great Acropolis complex, is the **Pirámide de los Cinco Pisos** (Five-Story Pyramid), which rises 102 ft. The man-made platform consists of five levels, each narrower than the one below it, terminating in a tiny temple crowned by a roof comb. Hieroglyphs carved into the vertical face of the 15 steps between each level describe astronomy and history, while the numerous stelae depict the opulent attire and adornment of the ruling class— quetzal feathers, jade pectorals, and skirts of jaguar skin. The **House of the Moon, Southwest Temple,** and **Northwest Temple,** plus **Puuc Courtyard** can be seen within this complex.

In 1992 Campeche archaeologist Antonio Benavides discovered that the Five-Story Pyramid was so constructed that, during certain dates of the year, the setting sun would illuminate the mask of the sun god, Itzamná, located inside one of the pyramid's rooms. This happens annually on May 1, 2, and 3—the beginning of the planting season for the ancient Maya, when they invoked the god to bring rain. It also occurs on August 7, 8, and 9, when the harvest was brought in and the Maya thanked the god for his help. Today, a local anthropologist, Elvira del Carmen Tello, stages an ancient Maya production at Edzná each May to commemorate the phenomenon. Check with the tourist office or travel desk at the Ramada Inn in Campeche City for more information.

Carved into **Building 414 or Temple of the Stone Masks** (as it is also called) of the Great Acropolis are some grotesque masks of the sun god with huge and sinister protruding eye sockets and crossed eyes, the effect of which is enhanced by the oversize tongues extending from the upper lips and large ear plugs. Local lore holds that Edzná, which means the House of the Gestures, or Grimaces, may have been named for these images. More recent theories claim the name comes from "Home of the Echo" since there is an acoustic effect between the main buildings of the site. Yet others say that it means "Home of the Itzáes." "Itzáes" refers to several Maya groups native to southwest Campeche.

There's also a **Small Acropolis** south of the great one where you can see a square filled with four buildings, each facing a cardinal point in the compass. The heaviest looking is the **Temple of the Stairway with Reliefs,** which has a stairway decorated with crude reliefs showing seated figures, faces, and jaguars. The architectural style of this acropolis relies heavily on the Petén and Puuc schools and were built between AD 800 and AD 1000.

A variety of architectural styles have been discerned at this site. The Petén style of northern Guatemala and Chiapas is reflected in the use of acropoli as bases for pyramids; of low-lying structures that contrast handsomely with soaring temples; and of corbeled arch roofs, richly ornamented stucco facades, and roof combs. The Río Bec style, which dominated much of Campeche, can be seen in the slender columns and exuberant stone mosaics. The multistory edifices, arched passageways, stone causeways, and hieroglyph-adorned stairways represent both the Chenes and Puuc styles.

If you're not driving, consider taking one of the inexpensive day trips offered by most travel agencies in Campeche; this is far easier than trying to get to Edzná by bus. If you do go by bus, be forewarned that you must walk about 1 km (½ mi) from the main road to the ruins. Check and double check with the driver about return buses—they are few and far between, and many tourists have been stranded until the next day. ✉ *Rte. 261 east from Campeche City for 44 km (27 mi) to Cayal, then Rte. 188 southeast for 18 km (11 mi),* ☎ *no phone.* 🎫 *$2, free Sun. and holidays.* ☉ *Daily 8–5.*

Hopelchén

㉕ *41 km (25 mi) north of the Edzná turnoff on Route 261.*

Since 1985 Hopelchén has been home to an immigrant colony of blond-haired, blue-eyed Mennonites who came from northern Mexico looking for arable land. (Every time the Mennonite colony gets too big, the elders send out settlers to other parts). These people are very tradition bound and still speak a Dutch-German dialect, although those who do business with outsiders learn Spanish. The Campeche group make and sell "Mennonite" cheese and they can often be seen hawking it on the streets and in restaurants in Campeche City. Under no circumstances should you buy it, as it is often made here with unpasteurized milk and can cause botulism.

Otherwise, Hopelchén—the name means Place of the Five Wells—is a traditional Maya town noted for the lovely Franciscan church built in honor of St. Francis of Padua in 1667. Corn, beans, tobacco, fruit, and henequen are cultivated in this rich agricultural center.

Bolonchén de Rejón

㉖ *34 km (21 mi) north of Hopelchén.*

Just short of the state line between Campeche and Yucatán and a few miles before Bolonchén de Rejón is the Grutas de Xtacumbilxunán caverns ("hidden women" in Maya), where legend says a Maya girl never came back after going into the caverns for water. In ancient times cenotes (sinkholes) deep in the extensive cave system provided an emergency water source during droughts. Only a few chambers are open to the public because the rock surfaces are dangerously slippery and the depth of the caverns is 240 ft. Visitors can admire the delicate limestone formations in the upper part of the cave on an easy, two-hour guided tour booked through a travel agency in the city of Campeche; there are no guides at the site. 🎫 *$2.* ☉ *Daily 8–5.*

Hochob

🔺 ㉗ *41 km (25 mi) south of Hopelchén.*

The small Maya ruin of Hochob is an excellent example of the Chenes architectural style, which flowered in the Classic period from about AD 200 to AD 900. Found throughout central and southern Campeche, Chenes-style temples are easily recognized by their elaborate stucco facades forming giant masks of jaguars, birds, or other creatures, with doorways representing the beasts' open jaws. Since work began at Hochob in the early 1980s, eight temples and palaces have been excavated at the site, including two that have been restored to their original grandeur. ⊠ *South of Hopelchén on Dzibalchén–Chenko road,* ☎ *no phone.* ⊡ *Free.* ⊙ *Tues.–Thurs. and weekends 8–5.*

Dzibilnocac

⛰ ㉘   *25 km (16 mi) east of Hochob.*

The rarely visited archaeological site of Dzibilnocac, reached by a good but unpaved road, was a fair-size ceremonial center between AD 250 and AD 900. Although at least seven temple pyramids have been located here, the only one that has been excavated is the **Palacio Principal,** an unusual, rounded, three-level pyramid resembling a smaller version of the one at Uxmal and combining elements of the Puuc and Chenes architectural styles. A one-room, square chamber at the top level is beautifully executed with dozens of Chaac curled noses carved into the outside walls and each wall has it's own open doorway. ⊠ *East of Hochob on Iturbide Rd.,* ☎ *no phone.* ⊡ *Free.* ⊙ *Daily 8–5.*

ROUTE 180 TO VILLAHERMOSA

Heading south from Campeche, Route 180 hugs the coast, offering a wonderful view of the Gulf of Mexico. The deep green sea is so shallow that the continental shelf is almost visible at low tide, and because waves and currents are rare, the gulf resembles a lake more than the vast body of water that it is.

Playa Bonita

㉙   *13 km (8 mi) south of Campeche City.*

The first beach south of Campeche City, Playa Bonita can be reached by public buses from the market (⊠ Circuito Baluartes between Calles 53 and 55); the buses depart daily (6 AM–11 PM). The beach has lockers, changing rooms, showers, and a snack bar, but is crowded on weekends and badly littered at all times. A few beaches are private property where trespassing is not allowed. This is the case with Playa San Lorenzo, which is about 5 km (3 mi) south of Playa Bonita. You are allowed to walk the 3-km (2-mi) trail between the two beaches, however.

Seybaplaya

㉚   *20 km (12 mi) south of Playa Bonita.*

Wooden motor launches fill the beach at the traditional fishing port of Seybaplaya; its palm-lined setting is probably the prettiest seascape on the Campeche coast. A couple of miles beyond lies **Payucán,** a beach with fine white sand and moderate waves. It has a campsite and a snack bar that only opens during holiday periods like Holy Week, Christmas Week, and July and August; otherwise, there are no facilities. There's a new paved road from Seyaplaya to Payucán.

Champotón

㉛   *35 km (22 mi) south of Seybaplaya.*

The highway curves through a hilly region before reaching Champotón's immensely satisfying vista of open seas. Champotón is a charming little town with a bridge, palapas right on the water, and plenty of swimmers and launches in sight. The Spaniards dubbed the outlying bay the *Bahía de la Mala Pelea,* or Bay of the Evil Battle, because it was here that the troops of the Spanish conqueror and explorer Hernández de Córdoba were trounced for the first time in Mexico in 1517 by belligerent Indians armed with arrows, slingshots, and darts.

The 17th-century Church of **Nuestra Señora de las Mercedes** and the ruins of the **Fortin (Small Fort) de San Luis** still stand in Champotón. This area, ideal for fishing and hunting, teems with shad and bass as well as deer, wild boar, doves, and quail, and is sustained by an economy based largely on chicle, water coconut, sugarcane, bananas, avocados, corn, and beans. The famous Champotón baby shrimp are harvested here.

Isla del Carmen

32 *115 km (71 mi) south of Champotón.*

It was on this barrier island protecting the lagoon from the gulf that the pirates who raided Campeche hid from 1663 until their expulsion in 1717. The island has served as a depot for everything from dyewoods and textiles to hardwoods, chicle, shrimp, and (for over 20 years) oil. Its major development is at **Ciudad del Carmen,** on the eastern end, now connected by two bridges to the mainland; the second, inaugurated in November 1994, eliminates an hour's detour around the lagoon when driving north.

There is a surprising variety of things to do on Isla del Carmen, which has several fine white-sand beaches with palm groves and shallow waters, excellent fishing (sailfish, swordfish, shrimp, oyster, and conch), water sports, restaurants, hotels, and even some nightlife. **Dolphins** can be spotted at Zacatal, a hotel on the lagoon side of the island; a Moorish 18th-century pavilion marks the center of **Zaragoza Park;** and the **Museum of Anthropology and History** (⊠ Av. Gobernadores 406, ☎ no phone), which in December 1997 moved to a restored colonial building that used to be a hospital, displays pre-Hispanic and pirate artifacts and has educational exhibits for children. Archaeological sites on the island include **Xicalango,** where Cortés's mistress, Malinche, eventually lived, and **Itzankanac,** where the last Aztec emperor, Cuauhtémoc, supposedly met his demise (although other sources place Itzankanac on the mainland). The tourist office can arrange for a guide to take visitors through the **Laguna de Terminos,** past mangroves and an estuary. There's a stop to see how oysters grow and a short visit to a crocodile farm to get a look at its most famous couple, "Sasha" and "Conan," who measure 9 ft each. Cataraman tours (arranged through the office), for up to 40 people, traverse the inner canals and go past lagoons and mangroves. The best beaches for swimming are **El Playon** and **Playa Benjamin.**

Dining and Lodging

$$ ✕ **El Cactus.** Locals and carnivores alike flock here when they want a change to feast on meat dishes like succulent rib eye with a baked potato dripping in butter or the equally popular filet mignon. (The entée menu is all meat dishes). For starters there's bone marrow or French onion soup and lastly, for dessert, light caramel custard or filling cheese pie. The outside of the restaurant resembles a faux adobe house with, you guessed it, cacti growing at the doorway. ⊠ *Calle 31 no. 132, Col. Cuauhtemoc,* ☎ *938/24986. AE, MC, V.*

$$ ✕ **Piamonte.** This is an exception to the rule that says hotel restaurants are bound to be inferior. The dining room at the Eurohotel serves some of Ciudad del Carmen's finest fare, featuring Italian pastas as well as seafood. Grilled, cooked, and oven-broiled lobster and shrimp from the nearby gulf get top billing with local oil entrepreneurs who frequently book business lunches. Soft music plays in the evening. ⊠ *Calle 22, No. 208,* ☎ *938/23044. AE, MC, V.*

$$ 🏨 **Eurohotel.** Geared to the Mexican business traveler, this contemporary, upscale hotel is close to the center of town and offers secretarial services and meeting rooms. It also affords lots of after-work relaxation

options, including a bar, pool, and club room where off-track betting is offered via satellite on U.S. sporting events. Standard modern guest rooms, which were repainted in 1997 in soft gray, blue, and cream colors, are air-conditioned, with cable TV and phones. ⊠ *Calle 22, No. 208, 1 block from Terminos lagoon,* ☎ *938/23044 or 938/23078,* FAX *938/23021. 80 rooms, 12 suites. Restaurant, coffee shop, air-conditioning, room service, business services, meeting rooms, free parking. AE, MC, V.*

$ ☷ **Hotel Zacarias.** This bare-bones downtown hotel does not provide phones in the rooms, but some quarters have air-conditioning and cable TV. Most of the older accommodations offer only sofa beds, but there are 18 rooms in a wing with standard-size beds. There's no restaurant but there are plenty to choose from on the plaza that's within walking distance. ⊠ *Calle 24, No. 58, on Plaza Principal,* ☎ *938/20121. 58 rooms. No credit cards.*

ALONG ROUTE 186 TOWARD CHETUMAL

Campeche's archaeological sites, particularly those near the Quintana Roo border, are attracting more attention from scientists and travelers alike. The vestiges of at least 10 little-known Maya cities lie hidden off Route 186 between Francisco Escárcega and Chetumal. Becán and the neighboring sites of Chicanná and Xpujil are just off Highway 186 near the Quintana Roo border, and you can now take a paved road all the way to Calakmul near the Guatemala border south of Xpujil, but the others are more difficult to reach; a four-wheel-drive vehicle—and much enthusiasm—are required. The first three sites are easily viewed in a day if you're en route between Escárcega and Chetumal; take another half day for Calakmul. The ruins at Hormiguero and Río Bec are reached by expeditions of several hours along four-wheel-drive-only roads on the edge of the Calakmul Biosphere Reserve. Both sites are best visited on guided Land Rover tours. A half-day Hormiguero trip or an all-day Río Bec expedition can be arranged a day in advance at the Ramada Ecovillage (☞ *below*), where you can also arrange a guide for Calakmul. For now this secluded but accessible area is perfect for those who want to get a sense of the ruins as they appear in the wild. This area is gradually being developed for visitors, with attempts made to minimize the impact of tourism on the surrounding areas. In fact Calakmul leads all other archaeological zones in the country with the installation of the first ecological public rest rooms. Men and women still have separate areas but within each are stalls with two different latrines, one for liquids and the others for solid waste. The waste material gets covered with sawdust and then it's used in organic farming. Other sites along the Río Bec route have followed suit already.

Becán

⛏ ㉝ *293 km (182 mi) southeast of Campeche, 132 km (82 mi) west of Chetumal.*

Becán, which means "path of the serpent" in Maya, may have served as a religious and ceremonial center as early as AD 150, based on the period in which its defensive moat was constructed. Most of Becán's temples date from AD 600 to AD 900. The site has some of Campeche's largest Maya buildings, connected by underground passages and secret rooms. A deep moat ½ km long (¼ mi long) surrounds the ruins, which have been extensively restored. A visitor center with snack bar and rest rooms has opened at this pristine site. ▣ *$2.* ☉ *Daily 8–5.*

Chicanná

 3 km (2 mi) east of Becán.

A small city of the same era as Becán, Chicanná (Maya for "house of the serpent's mouth") dates from the Late Classic period. The main temple at this intimate site has lovely sculpted reliefs and faces with long twisted noses caressing its facade. Masks most likely representing an earth monster are on the facades of several temples. The Chenes-style main temple is virtually identical to the one at Hochob, far to the north. A small snack shop with rest rooms has been added. ✉ $1.50. ☉ Daily 8–5.

Xpujil

 7 km (4½ mi) east of Chicanná.

Xpujil (or "cat's tail") comprises three large towers in one structure overlooking the jungle, along with several other building groups that have not yet been excavated. The site, which can be clearly seen from the highway, blends architectural elements of both the Chenes architectural style, characterized by elaborate facades with "monster mouth" doorways, and the Río Bec style, with facades decorated with massive false pyramids. A visitor center with a snack bar and rest rooms is now in operation. ✉ $1.50. ☉ Daily 8–5.

Lodging

$$ 🏨 **Ramada Ecovillage Resort.** Until recently the complete absence of overnight accommodations and the distance from major towns made visiting the Maya ruins in southern Campeche very difficult. The opening of this jungle lodge in early 1995 has changed that. The lodge's rooms, in two-story stucco duplexes with thatched roofs, are secluded in a rain forest. Each of the large units has a separate bedroom with one king-size or two double beds, overhead fan, plus one or two hammocks on a porch or balcony. Lush gardens surround the outdoor swimming pool. Solar energy powers the hot water, there's an artificial lagoon for water storage and an organic waste-treatment plant. There are no phones or TVs at the lodge, though public long-distance phones and fax service are available at the small village of Xpujil. ✉ Off Rte. 186 at Zona Arqueológico Xpujil, 3 km (2 mi) north of village of Xpujil, ☎ 981/62233 or 800/228–9898, ℻ 981/11618. Restaurant, bar, fans, pool. AE, MC, V.

$ 🏨 **Hotel Calakmul.** As a last resort this bare-bones place in town with the fancy name will do; there are doubles, triples, and singles—about half with private bath and the rest with shared bath. Clean rooms have white walls and beds and that's about all; all bathrooms have hot water. But you can't beat the $9–$19 room rates for the top-of-the-line unit. There's a restaurant on the premises that's open all day. Owner Sra. Maria Cabrera will see to it that you get a hot meal of meat or fish or her speciality mole poblano (rich, spicy chocolate sauce served over turkey leg) and local beer, wines, and liquors. ✉ Carretera Escárcega–Chetumal km. 153 in the town of Xpuhil, ☎ 983/29162. 14 rooms. Restaurant, free parking. No credit cards.

Hormiguero

 19 km (12 mi) southeast of Xpujil.

Hormiguero is Spanish for "anthill," referring to the looters' tunnels that honeycombed the ruins when archaeologists discovered them. The site has five temples, two of which have been excavated to reveal ornate facades covered with zoomorphic figures whose mouths are the doorways. During the rainy season the unpaved road from Xpujil is impassable. ✉ *Free*.

Río Bec

🏔 ③⑦ *15 km (9 mi) south of Xpujil, same distance from Hormiguero.*

The sprawling Río Bec archaeological zone covers nearly 78 square km (30 square mi) along the banks of the river of the same name. The zone includes five major ceremonial centers and 15 smaller temple groups, but although archaeologists have done extensive surveys of the area, little clearing or excavation has been done. The only structure that has been completely excavated and restored, known as **Río Bec B**, is a 55-ft-tall temple. Similar in design to the temples found at Becán, Xpujil, and other sites in the area, it typifies the so-called Río Bec architectural style with two false-pyramid towers at opposite edges of a long, low building whose front entrance is the mouth of a serpent. Ancient builders created miniaturized, impossibly steep stairways inside the towers and used an optical illusion known as forced perspective to give the towers the appearance of huge pyramids towering hundreds of feet. Experts now believe the center of the Río Bec culture was actually Calakmul (☞ *below*), about 95 km (59 mi) to the southeast, but the architectural style was given this name before Calakmul was discovered. ✉ *Free*.

Seeing all the main ceremonial centers at Río Bec requires about eight hours of hiking through difficult rain forest terrain. An all-day trip that includes Río Bec B and its unexcavated look-alike, Río Bec N, involves only a few miles of relatively easy hiking. Guide services, essential for this trip, can be arranged (at least a day in advance) at the Ramada Ecovillage (☞ *above*); at a travel agency in Campeche; or at Rancho Encantado at Bacalar, Quintana Roo (☞ Chapter 5).

Calakmul Biosphere Reserve

🏔 ③⑧ *70 km (43 mi) southwest of Xpujil.*

Remote Calakmul (Twin Towers) is in the isolated region near the Guatemala border. The area surrounding the ancient Maya city has been declared a biosphere reserve; with its 1.8 million acres, Calakmul is the second largest reserve of its kind on the continent next to Sian Ka'an (☞ Chapter 5). There are many species of flora and fauna, including some that are endangered. Among them are wildcats (jaguar, puma, ocelot), spider and howler monkeys, 329 different kinds of birds, and 120 varieties of orchids. The area was declared a protected biosphere reserve in 1989 and efforts have been made since then to control the damage being perpetuated by its inhabitants. As late as 1950, the region was not populated by humans. The Mexican government began colonizing it with Maya settlers from Tabasco who had lost their land to cattle barons. Later immigrants, who also lost their land to the cattle industry, came from Veracruz, and when the Chicosen volcano erupted in Chiapas in the early 1980s, another wave of farmers appeared. They live a marginal existence and dwell in adobe or corrugated-tin huts in very isolated communities, with only two schools serving them. About 25 communities of between 4,000 and 5,000 people live inside the reserve and another 2,500–3,000 people live just outside it. The slash-and-burn technique of farming—where parts of precious forests have been burned down to make way for crops—is probably the most dangerous threat to the reserve. Therefore, alternative means of making a living like beekeeping and pig farming have been introduced to the farmers, along with organic farming methods that will give higher yields on crops and thus prevent the clearing of more land for agriculture. To instill a sense of responsibility in saving the rain forest, educational programs on sustainable forest management are also continuously taking place in the communities.

The Escarcéga-Chetumal highway runs right through the reserve. Lying just south of the highway is the archaeological zone within the reserve. Although structures will be excavated, the dense jungle surrounding them will be left in its natural state. Extensive information on the site's ecosystem is presented in tours conducted by local guides. You have a better chance of getting an English-speaking guide if you hire one through a travel agency in Campeche City.

Archaeologists and anthropologists estimate that the region may once have been inhabited by more than 50,000 Maya, and have thus far mapped more than 6,250 structures ranging from small to large, including what may be the largest Maya building on the peninsula. More than 180 stelae have also been found. Twin pyramids or temples facing each other across a plaza, similar to those found at Tikal, Guatemala, have been discovered here. However, the sites' early Petén architectural style characterized by towering temples with long, sloping sides looks a little bulky but is closest to the graceful, aesthetically appealing temples at Tikal. Perhaps the most monumental discovery so far is a 1,000-year-old individual, found wrapped in animal skins (but not embalmed) and locked away in a royal tomb. The 1994 discovery is the first known example of this type of burial in the Maya world to date, and the remains are under study at the government's anthropology institute in Mexico City. However, some of the most exquisite finds—including six jade funeral masks—are on display at the Fuerte de San Miguel's Museum of the Maya in Campeche City (☞ *above*). The entrance road to the site was paved in 1996 and a standard module with snack bar, rest rooms, and bookshop was opened in the beginning of 1997. It's best to take a tour offered by the Ramada Ecovillage (☞ Xpujil, *above*) or to book one through a travel agency in the city of Campeche.

Calakmul was a formidable military power in its time. It was estimated to have been first settled around 1500 BC but now experts agree it was no earlier then 1000 BC. They also say it was probably the capital city of the mighty Serpent Head dynasty. The glyph with this symbol has been found on stelae in other parts of the ancient Maya empire, suggesting that Calakmul dominated a large number of tributary city-states. It reached the pinnacle of its power in the Late Classic period when it held sway over Palenque in Chiapas and superpower Tikal in Guatemala. Stelae under study also indicate that the new heads of tributary cities were obligated to journey to Calakmul to be formally consecrated in their new duties by the leader of the Serpent Head lineage. Epigraphers also have discovered inscriptions relating the defeat of Calakmul's most famous ruler, Jaguar Paw, at the hands of arch rival Tikal in AD 695. The city-state went into decline after this.

All visitors entering Calakmul must register at the entrance gate. From there vehicles drive about 10 minutes along a newly paved road to the parking area. Then it's a good 20-minute hike to the first building. The site is shrouded in thick rain forest, but paths with signposts lead to various temples. Only about a half dozen structures can be visited, including Temples II and VII—twin pyramids separated by an immense plaza. Temple II, the tallest so far at 175 ft, has to be climbed via a ragged rock incline as the steps have not been completely restored yet. It's worth it though, because the view from the top of the surrounding canopy of rain forest is spectacular; you can see into Guatemala 30 km (19 mi) away. A stone mask was uncovered on the facade of this temple in 1997 and is currently under study. The facade and steps of slightly smaller Temple I have been restored, so it's easier to climb. A pair of royal tombs has been extracted from here, one of a female regent. There's a stela at the base of the pyramid overlooking the plaza. Parts of temples are scattered around one of the rain forest paths, probably the work of grave robbers who got away with the choice pieces. It's hard to thwart these criminals since to do so would require a large corps of guards at the site, and there is no budget available for hiring them. This site is also perfect for bird-watchers. ⊠ *97 km (60 mi) east of Escárega to turnoff at Cohuas, then 65 km (40 mi) south to Calakmul.* ⊠ *$6.50 per car (more for larger vehicles), plus $1.50 per person.* ⊙ *Daily 8–5.*

El Tigre

 180 km (112 mi), 30 km (19 mi) from Escárcega.

El Tigre is difficult to reach and barely explored. The ruins may have been the site of Post-Classic Itzankanac, capital of the province of Acalán, where Spanish conquistador Cortés supposedly hanged Cuauhtémoc, the last Aztec emperor. El Tigre comprises a 656-ft-long ceremonial plaza and dozens of mounds in the jungle near Lake Salsipuedes and Vieja Lagoon in the Candelaria River basin. Hire a *cayuca* (dugout canoe) from one of the locals to take you from Candelaria across the river to the site. A four-wheel-drive vehicle is best for traversing the 30½ km (19 mi) of dirt road to the river from Francisco Escárcega. ⊠ *Fee at all sites when someone is there to collect it.*

CAMPECHE A TO Z

Arriving and Departing

By Bus

Bus assaults of passengers have been reported along Rte. 261 near Escarcéga in Campeche, both during the day and at night. Tourists have been the target of the robberies. Since mid-1997 the government has beefed up security forces along the highway, who also periodically stop buses to check for firearms and anything else that might be amiss.

ADO (⊠ Av. Gobernadores 289 at Calle 45, along Rte. 261 to Mérida, ☎ 981/62802), a first-class line, runs buses to Campeche City from Coatzacoalcos, Ciudad del Carmen, and Mérida every half hour, and from Mexico City, Puebla, Tampico, Veracruz, and Villahermosa regularly, but less frequently. The deluxe **Expreso del Caribe** (☎ 981/13973) travels between Campeche, Mérida, Villahermosa, and Cancún. Buses depart from the Plaza Ah-Kim-Pech on Avenida Pedro Sainz de Baranda 120. There is less desirable second-class service on **Autobuses del Sur** (☎ 981/63445) from Chetumal, Ciudad del Carmen, Escárcega, Mérida, Palenque, Tuxtla Gutiérrez, Villahermosa, and intermediate points throughout the Yucatán Peninsula.

By Car

Campeche can be reached from Mérida in about 1½ hours along the 160-km (99-mi) *via corta* (short way, Route 180). The alternative route, the 250-km (155-mi) *via larga* (long way, Route 261), takes at least three hours but crosses the major Maya ruins of Uxmal, Kabah, and Sayil. From Chetumal take Route 186 west to Francisco Escárcega, where you pick up Route 261 north; the drive takes about seven hours. Villahermosa is about six hours away if you drive inland via the town of Francisco Escárcega, but longer if you hug the gulf and cross the bridge at Ciudad del Carmen. There's a new four-lane toll road from

Campeche City to Champotón. One-way costs $3 and it shaves 20 km (12 mi) off the 68-km (42-mi) road. Look for the 180 CUOTA sign when leaving the city for the coast. There's a new paved, two-lane highway from Hopelchén to Xpuhil, actually the continuation of Route 269 south, which will get you to the Río Bec area and Calakmul much faster from Mérida (hooks up with Route 261 north) and easier from Campeche City if you want to bypass the coastal region.

By Plane
Aeromexico (☎ 981/65678) has one flight daily from Mexico City to Campeche City.

Getting Around

By Bus
The municipal bus system covers all of Campeche City, but you can easily visit the major sights on foot. Public buses run along Avenida Ruíz Cortines and cost under $1.

By Taxi
Taxis can be hailed on the street in Campeche City, or—more reliably—commissioned from the **main taxi stand** (⊠ Calle 8, between Calles 55 and 53, ☎ 981/62366 or 981/65230) or at stands by the bus stations and market. Because of the scarcity of taxis, it's quite common to share them with other people headed in the same direction as you. Don't be surprised to see one already occupied slow down to where you are standing if the cab driver thinks he can pick up another fare. A shared cab ride will cost under $1. If you have one to yourself, it's around $2.

Contacts and Resources

Banks
Campeche City banks are open weekdays 9–1. Those where you can exchange money include **Banamex** (⊠ Calle 53, No. 15, at Calle 10, ☎ 981/65251) and **Bancomer** (⊠ Av. 16 de Septiembre, No. 120, ☎ 981/66622).

Car Rental
There is a **Hertz** representative at the Torres de Cristal building in Campeche City (⊠ Av. Ruíz Cortines 112, ☎ 981/12106) and the airport (☎ 981/68848).

Emergencies
Throughout the state, call 06 locally in case of emergency.

Campeche City: Police (⊠ Av. Resurgimiento s/n, ½ block from Hotel Alhambra, ☎ 981/62329); **Red Cross** (⊠ Av. Resurgimiento s/n, ☎ 981/52411).

Guided Tours
Trolley tours of the city leave from the Plaza Principal daily at 9:30, 6, and 8. They last an hour, have a Spanish-speaking guide, and cost $1.

Emerald Planet (⊠ 4076 Crystal Court, Boulder, CO 80304, ☎ 303/541–9688 or 800/883–3260, FAX 303/449–7805) arranges 10-day group (minimum eight people) tours to the **Calakmul Reserve** to see the conservation projects such as beekeeping, organic gardening, women's program, and the local environmental educational program. Other activities include viewing orchids, birds, big mammals, and other wildlife. Mexico's **Pronatura** field personnel coordinate everything and hire a local biologist as the escort. Besides Calakmul the tour visits two other protected areas of the Yucatán peninsula—Celestún

and Sian Ka'an—and involves a lot of camping and hiking. There's also
a 10-day wildlife/archaeological tour that focuses entirely on the state
of Campeche, and a seven-day orchid tour, which includes Calakmul,
with its more than 100 species.The Calakmul projects' sponsors, the
Pronatura private conservation group (✉ Calle 1-D 254-A, Campestra, 99/443390 and 99/443580), receives support from several presti-
gious international conservation funds. It mainly acts as coordinator
to tours of this kind and receives a percentage of the booking revenue.
It will occasionally lead shorter overnight trips to Calakmul for groups.
However, these trips require advance reservations and an obligatory
donation.

Mail
The **post office** (✉ Av. 16 de Septiembre, between Calles 53 and 55, ☎
981/62134) in Campeche City is open weekdays 9–6, Saturday 9–1.

Medical Clinics
In Campeche City **Hospital General** (✉ Av. Central at Circuito Baluartes, ☎ 981/60920 or 981/64233) and **Social Security Clinic** (✉ Av.
Lopez Mateos and Circuito Baluartes, ☎ 981/65202) are both open
24 hours for emergencies.

Pharmacies
In Campeche City **Clínica Campeche** (✉ Av. Central 65, near the So-
cial Security Clinic, ☎ 981/65612) is open 24 hours. The **Farmacia Al-
hambra** in the Hotel Alhambra (✉ Av. Resurgimiento 85, between Av.
Universidad and Av. Augusto Melgar, ☎ 981/11246), open 7 AM–11
PM, will deliver to guests of other hotels.

Telephones
There are several public booths for making long-distance calls in
Campeche City: In addition to the ones at Avenida Gobernadores s/n
(8 AM–10 PM) and at the corner of Calle 12 at Calle 59 (9 AM–10 PM),
there are phones at the post office and all international courier service
offices.

Travel Agencies and Tour Operators
Campeche City: **American Express/VIPs** (✉ Prolongación Calle 59, Edificio Belmar, Depto. 5, ☎ 981/11010 or 981/11000, FAX 981/68333);
Destinos Maya (✉ Av. Miguel Aleman 162, Locale 106, ☎ 981/13726
or 713/440–0291 or 713/440–0253 in the U.S., FAX 981/10934); **Viajes Campeche** (✉ Calle 10, No. 339, ☎ 981/65233, FAX 981/62844).

Visitor Information
The **tourist office** (✉ Av. Ruiz Cortines s/n, across the street from the
Palacio de Gobierno, ☎ 981/65593 or 981/66829) is open weekdays
9–3 and 5–8. There's an information booth at the Baluarte de Santiago at the Botanical Gardens and the Baluarte de Santa Rosa (✉ Circuito Baluartes and Calle 14).

Ciudad del Carmen: The **tourist office** (✉ Palacio Municipal on the
main plaza, ☎ 938/21137) is open weekdays 9–3 and 6–9.

8 Portraits of the Yucatán Peninsula

Chronology of the Maya
and History of Yucatán

The Three Faces of the Yucatán

CHRONOLOGY OF THE MAYA AND HISTORY OF YUCATÁN

11,000 BC Hunters and gatherers settle in Yucatán.

Preclassic Period: 2000 BC–AD 200

2,000 BC Maya ancestors in Guatemala begin to cultivate corn and build permanent dwellings.

1500–900 BC The powerful and sophisticated Olmec civilization develops along the Gulf of Mexico in the present-day states of Veracruz and Tabasco. Primitive farming communities develop in Yucatán.

900–300 BC The Maya adopt the Olmecs' concepts of iconography, tribal confederacies, and small kingships as they move across the lowlands.

600 BC Edzná is settled. It will be inhabited for nearly 900 years before the construction of the large temples and palaces found there today.

400 BC– AD 100 Dzibilchaltún develops as an important center in Komchen, an ancient state north of present-day Mérida. Becán, in southern Campeche, is also settled.

300 BC– AD 200 New architectural elements, including the corbeled arch and roof comb, develop in Guatemala and spread into the Yucatán.

300 BC– AD 900 Edzná becomes a city; increasingly large temple-pyramids are built.

AD 200 A small temple is built on Isla Cancún.

Classic Period: 200–900

The calendar and the written word are among the achievements that mark the beginning of the Classic period. The architectural highlight of the period is large, stepped pyramids with frontal stairways topped by limestone and masonry temples, arranged around plazas and decorated with stelae (stone monuments), bas-reliefs, and frescoes. Each Maya city is painted a single bright color, often red or yellow.

200–600 Economy and trade flourish. Maya culture achieves new levels of scientific sophistication and some groups become warlike.

250–300 A defensive fortification ditch and earthworks are built at Becán.

300 The first structures are built at San Gervasio on Cozumel.

300–600 Kohunlich rises to dominate the forests of southern Quintana Roo.

400–1100 Cobá grows to be the largest city in the eastern Yucatán.

432 The first settlement is established at Chichén Itzá.

6th Century Influenced by the Toltec civilization of Teotihuacán in Central Mexico, larger and more elaborate palaces, temples, ball courts, roads, and fortifications are built in southern Maya cities, including Becán, Xpujil, and Chicanná in Campeche.

600–900 Northern Yucatán ceremonial centers become increasingly important as centers farther south reach and pass developmental climax; the influence of Teotihuacán wanes. Three new Maya architectural styles develop: Puuc (exemplified by Chichén Itzá and Edzná is the dominant style; Chenes (in northern Campeche, between the Puuc hills and the Río Bec area) is characterized by ornamental facades with serpent masks; and Río Bec (at Río Bec and Becán) features small palaces with high towers exuberantly decorated with serpent masks.

850–950   The largest pyramids and palaces of Uxmal are built. By 975, however, Uxmal and most other Puuc sites are abandoned.

Post-Classic Period: 900–1541

900–1050   The great Classic Maya centers of Guatemala, Honduras, and southern Yucatán are abandoned for unknown reasons.

circa 920   The Itzá, a Maya tribe from the Petén rain forest in Guatemala, establish themselves at Champotón and then at Chichén Itzá.

987   According to legend, Toltecs leave their capital at Tula in central Mexico under the leadership of an exiled priest-king believed to be an incarnation of Quetzalcóatl, the "feathered serpent" god. The Yucatec Maya recognize him as the incarnation of their snake god, Kukulcán, and he becomes the ruler of Chichén Itzá. The Toltecs will rule Chichén Itzá for two centuries, until 1185.

987–1007   The Xiu, a Maya clan from the southwest, settle near ruins of Uxmal.

1224   An Itzá dynasty known as Cocomes emerges as a dominant group in northern Yucatán, building their capital at Mayapán.

1224–44   The Cocomes force the Toltec rulers out of Chichén Itzá, but the Itzá Maya soon return to the abandoned city as squatters.

1263–1440   Mayapán, under the rule of Cocomes aided by Canul mercenaries from Tabasco, becomes the most powerful city-state in Yucatán. The league of Mayapán—including the key cities of Uxmal, Chichén Itzá, and Mayapán—is formed in northern Yucatán. Peace reigns for almost two centuries. To guarantee the peace, the rulers of Mayapán hold members of other Maya royal families as lifelong hostages.

1441   Maya cities under Xiu rulers sack Mayapán, ending centralized rule of the peninsula. Yucatán henceforth is governed as 18 petty provinces, with constant internecine strife. The Itzá return to Lake Petén Itzá in Guatemala and establish their capital at Tayasal (modern-day Flores), one of the last un-Christianized Maya capitals, which will not be conquered by the Spanish until 1692.

15th Century   The last ceremonial center on Cancún island is abandoned. Other Maya communities are developing along the Caribbean coast.

1502   A Maya canoe is spotted during Columbus's fourth voyage.

1511   Spanish sailors Jerónimo de Aguilar and Gonzalo Guerrero are shipwrecked off Yucatán's Caribbean coast and taken to a Maya village on Cozumel.

1517   Fernández de Córdoba discovers Isla Mujeres. Trying to sail around Yucatán, which he believes to be an island, Córdoba lands at Campeche, marking first Spanish landfall on the mainland. He is defeated by the Maya at Champotón.

1519   Hernán Cortés lands at Cozumel, where he rescues Aguilar. Guerrero chooses to remain on the island with his Maya family.

1527, 1531, 1541   Unsuccessful Spanish attempts to conquer Yucatán.

1540   Francisco de Montejo founds Campeche, the first Spanish settlement in Yucatán.

Colonial Period: 1541–1821

1542　Maya chieftains surrender to Montejo at T'ho; 500,000 Indians are killed during the conquest of Yucatán. Indians are forced into labor under the *encomienda* system, by which conquistadors are charged with their subjugation and Christianization. The Franciscans contribute to this process. Mérida is founded on the ruins of T'ho.

1543　Valladolid is founded on the ruins of Zací.

1546　A Maya group attacks Mérida, resulting in a five-month-long rebellion.

1562　Bishop Diego de Landa burns Maya codices at Maní.

1600　Cozumel is abandoned after smallpox decimates population.

1686　Campeche's city walls are built for defense against pirates.

1700　182,500 Indians account for 98% of Yucatán's population.

1736　Indian population of Yucatán declines to 127,000.

1761　The Cocom uprising near Sotuta leads to death of 600 Maya.

1771　The Fuerte (fort) de San Miguel is completed on a hill above Campeche, ending the pirates' reign of terror.

1810　Port of Sisal opens, ending Campeche's ancient monopoly on peninsular trade and its economic prosperity.

Postcolonial/Modern Period: 1821–Present

1821　Mexico wins independence from Spain by diplomatic means. Various juntas vie for control of the new nation, resulting in frequent military coups.

1823　Yucatán becomes a Mexican state encompassing the entire peninsula.

1839–42　American explorer John Lloyd Stephens visits Yucatán's Maya ruins and describes them in two best-selling books.

1840–42　Yucatecan separatists revolt in an attempt to secede from Mexico. The Mexican government quells the rebellion, reduces the state of Yucatán to one-third its previous size, creates the federal territories of Quintana Roo and Campeche, and recruits Maya soldiers into a militia to prevent further disturbance.

1846　Following years of oppression, violent clashes between Maya militiamen and residents of Valladolid launch the War of the Castes. The entire non-Indian population of Valladolid is massacred.

circa 1848　Twenty refugee families from the Caste War settle in Cozumel, which has been almost uninhabited for centuries. By 1890 Cozumel's population numbers 500.

1850　Following the end of the Mexican War with the United States in 1849, the Mexican army moves into the Yucatán to end the Indian uprising. The Maya flee into the unexplored forests of Quintana Roo. Military attacks, disease, and starvation reduce the Maya population of the Yucatán Peninsula to less than 10,000.

1863　Campeche achieves statehood.

1880–1914　Yucatán's monopoly on henequen, enhanced by plantation owner's exploitation of Maya peasants, leads to its Golden Age as one of the wealthiest states in Mexico. Prosperity will last until the beginning of World War II.

Waves of Middle Eastern immigrants arrive in Yucatán and become successful in commerce, restaurants, cattle ranching, and tourism.

1901 The Caste War virtually ends with the defeat of the Chan Santa Cruz Maya in Quintana Roo.

U.S. Consul Edward Thompson buys Chichén Itzá for $500 and spends the next three years dredging the Sacred Cenote for artifacts.

1902 Mexican President Porfirio Díaz asserts federal jurisdiction over the Territory of Quintana Roo to isolate rebellious pockets of Indians and increase his hold on regional resources.

1915–24 Felipe Carrillo Puerto, Socialist governor of Yucatán, institutes major reforms in land distribution, labor, women's rights, and education during Mexican Revolution.

1923–48 A Carnegie Institute team led by archaeologist Sylvanus Moreley restores the ruins of Chichén Itzá.

1935 Chan Santa Cruz rebels in Quintana Roo relinquish Tulum and sign a peace treaty.

1940–70 With collapse of the world henequen markets, Yucatán gradually becomes one of the poorest states in Mexico.

1968 Cancún is selected by FONATUR as the site of Mexico's largest tourist resort.

1974 Quintana Roo achieves statehood. Resort hotels open in Cancún.

1988 Hurricane Gilbert shuts down Cancún hotels and devastates the north coast of the Yucatán. The reconstruction is immediate. Within three years, the number of hotels on Isla Cancún triples.

1993 Quintana Roo's newly elected environmentalist governor, Mario Villanueva, toughens ecological protection in the state and orders a moratorium on new hotel construction on Cancún Island.

1994 Mexico joins the United States and Canada in NAFTA (North American Free Trade Association), which will phase out tariffs over a 15-year period.

Popular PRI presidential candidate Luis Donaldo Colosio is assassinated while campaigning in Tijuana. Ernesto Zedillo, an "old boy"–style PRI politician, replaces him and wins the election.

Zedillo, blaming the economic policies of his predecessor, devalues the peso in December.

1995 Recession sets in as a result of the peso devaluation. Scandals erupt about the assassination of Colosio; ex-President Carlos Salinas de Gortari moves to the United States.

1996 Mexico's economy, bolstered by a $28 billion bailout led by the United States, turns around, but the recovery is fragile. The opposition National Action Party (PAN), which is committed to conservative economic policies, gains strength. New details emerge of scandals within the former administration.

1997 Mexico's top antidrug official is arrested on bribery charges. The United States nonetheless recertifies Mexico as a partner in the war on drugs.

THE THREE FACES OF THE YUCATÁN

AS ANCIENT and mysterious as a stone idol, as stately as a cathedral, as sleek and modern as a sailboard slicing across a brilliant blue-green sea, the Yucatán Peninsula is a land with a complicated soul.

Vestiges of ancient Maya wisdom show in the eyes of country people carrying loads of wood along the roadside. A timeless innocence glows in the faces of children playing soccer amid the ruins of thousand-year-old ball courts and plunging merrily into cenotes, virtually bottomless water holes believed by their ancestors to possess mystical powers.

The ghost of Don Quixote dances in the faces of the men who drive *calesas*, old-fashioned horse-drawn carriages, along the traffic-choked Spanish Colonial streets of Mérida in competition with modern taxi cabs. The spirit of the conquistadors lives on in the cold, proud gaze of the bullfighters who keep Mexico's earlier tradition of blood ritual alive throughout the peninsula—even in that most modern of Yucatecan cities, Cancún.

The eyes of the tourists speaking a babel of languages up and down the seemingly endless beaches of Isla Cancún hide behind dark glasses—bloodshot, most likely, from a pre-dawn airline flight or a late-night tour of the local discos. International visitors are equal partners in the unique multicultural mix of the Yucatán Peninsula today: From Cancún on the east coast to Celestún on the gulf coast, tourism is by far the region's largest industry.

The palm-lined beaches, warm turquoise waters, and dazzling coral reefs along the Corridor Turistico, the stretch of Caribbean coastline from Cancún south, offer sufficient reason for millions of vacationers to come to the Yucatán each year—North Americans and Europeans to escape the winter cold, Mexicans to find respite from the summer heat. But beyond the realm of tourist resorts lies a land with a cultural heritage rich and mysterious.

Perhaps no civilization known to have inhabited Earth is more enigmatic and fascinating than that of the Maya.

We know that their accomplishments during the Classic period (AD 200–900) were profound. Besides the monumental architecture and artwork we can see today at Classic period sites, the Maya developed astronomy so advanced that some of their calculations did not become known to modern scientists until the 1930s. Their hieroglyphs were the only true written language used in the Western Hemisphere before Columbus. Their calendar, an ingenious refinement of the earlier Olmec calendar used by many ancient Mexican cultures, was more sophisticated than calendars used in Europe at the time. Their mathematics made use of the digit "zero," a concept unknown to European mathematicians in those days. And the Maya were probably the first people to discover the secret of cultivating corn. By freeing them from the need to wander in an endless, nomadic search for food, corn may have enabled the Maya to develop their sophisticated arts and sciences.

But who were these people? The early Mormon Church held that the Maya were the lost tribes of Israel. Some 19th-century scholars believed that their origins might lie in Egypt, Cambodia, or even the lost continent of Atlantis. In the 20th century there are those who theorize that the Maya were influenced by mystical prophecies or by "gods" from outer space.

Most modern archaeologists now agree that the Maya were a purely American Indian race who inhabited the Yucatán Peninsula from about 2000 BC and were the ancestors of the native people who live in the Yucatán today. Maya people also lived in the adjoining areas of present-day Belize, Guatemala, Honduras, El Salvador, and the Mexican state of Chiapas.

Still, the more that has been learned about the ancient Maya, the less certain experts have grown about the exact nature of their society. Were the Maya peace-loving or warlike? Were their rulers priests and artists or barbarian warlords? Did they sacrifice human beings to the gods, or was this solely a practice of Toltec invaders? Was it civil war, disease, famine, political collapse, environmental disaster, or urban decay that brought the Classic Maya civilization to an end? Archaeologists may argue endlessly about such matters. Touching the stones of lost cities with your own hands and letting ancient forest temples tug at your imagination, you can come up with your own answers.

Follow the highway for 142 km (88 mi) south of Cancún, and you will find yourself among the ruins of Tulum, an ideal introduction to the world of the ancient Maya. Here a temple known as El Castillo ("The Castle") stands silent watch atop jagged charcoal-gray cliffs at the highest point on the coast of the Yucatán Peninsula. The youngest restored archaeological zone in the Yucatán—its main temples were built 300 years after the fall of the Classic Maya empire—Tulum was the center of a seagoing culture that traded up and down the coast in long canoes nearly 800 years ago. At midday, fleets of tour buses from Cancún parade into the parking lot and camera-clicking multitudes seize the place like an invading army. Yet, even at the most crowded times, a profound sense of strangeness wraps Tulum.

CONSIDER, THEN, that the art and architecture of Tulum are pale imitations of the grandeur that can still be seen at the ruins of older, much larger Maya cities throughout the Yucatán Peninsula. Tulum tantalizes the traveler with just enough hints of ancient glory to make the idea of a trip to other Maya sites such as Cobá, Chichén Itzá, and Uxmal irresistible.

Less than an hour from Tulum, on a side road where few tour buses venture, Cobá could not be more different from its neighbor. As Tulum is a young site, Cobá is a very old one, perhaps one of the first Maya capitals on the Yucatán Peninsula. As Tulum's temples are small, graceless, and slightly crooked, Coba's are some of the tallest in the Yucatán. And as Tulum is compact enough to visit on a half-day excursion from Cancún, Cobá's ruins stand at the shoreline of several lakes and require miles of hiking along jungle trails.

If you have time to visit only one Maya ruin during a brief trip to the Yucatán, choose Chichén Itzá, the most magnificently restored of all ancient ruins on the peninsula, ranking alongside Egypt's Valley of the Kings and the temples of ancient Greece as one of the foremost wonders of the archaeological world. The enormous scale and intricate detail of the site, with its Roman-looking columns, its murals recording rituals of human sacrifice, and its giant, dragonlike stone heads carved in the style of the Toltecs who occupied this part of the peninsula in the late part of the Classic Maya era, is awe-inspiring.

If Tulum and Cobá are studies in contrast, so too are Chichén Itzá and Uxmal, which lies south of Mérida. Although the largest structures at both sites were built around the same time, Uxmal's architecture is purely Maya, free from any hint of the Toltec influences that characterize Chichén Itzá. Instead of Chichén's plumed serpent sculptures, sacrificial altars, and carvings of warrior heroes, Uxmal is ornamented with complex geometric designs and small, symbolic sculptures of turtles, parrots, rattlesnakes, and human faces peering from the jaws of beasts. There are few hieroglyphs or other physical clues to the history of Uxmal—so just let your imagination roam.

One of the few things archaeologists know for sure about Uxmal is that it was the center of a state known as the Puuc (Maya for "Hills"). Wide, limestone-paved ancient roadways, or *sacbeob,* connected Uxmal with smaller communities throughout the hill country. Several of the most impressive, including Kabah, Sayil, and Labná, lie within a few minutes' drive from Uxmal along winding roads that were paved in the late 1970s to make the ruins accessible for visitors. Ongoing restoration has transformed Kabah from rubble to majesty and keeps on revealing new temples down winding forest footpaths. Sayil and Labná, just a few miles apart, have been cleared but not extensively restored. Two of the most lavish palaces in the ancient Maya Yucatán have been excavated there.

Fascinating as it is, ancient civilization in the Yucatán is only one aspect of the region's complex historical and cultural tapestry. Whatever miracles or visions may have given rise to the high Maya civilization, whatever catastrophe may have brought about its decline and fall, cannot have been any more dramatic than the events that have swept the region since it became a Spanish colony nearly five centuries ago. Travelers in the Yucatán are never far from reminders of the Spanish Colonial era. Besides the more than 70 old Franciscan mission churches still in use in towns and villages throughout the region, the abandoned mansion houses of overgrown plantations are a familiar sight along Yucatán highways and back roads. In Mérida, as well as in the smaller cities of Valladolid and Campeche, most downtown buildings date back to colonial times.

IT BEGAN QUIETLY in 1511, when two shipwrecked Spanish sailors, Jerónimo de Aguilar and Gonzalo Guerrero, were washed up half-drowned on a beach near Tulum. The first Europeans ever to set foot on the American mainland, they were promptly captured by seagoing Maya traders who brought them to the island of Cozumel, which became their home for eight years. In 1519 Hernán Cortés stopped on Cozumel in the early days of the expedition that would end with the conquest of Mexico. Aguilar was rescued, but Guerrero chose to stay with his Maya wife and family. Aguilar became a military advisor to Spanish army expeditions in the Yucatán, while Guerrero counseled the Maya chiefs on how to resist the Spanish invaders.

Guerrero's advice must have been effective, because it took 21 years for conquistador Francisco de Montejo to establish the first permanent Spanish outpost in the Yucatán. This early settlement became Campeche, now the capital city of the state of the same name. Mérida, capital of the entire peninsula in colonial times and of the state of Yucatán today, was founded two years later, in 1542, and Chetumal, capital of Quintana Roo, in 1544. Montejo's mansion still stands in Mérida, across the *zócalo* (town square) from the cathedral and the government palace.

The Spanish conquest seemed to spell the end of the ancient Maya heritage. Franciscan missionaries, under the direction of notorious inquisition leader Bishop Diego de Landa, destroyed dozens of Maya temples and used the stones to build the imposing mission churches that still tower over many Maya villages today, including the great cathedral at Izamal, on the route

between Mérida and Chichén Itzá and still one of the Yucatán's most impressive sights. Landa also burned the sacred books used by the native priests; only four of these Maya books are known to have been saved from the flames. At the same time, smallpox and other epidemics wiped out half the Indian population of the peninsula and drove the survivors to regroup in new communities under church guidance. The ways of the ancient Maya were forgotten—or so the conquerors believed.

For a time the greatest problem facing the people of the Yucatán was piracy. As on the other side of the Atlantic, the British Navy fought the Spanish Armada for the right to colonize North America; England commissioned "privateers"—free-lance fighting ships—to rob Spanish gold shipments and loot Spanish seaport towns from Florida to Colombia. As lawlessness increased on the Caribbean sea route known as the Spanish Main, Dutch and French mercenaries as well as renegade Spaniards joined in the plunder.

The Yucatán became both a perfect hideout and an easy target. Campeche, its largest port city in colonial times, was sacked by pirates repeatedly despite the construction of the massive stone walls that still surround the old city today.

It was only after 1771, when two impregnable fortresses were built on the hills overlooking the city and the harbor, that pirates quit looting and burning Campeche. At the same time, the uninhabited north and east coasts provided safe havens for other infamous pirates including Jean Laffite, whose grave is in the small Yucatán fishing village of Dzilam de Bravo, and Edward "Blackbeard" Teach, who is credited with founding the isolated community of Punta Allen in what is now Quintana Roo's Sian Ka'an Biosphere Reserve.

Although they never intermarried as Indians and soldiers did in other parts of Mexico, for nearly three centuries the Spanish and Maya people of the Yucatán coexisted in peace—the Spanish as sugarcane plantation owners, the Maya as sharecroppers or church servants. But in 1821, following Mexico's declaration of independence from Spain, the new government banished the clergy, ending church protection of the Indians. Soon many Maya people found themselves brutalized as slaves. The anger that began to seethe would soon erupt in events so devastating that they would leave the Spanish Colonial culture of the Yucatán in ruins alongside the debris of the ancient Maya civilization.

After a failed 1840 attempt by civic leaders in the Yucatán to secede from Mexico and form an alliance with the breakaway republic of Texas, the Mexican government segmented the peninsula into thirds, with boundaries so straight that the three states—Yucatán on the north, Campeche on the west, and Quintana Roo on the east—look like a sliced pie. The government also established a militia of Maya army recruits in order to keep the region under federal control.

THE PLAN BACKFIRED when, in 1847, Maya soldiers turned their guns against their oppressors in history's bloodiest Indian war. The Maya people killed the entire Spanish-speaking population of the city of Valladolid, and every plantation owner in the Yucatán either fled or died. As the last remaining Spanish residents of the peninsula huddled within the besieged walls of Mérida, with the Maya insurgents poised to annihilate them, a strange thing happened: Maya astronomers announced that the time for planting had arrived. The rebel Maya army suddenly abandoned the siege of Mérida and went home to plant corn.

The conflict that became known as the War of the Castes—a reference to the complicated Spanish Colonial caste system, at this point reduced simply to Spanish versus Indian—dragged on for more than 50 years, until 1901. Except for Mexican army patrols, few Spanish-speaking people ever ventured far from the protection of the capital cities. The army systematically killed the Maya wherever they were found. By the end of the century, not only had the Spanish-speaking population of the Yucatán been reduced to half of what it had been in colonial times, but the Maya people had been almost wiped out; authorities believed that there were fewer than 300 living Maya left in the Yucatán.

But they were wrong. As many as 10,000 Indians had taken refuge deep in the forests of Quintana Roo, where, unknown to the Spanish, they had built a capital city called Chan Santa Cruz and returned to ancient Maya religious practices in newly built temples. The war ended with the Spanish capture of Chan Santa Cruz, which became the town of Felipe Carrillo Puerto. The memory of the War of the Castes lives on in rural areas of the Yucatán today in an undercurrent of distrust between the Maya and the Mexicans.

Outsiders' fascination with the Yucatán began in 1841 with the publication of *Incidents of Travel in Central America, Chiapas and Yucatán* by American explorer John Lloyd Stephens, the first popular account in English describing Maya ruins. The book and its sequel, *Incidents of Travel in Yucatán*, published two years later, ranked among the top best-sellers of their day. They would have sparked a wave of tourism in the mid-19th century had the War of the Castes not put the Yucatán off limits to gringos for the next half century.

Popular interest in the Yucatán was revived in 1901, when the U.S. Consul to Mérida, Edward Thompson, bought the ranch where the overgrown ruins of Chichén Itzá lay and proceeded to dredge the Sacred Cenote on his property. His discoveries—not only of huge quantities of Maya artifacts, but also of enough human skeletons to give rise to romantic legends about sacrificial virgins—were taken to Harvard University with so much fanfare that Maya artifacts came into high demand on the international art market. As the War of the Castes drew to an end, hordes of archaeologists and treasure hunters descended upon the Yucatán.

At the same time as the Maya civilization was being rediscovered, Mexican plantation owners were riding a wave of prosperity based on henequen, a plant fiber native to northern Yucatán used to make rope. Demand for rope boomed during World War I, which led to the financing of the construction of factories to strip the plants into fiber and railroad spurs to ship it to the seaport of Sisal. In a region whose economy had been destroyed by a protracted war, henequen built the elegant mansions along Mérida's Paseo de Montejo and created jobs for thousands of Maya.

But as synthetic rope materials were developed during World War II, the market for henequen collapsed, plunging landowners into bankruptcy. Plantations were abandoned and native laborers were without work. Famine swept the Yucatán, which once again became the poorest region of Mexico.

The region's terrible poverty was one reason the government decided to locate its most ambitious tourism project on the coast of the Yucatán. The ruins of Chichén Itzá and Uxmal, as well as the picturesque fishing villages, sparkling beaches, and lovely coral reefs of Cozumel and Isla Mujeres, had been attracting small numbers of adventurous travelers for decades. In 1968 FONART, the Mexican federal agency in charge of promoting resorts, ran a computer analysis and concluded that the most promising site in Mexico for development was an uninhabited barrier island the Maya people called *Can-Cun* (meaning "Bowl of Snakes").

THE ISLAND LIES ON the Caribbean, exactly the kind of turquoise, transparent, bathwater-warm sea people daydream about. And it has a unique beach. Scientists have found that its white sand contains snowflake-shape fossils of extinct microorganisms from Jurassic times, giving it a luxuriant, almost fluffy feel. Not far offshore, coral reefs at Punta Nizuc and Punta Cancún are havens for myriad colorful fish. On the side of Isla Cancún that faces the mainland lies a wild coastline where water flows from hidden freshwater springs to form a labyrinth of channels among the mangroves. Snowy egrets and great blue herons stand statue-like or glide overhead on silent wings.

FONART presented their plan for a mega-resort to more than 80 international luxury hotel corporations based in Mexico, the United States, Great Britain, Germany, and Japan: Mexico would build a huge international airport in the jungle and pave the highway all the way to Cancún, and the hotel chains would take care of the rest. Workers hacked away with machetes at the bushes to make way for construction.

The plan worked brilliantly. With the opening of the first hotels in 1974, the Yucatán Peninsula was transformed from the poorest region of Mexico to the wealthiest. Since then, Cancún has taken its place among the world's leading beach resort areas, in recent years drawing more international visitors than all other destinations in Mexico combined.

Tourism has overflowed Cancún's Zona Hotelería (Hotel Zone). It fills the cobblestone streets of Isla Mujeres with daily groups of sightseers. It has poured down the Caribbean coast along the segment of Highway 307 that slices straight through the jungle, flanking beaches and rocky points at a discreet distance for 140 km (87 mi) south of Cancún. It has spurred large-scale resort development on the island of Cozumel and along once-remote expanses of sand that have been transformed into hotel and recreation complexes at Playacar, Akumal, and Puerto Aventuras; this stretch of highway is now officially called the Corridor Turistico.

Yet this is no tropical paradise lost. Large-scale development is confined to a few, small glitzy pockets along the Corridor Turistico where the government has provided electricity, water, and other services. Far more of the coastline remains isolated. At plenty of remote, picture-perfect beaches along this route, the only accommodations are thatched-roof Maya-style huts with few modern conveniences. Other great beaches in the area are so little known that if you go there, yours may be the only footprints in the sand.

In the interior, from Chichén Itzá's souvenir stalls to the big public market in downtown Mérida, the Yucatán is a wonderland of traditional handicrafts, including beautifully embroidered dresses, hammocks, guayabera shirts, Panama hats, and carved-wood replicas of ancient Maya sculptures. Such items are rare and overpriced in Cancún and the Corridor Turistico, a government-designated free-trade zone where French perfumes, Italian designer fashions, Cuban cigars, and other international imports dominate the stores. Literally thousands of T-shirts celebrate beaches, tequila, the sea . . .

But not snakes. The tourist office assures us that the snakes that gave Cancún its name have all moved to the southern part of the state. The reptiles most often encountered on Isla Cancún these days are little lizard-like beasts called geckos, which bring good luck according to local belief. They also attract mosquitos and eat them—which may help explain why they are unofficial local mascots. Searching for that final reminder of your Yucatán vacation? Nothing says Cancún like a gecko T-shirt.

— Richard Harris

SPANISH VOCABULARY

Note: *Mexican Spanish differs from Castilian Spanish.*

English	Spanish	Pronunciation

Basics

English	Spanish	Pronunciation
Yes/no	Sí/no	see/no
Please	Por favor	pore fah-**vore**
May I?	¿Me permite?	may pair-**mee**-tay
Thank you (very much)	(Muchas) gracias	(moo-chas) grah-see-as
You're welcome	De nada	day **nah**-dah
Excuse me	Con permiso	con pair-**mee**-so
Pardon me/ what did you say	¿Como?/Mánde?	**coh**-mo/**mahn**-dey
Could you tell me?	¿Podría decirme?	po-**dree**-ah deh-**seer**-meh
I'm sorry	Lo siento	lo see-**en**-toe
Good morning!	¡Buenos días!	**bway**-nohs **dee**-ahs
Good afternoon!	¡Buenas tardes!	**bway**-nahs **tar**-dess
Good evening!	¡Buenas noches!	**bway**-nahs **no**-chess
Goodbye!	¡Adiós!/ ¡Hasta luego!	ah-dee-**ohss**/ ah-stah-**lwe**-go
Mr./Mrs.	Señor/Señora	sen-**yor**/sen-**yore**-ah
Miss	Señorita	sen-yo-**ree**-tah
Pleased to meet you	Mucho gusto	**moo**-cho **goose**-to
How are you?	¿Cómo está usted?	**ko**-mo es-**tah** oo-sted
Very well, thank you	Muy bien, gracias	**moo**-ee bee-**en**, **grah**-see-as
And you?	¿Y usted?	ee oos-**ted**
Hello (on the telephone)	Bueno	**bwen**-oh

Useful Phrases

English	Spanish	Pronunciation
Do you speak English?	¿Habla usted inglés?	**ah**-blah oos-**ted** in-**glehs**
I don't speak Spanish	No hablo español	no **ah**-blow es-pahn-**yol**
I don't understand (you)	No entiendo	no en-tee-**en**-doe
I understand (you)	Entiendo	en-tee-**en**-doe
I don't know	No sé	no **say**
I am American/ British	Soy americano(a)/ inglés(a)	soy ah-meh-ree-**kah**-no(ah)/in-**glace**(ah)
What's your name?	¿Cómo se llama usted?	**koh**-mo say **yah**-mah oos-**ted**
My name is . . .	Me llamo . . .	may **yah**-moh
What time is it?	¿Qué hora es?	keh **o**-rah es

It is one, two, three . . . o'clock	Es la una; son las dos, tres	es la **oo**-nah/sone lahs dose, trace
Yes, please/	Sí, por favor/	**see** pore fah-**vor**/
No, thank you	No, gracias	no **grah**-see-us
How?	¿Cómo?	**koh**-mo
When?	¿Cuándo?	**kwahn**-doe
This/Next week	Esta semana/ la semana que entra	**es**-tah seh-**mah**-nah/ lah say-**mah**-nah keh **en**-trah
Yesterday/today/ tomorrow	Ayer/hoy/mañana	ah-**yair**/oy/mahn-**yah**-nah
This morning/ afternoon	Esta mañana/ tarde	**es**-tah mahn-**yah**-nah/**tar**-day
Tonight	Esta noche	**es**-tah **no**-cheh
What?	¿Qué?	keh
What is it?	¿Qué es esto?	keh es **es**-toe
Why?	¿Por qué?	pore **keh**
Who?	¿Quién?	kee-**yen**
Where is . . . ?	¿Dónde está . . . ?	**dohn**-day es-**tah**
the bus stop?	la parada del autobús?	la pah-**rah**-dah del oh-toe-**boos**
the post office?	la oficina de correos?	la oh-fee-**see**-nah day koh-**reh**-os
the bank?	el banco?	el **bahn**-koh
the . . . hotel?	el hotel . . . ?	el oh-**tel**
the store?	la tienda . . . ?	la tee-**en**-dah
the cashier?	la caja?	la **kah**-hah
the . . . museum?	el museo . . . ?	el moo-**seh**-oh
the hospital?	el hospital?	el ohss-pea-**tal**
the elevator?	el ascensor?	el ah-**sen**-sore
the bathroom?	el baño?	el **bahn**-yoh
Here/there	Aquí/allá	ah-**key**/ah-**yah**
Open/closed	Abierto/cerrado	ah-be-**er**-toe/ ser-**ah**-doe
Left/right	Izquierda/derecha	iss-key-**er**-dah/ dare-**eh**-chah
Straight ahead	Derecho	der-**eh**-choh
Is it near/far?	¿Está cerca/lejos?	es-**tah sair**-kah/ **leh**-hoss
I'd like . . .	Quisiera . . .	kee-see-**air**-ah
a room	un cuarto/ una habitación	oon **kwahr**-toe/**oo**-nah ah-bee-tah-see-**on**
the key	la llave	lah **yah**-vay
a newspaper	un periódico	oon pear-ee-**oh**-dee-koh
a stamp	un timbre de correo	oon **team**-bray day koh-**reh**-oh
I'd like to buy . . .	Quisiera comprar . . .	kee-see-**air**-ah kohm-**prahr**
cigarettes	cigarrillo	ce-gar-**reel**-oh
matches	cerillos	ser-**ee**-ohs

a dictionary	un diccionario	oon deek-see-oh-**nah**-ree-oh
soap	jabón	hah-**bone**
a map	un mapa	oon **mah**-pah
a magazine	una revista	**oon**-ah reh-**veess**-tah
paper	papel	pah-**pel**
envelopes	sobres	**so**-brace
a postcard	una tarjeta postal	**oon**-ah tar-**het**-ah post-**ahl**
How much is it?	¿Cuánto cuesta?	**kwahn**-toe **kwes**-tah
It's expensive/cheap	Está caro/barato	es-**tah kah**-roh/bah-**rah**-toe
A little/a lot	Un poquito/mucho . . .	oon poh-**kee**-toe/**moo**-choh
More/less	Más/menos	mahss/**men**-ohss
Enough/too much/	Suficiente/de	soo-fee-see-**en**-tay/
Telephone	Teléfono	tel-**ef**-oh-no
Telegram	Telegrama	teh-leh-**grah**-mah
I am ill/sick	Estoy enfermo(a)	es-**toy** en-**fair**-moh(ah)
Please call a doctor	Por favor llame un médico	pore fa-**vor ya**-may oon **med**-ee-koh
Help!	¡Auxilio! ¡Ayuda!	owk-**see**-lee-oh/ah-**yoo**-dah
Fire!	¡Encendio!	en-**sen**-dee-oo
Caution!/Look out!	¡Cuidado!	kwee-**dah**-doh

Dining Out

A bottle of . . .	Una botella de . . .	**oo**-nah bo-**tay**-yah deh
A cup of . . .	Una taza de . . .	**oo**-nah **tah**-sah deh
A glass of . . .	Un vaso de . . .	oon **vah**-so deh
Ashtray	Un cenicero	oon sen-ee-**seh**-roh
Bill/check	La cuenta	lah **kwen**-tah
Bread	El pan	el pahn
Breakfast	El desayuno	el day-sigh-**oon**-oh
Butter	La mantequilla	lah mahn-tay-**key**-yah
Cheers!	¡Salud!	sah-**lood**
Cocktail	Un aperitivo	oon ah-pair-ee-**tee**-voh
Dinner	La cena	lah **seh**-nah
Dish	Un plato	oon **plah**-toe
Dish of the day	El platillo de hoy	el plah-**tee**-yo day oy
Enjoy!	¡Buen provecho!	bwen pro-**veh**-cho
Fixed-price menu	La comida corrida	lah koh-**me**-dah co-**ree**-dah
Fork	El tenedor	el ten-eh-**door**

Is the tip included?	¿Está incluida la propina?	es-**tah** in-clue-**ee**-dah lah pro-**pea**-nah
Knife	El cuchillo	el koo-**chee**-yo
Lunch	La comida	lah koh-**me**-dah
Menu	La carta	lah **cart**-ah
Napkin	La servilleta	lah sair-vee-**yet**-uh
Pepper	La pimienta	lah pea-me-**en**-tah
Please give me . . .	Por favor déme	pore fah-**vor day**-may
Salt	La sal	lah sahl
Spoon	Una cuchara	oo-nah koo-**chah**-rah
Sugar	El azúcar	el ah-**sue**-car
Waiter!/Waitress!	¡Por favor Señor/ Señorita!	pore fah-**vor** sen-**yor**/ sen-yor-**ee**-tah

INDEX

X = *restaurant*, 🏨 = *hotel*

WHEREVER YOU TRAVEL, *H*ELP IS NEVER FAR AWAY.

From planning your trip to providing travel assistance
along the way, American Express® Travel Service Offices
are always there to help.

Cancun

American Express Travel Service
Av. Tulum 208 Esq Agua
Supermanzana
98/84-19-99

Travel

http://www.americanexpress.com/travel

American Express Travel Service Offices are
found in central locations throughout Mexico.